The Mammoth Book of

CLASSIC
SCIENCE FICTION

Short Novels of the 1930s

The Mammoth Book of

CLASSIC
SCIENCE FICTION
Short Novels of the 1930s

Edited by Isaac Asimov,
Charles G. Waugh and Martin H. Greenberg

Robinson Publishing
London

Robinson Publishing
11 Shepherd House
Shepherd Street
London W1Y 7LD

First published in 1988 by Robinson Publishing

Collection copyright © Nightfall Inc.,
Martin H. Greenberg and
Charles G. Waugh, 1988

Cover illustration copyright © Les Edwards

0 948164 72 7

Printed by Wm. Collins & Sons Ltd., Glasgow

CONTENTS

CONTENTS

ACKNOWLEDGEMENTS

INTRODUCTION

Isaac Asimov
Science Fiction Finds Its Voice

There is no easy agreement as to when we might date the beginnings of science fiction (s.f.). There are those ambitious souls who lay claim to Plato's tale of Atlantis (*c.* 350 BC) as the origin and others even more all-embracing who wish to annex the Epic of Gilgamesh (*c.* 2400 BC).

This is simply, at least in my opinion, nonsense. Science fiction must involve itself with science and technology at least tangentially. It must deal with a society noticeably different from the real one of its time, and this difference must involve some change in the level of science and technology. If this is so, s.f. cannot predate popular awareness of the connection between advancing science and technology and social change, and that brings us up to the Industrial Revolution. Anything earlier is only fantasy even if it involves trips to the Moon, as does the *True History* (*c.* 150) of Lucian of Samosata.

There are those who accept this view and consider that s.f. dates back to the early decades of the nineteenth century. Some suggest Mary Shelley's *Frankenstein* (1818) as a beginning. Others feel that *Frankenstein* is more honestly classified as a 'Gothic tale' in the tradition of Horace Walpole's *The Castle of Otranto* (1765). Later examples that are often thought of as early s.f. might be labelled the same, notably the works of Poe and Hawthorne.

It might seem, then, that we ought to start true s.f. with Jules Verne's *Five Weeks in a Balloon* (1863). Verne wrote s.f. without Gothic trappings, and he was the first person to write s.f. almost exclusively, and to gain great popularity and wealth as a result. Certainly, 1863 as a beginning sounds good.

Yet we can present an argument against even this. Science fiction, whether it begins in 2400 BC, 150, 1818, or 1863, has always been a thin thread through literature generally. Relatively few authors have tried their hand at anything that can be called s.f. by even a liberal interpretation of the term, and even fewer have done so in truly popular fashion – Jules Verne and H.G. Wells are the two best we can name prior to the 1920s.

Why not then find a beginning to s.f. as a mass phenomenon? When did s.f. begin to be turned out in quantity, by first dozens, then scores, and then hundreds of writers? What set it on the road to where it is today, an extraordinarily popular literary phenomenon that has many first-rate luminaries. One need only mention Robert Heinlein, Arthur C. Clarke, Anne McCaffrey, Frank Herbert, Ray Bradbury, Ursula K. Le Guin – but modesty forbids my continuing.

Clearly, what is responsible for this is *magazine* science fiction (m.s.f.), which began with the first issue (April 1926) of *Amazing Stories* published by Hugo Gernsback.

There are those who scorn this, and object strenuously. Writers and critics who demand literary respectability for science fiction consider m.s.f. to have been a 'ghetto' which reduced s.f. to a variety of pulp fiction (i.e., magazines printing lurid stuff for semi-literates on cheap pulpwood paper), so befouling the genre as to cause mainstream writers to refuse to deal with the field.

There is something to this. Certainly, some 90 per cent of m.s.f. was indeed teenage childishness at first. (Remember Sturgeon's Law: 90 per cent of *everything* is crud.) Nevertheless, m.s.f. did create a forcing ground in which many youngsters sharpened their talents, when otherwise they would never have entered writing at all, or would have written something other than s.f. 'Literary' science fiction *never* made the field popular, although it made a very few writers popular. It was magazine science fiction that did the job, although it did have to crawl before it could walk, and walk before it could run.

To turn up one's nose at m.s.f., then, does the phenomenon a great injustice, and merely reveals the nose-up-turners to be pretentious pedants. (Some of these made their own name and fame in magazine science fiction to begin with, which catches them in the unlovely act of attempting to gain literary prestige by biting the hand that fed them.)

Let us, then, turn to magazine science fiction. It did not have an easy birth. It was precisely because the field was not popular and had few practitioners that there were not enough writers to support a monthly magazine. Gernsback had to depend on reprints of H.G. Wells and Jules Verne in his early issues and only gradually did new writers rally to the field.

These new writers were sometimes raw beginners whose skills were, as yet, small, and sometimes pulp writers who turned from their adventure yarns (or whatever) to try their hand at a new variety of pulp without much understanding of what s.f. really was. Consequently the magazine science fiction of the Twenties does not offer us much in the way of quality.

At that time, as in all times before or since, the longer the story, the better the quality on the whole (but only on the whole, for there were many notable exceptions, of course.) It is not surprising, then, that the one notable example of m.s.f. of the Twenties, was *The Skylark of Space*, a novel serialized in *Amazing Stories* in 1928.

Unfortunately, we cannot include novels in this collection but must confine ourselves to 'novellas', which are long stories that are short enough to be included in a single issue of a magazine. Since more novellas than novels can be published in the magazines simply out of consideration of length, some of the best writers in the field began to concentrate on novellas – as you will see when you read this book.

It was in the 1930s that magazine science fiction began to find its voice. Even where the writing remained 'pulpish' – that is, overwritten and unsubtle – ideas began to flourish and the minds of the readers were stretched.

In the Thirties, the leading s.f. magazine was *Astounding Stories*. It had begun with the January 1930 issue and had quickly outpaced *Amazing Stories*, both because it offered higher word-rates, and because its editor, Harry Bates, abandoned Gernsback's didacticism and emphasized action. With the March 1933 issue, however, at the depth of the Great Depression, William Clayton, the publisher, went bankrupt. The title was bought by Street & Smith publications, and the magazine was resurrected with the October 1933 issue, under the editorial direction of F. Orlin Tremaine.

Tremaine remained at the helm for four years, and his great contribution was the notion of 'thought-variant' stories – that is, stories featuring some startling new notion, or some unexpected variation of an old notion. These greatly pleased the readers and the magazine was never again threatened by failure.

As an outstanding example of a thought-variant, there is 'Sidewise in Time' by Murray Leinster (a pseudonym of William F. Jenkins), which was published in the June 1934 issue of

Astounding Stories. 'Sidewise in Time' was the first attempt to deal with the notion of parallel time-streams, of universes that, at key moments, could take one path or another, with all paths attaining some sort of existence. (Forty years later, physicists dealing with the more esoteric consequences of quantum mechanics are finding themselves forced to deal with this Leinsterian concept.)

Another unusual story of the Tremaine era, was 'Alas, All Thinking', written by Tremaine's editorial predecessor, Harry Bates. It appeared in the June 1935 issue of *Astounding Stories*. Bates did not write many stories, but the few he did write were good. 'Alas, All Thinking' is a chilling tale of evolutionary degeneration.

The outstanding writer of the Tremaine era was John W. Campbell, Jr. He began his career as a writer of 'super-science' stories, in imitation of E.E. Smith, and was second only to Smith in that field. But then, under the pseudonym of Don A. Stuart, he took to writing much more subtle stories, with surprisingly high literary and emotional content. His first of this type was the short story 'Twilight', appearing in the November 1934, *Astounding Stories*.

The longest and best Stuart story, however, was 'Who Goes There?' which appeared in the August 1938 issue of *Astounding Stories*. It is included here and if you have never read it before, I envy you, for you'll find it among the cleverest and most insidiously horrifying stories you have ever read. I won't say a word about the plot. You must find that out for yourself.

By the time that 'Who Goes There?' appeared, however, another revolution had taken place. Tremaine was promoted to a higher position and John W. Campbell himself, became editor of *Astounding Stories* in December 1937. He quickly changed the name of the magazine to *Astounding Science Fiction* and began to search for writers capable of achieving greater heights of literacy and greater fidelity in their description of science and scientists.

To begin with, of course, he had to use, and encourage the further development, of authors already in the field. Horace Gold had written several good stories for Tremaine under the pseudonym of Clyde Crane Campbell. Obviously, he could not use that pseudonym under the new dispensation. In the December 1938 issue of *Astounding Science Fiction* then, Gold's first story under his own name, 'A Matter of Form' appeared. This was an astonishingly realistic description of the adventures and misadventures of a man who was hampered (as the title indicates) by his form.

Another Tremaine author who was ripe for greatness was L. Sprague de Camp. His first published story had appeared in the September 1937, *Astounding Stories* and he has written numerous stories since. He was sound both in science and in history and was meticulous in his accuracy in both fields. Furthermore, he was one of the relatively few science fiction writers with a good sense of humor. He came into his own when Campbell introduced a sister-magazine to *Astounding Science Fiction*. The new magazine was *Unknown*, the first issue of which was March, 1939. It featured 'adult fantasy', as meticulous in its internal logic, as the stories in *Astounding Science Fiction*.

De Camp quickly became a mainstay of the magazine and his amusing 'Divide and Rule', with its peculiar but logical blend of medieval chivalry and modern technology, appeared in its second issue, April 1939.

Thus, we present ten of the best short novels of the Thirties.

THE SHADOW OUT OF TIME

H.P. Lovecraft

1

After twenty-two years of nightmare and terror, saved only by a desperate conviction of the mythical source of certain impressions, I am unwilling to vouch for the truth of that which I think I found in Western Australia on the night of July 17-18, 1935. There is reason to hope that my experience was wholly or partly an hallucination – for which, indeed, abundant causes existed. And yet, its realism was so hideous that I sometimes find hope impossible.

If the thing did happen, then man must be prepared to accept notice of the cosmos, and of his own place in the seething vortex of time, whose merest mention is paralyzing. He must, too, be placed on guard against a specific, lurking peril which, though it will never engulf the whole race, may impose monstrous and unguessable horrors upon certain venturesome members of it.

It is for this latter reason that I urge, with all the force of my being, a final abandonment of all the attempts at unearthing those fragments of unknown, primordial masonry which my expedition set out to investigate.

Assuming that I was sane and awake, my experience on that night was such as has befallen no man before. It was, moreover, a frightful confirmation of all I had sought to dismiss as myth and dream. Mercifully there is no proof, for in my fright I lost the awesome object which would – if real and brought out of that noxious abyss – have formed irrefutable evidence.

When I came upon the horror I was alone – and I have up to now told no one about it. I could not stop the others from digging in its direction, but chance and the shifting sand have so

1

far saved them from finding it. Now I must formulate some definite statement – not only for the sake of my own mental balance, but to warn such others as may read it seriously.

These pages – much in whose earlier parts will be familiar to close readers of the general and scientific press – are written in the cabin of the ship that is bringing me home. I shall give them to my son, Professor Wingate Peaslee of Miskatonic University – the only member of my family who stuck to me after my queer amnesia of long ago, and the man best informed on the inner facts of my case. Of all living persons, he is least likely to ridicule what I shall tell of that fateful night.

I did not enlighten him orally before sailing, because I think he had better have the revelation in written form. Reading and rereading at leisure will leave him with a more convincing picture than my confused tongue could hope to convey.

He can do anything that he thinks best with this account – showing it, with suitable comment, in any quarters where it will be likely to accomplish good. It is for the sake of such readers as are unfamiliar with the earlier phases of my case that I am prefacing the revelation itself with a fairly ample summary of its background.

My name is Nathaniel Wingate Peaslee, and those who recall the newspaper tales of a generation back – or the letters and articles in psychological journals six or seven years ago – will know who and what I am. The press was filled with the details of my strange amnesia in 1908–13, and much was made of the traditions of horror, madness, and witchcraft which lurked behind the ancient Massachusetts town then and now forming my place of residence. Yet I would have it known that there is nothing whatever of the mad or sinister in my heredity and early life. This is a highly important fact in view of the shadow which fell so suddenly upon me from *outside* sources.

It may be that centuries of dark brooding had given to crumbling, whisper-haunted Arkham a peculiar vulnerability as regards such shadows – though even this seems doubtful in the light of those other cases which I later came to study. But the chief point is that my own ancestry and background are altogether normal. What came, came from *somewhere else* – where, I even now hesitate to assert in plain words.

I am the son of Jonathan and Hannah (Wingate) Peaslee, both of wholesome old Haverhill stock. I was born and reared in Haverhill – at the old homestead in Boardman Street near Golden Hill – and did not go to Arkham till I entered Miskatonic

University as instructor of political economy in 1895.

For thirteen years more my life ran smoothly and happily. I married Alice Keezar of Haverhill in 1896, and my three children, Robert, Wingate and Hannah were born in 1898, 1900 and 1903, respectively. In 1898 I became an associate professor, and in 1902 a full professor. At no time had I the least interest in either occultism or abnormal psychology.

It was on Thursday, May 14, 1908, that the queer amnesia came. The thing was quite sudden, though later I realized that certain brief, glimmering visions of several hours previous – chaotic visions which disturbed me greatly because they were so unprecedented – must have formed premonitory symptoms. My head was aching, and I had a singular feeling – altogether new to me – that someone else was trying to get possession of my thoughts.

The collapse occurred about 10:20 A.M., while I was conducting a class in Political Economy VI – history and present tendencies of economics – for juniors and a few sophomores. I began to see strange shapes before my eyes, and to feel that I was in a grotesque room other than the classroom.

My thoughts and speech wandered from my subject, and the students saw that something was gravely amiss. Then I slumped down, unconscious, in my chair, in a stupor from which no one could arouse me. Nor did my rightful faculties again look out upon the daylight of our normal world for five years, four months, and thirteen days.

It is, of course, from others that I have learned what followed. I showed no sign of consciousness for sixteen and a half hours, though removed to my home at 27 Crane Street, and given the best of medical attention.

At 3 A.M. May 15 my eyes opened and I began to speak, but before long the doctors and my family were thoroughly frightened by the trend of my expression and language. It was clear that I had no remembrance of my identity and my past, though for some reason I seemed anxious to conceal this lack of knowledge. My eyes gazed strangely at the persons around me, and the flections of my facial muscles were altogether unfamiliar.

Even my speech seemed awkward and foreign. I used my vocal organs clumsily and gropingly, and my diction had a curiously stilted quality, as if I had laboriously learned the English language from books. The pronunciation was barbarously alien, whilst the idiom seemed to include both scraps of curious archaism and expressions of a wholly incomprehensible cast.

Of the latter, one in particular was very potently – even terrifiedly – recalled by the youngest of the physicians twenty years afterward. For at that late period such a phrase began to have an actual currency – first in England and then in the United States – and though of much complexity and indisputable newness, it reproduced in every least particular the mystifying words of the strange Arkham patient of 1908.

Physical strength returned at once, although I required an odd amount of reeducation in the use of my hands, legs, and bodily apparatus in general. Because of this and other handicaps inherent in the mnemonic lapse, I was for some time kept under strict medical care.

When I saw that my attempts to conceal the lapse had failed, I admitted it openly, and became eager for information of all sorts. Indeed, it seemed to the doctors that I lost interest in my proper personality as soon as I found the case of amnesia accepted as a natural thing.

They noticed that my chief efforts were to master certain points in history, science, art, language, and folklore – some of them tremendously abstruse, and some childishly simple – which remained, very oddly in many cases, outside my consciousness.

At the same time they noticed that I had an inexplicable command of many almost unknown sorts of knowledge – a command which I seemed to wish to hide rather than display. I would inadvertently refer, with casual assurance, to specific events in dim ages outside of the range of accepted history – passing off such references as a jest when I saw the surprise they created. And I had a way of speaking of the future which two or three times caused actual fright.

These uncanny flashes soon ceased to appear, though some observers laid their vanishment more to a certain furtive caution on my part than to any waning of the strange knowledge behind them. Indeed, I seemed anomalously avid to absorb the speech, customs, and perspectives of the age around me; as if I were a studious traveler from a far, foreign land.

As soon as permitted, I haunted the college library at all hours; and shortly began to arrange for those odd travels, and special courses at American and European Universities, which evoked so much comment during the next few years.

I did not at any time suffer from a lack of learned contacts, for my case had a mild celebrity among the psychologists of the period. I was lectured upon as a typical example of secondary personality – even though I seemed to puzzle the lecturers now and then with some bizarre symptoms or some queer trace of carefully veiled mockery.

Of real friendliness, however, I encountered little. Something in my aspect and speech seemed to excite vague fears and aversions in everyone I met, as if I were a being infinitely removed from all that is normal and healthful. This idea of a black, hidden horror connected with incalculable gulfs of some sort of *distance* was oddly widespread and persistent.

My own family formed no exception. From the moment of my strange waking my wife had regarded me with extreme horror and loathing, vowing that I was some utter alien usurping the body of her husband. In 1910 she obtained a legal divorce, nor would she ever consent to see me even after my return to normality in 1913. These feelings were shared by my elder son and my small daughter, neither of whom I have ever seen since.

Only my second son, Wingate, seemed able to conquer the terror and repulsion which my change aroused. He indeed felt that I was a stranger, but though only eight years old held fast to a faith that my proper self would return. When it did return he sought me out, and the courts gave me his custody. In succeeding years he helped me with the studies to which I was driven, and today, at thirty-five, he is a professor of psychology at Miskatonic.

But I do not wonder at the horror I caused – for certainly, the mind, voice, and facial expression of the being that awakened on May 15, 1908, were not those of Nathaniel Wingate Peaslee.

I will not attempt to tell much of my life from 1908 to 1913, since readers may glean all the outward essentials – as I largely had to do – from files of old newspapers and scientific journals.

I was given charge of my funds, and spent them slowly and on the whole wisely, in travel and in study at various centers of learning. My travels, however, were singular in extreme, involving long visits to remote and desolate places.

In 1909 I spent a month in the Himalayas, and in 1911 aroused much attention through a camel trip into the unknown deserts of Arabia. What happened on those journeys I have never been able to learn.

During the summer of 1912 I chartered a ship and sailed in the Arctic, north of Spitzbergen, afterward showing signs of disappointment.

Later in that year I spent weeks alone beyond the limits of previous or subsequent exploration in the vast limestone cavern systems of western Virginia – black labyrinths so complex that no retracing of my steps could even be considered.

My sojourns at the universities were marked by abnormally rapid assimilation, as if the secondary personality had an intelligence enormously superior to my own. I have found, also, that my rate of reading and solitary study was phenomenal. I could master every detail of a book merely by glancing over it as fast as I could turn the leaves; while my skill at interpreting complex figures in an instant was veritably awesome.

At times there appeared almost ugly reports of my power to influence the thoughts and acts of others, though I seemed to have taken care to minimize displays of this faculty.

Other ugly reports concerned my intimacy with leaders of occultist groups, and scholars suspected of connection with nameless bands of abhorrent elder-world hierophants. These rumors, though never proved at the time, were doubtless stimulated by the known tenor of some of my reading – for the consultation of rare books at libraries cannot be effected secretly.

There is tangible proof – in the form of marginal notes – that I went minutely through such things as the Comte d'Erlette's *Cultes des Goules*, Ludvig Prinn's *De Vermis Mysteriis*, the *Unausprechlichen Kulten* of von Junzt, the surviving fragments of the puzzling *Book of Eibon*, and the dreaded *Necronomicon* of the mad Arab Abdul Alhazred. Then, too, it is undeniable that a fresh and evil wave of underground cult activity set in about the time of my odd mutation.

In the summer of 1913 I began to display signs of ennui and flagging interest, and to hint to various associates that a change might soon be expected in me. I spoke of returning memories of my earlier life – though most auditors judged me insincere, since all the recollections I gave were casual, and such as might have been learned from my old private papers.

About the middle of August I returned to Arkham and reopened my long-closed house in Crane Street. Here I installed a mechanism of the curious aspect, constructed piecemeal by different makers of scientific apparatus in Europe and America, and guarded carefully from the sight of any one intelligent enough to analyze it.

Those who did see it – a workman, a servant, and the new housekeeper – say that it was a queer mixture of rods, wheels, and mirrors, though only about two feet tall, one foot wide, and one foot thick. The central mirror was circular and convex. All this is borne out by such makers of parts as can be located.

On the evening of Friday, September 26, I dismissed the housekeeper and the maid until noon of the next day. Lights burned in the house till late, and a lean, dark, curiously foreign-looking man called in an automobile.

It was about one A.M. that the lights were last seen. At 2:15 A.M. a policeman observed the place in darkness, but the stranger's motor still at the curb. By 4 o'clock the motor was certainly gone.

It was 6 o'clock that a hesitant, foreign voice on the telephone asked Dr. Wilson to call at my house and bring me out of a peculiar faint. This call – a long-distance one – was later traced to a public booth in the North Station in Boston, but no sign of the lean foreigner was ever unearthed.

When the doctor reached my house he found me unconscious in the sitting room – in an easy-chair with a table drawn up before it. On the polished top were scratches showing where some heavy object had rested. The queer machine was gone, nor was anything afterward heard of it. Undoubtedly the dark, lean foreigner had taken it away.

In the library grate were abundant ashes, evidently left from the burning of every remaining scrap of paper on which I had written since the advent of amnesia. Dr. Wilson found my breathing very peculiar, but after a hypodermic injection it became more regular.

At 11:15 A.M., September 27, I stirred vigorously, and my hitherto masklike face began to show signs of expression. Dr. Wilson remarked that the expression was not that of my secondary personality, but seemed much like that of my normal self. About 11:30 I muttered some very curious syllables – syllables which seemed unrelated to any human speech. I appeared, too, to struggle against something. Then, just after noon – the housekeeper and the maid having meanwhile returned – I began to mutter in English:

'– of the orthodox economists of that period, Jevons typifies the prevailing trend toward scientific correlation. His attempt to link the commercial cycle of prosperity and depression with the physical cycle of the solar spots forms perhaps the apex of – '

Nathaniel Wingate Peaslee had come back – a spirit of whose time scale was still Thursday morning in 1908, with the economics class gazing up at the battered desk on the platform.

2

My reabsorption into normal life was a painful and difficult process. The loss of over five years creates more complications than can be imagined, and in my case there were countless matters to be adjusted.

What I heard of my actions since 1908 astonished and disturbed me, but I tried to view the matter as philosophically as I could. At last, regaining custody of my second son, Wingate, I settled down with him in the Crane Street house and endeavoured to resume my teaching – my old professorship having been kindly offered me by the college.

I began work with the February 1914 term, and kept at it just a year. By that time I realized how badly my experience had shaken me. Though perfectly sane – I hoped – and with no flaw in my original personality, I had not the nervous energy of the old days. Vague dreams and queer ideas continually haunted me, and when the outbreak of the World War turned my mind to history I found myself thinking of periods and events in the oddest possible fashion.

My conception of *time* – my ability to distinguish between consecutiveness and simultaneousness – seemed subtly disordered; so that I formed chimaerical notions about living in one age and casting one's mind all over eternity for knowledge of past and future ages.

The War gave me strange impressions of remembering some of its far-off consequences – as if I knew how it was coming out and could look *back* upon it in the light of future information. All such quasi-memories were attended with much pain, and with a feeling that some artificial psychological barrier was set against them.

When I diffidently hinted to others about my impressions, I met with varied responses. Some persons looked uncomfortably at me, but men in the mathematics department spoke of new developments in those theories of relativity – then discussed only in learned circles – which were later to become so famous. Dr. Albert Einstein, they said, was rapidly reducing time to the status of a mere dimension.

But the dreams and disturbed feelings gained on me, so that I had to drop my regular work in 1915. Certain of the impressions were taking an annoying shape – giving me the persistent notion that my amnesia had formed some unholy sort of exchange; that the secondary personality had indeed been an intruding force from unknown regions, and that my own personality had suffered displacement.

Thus I was driven to vague and frightful speculations concerning the whereabouts of my true self during the years that another had held my body. The curious knowledge and strange conduct of my body's late tenant troubled me more and more as I learned further details from persons, papers, and magazines.

Queernesses that had baffled others seemed to harmonize terribly with some background of black knowledge which festered in the chasms of my subconsciousness. I began to search feverishly for every scrap of information bearing on the studies and travels of that other one during the dark years.

Not all of my troubles were as semi-abstract as this. There were the dreams – and these seemed to grow in vividness and concreteness. Knowing how most would regard them, I seldom mentioned them to any one but my son or certain trusted psychologists, but eventually I commenced a scientific study of other cases in order to see how typical or nontypical such visions might be among amnesia victims.

My results, aided by psychologists, historians, anthropologists and mental specialists of wide experience, and by a study that included all records of split personalities from the days of demoniac-possession legends to the medically realistic present, at first bothered me more than they consoled me.

I soon found that my dreams had, indeed, no counterpart in the overwhelming bulk of true amnesia cases. There remained, however, a tiny residue of accounts which for years baffled and shocked me with their parallelism to my own experience. Some of them were bits of ancient folklore; others were case histories in the annals of medicine; one or two were anecdotes obscurely buried in standard stories.

It thus appeared that, while my special kind of affliction was prodigiously rare, instances of it had occurred at long intervals ever since the beginning of men's annals. Some centuries might contain one, two, or three cases, others none – or at least none whose record survived.

The essence was always the same – a person of keen thoughtfulness seized with a strange secondary life and leading for a greater or lesser period an utterly alien existence typified at first by vocal and bodily awkwardness, and later by a wholesale acquisition of scientific, historic, artistic, and anthropological knowledge; an acquisition carried on with feverish zest and with a wholly abnormal absorptive power. Then a sudden return of the rightful consciousness, intermittently plagued ever after with vague unplaceable dreams suggesting fragments of some hideous memory elaborately blotted out.

And the close resemblance of those nightmares to my own – even in some of the smallest particulars – left no doubt in my mind of their significantly typical nature. One or two of the cases had an added ring of faint, blasphemous familiarity, as if I had heard of them before through some cosmic channel too morbid and frightful to contemplate. In three instances there was specific mention of such an unknown machine as had been in my house before the second change.

Another thing that worried me during my investigation was the somewhat greater frequency of cases where a brief, elusive glimpse of the typical nightmares was afforded to persons not visited with well-defined amnesia.

These persons were largely of mediocre mind or less – some so primitive that they could scarcely be thought of as vehicles for abnormal scholarship and preternatural mental acquisitions. For a second they would be fired with alien force – then a backward lapse, and a thin, swift-fading memory of unhuman horrors.

There had been at least three such cases during the past half century – one only fifteen years before. Had something been groping blindly through time from some unsuspected abyss in nature? Were these faint cases monstrous, sinister experiments of a kind and authorship utterly beyond sane belief?

Such were a few of the formless speculations of my weaker hours – fancies abetted by myths which my studies uncovered. For I could not doubt but that certain persistent legends of immemorial antiquity apparently unknown to the victims and physicians connected with recent amnesia cases, formed a striking and awesome elaboration of memory lapses such as mine.

Of the nature of the dreams and impressions which were growing so clamorous I still almost fear to speak. They seemed to savor of madness, and at times I believed I was indeed going mad. Was there a special type of delusion afflicting those who had suffered lapses of memory? Conceivably, the efforts of the subconsious mind to fill up a perplexing blank with pseudome-mories might give rise to strange imaginative vagaries.

This, indeed – though an alternative folklore theory finally seemed to me more plausible – was the belief of many of the alienists who helped me in my search for parallel cases, and who shared my puzzlement at the exact resemblances sometimes discovered.

They did not call the condition pure insanity, but classed it rather among neurotic disorders. My course in trying to track down and analyze it, instead of vainly seeking to dismiss or forget it, they heartily endorsed as correct according to the best psychological principles. I especially valued the advice of such physicians as had studied me during my possession by the other personality.

My first disturbances were not visual at all, but concerned the more abstract matters which I have mentioned. There was, too, a feeling of profound and inexplicable horror concerning myself. I developed a queer fear of seeing my own form, as if my eyes would find it something utterly alien and inconceivably abhorrent.

When I did glance down and behold the familiar human shape in quiet gray or blue clothing, I always felt a curious relief, though in order to gain this relief I had to conquer an infinite dread. I shunned mirrors as much as possible, and was always shaved at the barber's.

It was a long time before I correlated any of these diappointed feelings with the fleeting visual impressions which began to develop. The first such correlation had to do with the odd sensation of an external, artificial restraint on my memory.

I felt that the snatches of sight I experienced had a profound and terrible meaning, and a frightful connection with myself, but that some purposeful influence held me from grasping that meaning and that connection. Then came that queerness about the element of time, and with it desperate efforts to place the fragmentary dream glimpses in the chronological and spatial pattern.

The glimpses themselves were at first merely strange rather than horrible. I would seem to be in an enormous vaulted chamber whose lofty stone groinings were well nigh lost in the shadows overhead. In whatever time or place the scene might be, the principle of the arch was known as fully and used as extensively as by the Romans.

There were colossal, round windows and high, arched doors, and pedestals or tables each as tall as the height of an ordinary room. Vast shelves of dark wood lined the walls, holding what seemed to be volumes of immense size with strange hieroglyphs on their backs.

The exposed stonework held curious carvings, always in curvilinear mathematical designs, and there were chiseled inscriptions in the same characters that the huge books bore. The dark granite masonry was a monstrous megalithic type, with lines of convex-topped blocks fitting the concave-bottomed courses which rested upon them.

There were no chairs, but the tops of the vast pedestals were littered with books, papers, and what seemed to be writing materials – oddly figured jars of a purplish metal, and rods with stained tips. Tall as the pedestals were, I seemed at times able to view them from above. On some of them were great globes of luminous crystal serving as lamps, and inexplicable machines formed of vitreous tubes and metal rods.

The windows were glazed, and latticed with stout-looking bars. Though I dared not approach and peer out them, I could see from where I was the waving tops of singular fernlike growths. The floor was of massive octagonal flagstones, while rugs and hangings were entirely lacking.

Later, I had visions of sweeping through Cyclopean corridors of stone, and up and down gigantic inclined panes of the same monstrous masonry. There were no stairs anywhere, nor was any passageway less than thirty feet wide. Some of the structures through which I floated must have towered in the sky for thousands of feet.

There were multiple levels of black vaults below, and never-opened trapdoors, sealed down with metal bands and holding dim suggestions of some special peril.

I seemed to be a prisoner, and horror hung broodingly over everything I saw. I felt that the mocking curvilinear hieroglyphs on the walls would blast my soul with their message were I not guarded by a merciful ignorance.

Still later my dreams included vistas from the great round windows, and from the titanic flat roof, with its curious gardens, wide barren area, and high, scalloped parapet of stone, to which the topmost of the inclined planes led.

There were almost endless leagues of giant buildings, each in its garden, and ranged along paved roads fully two hundred feet wide. They differed greatly in aspect, but few were less than five hundred feet square or a thousand feet high. Many seemed so limitless that they must have had a frontage of several thousand feet, while some shot up to mountainous altitudes in the gray, steamy heavens.

They seemed to be mainly of stone or concrete, and most of them embodied the oddly curvilinear type of masonry noticeable in the building that held me. Roofs were flat and garden-covered, and tended to have scalloped parapets. Sometimes there were terraces and higher levels, and wide, cleared spaces amidst the gardens. The great roads held hints of motion, but in the earlier visions I could not resolve this impression into details.

In certain places I beheld enormous dark cylindrical towers which climbed far above any of the other structures. These appeared to be of a totally unique nature and showed signs of prodigious age and dilapidation. They were built of a bizarre type of square-cut basalt masonry, and tapered slightly toward their rounded tops. Nowhere in any of them could the least traces of windows or other apertures save huge doors be found. I noticed also some lower buildings – all crumbling with the weathering of aeons – which resembled these dark, cylindrical towers in basic architecture. Around all these aberrant piles of square-cut masonry there hovered an inexplicable aura of menace and concentrated fear, like that bred by the sealed trapdoors.

The omnipresent gardens were almost terrifying in their strangeness, with bizarre and unfamiliar forms of vegetation nodding over broad paths lined with curiously carven monoliths. Abnormally vast fern-like growths predominated – some green, and some of ghastly, fungoid pallor.

Among them rose great spectral things resembling calamites, whose bamboo-like trunks towered to fabulous heights. Then there were tufted forms like fabulous cycads, and grotesque dark-green shrubs and trees of coniferous aspect.

Flowers were small, colorless, and unrecognizable, blooming in geometrical beds and at large among the greenery.

In a few of the terrace and roof-top gardens were larger and more vivid blossoms of almost offensive contours and seeming to suggest artifical breeding. Fungi of inconceivable size, outlines, and colors speckled the scene in patterns bespeaking some unknown but well-established horticultural tradition. In larger gardens on the ground there seemed to be some attempt to preserve the irregularities of nature, but on the roofs there was more selectiveness, and more evidences of the topiary art.

The skies were almost always moist and cloudy, and sometimes I would seem to witness tremendous rains. Once in a while, though, there would be glimpses of the Sun – which looked abnormally large – and of the Moon, whose markings held a touch of difference from the normal that I could never quite fathom. When – very rarely – the night sky was clear to any extent, I beheld constellations which were nearly beyond recognition. Known outlines were sometimes approximated, but seldom duplicated; and from the position of the few groups I could recognize, I felt I must be in the Earth's southern hemisphere, near the Tropic of Capricorn.

The far horizon was always steamy and indistinct, but I could see that great jungles of unknown tree ferns, Calamites, Lepidodendro, and sigillaria lay outside the city, their fantastic frondage waving mockingly in the shifting vapours. Now and then there would be suggestions of motion in the sky, but these my early visions never resolved.

By the autumn of 1914 I began to have infrequent dreams of strange floatings over the city and through the regions around it. I saw interminable roads through forests of fearsome growths with mottled, fluted, and banded trunks, and past other cities as strange as the one which persistently haunted me.

I saw monstrous constructions of black or iridescent stone in glades and clearings where perpetual twilight reigned, and traversed long causeways over swamps so dark that I could tell but little of their moist, towering vegetation.

Once I saw an area of countless miles strewn with age-blasted basaltic ruins whose architecture had been like that of the few windowless, round-topped towers in the haunting city.

And once I saw the sea – a boundless, steamy expanse beyond the colossal stone piers of an enormous town of domes and arches.

3

As I have said, it was not immediately that these wild visions began to hold their terrifying quality. Certainly, many persons have dreamed intrinsically stranger things – things compounded of unrelated scraps of daily life, pictures, and reading, and arranged in fantastically novel forms by the unchecked caprices of sleep.

For some time I accepted the visions as natural, even though I had never before been an extravagant dreamer. Many of the vague anomalies, I argued, must have come from trivial sources too numerous to track down; while others seemed to reflect a common textbook knowledge of the plants and other conditions of the primitive world of a hundred and fifty million years ago – the world of the Permian or Triassic Age.

In the course of some months, however, the element of terror did figure with accumulating force. This was when the dreams began so unfailingly to have the aspect of memories, and when my mind began to link them with my growing abstract disturbances – the feeling of mnemonic restraint, the curious impressions regarding time, the sense of a loathsome exchange with my secondary personality of 1908-13, and, considerably later, the inexplicable loathing of my own person.

As certain definite details began to enter the dreams, their horror increased a thousandfold – until by October 1915, I felt I must do something. It was then that I began an intensive study of other cases of amnesia and visions, feeling that I might thereby objectivize my trouble and shake clear of its emotional grip.

However, as before mentioned, the result was at first almost exactly opposite. It disturbed me vastly to find that my dreams had been so closely duplicated; especially since some of the accounts were too early to admit of any geological knowledge – and therefore of any idea of primitive landscapes – on the subjects' part.

What is more, many of these accounts supplied very horrible details and explanations in connection with the visions of great buildings and jungle gardens – and other things. The actual sights and vague impressions were bad enough, but what was hinted or asserted by some of the other dreamers savored of madness and blasphemy. Worst of all, my own pseudomemory was aroused to wilder dreams and hints of coming revelations. And yet most doctors deemed my course, on the whole, an advisable one.

I studied psychology systematically, and under the prevailing stimulus my son Wingate did the same – his studies leading eventually to his present professorship. In 1917 and 1918 I took special courses at Miskatonic. Meanwhile, my examination of medical, historical, and anthropological records became indefatigable, involving travels to distant libraries, and finally including even a reading of the hideous book of forbidden lore in which my secondary personality had been so disturbingly interested.

Some of the latter were the actual copies I had consulted in my altered state, and I was greatly disturbed by certain marginal notations and ostensible *corrections* of the hideous text in a script and idiom which somehow seemed oddly unhuman.

These markings were mostly in the respective languages of the various books, all of which the writer seemed to know with equal, though obviously, academic facility. One note appended to von Junzt's *Unaussprechlichen Kulten*, however, was alarmingly otherwise. It consisted of certain curvilinear hieroglyphs in the same ink as that of the German corrections, but following no recognized human pattern. And these hieroglyphs were closely and unmistakably akin to the characters constantly met with in my dreams – characters whose meaning I would sometimes momentarily fancy I knew, or was just on the brink of recalling.

To complete my black confusion, many librarians assured me that, in view of previous examinations and records of consultation of the volumes in question, all of these notations must have been made by myself in my secondary state. This despite the fact that I was and still am ignorant of three of the languages involved. Piecing together the scattered records, ancient and modern, anthropological and medical, I found a fairly consistent mixture of myth and hallucination whose scope and wildness left me utterly dazed. Only one thing consoled me: the fact that the myths were of such early existence. What lost knowledge could have brought pictures of the Paleozoic or Mesozoic landscape into these primitive fables, I could not even guess; but the pictures had been there. Thus, a basis existed for the formation of a fixed type of delusion.

Cases of amnesia no doubt created the general myth pattern – but afterward the fanciful accretions of the myths must have reacted on amnesia sufferers and colored their pseudomemories. I myself had read and heard all the early tales during my memory lapse – my quest had amply proved that. Was it not natural, then, for my subsequent dreams and emotional impressions to become colored and molded by what my memory subtly held over from my secondary state?

A few of the myths had significant connections with other cloudy legends of the prehuman world, especially those Hindu tales involving stupefying gulfs of time and forming part of the lore of modern theosophists.

Primal myth and modern delusion joined in their assumption that mankind is only one – perhaps the least – of the highly evolved and dominant races of this planet's long and largely unknown career. Things of unconceivable shape, they implied, had reared towers to the sky and delved into every secret of nature before the first amphibian forbear of man had crawled out of the hot sea three hundred million years ago.

Some had come down from the stars; a few were as old as the cosmos itself; others had arisen swiftly from terrane germs as far behind the first germs of our life cycle as those germs are behind ourselves. Spans of thousands of millions of years, and linkages of other galaxies and universes, were spoken of. Indeed, there was no such thing as time in its humanly accepted sense.

But most of the tales and impressions concerned a relatively late race, of a queer and intricate shape, resembling no life form known to science, which had lived till only fifty million years before the advent of man. This, they indicated, was the greatest race of all because it alone had conquered the secret of time.

It had learned all things that ever were known or ever would be known on the Earth, through the power of its keener minds to project themselves into the past and future, even through gulfs of millions of years, and study the lore of every age. From the accomplishments of this race arose all legends of prophets, including those in human mythology.

In its vast libraries were volumes of texts and pictures holding the whole of Earth's annals – histories and descriptions of every species that had ever been or that ever would be, with full records of their arts, their achievements, their languages, and their psychologies.

With this aeon-embracing knowledge, the Great Race chose from every era and life form such thoughts, arts, and processes as might suit its own nature and situation. Knowledge of the past, secured through a kind of mind-casting outside the recognized senses was harder to glean than knowledge of the future.

In the latter case the course was easier and more material. With suitable mechanical aid a mind would project itself forward in time, feeling its dim, extrasensory way till it approached the desired period. Then, after preliminary trials, it would seize on the best discoverable representative of the highest of that period's life forms. It would enter the organism's brain and set up therein its own vibrations, while the displaced mind would strike back to the period of the displacer, remaining in the latter's body till a reverse process was set up.

The projected mind, in the body of the organism of the future, would then pose as a member of the race whose outward form it wore, learning as quickly as possible all that could be learned of the chosen age and its massed information and techniques.

Meanwhile the displaced mind, thrown back to the displacer's age and body, would be carefully guarded. It would be kept from harming the body it occupied, and would be drained of all its knowledge by trained questioners. Often it could be questioned in its own language, when previous quests into the future had brought back records of that language.

If the mind came from a body whose language the Great Race could not physically reproduce, clever machines would be made, on which the alien speech could be played as on a musical instrument.

The Great Race's members were immense rugose cones ten feet high, and with head and other organs attached to foot-thick distensible limbs spreading from the apexes. They spoke by the clicking or scraping of huge paws or claws attached to the end of two of their four limbs, and walked by the expansion and contraction of a viscous layer attached to their vast, ten-foot bases.

When the captive mind's amazement and resentment had worn off, and when – assuming that it came from a body vastly different from the Great Race's – it had lost its horror at its unfamiliar, temporary form, it was permitted to study its new environment and experience a wonder and wisdom approximating that of its displacer.

With suitable precautions, and in exchange for suitable services, it was allowed to rove all over the habitable world in titan airships or on the huge boat-like, atomic-engined vehicles which traversed the great roads, and to delve freely into the libraries containing the records of the planet's past and future.

This reconciled many captive minds to their lot; since none were other than keen, and to such minds the unveiling of hidden mysteries of Earth – closed chapters of inconceivable pasts and dizzying vortices of future time which include the years ahead of their own natural ages – forms always, despite the abysmal horrors often unveiled, the supreme experience of life.

Now and then certain captives were permitted to meet other captive minds seized from the future – to exchange thoughts with consciousnesses living a hundred or a thousand or a million years before or after their own ages. And all were urged to write copiously in their own languages of themselves and their respective periods such documents to be filed in the great central archives.

It may be added that there was one special type of captive whose privileges were far greater than those of the majority. These were the dying *permanent* exiles, whose bodies in the future had been seized by keen-minded members of the Great Race who, faced with death, sought to escape mental extinction.

Such melancholy exiles were not as common as might be expected, since the longevity of the Great Race lessened its love of life – especially among those superior minds capable of projection. From cases of the permanent projection of elder minds arose many of those lasting changes of personality noticed in later history – including mankind's.

As for the ordinary cases of exploration – when the displacing mind had learned what it wished in the future, it would build an apparatus like that which had started its flight and reverse the process of projection. Once more it would be in its own body in its own age while the lately captive mind would return to that body of the future to which it properly belonged.

Only when one or the other of the bodies had died during the exchange was this restoration impossible. In such cases, of course, the exploring mind had – like those of the death escapers – to live out of an alien-bodied life in the future; or else the captive mind – like the dying permanent exiles – had to end its days in the form and past age of the Great Race.

This fate was less horrible when the captive mind was also of the Great Race – a not infrequent occurrence, since in all its periods that race was intensely concerned with its own future. The number of dying permanent exiles of the Great Race was very slight – largely because of the tremendous penalties attached to displacements of future Great Race minds by the moribund.

Through projection, arrangements were made to inflict these penalties on the offending minds in their new future bodies – and sometimes forced reexchanges were effected.

Complex cases of the displacement of exploring or already captive minds by minds in various regions of the past had been known and carefully rectified. In every age since the discovery of mind projection, a minute but well-recognized element of the population consisted of Great Race minds from past ages, sojourning for a longer or shorter while.

When a captive mind of alien origin was returned to its own body in the future, it was purged by an intricate mechanical hypnosis of all it had learned in the Great Race's Age – this because of certain troublesome consequences inherent in the general carrying forward of knowledge in large quantities.

The few existing instances of clear transmission had caused, and would cause at known future times, great disasters. And it was largely in consequence of two cases of the kind – said the old myths – that mankind had learned what it had concerning the Great Race.

Of all things surviving physically and directly from that aeon–distant world, there remained only certain ruins of great stones in far places and under the sea, and parts of the text of the frightful Pnakotic Manuscripts.

Thus the returning mind reached its own age with only the faintest and most fragmentary vision of what it had undergone since its seizure. All memories that could be eradicated were eradicated, so that in most cases only a dream-shadowed blank stretched back to the time of the first exchange. Some minds recalled more than others, and the chance of joining of memories had at rare times brought hints of the forbidden past to future ages.

There probably never was a time when groups or cults did not secretly cherish certain of these hints. In the *Necronomicon* the presence of such a cult among human beings was suggested – a cult that sometimes gave aid to minds voyaging down the aeons from the days of the Great Race.

And, meanwhile, the Great Race itself waxed well-nigh omniscient, and turned to the task of setting up exchanges with the minds of other planets, and of exploring their pasts and futures. It sought likewise to fathom the past years and origin of that black, aeon-dead orb in far space whence its own mental heritage had come – for the mind of the Great Race was older than its bodily form.

The beings of a dying elder world, wise with the ultimate secrets, had looked ahead for a new world and species wherein they might have long life, and had sent their minds *en masse* into that future race best adapted to house them – the cone-shaped things that peopled our Earth a billion years ago.

Thus the Great Race came to be, while the myriad minds sent backward were left to die in the horror of strange shapes. Later the race would again face death, yet would live through another forward migration of its best minds into the bodies of others who had a longer physical span ahead of them.

Such was the background of intertwined legend and hallucination. When, around 1920, I had my researches in coherent shape, I felt a slight lessening of the tension which their earlier stages had increased. After all, and in spite of the fancies prompted by blind emotions, were not most of my phenomena readily explainable? Any chance might have turned my mind to dark studies during the amnesia – and then I read the forbidden legends and met the members of ancient and ill-regarded cults. That, plainly, supplied the material for the dreams and disturbed feelings which came after the return of memory.

As for the marginal notes in dream hieroglyphs and languages unknown to me, but laid at my door by librarians – I might easily have picked up a smattering of the tongues during my secondary state, while the hieroglyphs were doubtless coined by my fancy from descriptions in old legends, and afterward woven into my dreams. I tried to verify certain points through conversations with known cult leaders, but never succeeded in establishing the right connections.

At times the parallelism of so many cases in so many distant ages continued to worry me as it had at first, but on the other hand I reflected that the excitant folklore was undoubtedly more universal in the past than in the present.

Probably all the other victims whose cases were like mine had had a long and familiar knowledge of the tales I had learned only when in my secondary state. When these victims had lost their memory, they had associated themselves with the creatures of their household myths – the fabulous invaders supposed to displace men's minds – and had thus embarked upon quests for knowledge which they thought they could take back to a fancied, nonhuman past.

Then, when their memory returned, they reversed the associative process and thought of themselves as the former captive minds instead of as the displacers. Hence the dreams and pseudomemories following the conventional myth pattern.

Despite the seeming cumbrousness of these explanations, they came finally to supersede all others in my mind – largely because of the greater weakness of any rival theory. And a substantial number of eminent psychologists and anthropologists gradually agreed with me.

The more I reflected, the more convincing did my reasoning seem; till in the end I had a really effective bulwark against the visions and impressions which still assailed me. Suppose I did see strange things at night? These were only what I had heard and read of. Suppose I did have odd loathings and perspectives and pseudomemories? These, too, were only echoes of myths absorbed in my secondary state. Nothing that I might dream, nothing that I might feel, could be of any actual significance.

Fortified by this philosophy, I greatly improved in nervous equilibrium, even though the visions – rather than the abstract impressions – steadily became more frequent and more disturbingly detailed. In 1922 I felt able to undertake regular work again, and put my newly gained knowledge to practical use by accepting an instructorship in psychology at the university.

My old chair of political economy had long been adequately filled – besides which, methods of teaching economics had changed greatly since my heyday. My son was at this time just entering on the post-graduate studies leading to his present professorship, and we worked together a great deal.

4

I continued, however, to keep a careful record of the *outré* dreams which crowded upon me so thickly and vividly. Such a record, I argued, was of genuine value as a psychological document. The glimpses still seemed damnably like memories, though I fought off this impression with a goodly measure of success.

In writing, I treated the phantasmata as things seen; but at all other times I brushed them aside like any gossamer illusions of the night. I had never mentioned such matters in common conversation; though reports of them, filtering out as such things will, had aroused sundry rumors regarding my mental health. It is amusing to reflect that these rumors were confined wholly to laymen, without a single champion among physicians or psychologists.

Of my visions after 1914 I will here mention only a few, since fuller accounts and records are at the disposal of the serious student. It is evident that with time the curious inhibitions somewhat waned, for the scope of my visions vastly increased. They have never, though, become other than disjointed fragments seemingly without clear motivation.

Within the dreams I seemed gradually to acquire a greater and greater freedom of wandering. I floated through many strange buildings of stone, going from one to the other along mammoth underground passages which seemed to form the common avenues of transit. Sometimes I encountered those gigantic sealed trapdoors in the lowest level, around which such an aura of fear and forbiddenness clung.

I saw tremendous tessellated pools, and rooms of curious and inexplicable utensils of myriad sort. Then there were colossal caverns of intricate machinery whose outlines and purpose were wholly strange to me, and whose sound manifested itself only after many years of dreaming. I may here remark that sight and sound are the only senses I have ever exercised in the visionary world.

The real horror began in May 1915, when I first saw the living things. This was before my studies had taught me what, in view of the myths and case histories, to expect. As mental barriers wore down, I beheld great masses of thin vapor in various parts of the building and in the streets below.

These steadily grew more solid and distinct, till at last I could trace their monstrous outlines with uncomfortable ease. They seemed to be enormous, iridescent cones, about ten feet high and ten feet wide at the base, and made of some ridgy, scaly, semi-elastic matter. From their apexes projected four flexible, cylindrical members, each a foot thick, and of a ridgy substance like that of the cones themselves.

These members were sometimes contracted almost to nothing, and sometimes extended to any distance up to about ten feet. Terminating two of them were enormous claws or nippers. At the end of a third were four red, trumpetlike appendages. The fourth terminated in an irregular yellowish globe some two feet in diameter and having three great dark eyes ranged along its central circumference.

Surmounting this head were four slender gray stalks bearing flowerlike appendages, whilst from its nether side dangled eight greenish antennae or tentacles. The great base of the central cone was fringed with a rubbery, gray substance which moved the whole entity through expansion and contraction.

Their action, though harmless, horrified me even more than their appearance – for it is not wholesome to watch monstrous objects doing what one had known only human beings to do. These objects moved intelligently about the great rooms, getting books from the shelves and taking them to the great tables, or *vice versa*, and sometimes writing diligently with a peculiar rod gripped in the greenish head tentacles. The huge nippers were used in carrying books and in conversation – speech consisting of a kind of clicking.

The objects had no clothing, but wore satchels or knapsacks suspended from the top of the conical trunk. They commonly carried their head and its supporting member at the level of the cone top, though it was frequently raised or lowered.

The other three great members tended to rest downward at the sides of the cone, contracted to about five feet each, when not in use. From their rate of reading, writing, and operating their machines – those on the tables seemed somehow connected with thought – I concluded that their intelligence was enormously greater than man's.

Afterward I saw them everywhere; swarming in all the great chambers and corridors, tending monstrous machines in vaulted crypts, and racing along the vast roads in gigantic, boat-shaped cars. I ceased to be afraid of them, for they seemed to form supremely natural parts of their environment.

Individual difference amongst them began to be manifest, and a few appeared to be under some kind of restraint. These latter, though showing no physical variation, had a diversity of gestures and habits which marked them off not only from the majority, but very largely from one another.

They wrote a great deal in what seemed to my cloudy vision a vast variety of characters – never the typical curvilinear hieroglyphs of the majority. A few, I fancied, used our own familiar alphabet. Most of them worked much more slowly than the general mass of the entities.

All this time my own part in the dreams seemed to be that of a disembodied consciousness with a range of vision wider than the normal, floating freely about, yet confined to the ordinary avenues and speeds of travel. Not until August 1915, did any suggestions of bodily existence begin to harass me. I say harass, because the first phase was purely abstract, though infinitely terrible, association of my previously noted body-loathing with the scenes of my visions.

For a while my chief concern during dreams was to avoid looking down at myself, and I recall how grateful I was for the total absence of large mirrors in the strange rooms. I was mightily troubled by the fact that I always saw the great tables – whose height could not be under ten feet – from a level not below that of their surfaces.

And the the morbid temptation to look down at myself became greater and greater, till one night I could not resist it. At first my downward glance revealed nothing whatever. A moment later I perceived that this was because my head lay at the end of a flexible neck of enormous length. Retracting this neck and gazing down very sharply, I saw the scaly, rugose, iridescent bulk of a vast cone ten feet fall and ten feet wide at the base. That was when I waked half of Arkham with my screaming as I plunged madly up from the abyss of sleep.

Only after weeks of hideous repetition did I grow half reconciled to these visions of myself in monstrous form. In the dreams I now moved bodily among the other unknown entities, reading terrible books from the endless shelves and writing for hours at the great tables with a stylus managed by the green tentacles that hung down from my head.

Snatches of what I read and wrote would linger in my memory. There were horrible annals of other worlds and other universes, and of stirrings of formless life outside of all universes. There were records of strange orders of beings which had peopled the world in forgotten pasts, and frightful chronicles of grotesque-bodied intelligences which would people it millions of years after the death of the last human being.

I learned of chapters in human history whose existence no scholar of today has ever suspected. Most of these writings were in the language of the hieroglyphs; which I studied in a queer way with the aid of droning machines, and which was evidently an agglutinative speech with root systems utterly unlike any found in human languages.

Other volumes were in other unknown tongues learned in the same queer way. A very few were in languages I knew. Extremely clever pictures, both inserted in the records and forming separate collections, aided me immensely. And all the time I seemed to be setting down a history of my own age in English. On waking, I could recall only minute and meaningless scraps of the unknown tongues which my dream self had mastered, though whole phrases of the history stayed with me.

I learned – even before my waking self had studied the parallel cases or the old myths from which the dreams doubtless sprang – that the entities around me were of the world's greatest race, which had conquered time and had sent exploring minds into every age. I knew, too, that I had been snatched from my age, while another used my body in that age, and that a few of the other strange forms housed similarly captured minds. I seemed to talk, in some odd language of claw clickings, with exiled intellects from every corner of the solar system.

There was a mind from the planet we know as Venus, which would live incalculable epochs to come, and one from an outer moon of Jupiter six million years in the past. Of Earthly minds there were some from the winged, star-headed, half-vegetable race of paleogean Antartica; one from the reptile people of fabled Valusia; three from the furry prehuman Hyperborean worshippers of Tsathoggua; one from the wholly abominable Tcho-Tchos; two from the Arachnid denizens of Earth's last age; five from the hardy Coleopterous species immediately following mankind, to which the Great Race was someday to transfer its keenest minds *en masse* in the face of horrible peril; and several from different branches of humanity.

I talked with the mind of Yiang-Li, a philosopher from the cruel empire of Tsan-Chan, which is to come in 5,000 AD; with that of a general of the great-headed brown people who held South Africa in 50,000 BC; with that of a twelfth-century Florentine monk named Bartolomeo Corsi; with that of a king of Lomar who ruled that terrible polar land one hundred thousand years before the squat, yellow Inutos came from the west to engulf it.

I talked with the mind of Nug-Soth, a magician of the dark conquerors of 16,000 AD; with that of a Roman named Titus Cempronius Blaesus, who had been a quaestor in Sulla's time; with that of Khephnes, an Egyptian of the 14th Dynasty, who told me the hideous secret of Nyarlathotep; with that of a priest of Atlantis' middle kingdom; with that of a Suffolk gentleman of Cromwell's day, James Woodville; with that of a court astronomer of pre-Inca Peru; with that of the Australian physicist Nevel Kingston-Brown, who will die in 2,518 AD; with that of an archimage of vanished Yhe in the Pacific; with that of Theodotides, a Graeco-Bactrian official of 200 BC; with that of an aged Frenchman of Louis XIII's time named Pierre-Louis Montagny; with that of Crom-Ya, a Cimmerian chieftain of 15,000 BC; and with so many others that my brain cannot hold the shocking secrets and dizzying marvels I learned from them.

I awakened each morning in a fever, sometimes frantically trying to verify or discredit such information as fell within the range of modern human knowledge. Traditional facts took on new and doubtful aspects, and I marveled at the dream fancy which could invent such surprising addenda to history and science.

I shivered at the mysteries the past may conceal, and trembled at the menaces the future may bring forth. What was hinted in the speech of post-human entities of the fate of mankind produced such an effect on me that I will not set it down here.

After man there would be the mighty beetle civilization, the bodies of whose members the cream of the Great Race would seize when the monstrous doom overtook the elder world. Later, as the Earth's span closed, the transferred minds would again migrate through time and space – to another stopping place in the bodies of bulbous vegetable entities of Mercury. But there would be races after them, clinging pathetically to the cold planet and burrowing to its horror-filled core, before the utter end.

Meanwhile, in my dreams, I wrote endlessly in that history of my own age which I was preparing – half voluntarily and half through promises of increased library and travel opportunities – for the Great Race's central archives. The archives were in a colossal subterranean structure near the city's center, which I came to know well through frequent labors and consultations. Meant to last as long as the race, and to withstand the fiercest of Earth's convulsions, this titan repository surpassed all other buildings in the massive, mountainlike firmness of its construction.

The records, written or printed on great sheets of a curiously tenacious cellulose fabric were bound into books that opened from the top and were kept in individual cases of a strange, extremely light rustless metal of grayish hue, decorated with mathematical designs and bearing the title in the Great Race's curvilinear hieroglyphs.

These cases were stored in tiers of rectangular vaults – like closed, locked shelves – wrought of the same rustless metal and fastened by knobs with intricate turnings. My own history was assigned a specific place in the vaults of the lowest of vertebrate level – the section devoted to the cultures of mankind and of the furry and reptilian races immediately preceding it in Terrestrial dominance.

But none of the dreams ever gave me a full picture of daily life. All were the merest misty, disconnected fragments, and it is certain that these fragments were not unfolded in their rightful sequence. I have, for example, a very imperfect idea of my own living arrangements in the dream world; though I seem to have possessed a great stone room of my own. My restrictions as a prisoner gradually disappeared, so that some of the visions included vivid travels over the mighty jungle roads, sojourns in strange cities, and explorations of some of the vast, dark, windowless ruins from which the Great Race shrank in curious fear. There were also long sea voyages in enormous, many-decked boats of incredible swiftness, and trips over wild regions in closed, projectlike airships lifted and moved by electrical repulsion.

Beyond the wide, warm ocean were other cities of the Great Race, and on one far continent I saw the crude villages of the black-snouted, winged creatures who would evolve as a dominant stock after the Great Race had sent its foremost minds into the future to escape the creeping horror. Flatness and exuberant green life were always the keynote of the scene. Hills were low and sparse, and usually displayed signs of volcanic forces.

Of the animals I saw, I could write volumes. All were wild; for the Great Race's mechanical culture had long since done away with domestic beasts, while food was wholly vegetable or synthetic. Clumsy reptiles of great bulk floundered in steaming morasses, fluttered in the heavy air, or spouted in the seas and lakes; and among these I fancied I could vaguely recognize lesser, archaic prototypes of many forms – Dinosaurs, Pterodactyls, Itchthyosaurs, Labyrinthodonts, Plesiosaurs, and the like – made familiar through paleontology. Of birds or mammals there were none that I could discover.

The ground and swamps were constantly alive with snakes, lizards, and crocodiles, while insects buzzed incessantly among the lush vegetation. And far out at sea, unspied and unknown monsters spouted mountainous columns of foam into the vaporous sky. Once I was taken under the ocean in a gigantic submarine vessel with searchlights, and glimpsed some living horrors of awesome magnitude. I saw also the ruins of the incredible sunken cities, and the wealth of crinoid, brachiopod, coral, and ichthyic life which everywhere abounded.

Of the physiology, psychology, folkways, and detailed history of the Great Race my visions preserved but little information, and many of the scattered points I here set down were gleaned from my study of old legends and other cases rather than from my own dreaming.

For in time, of course, my reading and research caught up with and passed the dreams in many phases, so that certain dream fragments were explained in advance and formed verifications of what I had learned. This consolingly established my belief that similar reading and research, accomplished by my secondary self, had formed the source of the whole terrible fabric of pseudomemories.

The period of my dreams, apparently, was one somewhat less than 150,000,000 years ago, when the Paleozoic Age was giving place to the Mesozoic. The bodies occupied by the Great Race represented no surviving – or even scientifically known – line of Terrestrial evolution, but were of a peculiar, closely homogeneous, and highly specialized organic type inclining as much to the vegetable as to the animal state.

Cell action was of an unique sort almost precluding fatigue, and wholly eliminating the need of sleep. Nourishment, assimilated through the red trumpetlike appendages on one of the great flexible limbs, was always semifluid and in many aspects wholly unlike the food of existing animals.

The beings had but two of the senses which we recognize – sight and hearing, the latter accomplished through the flowerlike appendages on the gray stalks above their head. Of other and incomprehensible senses – not, however, well utilizable by alien captive minds inhabitating their bodies – they possessed many. Their three eyes were so situated as to give them a range of vision wider than the normal. Their blood was a sort of deep-greenish ichor of great thickness.

They had no sex, but reproduced through seeds or spores which clustered on their bases and could be developed only under water. Great, shallow tanks were used for the growth of their young – which were, however, reared only in small numbers on account of the longevity of individuals – four or five thousand years being the common life span.

Markedly defective individuals were quickly disposed of as soon as their defects were noticed. Disease and the approach of death were, in the absence of a sense of touch or of physical pain, recognized by purely visual symptoms.

The dead were incinerated with dignified ceremonies. Once in a while, as before mentioned, a keen mind would escape death by forward projection in time; but such cases were not numerous. When one did occur, the exiled mind from the future was treated with the utmost kindness till the dissolution of its unfamiliar tenement.

The Great Race seemed to form a single, loosely knit nation or league, with major institutions in common, though there were four definite divisions. The political and economic system of each unit was a sort of fascistic socialism, with major resources rationally distributed, and power delegated to a small governing board elected by the votes of all able to pass certain educational and psychological tests. Family organization was not over-stressed, though ties among persons of common descent were recognized, and the young were generally reared by their parents.

Resemblances to human attitudes and institutions were, of course, most marked in those fields where on the one hand highly abstract elements were concerned, or, where on the other hand there was a dominance of the basic, unspecialized urges common to all organic life. A few added likenesses came through conscious adoption as the Great Race probed the future and copied what it liked.

Industry, highly mechanized, demanded but little time from each citizen; and the abundant leisure was filled with intellectual and aesthetic activities of various sorts.

The sciences were carried to an unbelievable height of development, and art was a vital part of life, though at the period of my dreams it had passed its crest and meridian. Technology was enormously stimulated through the constant struggle to survive, and to keep in existence the physical fabric of great cities, imposed by the prodigious geologic upheavals of those primal days.

Crime was surprisingly scant, and was dealt with through highly efficient policing. Punishments ranged from privilege deprivation and imprisonment to death or major emotion wrenching, and were never administered without a careful study of the criminal's motivations.

Warfare, largely civil for the last few millennia though sometimes waged against reptilian and octopodic invaders, or against the winged, star-headed Old Ones who centered in the antarctic, was infrequent though infinitely devastating. An enormous army, using cameralike weapons which produced tremendous electrical effects, was kept on hand for purposes seldom mentioned, but obviously connected with the ceaseless fear of the dark, windowless elder ruins and of the great sealed trapdoors in the lowest subterranean levels.

This fear of the basalt ruins and trapdoors was largely a matter of unspoken suggestion – or, at most, of furtive quasi-whispers. Everything specific which bore on it was significantly absent from such books as were on the common shelves. It was the one subject lying altogether under a taboo among the Great Race, and seemed to be connected alike with horrible bygone struggles, and with that future peril which would someday force the race to send its keener minds ahead *en masse* in time.

Imperfect and fragmentary as were the other things presented by dreams and legends, this matter was still more bafflingly shrouded. The vague old myths avoided it – or perhaps all allusions had for some reason been excised. And in the dreams of myself and others, the hints were peculiarly few. Members of the Great Race never intentionally referred to the matter, and what could be gleaned came only from some of the more sharply observant captive minds.

According to these scraps of information, the basis of the fear was a horrible elder race of half polypous, utterly alien entities which had come through space from immeasurably distant universes and had dominated the Earth and three other solar planets about six hundred million years ago. They were only partly material – as we understand matter – and their type of consciousness and media of perception differed widely from those of Terrestrial organisms. For example, their senses did not include that of sight; their mental world being a strange, nonvisual pattern of impressions.

They were, however, sufficiently material to use implements of normal matter when in cosmic areas containing it; and they required housing – albeit of a peculiar kind. Though their senses could penetrate all material barriers, their substance could not; and certain forms of electrical energy could wholly destroy them. They had the power of aerial motion, despite the absence of wings or any other visible means of levitation. Their minds were of such texture that no exchange with them could be effected by the Great Race.

When these things had come to the Earth they had built mighty basalt cities of windowless towers, and had preyed horribly upon the beings they found. Thus it was when the minds of the Great Race sped across the void from that obscure, transgalactic world known in the disturbing and debatable Eltdown Shards as Yith.

The newcomers, with the instruments they created, had found it easy to subdue the predatory entities and drive them down to those caverns of inner earth which they had already joined to their abodes and begun to inhabit.

Then they had sealed the entrances and left them to their fate, afterward occupying most of their great cities and preserving certain important buildings for reasons connected more with superstition than with indifference, boldness, or scientific and historical zeal.

But as the aeons passed, there came vague, evil signs that the elder things were growing strong and numerous in the inner world. There were sporadic irruptions of a particularly hideous character in certain small and remote cities of the Great Race, and in some of the deserted elder cities which the Great Race had not peopled – places where the paths to the gulfs below had not been properly sealed or guarded.

After that greater precautions were taken, and many of the paths were closed forever – though a few were left with sealed trapdoors for strategic use in fighting the elder things if ever they broke forth in unexpected places.

The irruptions of the elder things must have been shocking beyond all description, since they had permanently colored the psychology of the Great Race. Such was the fixed mood of horror that the very aspect of the creatures was left unmentioned. At no time was I able to gain a clear hint of what they looked like.

There were veiled suggestions of a monstrous plasticity, and of temporary lapses of visibility, while other fragmentary whispers referred to their control and military use of great winds. Singular whistling noises, and colossal footprints made up of five circular toe marks, seemed also to be associated with them.

It was evident that the coming doom so desperately feared by the Great Race – the doom that was one day to send millions of keen minds across the chasm of time to strange bodies in the safer future – had to do with a final successful irruption of the elder beings.

Mental projections down the ages had clearly foretold such a horror, and the Great Race had resolved that none who could escape should face it. That the foray would be a matter of vengeance, rather than an attempt to reoccupy the outer world, they knew from the planet's later history – for their projections showed the coming and going of subsequent races untroubled by the monstrous entities.

Perhaps these entities had come to prefer Earth's inner abysses to the variable, storm-ravaged surface, since light meant nothing to them. Perhaps, too, they were slowly weakening with the aeons. Indeed, it was known that they would be quite dead in the time of the post-human beetle race which the fleeing minds would tenant.

Meanwhile, the Great Race maintained its cautious vigilance, with potent weapons ceaselessly ready despite the horrified banishing of the subject from common speech and visible records. And always the shadow of nameless fear hung about the sealed trapdoors and the dark, windowless elder towers.

5

That is the world of which my dreams brought me dim, scattered echoes every night. I cannot hope to give any true idea of the horror and dread contained in such echoes, for it was upon a wholly intangible quality – the sharp sense of pseudomemory – that such feelings mainly depended.

As I have said, my studies gradually gave me a defense against these feelings in the form of rational psychological explanations; and this saving influence was augmented by the subtle touch of accustomedness which comes with the passage of time. Yet in spite of everything the vague, creeping terror would return momentarily now and then. It did not, however, engulf me as it had before; and after 1922 I lived a very normal life of work and recreation.

In the course of years I began to feel that my experience – together with the kindred cases and the related folklore – ought to be definitely summarized and published for the benefit of serious students; hence, I prepared a series of articles briefly covering the whole ground and illustrated with crude sketches of some of the shapes, scenes, decorative motifs, and hieroglyphs remembered from the dreams.

These appeared at various times during 1928 and 1929 in the *Journal of the American Psychological Society*, but did not attract much attention. Meanwhile, I continued to record my dreams with the minutest care, even though the growing stack of reports attained vast proportions.

On July 10, 1934, there was forwarded to me by the Psychological Society the letter which opened the culminating and most horrible phase of the whole mad ordeal. It was postmarked Pilbarra, Western Australia, and bore the signature of one whom I found, upon inquiry, to be a mining engineer of considerable prominence. Enclosed were some very curious snapshots. I will reproduce the text in its entirety, and no reader can fail to understand how tremendous an effect it and the photographs had upon me.

I was, for a time, almost stunned and incredulous; for, although I had often thought that some basis of fact must underlie certain phases of the legends which had colored my dreams, I was none the less unprepared for anything like a tangible survival from a lost world remote beyond all imagination. Most devastating of all were the photographs – for here, in cold, incontrovertible realism, there stood out against a background of sand certain worn-down, water-ridged, storm-weathered blocks of stone whose slightly convex tops and slightly concave bottoms told their own story.

And when I studied them with a magnifying glass I could see all too plainly, amidst the betterings and pittings, the traces of those vast curvilinear designs and occasional hieroglyphs whose significance had become so hideous to me. But here is the letter, which speaks for itself:

49 Dampier St.,
Pilbarra, W. Australia,
May 18, 1934.

Prof. N.W. Peaslee,
c/o Am. Psychological Society,
30 E. 41st St.,
New York City, U.S.A.

MY DEAR SIR:

A recent conversation with Dr. E.M. Boyle of Perth, and some papers with your articles which he has just sent me, make it advisable for me to tell you about certain things I have seen in the Great Sandy Desert east of our gold field here. It would seem, in view of the peculiar legends about old cities with huge stonework and strange designs and hieroglyphs which you describe, that I have come upon something very important.

The blackfellows have always been full of talk about 'great stones with marks on them,' and seem to have a terrible fear of such things. They connect them in some way with their common racial legends about Buddai, the gigantic old man who lies asleep for ages underground with his head on his arm, and who will someday awake and eat up the world.

There are some very old and half forgotten tales of enormous underground huts of great stones, where passages lead down and down, and where horrible things have happened. The blackfellows claim that once some warriors, fleeing in battle, went down into one and never came back, but that frightful winds began to blow from the place soon after they went down. However, there usually isn't much in what these natives say.

But what I have to tell is more than this. Two years ago, when I was prospecting about five hundred miles east in the desert, I came on a lot of queer pieces of dressed stone perhaps $3 \times 2 \times 2$ feet in size, and weathered and pitted to the very limit.

At first I couldn't find any of the marks the blackfellows told about, but when I looked close enough I could make out some deeply carved lines in spite of the weathering. There were peculiar curves, just like what the blackfellows had tried to describe. I imagine there must have been thirty or forty blocks, some nearly buried in the sand, and all within a circle perhaps a quarter of a mile in diameter.

When I saw some, I looked around closely for more, and made a careful reckoning of the place with my instruments. I also took pictures of ten or twelve of the most typical blocks, and will enclose the prints for you to see.

I turned my information and pictures over to the government at Perth, but they have done nothing about them.

Then I met Dr. Boyle, who had read your articles in the *Journal of the American Psychological Society*, and, in time, happened to mention the stones. He was enormously interested and became quite excited when I showed him my snapshots, saying that the stones and the markings were just like those of the masonry you had dreamed about and seen described in legends.

He meant to write to you, but was delayed. Meanwhile, he sent me most of the magazines with your articles and I saw at once, from your drawings and descriptions, that my stones are certainly the kind you mean. You can appreciate this from the enclosed prints. Later on you will hear directly from Dr. Boyle.

Now I can understand how important all this will be to you. Without question we are faced with the remains of an unknown civilization older than any dreamed of before, and forming a basis for your legends.

As a mining engineer I have some knowledge of geology, and can tell you that these blocks are so ancient they frighten me. They are mostly sandstone and granite, though one is almost certainly made of a queer sort of cement or concrete.

They bear evidence of water action, as if this part of the world had been submerged and come up again after long ages – all since those blocks were made and used. It is a matter of hundreds of thousands of years – or Heaven knows how much more. I don't like to think about it.

In view of your previous diligent work in tracking down the legends and everything connected with them, I cannot doubt but that you will want to lead an expedition to the desert and make some archaeological excavations. Both Dr. Boyle and I are prepared to cooperate in such work if you – or organizations known to you – can furnish the funds.

I can get together a dozen miners for the heavy digging – the blackfellows would be of no use, for I've found that they have an almost maniacal fear of this particular spot. Boyle and I are saying nothing to others, for you very obviously ought to have precedence in any discoveries or credit.

The place can be reached from Pilbarra in about four days by motor tractor – which we'd need for our apparatus. It is somewhat west and south of Warburton's path of 1873, and one hundred miles southeast of Joanna Spring. We could float things up the De Grey River instead of starting from Pilbarra – but all that can be talked over later.

Roughly the stones lie at a point about 22° 3′ 14″ South Latitude, 125° 0′ 39″ East Longitude. The climate is tropical, and the desert conditions are trying.

I shall welcome further correspondence upon this subject, and am indeed keenly eager to assist in any plan you may devise. After studying your articles I am deeply impressed with the profound significance of the whole matter. Dr. Boyle will write later. When rapid communication is needed, a cable to Perth can be relayed by wireless.

Hoping profoundly for an early message,

Believe me,

Most faithfully yours,

ROBERT B.F. MACKENZIE

Of the immediate aftermath of this letter, much can be learned from the press. My good fortune in securing the backing of Miskatonic University was great, and both Mr. Mackenzie and Dr. Boyle proved invaluable in arranging matters at the Australian end. We were not too specific with the public about our objects, since the whole matter would have lent itself unpleasantly to sensational and jocose treatment by the cheaper newspapers. As a result, printed reports were sparing; but enough appeared to tell of our quest for reported Australian ruins and to chronicle our various preparatory steps.

Professor William Dyer of the college's geology department – leader of the Miskatonic Antarctic Expedition of 1930-31 – Ferdinand C. Ashley of the department of ancient history, and Tyler M. Freeborn of the department of anthropology – together with my son Wingate – accompanied me.

My correspondent, Mackenzie, came to Arkham early in 1935 and assisted in our final preparations. He proved to be a tremendously competent and affable man of about fifty, admirably well-read, and deeply familiar with all the conditions of Australian travel.

He had tractors waiting at Pilbarra, and we chartered a tramp steamer sufficiently small to get up the river to that point. We were prepared to excavate in the most careful and scientific fashion, sifting every particle of sand, and disturbing nothing which might seem to be in or near its original situation.

Sailing from Boston aboard the wheezy *Lexington* on March 28, 1935, we had a leisurely trip across the Atlantic and Mediterranean, through the Suez Canal, down the Red Sea, and across the Indian Ocean to our goal. I need not tell how the sight of the low, sandy West Australian coast depressed me, and how I detested the crude mining town and dreary gold fields where the tractors were given their last loads.

Dr. Boyle, who met us, proved to be elderly, pleasant and intelligent – and his knowledge of psychology led him into many long discussions with my son and me.

Discomfort and expectancy were oddly mingled in most of us when at length our party of eighteen rattled forth over the arid leagues of sand and rock. On Friday, May 31, we forded a branch of the De Grey and entered the realm of utter desolation. A certain positive terror grew on me as we advanced to this actual site of the elder world behind the legends – a terror, of course, abetted by the fact that my disturbing dreams and pseudomemories still beset me with unabated force.

It was on Monday, June 3, that we saw the first of the half-buried blocks. I cannot describe the emotions with which I actually touched – in objective reality – a fragment of Cyclopean masonry in every respect like the blocks in the walls of my dream buildings. There was a distinct trace of carving – and my hands trembled as I recognized part of a curvilinear decorative scheme made hellish to me through years of tormenting nightmare and baffling research.

A month of digging brought a total of some 1250 blocks in varying stages of wear and disintegration. Most of these were carven megaliths with curved tops and bottoms. A minority were smaller, flatter, plain-surfaced and square or octagonally cut – like those of the floors and pavements in my dreams – while a few were singularly massive and curved or slanted in such a manner as to suggest use in vaulting or groining, or as parts of arches or round window casings.

The deeper – and farther north and east – we dug, the more blocks we found – though we still failed to discover any trace of arrangement among them. Professor Dyer was appalled at the measureless age of fragments, and Freeborn found traces of symbols which fitted darkly into certain Papuan and Polynesian legends of infinite antiquity. The condition and scattering of the blocks told mutely of vertiginous cycles of time and geologic upheavals of cosmic savagery.

We had an airplane with us, and my son Wingate would often go up to different heights and scan the sand-and-rock waste for signs of dim, large-scale outlines – either difference of level or trails of scattered blocks. His results were virtually negative; for whenever he would one day think he had glimpsed some significant trend, he would on his next trip find the impression replaced by another equally insubstantial – a result of the shifting, wind-blown sand.

One or two of these ephemeral suggestions, affected me queerly and disagreeably. They seemed, after a fashion, to dovetail horribly with something I had dreamed or read, but which I could no longer remember. There was a terrible familiarity about them – which somehow made me look furtively and apprehensively over the abominable, sterile terrain.

Around the first week in July I developed an unaccountable set of mixed emotions about that general northeasterly region. There was horror, and there was curiosity – but more than that, there was a persistent and perplexing illusion of memory.

I tried all sorts of psychological expedients to get these notions out of my head, but met with no success. Sleeplessness also gained upon me, but I almost welcomed this because of the resultant shortening of my dream periods. I acquired the habit of taking long, lone walks in the desert late at night – usually to the north or northeast, whither the sum of my strange new impulses seemed subtly to pull me.

Sometimes, on these walks, I would stumble over nearly buried fragments of the ancient masonry. Though there were fewer visible blocks here than where we had started, I felt sure that there must be a vast abundance beneath the surface. The ground was less level than at our camp, and the prevailing high winds now and then piled the sand into fantastic temporary hillocks – exposing low traces of the elder stones while it covered other traces.

I was queerly anxious to have the excavations extend to this territory, yet at the same time dreaded what might be revealed. Obviously, I was getting into a rather bad state – all the worse because I could not account for it.

An indication of my poor nervous health can be gained from my response to an odd discovery which I made on one of my nocturnal rambles. It was on the evening of July 11, when the Moon flooded the mysterious hillocks with a curious pallor.

Wandering somewhat beyond my usual limits, I came upon a great stone which seemed to differ markedly from any we had yet encountered. It was almost wholly covered, but I stooped and cleared away the sand with my hands, later studying the object carefully and supplementing the Moonlight with my electric torch.

Unlike the other very large rocks, this one was perfectly square-cut, with no convex or concave surface. It seemed, too, to be of a dark basaltic substance, wholly dissimilar to the granite and sandstone and occasional concrete of the now familiar fragments.

Suddenly I rose, turned, and ran for the camp at top speed. It was a wholly unconscious and irrational flight, and only when I was close to my tent did I fully realize why I had run. Then it came to me. The queer dark stone was something which I had dreamed and read about, and which was linked with the uttermost horrors of the aeon-old legendry.

It was one of the blocks of that basaltic elder masonry which the fabled Great Race held in such fear – the tall, windowless ruins left by those brooding, half-material, alien things that festered in Earth's nether abysses and against whose windlike, invisible forces the trapdoors were sealed and the sleepless sentinels posted.

I remained awake all night, but by dawn realized how silly I had been to let the shadow of a myth upset me. Instead of being frightened, I should have had a discoverer's enthusiasm.

The next forenoon I told the others about my find, and Dyer, Freeborn, Boyle, my son, and I set out to view the anomalous block. Failure, however, confronted us. I had formed no clear idea of the stone's location and a late wind had wholly altered the hillocks of shifting sand.

6

I come now to the crucial and most difficult part of my narrative – all the more difficult because I cannot be quite certain of its reality. At times I feel uncomfortably sure that I was not dreaming or deluded; and it is this feeling – in view of the stupendous implications which the objective truth of my experience would raise – which impels me to make this record.

My son – a trained psychologist with the fullest and most sympathetic knowledge of my whole case – shall be the primary judge of what I have to tell.

First let me outline the externals of the matter, as those at the camp know them: On the night of July 17-18, after a windy day, I retired early but could not sleep. Rising shortly before eleven and afflicted as usual with that strange feeling regarding the northeastward terrain, I set out on one of my typical nocturnal walks, seeing and greeting only one person – an Australian miner named Tupper – as I left our precincts.

The Moon, slightly past full, shone from a clear sky, and drenched the ancient sands with a white, leprous radiance which seemed to me somehow infinitely evil. There was no longer any wind, nor did any return for nearly five hours, as amply attested by Tupper and others who saw me walking rapidly across the pallid, secret-guarding hillocks toward the northeast.

About 3:30 A.M., a violent wind blew up, waking everyone in camp and felling three of the tents. The sky was unclouded, and the desert still blazed with that leprous Moonlight. As the party saw to the tents my absence was noted, but in view of my previous walks this circumstance gave no one alarm. And yet, as many as three men – all Australians – seemed to feel something sinister in the air.

Mackenzie explained to Professor Freeborn that this was a fear picked up from blackfellow folklore – the natives having woven a curious fabric of malignant myth about the high winds which at long intervals sweep across the sands under a clear sky. Such winds, it is whispered, blow out of the great stone huts under the ground, where terrible things have happened – and are never felt except near places where the big marked stones are scattered. Close to four the gale subsided as suddenly as it had begun, leaving the sand hills in new and unfamiliar shapes.

It was just past five, with the bloated, fungoid Moon sinking in the west, when I staggered into camp – hatless, tattered, features scratched and ensanguined, and without my electric torch. Most of the men had returned to bed, but Professor Dyer was smoking a pipe in front of his tent. Seeing my winded and almost frenzied state, he called Dr. Boyle, and the two of them got me on my cot and made me comfortable. My son, roused by the stir, soon joined them, and they all tried to force me to lie still and attempt sleep.

But there was no sleep for me. My psychological state was very extraordinary – different from anything I had previously suffered. After a time I insisted upon talking – nervously and elaborately explaining my condition.

I told them I had become fatigued, and had lain down in the sand for a nap. There had, I said, been dreams even more frightful than usual – and when I was awakened by the sudden high wind my overwrought nerves had snapped. I had fled in panic, frequently falling over half-buried stones and thus gaining my tattered and bedraggled aspect. I must have slept long – hence the hours of my absence.

Of anything strange either seen or experienced I hinted absolutely nothing – exercising the greatest self-control in that respect. But I spoke of a change of mind regarding the whole work of the expedition, and urged a halt in all digging toward the northeast.

My reasoning was patently weak – for I mentioned a dearth of blocks, a wish not to offend the superstitious miners, a possible shortage of funds from the college, and other things either untrue or irrelevant. Naturally, no one paid the least attention to my new wishes – not even my son, whose concern for my health was very obvious.

The next day I was up and around the camp, but took no part in the excavations. I decided to return home as soon as possible for the sake of my nerves, and made my son promise to fly me in the plane to Perth – a thousand miles to the southwest – as soon as he had surveyed the region I wished let alone.

If, I reflected, the thing I had seen was still visible, I might decide to attempt a specific warning even at the cost of ridicule. It was just conceivable that the miners who knew the local folklore might back me up. Humoring me, my son made the survey that very afternoon, flying over all the terrain my walk could possibly have covered. Yet nothing of what I had found remained in sight.

It was the case of the anomalous basalt rock all over again – the shifting sand had wiped out every trace. For an instant I half regretted having lost a certain awesome object in my stark fright – but now I know that the loss was merciful. I can still believe my whole experience an illusion – especially if, as I devoutly hope, that hellish abyss is never found.

Wingate took me to Perth on July 20, though declining to abandon the expedition and return home. He stayed with me until the 25th, when the steamer for Liverpool sailed. Now, in the cabin of the *Empress*, I am pondering long and frantically upon the entire matter, and have decided that my son, at least, must be informed. It shall rest with him whether to diffuse the matter more widely.

In order to meet any eventuality I have prepared this summary of my background – as already known in a scattered way to others – and will now tell as briefly as possible what seemed to happen during my absence from the camp that hideous night.

Nerves on edge, and whipped into a kind of perverse eagerness by that inexplicable, dread-mingled, mnemonic urge toward the northeast, I plodded on beneath the evil, burning Moon. Here and there I saw, half shrouded by the sand, those primal Cyclopean blocks left from nameless and forgotten aeons.

The incalculable age and brooding horror of this monstrous waste began to oppress me as never before, and I could not keep from thinking of my maddening dreams, of the frightful legends which lay behind them, and of the present fears of natives and miners concerning the desert and its carven stones.

And yet I plodded on as if to some eldritch rendezvous – more and more assailed by bewildering fancies, compulsions, and pseudomemories. I thought of some of the possible contours of the lines of stones as seen by my son from the air, and wondered why they seemed at once so ominous and so familiar. Something was fumbling and rattling at the latch of my recollection, while another unknown force sought to keep the portal barred.

The night was windless, and the pallid sand curved upward and downward like frozen waves of the sea. I had no goal, but somehow plowed along as if with fate-bound assurance. My dreams welled up into the waking world, so that each sand-embedded megalith seemed part of endless rooms and corridors of prehuman masonry, carved and hieroglyphed with symbols that I knew too well from years of custom as a captive mind of the Great Race.

At moments I fancied I saw those omniscient, conical horrors moving about at their accustomed tasks, and I feared to look down lest I find myself one with them in aspect. Yet all the while I saw the sand-covered blocks as well as the rooms and corridors; evil, burning Moon as well as the lamps of luminous crystal; the endless desert as well as the waving ferns beyond the windows. I was awake and dreaming at the same time.

I do not know how long or how far – or indeed, in just what direction – I had walked when I first spied the heap of blocks bared by the day's wind. It was the largest group in one place that I had seen so far, and so sharply did it impress me that the visions of fabulous aeons faded suddenly away.

Again there were only the desert and the evil Moon and the shards of an unguessed past. I drew close and paused, and cast the added light of my electric torch over the tumbled pile. A hillock had blown away, leaving a low, irregularly round mass of megaliths and smaller fragments some forty feet across and from two to eight feet high.

From the very outset I realized that there was some utterly unprecedented quality about those stones. Not only was the mere number of them quite without parallel, but something in the sandworn traces of design arrested me as I scanned them under the mingled beams of the Moon and my torch.

Not that any one differed essentially from the earlier specimens we had found. It was something subtler than that. The impression did not come when I looked at one block alone, but only when I ran my eye over several almost simultaneously.

Then, at last, the truth dawned upon me. The curvilinear patterns on many of those blocks were closely related – parts of one vast decorative conception. For the first time in this aeon-shaken waste I had come upon a mass masonry in its old position – tumbled and fragmentary, it is true, but nonetheless existing in a very definite sense.

Mounting at a low place, I clambered laboriously over the heap; here and there clearing away the sand with my fingers, and constantly striving to interpret varieties of size, shape, and style and relationships of design.

After a while I could vaguely guess at the nature of the bygone structure, and at the designs which had once stretched over the vast surfaces of the primal masonry. The perfect identity of the whole with some of my dream glimpses appalled and unnerved me.

This was once a Cyclopean corridor thirty feet wide and thirty feet tall, paved with octagonal blocks and solidly vaulted overhead. There would have been rooms opening off on the right, and at the farther end one of those strange inclined planes would have wound down to still lower depths.

I started violently at these conceptions occurred to me, for there was more in them than the blocks themselves had supplied. How did I know that this level should have been far underground? How did I know that the plane leading upward should have been behind me? How did I know that the long subterrane passage to the Square of Pillars ought to lie on the left one level above me?

How did I know that the room of machines and the rightward-leading tunnel to the central archives ought to lie two levels below? How did I know that there would be one of those terrible metal-banded trapdoors at the very bottom four levels down? Bewildered by this intrusion from the dream world, I found myself shaking and bathed in a cold perspiration.

Then, as a last, intolerable touch, I felt that faint, insidious stream of cool air trickling upward from a depressed place near the center of the hugh heap. Instantly, as once before, my visions faded, and I saw again only the evil Moonlight, the brooding desert, and the spreading tumulus of paleogean masonry. Something real and tangible, yet fraught with infinite suggestions of nighted mystery, now confronted me. For that stream of air could argue but one thing – a hidden gulf of great size beneath the disordered blocks on the surface.

My first thought was of the sinister blackfellow legend of vast underground huts among the megaliths where horrors happened and great winds are born. Then thoughts of my own dreams came back, and I felt dim pseudomemories tugging at my mind. What manner of place lay below me? What primal, inconceivable source of old-age myth cycles and haunting nightmares might I be on the brink of uncovering?

It was only for a moment that I hesitated, for more than curiosity and scientific zeal was driving me on and working against my growing fear.

I seemed to move almost automatically, as if in the clutch of some compelling fate. Pocketing my torch, and struggling with a strength that I had not thought I possessed, I wrenched aside first one titan fragment of stone and then another, till there welled up a strong draft whose dampness contrasted oddly with the desert's dry air. A black rift began to yawn, and at length – when I had pushed away every fragment small enough to budge – the leprous Moonlight blazed on an aperture of ample width to admit me.

I drew out my torch and cast a brilliant beam into the opening. Below me was a chaos of tumbled masonry, sloping roughly down toward the north at an angle of about forty-five degrees, and evidently the result of some bygone collapse from above.

Between its surface and the ground level was a gulf of impenetrable blackness at whose upper edge were signs of gigantic, stress-heaved vaulting. At this point, it appeared, the desert's sands lay directly upon a floor of some titan structure of Earth's youth – how preserved through aeons of geologic convulsion I could not then and cannot now even attempt to guess.

In retrospect, the barest idea of a sudden lone descent into such a doubtful abyss – and at a time when one's whereabouts were unknown to any living soul – seems like the utter apex of insanity. Perhaps it was – yet that night I embarked without hesitancy upon such a descent.

Again there was manifest that lure and driving of fatality which had all along seemed to direct my course. With torch flashing intermittently to save the battery, I commenced a mad scramble down the sinister, Cyclopean incline below the opening – sometimes facing forward as I found good hand and foot holds, and at other times turning to face the heap of megaliths as I clung and fumbled more precariously.

In two directions beside me, distant walls of carven, crumbling masonry loomed dimly under the direct beams of my torch. Ahead, however, was darkness.

I kept no track of time during my downward scramble. So seething with baffling hints and images was my mind that all objective matters seemed withdrawn to incalculable distances. Physical sensation was dead, and even fear remained as a wraithlike, inactive gargoyle leering impotently at me.

Eventually I reached a level floor strewn with fallen blocks, shapeless fragments of stone, and sand and detritus of every kind. On either side – perhaps thirty feet apart – rose massive walls culminating in huge groinings. That they were carved I could just discern, but the nature of the carvings was beyond my perception.

What held me most was the vaulting overhead. The beam from my torch could not reach the roof, but the lower parts of monstrous arches stood out distinctly. And so perfect was their identity with what I had seen in countless dreams of the elder world, that I trembled actively for the first time.

Behind and high above, a faint luminous blur told of the distant Moonlight world outside. Some vague shred of caution warned me that I should not let it out of my sight, lest I have no guide for my return.

I now advanced toward the wall at my left, where the traces of carving were plainest. The littered floor was nearly as hard to traverse as the downward heap had been, but I managed to pick my difficult way.

At one place I heaved aside some blocks and kicked away the detritus to see what the pavement was like, and shuddered at the utter, fateful familiarity of the great octagonal stones whose buckled surface still held roughly together.

Reaching a convenient distance from the wall, I cast the searchlight slowly and carefully over its worn remnants of carving. Some bygone influx of water seemed to have acted on the sandstone surface, while there were curious incrustations which I could not explain.

In places the masonry was very loose and distorted, and I wondered how many aeons more this primal, hidden edifice could keep its remaining traces of form amidst Earth's heavings.

But it was the carvings themselves that excited me most. Despite their time-crumbled state, they were relatively easy to trace at close range; and the complete, intimate familiarity of every detail almost stunned my imagination. That the major attributes of this hoary masonry should be familiar, was not beyond normal credibility.

Powerfully impressing the weavers of certain myths, they had become embodied in a stream of cryptic lore which, somehow, coming to my notice during the amnesic period, had evoked vivid images in my subconscious mind.

But how could I explain the exact and minute fashion in which each line and spiral of these strange designs tallied with what I had dreamed for more than a score of years? What obscure, forgotten inconography could have reproduced each subtle shading and nuance which so persistently, exactly, and unvaryingly besieged my sleeping vision night after night?

For this was no chance of remote resemblance. Definitely and absolutely, the millennially ancient, aeon-hidden corridor in which I stood was the original of something I knew in sleep as intimately as I knew my own house in Crane Street, Arkham.

True, my dreams showed the place in its undecayed prime; but the identity was no less real on that account. I was wholly and horribly oriented.

The particular structure I was in was known to me. Known, too, was its place in that terrible elder city of dream. That I could visit unerringly any point in that structure or in that city which had escaped the changes and devastations of uncounted ages, I realized with hideous and instinctive certainty. What in Heaven's name could all this mean? How had I come to know what I knew? And what awful reality could lie behind those antique tales of the beings who had dwelt in this labyrinth of primordial stone?

Words can convey only fractionally the welter of dread and bewilderment which ate at my spirit. I knew this place. I knew what lay below me, and what had lain overhead before the myriad towering stories had fallen to dust and debris and the desert. No need now, I thought with a shudder, to keep that faint blur of Moonlight in view.

I was born betwixt a longing to flee and a feverish mixture of burning curiosity and driving fatality. What had happened to this monstrous megalopolis of old in the millions of years since the time of my dreams? Of the subterrene mazes which had underlain the city and linked all the titan towers, how much had still survived the writhings of Earth's crust?

Had I come upon a whole buried world of unholy archaism? Could I still find the house of the writing master, and the tower where S'gg'ha, the captive mind from the star-headed vegetable carnivores of Antarctica, had chiseled certain pictures on the blank spaces of the walls?

Would the passage at the second level down to the hall of the alien minds, be still unchoked and traversable? In that hall the captive mind of an incredible entity — a half-plastic denizen of the hollow interior of an unknown trans-Plutonian planet eighteen million years in the future — had kept a certain thing which it had modeled from clay.

I shut my eyes and put my hand to my head in a vain, pitiful effort to drive these insane dream fragments from my consciousness. Then, for the first time I felt acutely the coolness, motion, and dampness of the surrounding air. Shuddering, I realized that a vast chain of aeon-dead black gulfs must indeed be yawning somewhere beyond and below me.

I thought of the frightful chambers and corridors and inclines as I recalled them from my dreams. Would the way to the central archives still be open? Again that driving fatality tugged insistently at my brain as I recalled the awesome records that once lay cased in those rectangular vaults of rustless metal.

There, said the dreams and legends, had reposed the whole history, past and future, of the cosmic space-time continuum – written by captive minds from every orb and every age in the solar system. Madness, of course – but had I not now stumbled into a nighted world as mad as I?

I thought of the locked metal shelves, and of the curious knob twistings needed to open each one. My own came vividly into my consciousness. How often had I gone through that intricate routine of varied turns and pressures in the Terrestrial vertebrate section on the lowest level! Every detail was fresh and familiar.

If there was such a vault as I had dreamed of, I could open it in a moment. It was then that madness took me utterly. An instant later, and I was leaping and stumbling over the rocky debris toward the well-remembered incline to the depths below.

7

From that point forward my impressions are scarcely to be relied on – indeed, I still possess a final, desperate hope that they all form parts of some demonaic dream or illusion born of delirium. A fever raged in my brain, and everything came to me through a kind of haze – sometimes only intermittently.

The rays of my torch shot feebly into the engulfing blackness, bringing phantasmal flashes of hideously familiar walls and carvings, all blighted with the decay of ages. In one place a tremendous mass of vaulting had fallen, so that I had to clamber over a mighty mound of stones reaching almost to the ragged grotesquely stalactited roof.

It was all the ultimate apex of nightmare, made worse by the blasphemous tug of pseudomemory. One thing only was unfamiliar, and that was my own size in relation to the monstrous masonry. I felt oppressed by a sense of unwonted smallness, as if the sight of these towering walls from a mere human body was something wholly new and abnormal. Again and again I looked nervously down at myself, vaguely disturbed by the human form I possessed.

Onward through the blackness of the abyss I leaped, plunged and staggered – often falling and bruising myself, and once nearly shattering my torch. Every stone and corner of that demonaic gulf was known to me, and at many points I stopped to cast beams of light through choked and crumbling, yet familiar, archways.

Some rooms had totally collapsed; others were bare, or debris-filled. In a few I saw masses of metal – some fairly intact, some broken, and some crushed or battered – which I recognized as the colossal pedestals or tables of my dreams. What they could in truth have been, I dared not guess.

I found the downward incline and began its descent – though after a time halted by a gaping, ragged chasm whose narrowest point could not be much less than four feet across. Here the stonework had fallen through, revealing incalculable inky depths beneath.

I knew there were two more cellar levels in this titan edifice, and trembled with fresh panic as I recalled the metal-clamped trapdoor on the lowest one. There could be no guards now – for what had lurked beneath had long since done its hideous work and sunk into its long decline. By the time of the posthuman beetle race it would be quite dead. And yet, as I thought of the native legends, I trembled anew.

It cost me a terrible effort to vault that yawning chasm, since the littered floor prevented a running start – but madness drove me on. I chose a place close to the left-hand wall – where the rift was least wide and the landing spot reasonably clear of dangerous debris – and after one frantic moment reached the other side in safety.

At last, gaining the lower level, I stumbled on past the archway of the room of machines, within which were fantastic ruins of metal, half buried beneath fallen vaulting. Everything was where I knew it would be, and I climbed confidently over the heaps which barred the entrance of a vast transverse corridor. This, I realized, would take me under the city to the central archives.

Endless ages seemed to unroll as I stumbled, leaped, and crawled along that debris-cluttered corridor. Now and then I could make out carvings on the age-stained walls – some familiar, other seemingly added since the period of my dreams. Since this was a subterrene house-connecting highway, there were no archways save when the route led through the lower levels of various buildings.

At some of these intersections I turned aside long enough to look down well-remembered corridors and into well-remembered rooms. Twice only did I find any radical changes from what I had dreamed of – and in one of these cases I could trace the sealed-up outlines of the archway I remembered.

I shook violently, and felt a curious surge of retarding weakness as I steered a hurried and reluctant course through the crypt of one of those great windowless, ruined towers whose alien, basalt masonry bespoke a whispered and horrible origin.

This primal vault was round and fully two hundred feet across with nothing carved upon the dark-hued stonework. The floor was here free from anything save dust and sand, and I could see the apertures leading upward and downward. There were no stairs nor inclines – indeed, my dreams had pictured those elder towers as wholly untouched by the fabulous Great Race. Those who had built them had not needed stairs or inclines.

In the dreams, the downward aperture had been tightly sealed and nervously guarded. Now it lay open – black and yawning, and giving forth a current of cool, damp air. Of what limitless caverns of eternal light might brood below, I would not permit myself to think.

Later, clawing my way along a badly heaped section of the corridor, I reached a place where the roof had wholly caved in. The debris rose like a mountain, and I climbed up over it, passing through a vast, empty space where my torchlight could reveal neither walls nor vaulting. This, I reflected, must be the cellar of the house of the metal purveyors, fronting on the third square not far from the archives. What had happened to it I could not conjecture.

I found the corridor again beyond the mountain of detritus and stone, but after a short distance encountered a wholly choked place where the fallen vaulting almost touched the perilously sagging ceiling. How I managed to wrench and tear aside enough blocks to afford a passage, and how I dared disturb the tightly packed fragments when the least shift of equilibrium might have brought down all the tons of superincumbent masonry to crush me to nothingness, I do not know.

It was sheer madness that impelled and guided me – if, indeed, my whole underground adventure was not – as I hope – a hellish delusion or phase of dreaming. But I did make – or dream that I made – a passage that I could squirm through. As I wriggled over the mound of debris – my torch, switched continously on, thrust deeply in my mouth – I felt myself torn by the fantastic stalactites of the jagged floor above me.

I was now close to the great underground archival structure which seemed to form my goal. Sliding and clambering down the farther side of the barrier, and picking my way along the remaining stretch of corridor with handheld, intermittently flashing torch, I came at last to a low, circular crypt with arches – still in a marvellous state of preservation – opening off on every side.

The walls, or such parts of them as lay within reach of my torchlight, were densely hieroglyphed and chiseled with typical curvilinear symbols – some added since the period of my dreams.

This, I realized, was my fated destination, and I turned at once through a familiar archway on my left. That I could find a clear passage up and down the incline to all the surviving levels, I had, oddly, little doubt. This vast, Earth-projected pile, housing the annals of all the solar system, had been built with supernal skill and strength to last as long as the system itself.

Blocks of stupendous size poised with mathematical genius and bound with cements of incredible toughness had combined to form a mass as firm as the planet's rocky core. Here, after ages more prodigious than I could sanely grasp, its buried bulk stood in all its essential contours, the vast, dust-drifted floors scarce sprinkled with the litter elsewhere so dominant.

The relativity easy walking from this point onward went curiously to my head. All the frantic eagerness hitherto frustrated by obstacles now took itself out in a kind of febrile speed, and I literally raced along the low-roofed, monstrously well-remembered aisles beyond the archway.

I was past being astonished by the familiarity of what I saw. On every hand the great hieroglyphed metal shelf doors loomed monstrously; some yet in place, others sprung open, and still others bent and buckled under bygone geological stresses not quite strong enough to shatter the titan masonry.

Here and there a dust-covered heap beneath a gaping, empty shelf seemed to indicate where cases had been shaken down by the Earth tremors. On occasional pillars were great symbols and letters proclaiming classes and subclasses of volumes.

Once I paused before an open vault where I saw some of the accustomed metal cases still in position amidst the omnipresent gritty dust. Reaching up, I dislodged one of the thinner speciments with some difficulty, and rested it on the floor for inspection. It was titled in the prevailing curvilinear hieroglyphs, though something in the arrangement of the characters seemed subtly unusual.

The odd mechanism of the hooked fastener was perfectly well known to me, and I snapped up the still rustless and workable lid and drew out the book within. The latter, as expected, was some twenty by fifteen inches in area, and two inches thick; the thin metal covers opening at the top.

Its tough cellulose pages seemed unaffected by the myriad cycles of time they had lived through, and I studied the queerly pigmented, brush-drawn letters of the text — symbols unlike either the usual curved hieroglyphs or any alphabet known to human scholarship — with a haunting, half-aroused memory.

It came to me that this was the language used by a captive mind I had known slightly in my dreams — a mind from a large asteroid on which had survived much of the archaic life and lore of the primal planet whereof it formed a fragment. At the same time I recalled that this level of the archives was devoted to volumes dealing with the non-Terrestrial planets.

As I ceased poring over this incredible document, I saw that the light of my torch was beginning to fail, hence quickly inserted the extra battery I always had with me. Then, armed with the stronger radiance, I resumed my feverish racing through unending tangles of aisles and corridors — recognizing now and then some familiar shelf, and vaguely annoyed by the acoustic conditions which made my footfalls echo incongruously in these catacombs.

The very prints of my shoes behind me in the millennially untrodden dust made me shudder. Never before, if my mad dreams held anything of truth, had human feet pressed upon those immemorial pavements.

Of the particular goal of my insane racing, my conscious mind held no hint. There was, however, some force of evil potency pulling at my dazed will and buried recollection, so that I vaguely felt I was not running at random.

I came to a downward incline and followed it to profound depths. Floors flashed by me as I raced, but I did not pause to explore them. In my whirling brain there had begun to beat a certain rhythm which set my right hand twitching in unison. I wanted to unlock something, and felt that I knew all the intricate twists and pressures needed to do it. It would be like a modern safe with a combination lock.

Dream or not, I had once known and still knew. How any dream — or any scrap of unconsciously absorbed legend — could have taught me a detail so minute, so intricate, and so complex, I did not attempt to explain to myself. I was beyond all coherent thought. For was not this whole experience — this shocking familiarity with a set of unknown ruins, and this monstrously exact identity of everything before me with what only dreams and scraps of myth could have suggested – a horror beyond all reason?

Probably it was my basic conviction then – as it is now during my saner moments – that I was not awake at all, and that the entire buried city was a fragment of febrile hallucination.

Eventually, I reached the lowest level and struck off to the right of the incline. For some shadowy reason I tried to soften my steps, even though I lost speed thereby. There was a space I was afraid to cross on this last, deeply buried floor.

As I drew near it I recalled what thing in that space I feared. It was merely one of the metal-barred and closely guarded trapdoors. There would be no guards now, and on that account I trembled and tiptoed as I had done in passing through that black basalt vault where a similar trapdoor had yawned.

I felt a current of cold damp air, as I had felt there, and wished that my course led in another direction. Why I had to take the particular course I was taking, I did not know.

When I came to the space I saw that the trapdoor yawned wildly open. Ahead, the shelves began again, and I glimpsed on the floor before one of them a heap very thinly covered with dust, where a number of cases had recently fallen. At the same moment a fresh wave of panic clutched me, though for some time I could not discover why.

Heaps of fallen cases were not uncommon, for all through the aeons this lightless labyrinth had been racked by the heavings of Earth and had echoed at intervals to the deafening clatter of toppling objects. It was only when I was nearly across the space that I realized why I shook so violently.

Not the heap, but something about the dust of the level floor, was troubling me. In the light of my torch it seemed as if that dust were not as even as it ought to be – there were places where it looked thinner, as if it had been disturbed not many months before. I could not be sure, for even the apparently thinner places were dusty enough; yet certain suspicion of regularity in the fancied unevenness was highly disquieting.

When I brought the torchlight close to one of the queer places I did not like what I saw – for the illusion of regularity became very great. It was as if there were regular lines of composite impressions – impressions that went in threes, each slightly over a foot square, and consisting of five nearly circular three-inch prints, one in advance of the other four.

These possible lines of foot-square impression appeared to lead in two directions, as if something had gone somewhere and returned. They were, of course, very faint, and may have been illusions or accidents; but there was an element of dim, fumbling terror about the way I thought they ran. For at one end of them was the heap of cases which must have clattered down not long before, while at the other end was the ominous trapdoor with the cool, damp wind, yawning unguarded down to abysses past imagination.

8

That my strange sense of compulsion was deep and over-whelming is shown by its conquest of my fear. No rational motive could have drawn me on after that hideous suspicion of prints and the creeping dream memories it excited. Yet my right hand, even as it shook with fright, still twitched rhythmically in its eagerness to turn a lock it hoped to find. Before I knew it I was past the heap of lately fallen cases and running on tiptoe through aisles of utterly unbroken dust toward a point which I seemed to know morbidly, horribly well.

My mind was asking itself questions whose origin and relevancy I was only beginning to guess. Would the shelf be reachable by a human body? Could my human hand master all the aeon-remembered motions of the lock? Would the lock be undamaged and workable? And what would I do – what dare I do – with what – as I now commenced to realize – I both hoped and feared to find? Would it prove the awesome, brain-shattering truth of something past normal conception, or show only that I was dreaming?

The next I knew I had ceased my tiptoed racing and was standing still, staring at a row of maddeningly familiar hiero-glyphed shelves. They were in a state of almost perfect preservation, and only three of the doors in this vicinity had sprung open.

My feelings toward these shelves cannot be described – so utter and insistent was the sense of old acquaintance. I was looking high up a row near the top and wholly out of my reach, and wondering how I could climb to best advantage. An open door four rows from the bottom would help, and the locks of the closed doors formed possible holds for hands and feet. I would grip the torch between my teeth, as I had in other places where both hands were needed. Above all I must make no noise.

How to get down what I wished to remove would be difficult, but I could probably hook its movable fastener in my coat collar and carry it like a knapsack. Again I wondered whether the lock would be undamaged. That I could repeat each familiar motion I had not the least doubt. But I hoped the thing would not scrape or creak – and that my hand could work it properly.

Even as I thought these things I had taken the torch in my mouth and begun to climb. The projecting locks were poor supports; but as I had expected, the opened shelf helped greatly. I used both the swinging door and the edge of the aperture itself in my ascent, and managed to avoid any loud creaking.

Balanced on the upper edge of the door, and leaning far to my right, I could just reach the lock I sought. My fingers, half numb from climbing, were very clumsy at first; but I soon saw that they were anatomically adequate. And the memory rhythm was strong in them.

Out of unknown gulfs of time the intricate, secret motions had somehow reached my brain correctly in every detail – for after less than five minutes of trying there came a click whose familiarity was all the more startling because I had not consciously anticipated it. In another instant the metal door was slowly swinging open with only the faintest grating sound.

Dazedly I looked over the row of grayish case ends thus exposed, and felt a tremendous surge of some wholly inexplicable emotion. Just within reach of my right hand was a case whose curving hieroglyphs made me shake with a pang infinitely more complex than one of mere fright. Still shaking, I managed to dislodge it amidst a shower of gritty flakes, and ease it over toward myself without any violent noise.

Like the other case I had handled, it was slightly more than twenty by fifteen inches in size, with curved mathematical designs in low relief. In thickness it just exceeded three inches.

Crudely wedging it between myself and the surface I was climbing, I fumbled with the fastener and finally got the hook free. Lifting the cover, I shifted the heavy object to my back, and let the hook catch hold of my collar. Hands now free, I awkwardly clambered down to the dusty floor and prepared to inspect my prize.

Kneeling in the gritty dust, I swung the case around and rested it in front of me. My hands shook, and I dreaded to draw out the book within almost as much as I longed – and felt compelled – to do so. It had very gradually become clear to me what I ought to find, and this realization nearly paralyzed my faculties.

If the thing were there – and if I were not dreaming – the implications would be quite beyond the power of human spirit to bear. What tormented me most was my momentary inability to feel that my surroundings were a dream. The sense of reality was hideous – and again becomes so as I recall the scene.

At length I tremblingly pulled the book from its container and stared fascinatedly at the well-known hieroglyphs on the cover. It seemed to be in prime condition, and the curvilinear letters of the title held me in almost as hypnotized a state as if I could read them. Indeed, I cannot swear that I did not actually read them in some restraint and terrible access of abnormal memory.

I do not know how long it was before I dared to lift that thin metal cover. I temporized and made excuses to myself. I took the torch from my mouth and shut it off to save the battery. Then, in the dark, I collected my courage – finally lifting the cover without turning on the light. Last of all, I did indeed flash the torch upon the exposed page – steeling myself in advance to suppress any sound no matter what I should find.

I looked for an instant, then collapsed. Clenching my teeth, however, I kept silent. I sank wholly to the floor and put a hand to my forehead amidst the engulfing blackness. What I dreaded and expected was there. Either I was dreaming, or time and space had become a mockery.

I must be dreaming – but I would test the horror by carrying this thing back and showing it to my son if it were indeed a reality. My head swam frightfully, even though there were no visible objects in the unbroken gloom to swirl about me. Ideas and images of the starkest terror – excited by the vistas which my glimpse had opened up – began to throng in upon me and cloud my senses.

I thought of those possible prints in the dust, and trembled at the sound of my own breathing as I did so. Once again I flashed on the light and looked at the page as a serpent's victim may look at his destroyer's eyes and fangs.

Then, with clumsy fingers, in the dark, I closed the book, put it in its container, and snapped the lid and the curious, hooked fastener. This was what I must carry back to the outer world if it truly existed – if the whole abyss truly existed – if I, and the world itself, truly existed.

Just when I tottered to my feet and commenced my return I cannot be certain. It comes to me oddly – as a measure of my sense of separation from the normal world – that I did not even once look at my watch during those hideous hours underground.

Torch in hand, and with the ominous case under one arm, I eventually found myself tiptoeing in a kind of silent panic past the draft-giving abyss and those lurking suggestions of prints. I lessened my precautions as I climbed up the endless inclines, but could not shake off a shadow of apprehension which I had not felt on the downward journey.

I dreaded having to repass through that black basalt crypt that was older than the city itself, where cold drafts welled up from unguarded depths. I thought of that which the Great Race had feared, and of what might still be lurking – be it ever so weak and dying – down there. I thought of those five-circle prints and of what my dreams had told me of such prints – and of strange winds and whistling noises associated with them. And I thought of the tales of the modern blackfellows, wherein the horror of great winds and nameless ruins was dwelt upon.

I knew from a carven wall symbol the right floor to enter, and came at last – after passing that other book I had examined – to the great circular space with the branching archways. On my right, and at once recognizable, was the arch through which I had arrived. This I now entered, conscious that the rest of my course would be harder because of the tumbled state of the masonry outside the archive building. My new metal-cased burden weighed upon me, and I found it harder and harder to be quiet as I stumbled among debris and fragments of every sort.

Then I came to the ceiling-high mound of debris through which I had wrenched a scanty passage. My dread at wriggling through again was infinite, for my first passage had made some noise, and I now – after seeing those possible prints – dreaded sound above all things. The case, too, doubled the problem of traversing the narrow crevice.

But I clambered up the barrier as best I could, and pushed the case through the aperture ahead of me. Then, torch in mouth, I scrambled through myself - my back torn as before by stalactites.

As I tried to grasp the case again, it fell some distance ahead of me down the slope of the debris, making a disturbing clatter and arousing echoes which sent me into a cold perspiration. I lunged for it at once, and regained it without further noise – but a moment afterward the slipping of blocks under my feet raised a sudden and unprecedented din.

That din was my undoing. For, falsely or not, I thought I heard it answered in a terrible way from spaces far behind me. I thought I heard a shrill, whistling sound, like nothing else on Earth, and beyond any adequate verbal description. If so, what followed has a grim irony – save for the panic of this thing, the second thing might never have happened.

As it was, my frenzy was absolute and unrelieved. Taking my torch in my hand and clutching feebly at the case, I leaped and bounded wildly ahead with no idea in my brain beyond a mad desire to race out of these nightmare ruins to the waking world of desert and Moonlight which lay so far above.

I hardly knew it when I reached the mountain of debris which towered into the vast blackness beyond the caved-in roof, and bruised and cut myself repeatedly in scrambling up its steep slope of jagged blocks and fragments.

Then came the great disaster. Just as I blindly crossed the summit, unprepared for the sudden dip ahead, my feet slipped utterly and I found myself involved in a mangling avalanche of sliding masonry whose cannon-loud uproar split the black, cavern air in a deafening series of Earth-shaking reverberations.

I have no recollection of emerging from this chaos, but a momentary fragment of consciousness shows me as plunging and tripping and scrambling along the corridor amidst the clangor – case and torch still with me.

Then, just as I approached the primal basalt crypt I had so dreaded, utter madness came. For as the echoes of the avalanche died down, there became audible a repetition of that frightful alien whistling I thought I had heard before. This time there was no doubt about it – and what was worse, it came from a point not behind but *ahead of me*.

Probably I shrieked aloud then. I have a dim picture of myself as flying through the hellish basalt vault of the elder things, and hearing that damnable alien sound piping up from the open, unguarded door of limitless nether blackness. There was a wind, too – not merely a cool, damp draft, but a violent, purposeful blast belching savagely and frigidly from that abominable gulf whence the obscene whistling came.

There are memories of leaping and lurching over obstacles of every sort, with that torrent of wind and shrieking sound growing moment by moment, and seeming to curl and twist purposefully around me as it struck out wickedly from the spaces behind and beneath.

Though in my rear, that wind had the odd effect of hindering instead of aiding my progress; as if it acted like a noose or lasso thrown around me. Heedless of the noise I made, I clattered over a great barrier of blocks and was again in the structure that led to the surface.

I recall glimpsing the archway to the room of machines and almost crying out as I saw the incline leading down to where one of those blasphemous trapdoors must be yawning two levels below. But instead of crying out I muttered over and over to myself that this was all a dream from which I must soon awake. Perhaps I was in camp – perhaps I was at home in Arkham. As these hopes bolstered up my sanity I began to mount the incline to the higher level.

I knew, of course, that I had the four-foot cleft to recross, yet was too racked by other fears to realize the full horror until I came almost upon it. On my descent, the leap across had been easy – but could I clear the gap as readily when going uphill, and hampered by fright exhaustion, the weight of the metal case, and the anomalous backward tug of that demon wind? I thought of these things at the last moment, and thought also of the nameless entities which might be lurking in the black abysses below the chasm.

My wavering torch was growing feeble, but I could tell by some obscure memory when I neared the cleft. The chill blasts of wind and the nauseous whistling shrieks behind me were for the moment like a merciful opiate, dulling my imagination to the horror of the yawning gulf ahead. And then I became aware of the added blasts and whistling in front of me – tides of abomination surging up through the cleft itself from depths unimagined and unimaginable.

Now, indeed, the essence of pure nightmare was upon me. Sanity departed – and, ignoring everything except the animal impulse of flight, I merely struggled and plunged upward over the incline's debris as if no gulf had existed. Then I saw the chasm's edge, leaped frenziedly with every ounce of strength I possessed, and was instantly engulfed in a pandemoniac vortex of loathsome sound and utter, materially tangible blackness.

That is the end of my experience, so far as I can recall. Any further impressions belong wholly to the domain of phantasmago-ric delirium. Dream, madness, and memory merged wildly together in a series of fantastic, fragmentary delusions which can have no relation to anything real.

There was a hideous fall through incalculable leagues of viscous, sentient darkness, and a babel of noises utterly alien to all that we know of the Earth and its organic life. Dormant, rudimentary senses seemed to start into vitality within me, telling of pits and voids peopled by floating horrors and leading to sunless crags and oceans and teeming cities of windowless, basalt towers upon which no light ever shone.

Secrets of the primal planet and its immemorial aeons flashed through my brain without the aid of sight or sound, and there were known to me things which not even the wildest of former dreams had ever suggested. And all the while cold fingers of damp vapor clutched and picked at me, and that eldritch, damnable whistling shrieked fiendishly above all the alternations of babel and silence of whirlpools of darkness around.

Afterward there were visions of the Cyclopean city of my dreams – not in ruins, but just as I had dreamed of it. I was in my conical, nonhuman body again, and mingled with crowds of the Great Race and the captive minds who carried books up and down the lofty corridors and vast inclines.

Then, superimposed upon these pictures, were frightful, momentary flashes of a nonvisual consciousness involving desperate struggles, a writhing free from clutching tentacles of whistling wind, an insane, batlike flight through half-solid air, a feverish burrowing through the cyclone-whipped dark, and a wild stumbling and scrambling over fallen masonry.

Once there was a curious, intrusive flash of half sight – a faint, diffuse suspicion of bluish radiance far overhead. Then there came a dream of wind-pursued climbing and crawling – of wriggling into a blaze of sardonic moonlight through a jumble of debris which slid and collapsed after me amidst a morbid hurricane. It was the evil, monotonous beating of that maddening moonlight which at last told me of the return of what I had once known as the objective, waking world.

I was clawing prone through the sands of the Australian desert, and around me shrieked such a tumult of wind as I had never before known on our planet's surface. My clothing was in rags, and my whole body was a mass of bruises and scratches.

Full consciousness returned very slowly, and at no time could I tell just where delirious dream left off and true memory began. There had seemed to be a mound of titan blocks, an abyss beneath it, a monstrous revelation from the past, and a nightmare horror at the end – but how much of this was real?

My flashlight was gone, and likewise my metal case I may have discovered. Had there been such a case – or any abyss – or any mound? Raising my head, I looked behind me, and saw only the sterile, undulant sands of the desert.

The demon wind died down, and the bloated, fungoid moon sank reddeningly in the west. I lurched to my feet and began to stagger southwestward toward the camp. What in truth had happened to me? Had I merely collapsed in the desert and dragged a dream-racked body over miles of sand and buried blocks? If not, how could I bear to live any longer?

For, in this new doubt, all my faith in the myth-born unreality of my visions dissolved once more into the hellish older doubting. If that abyss was real, then the Great Race was real – and its blasphemous reachings and seizures in the cosmos-wide vortex of time were no myths or nightmares, but a terrible, soul-shattering actuality.

Had I, in full, hideous fact, been drawn back to a prehuman world of a hundred and fifty million years ago in those dark, baffling days of the amnesia? Had my present body been the vehicle of a frightful alien consciousness from paleogean gulfs of time?

Had I, as the captive mind of those shambling horrors, indeed known that accursed city of stone in its primordial heyday, and wriggled down those familiar corridors in the loathsome shape of my captor? Were those tormenting dreams of more than twenty years the offspring of stark, monstrous memories?

Had I once veritably talked with minds from reachless corners of time and space, learned the universe's secrets, past and to come, and written the annals of my own world for the metal cases of those titan archives? And were those others – those shocking elder things of the mad winds and demon pipings – in truth a lingering, lurking menace, waiting and slowly weakening in black abysses while varied shapes of life drag out their multimillennial courses on the planet's age-racked surface?

I do not know. If that abyss and what it held were real, there is no hope. Then, all too truly, there lies upon this world of man a mocking and incredible shadow out of time. But, mercifully, there is no proof that these things are other than fresh phases of my myth-born dreams. I did not bring back the metal case that would have been a proof, and so far those subterranean corridors have not been found.

If the laws of the universe are kind, they will never be found. But I must tell my son what I saw or thought I saw, and let him use his judgment as a psychologist in gauging the reality of my experience, and communicating this account to others.

I have said that the awful truth behind my tortured years of dreaming hinges absolutely upon the actuality of what I thought I saw in those Cyclopean, buried ruins. It has been hard for me, literally, to set down that crucial revelation, though no reader can have failed to guess it. Of course, it lay in that book within the metal case – the case which I pried out of its lair amidst the dust of a million centuries.

No eye had seen, no hand had touched that book since the advent of man to this planet. And yet, when I flashed my torch upon it in that frightful abyss, I saw that the queerly pigmented letters on the brittle, aeon-browned cellulose pages were not indeed any nameless hieroglyphs of Earth's youth. They were, instead, words of the English language in my own handwriting.

End of File: AB004P ... on Dir: 89

A MATTER OF FORM

Horace L. Gold

Gilroy's telephone bell jangled into his slumber. With his eyes grimly shut, the reporter flopped over on his side, ground his ear into the pillow and pulled the cover over his head. But the bell jarred on.

When he blinked his eyes open and saw rain streaking the windows, he gritted his teeth against the insistent clangor and yanked off the receiver. He swore into the transmitter – not a trite blasphemy, but a poetic opinion of the sort of man who woke tired reporters at four in the morning.

'Don't blame me,' his editor replied after a bitter silence. 'It was your idea. You wanted the case. They found another whatsit.'

Gilroy instantly snapped awake. 'They found another catatonic!'

'Over on York Avenue near Ninety-first Street, about an hour ago. He's down in the observation ward at Memorial.' The voice suddenly became low and confiding. 'Want to know what I think, Gilroy?'

'What?' Gilroy asked in an expectant whisper.

'I think you're nuts. These catatonics are nothing but tramps. They probably drank themselves into catatonia, whatever that is. After all, be reasonable, Gilroy; they're only worth a four-line clip.'

Gilroy was out of bed and getting dressed with one hand. 'Not this time, chief,' he said confidently. 'Sure, they're only tramps, but that's part of the story. Look . . . *hey*! You should have been off a couple of hours ago. What's holding you up?'

The editor sounded disgruntled. 'Old Man Talbot. He's seventy-six tomorrow. Had to pad out a blurb on his life.'

'What! Wasting time whitewashing that murderer, racketeer –'

'Take it easy, Gilroy,' the editor cautioned. 'He's got a half interest in the paper. he doesn't bother us often.'

'O.K. But he's still the city's one-man crime wave. Well, he'll kick off soon. Can you meet me at Memorial when you quit work?'

'In this weather?' The editor considered. 'I don't know. Your news instinct is tops, and if you think this is big – oh, hell . . . yes!'

Gilroy's triumphant grin soured when he ripped his foot through a sock. He hung up and explored empty drawers for another pair.

The street was cold and miserably deserted. The black snow was melting to grimy slush. Gilroy hunched into his coat and sloshed in the dirty sludge toward Greenwich Avenue. He was very tall and incredibly thin. With his head down into the driving swirl of rain, his coat flapping around his skinny shanks, his hands deep in his pockets, and his sharp elbows sticking away from his rangy body, he resembled an unhappy stork peering around for a fish.

But he was far from being unhappy. He was happy, in fact, as only a man with a pet theory can be when facts begin to fight on his side.

Splashing through the slush, he shivered when he thought of the catatonic who must have been lying in it for hours, unable to rise, until he was found and carried to the hospital. Poor devil! The first had been mistaken for a drunk, until the cop saw the bandage on his neck.

'Escaped post-brain-operatives,' the hospital had reported. It sounded reasonable, except for one thing – catatonics don't walk, crawl, feed themselves or perform *any* voluntary muscular action. Thus Gilroy had not been particularly surprised when no hospital or private surgeon claimed the escaped post-operatives.

A taxi driver hopefully sighted his agitated figure through the rain. Gilroy restrained an urge to hug the hackie for rescuing him from the bitter wind. He clambered in hastily.

'Nice night for a murder,' the driver observed conversationally.

'Are you hinting that business is bad?'

'I mean the weather's lousy.'

'Well, damned if it isn't!' Gilroy exclaimed sarcastically. 'Don't let it slow you down, though. I'm in a hurry. Memorial Hospital, quick!'

The driver looked concerned. He whipped the car out into the middle of the street and scooted through a light that was just an instant too slow.

Three catatonics in a month! Gilroy shook his head. It was a real puzzler. They couldn't have escaped. In the first place, if they had, they would have been claimed; and in the second place, it was physically impossible. And how did they acquire those neat surgical wounds on the backs of their necks, closed with two professional stitches and covered with a professional bandage? New wounds, too!

Gilroy attached special significance to the fact that they were very poorly dressed and suffered from slight malnutrition. But what was the significance? He shrugged. It was an instinctive hunch.

The taxi suddenly swerved to the curb and screeched to a stop. He thrust a bill through the window and got out. The night burst abruptly. Rain smashed against him in a roaring tide. He battered upwind to the hospital entrance.

He was soaked, breathless, half-repentant for his whim in attaching importance to three impoverished catatonics. He gingerly put his hand in his clammy coat and brought out a sodden identification card.

The girl at the reception desk glanced at it. 'Oh, a news-paperman! Did a big story come in tonight?'

'Nothing much,' he said casually. 'Some poor tramp found on York and Ninety-first. Is he up in the screwball ward?'

She scanned the register and nodded. 'Is he a friend of yours?'

'My grandson.' As he moved off, both flinched at the sound of water squishing in his shoes at each step. 'I must have stepped in a puddle.'

When he turned around in the elevator, she was shaking her head and pursing her lips maternally. Then the ground floor dropped away.

He went through the white corridor unhesitantly. Low, horri-ble moans came from the main ward. He heard them with academic detachment. Near the examination room, the sound of the rising elevator stopped him. He paused, turning to see who it was.

The editor stepped out, chilled, wet and disgusted. Gilroy reached down and caught the smaller man's arm, guiding him silently through the door and into the examination room. The editor sighed resignedly.

The resident physician glanced up briefly when they unobtru-sively took places in the ring of interns about the bed. Without effort, Gilroy peered over the heads before him, inspecting the catatonic with clinical absorption.

The catatonic had been stripped of his wet clothing, toweled, and rubbed with alcohol. Passive, every muscle absolutely relaxed, his eyes were loosely closed, and his mouth hung open in idiotic slackness. The dark line of removed surgical plaster showed on his neck. Gilroy strained to one side. The hair had been clipped. He saw part of a stitch.

'Catatonic, doc?' he asked quietly.

'Who are you?' the physician snapped.

'Gilroy . . . *Morning Post.*'

The doctor gazed back at the man on the bed. 'Its catatonia, all right. No trace of alcohol or inhibiting drugs. Slight malnutrition.'

Gilroy elbowed politely through the ring of interns. 'Insulin shock doesn't work, eh? No reason why it should.'

'Why shouldn't it?' the doctor demanded, startled. 'It always works in catatonia . . . at least, temporarily.'

'But it didn't in this case, did it?' Gilroy insisted brusquely.

The doctor lowered his voice defeatedly. 'No.'

'What's this all about?' the editor asked in irritation. 'What's catatonia, anyhow? Paralysis, or what?'

'It's the last stage of schizophrenia, or what used to be called dementia praecox,' the physician said. 'The mind revolts against responsibility and searches for a period in its existence when it was not troubled. It goes back to childhood and finds that there are childish cares; goes further and comes up against infantile worries; and finally ends up in a prenatal mental state.'

'But it's a gradual degeneration,' Gilroy stated. 'Long before the complete mental decay, the victim is detected and put in an asylum. He goes through imbecility, idiocy, and after years of slow degeneration, winds up refusing to use his muscles or brain.'

The editor looked baffled. 'Why should insulin shock pull him out?'

'It shouldn't!' Gilroy rapped out.

'It should!' the physician replied angrily. 'Catatonia is negative revolt. Insulin drops the sugar content of the blood to the point of shock. The sudden hunger jolts the catatonic out of his passivity.'

'That's right,' Gilroy said incisively. 'But this isn't catatonia! It's mighty close to it, but you never heard of a catatonic who didn't refuse to carry on voluntary muscular action. There's no salivary retention! My guess is that it's paralysis.'

'Caused by what?' the doctor asked bitingly.

'That's for you to say. I'm not a physician. How about the wound at the base of the skull?'

'Nonsense! It doesn't come within a quarter inch of the motor nerve. It's *cerias flexibilitas* ... waxy flexibility.' He raised the victim's arm and let go. It sagged slowly. 'If it were general paralysis, it would have affected the brain. He'd have been dead.'

Gilroy lifted his bony shoulders and lowered them. 'You're on the wrong track, doc,' he said quietly. 'The wound has a lot to do with his condition, and catatonia can't be duplicated by surgery. Lesions can cause it, but the degeneration would still be gradual. And catatonics can't walk or crawl away. He was deliberately abandoned, same as the others.'

'Looks like you're right, Gilroy,' the editor conceded. 'There's something fishy here. All three of them had the same wounds?'

'In exactly the same place, at the base of the skull and to the left of the spinal column. Did you ever see anything so helpless? Imagine him escaping from a hospital, or even a private surgeon!'

The physician dismissed the interns and gathered up his instruments preparatory to harried flight. 'I don't see the motive. All three of them were undernourished, poorly clad; they must have been living in substandard conditions. Who would want to harm them?'

Gilroy bounded in front of the doctor, barring his way. 'But it doesn't have to be revenge! It could be experimentation!'

'To prove what?'

Gilroy looked at him quizzically. 'You don't know?'

'How should I?'

The reporter clapped his drenched hat on backward and darted to the door. 'Come on, chief. We'll ask Moss for a theory.'

'You won't find Dr. Moss here,' the physician said. 'He's off at night, and tomorrow, I think, he's leaving the hospital.'

Gilroy stopped abruptly. 'Moss ... leaving the hospital!' he repeated in astonishment. 'Did you hear that, chief? He's a dictator, a slave driver and a louse. But he's probably the greatest surgeon in America. Look at that. Stories breaking all around you, and you're whitewashing Old Man Talbot's murderous life!' His coat bellied out in the wash of his swift, gaunt stride. 'Three catatonics found lying on the street in a month. That never happened before. They can't walk or crawl, and they have mysterious wounds at the base of their skulls. Now the greatest surgeon in the country gets kicked out of the hospital he built up to first place. And what do you do? You sit in the office and wire stories about what a swell guy Talbot is underneath his slimy exterior!'

The resident physician was relieved to hear the last of that relentlessly incisive, logical voice trail down the corridor. But he gazed down at the catatonic before leaving the room.

He felt less certain that it was catatonia. He found himself quoting the editor's remark – there definitely *was* something fishy there!

But what was the motive in operating on three obviously destitute men and abandoning them; and how had the operation caused a state resembling catatonia?

In a sense, he felt sorry that Dr. Moss was going to be discharged. The cold, slave-driving dictator might have given a good theory. That was the physician's scientific conscience speaking. Inside, he really felt that anything was worth getting away from that silkily mocking voice and the delicately sneering mouth.

At Fifty-fifth Street, Wood came to the last Sixth Avenue employment office. With very little hope, he read the crudely chalked signs. It was an industrial employment agency. Wood had never been inside a factory. The only job he could fill was that of apprentice upholsterer, ten dollars a week; but he was thirty-two years old and the agency would require five dollars immediate payment.

He turned away dejectedly, fingering the three dimes in his pocket. Three dimes – the smallest, thinnest American coins . . .

'Anything up there, Mac?'

'Not for me,' Wood replied wearily. He scarcely glanced at the man.

He took a last glance at his newspaper before dropping it to the sidewalk. That was the last paper he'd buy, he resolved; with his miserable appearance he couldn't answer advertisements. But his mind clung obstinately to Gilroy's article. Gilroy had described the horror of catatonia. A notion born of defeat made it strangely attractive to Wood. At least, the catatonics were fed and housed. He wondered if catatonia could be simulated . . .

But the other had been scrutinizing Wood. 'College man, ain't you?' he asked as Wood trudged away from the employment office.

Wood paused and ran his hand over his stubbled face. Dirty cuffs stood away from his fringing sleeves. He knew that his hair curled long behind his ears. 'Does it still show?' he asked bitterly.

'You bet. You can spot a college man a mile away.'

Wood's mouth twisted. 'Glad to hear that. It must be an inner light shining through the rags.'

'You're a sucker coming down here with an education. Down here they want poor slobs who don't known any better . . . guys like me, with big muscles and small brains.'

Wood looked up at him sharply. He was too well-dressed and alert to have prowled the agencies for any length of time. He might have just lost his job; perhaps he was looking for company. But Wood had met his kind before. He had the hard eyes of the wolf who preyed on the jobless.

'Listen,' Wood said coldly, 'I haven't a thing you'd want. I'm down to thirty cents. Excuse me while I sneak my books and toothbrush out of my room before the super snatches them.'

The other did not recoil or protest virtuously. 'I ain't blind,' he said quietly. 'I can see you're down and out.'

'Then what do you want?' Wood snapped ill-temperedly. 'Don't tell me you want a threadbare but filthy college man for company —'

His unwelcome friend made a gesture of annoyance. 'Cut out the mad-dog act. I was turned down on a job today because I ain't a college man. Seventy-five a month, room and board doctor's assistant. But I got the air because I ain't a grad.'

'You've got my sympathy,' Wood said, turning away.

The other caught up with him. 'You're a college grad. Do you want the job? It'll cost you your first week's pay . . . my cut, see?'

'I don't know anything about medicine. I was a code expert in a stockbroker's office before people stopped having enough money for investments. Want any codes deciphered? That's the best I can do.'

He grew irritated when the stranger stubbornly matched his dejected shuffle.

'You don't have to know anything about medicine. Long as you got a degree, a few muscles and a brain, that's all the doc wants.'

Wood stopped short and wheeled.

'Is that on the level?'

'Sure. But I don't want to take a deadhead up there and get turned down. I got to ask you the questions they asked me.'

In face of a prospective job Wood's caution ebbed away. He felt the three dimes in his pocket. They were exceedingly slim and unprotective. They meant two hamburgers and two cups of coffee, or a bed in some filthy hotel dormitory. Two thin meals and sleeping in the wet March air; or shelter for a night and no food . . .

'Shoot!' he said deliberately.

'Any relatives?'

'Some fifth cousins in Maine.'

'Friends?'

'None who would recognize me now.' He searched the stranger's face. 'What's this all about? What have my friends or relatives got to do –'

'Nothing,' the other said hastily. 'Only you'll have to travel a little. The doc wouldn't want a wife dragging along, or have you break up your work by writing letters. See?'

Wood didn't see. It was a singularly lame explanation; but he was concentrating on the seventy-five a month, room and *board* – food.

'Who's the doctor?' he asked.

'I ain't dumb.' The other smiled humorlessly. 'You'll go there with me and get the doc to hand over my cut.'

Wood crossed to Eighth Avenue with the stranger. Sitting in the subway, he kept his eyes from meeting casual, disinterested glances. He pulled his feet out of the aisle, against the base of the seat, to hide the loose, flapping right sole. His hands were cracked and scaly, with tenacious dirt deeply embedded. Bitter, defeated, with the appearance of a mature waif. What a chance there was of being hired! But at least the stranger had risked a nickel on his fare.

Wood followed him out at 103rd Street and Central Park West; they climbed the hill to Manhattan Avenue and headed several blocks downtown. The other ran briskly up the stoop of an old house. Wood climbed the steps more slowly. He checked an urge to run away, but he experienced in advance the sinking feeling of being turned away from a job. If he could only have his hair cut, his suit pressed, his shoes mended! But what was the use of thinking about that? It would cost a couple of dollars. And nothing could be done about his ragged hems.

'Come on!' the stranger called.

Wood tensed his back and stood looking at the house while the other brusquely rang the doorbell. There were three floors and no card above the bell, no doctor's white glass sign in the darkly curtained windows. From the outside it could have been a neglected boardinghouse.

The door opened. A man of his own age, about middle height, but considerably overweight, blocked the entrance. He wore a white laboratory apron. Incongruous in his pale, soft face, his nimble eyes were harsh.

'Back again?' he asked impatiently.

'It's not for me this time,' Wood's persistent friend said. 'I got a college grad.'

Wood drew back in humiliation when the fat man's keen glance passed over his wrinkled, frayed suit and stopped distastefully at the long hair blowing wildly around his hungry, unshaven face. There – he could see it coming: 'Can't use him.'

But the fat man pushed back a beautiful collie with his leg and held the door wide. Astounded, Wood followed his acquaintance into the narrow hall. To give an impression of friendliness, he stooped and ruffled the dog's ears. The fat man led them into a bare front room.

'What's your name?' he asked indifferently.

Wood's answer stuck in his throat. He coughed to clear it. 'Wood,' he replied.

'Any relatives?' Wood shook his head.

'Friends?'

'Not any more.'

'What kind of degree?'

'Science, Columbia, 1925.'

The fat man's expression did not change. He reached into his left pocket and brought out a wallet. 'What arrangement did you make with this man?'

'He's to get my first week's salary.' Silently, Wood observed the transfer of several green bills; he looked at them hungrily, pathetically. 'May I wash up and shave, doctor?' he asked.

'I'm not the doctor,' the fat man answered. 'My name is Clarence, without a mister in front of it.' He turned swiftly to the sharp stranger. 'What are you hanging around for?'

Wood's friend backed to the door. 'Well, so long,' he said. 'Good break for both of us, eh, Wood?'

Wood smiled and nodded happily. The trace of irony in the stranger's hard voice escaped him entirely.

'I'll take you upstairs to your room,' Clarence said when Wood's business partner had left. 'I think there's a razor there.'

They went out into the dark hall, the collie close behind them. An unshaded lightbulb hung on a single wire above a gate-leg table. On the wall behind the table an oval, gilt mirror gave back Wood's hairy, unkempt image. A worn carpet covered the floor to a door cutting off the rear of the house, and narrow stairs climbed in a swift spiral to the next story. It was cheerless and neglected, but Wood's conception of luxury had become less exacting.

'Wait here while I make a telephone call,' Clarence said.

He closed the door behind him in a room opposite the stairs. Wood fondled the friendly collie. Through the panel he heard Clarence's voice, natural and unlowered.

'Hello, Moss? . . . Pinero brought back a man. All his answers are all right . . . Columbia, 1925 . . . Not a cent, judging from his appearance . . . Call Talbot? For when? . . . O.K. . . . You'll get back as soon as you get through with the board? . . . O.K. . . . Well, what's the difference? You got all you wanted from them, anyhow.'

Wood heard the receiver's click as it was replaced and taken off again. Moss? That was the head of Memorial Hospital – the great surgeon. But the article about the catatonics hinted something about his removal from the hospital.

'Hello, Talbot?' Clarence was saying. 'Come around at noon tomorrow. Moss says everything'll be ready then . . . O.K., don't get excited. This is positively the last one! . . . Don't worry. Nothing can go wrong.'

Talbot's name sounded familiar to Wood. It might have been the Talbot that the *Morning Post* had written about – the seventy-six-year-old philanthropist. He probably wanted Moss to operate on him. Well, it was none of his business.

When Clarence joined him in the dark hall, Wood thought only of his seventy-five a month, room and board; but more than that, he had a job! A few weeks of decent food and a chance to get some new clothes, and he would soon get rid of his defeatism.

He even forgot his wonder at the lack of shingles and waiting-room signs that a doctor's house usually had. He could only think of his neat room on the third floor, overlooking a bright back yard. And a shave . . .

Dr. Moss replaced the telephone with calm deliberation. Striding through the white hospital corridor to the elevator, he was conscious of curious stares. His pink, scrupulously shaven, clean-scrubbed face gave no answer to their questioning eyes. In the elevator he stood with his hands thrust casually into his pockets. The operator did not dare to look at him or speak.

Moss gathered his hat and coat. The space around the reception desk seemed more crowded than usual, with men who had the penetrating look of reporters. He walked swiftly past.

A tall, astoundingly thin man, his stare fixed predatorily on Moss, headed the wedge of reporters that swarmed after Moss.

'You can't leave without a statement to the press, doc!' he said.

'I find it very easy to do,' Moss taunted without stopping.

He stood on the curb with his back turned coldly on the reporters and unhurriedly flagged a taxi.

'Well, at least you can tell us whether you're still director of the hospital,' the tall reporter said.

'Ask the board of trustees.'

'Then how about a theory on the catatonics?'

'Ask the catatonics.' The cab pulled up opposite Moss. Deliberately he opened the door and stepped in. As he rode away, he heard the thin man exclaim: 'What a cold, clammy reptile!'

He did not look back to enjoy their discomfiture. In spite of his calm demeanor, he did not feel too easy himself. The man on the *Morning Post*, Gilroy or whatever his name was, had written a sensational article on the abandoned catatonics, and even went so far as to claim they were not catatonics. He had had all he could do to keep from being involved in the conflicting riot of theory. Talbot owned a large interest in the paper. He must be told to strangle the articles, although by now all the papers were taking up the cry.

It was a clever piece of work, detecting the fact that the victims weren't suffering from catatonia at all. But the *Morning Post* reporter had cut himself a man-size job in trying to understand how three men with general paralysis could be abandoned without a trace of where they had come from, and what connection the incisions had on their condition. Only recently had Moss himself solved it.

The cab crossed to Seventh Avenue and headed uptown.

The trace of his parting smile of mockery vanished. His mobile mouth whitened, tight-lipped and grim. Where was he to get money from now? He had milked the hospital funds to a frightening debt, and it had not been enough. Like a bottomless maw, his researches could drain a dozen funds.

If he could convince Talbot, prove to him that his failures had not really been failures, that this time he would not slip up . . .

But Talbot was a tough nut to crack. Not a cent was coming out of his miserly pocket until Moss completely convinced him that he was past the experimental stage. This time there would be no failure!

At Moss's street, the cab stopped and the surgeon sprang out lightly. He ran up the steps confidently, looking neither to the left nor to the right, though it was a fine day with a warm yellow sun, and between the two lines of old houses Central Park could be seen budding greenly.

He opened the door and strode almost impatiently into the narrow, dark hall, ignoring the friendly collie that bounded out to greet him.

'Clarence!' he called out. 'Get your new assistant down. I'm not even going to wait for a meal.' He threw off his hat, coat and jacket, hanging them up carelessly on a hook near the mirror.

'Hey, Wood!' Clarence shouted up the stairs. 'Are you finished?'

They heard a light, eager step race down from the third floor.

'Clarence, my boy,' Moss said in a low, impetuous voice, 'I know what the trouble was. We didn't really fail at all. I'll show you . . . we'll follow exactly the same technique!'

'Then why didn't it seem to work before?'

Wood's feet came into view between the rails on the second floor. 'You'll understand as soon as it's finished,' Moss whispered hastily, and then Wood joined them.

Even the short time that Wood had been employed was enough to transform him. He had lost the defeatist feeling of being useless human flotsam. He was shaved and washed, but that did not account for his kindled eyes.

'Wood . . . Dr. Moss,' Clarence said perfunctorily.

Wood choked out an incoherent speech that was meant to inform them that he was happy, though he didn't know anything about medicine.

'You don't have to,' Moss replied silkily. 'We'll teach you more about medicine than most surgeons learn in a lifetime.'

It could have meant anything or nothing. Wood made no attempt to understand the meaning of the words. It was the hint of withdrawn savagery in the low voice that puzzled him. It seemed a very peculiar way of talking to a man who had been hired to move apparatus and do nothing but the most ordinary routine work.

He followed them silently into a shining, tiled operating room. He felt less comfortable than he had in his room; but when he dismissed Moss's tones as a characteristically sarcastic manner of speech, hinting more than it contained in reality, his eagerness returned. While Moss scrubbed his hands and arms in a deep basin, Wood gazed around.

In the center of the room an operating table stood, with a clean sheet clamped unwrinkled over it. Above the table five shadowless light globes branched. It was a compact room. Even Wood saw how close everything lay to the doctor's hand – trays of tampons, swabs and clamps, and a sterilizing instrument chest that gave off puffs of steam.

'We do a lot of surgical experimenting,' Moss said. 'Most of your work'll be handling the anesthetic. Show him how to do it, Clarence.'

Wood observed intently. It appeared simple – cut-ins and shut-offs for cyclopropane, helium and oxygen; watch the dials for overrich mixture; keep your eye on the bellows and water filter . . .

Trained anesthetists, he knew, tested their mixture by taking a few sniffs. At Clarence's suggestion he sniffed briefly at the whispering cone. He didn't know cyclopropane – so lightning-fast that experienced anesthetists are sometimes caught by it . . .

Wood lay on the floor with his arms and legs sticking up in the air. When he tried to straighten them, he rolled over on his side. Still they projected stiffly. He was dizzy with the anesthetic. Something that felt like surgical plaster pulled on a sensitive spot on the back of his neck.

The room was dark, its green shades pulled down against the outer day. Somewhere above him and toward the end of the room, he heard painful breathing. Before he could raise himself to investigate, he caught the multiple tread of steps ascending and approaching the door. He drew back defensively.

The door flung open. Light flared up in the room. Wood sprang to his feet – and found he could not stand erect. He dropped back to a crawling position, facing the men who watched him with cold interest.

'He tried to stand up,' the old one stated.

'What'd you think I'd do?' Wood snapped. His voice was a confused, snarling growl without words. Baffled and raging, he glared up at them.

'Cover him, Clarence,' Moss said. 'I'll look at the other one.'

Wood turned his head from the threatening muzzle of the gun aimed at him, and saw the doctor lift the man on the bed. Clarence backed to the window and raised the shade. Strong moonlight roused the man. His profile was turned to Wood. His eyes fastened blankly on Moss's scrubbed pink face, never leaving it. Behind his ears curled long, wild hair.

'There you are, Talbot,' Moss said to the old man. 'He's sound.'

'Take him out of bed and let's see him act like you said he would.' The old man jittered anxiously on his cane.

Moss pulled the man's legs to the edge of the bed and raised him heavily to his feet. For a short time he stood without aid; then all at once he collapsed to his hands and knees. He stared full at Wood.

It took Wood a minute of startled bewilderment to recognize the face. He had seen it every day of his life, but never so detachedly. The eyes were blank and round, the facial muscles relaxed, idiotic.

But it was his own face . . .

Panic exploded in him. He gaped down at as much of himself as he could see. Two hairy legs stemmed from his shoulders, and a dog's forepaws rested firmly on the floor.

He stumbled uncertainly toward Moss. 'What did you do to me?' he shouted. It came out in an animal howl. The doctor motioned the others to the door and backed away warily.

Wood felt his lips draw back tightly over his fangs. Clarence and Talbot were in the hall. Moss stood alertly in the doorway, his hand on the knob. He watched Wood closely, his eyes glacial and unmoved. When Wood sprang, he slammed the door, and Wood's shoulder crashed against it.

'He knows what happened,' Moss's voice came through the panel.

It was not entirely true. Wood knew something had happened. But he refused to believe that the face of the crawling man gazing stupidly at him was his own. It was, though. And Wood himself stood on the four legs of a dog, with a surgical plaster covering a burning wound in the back of his neck.

It was crushing, numbing, too fantastic to believe. He thought wildly of hypnosis. But just by turning his head, he could look directly at what had been his own body, braced on hands and knees as if it could not stand erect.

He was outside his own body. He could not deny that. Somehow he had been removed from it; by drugs or hypnosis, Moss had put him in the body of a dog. He had to get back into his own body again.

But how do you get back into your own body?

His mind struck blindly in all directions. He scarcely heard the three men move away from the door and enter the next room. But his mind suddenly froze with fear. His human body was complete and impenetrable, closed hermetically against his now-foreign identity.

Through his congealed terror, his animal tears brought the creak of furniture. Talbot's cane stopped in nervous, insistent tapping.

'That should have convinced even you, Talbot?' he heard Moss say. 'Their identities are exchanged without the slightest loss of mentality.'

Wood started. It meant – no, it was absurd! But it did account for the fact that his body crawled on hands and knees, unable to stand on its feet. It meant that the collie's identity was in Wood's body!

'That's O.K.,' he heard Talbot say. 'How about the operation part? Isn't it painful, putting their brains into different skulls?'

'You can't put them into different skulls,' Moss answered with a touch of annoyance. 'They don't fit. Besides, there's no need to exchange the whole brain. How do you account for the fact that people have retained their identities with parts of their brains removed?'

There was a pause. 'I don't know,' Talbot said doubtfully.

'Sometimes the parts of the brain that were removed contained nerve centers, and paralysis set in. But the identity was still there. Then what part of the brain contained the identity?'

Wood ignored the old man's questioning murmur. He listened intently, all his fears submerged in the straining of his sharp ears, in the overwhelming need to know what Moss had done to him.

'Figure it out,' the surgeon said. 'The identity must have been in some part of the brain that wasn't removed, that couldn't be touched without death. That's where it was. At the absolute base of the brain, where a scalpel couldn't get at it without having to cut through the skull, the three medullae, and the entire depth of the brain itself. There's a mysterious little body hidden away safely down there – less than a quarter of an inch in diameter – called the pineal gland. In some way it controls the identity. Once it was a third eye.'

'A third eye, and now it controls the identity?' Talbot exclaimed.

'Why not? The gills of our fish ancestors became the Eustachian canal that controls the sense of balance.

'Until I developed a new technique in removing the gland – by excising from beneath the brain instead of through it – nothing at all was known about it. In the first place, trying to get at it would kill the patient; and oral or intravenous injections have no effect. But when I exchanged the pineals of a rabbit and a rat, the rabbit acted like a rat, and the rat like a rabbit – within their limitations, of course. It's empiricism – it works, but I don't know why.'

'Then why did the first three act like . . . what's the word?'

'Catatonics. Well, the exchanges were really successful, Talbot; but I repeated the same mistake three times, until I figured it out. And by the way, get that reporter on something a little less dangerous. He's getting pretty warm. Excepting the salivary retention, the victims acted almost like catatonics, and for nearly the same reason. I exchanged the pineals of rats for the men's. Well, you can imagine how a rat would act with the relatively huge body of a man to control. It's beyond him. He simply gives up, goes into a passive revolt. But the difference between a dog's body and a man's isn't so great. The dog is puzzled, but at any rate he makes an attempt to control his new body.'

'Is the operation painful?' Talbot asked.

'There isn't a bit of pain. The incision is very small, and heals in a short time. And as for recovery – you can see for yourself how swift it is. I operated on Wood and the dog last night.'

Wood's dog's brain stampeded, refusing to function intelligently. If he had been hypnotized or drugged, there might have been a chance of his eventual return. But his identity had been violently and permanently ripped from his body and forced into that of a dog. He was absolutely helpless, completely dependent on Moss to return him to his body.

'How much do you want?' Talbot was asking craftily.

'Five million!'

The old man cackled in a high, cracked voice. 'I'll give you fifty thousand, cash,' he offered.

'To exchange your dying body for a young, strong, healthy one?' Moss asked, emphasizing each adjective with special significance. 'The price is five million.'

'I'll give you seventy-five thousand,' Talbot said with finality. 'Raising five million is out of the question. It can't be done. All my money is tied up in my . . . uh . . . syndicates. I have to turn most of the income back into merchandise, wages, overhead and equipment. How do you expect me to have five million in cash?'

'I don't,' Moss replied with faint mockery.

Talbot lost his temper. 'Then what are you getting at?'

'The interest on five million is exactly half your income. Briefly, to use your business terminology, I'm muscling into your rackets.'

Wood heard the old man gasp indignantly. 'Not a chance!' he rasped. 'I'll give you eighty thousand. That's all the cash I can raise.'

'Don't be a fool, Talbot,' Moss said with deadly calm. 'I don't want money for the sake of feeling it. I need an assured income, and plenty of it; enough to carry on my experiments without having to bleed hospitals dry and still not have enough. If this experiment didn't interest me, I wouldn't do it even for five million, much as I need it.'

'Eighty thousand!' Talbot repeated.

'Hang onto your money until you rot! Let's see, with your advanced angina pectoris, that should about six months from now, shouldn't it?'

Wood heard the old man's cane shudder nervously over the floor.

'You win, you cold-blooded blackmailer,' the old man surrendered.

Moss laughed. Wood heard the furniture creak as they rose and set off toward the stairs.

'Do you want to see Wood and the dog again, Talbot?'

'No. I'm convinced.'

'Get rid of them, Clarence. No more abandoning them in the street for Talbot's clever reporters to theorize over. Put a silencer on your gun. You'll find it downstairs. Then leave them in the acid vat.'

Wood's eyes flashed around the room in terror. He and his body had to escape. For him to escape alone would mean the end of returning to his own body. Separation would make the task of forcing Moss to give him back his body impossible.

But they were on the second floor, at the rear of the house. Even if there had been a fire escape, he could not have opened the window. The only way out was through the door.

Somehow he had to turn the knob, chance meeting Clarence or Moss on the stairs or in the narrow hall, and open the heavy front door – guiding and defending himself and his body!

The collie in his body whimpered baffledly. Wood fought off the instinctive fear that froze his dog's brain. He had to be cool.

Below, he heard Clarence's ponderous steps as he went through the rooms looking for a silencer to muffle his gun.

Gilroy closed the door of the telephone booth and fished in his pockets for a coin. Of all of mankind's scientific gadgets, the telephone booth most clearly demonstrates that this is a world of five feet nine. When Gilroy pulled a coin out of his pocket, his elbow banged against the shut door; and as he dialed his number and stooped over the mouthpiece, he was forced to bend himself into the shape of a cane. But he had conditioned his lanky body to adjust itself to things scaled below its need. He did not mind the lack of room.

But he shoved his shapeless felt hat on the back of his head and whistled softly in a discouraged manner.

'Let me talk to the chief,' he said. The receiver rasped in his ear. The editor greeted him abstractedly; Gilroy knew he had just come on and was scattering papers over his desk, looking at the latest. 'Gilroy, chief,' the reporter said.

'What've you got on the catatonics?'

Gilroy's sharply planed face wrinkled in earnest defeat. 'Not a thing, chief,' he replied hollowly.

'Where were you?'

'I was in Memorial all day, looking at the catatonics and waiting for an idea.'

The editor became sympathetic. 'How'd you make out?' he asked.

'Not a thing. They're absolutely dumb and motionless, and nobody around here has anything to say worth listening to. How'd you make out on the police and hospital reports?'

'I was looking at them just before you called.' There was a pause. Gilroy heard the crackle of papers being shoved around. 'Here they are – the fingerprint bureau has no records of them. No police department in any village, town or city recognizes their pictures.'

'How about the hospitals outside New York?' Gilroy asked hopefully.

'No missing patients.'

Gilroy sighed and shrugged his thin shoulders eloquently. 'Well, all we have is a negative angle. They must have been picked damned carefully. All the papers around the country printed their pictures, and they don't seem to have any friends, relatives or police records.'

'How about a human-interest story,' the editor encouraged; 'what they eat, how helpless they are, their torn, old clothes? Pad out a story about their probable lives, judging from their features and hands. How's that? Not bad, eh?'

'Aw, chief,' Gilroy moaned. 'I'm licked. That padding stuff isn't my line. I'm not a sob sister. We haven't a thing to work on. These tramps had absolutely no connection with life. We can't find out who they were, where they came from, or what happened to them.'

The editor's voice went sharp and incisive. 'Listen to me, Gilroy!' he rapped out. 'You stop that whining, do you hear me? I'm running this paper, and as long as you don't see fit to quit, I'll send you out after birth lists if I want to.'

'You thought this was a good story and you convinced me that it was. Well, I'm still convinced! I want these catatonics tracked down. I want to know all about them, and how they wound up behind the eight ball. So does the public. I'm not stopping until I *do* know. Get me?'

'You get to work on this story and hang onto it. Don't let it throw you! And just to show you how I'm standing behind you ... I'm giving you a blank expense account and your own discretion. Now track these catatonics down in any way you can figure out!'

Gilroy was stunned for an instant. 'Well, gosh,' he stammered, confused, 'I'll do my best, chief, I didn't know you felt that way.'

'The two of us'll crack this story wide open, Gilroy. But just come around to me with another whine about being licked, and you can start in as copy boy for some other sheet. Do you get me? That's final!'

Gilroy pulled his hat down firmly. 'I get you, chief,' he declared manfully. 'You can count on me right up to the hilt.'

He slammed the receiver on its hook, yanked the door open, and strode out with a new determination. He felt like the power of the press, and the feeling was not unjustified. The might and cunning of a whole vast metropolitan newspaper was ranged solidly behind him. Few secrets could hide from his searching probe.

All he needed was patience and shrewd observation. Finding the first clue would be hardest; after that the story would unwind by itself. He marched toward the hospital exit.

He heard steps hastening behind him and felt a light, detaining touch on his arm. He wheeled and looked down at the resident physician, dressed in streetclothes and coming on duty.

'You're Gilroy, aren't you?' the doctor asked. 'Well, I was thinking about the incisions on the catatonics' necks –'

'What about them?' Gilroy demanded alertly, pulling out a pad.

'Quitting again?' the editor asked ten minutes later.

'Not me, chief!' Gilroy propped his stenographic pad on top of the telephone. 'I'm hot on the trail. Listen to this. The resident physician over here at Memorial tipped me off to a real clue. He figured out that the incisions on the catatonics' necks aimed at some part of their brains. The incisions penetrate at a tangent a quarter of an inch off the vertebrae, so it couldn't have been to tamper with the spinal cord. You can't reach the posterior part of the brain from that angle, he says, and working from the back of the neck wouldn't bring you to any important part of the neck that can't be reached better from the front or through the mouth.

'If you don't cut the spinal cord with that incision, you can't account for general paralysis; and the cords definitely weren't cut.

'So he thinks the incisions were aimed at some part of the base of the brain that can't be reached from above. He doesn't know what part or how the operation would cause general paralysis.

'Got that? O.K. Well, here's the payoff:

'To reach the exact spot of the brain you want, you ordinarily take off a good chunk of skull, somewhere around that spot. But these incisions were predetermined to the last centimeter. And he doesn't know how. The surgeon worked entirely by measurements – like blind flying. He says only three or four surgeons in the country could've done it?'

'Who are they, you cluck? Did you get their names?'

Gilroy became offended. 'Of course, Moss in New York; Faber in Chicago; Crowninshield in Portland; maybe Johnson in Detroit.'

'Well, what're you waiting for?' the editor shouted. 'Get Moss!'

'Can't locate him. He moved from his Riverside Drive apartment and left no forwarding address. He was peeved. The board asked for his resignation and he left with a pretty bad name for mis管-nagement.'

The editor sprang into action. 'That leaves us four men to track down. Find Moss. I'll call up the other boys you named. It looks like a good tip.'

Gilroy hung up. With a half a dozen vast strides, he had covered the distance to the hospital exit, moving with ungainly, predatory swiftness.

Wood was in a mind-freezing panic. He knew it hindered him, prevented him from plotting his escape, but he was powerless to control the fearful darting of his dog's brain.

It would take Clarence only a short time to find the silencer and climb the stairs to kill him and his body. Before Clarence could find the silencer, Wood and his body had to escape.

Wood lifted himself clumsily, unsteadily, to his hind legs and took the doorknob between his paws. They refused to grip. He heard

Clarence stop, and the sound of scraping drawers came to his sharp ears.

He was terrified. He bit furiously at the knob. It slipped between his teeth. He bit harder. Pain stabbed his sensitive gums, but the bitter brass dented. Hanging on to the knob, he lowered himself to the floor, bending his neck sharply to turn. The tongue clicked out of the lock. He threw himself to one side, flipping back the door as he fell. It opened a crack. He thrust his snout in the opening and forced it wide.

From below, he heard the ponderous footfalls moving again. Wood stalked noiselessly into the hall and peered down the well of the stairs. Clarence was out of sight.

He drew back into the room and pulled at his body's clothing, backing out into the hall again until the dog crawled voluntarily. It crept after him and down the stairs.

All at once Clarence came out of a room and made for the stairs. Wood crouched, trembling at the sound of metallic clicking that he knew was a silencer being fitted to a gun. He barred his body. It halted, its idiot face hanging down over the step, silent and without protest.

Clarence reached the stairs and climbed confidently. Wood tensed, waiting for Clarence to turn the spiral and come into view.

Clarence sighted them and froze rigid. His mouth opened blankly, startled. The gun trembled impotently at his side, and he stared up at them with his fat, white neck exposed and inviting. Then his chest heaved and his larynx tightened for a yell.

But Wood's long teeth cleared. He lunged high, directly at Clarence, and his fangs snapped together in midair.

Soft flesh ripped in his teeth. He knocked Clarence over; they fell down the stairs and crashed to the floor. Clarence thrashed around, gurgling. Wood smelled a sudden rush of blood that excited an alien lust in him. He flung himself clear and landed on his feet.

His body clumped after him, pausing to sniff at Clarence. He pulled it away and darted to the front door.

From the back of the house he heard Moss running to investigate. He bit savagely at the doorknob, jerking it back awkwardly, terrified that Moss might reach him before the door opened.

But the lock clicked, and he thrust the door wide with his body. His human body flopped after him on hands and knees to the stoop. He hauled it down the steps to the sidewalk and herded it anxiously toward Central Park West, out of Moss's range.

Wood glanced back over his shoulder, saw the doctor glaring at them through the curtain on the door, and, in terror, he dragged his body in a clumsy gallop to the corner where he would be protected by traffic.

He had escaped death, and he and his body were still together; but his panic grew stronger. How could he feed it, shelter it, defend it against Moss and Talbot's gangsters? And how could he force Moss to give him back his body?

But he saw that first he would have to shield his body from observation. It was hungry, and it prowled around on hands and knees, searching for food. The sight of a crawling, sniffing human body attracted disgusted attention; before long they were almost surrounded.

Wood was badly scared. With his teeth, he dragged his body into the street and guided its slow crawl to the other side, where Central Park could hide them with its trees and bushes.

Moss had been more alert. A black car sped through a red light and crowded down on them. From the other side a police car shot in and out of traffic, its siren screaming, and braked beside Wood and his body.

The black car checked its headlong rush.

Wood crouched defensively over his body, glowering at the two cops who charged out at them. One shoved Wood away with his foot; the other raised his body by the armpits and tried to stand it erect.

'A nut – he thinks he's a dog,' he said interestedly. 'The screwball ward for him, eh?'

The other nodded. Wood lost his reason. He attacked, snapping viciously. His body took up the attack, snarling horribly and biting on all sides. It was insane, hopeless; but he had no way of communicating, and he had to do something to prevent being separated from his body. The police kicked him off.

Suddenly he realized that if they had not been burdened with his body, they would have shot him. He darted wildly into traffic before they sat his body in the car.

'Want to get out and plug him before he bites somebody?' he heard.

'This nut'll take a hunk out of you,' the other replied. 'We'll send out an alarm from the hospital.'

It drove off downtown. Wood scrambled after it. His legs

pumped furiously; but it pulled away from him, and other cars came between. He lost it after a few blocks.

The he saw the black car make a reckless turn through traffic and roar after him. It was too intently bearing down on him to have been anything but Talbot's gangsters.

His eyes and muscles coordinated with animal precision. He ran in the swift traffic, avoiding being struck, and at the same time kept watch for a footpath leading into the park.

When he found one, he sprinted into the opposite lane of traffic. Brakes screeched; a man cursed him in a loud voice. But he scurried in front of the car, gained the sidewalk, and dashed along the cement path until he came to a miniature forest of bushes.

Without hesitation, he left the path and ran through the woods. It was not a dense growth, but it covered him from sight. He scampered deep into the park.

His frightened eyes watched the carload of gangsters scour the trees on both sides of the path. Hugging the ground, he inched away from them. They beat the bushes a safe distance away from him.

While he circled behind them, creeping from cover to cover, there was small danger of being caught. But he was appalled by the loss of his body. Being near it had given him a sort of courage, even though he did not know how he was going to force Moss to give it back to him. Now, besides making the doctor operate, he had to find a way of getting near it again.

But his empty stomach was knotted with hunger. Before he could make plans he had to eat.

He crept furtively out of his shelter. The gangsters were far out of sight. Then, with infinite patience, he sneaked up on a squirrel. The alert little animal was observant and wary. It took an exhaustingly long time before he ambushed it and snapped its spine. The thought of eating an uncooked rodent revolted him.

He dug back into his cache of bushes with his prey. When he tried to plot a line of action, his dog's brain balked. It was terrified and maddened with helplessness.

There was good reason for its fear – Moss had Talbot's gangsters out gunning for him, and by this time the police were probably searching for him as a vicious dog.

In all his nightmares he had never imagined any so horrible. He was utterly impotent to help himself. The forces of law and crime were ranged against him; he had no way of communicating the fact that he was a man to those who could possibly help him; he was completely inarticulate; and besides, *who* could help him, except Moss? Suppose he *did* manage to evade the police, the gangsters, and sneaked past a hospital's vigilant staff, and somehow succeeded in communicating . . .

Even so, only Moss could perform the operation!

He had to rule out doctors and hospitals; they were too routinized to have much imagination. But, more important than that, they could not influence Moss to operate.

He scrambled to his feet and trotted cautiously through the clumps of brush in the direction of Columbus Circle. First, he had to be alert for police and gangsters. He had to find a method of communicating – but to somebody who could understand him and exert tremendous pressure on Moss.

The city's smells came to his sensitive nostrils. Like a vast blanket, covering most of them, was a sweet odor that he identified as gasoline vapor. Above it hovered the scent of vegetation, hot and moist; and below it, the musk of mankind.

To his dog's perspective, it was a different world, with a broad, distant, terrifying horizon. Smells and sounds formed scenes in his animal mind. Yet it was interesting. The pad of his paws against the soft, cushioned ground gave him an instinctive pleasure; all the clothes he needed, he carried on him; and food was not hard to find.

While he shielded himself from the police and Talbot's gangsters, he even enjoyed a sort of freedom – but it was a cowardly freedom that he did not want, that was not worth the price. As a man, he had suffered hunger, cold, lack of shelter and security, indifference. In spite of all that, his dog's body harbored a human intelligence; he belonged on his hind legs, standing erect, living the life, good or bad, of a man.

In some way he must get back to that world, out of the solitary anarchy of animaldom. Moss alone could return him. He must be forced to do it! He must be compelled to return the body he had robbed!

But how would Wood communicate, and who could help him?

Near the end of Central Park, he exposed himself to overwhelming danger.

He was padding along a path that skirted the broad road. A cruising black car accelerated with deadly, predatory swiftness and sped abreast of him. He heard a muffled *pop*. A bullet hissed an inch over his head.

He ducked low and scurried back into the concealing bushes. He snaked nimbly from tree to tree, keeping obstacles between him and the line of fire.

The gangsters were out of the car. He heard them beating the brush for him. Their progress was slow, while his fleet legs pumped three hundred yards of safety away from them.

He burst out of the park and scampered across Columbus Circle, reckless of traffic. On Broadway he felt more secure, hugging the buildings with dense crowds between him and the street.

When he felt certain that he had lost the gangsters, he turned west through one-way streets, alert for signs of danger.

In coping with physical danger, he discovered that his animal mind reacted instinctively and always more cunningly than a human brain.

Impulsively, he cowered behind stoops, in doorways, behind any sort of shelter, when the traffic moved. When it stopped, packed tightly, for the light, he ran at topnotch speed. Cars skidded across his path, and several times he was almost hit; but he did not slow to a trot until he had zigzagged downtown, going steadily away from the center of the city, and reached West Street, along North River.

He felt reasonably safe from Talbot's gangsters. But a police car approached slowly under the express highway. He crouched behind an overflowing garbage can outside a filthy restaurant. Long after it was gone, he cowered there.

The shrill wind blowing over the river and across the covered docks picked a newspaper off the pile of garbage and flattened it against the restaurant window.

Through his animal mind, frozen into numbing fear, he remembered the afternoon before – standing in front of the employment agency, talking to one of Talbot's gangsters.

A thought had come to him then; that it would be pleasant to be a catatonic instead of having to starve. He knew better now. But . . .

He reared to his hind legs and overturned the garbage can. It fell with a loud crash, rolling down toward the gutter, spilling refuse all over the sidewalk. Before a restaurant worker came out, roaring abuse, he pawed through the mess and seized a twisted newspaper in his mouth. It smelled of sour, rotting food, but he caught it up and ran.

Blocks away from the restaurant, he ran across a wide, torn lot, to cover behind a crumbling building. Sheltered from the river wind, he straightened out the paper and scanned the front page.

It was a day old, the same newspaper that he had thrown away before the employment agency. On the left column he found the catatonic story. It was signed by a reporter named Gilroy.

Then he took the edge of the sheet between his teeth and backed away with it until the newspaper opened clumsily, wrinkled, at the next page. He was disgusted by the fetid smell of putrifying food that clung to it; but he swallowed his gorge and kept turning the huge, stiff, unwieldy sheets with his inept teeth. He came to the editorial page and paused there, studying intently the copyright box.

He set off at a fast trot, wary against danger, staying close to walls of buildings, watching for cars that might contain either gangsters or policemen, darting across streets to shelter – trotting on . . .

The air was growing darker, and the express highway cast a long shadow. Before the sun went down, he covered almost three miles along West Street, and stopped not far from the Battery.

He gaped up at the towering *Morning Post* Building. It looked impregnable, its heavy doors shut against the wind.

He stood at the main entrance, waiting for somebody to hold a door open long enough for him to lunge through it. Hopefully, he kept his eyes on an old man. When he opened the door, Wood was at his heels. But the old man shoved him back with gentle firmness.

Wood bared his fangs. It was his only answer. The man hastily pulled the door shut.

Wood tried another approach. He attached himself to a tall, gangling man who appeared rather kindly in spite of his intent face. Wood gazed up, wagging his tail awkwardly in friendly greeting. The tall man stooped and scratched Wood's ears, but he refused to take him inside. Before the door closed, Wood launched himself savagely at the thin man and almost knocked him down.

In the lobby, Wood darted through the legs surrounding him. The tall man was close behind, roaring angrily. A frightened stampede of thick-soled shoes threatened to crush Wood; but he twisted in and out between the surging feet and gained the stairs.

He scrambled up them swiftly. The second-floor entrance had plateglass doors. It contained the executive offices.

He turned the corner and climbed up speedily. The stairs narrowed, artificially illuminated. The third and fourth floors were printing-plant rooms; he ran past; clambered by the business offices, classified advertising. . . .

At the editorial department he panted before the heavy fire door, waiting until he regained his breath. Then he gripped the knob between his teeth and pulled it around. The door swung inward.

Thick, bitter smoke clawed his sensitive nostrils; his ears flinched at the clattering, shouting bedlam.

Between rows of littered desks, he inched and gazed around hopefully. He saw abstract faces, intent on typewriters that rattled out stories; young men racing around to gather batches of papers; men and women swarming in and out of the elevators. Shrewd faces, intelligent and alert. . . .

A few had turned for an instant to look at him as he passed, then turned back to their work, almost without having seen him.

He trembled with elation. These were the men who had the power to influence Moss, and the acuteness to understand him! He squatted and put his paw on the leg of a typing reporter, staring up expectantly. The reporter stared, looked down agitatedly, and shoved him away.

'Go on, beat it!' he said angrily. 'Go home!'

Wood shrank back. He did not sense danger. Worse than that, he had failed. His mind worked rapidly: suppose he *had* attracted interest, how would he have communicated his story intelligibly? How could he explain in the equivalent of words?

All at once the idea exploded in his mind. He had been a code translator in a stockbroker's office. . . .

He sat back on his haunches and barked, loud, broken, long and short yelps. A girl screamed. Reporters jumped up defensively, surged away in a tightening ring. Wood barked out his message in Morse, painful, slow, straining a larynx that was foreign to him. He looked around optimistically for someone who might have understood.

Instead, he met hostile, annoyed stares – and no comprehension.

'That's the hound that attacked me!' the tall, thin man said.

'Not for food, I hope,' a reporter answered.

Wood was not entirely defeated. He began to bark his message again; but a man hurried out of the glass-enclosed editor's office.

'What's all the commotion here?' he demanded. He sighted Wood among the ring of withdrawing reporters. 'Get that damned dog out of here!'

'Come on – get him out of here!' the thin man shouted.

'He's a nice, friendly dog. Give him the hypnotic eye, Gilroy.'

Wood stared pleadingly at Gilroy. He had not been understood, but he had found the reporter who had written the catatonic articles! Gilroy approached cautiously, repeating phrases calculated to sooth a savage dog.

Wood darted away through the rows of desks. He was so near to success – he only needed to find a way of communicating before they caught him and put him out!

He lunged to the top of a desk and crashed a bottle of ink to the floor. It splashed into a dark puddle. Swiftly, quiveringly, he seized a piece of white paper, dipped his paw into the splotch of ink, and made a hasty attempt to write.

His surge of hoped died quickly. The wrist of his forepaw was not the universal joint of a human being; it had a single upward articulation! When he brought his paw down on the paper, it flattened uselessly, and his claws worked in a unit. He could not draw back three to write with one. Instead, he made a streaked pad print.

Dejectedly, rather than antagonize Gilroy, Wood permitted himself to be driven back into an elevator. He wagged his tail clumsily. It was a difficult feat, calling into use alien muscles that he employed with intellectual deliberation. He sat down and assumed a grin that would have been friendly on a human face; but, even so, it reassured Gilroy. The tall reporter patted his head. Nevertheless, he put him out firmly.

But Wood had reason to feel encouraged. He had managed to get inside the building and had attracted attention. He knew that a newspaper was the only force powerful enough to influence Moss, but there was still the problem of communication. How would he solve it? His paw was worthless for writing, with its single articulation; and nobody in the office could understand Morse code.

He crouched against the white cement wall, his harried mind darting wildly in all directions for a solution. Without a voice or prehensile fingers, his only method of communication seemed to be barking in code. In all that throng, he was certain there would be one to interpret it.

Glances *did* turn to him. At least, he had no difficulty in arousing interest. But they were uncomprehending looks.

For some moments he lost his reason. He ran in and out of the deep, hurrying crowd, barking his message furiously, jumping up at men who appeared more intelligent than others, following them short distances until it was overwhelmingly apparent that they did not understand, then turning to other men, raising an ear-shattering din of appeal.

He met nothing but a timid pat or frightened rebuffs. He stopped his deafening yelps and cowered back against the wall, defeated. No one would attempt to interpret the barking of a dog in terms of code. When he was a man, he would probably have responded in the same way. The most intelligible message he could hope to convey by his barking was simply the fact that he was trying to attract interest. Nobody would search for any deeper meaning in a dog's barking.

He joined the traffic hastening toward the subway. He trotted along the curb, watchful for slowing cars, but more intent on the strewing of rubbish in the gutter. He was murderously envious of the human feet around him that walked swiftly and confidently to a known destination; smug, selfish feet, undeviating from their homeward path to help him. Their owners could convey the finest shadings and variations in emotion, commands, abstract thought, by speech, writing, print, through telephone, radio, books, newspapers. . . .

But his voice was only a piercing, inarticulate yelp that infuriated human beings; his paws were good for nothing but running; his pointed face transmitted no emotions.

He trotted along the curbs of three blocks in the business district before he found a pencil stump. He picked it up in his teeth and ran to the docks on West Street, though he had only the vague outline of a last experiment in communication.

There was plenty of paper blowing around in the river wind, some of it even clean. To the stevedores, waiting at the dock for the payoff, he appeared to be frisking. A few of them whistled at him. In reality, he chased the flying paper with deadly earnestness.

When he captured a piece, he held it firmly between his forepaws. The stub of pencil was gripped in the even space separating his sharp canine fangs.

He moved the pencil in his mouth over the sheet of paper. It was clumsy and uncertain, but he produced long, wavering block letters. He wrote: 'I AM A MAN.' The short message covered the whole page, leaving no space for further information.

He dropped the pencil, caught up the paper in his teeth, and ran back to the newspaper building. For the first time since he had escaped from Moss, he felt assured. His attempt at writing was crude and unformed, but the message was unmistakably clear.

He joined a group of tired young legmen coming back from assignments. He stood passively until the door was opened, then lunged confidently through the little procession of cub reporters. They scattered back cautiously, permitting him to enter without a struggle.

Again he raced up the stairs to the editorial department, put the sheet of paper down on the floor, and clutched the doorknob between his powerful teeth.

He hesitated for only an instant, to find the cadaverous reporter. Gilroy was seated at a desk, typing out his article. Carrying his message in his mouth, Wood trotted directly to Gilroy. He put his paw on the reporter's sharp knee.

'What the hell!' Gilroy gasped. He pulled his leg away startedly and shoved Wood away.

But Wood came back insistently, holding his paper stretched out to Gilroy as far as possible. He trembled hopefully until the reporter snatched the message out of his mouth. Then his muscles froze, and he stared up expectantly at the angular face, scanning it for signs of growing comprehension.

Gilroy kept his eyes on the straggling letters. His face darkened angrily.

'Who's being a wise guy here?' he shouted suddenly. Most of the staff ignored him. 'Who let this mutt in and gave him a crank note to bring to me? Come on – who's the genius?'

Wood jumped around him, barking hysterically, trying to explain.

'Oh, shut up!' Gilroy rapped out. 'Hey, copy! Take this dog down and see that he doesn's get back in! He won't bite you.'

Again Wood had failed. But he did not feel defeated. When his hysterical dread of frustration ebbed, leaving his mind clear and analytical, he realized that his failure was only one of degree. Actually, he had communicated, but lack of space had prevented him from detailed clarity. The method was correct. He only needed to augment it.

Before the copy boy cornered him, Wood swooped up at a pencil on an empty desk.

'Should I let him keep the pencil, Mr. Gilroy?' the boy asked.

'I'll lend you mine, unless you want you arm snapped off,' Gilroy snorted, turning back to his typewriter.

Wood sat back and waited beside the copy boy for the elevator to pick them up. He clenched the pencil possessively between his teeth. He was impatient to get out of the building and back to the lot on West Street, where he could plan a system of writing a more explicit message. His block letters were unmanageably huge and shaky; but, with the same logical detachment he used to employ when he was a code translator, he attacked the problem fearlessly.

He knew that he could not use the printed or written alphabet. He would have to find a substitute that his clumsy teeth could manage, and that could be compressed into less space.

Gilroy was annoyed by the collie's insistent returning. He crumpled the enigmatic, unintelligible note and tossed it in the wastebasket, but beyond considering it as a practical joke, he gave it no further thought.

His long, large-jointed fingers swiftly tapped out the last page of his story. He ended it with a short line of zeros and dashes, gathered a sheaf of papers, and brought it to the editor.

The editor studied the lead paragraph intently and skimmed hastily through the rest of the story. He appeared uncomfortable.

'Not bad, eh?' Gilroy exulted.

'Uh – what?' The editor jerked his head up blankly. 'Oh. No, it's pretty good. Very good, in fact.'

'I've got to hand it to you,' Gilroy continued admiringly. 'I'd have given up. You know – nothing to work on, just a bunch of fantastic events with no beginning and no end. Now, all of a sudden, the cops pick up a nut who acts like a dog and has an incision like the catatonics. Maybe it isn't any clearer, but at least we've got something actually happening. I don't know – I feel pretty good. We'll get to the bottom – '

The editor listened abstractedly, growing more uneasy from sentence to sentence. 'Did you see the latest case?' he interrupted.

'Sure. I'm in soft with the resident physician. If I hadn't been following this story right from the start, I'd have said the one they just hauled in was a genuine screwball. He goes bounding around on the floor, sniffs at things, and makes a pathetic attempt to bark. But he has an incision on the back of his neck. It's just like the others – even has two professional stitches, and it's the same number of millimeters away from the spine. He's a catatonic, or whatever we'll have to call it now – '

'Well, the story's shaping up faster than I thought it would,' the editor said, evening the edges of Gilroy's article with ponderous care. 'But – ' His voice dropped huskily. 'Well, I don't know how to tell you this, Gilroy.'

The reporter drew his brows together and looked at him obliquely. 'What's the hard word this time?' he asked, mystified.

'Oh, the usual thing. You know. I've got to take you off this story. It's too bad, because it was just getting hot. I hated to tell you, Gilroy; but, after all, what the hell. That's part of the game.'

'It is, huh?' Gilroy flattened his hands on the desk and leaned over them resentfully. 'Whose toes did we step on this time? Nobody's. The hospital has no kick coming. I couldn't mention names because I didn't know any to mention. Well, then, what's the angle?'

The editor shrugged. 'I can't argue. It's a front-office order. But I've got a good lead for you to follow tomorrow – '

Savagely, Gilroy strode to the window and glared out at the darkening street. The business department wasn't behind the order, he reasoned angrily; they weren't getting ads from the hospital. And as for the big boss – Talbot never interfered with policy, except when he had to squash a revealing crime story. By eliminating the editors, who yielded an inch when public opinion demanded a mile, the business department, who fought only when advertising was at stake, Gilroy could blame no one but Talbot.

Gilroy tapped his bony knuckles impatiently against the window encasement. What was the point of Talbot's order? Perhaps he had a new way of paying off traitors. Gilroy dismissed the idea immediately; he knew Talbot wouldn't go to that expense and risk possible leakage when the old way of sealing a body in a cement block and dumping it in the river was still effective and cheap.

'I give up,' Gilroy said without turning around. 'I can't figure out Talbot's angle.'

'Neither can I,' the editor admitted.

At this confession, Gilroy wheeled. 'Then you *know* it's Talbot!'

'Of course. Who else could it be? But don't let it throw you, pal.' He glanced around cautiously as he spoke. 'Let this catatonic yarn take a rest. Tomorrow you can find out what's behind this bulletin that Johnson phoned in from City Hall.'

Gilroy absently scanned the scribbled note. His scowl wrinkled into puzzlement.

'What the hell is this? All I can make out of it is the A.S.P.C.A. and dog lovers are protesting to the mayor against organized murder of brown-and-white collies.'

'That's just what it is.'

'And you think Talbot's gang is behind it, naturally?' When the editor nodded, Gilroy threw up his hands in despair. 'This gang stuff is getting too deep for me, chief. I used to be able to call their shots. I knew why a torpedo was bumped off, or a crime was pulled; but I don't mind telling you that I can't see why a gang boss wants a catatonic yarn hushed up, or sends his mob around plugging innocent collies. I'm going home . . . get drunk –'

He stormed out of the office. Before the editor had time to shrug his shoulders, Gilroy was back again, his deep eyes blazing furiously.

'What a pair of prized dopes we are, chief!' he shouted. 'Remember that collie – the one that came in with a hunk of paper in his mouth? We threw him out, remember? Well, *that's*

*the hound Talbot's gang is out gunning for! He's trying to carry
messages to us!'*

'Hey, you're right!' The editor heaved out of the chair and
stood uncertainly. 'Where is he?'

Gilroy waved his long arms expressively.

'Then come on! To hell with hats and coats!'

They dashed into the staff room. The skeleton night crew
loafed around, reading papers before moping out to follow up
undeveloped leads.

'Put those papers down!' the editor shouted. 'Come on with
me – every one of you.'

He herded them, baffled and annoyed, into the elevator. At the
entrance to the building, he searched up and down the street.

'He's not around, Gilroy. All right, you deadbeats, divide up
and chase around the streets, whistling. When you see a brown-
and-white collie, whistle to him. He'll come to you. Now beat it
and do as I say.'

They moved off slowly. 'Whistle?' one called back anxiously.

'Yes, whistle!' Gilroy declared. 'Forget your dignity. Whistle!'

They scattered, whistling piercingly the signals that are supposed to attract dogs. The few people around the business
district that late were highly interested and curious, but Gilroy
left the editor whistling at the newspaper building, while he
whistled toward West Street. He left the shrill calls blowing
away from the river, and searched along the wide highway in the
growing dark.

For an hour he pried into dark spaces between the docks,
patiently covering his ground. He found nothing but occasional
longshoremen unloading trucks and a light uptown traffic. There
were only homeless, prowling mongrels and starving drifters: no
brown-and-white collie.

He gave up when he began to feel hungry. He returned to the
building hoping the others had more luck, and angry with
himself for not having followed the dog when he had the chance.

The editor was still there, whistling more frantically than ever.
He had gathered a little band of inquisitive onlookers, who
waited hopefully for something to happen. The reporters were
also returning.

'Find anything?' the editor paused to ask.

'Nope. He didn't show up here?'

'Not yet. Oh, he'll be back, all right. I'm not afraid of that.'
And he went back to his persistent whistling, disregarding stares
and rude remarks. He was a man with an iron will. He sneered

openly at the defeated reporters when they slunk past him into the building.

In the comparative quiet of the city, above the editor's shrills, Gilroy heard swiftly pounding feet. He gazed over the heads of the pack that had gathered around the editor.

A reporter burst into view, running at top speed and doing his best to whistle attractively through dry lips at a dog streaking away from him.

'Here he comes!' Gilroy shouted. He broke through the crowd and his long legs flashed over the distance to the collie. In his excitement, empty, toneless wind blew between his teeth; but the dog shot straight for him just the same. Gilroy snatched a dirty piece of paper out of his mouth. Then the dog was gone, toward the docks; and a black car rode ominously down the street.

Gilroy half started in pursuit, paused, and stared at the slip of paper in his hand. For a moment he blamed the insufficient light, but when the editor came up to him, yelling blasphemy for letting the dog escape, Gilroy handed him the unbelievable note.

'That dog can take care of himself,' Gilroy said. 'Read this.'

The editor drew his brows together over the message. It read:

;;;;,; ;;:··..;,·. ;;;. ..";:, .;:...··..,;;." ..::;".",;.. "..;
".".;. .:;.:;".,"""' ";.;; ..·.";,..·;;.. ":.";;;; ..";:,;;

'Well, I'll be damned!' the editor exclaimed. 'Is it a gag?'

'Gag, my eye!'

'Well, I can't make head or tail of it!' the editor protested.

Gilroy looked around undeterminedly, as if for someone to help them. 'You're not supposed to. It's a code message.' He swung around, stabbing an enormously long, knobbed finger at the editor. 'Know anyone who can translate code – cryptograms?'

'Uh – let's see. How about the police, or the G-men – '

Gilroy snorted. 'Give it to the bulls before we know what's in it!' He carefully tucked the crudely penciled noted into his breast pocket and buttoned his coat. 'You stick around outside here, chief. I'll be back with the translation. Keep an eye out for the pooch!'

He loped off before the editor could more than open his mouth.

In the index room of the Forty-second Street Library, Gilroy crowded into the telephone booth and dialed a number. His eyes ached and he had a dizzy headache. Close reasoning always scrambled his wits. His mind was intuitive rather than ploddingly analytical.

'Executive office, please,' he told the night operator. 'There must be somebody there. I don't care if it's the business manager himself, I want to speak to somebody in the executive office. I'll wait.' He lolled, bent into a convenient shape, against the wall. 'Hello. Who's this? . . . Oh, good. Listen, Rothbart, this is Gilroy. Do me a favor, huh? You're nearest the front entrance. You'll find the chief outside the door. Send him into the telephone, and take his place until he gets through. While you're out there, watch for a brown-and-white collie. Nab him if he shows up and bring him inside . . . Will you? . . . Thanks!'

Gilroy held the receiver to his ear, defeatedly amusing himself by identifying the sounds coming over the wire. He was no longer in a hurry, and when he had to pay another nickel before the editor finally came to the telephone, he did not mind.

'What's up, Gilroy?' the editor asked hopefully.

'Nothing, chief. That's why I called up. I went through a military code book, some kids's stuff, and a history of cryptography through the ages. I found some good codes, but nobody seems to've thought of this punctuation code. Ever see the Confederate cipher? Boy, it's a real dazzler – wasn't cracked until after the Civil War was over! The old Greeks wound strips of paper around identical sticks. When they were unrolled, the strips were gibberish, around the sticks, the words fell right into order.'

'Cut it out,' the editor snapped. 'Did you find anything useful?'

'Sure. Everybody says the big clue is the table of frequency – the letters used more often than others. But, on the other hand, they say that in short messages, like ours, important clues like the single words "a" and "I", bigrams like "am", "as", and even trigrams like "the" or "but", are often omitted entirely.'

'Well, that's fine. What're you going to do now?'

'I don't know. Try the cops after all, I guess.'

'Nothing doing,' the editor said firmly. 'Ask a librarian to help.'

Gilroy seized the inspiration. He slammed down the receiver and strode to the reference desk.

'Where can I get hold of somebody who knows cryptograms?' he rasped.

The attendant politely consulted his colleagues. 'The guard of the manuscript room is pretty good,' he said, returning. 'Down the hall –'

Gilroy shouted his thanks and broke into an ungainly run, ignoring the attendant's order to walk. At the manuscript room he clattered the gate until the keeper appeared and let him in.

'Take a look at this,' he commanded, flinging the message on a table.

The keeper glanced curiously at it. 'Oh, cryptogram, eh?'

'Yeah. Can you make anything out of it?'

'Well, it looks like a good one,' the guard replied cautiously, 'but I've been cracking them all for the last twenty years.' They sat down at the table in the empty room. For some time the guard stared fixedly at the scrawled note. 'Five symbols,' he said finally. 'S colon, period, comma, colon, quotation marks. Thirteen word units, each with an even number of symbols. They must be used in combinations of two.'

'I figured that out already,' Gilroy rapped out. 'What's it *say*?'

The guard lifted his head, offended. 'Give me a chance. Bacon's code wasn't solved for three centuries.'

Gilroy groaned. He did not have so much time on his hands.

'There's only thirteen word units here,' the guard went on, undaunted by the Bacon example. 'Can't use frequency, bigrams or trigrams.'

'I know that already,' Gilroy said hoarsely.

'Then why'd you come to me if you're so smart?'

Gilroy hitched his chair away. 'O.K., I won't bother you.'

'Five symbols to represent twenty-six letters. Can't be. Must be something like the Russian nihilist code. They can represent only twenty-five letters. The missing one is either "q' or "j', most likely, because they're not used much. Well, I'll tell you what I think.'

'What's that?' Gilroy demanded, all alert.

'You'll have to reason *a priori*, or whatever it is.'

'Any way you want,' Gilroy sighed. 'Just get on with it.'

'The square root of twenty-five is five. Whoever wrote this note must've made a square of letters, five wide and five deep. That sounds right.' The guard smiled and nodded cheerfully. 'Possible combinations in a square of twenty-five letters is . . . uh . . . 625. The double symbols must identify the lines down and across. Possible combinations, twenty-five. Combinations all told . . . hmmm . . . 15,625. Not so good. If there's a key word, we'll have to search the dictionary until we find it. Possible combinations, 15,625 multiplied by the English vocabulary – that is, if the key word *is* English.'

Gilroy raised himself to his feet. 'I can't stand it,' he moaned. 'I'll be back in an hour.'

'No, don't go,' the guard said. 'You've been helping me a lot. I don't think we'll have to go through more than 625 combinations at the most. That'll take no time at all.'

He spoke, of course, in relative terms. Bacon code, three centuries; Confederate code, fifteen years; wartime Russian code, unsolved. Cryptographers must look forward to eternity.

Gilroy seated himself, while the guard plotted a square:

```
:  ”  ,  .  :  ;
a  b  c  d  e  ”
f  g  h  i  j  ,
k  l  m  n  o  .
p  r  s  t  u  :
v  w  x  y  z
```

The first symbol combination, two semicolons, translated to 'a', by reading down the first line, from the top semicolon, and across from the side semicolon. The next, a semicolon and a comma, read 'l'. He went on in this fashion until he screwed up his face and pushed the half-completed translation to Gilroy. It read:

'akdd kyoiztou kp tbo eztztkprepd'

'Does it make sense to you?' he asked anxiously.

Gilroy strangled, unable to reply.

'It could be Polish,' the guard explained, 'or Japanese.'

The harassed reporter fled.

When he returned an hour later, after having eaten and tramped across town, nervously chewing cigarettes, he found the guard defended from him by a breastwork of heaped papers.

'Does it look any better?' Gilroy asked hoarsely.

The guard was too absorbed to look up or answer. By peering over his shoulder, Gilroy saw that he had plotted another square. The papers on the table were covered with discarded letter keys; at a rough guess, Gilroy estimated that the keeper had made over a hundred of them.

The one he was working with had been formed as the result of methodical elimination. His first square the guard had kept, changing the positions of the punctuation marks. When that had failed, he altered his alphabet square, tried that, and reversed his punctuation marks once more. Patient and plodding the guard had formed this square:

```
             ,  .  ;  ”  :
             z  u  o  j  e  ,
             y  t  n  i  d  .
             x  s  m  h  c  ;
             w  r  l  g  b  ”
             v  p  k  f  a  :
```

Without haste, he counted down under the semicolon and across from the side semicolon, stopping at 'm'. Gilroy followed him, nodding at the result. He was faster than the old guard at interpreting the semicolon and comma – 'o'. The period and semicolon, repeated twice, came to 'ss'. First word: 'moss'.

Gilroy straightened up and took a deep breath. He bent over again and counted down and across with the guard, through the whole message, which the old man had lined off between every two symbols. Completed, it read,

;;|;;|.;|.;| ;;|.:|.;|.”|::|..|.;|.:| ;;|;.| ..|”;|.;| :;|::|..|.::|..|;;|;.|”.|.;;|.;|
moss   **operated**   **on**   **the**   **catatonics**

..|::|;.”|;;|..| ”.|.;| ”:|.”.|;.|::|;.|:;|”.|;.|”’”| ”;|.”.|;;| .:|.”|;;|..|:;|:;|..|
talbot   **is**   **financing**   **him**   **protect**

;;|:.| ”:|.”|:.|;;| ..|”;|.;|;;|
me   **from**   **them**

'Hmmm,' the guard mused. 'That makes sense, if I knew what it meant.'

But Gilroy had snatched the papers out of his hand. The gate clanged shut after him.

Returning to the office in a taxi, Gilroy was not too joyful. He rapped on the inside window. 'Speed it up! I've seen the sights.'

He thought, if the dog's been bumped off, good-by catatonic story! The dog was his only link with the code writer.

Wood slunk along the black, narrow alleys behind the wholesale fruit markets on West Street. Battered cans and crates of rotting fruit made welcome obstacles and shelters if Talbot's gangsters were following him.

He knew that he had to get away from the river section. The gangsters must have definitely recognized him; they would call Talbot's headquarters for greater forces. With their speedy cars they could patrol the borders of the district he was operating in, and close their lines until he was trapped.

More important was the fact that reporters had been sent out to search for him. Whether or not his simple code had been deciphered did not matter very much; the main thing was that Gilroy at last knew he was trying to communicate with him.

Wood's unerring animal sense of direction led him through the maze of densely shadowed alleys to a point nearest the newspaper office. He peered around the corner, up and down the street. The black gang car was out of sight. But he had to make an unprotected dash of a hundred yards, in the full glare of the streetlights, to the building entrance.

His powerful leg muscles gathered. He sped over the hard cement sidewalk. The entrance drew nearer. His legs pumped more furiously, shortening the dangerous space more swiftly than a human being could; and for that he was grateful.

He glimpsed a man standing impatiently at the door. At the last possible moment, Wood checked his rush and flung himself toward the thick glass plate.

'There you are!' the editor cried. 'Inside – quick!'

He thrust open the door. They scurried inside and commandeered an elevator, then ran through the newsroom to the editor's office.

'Boy, I hope you weren't seen! It'd be curtains for both of us.'

The editor squirmed uneasily behind his desk, from time to time glancing disgruntledly at his watch and cursing Gilroy's long absence. Wood stretched out on the cold floor and panted. He had expected his note to be deciphered by then, and even hoped to be recognized as a human being in a dog's body. But he realized that Gilroy probably was still engaged in decoding it.

At any rate he was secure for a while. Before long, Gilroy would return; then his story would be known. Until then he had patience.

Wood raised his head and listened. He recognized Gilroy's characteristic pace that consumed at least four feet at a step. Then the door slammed open and shut behind the reporter.

'The dog's here, huh? Wait'll you take a look at what I got!'

He threw a square of paper before the editor. Wood scanned the editor's face as he eagerly read it. He ignored the vast hamburger that Gilroy unwrapped for him. He was bewildered by Gilroy's lack of more than ordinary interest in him; but perhaps the editor would understand.

'So that's it! Moss and Talbot, eh? It's getting a lot clearer.'

'I get Moss's angle,' Gilroy said. 'He's the only guy around here who could do an operation like that. But Talbot – I don't get his game. And who sent the note – how'd he get the dope – where is he?'

Wood almost went mad with frustration. He could explain; he knew all there was to be known about Talbot's interest in Moss's experiment. The problem of communication had been solved. Moss and Talbot were exposed; but he was as far as ever from regaining his own body.

He had to write another cipher message – longer, this time, and more explicit, answering the questions Gilroy raised. But to do that – he shivered. To do that, he would have to run the gang patrol; and his enciphering square was in the corner of the lot. It would be too dark. . . .

'We've got to get him to lead us to the one who wrote the message,' Gilroy said determinedly. 'That's the only way we can corner Moss and Talbot. Like this, all we have is an accusation and no legal proof.'

'He must be around here somewhere.'

Gilroy fastened his eyes on Wood. 'That's what I think. The dog came here and barked, trying to get us to follow him. When we chased him out, he came back with a scrawled note about a half-hour later. Then he brought the code message within another hour. The writer must be pretty near here. After the dog eats, we'll –' He gulped audibly and raised his bewildered gaze to the editor. Swiftly, he slipped off the edge of the desk and fumbled in the long hair on Wood's neck. 'Look at that, chief – a piece of surgical plaster. When the dog bent his head to eat, the hair fell away from it.'

'And you think he's a catatonic.' The editor smiled pityingly and shook his head. 'You're jumpy, Gilroy.'

'Maybe I am. But I'd like to see what's under the plaster.'

Wood's heart pumped furiously. He knew that his incision was the precise duplicate of the catatonics', and if Gilroy could see it, he would immediately understand. When Gilroy picked at the plaster, he tried to bear the stabbing pain; but he had to squirm away. The wound was raw and new, and the deeply rooted hair was firmly glued to the plaster. He permitted Gilroy to try again. The sensation was far too fierce; he was afraid the incision would rip wide open.

'Stop it,' the editor said squeamishly. 'He'll bite you.'

Gilroy straightened up. 'I could take it off with some ether.'

'You don't really think he was operated on, do you? Moss doesn't operate on dogs. He probably got into a fight, or one of Talbot's torpedoes creased him with a bullet.'

The telephone bell rang insistently. 'I'd still like to see what's under it,' Gilroy said as the editor removed the receiver. Wood's hopes died suddenly. He felt that he was to blame for resisting Gilroy.

'What's up, Blaine?' the editor asked. He listened absorbedly, his face darkening. 'O.K. Stay away if you don't want to take a chance. Phone your story in to the rewrite desk.' He replaced the receiver and said to Gilroy: 'Trouble, plenty of it. Talbot's gang cars are cruising around the district. Blaine was afraid to run them. I don't know how you're going to get the dog through.'

Wood was alarmed. He left his meal unfinished and agitated toward the door, whimpering involuntarily.

Gilroy glanced curiously at him. 'I'd swear he understood what you said. Did you see the change that came over him?'

'That's the way they react to voices,' the editor said.

'Well, we've got to get him to his master.' Gilroy mused, biting the inside of his cheek. 'I can do it – if you're in with me.'

'Of course I am. How?'

'Follow me.' Wood and the editor went through the news-room on the cadaverous reporter's swift heels. In silence they waited for an elevator, then descended to the lobby. 'Wait here beside the door,' Gilroy said. 'When I give the signal, come running.'

'What signal?' the editor cried, but Gilroy had loped into the street and out of sight.

They waited tensely. In a few minutes a taxi drew up to the curb and Gilroy opened the door, sitting alertly inside. He watched the corner behind him. No one moved for a long while; then a black gang car rode slowly and vigilantly past the taxi. An automatic rifle barrel glinted in the yellow light. Gilroy waited until a moment after it turned into West Street. He waved his arms frantically.

'Step on it!' Gilroy ordered harshly. 'Up West Street!'

The editor scooped Wood up in his arms, burst open the door, and darted across the sidewalk into the cab.

The taxi accelerated suddenly. Wood crouched on the floor, trembling, in despair. He had exhausted his ingenuity and he was as far as ever from regaining his body. They expected him to lead them to his master; they still did not realize that he had written the message. Where should he lead them – how could he convince them that he was the writer?

'I think this is far enough,' Gilroy broke the silence. He tapped on the window. The driver stopped. Gilroy and the editor got out, Wood following indecisively. Gilroy paid and waved the driver away. In the quiet of isolation of the broad commercial highway, he bent his great height to Wood's level. 'Come on, boy!' he urged. 'Home!'

Wood was in a panic of dismay. He could think of only one place to lead them. He set off at a slow trot that did not tax them. Hugging the walls, sprinting across streets, he headed cautiously downtown.

They followed him behind the markets fronting the highway, over a hemmed-in lot. He picked his way around the deep, treacherous foundation of a building that had been torn down, up and across piles of rubbish, to a black-shadowed clearing at the lot's end. He halted passively.

Gilroy and the editor peered around into the blackness. 'Come out!' Gilroy called hoarsely. 'We're your friends. We want to help you.'

When there was no response, they explored the lot, lighting matches to illuminate dark corners of the foundation. Wood watched them with confused emotions. By searching in the garbage heaps and the crumbling walls of the foundation, they were merely wasting time.

As closely as possible in the dark, he located the site of his enciphering square. He stood near it and barked clamorously. Gilroy and the editor hastily left their futile prodding.

'He must've seen something,' the editor observed in a whisper.

Gilroy cupped a match in his hand and moved the light back and forth in the triangular corner of the cleared space. He shrugged.

'Not around there,' the editor said. 'He's pointing at the ground.'

Gilroy lowered the match. Before its light struck the ground, he yelped and dropped it, waving his burned fingers in the cool air. The editor murmured sympathy and scratched another match.

'Is this what you're looking for – a lot of letters in a square?'

Wood and Gilroy crowded close. The reporter struck his own match. In its light he narrowly inspected the crudely scratched encoding square.

'Be back in a second,' he said. It was too dark to see his face, but Wood heard his voice, harsh and strained. 'Getting flashlight.'

'What'll I do if the guy comes around?' the editor asked hastily.

'Nothing,' Gilroy rasped. 'He won't. Don't step on the square.'

Gilroy vanished into the night. The editor struck another match and scrutinized the ground with Deerslayer thoroughness.

'What the hell did he see?' he pondered. 'That guy –' He shook his head defeatedly and dropped the match.

Never in his life had Wood been so passionately excited. What *had* Gilroy discovered? Was it merely another circumstantial fact, like his realization that Talbot's gangsters were gunning for Wood; or was it a suspicion of Wood's identity? Gilroy had replied that the writer would not reappear, but that could have meant anything or nothing. Wood frantically searched for a way of finally demonstrating who he really was. He found only a negative plan – he would follow Gilroy's lead.

With every minute that passed, the editor grew angrier, shifting his leaning position against the brick wall, pacing around. When Gilroy came back, flashing a bright cone of light before him, the editor lashed out.

'Get it over with, Gilroy. I can't waste the whole night. Even if we do find out what happened, we can't print it –'

Gilroy ignored him. He splashed the brilliant ray of his huge five-celled flashlight over the enciphering square.

'Now look at it,' he said. He glanced intently at Wood, who also obeyed his order and stood at the editor's knee, searching the ground. 'The guy who made that square was very cautious – he put his back to the wall and faced the lot, so he wouldn't be taken by surprise. The square is upside-down to us. No, wait!' he said sharply as the editor moved to look at the square from its base. 'I don't want your footprints on it. Look at the bottom, where the writer must've stood.'

The editor stared closely. 'What do you see?' he asked puzzledly.

'Well, the ground is moist and fairly soft. There should be footprints. There are. *Only they're not human!*'

Raucously, the editor cleared his throat. 'You're kidding.'

'*Gestalt*,' Gilroy said, almost to himself, 'the whole is greater than the sum of its parts. You get a bunch of unconnected facts, all apparently unrelated to each other. Then suddenly one fact pops up – it doesn't seem any more important than the others – but all at once the others click into place, and you get a complete picture.'

'What are you mumbling about?' the editor whispered anxiously.

Gilroy stooped his great height and picked up a yellow stump of pencil. He turned it over in his hand before passing it to the editor.

'That's the pencil this dog snatched before we threw him out. You can see his teethmarks on the sides, where he carried it. But

there're teethmarks around the sharpened end. Maybe I'm nuts –'
He took the dirty code message out of his inside breast pocket and
smoothed it out. 'I saw these smudges the minute I looked at the
note, but they didn't mean anything to me then. What do you
make of them?'

The editor obediently examined the note in the glare of the
flash. 'They could be palmprints.'

'Sure – a baby's,' Gilroy said witheringly. 'Only they're not.
We both know they're pawprints, the same as are at the bottom
of the square. You know what I'm thinking. Look't the way the
dog is listening.'

Without raising his voice, he half turned his head and said quite
casually, 'Here comes the guy who wrote the note, right behind
the dog.'

Involuntarily, Wood spun round to face the dark lot. Even his
keen animal eyes could detect no one in the gloom. When he lifted
his gaze to Gilroy, he stared full into grim, frightened eyes.

'Put that in your pipe,' Gilroy said tremendously. 'That's the
reaction to the pitch of my voice, eh? You can't get out of it, chief.
We've got a werewolf on our hands, thanks to Moss and Talbot.'

Wood barked and frisked happily around Gilroy's towering
legs. He had been understood!

But the editor laughed, a perfectly normal, humorous, unconvinced laugh. 'You're wasting your time writing for a newspaper,
Gilroy –'

'O.K., smart guy,' Gilroy replied savagely. 'Stop your cackling
and tell me the answer to this –

'The dog comes into the newsroom and starts barking. I though
he was just trying to get us to follow him; but I never heard a dog
bark in long and short yelps before. He ran up the stairs, right
past all the other floors – business office, advertising department,
and so on – to the newsroom, because that's where he wanted to
go. We chased him out. He came back with a scrawled note,
saying: "I am a man.' Those four words took up the whole page.
Even a kid learning how to write wouldn't need so much space.
But if you hold the pencil in your mouth and try to connect the
bars of letters, you'd have written letters something like the ones
on the note.

'He needed a smaller system of letters, so he made up a simple
code. But he'd lost his pencil. He stole one of ours. Then he came
back, watching out for Talbot's gang cars.

'There aren't any footprints at the bottom of this square – only
a dog's pawprints. And there're two smudges on the message,

where he put his paws to hold down the paper while he wrote on it. All along he's been listening to every word we said. When I said in a conversational tone that the writer was standing behind him, he whirled around. Well?'

The editor was still far from convinced. 'Good job of training –'

'For a guy I used to respect, you certainly have the brain of a flea. Here – I don't know you name,' he said to Wood. 'What would you do if you had Moss here?'

Wood snarled.

'You're going to tell us where to find him. I don't know how, but you were smart enough to figure out a code, so you can figure out another way of communicating. Then you'll tell us what happened.'

It was Wood's moment of supreme triumph. True, he didn't have his body yet, but now it was only a matter of time. His joy at Gilroy's words was violent enough to shake the editor's literal, unimaginative mind.

'You still don't believe it,' Gilroy accused.

'How can I?' the editor cried plaintively. 'I don't even know why I'm talking to you as if it could be possible.'

Gilroy probed in a pile of rubbish until he recovered a short piece of wood. He quickly drew a single lin of small alphabetical symbols. He threw the stick away, stepped back and flashed the light directly at the alphabet. 'Now spell out what happened.'

Wood sprang back and forth before the alphabet, stopping at the letters he required and indicating them by pointing his snout down.

'T-a-l-b-o-t w-a-n-t-e-d a y-o-u-n-g h-e-a-l-t-h-y b-o-d-y M-o-s-s s-a-i-d h-e c-o-u-l-d g-i-v-e i-t t-o h-i-m –'

'Well, I'll be damned!' the editor blurted.

After that exclamation there was silence. Only the almost inaudible padding of Wood's paws on the soft ground, his excited panting, and the hoarse breathing of the men could be heard. But Wood had won!

Gilroy sat at the typewriter in his apartment; Wood stood beside his chair and watched the swiftly leaping keys; but the editor stamped nervously up and down the floor.

'I've wasted half the night,' he complained, 'and if I print this story I'll be canned. Why, damn it, Gilroy – how do you think the public'll take it if I can't believe it myself?'

'Hmmm,' Gilroy explained.

'You're sacrificing our job. You know that, don't you?'

'It doesn't mean that much to me,' Gilroy said without glancing up. 'Wood has to get back his body. He can't do it unless we help him.'

'Doesn't that sound ridiculous to you? "He has to get back his body." Imagine what the other papers'll do to that sentence!'

'Gilroy shifted impatiently. 'They won't see it,' he stated.

'Then why in hell are you writing the story?' the editor asked, astounded. 'Why don't you want me to go back to the office?'

'Quiet! I'll be through in a minute.' He inserted another sheet of paper and his flying fingers covered it with black, accusing words. Wood's mouth opened in a canine grin when Gilroy smiled down at him and nodded his head confidently. 'You're practically walking around on your own feet, pal. Let's go.'

He flapped on his coat and carelessly dropped a battered hat on his craggy head. Wood braced himself to dart off. The editor lingered.

'Where're we going?' he asked cautiously.

'To Moss, naturally, unless you can think of a better place.'

Wood could not tolerate the thought of delay. He tugged at the leg of the editor's pants.

'You bet I can think of a better place. Hey, cut it out, Wood – I'm coming along. But, hell, Gilroy! It's after ten. I haven't done a thing. Have a heart and make it short.'

With Gilroy hastening him by the arm and Wood dragging at his leg, the editor had to accompany them, though he continued his protests. At the door, however, he covered Wood while Gilroy hailed a taxi. When Gilroy signaled that the street was clear, he ran across the sidewalk with Wood bundled in his arms.

Gilroy gave the address. At its sound, Wood's mouth opened in a silent snarl. He was only a short distance from Moss, with two eloquent spokesmen to articulate his demands, and, if necessary, to mobilize public opinion for him! What would Moss do against that power?

They rode up Seventh Avenue and along Central Park West. Only the editor felt that they were speeding. Gilroy and Wood fretted irritably at every stop signal.

At Moss's street, Gilroy cautioned the driver to proceed slowly. The surgeon's house was guarded by two loitering black cars.

'Let us out at the corner,' Gilroy said.

They scurried into the entrance of a rooming house.

'Now what?' the editor demanded. 'We can't fight past them.'

Wood shook his head negatively. There was no entrance through the rear.

'Then the only way is across the roofs,' Gilroy determined. He put his head out and scanned the buildings between them and Moss. 'This one is six stories, the next two five, the one right next to Moss's is six, and Moss's is three. We'll have to climb up and down fire escapes and get in through Moss's roof. Ready?'

'I suppose so,' the editor said fatalistically.

Gilroy tried the door. It was locked. He chose a bell at random and rang it vigorously. There was a brief pause; then the tripper buzzed. He thrust open the door and burst up the stairs, four at a leap.

'Who's there?' a woman shouted down the stairwell.

They galloped past her. 'Sorry, lady,' Gilroy called back. 'We rang your bell by mistake.'

She looked disappointed and rather frightened; but Gilroy anticipated her emotion. He smiled and gayly waved his hand as he loped by.

The roof door was locked with a stout hook that had rusted into its eye. Gilroy smashed it open with the heel of his palm. They broke out onto a tarred roof, chill and black in the overcast, threatening night.

Wood and Gilroy discovered the fire escape leading to the next roof. They dashed for it. Gilroy tucked Wood under his left arm and swung himself over the anchored ladder.

'This is insane!' the editor said hoarsely. 'I've never done such a crazy thing in my life. Why can't we be smart and call the cops?'

'Yeah?' Gilroy sneered without stopping. 'What's your charge?'

'Against Moss? Why –'

'Think about it on the way.'

Gilroy and Wood were on the next roof, waiting impatiently for the editor to descend. He came down quickly but his thoughts wandered.

'You can charge him with what he did. He made a man into a dog.'

'That would sound swell in the indictment. Forget it. Just walk lightly. This damned roof creaks and lets out a noise like a drum.'

They advanced over the tarred sheets of metal. Beneath them, they could hear their occasionally heavy tread resound through hollow rooms. Wood's claws tapped a rhythmic tattoo.

They straddled over a low wall dividing the two buildings. Wood sniffed the air for enemies lurking behind chimneys, vents and doors. At instants of suspicion, Gilroy briefly flashed his light ahead. They climbed up a steel ladder to the six-story building adjoining Moss's.

'How about a kidnap charge?' the editor asked as they stared down over the wall at the roof of Moss's building.

'Please don't annoy me. Wood's body is in the observation ward at the hospital. How're you going to prove that Moss kidnapped him?'

The editor nodded in the gloom and searched for another legal charge. Gilroy splashed his light over Moss's roof. It was unguarded.

'Come on, Wood,' he said, inserting the flashlight in his belt. He picked up Wood under his left arm. In order to use his left hand in climbing, he had to squeeze Wood's middle in a stranglehold.

The only thing Wood was thankful for was that he could not look at the roof three stories below. Gilroy held him securely, tightly enough for his breath to struggle in whistling gasps. His throat knotted when Gilroy gashed his hand on a sharp sliver of dry paint scale.

'It's all right,' Gilroy hissed reassuringly. 'We're almost there.'

Above them, he saw the editor clambering heavily down the insecurely bolted ladder. Between the anchoring plates it groaned and swayed away from the unclean brick wall. Rung by rung they descended warily, Gilroy clutching for each hold, Wood suspended in space and helpless – both feeling their hearts drop when the ladder jerked under their weight.

The Gilroy lowered his foot and found the solid roof beneath it. He grinned impetuously in the dark. Wood writhed out of his hold. The editor cursed his way down to them.

He followed them to the rear fire escape. This time he offered to carry Wood down. Swinging out over the wall, Wood felt the editor's muscles quiver. Wood had nothing but a miserable animal life to lose, and yet even he was not entirely fearless in the face of the hidden dangers they were braving. He could sympathize with the editor, who had everything to lose and did not wholly believe that Wood was not a dog. Discovering a human identity in an apparently normal collie must have been a staggeringly hard fact for him to swallow.

He set Wood down on the iron bars. Gilroy quickly joined them, and yanked fiercely at the top window. It was locked.

'Need a jimmy to pry it open,' Gilroy mused. He fingered the edges of the frame. 'Got a knife on you?'

The editor fished absentmindedly through his pockets. He brought out a handful of keys, pencil stubs, scraps of paper, matches, and a cheap sheathed nail file. Gilroy snatched the file.

He picked at the putty in the ancient casement with the point. It chipped away easily. He loosened the top and sides.

'Now,' he breathed. 'Stand back a little and get ready to catch it.'

He inserted the file at the top and levered the glass out of the frame. It stuck at the bottom and sides, refusing to fall. He caught the edges and lifted it out, laying it down noiselessly out of the way.

'Let's go.' He backed in through the empty casement. 'Hand Wood through.'

They stood in the dark room, under the same roof with Moss. Wood exultantly sensed the proximity of the one man he hated – the one man who could return his body to him. 'Now!' he thought. '*Now!*'

'Gilroy,' the editor urged, 'we can charge Moss with vivisection.'

'That's right,' Gilroy whispered. But they heard the doorknob rattle in his hand and turn cautiously.

'Then where're you going?' the editor rasped in a panic.

'We're here,' Gilroy replied coolly. 'So let's finish it.'

The door swung back; pale weak light entered timidly. They stared down the long, narrow, dismal hall to the stairs at the center of the house. Down those stairs they would find Moss.

Wood's keen animal sense of smell detected Moss's personal odor. The surgeon had been there not long before.

He crouched around the stairhead and cautiously lowered himself from step to step. Gilroy and the editor clung to the banister and wall, resting the bulk of their weight on their hands. They turned the narrow spiral where Clarence had fatally encountered the sharpness of Wood's fangs, down to the hall floor where his fat body had sprawled in blood.

Distantly, Wood heard a cane tap nervously, momentarily; then it stopped at a heated, hissed command that scarcely carried even to his ears. He glanced up triumphantly at Gilroy, his deep eyes glittering, his mouth grinning savagely, baring the red tongue lolling in the white, deadly trap of fangs. He had located and identified the sounds. Both Moss and Talbot were in a room at the back of the house.

He hunched his powerful shoulders and advanced slowly, stiff-legged, with the ominous air of all meat hunters stalking prey from ambush. Outside the closed door he crouched, muscles gathered for the lunge, his ears flat back along his pointed head to protect them from injury. But they heard muffled voices inaudible to men's dulled senses.

'Sit down, doc,' Talbot said. 'The truck'll be here soon.'

'I'm not concerned with my personal safety,' Moss replied tartly. 'It's merely that I dislike inefficiency, especially when you claim –'

'Well, it's not Jake's fault. He's coming back from a job.'

Wood could envision the faint sneer on Moss's scrubbed pink face. 'You'll collapse any minute within the next six months, but the acquisitive nature is as strong as ever in you, isn't it, Talbot? You couldn't resist the chance of making a profit, and at a time like this!'

'Oh, don't lose your head. The cata-whatever-you-call-it can't talk and the dog is probably robbing garbage cans. What's the lam for?'

'I'm changing my residence purely as a matter of precaution. You underestimate human ingenuity, even limited by a dog's inarticulateness.'

Wood grinned up at his comrades. The editor was dough-faced, rigid with apprehension. Gilroy held a gun and his left hand snaked out at the doorknob. The editor began an involuntarily motion to stop him. The door slammed inward before he completed it.

Wood and Gilroy stalked in, sinister in their grim silence. Talbot merely glanced at the gun. He had stared into too many black muzzles to be frightened by it. When his gaze traveled to Wood his jaw fell and hung open, trembling senilely. His constantly fighting lungs strangled. He screamed, a high, tortured wail, and tore frantically at his shirt, trying to release his chest from crushing pressure.

'An object lesson for you, Talbot,' Moss said without emotion. 'Do not underestimate an enemy.'

Gilroy lost his frigid attitude. 'Don't let him strangle. Help him.'

'What can I do?' Moss shrugged. 'It's angina pectoris. Either he pulls out of the convulsions by himself – or he doesn't. I can't help. But what did you want?'

No one answered him. Horrified, they were watching Talbot go purple in his death agony, lose the power of shrieking, and tear at his chest. Gilroy's gun hand was limp; yet Moss made no attempt to escape. The air rattled through Talbot's predatory nose. He fell in a contorted heap.

Wood felt sickened. He knew that in self-preservation doctors had to harden themselves, but only a monster of brutal callousness could have disregarded Talbot's frightful death as if it had not been going on.

'Oh, come now, it isn't as bad as all that,' Moss said acidly.

Wood raised his shocked stare from the rag-doll body to Moss's hard, unfearful eyes. The surgeon had made no move to defend himself, to call for help from the squad of gangsters at the front of the house. He faced them with inhuman prepossession.

'It upsets your plans,' Gilroy spat.

Moss lifted his shoulders, urbanely, delicately disdainful. 'What difference should his death make to me? I never cared for his company.'

'Maybe not, but his money seemed to smell O.K. to you. He's out of the picture. He can't keep us from printing this story now.' Gilroy pulled a thin folded typescript from his inside breast pocket and shoved it out at Moss.

The surgeon read it interestedly, leaning casually against a wall. He came to the end of the short article and read the lead paragraph over again. Politely, he gave it back to Gilroy.

'It's very clear,' he said. 'I'm accused of exchanging the identities of a man and a dog. You even describe my alleged technique.'

'"Alleged"!' Gilroy roared savagely. 'You mean you deny it?'

'Of course. Isn't it fantastic?' Moss smiled. 'But that isn't the point. Even if I admitted it, how do you think I could be convicted on such evidence? The only witness seems to be the dog you call Wood. Are dogs allowed to testify in court? I don't remember, but I doubt it.'

Wood was stunned. He had not expected Moss to brazen out the charge. An ordinary man would have broken down, confronted by their evidence.

Even the shrinking editor was stung into retorting: 'We have proof of criminal vivisection!'

'But no proof that I was the surgeon.'

'You're the only one in New York who could've done that operation.'

'See how far that kind of evidence will get you.'

Wood listened with growing anger. Somehow they had permitted Moss to dominate the situation, and he parried their charges with cool, sarcastic deftness. No wonder he had not tried to escape! He felt himself to be perfectly safe. Wood growled, glowering hatred at Moss. The surgeon looked down contemptuously.

'All right, we can't convict you in court,' Gilroy said. He hefted his gun, tightening his finger on the trigger. 'That's not what we want, anyhow. This little scientific curiosity can make you operate on Wood and transfer his identity back to his own body.'

Moss's expression of disdain did not alter. He watched Gilroy's tensing finger with an astonishing lack of concern.

'Well, speak up,' Gilroy rasped, waving the gun ominously.

'You can't force me to operate. All you can do is kill me, and I am as indifferent to my own death as I was to Talbot's.' His smile broadened and twisted down at the corners, showing his teeth in a snarl that was the civilized, overrefined counterpart of Wood's. 'Your alleged operation interests me, however. I'll operate for my customary fee.'

The editor pushed Gilroy inside and hurriedly closed the door. 'They're coming,' he chattered. 'Talbot's gangsters.'

In two strides Gilroy put Moss between him and the door. His gun jabbed rudely into Moss's unflinching back. 'Get over on the other side, you two, so the door'll hide you when it swings back,' he ordered.

Wood and the editor retreated. Wood heard steps along the hall, then a pause, and a harsh voice shouted: 'Hey, boss! Truck's here.'

'Tell them to go away,' Gilroy said in a low, suppressed tone.

Moss called, 'I'm in the second room at the rear of the house.'

Gilroy viciously stabbed him with the gun muzzle. 'You're asking for it. I said tell them to go away!'

'You wouldn't dare to kill me until I've operated –'

'If you're not scared, why do you want them? What's the gag?'

The door flung open. A gangster started to enter. He stiffened, his keen, battle-trained eyes flashing from Talbot's twisted body to Moss, and to Gilroy, standing menacingly behind the surgeon. In a swift, smooth motion a gun leaped from his armpit holster.

'What happened to the boss?' he demanded hoarsely. 'Who's he?'

'Put your gun away, Pinero. The boss died of a heart attack. That shouldn't surprise you – he was expecting it any day.'

'Yeah, I know. But how'd that guy get in?'

Moss stirred impatiently. 'He was here all along. Send the truck back. I'm not moving. I'll take care of Talbot.'

The gangster looked uncertain, but, in lieu of another commander, he obeyed Moss's order. 'Well, O.K. if you say so.' He closed the door.

When Pinero had gone down the hall, Moss turned to face Gilroy.

'You're not scared – much!' Gilroy said.

Moss ignored his sarcastic outburst. 'Where were we?' he asked. 'Oh, yes. While you were standing there shivering, I had time to think over my offer. I'll operate for nothing.'

'You bet you will!' Gilroy wagged his gun forcefully.

Moss sniffed at it. 'That has nothing to do with my decision. I have no fear of death, and I'm not afraid of your evidence. If I do operate, it will be because of my interest in the experiment.' Wood intercepted Moss's speculative gaze. It mocked, hardened, glittered sinisterly. 'But of course,' Moss added smoothly, 'I will definitely operate. In fact, I insist on it!'

His hidden threat did not escape Wood. Once he lay under Moss's knife it would be the end. A slip of the knife – a bit of careful carelessness in the gas mixture – a deliberately caused infection – and Moss would clear himself of the accusation by claiming he could not perform the operation, and therefore he was not the vivisectionist. Wood recoiled, shaking his head violently from side to side.

'Wood's right,' the editor said. 'He knows Moss better. He wouldn't come out of the operation alive.'

Gilroy's brow creased in an uneasy frown. The gun in his hand was a futile implement of force; even Moss knew he would not use it – could not, because the surgeon was only valuable to them alive. His purpose had been to make Moss operate. Well, he thought, he had accomplished that purpose. Moss offered to operate. But all four knew that under Moss's knife, Wood was doomed. Moss had cleverly turned the victory to utter rout.

'Then what the hell'll we do?' Gilroy exploded savagely. 'What do you say, Wood? Want to take the chance, or keep on in a dog's body?'

Wood snarled, backing away.

'At least, he's still alive,' the editor said fatalistically.

Moss smiled, protesting with silken mockery that he would do his best to return Wood's body.

'Barring accidents,' Gilroy spat. 'No soap, Moss. He'll get along the way he is, and you're going to get yours.'

He looked grimly at Wood, jerking his head significantly in Moss's direction.

'Come on, chief,' he said, guiding the editor through the door and closing it. 'These old friends want to be alone – lot to talk over –'

Instantly, Wood leaped before the door and crouched there menacingly, glaring at Moss with blind, vicious hatred. For the first time, the surgeon dropped his pose of indifference. He inched cautiously around the wall toward the door. He realized suddenly that this was an animal . . . .

Wood advanced, cutting off his line of retreat. Mane bristling, head lowered ominously between blocky shoulders, bright gums showing above white curved fangs, Wood stalked over the floor, stiff-jointed, in a low, inexorably steady rhythm of approach.

Moss watched anxiously. He kept looking up at the door in an agony of longing. But Wood was there, closing the gap for the attack. He put up his hands to thrust away . . . .

And his nerve broke. He could not talk down mad animal eyes as he could a man holding a gun. He darted to the side and ran for the door.

Wood flung himself at the swiftly pumping legs. They crashed against him, tripped. Moss sprawled face down on the floor. He crossed his arms under his head to protect his throat.

Wood slashed at an ear. It tore, streaming red. Moss screeched and clapped his hands over his face, trying to rise without dropping his guard. But Wood ripped at his fingers.

The surgeon's hands clawed out. He was kneeling, defenseless, trying to fight off the rapid, aimed lunges – and those knifelike teeth . . . .

Wood gloated. A minute before, the scrubbed pink face had been aloof, sneering. Now it bobbed frantically at his eye level, contorted with overpowering fear, blood flowing brightly down the once scrupously clean cheeks.

For an instant, the pale throat gleamed exposed at him. It was soft and helpless. He shot through the air. His teeth struck at an angle and snatched – the white flesh parted easily. But a bony structure snapped between his jaws as he swooped by.

Moss knelt there after Wood had struck. His pain-twisted face gaped imbecilically, hands limp at his sides. His throat poured a red flood. Then his face drained to a ghastly lack of color and he pitched over.

He had lost, but he had also won. Wood was doomed to live out his life in a dog's body. He could not even expect to live his own life span. The average life of a dog is fifteen years. Wood could expect perhaps ten years more.

In his human body, Wood had found it difficult to find a job. He had been a code expert; but code experts, salesmen and apprentice workmen have no place in a world of shrinking markets. The employment agencies are glutted with an oversupply of normal human intelligences housed in strong, willing, expert human bodies.

The same normal human intelligence in a handsome collie's body had a greater market value. It was a rarity, a phenomenon to be gaped at after a ticket had been purchased for the privilege.

'Men've always had a fondness for freaks,' Gilroy philosophized on their way to the theater where Wood had an engagement. 'Mildly amusing freaks are paid to entertain. The really funny ones are given seats of honor and power. Figure it out, Wood. I can't. Once we get rid of our love of freaks and put them where they belong, we'll have a swell world.'

The taxi stopped in a sidestreet, at the stage entrance. Lurid red-and-yellow posters, the size of cathedral murals, plastered the theater walls; and from them smirked prettified likenesses of Wood.

'Gosh!' their driver gasped. 'Wait'll my kids hear about this. I drove the Talkin' Dog! Gee, is that an honor, or ain't it?'

On all sides, pedestrians halted in awe, taxis stopped with a respectful screech of brakes; then an admiring swarm bore down on him.

'Isn't he *cute*?' women shrieked. 'So *intelligent*-looking!'

'Sure,' Wood heard their driver boast proudly, 'I drove him down here. What's he like?' His voice lowered confidentially. 'Well, the guy with him — his manager, I guess — he was talkin' to him just as intelligent as I'm talkin' to you. Like he could understand ev'y word.'

'Bet he could, too,' a listener said definitely.

'G'on,' another theorized. 'He's just trained, like Rin-tin-tin, on'y better. But he's smart all right. Wisht I owned him.'

The theater-district squad broke through the tangle of traffic and formed a lane to the stage door.

'Yawta be ashamed ayehselves,' a cop said. 'All this over a mutt!'

Wood bared his fangs at the speaker, who retreated defensively.

'Wise guy, huh?' the mob jeered. 'Think he can't understand?'

It was a piece of showmanship that Wood and Gilroy had devised. It never failed to find a feeder in the form of an officious policeman and a response from the crowd.

Even in the theater, Wood was not safe from overly enthusiastic admiration. His fellow performers persisted in scratching his unitching back and ears, cooing and burbling in a singularly unintelligent manner.

The thriller that Wood had made in Hollywood was over; and while the opening acts went through their paces, Wood and Gilroy stood as far away from the wings as the theater construction would permit.

'Seven thousand bucks a week, pal,' Gilroy mused over and over. 'Just for doing something that any mug out in the audience can do twice as easily. Isn't that the payoff?'

In the year that had passed, neither was still able to accustom himself to the mounting figures in their bankbooks. Pictures, personal appearances, endorsements, highly fictionized articles in magazines – all at astronomical prices. . . .

But he could never have enough money to buy back the human body he had starved in.

'O.K., Wood,' Gilroy whispered. 'We're on.'

They were drummed onto the stage with deafening applause. Wood went through his routine perfunctorily. He identified objects that had been named by the theater manager, picking them out of a heap of piled objects.

Ushers went through the aisles, collecting questions the audience had written on slips of paper. They passed them up to Gilroy.

Wood took a long pointer firmly in his mouth and stood before a huge lettered screen. Painfully, he pointed out, letter by letter, the answers to the audience's questions. Most of them asked about the future, market tips, racing information. A few seriously probed his mind.

White light stabbed down at him. Mechanically, he spelled out the simple answers. Most of his bitterness had evaporated; in its place was a dreary defeat, and dull acceptance of his dog's life. His bankbook had six figures to the left of the decimal – more than he had ever conceived of, even as a distant utopian possibility. But no surgeon could return his body to him, or increase his life expectancy of less than ten years.

Sharply, everything was washed out of sight; Gilroy, the vast alphabet screen, the heavy pointer in his mouth, the black space smeared with pale, gaping blobs of faces, even the white light staring down. . . .

He lay on a cot in a long ward. There was no dream-like equality of illusion in the feel of smooth sheets beneath and above him, or in the weight of blankets resting on his *outstretched* body.

And independently of the rest of his hand, his *finger* moved in response to his will. Its nail scratched at the sheet, loudly, victoriously.

An intern, walking through the ward, looked around for the source of the gloating sound. He engaged Wood's eyes that were glittering avidly, deep with intelligence. Then they watched the scratching finger.

'You're coming back,' the intern said at last.

'I'm coming back.' Wood spoke quietly, before the scene vanished and he heard Gilroy repeat a question he had missed.

He knew then that the body-mind was a unit. Moss had been wrong; there was more to identity than that small gland, something beyond the body. The forced division Moss had created was unnatural; the transplanted tissue was being absorbed, remodeled. Somehow, he knew these returns to his natural identity would recur, more and more – till it became permanent – till he became human once more.

JANE BROWN'S BODY

Cornell Woolrich

Three o'clock in the morning. The highway is empty, under a malignant moon. The oil drippings make the roadway gleam like a blue-satin ribbon. The night is still but for a humming noise coming up somewhere behind a rise of ground.

Two other, fiercer, whiter moons, set close together, suddenly top the rise, shoot a fan of blinding platinum far down ahead of them. Headlights. The humming burgeons into a roar. The touring car is going so fast it sways from side to side. The road is straight. The way is long. The night is short.

The man hunched at the wheel is tense; his eyes are fixed unblinkingly on the hem of the black curtain that the headlights roll up before him. His eyes are like two little lumps of coal. His face is brown; his hair is white. His figure is gaunt, but there is power in the bony wrists that grip the wheel, and power in the locked jaws that show white with their own tension.

The speedometer needle flickers a little above eighty . . . .

The rear-view mirror shows a very tired young woman napping on the back seat. Her legs are tucked up under her, and the laprobe has been swathed around her from the waist down. One black-gloved hand is twisted in the looped cord dangling from the side of the car; it hangs there even as she sleeps, of its own weight. She sways with a limpness, a lack of reflex-resistance, that almost suggests an absence of life.

She has on a tiny pillbox hat with a fine-meshed veil flaring out all around below it. The wind keeps pushing it back like a film across her face. The contact of her nose makes a funny little knob on it. It should billow out at that point with her breathing, at such close contact. It doesn't, just caves in as though she were sucking it through parted lips. She sleeps with her mouth slightly open.

The moon is the only thing that keeps up with this careening

119

car, grinning down derisively on it all the way, mile after mile, as though to say, 'I'm on to you!'

A scattering of pinpoint lights shows up in the blackness ahead. A town or village straddling the highway. The indicator on the speedometer begins to lose ground. The man glances in his mirror at the girl, a little anxiously as if this oncoming town were some kind of test to be met.

An illuminated road sign flashes by.

CAUTION!

MAIN STREET AHEAD – SLOW UP

The man nods grimly, as if agreeing with that first word. But not in the way it is meant.

The lights grow bigger, spread out on either side. Street lights peer out here and there among the trees. The highway suddenly sprouts a plank sidewalk on each side of it. Dark store-windows glide by.

With an instinctive gesture, the man dims his lights from blinding platinum to just a pale wash. A lunch-room window drifts by.

The lights of a big bus going his way wink just ahead. He makes ready to swerve out and get past it. And then there is an unlooked-for complication. A railroad right-of-way bisects the main street here. Perhaps no train has passed all night until now. Perhaps no other will pass until morning. Five minutes sooner, five minutes later, and he could have avoided the delay. But just as car and lighted bus approach, side by side, a bells starts ringing, zebra-striped barriers weighted with red lanterns are slowly lowered, and the road is blocked off. The two cars are forced to halt abreast while a slow procession of freight cars files endlessly by. Almost simultaneously, a large milk-truck has turned in behind him from the side-road, sealing him in.

The lights of the bus shine into the car and fall on the sleeping woman. There is only one passenger in the bus, but he is on the near side, and he looks idly out the window into the neighbouring machine. His eye drops to the sleeping woman and remains there, as any man's would.

There is terrible rigidity about the man at the wheel now. White shows over his knuckles. His eyes are glued on the mirror, in which he can see the bus passenger gazing casually into the rear of his car. A shiny thread starts down his face, catches in one of its leathery furrows. Sweat. A second one follows. His chest is rising and falling under his coat and he breathes as if he has been running.

The man at the bus window keeps looking at the woman, looking at her. He doesn't mean anything by it, probably. There's nothing else for him to look at. Why shouldn't he look at a woman, even a sleeping one? She must be beautiful under that veil. Some men are born starers-at-women, anyway.

But as the endless freight cars click by ahead, as the long scrutiny keeps on, one of the white-knuckled hands on the wheel is moving. It leaves the polished wooden rim, drops to its owner's lap. The whiteness goes out of it. It starts crawling up under his coat, buries itself between the buttoned halves, comes out again, white over the knuckles again, gripping an automatic.

His eyes have never once left the rear-view mirror, never once left the reflection of the bus-passenger's face. He acts as if he is waiting for some expression to come into it. Some certain, telltale expression. He acts as if, then, he will do something with that gun on his lap.

But the caboose has finally terminated the endless chain of freight cars, the bell stops ringing, the barriers slowly rise. The bus driver unlumbers his clutch, the line of lighted windows start to edge forward. The gun vanishes, the hand that held it returns to the wheel empty. A moment later bus, and passenger, and face have all spurted ahead. The touring car hangs back a moment, to give it a good start. The milk truck signals impatiently for clearance, then cuts out around the obstacle, lurches ahead.

The leathery-faced man at the wheel has his under lip thrust out, expelling hot breath of relief up past his own face. He touches the two liquid threads the drops of sweat left on his face, blots them.

He goes on into the night, along the arrow-straight highway, under the peering moon. The lady sways and dreams, and puckers her veil in.

A long slow rise begins, and now the car starts to buck when he gives it the accelerator. He looks at the gauge; his gas is dwindling fast. The tan washes out of his face for a moment. He's on a main road, after all. All he has to do is pull over, wait for a tow-line, if he runs out of gas. Why that fleeting panic on his face?

He nurses the car forward on the dregs of gas remaining. Zigzags it from side to side of the highway, to lessen the incline that might defeat it. It goes by fits and starts, slower all the time, but he's near the crest now. If he can only reach it, he can coast down the dip on the other side without an engine.

The car creeps up over the rise, hesitates, about to stall. Before him the road dips downward under the moon for miles. In the distance a white glow marks a filling station. He maneuvers the wheel desperately in and out, the momentum of the descent catches at the machine, and a moment later it's coasting along at increasing speed.

The filling station blazes nearer, an aurora borealis in the middle of the dark countryside. He dare not go past, yet he's very tense as the car rolls within the all-revealing light. He glances anxiously in the mirror. He wonders about the window shades, but leaves them the way they are. There's nothing that draws the human eye quicker than a suggestively lowered shade.

He turns aside, inches up the runway, brakes to a stop. An attendant jumps over.

'Five', he says, and sits there watching the man hook up the pipeline. Watching him with utter absorption. The gun is in his lap again, bedded under the hem of his coat.

The grease monkey approaches the front window. 'Wash your windows, chief?'

The driver stretches his lips into a grin. 'Leave 'em.'

The monkey grins back, and his eyes wander on past the driver to the girl in the back of the car, rest there for a minute.

'Dead tired,' the man at the wheel says. 'Here's your money; keep the change.' The car moves out of the yellow radiance into the sheltering gloom again. Secrecy wells up into its interior once more, like India ink.

The flabbergasted attendant is shouting something after him. 'Hey, mister, that's a twenty-dollar bill you –'

The car is racing along again now. The man at the wheel tenses. What's that peppering sound coming up behind him? A small, single beam of light is seesawing after him. If the man was frightened by the bus and by the filling station, what word can describe the look on his face now, as his mirror shows him a state policeman on his tail? Teeth bared in a skull-like flash, he fights down an impulse to open up, to try to race for it. He pulls over to the side, slows, stops. Again the gun comes out, and again it is bedded under his thigh with the butt protruding in readiness on the side away from the window. Then he sits grinding his fist into the hollow of his other hand.

The motorcycle flashes by, loops awkwardly around, comes back. The rider gets off, walks over, planks his foot down heavily on the runningboard. He ducks his head, leers in at him, beetle-browed.

'What's your hurry, fellow? I clocked you at eighty.'

'Eighty-four,' corrects the leathery-faced man, with a dangerous quietness that cannot be mistaken for humility.

'Well, fifty's the limit around here. Lemme see your license.'

The driver takes out his license with his left hand; the right is lying idly beside his right thigh, on cold black metal.

The state cop reads by the dashboard light, leaning even further in to do so. His own weapon is way out behind at his hip; the window frame would block his elbow in a sudden reach. 'Anton Denholt. Doctor, eh? I'm surprised at you, all the more reason you oughta have more sense! Next state, too, huh? You people are the ones give us the most trouble. Well, you're in my state now, get that; you didn't quite make that state-line marker down there – '

Denholt glances along the road as if he hadn't seen the marker before. 'I didn't try to,' he says in that same toneless voice.

The cop nods thoughtfully. 'I guess you could have at that,' he admits. 'What were you doing eight-four for – ?'

Perhaps Denholt can't stand waiting for the man to discover the girl sleeper in the back, perhaps his nerves are so frayed by now that he'd rather call attention to her himself and get it over with. He jerks his head toward the back seat. 'On her account', he says. 'Every minute counts.'

The cop peers back. 'She sick, Doc?' he asks, a little more considerately.

Denholt says, 'It's a matter of life and death.' And again he is speaking the absolute truth, far more than the trooper can guess.

The cop begins to look apologetic. 'Why didn't you say so? There's a good hospital at Rawling. You must have passed by there an hour ago. Why didn't you take her there?'

'No. I can make it where I'm going, if you'll only let me be on my way. I want to get her home before the baby – '

The cop gives a low whistle. 'No wonder you were burning up the road!' He slaps his book closed, hands Denholt back his license. 'You want an escort? You'll make better time. My beat ends at that marker down there, but I can put in a call for you –'

'No, thanks,' says Denholt blandly. 'I haven't much further to go.'

The touring car glides off. There is a sort of fatalism in Denholt's attitude now, as he urges the car back to high speed. What else can happen to him, after what just did? What else is there to be afraid of – now?

Less than forty miles past the state line, he leaves the great transcontinental highway and turns off into a side road, a 'feeder'. Presently it begins to take a steady upgrade, into the foothills of a chain of mountains. The countryside changes, becomes wilder, lonelier. Trees multiply to the thickness of woodlands. The handiwork of man, all but the roadway itself, slowly disappears.

He changes his course a second time, leaves the feeder for what is little better than an earth-packed trail, sharply tilted, seldom used. The climb is steady. Through occasional breaks in the trees of the thickly wooded slopes that support the trail, he can see the low country he has left below, the ribbon of the trunkroad he was on, an occasional winking light like a glow-worm toiling slowly along it. There are hairpin turns; over-hanging branches sway back with a hiss as he forces his way through. He has to go much slower here, but he seems to know the way.

A barbed-wire fence leaps suddenly out from nowhere, begins to parallel the miserable road. Four rungs high, each rung three strands in thickness, viciously spined, defying penetration by anything but the smallest animals. Strange, to want privacy that badly in such an out-of-the-way place. A double gate sidles along in it, double-padlocked, and stops abreast of him as his car comes to a halt. A placard beside it reads in the diamond-brightness of the headlights: 'Private Property. Keep Out.' A common-enough warning, but strange to find it here in this mountain fastness. Even, somehow, sinister.

He gets out, opens both padlocks, edges the freed halves of the gate inward with his shoe. Instantly a jarring, jangling sound explodes from one of the trees nearby. An alarm bell, wired to the gate. Its clang is frightening in this dark silence. It too spells lack of normality, seems the precaution of a fanatic.

The car drives through, stops while the man closes and fastens the prickly gate behind it. The bell shuts off; the stillness is deafening by contrast. The car goes on until the outline of a house suddenly uptilts the searching headlight-beams, log-built, sprawling, resembling a hunting-lodge. But there's no friend-liness to it. There is something ominous and forbidding about its look, so dark, so forgotten, so secretive-looking. The kind of a house that has a maw to swallow with – a one-way house, that you feel will never disgorge any living thing that enters it. Leprous in the moonlight festering on its roof. And the two round sworls of light played by the heads of the car against its side, intersecting, form a pear-shaped oval that resembles a gleaming skull.

The man leaves the car again, jumps up under a sort of a shed arrangement sheltering the main entrance. Metal clashes and a black opening yawns. He vanishes through it, while pulsing bright-beamed car and sleeping lady wait obediently outside.

Light springs up within – the yellow-green wanness of coal-oil, shining out through the door to make the coal-black tree-trunks outside seem even blacker. The place looks eerier than ever now.

Homecoming?

The man's shadow lengthens, blacks out of the doorway, and he's ready to receive the patient lady. He kills the engine, opens the rear door and reaches in for her with outstretched arms. He disengages her dangling wrist from the intertwined support-strap, brushes off the laprobe, cradles her body in upturned arms, and waddles inside with her, like someone carrying something very precious. The door bangs shut behind him at a backward thrust of his heel, and darkness swallows up the world outside.

2

He carries her through the building into an extension hidden from view from the outside. There is a distinct difference between it and the rest of the rambling structure. Its walls are not log, but brick, covered with plaster, that must have been hauled to this inaccessible place at great trouble and expense. It's wired for electricity, current supplied by a homemade generator. Dazzling, clinical-white lights beats down from above in here. And there are no chairs here, no rough-hewn tables, anything like that. Instead, retorts and bunsen-burners. A zinc operating table. Solution pans. A glass case of instruments. And across one entire side of the room a double tier of mesh cages, each containing a rabbit.

He comes in swiftly with his burden, puts her down on the zinc table. She never stirs. He turns back and closes the door, bolts it both at top and bottom. He strips off coat and shirt and undershirt, slips into a surgeon's white jacket. He takes a hypodermic needle out of the instrument case, drops it into a pan of antiseptic solution, lights a flame under it. Then he goes back to the table.

The girl's figure has retained the double-up position it held all during the long ride; it lies on her side, legs tucked-up under her as they were on the car-seat, arm thrust out, wrist dangling just as the strap held it. Denholt seems to have expected this, yet he frowns just a little. He tries to straighten out the stiffened limbs; they resist him. Not all his strength can force them into a straight line with the torso. He begins to do what he has to do with frantic haste, as if every moment was both an obstacle and a challenge.

This is so. For rigor is setting in; the sleeping lady has been dead the better part of the night. . . .

Denholt tears her things off arm over arm, with motions like an overhand swimmer. Hat and veil, black dress, shoes, hosiery, fall about the floor.

The girl was evidently pretty; she must have been quite young too. The rouge she put on in life still frames her parted lips. Her figure is slim and shapely, unmarred by wounds. There is no blood on her at all. That is important. Denholt races up with a jar of alcohol, douses it all over her with a great slapping splash.

He seizes the hypo from the scalding pan, hurriedly fills the barrel at a retort of colorless liquid, turns the huddled dripping figure over on its face, sweeps the nape-hair out of the way with one hand. He poises the needle at the base of the skull, looks briefly at the whitewashed ceiling as though in prayer, presses the plunger home.

He stands back, lets the hypo fall with a clash. It breaks, but that doesn't matter; if it has failed, he never wants to use one again.

The needle's tiny puncture doesn't close up as it would in living tissue; it remains a visible, tiny, black pore. He takes a wad of cotton, holds it pressed there, to keep the substance just injected from trickling out again. He is trembling all over. And the seconds tick into minutes.

Outside it must be dawn, but no light penetrates the sealed-up laboratory. It must be dawn, and the last breath went out of his body on the table – how long before? Irretrievably gone from this world, as dead as though she had lived a thousand years ago. Men have cut the Isthmus of Panama and joined the two oceans; they have bored tunnels that run below rivers; built aluminium planes that fly from Frisco to Manila; sent music over the air and photographs over wires; but never, when the heart-beat of their own kind has once stopped, never when the spark of life has fled, have they been able to reanimate the mortal clay with that commonest yet most mysterious of all processes; the vital force. And this man thinks he can – this man alone, out of all the world's teeming billions!

Five minutes that are centuries have gone by. There has been no change in her face or body. He lifts the wad of cotton now because his thumb and forefinger ache from holding it so steadily. And then –

The black puncture has vanished. The indented skin has closed up to erase it. Denholt tries to tell himself that this is due to the moisture of the serum itself or to the pressure of his fingers; but he knows that only life can do that – neither moisture nor pressure if there isn't life. Shrinking from facing disappointment, he whispers aloud: 'It's still there; I don't see it, that's all. My eyes aren't sharp enough.'

Tottering, he moves around the zinc table, picks up a small mirror, comes back with it. He turns her head slightly, holds the glass to the rigid mouth. Something wavers across it, too nebulous for the eye to discern at first. It comes again, stronger. Like a flurry. The glass mists, then clears. Then it mists once more, unmistakably now.

'The nervous exudation of my own fingers, holding it,' he whispers. But he knows better. He drops the mirror as he did the needle. It clashes and shivers into pieces. But it has told him all it could.

There remains the heart to go by. If breath has done that to the glass, the heart will show it. Without the heart, no breath.

He turns her over completely now, on her back once more. His hand slowly descends to her chest, like a frightened bird spiraling to rest. It leaps up again spasmodically, as though it has received a galvanic shock at what it felt. Not alone a vibration, but warmth. Warmth slowly diffusing around the region of the heart; a lessening of the stone coldness that grips the body elsewhere. The whole chest cavern is slowly rising and falling. The heart is alive, has come back to life, in a dead body. And life is spreading, catching on!

Awed almost beyond endurance – even though he has given up his whole life for this, believing he *could* accomplish it, believing some day it *would* happen – he collapses to his knees, buries his head against the side of the table, sobs broken-heartedly. For extreme joy and extreme sorrow are indistinguishable beyond a certain point. Denholt is a very humble, a very terrified man, at the moment, almost regretting what he has done – he has set God's law at bay, he knows it. Pride, triumph, the overweening egotism that spells complete insanity will come later.

He rouses himself presently. She stills needs help, attention, or he may lose her again. How often that happened with the rabbits until he learned what to do. The warm radiations from the heart have spread all over the body now, and it is a greater warmth than that of his own body. A ruddy flush, a fever-redness, has replaced the dead-white hue, especially over the heart and on the face and throat. It needs a furnace-temperature like this to cause the once-stagnant blood to circulate anew. He snatches up a thermometer, applies it. One hundred and five degrees, high enough to kill her all over again a second time. But death must be burned out and new life infused at molten heat, for this is not biological birth – but pure chemistry.

He must work fast.

He opens the door of the electric refrigerator, removes a pail of finely chopped ice he had prepared. The fearful heat of almost-boiling blood must be offset or it will destroy her before she has begun again to live. He wraps a rubber sheet around her, packs her body with the chopped ice, rolls her tightly up in it. He tests her temperature repeatedly. Within five minutes it has gone down considerably. The ice has all melted, as if placed on a hot stove. As he opens the sheet streams of water trickle out of the four corners. But the heart and the lungs are still going, the first danger has been met and overcome, the process of revivification has not in itself destroyed her. A delirious groan escaping her lips is the first sound she makes in this second life of hers; a feverish tossing from side to side the first movement. She is in full delirium. But delirium is the antithesis of death; it is the body's struggle to survive.

The laboratory has done all it can for her; from now on it is a matter of routine medical care, nursing, as in an ordinary illness. He wraps her in a thick blanket, unbolts the door, removes her from the cold zinc table and carries her to a bed in a room in another part of the house.

All through the long hours of the day he sits by her, as a mother sits by her only child in mortal illness, counting each breath she takes, feeling her pulse, helping her heart-action with a little digitalis, pouring a little warm milk and brandy down her parched throat from time to time. Watching, waiting, for the second great mystery to unfold itself. A mystery as great or greater than the one he has already witnessed. Will reason return full-panoplied, or will the brain remain dead or crippled in an otherwise living body? Will she be some inarticulate, idiot thing better left unrevived? Or will she remember who she was, what went before – be the first human to bridge the gap of death, to tell the living what awaits them on the other side of the shadowy border?

All through the day the fever-reaction induced by the serum continues – and unconsciousness with it – but she lives. Undeniably she lives! At nightfall the fever increases a little, but then all fevers do; any doctor knows that. At midnight of the second night, a full twenty-four hours after she died, there is a sudden, unexpected break in her heavy breathing, and before the watcher has quite realized it, her eyes are wide open for the first time. She has regained consciousness! For the first time he sees the color of her eyes – as the lids go up. Blue eyes, that have seen death, now looking into his. Calmly, undilated, unfrightened, peaceful.

He hastily takes her temperature. Normal. The serum has at last been accepted by her system. All that remains now is the answer to the second mystery. In medieval terms, has he saved her soul as well as her body? In modern scientific ones, have the accumulated memories of the past existence been carried over into this one, or were her brain cells damaged beyond repair?

The blue eyes fix themselves on him, stare unblinkingly. He says softly, almost afraid of the sound of his own voice, 'Good evening.' The blue eyes continue to stare. He waits, trembling. He knows that she was an American, knew the language. He whispers it over again, 'Good evening, young lady.'

A change is coming over her face. The staring blue eyes fill with tears that presently overflow and stream down her face. The eyes themselves narrow in a squint. The lips that knew rouge, cigarettes, and men's kisses, pucker into infant's whimper. A feeble bleating cry, the wail of a new-born child, escapes from her. The wordless, pitiful sound that any nursery knows.

The shock, the disappointment, is terrific; his gaunt face pales, he clutches his chair to keep from slumping off it, lets out a long sighing breath. Then presently, somewhat recovered, he takes out a shiny gold watch from his pocket, dangles it before her eyes. The light flashes from it. The tears stop, the wailing breaks off short. Her eyes sparkle with interest. She reaches towards it with ten fingers whose nails still bear adult nail lacquer; her mouth wreathes in an infantile grin. She says, 'Da!' and crows with pleasure. Reason is back – at least in its primary stages. For if she were a new-born infant, this would be a highly precocious reaction. Her faculties are intact. It is not as bad as he thought.

He will have to teach her to speak, to walk all over again, as one does any child, that is all. Intelligence has returned, but not memory. Her memory went into the grave. He murmurs to himself, 'Her body is twenty-two, but she is in the infancy of her second life. I will call her Nova, the New One.' He rubs his hands over his eyes.

Exhausted by his long vigil he slumps to the floor beside the bed, goes to sleep with his head resting against its edge. Above him the resurrected woman's hands stray gropingly to his thick white hair, clutch playfully at it like a child in its crib . . . .

3

The plane is a hopeless wreck, and even in the act of crawling out into the blinding rain, Penny O'Shaughnessy wonders dazedly why he's still alive. Dazedly, but briefly. O'Shaughnessy is not the kind to waste time wondering. Just one more lucky break, he supposes. His whole adult life has been an unbroken succession of them. His given nickname itself is a token of this, dating from the time he was sighted flying in from the open Caribbean after a particularly devastating hurricane had turned half the Lesser Antilles upside down.

'I just went up over it and waited till it went by below,' he explained, alighting midst the splinters of the airport hangar.

'A bad penny always turns up,' someone muttered incredulously.

Who else had ever met the business-end of a bolt of lightning in midflight, as he had just now, flying blind through a storm, lost a wing, managed to come down still alive even if it is on a wooded mountainside, to cut the contact at the moment of crashing so that he wasn't roasted alive, and crawl out with just a wrenched shoulder and a lot of cuts and bruises? He couldn't bail out because he was flying too low, hoping for a break through the clouds through which to spot something flat enough to come down on; he doesn't like bailing out anyway, hates to throw away a good plane.

This one lying all over the side of the mountain around him is not so good any more, he has to admit. The first thing he does is feel in his pocket, haul out a rabbit's foot, and stroke it twice. Then he straightens up, hobbles a short distance further from the wreck, turns to survey it. Almost instantly the lightning, which already stunned him once in the air, strikes a nearby tree with a bang and a shower of sparks. It cracks, comes down with a propeller-like whirr of foliage, and flattens what's left of his engine into the ground.

'All right, you don't like my crate,' O'Shaughnessy grumbles, with a back-arm swing at the elements in general. 'I believed you the first time!'

He trudges off, neck bowed against the rain, which forms a solid curtain around him. He hasn't the faintest idea where he is, because he was flying blind a full forty minutes before the crash. There is no visibility to speak of, just a pall of rain and mist, with the black silhouettes of trees peering through all around. The sharp slant of the ground tells him he's on the mountainside. He takes the downgrade; people, houses, are more often to be found in valleys than on mountains.

The ground is muddy soup around him; he doesn't walk as much as skid on his heels from tree trunk to tree trunk, using them as brakes to prevent a headlong fall. Rain water gets in between clothes and skin; the cuts and welts tingle; the wrenched shoulder pounds, and the thickening of the gloom around him tells him it is night.

'All set,' he mutters, 'to spend a quiet evening at home!'

The tree trunks blend into the surrounding darkness, and it gets harder to aim for them each time; he has to ski-jump blindly and coast with outspread arms, hoping one will stop him before he lands flat on his face. He misses one altogether – or else it isn't there in the first place – goes skittering down in axle-grease mud, wildly spiraling with his arms to keep his balance, and finally flattens into something that rasps and stings. A barbed-wire fence.

All the air has been knocked out of his stomach, and one of the wicked spines just missed his left eye, taking a gouge at his brow instead. But more than that, the jar he has thrown into the thing has set off an electric alarm bell somewhere up in one of the trees nearby. Its clamor blasts through the steady whine and slap of the rain.

His clothing has caught in ten different places, and skin with it in half of them. As he pulls himself free, swearing, and the vibrations of the obstacle lessen, the alarm breaks off. He kicks the fence vengefully with his foot, and this elicits an added spasm or two from the bell-battery, then once more it stops.

He is too preoccupied for a minute rubbing his gashes with his bare hands and wincing, to proceed with an investigation of this inhospitable barrier. Suddenly a rain-washed glow of murky light is wavering toward him on the other side of the fence, zigzagging uncertainly as though its bearer were picking his way.

'What the – ' Somebody living up here in this forsaken place?

The light stops flush against the fence directly opposite where he is standing and behind it he can make out a hooded, cloaked figure. O'Shaughnessy must be practically invisible behind the rain-mist and darkness.

'That yours?' he growls, balling a fist at the fence. 'Look what it did to me! Come out here and I'll – !'

A musical voice from below the hood speaks softly: 'Who are you? Why are you here?'

'A girl!' O'Shaughnessy gasps, and the anger leaves his voice. 'Sorry, I couldn't make you out. Didn't mean to tear loose that way, but I'm clawed up.' He stares at her for a long minute. Twenty-three, pretty, he can see that much. Blue eyes gaze levelly back at him from under the hood she is wearing as he steps up closer to the fence. 'I cracked up further back along the mountain, the plane came down – '

'What's a plane?' she asks, round-eyed.

His jaw drops slightly and he stares at her with disapproval, thinks she is trying to be cute or something. He keeps waiting for the invitation to shelter that a dog would be given, in such weather, at such an out-of-the-way place as this. It isn't forthcoming.

'Got a house back there?' he says finally.

She nods, and drops of rain fly off her hood. 'Yes, straight back there.' Just that, answered as asked.

He says with growing impatience, 'Well, won't you let me in a few minutes? I won't bite you!' The reason he thinks she's playing a part, knows better, is that her voice is city bred, not like a mountain girl's.

She says helplessly, 'It's locked and *he* has the keys. No one ever came here before, so I don't know what to do. I can't ask him because he's in the laboratory, and I'm not allowed to disturb him when he's in there.'

'Well, haven't you got a telephone I can use at least?'

'What's a telephone?' she wants to know, without a trace of mockery.

This time O'Shaughnessy flares up. Enough is enough. 'What kind of a person are you anyway? All right, keep your shelter. I'm not going to stand here begging. Would it be too much to tell me which direction the nearest road or farmhouse is from here, or would you rather not do that either?'

'I don't know,' she answers. 'I've never been outside this' – indicating the fence – 'never been out there where you're standing.'

It's beginning to dawn on him that she's not trying to make fun of him. He senses some mystery about her, and this whole place, but what it is he can't imagine. 'Who lives here with you?' he asks curiously.

'Papa,' she answers simply.

She's already been missed, for a voice shouts alarmedly: 'Nova! Nova, where are you?' And a second lantern looms toward them, zigzagging hurriedly through the mist. A blurred figure emerges, stops short in fright at sight of the man outside the barrier, nearly drops the lantern. 'Who's that? Who are You? How'd you get here?' The questions are almost panic-stricken.

'Papa,' thinks O'Shaughnessy, 'doesn't like company. Wonder why?' He explains his situation in a few brief words.

The man comes closer, motions the girl back as though O'Shaughnessy were some dangerous animal in a zoo-cage. 'Are you alone?' he asks, peering furtively around.

O'Shaughnessy has never lacked self-assertiveness with other men, quite the reverse. 'Who'd you think I had with me, the Lafayette Escadrille?' he says bluntly. 'Why so cagy, mister? Got a guilty conscience about something? Or are you making mash back there? Did you ever hear of giving a stranger shelter?' He swipes accumulated raindrops off his jaw and flicks them disgustedly down.

The hooded girl is hovering there in the background, looking uncertainly from one to the other. The man with the lantern gives a forced laugh. 'We're not trying to hide anything. We're not afraid of anything. You're mistaken,' he protests. A protest that rings about as true as a lead quarter to O'Shaughnessy's experienced ears. 'I wouldn't for the world want you to – er, go away from here spreading stories that there's anything strange about this place – you know how folks talk, first thing you know they'll be coming around snooping – '

'So that's it,' says O'Shaughnessy within his chest.

The man on the other side of the fence has taken a key out, is jabbing it hurriedly at the padlocks. So hurriedly that now he almost seems afraid of O'Shaughnessy will get away before he can get the gate open. 'Er – won't they send out and look for you, when they find out you're overdue at the airport?'

O'Shaughnessy snaps briefly, 'I wasn't expected anywhere. I was flying my own time; the crate belonged to me. What d'ye think, I'm somebody's errand-boy, or one of these passenger-plane pilots?' He expectorates to show his contempt, his independence.

The black shoe-button eyes opposite him gleam, as though this is an eminently satisfactory situation, as though he couldn't ask for a better one. He swings the gate halves apart. 'Come in,' he urges with bleated insistence. 'Come in by all means! Get back in the house, Nova, you'll get soaked – and see that you close *that* door! I'm Doctor Denholt, sir, and please don't think there's anything strange about us here.'

'I do already,' says O'Shaughnessy, bluntly, as he steps through the enclosure. He cocks his head at the renewed blare of the alarm bell.

Denholt hastily closes and refastens the gate, shutting off the clangor. 'Just an ordinary precaution, we're so cut off here,' he explains.

O'Shaughnessy refrains from further comment; he is on this man's domain now. He has one iron-clad rule, like an Arab: Never abuse hospitality. 'I'm O'Shaughnessy,' he says. They shake hands briefly. The doctor's hand is slender and flexible, that of a skilled person. But it is soft, too, and there is a warning of treachery in that pliability.

He leads his uninivited guest into the lamp-lighted house, which looks mighty good to O'Shaughnessy, warm and dry and cheerful in spite of its ugly, rustic furniture. The girl has discarded her cape and hood; O'Shaughnessy glimpses here in the main room, crouched before the clay-brick fireplace readying a fire, as Denholt ushers him into his own bedroom. Her hair, he sees now, is long and golden; her feet are stockingless in home-made deerskin moccasins, her figure slim and childlike in a cheap little calico dress.

At the rear of the room is a door tightly closed. They flyer's trained eyes, as they flicker past it, notice two things. It is metal, specially constructed, unlike the crude plank-panels of the rest of the house. A thread of platinum-bright light outlines it on three sides, too intense to be anything but high-voltage electricity. Electricity in there, coal-oil out here.

He hears the girl: 'He's in the laboratory, I'm not allowed to disturb him when he's in there.'

He hears the man: 'See that you close *that* door.'

He says to himself: 'I wonder what's in back of there.'

In Denholt's sleeping-quarters he peels off his drenched things, reveals a body of livid welts, barbed-wire lacerations, and black grease smudges. His host purses his lips in long-forgotten professional inspection. 'You *are* pretty badly scraped up! Better let me fix up some of those cuts for you, that barbed-wire's liable to be rusty. Just stand there where you are a minute.' He takes the water-logged clothing outside to the girl.

O'Shaughnessy crooks a knowing eyebrow at himself, waiting there. 'Why not in the laboratory, where he keeps all his stuff and the light's better? See no evil, think no evil, I guess.'

Denholt hurries back with hot water, dressings, antiseptic. O'Shaughnessy flinches at the searing touch of it, grins shame-facedly even as he does so, 'Can't take it any more, I guess. In Shanghai once I had to have a bad tooth pulled by a local dentist; his idea of an anaesthetic was to have his daughter wave a fan at me while he hit it out with a mallet and steel bar.'

'Did you yell?'

'Naw. Ashamed to in front of a girl.'

He catches Denholt staring with a peculiar intentness at his bared torso and muscular shoulders. 'Pretty husky, aren't you?' the doctor remarks, offhandedly. But something chilly passes down the flyer's back at the look that goes with the words. O'Shaughnessy wonders what it means. Or do all doctors look at you that way, sort of calculatingly, as though you'd do nicely for some experiment they had in mind?

'Yep,' he answers almost challengingly, 'I guess I can take care of myself all right if I have to.'

Denholt just looks at him with veiled guile.

4

Outside afterward, at the rough pine-board table set in the cheerful glow of the blazing hearth, Denholt's borrowed clothes on him, he has a better chance to study the girl at closer range. There is nothing strange about in her the least; she is all youthful animation, her face flushed with the excitement of having a stranger at their board; sits there devouring him with her eyes, as if she never saw an outsider before. But in her talk and in her movements there is perfect rhythm, harmony, coordination, balance, call it what you will; she is an utterly normal young girl.

The old man on the other hand – O'Shaughnessy char-acterizes him mentally thus – the old man has this brooding light in his eyes, is spasmodic and disconnected in his talk and gestures. The isolation, the years of loneliness, have done that to him perhaps, O'Shaughnessy thinks.

'All right,' he says to himself, 'that's his own business. But why does he keep a lovely kid like that cooped up here? Never heard of a plane, a telephone. What's he trying to do to her? Darned shame!'

Denholt catches him watching the girl. 'Eat,' he urges, 'eat up, man. You need strength after what you went through.'

The flyer grins, obeys. Yet something about the way it was said, the appraising look that went with it, makes him feel like a fowl being fattened for slaughter. He shakes his head baffledly.

Lightning keeps flaring like flashlight-powder outside the windowpanes every half-minute or so; there is an incessant roll of celestial drums all up and down the mountainside, so deep that O'Shaughnessy can feel it in his chest at times; the rain on the roof sounds like a steak frying.

Denholt is staring abstractedly into his plate, fingers drumming soundlessly on the table. O'Shaughnessy turns to the girl, to break the silence. 'Have you lived here long?'

'Two years.'

His eyebrows move a little, upward. She doesn't know what a plane is, a phone? 'Where'd you live before then?'

'I was born here,' she answers shyly.

He thinks she's misunderstood. 'You look older than two to me,' he says with a laugh.

The point seems to baffle her too, as if it has never occurred to her before. 'That's as far back as I can remember,' she says slowly. 'Last spring, and the spring before, when I was learning to talk and walk – that's two years, isn't it? How long ago did you learn to talk?'

He can't answer; a chunk of rabbit has gone down whole; he's lucky he doesn't choke. But it isn't the bolted rabbit that stiffens the hairs on the back of his neck, puts a needle of fear through his heart.

'That'll do, Nova,' says Denholt sharply. There's a strain around the eyes. His fork drops with a clash, as if he has just had a fright. 'You'll find – er, some cigarettes in a drawer in my bedroom for Mr. O'Shaughnessy.' And as soon as she's left the table, he leans forward confidentially toward the flyer. 'I'd better give you a word of explanation. She's not quite – right.' He touches his own head. 'That's why – the fence and all that. I keep her secluded up here with me, it's more humane you know. Don't take anything she says too seriously.'

O'Shaughnessy won't commit himself on this point, not even by a monosyllable. Just looks at his host, keeps his own counsel. It sounds reasonable enough, Lord knows, but he can't forget the girl's clear, sane eyes, nor Denholt's hungry, probing, almost gloating, stare. If anyone is crazy in this house – the little chill plays on his spine once more, and his flesh crawls under the borrowed clothes.

They have very little to say to one another, after that, while they sit there puffing away and the fire in the hearth slowly dies down into itself. The girl is in the adjoining room, washing the dishes. The waning fire throws the two men's shadows on the walls, long and wavering. Denholt's in particular, looks like that of a monster breathing smoke out of its nostrils. O'Shaughnessy grins a little at the idea.

He crushes out his cigarette. 'Well,' he says, 'looks like the storm'll keep up all night. Guess I better make a break for it.'

Denholt stiffens, then smiles. 'You're not thinking of leaving *now*? You'll spend the rest of the night wandering around in circles out there in the dark! Wait till daylight at least, maybe it'll let up by then. There's an extra room back there, you won't be any trouble at all.'

The girl says from the doorway, almost frightenedly, 'Oh, please, don't go yet, Mr. O'Shaughnessy! It's so nice having you.'

She waits for his answer.

O'Shaughnessy gives them both a long look in turn. Then he uncrosses his long legs, recrosses them the other way around. 'I'm staying, then,' he says quietly.

Denholt gets up. 'I've a little work to finish – something I was in the midst of when – er, your arrival interrupted me. If you'll excuse me for a few minutes – You can go to bed any time you feel like it.' And then, with a covert glance toward the kitchen doorway, 'Just bear in mind what I said. Don't take anything she says too seriously.'

The girl comes in after the doctor has gone, sits shyly down on the opposite side of the cleared table. That strange hungry look of hers rests steadily on his face, as if she never had seen anyone like him before.

'I'm glad you're staying,' she murmurs finally. 'I wanted you to because – well, maybe if you're here, I won't have to take my injection.'

O'Shaughnessy droops his lids a little. 'What kind of an injection?' he says with almost somnolent slowness.

She turns her hand up, down again. 'I don't know, I only know I have to take them. About once a month. He says it's bad for me if I miss any. Tomorrow would be the day, if you hadn't come.' She screws up her eyes at him pathetically. 'I don't like them, because they hurt so, and they make me feel so ill afterward. Once I tried to run away, but I couldn't get through the fence.'

There's something a little flinty in O'Shaughnessy's eyes that wasn't there before. 'And what'd he do when he caught you?' His own hand on the table flexes a little.

'Oh, nothing. Just talked to me, told me I had to have them whether I liked it or not. He said it was for my own sake he gives them to me. He said if I went too long without getting one — '

'What would happen?'

'He didn't say. Just said something pretty awful.'

O'Shaughnessy growls to himself deep in his throat. Drugging, eh? Maybe that's why she can't remember further back than two years, and why she says such weird things from time to time. But on second thought, it can't be that, either. The infrequency of the injections argue against it. There wouldn't be pain, if it were some kind of a drug. And if it were something able to affect her memory of the far past, why not the recent past as well? O'Shaughnessy's no medical man, but he's knocked around enough to know a little something; in the Orient and South America he's seen the telltale traces of almost every known narcotic under the sun. There is absolutely no sign of it about Nova. She is as fresh as that rain falling from the sky outside.

He only asks her one question, to make sure. 'Do you dream — dream about pretty things — after you've had one of these shots?'

'No,' she shudders, 'I feel like I'm all on fire. I woke up once and there was all ice around me — '

Not a drug, then. Maybe he has Denholt all wrong; maybe she really does need these treatments — vaccine or serum it sounds like — maybe she had some ghastly illness that robbed her of her memory, the use of her limbs, two years ago, and these injections are to speed her recovery, guard her against a relapse. Still, Denholt did try to pass her off as mentally unbalanced, when she isn't at all. No, there's something the man is up to — something secret and — and ugly. The barbed-wire fence, the alarm-bell show that too. Why bring her way up here when she could have far better care and attention — *if* she needs any — at a hospital in one of the big cities?

'Did you really mean what you said about only learning to walk and talk the spring before last?'

'Yes,' she says. 'I'll show you one of the copy-books he taught me out of.' She comes back with a dog-eared primer.

He thumbs through it. 'C is for Cat. Does-the-Cat-see-the-Rat?' He closes it, more at sea than ever.

'Were you as big as now when he taught you to walk?'

'Yes. I wore this same dress I have on now, that's how I can tell. I learned by myself, mostly. He used to put me down on the floor over there by the wall, and then put a lump of sugar on a chair all the way across the room, and coax me to walk over to get it. If I crawled on my hands and knees, he wouldn't let me have the sugar. After awhile I got so I could stand up straight – '

'Stop!' he says, with a sudden sharp intake of breath. 'It's enough to make a person go crazy just trying to figure out! There's – there's craziness in it somewhere! And I know on whose part. Not yours! God knows what he did to you the first twenty years of your life to make you forget everything you should have known – '

She doesn't answer. She can't seem to understand what he means. But her eyes show fright at the force of his speech. He sees he may do more harm than good by telling her other people aren't like she is. She's grown up, and she's been held here in some kind of mental thralldom – that's the closest he can get to the answer. And the man that would do that to another human being is a monster and a maniac.

His voice hoarse with pity and anger, he says, 'Tell me now, did you ever see any other man but me and the doctor before in your life?'

'No,' she breathes, 'that's why I like you so much.'

'Didn't you even ever see another girl – have someone like yourself around you to talk with?'

'No,' she murmurs again. 'Only him. No one else at all.'

He rises as if he can't stand any more of it, takes three quick turns around his chair, raises it, bangs it down again.

She watches him timidly, not speaking, with just that fright in her eyes. He slumps down in his chair again, looks at her broodingly. Somehow he knows he's going to take her with him when he leaves, and he wonders if he has any right to. What'll he do with her afterward – turn her loose like a lamb among wolves? Drag her around with him from bar to cantina to bistro, when he's not up in the air risking his neck for some Chinese war lord or Nicaraguan outlaw? His kind of life – At least she has peace here, and a sort of security.

The bolts shoot back behind the laboratory door. He sees her glance past him, but doesn't turn his head to look. On the wall opposite Denholt's long wavering silhouette appears more

ominous now than before. Madman, criminal, samaritan –
which? Playing the role of God to this girl – in some obscure way
that O'Shaughnessy cannot fathom even yet – which he has no
right to do. Better the cantinas and the tropical hell-holes of his
own life. If she has anything in her, she'll rise above them; this way
she hasn't even a chance to do that.

Her quick whisper reaches him while Denholt is in the act of
closing the door after him. 'Don't let him give me another
injection. Maybe if *you* ask him not to he'll listen to you!'

'You've had your last!' O'Shaughnessy says, decisively.

Denholt approaches the table, looks suspiciously from one to
the other. Then a smile crosses his face. 'Still up, eh? How about a
nice hot toddy for both of us before we turn in?' Nova makes a
move to leave her chair and he quickly forestalls her. 'I'll fix it
myself.'

O'Shaughnessy doesn't miss that. He stares up into the other's
face, takes his time about answering. 'Why not?' he says, finally,
jutting out his chin.

Denholt goes into the kitchen. O'Shaughnessy can see him
pouring whiskey into two tumblers, spooning sugar, from where
he is. The doctor keeps looking obliquely out at him from time to
time, with a sort of smirk of satisfaction on his face.

O'Shaughnessy says quietly to the girl, sitting there feasting her
eyes on him with a doglike devotion: 'Go over there to my coat,
hanging up over the fireplace. You'll find an oilsilk packet in the
inside pocket, full of papers and things. Take the papers out and
just bring me the folder. Don't let him see you.'

He thrusts the moisture-proof oblong down just under the
collar of his shirt, buttons the neck over it, stretches the collarband
out as far as it will go, to create a gap. Then he bends forward a
little, sticks his elbows on the table, rests his chin on his hands. His
upthrust arms obscure his chest and neck. He drawls something
she doesn't understand – one more of the many incomprehensible
things he is always saying: 'I can smell a Mickey a mile away.'

Denholt comes in with the two toddies, says to her, 'You'd
better go to your room now, Nova, it's getting late, and you're
going to need all your strength. *Tomorrow*, you know.'

She shivers when she hears that, slowly withdraws under the
compulsion of Denholt's stare, sending appealing looks at
O'Shaughnessy. A door closes after her somewhere in the back.

Denholt has noticed the telegraphic communication betweem
them. 'I don't know what my ward has been telling you – ' he
begins.

O'Shaughnessy is not showing his cards yet. 'Not a thing, Doc,' he says. 'Not a thing. Why? Is there something she *could* tell me?'

'No, no, of course not,' Denholt covers up hastily. 'Only – er, she gets delusions about injections and things. That's why I don't allow her in the laboratory any more. She caught me giving a rabbit an injection one day, and she'd be perfectly capable of telling you that it was *she* I gave it to, and what's more, believing it herself. Let's drink up, shall we?'

He hands his guest one of the two glasses. O'Shaughnessy takes it with one hand, keeps the other cupped along the line of his jaw. He hoists it an eighth of an inch. 'Here's to *tomorrow*.'

Denholt's piercing gaze transfixes him for a minute. Then, he relaxes into a slow, derisive smile. 'Here's to *tonight*,' he contradicts, 'tomorrow will take care of itself.'

O'Shaughnessy thrusts the rim of his glass up under his lower lip, slowly levels it until it is horizontal – and empty. The forked hand supporting his chin is between it and Denholt. He's a sloppy drinker, the collar of his shirt gets a little wet. . . .

The yellow-green of the doctor's oil lamp recedes waveringly from the doorway of the bedroom O'Shaughnessy is to occupy. Pitch blackness wells up all around, cut by an occasional calcium-flare of lightning outside the high, small window. The flashes are less frequent now and the rain has let up.

O'Shaughnessy is lying flat on his back, on the rickety cot. He has left on his trousers and shirt. Denholt said, perhaps, with ghastly double meaning, 'I'm sure you'll be dead to the world in no time at all!' as he went out just now. The first thing the flyer does, as the waning lamp glow finally snuffs out altogether and a door closes somewhere in the distance, is to take out the bulging waterlogged oil-silk envelope from his shirt and let its contents trickle silently onto the floor.

The rustle of the slackening rain outside begins to lull his senses before he knows it. The ache of his wrenched shoulder lessens, is erased by oncoming sleep. The lids of his eyes droop closed. He catches them the first time, holds them open by sheer willpower. Not a sound, not a whisper comes to help him keep awake. The lonely mountain house is deathly still; only the rain and the far-off thunder sound outside. The girl's story begins to take on a dream-like quality, unreal, remote, fantastic –

The muffled creak of a pinewood floor-board, somewhere just beyond the open door of his room, jerks his senses awake. At first he thinks he's still at the stick of his plane, makes vague motions to keep from going into a tailspin . . . Then he remembers where he is.

Twenty minutes, half an hour, an hour maybe, since Denholt's murky lamp-glow flickered away from the door. Maybe even more than that. O'Shaughnessy swears at himself mentally for fading out like this. But it's all right; if this is it now –

It must be deep in the night. There's no rain now any more, just the plink of loose drops as they detach themselves one by one from the eaves. A pale silver radiance, little more than a phantom glint, is coming through the window up over him. Dawn? No, a late moon, veiled by the last of the storm clouds.

The creak is repeated, closer at hand, a little more distinct this time. He can hear breathing with it. Outstretched there on the cot, he begins drawing up his knees closer to his body, tensing himself for the spring. What'll *he* have – a knife, a gun, some viciously-keen surgical instrument? O'Shaughnessy widens his arms, into a sort of simulation of a welcoming embrace. The dark hides the great fists, the menacing grin at his mouth.

Something comes over the threshold. O'Shaughnessy can *sense* the stirring of air at its furtive passage, rather than see or hear anything. There's a widespread footfall within the room itself. A blur of motion glides momentarily through the wan silvery light, which isn't strong enough to focus it clearly, into the concealing dark on his side of it.

There's a clang from the bucked cot-frame, the upward fling of a body, a choked sound of fright as a pair of arms lash out in a bear-hug. In the soft purring tones of a tea-kettle O'Shaughnessy's voice pours out unprintable maledictions.

Her softness warns him just in time, before he's done more than pinion her arms fast and drive all the breath out of her body. 'Don't,' she pants, 'it's me.' His arms drop away, he blows out breath like a steam-valve, the reaction staggers him back a step to the wall, off balance. 'You! Why didn't you whisper a warning? I was – '

'I was afraid he'd hear me. He's in the laboratory. He left the door open behind him and I've been watching him from outside in the dark – '

'What's he think he's going to do, give you one of them shots again?'

'No, it's you – he's going to do something to you. I don't know what! He took your coat in there, and took all the papers in it and burned them. Then he – he lit flames under all those big glass things, and put a needle in a pan to soak, like he does with

me. But this time had has a silk cord in there with him, and he
made a big loop in it and measured it round his own neck first,
then took it off again and practiced throwing it and pulling it
tight. He's got a big black thing in there too, you hold it this way
and point it – '

'A gun,' says O'Shaughnessy softly, mockingly. 'He's not
missing any bets, is he? Knockout drops, a noose, a positive.
How's he fixed for hand grenades?'

She puts the flats of her hands against his chest. 'Don't stay,
please! I don't want – things like that to happen to you! Go
before he gets through! He's awfully quick and strong, you
ought to see how he ran after me that time when I tried to get to
the fence! Maybe you can sneak by outside the door without his
seeing you, or get out one of the windows – Don't stand there
without moving like that! Please don't wait. That's why I came
in here to you. There's steam coming from the pan the needle's in
already. I saw it!' And then, in a low heartbroken wail, 'Aren't
you going to go?'

Instead he sits down on the edge of the cot, leisurely puts on
the soiled canvas shoes Denholt has lent him. Reaches toward
her, draws her over, and stands her before him.

'Nova, d'you like me?' he says.

'I like you very much.'

He rubs his hair awry with one hand, as though at his wits'
end. 'Don't be givin' me any blarney now. D'you want to marry
me?'

'What's marry?'

'I ought to be shot,' he says softly to himself. 'Well – d'you
want to be with me always, go wherever I go, tell me how good I
am when I'm good, buck me up when I'm down in the dumps –
and one of these days, pretty soon, wear black for me?'

'Yes,' she says softly. 'I want to be near you. If that's to marry,
then that's what I want.'

He puts out his hand at her. 'Shake, Mrs. O'Shaughnessy!
Now let's get out of here.' He goes over to the door, looks out at
the distant bar of light escaping across their path from the open
laboratory-door. 'Got anything you want to bring with you?
You're standing in the middle of your wardrobe right now, I
guess. Got any idea where he keeps that key?'

'The one to the padlock on the gate outside? In the pockets of
his coat, I guess; he always seems to reach in there for it. He
hasn't got it on, though; he's got on that white thing he wears in
the laboratory. It must be in the room where he sleeps.'

'Okay, we'll try lifting it. I wouldn't mind roughing that bird up, only I don't want anything to happen to you. He's probably got an aim, with that gun of his, like a cockeyed nervewreck with palsy. Stick close behind me.'

5

They glide through the velvety dark, O'Shaughnessy in the lead, the girl behind him, keeping contact with her fingers resting lightly against the back of his shoulder. The vague outline of the room doorway seems to move toward them, not they toward it, to come abreast, to slip past. Ahead there is just that bar sinister of bleaching whiteness, falling across the floor of the main room and leaping up one wall.

'Gotta watch these boards,' he breathes across his shoulder, 'you woke me up getting in here, and you don't weigh what I do.' The touch of her fingers against his back tells him she's shaking all over. 'It's all right. You're with me now.'

A board whimpers a little, and he gets off it with a catlike litheness before it goes into a full-bodied creak. The gash of laboratory whiteness comes slowly nearer, outlining the angles of things even beyond its own radius. This house, he thinks, is as black physically as it is in spirit. Little tinkering, puttering sounds become audible from the still-distant laboratory, magnified in the stillness. Mania at its preparations.

She signals with her fingertips, abreast of an open door. 'In here?' he whispers. They turn aside and glide through. 'Stand here right beside the door where I can find you again. I'll see if I can locate his coat.'

He does after a lot of cautious circling and navigation; it is hanging from a peg in the wall. He finds the key very quickly, though to her it must seem forever that he's standing there fumbling with the coat. He slips back to her, jaunty with his own peculiar jauntiness even in this eerie situation. 'Got it. Now here we go.'

Outside again. Step by step through the silence and the blackness, the triangular wedge of white ahead the only visible thing. A board barks treacherously under him, this time before he can withdraw his foot. They stand rigid, while the echoes move into the night. The tinkering has stopped abruptly. Questioning silence from the laboratory now. O'Shaughnessy nudges her with his elbow, and they draw in against the wall.

Not a sound from the laboratory. The bar of escaping light, narrow as a candlestick until now, slowly, insinuatingly, broadens out fan-shaped as the door behind it silently widens. A silhouette bisects it, Denholt's outline thrown before him over the floor and up the wall, rigid, standing just within the opening, listening.

The grin has come back to O'Shaughnessy's face; he reaches behind him and squeezes her throbbing wrist reassuringly. It seems so long ago that he was last afraid of anything. Seventeen, was he then? Eighteen? Sometimes he thinks he's missing a lot by being like this – fear gives life a fillip. He wonders how it is he lost it all, and what there is – if anything – ever to bring it back.

One thing's sure, she's being afraid for the both of them, and plenty left over; her pulse is a whipcord under the thumb that is holding her wrist.

The silhouette moves at last, begins to recede within the lighted room. The noise that conjured it up, like a genie out of a bottle, hasn't been repeated. The tinkerings and drippings resume where they left off. Only the path of light remains wider than before, a ticklish gap to bridge undiscovered. When they are almost abreast of it and can hear Denholt's breathing inside. O'Shaughnessy stops, gropes behind him, draws Nova around in front of him. He transfers the padlock key to her palm, closes her fingers over it. 'I want to be sure you make that gate, no matter what. Take a deep breath and get across that lighted place. Don't be afraid, I'm right here backing you up.'

She edges forward, cranes her neck toward the open door. Apparently Denholt's back is toward it. She takes a quick soundless sidestep, with instinctive feminine deftness, and is on the other side of the luminous barrier. He can see her there anxiously waiting for him to join her.

A moment later he is beside her again, bringing with him a quick bird's-eye glimpse of white-coated form bent over, laboriously pouring something from a retort into a hypodermic-barrel. In the background a pair of operating tables, not just one. One an improvised one – planks bridging two chairs, with a rubber sheet draped over them. 'Double-header coming up,' thinks O'Shaughnessy. 'Rain – no game.'

She is tugging insistently at his arm, but he is suddenly resistant, immobile. She turns her face up toward his. 'O'Shaughnessy, come on! Any minute he's – '

'My rabbit's foot. He's got it in there with him, in my coat. I couldn't go without it – '

'O'Shaughnessy, he'll kill you.'

'Him and what sextet? Get over there to the door, kid, and start working on it. I want you in the clear in case that gun of his starts going boom. I've got to go in after my lucky paw, no two ways about it.' He has to jog her, push her slightly, to get her to tear herself away from him. Finally she slips off in the dark with a little whimper of protest. He waits there until a faint clicking comes from the main door. Then a bolt grates miserably as she clears it, and there is sudden, startled silence from within the gleaming laboratory.

O'Shaughnessy, muscles taut as wires, rounds the angle of the doorframe, unhurried, casual. Digs a thumb at the man in the white jacket who has just whirled to face the door. 'My coat, Doc. I'm leaving.'

Denholt had just finished putting down the loaded needle he was preparing. The gun the girl mentioned is on the table, but under his hand already.

'So you think you're leaving? You're very foolish, my friend. It would have been easier to sleep, the way I meant you to. No fright, no last-minute agony. You would not have seen your own death.'

'No fright, no agony this way either.' O'Shaughnessy calmly reaches for his coat, extracts the charm, stuffs it into his trouser pocket. 'Don't be so handy burning my identification papers next time,' he says, 'or I'll slap your head all the way around your neck – '

The gun is up now, level with his chest.

Behind them in the darkness the heavy outer door swings open with a grinding whirr. Denholt takes a quick step forward. O'Shaughnessy doesn't move from before him, blocking his way. He's flexing his wrists slightly, in and out.

A patter of quick, light footsteps recedes outside in the open, flying over the clayey rain-wet ground.

'Who's that?'

'Who should it be? That's the girl. I'm taking her with me.'

Denholt's face is a sudden mask of dismay. 'You can't!' he cries shrilly. 'You don't know what it means, you fool! You can't take her out into the world with you! She's got to stay here, she needs *me*!' He raises his voice to a frenzied shout. 'Nova! Come back here!'

'That's your story and you're stuck with it.' O'Shaughnessy raises his own voice, in a bull ramble. He shifts dead-center in front of the leveled gun, to keep Denholt from snaking past around him.

'Get out of my way, or I'll shoot you dead. I didn't want to puncture your skin, damage any vital organ, but if I have to, you're the loser! Nothing can bring you back then, do you hear me, nothing can bring you back! You'll *stay* dead!'

O'Shaughnessy just stands, crouched a little, measuring him with his eyes. O'Shaughnessy is a gambler; he senses a reluctance on Denholt's part to shoot him, and he plays on it for what it's worth. Instead of giving ground before the weapon, he takes a sidling step in, and another.

The alarm-bell begins ringing somewhere off in the dripping trees . . . She's got the last barrier open, she's made it.

A sudden taut cord down the side of Denholt's neck reveals to O'Shaughnessy the muscular signal sent down to his unseen trigger finger. He swerves like a drunk. A foreshortened bar of orange, like a tube-light, seems to solder the two of them together for a second. Noise and smoke come later. O'Shaughnessy isn't aware of pain, only knows that he's been hit somewhere and mustn't be hit any more. He has the gun hand in his own now, ten fingers obeying two different brains, clutching a single weapon. It goes off again, and again, and again – four, five, six times.

O'Shaughnessy is hitting Denholt on the side of his head with his free arm, great, walloping, pile-driver blows. The two of them stagger together, like partners in a crazy dance. Glass is breaking all around them. Gray smoke from the six shots, pink-and-white dust from the chipped brick-and-plaster walls, swirl around them in a rainbow haze. Something vividly green flares up from one of the overturned retorts, goes right out again. O'Shaughnessy tears the emptied gun away, flings it off somewhere. More breaking glass, and this time a tart pungent smell that makes the nostrils sting. The crunch of pulverized tube glass underfoot makes it sound as if they were scuffling in sand or hard-packed snow.

O'Shaughnessy can't hit with his left arm, he notices; the shoulder blocks off the brain-message each time. He just uses that arm to hold Denholt where his right-hand blows can find him. He has lost track of the other's left hand for a moment, it comes back again around his body from somewhere, with a warning flash to it. Scalpel or something.

O'Shaughnessy dives, breaks, puts space between them. A downward hiss misses his chest barrel, he pounces, traps the arm before it can come up again, vises it between his own arm and upthrust thigh, starts forcing it out of joint. The thing drops with a musical ting! He scuffs it aside, takes a quick step back to get driving-force, sends a shattering haymaker in. Denholt topples, skids through broken tube-glass, lies there stunned, tilted on one elbow.

O'Shaughnessy, his shoulder throbbing with pain like a bass drum, pants grimly: 'Now – got it through your head I'm taking her?' He turns and shuffles unsteadily toward the door.

Denholt is trying to struggle up, gabbling: 'You're taking her to her death!'

The alarm bell keeps pealing, waiting. O'Shaughnessy stumbles out of the laboratory, on through the darkness toward the front door. Cool, dank, before-dawn air swirls about him. He turns and sees Denholt outlined there behind him in the lighted doorway, where he has dragged himself, hanging weakly onto the frame, holding up one arm in imprecation – or in warning.

'Remember what I'm saying. You're dooming her. This is the thirtieth of June – remember this date, remember it well! You'll know, you'll know soon enough! You'll come crawling back to me – with her – begging me to help you! You'll get down on your bended knees to me, you'll grovel at my feet – that'll be my hour!'

'Have another shot – on me,' O'Shaughnessy growls back from the darkness under the trees.

'You're not taking her out to life, you're taking her out to her death – the most awful death a human being ever experienced!'

The shrieking, maddened voice dwindles away behind him in the house, and he can make out Nova waiting tremblingly for him at the opened barbed-wire barrier. He stumbles to her through the mud of the storm-wrack, holding his bullet-seared shoulder. He grins and drawls in that quiet way of his above the slackening noise of the exhausted alarm-bell: 'H'lo, Mrs. O'Shaughnessy. Shall we go now?'

He takes her arm.

6

O'Shaughnessy, dickering with a man named Tereshko at the bar of the Palmer House, Chicago, excuses himself, steps into a booth to call his North Side flat.

'Why not have your wife join us for dinner?' Tereshko says. 'Say, at the Chez Paree. We can talk business to music just as well as here.'

'Great,' says O'Shaughnessy. Business after all is a form of warfare; you bring all your available weapons to bear. If you don't you're a fool. You could call Nova O'Shaughnessy's illuminating beauty that of a star-shell. If he uses it to help dazzle this wary gentleman he is trying to dent, it doesn't mean he values it any the less himself.

So he says into the phone: 'Nova, I want you to meet me at Chez Paree. I've got a man with me. He's looking for a pilot, and he's talking big money, so be as beautiful as you can. Take a cab, honey.' Nova is still new to the city streets. 'Just one thing. Any offer under seventy-five hundred and you give me a look, much as to say, "Isn't he funny?" Get it? And not a word about – that place on the mountain, of course.'

At the Paree they order a table for three. They've been drinking a good deal, and Tereshko is beginning to show it. He isn't drunk but he loses some of his caginess. Loosens up, so to speak.

'You had much experience locating mining claims from the air?' he resumes.

'No, just flying. But as I understand it, all you want is to be piloted up there, so you can look them over yourself. I can guarantee to do that for you. All I need's the general direction and plenty of gas.'

It's obvious that money isn't the hitch. This Tereshko has that written all over him, in a flashy uncouth sort of way. His hesitancy – and O'Shaughnessy is a good judge of men's motives – seems to stem from caution, as though he wants to make sure whom he's dealing with first before he puts all his cards on the table. He can't doubt by now that O'Shaughnessy's an experienced enough flier to get him anywhere he wants to go, after the clippings and documents he's been showing him all afternoon long.

'Of course,' Tereshko feels his way, offering the applicant a cigarette out of a platinum case with an emerald catch, 'what I'm mainly interested in is to see that the whole undertaking is kept strictly between ourselves. I don't want known to anyone what its object or destination is. No one at all, is that clear? Not even after it's been wound up.'

'I can give you a guarantee on that too. I'm no loudspeaker.'

'No, you seem like the sort that minds his own business – that's why I approached you in the first place.' He – very unwisely – signals for another drink.

Tereshko relaxes still further. 'I don't mind telling you,' he admits, 'that that whole mine-location business was just camouflage. What I'm looking for is already mined and minted, only it was put back in the ground. And it's all the way around the compass from where I said. Not British Columbia at all, but in one of the Florida keys, we think. Maybe one of the Bahamas. I suppose that gives you the clue. Well, it looks like you're our man, so there's no harm in your knowing.'

'Pirate stuff, eh?'

'Yes and no,' says Tereshko. 'Certainly was a pirate all right, but he dates from prohibition days and not Captain Kidd's time. Guess you know who I mean now.'

O'Shaughnessy doesn't, but it doesn't cost anything to let the other think so.

'He won't get out until, let's see – ' A pecan-sized diamond flames as he figures on his fingers. '1948, or is it '50? Hell, he was a great guy and all that,' he goes on by way of self-excuse, 'but you can't blame the rest of us. After all, we're getting older every day. He got his, why shouldn't we get ours? He's served two years of his sentence – why should we wait?'

'Then you have no right to it?'

'Any more than he had!' snaps the other. 'It's nobody's money. It don't even belong to the saps he got it from, because he gave 'em needle-beer for it at four bits a throw.'

'One way of looking at it,' says O'Shaughnessy non-committally.

'What other way of looking at it is there? Is it doing anybody any good lying where it is in the ground? We wouldn't have to go to all this trouble only – you see banks were no good, nor safe-deposit boxes nor anything else, because his trouble was – Government trouble. He musta seen it coming up. We didn't, but he musta, because we all remember how just before it happened he went off on a cruise down Florida waters in his motor yacht. Just him and a small crew to run the thing for him and, oh yes, some girl he was playing around with at the time. None of *us*, not one of us. We all thought that was funny, too, because he was a guy loved company. Until then he'da caught cold without the bunch of us being around him all the time. Well funnier still, just before turning back they touch at Havana. Him and this dame go ashore and nobody else's allowed to leave the boat. Then, on very sudden orders from him, the yacht leaves Havana – without him and the girl coming back to it. It's supposed to pick them up later at Bimini or something. It was never seen in one piece again. A piece of charred wood was picked up later with its name on it. Must have been destroyed at sea by an explosion, and not a soul aboard escaped alive. Funny, huh, to send it on ahead like that, when it could have waited right in the harbour for them? They were the only two it had to cater to.'

'Funny is right, but not for laughing,' O'Shaughnessy agrees.

'Just when we were getting out our black neckties and armbands, a cable comes from him. "Hope you're not worried, I'm okay, taking the next plane north, and wasn't that a terrible accident?" Thirty days later to the hour, Uncle Sam jumps on his neck and – ' He pinches his fingers together, kisses them, flies them apart. 'How much turned up, when the smoke had cleared away? Five grand. Why, he used to carry as much as that around in his pocket for change! Does it look like I'm right, or does it look like I'm right? Every other lead we've had since then has petered out. It took us long enough to tumble, but now I think we've got it added up right. Now, d'you think you can help us swing it?'

O'Shaughnessy shrugs. 'What's hard about it? I can taxi you around for a a month, two months, as long as it takes you to locate it. An amphibian is the answer, of course. Now there's this: you'll have to stake me to the plane. I banged my own up week before last – that's when I got this busted shoulder. Don't get the idea I can't fly – lightning butted in, that was all.'

'We'll provide you with the plane,' Tereshko assures him. 'You shop around and pick up what you think you'll need, and you can keep it, as an extra bonus, when we get back.'

'Just how long will I last after that to enjoy the use of it?' wonders O'Shaughnessy knowingly. But that isn't really a deterrent – people have thought they'd get rid of him, once he's served his purpose, before now – and haven't made a go of it. These fellows'll find that out too.

'The wren would come in handy for a guide – did you ever think of contacting her?' he says thoughtfully.

'Did we think?' scoffs the other. 'His cell door wasn't closed behind him yet before we started to put on the pressure. Well we put it on too heavy. We had her figured all wrong. It just happens she was one of those innocent babes, hadn't known what it was all about until the lid blew off – musta thought he made his dough in stocks and bonds or something.'

O'Shaughnessy makes that derisive sound with his lips commonly known as the raspberry.

'No, that's what we thought too,' Tereshko assures him, 'but it was on the level. He used to tell us everything was on the up-and-up between them – you know what I mean, and she wasn't really his moll. . . . He called her his madonna – '

'Machine-gun madonna,' chuckles O'Shaughnessy.

'He was going to marry her. She was only a kid, seventeen or something like that. Well, between the shock of finding out who she'd been mixed up with, and us putting the pressure on her, the poor dame never had a chance. She claimed she didn't know anything that went on during that cruise. So then we lock her up in a dark garage overnight, to frighten her into talking. We frightened her all right, but not into talking. Just our luck – he'd never let her cut her hair, said she looked like an angel with it long. So she has a hairpin to unlock the engines of all the cars in there – and there was about six of them – and starts them all turning over and breathes the monoxide until she's gone. With a kitten he gave her still in her arms.'

'Fine note.' O'Shaughnessy scowls sympathetically. Not with them, but with the harried, friendless girl in the garage.

Tereshko grins.

'Yeah, ain't it? Of all the dirty tricks! We hadda leave her in there all next day. Then we sneaked her out after dark, carried her miles away, and planted her somewhere else. I never even read about them finding her. If they did, they never tumbled to who she was, not a word about it came out in the pa – '

'Here's my wife,' O'Shaughnessy interrupts, standing up. He's sighted across Tereshko's shoulder as she comes in from the street just then, stands there a second, looks around. She's something to look at, as she locates them, starts over toward them, with a smile for him on her face.

Tereshko, whose chair is facing the other way, follows him to his feet, turning around to greet her as he does so.

O'Shaughnessy is saying, 'Nova, meet Mr. Vincent Tereshko.'

There's a tinkle as Tereshko's cocktail glass hits the floor. There's a peculiar hiss at the same time, like an overheated radiator, or an inner tube deflating. Tereshko sort of reels back, the low top of the chair he has just risen from catches him across the spine, he goes over it, dumping the back of his head onto the soft padded seat, and then he and chair alike roll over sideward to the floor. Instantly he scrambles up again, gives a hoarse cry that sounds like, 'No! Get away from me! You're not real.'

He makes flailing motions with both arms, buffeting the air before him, then turns and runs through the foyer and out into the street.

They come out of their trance after awhile, not right away.

'Well, I'll be a – Did you see that? What bit him? A minute ago
he's sitting here chatting with me, then all at once he goes
haywire.'

'It was – me,' she says wonderingly, still staring after
Tereshko.

He flips his head impatiently at such an idea. 'Nah, how could
it have been you? Talk sense. You're not used to crowds yet,
every time anyone looks at you you think something's the
matter.' He can't, after all, really tell who or what Tereshko saw.

'It was, O'Shaughnessy,' she insisted troubledly. 'He was
looking right at me, right into my face. Something must be the
matter with me! Is there anything wrong with the way I look?
Because that's the second time tonight that's happened – '

He turns to her, startled. 'Second! What d'you mean?'

'Just now, outside the door. There was a man sitting waiting
in a limousine for someone, and as I got out of my cab, he turned
around and looked at me, and then he – he gave a yell like this
one did, and started off, tearing down the street a mile a minute
as if he'd seen a ghost – '

O'Shaughnessy looks puzzled.

'Turn around a minute. Lemme see,' he says. Then as she
slowly revolves before him: 'You're okay from every angle. I
don't see anything about you to scare grown men out of their
wits. He musta seen somebody or something in back of you that
did that to him. The heck with it. Let's go home. It looks like the
deal's off, and I'm just as satisfied. It had a bad smell to it from
the beginning.'

Seventy-two hours go by, the lull before the storm. Then, the
third night after that, he happens to come back to the flat earlier
than usual. He's down to his last few dollars, and he's been
tramping around all day trying to make connections. But
free-lance pilots, flying soldiers of fortune, don't seem to be in
great demand at the moment. He has her to look after now. . . .

He spots her standing at the curb in front of their house, as he
rounds the corner. She's looking for a taxi. She signals one, and
just as she's on the point of getting in, he shouts: 'Hey Nova!
What's the idea?' and comes running up just in time.

She seems astonished to see him. Not confused, just
astonished.

'I'm sorry it took me so long. I didn't mean to keep you
waiting like that. Is that why you changed your mind and came
back here instead? You're not sore, are you. O'Shaughnessy?'

He says: 'What're you talking about? Sore about what?'

'Why, because I'm half an hour late in meeting you.'

'Who told you to meet me?'

She's more astonished than ever. 'Why, you did! You tele-
phoned me over an hour ago and said to take a taxi and come
out and meet you at –'

He takes a look around him up and down the street. 'Come on
upstairs,' he says crisply. 'Never mind, driver, we don't want
you.' And upstairs: 'What else did I say?'

'You told me to come as quickly as I could, that's all.'

'Don't you know my voice on the wire?'

'I've never heard anybody else's but yours, so I thought it was
you again. You sounded a little far-off, that's all.'

'Well, it wasn't me. And I'm wondering who it was. Listen
Nova, honey, don't go out any more by yourself after this. I'll
give you a password over the phone from now on. Barbed wire,
how'll that be? If you don't hear me say barbed wire, you'll
know it isn't me.'

'Yes, O'Shaughnessy.'

The following evening, when he comes back, he has trouble
getting in. His latchkey works, but she has something shoved up
against the door on the inside, a chair inserted under the knob,
maybe. It doesn't hold him very long, and she's standing there in
the middle of the room shaking like a leaf.

'What'd you do that for?' he asks. 'And how'd that hole get in
the door, over the lock?'

She runs over and hangs on tight. 'They called again. They
said it was you, but I knew it wasn't because they didn't say
barbed wire.'

'They try to get you to come out again?'

'No, they didn't. They said, "We've got a message for you
from Benny." Who's Benny?'

O'Shaughnessy just looks at her, eyes narrowing.

'Then they said, "Oh, so your torch went out?" Then they
laughed and they said, "Where'd you get hold of the mick?"
What's a mick?'

'Me,' he says slowly, wondering. 'Anything else?'

She shakes her head dazedly. 'I couldn't make head or tail of
it. They said, "You sure put one over on us, didn't you? It was a
good gag while it lasted, but it's run out now. We'll be seeing
you."

'Then what?'

'Oh, O'Shaughnessy, I was so scared. I didn't know where to
get hold of you, except you were downtown in the Loop

somewhere. I locked the door and I hid in the closet, just left it open on a crack. In about half an hour, all of a sudden I could the doorknob slowly turning, as if someone was out there trying it. Then when that wouldn't work the bell started to ring, and a voice said thickly, "It's me, babe. Let me in, I forgot my key." But I knew it wasn't you. I got way in the far corner of the closet and pulled all the clothes over me – '

Meanwhile he's taken his gun out of the valise where he keeps it and is checking it over, his wrists trembling a little with rage. That's a man's vital spot, the helpless thing he loves.

She goes on:

'Then something went *pokk* right into the door and came through on this side. I couldn't stand it any more, I was afraid they'd come in and get me. I ran out of the closet and climbed out that window there onto the fire escape and got into the flat next door and begged the lady to hide me. I told her someone was trying to break into our flat, and she started to call the police, but by that time they'd gone. I could hear feet scuttling down the stairs, a whole lot of them, and a big car driving off outside – '

Walking back and forth, trying to dope it out, tapping the muzzle of his gun against his palm, he says, 'Listen kid, I don't know what we're up against, it may be just a false alarm, but – Shooting a bullet-hole through your door in broad daylight makes it look like the McCoy. If I could only figure what it was all about! It's no one in *my* life. I've made enough enemies, heaven knows, but not in this country. Nova, tell me the truth – were you ever in Chicago before?' He stands still and looks at her.

'Never, O'Shaughnessy, never, until we came here two weeks ago. I don't know anyone here but you. I've never spoken to anyone but you the whole time we've been here. You've got to believe me!'

He does, how could he help it?

But then, what is it? What would you call it anyway? If he had anything, he'd say it had the earmarks of an attempted snatch, for ransom. Mistaken identity? Yes, but who do they take her to be? The whole thing's a maze. He wonders if he ought to give it to the police to handle for him. But then, what can he tell them? Somebody impersonated me on the phone to my wife, somebody tried to break into my flat while I was out. It doesn't stack up to much when you put it that way. And he's an individualist, anyway, used to being on his own. When it comes to anything threatening Nova, he'd rather take care of her himself.

Tereshko rings up unexpectedly that night. 'This is Tereshko, O'Shaughnessy,' he says. 'I'm down on lower State Street. I'd like to conclude that transaction we were talking over. Can you run down and meet me for ten minutes or so?'

'What happened to you the other night? Something seemed to frighten you.'

A phony laugh. 'Me? Not at all. I got kinda sick all of a sudden, and beat it for the street.'

O'Shaughnessy motions Nova over, puts the receiver to her ear and whispers: 'This the same voice you heard the other times?'

She listens, shakes her head.

So he says into the phone: 'Frankly, the deal's off, count me out.'

Tereshko doesn't seem very perturbed, perhaps he doesn't realize how much he revealed that night. 'Sorry you feel that way, but you know best. Come down anyway for a drink, to show there's no hard feeling. Come alone.'

O'Shaughnessy decides then and there that he will, to see what this is all about. That first night Tereshko was all for having Nova join them. Tonight he wanted O'Shaughnessy to come down alone. Does Tereshko want Nova left alone in the flat? Is *he* the one behind all this? Nothing like finding out. he says, 'Get your hat.' And on the street, a couple of blocks away: 'You've never been to a movie, have you? Well, you're going to one now.'

He buys two seats, takes her in, finds a place for her. 'Now don't move from there till I come back and get you!' As if she were a child.

'Yes, O'Shaughnessy.'

There is no sign of Tereshko at the taproom where they were supposed to meet. O'Shaughnessy waits ten minutes, leaves, goes back and gets Nova. He fingers the gun in his pocket as they near their flat. 'So now,' he says to himself grimly, 'I think I know *who* I'm up against – if not why.'

The flat door falls back unfastened before them. They give one another a look. 'I thought – I saw you lock it after us when we left,' she whispers.

'You thought right,' he says grimly. He goes in first, gun bared.

No one there. 'Must have blown open,' he says. 'Maybe sneak thieves.'

This alarms her. 'My clothes! All the pretty things you gave me!' He grins a little at the woman of it, while she runs to the closet to find out. She comes out again as puzzled as ever.

'Anything missing?'

'No, but – I don't remember *this* being on here before.' She's holding one up to show him. A large lily is pinned to the front of it!

'Maybe it came that way and you've forgotten it.'

She strokes it with her fingers. 'But it's alive. They don't put *live* ones on them.'

Even he knows that. He aslo knows what lilies stand for as a rule. He softly starts to whistle a bar or two. 'Chicago, Chicago, I'll show you around – '

7

Some church-belfry on the other side of the river bongs twelve times. 'Got everything in?' he says quietly. 'I'll carry the bags down. You put out the lights.'

She tiptoes submissively down the stairs after him. 'I don't know how far we can get on five bucks,' he remarks, 'but it's a cinch I can't leave you up there by yourself any more in the daytime, and I can't drag you all over town with me either. Maybe we can get a room on the other side of the city – '

Just inside the doorway he puts down the bags, motions her to stand by them a minute. He saunters out ahead, carefully casual. Peers up one way, down the other. Nothing. The street's dead to the world.

Then suddenly, from nowhere, *ping*! Something flicks off the wall just behind him, flops at his feet like a dead bug. He doesn't bend down to look closer, he can tell what kind of bug it is all right. He's seen that kind of bug before, plenty of times. No flash, no report, to show which direction it came from. Silencer, of course.

He hasn't moved. *Fsssh*! and a bee or wasp in a hurry strokes by his cheek, tingles, draws a drop of slow blood. Another *pokk*! from the wall, another bug rolling over. The insect-world seems very streamlined, very self-destructive, tonight.

He takes a wary step back, slips inside the doorway again, still facing front. If he could only spot the flash, see where it was coming from, he could send them a few back. Meanwhile, he's half-in, half-out of the iron-grilled, thick, glass street door.

There's an anvil-like sound, and the warped spokes of a wheel slow up in the glass, centering in a neat, round hole. Powdery stuff like dandruff dusts his shoulder. Another bug has dropped inside the hallway.

Hands are gripping at his coat, pulling at him from behind. 'O'Shaughnessy, don't – you'll kill yourself standing there like that! Think of *me*!'

'Douse that bulb back there, swat it with your handbag – I want to see if I can catch the flashes.'

But she won't do it, and that traps him into going back and doing it himself. Then her arms wind around him when she gets him back there at the far end of the hallway, and she clings for dear life.

'No! No! I won't let you – What good'll you be to me dead? What'll become of me?' He gives in at last – it's either that or drag her bodily after him back to the entrance clinging like a barnacle.

'All right, all right. There must be a back way out of here.'

But, at the outlet to the electric-lighted basement passageway, as he emerges in advance of her – there are again winged insects on the loose, spitting off the wall. 'Wait a minute!' he says, cutting short her plaintive remonstrances. 'I think I caught the flash that time! Along the edge of the roof on that next house. Wait'll it comes again.' And cuts his hand at her backhand. 'The bulb. The bulb.' This time she obeys, blackness inks the passage behind him.

He draws and slowly raises this gun, standing perfectly still, face tilted to the sky. Gambler's odds: his life against the chances of hitting a powder-flash six stories up. His left thumbnail scrapes past the rabbit foot imbedded in his vest-pocket, half absent-mindedly.

A winking gleam just over the cornice up there, a flare from his own gun as fire draws fire. A chipping of the stonework just over and behind his head, and then something black and gangling falling clumsily down six stories, a blur against the gray gloom of the walls. A sickening thud against cement, just out of sight behind the eight-foot dividing fence.

More flashes up there, six in a row, and a sound like hail or gravel down where they are. But O'Shaughnessy's already back inside the sheltering passageway. 'It won't work. There's still a second one up there, and we could never get over that eight-foot fence alive. They seem to be doing this up in style. Come on back up to the flat.'

She goes up the inner stairs with her hands shielding her face. 'That fall. I hope he was dead before – he landed.'

'That evens the score a litte,' he says unsentimentally. 'They that live by the sword – '

Night in a Chicago flat. He says: 'The door's locked, and I'm here with Buster. You try to get a little sleep, honey, your old man'll look after you.'

'But promise me you'll stay up here with me, you won't go down there again.'

'I promise.'

So, fully dressed, she lies there on the bed, and after a while she sleeps, while he stands guard at the shade-drawn window, gun in hand, the spark of his cigarette held carefully behind his back.

A milkman comes and never dreams the muzzle of a gun is four inches away from his head on the other side of the door as he stoops to set down a bottle of milk. Nova sleeps on, like a child. Night in a Chicago flat.

Three hours after daylight they're ready to leave. There are enough people on the streets now to give them a chance. If they don't get out now, they never will. This net that's been meshed loosely around them all night will be pulled tight by the time darkness comes a second time. They want him out of the way, but they want her alive. That much he's sure of.

Just before they go, he murmurs, 'There's a cab been standing there ever since dawn, probably all night, just past the next corner. There's no public hack-stand at that spot, either.'

'Do you think that's – them?'

'I don't give a hoot whether it is or not, I can't breathe in here any more, I've got to get out in the open! Stick close behind me, and if I tumble, you keep going. I've been shot at before. I'm a bad penny that always turns up again.'

But then, as he puts his hand out to the doorknob, a sudden rigidity, as though some indefinable sound has reached him from outside it. 'There's someone out there,' he breathes.

She winces. 'We're too late.'

He motions her behind him, shielding her; reaches out and does something to the lock, levels his gun. 'It's open,' he calls out. 'Come in at your own risk.'

Nothing for a minute. Then very slowly it starts to fall back toward them.

'Quicker than that or I'll shoot!' He kicks it the rest of the way with the edge of his foot.

The trembling upraised arms are the first things they see. And the empty background behind the solitary figure. O'Shaughnessy takes a step backward, propelling her with him, not in retreat but to give himself elbow-room.

The face is Oriental, Chinese. Spectacles and close-cropped hair. Hat fallen off just now at the unexpected welcome.

O'Shaughnessy: 'This is the place you wanted?'

'Yes, if you will permit me to mop my forehead – '

'You warm?'

'No, but my reception was.'

'All right, close the door behind you. We've been a little draughty here all night.'

The visitor bows nervously. 'Allow me to introduce myself – '

'You're on the air.'

'I am Lawrence Lee, American name. I have come to offer you interesting proposition – '

'I just had one, thanks, a couple days ago.'

'I had great trouble finding you – '

'You're going to have even greater losing me, if this is a come-on.'

'I represent the illustrious Benevolent-Wisdom Yang. His recruitment-agent in United States. He has ordered a shipment of lovely planes, and needs someone who will know how to make them work. Your reputation has reached our ears. Can I offer you post on generalissimo's staff?'

O'Shaughnessy, gun stilll bared, sticks his left hand in his pocket, pulls it out again, lets the lining trail after it. 'You make it sound interesting – up to a point.'

'Five hundred dollars American, a week.'

'I'm no greenhorn, I've been in China before. I'm O'Shaughnessy of Winnipeg, he can't get another like me. The coolies used to bow down and worship in their rice-paddies whenever I passed overhead.' That he can stand and bargain like this, when both their lives are hanging by a thread, is – well, just part of his being O'Shaughnessy.

'Two thousand, p'aps?'

'More like it.' He turns to her, still huddled behind him. 'Shall we do it, just for the fun of it?' Then, with a grin to the emissary, 'Yang would not, I take it, be interested in a dead pilot?'

The agent, with Oriental lack of humor: 'Dead pilot could not handle planes satisfactorily.'

'Well, I may have a little trouble getting through alive from here to the Northwest Station. I can't promise you I will.' She shudders at this point, clings closer. 'However, that's my look-out. You leave two through tickets for Frisco on tap for us at the ticket office, and if I don't show up to claim them, you can always get a refund from the railroad – and another pilot.'

'Today-train agreeable? Shall do. Boat-tickets will be waiting
in Frisco at N.Y.K. Line office. And for binder, one thousand
advance suitable?'

O'Shaughnessy says in Chinese, 'I could not wound your
generosity by refusing.' Then in English, 'Carry your hat in your
hand leaving here, so your face can be seen clearly.'

The envoy bows himself out. 'Happy comings-down.'

When they're alone once more, he says to her: 'Shanghaiho.
The Coast Limited leaves at eleven, so we've got just one hour to
make it.'

'But how are we going to get out of here?'

'I don't know yet, but we are.' He goes back to the window,
peers narrowly down through the gap of the drawn shade.
'There goes Confucius without anyone stopping him; I guess
they didn't tie him up with me.' Then, 'Who's that fat woman
walking up and down out there with a poodle?'

'Oh, that's the lady in the rear flat I climbed into yesterday.
She always airs her dogs like that regularly every morning.'

'Dogs? She's only got one there.'

'She's got two in the flat. She has to take them down in relays
because they fight.'

'I've got it now!' he says. 'Wait'll she comes upstairs again.'

'What are you going to do?'

'You're going to take the next one down. I'm going to see that
you get to the station and safely aboard that train first of all. I'll
stall them off here, you call me back as soon as you get there.
Then I'll make a break for it myself – '

'Leave you – ' she wails.

'I'm giving the orders in this ground crew. Here she comes
now.' He goes to the door, stops her, brings her in with him.
She's globular and baby-faced, with carefully gilded hair under a
large cartwheel hat that flops around her face.

'Do you want to do something for us? I've got to get my wife
out of the building and I can't do it openly – we're being
watched. Will you lend her your hat and coat and dog? Your
other dog.'

'I'll gladly lend my hat and coat, but Fifi – my little Fifi –
who'll bring her back?'

'She'll turn her over to the station master for you, you can call
for her later. I tell you her life's in danger. Do this, won't you?'

'Yes,' she says, looking at Nova. 'I think I understand. I was
sure I'd seen your face somewhere before – in the paper, you
know. Tell me, what was he like? Was he as bad as they said? I

heard he used to make people stand with their feet in buckets of cement – '

'Skip it,' says O'Shaughnessy, 'you've got your wires crossed.'

It only takes a couple of minutes for the change. The wide-brimmed concealing hat hides everything but Nova's chin. He ties a couple of pillows around her with cord, one in front and on in back, under the coat, apologizing, 'No offense,' to the woman as he does so.

'That's all right,' she sighs. 'I know I've filled out.'

The fat lady stays up in their flat; she thinks it will be a good idea to give them a glimpse of her passing back and forth behind the windows. Make them think Nova's there. For this purpose they raise the shades once more. He goes down to the lower hall with Nova and the dog. Their parting is a mixture of comedy and tension. 'I'll be standing here behind the door covering you with my gun. Don't be frightened. Imitate her waddle. Walk slow and keep you eye on the dog, like she does. Give yourself a good two blocks before you jump for it. And don't drop those pillows to the sidewalk, whatever you do!'

'Oh, O'Shaughnessy, if you don't show up, I'm going to die.'

'I'll be there with bells on.'

The bulky, padded figure eases out through the door, minces after the dog, straining at its leash. He edges up slantwise against the door, screened by an abutment of the hall wall, peering out after her, gun ready, until she passes from his radius of vision. Then quickly chases upstairs where the window will give him a wider perspective.

The dog stops. The figure under the concealing hat brim stands patiently by. They go on again a few yards. They stop again. 'Darn dog!' he chafes, sweating with impatience in the hollows of his hands. Finally, almost imperceptibly, by fits and starts, she's progressed around the corner and out of sight.

He glues his eyes on the motionless taxi now. That street she just went up is a continuation of the one it's on. If it makes a move, starts out after her suddenly, he'll know –

Slow tense minutes. She must be a block away now. The cab's still standing. She ought to be off the streets by this time, safely installed in a cab, whirling toward the station. They've put it over!

He takes a deep breath of released tension, steps back into the room away from the window. The worst's over, she's made it. All that left now is to sit tight until she calls him to let him know she's reached the station. Fifteen minutes ought to do the trick, making every allowance for traffic-hitches and lights.

He sits there smoking calmly, waiting. The fat lady is still there in the flat. This, to her, is romance with a capital R. She's enjoying it more than a box of marshmallows. She's eating it up.

And then in a flash, before he quite knows how it's happened, seventeen minutes have passed, and the call is two minutes overdue, and the calmness is going out with every noseful of smoke he's expelling.

Twenty minutes. He throws down his cigarette, and takes three or four quick turns around the room. 'She should have called by now,' he says.

'Yes, she should have,' agrees the fat lady. 'It doesn't take that long to get from here to the Northwest Station.'

Twenty-five minutes, half an hour. 'Maybe the phone's out of order – ' But he's afraid to get on and test it, afraid to block her call. He shakes his fist at it helplessly.

He's prowling back and forth like a lion with distemper now. There's a shiny streak down one side of his face. 'I shouldn't have let her go ahead – I ought to be hung! Something's gone wrong. I can't stand this any more!' he says with a choked sound. 'I'm starting now – '

'But how are you – '

'Spring for it and fire as I go if they try to stop me.' And then as he barges out, the fat lady waddling solicitiously after him, 'Stay there; take it if she calls – tell her I'm on the way – '

He plunges straight at the street-door from all the way back in the hall, like a fullback headed for a touchdown. That's the best way. Gun bedded in his pocket, but hand gripping it ready to let fly through lining and all. He slaps the door out of his way without slowing and skitters out along the building, head and shoulders defensively lowered.

It *was* the taxi, you bet. No sound from it, at least not at this distance, just a thin bluish haze slowly spreading out around it that might be gas-fumes if its engine were turning; and at his end a long row of dun-colored spurts – of dust and stone-splinters – following him along the wall of the flat he's tearing away from. Each succeeding one a half yard too far behind him, smacking into where he was a second ago. And they never catch up.

He rounds the corner unscathed, spins like a dervish on one leg, brakes with the other, snaps a shot back at the cab, mist-haloed now, which is just getting into gear; and slipping out away from the curb. Glass tinkles faintly back there – he got the windshield maybe – and he sees the cab lurch crazily for a minute, as though more than glass got the bullet.

Then he sprints up the street without waiting to see any more. His own shots make plenty of noise, and the vicinity is coming to shocked life around him. Nothing in sight though that's any good to him – a slow-moving truck, a laundry-wagon. But music somewhere ahead – a cab radio – and he steers toward the sound, locates it just around the next corner, is in and on the way almost between two notes of a single bar. At the wheel himself.

The driver rears up in consternation in the back, holding a handful of pinochle cards, shrieks, 'Hey! what's the – '

'All right, climb around here and take it – I'm in a hurry, got no time to lower the gangplank!'

'What about these other guys?' The back of the cab is alive with shanghaied card-playing cab drivers.

'They'll have to come along for the ride.' Two blocks behind the other cab has showed up, is putting on a burst of speed. O'Shaughnessy warns, as the driver crawls over his lap: 'I want you to keep that cab back there where it belongs – zig-zag, I don't care what you do – but lose it. It means your back-tires if you don't!'

The rear-view mirror suddenly spatters into crystal confetti.

'See, what'd I tell you? Left, left, get offa here, don't stay in a straight line with 'em!'

The driver says, 'What *you* done? I don't like this!' He takes a turn that nearly lands them axle-shafts in air.

A series of two-wheel turns, and a combination of lights in their favor – the rabbit's foot must be working again – closing down after them like portcullises each time. They shake them off.

It's twelve-and-a-half minutes before train time when he jumps down at the Northwest Station, slaps one of Lawrence Lee's sawbucks in through the cab-window and dives inside.

At the barrier: 'Tickets, please!'

'Wasn't one left here for me with you?'

'Nope.'

'My wife must have taken them through to the train with her, then, Didn't you see her – pretty blonde, big floppy hat – ?'

'All blondes are pretty to me, haven's seen a bad-looking one so far today – '

'Buddy, I'm not interested in your love life, I wanna get through here to see if I can find her – '

'Hey, come back here!'

The agony of that wild, headlong plunge into car after car, calling: 'Nova! Nova!' from the vestibule of each one. No sign of her. Upstairs again at a mile a minute, nearly knocking over the gateman a second time – eight minutes to train-time now.

At the ticket-window, 'Two for the Coast – O'Shaughnessy – were they picked up?'

'Nope, here they are waiting for you.'

Uncalled for! She never got here, then! Seven minutes to find her, in a city of four million people! Outside again, and looking around him dazed. Dazed – and dangerous – and yet helpless. Ready to give this town something to be tough about, but not knowing where to start in – Instinctively touching the rabbit's foot, that habit of his. And then – like a genie at the summons of Aladdin's lamp – a redcap, haphazardly accosting him in line of duty. One out of the dozens swarming all over the place, but the right one, the right one out of all of them!

'Cab, boss?'

'No. Wait, George – blonde lady, big droopy hat, did you see anyone like that drive up here at all the past half-hour or so?'

'Li'l dog with a haircut 'cepting on its ankles?'

'Yes! Yes!' He grabs the guy by both shoulders. 'Hurry up and tell me, for Pete's sake!'

The redcap shows his teeth.

'That sho' was a dirty trick that lady have played on her. She done come away without bringin' no change fo' her cab fare, and the driver he wouldn't listen to her no-how, he turn around and take her to the police station.'

'Which?'

'Neares' one, I reckon.'

And there she is when he tears in a couple minutes later, sitting on a bench under the desk-sergeant's eye, dog and all. Driver, too.

'We've been trying to reach you, young fellow.' The sergeant clears his throat meaningly, winks at O'Shaughnessy to show he won't give him away. Wife starting on a vacation, somebody else answering the phone; *he* understands. 'Couldn't seem to get you.'

'How much is it? We've got a train to make.'

'Two dollas and twenny cents,' says the driver.

'Here it is. And here's a little something extra – ' Wham! and the driver nearly brings down the rear wall of the room as he lands onto it.

Then he's outside with her again, minus dog and pillows now, in another machine, tearing back to the station. Three minutes to spare. He doesn't notice as he jumps down that the cab ahead of theirs, the one that's just pulled into the driveway before them, has a shattered windshield.

They don't have to be mind-readers, these others, to figure out where he and she will head for. If they're on their way out of town, that means one of the stations. They've cased the La Salle Street Station first, now this one.

He starts her through the big vaulted place at a quick trot. Then suddenly a shout somewhere behind them, 'There they are!' and five men are streaming in after them, one with a bloody bandage over his head.

O'Shaughnessy daren't shoot; the station's alive with people crisscrossing the line of fire. His pursuers can't either; not that the risk of hitting somebody else would deter them, but they're sprinting after him too fast to stop for aim. A redcap goes keeling over, and one of the rodmen topples over a piece of hand-luggage the porter dropped, goes sliding across the smooth floor on his stomach. And above it all the amplifier blaring out remorselessly, 'Coast Limited – Kansas City – Denver – Salt Lake City – San Francisco! 'Board!'

He wedges her through the closing barrier, throws the tickets at the gateman. A shot, and looking back he can see the uniformed figure at the gate toppling, even while the gateman still tries to wedge it closed. A young riot is taking place back there, shouts, scuffling, station-guards' clubs swinging. But one figure squeezes through, detaches itself, comes darting after him, gun out. Tereshko.

O'Shaughnessy shoves her into a car vestibule. 'Get on, kid. Be right with you.' The train is already giving its first few preliminary hitches – forward.

Tereshko's gun flames out as he comes on; the shot hits the L of El Dorado, the Pullman's gold-lettered name, slowly slipping past behind O'Shaughnessy's back. Tereshko never had a chance for another shot. O'Shaughnessy closes in bare-handed; his fist swings out, meets Tereshko half way as he crashes into it, lands him spread-eagled on the platform. The gun goes flying up in a foreshortened arc, comes down again with a clank, and fires innocuously.

O'Shaughnessy flicks him a derisive salute from over one ear. 'I gotta make a train, or I'd stay and do it right!' He turns and catches the hand-rail of the next-to-the-last vestibule as it glides by, swings himself aboard. Tereshko stands staring blurredly down his own nose at the dwindling observation-platform of the Coast Limited.

O'Shaughnessy sinks wearily down in the seat beside Nova, and as she shrinks into the protective angle of his outstretched arm, he tells her grimly: 'You're O'Shaughnessy's girl for keeps. Let 'em try to take you away from me now!'

8

O'Shaughnessy, minutes after his Bellanca has kissed the hard-packed earth of the Shanghai municipal airport, is already on one of the airport phones asking for the Broadway Mansions. Seven weeks out of Shanghai, seven weeks back in the red mountains of Szechuan, China's 'wild west', piloting the great General Yang around, dropping a few well-placed bombs for him, and trans-shipping machine-gun parts inland from below Ichang, which is as far as the river boats can go. No commission in Yang's fighting-forces, nothing like that – just his own crate, his own neck, payment in American gold dollars, and a leave of absence whenever he feels like it, which happens to be right now. Seven weeks is a plenty long time.

He's still in the crumpled slacks and greasy khaki shirt he left the interior in, but under them a triple-tiered money-belt, twice around the chest and once across the waist, packed with good solid chunky gold eagles, outlawed at home now but as good as ever over here. Fifteen-thousand dollars' worth; two thousand a week salary, and a thousand bonus for obliterating a caterpillar tank that General Yang didn't like the looks of. Not bad, two thousand a week. But seven weeks is still a long time, any way you look at it.

Her voice comes over the wire throbbing with expectancy; every time it's rung she's hoped it was he – and now at last it is.

'O'Shaughnessy.' A love song in one word. She's never called him by anything but that.

'Just grounded. I've brought back fifteen-thousand-worth of red paint with me. Turn the shower on, lay out my dude-clothes, and get ready for a celebration!'

He just lingers long enough to see his plane put to bed properly, then grabs a cab at the airport-gate. 'The Settlement,' and forgetting that he's not inland any more, that Shanghai's snappier than Chicago, 'Chop-chop.'

'Sure, Mike,' grins the slant-eyed driver. 'Hop in.'

A change has come over the city since he went away, he can feel that the minute they hit the outskirts, clear the congested native sections, and cross the bridge into the Settlement. Shanghai is already tuning-up for its oncoming doom, without knowing it. A city dancing on the brink of the grave. There's an electric tension in the air, the place never seemed so gay, so hectic, as tonight; the roads opening off the Bund a welter of blinking, flashing neon lights, in ideographs and Latin letters alike, as far as the eye can see. Traffic hopelessly snarled at every crossing, cops piping on their whistles, packed sidewalks, the blare of saxophones coming from taxi-dance mills, and overhead the feverish Oriental stars competing with intercrossed search-light beams from some warships or other on the Whang-poo. Just about the right town and the right night to have fifteen thousand bucks in, all at one time.

He says: 'Hold it, Sam,' in front of a jewelry store in Bubbling Well Road, lopes in, comes out again with a diamond solitaire in his pocket.

The skyscraper Mansions shows up, he vaults out, counts windows up to the tenth floor, three over from the corner. Brightly lighted, waiting for him. Shies a five-dollar bill at the driver.

The elevator seems to crawl up; he feels like getting out and pushing. A pair of Englishmen stare down their noses at his waste rag outfit. The rush of her footsteps on one side of the door matches his long stride on the other.

'I'd recognize your step with cotton in my ears!'

'Watch it, you'll get fuel-oil all over you!'

They go in together in a welter of disjointed expressions, such as any pair might utter. 'I thought you were never coming back this time!'

'Boy, you certainly made time getting dressed. All set to go, aren't you?'

As a matter of fact she isn't, it's her gloves that mislead him. She has on a shimmery silver dress, but no shoes. Her hair is still down too.

He laughs. 'What do you do, put on your gloves before your shoes?'

A shadow of something passes across her face. Instantly she's smiling again. 'Just knowing you were back got me so rattled – '

He takes a quick shower, jumps into his best suit. Comes in on her just as she is struggling into a pair of silver dancing shoes – just in time to catch the expression of livid agony on her pretty face. She quickly banishes it.

'Matter – too tight? Wear another pair – '

'No, no, it isn' that. They're right for me – my feet got a little swollen wearing those Chinese things all day.'

He lets it go. 'Come on, where'll it be? Astor House, American Club, Jockey Club?' He laughs again as she drenches herself with expensive perfume, literally empties the bottle over herself. 'Incidentally, I think we'll move out of here. Something seems to be the matter with the drains in this apartment, you can notice a peculiar musty odor inside there – decay –'

The haunted look of a doomed thing flickers in her eyes. She takes his arm with desperate urgency. 'Let's – let's go. Let's get out into the open, O'Shaughnessy. It's such a lovely night, and you're back, and – life is so short!'

That air of electric tension, of a great city on the edge of an abyss, is more noticeable than ever at the White Russian cabaret called, not inappropriately, 'New York.' You wouldn't know you were in China. An almond-eyed platinum-blonde has just finished wailing, with a Mott Street accent. 'You're gonna lose your gal.'

O'Shaughnessy leads Nova back to the table apologizing. 'I knew I wasn't cut out for dancing, but I didn't know how bad I was until I got a look at your face just now. All screwed up like you were on the rack. Kid, why didn't you speak up – '

'It wasn't you, O'Shaughnessy,' she gasps faintly. 'My – my feet are killing me – '

'Well, I've got something here that'll cure that. We don't get together often, Mrs. O'Shaughnessy, but when we do – the sky's the limit.' He takes the three-thousand-dollar ring out of his pocket, blows on it, shows it to her. 'Take off your glove, honey, and lemme see how this headlight looks on your finger – '

Her face is a white, anguished mask. He reaches toward her right hand. 'Go ahead, take the glove off.'

The tense, frightened way she snatches it back out of his reach gives her away. He tumbles. The smile slowly leaves his face. 'What's the matter – don't you want my ring? You trying to cover up something with those gloves? You fixed your hair with them on, you powdered your nose with them on – What's under them? Take 'em off, let me see.'

'No, O'Shaughnessy. No!'

His voice changes. 'I'm your husband, Nova. Take off those gloves and let me see your hands!'

She looks around her agonized. 'Not here, O'Shaughnessy! Oh, not here!'

She sobs deep in her throat, even as she struggles with one glove. Her eyes are wet, pleading. 'One more night, give me one more night,' she whispers brokenly. 'You're leaving Shanghai again in such a little while. Don't ask to see my hands. O'Shaughnessy, if you love me. . . .'

The glove comes off, flops loosely over, and there's suddenly horror beating into his brain, smashing, pounding, battering. He reels a little in his chair, has to hold onto the edge of the table with both hands, at the impact of it.

A clawlike thing – two of the finger extremities already bare of flesh as far as the second joint; two more with only shriveled, bloodless, rotting remnants of it adhering, only the thumb intact, and that already unhealthy-looking, flabby. A dead hand – the hand of a skeleton – on a still-living body. A body he was dancing with only a few minutes ago.

A rank odor, a smell of decay, of the grave and of the tomb, hovers about the two of them now.

A woman points from the next table, screams. She's seen it, too. She hides her face, cowers against her companion's shoulder, shudders. Then he sees it too. His collar's suddenly too tight for him.

Others see it, one by one. A wave of impalpable horror spreads centrifugally from that thing lying there in the blazing electric light on O'Shaughnessy's table. The skeleton at the feast!

She says forlornly, in the stunned stillness: 'You wanted me to wear your ring, O'Shaughnessy –' and slips it over that denuded bone protruding like a knobby spine from her hand. Loosely, like a hoop, it falls down to the base of the thing, hangs there, flashing prismatically, in an inconceivable horror. Diamonds for the dead.

The spell breaks; the glitter of the diamond perhaps does it, shattering the hypnosis, freeing him. So lifelike there, so out of place. Not a word has passed between them, but for that one lament of hers. He seizes her to him suddenly, their two chairs go over, their champagne glasses crash to the floor. He pulls out a wing of his coat, wraps it concealing around the thing that was once her hand, clutches it to him, hurries her out of the place, his arm protectively about her. The flash of a silver dress, a whiff of gardenia, a hint of moldy, overturned earth, as they go by, and the dead has been removed from among the living. The ring drops off the insufficient bone-silver that carries it, rolls unheeded across the floor.

'Not so fast, O'Shaughnessy,' she pleads brokenly. 'My feet too – they're that way. My knees. My side, where the ribs are. It's coming out all over me.'

And then, in the cab hurtling them through the mocking constellations that were the Bund an hour ago, she says: 'Life was swell, though, while it lasted. Just knowing you has made – well, everything.'

He says again what he said before: 'No one is going to take you away from me!'

The English doctor says, 'Looks rather bad, y'know old man.'

O'Shaughnessy, white-lipped, growls out something. . . .

The German doctor says, 'Neffer before haff I such a thing seen. This case will become zenzational – '

'The case will, but what about her, that's what I want to know?'

'My *gut* man – '

'I get it. Send the bill around – !'

The American doctor says, 'There's just a slim chance – what you might call a thousand-to-one shot, that chaulmoogra oil might benefit her.'

'I thought you said it wasn't leprosy?'

'It isn't. It may be some Chinese disease none of us have ever heard of before. She seems to be *dying alive*. Her bodily functions are unimpaired, the X-rays show; whatever it is seems to be striking on the surface. If it continues unchecked – and there doesn't seem to be anything we can do to stop it – the whole skeletal structure will be revealed – you'll have an animated corpse on your hands! And then of course . . . death.'

The French doctor – the French, they are a very logical race and made good doctors – says: 'M'sieu, they have all been on the wrong track – '

O'Shaughnessy's wan face lights up. 'What can you tell me?'

'I can tell you only this: there is no hope. Your wife is lost to you. If you are a merciful man – I do not give you this advice as doctor, I give it to you as one husband to another – you will go to one of the opium houses of Chapei, buy a quantity sufficient for *two* at least – '

O'Shaughnessy says in a muffled voice, 'I'm no quitter. I'll beat this rap.'

There's pity in the Frenchman's face. 'Go to Chapei, *mon ami*. Go tonight. I say this for the sake of your own sanity. Your mind will crumble at the sight of what it will have to behold in a few more weeks.'

O'Shaughnessy says the name of his Maker twice, puts his arm up swiftly over his face. The doctor's hand comes to rest on his shoulder. 'I can see what led them astray; the others. They sought for disease. There is no disease there. No malady. No infection. It is not that; it is the state of death, itself, that has her.

How shall I say? This flesh that rots, drops away, is, paradoxically, healthy tissue. My microscopes do not lie. Just as, let us say, a person who has been shot dead by a bullet is otherwise a healthy person. But he lies in his grave and nature dissolves his flesh. That is what we have here. The effect without the cause – '

O'Shaughnessy raises his head after a while, gets up, moves slowly toward the door. 'You, at least,' he says, ' are a square shooter. All right, medical science tells me she's as good as dead. I'm not licked yet. There's a way.'

The doctor shrugs gloomily. 'How? What way is there? Lourdes, you are thinking of?'

'An awful way,' O'Shaughnessy says, 'but a way.'

He stumbles out into the bright sunlight of the Concession, roams around hopelessly. Along the Avenue of the Two Republics, bordering the French Concession, he finds himself beginning to tremble all over, suddenly.

Fear! Fear again, for the first time since his 'teens. Fear, that he thought he would never know any more. Fear that no weapon, no jeopardy, no natural cataclysm, has ever been able to inspire until now. And now here it is running icily through him in the hot Chinese noon. Fear for the thing he loves, the only fear that can ever wholly cow the reckless and the brave.

Fear of the Way, the Way that he mentioned to the doctor. Fear of the implication involved in it. A mad voice howling in the darkness sounds in his ears again: 'You'll come crawling back to me, begging me to help! *That'll be my hour!*' Oh, not that his own life will assuredly be forfeit as part of the bargain, that isn't what makes him tremble. Nor any amount of pain and horror that vindictive mania can devise. He can stand it with a smile, to give her an hour, a day, or a week of added life. It's what will come after, what she must face alone without him, once he's out of the way. The barbed-wire fence – cooped up with a madman; kept trapped like an animal in a cage, after having known the world. Better if he'd left her as he'd found her. . . .

But that's the Way, and there is no other. And once his mind's made up, the trembling and aimless walking stops, and he can look doom in the face without flinching.

He has their boat-tickets in his pocket when he goes back to the Mansions. All down the corridor, from the elevator-shaft to their door, there's that cloying odor of perfumery – to conceal another, different one.

She's propped up in bed, a native *amuh* sitting by her fanning her. He stops short in surprise. The screwy clock of this bedevilment seems to have spun backward again to that awful night, when he first came out of the interior – and didn't know yet. For she's beautiful there, composed, placid again, expressionless as a wax doll, the stigma of the knowledge of approaching doom erased from her face.

'The mask came,' she says through it, in a slightly resonant voice. Her own features, reproduced by a clever Chinese craftsman, at her terrified request – before anything happens to them. Not for herself, this, for the man who stands there looking at her – the man whom life and love have laughed at, the man to whom life and love and laughter, too, have been denied.

He gestures the Chinese woman out of the room.

When they're alone Nova asks, as tonelessly as though she were asking what the weather was like, 'Any hope?'

'Not here.' It's not the first time it's been asked and answered that way, so there's no shock to it any more.

He sees a small canvas bag upon the table beside her bed. 'What's that?'

'Another agent of Yang was here while you were out. He left this bag of gold, and a thinly veiled threat that your tea will be bitter if you don't report back soon. They think you've run out on them. Better go back, O'Shaughnessy.'

'Not a chance, darling. I've sold my plane. We're taking the early morning back to the States. I'm taking you back to Denholt.'

She is silent for a long minute. He can see her shivering through the thick, brocaded, Chinese jacket, pretty much the way he was, out in the sun-baked streets.

He sits down beside her. 'You've knocked around with me now for almost a year. You've talked to lots of other girls your age. You must have found out by now that none of them learned to walk and talk as late as you did. Something happened to you, and there's only one man alive knows what it was and what's to be done about it. Those injections – can't you see that he was keeping you alive in some way? It's our only chance, we've got to go back there, we've got to get more of his stuff.' And bitterly, as he hauls out a valise and tosses up the lid, 'O'Shaughnessy wasn't so smart. O'Shaughnessy knows when he's licked. . . .'

Down the Whangpoo to the Yangste, and out into the China Sea. A race against time now. A race against death. And the odds are so tall against them. The widest body of water in the world to cross. Then a whole continent afterward from west to east. Three weeks at the very least. Can she hold out that long by sheer will-power? Or have they waited too long, like fools? Then too, how can he be sure there is help waiting at the end of the long journey, even the help that they both dread so? Suppose Denholt is gone. How to locate him again in time? He may be in a strait jacket at this very moment, unable to tell a serum from a split of White Rock. The odds are pretty steep. But — at least there *are* odds.

She sits in a deck chair covered up to her chin in a steamer rug; her beautiful masked face above it never smiles, never frowns, never changes — just the eyes alive and the voice. He haunts the chart that marks their daily progress. Comes back to it a hundred times a day, says prayers before it while it lengthens a pitiful notch at a time, in red ink across the graph.

Kobe. Bad news. A Japanese English-language paper has picked up the story from something that must have come out in Shanghai after they left. Fright sounds through the mask. 'It's — it's leaked out already. Here, Beautiful girl stricken with living death. First case of its kind on record. Being rushed home by husband — '

She makes a small, plaintive sound. 'Don't you see? The papers in America will pick it up, follow it through, play it up. And your name's here. *They*, whoever they were, they'll know it means us, they'll find out we're coming back. They'll be waiting for us to land, they'll — we'll never make it. Oh, let's turn back, O'Shaughnessy! Let me die in China — what's the difference where it is? I've brought you enough grief, don't let me be the cause of — '

He takes her in his arms and holds her tight. 'You don't seem to think much of my ability to take care of us.'

She makes a thoughtless gesture to reach out and clasp his hand understandingly; but she remembers and draws the gloved claw back again.

Days pass. The story has circulated now, and turned the ship into a buzzing beehive of curiosity. People find excuses to go by her on the deck, just so they can turn and stare. O'Shaughnessy overhears two men bet that she won't reach Frisco alive. She tries to smoke a cigarette through the lips of the mask one afternoon, to buoy up his spirits a little. Smoke comes out of her hair-line, under her chin, before her ears. A steward drops a loaded bouillon-tray at the sight of her. Nova stays in her cabin after that.

9

Three thousand years later they're at Honolulu. Leis and steel guitars above deck; and below, something that scarcely stirs, that lies still now, saturated with cologne, smothered with fresh-cut flowers as though she were already on her bier. It's too painful to force the fleshless footbones to support her tottering body any more, even swathed in bandages, except for a few moments at a time. Reporters try to get in to see her; O'Shaughnessy has to swing his fists to get them to keep their distance.

Out to sea again, on the last leg of the trip. Sometimes he bends down, whispers low, like a prizefighter's second in his corner when the bout's going against him: 'You can make it. Just a little longer, honey. Do it for O'Shaughnessy.' Sometimes, in the depths of the night, he goes up on the boatdeck, shakes his fist – at what? The ship, the limitless ocean, the elusive horizon that never comes any nearer, the stars overhead that don't give a rap?

The rabbit's paw has hardly been out of his palm the whole way over. All the pelt's worn off it with his stroking. His thumb has developed an ineradicable habit of turning inward on itself, circling his palm. 'You and me,' he says to it grimly. 'We'll do the trick.'

Frisco at last. And the anchor plunges into the waters of the bay – they've made it – ! The three of them, he and she and the rabbit's foot. There's still a voice behind that mask – faltering, weak, but alive. Still living eyes behind those immobile eyeholes with their double tier of lashes – real and artificial.

He's wirelessed ahead from the Islands for a cabin plane, and it's tuned up and waiting at the airport over in Oakland. He gets Nova through the gang of reporters clogging the deck, has her carried down the gangplank on a stretcher while flashlights go off around her like a constellation. Into a car outside the Customs House, while the newsmen like a pack of hounds in full cry swarm around them, yapping. But there's one man who doesn't pepper him with questions, doesn't say a word – just takes a good look at the beautiful graven face being transferred from stretcher to car, and then dives into the nearest phone-booth. O'Shaughnessy isn't near enough to overhear him ask for long-distance. . . .

And then the plane, with a relief pilot to spell O'Shaughnessy. Up and due east. 'And we don't come down again for snow or rain or fog or engine-trouble until you hit Louisville,' says O'Shaughnessy.

All through the day they hurl through space. 'You got that Kentucky map I asked you to get hold of?'

He locates the mountain on it finally, draws a big ring around it. 'Here's where we come down, inside that circle.'

'But on what? How do we know what's there? It'll be dark long before we make it,' the relief pilot protests.

'Here's where we come down,' is O'Shaughnessy's remorseless answer, 'if we splinter into match wood. Here, right on the perimeter, where this feeder branches off from the trunk-highway on the west and climbs up. That's as close as we can get.'

'Radio ahead, contact one of the towns near there to have something waiting for you at that point, otherwise you may be held up for hours.'

'Yeah, that's it,' nods O'Shaughnessy. He starts calling the county seat.

Nova shakes her head. He bends down close to hear what she wants to say. 'That may bring *them* down on us, if you mention the place – tip them off where we're going to land.'

'How can they beat our time in, unless they're already somewhere around there?'

'But that's it, they may be. You wirelessed him from Honolulu and mentioned a chart of this one county. They may have intercepted that message. They're likely to be within reach of your set, and this'll bring them right to the exact spot.'

'Then that'll bring them grief!' is all he says. He fiddles with the dials 'Hello, Wellsville? This is a private chartered plane coming your way, with a desperately ill passenger on board. We need ground transport badly. . . .'

'Hello, this is Wellsville. This is Wellsville. There are no facilities here.'

'I'm not asking for hospitalization. All I want is ground transport. I want a car where Route 19 bisects the highway.'

'Well – I dunno – '

'Have you been reading the papers lately?' O'Shaughnessy barks. 'This is Penny O'Shaughnessy – Yes, yes, the "Dying Alive Girl", if you insist! Now do I get a car at that particular spot?'

'I'll start out now.'

'We don't want any publicity. Come alone. We should be there by ten. Tilt your headlights upward to guide us, keep snapping them off and on at two-minute intervals, we're going to have to land in pitch-darkness. If we live through it, be ready to start off at a moment's notice. Don't let us down, there's a human life at stake. This is her last chance.'

Louisville, an hour after dark, is a carpet of gilt thumb-tacks below them, with straight, twinkling lines like strings of beads leading out from it. Southeastward now, toward the Tennessee state-line.

At nine a continuous line of little pinpoints, stretched straight as an arrow, shows up below. They follow it, flying so low now the twinkling lights of an occasional car crawling along it seems to be right under them. Then, in thirty, forty minutes, a firefly down there in the dark fields, going off, on, off, on.

O'Shaughnessy clutches his pilot jubilantly by the shoulder. 'See it? Here, gimme the controls – I *couldn't* go wrong, not this late in the game!'

Around and around in a narrowing spiral. Then way out, and around, and in again in a straight swoop that barely seems to skim the roof of the waiting car. 'Hold on!' he warns, and slaps the pocket holding the rabbit's foot. The earth comes up flat like a blackboard. A jolt, a rise, a dip, another bump, a short stretch of wobbly taxiing, a shudder, and he cuts off his engine.

The car, waiting off across the field, has lowered its headlights to guide them. Carrying her between them they waver toward it up a thinly-talcumed path of light-motes. A rail fence shows up. 'All right, driver! You in the car!' shouts O'Shaughnessy. 'Come out here and give us a hand over this!'

A figure jumps out, hurries to meet them on the outside of the fence.

They ease her over the top rail, the newcomer holding her in both arms until O'Shaughnessy can scramble over and relieve him.

They pass her into the back of the car. Then suddenly, a dark motionless outline shows up a little way up the sideroad, under shadowing trees that all but blot it out – materializes into a second car, unlighted, stalled, apparently deserted.

The plane pilot, who has been standing off to one side, looking on, cries out: 'Hey, there's a guy lying here at the side of the road, out – '

'Take it easy pal,' an unseen voice purrs. An orange hyphen flicks toward the pilot from somewhere just behind the car. A report shatters the crossroads' stillness, and the pilot leans over toward the road, as though he saw a coin lying there and was languidly about to pick it up.

O'Shaughnessy doesn't wait for him to complete the fall. He whirls back toward Nova, flings out his arms to keep her from going into his car that is a trap. The blurred oval of a second face, not that of the man who helped to carry her to it, looms at him in the dark, above her body.

'No, you don't,' a voice says blandly, 'she's coming with us – we're taking up where we left off that night – and she ain't fooling us this time!'

A second red-orange spearhead leaps straight at O'Shaughnessy. The whole world seems to stand still. Then the gun behind it crashes, and there's a cataclysm of pain all over him, and a shock goes through him as if he ran head-on into a stone wall.

A voice from the car says blurredly, while the ground rushes up to meet him, 'Finish him up, you guys! I'm getting so I don't trust their looks no more, no matter how stiff they act!'

Three comets seem to dart down at him as he lies there on the ground. Asphalt-grits fly up beside his skull. A hot wire creases his side while something that feels like a mallet pounds his shoulder. He can feel his mouth opening; he must be trying to say something.

Far away, from some low-flying soundless plane in the skies, a pair of voices reach him. 'Did you hear where they were headed for?'

'Yeah, and it sounds like a swell idea – '

High up over him the chattering motor swells into a roar, the air he is trying to breathe is sucked away from him along the ground, grit and road-dust swirl over him. God, they're flying low! What're they trying to do – ? Looking down his own body can see a red light poised momentarily on the toe of his shoe. Then it dips below it, and it's gone. And he's alone there, with the unconscious pilot lying a little way off for company, and some other guy he's never even seen, only spoken to over the radio.

He wants to sleep so badly – dying they call it – and he can't. Something's bothering him to keep him awake. Something that won't let him alone. Not about Nova, not about the still pilot either. Something about this other, strange guy.

And then he remembers. The guy has a car, that's what it is. The guy brought a car here. The guy is dead now, but the car is still standing there, back a little ways under some trees. He saw it himself.

He's got to get into that car. He may be half-dead, but cars don't die; it'll get him wherever he wants to go, good as ever. And where he wants to go is just where Nova is, no matter where.

He rolls over on his face first. And a lot of hot wet stuff comes out on his shoulder and his chest and hip. That makes everything come alive again and hurt like blazes. He starts pulling himself around the other way, with his good arm and shoulder for a propeller, like something maimed that ought to be put out of its misery with a big stick.

Then when he gets all the way around in a half circle, there's the car, with the pilot and the other guy for milestones leading to it. He starts dragging himself toward it. He can tell it's no use trying to get up on his feet.

He comes up to the pilot first, rests full length beside him a minute, reaches out, shakes him a little.

Frazier moans a little – almost a bleat – stirs a little.

O'Shaughnessy inches on toward the car. Like a caterpillar goes, contracting in the middle, expanding again, contracting, expanding. Like a caterpillar someone's stepped on, though. He leaves a moist trail behind him along the asphalt roadbed.

It's easy to rear up as high as the running-board, but above that there's a long unbroken stretch of glossy tonneau up to the door handle. He makes it, on the heels of his hands and the points of his elbows, using them for grips, like vacuum cups. The window's down, luckily, and a hand on the sill of the frame keeps him up. He falls, sprawling, into the seat.

Light funnels out of the dead headlights again, across the two men on the ground. He jockeys slowly around, then straightens out.

The rush of air through the open windows clears some of the cobwebs from his bullet-stunned mind. He knows where they went, and where to follow. 'Did you hear where they were heading for?' the first voice had said. And the second answered, 'Sounds like a swell idea.'

The dirt-packed mountain-detour branches off at last, and the new-made treads of the car ahead are plainly visible along it. It's a hard trail to tackle, with just one good arm to steady the wheel by, and a grade like a loose plank tilted before your face, and obscuring branches and foliage whistling in at you through the windows.

The barbed-wire fence starts up beside him after awhile. He wonders if Denholt still lives behind it. The scooped-out hollows of their ruts are still before him, plain as day, and broken branches hanging down at right-angles. The fence suddenly crumples into the ground, and a big gap torn in it where the gate used to be, where he remembers it, shows him how they got in.

He turns in after them, brakes only when their own car, broad side to him, blocks further progress. Beyond, the house shows palely against his partly-deflected headlights. He gets out, bangs the car door after him out of habit, lurches over to their car, steadies himelf against it for a moment. Caution is for the healthy. He laughs sort of crazily and stamps onto the wooden porch. He hangs onto the door-frame for a minute, then goes on through the unguarded opening.

They haven't even closed the door after them, they're so sure they've left all opposition dead behind them where the highway crosses Route 19. That white light from the laboratory is streaming out to guide him. They're in there, all of them; he can hear their voices as he comes draggingly nearer. One voice, raised above the others, strident threatening.

'Don't tell us you don't know what we mean! Why the barbed-wire fence and all the trimmings, if it ain't around here somewhere? Why was the Brown girl, here, heading this way so fast with that guy she calls her husband? And a nifty place, if there ever was one! Here we was thinking it was somewhere down in the Florida keys all the time! That's just like the Boss, goes off on a cruise in one direction to cover up, sends the do-re-mi in another. He was always smart that way, always doing things like that. Now *you* be smart.'

'There's no money here. I don't know who you are, what brings you here, but there's no money here. Only the – the results of a lifetime of – For God's sake, be careful!'

That's Denholt's voice. Already O'Shaughnessy has reached the threshold by now and stands there looking in at them like an apparition, unnoticed. Their backs are all to him, even Nova's, gripped cruelly between two of them, held upright. Only Denholt is facing his way, at bay against the far wall.

Even from behind, O'Shaughnessy can spot one of those backs, Tereshko.

10

He is standing near a retort filled with colorless fluid; as Denholt's frantic warning singles it out, his elbow has just grazed it, caused it to teeter. The plea has exactly the opposite effect it was intended to; it is something precious to that old crank standing there before him, so his impulse is to destroy it forthwith. He deliberately completes the shove, sweeps it off the trestle it rests on. 'Nuts with all this junk y'got here! This is a phony front. Who y'think y'kidding?'

The retort shivers into pieces on the floor. Its contents flood out, spread, dissipate beyond recovery.

Denholt lets out a hoarse, anguished cry. And leaps at the wanton destroyer of his whole life's work. Tereshko's gun raps out almost perfunctorily; smoke blooms between them; Denholt staggers, turns around the other way, then goes down to his knees slowly like a penitent in prayer.

They hear him say, in the brief sentence: 'Yes, it's better this way – now.' Then he falls forward on his face.

O'Shaughnessy's leap for Tereshko crashes through the rearguard, sends the four behind Tereshko lurching off-balance. Nova released, totters aside, keeps herself from falling against the edge of the operating table. They whirl, see who faces them and forget, in their utter disbelief, to use their guns. Tereshko goes down backward, his neck caught in the grip of O'Shaughnessy's arm, while the Irishman's other fist is pounding, flailing, slashing, into the side of Tereshko's head and ribs.

The struggle doesn't last long; it's too unequal. Their momentary surprise overcome, they close in on him. The well-directed slice of a gun-butt slackens the good arm; it's easy to pry the disable one from around the racketeer's collar.

Tereshko is trembling with his anger. 'Now *him* again!' he protests, as though at an injustice. 'All they do is die and then get up and walk around again! What'sa matter, you guys using spitballs for slugs? No, don't kick at him, that'll never do it – I think the guy has nine lives!'

'Wait!' The mask has spoken, and they turn in awe at the impassive face looking at them. Face that lies now if it never did before – so calm, so untroubled, so serene, at the scene before it. 'What is it you want of us – of me? Why do you hound us like this? What have we ever done to you?'

Tereshko sneers, 'You're Benedetto's girl, ain't you? You're Jane Brown, ain't you? You oughta know what we want of you. We did his dirty work for seven long years, you just come in on the pay-off at the end. Where's the profits of those seven years, when two bits out of every fifty-cent glass of beer drunk east of the Mississippi went into his pockets? Where's the million and a quarter dollars in gold and Federal Reserve notes that dropped from sight when he was arrested?'

'I never saw or knew Benedetto,' says the mask slowly.

'You lying tomato! I'm looking right at the face he used to kiss in front of all of us. I'm looking right at the face that stood in a diamond frame on his bureau, every time I went in there to make a report. I'm hearing the voice that used to call him Benny-boy, I'm seeing the eyes that cried when he got sent away – Oh no! You're Jane Brown, all right.'

Glove hands rise from the enfolding cloak, undo tiny straps

behind the ears, below the golden hair on top of the head. 'Look closer still – and tell me if I'm Benedetto's girl – if I'm Jane Brown!' The face drops off – a shell – and yet repeats itself, identical, still unravaged, only paler, beneath.

They gasp in surprise. And then in the midst of a deep silence, Tereshko says: 'All right, that's a mask – so what?' but his voice trembles a little.

Her hands flutter up and down the cloak fastenings, seize it to throw it open. 'Look closer,' she says, 'and tell me if you know me!'

'No, Nova – don't!' O'Shaughnessy cries from the floor.

She says softly: 'Close your eyes, O'Shaughnessy, and keep them closed, if you love me. For no love could survive this – no love in all the world.'

Dumbly obedient, he holds his hands there in front of his eyes. A rustle of Nova's cloak, a swirl of air as it flies back. A choking sound from someone near him. A gun thudding to the floor. Then a wild, terrible scream – a sudden rush of feet, five pairs of them, around and past him and toward the door. A stampede of mortal terror.

'Get away from me! What – are you?'

Above it all, her voice, serene, sepulchral. 'Now – am I Benedetto's girl – am I anyone's girl any more?'

Across the wooden floor of the front of the house rushes the retreat of scuffling shoe-leather. A door bangs. The motor of their car comes to life – gears clash and scream. The car sound dies away – then suddenly comes a far-off crash carried thinly on the still night. One dim, final cry of pain and death – and dead silence drops at last like a curtain on a play. Within the room, for long minutes, there is no movement.

'They must have gone off the road,' O'Shaughnessy says tautly. His hands fall from before his eyes, and Nova's cloak is closed again. How close to death she must be, he thinks, to drive the living to their own deaths in wild flight just from the look of her.

A gun, dropped there on the laboratory floor, is all that's left of them. O'Shaughnessy toes it aside and it skitters across the room. Painfully, inch by inch, he hauls himself over beside Denholt, lifts the scientist's head and shoulders in his arms. Denholt's eyes, still alive, turn toward him.

O'Shaughnessy's voice rasps like a file. 'You've got to save her. Got to! Kill me if I've wronged you – but I've brought her back to you – you're the only one who can do anything. . . . Denholt, can you hear me?'

The dying man nods, points helplessly to the shattered retort, the evaporating stain on the floor.

'Was that it – ?' O'Shaughnessy shakes him wildly in his fright. 'There must be more. That can't be all! Can't you tell me how to make more?'

A sigh filters through the parted lips. 'No time.'

'Haven't you got it written down?'

A feeble shake of the head. 'Afraid to – Jealous someone else would steal it from me – '

O'Shaughnessy's bony hands claw at Denholt's shoulders. 'But you can't mean – that she's got to die. That there isn't anything you with your knowledge or I with my love can do for her – anything at all – ?' Something, like a cold hand, closes his throat. Something else, like little needles, pricks his eyes until the lashes are moistened. Nova, standing there motionless, slowly droops her head.

A thin tensile hand grips O'Shaughnessy's arm to arrest his attention. A hand that must have been very strong once. 'Wait. Lean down closer, so you can hear me – I was filling a hypo – for one of the rabbits – when they broke in. I don't remember what became – Look around, see if you can find it – Enough for one injection, if it's intact – hurry, it's getting dark, I'm going fast.'

But before he does look for it, before he makes a move, he remembers to touch that mascot in his pocket, the rabbit's foot. 'Help me,' he says to her then, 'you know what it looks like, you used to see enough of them – '

She raises her head, steps aside – and there it is behind her, lying on the operating table. A previous liquid glinting within its transparent barrel.

Then he's down again beside the dying man, holding it before his dimming eyes.

'Yes, that's it. All there is left now. It'll be lost forever in a few more minutes when I go. I'm taking it with me – after what I've seen tonight of human nature, too much power for evil in it – it's better, for our own sakes, the way Nature ordered it – '

'Shall I lift you up, do you think you can stand long enough to –'

'No time.' He motions to Nova, weakly. She draws near. 'Recline on the floor here, where I can reach you – ' Then to O'Shaughnessy, 'Sweep the hair from the base of her head. Hold my arm at the elbow, steady it – '

The needle falls, emptied.

O'Shaughnessy murmurs, staring dully at the floor: 'A month more – this'll give her. Maybe I'm a fool to have done it. What torture that month is going to be – knowing now our only chance is gone. Well, maybe that French doctor was right. . . .'

Again that hand on his arm. 'Listen – She will be ill, very ill, for twenty-four hours. The reaction. Keep ice packed around her until the temperature goes down. Then – after that – the injection will arrest it for a while. It can't mend what's already happened – but it will give you that one month. Maybe a little – longer. I am sorry that I can't give you more – or any real hope at all.'

Then whatever was human and compassionate in Denholt dies out, and the scientist replaces the man. 'I want you to know why I failed. I must tell someone. I brought everything in her to life – but the blood. That was dead, stayed dead. As it circulated in her veins it carried death through her body. The injections I gave her held that flowing decay at bay – no more.

'I didn't realize that – I do now. The chemical composition of the blood changed in death – nothing I have done restored it. It would always defeat the serum – eventually. She was not really alive in her own right; she was being kept alive by a sort of artificial combustion introduced into her system at periodic intervals.'

O'Shaughnessy's eyes glare dully. 'You had no right,' he says. 'You had no right to do it. It wasn't fair to her or to me – or' – and he smiles ruefully – 'even to those fear-crazy gunmen who are smeared all over your mountainside right now. You tried to bring life, Denholt – and you've got nothing but death on your hands.'

The pale, almost lifeless lips flicker in a ghastly smile. 'My death, too,' he whispers. He struggles to rise in O'Shaughnessy's arms. And there is a pitiful attempt at self-justification. 'If you hadn't come along, O'Shaughnessy – who can say? None of this – would have been. And yet, you represented the human element – the thing I didn't reckon on. Yes. It was the blood that defeated me – the passionate warm blood of men and women, hungry and greedy and alive – the blood I couldn't put into Jane Brown's body. . . .'

O'Shaughnessy's shoulder still throbs with pain and there is blood trickling down the arm inside the sleeve, coming out below the cuff, oozing over his wrist and his hands. O'Shaughnessy stares at it dully and remembers Denholt's last words; and then suddenly strength comes to him to do the thing he must do. There is a car outside and down below a plane waiting. And there is Nova, her pale face flushed and hectic with the fever, her eyes flickering closed, her breathing labored. And here – here, you crazy gods of Fate, is O'Shaughnessy, the man who hasn't been afraid, not for himself anyway, since he was eighteen. Yes, all the pieces of the mosaic are here to hand, and the pattern has just fallen into place in O'Shaughnessy's mind.

He is a little light-headed, and giddy, but there is a hard core of will in his brain. He can stand now, where before he could only crawl like a snake with its spine crushed. He scoops Nova up in his arms, totters for one step with her, before his walk is firm and steady.

Nova's head stirs against his shoulder. Her eyes are open. 'What are we to do now?' she murmurs, with the fever heat thickening her tones.

'What does it matter?' O'Shaughnessy says. He doesn't want to tell her, doesn't want her to know. 'I'm with you, Jane.'

He says that to show her that he can call her by her right name without feeling, that he doesn't hold Jane Brown against her. But she won't let him. That name isn't hers.

'My name,' she says, childlike, 'is Nova. Nova – O'Shaughnessy.'

She doesn't speak again all the time he is putting her into the car, where she slumps against the cushions like a rag doll, no more than half conscious, or while they are driving down the mountain-side, or even while he carries her to the plane that is still standing there.

He goes, a little more unsteadily now, to kneel beside the wounded pilot.

'How you feeling?' O'Shaughnessy's words are jerky.

The pilot nods. 'I'm okay, I guess. Feels like just a nick.'

'That's all right, then,' O'Shaughnessy says. He pushes a wad of bills into Frazier's hands, helps the man to sit up. 'I'm going to take your plane. I'm glad you're feeling okay, because I'd have to take the plane anyway – only it's nice that I don't have to leave you here dying. You can use the car there.'

Wrinkles of worry blossom at the corners of the relief pilot's eyes. 'You sound kinda crazy to me – what happened up there? What's this money for?'

'That's to square you for the plane – in case. . . . Well, just in case.'

Then he is gone, weaving across the uneven ground. Frazier gets up and wobbles after him. 'Hi, wait a minute. The propeller –'

In a few minutes, his hands are on the blades and from inside the plane-cabin O'Shaughnessy's voice is calling, 'Contact,' and

Frazier yanks, the propeller spins. Frazier falls back and the plane taxis jerkily with a sputtering roar of the engine.

O'Shaughnessy somehow negotiates a take-off from an impossibly tip-tilted angle, and Frazier stands there watching, jaw dropped, until the black of the sky and the distance have inked out the tiny plane lights.

'Screwball,' he mutters and paws the sweat from his face.

O'Shaughnessy's hard-knuckled hands grasp the stick hard. Thunder rumbles above the roar of the motor; lightning stabs the darkness. Rain begins to slash down around the plane.

O'Shaughnessy remembers another storm, another plane, another night; and he glances at the girl beside him. She seems to sense his gaze upon her, her eyes open; her lips would speak but the fever that is burning through her won't let the words come. They are in her eyes, though, as plain as any words could be, and her whole heart is with them. No question there at all, just courage and confidence.

'I brought you into this,' he says – to those eyes. 'Now I'm taking you out of it. There's no place in it for us any longer.'

Her fingers inside the glove tighten on his hand convulsively as if to say: 'Alone, O'Shaughnessy? Must I go alone?'

At least that's the way he figures it, for he says quickly: 'With me, honey. Together.'

The pressure of the fingers relaxes, then tightens, but more steadily this time, reassured and reassuring. That's her way of saying:

'All right, O'Shaughnessy. It's all right with me.'

Her face blurs in O'Shaughnessy's eyes; he begins to whistle a silly tune that even he can't hear, and somehow it is comforting. Lightning strikes again and a louder crash of thunder. A gust of wind rocks the plane. The black bulk of a granite ridge that looks like a giant comber whipped up by a typhoon and frozen by the hands of God shows up ahead and a little below.

O'Shaughnessy's hand blunders out to take Nova's gloved one in his own. She whimpers a little, and stirs. O'Shaughnessy slides the stick forward, the plane tilts sharply down; the mountainside, rocky and desolate, seems to be reaching up for them, but in these seconds they are alone, the two of them, with the sky and the storm.

It takes will power and nerve to hold the stick that way, to keeps his eyes open and watch the rocky face of the cliff, pine-bearded, rush up at them. O'Shaughnessy's mouth flattens, his face goes white. And then in that final fraction of a moment, he laughs, a little crazily – a laugh of defiance, of mocking farewell, and somehow, of conquest.

'Here we go, baby!' he shouts, teeth bared. 'Now I'm going to find out what it really feels like to fly into the side of a mountain! . . .'

There is only the storm to hear the smash of the plane as it splinters itself against the rock – and the storm drowns the sound out with thunder, just as the lightning turns pale the flame that rises, like a hungry tongue, from the wreckage.

WHO GOES THERE?

John W. Campbell, Jr.

1

The place stank. A queer, mingled stench that only the ice-buried cabins of an antarctic camp know, compounded of reeking human sweat, and the heavy, fish-oil stench of melted seal blubber. An overtone of liniment combatted the musty smell of sweat-and-snow-drenched furs. The acrid odor of burnt cooking fat, and the animal, not-unpleasant smell of dogs, diluted by time, hung in the air.

Lingering odors of machine oil contrasted sharply with the taint of harness dressing and leather. Yet, somehow, through all that reek of human beings and their associates – dogs, machines, and cooking – came another taint. It was a queer, neck-ruffling thing, a faintest suggestion of an odor alien among the smells of industry and life. And it was a life-smell. But it came from the thing that lay bound with cord and tarpaulin on the table, dripping slowly, methodically onto the heavy planks, dank and gaunt under the unshielded glare of the electric light.

Blair, the little bald-pated biologist of the expedition, twitched nervously at the wrappings, exposing a clear, dark ice beneath and then pulling the tarpaulin back into place restlessly. His little birdlike motions of suppressed eagerness danced his shadow across the fringe of dingy gray underwear hanging from the low ceiling, the equatorial fringe of stiff, graying hair around his naked skull a comical halo about the shadow's head.

Commander Garry brushed aside the lax legs of a suit of underwear, and stepped toward the table. Slowly his eyes traced around the rings of men sardined into the Administration Building. His tall, stiff body straightened finally, and he nodded. 'Thirty-seven. All here.' His voice was low, yet carried the clear authority of the commander by nature, as well as by title.

'You know the outline of the story back of that find of the Secondary Pole Expedition. I have been conferring with Second-in-Command McReady, and Norris, as well as Blair and Dr. Copper. There is a difference of opinion, and because it involves the entire group, it is only just that the entire Expedition personnel act on it.

'I am going to ask McReady to give you the details of the story, because each of you has been too busy with his own work to follow closely the endeavors of the others. McReady?'

Moving from the smoke-blued background, McReady was a figure from some forgotten myth, a looming, bronze statue that held life, and walked. Six feet four inches he stood as he halted beside the table, and with a characteristic glance upward to assure himself of room under the low ceiling beams, straightened. His rough, clashingly orange windproof jacket he still had on, yet on his huge frame it did not seem misplaced. Even here, four feet beneath the drift-wind that droned across the antarctic waste above the ceiling, the cold of the frozen continent leaked in, and gave meaning to the harshness of the man. And he was bronze – his great red-bronze beard, the heavy hair that matched it. The gnarled, corded hands gripping, relaxing, gripping and relaxing on the table planks were bronze. Even the deep-sunken eyes beneath heavy brows were bronzed.

Age-resisting endurance of the metal spoke in the cragged heavy outlines of his face, and the mellow tones of the heavy voice. 'Norris and Blair agree on one thing; that animal we found was not – terrestrial in origin. Norris fears there may be danger in that; Blair says there is none.

'But I'll go back to how, and why we found it. To all that was known before we came here, it appeared that this point was exactly over the South Magnetic Pole of Earth. The compass does point straight down here, as you all know. The more delicate instruments of the physicists, instruments especially designed for this expedition and its study of the magnetic pole, detected a secondary effect, a secondary, less powerful magnetic influence about eighty miles southwest of here.

'The Secondary Magnetic Expedition went out to investigate it. There is no need for details. We found it, but it was not the huge meteorite or magnetic mountain Norris had expected to find. Iron ore is magnetic, of course; iron more so – and certain special steels even more magnetic. From the surface indications, the secondary pole we found was small, so small that the magnetic effect it had was preposterous. No magnetic material conceivable could have that effect. Soundings through the ice indicated it was within one hundred feet of the glacier surface.

'I think you should know the structure of the place. There is a broad plateau, a level sweep that runs more than 150 miles due south from the Secondary Station, Van Wall says. He didn't have time or fuel to fly farther, but it was running smoothly due south then. Right there, where that buried thing was, there is an ice-drowned mountain ridge, a granite wall of unshakable strength that has damned back the ice creeping from the south.

'And four hundred miles due south is the South Polar Plateau. You have asked me at various times why it gets warmer here when the wind rises, and most of you know. As a meteorologist I'd have staked my word that no wind could blow at -70 degrees; that no more than a five-mile wind could blow at -50; without causing warming due to friction with ground, snow and ice and the air itself.

'We camped there on the lip of that ice-drowned mountain range for twelve days. We dug our camp into the blue ice that formed the surface, and escaped most of it. But for twelve consecutive days the wind blew at forty-five miles an hour. It went as high as forty-eight, and fell to forty-one at times. The temperature was -63 degrees. It rose to -60 and fell to -68. It was meteorologically impossible, and it went on uninterruptedly for twelve days and twelve nights.

'Somewhere to the south, the frozen air of the South Polar Plateau slides down from that 18,000-foot bowl, down a mountain pass, over a glacier, and starts north. There must be a funneling mountain chain that directs it, and sweeps it away for four hundred miles to hit that bald plateau where we found the secondary pole, and 350 miles farther north reaches the Antarctic Ocean.

'It's been frozen there since Antarctica froze twenty million years ago. There never has been a thaw there.

'Twenty million years ago Antarctica was beginning to freeze. We've investigated, though and built speculations. What we believe happened was about like this.

'Something came down out of space, a ship. We saw it there in the blue ice, a thing like a submarine without a conning tower or directive vanes, 280 feet long and 45 feet in diameter at its thickest.

'Eh, Van Wall? Space? Yes, but I'll explain that better later.' McReady's steady voice went on.

'It came down from space, driven and lifted by forces men haven't discovered yet, and somehow – perhaps something went wrong then – it tangled with Earth's magnetic field. It came south here, out of control probably, circling the magnetic pole. That's a savage country there; but when Antarctica was still freezing, it must have been a thousand times more savage. There must have been blizzard snow, as well as drift, new snow falling as the continent glaciated. The swirl there must have been particularly bad, the wind hurling a solid blanket of white over the lip of that now-buried mountain.

'The ship struck solid granite head-on, and cracked up. Not every one of the passengers in it was killed, but the ship must have been ruined, her driving mechanism locked. It tangled with Earth's field, Norris believes. No thing made by intelligent beings can tangle with the dead immensity of a planet's natural forces and survive.

'One of its passengers stepped out. The wind we saw there never fell below forty-one, and the temperature never rose above -60. Then – the wind must have been stronger. And there was drift falling in a solid sheet. The *thing* was lost completely in ten paces.' He paused for a moment, the deep, steady voice giving way to the drone of wind overhead and the uneasy, malicious gurgling in the pipe of the galley stove.

Drift – a drift-wind was sweeping by overhead. Right now the snow picked up by the mumbling wind fled in level, blinding lines across the face of the buried camp. If a man stepped out of the tunnels that connected each of the camp buildings beneath the surface, he'd be lost in ten paces. Out there, the slim, black finger of the radio mast lifted three hundred feet into the air, and at its peak was the clear night sky. A sky of thin, whining wind rushing steadily from beyond to another beyond under the licking, curling mantle of the aurora. And off north, the horizon flamed with queer, angry colors of the midnight twilight. That was Spring three hundred feet above Antarctica.

At the surface – it was white death. Death of a needle-fingered cold driven before the wind, sucking heat from any warm thing. Cold – and white mist of endless, everlasting drift, the fine, fine particles of licking snow that obscured all things.

Kinner, the little, scar-faced cook, winced. Five days ago he had stepped out to the surface to reach a cache of frozen beef. He had reached it, started back – and the drift-wind leapt out of the south. Cold, white death that streamed across the ground blinded him in twenty seconds. He stumbled on wildly in circles. It was half an hour before rope-guided men from below found him in the impenetrable murk.

It was easy for man – or *thing* – to get lost in ten paces.

'And the drift-wind then was probably more impenetrable than we know.' McReady's voice snapped Kinner's mind back. Back to the welcome, dank warmth of the Ad Building. 'The passenger of the ship wasn't prepared either, it appears. It froze within ten feet of the ship.

'We dug down to find the ship, and our tunnel happened to find the frozen – animal. Barclay's ice-ax struck its skull.

'When we saw what it was, Barclay went back to the tractor, started the fire up and when the steam pressure built, sent a call for Blair and Dr. Copper. Barclay himself was sick then. Stayed sick for three days, as a matter of fact.

'When Blair and Copper came, we cut out the animal in a block of ice, as you see, wrapped it and loaded it on the tractor for return here. We wanted to get into that ship.

'We reached the side and found the metal was something we didn't know. Our beryllium-bronze, non-magnetic tools wouldn't touch it. Barclay had some tool-steel on the tractor, and that wouldn't scratch it either. We made reasonable tests – even tried some acid from the batteries with no results.

'They must have had a passivating process to make magnesium metal resist acid that way, and the alloy must have been at least ninety-five percent magnesium. But we had no way of guessing that, so when we spotted the barely opened lock door, we cut around it. There was clear, hard ice inside the lock, where we couldn't reach it. Through the little crack we could look in and see that only metal and tools were in there, so we decided to loosen the ice with a bomb.

'We had decanite bombs and thermite. Thermite is the ice-softener; decanite might have shattered valuable things, where the thermite's heat would just loosen the ice. Dr. Copper, Norris and I placed a twenty-five-pound thermite bomb, wired it, and took the connector up the tunnel to the surface, where Blair had the steam tractor waiting. A hundred yards the other side of that granite wall we set off the thermite bomb.

'The magnesium metal of the ship caught of course. The glow of the bomb flared and died, then it began to flare again. We ran back to the tractor, and gradually the glare built up. From where we were we could see the whole ice-field illuminated from beneath with an unbearable light; the ship's shadow was a great, dark cone reaching off toward the north, where the twilight was just about gone. For a moment it lasted, and we counted three other shadow-things that might have been other – passengers –

frozen there. Then the ice was crashing down and against the ship.

'That's why I told you about that place. The wind sweeping down from the Pole was at our backs. Steam and hydrogen flame were torn away in white ice-fog; the flaming heat under the ice there was yanked away toward the Antarctic Ocean before it touched us. Otherwise we wouldn't have come back, even with the shelter of that granite ridge that stopped the light.

'Somehow in the blinding inferno we could see great hunched things – black bulks. They shed even the furious incandescence of the magnesium for a time. Those must have been the engines, we knew. Secrets going in blazing glory – secrets that might have given Man the planets. Mysterious things that could lift and hurl that ship – and had soaked in the force of the Earth's magnetic field. I saw Norris' mouth move, and ducked. I couldn't hear him.

'Insulation – something – gave way. All Earth's field they'd soaked up twenty million years before broke loose. The aurora in the sky above licked down, and the whole plateau there was bathed in cold fire that blanketed vision. The ice-ax in my hand got red hot, and hissed on the ice. Metal buttons on my clothes burned into me. And a flash of electric blue seared upward from beyond the granite wall.

'Then the walls of ice crashed down on it. For an instant it squealed the way dry ice does when it's pressed between metal.

'We were blind and groping in the dark for hours while our eyes recovered. We found every coil within a mile was fused rubbish, the dynamo and every radio set, the earphones and speakers. If we hadn't had the steam tractor, we wouldn't have gotten over the Secondary Camp.

'Van Wall flew in from Big Magnet at sun-up, as you know. We came home as soon as possible. That is the history of – that.' McReady's great bronze beard gestured toward the thing on the table.

2

Blair stirred uneasily, his little, bony fingers wriggling under the harsh light. Little brown freckles on his knuckles slid back and forth as the tendons under the skin twitched. He pulled aside a bit of the tarpaulin and looked impatiently at the dark ice-bound thing inside.

McReady's big body straightened somewhat. He'd ridden the rocking, jarring steam tractor forty miles that day, pushing onto Big Magnet here. Even his calm will had been passed by the anxiety to mix again with humans. It was lone and quiet out there in Secondary Camp, where a wolf-wind howled down from the Pole. Wolf-wind howling in his sleep – winds droning and the evil, unspeakable face of that monster leering up as he'd first seen it through clear, blue ice, with a bronze ice-ax buried in its skull.

The giant meteorologist spoke again. 'The problem is this. Blair wants to examine the thing. Thaw it out and make micro slides of its tissues and so forth. Norris doesn't believe that is safe, and Blair does. Dr. Copper agrees pretty much with Blair. Norris is a physicist, of course, not a biologist. But he makes a point I think we should all hear. Blair has described the microscopic life-forms biologists find living, even in this cold and inhospitable place. They freeze every winter, and thaw every summer – for three months – and live.

'The point Norris makes is – they thaw, and live again. There must have been microscopic life associated with this creature. There is with every living thing we know. And Norris is afraid that we may release a plague – some germ disease unknown to Earth – if we thaw those microscopic things that have been frozen there for twenty million years.

'Blair admits that such micro-life might retain the power of living. Such unorganized things as individual cells can retain life for unknown periods, when solidly frozen. The beast itself is as dead as those frozen mammoths they find in Siberia. Organized, highly developed life-forms can't stand that treatment.

'But micro-life could. Norris suggests that we may release some disease-form that man, never having met it before, will be utterly defenseless against.

'Blair's answer is that there may be such still-living germs, but that Norris has the case reversed. They are utterly nonimmune to man. Our life-chemistry probably – '

'Probably!' The little biologist's head lifted in a quick, birdlike motion. The halo of gray hair about his bald head ruffled as though angry. 'Heh, one look – '

'I know,' McReady acknowledge. 'The thing is not Earthly. It does not seem likely that it can have a life-chemistry sufficiently like ours to make cross-infection remotely possible. I would say that there is no danger.'

McReady looked toward Dr. Copper. The physician shook his head slowly. 'None whatever,' he asserted confidently. 'Man cannot infect or be infectd by germs that live in such comparatively close relatives as the snakes. And they are, I assure you,' his clean-shaven face grimaced uneasily, '*much* nearer to us than – *that*.'

Vance Norris moved angrily. He was comparatively short in this gathering of big men, some five feet eight, and his stocky, powerful build tended to make him feel shorter. His black hair was crisp and hard, like short, steel wires, and his eyes were the gray of fractured steel. If McReady was a man of bronze, Norris was all steel. His movements, his thoughts, his whole bearing had the quick, hard impulse of a steel spring. His nerves were steel – hard, quick acting – swift corroding.

He was decided on his point now, and he lashed out in its defense with a characteristic quick, clipped flow of words. 'Different chemistry be damned. That thing may be dead – or, by God, it may not – but I don't like it. Damn it, Blair, let them see the monstrosity you are petting over there. Let them see the foul thing and decide for themselves whether they want that thing thawed out in this camp.

'Thawed out, by the way. That's got to be thawed out in one of the shacks tonight, if it is thawed out. Somebody – who's watchman tonight? Magnetic – oh, Connant. Cosmic rays tonight. Well, you get to sit with that twenty-million-year-old mummy of his. Unwrap it, Blair. How the hell can they tell what they are buying, if they can't see it? It may have a different chemistry. I don't care what else it has, but I know it has something I don't want. If you can judge by the look on its face – it isn't human so maybe you can't – it was annoyed when it froze. Annoyed, in fact, is just about as close as an approximation of the way it felt, as crazy, mad, insane hatred. Neither one touches the subject.

'How the hell can these birds tell what they are voting on? They haven't seen those three red eyes and that blue hair like crawling worms. Crawling – damn, it's crawling there in the ice right now!

'Nothing Earth ever spawned had the unutterable sublimation of devastating wrath that thing let loose in its face when it looked around its frozen desolation twenty million years ago. Mad? It was mad clear through – searing, blistering mad!

'Hell, I've had bad dreams ever since I looked at those three red eyes. Nightmares. Dreaming the thing thawed out and came to life – that it wasn't dead, or even wholly unconscious all those twenty million years, but just slowed, waiting – waiting. You'll dream, too, while that damned thing that Earth wouldn't own is dripping, dripping in the Cosmos House tonight.

'And, Connant,' Norris whipped toward the cosmic ray specialist, 'won't you have fun sitting up all night in the quiet. Wind whining above – and that thing dripping – ' he stopped for a moment, and looked around.

'I know. That's not science. But this is, it's psychology. You'll have nightmares for a year to come. Every night since I looked at that thing I've had 'em. That's why I hate it – sure I do – and don't want it around. Put it back where it came from and let it freeze for another twenty million years. I had some swell nightmares – that it wasn't made like we are – which is obvious – but of a different kind of flesh that it can really control. That it can change its shape, and look like a man – and wait to kill and eat –

'That's not a logical argument. I know it isn't. The thing isn't Earth-logic anyway.

'Maybe it has an alien body-chemistry, and maybe its bugs do have a different body-chemistry. A germ might not stand that, but, Blair and Copper, how about a virus? That's just an enzyme molecule, you've said. That wouldn't need anything but a protein molecule of any body to work on.

'And how are you so sure of that, of the million varieties of microscopic life it may have, *none* of them are dangerous. How about diseases like hydrophobia – rabies – that attack any warm-blooded creature, whatever its body-chemistry may be? And parrot fever? Have you a body like a parrot, Blair? And plain rot – gangrene – necrosis if you want? *That* isn't choosy about body chemistry!'

Blair looked up from his puttering long enough to meet Norris' angry, gray eyes for an instant. 'So far the only thing you have said this thing gave off that was catching was dreams. I'll go so far as to admit that.' An impish, slightly malignant grin crossed the little man's seamed face. 'I had some, too. So. It's dream-infectious. No doubt an exceedingly dangerous malady.

'So far as your other things go, you have a badly mistaken idea about viruses. In the first place, nobody has shown that the enzyme-molecule theory, and that alone, explains them. And in the second place, when you catch tobacco mosaic or wheat rust, let me know. A wheat plant is a lot nearer your body-chemistry than this other-world creature is.

'And your rabies is limited, strictly limited. You can't get it from, nor give it to, a wheat plant or a fish – which is a collateral descendant of a common ancestor of yours. Which this, Norris, is not.' Blair nodded pleasantly toward the tarpaulined bulk on the table.

'Well, thaw the damned thing in a tub of formalin if you must. I've suggested that – '

'And I've said there would be no sense in it. You can't compromise. Why did you and Commander Garry come down here to study magnetism? Why weren't you content to stay at home? There's magnetic force enough in New York. I could no more study the life this thing once had from a formalin-pickled sample than you could get the information you wanted back in New York. And – if this one is so treated, *never in all time to come can there be a duplicate*! The race it came from must have passed away in the twenty million years it lay frozen, so that even if it came from Mars then, we'd never find its like. And – the ship is gone.

'There's only one way to do this – and that is the best possible way. It must be thawed slowly, carefully, and not in formalin.'

Commander Garry stood forward again, and Norris stepped back muttering angrily. 'I think Blair is right, gentlemen. What do you say?'

Connant grunted. 'It sounds right to us, I think – only perhaps he ought to stand watch over it while it's thawing.' He grinned ruefully, brushing a stray lock of ripe-cherry hair back from his forehead. 'Swell idea, in fact – if he sits up with his jolly little corpse.'

Garry smiled slightly. A general chuckle of agreement rippled over the group. 'I should think any ghost it may have had would have starved to death if it hung around here that long, Connant,' Garry suggested. 'And you look capable of taking care of it. "Ironman" Connant ought to be able to take out any opposing players, still.'

Connant shook himself uneasily. 'I'm not worrying about ghosts. Let's see that thing. I –'

Eagerly Blair was stripping back the ropes. A single throw of the tarpaulin revealed the thing. The ice had melted somewhat in the heat of the room, and it was clear and blue as thick, good glass. It shone wet and sleek under the harsh light of the unshielded globe above.

The room stiffened abruptly. It was face up there on the plain, greasy planks of the table. The broken haft of the bronze ice-ax was still buried in the queer skull. Three mad, hate-filled eyes blazed up with a living fire, bright as fresh-spilled blood, from a race ringed with a writhing, loathsome nest of worms, blue, mobile worms that crawled where hair should grow –

Van Wall, six feet and two hundred pounds of ice-nerved pilot, gave a queer, strangled gasp, and butted, stumbled his way out to the corridor. Half the company broke for the doors. The others stumbled away from the table.

McReady stood at one end of the table watching them, his great body planted solid on his powerful legs. Norris from the opposite end glowered at the thing with smouldering hate. Outside the door, Garry was talking with half a dozen of the men at once.

Blair had a tack hammer. The ice that cased the thing *schluffed* crisply under its steel claw as it peeled from the thing it had cased for twenty thousand thousand years –

3

'I know you don't like the thing, Connant, but it just has to be thawed out right. You say leave it as it is till we get back to civilization. All right, I'll admit your argument that we could do a better and more complete job there is sound. But – how are we going to get this across the Line? We have to take this through one temperature zone, the equatorial zone, and halfway through the other temperature zone before we get it to New York. You don't want to sit with it one night, but you suggest, then, that I hang its corpse in the freezer with the beef?' Blair looked up from his cautious chipping, his bald freckled skull nodding triumphantly.

Kinner, the stocky, scar-faced cook, saved Connant the trouble of answering. 'Hey, you listen, mister. You put that thing in the box with the meat, and by all the gods there ever were, I'll put you in to keep it company. You birds have brought everything movable in this camp in onto my mess tables here already, and I had to stand for that. But you go putting things like that in my meat box, or even my meat cache here, and you cook your own damn grub.'

'But, Kinner, this is the only table in Big Magnet that's big enough to work on,' Blair objected. 'Everybody's explained that.'

'Yeah, and everybody's brought everything in here. Clark brings his dogs every time there's a fight and sews them up on that table. Ralsen brings in his sledges. Hell, the only thing you haven't had on that table is the Boeing. And you'd 'a' had that in if you coulda figured a way to get it through the tunnels.'

Commander Garry chuckled and grinned at Van Wall, the huge Chief Pilot. Van Wall's great blond beard twitched suspiciously as he nodded gravely to Kinner. 'You're right, Kinner. The aviation department is the only one that treats you right.'

'It does get crowded, Kinner,' Garry acknowledged. 'But I'm afraid we all find it that way at times. Not much privacy in an antarctic camp.'

'Privacy? What the hell's that? You know, the thing that really made me weep, was when I saw Barclay marchin' through here chantin' "The last lumber in the camp! The last lumber in the camp!" and carryin' it out to build that house on his tractor. Damn it, I missed that moon cut in the door he carried out more'n I missed the sun when it set. That wasn't just the last lumber Barclay was walkin' off with. He was carryin' off the last bit of privacy in this blasted place.'

A grin rode even on Connant's heavy face as Kinner's perennial, good-natured grouch came up again. But it died away quickly as his dark, deepset eyes turned again to the red-eyed thing Blair was chipping from its cocoon of ice. A big hand ruffed his shoulder-length hair, and tugged at a twisted lock that fell behind his ear in a familiar gesture. 'I know that cosmic ray shack's going to be too crowded if I have to sit up with that thing,' he growled. 'Why can't you go on chipping the ice away from around it – you can do that without anybody butting in, I assure you – and then hang the thing up over the powder-plant boiler? That's warm enough. It'll thaw out a chicken, even a whole side of beef, in a few hours.'

'I know,' Blair protested, dropping the tack hammer to gesture more effectively with his bony, freckled fingers, his small body tense with eagerness, 'but this is too important to take any chances. There never was a find like this; there never can be again. It's the only chance men will ever have, and it has to be done exactly right.

'Look, you know how the fish we caught down near the Ross Sea would freeze almost as soon as we got them on deck, and come to life again if we thawed them gently? Low forms of life aren't killed by quick freezing and slow thawing. We have – '

'Hey, for the love of Heaven – you mean that damned thing will come to life!' Connant yelled. 'You get the damned thing – Let me at it! That's going to be in so many pieces – '

'No! *No*, you fool – ' Blair jumped in front of Connant to protect his precious find. 'No. Just *low* forms of life. For Pete's sake let me finish. You can't thaw higher forms of life and have them come to. Wait a moment now – hold it! A fish can come to after freezing because it's so low a form of life that the individual cells of its body can revive, and that alone is enough to reestablish life. Any higher forms thawed out that way are dead. Though the individual cells revive, they die because there must be organization and cooperative effort to live. That cooperation cannot be reestablished. There is a sort of potential life in any uninjured, quick-frozen animal. But it can't – can't under any circumstances – become active life in higher animals. The higher animals are too complex, too delicate. This is an intelligent creature as high in its evolution as we are in ours. Perhaps higher. It is as dead as a frozen man would be.'

'How do you know?' demanded Connant, hefting the ice-ax he had seized a moment before.

Commander Garry laid a restraining hand on his heavy shoulder. 'Wait a minute, Connant. I want to get this straight. I agree that there is going to be no thawing of this thing if there is the remotest chance of its revival. I quite agree it is much too unpleasant to have alive, but I had no idea there was the remotest possibility.'

Dr. Copper pulled his pipe from between his teeth and heaved his stocky, dark body from the bunk he had been sitting in. 'Blair's being technical. That's dead. As dead as the mammoths they find frozen in Siberia. We have all sorts of proof that things don't live after being frozen – not even fish, generally speaking – and no proof that higher animal life can under any circumstances. What's the point, Blair?'

The little biologist shook himself. The little ruff of hair standing out around his bald pate waved in righteous anger. 'The point is,' he said in an injured tone, 'that the individual cells might show the characteristics they had in life if it is properly thawed. A man's muscle cells live many hours after he has died. Just because they live, and a few things like hair and fingernail cells still live, you wouldn't accuse a corpse of being a zombie, or something.

'Now if I thaw this right, I may have a chance to determine what sort of world it's native to. We don't, and can't know by any other means, whether it came from Earth or Mars or Venus or from beyond the stars.

'And just because it looks unlike men, you don't have to accuse it of being evil, or vicious or something. Maybe that expression on its face is its equivalent to a resignation to fate.

White is the color of mourning to the Chinese. If men can have different customs, why can't a so-different race have different understandings of facial expressions?'

Connant laughed softly, mirthlessly. 'Peaceful resignation! If that is the best it could do in the way of resignation, I should exceedingly dislike seeing it when it was looking mad. That face was never designed to express peace. It just didn't have any philosophical thoughts like peace in its make-up.

'I know it's your pet – but be sane about it. That thing grew up on evil, adolesced slowly roasting alive the local equivalent of kittens, and amused itself through maturity on new and ingenious torture.'

'You haven't the slightest right to say that,' snapped Blair. 'How do you know the first thing about the meaning of a facial expression inherently inhuman? It may well have no human equivalent whatever. That is just a different development of Nature, another example of Nature's wonderful adaptability. Growing on another, perhaps harsher world, it has different form and features. But it is just as much a legitimate child of Nature as you are. You are displaying that childish human weakness of hating the different. On its own world it would probably class you as a fish-belly, white monstrosity with an insufficient number of eyes and a fungoid body pale and bloated with gas.

'Just because its nature is different, you haven't any right to say it's necessarily evil!'

Norris burst out a single, explosive, 'Haw!' He looked down at the thing. 'May be that things from other worlds don't *have* to be evil just because they're different. But that thing *was*! Child of Nature, eh? Well, it was a hell of an evil Nature.'

'Aw, will you mugs cut crabbing at each other and get the damned thing off my table?' Kinner growled. 'And put a canvas over it. It looks indecent.'

'Kinner's gone modest,' jeered Connant.

Kinner slanted his eyes up to the big physicist. The scarred cheek twisted to join the line of his tight lips in a twisted grin. 'All right, big boy, and what were you grousing about a minute ago? We can set the thing in a chair next to you tonight, if you want.'

'I'm not afraid of its face,' Connant snapped. 'I don't like keeping a wake over its corpse particularly, but I'm going to do it.'

Kinner's grin spread. 'Uh-huh.' He went off to the galley stove and shook down ashes vigorously, drowning the brittle chipping of the ice as Blair fell to work again.

4

'*Cluck,*' reported the cosmic-ray counter, '*cluck-burrrp-cluck.*'

Connant started and dropped his pencil.

'Damnation.' The physicist looked toward the far corner, back at the Geiger counter on the table near that corner. And crawled under the desk at which he had been working to retrieve the pencil. He sat down at his work again, trying to make his writing more even. It tended to have jerks and quavers in it, in time with the abrupt proud-hen noises of the Geiger counter. The muted whoosh of the pressure lamp he was using for illumination, the mingled gargles and bugle calls of a dozen men sleeping down the corridor in Paradise House formed the background sounds for the irregular, clucking noises of the counter, the occasional rustle of falling coal in the copper-bellied stove. And a soft, steady *drip-drip-drip* from the thing in the corner.

Connant jerked a pack of cigarettes from his pocket, snapped it so that a cigarette protruded, and jabbed the cylinder into his mouth. The lighter failed to function, and he pawed angrily through the pile of papers in search of a match. He scratched the wheel of the lighter several times, dropped it with a curse and got up to pluck a hot coal from the stove with the coal tongs.

The lighter functioned instantly when he tried it on returning to the desk. The counter ripped out a series of chuckling guffaws as a burst of cosmic rays struck through to it. Connant turned to glower at it, and tried to concentrate on the interpretation of data collected during the past week. The weekly summary –

He gave up and yielded to curiosity, or nervousness. He lifted the pressure lamp from the desk and carried it over to the table in the corner. Then he returned to the stove and picked up the coal tongs. The beast had been thawing for nearly eighteen hours now. He poked at it with an unconscious caution; the flesh was no longer hard as armor plate, but had assumed a rubbery texture. It looked like wet, blue rubber glistening under the droplets of water like little round jewels in the glare of the gasoline pressure lantern. Connant felt an unreasoning desire to pour the contents of the lamp's reservoir over the thing in its box and drop the cigarette into it. The three red eyes glared up at him sightlessly, the ruby eyeballs reflecting murky, smoky rays of light.

He realized vaguely that he had been looking at them for a very long time, even vaguely understood that they were no longer sightless. But it did not seem of importance, of no more importance than the labored, slow motion of the tentacular things that sprouted from the base of the scrawny, slowly pulsing neck.

Connant picked up the pressure lamp and returned to his chair. He sat down, staring at the pages of mathematics before him. The clucking of the counter was strangely less disturbing, the rustle of the coals in the stove no longer distracting.

The creak of the floorboards behind him didn't interrupt his thoughts as he went about his weekly report in an automatic manner, filling in columns of data and making brief, summarizing notes.

The creak of the floorboards sounded nearer.

5

Blair came up from the nightmare-haunted depths of sleep abruptly. Connant's face floated vaguely above him; for a moment it seemed a continuance of the wild horror of the dream. But Connant's face was angry, and a little frightened. 'Blair — Blair you damned log, wake up.'

'Uh — eh?' the little biologist rubbed his eyes, his bony, freckled finger crooked to a mutilated child-fist. From surrounding bunks other faces lifted to stare down at them.

Connant straightened up. 'Get up — and get a lift on. Your damned animal's escaped.'

'Escaped — what!' Chief Pilot Van Wall's bull voice roared out with a volume that shook the walls. Down the communication tunnels other voices yelled suddenly. The dozen inhabitants of Paradise House tumbled in abruptly, Barclay, stocky and bulbous in long woolen underwear, carrying a fire extinguisher.

'What the hell's the matter?' Barclay demanded.

'Your damned beast got loose. I fell asleep about twenty minutes ago, and when I woke up, the thing was gone. Hey, Doc, the hell you say those things can't come to life. Blair's blasted potential life developed a hell of a lot of potential and walked out on us.'

Copper stared blankly. 'It wasn't — Earthly,' he sighed suddenly. 'I — I guess Earthly laws don't apply.'

'Well, it applied for leave of absence and took it. We've got to find it and capture it somehow.' Connant swore bitterly, his deepset black eyes sullen and angry. 'It's a wonder the hellish creature didn't eat me in my sleep.'

Blair started back, his pale eyes suddenly fear-struck. 'Maybe it di – er – uh – we'll have to find it.'

'You find it. It's your pet. I've had all I want to do with it, sitting there for seven hours with the counter clucking every few seconds, and you birds in here singing night-music. It's a wonder I got to sleep. I'm going through to the Ad Building.'

Commander Garry ducked through the doorway, pulling his belt tight. 'You won't have to. Van's roar sounded like the Boeing taking off downwind. So it wasn't dead?'

'I didn't carry it off in my arms, I assure you,' Connant snapped. 'The last thing I saw, the split skull oozing green goo, like a squashed caterpillar. Doc just said our laws don't work – it's unearthly. Well, it's an unearthly monster, with an unearthly disposition, judging by the face, wandering around with a split skull and brains oozing out.' Norris and McReady appeared in the doorway, a doorway filling with other shivering men. 'Has anybody seen it coming over here?' Norris asked innocently. 'About four feet tall – three red eyes – brains oozing out – Hey, has anybody checked to make sure this isn't a cracked idea of humor? If it is, I think we'll unite in tying Blair's pet around Connant's neck like the Ancient Mariner's albatross.'

'It's no humor,' Connant shivered. 'Lord, I wish it were. I'd rather wear – ' He stopped. A wild, weird howl shrieked through the corridors. The men stiffened abruptly, and half turned.

'I think it's been located,' Connant finished. His dark eyes shifted with a queer unease. He darted back to his bunk in Paradise House, to return almost immediately with a heavy .45 revolver and an ice-ax. He hefted both gently as he started for the corridor toward Dogtown.

'It blundered down the wrong corridor – and landed among the huskies. Listen – the dogs have broken their chains – '

The half-terrorized howl of the dog pack had changed to a wild hunting melee. The voices of the dogs thundered in the narrow corridors, and through them came a low rippling snarl of distilled hate. A shrill of pain, a dozen snarling yelps.

Connant broke for the door. Close behind him, McReady, then Barclay and Commander Garry came. Other men broke for the Ad Building, and weapons – the sledge house. Pomroy, in charge of the Big Magnet's five cows, started down the corridor in the opposite direction – he had a six-foot-handled, long-tined pitchfork in mind.

Barclay slid to a halt, as McReady's giant bulk turned abruptly away from the tunnel leading to Dogtown, and vanished off at an angle. Uncertainly, the mechanician wavered a moment, the fire extinguisher in his hands, hesitating from one side to the other. Then he was racing after Connant's broad back. Whatever McReady had in mind, he could be trusted to make it work.

Connant stopped at the bend in the corridor. His breath hissed suddenly through his throat. 'Great God – ' The revolver exploded thunderously; three numbing, palpable waves of sound crashed through the confined corridors. Two more. The revolver dropped to the hard-packed snow of the trail, and Barclay saw the ice-ax shift into defensive position. Connant's powerful body blocked his vision, but beyond he heard something mewing and, insanely, chuckling. The dogs were quieter; there was a deadly seriousness in their low snarls. Taloned feet scratched at hard-packed snow, broken chains were clinking and tangling.

Connant shifted abruptly, and Barclay could see what lay beyond. For a second he stood frozen, then his breath went out in a gusty curse. The Thing launched itself at Connant, the powerful arms of the man swung the ice-ax flat-side first at what might have been a head. It crunched horribly, and the tattered flesh, ripped by a half-dozen savage huskies, leapt to its feet again. The red eyes blazed with an unearthly hatred, an unearthly, unkillable vitality.

Barclay turned the fire extinguisher on it; the blinding, blistering stream of chemical spray confused it, baffled it, together with the savage attacks of the huskies, not for long afraid of anything that did, or could live, and held it at bay.

McReady wedged men out of his way and drove down the narrow corridor packed with men unable to reach the scene. There was a sure foreplanned drive to McReady's attack. One of the giant blowtorches used in warming the plane's engines was in his bronze hands. It roared gustily as he turned the corner and opened the valve. The mad mewing hissed louder. The dogs scrambled back from the three-foot lance of blue-hot flame.

'Bar, get a power cable, run in it somehow. And a handle. We can electrocute this – monster, if I don't incinerate it.' McReady spoke with an authority of planned action. Barclay turned down the long corridor to the power plant, but already before him Norris and Van Wall were racing down.

Barclay found the cable in the electrical cache in the tunnel wall. In a half minute he was hacking at it, walking back. Van Wall's voice rang out in warning shout of 'Power!' as the emergency gasoline-powered dynamo thudded into action. Half a dozen other men were down there now; the coal, kindling were going into the firebox of the steam power plant. Norris, cursing in a low, deadly monotone, was working with quick, sure fingers on the other end of Barclay's cable, splicing a contactor into one of the power leads.

The dogs had fallen back when Barclay reached the corridor bend, fallen back before a furious monstrosity that glared from baleful red eyes, mewing in trapped hatred. The dogs were a semi-circle of red-dipped muzzles with a fringe of glistening white teeth, whining with a vicious eagerness that near matched the fury of the red eyes. McReady stood confidently alert at the corridor bend, the gustily muttering torch held loose and ready for action in his hands. He stepped aside without moving his eyes from the beast as Barclay came up. There was a slight, tight smile on his lean, bronzed face.

Norris' voice called down the corridor, and Barclay stepped forward. The cable was taped to the long handle of a snow shovel, the two conductors split and held eighteen inches apart by a scrap of lumber lashed at right angles across the far end of the handle. Bare copper conductors, charged with 220 volts, glinted in the light of pressure lamps. The Thing mewed and hated and dodged. McReady advanced to Barclay's side. The dogs beyond sensed the plan with the almost telepathic intelligence of trained huskies. Their whining grew shriller, softer, their mincing steps carried them nearer. Abruptly a huge night-black Alaskan leapt onto the trapped thing. It turned squalling saber-clawed feet slashing.

Barclay leapt forward and jabbed. A weird, shrill scream rose and choked out. The smell of burnt flesh in the corridor intensified; greasy smoke curled up. The echoing pound in the gas-electric dynamo down the corridor became a slogging thud.

The red eyes clouded over in a stiffening, jerking travesty of a face. Armlike, leglike members quivered and jerked. The dogs leapt forward, and Barclay yanked back his shovel-handled weapon. The thing on the snow did not move as gleaming teeth ripped it open.

6

Garry looked about the crowded room. Thirty-two men, some tensed nervously standing against the wall, some uneasily relaxed, some sitting, most perforce standing as intimate as sardines. Thirty-two, plus the five engaged in sewing up wounded dogs, made thirty-seven, the total personnel.

Garry started speaking. 'All right, I guess we're here. Some of you – three or four at most – saw what happened. All of you have seen that thing on the table, and can get a general idea. Anyone hasn't, I'll lift – ' His hand strayed to the tarpaulin bulking over the thing on the table. There was an acrid odor of singed flesh seeping out of it. The men stirred restlessly, hasty denials.

'It looks rather as though Charnauk isn't going to lead any more teams,' Garry went on. 'Blair wants to get at this thing, and make some more detailed examination. We want to know what happened, and make sure right now that this is permanently, totally dead. Right?'

Connant grinned. 'Anybody that doesn't can sit up with it tonight.'

'All right then, Blair, what can you say about it? What was it?' Garry turned to the little biologist.

'I wonder if we ever saw its natural form,' Blair looked at the covered mass. 'It may have been imitating the beings that built that ship – but I don't think it was. I think that it was its true form. Those of us who were up near the bend saw the thing in action; the thing on the table is the result. When it got loose, apparently, it started looking around Antarctica still frozen as it was ages ago when the creature first saw it – and froze. From my observations while it was thawing out, and the bits of tissue I cut and hardened then, I think it was native to a hotter planet than Earth. It couldn't, in its natural form, stand the temperature. There is no life-form on Earth that can live in Antarctica during the winter, but the best compromise is the dog. It found the dogs, and somehow got near enough to Charnauk to get him. The others smelled it – heard it – I don't know – anyway they went wild, and broke chains, and attacked it before it was finished. The thing we found was part Charnauk, queerly only half-dead, part Charnauk half-digested by the jellylike protoplasm of that creature, and part the remains of the thing we originally found, sort of melted down to the basic protoplasm.

'When the dogs attacked it, it turned into the best fighting thing it could think of. Some other-world beast apparently.'

'Turned,' snapped Garry. 'How?'

'Every living thing is made up of jelly – protoplasm and minute, submicroscopic things called nuclei, which control the bulk, the protoplasm. This thing was just a modification of that same world-wide plan of Nature; cells made up of protoplasm, controlled by infinitely tinier nuclei. You physicists might compare it – an individual cell of any living thing – with an atom; the bulk of the atom, the space-filling part, is made up of the electron orbits, but the character of the thing is determined by the atomic nucleus.

'This isn't wildly beyond what we already know. It's just a modification we haven't seen before. It's as natural, as logical, as any other manifestation of life. It obeys exactly the same laws. The cells are made of protoplasm, their character determined by the nucleus.

'Only, in this creature, the cell nuclei can control those cells *at will*. It digested Charnauk, and as it digested, studied every cell of his tissue, and shaped its own cells to imitate them exactly. Parts of it – parts that had time to finish changing – are dog-cells. But they don't have dog-cell nuclei.' Blair lifted a fraction of the tarpaulin. A torn dog's leg, with stiff gray fur protruded. 'That, for instance, isn't dog at all; it's imitation. Some parts I'm uncertain about; the nucleus was hiding itself, covering up with dog-cell imitation nucleus. In time, not even a microscope would have shown the difference.'

'Suppose,' asked Norris bitterly, 'it had had lots of time?'

'Then it would have been a dog. The other dogs would have accepted it. We would have accepted it. I don't think anything would have distinguished it, not microscope, nor X-ray, nor any other means. This is a member of a supremely intelligent race, a race that has learned the deepest secrets of biology, and turned them to its use.'

'What was it planning to do?' Barclay looked at the humped tarpaulin.

Blair grinned unpleasantly. The wavering halo of thin hair round his bald pate wavered in a stir of air. 'Take over the world, I imagine.'

'Take over the world! Just it, all by itself?' Connant gasped. 'Set itself up as a lone dictator?'

'No,' Blair shook his head. The scalpel he had been fumbling in his bony fingers dropped; he bent to pick it up, so that his face was hidden as he spoke. 'It would become the population of the world.'

'Become – populate the world? Does it reproduce asexually?'

Blair shook his head and gulped. 'It's – it doesn't have to. It weighed eighty-five pounds. Charnauk weighed about ninety. It would have become Charnauk, and had eighty-five pounds left, to become – oh, Jack for instance, or Chinook. It can imitate anything – that is, become anything. If it had reached the Antarctic Sea, it would have become a seal, maybe two seals. They might have attacked a killer whale, and become either killers, or a herd of seals. Or maybe it would have caught an albatross, or a skua gull, and flown to South America.'

Norris cursed softly. 'And every time it digested something, and imitated it – '

'It would have had its original bulk left, to start again,' Blair finished. 'Nothing would kill it. It has no natural enemies, because it becomes whatever it wants to. If a killer whale attacked it, it would become a killer whale. If it was an albatross, and an eagle attacked it, it would become an eagle. Lord, it might become a female eagle. Go back – build a nest and lay eggs!'

'Are you sure that thing from hell is dead?' Dr. Copper asked softly.

'Yes, thank Heaven,' the little biologist gasped. 'After they drove the dogs off, I stood there poking Bar's electrocution thing into it for five minutes. It's dead and – cooked.'

'Then we can only give thanks that this is Antarctica, where there is not one, single, solitary, living thing for it to imitate, except these animals in camp.'

'Us,' Blair giggled. 'It can imitate us. Dogs can't make four hundred miles to the sea; there's no food. There aren't any skua gulls to imitate at this season. There aren't any penguins this far inland. There's nothing that can reach the sea from this point – except us. We've got brains. We can do it. Don't you see – *it's got to imitate us – it's got to be one of us – that's the only way it can fly an airplane – fly a plane for two hours, and rule – be – all Earth's inhabitants*. A world for the taking – *if it imitates us*!

'It didn't know yet. It hadn't had a chance to learn. It was rushed – hurried – took the thing nearest its own size. Look – I'm Pandora! I opened the box! And the only hope that can come out is – that nothing can come out. You didn't see me. I did it. I fixed it. I smashed every magneto. Not a plane can fly. Nothing can fly.' Blair giggled and lay down on the floor crying.

Chief Pilot Van Wall made for the door. His feet were fading echoes in the corridors as Dr. Copper bent unhurriedly over the little man on the floor. From his office at the end of the room he brought something and injected a solution into Blair's arm. 'He might come out of it when he wakes up,' he sighed, rising. McReady helped him lift the biologist onto a nearby bunk. 'It all depends on whether we can convince him that thing is dead.'

Van Wall ducked into the shack, brushing his heavy blond beard absently. 'I didn't think a biologist would do a thing like that up thoroughly. He missed the spares in the second cache. It's all right. I smashed them.'

Commader Garry nodded. 'I was wondering about the radio.'

Dr. Copper snorted. 'You don't think it can leak out on a radio wave do you? You'd have five rescue attempts in the next three months if you stop the broadcasts. The thing to do is to talk loud and not make a sound. Now I wonder – '

McReady looked speculatively at the doctor. 'It might be like an infectious disease. Everything that drank any of its blood – '

Copper shook his head. 'Blair missed something. Imitate it may, but is has, to a certain extent, its own body chemistry, its own metabolism. If it didn't, it would become a dog – and be a dog and nothing more. It has to be an imitation dog. Therefore you can detect it by serum tests. And its chemistry, since it comes from another world, must be so wholly, radically different that a few cells, such as gained by drops of blood, would be treated as disease germs by the dog, or human body?'

'Blood – would one of those imitations bleed?' Norris demanded.

'Surely. Nothing mystic about blood. Muscle is about 90% water; blood differs only in having a couple percent more water, and less connective tissue. They'd bleed all right,' Copper assured him.

Blair sat up in his bunk suddenly. 'Connant – where's Connant?'

The physicist moved over toward the little biologist. 'Here I am. What do you want?'

'Are you?' giggled Blair. He lapsed back into the bunk contorted with silent laughter.

Connant looked at him blankly. 'Huh? Am I what?'

'*Are* you there?' Blair burst into gales of laughter. '*Are* you Connant? The beast wanted to be *man* – not a dog –'

7

Dr. Copper rose wearily from the bunk, and washed the hypodermic carefully. The little tinkles it made seemed loud in the packed room, now that Blair's gurgling laughter had finally quieted. Copper looked toward Garry and shook his head slowly. 'Hopeless, I'm afraid. I don't think we can ever convince him the thing is dead now.'

Norris laughed uncertainly. 'I'm not sure you can convince me. Oh, damn you, McReady.'

'McReady?' Commander Garry turned to look from Norris to McReady curiously.

'The nightmares,' Norris explained. 'He had a theory about the nightmares we had at the Secondary Station after finding that thing.'

'And that was?' Garry looked at McReady levelly.

Norris answered for him, jerkily, uneasily. 'That the creature wasn't dead, had a sort of enormously slowed existence, an existence that permitted it, nonetheless, to be vaguely aware of the passing of time, of our coming, after endless years. I had a dream it could imitate things.'

'Well,' Copper grunted, 'it can.'

'Don't be an ass,' Norris snapped. 'That's not what's bothering me. In the dream it could read minds, read thoughts and ideas and mannerisms.'

'What's so bad about that? It seems to be worrying you more than the thought of the joy we're going to have with a madman in an antarctic camp.' Copper nodded toward Blair's sleeping form.

McReady shook his great head slowly. 'You know that Connant is Connant, because he not merely looks like Connant – which we're beginning to believe the beast might be able to do – but he thinks like Connant, moves himself around as Connant does. That takes more than merely a body that looks like him; that takes Connant's own mind, and thoughts and mannerisms. Therefore, though you know that the thing might make itself *look* like Connant, you aren't much bothered, because you know it has a mind from another world, a totally unhuman mind, that couldn't possibly react and think and talk like a man we know, and do it so well as to fool us for a moment. The idea of the creature imitating one of us is fascinating, but unreal, because it is too completely unhuman to deceive us. It doesn't have a human mind.'

'As I said before,' Norris repeated, looking steadily at McReady, 'you can say the damnedest things at the damnedest times. Will you be so good as to finish that thought – one way or the other?'

Kinner, the scar-faced expedition cook, had been standing near Connant. Suddenly he moved down the length of the crowded room toward his familiar galley. He shook the ashes from the galley stove noisily.

'It would do it no good,' said Dr. Copper, softly as though thinking out loud, 'to merely look like something it was trying to imitate; it would have to understand its feelings, its reactions. It *is* unhuman; it has powers of imitation beyond any conception of man. A good actor, by training himself, can imitate another man, another man's mannerisms, well enough to fool most people. Of course no actor could imitate so perfectly as to deceive men who had been living with the imitated one in the complete lack of privacy of an antarctic camp. That would take a superhuman skill.'

'Oh, you've got the bug, too?' Norris cursed softly.

Connant standing alone at one end of the room, looked about him wildly, his face white. A gentle eddying of the men had crowded them slowly down toward the other end of the room, so that he stood quite alone. 'My God, will you two Jeremiahs shut up?' Connant's voice shook. 'What am I? Some kind of microscopic specimen you're dissecting? Some unpleasant worm you're discussing in the third person?'

McReady looked up at him; his slowly twisting hands stopped for a moment. 'Having a lovely time. Wish you were here. Signed: Everybody.

'Connant, if you think you're having a hell of a time, just move over on the other end for a while. You've got one thing we haven't, you know what the answer is. I'll tell you this, right now you're the most feared and respected man in Big Magnet.'

'Lord, I wish you could see your eyes,' Connant gasped. 'Stop staring, will you! What the hell are you going to do?'

'Have you any suggestions, Dr. Copper?' Commander Garry asked steadily. 'The present situation is impossible.'

'Oh, is it?' Connant snapped. 'Come over here and look at that crowd. By Heaven, they look exactly like that gang of huskies around the corridor bend. Benning, will you stop hefting that damned ice-ax?'

The coppery blade rang on the floor as the aviation mechanic nervously dropped it. He bent over and picked it up instantly, hefting it slowly, turning it in his hands, his brown eyes moving jerkily about the room.

Copper sat down on the bunk beside Blair. The wood creaked noisily in the room. Far down a corridor, a dog yelped in pain, and the dog drivers' tense voices floated softly back. 'Microscopic examination,' said the doctor thoughtfully, 'would be useless, as Blair pointed out. Considerable time has passed. However, serum tests would be definitive.'

'Serum tests? What do you mean exactly?' Commander Garry asked.

'If I had a rabbit that had been injected with human blood – a poison to rabbits, of course, as is the blood of any animal save that of another rabbit – and the injections continued in increasing doses for some time, the rabbit would be human-immune. If a small quantity were drawn off, allowed to separate in a test tube, and to the clear serum, a bit of human blood were added, there would be a visible reaction, proving the blood was human. If cow, or dog blood were added – or any protein material other than that one thing, human blood – no reaction would take place. That would prove definitely.'

'Can you suggest where I might catch a rabbit for you, Doc?' Norris asked. 'That is, nearer than Australia, we don't want to waste time going that far.'

'I know there aren't any rabbits in Antarctica,' Copper nodded, 'but that is simply the usual animal. Any animal except man will do. A dog for instance. But it will take several days, and due to the greater size of the animal, considerable blood. Two of us will have to contribute.'

'Would I do?' Garry asked.

'That will make two,' Copper nodded. 'I'll get to work on it right away.'

'What about Connant in the meantime,' Kinner demanded. 'I'm going out that door and head off for the Ross Sea before I cook for him.'

'He may be human – ' Copper started.

Connant burst out in a flood of curses. 'Human! *May* be human, you damned sawbones! What in hell do you think I am?'

'A monster,' Copper snapped sharply. 'Now shut up and listen.' Connant's face drained of color and he sat down heavily as the indictment was put in words. 'Until we know – you know as well as we do that we have reason to question the face, and only you know how that question is to be answered – we may reasonably be expected to lock you up. If you are – unhuman – you're a lot more dangerous than poor Blair there, and I'm going to see that he's locked up thoroughly. I expect that his next stage will be a violent desire to kill you, all the dogs, and probably all of us. When he wakes, he will be convinced we're all unhuman, and nothing on the planet will ever change his conviction. It would be kinder to let him die, but we can't do that, of course. He's going in one shack, and you can stay in Cosmos House with your cosmic apparatus. Which is about what you'd do anyway. I've got to fix up a couple of dogs.'

Connant nodded bitterly. 'I'm human. Hurry that test. Your eyes – Lord, I wish you could see your eyes staring – '

Commander Garry watched anxiously as Clark, the dog-handler, held the big brown Alaskan husky, while Copper began the injection treatment. The dog was not anxious to cooperate; the needle was painful, and already he'd experienced considerable needle work that morning. Five stitches held closed a slash that ran from his shoulder, across his ribs, halfway down his body. One long fang was broken off short; the missing part was to be found half buried in the shoulder bone of the monstrous thing on the table in the Ad Building.

'How long will that take?' Garry asked, pressing his arm gently. It was sore from the prick of the needle Dr. Copper had used to withdraw blood.

Copper shrugged. 'I don't know, to be frank. I know the general method. I've used it on rabbits. But I haven't experimented with dogs. They're big, clumsy animals to work with; naturally rabbits are preferable, and serve ordinarily. In civilized places you can buy a stock of human-immune rabbits from suppliers, and not many investigators take the trouble to prepare their own.'

'What do they want with them back there?' Clark asked.

'Criminology is one large field. A says he didn't murder B, but that the blood on his shirt came from killing a chicken. The State makes a test, then it's up to A to explain how it is the blood reacts on human-immune rabbits, but not on chicken-immunes.'

'What are we going to do with Blair in the meantime?' Garry asked wearily. 'It's all right to let him sleep where he is for a while, but when he wakes up – '

'Barclay and Benning are fitting some bolts on the door of Cosmos House,' Copper replied grimly. 'Connant's acting like a gentleman. I think perhaps the way the other men look at him makes him rather want privacy. Lord knows, heretofore we've all of us individually prayed for a little privacy.'

Clark laughed bitterly. 'Not any more, thank you. The more the merrier.'

'Blair,' Copper went on, 'will also have to have privacy – and locks. He's going to have a pretty definite plan in mind when he wakes up. Ever hear the old story of how to stop hoof-and-mouth disease in cattle?'

Clark and Garry shook their heads silently.

'If there isn't any hoof-and-mouth disease, there won't be any hoof-and-mouth disease,' Copper explained. 'You get rid of it by killing every animal that exhibits it, and every animal that's been near the diseased animal. Blair's a biologist, and knows that story. He's afraid of this thing we loosed. The answer is probably pretty clear in his mind now. Kill everybody and everything in this camp before a skua gull or a wandering albatross coming in with the spring chances out this way – catches the disease.'

Clark's lips curled in a twisted grin. 'Sounds logical to me. If things get too bad – maybe we'd better let Blair get loose. It would save us committing suicide. We might also make something of a vow that if things get bad, we see that that does happen.'

Copper laughed softly. 'The last man alive in Big Magnet – wouldn't be a man,' he pointed out. 'Somebody's got to kill those – creatures that don't desire to kill themselves, you know. We don't have enough thermite to do it all at once, and the decanite explosive wouldn't help much. I have an idea that even small pieces of one of those things would be self-sufficient.'

'If,' said Garry thoughtfully, 'they can modify their protoplasm at will, won't they simply modify themselves to birds and fly away? They can read all about birds, and imitate their structure without even meeting them. Or imitate, perhaps, birds of their home planet.'

Copper shook his head, and helped Clark to free the dog. 'Man studied birds for centuries, trying to learn how to make a machine to fly like them. He never did do the trick; his final success came when he broke away entirely and tried new methods. Knowing the general idea, and knowing the detailed structure of wing and bone and nerve-tissue is something far, far different. And as for other-world birds, perhaps, in fact very probably, the atmospheric conditions here are so vastly different that their birds couldn't fly. Perhaps, even, the being came from a planet like Mars with such a thin atmosphere that there were no birds.'

Barclay came into the building, trailing a length of airplane control cable. 'It's finished, Doc. Cosmos House can't be opened from the inside. Now where do we put Blair?'

Copper looked toward Garry. 'There wasn't any biology building. I don't know where we can isolate him.'

'How about East Cache?' Garry said after a moment's thought. 'Will Blair be able to look after himself – or need attention?'

'He'll be capable enough. We'll be the ones to watch out,' Copper assured him grimly. 'Take a stove, a couple of bags of coal, necessary supplies and a few tools to fix it up. Nobody's been out there since last fall, have they?'

Garry shook his head. 'If he gets noisy – I thought that might be a good idea.'

Barclay hefted the tools he was carrying and looked up at Garry. 'If the muttering he's doing now is any sign, he's going to sing away the night hours. And we won't like his song.'

'What's he saying?' Copper asked.

Barclay shook his head. 'I didn't care to listen much. You can if you want to. But I gathered that the blasted idiot had all the dreams McReady had, and a few more. He slept beside the thing when we stopped on the trail coming in from Secondary Magnetic, remember. He dreamt the thing was alive, and dreamt more details. And – damn his soul – knew it wasn't all dream, or had reason to. He knew it had telepathic powers that were stirring vaguely, and that it could not only read minds, but project thoughts. They weren't dreams, you see. They were stray thoughts that thing was broadcasting, the way Blair's broadcasting his thoughts now – a sort of telepathic muttering in his sleep. That's why he knew so much about its powers. I guess you and I, Doc, weren't so sensitive – if you want to believe in telepathy.'

'I have to,' Copper sighed. 'Dr. Rhine of Duke University has shown that it exists, shown that some are much more sensitive than others.'

'Well, if you want to learn a lot of details, go listen in on Blair's broadcast. He's driven most of the boys out of the Ad Building; Kinner's rattling pans like coal going down a chute. When he can't rattle a pan, he shakes ashes.

'By the way, Commander, what are we going to do this spring, now the planes are out of it?'

Garry sighed. 'I'm afraid our expedition is going to be a loss. We cannot divide our strength now.'

'It won't be a loss – if we continue to live, and come out of this,' Copper promised him. 'The find we've made, if we can get it under control, is important enough. The cosmic ray data, magnetic work, and atmospheric work won't be greatly hindered.'

Garry laughed mirthlessly. 'I was just thinking of the radio broadcasts. Telling half the world about the wonderful results of our exploration flights, trying to fool men like Byrd and Ellsworth back home there that we're doing something.'

Copper nodded gravely. 'They'll know something's wrong. But men like that have judgment enough to know we wouldn't do tricks without some sort of reason, and will wait for our return to judge us. I think it comes to this: men who know enough to recognize our deception will wait for our return. Men who haven't discretion and faith enough to wait will not have the experience to detect any fraud. We know enough of the conditions here to put through a good bluff.'

'Just so they don't send "rescue" expeditions,' Garry prayed. 'When – if – we're ever ready to come out, we'll have to send word to Captain Forsyth to bring a stock of magnetos with him when he comes down. But – never mind that.'

'You mean if we don't come out?' asked Barclay. 'I was wondering if a nice running account of an eruption or an earthquake via radio – with a swell windup by using a stick of decanite under the microphone – would help. Nothing, of course, will entirely keep people out. One of those swell, melodramatic "last-man-alive-scenes' might make 'em go easy though.'

Garry smiled with genuine humor. 'Is everybody in camp trying to figure that out, too?'

Copper laughed. 'What do you think, Garry? We're confident we can win out. But not too easy about it, I guess.'

Clark grinned up from the dog he was petting into calmness. 'Confident, did you say, Doc?'

8

Blair moved restlessly around the small shack. His eyes jerked and quivered in vague, fleeting glances at the four men with him; Barclay, six feet tall and weighing over 190 pounds; McReady, a bronze giant of a man; Dr. Copper, short, squatly powerful; and Benning, five feet ten of wiry strength.

Blair was huddled up against the far wall of the East Cache cabin, his gear piled up in the middle of the floor beside the heating stove, forming an island between him and the four men. His bony hands clenched and fluttered, terrified. His pale eyes wavered uneasily as his bald, freckled head darted about in birdlike motion.

'I don't want anybody coming here. I'll cook my own food,' he snapped nervously. 'Kinner may be human now, but I don't believe it. I'm going to get out of here, but I'm not going to eat any food you send me. I want cans. Sealed cans.'

'OK, Blair, we'll bring 'em tonight,' Barclay promised. 'You've got coal, and the fire's started. I'll make a last – ' Barclay started forward.

Blair instantly scurried to the farthest corner. 'Get out! Keep away from me, you monster!' the little biologist shrieked, and tried to claw his way through the wall of the shack. 'Keep away from me – keep away – I won't be absorbed – I won't be – '

Barclay relaxed and moved back. Dr. Copper shook his head. 'Leave him alone, Bar. It's easier for him to fix the thing himself. We'll have to fix the door, I think – '

The four men let themselves out. Efficiently, Benning and Barclay fell to work. There were no locks in Antarctica; there wasn't enough privacy to make them needed. But powerful screws had been driven in each side of the door frame, and the spare aviation control cable, immensely strong, woven steel wire, was rapidly caught between them and drawn taut. Barclay went to work with a drill and a key-hole saw. Presently he had a trap cut in the door through which goods could be passed without unlashing the entrance. Three powerful hinges from a stock crate, two hasps and a pair of three-inch cotter pins made it proof against opening from the other side.

Blair moved about restlessly inside. He was dragging something over to the door with panting gasps, and muttering frantic curses. Barclay opened the hatch and glanced in, Dr. Copper peering over his shoulder. Blair had moved the heavy bunk against the door. It could not be opened without his cooperation now.

'Don't know but what the poor man's right at that,' McReady sighed. 'If he gets loose, it is his avowed intention to kill each and all of us as quickly as possible, which is something we don't agree with. But we've something on our side of that door that is worse than a homocidal maniac. If one or the other has to get loose, I think I'll come up and undo these lashings here.'

Barclay grinned. 'You let me know, and I'll show you how to get these off fast. Let's go back.'

The sun was painting the northern horizon in multicolored rainbows still, though it was two hours below the horizon. The field of drift swept off to the north, sparkling under its flaming colors in a million reflected glories. Low mounds of rounded white on the northern horizon showed the Magnet Range was barely awash above the sweeping drift. Little eddies of wind-lifted snow swirled away from their skies as they set out toward the main encampment two miles away. The spidery finger of the broadcast radiator lifted a gaunt black needle against the white of the Antarctic continent. The snow under their skis was like fine sand, hard and gritty.

'Spring,' said Benning bitterly, 'is come. Ain't we got fun! And I've been looking forward to getting away from this blasted hole in the ice.'

'I wouldn't try it now, if I were you.' Barclay grunted. 'Guys that set out from here in the next few days are going to be marvelously unpopular.'

'How is your dog getting along, Dr. Copper?' McReady asked. 'Any results yet?'

'In thirty hours? I wish there were. I gave him an injection of my blood today. But I imagine another five days will be needed. I don't know certainly enough to stop sooner.'

'I've been wondering – if Connant were – changed, would he have warned us so soon after the animal escaped? Wouldn't he have waited long enough for it to have a real chance to fix itself? Until we woke up naturally?' McReady asked slowly.

'The thing is selfish. You didn't think it looked as though it were possessed of a store of the higher justices, did you?' Dr. Copper pointed out. 'Every part of it is all of it, every part of it is all for itself, I imagine. If Connant were changed, to save his skin, he'd have to – but Connant's feelings aren't changed; they're imitated perfectly, or they're his own. Naturally, the imitation, imitating perfectly Connant's feelings, would do exactly what Connant would do.'

'Say, couldn't Norris or Vane give Connant some kind of a test? If the thing is brighter than men, it might know more physics than Connant should, and they'd catch it out,' Barclay suggested.

Copper shook his head wearily. 'Not if it reads minds. You can't plan a trap for it. Vane suggested that last night. He hoped it would answer some of the questions of physics he'd like to know answers to.'

'This expedition-of-four idea is going to make life happy.' Benning looked at his companions. 'Each of us with an eye on the other to make sure he doesn't do something – peculiar. Man, aren't we going to be a trusting bunch! Each man eyeing his neighbors with the grandest exhibition of faith and trust – I'm beginning to know what Connant meant by "I wish you could see your eyes." Every now and then we all have it, I guess. One of you looks around with a sort of "I-wonder-if-the-other-*three*-are-look." Incidentally, I'm not excepting myself.'

'So far as we know, the animal is dead, with a slight question as to Connant. No other is suspected,' McReady stated slowly. 'The "always-four" order is merely a precautionary measure.'

'I'm waiting for Garry to make it four-in-a-bunk,' Barclay sighed. 'I thought I didn't have any privacy before, but since that order –'

9

None watched more tensely than Connant. A little sterile glass
test tube, half filled with straw-colored fluid. One – two – three
–four – five drops of the clear solution Dr. Copper had prepared
from the drops of blood from Connant's arm. The tube was
shaken carefully, then set in a beaker of clear, warm water. The
thermometer read blood heat, a little thermostat clicked noisily,
and the electric hotplate began to glow as the lights flickered
slightly. Then – little white flecks of precipitation were forming,
snowing down in the clear straw-colored fluid. 'Lord,' said
Connant. He dropped heavily into a bunk, crying like a baby.
'Six days – ' Connant sobbed, 'six days in there – wondering if
that damned test would lie – '

Garry moved over silently, and slipped his arm across the
physicist's back.

'It couldn't lie,' Dr. Copper said. 'The dog was human-
immune – and the serum reacted.'

'He's – all right?' Norris gasped. 'Then – the animal is dead –
dead forever?'

'He is human,' Copper spoke definitely, 'and the animal is
dead.'

Kinner burst out laughing, laughing hysterically. McReady
turned toward him and slapped his face with a methodical
one-two, one-two action. The cook laughed, gulped, cried a
moment, and sat up rubbing his cheeks, mumbling his thanks
vaguely. 'I was scared. Lord, I was scared – '

Norris laughed brittely. 'You think we weren't, you ape? You
think maybe Connant wasn't?'

The Ad Building stirred with a sudden rejuvenation. Voices
laughed, the men clustering around Connant spoke with
unnecessarily loud voices, jittery, nervous voices relievedly friendly again. Somebody called out a suggestion, and a dozen
started for their skis. Blair, Blair might recover – Dr. Copper
fussed with his test tubes in nervous relief, trying solutions. The
party of relief for Blair's shack started out the door, skis clapping
noisily. Down the corridor, the dogs set up a quick yelping howl
as the air of excited relief reached them.

Dr. Copper fussed with his tubes. McReady noticed him first,
sitting on the edge of the bunk, with two precipitin-whitened test
tubes of straw-colored fluid, his face whiter than the stuff in the
tubes, silent tears slipping down from horror-widened eyes.

McReady felt a cold knife of fear pierce through his heart and freeze in his breast. Dr. Copper looked up. 'Garry,' he called hoarsely. 'Garry, for God's sake, come here.'

Commander Garry walked toward him sharply. Silence clapped down on the Ad Building. Connant looked up, rose stiffly from his seat.

'Garry – tissue from the monster – precipitates, too. It proves nothing. Nothing – but the dog was monster-immune too. That *one of the two contributing blood – one of us two,* you and I, Garry *– one of us is a monster.*'

10

'Bar, call back those men before they tell Blair,' McReady said quietly. Barclay went to the door; faintly his shouts came back to the tensely silent men in the room. Then he was back.

'They're coming,' he said. 'I didn't tell them why. Just that Dr. Copper said not to go.'

'McReady,' Garry sighed, 'you're in command now. May God help you. I cannot.'

The bronzed giant nodded slowly, his deep eyes on Commander Garry.

'I may be the one,' Garry added. 'I know I'm not, but I cannot prove it to you in any way. Dr. Copper's test has broken down. The fact that he showed it was useless, when it was to the advantage of the monster to have that uselessness not known, would seem to prove he was human.'

Copper rocked back and forth slowly on the bunk. 'I know I'm human. I can't prove it either. One of us two is a liar, for that test cannot lie, and it says one of us is. I gave proof that the test was wrong, which seems to prove I'm human, and now Garry has given that argument which proves me human – which he, as the monster, should not do. Round and round and round and round and – '

Dr. Copper's head, then his neck and shoulders began circling slowly in time to the words. Suddenly he was lying back on the bunk, roaring with laughter. 'It doesn't have to prove *one* of us is a monster! It doesn't have to prove that at all! Ho-ho. If we're *all* monsters it works the same – we're all monsters – all of us – Connant and Garry and I – and all of you.'

'McReady,' Van Wall, the blond-bearded Chief Pilot, called softly, 'you were on the way to an M.D. when you took up meteorology, weren't you? Can you make some kind of test?'

McReady went over to Copper slowly, took the hypodermic from his hand, and washed it carefully in ninety-five percent alcohol. Garry sat on the bunk edge with wooden face, watching Copper and McReady expressionlessly. 'What Copper said is possible,' McReady sighed. 'Van, will you help here? Thanks.' The filled needle jabbed into Copper's thigh. The man's laughter did not stop, but slowly faded into sobs, then sound sleep as the morphia took hold.

McReady turned again. The men who had started for Blair stood at the far end of the room, skis dripping snow, their faces as white as their skis. Connant had lighted a cigarette in each hand; one he was puffing absently, and staring at the floor. The heat of the one in his left hand attracted him and he stared at it and the one in the other hand stupidly for a moment. He dropped one and crushed it under his heel slowly.

'Dr. Copper,' McReady repeated, 'could be right. I know I'm human – but of course can't prove it. I'll repeat the test for my own information. Any of you others who wish to may do the same.'

Two minutes later, McReady held a test tube with white precipitin settling slowly from straw-colored serum. 'It reacts to human blood too, so they aren't both monsters.'

'I didn't think they were,' Van Wall sighed. 'That wouldn't suit the monster either; we could have destroyed them if we knew. Why hasn't the monster destroyed us, do you suppose? It seems to be loose.'

McReady snorted. Then laughed softly. 'Elementary, my dear Watson. The monster wants to have life-forms available. It cannot animate a dead body, apparently. It is just waiting – waiting until the best opportunities come. We who remain human, it is holding in reserve.'

Kinner shuddered violently. 'Hey. Hey, Mac. Mac, would I know if I was a monster? Would I know if the monster had already got me? Oh Lord, I may be a monster already.'

'You'd know,' McReady answered.

'But we wouldn't,' Norris laughed shortly, half hysterically.

McReady looked at the vial of serum remaining. 'There's one thing this damned stuff is good for, at that,' he said thoughtfully. 'Clark, will you and Van help me? The rest of the gang better stick together here. Keep an eye on each other,' he said bitterly. 'See that you don't get into mischief, shall we say?'

McReady started down the tunnel toward Dogtown, with Clark and Van Wall behind him. 'You need more serum?' Clark asked.

McReady shook his head. 'Tests. There's four cows and a bull, and nearly seventy dogs down there. This stuff reacts only to human blood and – monsters.'

11

McReady came back to the Ad Building and went silently to the wash stand. Clark and Van Wall joined him a moment later. Clark's lips had developed a tic, jerking into sudden, unexpected sneers.

'What did you do?' Connant exploded suddenly. 'More immunizing?'

Clark snickered, and stopped with a hiccough. 'Immunizing. Haw! Immune all right.'

'That monster,' said Van Wall steadily, 'is quite logical. Our immune dog was quite all right, and we drew a little more serum for the tests. But we won't make any more.'

'Can't – can't you use one man's blood on another dog – ' Norris began.

'There aren't,' said McReady softly, 'any more dogs. Nor cattle, I might add.'

'No more dogs?' Benning sat down slowly.

'They're very nasty when they start changing,' Van Wall said precisely. 'But slow. That electrocution iron you made up, Barclay, is very fast. There is only one dog left – our immune. The monster left that for us, so we could play with our little test. The rest – ' He shrugged and dried his hands.

'The cattle – 'gulped Kinner.

'Also. Reacted very nicely. They look funny as hell when they start melting. The beast hasn't any quick escape, when it's tied in dog chains, or halters, and it had to be to imitate.'

Kinner stood up slowly. His eyes darted around the room, and came to rest horribly quivering on a tin bucket in the galley. Slowly, step by step, he retreated toward the door, his mouth opening and closing silently, like a fish out of water.

'The milk – ' he gasped. 'I milked 'em an hour ago – ' His voice broke into a scream as he dived through the door. He was out on the ice cap without windproof or heavy clothing.

Van Wall looked after him for a moment thoughtfully. 'He's probably hopelessly mad,' he said at length, 'but he might be a monster escaping. He hasn't skis. Take a blow torch – in case.'

The physical motion of the chase helped them; something that needed doing. Three of the other men were quietly being sick.

Norris was lying flat on his back, his face greenish, looking steadily at the bottom of the bunk above him.

'Mac, how long have the – cows been not-cows – '

McReady shrugged his shoulders hopelessly. He went over to the milk bucket, and with his little tube of serum went to work on it. The milk clouded it, making certainty difficult. Finally he dropped the test tube in the stand, and shook his head. 'It tests negatively. Which means either they were cows then, or that, being perfect imitations, they gave perfectly good milk.'

Copper stirred restlessly in his sleep and gave a gurgling cross between a snore and a laugh. Silent eyes fastened on him. 'Would morphia – a monster – ' somebody started to ask.

'Lord knows,' McReady shrugged. 'It affects every Earthly animal I know of.'

Connant suddenly raised his head. 'Mac! The dogs must have swallowed pieces of the monster, and the pieces destroyed them! The dogs were where the monster resided. I was locked up. Doesn't that prove – '

Van Wall shook his head. 'Sorry. Proves nothing about what you are, only proves what you didn't do.'

'It doesn't do that,' McReady sighed. 'We are helpless because we don't know enough, and so jittery we don't think straight. Locked up! Ever watch a white corpuscle of blood go through the wall of a blood vessel? No? It sticks out a pseudopod. And there it is – on the far side of the wall.'

'Oh,' said Van Wall unhappily. 'The cattle tried to melt down, didn't they? They could have melted down – become just a threat of stuff and leaked under a door to re-collect on the other side. Ropes – no – no, that wouldn't do it. They couldn't live in a sealed tank or – '

'If,' said McReady, 'you shoot it through the heart, and it doesn't die, it's a monster. That's the best I can think of, offhand.'

'No dogs,' said Garry quietly, 'and no cattle. It has to imitate men now. And locking up doesn't do any good. Your test might work, Mac, but I'm afraid it would be hard on the men.'

12

Clark looked up from the galley stove as Van Wall, Barclay, McReady, and Benning came in, brushing the drift from their clothes. The other men jammed into the Ad Building continued studiously to do as they were doing, playing chess, poker, reading. Ralsen was fixing a sledge on the table; Vane and Norris had their heads together over magnetic data, while Harvey read tables in a low voice.

Dr. Copper snored softly on the bunk. Garry was working with Dutton over a sheaf of radio messages on the corner of Dutton's bunk and a small fraction of the radio table. Connant was using most of the table for cosmic ray sheets.

Quite plainly through the corridor, despite two closed doors, they could hear Kinner's voice. Clark banged a kettle onto the galley stove and beckoned McReady silently. The meteorologist went over to him.

'I don't mind the cooking so damn much,' Clark said nervously, 'but isn't there some way to stop that bird? We all agreed that it would be safe to move him into Cosmos House.'

'Kinner?' McReady nodded toward the door. 'I'm afraid not. I can dope him, I suppose, but we don't have an unlimited supply of morphia, and he's not in danger of losing his mind. Just hysterical.'

'Well, we're in danger of losing ours. You've been out for an hour and a half. That's been going on steadily ever since, and it was going for two hours before. There's a limit, you know.'

Garry wandered over slowly, apologetically. For an instant, McReady caught the feral spark of fear – horror – in Clark's eyes, and knew at the same instant it was in his own. Garry – Garry or Copper, was certainly a monster.

'If you could stop that, I think it would be a sound policy, Mac,' Garry spoke quietly. 'There are – tensions enough in this room. We agreed that it would be safer for Kinner in there, because everyone else in camp is under constant eyeing.' Garry shivered slightly. 'And try, try in God's name, to find some test that will work.' McReady sighed. 'Watched or unwatched, everyone's tense. Blair's jammed the trap so it won't open now. Says he's got food enough, and keeps screaming "Go away, go away – you're monsters. I won't be absorbed. I won't. I'll tell men when they come. Go away." So – we went away.'

'There's another test?' Garry pleaded.

McReady shrugged his shoulders. 'Copper was perfectly right. The serum test could be absolutely definitive if it hadn't been – contaminated. But that's the only one dog left, and he's fixed now.'

'Chemicals? Chemical tests?'

McReady shook his head. 'Our chemistry isn't that good. I

tried the microscope you know.'

Garry nodded. 'Monster-dog and real dog were identical. But – you've got to go on. What are we going to do after dinner?'

Van Wall had joined them quietly. 'Rotation sleeping. Half the crowd sleep; half stay awake. I wonder how many of us are monsters? All the dogs were. We thought we were safe, but somehow it got Copper – or you.' Van Wall's eyes flashed uneasily. 'It may have gotten every one of you – all of you but myself may be wondering, looking. No, that's not possible. You'd just spring then, I'd be helpless. We humans must somehow have the greater numbers now. But –' he stopped.

McReady laughed shortly. 'You're doing what Norris complained of in me. Leaving it hanging. "But if one more is changed – that may shift the balance of power." It doesn't fight. I don't think it ever fights. It must be a peaceable thing, in its own – inimitable – way. It never had to, because it always gained its end otherwise.'

Van Wall's mouth twisted in a sickly grin. 'You're suggesting then, that perhaps it already *has* the greater numbers, but is just waiting – waiting, all of them – all of you, for all I know – waiting till I, the last human, drop my wariness in sleep. Mac, did you notice their eyes, all looking at us.'

Garry sighed. 'You haven't been sitting here for four straight hours, while all their eyes silently weighed the information that one of us two, Copper or I, is a monster certainly – perhaps both of us.'

Clark repeated his request. 'Will you stop that bird's noise? He's driving me nuts. Make him tone down, anyway.'

'Still praying?' McReady asked.

'Still praying,' Clark groaned. 'He hasn't stopped for a second. I don't mind his praying if it relieves him, but he yells, he sings psalms and hymns and shouts prayers. He thinks God can't hear well way down here.'

'Maybe he can't,' Barclay grunted. 'Or he'd have done something about this thing loosed from hell.'

'Somebody's going to try that test you mentioned, if you don't stop him,' Clark stated grimly. 'I think a cleaver in the head would be as positive a test as a bullet in the heart.'

'Go ahead with the food. I'll see what I can do. There may be something in the cabinets.' McReady moved wearily toward the corner Copper had used as his dispensary. Three tall cabinets of rough boards, two locked, were the repositories of the camp's medical supplies. Twelve years ago, McReady had graduated, had started for an internship, and been diverted to meteorology. Copper was a picked man, a man who knew his profession thoroughly and modernly. More than half the drugs available were totally unfamiliar to McReady; many of the others he had forgotten. There was no huge medical library here, no series of journals available to learn the things he had forgotten, the elementary, simple things to Copper, things that did not merit inclusion in the small library he had been forced to content himself with. Books are heavy, and every ounce of supplies had been freighted in by air.

McReady picked a barbiturate hopefully. Barclay and Van Wall went with him. One man never went anywhere alone in Big Magnet.

Ralsen had his sledge put away, and the physicists had moved off the table, the poker game broken up when they got back. Clark was putting out the food. The click of spoons and the muffled sounds of eating were the only sign of life in the room. There were no words spoken as the three returned; simply all eyes focused on them questioningly while the jaws moved methodically.

McReady stiffened suddenly. Kinner was screeching out a hymn in a hoarse, cracked voice. He looked wearily at Van Wall with a twisted grin and shook his head. 'Uh-uh.'

Van Wall cursed bitterly, and sat down at the table. 'We'll just plumb have to take that till his voice wears out. He can't yell like that forever.'

'He's got a brass throat and a cast-iron larynx,' Norris declared savagely. 'Then we could be hopeful, and suggest he's one of our friends. In that case he could go on renewing his throat till doomsday.'

Silence clamped down. For twenty minutes they ate without a word. Then Connant jumped with an angry violence. 'You sit as still as a bunch of graven images. You don't say a word, but oh, Lord, what expressive eyes you've got. They roll around like a bunch of glass marbles spilling down a table. They wink and blink and stare – and whisper things. Can you guys look somewhere else for a change, please?'

'Listen, Mac, you're in charge here. Let's run movies for the rest of the night. We've been saving those reels to make 'em last. Last for what? Who is it's going to see those last reels, eh? Let's see 'em while we can, and look at something other than each other.'

'Sound idea, Connant. I, for one, am quite willing to change this in any way I can.'

'Turn the sound up loud, Dutton. Maybe you can drown out the hymns,' Clark suggested.

'But don't,' Norris said softly, 'don't turn off the lights altogether.'

'The lights will be out.' McReady shook his head. 'We'll show all the cartoon movies we have. You won't mind seeing the old cartoons will you?'

'Goody, goody – a moom-pitcher show. I'm just in the mood.' McReady turned to look at the speaker, a lean, lanky New Englander, by the name of Caldwell. Caldwell was stuffing his pipe slowly, a sour eye cocked up to McReady.

The bronze giant was forced to laugh. 'OK, Bart, you win. Maybe we aren't quite in the mood for Popeye and trick ducks, but it's something.'

'Let's play Classifications,' Caldwell suggested slowly. 'Or maybe you call it Guggenheim. You draw lines on a piece of paper, and put down classes of things – like animals, you know. One for "H" and one for "U" and so on. Like "Human" and "Unknown" for instance. I think that would be a hell of a lot better game. Classification, I sort of figure, is what we need right now a lot more than movies. Maybe somebody's got a pencil that he can draw lines with, draw lines between the "U" animals and the "H" animals for instance.'

'McReady's trying to find that kind of a pencil,' Van Wall answered quietly, 'but, we've got three kinds of animals here, you know. One that begins with "M". We don't want any more.'

'Mad ones, you mean. Uh-huh. Clark, I'll help you with those pots so we can get our little peep show going.' Caldwell got up slowly.

Dutton and Barclay and Benning, in charge of the projector and sound mechanism arrangements, went about their job silently, while the Ad Building was cleared and the dishes and pan disposed of. McReady drifted over toward Van Wall slowly, and leaned back in the bunk beside him. 'I've been wondering, Van,' he said with a wry grin, 'whether or not to report my ideas in advance. I forgot the "U" animal' as Caldwell named it, could read minds. I've a vague idea of something that might work. It's too vague to bother with, though. Go ahead with your show, while I try to figure out the logic of the thing. I'll take this bunk.'

Van Wall glanced up, and nodded. The movie screen would be practically on a line with this bunk, hence making the pictures least distracting here, because least intelligible. 'Perhaps you should tell us what you have in mind. As it is, only the unknowns know what you plan. You might be – unknown before you got it into operation.'

'Won't take long, if I get it figured out right. But I don't want any more all-but-the-test-dog-monsters things. We better move Copper into this bunk directly above me. He won't be watching the screen either.' McReady nodded toward Copper's gently snoring bulk. Garry helped them lift and move the doctor.

McReady leaned back against the bunk, and sank into a trance, almost, of concentration, trying to calculate chances, operations, methods. He was scarcely aware as the others distributed themselves silently, and the screen lit up. Vaguely Kinner's hectic, shouted prayers and his rasping hymn-singing annoyed him till the sound accompaniment started. The lights were turned out, but the large, light-colored area of the screen reflected enough light for ready visibility. It made men's eyes sparkle as they moved restlessly. Kinner was still praying, shouting, his voice a raucous accompaniment to the mechanical sound. Dutton stepped up the amplification.

So long had the voice been going on, that only vaguely at first was McReady aware that something seemed missing. Lying as he was, just across the narrow room from the corridor leading to Cosmos House, Kinner's voice had reached him fairly clearly, despite the sound accompaniment of the pictures. It struck him abruptly that it had stopped.

'Dutton, cut that sound,' McReady called as he sat up abruptly. The pictures flickered a moment, soundless and strangely futile in the sudden, deep silence. The rising wind on the surface above bubbled melancholy tears of sound down the stove pipes. 'Kinner's stopped,' McReady said softly.

'For God's sake start that sound then; he may have stopped to listen,' Norris snapped.

McReady rose and went down the corridor. Barclay and Van Wall left their places at the far end of the room to follow him. The flickers bulged and twisted on the back of Barclay's gray underwear as he crossed the still-functioning beam of the projector. Dutton snapped on the lights, and the pictures vanished.

Norris stood at the door as McReady had asked. Garry sat down quietly in the bunk nearest the door, forcing Clark to make room for him. Most of the others had stayed exactly where they were. Only Connant walked slowly up and down the room, in steady, unvarying rhythm.

'If you're going to do that, Connant,' Clark spat, 'we can get along without you altogether, whether you're human or not. Will you stop that damned rhythm?'

'Sorry.' The physicist sat down in a bunk, and watched his toes thoughtfully. It was almost five minutes, five ages, while the wind made the only sound, before McReady appeared at the door.

'Well,' he announced, 'haven't got enough grief here already. Somebody's tried to help us out. Kinner has a knife in his throat, which was why he stopping singing, probably. We've got monsters, madmen and murderers. Any more "M"s' you can think of, Caldwell? If there are, we'll probably have 'em before long.'

13

'Is Blair loose?' someone asked.

'Blair is not loose. Or he flew in. If there's any doubt about where our gentle helper came from – this may clear it up.' Van Wall held a foot-long, thin-bladed knife in a cloth. The wooden handle was half burnt, charred with the peculiar pattern of the top of the galley stove.

Clark stared at it. 'I did that this afternoon. I forgot the damn thing and left it on the stove.'

Van Wall nodded. 'I smelled it, if you remember. I knew the knife came from the galley.'

'I wonder,' said Benning, looking around at the party warily, 'how many more monsters have we? If somebody could slip out of his place, go back of the screen to the galley and then down to the Cosmos House and back – he did come back, didn't he? Yes – everybody's here. Well, if one of the gang could do all that – '

'Maybe a monster did it,' Garry suggested quietly.

'There's that possibility.'

'The monster, as you pointed out today, has only men left to imitate. Would he decrease his – supply, shall we say?' Van Wall pointed out. 'No, we just have a plain, ordinary louse, a murderer to deal with. Ordinarily we'd call him an "inhuman murderer" I suppose, but we have to distinguish now. We have inhuman murderers, and now we have human murderers. Or one at least.'

'There's one less human,' Norris said softly. 'Maybe the monsters have the balance of power now.'

'Never mind that,' McReady sighed and turned to Barclay. 'Bar, will you get your electric gadget? I'm going to make certain –'

Barclay turned down the corridor to get the pronged electrocuter, while McReady and Van Wall went back toward Cosmos House. Barclay followed them in some thirty seconds.

The corridor to Cosmos House twisted, as did nearly all corridors in Big Magnet, and Norris stood at the entrance again. But they heard, rather muffled, McReady's sudden shout. There was a savage flurry of blows, a dull *ch-thunk, shluff* sounds. 'Bar – Bar – ' And a curious, savage mewing scream, silenced before even quick-moving Norris had reached the bend.

Kinner – or what had been Kinner – lay on the floor, cut half in two by the great knife McReady had had. The meteorologist stood against the wall, the knife dripping red in his hand. Van Wall was stirring vaguely on the floor, moaning, his hand half-consciously rubbing at his jaw. Barclay, an unutterably savage gleam in his eyes, was methodically leaning on the pronged weapon in his hand, jabbing – jabbing, jabbing.

Kinner's arms had developed a queer, scaly fur, and the flesh had twisted. The fingers had shortened, the hand rounded, the fingernails become three-inch long things of dull red horn, keened to steel-hard, razor-sharp talons.

McReady raised his head, looked at the knife in his hand and dropped it. 'Well, whoever did it can speak up now. He was an inhuman murderer at that – in that he murdered an inhuman. I swear by all that's holy, Kinner was a lifeless corpse on the floor here when we arrived. But when It found we were going to jab It with the power – It changed.'

Norris stared unsteadily. 'Oh, Lord, those things can act. Ye gods – sitting in here for hours, mouthing prayers to a God it hated! Shouting hymns in a cracked voice – hymns about a Church it never knew. Driving us mad with its ceaseless howling –

'Well. Speak up, whoever did it. You didn't know it, but you did the camp a favor. And I want to know how in blazes you got out of the room without anyone seeing you. It might help in guarding ourselves.'

'His screaming – his singing. Even the sound projector couldn't drown it.' Clark shivered. 'It was a monster.'

'Oh,' said Van Wall in sudden comprehension. 'You *were* sitting right next to the door, weren't you? And almost behind the projection screen already.'

Clark nodded dumbly. 'He – it's quiet now. It's a dead – Mac, your test's no damn good. It was dead anyway, monster or man, it was dead.'

McReady chuckled softly. 'Boys, meet Clark, the only one we know is human! Meet Clark, the one who proves he's human by trying to commit murder – and failing. Will the rest of you please refrain from trying to prove you're human for a while? I think we may have another test.'

'A test!' Connant snapped joyfully, then his face sagged in disappointment. 'I suppose it's another either-way-you-want-it.'

'No,' said McReady steadily. 'Look sharp and be careful. Come into the Ad Building. Barclay, bring your electrocuter. And somebody – Dutton – stand with Barclay to make sure he does it. Watch every neighbor, for by the Hell these monsters came from, I've got something, and they know it. They're going to get dangerous!'

The groups tensed abruptly. An air of crushing menace entered into every man's body, sharply they looked at each other. More keenly than ever before – *is that man next to me an inhuman monster?*

'What is it?' Garry asked, as they stood again in the main room. 'How long will it take?'

'I don't know, exactly,' said McReady, his voice brittle with angry determination. 'But I *know* it will work, and no two ways about it. It depends on a basic quality of the *monsters*, not on us. "*Kinner*" just convinced me.' He stood heavy and solid in bronzed immobility, completely sure of himself again at last.

'This,' said Barclay, hefting the wooden-handled weapon tipped with its two sharp-pointed, charged conductors, 'is going to be rather necessary, I take it. Is the power plant assured?'

Dutton nodded sharply. 'The automatic stoker bin is full. The gas power plant is on standby. Van Wall and I set it for the movie operation – and we've checked it over rather carefully several times, you know. Anything those wires touch, dies,' he assured them grimly. 'I know that.'

Dr. Copper stirred vaguely in his bunk, rubbed his eyes with fumbling hand. He sat up slowly, blinked his eyes blurred with sleep and drugs, widened with an unutterable horror of drug-ridden nightmares. 'Garry,' he mumbled, 'Garry – listen. Selfish – from hell they came, and hellish shellfish – I mean self – Do I? What do I mean?' He sank back in his bunk, and snored softly.

McReady looked at him thoughtfully. 'We'll know presently,' he nodded slowly. 'But selfish is what you mean, all right. You may have thought of that, half-sleeping, dreaming there. I didn't stop to think what dreams you might be having. But that's all right. Selfish is the word. They must be, you see.' He turned to the men in the cabin, tense, silent men staring with wolfish eyes each at his neighbor. 'Selfish, and as Dr. Copper said – *every part is a whole*. Every piece is self-sufficient, an animal in itself.

'That, and one other thing, tell the story. There's nothing mysterious about blood; it's just as normal a body tissue as a piece of muscle, or a piece of liver. But it hasn't so much connective tissue, though it has millions, billions of life cells.'

McReady's great bronze beard ruffled in a grim smile. 'This is satisfying, in a way. I'm pretty sure we humans still outnumber you – others. Others standing here. And we have what you, your other-world race, evidently doesn't. Not an imitated, but a bred-in-the-bone instinct, a driving, unquenchable fire that's genuine. We'll fight, fight with a ferocity you may attempt to imitate, but you'll never equal! We're human. We're real. You're imitations, false to the core of your every cell.'

'All right. It's a showdown now. *You* know. You, with your mind reading. You've lifted the idea from my brain. You can't do a thing about it.

'Standing here –

'Let it pass. Blood is tissue. They have to bleed; if they don't bleed when cut, then by Heaven, they're phoney from hell! If they bleed – then that blood, separated from them, is an individual – *a newly formed individual in its own right, just as they – split, all of them, from one original – are individuals!*

'Get it, Van? See the answer, Bar?'

Van Wall laughed very softly. 'The blood – the blood will not obey. It's a new individual, with all the desire to protect its own life that the original – the main mass from which it was split – has. The *blood* will live – and try to crawl away from a hot needle, say!'

McReady picked up the scalpel from the table. From the cabinet, he took a rack of test tubes, a tiny alcohol lamp, and a length of platinum wire set in a little glass rod. A smile of grim satisfaction rode his lips. For a moment he glanced up at those around him. Barclay and Dutton moved toward him slowly, the wooden-handled electric instrument alert.

'Dutton,' said McReady, 'suppose you stand over by the splice there where you've connected that in. Just make sure no – thing pulls it loose.'

Dutton moved away. 'Now, Van, suppose you be first on this.'

White-face, Van Wall stepped forward. With a delicate precision, McReady cut a vein in the base of his thumb. Van Wall winced slightly, then held steady as a half inch of bright blood collected in the tube. McReady put the tube in the rack, gave Van Wall a bit of alum, and indicated the iodine bottle.

Van Wall stood motionlessly watching. McReady heated the platinum wire in the alcohol lamp flame, then dipped it into the tube. It hissed softly. Five times he repeated the test. 'Human, I'd say,' McReady sighed, and straightened. 'As yet, my theory hasn't been actually proven – but I have hopes. I have hopes.

'Don't, by the way, get too interested in this. We have with us some unwelcome ones, no doubt. Van, will you relieve Barclay at the switch? Thanks. OK, Barclay, and may I say I hope you stay with us? You're a damned good guy.'

Barclay grinned uncertainly; winced under the keen edge of the scalpel. Presently, smiling widely, he retrieved his long-handed weapon.

'Mr. Samuel Dutt – *Bar*!'

The tensity was released in that second. Whatever the hell the monsters may have had within them, the men in that instant matched it. Barclay had no chance to move his weapon, as a score of men poured down on the thing that had seemed Dutton. It mewed, and spat, and tried to grow fangs – and was a hundred broken, torn pieces. Without knives, or any weapon save the brute-given strength of a staff of picked men, the thing was crushed, rent.

Slowly they picked themselves up, their eyes smouldering, very quiet in their motions. A curious wrinkling of their lips betrayed a species of nervousness.

Barclay went over with the electric weapon. Things smouldered and stank. The caustic acid Van Wall dropped on each spilled drop of blood gave off tickling, cough-provoking fumes.

McReady grinned, his deepset eyes alight and dancing.'Maybe,' he said softly, 'I underrated man's abilities when I said nothing human could have the ferocity in the eyes of that thing we found. I wish we could have the opportunity to treat in a more befitting manner these things. Something with boiling oil, or melted lead in it, or maybe slow roasting in the power boiler. When I think what a man Dutton was –

'Never mind. My theory is confirmed by – by one who knew? Well, Van Wall and Barclay are proven. I think, then, that I'll try to show you what I already know. That I, too, am human.' McReady swished the scalpel in absolute alcohol, burned it off the metal blade, and cut the base of his thumb expertly.

Twenty seconds later he looked up from the desk at the waiting men. There were more grins out there now, friendly grins, yet withal, something else in the eyes.

'Connant,' McReady laughed softly, 'was right. The huskies watching that thing in the corridor bend had nothing on you. Wonder why we think only the wolf blood has the right to ferocity? Maybe on spontaneous viciousness a wolf takes tops, but after these seven days – abandon all hope, ye wolves who enter here!

'Maybe we can save time. Connant, would you step for – '

Again Barclay was too slow. There were more grins, less tensity still, when Barclay and Van Wall finished their work.

Garry spoke in a low, bitter voice. 'Connant was one of the finest men we had here – and five minutes ago I'd have sworn he was a man. Those damnable things are more than imitation.' Garry shuddered and sat back in his bunk.

And thirty seconds later, Garry's blood shrank from the hot platinum wire, and struggled to escape the tube, struggled as frantically as a suddenly feral, red-eyed, dissolving imitation of Garry struggled to dodge the snake-tongue weapon Barclay advanced at him, white-faced and sweating. The Thing in the test tube screamed with a tiny, tinny voice as McReady dropped it into the glowing coal of the galley stove.

14

'The last of it?' Dr. Copper looked down from his bunk with bloodshot, saddened eyes. 'Fourteen of them – '

McReady nodded shortly. 'In some ways – if only we could have permanently prevented their spreading – I'd like to have even the imitations back. Commander Garry – Connant – Dutton – Clark – '

'Where are they taking those things?' Copper nodded to the stretcher Barclay and Norris were carrying out.

'Outside. Outside on the ice, where they've got fifteen smashed crates, half a ton of coal, and presently will add ten gallons of kerosene. We've dumped acid on every spilled drop, every torn fragment. We're going to incinerate those.'

'Sounds like a good plan.' Copper nodded wearily. 'I wonder, you haven't said whether Blair – '

McReady started. 'We forgot him? We had so much else! I wonder – do you suppose we can cure him now?'

'If – ' began Dr. Copper, and stopped meaningly.

McReady started a second time. 'Even a madman. It imitated Kinner and his praying hysteria – ' McReady turned toward Van

Wall at the long table. 'Van, we've got to make an expedition to Blair's shack.'

Van looked up sharply, the frown of worry faded for an instant in surprised remembrance. Then he rose, nodded. 'Barclay better go along. He applied the lashings, and may figure how to get in without frightening Blair too much.'

Three quarters of an hour, through -37° cold, while the aurora curtain bellied overhead. The twilight was nearly twelve hours long, flaming in the north on snow like white, crystalline sand under their skis. A five-mile wind piled it in drift-lines pointing off to the northwest. Three quarters of an hour to reach the snow-buried shack. No smoke came from the little shack, and the men hastened.

'Blair!' Barclay roared into the wind and when he was still a hundred yards away. 'Blair!'

'Shut up,' said McReady softly. 'And hurry. He may be trying a lone hike. If we have to go after him – no planes, the tractors disabled – '

'Would a monster have the stamina a man has?'

'A broken leg wouldn't stop it for more than a minute,' McReady pointed out.

Barclay gasped suddenly and pointed aloft. Dim in the twilit sky, a winged thing circled in curves of indescribable grace and ease. Great white wings tipped gently, and the bird swept over them in silent curiosity. 'Albatross – 'Barclay said softly. 'First of the season, and wandering way inland for some reason. If a monster's loose – '

Norris bent down on the ice, and tore hurriedly at his heavy, windproof clothing. He straightened, his coat flapping open, a grim blue-metaled weapon in his hand. It roared a challenge to the white silence of Antarctica.

The thing in the air screamed hoarsely. Its great wings worked frantically as a dozen feathers floated down from its tail. Norris fired again. The bird was moving swiftly now, but in an almost straight line of retreat. It screamed again, more feathers dropped, and with beating wings it soared behind a ridge of pressure ice, to vanish.

Norris hurried after the others. 'It won't come back,' he panted.

Barclay cautioned him to silence, pointing. A curiously, fiercely blue light beat out from the cracks of the shack's door. A very low, soft humming sounded inside, a low, soft humming and a clink and click of tools, the very sounds somehow bearing a message of frantic haste.

McReady's face paled. 'Lord help us if that thing has – ' He grabbed Barclay's shoulder, and made snipping motions with his fingers, pointing toward the lacing of control cables that held the door.

Barclay drew the wire cutters from his pocket, and kneeled soundlessly at the door. The snap and twang of cut wires made an unbearable racket in the utter quiet of the Antarctic hush. There was only that savage, sweetly soft hum from within the shack, and the queerly, hectically clipped clicking and rattling of tools to drown their noises.

McReady peered through a crack in the door. His breath sucked in huskily and his great fingers clamped cruelly on Barclay's shoulder. The meteorologist backed down. 'It isn't,' he explained very softly, 'Blair. It's kneeling on something on the bunk – something that keeps lifting. Whatever it's working on is a thing like a knapsack – and it lifts.'

'All at once,' Barclay said grimly. 'No. Norris, hang back, and get that iron of yours out. It may have – weapons.'

Together, Barclay's powerful body and McReady's giant strength struck the door. Inside, the bunk jammed against the door screeched madly and crackled into kindling. The door flung down from broken hinges, the patched lumber of the doorpost dropping inward.

Like a blue rubber-ball, a Thing bounced up. One of its four tentacle-like arms looped out like a striking snake. In a seven-tentacled hand a six-inch pencil of winking, shining metal glinted and swung upward to face them. Its line-thin lips twitched back from snake-fangs in a grin of hate, red eyes blazing.

Norris' revolver thundered in the confined space. The hate-washed face twitched in agony, the looping tentacle snatched back. The silvery thing in its hand a smashed ruin of metal, the seven-tentacled hand became a mass of mangled flesh oozing greenish-yellow ichor. The revolver thundered three times more. Dark holes drilled each of the three eyes before Norris hurled the empty weapon against its face.

The Thing screamed in feral hate, a lashing tentacle wiping at blinded eyes. For a moment it crawled on the floor, savage tentacles lashing out, the body twitching. Then it staggered up again, blinded eyes working, boiling hideously, the crushed flesh sloughing away in sodden gobbets.

Barclay lurched to his feet and dove forward with an ice-ax. The flat of the weighty thing crushed against the side of the head.

Again the unkillable monster went down. The tentacles lashed out, and suddenly Barclay fell to his feet in the grip of a living, livid rope. The thing dissolved as he held it, a white-hot band that ate into the flesh of his hands like living fire. Frantically he tore the stuff from him, held his hands where they could not be reached. The blind Thing felt and ripped at the tough, heavy, windproof cloth, seeking flesh – flesh it could convert –

The huge blowtorch McReady had brought coughed solemnly. Abruptly it rumbled disapproval throatily. Then it laughed gurglingly, and thrust out a blue-white, three-foot tongue. The Thing on the floor shrieked, flailed out blindly with tentacles that writhed and withered in the bubbling wrath of the blowtorch. It crawled and turned on the floor, it shrieked and hobbled madly, but always McReady held the blowtorch on the face, the dead eyes burning and bubbling uselessly. Frantically the Thing crawled and howled.

A tentacle sprouted a savage talon – and crisped in the flame. Steadily McReady moved with a planned, grim campaign. Helpless, maddened, the Thing retreated from the grunting torch, the caressing, licking tongue. For a moment it rebelled, squalling in inhuman hatred at the touch of the icy snow. Then it fell back before the charring breath of the torch, the stench of its flesh bathing it. Hopelessly it retreated – on and on across the Antarctic snow. The bitter wind swept over it, twisting the torch-tongue; vainly it flopped, a trail of oily, stinking smoke bubbling away from it –

McReady walked back toward the shack silently. Barclay met him at the door. 'No more?' the giant meteorologist asked grimly.

Barclay shook his head. 'No more. It didn't split?'

'It had other things to think about,' McReady assured him. 'When I left it, it was a glowing coal. What was it doing?'

Norris laughed shortly. 'Wise boys, we are. Smash magnetos, so planes won't work. Rip the boiler tubing out of the tractors. And leave that Thing alone for a week in this shack. Alone and undisturbed.'

McReady looked in at the shack more carefully. The air, despite the ripped door, was hot and humid. On a table at the far end of the room rested a thing of coiled wires and small magnets, glass tubing and radio tubes. At the center a block of rough stone rested. From the center of the block came the light that flooded the place, the fiercely blue light bluer than the glare of an electric arc, and from it came the sweetly soft hum. Off to one side was another mechanism of crystal glass, blown with an incredible neatness and delicacy, metal plates and a queer, shimmery sphere of insubstantiality.

'What is that?' McReady moved nearer.

Norris grunted. 'Leave it for investigation. But I can guess pretty well. That's atomic power. That stuff to the left – that's a neat little thing for doing what men have been trying to do with hundred-ton cyclotrons and so forth. It separates neutrons from heavy water, which he was getting from the surrounding ice.'

'Where did he get all – oh. Of course. A monster couldn't be locked in – or out. He's been through the apparatus caches.' McReady stared at the apparatus. 'Lord, what minds that race must have – '

'The shimmery sphere – I think it's a sphere of pure force. Neutrons can pass through any matter, and he wanted a supply reservoir of neutrons. Just project neutrons against silica – calcium – beryllium – almost anything, and the atomic energy is released. That thing is the atomic generator.'

McReady plucked a thermometer from his coat. 'It's 120° in here, despite the open door. Our clothes have kept the heat out to an extent, but I'm sweating now.'

Norris nodded. 'The light's cold. I found that. But it gives off heat to warm the place through that coil. He had all the power in the world. He could keep it warm and pleasant, as his race thought of warmth and pleasantness. Did you notice the light, the color of it?'

McReady nodded. 'Beyond the stars is the answer. From beyond the stars. From a hotter planet that circled a brighter, bluer sun they came.'

McReady glanced out the door toward the blasted, smoke-stained trail that flopped and wandered blindly off across the drift. 'There won't be any more coming. I guess. Sheer accident it landed here, and that was twenty million years ago. What did it do all that for?' He nodded toward the apparatus.

Barclay laughed softly. 'Did you notice what it was working on when we came? Look.' He pointed toward the ceiling of the shack.

Like a knapsack made of flattened coffee tins, with dangling cloth straps and leather belts, the mechanism clung to the ceiling. A tiny, glaring heart of supernal flame burned in it, yet burned through the ceiling's wood without scorching it. Barclay walked over to it, grasped two of the dangling straps in his hands, and pulled it down with an effort. He strapped it about his body. A slight jump carried him in a weirdly slow arc across the room.

'Antigravity,' said McReady softly.

'Antigravity,' Norris nodded. 'Yes, we had 'em stopped, with no planes, and no birds. The birds hadn't come – but it had coffee tins and radio parts, and glass and the machine shop at night. And a week – a whole week – all to itself. America is a single jump – with antigravity powered by the atomic energy matter.

'We had 'em stopped. Another half hour – it was just tightening these straps on the device so it could wear it – and we'd have stayed in Antarctica, and shot down any moving thing that came from the rest of the world.'

'The albatross – 'McReady said softly. 'Do you suppose – '

'With this thing almost finished? With that death weapon it held in its hand?'

'No, by the grace of God, who evidently does hear very well, even down here, and the margin of half an hour, we keep our world, and the planets of the system, too. Antigravity, you know, and atomic power. Because They came from another sun, a star beyond the stars. *They* came from a world with a bluer sun.'

SIDEWISE IN TIME

Murray Leinster

Looking back, it seems strange that only James Minott figured the thing out in advance. The indications were more than plain. In early December Professor Michaelson announced his finding that the speed of light was not an absolute—could not be considered invariable. That, of course, was one of the first indications of what was to happen. A second indication came on February 15th, when at 12:40 P.M. Greenwich mean time, the sun suddenly shone blue-white and the enormously increased rate of radiation raised the temperature of the earth's surface by twenty-two degrees Fahrenheit in five minutes. At the end of the five minutes, the sun went back to its normal rate of radiation without any other symptom of disturbance. A great many bids for scientific fame followed, of course, but no plausible explanation of the phenomenon accounted for a total lack of after-disturbances in the sun's photosphere.

For a third clear forerunner of the events of June, on March 10th, the male giraffe in the Bronx Zoological Park, in New York, ceased to eat. In the nine days following, it changed its form, absorbing all its extremities, even its neck and head, into an extraordinary, egg-shaped mass of still-living flesh and bone which on the tenth day began to divide spontaneously and on the twelfth was two slightly pulsating fleshy masses. A day later still, bumps appeared on the two masses, They grew, took form and design, and twenty days after the beginning of the phenomenon were legs, necks, and heads. Then two giraffes, both male, moved about the giraffe enclosure. Each was slightly less than half the weight of the original animal. They were identically marked. And they ate and moved and in every way seemed normal though immature animals. An exactly similar occurrence was reported from the Argentine Republic, in which a steer from the pampas was going through the same extraordinary method of reproduction under the critical eyes of Argentine scientists.

Nowadays it seems incredible that the scientists of the time should not have understood the meaning of these oddities. We now know something of the type of strain which produced them, though they no longer occur. But between January and June the news-services of the nation were flooded with items of similar import. For two days the Ohio River flowed upstream. For six hours the trees in Euclid Park, in Cleveland, lashed their branches madly as if in a terrific storm, though not a breath of wind was stirring. And in New Orleans, near the last of May, fishes swam up out of the Mississippi River through the air, proceeded to 'drown' in the air which inexplicably upheld them, and then turned belly-up and floated placidly in an imaginary water-level some fifteen feet above the pavements of the city.

But it seems clear enough that Minott was the only man in the world who guessed the meaning of these now clear-cut indications of later events. He was then an instructor in mathematics on the faculty of Robinson College, in Fredericksburg, Virginia. We know that he anticipated very nearly every one of the happenings which we still only partly understand, though they affected every human being in our world—and in other worlds most of us have never dreamed could exist.

He made no attempt to share his knowledge with the rest of us. At first glance it seems unbelievable, but actually the attempt would have been useless. He was merely an instructor—not even a full professor—in what can only be called a jerkwater college. He had no scientific reputation, and even his fellow faculty members and all his former instructors at Johns Hopkins University considered him brash, cocky, unreliable, and thoroughly in need of having his ears pinned back. They would have taken great pleasure in putting him in his place. Had he attempted to publicize his foreknowledge he would surely have been firmly deprived of any chance at a hearing. His mathematics, in any case, were undoubtedly so far advanced that only a very limited number of people would have been able to understand them—as was the case with Einstein's relativity theory at the beginning—and there could be no experimental proof except the universal experience which came later.

Even had he tried to use the preliminary signs—noted above—as proofs of his explanation and mathematics, he would have been considered insane.

And yet he knew. Whether his first clue was Michaelson's

report on the variable velocity of light, which proved the existence of strains of a sort never before reported–the speed of light has now ceased to be variable, by the way–or whether another of the eccentric variations in natural law suggested his calculations, we cannot even guess. But he knew what was going to happen before it did. He knew it so thoroughly that he had calculated our chances of survival at one in four. Which pessimistic estimate alone would have caused him to be shouted down instantly had he offered his knowledge ahead of time.

In any event, he made no effort to give warning. He brought revolvers and books. He had sandwiches prepared for the greatest danger that has ever existed, anywhere, and for the most exotic enterprise any man ever attempted. Maybe he succeeded. We shall never know.

The main features of his life are well enough established. He was the son of a small farmer in West Virginia, with no history of previous genius in his family. He attended a rural grammar and consolidated high school, and seems to have annoyed each and every teacher with whom he came in contact. he worked his way through John Hopkins University, in Baltimore, displaying the same talent for unpopularity. He had brains. We know that now! But he was aware of them too, and so pushingly ambitious to prove and use them that he aroused antagonism wherever he went. The story is now classic, of the term-paper he submitted in his junior year, covering a problem in the calculus of probability. He solved the problem in wholly orthodox fashion, and added a scornful note:

'*The above is what I was supposed to do to get a good grade. It happens to be idiotically wrong. The problem should be solved as below:*'

And then he re-stated the problem in a fashion of which his instructor could not make head or tail, and got an answer normal mathematics would not justify. The term-paper was preserved by accident, and after his genius had been proved it was closely studied. The result is that Minott's Equation is now regarded with reverence and has changed the whole mathematical treatment of some aspects of probability.

The world lost a great deal through the sheer unamiability of Minott's character. He was embittered by his own impatience, frustrated by his own intelligence, and undoubtedly cursed with an ambition not seemly in an instructor of mathematics at Robinson College, Fredericksburg. Perhaps if he had had normal emotional ties the world would have benefited. Perhaps he would have, also. But it is useless to guess. We do know that if we had the notes he burned on the night of June 4th our mathematics would be so greatly advanced as to be practically a new science bringing all knowledge into a new unity. The few unburned scraps found in the fireplace of his living-room have given tantalizing glimpses of that science. They are invaluable. Some partly-burned fragments have been infuriating in their incompleteness. But he must have taken his most valuable notes with him, into that unguessed-at place where he may still live and work.

He would be amused at the diligence with which his least-considered scribble is now discussed by men who would have ignored him before. Perhaps—it is quite possible—he may have invented a word for the scope of the catastrophe we escaped. We have no word for it as yet. There is no term which can indicate a disaster in which not only the earth but our whole solar system would have been destroyed. Not only our solar system but our galaxy. Not only our galaxy but every other island universe in all the space we know. And even more than that, the destruction of time itself, meaning not only the obliteration of present and future, but even the annihilation of the past so that it would never have been. And then, besides, all those other strange states of existence we now know of, those other universes, those other pasts and presents and futures—all to be shattered into nothingness. There is no word for such a catastrophe!

It would be interesting to know what Minott termed it to himself as he coolly prepared to take advantage of the one chance in four of survival if that should be the one to eventuate. But it is easier merely to wonder how he felt when the morning of June 5th dawned. We do not know, of course. We cannot know. All we can be certain of is how we felt—and what happened.

It was 7:30 A.M. of June 5th. The city of Joplin, Missouri, awakened from a comfortable, summernight sleep. Dew glistened upon grass blades and leaves and the filmy webs of morning-spiders glittered like diamond-dust in the early sunshine. In the most easterly suburb a high-school boy, yawning, came somnolently out of his house to mow the lawn before school-time. A rather rickety family car roared, a block away. It back-fired, stopped, roared again, and throttled down to a steady, waiting hum. The voices of children sounded among the houses. A colored wash-woman appeared, striding beneath the trees which lined this strictly residential street. From an upper window a radio blatted: '–*one, two, three, four! Higher, now!– three, four! Put your weight into it!–two, three, four!* . . . ' The radio suddenly squawked and began to emit an insistent, mechanical shriek which changed again to a squawk and then a terrific sound as of all the static of ten thousand thunder-storms on the air at once. Then it was silent.

The high-school boy leaned mournfully on the push-bar of the lawn-mower. At the instant the static ended, the boy sat down suddenly on the dew-wet grass. The colored woman reeled and grabbed frantically at the nearest tree-trunk. The basket of wash toppled and spilled in a snowstorm of starched, vari-colored clothing. Howls of terror from chidren. Sharp shrieks from women. '*Earthquake! Earthquake!*' Figures appeared running, pouring out of houses. Someone fled out to a sleeping porch, slid down a supporting column, and in his pajamas tripped over a rose-bush. In seconds, it seemed, the entire population of the street was out-of-doors.

And then there was a queer, blank silence. There was no earthquake. No house had fallen. No chimney had cracked. Not so much as a dish or window-pane had made a sound in smashing. The senstaion every human being had felt was not an actual shaking of the ground. There had been movement, yes, and of the earth, but no such movement as any human being had ever dreamed of before. These people were to learn of that movement much later. Now they stared blankly at each other.

And in the sudden, dead silence broken only by the hum of an idling car and the wail of a frightened baby, a new sound became audible. It was the tramp of marching feet. With it came a curious clanking and clattering noise. And then a barked command, which was definitely not in the English language.

Down the street of a subrub of Joplin, Missouri, came a file of spear-armed, shield-bearing soldiers, in the short, skirtlike dress of ancient Rome. They wore helmets upon their heads. They peered about as if they were as blankly amazed as the citizens of Joplin who regarded them. A long column of marching men came into view, every man with shield and spear and the indefinable air of being used to just such weapons.

They halted at another barked order. A wizened short man with a short-sword snapped a question at the staring citizens. The high-school boy jumped. The wizened man roared his question again. The high-school boy stammered, and painfully formed syllables with his lips. The wizened man grunted in satisfaction. He talked, articulating clearly if impatiently. And the high-school boy turned dazedly to the other Americans.

'He wants to know the name of this town,' he said, disbelieving his own ears. 'He's talking Latin, like I learn in school. He says this town isn't on the roadmaps, and he doesn't know where he is. But all the same he takes possession of it in the name of the Emperor Valerius Fabricius, emperor of Rome and the far corners of the earth.' And then the school-boy stuttered. 'He–he says these are the first six cohorts of the Forty-Second Legion, on garrison duty in Messalia. That–that's supposed to be two days march up that way.'

He pointed in the direction of St. Louis.

The idling motor-car roared suddenly into life. Its gears whined and it came rolling out into the street. Its horn honked peremptorily for passage through the shield-clad soldiers. They gaped at it. It honked again and moved toward them.

A roared order, and they flung themselves upon it, spears thrusting, short-swords stabbing. Up to this instant there was not one single inhabitant of Joplin who did not believe the spear-armed soldiers motion-picture actors, or masqueraders, or something else equally insane but credible. But there was nothing make-believe about their attack on the car. They assaulted it as if it were a strange and probably deadly beast. They flung themselves into battle with it in a grotesquely reckless valor.

And there was nothing at all make-believe in the thoroughness and completeness with which they speared Mr. Horace B. Davis, who had only intended to drive down to the cotton-brokerage office of which he was chief clerk. They thought he was driving this strange beast to slaughter them, and they slaughtered him instead. The high-school boy saw them do it, growing whiter and whiter as he watched. When a swordsman approached the wizened man and displayed the severed head of Mr. Davis, with the spectacles dangling grotesquely from one ear, the high-school boy fainted dead away.

It was sunrise of June 5th. Cyrus Harding gulped down his breakfast in the pale gray dawnlight. He had felt very dizzy and sick for just a moment, some little while since, but he was himself again now. The smell of frying filled the kitchen. His wife cooked. Cyrus Harding ate. he made noises as he emptied his plate. His hands were gnarled and work-worn, but his expression was of complacent satisfaction. He looked at a calendar hung on the wall, a Christmas sentiment from the Bryan Feed and Fertilizer Company, in Bryan, Ohio.

'Sheriff's goin' to sell out Amos today,' he said comfortably. 'I figger I'll get the north forty cheap.'

His wife said tiredly:

'He's been offerin' to sell it to you for a year.'

'Yep,' agreed Cyrus Harding more complacently still. 'Comin' down on the price, too. But nobuddy'll bid against me at the sale. They know I want it bad, an' I ain't a good neighbor to have when somebuddy takes somethin' from under my nose. Folks know it. I'll git it a lot cheaper'n Amos offered it to me for. He wanted to sell it t'meet his int'rest an' hol' on another year. I'll git it for half that.'

He stood up and wiped his mouth. He strode to the door.

'That hired man shoulda got a good start with his harrowin','' he said expansively. 'I'll take a look an' go over to the sale.'

He went to the kitchen door and opened it. Then his mouth dropped open. The view from this doorway was normally that of a not-especially neat barnyard, with beyond it farmland flat as a floor, cultivated to the very fence-rails, with a promising crop of corn as a border against the horizon.

Now the view was quite otherwise. All was normal as far as the barn. But beyond the barn was delirium. Huge, spreading tree-ferns soared upward a hundred feet. Lacy, foliated branches formed a roof of incredible density above sheer jungle such as no man on earth had ever seen before. The jungles of the Amazon basin were park-like by comparison with its thickness. It was a riotous tangle of living vegetation in which growth was battle, and battle was life, and life was deadly, merciless conflict. No man could have forced his way ten feet through such a wilderness. From it came a fetid exhalation which was part decay and part lush rank growing things, and part the overpowering perfumes of glaringly vivid flowers. It was jungle such as paleobotanists have described as existing in the Carboniferous Period; as the source of our coal-beds.

'It—it ain't so!' said Cyrus Harding weakly. 'It—ain't so!'

His wife did not reply. She had not seen. Wearily, she began to clean up after her lord and master's meal.

He went down the kitchen steps, staring and shaken. he moved toward this impossible apparition which covered his crops. It did not disappear as he neared it. He went within twenty feet of it and stopped, still staring, still unbelieving, beginning to entertain the monstrous supposition that he had gone insane.

Then something moved in the jungle. A long, snaky neck, feet thick at its base and tapering to a mere sixteen inches behind a head the size of a barrel. The neck reached out the twenty feet to him. Cold eyes regarded him abstractedly. The mouth opened. Cyrus Harding screamed.

His wife raised her eyes. She looked through the open door and saw the jungle. She saw the jaws close upon her husband. She saw the colossal, abstracted eyes half-close as Something gulped, and partly choked, and swallowed. She saw a lump in the monstrous neck move from the relatively slender portion just behind the head to the enormous mass of flesh where the neck joined its unseen body. She saw the head withdraw into the jungle and be instantly lost to sight.

Cyrus Harding's widow went very pale. She put on her hat and walked subduedly out of the front door. She began to walk steadily toward the house of the nearest neighbor. As she went, she said composedly to herself:

'It's come. I've gone crazy. They'll have to put me in an asylum. But I won't have to stand him any more. *I won't have to stand him any more!*'

And at 10:30 A.M. on the morning of June 5th, Instructor James Minott of Robinson College turned upon the party of students with a revolver in each hand. Gone was the appearance of the dour young instructor whose most destructive possibility was a below-passing mark in Math. He had guns in his hands now, instead of chalk or pencil, and his eyes were glowing even as he smiled frostily. The four girls gasped. The young men, accustomed to see him only in a class-room, realized that not only could he use the weapons in his hands, but that he would. And suddenly they respected him as they would respect—say—a burglar or a prominent gangster or a well-known murderer. He was raised far above the level of a mathematics instructor. He became instantly a leader, and by virtue of his weapons, even a ruler.

'As you see,' said Minott evenly, 'I have anticipated the situation in which we find ourselves. At any moment, to be sure, we and all the human race may be wiped out with a completeness of which you can form no idea. But we may survive, and I am prepared equally to be wiped out or to make the most of my chance of survival—if we live.'

He looked steadily from one to another of the students who had followed him to explore the extraordinary appearance of a sequoia forest north of Fredericksburg.

'I know what has happened,' said Minott coolly. 'I also know what is likely to happen. And I know what I intend to do about it. Any of you who are prepared to follow me can say so. Any of you who objects—well—I can't have mutinies! I'll shoot him!'

'But Mr. Minott,' said Blake nervously, 'we ought to get the girls home—'

'They will never go home,' said Minott calmly. 'Neither will you nor any of the rest of us. As soon as you're quite convinced that I'm ready to use these weapons, I'll tell you what's happened and what it means. I've been preparing for it for weeks.'

It was noon of June 5th. The cell-door opened and a very grave, whiskered man in a curious gray uniform came in. He tapped the prisoner gently on the shoulder.

'I'm Doctor Holloway,' he said encouragingly. 'Army Medical Corps. Suppose you tell me, suh, just what happened t'you? I'm right sure it can all be straightened out.'

The prisoner sputtered:

'Why—why—dammit,' he protested. 'I drove down from Louisville this morning. I had a dizzy spell and—well—I must have missed my road, because suddenly I noticed that everything around me was unfamiliar. And then a man in a gray uniform yelled at me, and a minute later he began to shoot, and the first thing I knew they'd arrested me for having the American flag painted on my car! I'm a traveling salesman for the Uncle Sam Candy-Bar Company! Dammit, it's funny when a man can't fly his own country's flag—'

'In your own country, of co'se,' assented the doctor, comfortingly. 'But you must know, suh, that we don't allow any flag but ouah own to be displayed heah. You violated ouah laws, suh.'

'Your laws!' The prisoner stared blankly. 'What laws? Where in the United States is it illegal to fly the American flag?'

'Nowheah in the United States, suh.' The doctor smiled. 'You must have crossed ouah border unawares, suh. I will be frank, an' admit that it was suspected you were insane. I see now that it was just a mistake.'

'Border—United—' The prisoner gasped. 'I'm not in the United States? I'm not? The where in hell am I?'

'Ten miles, suh, within the borders of the Confederacy,' said the doctor, and laughed. 'A queer mistake, suh, but theah was no intention of insult. You'll be released at once. Theah is enough tension between Washington an' Richmond without another border incident to upset ouah hot-heads.'

'Confederacy?' The prisoner choked. 'You can't—you don't mean the Confederate States—'

'Of co'se, suh. The Confederate States of North America. Why not?'

The prisoner gulped.

'I—I've gone mad!' he stammered. 'I must be mad! There was Gettysburg—there was—'

'Gettysburg? Oh, yes!' The doctor nodded indulgently. 'We are very proud of ouah history, suh. You refer to the battle in the War of Separation, when the fate of the Confederacy rested on ten minutes time. I have often wondered what would have been the result if Pickett's charge had been driven back. It was Pickett's charge that gained the day for us, suh. England recognized the Confederacy two days later, France in another week, an' with unlimited credit abroad we won out. But it was a tight squeeze, suh!'

The Prisoner gasped again. He stared out of the window. And opposite the jail stood an unquestionable court-house. Upon the court-house stood a flagpole. And spread gloriously in the breeze above a government building—floated the Stars and Bars of the Confederacy!

It was night of June 5th. The post-master of North Centerville, Massachusetts, came out of his cubbyhole to listen to the narrative. The pot-bellied stove of the general store sent a comfortable, if unnecessary glow about. The eyewitness chuckled.

'Yeah. They come around the cape, thirty or forty of 'em in a boat all o' sixty feet long with a crazy square sail drawin'. Round things in the gun'le like—shields. An' rowin' like hell. They stopped when they saw the town an' looked s'prised. Then they hailed us, talkin' some lingo that wa'n't American. Ole Peterson, he near dropped his line, with a fish on it too. Then he tried t' talk back. They hadda lotta trouble understandin' him, or made out to. Then they turned around an' rowed back. Actors or somethin', tryin' to play a joke. It fell flat, though. Maybe some o' those rich folks up the coast pullin' it. Ho! Ho! Ole says they was talkin' a funny, old-fashioned Skowegian. They told him they was from Leifsholm, or somethin' like that, just up the coast. That they couldn't make out how our town got here. They'd never seen it before! Can y' imagine that? Ole says they were Vikin's, an' they called this place Vinland, an' says—My Gawd! What's that?'

A sudden hubbub arose in the night. Screams. Cries. A shot-gun boomed dully. The loafers in the general store crowded out on the porch. Flames rose from half a dozen places on the water-front. In their light could be seen a full dozen serpent-ships, speeding for the shore, propelled by oars. Firelight glinted on swords, on shields. A woman screamed as a huge, yellow-maned man seized her. His brazen helmet and shield glittered. He was laughing. Then a figure in overalls hurtled toward the blond giant, an axe held threateningly—

The giant cut him down with an already dripping blade and roared. Men rushed to him and they plunged on to loot and burn. More of the armoured figures leaped to the sand from another beached ship. Another house roared flames sky-ward . . . .

Tall trees rose around the party. Giant trees. Magnificent trees. They towered two hundred and fifty feet into the air, and their air of venerable calm was at once the most convincing evidence of their actuality, and the most improbable of all the things which had happened in the neighborhood of Fredericksburg, Virginia. The little group of people sat their horses affrightedly beneath the monsters of the forest. Minott regarded them estimatingly, these three young men and four girls, all students of Robinson College.

Minott was now no longer the faculty-member in charge of a party of exploration, but a definitely ruthless leader.

At eight-thirty A.M. on June 5th the inhabitants of Fredericksburg had felt a curious, unanimous dizziness. It passed. The sun shone brightly. There seemed to be no noticeable change in any of the facts of everyday existence. But within an hour, the sleepy little town was buzzing with excitement. The road to Washington—Route One on all road-maps—ceased abruptly some three miles north. A colossal, a gigantic forest had appeared magically to block the way. Telegraphic communication with Washington had ceased. Even the Washington broadcasting stations were no longer on the air. The trees of the extraordinary forest were tall beyond the experience of any human being in town. They looked like the photographs of the giant sequoias on the Pacific Coast, but—well—the thing was simply impossible.

In an hour and a half, instructor Minott had organized a party of sight-seers among the students. He seemed to pick his party with a queer definiteness of decision. Three young men and four girls. They would have piled into a rickety car owned by one of the boys, but Minott negated the idea.

'The road ends at the forest,' he said, smiling. 'I'd rather like to explore a magic forest. Suppose we ride horseback? I'll arrange for horses.'

In ten minutes the horses appeared. The girls had vanished to get into riding-breeches or knickers. They noted appreciatively on their return that besides the saddles, the horses had saddle-bags slung in place. Again Minott smiled.

'We're exploring,' he said humorously. 'We must dress the part. Also, we'll probably want some lunch. And we can bring back specimens for the botanical lab to look over.'

They rode forth; the girls thrilled, the young men pleased and excited, and all of them just a little bit disappointed at finding themselves passed by motorcars which whizzed by as all Fredericksburg went to look at the improbable forest ahead.

There were cars by hundreds where the road abruptly ended. A crowd stared at the forest. Giant trees, their roots fixed firmly in the ground. Undergrowth here and there. Over it all, an aspect of peace and utter serenity—and permanence. The watching crowd hummed and buzzed with speculation, with talk. The thing they saw was impossible. It could not have happened. This forest could not possibly be real. They were regarding some sort of mirage.

But as the party of riders arrived, half a dozen daring men came out of the forest. They had dared to enter it. Now they returned, still incredulous of their own experience, bearing leaves and branches and one of them certain small berries unknown on the Atlantic Coast.

A State Police officer held up his hand as Minott's party went toward the edge of the forest.

'Look here!' he said. 'We been hearin' funny noises in there. I'm stoppin' anybody else from goin' in until we know what's what.'

Minott nodded.

'We'll be careful. I'm a faculty member of Robinson College. We're going in after some botanical specimens. I have a revolver. We're all right.'

He rode ahead. The State policeman, without definite orders for authority, shrugged his shoulders and bent his efforts to the prevention of other attempts to explore. In minutes, the eight horses and their riders were out of sight.

That was now three hours past. For three hours, Minott had led his charges a little south of north-east. In that time they saw no dangerous animals. They saw some–many–familiar plants. They saw rabbits in quantity, and once a slinking gray form which Tom Hunter, who was majoring in zoology, declared was a wolf. There are no wolves in the vicinity of Fredericksburg, but neither are their sequoias. And the party had seen no signs of human life, though Fredericksburg lies in farming country which is thickly settled. In three hours the horses must have covered between twelve and fifteen miles, even through the timber. It was just after sighting a shaggy beast which was unquestionably a woodland buffalo–extinct east of the Rockies as early as 1820– that young Blake protested uneasily against further travel.

'There's something awfully queer, sir,' he said awkwardly. 'I don't mind experimenting as much as you like, sir, but we've got the girls with us. If we don't start back pretty soon, we'll get in trouble with the dean!'

And then Minott drew his two revolvers and very calmly announced that none of them would ever go back. That he knew what had happened and what could be expected. And he added that he would explain as soon as they were convinced he would use his revolvers in case of a mutiny.

'Call us convinced now, sir,' said young Blake. He was a bit pale about the lips, but he hadn't flinched. In fact, he'd moved to be between Maida Haynes and the gun-muzzle. 'We'd like very much to know how all these trees and plants, which ought to be three thousand miles away, happen to be growing in Virginia without any warning. Especialy, sir, we'd like to know how it is that the topography underneath all this brand-new forest is the same. The hills trend the same way they used to, but everything that ever was on them has vanished, and something else is in its place.'

Minott nodded approvingly.

'Splendid, Blake!' he said warmly. 'Sound observation! I picked you because you're well spoken of in geology, even though there were–er–other reasons for leaving you behind. Let's go on over the next rise. Unless I'm mistaken, we should find the Potomac in view. Then I'll answer any questions you like. I'm afraid we've a good bit more of riding to do today.'

Reluctantly, the eight horses breasted the slope. They scrambled among underbush. It was queer that in three hours they had seen not a trace of a road leading anywhere. But up at the top of the hill there was a road. It was a narrow, wandering cart-track.

Without a word, every one of the eight riders turned their horses to follow it. It meandered onward for perhaps a quarter of a mile. It dipped suddenly. And the Potomac lay before and below them.

Then seven of the eight riders exclaimed. There was a settlement upon the banks of the river. There were boats in harbor. There were other boats in view beyond; two beating down from the long reaches upstream, and three others coming painfully up from the direction of Chesapeake Bay. But neither the village nor the boats should have been upon the Potomac River. The village was small and mud-walled. Tiny, blue-clad figures moved about the fields outside. The buildings, the curving lines of the roofs, and more especially the unmistakable outline of a sort of temple near the center of the fortified hamlet—these were Chinese. The boats in sight were junks, save that their sails were cloth instead of slatted bamboo. The fields outside the squat mud walls were cultivated in a fashion altogether alien. Near the river, where marsh flats would be normal along the Potomac, rice-fields intensely worked spread out instead.

Then a figure appeared nearby. Wide hat, wadded cotton-padded jacket, cotton trousers, and clogs, it was Chinese peasant incarnate, and all the more so when it turned a slant-eyed, terror-stricken face upon them and fled squawking. It left a monstrously heavy wooden yoke behind, from which dangled two buckets filled with berries it had gathered in the forest.

The riders stared. There was the Potomac. But a Chinese village nestled beside it, Chinese junks plied its waters . . . .

'I—I think,' said Maida Haynes unsteadily, 'I—think I've—gone insane. Haven't I?'

Minott shrugged. He looked disappointed but queerly resolute.

'No,' he said shortly. 'You're not mad. It just happens that the Chinese happened to colonize America first. It's been known that Chinese junks touched the American shore—the Pacific Coast, of course—long before Columbus. Evidently they colonized it. They may have come all the way overland to the Atlantic, or maybe around by Panama. In any case, this is a Chinese continent now. This isn't what we want. We'll ride some more.'

The fleeing, squawking figure had been seen from the village. A huge, discordant gong began to sound. Figures fled toward the walls from the fields round about. The popping of fire-crackers began, with a chorus of most intimidating yells.

'Come on!' said Minott sharply. 'We'd better move!'

He wheeled his horse about and started off at a canter. By instinct, since he was the only one who seemed to have any definite idea what to do, the others flung after him.

And as they rode, suddenly the horses staggered. The humans atop them felt a queer, queazy vertigo. It lasted only for a second, but Minott paled a little.

'Now we'll see what's happened,' he said composedly. 'The odds are still fair, but I'd rather have had things stay as they were until we'd tried a few more places . . .

That same queazy vertigo affected the staring crowd at the end of the road leading north from Fredericksburg. For perhaps a second they felt an unearthly illness, which even blurred their vision. Then they saw clearly again. And in an instant they were babbling in panic, starting their motor-cars in terror, some of them fleeing on foot.

The sequoia forest had vanished. In its place was a dreary waste of glittering white; stumpy trees buried under snow; rolling ground covered with a powdery, glittering stuff. . . .

In minutes dense fog shut off the view, as the warm air of a Virginia June morning was chilled by that frigid coating. But in minutes, too, the heavy snow began to melt. The cars fled away along the concrete road, and behind them an expanding belt of fog spread out—and the little streams and runlets filled with a sudden surplus of water, and ran more swiftly, and rose. . . .

There were only sparse trees and a tall, canelike grass. The ground was still rolling, but the air was misty. Clear vision was not possible for a very long distance. Still, the topography in terms of hills and valleys had not changed. But they saw a tapir—it looked like a pigmy elephant at first glance—and they had seen other things that looked human, but weren't. So two of the young men rode on ahead, watching lest there should be anything hidden in the breast-high grass, and Minott followed with the four girls, and another of the students followed twenty yards behind.

'I don't like this,' said Minott coldly. 'Not at all. But we'll keep going.'

Lucy Blair rode beside him on one hand. He'd shown her how to use a revolver. Maida Haynes rode on the other.

'What were those—things we saw?' asked Lucy shakenly. 'They—looked human. Were they, really?'

'Depends, on what you mean by human,' said Minott. 'If you mean *homo sapiens*—our species—probably not. The human family had a number of species, like the equine and feline families. There was Neanderthal man and Java man and so on.

Homo sapiens wiped them out, in the world we came from. But in the history of this particular place the battle may have gone the other way.'

Maida Haynes licked her lips. She was terribly tense.

'History,' she said in a queer voice. 'What has that to do with—what's happening to us? I—I still think I'm dreaming. I—I must be!'

'I think I'm dreaming too,' said Lucy. 'And I'm scared too, but so far it's rather wonderful. I—think I'll get over being too scared, in time.'

One of the two figures on ahead swerved to one side. He rode cautiously, and reined in, and then turned his horse and came racing back to Minott.

'Some of those—creatures lying in wait there,' he said through chattering lips. 'The—funny things that look like men. What'll we do?'

Minott considered coldly.

'If we planned to stay here,' he said presently, without emotion, 'we'd charge them and kill enough of them to teach a needed lesson. But we don't intend to stay here. It isn't worth the risk or trouble. We'd gain nothing. Swing wide of them. If they try to follow us we'll shoot one or two.'

Harris sent his horse plunging back to join young Blake. They changed course. Beastly howlings arose from a spot they would now avoid. Loping, bouncing figures with long brown shaggy hair went leaping and bounding to intercept them. The figures carried clubs and spears.

Minott very calmly drew a revolver. He aimed and fired six times. A creature screamed up ahead. Its fellows fled away, howling. The wounded creature thrashed and shrieked. Then it suddenly made bubbling sounds and was still. Minott reloaded his revolver.

'You—killed it!' gasped Maida, horrified.

'To be sure,' said Minott casually. 'Killing one made the others run away. If they'd attacked us we'd have had to kill several, and it would have used up a good deal of ammunition.

'Intelligence isn't at a premium here,' said Minott. 'We can't make much of this environment!'

He made no other comment. Far, far away, the misty air seemed to grow thicker. There was a white fog before them. It seemed to stretch out of sight on either hand. They rode toward it.

Lucy Blair said suddenly:

'Do you really think we'll come upon a civilization where we'll be welcomed, Mr. Minott?'

'Naturally!' His tone was dry. 'I did not plan this expedition without some definite ideas!'

'And do you think we will — we will —'.

'Rule it?' He said more dryly still: 'I assure you that I will rule it. I need only to be received—to be accepted—in a community not too far advanced in culture, but a shade above savagery. Given that foothold, I can use my special knowledge to its full value. I need only a society still fluid, still malleable, not yet frozen in a pattern of conventional stability. I will end by ruling it. In our own culture, man is only afraid of losing what he has. I can do nothing with such people. But give me men who want what they have not, and I can give it to them! I can make them prosper as if by magic!'

'By mathematics?' asked Lucy dubiously.

He smiled faintly.

'You might call it that,' he said ironically. 'But by your definition mathematics is only a form of integration dealing with quantity. Logic is a form of integration which deals with ideas but not with quantity. There can be—there is!—a form of integration which deals with both and more besides. I discovered it. It is useless in our time, of course. It would upset too much that is solidly established. But it is as precise in its operation as either mathematics or logic. And I assure you that it will give me as much advantage in all dealings with men of a proper culture, as the ability to count gives in dealings with savages who cannot.'

Lucy Blair looked at him oddly.

'That sounds like pure intellectuality. You act like something else entirely. Do you know, I've always thought you were lonely?'

. 'I always have been,' said Minott bitterly. 'I always will be. But I shall do things to make up for it now! Let me find just one community of men who are restless and desirous, and I will remake it, remould it, rule and guide it, and—'

But then he stopped. Lucy did not look shocked. She said interestedly:

'And how do we fit into that?'

'You will help me,' he said calmly. 'All of you. You have no choice, of course, but you will have such rewards as you cannot now imagine. I won't need to force any of you. You'll have no choice. But you will be glad, I think.'

'But it's—preposterous—' protested Maida, shrilly, 'not to—not to be able to go home again—'

'You will marry,' said Minott practically. 'Then you won't mind. Even that, though, will be of your own choice. Of course. You won't find semi-savages interesting, any more than any of the rest of us would. You'll do all right.'

The two girls stared at each other. There were four girls. Three students—and Minott.

'Yes,' he said matter-of-factly. 'I shall marry one of you. The most suitable for my plans. I shall want an intelligent empress.'

But then he spurred ahead. The fog-bank before them spread one horizon to the other. As the horses went uneasily into it, the air turned icy cold.

The ferryboat from Berkeley, California, ploughed valorously through the fog. Its whistle howled mournfully at the proper intervals. Up in the pilot-house, the skipper said confidentially:

'I tell you, I had the funniest feelin' of my life, just now. I was dizzy an' sick all over, like seasick an' drunk together.'

The mate said abstractedly:

'Me too, a little while ago. Somethin' we ate, prob'ly. Say, that's funny!'

'What?'

'Was a lot o' traffic in the harbor just now. Whistlin'. I ain't heard a whistle for minutes. Listen!'

Both men strained their ears. There was the rhythmic shudder of the vessel, itself a sound produced by the engines. There were fragmentary voice-noises from the passenger-deck below. There was the wash of water by the ferryboat's bow. There was nothing else. Nothing at all.

'Funny!' said the skipper.

'Dam' funny!' agreed the mate.

The ferryboat went on. The fog cut down all visibility to a radius of perhaps two hundred feet.

'Funniest thing I ever saw!' said the skipper worriedly. He reached for the whistle-cord and the mournful bellow of the horn resounded. 'We're near our slip, though. I wish . . .'

With a little chugging, swishing sound a steam-launch came out of the mist. It sheered off, the men in it staring blankly at the huge bulk of the ferry. It made a complete circuit of the big, clumsy craft. Then someone stood up and bellowed unintelligibly in the launch. He bellowed again. He was giving an order. He pointed to the flag at the stern of the launch—it was an unfamiliar flag—and roared furiously.

'What the hell's the matter with that guy?' wondered the mate.

A little breeze blew suddenly. The fog began to thin. The faintly brighter spot which was the sun overhead grew bright indeed. Faint sunshine struggled through the fog-bank. The wind drove the fog back before it—and the bellowing man in the steam-launch grew purple with rage as his orders went unheeded.

Then, quite abruptly, the last wisps of vapor blew away. San Francisco stood revealed. But—San Francisco? This was not San Francisco! It was a wooden city. A small city. A dirty city with narrow streets and gas street-lamps and four monstrous, barrack-like edifices fronting the harbor. Nob Hill stood, but it was barren of dwellings. And—

'My Gawd!' said the mate of the ferryboat.

He was staring at a colossal mass of masonry, four-square and huge, which rose to a gigantic spiral-fluted dome. A strange and alien flag fluttered in the breeze above certain buildings. Figures moved in the streets. There were motor-cars, but they were clumsy and huge. The mate's eyes rested upon a horse-drawn carriage. It was drawn by three horses abreast, and they were either so trained or so check-reined that only the center one faced straight ahead. The necks of the other two were arched outward in the fashion of Tsarist Russia.

But that was natural enough, after all. When an interpreter could be found, the mate and skipper were savagely abused for entering the harbor of Novo Skevsky without obeying the ordinances in force by ukase of the Tsar Alexis of All the Russias. Those rules, they learned, were enforced with special rigor in all the Russian territory in America, from Alaska on south.

The eight riders were every one very pale. Even Minott seemed shaken but no less resolute when he drew rein.

'I imagine you will all be satisfied now,' he said composedly. 'Blake, you're the geologist of the party. Doesn't the shore-line there look familiar?'

Young Blake nodded. He was very white indeed. He pointed to the stream.

'Yes. The falls, too. This is the site of Fredericksburg, sir, where we were this morning. There is where the main bridge was—or will be. The main highway to Richmond should run—' He licked his lips. 'It should run where that very big oak-tree is standing. The Princess Anne Hotel should be on the other side of

that hill. I—I would say, sir, that somehow we've gone backwards
in time or else forward into the future. It sounds insane, but I've
been trying to figure it out . . . '

Minott nodded coolly.

'Very good. This is the site of Fredericksburg, to be sure. But
we have not traveled backward or ahead in time. I hope that you
noticed where we came out of the sequoia forest. There seems to
be a sort of fault along that line, which it may be useful to
remember.' He paused. 'We're not in the past or the future,
Blake. We've traveled sidewise, in a sort of oscillation from one
time-path to another. We happen to be in a—well—in a part of
time where Fredericksburg has never been built, just as a little
while since we were where the Chinese occupy the American
continent. I think we'd better have lunch.'

He dismounted. The four girls tended to huddle together.
Maida Haynes teeth chattered. Blake moved to the horses'
heads.

'Don't get rattled,' he said urgently. 'We're here, wherever it
is. Mr. Minott is going to explain things fully in a minute. Since
he knows what's what, we're in no danger. Climb off your
horses and let's eat. I'm hungry as a bear. Come on, Maida!'

Maida Haynes dismounted. She managed a rather shaky
smile.

'I'm—afraid of—him.' she said in a whisper. 'More than—
anything else—stay close to me, please'

Blake frowned. Minott said dryly:

'Look in your saddle-bags and you'll find sandwiches. Also
you'll find firearms. You young men had better arm yourselves.
Since there's now no conceivable hope of getting back to the
world we know, I think you can be trusted with weapons.'

Young Blake stared at him, then silently investigated his own
saddle-bags. He found two revolvers, with what seemed an
abnormally large supply of cartridges. He found a mass of paper,
which turned out to be books with their cardboard backs torn
off. He glanced professionally at the revolvers and slipped them
in his pockets. He put back the books.

'I appoint you second in command, Blake,' said Minott, more
dryly than before. 'You understand nothing, but you want to
understand. I made no mistake in choosing you, despite my
reasons for leaving you behind. Sit down, and I'll tell you what
happened!'

With a grunt and a puffing noise, a small black bear broke
cover and fled across a place where only that morning a highly

elaborate filling-station had stood. The party started, then relaxed. The girls suddenly started to giggle foolishly, almost hysterically. Minott bit calmly into a sandwich and said pleasantly:

'I shall have to talk mathematics to you, but I'll try to make it more palatable than my class-room lectures have been. You see, everything that has happened can only be explained in terms of mathematics, and more especially certain concepts in mathematical physics. You young ladies and gentlemen being college men and women, I shall have to phrase things very simply, as for ten-year-old children. Hunter, you're staring. If you actually see something, such as an Indian, shoot at him and he'll run away. The probabilities are that he never heard the report of a firearm. We're not on the Chinese continent now.'

Hunter gasped, and fumbled at his saddle-bags. While he got out the revolvers in it, Minott went on imperturbably:

'There has been an unheaval of nature, which still continues. But instead of a shaking and jumbling of earth and rocks, there has been a shaking and jumbling of space and time. I go back to first principles. Time is a dimension. The past is one extension of it, the future is the other, just as east is one extension of a more familiar dimension and west is its opposite. But we ordinarily think of time as a line, a sort of tunnel, perhaps. We do not make that error in the dimensions about which we think daily. For example, we know that Annapolis, King George Court House, and—say—Norfolk are all to eastward of us. But we know that in order to reach any of them, as a destination, we would have to go not only east but north or south in addition. In imaginative travels into the future, however, we never think in such a commonsense fashion. We assume that the future is a line instead of a coordinate, a path instead of a direction. We assume that if we travel to futureward there is but one possible destination. And that is as absurd as it would be to ignore the possibility of traveling to eastward in any other line than due east, forgetting that there are north-east and south-east and a large number of intermediate points.'

Young Blake said slowly:

'I follow you, sir, but it doesn't seem to bear—'

'On our problem? But it does!' Minott smiled, showing his teeth. He bit into his sandwich again. 'Imagine that I came to a fork in a road. I flip a coin to determine which fork I shall take. Whichever route I follow, I shall encounter certain landmarks, and certain adventures. But they will not be the same, whether landmarks or adventures. In choosing between the forks of the road I choose not only between two sets of landmarks I could encounter, but between two sets of events. I choose between paths, not only on the surface of the earth, but in time. And as those paths upon earth may lead to two different cities, so those paths in the future may lead to two entirely different futures. On one of them may lie opportunities for riches. On the other may lie the most prosaic of hit-and-run accidents which will leave me a mangled corpse, not only upon one fork of a highway in the state of Virginia, but upon one fork of a highway in time. In short, I am pointing out that there is more than one future we can encounter, and with more or less absence of deliberation we choose among them. But the futures we fail to encounter, upon the roads we do not take, are just as real as the landmarks upon those roads. We never see them, but we freely admit their existence.'

Again it was young Blake who protested:

'All this is interesting enough, sir, but still I don't see how it applies to our present situation.'

Minott said impatiently:

'Don't you see that if such a state of things exists in the future, that it must also have existed in the past? We talk of three dimensions and one present and one future. There is a theoretic necessity—a mathematical necessity—to assume more than one future. There are an indefinite number of possible futures, any one of which we would encounter if we took the proper 'forks' in time. There are any number of destinations to eastward. There are any number to futureward. Start a hundred miles west and come eastward, choosing your paths on earth at random, as you do in time. You may arrive here. You may arrive to the north or south of this spot, and still be east of your starting-point. Now start a hundred years back instead of a hundred miles west!'

Groping, young Blake said fumblingly:

'I think you're saying, sir, that—well as there must be any number of futures, there must have been any number of pasts besides those written down in our histories. And—and it would follow that there are any number of what you might call "presents."'

Minott gulped down the last of his sandwich and nodded.

'Precisely! And today's convulsion of nature has jumbled them, and still upsets them from time to time. The Northmen once colonized America. In the sequence of events which mark the pathway of our own ancestors through time, that colony failed. But along another path through time that colony throve and flourished. The Chinese reached the shores of California. In the path our ancestors followed through time, nothing developed from the fact. But this morning we touched upon the pathway in which they have colonized and conquered the continent, though from the fear that one peasant we saw displayed, they have not wiped out the Indians as our ancestors did. Somewhere the Roman Empire still exists, and may not improbably rule America as it once ruled Britain. Somewhere, the conditions causing the glacial period still obtain and Virginia is buried under a mass of snow. Somewhere even the Carboniferous Period may exist. Or to come more closely to the present we know, somewhere there is a path through time in which Pickett's charge at Gettysburg went desperately home, and the Confederate States of America is now an independent nation with a heavily fortified border and a chip-on-the-shoulder attitude toward the United States.'

Blake alone had asked questions, but the entire party had been listening open-mouthed. Now Lucy Blair said:

'But–Mr. Minott, where are we now?'

'We are probably,' said Minott, smiling, 'in a path of time in which America has never been discovered by white men. That isn't a very satisfactory state of things. We're going to look for something better. We wouldn't be comfortable in wigwams, with skins for clothing. So we shall hunt for a more congenial environment. We will have some weeks in which to do our searching, I think. Unless, of course, all space and time is wiped out by the cause of our predicament.'

Tom Hunter stirred uncomfortably.

'We haven't traveled backward or forward in time, then.'

'No,' repeated Minott. He got to his feet. 'That odd nausea we felt seems to be caused by travel sidewise in time. It's the symptom of a time-oscillation. We'll ride on and see what other worlds await us. We're a rather well-qualified party for this sort of exploration. I chose you for your training. Hunter, zoology. Blake, engineering and geology. Harris–' He nodded to the rather undersized young man, who flushed at being noticed. :– Harris is quite a competent chemist, I understand. Miss Ketterline is a capable botanist. Miss Blair–'

Madia Haynes rose slowly.

'You anticipated all this, Mr. Minott, and yet you brought us into it. You–you said we'll never get back home. Yet you deliberately arranged it. What–What was your motive? What did you do it for?'

Minott climbed into the saddle. He smiled, but there was bitterness in his smile.

'In the world we know,' he told her, 'I was an instructor in mathematics in a small and unconsidered college. I had absolutely no chance of ever being more than a professor of mathematics in a small and unconsidered college. In this world I am, at least, the leader of a group of reasonably intelligent young people. In our saddle-bags are arms and ammunition and—more important—books of reference for our future activities. We shall hunt for and find a civilization in which our technical knowledge is at a premium. We shall live in that world—if all time and space is not destroyed—and use our knowledge.'

Maida Haynes said:

'But again—what for?'

'To conquer it!' said Minott in sudden fierceness. 'To conquer it! We eight will rule a world as no world has been ruled since time began! I promise you that when we find the environment we seek, you will have wealth by millions, slaves by thousands, every luxury and all the power human beings could desire!'

Blake said evenly:

'And you, sir? What will you·have?'

'Most power of all,' said Minott steadily. 'I shall be the emperor of the world!'

He turned his back to them and rode off to lead the way. Maida Haynes was deathly pale as she rode close to Blake. Her hand closed convulsively upon his arm.

'J-jerry!' she whispered. 'I'm—frightened!'

But Lucy Blair rode onward with an odd, excited smile on her face.

The boy ran shouting up to the village. *'Hey, Grampa! Hey, Grampa! Lookit the birds!'* He pointed as he ran. A man looked idly, and stood transfixed. A woman stopped, and stared. Lake Superior glowed bluely off to westward, and the little village most often turned its eyes in that direction. Now though, as the small boy ran shouting of what he had seen, men stared,and women marveled, and the children ran and shouted and whooped in the instinctive excitement of childhood at anything which entrances grown-ups.

Over the straggly pine forests birds were coming. They came in great dark masses. Not by dozens, or by hundreds, or even by thousands. They came in millions, in huge dark clouds which literally obscured the sky. There were two huge flights in sight at the boy's first shouting. There were six in view before he had reached his home and was panting a demand that his elders come and look. And there were others, incredible numbers of others, sweeping onward straight over the village.

Dusk fell abruptly as the first flock passed overhead. The whirring of wings was loud. It made people raise their voices as they asked each other what such birds could possibly be. Daylight again, and again darkness as the flocks poured on. The size of each flock was to be measured not in feet or yards, but in miles of front. Two—three miles of birds, flying steadily in a single enormous mass some four miles deep. Another such mass, and another, and another . . .

'What are they, Grampa? There must be millions of 'em!'

Somewhere, a shot-gun went off. Small things dropped from the sky. Another gun-shot, and another. A rain of bird-shot went up from the village into the mass of whirring wings. And crazily careening small bodies fell down among the houses . . . .

Grampa examined one of them, smoothing its rumpled plumage. He exclaimed. He gasped in excitement.

'It's a wild pigeon! What they used t' call passenger pigeons! Back in '78 there was these birds by billions. Folks said a billion was killed in Michigan that one year! But they' gone now. They' gone like the buffalo. There ain't any more.'

The sky was dark with birds above him. A flock four miles wide and three miles long literally made lights necessary in the village. The air was filled with the sound of wings. Droppings fell like snow. The passenger pigeon had returned to a continent from which it had been absent for more than fifty years. Flocks of passenger pigeons flew overhead in thick masses equalling those seen by Audubon in 1813, when he computed the pigeons flight above Kentucky at hundreds of billions in number. In flocks that were literally innumerable they flew to westward. The sun set, and still the air was filled with the sound of their flying. For hours after darkness fell, the whirring of wings continued without ceasing.

A great open fire licked at the rocks against which it had been built. The horses cropped uneasily at herbage nearby. The smell of fat meat cooking was undeniably savory, but one of the girls blubbered gustily on a bed of leaves. Harris tended the cookery. Tom Hunter brought wood. Blake stood guard a little beyond the firelight, revolvers ready, staring off into the blackness. Minott pored over a topographical map of Virginia. Lucy Blair tried to comfort the blubbering girl.

'Supper's ready,' said Harris. He made even that announcement seem somehow shy and apolegetic.

Minott put down his map. Tom Hunter began to cut great chunks of steaming meat from the haunch of venison. He put them on slabs of bark and began to pass them around. Minott reached out his hand and took one of them. He ate with obvious appetite. He seemed to have abandoned his preoccupation the instant he laid down his map. He was displaying the qualities of a capable leader.

'Hunter,' he observed, 'after you've eaten that stuff, you might relieve Blake. We'll arrange reliefs for the rest of the night. By the way, you men mustn't forget to wind your watches. We'll need to rate them, ultimately.'

Hunter gulped down his food and moved out to Blake's hiding-place. They exchanged low-toned words. Blake came back to the fire. He took the food Harris handed him and began to eat it. he looked at the blubbering girl on the bed of leaves.

'She's just scared,' said Minott. 'Barely slit the skin on her arm. But it is upsetting for a senior at Robinson College to be wounded by a flint arrow-head.'

Blake nodded.

'I heard some noises off in the darkness,' he said curtly. 'I'm not sure, but my impression was that I was being stalked. And I thought I heard a human voice.'

'We may be watched,' admitted Minott. 'But we're out of the path of time in which those Indians tried to ambush us. If any of them followed, they're too bewildered to be very dangerous.'

'I hope so,' said Blake.

His manner was devoid of cordiality, yet there was no exception to be taken to it. From his standpoint, Minott had deliberately gotten the party into a predicament from which there seemed to be no possibility of escape. He had organized it to get it into just that predicament. He was unquestionably the leader of the party, despite his action. Blake made no attempt to undermine his leadership. But Blake himself had some qualifications as a leader, young as he was. Perhaps the most promising of them was the fact that he made no attempt to exercise his talents until he knew as much as Minott of what was to be looked for: what was to be expected. He listened sharply, and then said:

'I think we've digested your lesson of this morning, sir. But—how long is this scrambling of space and time to continue? We left Fredericksburg and rode to the Potomac. It was Chinese territory. We rode back to Fredericksburg, and it wasn't there. Later we hit a highly primitive area with ape-men in it, and then a glacial area, and afterward we encountered Indians who let loose a flight of arrows at us and wounded Bertha Ketterline in the arm. We were nearly out of range at the time, though.'

'They were scared,' said Minott. 'They'd never seen horses before. Our white skins probably upset them, too. And then our guns, and the fact that I killed one, should have chased them off.'

'But—what happened to Fredericksburg. We rode away from it. Why couldn't we ride back?'

'The scrambling process has kept up,' said Minott dryly. 'You remember that queer vertigo? We've had it several times today, and every time, as I see it, there's been an oscillation of the earth we happened to be on. Hm . . . Look!'

He got up and secured the map over which he had been poring. He brought it back and pointed to a heavy penciled line.

'Here's a map of Virginia in our time. The Chinese continent appeared just about three miles north of Fredericksburg. The line of demarcation was, I consider, the line along which the giant sequoias appeared. While in the Chinese time we felt that giddiness and rode back toward Fredericksburg. We came out of the sequoia forest at the same spot as before. I made sure of it. But the continent of our time was no longer there. We rode east and before we reached the border of King George County there was another abrupt change in the vegetation. From a pine country to canelike grass and primitive trees and tapirs and ape-men, which are not exactly characteristic of this part of the world in our time. We saw no signs of any civilization. We turned south, and ran into that heavy fog and the snow beyond it. Evidently, there's a section of a time-path in which Virginia is still subject to a glacial climate.'

Blake nodded. He listened again. Then he said:

'You've three sides of an—an island of time marked there.'

'Just so,' agreed Minott. 'Exactly! In the scrambling process, the oscillating process, there seem to be natural 'faults' in the surface of the earth. Relatively large areas seem to shift back and forth as units from one time-path to another. In my own mind, I've likened them to elevators with many stories. We were on the Fredericksburg 'elevator,' or that section of our time-path, when it shifted. We rote off it onto the Chinese continent. While there, the section we started from shifted again, to another time altogether. When we rode back to where it had been—well—the town of Fredericksburg was in another time-path altogether.'

Blake said sharply:

'Listen!'

A dull, dull mutter sounded far to the north. It lasted for an instant, and died away. There was a crashing of bushes nearby and a monstrous animal stepped alertly into the firelight. It was an elk, but such an elk! It was a giant, a colossal creature. One of the girls cried out affrightedly, and it turned and crashed away into the underbrush.

'There are no elk in Virginia,' said Minott dryly.

Blake said sharply again:

'Listen!'

Again that dull muttering to the north. It grew louder, now. It was an airplane motor. It increased in volume from a dull mutter to a growl, from a growl to a roar. Then the plane shot overhead, the navigation-lights on its wings glowing brightly. It banked steeply and returned. It circled overhead, with a queer effect of helplessness. And then suddenly it dived down . . .

'An aviator from our time,' said Blake, staring toward the sound. 'He saw our fire. He's going to try to make a crash landing in the dark . . . .'

The motor cut off. An instant in which there was only the crackling of the fire and the whistling of wind around gliding surfaces off there in the night. Then a terrific thrashing of branches. A crash . . .

Then a flare of flame. A roaring noise, and the lurid yellow of gasoline-flames spouting skyward.

'Stay here!' snapped Blake. He was on his feet in an instant. 'Harris, Minott! Somebody has to stay with the girls! I'll get Hunter and go help!'

He plunged off into the darkness, calling to Hunter. The two of them forced their way through the underbrush. Minott scowled and got out his revolvers. Still scowling, he slipped out of the firelight and took up the guard-duty Hunter had abandoned.

A gasoline-tank exploded, off there in the darkness. The glare of the fire grew intolerably vivid. The sound of the two young men racing through undergrowth became fainter and died away.

A long time passed. A very long time. Then, very far away, the sound of thrashing bushes could be heard again. The gasoline-flare dulled and dimmed. Figures came slowly back. They moved as if they were carrying something very heavy. They stopped beyond the glow of light from the campfire. Then Blake and Hunter reappeared, alone.

'He's dead,' said Blake curtly. 'Luckily, he was flung clear of the crash before the gas-tanks caught. He came back to consciousness for a couple of minutes before he—died. Our fire was the only sign of human life he'd seen in hours. We brought him over here. We'll bury him in the morning.'

There was silence. Minott's scowl was deep and savage as he came back to the firelight.

'What—what did he say?' asked Maida Haynes.

'He left Washington at five this afternoon,' said Blake shortly. 'From our time, or something like it. All of Virginia across the Potomac vanished at four-thirty, and virgin forest took its place. He went out to explore. At the end of an hour he came back, and Washington was gone. In its place was a fog-bank, with snow underneath. He followed the Potomac down and saw palisaded homesteads with long, oared ships drawn up on shore.'

'Vikings—Norsemen!' said Minott in satisfaction.

'He didn't land. He swept down, following the edge of the bay. He looked for Baltimore. Gone. Once, he's sure, he saw a city, but he was taken sick at about that time and when he recovered, it had vanished. He was heading north again and his gasoline was getting low when he saw our fire. He tried for a crash landing. He'd no flares with him. He crashed—and died.'

'Poor fellow!' said Lucy shakenly.

'The point is,' said young Blake, 'that Washington was in our present time at about four-thirty today. We've got a chance, though a slim one, of getting back! We've got to get to the edge of one of these blocks that go swinging through time, the edge of what Mr. Minott calls a 'time-fault,' and watch it! When the shifts come, we explore as quickly as we can. We've no great likelihood, perhaps, of getting back exactly to our own period, but we can get nearer to it than we are now! Mr. Minott said that somewhere the Confederacy exists. Even that, among people of our own race and speaking our own language, would be better than to be marooned forever among Indians, or among Chinese or Norsemen.'

Minott said harshly:

'Blake, we'd better have this out right now! I give the orders in this party! You jumped quickly when the plane crashed, and you gave orders to Harris and to me, I let you get away with it, but we can have but one leader. I am that leader! See you remember it!'

Blake swung about. Minott had a revolver bearing on his body.

'And you are making plans for a return to our time,' he went on savagely. 'I won't have it! The odds are still that we'll all be killed. But if I do live, I mean to take advantage of it! And my plans do not include a return to an instructorship in mathematics at Robinson College!'

'Well?' said Blake coolly. 'What of it, sir?'

'Just this! I'm going to take your revolvers. I'm going to make the plans and give the orders hereafter. We are going to look for the time-path in which a Viking civilization thrives in America. We'll find it, too, because these disturbances will last for weeks yet. And once we find it, we will settle down among those Norsemen and when space and time are stable again I shall begin the formation of my empire! And you will obey orders or you'll be left afoot while the rest of us go on.'

Blake said very quietly indeed:

'Perhaps, sir, we'd all prefer to be left to our own destinies rather than be merely the tools by which you attain to yours.'

Minott stared at him an instant. His lips tensed.

'It is a pity,' he said coldly. 'I could have used your brains, Blake. But I can't have mutiny. I shall have to shoot you.'

His revolver came up remorselessly.

The British Acadamy of Sciences was in extraordinary session to determine the cause of various untoward events. Its members were weary, bleary-eyed, but still conscious of their dignity and the importance of their task. A venerable, whiskered physicist spoke with fitting definiteness and solemnity.

'. . . And so, gentlemen, I see nothing more that remains to be said. The extraordinary events of the past hours seem to follow from certain facts about our own closed space. The gravitational fields of point 10^{79} particles of matter will close space about such an aggregation. No cosmos can be larger. No cosmos can be smaller. And if we envision the creation of such a cosmos we will observe its galaxies vanish at the instant the 10^{79}th particle adds its own mass to those which were present before it. However, the fact that space has closed about such a cosmos does not imply its annihilation. It means merely its separation from its original space, the isolation of itself in space and time because of the curvature of space due to its gravitational field. And if we assume the existence of more than one area of closed space, we assume in some sense the existence of a hyper? – ? space separating the closed spaces; hyper-spatial coordinates which mark their relative hyper-spatial positions; hyper–'

A gentleman with even longer and whiter whiskers than the speaker said in a loud and decided voice:

'Fiddlesticks! Stuff and nonsense!'

The speaker paused. He glared.

'Sir! Do you refer—'

'I do!' said the gentleman with the longer and whiter whiskers. 'It is stuff and nonsense! Next you'd be saying that in this hyper-space of yours the closed spaces would be subject to hyper-laws, revolve about each other in hyper-orbits regulated by hyper-gravitation, and undoubtedly at times there would be hyper-earthtides or hyper-collisions, producing decidedly hyper-catastrophes!'

'Such, sir,' said the whiskered gentleman on the rostrum, quivering with indignation, 'such is the fact, sir!'

'Then the fact,' rejoined the scientist with the longer and whiter whiskers, 'the fact, sir, makes me sick!'

And as if to prove it, he reeled. But he was not alone in reeling. The entire venerable assembly shuddered in abrupt, nauseating vertigo. And then the British Academy of Sciences adjourned without formality and in a panic. It ran away. Because abruptly there was no longer a rostrum nor any end to its assembly-hall. Where their speaker had been was open air. In the open air was a fire. About the fire were certain brutish figures incredibly resembling the whiskered scientists who fled from them. They roared at the fleeing, venerable men. Snarling, wielding crude clubs, they plunged into the hall of the British Academy of Sciences. It is known that they caught one person—a biologist of highly eccentric views. It is believed that they ate him.

But it has long been surmised that some, at least, of the extinct species of humanity such as the Piltdown and Neanderthal men were cannibals. If in some pathway of time they happened to exterminate their more intelligent rivals—if somewhere *pithecanthropus erectus* survives and *homo sapiens* does not—well, in that pathway of time cannibalism is the custom of society.

With a gasp, Maida Haynes flung herself before Blake. But Harris was even quicker. Apologetic and shy, he had just finished cutting a smoking piece of meat from the venison haunch. He threw it, swiftly, and the searing mass of stuff flung Minott's hand aside at the same instant that it burned it painfully.

Blake was on his feet, his gun out.

'If you pick up that gun sir,' he said rather breathlessly but with unquestionable sincerity, 'I'll but a bullet through your arm!'

Minott swore. He retrieved the weapon with his left hand and thrust it in his pocket.

'You young fool!' he snapped. 'I'd no intention of shooting you. I did intend to scare you thoroughly! Harris, you're an ass! Maida—I shall discuss your action later! The worst punishment I could give the lot of you would be to leave you to yourselves!'

He stalked out of the firelight and off into the darkness. Something like consternation came upon the group. The flow of fire where the plane had crashed flickered fitfully. The base of the dull-red light seemed to widen a little.

'That's the devil!' said Hunter uneasily. 'He does know more about this stuff than we do. If he leaves us, we're messed up!'

'We are,' agreed Blake grimly. 'And perhaps if he doesn't.'

Lucy Blair said:

'I—I'll go and talk to him. He—used to be nice to me in class. And—and his hand must hurt terribly. It's burnt.'

She moved away from the fire, a long and angular shadow going on before her. Minott's voice came sharply.

'Go back! There's something moving out here!'

Instantly after, his revolver flashed. A howl arose, and the weapon flashed again and again. Then there were many crashings. Figures fled. Minott came back to the firelight scornfully.

'Your leadership is at fault, Blake,' he commented sardonically. 'You forgot about a guard. And you were the man who thought he heard voices! They've run away now, though. Indians of course.'

Lucy Blair said hesitantly:

'Could I—could I do something for your hand? It's burnt . . . '

'What can you do?' he asked angrily.

'There's some fat,' she told him. 'Indians used to dress wounds with bear-fat. I suppose deer-fat would do as well.'

He permitted her to dress the burn, though it was far from a serious one. She begged handkerchiefs from the others to complete the job. There was distinct uneasiness all about the campfire. This was no party of adventurers, prepared for anything. It had started out as an outing of undergraduates. Minott scowled as Lucy Blair worked on his hand. Harris looked as apologetic as possible, because he had made the injury. Bertha Ketterline blubbered—less noisily, now, because nobody paid her any attention. Young Blake frowned meditatively at the fire.

The horses moved uneasily. Bertha Ketterline, between her blubberings, sneezed. Lucy felt her eyes smarting. She was the first one to see the spread of the blaze started by the gas-tanks of the aeroplane. Her cry of alarm roused the others.

The plane has crashed a good mile from the campfire. The blazing of its tanks had been fierce but brief. The burning of the wings and chassis-fabric had been short, as well. The fire had died down to seeming dull embers. But there were more than embers ablaze out there now.

The fire had died down, to be sure, but only that it might spread among thick and tangled underbush. It had spread widely on the ground before some climbing vine, blazing, carried flames up to resinous pine–branches overhead. A small but steady wind was blowing. And as Lucy looked off to see the source of smoke which stung her eyes, one tall tree was blazing, a long line of angry red flame crept along the ground, and then at two more, –three more–a dozen points bright fire roared upward toward the sky.

The horses snorted and reared. Minott snapped:

'Harris! Get the horses! Hunter, see that the girls get mounted, and quickly!'

He pointedly gave Blake no orders. He pored intently over his map as more trees and still more caught fire and blazed upward. He stuffed it in his pocket. Blake calmly rescued the haunch of venison, and when Minott sprang into the saddle among the snorting, scared horses, Blake was already by Maida Haynes' side, ready to go.

'We ride in pairs,' said Minott curtly. 'A man and a girl. You men, look after them. I've a flashlight. I'll go ahead. We'll hit the Rappahannock River sooner or later, if we don't get around the fire first–and if we can keep ahead of it.'

They topped a little hillock and saw more of the extent of their danger. In a half-mile of spreading, the fire had gained three times as much breadth. And to their right, the fire even then roared in among the trees of a forest so thick as to be jungle. The blaze fairly raced through it as if the fire made its own wind, which in fact it did. To their left it crackled fiercely in under-brush which, as they fled, blazed higher.

And then, as if to add mockery to their very real danger, a genuinely brisk breeze sprang up suddenly. Sparks and blazing bits of leaves, fragments of ash and small, unsubstantial coals began to fall among them. Bertha Ketterline yelped suddenly as a tiny live coal touched the flesh of her cheek. Harris' horse squealed and kicked as something singed it. The eight of them galloped madly ahead. Trees rose about them. The white beam of Minott's flashlight seemed almost ludicrous in the fierce red glare from behind, but at least it showed the way.

Something large and dark and clumsy lumbered cumbersomely into the space between Grady's statue and the post-office building. The arc-lights showed it clearly, and it was not anything which should be wandering in the streets of Atlanta, Georgia, at any hour of the day or night. A taxicab chauffeur saw it, and nearly tore off a wheel in turning around to get away. A policeman saw it, and turned very pale as he grabbed at his beat-telephone to report it. But there had been too many queer things happening this day for him to suspect his own sanity, and the *Journal* had printed too much news from elsewhere for him to disbelieve his own eyes.

The Thing was monstrous, reptilian, loathsome. It was eighty feet long, of which at least fifty was head and tail and the rest flabby-fleshed body. It may have weighed twenty-five or thirty tons, but its head was not much larger than that of a rather large horse. That tiny head swung about stupidly. The Thing was bewildered. It put down a colossal foot—and water gushed up from a broken water-main beneath the pavement. The Thing did not notice. It moved vaguely, exhaling a dank and musty odor.

The clang of police-emergency cars and the scream of fire-engine sirens filled the air. An ambulance flashed into view—and was struck by a balancing sweep of the mighty tail. The ambulance careened and crashed.

The Thing uttered a plaintive cry, ignoring the damage its tail had caused. The sound was like that of a bleat, a thousand times multiplied. It peered ceaselessly around, seeming to feel trapped by the tall buildings about it, but it was too stupid to retrace its steps for escape.

Somebody screamed in the distance as police-cars and fire-engines reached the spot where the first Thing swayed and peered and moved in quest of escape. Two other Things, smaller than the first, came lumbering after it. Like it, they had monstrous bodies and disportionately tiny heads. One of them blundered stupidly into a hook-and-ladder truck. Truck and beast went down, and the beast bleated like the first.

Then some fool began to shoot. Other fools joined in. Steel—jacketed bullets poured into the mountains of reptilian flesh. Police sub-machine-guns raked the monsters. Those guns were held by men of great daring, who could not help noting the utter stupidity of the Things out of the great swamp which had appeared where Inman Park used to be.

The bullets stung. They hurt. The three beasts bleated and tried bewilderedly and very clumsily indeed to escape. The largest tried to climb a five-story building, and brought it down in sheer wreckage.

Before the last of them was dead—or rather, before it ceased to move its great limbs, because the tail moved jerkily for a long time and its heart was still beating spasmodically when loaded on a city dump-cart next day—before the last of them was dead they had made sheer chaos of three blocks of business buildings in the heart of Atlanta, had killed seventeen men—and the best testimony is that they made not one attempt to fight. Their whole and only thought was to escape. The destruction they wrought and the deaths they caused were due to their clumsiness and stupidity.

The leading horses floundered horribly. They sank to their fetlocks in something soft and spongy. Bertha Ketterline squawked in terror as her mount's motion changed. Blake said crisply in the blackness:

'It feels like ploughed ground. Better use the light again, Mr. Minott!'

The sky behind them glowed redly. The forest fire still trailed them. For miles of front, now, it shot up sparks and flame and a harsh red glare which illumined the clouds of its own smoke.

The flashlight stabbed at the earth. The ground was ploughed. It was softened by the hands of men. Minott kept the light on as little gasps of thankfulness arose. Then he said sardonically:

'Do you know what this crop is? It's lentils. Are lentils grown in Virginia? Perhaps! We'll see what sort of men these may happen to be!'

He swung to follow the line of the furrows. Tom Hunter said miserably:

'If that's ploughed ground, it's a dam' shallow furrow. A one-horse plough'd throw up more dirt than that!'

A light glowed palely in the distance. Every person in the party saw it at the same instant. As if by instinct, the head of every horse swerved for it.

'We'll want to be careful,' said Blake quietly. 'These may be Chinese, too.'

The light was all of a mile distant. They moved over the ploughed ground cautiously . . . .

Suddenly the hoofs of Lucy Blair's horse rang on stone. The noise was startlingly loud. Other horses, following hers, clattered thunderously. Minott flashed down the light again. Dressed stone. Cut stone. A roadway built of dressed stone blocks, some six or eight feet wide. Then one of the horses shivered and snorted. It pranced agitatedly, edging away from something on the road. Minott swept the flashlight beam along the narrow way.

'The only race,' he said dryly, 'that ever built roads like these was the Romans. They made their military roads like this. But they didn't discover America that we know of.'

The beam touched something dark. It came back and steadied. One of the girls uttered a stifled exclamation. The beam showed dead men. One was a man with shield and sword and a helmet such as the soldiers of ancient Rome are pictured as having worn. He was dead. Half his head had been blown off. Lying atop him there was a man in a curious gray uniform. He had died of a sword-wound.

The beam searched around. More bodies. Many Roman-accoutred figures. Four or five men in what looked remarkably like the uniform that might be worn by soldiers of the Confederate Army—if a Confederate Army could be supposed to exist.

'There's been fighting,' said Blake, composedly. 'I guess somebody from the Confederacy—that time-path, say—started to explore what must have seemed a damned strange happening. And these Romans—if they're Romans—jumped them.'

Something came shambling through the darkness. Minott threw the flash-beam upon it. It was human, yes. But it was three parts naked, and it was chained, and it had been beaten horribly, and there were great sores upon its body from other beatings. It was bony and emaciated. The insensate ferocity of sheer despair marked it. It was brutalized by its sufferings until it was just human, barely human, and nothing more.

It squinted at the light, too dull of comprehension to be afraid.

Then Minott spoke, and at his words it automatically groveled in the dirt. Minott spoke harshly, in half-forgotten Latin, and the groveling figure mumbled words which had been barbarous Latin to begin with, and through it bruised lips were still further mutilated.

'It's a slave,' said Minott coldly. 'Strange men—Confederates, I suppose—came from the north today. They fought and killed some of the guards at this estate. This slave denies it, but I imagine he was heading north in hopes of escaping to them. When you think of it, I suppose we're not the only explorers to be caught out of our own time-path by some shift or another.'

He growled at the slave and rode on, still headed for the distant light.

'What—what are you going to do? asked Maida faintly.

'Go on to the villa yonder and ask questions,' said Minott dryly. 'If Confederates hold it, we'll be well received. If they don't, we'll still manage to earn a welcome. I intend to camp along a time-fault and cross over whenever a time-shift brings a Norse settlement in sight. Consequently, I want exact news of places where they've been seen, if such news is to be had.'

Maida Haynes pressed close to Blake. He put a reassuring hand on her arm as the horses trudged on over the soft ground. The fire-light behind them grew brighter. Occasional resinous, coniferous trees flared upward and threw fugitive red glows upon the riding figures. But gradually the glare grew steadier and stronger. The white walls of a rambling stucco house became visible. Out-buildings. Barns. A monstrous structure which looked startingly like a barracks.

It was a farm, an estate, a Roman villa transplanted to the very edge of a wilderness. It was—Blake remembered vaguely—like a picture he had once seen of a Roman villa in England, restored to look as it had looked before Rome withdrew her legions from Britain and left the island to savagery and darkness. There were small mounds of curing hay about them, though which the horses picked their way. Blake suddenly wrinkled his nostrils suspiciously. He sniffed . . . .

Maida pressed close to him. Her lips formed words. Lucy Blair rode close to Minott, glancing up at him from time to time. Harris rode apologetically beside Bertha Ketterline, and Bertha sat her horse as if she were saddle-sore. Tom Hunter clung close to Minott as if for protection, leaving Janet Thompson to look out for herself.

'J-Jerry,' said Maida. 'What—what do you think?'

'I don't like it,' admitted Blake in a low tone. 'But we've got to tag along. I think I smell—'

Then a sudden swarm of figures leaped at the horses. Wild figures, naked figures, sweaty and reeking and almost maniacal figures, some of whom clanked chains as they leaped. A voice bellowed orders at them from a distance, and a whip cracked ominously.

Before the struggle ended, there were just two shots fired. Minott fired them both and wheeled about . . . Then a horse streaked away, and Bertha Ketterline was bawling plaintively, and Tom Hunter babbled hysterically, and Harris swore with complete lack of his customary air of apology.

Blake seemed to be buried under a mass of foul bodies like the rest, but he rasped at his captors in an authoritative tone. They fell away from him, cringing as if by instinct. And then torches appeared suddenly and slaves appeared in their light, slaves of every possible degree of filth and degradation, of every possible racial mixture, but unanimous in a desperate abjectness before their master amid the torch-bearers.

He was a short, fat man, in an only slightly modified toga. he drew it close about his body as the torch-bearers held their flares close to the captives. The torchlight showed the captives, to be sure, but also it showed the puffy, self-indulgent and invincibly cruel features of the man who owned these slaves and the villa. By his pose and the orders he gave in a curiously corrupt Latin, he showed that he considered he owned the captives too.

The deputy from Aisne-le-Sur decided that it had been very wise indeed for him to walk in the fresh air. Paris at night is stimulating. That curious attack of vertigo had come of too much champagne. The fresh air had dispelled the fumes. But it was odd that he did not know exactly where he was, though he knew his Paris well. These streets were strange. The houses were unlike any that he remembered ever having seen before. In the light of the street-lamps—and they were unusual, too!—there was a certain unfamiliar quality about their architecture. He puzzled over it, trying to identify the peculiar *flair* these houses showed.

He became impatient. After all, it was necessary for him to return home some time, even though his wife . . . The deputy from Aisne-le-Sur shrugged. Then he say bright lights ahead. He hastened his steps. A magnificent mansion, brilliantly illuminated.

The clattering of many hoofs. A cavalry escort, forming up before the house. A pale young man emerged, escorted by a tall, fat man who kissed his hand as if in an ecstasy of admiration. Dismounted cavalrymen formed a lane from the gateway to the car. Two young officers followed the pale young man. They were ablaze with decorations. The deputy from Aisne-le-Sur noted subconsciously that he did not recognize their uniforms. The car-door was open and waiting. There was some oddity about the car, but the deputy could not see clearly just what it was.

There was much clicking of heels. Steel blades at salute. The pale young man patiently allowed the fat man to kiss his hand again. He entered the car. The two bemedaled young officers climbed in after him. The car rolled away. Instantly, the cavalry escort clattered with it, before it, behind it, all around it . . . .

The fat man stood on the sidewalk, beaming and rubbing his hands together. The dismounted cavalrymen swung to their saddles and trotted briskly after the others.

The deputy from Aisne-le-Sur stared blankly. He saw another pedestrian, halted like himself to regard the spectacle. He was disturbed by the fact that this pedestrian was clothed in a fashion as perturbingly unfamiliar as these houses, and the spectacle he had witnessed.

'Pardon, *m'sieur,*' said the deputy from Aisne-le-Sur. 'I do not recognize my surroundings. would you tell me—'

'The house,' said the other, caustically, 'is the hotel of M. Le Duc de Montigny. It is possible that one does not know of M. le Duc? Or more especially of Madame la Duchesse, and what she is and where she lives?'

The deputy from Aisne-le-Sur blinked.

'Montigny?—Montigny? No,' he confessed. 'And the young man of the car, whose hand was kissed by—'

'Kissed by M. le Duc?' The stranger stared frankly. '*Mon dieu!* where have you come from that you do not recognize Louis the Twentieth? He has but departed from a visit to Madame his mistress.'

'Louis—Louis the Twentieth!' stammered the deputy from Aisne-le-Sur. 'I—I do not understand!'

'Fool!' said the stranger impatiently, 'that was the King of France, who succeeded his father as a child of ten and has been free of the regency for but six months—and already ruins France!'

The long-distance operator plugged in with a shaking hand, '*Number please . . . I am sorry, sir, but we are unable to connect you with Camden . . . . The lines are down . . . . I am sorry, sir, but we are unable to connect you with Jenkinstown. The lines are down . . . . Very sorry, sir.*'

Another call buzzed and lighted up.

'*Hello . . . I am sorry, sir. We are unable to connect you with Dover. The lines are down . . . .*' Her hands worked automatically. '*Hello . . . I am sorry, but we are unable to connect you with New York. The lines are down . . . . No, sir. We cannot route it by Atlantic City. The lines are down . . . . Yes, sir, I know the telegraph companies cannot guarantee delivery . . . . No, sir, we cannot reach Pittsburg, either, to get a message through . . .*' Her voice quivered. '*No, sir, the lines are down to Scranton . . . . And Harrisburg too. Yes, sir . . . . I am sorry, but we cannot get a message of any sort out of Philadelphia in any*

direction . . . . We have tried to arrange communication by
radio, but no calls are answered . . . .'

She covered her face with her hands for an instant. Then she
plugged in and made a call herself.

'Minnie! Haven't they heard anything? . . . Not anything? . . .
. What? They phoned for more police? . . . The–the operator out
there says there's fighting? . . . She hears a lot of shooting? . . .
What is it, Minnie? Don't they even know? . . . They–they're
using the armored cars from the banks to fight with, too? . . .
But what are they fighting? What? . . . My folks are out there,
Minnie! My folks are out there!'

The doorway of the slave-barracks closed and great bars
slammed against its outer side. Reeking, foul, unbreathable air
closed about them like a wave. Then a babbling of voices all
about. The clanking of chains. The rustling of straw, as if
animals moved. Someone screeched; howled above the others.
He began to gain the ascendancy. There was almost some
attention paid to him, though a minor babbling continued all
about.

Maida said in a strained voice:

'I–I can catch a word here and there. He's–telling these other
slaves how we were captured. It's–Latin–of sorts.'

Bertha Ketterline squalled suddenly, in the absolute dark.

'Somebody touched me!' she bawled. 'A man!'

A voice spoke humorously, somewhere near. There was
laughter. It was the howled laughter of animals. Slaves were
animals, according to the Roman notion. A rustling noise, as if
in the noisome freedom of their barracks the utterly brutalized
slaves drew nearer to the newcomers. There could be sport with
new-captured folk, not yet degraded to their final status.

Lucy Blair cried out in a stifled fashion. There was a sharp,
incisive *'crack.'* Somebody fell. More laughter.

'I knocked him out!' snapped Blake. 'Harris! Hunter! Feel
around for something we can use as clubs! These slaves intend to
haze us, and in their own den there's no attempt to control them!
Even if they kill us they'll only be whipped for it. And the girls–'

Something, snarling, leaped for him in the darkness. The
authoritative tone of Blake's voice was hateful. A yapping sound
arose. Other figures closed in. Reduced to the status of animals,
the slaves of the Romans behaved as beasts when locked in their
monster kennel. The newcomers were hateful if only because
they had been freemen, not slaves. The women were clean and

they were frightened—and they were prey. Chains clanked ominously. Foul breaths tainted the air. The reek of utter depravity, of human beings brought lower than beasts—who at least do not foul their own dens—filled the air. It was utterly dark.

Bertha Ketterline began to blubber noisily. There was the sudden savage sound of a blow meeting flesh. Then pandemonium, and battle, and the sudden terrified screams of Lucy Blair. . . . The panting of men who fought. The sound of blows. A man howled. Another shrieked curses. A woman screamed shrilly . . . .

'*Bang! Bang! Bang-bang!*' Shots outside, a veritable fusillade of them. Running feet. Shouts. The bars at the doorway fell. The great doors opened, and men stood in the opening with whips and torches, bellowing for the slaves to come out and attack something yet unknown. They were being called from their kennel like dogs. Four of the whip-men came inside, flogging the slaves out, while the sound of shots continued. The slaves shrank away, or bounded howling for the open air. But there were three of them who would never shrink or cringe again.

Blake and Harris stood embattled in a corner of the slave-shed. Blake held a heavy beam in a desperate readiness for further battle. Harris, likewise, held a clumsy club. With torch-light upon him, his air of savage defiance turned to one of quaint apology for the dead slave at his feet. And Hunter and two of the girls competed in stark panic for a position behind him. Lucy Blair, dead-white, stood backed against a wall, a jagged fragment of gnawed bone held dagger-wise.

The whips lashed out at them. Voices snarled at them. The whips again . . . Blake struck out furiously, a huge welt across his face. . . .

And revolvers cracked at the great door. Minott stood there, a revolver in each hand, his eyes blazing. A torch-bearer dropped, and the torches flared smokily in the foul mud of the flooring.

'All right,' said Minott fiercely. 'Come on out!'

Hunter was the first to reach him, babbling and gasping. There was sheer uproar all about. A huge grain-shed roared upward in flames. Figures rushed crazily all about it. From the flames came another explosion, then two, then three more.

'Horses over here by the stables,' said Minott, his face dead-white and very deadly indeed. 'They haven't unsaddled them. The stable-slaves haven't figured out the cinches yet. I put some revolver-bullets in the straw when I set fire to the grain-shed. They're going off from time to time.'

A figure with whip and dagger raced around an out-building and confronted them. Minott shot him down. Blake said hoarsely:

'Give me a revolver, Minott! I want to—'

'Horses first!' snapped Minott.

They raced into a courtyard. Two shots. The slaves fled, howling. Out of the courtyard, bent low in the saddle. They swept close to the villa itself. On a little raised terrace before it raged a stout man in an only slightly modified toga. A slave groveled before him. He kicked the abject figure and strode out, shouting commands in a voice that cracked with his fury. The horses loomed up and he shook his fists at the riders, purple with wrath, incapable of fear because of his beastly rage.

Minott shot him dead, swung off his horse, and stripped the toga from him. He flung it to Lucy.

'Take this!' he said savagely. 'By God, I could kill . . . '

There was now no question of his leadership. he led the retreat from the villa. The eight horses headed north again, straight for the luridly flaming forest.

They stopped once more. Behind them, another building of the estate had caught from the first. Sheer confusion ruled. The slaughter of the master disrupted all organization. The roof of the slave-barracks caught. Screams and howls of pure panic reached even the fugitives. Then there were racing, maddened figures rushing here and there in the glare of the fires. . . . Suddenly there was fighting. A howling ululation arose . . . .

Minott worked savagely, stripping clothing from the bodies slain in that incredible, unrecorded conflict of Confederate soldiers and Roman troops, in some unguessable pathway of space and time. Blake watched behind, but Minott curtly commanded the salvaging of rifles and ammunition from the dead Confederates—if they were Confederates.

And as Hunter, still gasping hysterically, took the load of yet unfamiliar weapons upon his horse, the eight felt a certain incredible, intolerable vertigo and nausea. The burning forest ahead vanished from their sight. Instead, there was darkness. A noisome smell came down-wind; dampness and strange, over-powering perfumes of monstrous colored flowers . . . . Some-thing huge and deadly bellowed, in the space before them which smelled like a monstrous swamp.

The liner *City of Baltimore* ploughed through the open sea in the first pale light of dawn. The skipper, up on the bridge, wore a worried frown. The radio operator came up. He carried a sheaf of radiogram forms. His eyes were blurry with loss of sleep.

'Maybe it was me, sir,' he reported heavily. 'I felt awful funny for a while last night, an' then all night long I couldn't raise a station. I checked everything an' couldn't find anything wrong. But just now I felt awful sick an' funny for a minute, an' when I come out of it the air was full o' code. Here's some of it. I don't understand how I coulda been sick so I couldn't hear code, sir, but–'

The skipper said abruptly:

'I had that sick feeling too. Dizzy. So did the man at the wheel. So did everybody. Give me the messages.'

'. . . *News flash. Half of London disappeared at 2:00* A.M. *this morning. . . . ' ' . . . S.S.* Manzanillo *reporting. Sea-serpent which attacked this ship during the night and seized four sailors returned and was rammed five minutes ago. It seems to be dying. Our bow badly smashed. Two forward compartments flooded. . . . ' ' . . . Warning to all mariners. Pack ice seen floating fifty miles off New York harbor. . . . ' ' . . . news flash. Madrid, Spain, has undergone inexplicable change. All buildings formerly known now unrecognizable from the air. Airfields have vanished. Mosques seem to have taken the place of churches and cathedrals. A flag bearing the crescent floats . . . ' ' . . . European population of Calcutta seems to have been massacred. S.S.* Carib *reports harbor empty, all signs of European domination vanished, and hostile mobs lining shore . . . '*

The skipper of the *City of Baltimore* passed his hand over his forehead. He looked uneasily at the radio operator.

'Sparks,' he said gently, 'you'd better go see the ship's doctor. Here! I'll detail a man to go with you.'

'I know,' said Sparks bitterly. 'I guess I'm nuts, all right! But that's what came through!'

He marched away with his head hanging, escorted by a sailor. A little speck of smoke appeared dead ahead. It became swiftly larger. With the combined speed of the two vessels, in a quarter of an hour the other ship was visible. In half an hour it could be made out clearly. It was long, and low, and painted black, but the first incredible thing was that it was a paddle-steamer, with two sets of paddles instead of one, and the after set revolving more swiftly than the forward.

The skipper of the *City of Baltimore* looked more closely through his glasses, and nearly dropped them in stark amazement. The flag flying on the other ship was black and white only.

A beam wind blew it out swiftly. A white deaths-head, with two crossed bones below it. The traditional flag of piracy!

Signals-flags fluttered up in the rigging of the other ship. The skipper of the *City of Baltimore* gazed at them, stunned.

'Gibberish!' he muttered. 'It don't make sense! They aren't International Code. Not the same flags at all!'

Then a gun spoke. A monstrous puff of black-powder smoke billowed over the other ship's bow. A heavy shot crashed into the forepart of the *City of Baltimore*. An instant later it exploded.

'I'm crazy too!' said the skipper dazedly.

A second shot. A third and fourth. The black steamer sheered off and started to pound the *City of Baltimore* in a business-like fashion. Half the bridge went overside. The forward cargo-hatch blew up with a cloud of smoke from an explosion underneath.

Then the skipper came to. He roared orders. The big ship heeled as it came around. It plunged forward at vastly more than its normal cruising speed. The guns on the other ship doubled and redoubled their rate of fire. Then the black ship tried to dodge. But it had not time.

The *City of Baltimore* rammed it. At the very last moment the skipper felt certain of his own insanity. But it was too late to save the other ship then. The *City of Baltimore* cut it in two.

The pale gray light of dawn filtered down through an incredible thickness of foliage. it was a subdued, a tiny feeble twilight when it reached the earth where a tiny campfire burned. The fire gave off thick smoke from water-soaked wood. Hunter tended it, clad in ill-assorted remnants of a gray uniform. Harris worked patiently at a rifle, trying to understand exactly how it worked. It was unlike any rifle with which he was familiar. The bolt-action was not really a bolt-action at all, and he'd noticed that there was no rifling in the barrel. He was trying to understand how the long bullet was made to revolve. Harris, too, had substituted Confederate gray for the loin-cloth flung him for sole covering when with the others he was thrust into the slave-pen of the Roman villa. Minott sat with his head in his hands, staring at the opposite side of the stream. On his face was all bitterness.

Lucy Blair darted furtive, somehow wistful glances at him. Presently she moved to sit beside him. She asked him an anxious question. The other two girls sat by the fire. Bertha Ketterline was slouched back against a tree-fern trunk. Her head had fallen back. She snored. With the exception of Blake, all of them were barefoot. Those who had been enslaved had, of course, been plundered of all their possessions.

Blake came back to the fire. He nodded across the little stream.

'We seem to have come to the edge of a time-fault, sir,' he observed hopefully. 'This side of the stream is definitely carboniferous-period vegetation. The other side isn't as primitive, but it isn't of our time, anyhow. Mr Minott!'

Minott lifted his head.

'Well?' he demanded.

'We've been here for hours, sir,' said Blake. 'And there's been no further change in time-paths that we've noticed. Is it likely that the scrambling of time and space is ended, sir? If it has, and the time-paths stay jumbled, we'll never find our world intact, of course, but as you said, we can hunt for colonies or even cities of our own kind of people.'

Minott shrugged.

'I expect,' he said deliberately, 'that the oscillations of time-paths will keep up for at least two weeks—if we aren't all annihilated.'

Lucy Blair said something in a low tone. She regarded him worshipfully.

'No,' he snapped. 'I find that I am a fool—or I was!—I thought that young men, at least, even of Robinson College, would want things they did not have! But they're already frozen into the pattern of law-abiding citizens. They'd be useless. That business at the villa was proof enough! Attacked, what did they do? They used their fists! Beautiful, civilized, tame-animal thinking! They'd be no good to me! I was the only one who fired a pistol! They didn't have time to think—so they fought like little boys!'

Lucy murmured again. Minott glowered.

'I am a faculty member of Robinson College,' he said in exquisite sarcasm. 'You students are in my care. I'd make kings of the men—I'd make them lords of men and nations!—but they want to go back and be insurance salesmen. So back they go!'

'Really, sir,' said Blake defensively.

'Hush!' said Lucy. 'He's going to explain to you so you can tell everybody what's happened. Listen!'

Blake had already unconsciously reassumed some of his former respectful manner. His capture and scornful dismissal to the status of slave had shaken all his self-confidence. Before, he had felt himself not only a member of a superior race, but as a college student a superior member of that race. In being enslaved he had been both degraded and scorned. His vanity was still gnawed at by that memory, and his self-confidence shattered by the fact that he had been able to kill two utterly brutalized slaves in the slave-barracks, without in the least contributing to his own freedom. Now he winced at the scorn in Minott's voice.

'We—we know that gravity warps space,' said Minott harshly. 'From observation we have been able to discover the amount of warping produced by a given mass. We can calculate the mass necessary to warp space so that it will close in completely, making a closed universe which is unreachable and undetectable in any of the dimensions we know. We know, for example, that if two gigantic star-masses of a certain combined mass were to rush together, at the instant of their collision there would not be a great cataclysm. They would simply vanish. But they would not cease to exist. They would merely cease to exist in our space and time. They would have created a space and time of their own.'

Harris said apologetically:

'Like crawling in a hole and pulling the hole in after you. I read something like that in a Sunday supplement, once, sir.'

Minott nodded. He went on scornfully.

'Now, imagine that two such universes have been formed. They are both invisible from the space and time in which they originated. Each exists in its own space and time, just as our universe does. But each must also exist in a certain—well—hyper-space, because if closed spaces are separated, there must be some sort of something in between them, else they would be together.'

'Really,' said Blake, 'You're talking about something we can infer, but ordinarily can't possibly learn anything about by observation.'

'I did!' said Minott. 'From published observations! If our space is closed, we must assume that there are other closed spaces. And don't forget that other closed spaces would be as real—are as real—as our closed space is.'

'But what does it mean?' asked Blake.

'If there are other closed spaces like ours, and they exist in a common medium—the hyper-space from which they and we alike are sealed off—they might be likened to—say—stars and planets in our space, which are separated by space and yet affect each other through space. Since these various closed spaces are separted by a logically necessary hyper-space, it is at least probable that they should affect each other through that hyper-space.'

Blake said slowly:

'Then these shiftings of time-paths—well—they're the result of something on the order of tidal strains? If another star got close to the sun, our planets would crack up from tidal strains alone. You're suggesting that another closed space has gotten close to our closed space in hyper-space. . . . It's awfully confused, sir.'

'I have calculated it,' said Minott harshly. 'The odds are three to one that space and time and universe, every star and every galaxy in the skies, will be obliterated in one monstrous destruction when even the past will never have been! But there is one chance in four, and I planned to take full advantage of it. I planned—I planned—'

Then he stood up suddenly. His figure straightened. He struck his hands together savagely.

'By God, it can still be done if you're more than worms! We have arms! We have books, technical knowledge, formulas—the cream of the technical knowledge of earth packed in our saddle-bags! Listen to me! We cross this stream now! When the next change comes, we strike across whatever time-path takes the place of this. We make for the Potomac, where that aviator saw Norse ships drawn up! I have Anglo-Saxon and early Norse vocabularies in the saddle-bags! We'll make friends with them! We'll teach them! We'll lead them! We'll make ourselves masters of the world—'

Harris said apologetically:

'I'm sorry, sir, but I promised Bertha I'd take her home, if it was humanly possible. I have to do it. I can't join you in becoming an emperor, even if the breaks are right.'

Minott scowled at him.

'Hunter?'

'I—I'll do as the others do,' said Hunter uneasily. 'I—I'd rather go home. . . . '

'Fool!' snarled Minott.

Lucy Blair said loyally:

'I—I'd like to be an empress, Mr. Minott'

Maida Haynes stared at her. She opened her mouth to speak. Blake absently pulled a revolver from his pocket and looked at it meditatively as Minott clenched and unclenched his hands. The veins stood out on his forehead. He began to breathe heavily.

'Fools!' he roared. 'Fools! You'll never be more than shoe-clerks or professors! Yet you throw away—'

Swift, sharp, agonizing vertigo smote them all. The revolver fell from Blake's hands. He looked up. Familiar pine and fields. More—houses, Familiar ones. A dead silence fell. They hardly dared to breathe. Then Blake said shakily:

'That—' He swallowed. 'That is King George Court House, in King George County, in Virginia, in our time I think—Hell! Let's get across that stream!'

He feverishly seized Maida. He carried her toward the stream in his arms. Minott said desperately:

'Wait!'

He looked at them in a sort of bitter hope.

'I offer you, for the last time—I offer riches, power—lordships—everything that any man could long for—'

Blake waded across and put Maida safely down upon the shore. Hunter was splashing frantically through the shallow water. Blake splashed back. He rounded up the horses, in trembling haste. He loaded the salvaged weapons over a saddle. He shepherded the three remaining girls across. Hunter was out of sight. He had fled toward the painted buildings of the village. Blake drove the horses across. Minott watched. His eyes blazed with scorn.

'Better come along,' said Blake, generously.

'And be an instructor in mathematics?' Minott laughed. 'No! I stay here!'

Blake considered. Minott was a strange, an unprepossessing figure. Standing against the background of a carboniferous jungle, he was even pitiable—to Blake. But he was utterly contempuous of the younger men.

'Wait, sir,' said Blake in conscious nobility.

He stripped the saddle-bags from six of the horses. He heaped them on the remaining two. He led them back across the stream. Minott regarded him with implacable scorn.

'You'll graduate,' he said, biting off each word separately. 'You'll get a job. You'll spend your life paying bills, when you could have sailed a long-ship! You'll be a pedestrian—when you could have been a king. But I won't! I may die, but if I don't—'

Blake shrugged. He went back across the stream and remounted. Lucy Blair looked doubtfully at the lonely figure of Minott, whom probably nobody else in all the world had ever admired.

A faint, almost imperceptible dizziness affected all of them. It passed. By instinct they looked back at the tall jungle. It stood unchanged. Minott laughed at them. Bitterly.

'I—I've got something to say to him!' panted Lucy Blair suddenly. 'D-don't wait for me!'

She rode for the stream. Again that faint, nearly imperceptible dizziness. Lucy slapped her horse's flank frantically. Maida cried:

'Come back, Lucy! It's going to shift—'

'That's what I want,' cried Lucy joyfully, over her shoulder. 'I mean to stay—'

She was half-way across the stream. More than half-way. Then the vertigo struck all of them.

Everyone knows the rest of the story. For two weeks longer there were still occasional shiftings of the time-paths. But gradually, it became noticeable that the number of 'time-faults'—in Minott's phrase—were decreasing in number. At the most drastic period, it has been estimated that no less than twenty-five per cent of the whole earth's surface was at a given moment at some other time-path than its own. We do not know of any portion of the earth which did not vary from its own time-path at some period of the disturbance.

That means, of course, that practically one hundred per cent of the earth's population encountered the conditions caused by the earth's extraordinary oscillations sidewise in time. Our scientists are no longer quite as dogmatic as they used to be. The dialectics of philosophy have received a serious jolt. Basic ideas in botany, zoology, and even philology have been altered by the new facts made available by our unintended travels.

Because of course it was the fourth chance which happened, and the earth survived. In our time-path, at any rate. The six survivors of Minott's exploring-party reached King George Court House barely a quarter of an hour after the time-shift which carried Minott and Lucy Blair out of our space and time forever. Blake and Harris searched for a means of transmitting the information they possessed to the world at large. Through a lonely radio amateur a mile from the village, they sent out Minott's theory on short waves. Shorn of Minott's pessimistic analysis of the probabilities of survival, it went swiftly to every part of the world then in its proper relative position. It was valuable, in that it checked explorations in force which in some places had been planned. It prevented, for example, a punitive military expedition from going beyond a time-fault in Georgia, past which a scalping-party of Indians from an uncivilized America had retreated. It prevented the dispatch of a squadron of destroyers to find and sieze Leifsholm, from which a Viking foray had been made upon North Centerville, Massachusetts. A squadron of mapping planes was recalled from reconnaissance work above a carboniferous swamp in West Virginia, just before the time-shift which would have isolated them forever.

Some things, though, no knowledge could prevent. It has been estimated that no less than five thousand daring persons in the United States are missing from their own space and time through having adventured into the strange landscapes which appeared so suddenly. Many must have perished. Some, we feel sure, have come in contact with one or another of the distinct civilizations we now know to exist. Conversely, we have gained inhabitants from other time-paths. Two cohorts of the Twenty-Second Roman Legion were left upon our soil near Ithaca, New York. Four families of Chinese peasants essayed to pick berries in what they considered a miraculous strawberry patch in Virginia, and remained there when that section of ground returned to its proper *milieu*. A Russian village remains in Colorado. A French trading settlement in the—in their time undeveloped—Middle West. A part of the northern herd of buffalo has returned to us, two hundred thousand strong, together with a village of Cheyenne Indians who had never seen either horses or firearms. The passenger pigeon, to the number of a billion and a half birds, has returned to North America.

But our losses are heavy. Besides those daring individuals who were carried away upon the strange territories they were exploring, there are the overwhelming disasters affecting Detroit, and Tokyo, and Rio de Janeiro. The last two we understand. When the causes of oscillation sidewise in time were removed, most of the earth-sections returned to their proper positions in their own time-paths. But not all. There is a section of Post-Cambrian jungle left in eastern Tennessee. The Russian village in Colorado has been mentioned, and the French trading-post in the Middle West. In some cases sections of the oscillating time-paths remained in new positions, remote from their points of origin.

That is the cause of the utter disappearance of Rio and Tokyo. Where Rio stood an untouched jungle remains. It is of our own geological period, but it is simply from a path in time in which Rio de Janeiro never happened to be built. On the site of Tokyo stands a forest of extraordinarily primitive type, about which botanists and paleontologists still debate. Somewhere, in some space and time, Tokyo and Rio yet exist and their people still live on. But Detroit . . . .

We still do not understand what happened to Detroit. It was upon an oscillating segment of earth. It vanished from our time, and it returned to our time. But its inhabitants did not come back with it. The city was empty; deserted as if the hundreds of thousands of human beings who lived in it had simply evaporated into the air. There have been some few signs of struggle seen, but they may have been the result of panic. The city of Detroit returned to its own space and time untouched, unharmed, unlooted and undisturbed. But no living thing, not even a domestic animal or a caged bird, was in it when it came back. We do not understand that at all.

Perhaps if Minott had returned to us, he could have guessed at the answer to the riddle. What fragmentary papers of his that have been shown to refer to the time-upheaval have been of inestimable value. Our whole theory of what happened depends upon the papers Minott left behind as too unimportant to bother with–plus, of course, Blake's and Harris' account of his explanations to them. Tom Hunter can remember little that is useful. Maida Haynes has given some worth-while data, but it covers ground we have other observers for. Bertha Ketterline also reports very little.

The answers to a myriad problems yet elude us, but in the saddle-bags given to Minott by Blake as preparation for his desperate journey through space and time, the solutions to many must remain. Our scientists labor diligently to understand and to elaborate the figures Minott thought of trivial significance. And throughout the world many, many minds turn longingly to certain saddle-bags, loaded on a led horse, following Minott and Lucy Blair through unguessable landscapes, to unimaginable adventures, with revolvers and text-books as their armament for the conquest of a world.

ALAS, ALL THINKING

Harry Bates

1

Strictly confidential. (This is dynamite! Be careful who sees it!)

From: Charles Wayland.

To: Harold C. Pendleton, Chairman of the Human Salvage Section of the National Lunacy Commission.

Subject: Report on the conversations and actions of Harlan T. Frick on the night of June 7, 1963.

Method: I used the silent pocket dictograph you gave me; and my report is a literal transcription of the record obtained, with only such additions of my own as are needed to make it fully intelligible.

Special Notes: (a) The report, backed by the dictograph record, may be considered as one-third of the proof that your 'amateur neurosis detective' Wayland is not himself a subject for psychopathic observation, since this fantastic report can be corroborated in all its details by Miles Matson, who was with us that night, and would be, I think, by Frick himself.

(b) Pending any action by you, I have cautioned both Matson and Frick to maintain absolute silence with regard to the conversation and events covered. They may be trusted to comply.

(c) So that you may follow the report more intelligently, I feel that it is necessary to say here, in advance, that Frick will be proved to be wholly sane, but that never again may his tremendous talents be utilized for the advancement of science. As his friend, I have to recommend that you give up all hope of salvaging him, and leave him to go his prodigal, pleasure-seeking way alone. You might think of him as a great scientist who has died. He is reasonable, but human, and I see his waste of his life as humanly reasonable. You will see, too.

Report: The amazing events of the evening started in a manner commonplace enough at the Lotus Gardens, where I had made a dinner engagement with Frick and our old mutual friend, Miles Matson, chemist and recent author of an amusing mathematical theory of inverse variables as applied to feminine curves, which Frick had expressed a desire to hear. I should have preferred to observe Frick alone, but was not sure that alone I would be able to hold the interest of his restless, vigorous mind for a third time within two weeks. Ten minutes of boredom and my psychological observations would come to a sudden end, and you would have to find and impress someone else to do your psychological sleuthing.

I got to our reserved table fifteen minutes early to get settled, set up the dictograph in my pocket, and review for the last time my plans. I had three valuable leads. I had discovered (see my reports of May 26th and May 30th) peculiar, invariable, marked emotional reactions in him when the words 'brains', 'human progress', and 'love' were mentioned. I was sure that this was symptomatic. And I hoped to get nearer the roots of his altered behavior pattern by the common method of using a prepared and memorized list of words, remarks, and questions, which I would spring on him from time to time.

I could only trust that Frick was not too familiar with psychoanalysis, and so would not notice what I was doing.

I confess that for a moment while waiting I was swept with the feeling that it was hopeless, but I soon roused from that. One can do no more than try, and I was going to try my hardest. With another I might have been tempted to renege, but never with Frick. For he was my old friend of college days, and so eminently worth saving! He was still so young; had so much to give to mankind!

I guessed once more at the things that might have altered his pattern so. A physicist, perhaps the most brilliant and certainly the most promising in the world, enters his laboratory after his graduation from college and for eleven years hardly so much as sticks his nose outside its door. All the while he sends from it a stream of discoveries, new theories, and integrations of old laws the like of which has never before been equaled; and then this same physicist walks out of his laboratory, locks the door, shuns the place, and for two years devotes himself with casual abandon to such trivialisms of the modern idler as golfing, clothes, travel, fishing, nightclubs, and so on. Astounding is a weak word for this spectacle. I could think of nothing that would remotely suit.

Miles Matson arrived a minute early–which was, for him, a phenomenon, and showed how the anticipation of dining with Frick had affected him. Miles is forty-five, short, solid, bald–but then I needn't describe him.

'He'll come?' were his first words, before seating himself on the other side of the table.

'I think so,' I assured him, smiling a little at his apparent anxiety. He looked a little relieved, and fished from the jacket of his dinner clothes that abominable pipe he smokes whenever and wherever he pleases, and be damned to frowning head waiters. He lighted it, took a few quick puffs, then leaned back, smiled, and volunteered frankly, 'Charles, I feel like a little boy about to have dinner with the principal of his school.'

I could understand that, for most scientists would feel that way where Frick was concerned. I smiled, too, and chaffed him.

'What–you and that pipe intimidated by a mere playboy?'

'No–by the mystery behind the playboy,' was his serious rejoinder. 'What's your guess at the solution? Quick, before he comes,' he asked earnestly.

I shrugged my shoulders. Miles, of course, was not in my confidence.

'Could it be a woman?' he went on. 'I haven't heard of any one woman. A disappointment in his work? Some spoiled-child reaction? Is he crazy'? What's made the change?'

If I only knew!

'Frick, further than any man alive, has touched out to the infinite unknowable,' he continued almost grumbling, 'and I want to know how such a man can trade his tremendous future for a suit of evening clothes!'

'Perhaps he is just relaxing a little,' I suggested with a smile.

'Ah, of course–relaxing,' he answered sarcastically. 'For two years!'

I knew at once Frick had heard what we had been saying, for at that moment I looked up and around just in time to see him, lean and graceful in his dinner clothes, his mouth twisted with amusement, stepping past the head waiter to his place at the table. Miles and I rose; and we must have shown confusion, for one simply did not mention that topic in Frick's hearing. But he showed no offense–indeed, he seemed in unusually good spirits– for he lightly acknowledged our greeting, waved us back in our places, and, seating himself, added to our dialogue.

'Yes, for two years. I will for forty-two more!'

This opening of the conversation threw me unexpectedly off

stride, but I remembered to switch on the dictograph, and then siezed the opportunity to ask what otherwise I would never have dared.

'Why?'

Still he showed no offense, but instead, surprisingly, indulged in a long, low chuckle that seemed to swell up as from a spring of inexhaustible deliciousness. He answered cryptically, bubblingly, enjoying our puzzlement with every word.

'Because Humpty Dumpty had a great fall. Because thought is withering, and sensation sweet. Because I've recovered my sense of humor. Because 'why' is a dangerous word, and makes people unhappy. Because I have had a glimpse of the most horrible cerebral future. Yes!' He laughed, paused for a moment, then said in a lower voice with dramatic impressiveness, 'Would you believe it? I have terminated the genus Homo Sapiens.'

2

He was not drunk, and, as you will see, not crazy—though I would not have bet any money on it just then. His mood was only one of extraordinary good humor. Vastly amused at our reaction to his wild words, he allowed himself to shock us, and did it again and again. I might say here that it is my opinion that all the revelations of the night were, in the main, the result of Frick's sudden notion to shock us, and that no credit whatever is due me and my intended plan of psychological attack.

Miles' face showed blank dismay. Frick ceased chuckling and his gray eyes gleaming, enjoyed our discomfiture in quiet for a moment. Then he added, 'No. Strictly speaking, there is one piece of unfinished business. A matter of one murder. I was sort of dallying with the idea of committing it tonight, and finishing off the whole affair. Would you two like to be in on it?'

Miles looked as if he would like to excuse himself. He coughed, smiled unhappily, glanced doubtfully at me. I at once decided that if Frick was going to attempt murder, I was going to be on hand to prevent it. I suppose that the desperate resolution showed in my face, for Frick, looking at me, laughed outright. Miles then revived enough to smile wanly at Frick and suggest he was joking. He added, 'I'm surprised that anyone with the brains you have should make so feeble a joke?'

At the word 'brains' Frick almost exploded.

'Brains!' he exclaimed. 'Not me! I'm dumb! Dumb as the

greasy-haired saxophone player over there! I understand that I used to have brains, but that's all over; it's horrible; let's not think about it. I tell you I'm dumb, now—normally, contentedly dumb!'

Miles did not know how to understand Frick any more than did I. He reminded him, 'You used to have an I.Q. of 248–'

'I've changed!' Frick interrupted. He was still vehement, but I could see that he was full of internal amusement.

'But no healthy person's intelligence can drop much in the course of a few years,' Miles objected strongly.

'Yes—I'm dumb!' Frick reiterated.

My opportunities lay in keeping him on the subject. I asked him, 'Why have you come to consider the possession of brains such an awful thing?'

' "Ah, to have seen what I have seen, know what I know"!' he quoted.

Miles showed irritation. 'Well, then, let's call him dumb?' he said, looking at me. 'To insist on such a stupid jest?'

I took another turn at arousing Frick. 'You are, of course, speaking ironically out of some cryptic notion that exists only in your own head; but whatever this notion, it is absurd. Brains in quantity are the exclusive possession of the human race. They have inspired all human progress they have made us what we are today, masters of the whole animal kingdom, lords of creation. Two other things have helped—the human hand and human love; but even above these ranks the human brain. You are only ridiculous when you scoff at its value.'

'Oh, love and human progress!' Frick exclaimed, laughing. 'Charles, I tell you brains will be the ruination of the human race,' he answered with great delight.

'Brains will be the salvation of the human race!' Miles contradicted with heat.

'You make a mistake, a very common mistake, Miles,' Frick declared, more seriously. 'Charles is of course right in placing man at the top of creation, but you're very wrong in assuming he will always remain there. Consider. Nature made the cell, and after a time the cell became a fish; and that fish was the lord of creation. The very top. For a while. For just a few million years. Because one day a fish crawled out of the sea and set about becoming a reptile. He became a magnificent one. Tyrannosaurus Rex was fifty feet long, twenty high; he had teeth half a foot long, and feet armed with claws that were terrible. No other creature could stand against him; he had speed, size, power and ferocity; *he* became the lord of creation.

'What happened to the fish? He had been the lord of creation, but, well, he never got anywhere. What of Tyrannosaurus Rex? He, too, was the lord of creation, but he, alas, is quite, quite extinct.

'Nature tried speed with the fish, then size with the saurians. Neither worked; the fish got stuck, the saurian died off. But did she quit experimenting at that? Not at all—she tried mobility, and we got the monkey. The first monkey swung from limb to limb screeching, 'I am the lord of creation!' and, by Jove, he was! But he could not know that one day, after a few millions of years, one of his poor relations would go down on the ground, find fire, invent writing, assume clothing, devise modern inconveniences, discover he had lost his tail, and crow, 'Behold, I am the lord of creation!'

'Why did this tailless monkey have his turn? Because his makeup featured brains? You will bellow yes—but I hear Mother Nature laughing at you. For you are only her *latest* experiment! The lord of creation! That you are—but only for a little while! Only for a few million years!'

Frick paused, his eyes flashed, his nostrils distended contemptuously. 'How dare man be so impertinent as to assume nature has stopped experimenting!' he exclaimed at length.

In the quiet which followed this surprising outburst I could see Miles putting two and two together. But he took his time before speaking. He relighted his pipe and gave it a good, fiery start before removing it from his mouth and saying, almost in a drawl, 'It amounts to this, then. Anticipating that nature is about to scrap brains and try again along new lines, you choose to attempt immortality by denying your own undoubted brains and trying to be the first to jump in the new direction.'

Frick only laughed. 'Wrong again, Miles,' he said 'I'm just standing pat.'

'To go back a little,' I said to Frick; 'it seems to me you're assuming far too much when you tell us that the human race is not the last, but only the most recent of nature's experiments.'

The man acted almost shocked. 'But have you forgotten what I told you just a little while ago? I said I have *terminated* the genus Homo Sapiens!'

Miles snorted with disgust. I was alarmed. Miles tried sarcasm. 'Have you and Mother Nature already decided, then, what the next lord of creation is to be?'

'I myself have nothing to say about it,' Frick replied with assumed naiveté, 'nor do I know what it will be. I could find out, but I doubt if I ever shall. It's much more fun not to know—don't you think? Though, if I had to guess,' he added, 'I should say she will feature instinct.'

This was too much for Miles. He started to rise, saying, as he pushed his chair back, 'This is enough. You're either crazy or else you're a conceited fool! Personally, I think it's both!'

But Frick held him with a gesture, and in a voice wholly sincere said, 'Sit down, Miles; keep your shirt on. You know very well I neither lie nor boast. I promise to prove everything I have said.'

Miles resumed his seat and looked at Frick almost sneeringly as he went on.

'You're quite right about my being a fool, though. I was one; oh, a most gorgeous fool! But I am not conceited. I am so little conceited that I offer to show you myself in what must surely be the most ridiculous situation that a jackass or a monkey without a tail has ever been in. I'll exchange my dignity for your good opinion; you'll see that I'm not crazy; and then we'll have the most intelligent good laugh possible to Genus Homo. Yes? Shall we?'

Miles gave me a look which clearly expressed his doubt of Frick's sanity. Frick, seeing, chuckled and offered another inducement.

'And I'll throw in, incidentally, a most interesting murder'

Our friend was completely disgusted. 'We came here to eat,' he said. 'Let's get it over with.' And with the words he picked up the menu which had been lying in front of him all this time. Frick looked at me.

'I'm not hungry,' he said, 'Are you?'

I wasn't. I shook my head.

'Shall we two go, then?'

I hesitated. I was not overanxious to accompany, alone, a madman on a mission of murder. But I caught Miles' eye, and like the noble he is, he said he'd come too. Frick smiled softly.

3

Ten minutes later we had made the short flight along the north shore to Glen Cove, where Frick has his estate, and were escorted by him into a small, bare room on the second floor of the laboratory building which adjoins his beautiful home.

While we stood there wondering, Frick went into an adjoining room and returned with two chairs, and then, in two more trips, with a third chair and a tray on which rested a large thermos bottle and a tea service for three. The chairs he arranged facing each other in an intimate group, and the tray he set on the floor by the chair he was to take himself.

'First I have to tell a rather long story.' he explained. 'The house would be more comfortable, but this room will be more convenient.'

Frick was now a changed man. His levity of before was gone; tense, serious lines appeared on his rugged face; his great head lowered with the struggle to arrange thoughts that were difficult, and perhaps painful, to him. When he spoke, it was softly, in a voice likewise changed.

My dictograph was still turned on.

'Charles, Miles,' Frick began, 'forgive me for my conduct back in the Gardens. I had so much on my mind, and you were so smugly skeptical, that the inclination to overpower you with what I know was irrestible. I had not expected to make any of these revelations to you. I offered to on impulse; but do not fear, I shall not regret it. I think—I see now that I have been carrying a very heavy load—

'What I have to say would fill a large book, but I will make it as short as I can. You will not believe me at first, but please be patient, for proof will eventually be forthcoming. Every single thing I said to you is true, even to the murder I must commit—'

He paused, and seemed to relax, as if tired. Unknown black shadows closed over my heart. Miles watched him closely, quite motionless. We waited. Frick rubbed the flat of his hand slowly over his eyes and forehead, then let it drop.

'No,' he said at length, 'I have never been conceited. I don't think so. But there was a time when I was very proud of my intelligence. I worked; I accomplished things that seemed to be important; I felt myself a leader in the rush of events. Work was enough, I thought; brain was the prime tool of life; and with my brain I dared try anything. Anything! I dared try to assemble the equation of a device that would enable me to peer into the future! And when I thought I had it, I started the construction for that device! I never finished it, and I never shall, now; but the attempt brought Pearl to me—

'Yes,' he added, as if necessary that he convince himself, 'I am certain that had I not attempted that, Pearl would not have come. Back through the ages she has somehow felt me out—don't ask me how, for I don't know—and through me chose to enter for a brief space this, our time.

'I was as surprised as you would have been. I was working in this very room, though then it was twice as large and fairly cluttered with clumsy apparatus I have since had removed. I had been working feverishly for months; I was unshaven, red-eyed and dirty—and there, suddenly, she was. Over there, beyond that door at which I'm pointing. She was in a golden-glowing cylinder whose bottom hung two feet off the floor. For a moment she stood suspended there; and then the glow disappeared and she stepped through to the floor.

'You do not believe me? Well of course, I don't expect you to. But there will be proof. There will be proof.

'I was surprised, but somehow I wasn't much frightened. The person of my visitor was not intimidating. She was just a barefooted young woman, very slender, of average height, clad in a shiny black shift which reached her knees. I cannot say she was well formed. Her body was too thin, her hips too narrow, her head too large. And she was miles from being pretty. Her hair and eyes were all right; they were brown; but her face was plain and flat, with an extraordinary and forbidding expression of dry intellectuality. The whole effect of her was not normal, yet certainly not weird; she was just peculiar, different—baroque.

'She spoke to me in English. In nonidiomatic English with the words run together and an accent that was atrocious! She asked severely, 'Do you mind too much this intrusion of mine?'

'Why—why no!' I said when I had recovered from the shock of the sound of her speech. 'But are you real, or just an illusion?'

'I do not know,' she replied. 'That is a tremendous problem. It has occupied the attention of our greatest minds for ages. Excuse me, sir.' And with these last words she calmly sat herself down on the floor, right where she was, and appeared to go off into deep thought!

'You can imagine my astonishment! She sat there for a full two minutes, while I gaped at her in wonder. When she rose again to her feet she finished with, 'I do not know. It is a tremendous problem.'

'I began to suspect that a trick was being played on me, for all this was done with the greatest seriousness.

'Perhaps there is a magician outside,' I suggested.

'I am the magician,' she informed me.

'Oh!' I said ironically. 'I understand everything now.'

'Or no, fate is the magician,' she went on as if in doubt. 'Or no, I am—a very deep problem—' Whereupon she sat down on the floor and again went off into meditation!

'I stepped around her, examining her from all angles, and, since she was oblivious to everything outside of herself, I made a cursory examination of the thing she had come in on. It looked simple enough—a flat, plain, circular box, maybe four feet in diameter and six inches deep, made of some sort of dull-green metal. Fixed to its center, and sticking vertically upward, was a post of the same stuff capped with a plate containing a number of dials and levers. Around the edge of the upper surface of the box was a two-inch bevel of what seemed to be yellow glass. And that was all—except that the thing continued to remain fixed in the air two feet off the floor!

'I began to get a little scared. I turned back to the girl and again looked her over from all sides. She was so deep in her thoughts that I dared to touch her. She was real, all right!

'My touch brought her to her feet again.

'You have a larger head than most men,' she informed me.

'Who are you anyway?' I asked with increasing amazement. She gave me a name that it took me two days to memorize, so horrible was its jumble of sounds. I'll just say here that I soon gave her another—Pearl—because she was such a baroque—and by that name I always think of her.

' How did you get in?' I demanded.

'She pointed to the box.

'But what is it?' I wanted to know.

'You have no name for it,' she replied. 'it goes to yesterday, to last year, to the last thousand years—like that,'

'You mean it's a time traveler?' I asked, astounded. 'That you can go back and forth in time?'

'Yes,' she answered, 'I stopped to see you, for you are something like me.'

'You wouldn't misinform me?' I asked sarcastically, feeling I must surely be the victim of some colossal practical joke.

'Oh, no, I would not misinform you,' she replied aridly.

'I was very skeptical. 'What do you want here?' I asked.

'I should like you to show me the New York of your time. Will you, a little?'

'If you'll take me for a ride on that thing, and it works, I'll show you anything you want,' I answered, still more skeptical.

'She was glad to do it.

'Come,' she commanded. I stepped gingerly up on the box. 'Stand here, and hold on to this,' she went on, indicating the rod in the center. I did so, and she stepped up to position just opposite me, and very close. I was conscious of how vulnerable I was if a joke was intended.

'You must not move,' she warned me. I assured her I would not. 'Then, when do you want to go?'

'A week back,' I said at random, with, in spite of everything, a creeping sensation going up and down my spine.

'That will do,' she decided; and again she warned me not to move. Then her hands went to the controls.

'A golden veil sprang up around us and the room grew dim through it, then disappeared. A peculiar silence came over me, a silence that seemed not so much outside of me as within. There was just a second of this, and then I was again looking into the room through the golden veil. Though it dimmed the light I could clearly make out the figure of a man stretched full length on the floor working on the underpart of a piece of apparatus there.

'It's I!' I exclaimed, and every cell in my body leaped at the miracle of it. That this could be! That I could be standing outside of myself looking at myself! That last week had come back, and that I, who already belonged to a later time, could be back there again in it! As I peered, thoughts and emotions all out of control, I saw happen a thing that stilled the last thin voice of inward doubt.

'The man on the floor rolled over, sat up, turned his face—my face—toward us, and, deep in thought, gently fingered a sore place on his head—from a bump that no one, positively, knew anything about. Trickery seemed excluded.

'But a contradictory thing occurred to me. I asked Pearl, 'Why doesn't he see us, since he's looking right this way? I never saw anything at the time.'

'It is only in the next stage toward arriving that we can be seen,' she explained with her hands still on the controls. 'At this moment I'm keeping us unmaterialized. This stage is extremely important. If we tried to materialize within some solid, and not in free space, we should explode.

'Now, let us return,' she said. 'Hold still,'

'The room disappeared; the peculiar silence returned; then I saw the room again, dim through the golden veil. Abruptly the veil vanished and the room came clear; and we stepped down on the floor on the day we had left.

'My legs were trembling so as to be unreliable. I leaned against a table, and my amazing visitor, as it seemed her habit, sat down on the floor.

'That was my introduction to Pearl.'

4

Frick rose and walked to the far corner of the room and back. The thoughts in his mind were causing some internal disturbance, that was obvious.

I prayed that my dictograph was working properly!

When Frick sat down again he was calmer. Not for long could any emotion sweep out of control his fine mind and dominating will. With a faint smile and an outflung gesture of his arm he said, 'That was the beginning!'

Again he paused, and ended it with one of his old chuckles. 'I showed Pearl New York. I showed her!

'Charles, Miles, there is just too much,' he resumed at a tangent, shaking his head. 'There is a tendency to go off into details, but I'll try to avoid it. Maybe some other time. I want to be brief, just now.

'Well, I got her some clothes and showed her New York City. It was a major experience. For she was not your ordinary out-of-towner, but a baroque out of far future time. She had learned our language and many of our customs; she was most amazingly mental; and yet, under the difficult task of orienting herself to what she called our crudeness, she exhibited a most delicious naiveté.

'I showed her my laboratory and explained the things I had done. She was not much interested in that. I showed her my house, others too, and explained how we of the twentieth century live.

'Why do you waste your time acquiring and operating gadgets?' she would ask. She liked that word 'gadgets'; it became her favourite. By it she meant electricity, changes of clothing, flying, meals in courses, cigarettes, variety of furniture, even the number of rooms in our homes. She'd say, 'You are a superior man for this time; why don't you throw out all your material luxuries so as to live more completely in the realms of the mind?'

'I would ask her what standard she judged our civilization against; but whenever I did that she'd always go obscure, and say she guessed we were too primitive to appreciate the higher values. She consistently refused to describe the sort of civilization she had come from; though, toward the end, she began promising me that if I were a good guide, and answered all her questions, she might—only might—take me there to see it. You can imagine I was a good guide!

'But meanwhile, I got nothing but my own inferences; and what an extraordinary set I acquired from her questions and reactions! You make your own set as I go along!

'I showed her New York. She'd say, 'But why do the people hurry so? Is it really necessary for all those automobiles to keep going and coming? Do the people *like* to live in layers? If the United States is as big as you say it is, why do you build such high buildings? What is your reason for having so few people rich, so many people poor?' It was like that. And endless.

'I took her to restaurants. 'Why does everybody take a whole hour just to eat?' I told her that people enjoyed eating; it seemed not to have occurred to her. 'But if they spent only a few minutes at it they'd have much more time for meditation!' I couldn't but agree.

'I took her to a nightclub. 'Why do all those men do all the carrying, and those others all the eating?' I explained that the first were waiters, the latter guests. 'Will the guests have a turn at carrying?' I told I thought so, some day.

'Is that man a singing waiter?'

'No, only a crooner.'

'Why do those men with the things make such an awful noise?'

'Because dance bands get paid for making it.'

'It must be awfully hard on them.' I told her I hoped so. 'Are those people doing what you call dancing?'

'Yes.'

'Do they like to do it?'

'Yes.'

'The old ones, too?'

'I doubt it.'

'Then why do they do it?' I didn't know. At the end she asked me almost poignantly, 'Don't they *ever* spend any time in meditation?' and I had to express my doubts.

'In our little jaunts it became increasingly clear to her that there was very little meditation being done in New York. It was the biggest surprise that our civilization gave her.

'However, she continued to indulge her peculiar habit of going off into meditation when something profound, or interesting, or puzzling came to her attention; and the most extraordinary thing about it was that she had to sit down at it, no matter where she was. If there was a chair handy, all right, but if not, she would plunk right down on the floor, or, ouside, even in the street! This was not so bad when we were alone, but once it happened under

Murphy's flagpole in Union Square as we stood observing the bellowings of a soap-box orator, and once again in Macy's, where we lingered a moment listening to a demonstrator with the last word possible in beauty preparations. It was quite embarrassing! Toward the end I grew adept in detecting signs of the coming descent and was fairly successful in holding her up!

'In all the six days I spent showing Pearl New York, not once did she show any emotion other than that of intellectual curiosity; not once did she smile; not once did she so much as alter the dry expression on her face. And *this*, my friends, was the creature who became a student and an exponent of love!

'It bears on my main theme, so I will tell you in some detail about her experiences with love, or what she thought was love.

'During the first three days she did not mention the word; and from what I know of her now, I can say with surety that she was holding herself back. During those three days she had seen one performance of *Romeo and Juliet,* had read two romantic novels containing overwhelming love themes, had observed everywhere the instinct for young people to seek each other out, had seen two couples kiss while dancing, had seen the fleet come in and the sailors make for Riverside Drive, and had heard I don't know how many hours of crooning on radio broadcasts.

'After all this, one day in my drawing room, she suddenly asked me, 'What is this love that everyone is always talking about?'

'Never dreaming of the part love was to play between us, I answered simply that it was nature's device to make mature humans attractive to each other and ensure the arrival of offspring and the maintenance of the race. That, it seems, is what she thought it was, but what she couldn't understand was why everybody made such a to-do about it. Take kissing, for instance. That was when a male and a female pushed each other on the lips. Did they like that? I assured her they did. Was it, since they held it so long, a kind of meditation? Well, no, not exactly. Would I try it with her?

'Don't smile yet, you two—that's nothing! Wait! Anyway, you wouldn't want me to spoil my chances of being taken for a visit to her own time, would you?

'Well, we kissed. She stood on tiptoe, her dry face looking up at mine, her arms stiffly at her sides, while I bent down, my sober face looking down at hers, and my arms stiffly at my sides. We both pushed; our lips met; and we stayed that way a little. Then almost maintaining contact, Pearl asked me, 'Is it supposed to sort of scrape?' I assured her it was—something like a scrape. After a moment she said, 'Then there's a great mystery here, somewhere—' And damned if she didn't squat right down on the floor and go off into a think! I couldn't keep a straight face, so I bounced out of the room; and when I returned several minutes later there she was still meditating on her kiss. *O tempora!*

'That kiss happened on the third day, and she stayed six, and for the remainder of her visit in our time she said not one thing more about this thing called love—which told me it was a mystery always on her mind, for she asked questions by the score about every other conceivable thing.

'But I also knew from another thing. For the three days following that kiss she went innumerable times to my radio and tuned in dance and vocal programs whose songs would, of course, inevitably be about love. She fairly saturated herself with love's and above's, star's and are's, blue's and you's, June's and moon's. What a horrible flock of mangy clichés must have come to flap around in her mental—all too mental—mind! What peculiar notions about love they must have given her!

'But enough of that phase. You have an idea. You have seen Pearl in New York, tasting love. Six nights to the very hour after she first appeared to me I stood again on the round base of the time traveler, and this time I accompanied her forward to her time. I do not know how far in the future that was, but I estimate it to be around three million years.'

5

Frick paused, rose, and, without asking us if we wanted any, served some cold tea from the thermos bottle by his chair. This time we were glad to have it.

By then I was as close to fully believing as was, I think, Miles. We wasted little time over the tea, but, considerably refreshed and extremely eager with anticipations of what would follow, leaned forward and were again lost in Frick's extraordinary story.

'The trip forward took what seemed to be only half a minute, and I believe it might have been instantaneous but for the time needed to bring the machine to a stop on exactly the right day. As before, the passage was a period of ineffable silence; but I was aware that all the time Pearl fingered the controls. Very suddenly I saw we were in a dimly lighted room; with equal suddenness the golden screen vanished and normal daylight took its place. We had arrived.

'I stepped off the traveler and looked curiously about. We were in a small place, the walls of which were partitions which projected perhaps ten feet up toward a very high ceiling. Everything I could see was made of an ugly, mud-yellow metallic substance, and everything seemed to be built on the square. Light entered from large windows on all sides. The section of the great room in which we had arrived was bare of everything but our traveler. I saw that this time it rested firmly on the floor—a very dirty floor.

'I suppose it would be superfluous to paint the tremendous state of excitement and curiosity I was in. To be the only man of our time to have voyaged forward! To be the only one allowed to see the human race in marvelous maturity! What honor, glory, luck that such an unmerited distinction should fall upon me! Every atom of my body was living and tingling at that moment. I was going to drink in and remember everything that crossed my senses.

'I was full of questions at once, but Pearl had warned me not to talk. She had told me that there were several caretakers from whose sight I was to remain hidden; and now the first thing she did was to put her finger to her lips and peer down the corridor outside. She listened a moment, then stepped out and beckoned me to follow.

'I did—and all but exclaimed out loud to see that the corridor was carpeted with fine dust fully an inch deep!

'How could this be an important building of so advanced an age? For surely that building was important, to house, as it did, so marvelous a device as the traveler!

'But I had no time for wonderment, for Pearl led me rapidly toward the far side of the great room. At our every step clouds of dust billowed out on each side, so that a hasty glance behind showed such diffusion of it that all there was hidden. The corridor was quite wide, and ran lengthwise of the building on one side of the center. At varying distances we passed doorways, all of them closed, and at the end we turned to the left, to come quickly to a high, wide door. It was open, and golden sunlight was shining through. For a second Pearl held me back while she peered around the edge, then, taking me by the hand, she led me out into our world of the future.

'What would you have expected to see, Charles? You, Miles? Towering buildings, perhaps, transversed on their higher levels by aerial traffic ways? And crowds of people strangely mannered and curiously dressed? And mysterious-powered aerial carriers? And parks? And flowers? And much use of metal and synthetic marble? Well, of these there was nothing. My eyes looked out over a common, ordinary, flat, 1963 field. In the distance were some patches of trees; nearby were some wild grass, low bushes, and millions of daisies; and that was all!

'My first thought was that Pearl had made some mistake in our time of destination, and when I sought her face, and saw that this was only what she expected, I grew alarmed. She misread my thoughts, though, and saying 'Don't be afraid' led me along a wide walk to a corner of the building, where she peeped around the edge, and, apparently satisfied with what she found, stepped forth and motioned me to follow. Then she spoke:

'Here we are,' she said .

'Before me stretched the same sort of landscape as on the other quarter, except that here the immediate field was tenanted with a square block of large metallic boxes, six on a side, and each separated by about ten yards from its neighbors.

'I suppose I stood there and gaped. I didn't understand, and I told Pearl as much. Her tone in replying came as near surprise as I ever heard it.

'Not understand? she asked. 'What do you mean? Isn't this just about what you expected?'

'Eventually I found words. 'But where is your city?' I asked.

'There,' she answered, with a gesture of her arm toward the boxes.

'But the people!' I exclaimed.

'They are inside.'

'But I–I–there's something wrong!' I stammered. 'Those things are no city, and they couldn't hold ten people apiece!'

'They hold only one apiece,' she informed me with dignity.

'I was completely flabbergasted. 'Then–then your total population is–'

'Just thirty-six, out here; or, rather, thirty-five, for one of us has just died.'

'I thought I saw the catch. 'But how many have you that aren't out here?'

'Just us younger ones–four, including myself,' she answered simply. She added, 'And, of course, the two who are not yet born.'

'All before this had turned my head; her last statement came near turning my stomach. Clutching at straws, I blurted out, 'But this is just a small community; the chief centers of your population lie elsewhere?'

'No,' she corrected levelly, 'this is the only center of our civilization. All human beings are gathered here.' She fixed me with her dry gaze. 'How primitive you are!' she said, as a zoologist might, looking at a threadworm. 'I see that you expected numbers, mere numbers. But I suppose that a comparative savage like you might be expected to prefer quantity of life to quality of life.

'We have here quality,' she went on with noble utterance, 'the finest of the finest, for ten thousand generations. Nature has need of quantity in her lower orders, but in allowing the perfection of such towering supermen as are my friends out here she has indulged in the final luxury of quality.

'Nor is that all. With quality we have at last achieved simplicity, and in the apotheosis of humanity these two things are the ultimates.'

'All I could do was mumble that simplicity was too weak a word.'

Frick stopped here, laughed, and rose. 'She had my mind down and its shoulders touching! And from that moment–I assure you, my friends–the whole thing began to amuse me.'

He took a few steps about the room, laughing silently; then, leaning with one shoulder against the wall, he went on.

'Pearl was on an awfully high horse, there, for a moment, but she soon dismounted and considered what she might offer for my entertainment. She expressed polite regret that her civilization contained so little for me to see with my eyes. She implied that the vast quantities of intellectual activity going on would be far past my understanding.

'I asked, then, if there was any way I might have a peep at their quality group in action; and to this she replied that her countrymen never came together in groups, and neither did they indulge in actions, but that it would be easy to show me one or two of the leading citizens.

'I of course told her I did not want her to run a risk of getting in trouble, but she assured me there was no danger of that. The guardians of the place–they were the three other 'younger ones' she had just mentioned–were quiet somewhere, and as for the adults, 'They,' she said, 'will be able neither to see nor hear you.'

'Well, she showed me two. And merciful heavens!'

Frick laughed so that for a moment he could not go on. Miles by now was reflecting Frick's every mood, and would smile in anticipation when he laughed. I suppose I was doing the same. We were both completely under Frick's spell.

'She escorted me openly across the field to the nearest box, and I remember that on the way I got a bur in my ankle which I stopped to remove. I found from close up that the boxes were about ten feet square and made of the same ugly yellow metal used in the big building. The upper part of each side had a double row of narrow horizontal slits, and in the middle of each front side there was a closely fitted door. I was remembering Pearl's promise that they would be able neither to see nor to hear me, so I was alarmed when without ceremony she opened the door and half pushed me in.

'What I saw! I was so shocked that, as Pearl told me later, I gasped out an involuntary 'Oh!' and fairly jumped backward. Had she not been right behind and held me, I might have run. As it was I remained, hypnotized by sight of what met my eyes, trembling, and I think gagging.

'I saw a man; or some kind of a man. He sat right in front of me, nude from the waist up, and covered as the floor was covered from the waist down. How shall I adequately describe him!

'He was in some ways like an unwrapped mummy, except that a fallen-in mummy presents a fairly respectable appearance. And then he was something like a spider—a spider with only three legs. And again, looking quickly, he was all one gigantic head, or at least a great mass of whose parchment surface appeared a little round two-holed knoll where the nose customarily is, lidded caverns where the eyes belong, small craters where the ears commonly are, and, on the underside, a horrible, wrinkled, half-inch slit, below which more parchment backed almost horizontally to a three-inch striated and, in places, bumpy pipe.

'By not the slightest movement of any kind did the monster show he knew I was there. He sat on a high dais; his arms were only bones converging downward; his body, only half the usual thickness, showed every rib and even, I think, the front side of some of his vertebrae; and his pipe of a neck, unable alone to support his head, gave most of that job to two curved metal pieces that came out of the wall.

'He had a musty smell.

'And, final horror, the stuff that covered him to the waist was dust; and there were two inches of dust on the top of his head and lesser piles of it on every little upper surface!

6

'It was horrible; but I swear that as I stood there goggling at him he began to strike me funny. It grew on me, until I think I should have laughed in the old gent's face had I not been restrained by a slight fear that he might in some way be dangerous.

'Goodness knows what all I thought of as I stood there. I know I eventually asked Pearl, for caution's sake:

'You're sure he can't see or hear me?'

'She told me he could not.

'I was not surprised; he looked too old for such strenuous activities. I scrutinized him, inch by inch. After a little I announced with conviction, 'He's dead! I'm sure of it!'

'She assured me he was not.

'But look at the dust! He can't have moved for years!'

'Why should he move?' she asked.

'That stopped me for a little.

'But—but,' I stammered eventually, 'he's as good as dead! He's not doing anything!'

'He certainly is doing something,' was her dignified correction. 'He's meditating.'

'All I could think to say was 'Good night!'

'At that, Pearl turned on me reproachfully. 'Your attitude is bestial,' she said, 'I have done you the honor of bringing you to witness the highest flowering of the human race, and you act like a pig. Life can hold nothing more beautiful than this man you see here; he is the ultimate in human progress, one who is in truth perfection, whose every taint of animal desire has been cleaned away, who is the very limit in the simplicity of his life and the purity of his thoughts and intentions.'

'Not to miss anything, she added, 'He embodies the extension of every quality that makes for civilization; he's reached the logical end of man's ambitious climb up from the monkey.'

'My Lord!' I said. 'Here's a dead end!'

'For myself, I sum it all in five words,' she went on nobly: 'He leads the mental life.'

'After a little my emotions suddenly got out of control. 'Does—does he *like* it?' I blurted out. But that was a mistake. I tried, 'Do you mean to imply he spends his life sitting here and thinking?'

'Pure living and high thinking' she put it.

'No living, I'm thinking!' I retorted. 'What does he think of?'

'He is probably our greatest aesthetician,' she answered proudly. 'It's a pity you can't know the trueness and beauty of his formulations.'

'How do you know they are beautiful?' I asked with my primitive skepticism.

'I can hear his thoughts, of course,' was the answer.

'This surprising statement started me on another string of questions, and when I got through I had learned the following: This old bird and the others could not hear me think because my intellectual wave length was too short for their receivers; that Pearl, when talking and thinking with me, was for the same reason below their range; and that Pearl shared with the old guys the power of tuning in or out of such private meditations or general conversations as might be going on.

'We utilize this telepathic faculty,' Pearl added, 'in the education of our young. Especially the babies, while they are still unborn. The adults take turns in tutoring them for their cells. I, it happens, was a premature baby—only eleven months—so I missed most of my prenatal instruction. That's why I'm different from the others here, and inferior. Though they say I was bad material all the way back from conception.'

'Her words made my stomach turn over, and the sight of that disproportioned cadaver didn't help it any, either. Still I stood my ground and did my best to absorb every single detail.

'While so engaged I saw one of the most fantastic things yet. The nasty little slit of a mouth under our host's head slowly separated until it revealed a dark and gummy opening; and as it reached its maximum I heard a click behind my back and jumped to one side just in time to see a small gray object shoot from a box fastened to the wall, and, after a wide arc through the air, make a perfect landing in the old gentleman's mouth!

'He felt the need for some sustenance,' Pearl explained. 'Those pellets contain his food and water. Naturally he needs very little. They are ejected by a mechanism sensitive to the force of his mind waves.'

'Let me out,' I said.

'We went out into the clean, warm sunshine. How sweet that homely field looked! I sat down on the grass and picked a daisy. It was not one whit different from those of my own time, at home.

'Pearl sat down beside me.

'We now have an empty cell,' she said, 'but one of our younger men is ready to fill it. He has been waiting until we installed a

new and larger food receptacle—one that will hold enough for
seventy-five years without refilling. We've just finished. It is, of
course, the young of our community who take care of the elders
by preparing the food pellets and doing what other few chores
are necessary. They do this until they outgrow the strength of
their bodies and can no longer get around—when they have the
honor of maturity and may take their place in one of the cells.'

'But how in the devil do creatures like—like that in there,
manage to have children?' I had to ask.

'Oh, I know what you mean, but you've got the wrong idea,'
came her instant explanation. 'That matter is attended to while
they are still comparatively young. From the very beginning the
young are raised in incubators.'

'I have always had a quick stomach—and she insisted on trying
to prove it!

'With us, it takes fifteen months,' she went along. 'We have
two underway at present. Would you like to see them?'

'I told her that I would see them, but that I would not like it.
'But first,' I asked, 'if you don't mind, show me one other of
these adults of yours. I—I—I can't get over it. I still can't quite
believe it.'

'She said she would. A woman. And at that we got up and she
led me to the next cell.

'I did not go in. I stood outside and took one look at the
inmate through the door. Horrible! Female that she was, it was
at that moment I first thought what a decent thing it would
be—yes, and how pleasant—to hold each one of the necks of those
cartoons of humankind in the ring of my two strong hands for a
moment—

'But I was a trusted visitor, and such thoughts were not to be
encouraged. I asked Pearl to lead on to the incubators.

'We had left the block of cells and were rounding the corner of
the building when Pearl stopped and pulled me back. Apparently
she had gotten some thought warning just in time, for in a
moment three outlandish figures filed out of the very door of the
big building that we had been making for. All wore black shiny
shifts like Pearl's, and they were, very obviously, young flowers
of Genus Homo in full perfection.

'The first was the size, but had not nearly the emaciated
proportions, of the old aesthetician, and his great bald head
wabbled precariously on his outrageous neck as he made his
uncertain way along. The second—a girl, I think—was smaller,
younger, stronger, but she followed her elder at a respectful

distance in the same awful manner. The third in the procession was a male, little more than a baby, and he half stumbled after the others in his own version of their caricature of a walk.

'They walked straight out into the field; and do you know, that little fellow, pure monster in appearance, ugly as ultimate sin, did a thing that brought tears to my eyes. As he came to the edge of the walk and stepped off into the grass, he bent laboriously over and plucked a daisy—and looked at it in preoccupied fashion as he toddled on after the others!

'I was much relieved that they had not discovered us, and so was Pearl. As soon as they were a safe distance away, she whispered to me, 'I had to be careful. They all can see, and the two younger ones still can hear.'

'What are they going to do out there?' I asked.

'Take a lesson in metaphysics,' she answered, and almost with her words the first one sat down thoughtfully out in the middle of the field—to be followed in turn by the second and even the little fellow!

'The tallest one, Pearl informed me, 'is the one who is to take a place in the vacant cell. He had better do it soon. It's becoming dangerous for him to walk about. His neck's too weak.'

'With care we edged our way up and into the building, but this time Pearl conducted me along the corridor on the other side. The dust there was as thick as in the first, except along the middle, where many footprints testified to much use. We came to the incubators.

'There I saw them. I saw them; I made myself look at them; but I tell you it was an effort! I—I think, if you don't mind, I won't describe them. You know—my personal peculiarity. They were wonderful. Curvings of glass and tubes. Two, in them. Different stages. I left right away; went back to the front door; and in a few minutes felt better.

'Pearl, of course, had to come after me and try to take me back; and I noticed an amusing thing. The sight of those coming babies had a sort of maternal effect on her! I swear it! For she *would* talk about them; and before long she timidly—ah, but as dryly as ever!—suggested that we attempt a kiss!—only she forgot the word and called it a scrape. Ye gods! Well, we scraped—exactly as before—and that, my friends, was the incident which led straight and terribly to the termination of the genus Homo Sapiens!

'You could never imagine what happened. It was this, like one-two-three: Pearl and I touched lips; I heard a soft, weird cry behind me; I wheeled; saw, in the entrance, side by side, the three creatures, I had thought were safely out in the field getting tutored; saw the eldest's face contort, his head wabble; heard a sharp snap; and then in a twinkling he had fallen over on the other two; and when the dust had settled we saw the young flowers of perfect humanity in an ugly pile, and they lay still, quite still, with, each one, a broken neck!

'They represented the total stock of the race, and they were dead, and I had been the innocent cause!

'I was scared; but how do you think their death affected Pearl? Do you think she showed any sign of emotion? She did not. She ratiocinated. She was sorry of course—so her words said—the tallest guy had been such a beautiful soul!—a born philosopher!—but it had happened; there was nothing to do about it except remove the bodies, and now it was up to her alone to look after the incubators and that cemetery of thinkers.

'But first,' she said, 'I'd better take you back to your time.'

'But no!' I said, and I invented lots of reasons why I'd better stay a little. Now that there was no one to discover my presence I more than ever did not want to go. There were a hundred things I wanted to study—the old men, how they functioned, the conditions of the outside world, and so on—but particularly, I confess, I wanted to examine the contents of that building. If it could produce a time traveler, it must contain other marvels, the secrets of which I might be able to learn and take back home with me.

'We went out into the sun and argued, and my guide did a lot of squatting and meditating, and in the end I won out. I could stay three days.

'On the afternoon of the first day something went wrong with the incubators, and Pearl came hurrying to tell me in her abstracted fashion that the two occupants, the last hopes of the human race, were dead.

'She did not know it, but I had done things to the mechanisms of the incubators.

'I had murdered those unborn monsters—

'Charles, Miles, let's have some more tea.'

7

Frick went over to the thermos bottle, poured for us, returned it to the floor, and resumed his chair. We rested for several minutes, and my dictograph shows that again not a word was spoken. I will not try to describe my thoughts except to say that the break in the tension had found me in need of the stimulation I was given.

When Frick resumed, it was suddenly, with unexpected bitterness and vehemence.

'Homo Sapiens had become a caricature and an abomination!' he exclaimed. 'I did not murder those unborn babies on impulse, nor did I commit my later murders on impulse. My actions were considered; my decisions were reached after hours of the calmest, clearest thinking I have ever done; I accepted full responsibility, and I still accept it!

'I want now to make a statement which above all I want you to believe. It is this. At the time I made up my mind to destroy those little monsters, and so terminate Genus Homo, I expected to bring Pearl back to live out her years in our time. That was the disposition I had planned for her. Her future did not work out that way. To put it baldly, Mother Nature made the most ridiculous ass of all time out of me; but remember, in justice to me, that the current of events got changed *after* my decision.

'I have said that Pearl took the death of the race's only young stock in her usual arid manner. She certainly did; but, as I think back over those days, it seems to me she did show a tiny bit, oh, a most infinitesimal amount, of feeling. That feeling was directed wholly toward me. You may ask how she could differ temperamentally—and physically—from those others, but I can only suggest that the enigma of her personal equation was bound up in the unique conditions of her birth. As she said, she may have been 'bad material' to start with. Then, something had gone wrong with an incubator; she was born after only eleven months; was four months premature; had received remote prenatal tutoring for that much less time; and had functioned in a different and far more physical manner much earlier, and with fewer built-in restraints, than the others.

'It was this difference in her, this independence and initiative, that caused her to find the time traveler, the unused and forgotten achievement of a far previous age. It was this difference that allowed her to dare use it in the way we know. And it was this difference—now I am speaking chiefly of her *physical* difference—that gave rise in me to the cosmic ambitions which took me from farce to horror, and which I will now try to describe.

'Toward the evening of the second day we sat out on the wold grass before that corroboree of static philosophers and discussed the remaining future of the human race.

'I argued, since there was no one else to look after them now, and since they could live only as long as she lived, it was clear that the best thing—and, in the event of accident to her, the most humane thing—would be for me to kill them all as painlessly as possible and take her back to my time to live.

'I need not mention the impossibility of there being any more descendants from them.

'But for the only time during all the period I knew her she refused to face the facts. She wouldn't admit a single thing; I got nowhere; argue and plead as I would, all she would say, over and over, was that it was a pity that the human race had to come to an end. I see now that I was dense to take so long to get what she was driving at. When I did finally get it I nearly fell over backward in the grass.

'My friends, she was delicately hinting that I was acceptable to her as the father of a future race!

'Oh, that was gorgeous! I simply couldn't restrain my laughter; I had to turn my back; and I had a devil of a time explaining what I was doing, and why my shoulders shook so. To let her down easily, told her I would think it over that night and give her my decision in the morning. And that was all there was to it at the time.

'Now comes the joke; now comes the beginning of my elevation to the supreme heights of asshood, and you are at liberty to laugh as much as you please. That night, under the low-hung stars of that far future world, I *did* decide to become the father of a future race! Yes—the single father of ultimate humanity!

'That night was perhaps the most tremendous experience of my life. The wide thinking I did! The abandoned planning! What were not the possibilities of my union with Pearl! She, on her side, had superb intellectuality, was the product of millions of years' culture; while I had emotion, vitality, the physicalness that she and the withered remains of her people lacked! Who might guess what renaissance of degenerated humanity our posterity might bring! I walked, that night; I shouted; I laughed; I cried. I was to become a latter-day god! I spent emotion terrifically; it could not last till dawn; morning found Pearl waking me, quite wet with dew, far out in the hills.

'I had settled everything in my mind. Pearl and I would mate, and nature would take her course; but there was one prime condition. There would have to be a house-cleaning, first. Those cartoons of humanity would have to be destroyed. They represented all that was absurd and decadent; they were utterly without value; they were a stench and an abomination. Death to the old, and on with the new!

'I told Pearl of my decision. She was not exactly torrid with gratitude when she heard me say I would make her my wife, but she did give some severely logical approval, and that was something. She balked, however, at my plan to exterminate her redoubtable exponents of the mental life. She was quite stubborn.

'All that day I tried to convince her. I pointed out the old folks' uselessness, but she argued they were otherwise: that usefulness gives birth to the notion of beauty; that, therefore, beauty accompanies usefulness; and that because the old gentlemen were such paragons of subjective beauty they were, therefore, paragons of usefulness. I got lost on that airy plane of reasoning. I informed her that I, too, was something of an aesthetician, and that I had proved to myself they smelled bad and were intolerable; and how easy it would be to exterminate them!—how slender their hold on life!

'Nothing doing. At one time I made the mistake of trying vile humor. Here's a splendid solution of the in-law problem! As if she could be made to smile! She made me explain what I had meant! And this seemed to give her new thinking material, and resulted in her going down into squat-thinks so often that I was almost ready to run amok.

'I suppose there must be a great unconscious loyalty to race in humans, for even in that attenuated time Pearl, unsentimental as she always was, doggedly insisted that they be allowed to live out their unnatural lives.

'I never did persuade her. I forced her. Either they had to go or I would. Late that night she gave me her permission.

'I awoke the morning of the fourth day in glorious high spirits. This was the day that was to leave me the lord of creation! I was not at all disturbed that it entailed my first assuming the office of high executioner. I went gaily to meet Pearl and asked her if she had settled her mind for the work of the day. She had. As we breakfasted on some damnable stuff like sawdust we talked over various methods of extermination.

'Oh, I was in splendid spirits! To prove to Pearl that I was a just executioner, I offered to consider the case of each philostatician separately and to spare any for whom extenuating circumstances could be found. We started on the male monster of my first day. Standing before him in his cell I asked Pearl, 'What good can you say of this alleged aesthetician?'

'He has a beautiful soul,' she claimed.

'But look at his body!'

'You are no judge,' she retorted. 'And what if his body does decay?–his mind is eternal.'

'What's he meditating on?'

'Pearl went into a think. After a moment she said, 'A hole in the ground.'

'Can you interpret his thoughts for me?' I asked.

'It is difficult, but I'll try,' she said. After a little she began tonelessly, 'It's a hole. There is something–a certain something about it–Once caught my leg in one–I pulled. Yes, there is something– ineffable–So-called matter around–air within– Holes–depth– moisture–leaks–juice – Yes, it is the *idea* of a hole– Hole–inverse infinity–holiness–'

'That'll do!' I said–and pulled the receptacle of all this wisdom suddenly forward. There was a sharp crack, like the breaking of a dry stick, and the receptacle hung swaying pendulously against his ribs. 'Justice!' I cried.

'The old woman was next. 'What's there good about her?' I asked.

'She is a mother,' Pearl replied.

'Enough!' I cried, and the flip of my arm was followed by another sharp crack. 'Justice to the mother who bore Homo Sapiens! Next!'

'The next was an awful-looking wreck–worse than the first. 'What good can you say of him?' I asked.

'He is a great scientist.'

'Can you interpret his thoughts?'

'Pearl sank and thought. 'Mind force,' she said tonelessly. 'How powerful–mm–yes, powerful– Basis of everything living–mm–really is everything–no living, all thinking–in direct proportion as it is not, there is nothing– Mm, yes, everything is relative, but everything together makes unity–therefore, we have a relative unit–or, since the reverse is the other half of the obverse, the two together equal another unity, and we get the equation: a relative unit equals a unit of relativity– Sounds as if it might mean something. Einstein was a primitive. I agree with Wlyxzso. He was a greater mind than Yutwlxi. And so it is proved that mind always triumphs over matter–'

'Proved!' I said–and crack went his neck! 'Justice!' I cried. 'Next!'

'The next, Pearl told me, was a metaphysician. 'Ye gods,' I cried, 'don't tell me that among this lot of supermetaphysicians there is a specialist and an ultra. What's he thinking?'

'But this time poor Pearl was in doubt. 'To tell the truth, we're not sure whether he thinks or not,' she said, 'or whether he is alive or dead. Sometimes we seem to get ideas so faint that we doubt if we really hear them; at others there is a pure blank.'

'Try,' I ordered. 'Try hard. Every last dead one must have his chance to be killed.'

'She tried. Eventually she said, 'I really think he is alive—Truth—air—truth firmly rooted high in air—ah, branching luxuriantly down toward earth—but never touching, so I cannot quite reach the branches, though I so easily grasp the roots—'

'Crack! went his neck.

'I cracked a dozen others. It got easier all the time. Then Pearl presented me to the prize of the collection. He had a head the size of a bushel basket.

'What good can you say of him?'

'He is the greatest of us all, and I do beg that you will spare him,' was her reply. 'I don't know what his speciality is, but everyone here regarded him so highly!'

'What is he thinking?' I asked.

'That's it,' she replied. 'No one knows. From birth he has never spoken; he used to drool at the mouth; no one has been able to detect any sign of cerebration. We put him in a cell very early. One of us gave an opinion that he was a congenital hydrocephalic idiot, but that was an error of judgment, for the rest of us have always been sure that his blankness is only apparent. His meditations are simply beyond our gross sensibilities. He no doubt ponders the uttermost problems of infinity.'

'Try,' I said. 'Even he gets his chance.'

'Pearl tried, and got nothing. Crack! went his neck.

'And so it went. One by one, with rapid dispatch, and with a gusto that still surprises me when I think of it, I rid the earth of its public enemies. By the time the sun was high in the heavens the job was complete, and I had become the next lord of creation!

8

'The effect of the morning's work sent Pearl into a meditation that lasted for hours. When she came out of it she seemed her usual self; but inside, as I know now, something was changed, or, let us say, accelerated; and when this acceleration had reached a certain point my goosish ambition was ignominiously cooked. Ah, and very well cooked! Humorous and serious — I was well done on both sides!

'But realization of my final humiliation came late and suddenly. My thoughts were not at all on any danger like that, but on millions of darling descendants in whose every parlor would hang my picture, when Pearl came out of her extended trance.

'I had decided to be awfully nice to her – a model father even if not the perfect lover – so it was almost like a courtier that I escorted her out on the field and handed her over to a large stone, where she promptly sat and efficiently asked what I wanted. I imagined she showed a trace of disappointment when I told her I only wished to talk over some arrangements relative to our coming civilization; but she made no remark, let me paint a glowing picture of the possibilities, and agreed with me on the outlines of the various plans I had formed.

'I was in a hurry. I asked her if she desired to slip back to my time to have the ceremony performed.

'This offer was, I thought, a delicate gesture on my part. She came back with what amounted to a terrific right to the heart. She said severely, 'Yes, Frick, I will marry you, but first, you must court me.'

'Observe, now, Miles, and you, Charles, my rapid ascent to asshood's most sublime peak. Countless other men have spent their lives trying to attain that dizzy height; a few have almost reached its summit, but it remained for me, the acting lord of creation, to achieve it. For – there was nothing else to do about it – I began to court her!

'Hold my hand,' she said – and I held her hand. She thought. 'Tell me that you love me,' she required. I told her that I loved her. 'But look at me when you say it,' she demanded – and I looked into her fleshless face with the thin lips that always reminded me of an alum and said again that I loved her. Again she took thought, and I got the impression that she was inspecting her sensations. 'Kiss me,' she ordered; and when I did she slid to the ground in a think!

'There are mysteries in there somewhere,' she said when I pulled her up. 'I shall have to give a great deal of thought to them.'

'I was in a hurry! I told her – Lord forgive me! – that she was clearly falling in love with me! And within herself she found something – I can't imagine what – that encouraged the idea. I struck while the iron was – well, not at absolute zero.

'Oh, come on,' I urged her. 'You see how we love each other; let's get married and get it over with.'

'No, you'll have to court me,' she answered, and I'll swear she was being coy. 'And court me for a long time, too,' she added. I found out all about it, in your time. It takes months.'

'This was terrible! 'But why wait? Why? We love each other. Look at Romeo and Juliet! Remember?'

'I liked that young man Rudy better,' she came back at a tangent.

'You mean the man in the nightclub?' I asked.

'Yes,' she answered. 'He seemed to be singing just to me.'

'Not singing – crooning!' I corrected irritably.

'Yes, crooning,' she allowed. 'You croon to me, Frick.'

'Imagine it! Me, of all people; she, of all people; and out in the middle of that field in broad daylight!

'But did I croon? I crooned. You have not seen me at the heights yet!

'More,' she said abstractedly. 'I think I feel something.'

'I crooned some more.

'Something with love and above in it,' she ordered.

'I made up something with love and above in it.

'And something with you and true,' she went on.

'I did it.

'Now kiss me again.'

'And I did that!

'Thank Heaven she flopped into another think! I escaped to the woods while she was unconscious, and did not see her again till the next day.

'My friends, this was the ignoble pattern of my life for the two weeks that followed.

'I suffered; how I suffered! There I was, all a-burning to be the author of a new civilization, luxuriating in advance at thought of titanic tasks complete; and there she was, surely the most extraordinary block to superhuman ambition that ever was, forever chilling my ardor, ruthlessly demanding to be courted! I held hands with her all over that portion of time; I gazed into her eyes at the tomb of old Hydrocephalus himself; I crooned to her at midnight; and I'll bet that neighborhood was pitted for years in the places she suddenly sat down to meditate on in the midst of a kiss!

'She had observed closely – all too closely – the technique of love overtures here in our time; and noted particularly the effect on the woman, so she must needs always be going off into a personal huddle to see if, perhaps, she was beginning to react in the desired manner!

'Ah, there was brains! How glad I am that I'm dumb!

'I began to lose weight and go around tired. I saw that our courtship could go on forever. But she saved me with an idea she got out of one of those novels she had read. She told me one rainy morning, brightly, that it might be a good thing if we did not see each other for a couple of months. She had so very, very much to think over, and, incidentally, how sorry she was for her poor countrymen who had died without dreaming life could hold such wealth of emotional experience as she had accumulated from me!

'By then I was as much as ever in a rush to get my revised race off under their own power, but I was physically so exhausted that my protests lacked force, and I had to give in. So we made all arrangements and had our last talk. It was fully understood that I was to come back in two months and take her as my bride. She showed me how to operate the traveler. I set the controls, and in a matter of a minute I was back here in this room.

'But I tricked her. That is, in a sense. For I didn't wait two months. The idea occurred to me to straddle that period in the traveler – so in only another minute I was materializing in the time two months away that I was to call back and claim her! I was thankful for that machine, for the long ordeal had left my body weak and my nerves frazzled, and I don't know how I could have stood so long a delay. You see, I was in such a hurry!

'Ah, had I known! The catastrophe was already upon me! Note its terrible, brief acceleration!

'When I arrived, all was exactly as before. The great building was as dusty, the community as deserted, the block of cells just as morbid as when I left. Only the fields had changed I found Pearl sitting before the tomb of Hydrocephalus, meditating.

'I'm surprised to find you back so soon,' were her words of greeting. 'It seems only a week.'

'Did you have a good time, my Pearl-of-great-price?' I asked tenderly. (She had come to insist on that name. Once, near despair, I had used it with a different meaning, and afterward she required me to lash myself with it whenever I addressed her.)

'It was a period of most interesting integration,' she replied. 'In fact, it has been a precious experience. But I have come to realize that we were hasty in terminating the noble lives of my fellow men.'

'This was ominous! I made her go for a walk in the fields with me. Three times on the way out she found things I lightly mentioned to be problems requiring immediate squatting and meditating!

'I sensed that this was the crisis, and it was. I threw all my resources into an attempt to force immediate victory. I held her hands with one of mine, hooked my free arm around her waist, placed my lips to hers and crooned, 'Marry me right now, darling! I can't wait! I love you, I adore you, I am quite mad over you!' -and damn it, at the word mad she squatted!

'I picked her up and tried it again, but like clockwork, on the word mad she went down again. Oh, I was mad over her, all right!

'I was boiling! You see, I had to hurry so! She was changing right under my nose!

'I fairly flew back to the time machine. I was going to learn once and for all what my future with regard to a potential human race was to be. I set its dials one year ahead.

'This time I found Pearl in the vacant cell. She was distinctly older, dryer, thinner, and her head was larger in size. She sat on the dais as had the others; and there was a light dust on her clothing –

'It is strange that you should come at this moment,' she said in a rusty voice. 'I was thinking of you.'

'With the last word she closed her eyes – so she should not see me, only think of me. I saw that the food box was full. Despair in my heart. I went back to the traveler.

'For a long time I hesitated in front of it. I was close to the bottom. The change had happened so quickly! To Pearl it took a year, to me, only an hour; yet her acts were as fixed, her character as immutable, as if they had been petrified under the weight of a millennium.

'I nerved myself for what I had to do. Suddenly, recklessly, I jumped on the traveler, set it for seventy years ahead, and shot forth into time.

'I saw Pearl once more. I hardly recognized her in the monster who sat on the dais in her cell. Her body was shriveled. Her head had grown huge. Her nose had subsided. Her mouth was a nasty, crooked slit. She sat in thick dust, and there was an inch of it where there had once been brown hair, and more on every little upper surface.

'She had a musty smell!

'She had reverted to type. She had overcome the differentness of her start and was already far down the nauseating road which overbrained humanity has yet to go.

'As I stood looking at her, her eyelids trembled a little, and I felt she knew I was there. It was horrible; but worse was to come. The mouth, too, moved; it twisted; opened; and out of it came an awful creak.

'Tell me that you love me.'

'I fled back to my time!'

9

Frick's long narrative had come to a close, but its end effect was of such sudden horror that Miles and I could not move from the edges of our chairs. In the silence Frick's voice still seemed to go on, exuberant, laughing, bitter, flexing with changing moods. The man himself sat slumped back in his chair, head low, drained of energy.

We sat this way long minutes, each with his thoughts, and each one's thoughts fixing terribly on the thing we knew Frick was going to do and which we would not ask him not to do. Frick raised his head and spoke, and I quivered at the implication of his words.

'The last time she had food for only five years,' he said.

Out of the depths of me came a voice, answering, 'It will be an act of mercy.'

'For you,' Frick said. 'I shall do it because she is the loathsome last.'

He got up; fixed us in turn with bitter eyes.

'You will come?' he asked.

We did not answer. He must have read our assent in our eyes. He smiled sardonically.

He went over to the door he had pointed out, unlocked it with a key from his pocket, pulled its heavy weight open, entered, switched on a light. I got up and followed, trembling, Miles after me.

'I had the traveler walled up,' Frick said. 'I have never used it since.'

I saw the machine. It was as he had described it. It hung in nothingness two feet off the floor! For a moment I lacked the courage to step on, and Frick pushed me up roughly. He was beginning to show the excitement which was to gather such momentum.

Miles stepped up promptly, and then Frick himself was up, hands on the controls. 'Don't move!' he cried – and then the room was dim goldenness, then nothing at all, and I felt permeated with fathomless silence.

Suddenly there was the goldenness again, and just as suddenly it left. We were in a small dark room. It was night.

I wondered if she knew we were coming.

We went to her silently, prowlers in infinity, our carpet the dust of ages. A turn, a door – and there was field land asleep under the pale wash of a gibbous moon. A walk, a turn – and there were the thirty six sepulchers of the degenerate dead. One not quite dead.

I was as in a dream.

Through the tall grass we struck, stealthily, Frick in the van like a swiftstalking animal. Straight through the wet grass he led us, though it clung to our legs as if to restrain us from our single purpose. Straight in among those silent sepulchers we went. Nature was nodding; her earth stretched out everywhere oblivious; and the ages to come, they did not care. Nor cared the mummied tenants of each tomb around us. Not now, with their heads resting on their ribs. Only Frick did, very much. He was a young humanity's agent before an old one's degradation. Splendidly, he was judge and executioner.

He slowed down before the sepulcher where was one who was yet alive. He paused there; and I prayed. An intake of breath, and he pulled open the door and entered. Dreadfully, Miles, then I, edged in after.

The door swung closed.

The tomb was a well of ink. Unseen dust rose to finger my throat. There was a musty smell! I held my breath, but my heart pounded on furiously. Ever so faintly through the pressing silence I heard the pounding of two others.

Could it be possible that a fourth heart was weakly beating there?

Faint sounds of movement came from my left. An arm brushed my side, groping. I heard a smothered gasp; I think it was Miles. Soon I had to have air, and breathed, in catches. I waited, straining my eyes toward where, ahead, there might have been a deeper blackness through the incessant gloom.

Silence. Was Frick gathering courage? I could *feel* him peering beside me there, afraid of what he had to see.

I knew a moment when the suspense became intolerable, and in that moment it was all over. There was a movement, a scratch, a match spluttered into light; for one eternal second I looked through a dim haze of dust on a mummied monstrosity whose eyelids moved! – and then darkness swept over us again, and there was a sharp crack, as of a broken stick, and I was running wildly with Death itself at my heels through the graveyard of a race to the building where lay our traveler.

In minutes we were back in our own time; in a few more Frick had blown up the traveler and I was out of the laboratory making for the Sound, sharp on my mind, as I went, the never-to-be-forgotten picture of Miles as he had raced behind me blurting, 'She blinked! Oh she blinked!' and that other, striding godlike in the rear, a little out of his head at the moment, who waved his arms over that fulfilled cemetery and thundered,

'*Sic transit gloria mundi!*'

SEEKER OF TOMORROW

E.F. Russell and L.T. Johnson

The Venusian city of Kar shimmered beneath an inverted bowl of blue glory. It was a perfect day for a civic demonstration such as the welcoming home of the first expedition to Earth in many centuries. Citizens appreciated the cooperation of the weather; Liberty Square was packed with a murmuring, multicolored concourse that swirled in kaleidoscopic patterns. Something shrieked in the vault of space; the kaleidoscope turned uniformly pink as five hundred thousand faces lifted to the sky.

High in the stratosphere appeared a pair of metallic pencils, their rear ends vomiting crimson flames. Sound waves from the rocket tubes fleeted downward, bounced from the eardrums of the expectant crowd. The pencils swelled; the crimson spread along their under surfaces as the retarding rockets belched with maximum power. In a short time the objects had resolved themselves into long, streamlined space ships.

With startling suddenness they loomed hugely to the view, sinking behind the mighty mass of university building. They seemed to pause for a moment, while the great, circular ports in their sides stared over the edge of the roof at the mob beneath. Then they were gone. Came one tremendous, reverberating crash succeeded by a moment's perfect silence. The great audience found tongues, broke into a babble of sound, as, with one accord, it stretched itself into a stream of individuals rushing along University Avenue toward the Kar Airport.

The landing field of Kar Airport presented a scene of utmost confusion. To one side lay the space ships surrounded by a shouting, struggling mob. The uproar was loudest at the point where the overwhelmed City Guards had reformed themselves into a wedge and were desperately battling their way through the barrier of bodies.

Babbling and bawling arose into a crescendo when it was

perceived that the nearer space ship was opening its bow door. Steadily, the circular piece of metal revolved along its worm, retreating more and more into the shadow. A final half-revolution and it was drawn into the interior of the ship, while the form of a man appeared in the gap thus left.

The crowd bellowed itself red in the face: 'Urnas Karin! Urnas Karin!'

Karin acknowledged the shouts and raised his hand for silence. Half the crowd hissed for silence, while the other half continued to bawl. The hissers reproved the bawlers and the bawlers answered back. Somebody pushed somebody and somebody else resented it. A woman fainted, collapsed, and a little man ten yards away was struck on the cranium by way of retaliation. In a flash, fifty different individuals assumed fifty different versions of what they regarded as a menacing pose. A hidden dog yelped, as somebody trod on it, and from the back of the crowd a piercing voice shrilled, 'Woopsey! Woopsey!'

Immediately the crowd laughed; an ugly situation passed away and silence fell.

Karin jumped to the ground, followed by twenty of his companions from inside the ship. A small platform, about twice man-height, stood near. Karin mounted and let his sharp eyes pass over the waiting audience. A uniformed guard placed before him a small ebony box mounted on a tripod. He waved away the guard, stood before the box and spoke.

'My friends,' he said, his voice pleasantly magnified by the disseminator he was using, 'your marvelous welcome is a reward in itself. I thank you; and again, on behalf of my colleagues, I thank you! Now, I am sure that you are all fairly bursting to know whether this expedition has made any startling discoveries upon our Mother Planet.' He paused and smiled, as the crowd signified with a roar that it *was* fairly bursting.

'Well I am afraid that our story is far too long to narrate in detail. Let it suffice if I tell you that we did not find a trace of civilization of those who were our ancestors. The great cities, they mighty machines that once were theirs have crumbled into the dust and have been obliterated completely by the foot of Time. Old Mother Earth is airless, waterless, and lifeless, thoroughly and completely.

'But we did make one most remarkable discovery.' He hesitated for a tantalizing minute. 'We found the body of a prehistoric man! It was truly an amazing discovery. There, upon a world so ancient that every artificial mark had been smoothed away, atmosphere had leaked off into space, and even axial rotation had ceased, lay the body of this man.

'Examination of the corpse disclosed the seemingly impossible fact that life had departed from it not more than fifty hours previously. Fortunately, we had with us, as part of our standard first-aid equipment, a normality chamber. We placed the corpse therein, warmed it, liquefied the blood and have succeeded in bringing it safely home in a condition that gives us good cause to hope that the experts in our Institute of Medicine and Surgery will be able to resuscitate it.

'The body of this man is in perfect condition. The cause of death, literally, was lack of breath. He appears to belong to a period placed several thousands of years before our ancestors departed from the dying Earth and settled here on Venus, a period so far back in time that our history reels do not talk of it. Why, his head is covered with hair and he even has hairs upon his chest and legs!

'The ability of scientists, in this our most progressive time, to revive the dead in cases where death is not due to old age and is not accompanied by serious injury is a marvel too well known to need emphasis by me. Possibly there are some people here who would not be with us but for the miracles performed by our most able men and women.' He was interrupted by several cries of assent.

'I feel that there is a most excellent chance of the institute bringing this man back to life and permitting him to tell us his story with his own lips. If my hopes prove to be justified, I intend to make an official request to Orca Sanla, chairman of the stereo-vision committee, that this lone inhabitant of a long-dead planet be allowed to stand before the screen at Kar Stereo Station and give to our world an explanation of circumstances which, to be quite candid with you, we regard as absolutely inexplicable.' Karin turned and gestured toward a burly individual standing in the front rank of his scores of followers.

'In any case, you will receive entertainment tonight. Olaf Morga, aided by his brother Reca, who is on our companion ship, has made a complete pictorial record of our venture from the time we departed from Kar to the time we left Earth. The record is being dispatched to the K.S. Station and will be radiated from sunset this evening.'

Karin started to descend as a storm of cheering broke out. A woman in the center of the crowd screamed, 'Belt!'

The word was caught up by a thousand others; ere Karin had placed his foot upon the topmost step the whole mob was roaring, 'The belt! We want the belt!'

Morga and Karin exchanged smiles. The latter returned to the center of the platform, slowly and deliberately unbuckling the flexible metal belt encircling his middle. He held it loosely by one end, while the crowd danced with excitement.

Suddenly he whirled it above his head, flung it upward and out. It snaked through the air toward where the throng clustered thickest. Half a hundred men leaped for it as it fell. Then it vanished beneath a mass of human beings all fighting madly for the prized souvenir.

Quick to profit by the diversion, the city guards cleared a path from the rocket ships to the control tower. Karin and his crew, together with the crew of the sister ship, sped along the path, entered the tower. The crowd swarmed out of the airport field, poured in a colorful torrent down University Avenue and put a test load on the moving roadways to the suburbs.

Dusk fell over Venus. The stars set in a moonless sky penetrated the thick veil of atmosphere just sufficiently to paint faint glimmers of steely brightness upon the sides of two voyagers of interplanetary space. Side by side, in a littered field, the rocket ships slept.

2

Two months later, Bern Hedan, the man who got the buckle of the belt, fiddled with the controls of his stereo set and cursed. The brandnew pan-selenite screen of the set displayed, in natural colors and with stereoscopic effect, the final stage of transformation of a sample of Venusian pond life. A hidden announcer betrayed the fact that Sanla's myrmidons regarded a dirge played upon an asthmatic oboe as fit accompaniment to the tri-monthly acrobatics of a frog-faced fish.

'By the death of Terra!' he ejaculated, using the most fearful oath his imagination could conceive at the moment. 'I pay fifty-five yogs down and twelve more every high tide to be the owner of the set. I pay exorbitant bills for power to operate it; I produce eighteen yogs per annum for the right to make use of that which I have purchased—or am purchasing.' He gestured to nothing in particular and talked aloud. He was very fond of talking to himself.

Common-sense views appealed to him. 'And what do we get for this outrageous expenditure? What do we get, I say? Pictorial demonstrations of the domestic habits of red-hammed Venusian baboons accompanied by the noise of wailing catgut. Or the amatory adventures of a deep-sea worm who pays court to somebody's symphony for ten harmonicas. Bah!'

He wound savagely at the coordinating handle protruding from the front of the stereo cabinet. The screen dimmed, clouded over, then cleared and depicted a new scene. It was an interior view of the Hall of Debate in the city of Newlondon. Two men were seated upon chairs placed on a semicircular stage, facing a great auditorium packed with people from floor to ceiling. A third individual stood upon the stage facing a stereo screen. Bern Hedan noticed that a mirror suspended on the wall at the rear of this stage was responsible for the peculiar effect of showing the transmission screen in his own screen, giving him a double image of the three people on the stage.

The stereo announcer was saying, 'This evening you have heard and seen an extremely interesting and most instructive debate upon the subject of another Great Migration. You all know the reasons why the human race was compelled to make use of its discovery of the means of traveling through cosmic space by indulging in a wholesale move to our present abode–Venus. The symptoms of planetary senile decay, such as loss of atmosphere, loss of orbital velocity, and speed of axial rotation, became so alarming that eventually it was obvious that Earth's characteristics were altering faster than humanity could accommodate itself to the change. Earth's days were numbered–from the human viewpoint, at least. Venus was a suitable habitat for our forefathers, ourselves, and our children's children, and the means to get to Venus were at hand.

'The question that has been discussed tonight has been, to put it briefly: "Will history repeat itself?" In the course of time, somewhere in the distant future, our planet's fate will duplicate that of Earth. We may not like to think of it, but it is a fact, a perfectly natural fact, an inevitable one. Will Venusians die with Venus, or shall there be another Great Migration?' He signed with his hand to the man seated on his right-hand side.

'The pessimist thinks we are doomed for the reasons he has given you, the most unanswerable of which is that the next foothold in space is the planet Mercury--and Mercury is quite uninhabitable by human beings.' He signed to the opposite side. 'The optimist believes that humanity shall never disappear from creation, mainly because of our steady scientific advancement, which, he has said, will enable us to perfect the art of space travel to such a degree that we shall have the choice of a dozen worlds long before our present one has grown uncomfortable.

'This concludes the debate between Leet Horis of Kar and Reca Morga of the Newlondon Debating Society.' He stood staring into the transmission screen while the auditorium thundered with applause.

'Now we come to the event to which all Venus has been looking forward with the keenest anticipation. Since the Kar Institute successfully resuscitated the prehistoric man two months ago, the entire world has been waiting to hear his story. There has been some comment about this delay of two months, which I am now to tell you was due to the fact that the revival of this man was not, in itself, enough to justify his immediate appearance. He needed a period of convalescence, during which he has learned how to speak our language. You will find that he can speak with fair fluency, the reason for this being that his own language proved to be the root of ours.'

Bern Hedan adjusted the clarity knob of his set, making the screen depict the stage more sharply. He moved an easy-chair before the stereo, sat in it and switched on the automatic head-scratcher. Soothed by the restfulness of the cushions and the gentle rubs and tickles of the scratcher, he prepared to listen with tolerance.

Seen in the screen, the pair of debaters left the stage. The announcer walked to the rear, opened a door and, with a dramatic air, ushered in the prehistoric man. The man stood directly in front of the screen and studied twelve thousand Venusians. Two hundred million Venusians studied the man.

The Venusians felt slightly disappointed. The object of their examination did not look as though he lived in trees and ate nuts. His head was covered with disgusting hair, but otherwise he looked quite normal. He stood six feet in height; his eyes were dark, alert, his face intellectual even by Venusian standards of judgment. A woven *silvoid karossa* hung from his shoulders; the inevitable Venusian belt encircled his middle. He seemed to be quite at ease; it was evident that he did not agree with his audience in giving his own personality a purely antiquarian value.

'It is my privilege,' said the announcer, 'to introduce to you Glyn Weston, the man from A.D. 2007—a date placed approximately seventy thousand years before the Great Migration, about one hundred and fifty thousand years from today.' Murmurs of surprise rippled around the serried rows of seats.

'Glyn Weston has told his story to the university board at Kar; he has made a most valuable contribution to the pages of ancient history. I shall now request him to repeat his narrative, and I think that after you have heard what he has to say you will agree that this voice from the past has recounted the most amazing tale ever to be projected over the stereo. *Glyn Weston!'*

3

My friends, began Weston, speaking in a pleasantly modulated voice, there is one thing I must say before I tell you my story. God's greatest gift to man is life. I cannot say that you have given me life, but to the remarkable abilities of your wonderful civilization I owe the restoration of that which was snatched from me – *life!* The poor and faulty power of speech is quite inadequate to convey to you the gratitude I feel. I want every one of you to know how deeply I appreciate what has been done for me by Venusian science.

(A roar of applause shook the auditorium. The audience decided that it was to listen to a man and not to a savage.)

As you have been informed, my name is Glyn Weston. My age I do not know; the reason will become apparent later in my story. In the period that is called mine, if any particular period can be so called, I was a physicist.

My work commenced at the age of twenty-eight, when I was fortunate enough to inherit a very large sum of money. I was then assistant to the famous Professor Vanderveen, astrophysicist at the Glasgow Observatory. For many years my hobby had been the study of the work of McAndrew, popularly called 'The Death-ray Man.'

McAndrew was a scientist of the previous decade. His life's work had advanced that of certain mathematicians and physicists of the twentieth century, most particularly Einstein, Graham, Forrest and Schweil. He was the world's most authoritative exponent of the space-time concept, and like many other geniuses, he died discredited by his contemporaries because he had asserted that it would be found possible to travel in time, to move through time into the future.

Schweil, with whom McAndrew had been coworker, had shown that time was not an independent concept but an aspect of motion. There could be no time without motion – no motion without time.

This may seem rather obscure to some of you, but it really is quite simple. Try to imagine time without motion; consider the means whereby you estimate time. The two cannot be separated, for they are merely different aspects of the same thing. McAndrew's life was dedicated to discovering the true relationship between these aspects and, if I may put it so, to defining the 'difference.'

His work was crowned with success two years before his death. Working upon the theory that the velocity of motion and the rate of time invariably maintained a constant parallel, he evolved a ray with which he made a number of objects vanish. It was his claim that the ray speeded up the velocity of electronic motion, causing the atoms to experience time at a faster rate and thus forcing the objects into the future. Of course, he was laughed at.

His discovery was described in the absurdest terms, such as 'the automatic disintegrator' and 'the death ray.' McAndrew left his data in the safe-keeping of the only scientist who believed in him. That scientist was Vanderveen, my superior.

Vanderveen was in his late fifties when he caught the torch cast by the fallen McAndrew. During my association with him he gave me constant, almost fatherly, encouragement. My interest in McAndrew pleased him immensely. When I received my inheritance I told him that it was my desire to use it in carrying on from where McAndrew had left off.

'Weston,' he said, placing a hand upon my shoulder, 'I have prayed that this should be your ambition. McAndrew, alas! found in me a dog too old to learn new tricks. But as for you – you are young.'

Thus the seed was sown. But Vanderveen did not live to see the crop. Twenty-two years later I became the human subject of a time-travel experiment. I had set up my laboratory in the wilds of the Peak District of Derbyshire, in England, where work could be carried on with the mimimum of interference. From this laboratory I had dispatched into the unknown, presumably the future, a multitude of objects, including several live creatures such as rats, mice, pigeons and domestic fowl. In no case could I bring back anything I had made to vanish. Once gone, the subject was gone forever. There was no way of discovering exactly where it had gone. There was nothing but to take a risk and go myself.

To this end I designed an air-tight time-travel room and had it fabricated immediately. The room was capable of holding the much perfected Schweil-McAndrew ray projector, myself and a quantity of material I considered necessary to take with me. The projector fitting was designed so that the entire room, with all its contents, would vanish immediately as the ray was turned on. I knew, of course, that if this room actually transported me into the future it was imperative that I take into account the possible alteration of ground contours over the period of time I covered. It would be foolhardy to experiment at a point where the ground might rise and leave me embedded yards below Earth's surface. So I hired a field upon a hilltop nine miles northwest of Bakewell – a very lonely spot – and equipped the roof beams with a parachute of my own design, to thwart an opposite possibility.

Upon the fourteenth of April, A.D. 1998, all was prepared for the great test. My financial affairs had been settled with an eye to the future in more ways than one. The time-travel room, lavishly set with windows and looking like a very large telephone kiosk, stood waiting in the middle of Farmer Wright's field. As I walked toward it, not knowing what Fate held in store for me, I thought what an incongruous object it looked standing amid the furrows. Without the slightest hesitation, I unlocked the door, stepped inside and relocked it, started the air-purifying apparatus, took one last look at Earth, fresh with the aura of spring, and closed the projector switch.

4

The sensation of being under the influence of the rays was weird in the extreme. My mind seemed to be emptied of all thoughts, retaining only alternating impressions of roughness and smoothness, stickiness and gloss, for all the world as if the very nature of my brain material was swaying between a pseudo-fibrousness like that of pulled toffee and a satisfying softness like that of a newly rolled ball of putty. A veil of mist came between myself and the world I strained my eyes to see. The mist was elusive, intangible. Some temporary optical fault intervened to defeat all my efforts to decide whether this mist lay over the windows of the room or was coating my own eyeballs.

A sudden panic assailed me, and I pressed down the switch handle to which my right hand was still clinging. A sensation of immense strain racked my body from hair to toes, my blood vessels fizzed as if their contents had been replaced with soda water. The fugitive mist was whisked away like the gauzy veil of an oriental dancer. I felt as sick as a dog.

My key clicked in the lock of the door. I stepped outside and looked around. Everything looked exactly as I had left it. The field was still furrowed; a few trees and bushes were displaying their awareness of spring; the sky was still cloudy, the air as stimulating as before. My experiment had failed.

It was a miserable man who wended his way along the lonely lanes to his laboratory. I remember that birds were singing, but I did not hear them – at the moment; early flowers were adding their sweet beauty to this ugly world of mine and I did not see them – just then.

Mentally cursing my lack of foresight in not parking my car in the hired field, I turned a bend in the road and began to climb a hill lying between the field and the laboratory. A farm laborer emerged from a lane to my left and trudged along behind me. He increased his pace, caught up to me and requested the time. He was an old man of the garrulous type and, to my mind, his question was merely an excuse for a conversation. Nevertheless, I lugged at my gold chain and glanced at the cheap timepiece hooked upon its end.

'I'm sorry,' I said, 'my watch has stopped.'

'So has mine,' he responded. 'Guess I'll have to get it on the wireless when I land home.' He lighted a cigarette and climbed up the hill in silence for a little while. 'What d'you think of the great rocket flight?' he asked suddenly.

I had some difficulty in gathering my wits, and had to make a definite mental effort before I could reply. Somehow, I managed to recall the sensational flight across the Channel of Robert Clair. This had been hailed as the first really successful experiment with a man-carrying rocket. If I remembered rightly, the event had taken place at least a month before. The science of rocketry held the interest of only a very small number of people; it was strange that this old man should still betray an interest in such an event placed a month earlier. Courtesy demanded a reply.

'Merely another step in the inevitable march of progress,' I answered.

'D'you think they'll ever get to the Moon?'

'Who can tell,' I said evasively.

'Well, they're talking about it; they're talking about it,' he persisted. 'I was reading in the papers only the other day that some professor had worked out how long it would take to get to Venus, how a suitable rocket could be built and how much it would cost. Always thought Venus was a naked woman, not a planet. Shows how knowledge has advanced since my younger days.'

'Ah! it is the fate of all of us to be considered ignorant by later standards,' I soothed.

'What's the world coming to?' he demanded, puffing furiously at his cigarette. 'What with steam engines, then motor cars, airplanes and them auto-whatyamacallits that look like windmills and have got no wings, stratosphere planes — and now rockets! I remember when I was a kid there was a furor in the papers because Ginger Leacock circum — circum — went right round the world without a stop, in one of them crazy old stratosphere planes. They've gone round six times since then and aren't satisfied with that! So they've started meddling with rockets.

'First of all some maniac hops over a house and breaks his neck. They called him 'a martyr to science.' Then another idiot who wants to be a martyr rockets across the Channel and breaks both his legs. Not to be outdone, another fool starts out from Dublin and plunges clean through a skyscraper in New York, smearing himself all — '

'Here!' I interrupted. 'What the devil are you talking about?'

'Rockets,' he replied, startled. 'And now when they can get from here to New Zealand in twenty-four hours, including stops, or eighteen hours without, what *I* say is — '

'Will you listen to me,' I shouted, grabbing him by the shoulders. 'What, in Heaven's name, are you talking about?'

'No offense, guv'nor, no offense!' he said nervously, trying to draw back. 'I didn't mean anything, really I didn't!'

'Of course there's no offense,' I roared. Then, realizing that my behavior was making the man nervous, I calmed myself and continued in a quieter tone. 'You must pardon me. This subject you have been talking about is one that interests me very considerably and, for certain reasons, I have been out of touch with the news concerning it. My foolish excitement was caused by your mention of a rocket flight to New York. Will you tell me when that flight took place?'

'Now let me see!' Apparently reassured, he stood and contemplated the skies while he exercised his memory. 'As near as I can guess it was the late summer of 2004.'

'What year?'

'2004,' he repeated.

'And when was this great rocket flight to which you alluded in the beginning?' I asked, making a tremendous effort to control myself.

'Yesterday.'

'You will think this a strange question,' I told him, ' but there is nothing seriously wrong with me. I am suffering from a slight trouble with my memory. Now tell me, what day was yesterday?'

He looked sympathetic, pulled a folded newspaper from his left pocket, opened it with deliberation and handed it to me. A two-inch streamer was spread across the top of the front page. It said 'NEW ROCKET RECORD.' Beneath appeared: 'TO N.Z. IN EIGHTEEN HOURS – Lampson Crashes In Hawkes Bay.' I took little notice of this news, red-hot though it was. My eyes searched eagerly along the top. There it stood in plain, indisputable print: 'DAILY VOICE – May 22, 2007.'

Before the startled native had time to move, I had seized him and kissed him. I flung his paper into the air and caught it with a mighty kick as it came down. I whoopee-e-ed at the top of my voice and danced a fandango in the roadway. My hat fell off and rolled without hindrance into a ditch; my watch jumped out of my pocket and danced in sympathy at the end of its chain. My time-travel experiment had *succeeded!* For a space of five minutes I went stark, staring mad, while my erstwhile companion, forgetting the dignity of age and his rheumatism, galloped up the hill like a hunted deer and vanished over the crest.

5

The remarkable feat of making a short trip through time had an effect upon me totally different from what I would have prophesied a few years before. I did not rush, flushed with triumph, to place the news before an astounded world. On the contrary, I became as suspicious and as secretive as any village miser. My desire for fame and the respect of the scientific world faded away, being replaced by a curiosity so insatiable that each today became a mere period of speculation about tomorrow. The future had grasped me like a vicious drug.

Formerly, I was secretive because I was determined not to permit my work to fall into unworthy hands. Now, the motive was fear of being deprived of the means to satisfy my desire to explore the future as thoroughly as possible.

From every point of view it seemed highly desirable that my next venture be undertaken at once. My personal fortune became a matter of little moment; my money was cached securely – but not securely enough to withstand the onslaught of time. I came to the conclusion that I could afford to ignore the fate of my worldly possessions; it was not likely that I could claim them at a distant date.

In the quiet atmosphere of the dust-covered laboratory, I thought it over. The time-travel room must be removed as soon as possible. Heavens alone knew what weird story had been told by my late companion upon his return home, what curious eyes and prying fingers would explore the object in Wright's field. Come to that, I did not know whether the field still belonged to Farmer Wright. The owner, whoever he might be, could arbitrarily uproot the trespasser upon his property. My next move must be made that night.

It was an hour after sunset when I entered the time-travel room and locked the door preparatory to my second adventure. My stomach was empty; the laboratory had been devoid of food and nothing had passed my lips for several hours. I consoled myself with a nine-year-old cigarette – still fresh! Faint streamers of light still permeated the sky in the direction of Staffordshire; a crescent moon hung low and stars twinkled clearly. The cigarette surrendered its last fragrant puff. I stamped on it and said, 'Good-by, 2007!'

With my hand on the switch, I hesitated. On the last occasion the switch had been closed between six and ten seconds, as near as I could estimate, and I had covered nine years. Was the distance traveled in direct proportion to the time the switch closed? Would I drop dead when the rays carried me to the very day that Nature intended to be the day of my death, or, whether it seemed logical or not, could one travel past what should be one's day of death? Silence answered my unspoken questions. There was nothing for it but to find out. It was a straight issue of success or suicide. I rammed home the switch with exaggerated determination. The die was cast!

I shall not weary you with another description of the sickness that I have called time nausea. The rays operated for a period about ten times longer than the last occasion – about one minute. Then the switch was opened; my body was subjected to a powerful but momentary strain and I had arrived. The key clicked in the door lock; the door swung inward. With my eyes raised to the distant hills, I stepped out. Something snatched at my unwary feet and I fell upon my face. Regaining my feet, I discovered that the time-travel room was sunk into the soil to a depth of six inches; I had been tripped by the step of earth outside the door. It was fortunate that I had not fitted the time-travel room with an outward-opening door and thus imprisoned myself.

Looking around me, the first thing I noticed was that the field was uncultivated. A few miserable trees and bushes displayed their last tattered rags of brownish foliage. The sky was gray, angry and overcast; I concluded that it was late autumn or early winter. There was not a soul in sight as I paced across the field toward the lane.

Reaching a stone wall, about four feet in height, I mounted it and surveyed the distant horizon and the intervening terrain. There was not a sign of life or human habitation. My eyes roamed eagerly around, caught a glimpse of an inexplicable shape in the mid-distance, about four miles away. I took out my spectacles, polished them and adjusted them carefully on my nose. The object was a huge hemisphere of drab color.

The edifice, if such it was, bulged from the top of a tor like a wart upon an Earthly nose. It lay in the opposite direction from where my laboratory stood, or had once stood. I felt very hungry; my stomach suggested that this, the only artificiality on the landscape, held promise of food. I jumped down from the wall and trudged in the general direction of the distant tor.

Maintaining a rapid pace for the best part of an hour brought me to within a few hundred yards of the object, which had resolved itself into a great, smooth hump of concrete about one thousand feet in diameter by five hundred feet in height. There seemed to be a large hole in its top. I did not get a chance to pause and examine it before proceeding nearer; I hesitated in my stride and a voice materialized out of the air behind me. It spoke in accents curiously clipped, somewhat as the Scottish speak, briefly and to the point. It said, 'Keep it up!'

I whirled around. Facing me was a man in dark-brown clothes cut in the manner of a compromise between an engineer's dungarees and a soldier's uniform. A helmet, nothing more than a dull metal skull-cap, rested on his head; his hands grasped and pointed at me an object bearing only the faintest resemblance to a rifle. His attire was quite devoid of decoration; it made him look like something between an infantryman and a plumber.

'Where did you come from?' I exclaimed.

'Under a gooseberry bush,' said he, grinning broadly. 'Where did you?'

'From the year 2007.'

'Indeed! Then the past is rising up against us!' A tinge of sarcasm suffused his voice, but he appeared to be an intelligent fellow.

'You must believe me,' I argued. 'My tale is very long, but when you have heard it you will find it –'

'Very plausible!' he interrupted. 'If you're a better liar than most of us, you must be good. Now, get going. You can tell us all about how you saved the world in 2300 when you get inside.'

'2300! Did you say 2300?' I tried to clutch his arm.

He placed the muzzle of his weapon against my middle. 'Of course I said 2300. Move those feet of yours a little more and your tongue a little less. And, just in case you want to keep up the play Methuselah, may I anticipate a question by informing you that this is the year of disgrace 2486?'

'Good heavens!' I cried, turning and moving up the hill. 'I've jumped nearly four centuries!'

'Right out of the frying pan into the fire,' my companion remarked.

'Why, what d'you mean?'

'Exactly what I said,' he answered, his face taking on a sardonic expression. 'You may be a good jumper, but you're a darned poor picker. Why didn't you jump a little less or a good bit more? The jumper who picks on this year is crazy. Hell, I knew you were crazy anyway!'

'Yes, but—'

'Walk on, jumper, walk on!' he commanded. 'I don't want to use my economy gun on a white man, even if he is cracked.'

'Why d'you call your weapon an "economy gun"?' I asked him.

He heaved a sigh. 'Well, if you must talk, and if you must pretend ignorance of commonplace things, it's because it uses poisoned darts propelled by compressed air and thus saves expenditure of explosives that are sorely needed elsewhere.'

I was about to ask him where the explosives were needed, and for what purpose, when I found that we had arrived at the foot of the concrete mound and were facing a metal door set in its side.

My companion touched the door and slid aside a small trap set in its center, revealing a fluorescent screen behind. He faced the screen and spoke. 'Number KH.32851B4, with a gentleman from the year 2007.'

6

The door opened silently. We entered. Facing us was a long passage indirectly illuminated from slots set in the sides. With synchronized step, which aggravated me and which I vainly tried to break, we marched down the passage, turned to the right at the bottom, *clump-clump-clumped* along a concrete corridor and entered a large room.

A leather-skinned, mustached individual looked up from his desk. 'What do you want?' he snapped.

'Food,' I answered, briefly.

'Bring him food,' he said, addressing my guardian. Turning to me, he said, 'Sit.'

A high cube of red rubber squatted on the floor behind me. I seated myself on it gingerly. It was an air cushion and it felt luxurious. The man behind the desk leaned forward, switched on an instrument bearing a vague resemblance to the old-time voice recorders. He stroked his mustache and looked me over.

'Name?' he demanded.

'Professor Glyn Weston.'

'Professor, eh? Of what seat of learning?'

'Originally of Glasgow Observatory; since then I have been working in my own laboratory, about nine miles from here.'

'There is no laboratory within a dozen miles of here,' he said acidly.

'My laboratory was within nine miles of here in the year 2007,' I replied, doggedly.

'In 2007! How old are you then?'

'From one point of view I am a little over fifty, from another I am nearly five hundred.'

'Absurd!' he exclaimed. 'Obviously absurd!'

'There is an explanation for this seeming absurdity. In the year 2007 I was the first man to have made a trip in time—that is to say, into the future. I had traveled to that year from 1998. The experiment has been repeated. This is the result—I am here!'

'Hah!' He rubbed one side of his nose with a forefinger and regarded me queerly. 'The popularity of science fiction has made the subject of time travel quite familiar to us. But time travel is impossible.'

'Why?' I asked.

'It is illogical.'

'Life is illogical; earthquakes are illogical.'

'True,' he agreed. 'From some aspects that is profoundly true. But can you reconcile yourself with the idea of shaking hands with your ancestors a few centuries before you are born?'

'No—that would be really illogical. My experiments have shown me that time can be traveled in one direction only—and that is forward, into the future. There can be no returning, no motion into the past by as much as a fraction of one second.'

He stood up, moved away from his desk toward a corner bookcase, searched along the serried volumes and pulled out a large, black tome. He ruffled its pages. Turning to me, with the book open in his hand, he questioned me. 'What was the population of Bakewell in 2007?'

'I cannot tell you,' I replied. 'I spent very little time in that year. But in 1998 it was about 4,500.'

'Hm-m-m! Who was the Premier of Great Britain?'

'Richard Grierson.'

'Correct! Clair flew the Channel that year. Who designed his rocket?'

'The German astronautical experimenter, Fritz Loeb.'

'Again correct!'

'Listen to me,' I begged. 'If that's some sort of ancient encyclopedia you've got there, please turn up the time concept and see who wrote books about it.'

He wet a finger, searched through the pages of his book. Placing it on the desk, he grabbed another and searched through that also. Four books were explored before he found what was wanted.

'Here we are. By the way, my name is Captain Henshaw,' he added, as an afterthought. 'Let me see, Schweil, Herman, philos. Dutch "Der something-or-other"; Schweil again, with another book; McAndrew, Fergus, "Space-Time Coordinates"; McAndrew again, "Time-Motion Relationship"; Weston Glyn— well I'm a yellow man! – Weston, Glyn, "Atomic Acceleration In the Time Stream"; again: Weston, Glyn, "Schweil-McAndrew Theories simplified." Another and another; one, two, three, four, five, six! Glyn Weston—that's *you!*'

'And I can prove it,' I said, feeling supremely satisfied that my work had been recorded over five centuries.

'How?' asked Captain Henshaw.

'My time-travel room stands awaiting your inspection at a place that I can describe to you only as Farmer Wright's field. It is an hour's walk from here.'

A door to my left-hand side opened suddenly. A uniformed man appeared wheeling a dinner wagon constructed of bright metal tubes and mounted upon doughnut-tired castors. He twisted the wagon dexterously, turning it before my seat, lifted a well-loaded tray from the top and, with the casual air of an expert conjurer, drew four telescopic legs from its underside. Adjusting the contraption to a nicety, he stepped backward, flourished a cloth and bowed with an impudent grin.

'You must be hungry after five hundred years of abstention!' he said. Throwing another grin at Henshaw he marched from the room.

'To be perfectly candid with you,' said Henshaw, as I commenced the welcome meal, 'Your story is too utterly ridiculous to believe, despite the evidence you have to offer. Now don't think that I am about to call you a liar, for I am not. All that I can say is that I intend to keep an open mind about the matter until I've had the opportunity to examine this magic kiosk of yours, and I am going to take a look at it immediately after my spell of duty ends, in about two hours' time.'

'You are welcome,' I mumbled with full mouth, waving a fork in the air.

'After I've taken a look at your gadget, I'll make a report to Manchester. My superiors can then decide how to treat you.'

'Sounds threatening,' I remarked, chewing rapidly.

'And, just in case your story happens to be true in every respect, is there anything you would like to know?'

'Yes!' I speared a potato. 'Where am I?'

'You are inside No.37 Interceptor Fortress.' He moved from his desk and began to pace the room.

'No. 37 what?' I asked with sudden energy.

'Interceptor Fortress,' he repeated. 'There is a war on.'

'A war!' I echoed, feebly.

'The biggest and most ferocious war the world has known. It has been on for the last five years and looks like lasting for the next five. One-tenth of Earth's population has been wiped out, obliterated. The Metropolis, which was called 'London' in your time, no longer exists except as a great area of shattered bricks, slates, and concrete, which harbor the bones of those they harbored in life. If you can travel in time, as you say you can, you will live to curse the invention that plunged you into the present day.' Henshaw's face grew bitter, his voice hoarse.

'With whom is Britain fighting?' I asked, my dinner almost forgotten.

'There is no Britain,' Henshaw answered. 'The name was given up two centuries ago. There is no British Empire, either. You are now living in England, which is a self-ruling state and part of the White World, just as Scotland, Ireland, Australia, Germany, Russia, and all the others are part of the White World. The Earth of today has only three divisions: the White World, the Yellow World, and the Brown World.

'The Brown World is the smallest and most insignificant of the three. It includes the so-called black races and is neutral—up to the moment. The White and Yellow Worlds are decimating each other to assert their right to breed regardless of the room available. But I am disturbing your meal; please finish it and I will take you to the tele-scan room. There I can show you something of the war.'

My mind pestered by a dozen vagrant thoughts, I ate in silence, while Henshaw fidgeted before the bookcase, taking out volumes and putting them back again. Eventually, the meal came to an end. I drank the last drop of liquid, munched the last fragment of biscuit and arose.

Henshaw signed toward the door through which I had entered. We passed through it, moved down a long corridor, through another door, up a corkscrew staircase into another corridor, reached its end and found ourselves in a long, rectangular room set under the roof of the fortress.

'This is the telescan room.' said Henshaw.

7

The walls and floor of the room were littered with a mass of instruments and equipment. Four men were moving about in the jumble, occupying themselves with various jobs, while, at the distant end, two more were seated at what I deduced to be control boards of some description. The most prominent object was a great glass disk secured in a metal frame in the center of the floor. The disk was tilted slightly out of the horizontal, had a mirror surface and bore a strong resemblance to the astronomical reflectors of my own day.

Henshaw produced a chair from somewhere. Placing it near the mirror, he bade me be seated, moved to the men at the control boards and held a brief conversation with them. He returned and stood by my chair.

'This telescan was the result of permitting amateur shortwave experimenters to play with television. It is much too complicated to explain to you here but, to put it briefly, a beam is directed into the sky, passed through the Heaviside and Appleton Layers and rebounds from the Grocott Layer, which lies at an altitude of about eight hundred miles. The beam then returns to Earth and catches the scene at its striking place.

'It bounces right round the Earth, registering the scene wherever it happens to strike; the first impression is the strongest, and when we pick up the beam again we have no great difficulty in tuning out the confusion of underlying scenes, leaving the first clear and sharp. The operators are now trying to angle the beam to give us a view of the Metropolis. We should get results any second.'

Even as he spoke, the mirrored disk came to life with startling suddenness. There was no preliminary clouding or blur. One moment the surface was devoid of all but glitter; the next movement it depicted a scene with astonishing clarity. I leaned forward and looked at it.

A ruined road, pitted with ragged craters, passed through an area filled with hummocks of crushed building material. Carefully though I searched, I could not perceive one place where two bricks still clung together, neither could I find a single unbroken brick. The scene maintained a harrowing uniformity from the foreground to the background, a square mile of pathetic evidence.

Nothing stirred in that dismal scene; no step was taken where once ten million pairs of feet had trod; no voice was raised where the voices of children once were raised in play. A lump came in my throat, as I realized that the Metropolis – dear old London – was no more. It lay like a great, gray scar upon what I still imagined as the sweet green face of Mother Earth; it lay like a scar upon the soul of humanity.

The mirror altered its focus as the men at the end of the room manipulated their controls. The nearest end of the road seemed to rise toward me and show itself in greater detail. I saw bones protruding from a mound of dirt fifty yards from a large crater; near the legs lay the flattened skeleton of a dog. Henshaw bent his head forward, rubbed his chin with a harsh, scratching sound and spoke.

'Before you lies one of the most heart-rending incidents of the war. The dog refused to leave its stricken master. It stayed there until it starved to death. Thousands of people watched its long, drawn-out act of devotion, watched it through the telescan with curses and tears born of helplessness. Flight Lieutenant O'Rourke, disobeying orders, made a mad attempt to rescue the dog about the time its belly disappeared into its ribs. He was brought down by a Yellow squadron. His rocket plane is mixed with the dust of the Marble Arch. God rest a gallant gentleman!'

'Are the Yellows winning?' I asked, feeling sick at heart.

'No, I would not say that. Warfare has now reached the stage of perfection where nobody wins and everybody loses. The Metropolis, or what is left of it, is in no worse condition than Kobe and Tokyo. The campaign consists of a series of destructive assaults, followed by equally destructive retaliation; there have been no prolonged battles such as featured the past, just a delivering of rapid blows by one side or the other. The end of this great city was the result of such a blow; the end of Tokyo was our reply. Come, we'll take a look at your time-travel room.'

With that I arose. We departed from the telescan room, retraced our steps through the corridors and came to the metal door. It opened silently as we reached it, revealing a small, streamlined vehicle standing on the path outside. Henshaw struggled to get his long legs beneath the steering wheel, while I took a seat by his side. Slamming the off-side door, Henshaw pressed a button protruding from the wheel boss. A smooth whir came from beneath the bonnet and we were off.

'Don't take the telescan picture too much to heart,' said Henshaw, juggling with the wheel. 'We received warning of that raid from our very excellent espionage service and managed to evacuate nine-tenths of the population in time. The remaining tenth was wiped out, but the death roll was not as large as the picture suggests.'

'What caused the damage?' I asked.

'Bombs — high-explosive bombs dropped from the stratosphere air-planes and also from rocket ships flying at tremendous heights. The next raid will be upon Manchester or Sheffield, for these are now the southernmost towns of importance, also centers of the armaments industry. Our fortress is one of a chain strung across the Derbyshire hills to protect Manchester. We cannot prevent a raid, but we can administer severe punishment with our rocket shells and our aerial torpedoes, which can ascend to very great heights, the latter by means of power picked up from the North Radiation Station.'

'The Continent must have dropped in for it!' I offered.

'Not so much as you would think,' he replied. 'The opposing forces have vented their spite on what they consider to be the nerve centers of the enemy; thus England and Japan are the favorite targets. Neither side keeps its air fleet for purposes of defence but for retaliation. That is why these fortresses are very important — they are one of the few defense concessions wrung from the powers that be who worship the policy of attack, attack and again attack.' He jerked at the steering wheel, avoided the curve of a stone wall and continued in a voice that grew more bitter.

'I am not looking forward to the next raid with eager anticipation. Information has reached us, from certain sources, telling that the Yellows have perfected a disintegrator bomb, the result of some nosey scientist occupying himself with the problem of how solar radiation is maintained. I understand that the bomb drops, bursts, upsets the stability of surrounding matter and causes it to burn itself away.

'The process does not continue indefinitely, but only as long as the original energy in the bomb lasts; the bigger the bomb the greater the area of matter affected. The process was described to me as "readjustment of electronic balance," and I believe that it takes place at a rate that will trap all but champion sprinters.'

The car went over the crest of a hill. A field came into view. Simultaneously, we saw the time-travel room. We shot down a slight slope toward it, took an equally slight rise and came to rest beside the wall from which I had viewed the distant fortress. Henshaw squirmed from his seat, took out a watch and glanced at its dial.

'Four minutes – not so bad considering the state of the road.'

'You've averaged about sixty miles per hour,' I told him. 'What sort of motor is this?' I asked, gesturing to the car.

'Electric. Runs on Freimeyer high-capacity batteries employing silver-tantalum alloy plates.' He vaulted the wall, stared at the object in midfield. 'So that's the magic box, eh? Let's go and put a penny in.'

I climbed the wall. We started for the room together. Henshaw stroked at his mustache, an expression of keen interest in his face. The turf was damp and slippery beneath our feet. We had covered half the distance to the room when a hoarse whistle ran over the hills and echoed in the valleys. Henshaw stopped abruptly. The whistle ended, then was succeeded by six short toots.

Henshaw whirled around, grabbed me by the arm, pulled me toward the car. 'By the Mandarin's Button,' he roared, his face red with excitement, *'a raid!* Did you hear the siren? It's a raid warning from the fortress. We must return at once! Put a move on, for Heaven's sake! There's not a second to lose.'

We ran toward the wall. Twenty yards from it I slid, staggered with wildly waving arms, slid again and fell upon the flat of my back with force that knocked the breath from my body. Henshaw, half a dozen jumps ahead, skidded in a circle, returned, and grasped my hands, preparatory to helping me up.

'Look!' I gasped weakly, my eyes bulging at the sky. *'Look!'*

About a mile away, coming in our direction at a fast pace, was a golden-colored air machine shaped like a bullet, small, stubby wings protruding from its sides, a long tail of fire streaming from its rear. it looked sinister, threatening; my heart turned to ice.

'By Hades! A fighting scout of the Yellows,' shouted Henshaw. 'He's got us spotted and intends to have a little amusement. Run like the very devil. We're as good as dead men already.'

So saying, he gave a tremendous heave that swung me to my feet. I clutched his shoulders. We swayed about like a pair of adagio dancers, slipped and went down together. Somebody rattled a piece of rock in a monster can; a roar swept overboard; a flood of hot air washed our recumbent bodies. We regained our feet. The scout had passed us by a mile and was nosing upward in a great loop. The car was a smoking ruin.

'He's coming back for us,' Henshaw screamed. 'We're done. There's nowhere we can hide!'

'Heaven help – ' I commenced, then paused as a thought struck me. 'The time-travel room! Come on. We can make it with luck. We'll be safe there.'

8

I turned, made for the center of the field, arms working like pistons, my pace hampered by fear of falls. Henshaw raced beside me, his chest laboring, his face livid.

Despite the telling pace, he found breath enough to ask a question as he ran. 'What good will it do to get into that thing? He'll simply blow it sky high!'

'Wait and see!' I grunted.

A noise grew loud behind us, filling us with fear that added to our speed. With surprising suddenness, the scout roared overhead followed by its wake of heated air. A terrific blast came somewhere in the rear. Henshaw looked over his shoulder.

'A disintegrator bomb!' he shouted. 'It's eating toward us like greased lightning. Run! Run as you've never run before!'

My protesting feet increased their speed. The total distance from the wall to the room was a bare five hundred yards. I would not have believed that such a distance could be so punishing. Thirty yards separated us from the time-travel room; it seemed like thirty miles. The distance already covered told in this final stage; we did not run it; we reeled it.

Henshaw, ahead of me, reached the room and tugged madly at the door, as a sensation of heat penetrated to the back of my legs. He danced with excitement as he pulled in vain. I sobbed out to him *'Push! Push!'* and he fell headlong inside. A fraction of a second later I staggered through the open door, turned and saw the earth literally melting and boiling within a yard of the step. We were barely in time.

Without further ado, I slammed the door and closed the switch of the ray apparatus. Red flames jumped upward and peered at us through the windows; a film of mist blotted them out. My body tingled with the old, familiar sensation and, as I breathed a prayer of thankfulness, the whole room fell over on its side. My head struck a projection on the wall. Frantically, I tightened my grip upon the switch as I slipped into unconsciousness.

The period of stupor did not last long – or it did not seem to. I came to my senses, jerked out a hand in search of the switch, found it and pulled it.

Somebody said, 'Ouch!'

I sat up hastily. I was in bed!

My astonishment can be well imagined. I was in bed; there was not the slightest doubt about that. I stroked and felt the clothes, studied the weave of them and pinched myself. There was nothing else for it: definitely, beyond all dispute, I was sitting up in bed clad in a crimson nightgown.

A half-seen movement to one side drew my attention that way. I rubbed my eyes and looked again. Standing beside the bed, his face expressive of kindly solicitude, was a bald-headed man garbed in rompers of brilliant hue. His forehead was high, his eyes large, liquid and brown, his mouth and chin small, almost womanly. Suspended from a chain encircling his neck was a plated instrument which, I guessed, had taken the tug that brought forth the 'Ouch!'

I stared at him. He contemplated me with quiet serenity.

'Where am I?' I asked weakly, making use of the conventional phrase under such circumstances.

'You are within my house situated in the city of Leamore,' he answered in a pleasantly modulated voice, 'and the year is 772 by the new reckoning, or 34656 by the old. You have leaped a chasm of time representing about thirty-two thousand years!'

'How did you know that I am a time traveler?' I demanded.

'Because your time-traveling device materialized out of thin air before the eyes of a half a hundred citizens. You chose the center of a busy road as your arriving point. Dozens of people witnessed the phenomenon which, in the far past, undoubtedly would have been given a supernatural explanation. Our solution was that you had traveled through time: a simple solution seeing that your feat is the second within the last five centuries. Finally, your companion confirmed our – '

'Henshaw!' I interrupted, realizing that I had had company on my time trip. 'Henshaw – Where is he?'

'He is having his hair plucked,' was the amazing response.

'Hair plucked! *Hair!* Why? What?' My mind relapsed into confusion at this nonsensical twist in the conversation. For the second time I pinched myself to make sure I was not asleep. The man in the blue rompers smiled as he noted the effect of his words. Seating himself on the edge of the bed, he hugged a knee and continued.

'Your friend appears to be a person accustomed to making quick decisions. It is scarcely thirty minutes since your time-conquering device staged its dramatic appearance, yet already he has discovered that, according to present-day conventions, hair is regarded as not nice. Apparently he is determined to look nice at all costs, so he is having his hair removed by a painless method of extraction. We are depriving him of his mustache and head covering. The bristles on his face will have to grow longer before we can deal with them.'

'Well, I'm damned!' I exploded. 'Henshaw – the blessed goat! I boost him through a multitude of centuries and what happens? He rushes into a beauty parlor leaving me to expire in bed.' Indignation brought me out of the bed and to my feet. 'In a crimson nightgown!' I added.

My companion laughed aloud. 'No fear of you expiring just yet,' he assured me. 'You received a nasty bump from which you will recover very soon. As for the nightgown, as you call it, we put you into it after giving you a much-needed bath, while we looked around for some suitable clothes.'

'What's wrong with my own clothes?' I demanded.

'They have been burned; your friend's have been burned, also. The contents of your pockets have been fumigated; so has your time-travel room. This is a hygienic world you've stepped into. We don't mind your coming here, but we object, in the strongest possible manner, to your importing large quantities of germs of types that we have gone to considerable pains to eliminate. We like you; we like your friend; we *don't* like your passengers.'

'Sorry!' I said, humbly.

'It's quite all right,' he answered, releasing his knee and standing up. 'Perhaps I have been too blunt. The apology should be mine.' He walked across the room, pressed a button. A panel in the wall slid silently downward. Behind lay a recessed wardrobe. He reached inside, produced a complete outfit of clothing made of some material resembling silk, tossed them onto the bed.

Removing the crimson wrap with secret relief, I commenced to put on the apparel. The soft, almost dainty material enveloped my bathed, refreshed body pleasantly. There was not a button in the outfit. Everything fastened with a sort of glorified zipper. I pulled on one strangely cut garment after another, zipped them tight and, in the end, stood before a mirror regarding myself attired in emerald-green rompers, green socks and sandals to match, a green tricorn hat cocked rakishly on my head. I stared into the mirror, thinking it depicted the biggest fool alive.

'How do you like it?' questioned the onlooker.

'Not so bad. All I want now is the cat.'

'The cat?' he repeated, mystified.

'Yes, the cat. I look like the principal boy in Dick Whittington.'

'Dick Whittington?' he muttered.

'You wouldn't know about that – let it pass!' I tried the tricorn at a different angle; the result was an abomination. Finally, I gave it up. If all of them dressed like this, an extra idiot wouldn't be noticed.

'Well, I'm ready, Mr. – Mr. –'

'Ken Melsona is my name,' he responded.

'And Glyn Weston is mine.' We shook hands. Melsona opened a door, led the way down a passage to another door, which sank at the pressure of a button. Outside lay the street. Conscious of my unfamiliar garb, I hesitated; Melsona, dressed like Little Boy Blue, stepped boldly out. I followed.

9

Before me stretched a scene so unexpected I stopped and gasped. Between the pavement curbs ran a moving roadway, smooth, soft-surfaced, flowing evenly from west to east. It was divided into three sections, all travelling in the same direction, the outer sections at about five miles per hour, the middle section at about ten. Hundreds of people clothed in gaudy colors stood and chatted on the road or stepped from one section to another, all carried along steadily like an array of targets in a gypsy shooting gallery. The total width of the roadway was about one hundred feet; fixed, mosaic-patterned pavements bordered it.

Picturesque villas set in lavish, well-cultivated gardens lined the roadway on both sides. Ornamental trees of every size and color, drilled and trimmed into every conceivable shape, sprouted from the pavements at intervals of thirty yards. It was a beautiful sight indeed, the most beautiful I had ever seen. The road deserved the name of Boulevard of Heaven.

Melsona made for the nearest-moving section of roadway, warning me to step on it while facing the direction of motion. We passed over to the middle section, stood upon it, side by side, and glided to the east. I felt as pleased as a kid at a fair.

'Let us call at one or two shops,' suggested my guide. 'Then we can pick up your companion – er – Henshaw you said his name was, didn't you?'

I mumbled an affirmative, my eyes roaming busily over the scenery and the accompanying crowd of road-riders, my mind inveigled by the novelty of it all.

We swept along for the best part of a mile, before Melsona nudged me into attention, dexterously transferred himself to the right-hand slow track, crossed it and gained the pavement. With me tagging behind, he made a beeline for a section of half a dozen shops, entering one displaying a mass of goods I had not the time to examine. A man and a woman, both brightly clad and equally bald, advanced eagerly at our entrance.

'Pray serve this gentleman,' said Melsona, making a patronizing wave in my direction.

'Ah, certainly, it is a pleasure,' purred the male assistant, washing his hands with invisible soap. 'What is the gentleman's need?'

'Money,' I said, succinctly.

'Money!' he parroted. 'Money! What a strange request! It is obtainable, of course, but you will have to apply to a collector.'

'Then how the devil can I – '

'It's quite all right,' Melsona interrupted. 'All you have got to do is to ask for whatever you require. If this shop has it, you will get it; if it hasn't, then some other shop may stock it.'

'Ask and it shall be given unto you,' I quoted. The idea sounded crazy to me, but who was I to question the economics of this age? 'Cigarettes,' I said, hopefully.

The words were no sooner out of my mouth than the lady assistant darted to a shelf, beating her confrere by a foot, grabbed a dozen packages of assorted size and shape and placed them on the counter. My eyes stared in astonishment and delight. They were packets of cigarettes. I took one of the biggest. The lady wanted to know whether she could provide me with anything else. I asked her for a cigarette case and got it. I asked her for an automatic lighter. She provided me with a replica of the instrument dangling from Melsona's neck, which I had mistaken for the switch. I spent thirty minutes in that shop, emerging convinced that I had stepped into Utopia.

We stood on the pavement outside. I opened my cigarette packet, placed a welcome tube between my lips, and Melsona showed me how to use the lighter. It was shaped like an elongated fir cone, made of metal and affixed to the conventional neck chain. One merely squeezed it. A small lid in the wide end popped open, revealing a glowing filament underneath. I lighted it, inhaling the fragrant smoke with indescribable satisfaction.

'How long will this last?' I asked, studying the flowing end of the lighter curiously.

'For the whole of your lifetime,' answered Melsona. 'It's –' He looked upward suddenly, as a loud noise thundered down from the clouds. 'Look! There's a world-trip liner!'

Overhead soared a titanic cigar, silvery-colored, flame-girt, awe-inspiring. The circumstances made it hard to grasp the true perspective. I judged the monster to be about a mile in length and a tenth of a mile in diameter. Poised high above the thin, almost transparent clouds, it was truly a majestic sight, its conical nose pointed toward the Sun setting in the west, its tail vomiting spears of flame that spread, lightened and resolved into an enormous fan of vapor.

It was moving at a height of at least seven miles, yet its size and the wonderful clearness of the atmosphere made the rows of circular ports along its sides easily discernible. Barraging the whole city of Leamore with a bombardment of sound, it sped swiftly to the west, its tremendous bulk dwarfing the antlike humans responsible for its fabrication.

'What do you think of that?' asked Melsona, proudly.

'It's magnificent! It's marvelous!' I said.

A shout drew our eyes to the roadway. A man standing on the distant five-mile track waved madly, rushed in our direction, trod on the edge of the intervening ten-mile track and executed an incomplete cartwheel. With the road rushing onward beneath him, he rolled full length in the contrary direction, mowing down people by the dozen. Still rolling, he broke out of a knot of recumbent forms, revolved across the track and tried to regain his feet on the very verge.

He stood up, for a fraction of a second, with one foot on the middle track and one foot on the nearer five-mile track; then the difference in speed overcame him. He chose the five-mile track and sat on it, hard. He passed us, as we gazed with interest, lying flat on his back, his feet in the air. Fifty yards along the road he gained the safety of the pavement with a sudden, acrobatic movement, turned and dashed toward us.

As he neared, I perceived that he was darker in complexion than most of the people I had seen. His rompers were a horrible yellow above the waist and black below; his socks were of black; his sandals black with yellow piping. A yellow pork-pie hat was rammed squarely on his head; a yellow tassel hung from the center of its crown and dangled over his left ear.

He came up to us, his face beaming with pleasure, and smacked me heartily on the back. I studied him closely. He was as hairy as an egg.

'I don't believe it,' I said, flatly.

'I can hardly believe it when I look at you,' he retorted.

'Then how did you recognize me?'

'Because yours is the only monkey nut in the whole wide world.' He took a pace back and surveyed me from head to heel. 'The only original Robin Hood, as I live and breathe,' he said. 'How d'you like my rig?' He spread his arms and slowly rotated before us.

'I would rather not say,' I said, averting my eyes from the bilious yellow; 'Justice can be pronounced only in vulgar terms.'

'Jealous!' was his laughing comment. 'Personally, I think attire such as this lends color to life. If I've any fault to find, it is only the trouble it creates in distinguishing sahibs from memsahibs. So you've been shopping, huh?' He jabbed a finger at the lighter suspended from my neck. 'And how do you like this moneyless world?'

'Seeing you know about the money, or lack of it, it's evident you've been shopping,' I commented.

'Oh, no,' he assured us. 'I went to pay the hair-plucker and he acted like one thunderstruck. Then I found out about the money. Wistfully, he said he would like an odd coin if I had one to give away. So I let him run through my purse, which I had swiped when they grabbed my clothes to burn them. His eyes stood out like organ stops when he saw what I had: eighteen dollars and forty-seven cents in good old White money.'

'*White* money?' I queried.

'Of course. You didn't think I'd have money from your age, did you? Well, he raked through the lot and picked out a half-dollar piece which was the oldest-dated coin there. He was as pleased as a dog with two tails. I asked him what he was going to do with it. You would never guess what he said.'

'What?' I encouraged him.

'I've not yet been able to make up my mind whether I'm mentally deficient or all this world's daft but me. Believe it or not, he said he was going to swap that half dollar for a *glass fish!*'

'A glass fish!' I echoed incredulously.

'Now what the deuce would he want with that?' Henshaw continued. 'A live fish would be bad enough, a dead fish better, but a glass fish!'

'That can be explained,' Melsona interjected. 'You see, this world has progressed so far that one great problem is how to keep people occupied. There is no monetary system; everything can be had for the mere asking. All work, manufacturing and the like, is carried on by volunteers, but so efficient are our methods that there is never enough work for all the people who want it. Inhabitants of this world have to fill up a very large amount of spare time somehow or other; consequently, work, once a curse, is now a godsend.

'How do our citizens spend their spare time? I will tell you. A little less than half devote themselves to science, a little more than half devote themselves to art. People invent things or create things, and everybody tries to make his work individualistic or superior to that of others.

'People dispose of the unwanted products of their own handicrafts by placing them in the shops for disposal to the persons who ask for them. The greatest shame any citizen can feel is when one of his products stands waiting in a shop for months. The greatest triumph he can experience is when so many clamor for one of his works that it has to be disposed by means of drawing lots.

'People who collect the work of any particular artist or have a special desire to acquire one of his works can obtain them in three ways: they can get them from a shop for the asking, if the shop happens to have them; or, if the artist is so popular his work never reaches a shop, they can apply to the artist to join with other applicants in drawing lots for his work; or, if the artist happens to be a collector himself they can barter with him.

'This explains your man's intention of changing a coin for a glass fish. Coins of your age are not rare; they are absolutely unknown and, therefore, of incalculable pleasure to a collector. One of our most prominent collectors of these old trading tokens is Torquilea, who is Earth's greatest glass artist. I would like you to see an example of his work. Come with me.'

10

Following Melsona's lead we marched along the pavement in the opposite direction to the motion of the road. A lively conversation was maintained; it consisted mainly of questions by Henshaw and myself, and Melsona's answers. We gathered that a system of moving roadways radiated like the spokes of a wheel from the center of Leamore to its outskirts, that roads ran inward and outward alternately, that people who wanted to travel in the opposite direction to a road's motion either walked along the pavements or cut through a side street to the next road. This road ran to the center of the city; if Nelson was returning home from the centre and did not care to walk, he just took the adjacent road, which ran outward, and entered his house by the back way. All roads exceeding thirty meters in width were moving roads; narrower roads were stable. The whole system of transport was absurdly simple.

Melsona was explaining to us that private air machines and wheeled vehicles existed in large numbers, but were not allowed to enter into, or fly over, any city, confining their activities to the terrain between towns. Just then we passed an open-air café. We did not go far past; with one accord, we retraced our steps, entered and claimed a table.

'– thus only the great liners bound for city airports are permitted to pass over occupied areas,' said Melsona, finishing his conversation. 'What will you have?'

'Beef,' said Henshaw.

'Beef? What is that?'

'Meat,' said Henshaw, licking his lips, and easing the belt around his rompers. An expression of ineffable disgust appeared on Melsona's face.

'I was only joking,' Henshaw assured him, quick-wittedly. 'I'll have whatever you recommend.'

Melsona's expression suggested that he did not regard the joke as being in the best of taste. He scribbled on a pad framed in the table's center, rammed his foot on a pedal protruding from the floor. The table sank downward, leaving us gaping into a shaft between our feet. After a short pause the table rose into view, settled before us with its top bearing the three meals ordered. We set to. The food was strange, but satisfying.

Eventually, feeling like a new man, I left the table and, with my companions, continued along the pavement. I fell into a reverie, thinking how queer it was that my previous meal was only a few hours before – or was it thousands of years? We had walked for about ten minutes, when Melsona stopped so suddenly that, still buried in my thoughts, I bumped into him. He pointed to the garden of a beautiful villa.

'Here's a fine sample of Torquilea's work,' he remarked. 'Come inside and take a look at it.' Without hesitation, he opened the gate and stepped into the garden, telling us that our interested inspection would be regarded as most flattering both by the artist and the owner. He led us to an object standing in the middle of the lawn. We looked at it in silence. It was divine; there was no other word for it.

A mass of colored marble, onyx, agate and lapis lazuli, ingeniously arranged, arose to a height of ten or twelve feet. Over it flowed a mock waterfall of glass so realistic one was shocked by the lack of noise. So superb was the artist's cunning that even the grain of the underlying stone had been utilized to create an impression of subsurface swirls. Embedded in the glass, by what means I could not determine, were bubbles and shadows and vague flickers of light making a perfect simulation of live and dancing water.

The fall broke at the bottom, eddying and spraying among the colored rocks, while here and there little drops of spray hung glistening in various cracks and crannies. A pair of glass salmon were leaping the fall. By looking closer I could discern that several fine wires held them suspended in midair, but so accurately were they formed by the fingers of genius it was hard to believe that the wand of some modern Merlin had not fixed them thus when in full enjoyment of vibrant life.

Henshaw removed his pork-pie and said, 'I take off my hat to this!'

'It was indeed a great triumph for Torquilea,' Melsona told us. 'No less than twenty-seven thousand persons drew lots to decide who should have this particular masterpiece.'

He looked wistfully at Henshaw. 'Torquilea is crazy about old coins. Only the other day I saw one of his works that will soon be given to somebody. It was simply a small bowl containing a seashore pool in glass. Sand and pebbles lay over its bottom; a pair of semi-transparent shrimps sported in its depths; a strand of green seaweed grew from a small rock on which bloomed a beautiful sea anemone with all its tentacles fully extended. It was a reproduction of nature so truthful, so marvelous, one half expected ripples on the surface of the glass. Torquilea is the happiest of men to have his work so eagerly sought after. I am sure he would consider an exchange.'

Henshaw took the hint. Fishing out a coin, he handed it to Melsona, telling him to put it to the best use on behalf of us all. This grouping together of us three seemed to please Melsona immensely. He accepted the gift with glee, announcing that he would interview Torquilea at the first opportunity.

Darkness had fallen several hours when we returned to Melsona's house for rest and sleep. We had ridden half the roads of Leamore, explored many shops and buildings, seen many marvels and had been introduced to so many people we could not remember more than a couple of them. Melsona, continuing in his voluntary capacity of city guide, had conducted us hither and thither, declaring himself to be the luckiest of men because our arrival had provided him with the means to use up leisure hours. His conversation, under the continual urge of our questions, informed us of a number of remarkable facts.

We found, first of all, that the day was much longer than in my time, and that Earth's axial rotation was slowing down at such a rate scientists estimated it would cease altogether in another twenty to thirty thousand years. The phenomenon dated from the arrival of The Invader, which time inaugurated the new calendar and made this the year 772 N.R.; the letters N.R. standing for 'new reckoning.'

The Invader, we were informed, was a planet about twice the size of Jupiter, which had come through interstellar space, cleaved a path through the solar system and vanished into the cosmos. It passed between the orbits of Mars and the asteroid belt, its influence upsetting the normal balance of half the system, making the paths of the asteroids, Mars and Earth much more eccentric, capturing and taking with it two members of the Trojan group of asteroids.

We were told that Venus had been reached by rocket ships about fifty years after The Invader had passed, that interplanetary travel was still so difficult, so risky, that the present population of Venus was not more than twelve thousand, and that for every individual who had reached the planet safely another had been killed in the attempt.

Earth's population had not altered in number for the last ten thousand years; all Earth acknowledged a central government situated in Osmia, and the social system was Pallarism. We found that Osmia was on the site of the city I had known as Constantinople, and that the 'ism' favored at the moment was based on the theories of a philosopher named Palla, who had lived about 22,800 O.R.

Our stomachs warmed with a late supper, our minds filled with memories of the day's explorations, we went to bed. With quiet deference to my taste, our host had laid upon my bed what looked like a black bathing costume. The crimson nightgown had been transferred to Henshaw's bed. Henshaw came into my room to get my opinion of how he looked prepared for slumber. I fell asleep murmuring a description he could not hear.

11

The following four days I count the most pleasant I have experienced. We travelled extensively with our host, becoming completely at home in this strange new world. Upon the morning of the fifth day we were riding on the center track of the Derby Highway, toward the outskirts of the city, when Melsona whistled to an old man walking along the pavement in the opposite direction. The old man stopped, Melsona transferred to the slow track, then to the pavement. We followed.

'This is Senior Glen Moncho,' he introduced us. 'Senior is a title we have for very learned men,' he added in explanation.

'Like professor,' I suggested.

'Exactly. This is Senior Glyn Weston and Captain Henshaw.' He smiled as we shook hands in turn. 'The senior is our most prominent historian. I thought he would have a special interest in meeting you.'

Henshaw was quick to seize the opportunity. He asked, 'Who won the White-Yellow War of 2481 to 2486?'

'The women,' replied the senior promptly.

'The women!' Henshaw looked dazed.

'The war lasted nine years, not five,' the senior continued. 'It was brought to an end by a militant organization of women who, first of all, refused to bear any more children, then deserted the munitions factories, causing both sides to withdraw great numbers of men to replace them, and, finally, took up arms and assassinated the individuals whom they considered to be the key men of the war. The conflict was the direct cause of the world matriarchy that held sway for the next three thousand years.'

'Well, I'm a dirty soldier!' cried Henshaw.

'So you're the famous time traveler,' said the senior, turning to me. 'I've heard a lot about you over the newscast. I understand that you are to be invited to the Annual Convention of Scientists to be held in Metro a week hence. It would be very interesting if you could bring your travel apparatus with you.'

'Now isn't that curious!' I said. 'I've been here several days and it has never occurred to me to inquire what has happened to the device.'

'It is quite safe,' said Melsona. 'It was carried along on the road while you were being taken into my house. It was rescued and placed in the Science Museum until such time as you wish to have it.'

'Good,' I responded. 'Would you like to go and see it?' Both Senior Moncho and Melsona indicated their eagerness to inspect the time-travel room. We cut through a side street to the next road, moving inward, stood upon an outer five-mile track and glided cityward.

'The most curious thing about time travel,' I said to the senior, 'is how it alters one's ideas. For instance, one would think that I have defeated Nature by living for thousands of years but, as a time traveller, I know that I have not. Actually, I am about a week older than when first I started my experiment. I now know that Nature has fixed the date of my end, not in terms of years of human computation but in terms of years of my life. I shall die a certain number of *my own years* after my birth, regardless of how that number of years may be divided out, or distributed over the future.'

'There is one point which, to my mind, is even more curious,' the senior remarked. 'How is it that we, with our great civilization, our enormous interest in every branch of science, have not been able to solve the problem which already has been solved by two who antedate us by thousands of years?'

'Henshaw hasn't solved it,' I told him.

'I was not referring to Henshaw, but to your predecessor.'

'My predecessor?' I failed to grasp the meaning.

'I told you that time traveling was known to us,' put in Melsona. 'I told you when first we met that it had been accomplished before.'

I searched my memory and found that I did have a vague recollection of his mentioning something of the sort. It had escaped me at the time, as I had felt rather confused.

'When Schweil turned up, claiming that –'

'Schweil!' I shouted at the top of my voice. 'Did you say *Schweil?*'

'Yes!' answered the senior, looking very startled. 'When he turned up claiming he had come originally from about your time, he was laughed at, and was –'

'Tell me,' I interrupted, 'from what year did he claim to come?'

'Let me see.' He studied the ground and thought for an exasperatingly long time. 'It was nineteen hundred and forty-four, I think.'

'That's it!' I howled, literally shaking with excitement. 'That's it!' Surrounding people stared at me as if they thought I was mad. I was making an exhibition of myself and didn't care.

'Did you know him?' asked the senior, a soothing note in his voice.

'No. He died a few years before I was born. Or he was believed to have died. He set out in his private airplane with the avowed intention of attending a scientific congress in New York. He vanished. The wreckage of his plane reached the shores of Nova Scotia a month later. He was rather eccentric, not very popular, and some people suggested that it was a plain case of suicide. His theories, and those of his successor, were used by me. What happened to him? Where is he? Please tell me about him – everything you know.'

The senior looked overwhelmed, took a deep breath and said, 'In 312 N.R., four hundred and sixty years ago, this man Schweil appeared on the outskirts of Metro, our great city on the Thames, and claimed that he had traveled through time from the past. His machine took the form of a dull metal sphere about three meters in diameter. Despite his atavistic characteristics, he was not believed. His machine was examined and pronounced a hoax.

'He was in the unfortunate position of not being able to prove his assertions, except by giving a practical demonstration and thus removing himself from the very people who were to be convinced, for he told us that though one could travel into the future there could be *no* motion into the past.'

'Quite correct,' I said, hanging on every word.

'He was very bitter. According to him ours was the eighth era he had visited and in not a single one of them had he been believed. In the end, he emigrated to Venus, taking his metal sphere with him. He lived there for nearly a year, then managed to convince us that his claims were justified. He did it by stepping into his sphere and vanishing before the eyes of a thousand colonists. He has not returned. We have seen nothing of him since.'

'He has traveled forward,' I said, jumping about like a cat on hot bricks. 'He has traveled forward. Oh, if only I could meet him! A man from my own time, a fit companion for my travels! I *must* meet him! I must find him somehow! He awaits me somewhere in the tomorrow. I must seek him! My travel room must be transported to Venus at once!' So saying, in my crazy excitement I jumped on to the faster center track and rushed along it, my mind filled with only one thought: to get to the Science Museum as soon as possible and arrange for the transport of the room.

The exertion of running must have calmed my mind. Half a mile along the road I transferred myself to the pavement and waited for the others to catch up with me. They came stringing along breathlessly, first Henshaw, then Melsona, the senior a bad last and finding the going hard.

Together we entered the Museum, where Melsona inquired where my room had been placed. Following his lead, we reached it on the top floor. By this time I had cooled enough to remember that my companions wanted to examine it. I opened the door and proceeded to explain to them how the ray apparatus worked and the theories it made use of.

The room seemed to have suffered slight damage. The outside corners were badly scratched and dented; one of the windows was cracked. I pulled out the valves and ray tube, held them up to the light and examined them, replacing them when I found them still in excellent condition.

I went over the whole apparatus, adjusting a cable here and tightening a terminal there. For several minutes I pottered about like a mother attending to her babe. I was in the act of bending down to examine a McAndrew vibrator contact when a nausea overcame me and the contact blurred before my gaze.

12

I straightened, saw the windows framing a semitransparancy in which a vague shadow danced, flickered, then disappeared like the flame of a snuffed candle. Panic overcame me, as a familiar mist obscured my sight. I realized what had happened. By some means the projector had come into operation.

Frantically, I searched the enveloping haze for the switch. The rapidly alternating impressions of smoothness and fibrousness fuddled my mind. I searched like a drunken man looking for he knew not what. Everything my hand touched I pulled. I tugged at unseen objects that refused to move. I heaved upon things that came out and sprang back again.

For how long I acted thus I do not know. I grew frantic at the knowledge that my last sweet world was receding rapidly into the irreclaimable past. I commenced to kick wildly in every direction. A crash of glass, followed by a sensation of strain, rewarded my efforts. The mist cleared, leaving me gazing at a broken valve. The time-travel room had come to rest.

A heavy vapor coated the inside surfaces of the windows. My attention was attracted by a loud, hissing sound. I was astounded to discover air rushing outward through the gap in the partly open door. I closed the door tightly, turned the petcock of the spare oxygen bottle, rubbed moisture from the windowpanes and looked out.

The scene before my eyes was most depressing: a smooth, even expanse of dirt and dust extended to the horizon without break. The sky to one side was sparkled with white light, to the other it loomed a dark, ominous purple. One glance told me that the world of this day was airless, deserted, dead. Horror took command of me with the knowledge that my hours were numbered. Death awaited me without – and within!

Hours later, with the precious oxygen still dribbling away, I stared gloomily through the windows of my room, noting that the sky had not changed in the slightest degree and that apparently I was stationed in a zone of perpetual twilight. Even as I watched, some instinct drew my attention to the far horizon. There, in a majestic curve, swooped a colossal space ship, its sleek body glistening, its tail plumed with fire. My heart leaped as I followed its line of flight until it dipped to an invisible landing place just over the edge of the Earth.

It did not occur to me to wonder why a space ship should fly over an airless world. The idea that I might be the victim of my own delusion never entered my head. I folded a handkerchief to form a pad, secured it over the end of the nearly empty oxygen bottle and opened the door. Ramming the pad against my nostrils, I ran toward the horizon –

For endless miles I seemed to run with heaving chest, thudding heart and whirling brain. My tongue swelled in my mouth; my eyes protruded painfully; I ceased to see. Whether I was moving in a straight line or in circles, I did not know or care. The main thing was to keep moving. Delirium became my master; I moved, moved, moved like an automaton.

I must have dropped the oxygen bottle; I must have fallen and died. But I have no recollection of it. My last memory of Earth is that of fleeing on leaden feet like one chased by phantoms in a nightmare. You know the rest of my story. I came to my senses lying in the resuscitation room at Kar Institute, my body racked with pain, my pulses throbbing in sympathy with the beating of a mechanical heart suspended over my chest.

What next? You are entitled to know. It is my intention to spend a little while touring your beautiful world. I wish to see the sights, to study your customs. With much interest I have learned that the immense amount of work resulting from the Great Migration has caused many radical changes from the world I visited last. I want to read about the Great Migration to learn all there is to learn about this remarkable epic in human history, to know the nature of the changes it has brought about such as, for instance, your return to a monetary system.

Then I shall set to work and build myself another time-travel room. I shall do this because I am going to find my age-compatriot Schweil. We need each other. Would you like to know how I expect to accomplish this? Let me tell you.

I shall make a series of very short jumps into the future and from them I shall derive the data necessary for certain calculations which, when completed, will enable me to set out for a predetermined date. If Schweil has not turned up by then, I shall leave a message for him making an appointment far into the future, and will then depart for that date. When Schweil arrives, and gets my message, he will travel to the same date. Thus we shall meet at a rendezvous in futurity.

I have no doubt that the scheme will work, if only Schweil is given my message. You will have to look for him. I am sure that already he has returned a dozen times since last he was heard of. Because of his previous receptions, knowing his character as I do, I can tell you he is likely to return secretly, without publicity.

You can assist me! All I ask of you is that you keep my story and my message ever fresh!

The stereo announcer padded softly in the direction of the transmission screen. The auditorium was a mass of eyes fixed intently on one central figure. With an abrupt movement, Glyn Weston, the 'Seeker of Tomorrow,' left the stage.

DAWN OF FLAME

Stanley G. Weinbaum

1

The World

Hull Tarvish looked backward but once, and that only as he reached the elbow of the road. The sprawling little stone cottage that had been home was visible as he had seen it a thousand times, framed under the cedars. His mother still watched him, and two of his younger brothers stood staring down the mountainside at him. He raised his hand in farewell, then dropped it as he realized that none of them saw him now; his mother had turned indifferently to the door, and the two youngsters had spied a rabbit. He faced about and strode away, down the slope out of Ozarky.

He passed the place where the great steel road of the Ancients had been, now only two rusty streaks and a row of decayed logs. Beside it was the mossy heap of stones that had been an ancient structure in the days before the Dark Centuries, when Ozarky had been a part of the old state of M'souri. The mountain people still sought out the place for squared stones to use in building, but the tough metal of the steel road itself was too stubborn for their use, and the rails had rusted quietly these three hundred years.

That much Hull Tarvish knew, for they were things still spoken of at night around the fireplace. They had been mighty sorcerers, those Ancients; their steel roads went everywhere, and everywhere were the ruins of their towns, built, it was said, by magic that lifted weights. Down in the valley, he knew, men were still seeking that magic; once a rider had stayed by night at the Tarvish home, a little man who said that in the far south the

367

secret had been found, but nobody ever heard any more of it.

So Hull whistled to himself, shifted the rag bag on his shoulder, set his bow more comfortably on his mighty back, and trudged on. That was why he himself was seeking the valley; he wanted to see what the world was like. He had been always a restless sort, not at all like the other six Tarvish sons, nor like the three Tarvish daughters. They were true mountainies, the sons great hunters, and the daughters stolid and industrious. Not Hull, however; he was neither lazy like his brothers nor stolid like his sisters, but restless, curious, dreamy. So he whistled his way into the world, and was happy.

At evening he stopped at the Hobel cottage on the edge of the mountains. Away before him stretched the plain, and in the darkening distance was visible the church spire of Norse. That was a village; Hull had never seen a village, or no more of it than this same distant steeple, shaped like a straight white pine. But he had heard all about Norse, because the mountanies occasionally went down there to buy powder and ball for their rifles, those of them who had rifles.

Hull had only a bow. He didn't see the use of guns; powder and ball cost money, but an arrow did the same work for nothing, and that without scaring all the game a mile away.

Morning he bade goodbye to the Hobels, who thought him, as they always had, a little crazy, and set off. His powerful, brown bare legs flashed under his ragged trousers, his bare feet made a pleasant *soosh* in the dust of the road, the June sun beat warm on his right cheek. He was happy; there never was a pleasanter world than this, so he grinned and whistled, and spat carefully into the dust, remembering that it was bad luck to spit toward the sun. He was bound for adventure.

Adventure came. Hull had come down to the plain now, where the trees were taller than the scrub of the hill country, and where the occasional farms were broader, well tilled, more prosperous. The trail had become a wagon road, and here it cut and angled between two lines of forest. And unexpectedly a man – no, two men – rose from a log at the roadside and approached Hull. He watched them; one was tall and light-haired as himself, but without his mighty frame, and the other was a head shorter, and dark. Valley people, surely, for the dark one had a stubby pistol at his belt, wooden-stocked like those of the Ancients, and the tall man's bow was of glittering spring steel.

'Ho, mountainy!' said the dark one. 'Where going?'

'Norse,' answered Hull shortly.

'What's in the bag?'

'My tongue,'* snapped the youth.

'Easy, there,' grunted the light man. 'No offense, mountainy. We're just curious. That's a good knife you got. I'll trade it.'

'For what?'

'For lead in your craw,' growled the dark one. Suddenly the blunt pistol was in his hand. 'Pass it over, and the bag too.'

Hull scowled from one to the other. At last he shrugged, and moved as if to lift his bag from his shoulders. And then, swift as the thrust of a striking diamondback, his left foot shot forward, catching the dark one squarely in the pit of his stomach, with the might of Hull's muscles and weight behind it.

The man had breath for a low grunt; he doubled and fell, while his weapon spun a dozen feet away into the dust. The light one sprang for it, but Hull caught him with a great arm about his throat, wrenched twice, and the brief fight was over. He swung placidly on toward Norse with a blunt revolver primed and capped at his hip, a glistening spring-steel bow on his shoulder, and twenty-two bright tubular steel arrows in his quiver.

He topped a little rise and the town lay before him. He stared. A hundred houses at least. Must be five hundred people in the town, more people than he'd ever seen in his life altogether. He strode eagerly on, goggling at the church that towered high as a tall tree, at the windows of bits of glass salvaged from ancient ruins and carefully pieced together, at the tavern with its swinging emblem of an unbelievably fat man holding a mammoth mug. He stared at the houses, some of them with shops before them, and at the people, most of them shod in leather.

He himself attracted little attention. Norse was used to the mountainies, and only a girl or two turned appraising eyes toward his mighty figure. That made him uncomfortable, however; the girls of the mountains giggled and blushed, but never at that age did they stare at a man. So he gazed defiantly back, letting his eyes wander from their bonnets to the billowing skirts above their leather strap-sandals, and they laughed and passed on.

Hull didn't care for Norse, he decided. As the sun set, the houses loomed too close, as if they'd stifle him, so he set out into the countryside to sleep. The remains of an ancient town bordered the village, with its spectral walls crumbling against the

---

* Idiom of the second century of the Enlightenment. To have 'one's tongue in the bag' was to refuse to answer questions.

west. There were ghosts there, of course, so he walked farther, found a wooded spot, and lay down, putting his bow and the steel arrows into his bag against the rusting effect of night-dew. Then he tied the bag about his bare feet and legs, sprawled comfortably, and slept with his hand on the pistol grip. Of course there were no animals to fear in these woods save the wolves, and they never attacked humans during the warm parts of the year, but there were men, and *they* bound themselves by no such seasonal laws.

He awoke dewy wet. The sun shot golden lances through the trees, and he was ravenously hungry. He ate the last of his mother's brown bread from his bag, now crumbled by his feet, and then strode out to the road. There was a wagon creaking there, plodding northward; the bearded, kindly man in it was glad enough to have him ride for company.

'Mountainy?' he asked.

'Yes.'

'Bound where?'

'The world,' said Hull.

'Well,' observed the other, 'it's a big place, and all I've seen of it much like this. All except Selui. That's a city. Yes, that's a city. Been there?'

'No.'

'It's got,' said the farmer impressively, 'twenty thousand people in it. Maybe more. And they got ruins there the biggest you ever saw. Bridges. Buildings. Four – five times as high as the Norse church, and at that they're fallen down. The Devil knows how high they used to be in the old days.

'Who lived in 'em?' asked Hull.

'Don't know. Who'd want to live so high up it'd take a full morning to climb there? Unless it was magic. I don't hold much with magic, but they do say the Old People knew how to fly.'

Hull tried to imagine this. For a while there was silence save for the slow clump of the horses' hooves. 'I don't believe it,' he said at last.

'Nor I. But did you hear what they're saying in Norse?'

'I didn't hear anything.'

'They say,' said the farmer, 'that Joaquin Smith is going to march again.'

'Joaquin Smith!'

'Yeah. Even the mountainies know about him, eh?'

'Who doesn't?' returned Hull. 'Then there'll be fighting in the south, I guess. I have a notion to go south.'

'Why?'

'I like fighting,' said Hull simply.

'Fair answer,' said the farmer, 'but from what folks say, there's not much fighting when the Master marches. He has a spell; there's great sorcery in N'Orleans, from the merest warlock up to Martin Sair, who's blood-son of the Devil himself, or so they say.'

'I'd like to see his sorcery against the mountainy's arrow and ball,' said Hull grimly. 'There's none of us can't spot either eye at a thousand paces, using rifle. Or two hundred with arrow.'

'No doubt; but what if powder flames, and guns fire themselves before he's even across the horizon? They say he has a spell for that, he or Black Margot.'

'Black Margot?'

'The Princess, his half-sister. The dark witch who rides beside him, the Princess Margaret.'

'Oh – but why Black Margot?'

The farmer shrugged. 'Who knows? It's what her enemies call her.'

'Then so I call her,' said Hull.

'Well, I don't know,' said the other. 'It makes small difference to me whether I pay taxes to N'Orleans or to gruff old Marcus Ormiston, who's eldarch of Ormiston village there.' He flicked his whip toward the distance ahead, where Hull now descried houses and the flash of a little river. 'I've sold produce in towns within the Empire, and the people of them seemed as happy as ourselves, no more, no less.'

'There is a difference, though. It's freedom.'

'Merely a word, my friend. They plow, they sow, they reap, just as we do. They hunt, they fish, they fight. And as for freedom, are they less free with a warlock to rule them than I with a wizened fool?'

'The mountanies pay taxes to no one.'

'And no one builds them roads, nor digs them public wells. Where you pay little you get less, and I *will* say that the roads within the Empire are better than ours.'

'Better than this?' asked Hull, staring at the dusty width of the highway.

'Far better. Near Memphis town is a road of solid rock, which they spread soft through some magic, and let harden, so there is neither mud nor dust.'

Hull mused over this. 'The Master,' he burst out suddenly, 'is he really immortal?'

The other shrugged. 'How can I say? There are great sorcerers in the southlands, and the greatest of them is Martin Sair. But I do know this, that I have seen sixty two years, and as far back as memory goes there was always Joaquin Smith in the south, and always an Empire gobbling cities as a hare gobbles carrots. When I was young it was far away, now it reaches close at hand; that is all the difference. Men talked of the beauty of Black Margot then as they do now, and of the wizardry of Martin Sair.'

Hull made no answer, for Ormiston was at hand. The village was much like Norse save that it huddled among low hills, on the crest of some of which loomed ancient ruins. At the rear side his companion halted, and Hull thanked him as he leaped to the ground.

'Where to?' asked the farmer.

Hull thought a moment. 'Selui,' he said.

'Well, it's a hundred miles, but there'll be many to ride you.'

'I have my own feet,' said the youth. He spun suddenly about at a voice across the road: 'Hi! Mountainy!'

It was a girl. A very pretty girl, slim waisted, copper-haired, blue eyed, standing at the gate before a large stone house. 'Hi!' she called. 'Will you work for your dinner?'

Hull was ravenous again. 'Gladly!' he cried.

The voice of the farmer sounded behind him. 'It's Vail Ormiston, the dotard eldarch's daugher. Hold her for a full meal, mountainy. My taxes are paying for it.'

But Vail Ormiston was above much converse with a wandering mountain-man. She surveyed his mighty form approvingly, showed him the logs he was to quarter, and then disappeared into the house. If, perchance, she peeped out through the clearest of the ancient glass fragments that formed the window, and if she watched the flexing muscles of his great bare arms as he swung the axe – well, he was unaware of it.

So it happened that afternoon found him trudging toward Selui with a hearty meal inside him and three silver dimes in his pocket, ancient money, with the striding figure of the woman all but worn away. He was richer than when he had set out by those coins, by the blunt pistol at his hip, by the shiny steel bow and arrows, and by the memory of the copper hair and blue eyes of Vail Ormiston.

2
Old Einar

Three weeks in Selui had served to give Hull Tarvish a sort of speaking acquaintancy with the place. He no longer gaped at the skypiercing ruins of the ancient city, or the vast fallen bridges, and he was quite at home in the town that lay beside it. He had found work easily enough in a baker's establishment, where his great muscles served well; the hours were long, but his pay was munificent – five silver quarters a week. He paid two for lodging, and food – what he needed beyond the burnt loaves at hand from his employment – cost him another quarter, but that left two to put by. He never gambled other than a wager now and then on his own marksmanship, and that was more profitable than otherwise.

Ordinarily Hull was quick to make friends, but his long hours hindered him. He had but one, an incredibly old man who sat at evening on the step beyond his lodging, Old Einar. So this evening Hull wandered out as usual to join him, staring at the crumbling towers of the Ancients glowing in the sunset. Trees sprung on many, and all were green with vine and tussock and the growth of wind-carried seeds. No one dared build among the ruins, for none could guess when the great tower might come crashing down.

'I wonder,' he said to Old Einar, 'what the Ancients were like. Were they men like us? Then how could they fly?'

'They were men like us, Hull. As for flying – well, it's my belief that flying is a legend. See here; there was a man supposed to have flown over the cold lands to the north and those to the south, and also across the great sea. But this flying man is called in some accounts Lindbird and in others Bird, and surely one can see the origin of such a legend. The migrations of birds, who cross land and seas each year, that is all.'

'Or perhaps magic,' suggested Hull.

'There *is* no magic. The Ancients themselves denied it, and I have struggled through many a moldy book in their curious, archaic tongue.'

Old Einar was the first scholar Hull had ever encountered. Though there were many during the dawn of that brilliant age called the Second Enlightenment, most of them were still within the Empire. John Holland was dead, but Olin was yet alive in the world, and Kohlmar, and Jorgensen, and Teran, and Martin

Sair, and Joaquin Smith the Master. Great names – the names of demigods.

But Hull knew little of them. 'You can read!' he exclaimed. 'That in itself is a sort of magic. And you have been within the Empire, even in N'Orleans. Tell me, what is the Great City like? Have they really learned the secrets of the Ancients? Are the Immortals truly immortal? How did they gain their knowledge?'

Old Einar settled himself on the step and puffed blue smoke from his pipe filled with the harsh tobacco of the region. 'Too many questions breed answers to none,' he observed. 'Shall I tell you the true story of the world, Hull – the story called History?'

'Yes. In Ozarky we spoke little of such things.'

'Well,' said the old man comfortably, 'I will begin then, at what to us is the beginning, but to the Ancients was the end. I do not know what factors, what wars, what struggles, led up to the mighty world that died during the Dark Centuries, but I do know that three hundred years ago the world reached its climax. You cannot imagine such a place. Hull. It was a time of vast cities, too – fifty times as large as N'Orleans with its hundred thousand people.'

He puffed slowly. 'Great steel wagons roared over the iron roads of the Ancients. Men crossed the oceans to east and west. The cities were full of whirring wheels, and instead of the many little city-states of our time, there were giant nations with thousands of cities and a hundred million – a hundred and fifty million people.'

Hull stared. 'I do not believe there are so many people in the world,' he said.

Old Einar shrugged. 'Who knows?' he returned. 'The ancient books – all too few – tell us that the world is round, and that beyond the seas lie one, or several continents, but what races are there today not even Joaquin Smith can say.' He puffed smoke again. 'Well, such was the ancient world. These were warlike nations, so fond of battle that they had to write many books about the horrors of war to keep themselves at peace, but they always failed. During the time they called their twentieth century there was a whole series of wars, not such little quarrels as we have so often between our city-states, nor even such as that between the Memphis League and the Empire, five years ago. *Their* wars spread like storm clouds around the world, and were fought between millions of men and unimaginable weapons that flung destruction a hundred miles, and with ships on the seas, and with gases.'

'What's gases?' asked Hull.

Old Einar waved his hand so that the wind of it brushed the youth's brown cheek. 'Air is a gas,' he said. 'They knew how to poison the air so that all who breathed it died. And they fought with diseases, and legend says that they fought also in the air with wings, but that is only legend.'

'Diseases!' said Hull. 'Diseases are the breath of Devils, and if they controlled Devils they used sorcery, and therefore they knew magic.'

'There *is* no magic,' reiterated the old man. '*I* do not know how they fought each other with diseases, but Martin Sair of N'Orleans knows. That was *his* study, not mine, but I know there was no magic in it.' He resumed his tale. 'So these great fierce nations flung themselves against each other, for war meant more to them than to us. With us it is something of a rough, joyous, dangerous game, but to them it was a passion. They fought for any reason, or for none at all save the love of fighting.'

'*I* love fighting,' said Hull.

'Yes, but would you love it if it meant simply the destroying of thousands of men beyond the horizon? Men you were never to see?'

'No. War should be man to man, or at least no farther than the carry of a rifle ball.'

'True. Well, some time near the end of their twentieth century, the ancient world exploded into war like a powder horn in a fire. They say every nation fought, and battles surged back and forth across seas and continents. It was not only nation against nation, but race against race, black and white and yellow and red, all embroiled in a titanic struggle.'

'Yellow and red?' echoed Hull. 'There are a few black men called Nigs in Ozarky, but I never heard of yellow or red men.'

'I have seen yellow men,' said Old Einar. 'There are some towns of yellow men on the edge of the western ocean, in the region called Friscia. The red race, they say, is gone, wiped out by the plague called the Grey Death, to which they yielded more readily than the other races.'

I have heard of the Grey Death,' said Hull. 'When I was very young, there was an old, old man who used to say that his grand-father had lived in the days of the Death.'

Old Einar smiled. 'I doubt it, Hull. It was something over two and a half centuries ago. However,' he resumed, 'the great ancient nations were at war, and as I say, they fought with diseases. Whether some nation learned the secret of the Grey

Death, or whether it grew up as a sort of cross between two or more other diseases, I do not know. Martin Sair says that diseases are living things, so it may be so. At any rate, the Grey Death leaped suddenly across the world, striking alike at all people. Everywhere it blasted the armies, the cities, the country-side, and of those it struck, six out of every ten died. There must have been chaos in the world; we have not a single book printed during that time, and only legend tells the story.

'But the war collapsed. Armies suddenly found themselves unopposed, and then were blasted before they could move. Ships in mid-ocean were stricken, and drifted unmanned to pile in wreckage, or to destroy others. In the cities the dead were piled in the streets, and after a while, were simply left where they fell, while those who survived fled away into the country. What remained of the armies became little better than roving robber bands, and by the third year of the plague there were few if any stable governments in the world.'

'What stopped it?' asked Hull.

'I do not know. They end, these pestilences. Those who take it and live cannot take it a second time, and those who are somehow immune do not take it at all, and the rest—die. The Grey Death swept the world for three years; when it ended, according to Martin Sair, one person in four had died. But the plague came back in lessening waves for many years; only a pestilence in the Ancient's fourteenth century, called the Black Death, seems ever to have equalled it.

'Yet its effects were only beginning. The ancient transport system had simply collapsed, and the cities were starving. Hungry gangs began raiding the countryside, and instead of one vast war there were now a million little battles. The weapons of the Ancients were everywhere, and these battles were fierce enough, in all truth, though nothing like the colossal encounters of the great war. Year by year the cities decayed until by the fiftieth year after the Grey death, the world's population had fallen by three-fourths, and civilization was ended. It was barbarism now that ruled the world, but only barbarism, not savagery. People still remembered the mighty ancient civili-zation, and everywhere there were attempts to combine into the old nations, but these failed for lack of great leaders.'

'As they should fail,' said Hull. 'We have freedom now.'

'Perhaps. By the first century after the Plague, there was little left of the Ancients save their ruined cities where lurked robber bands that scoured the country by night. They had little interest in anything save food or the coined money of the old nations, and they did incalculable damage. Few could read, and on cold nights it was usual to raid the ancient libraries for books to burn, and to make things worse, fire gutted the ruins of all cities, and there was no organized resistance to it. The flames simply burned themselves out, and priceless books vanished.'

'Yet in N'Orleans they study, don't they?' asked Hull.

'Yes, I'm coming to that. About two centuries after the Plague—a hundred years ago, that is—the world had stabilized itself. It was much as it is here today, with little farming towns and vast stretches of deserted country. Gunpowder had been rediscovered, rifles were used, and most of the robber bands had been destroyed. And then, into the town of N'Orleans, built beside the ancient city, came young John Holland.

'Holland was a rare specimen, anxious for learning. He found the remains of an ancient library and began slowly to decipher the archiac words in the few books that had survived. Little by little others joined him, and as the word spread slowly, men from other sections wandered in with books, and the Academy was born. No one taught, of course; it was just a group of studious men living a sort of communistic, monastic life. There was no attempt at practical use of the ancient knowlege until a youth named Teran had a dream—no less a dream than to recondition the centuries-old power machines of N'Orleans, to give the city the power that travels on wires!'

'What's that?' asked Hull. 'What's that, Old Einar?'

'You wouldn't understand, Hull. Teran was an enthusiast; it didn't stop him to realize that there was no coal or oil to run his machines. He believed that when power was needed, it would be there, so he and his followers scrubbed and filed and welded away, and Teran was right. When he needed power, it was there.

'This was the gift of a man named Olin, who had unearthed the last, the crowning secret of the Ancients, the power called atomic energy. He gave it to Teran, and N'Orleans became a miracle city where lights glowed and wheels turned. Men came from every part of the continent to see, and among these were two called Martin Sair and Joaquin Smith, come out of Mexico with the half-sister of Joaquin, the Satanically beautiful being sometimes called Black Margot.

'Martin Sair was a genius. He found his field in the study of medicine, and it was less than ten years before he had uncovered the secret of the hard rays. He was studying sterility but he found—immortality!'

'Then the Immortals *are* immortal!' murmured Hull.

'It may be, Hull. At least they do not seem to age, but – Well, Joaquin Smith was also a genius, but of a different sort. He dreamed of the re-uniting of the peoples of the country. I think he dreams of even more, Hull; people say he will stop when he rules a hundred cities, but I think he dreams of an American Empire, or' – Old Einar's voice dropped – a world Empire. At least, he took Martin Sair's immortality and traded it for power. The Second Enlightenment was dawning and there was genius in N'Orleans. He traded immortality to Kohlmar for a weapon, he offered it to Olin for atomic power, but Olin was already past youth, and refused, partly because he didn't want it, and partly because he was not entirely in sympathy with Joaquin Smith. So the Master seized the secret of the atom despite Olin, and the Conquest began.

'N'Orleans, directly under the influence of the Master's magnetic personality, was ready to yield, and yielded to him cheering. He raised his army and marched north, and everywhere cities fell or yielded willingly. Joaquin Smith is magnificent, and men flock to him, cities cheer him, even the wives and children of the slain swear allegiance when he forgives them in that noble manner of his. Only here and there men hate him bitterly, and speak such words as tyrant, and talk of freedom.'

'Such are the mountanies,' said Hull.

'Not even the mountainies can stand the ionic beams that Kohlmar dug out of ancient books, nor the Erden resonator that explodes gunpowder miles away. I think that Joaquin Smith will succeed, Hull. Moreover, I do not think it entirely bad that he should, for he is a great ruler, and a bringer of civilization.'

'What are they like, the Immortals?'

'Well, Martin Sair is as cold as mountain rock, and the Princess Margaret is like black fire. Even my old bones feel younger only to look at her, and it is wise for young men not to look at her at all, because she is quite heartless, ruthless, and pitiless. As for Joaquin Smith, the Master–I do not know the words to describe so complex a character, and I know him well. He is mild, perhaps, but enormously strong, kind or cruel as suits his purpose, glitteringly intelligent, and dangerously charming.'

'You *know* him!' echoed Hull, and added curiously, 'What is your other name, Old Einar, you who know the Immortals?'

The old man smiled. 'When I was born,' he said, 'my parents called me Einar *Olin*.'

3
The Master Marches

Joaquin Smith was marching. Hull Tarvish leaned against the door of File Ormson's iron worker's shop in Ormiston, and stared across the fields and across the woodlands, and across to the blue mountains of Ozarky in the south. There is where he should have been, there with the mountainy men, but by the time the tired rider had brought the news to Selui, and by the time Hull had reached Ormiston, it was already too late, and Ozarky was but an outlying province of the expanding Empire, while the Master camped there above Norse, and sent representations to Selui.

Selui wasn't going to yield. Already the towns of the three months old Selui Confederation were sending in their men, from Bloom'ton, from Cairo, even from distant Ch'cago on the shores of the saltless sea Mitchin. The men of the Confederation hated the little slender, dark Ch'cagoans, for they had not yet forgotten the disastrous battle at Starved Rock, but any allies were welcome against Joaquin Smith. The Ch'cagoans were good enough fighters, too, and heart and soul in the cause, for if the Master took Selui, his Empire would reach dangerously close to the saltless seas, spreading from the ocean on the east to the mountains on the west, and north as far as the great confluence of the M'sippi and M'souri.

Hull knew there was fighting ahead, and he relished it. It was too bad that he couldn't have fought in Ozarky for his own people, but Ormiston would do. That was his home for the present, since he'd found work here with File Ormson, the squat iron-worker, broad-shouldered as Hull himself and a head shorter. Pleasant work for his mighty muscles, though at the moment there was nothing to do.

He stared at the peaceful countryside. Joaquin Smith was marching, and beyond the village, the farmers were still working in their fields. Hull listened to the slow Sowing Song:

This is what the ground needs:
First the plow and then the seeds,
Then the harrow and then the hoe,
And rain to make the harvest grow.

This is what the man needs:
First the promises, then the deeds,
Then the arrow and then the blade,
And last the digger with his black spade.

This is what his wife needs:
First a garden free of weeds,
Then the daughter, and then the son,
And a fireplace warm when the work is done.

This is what his son needs: —

Hull ceased to listen. They were singing, but Joaquin Smith was marching, marching with the men of a hundred cities, with his black banner and its golden serpent fluttering. That serpent, Old Einar had said, was the Midgard Serpent, which ancient legend related had encircled the earth. It was the symbol of the Master's dream, and for a moment Hull had a stirring of sympathy for that dream.

'No!' he growled to himself. 'Freedom's better, and it's for us to blow the head from the Midgard Serpent.'

A voice sounded at his side. 'Hull! Big Hull Tarvish! Are you too proud to notice humble folk?'

It was Vail Ormiston, her violet eyes whimsical below her smooth copper hair. He flushed; he was not used to the ways of these valley girls, who flirted frankly and openly in a manner impossible to the shy girls of the mountains. Yet he – well, in a way, he liked it, and he liked Vail Ormiston, and he remembered pleasantly an evening two days ago when he had sat and talked a full three hours with her on the bench by the tree that shaded Ormiston well. And he remembered the walk through the fields when she had shown him the mouth of the great ancient storm sewer that had run under the dead city, and that still stretched crumbling for miles underground toward the hills, and he recalled her story of how, when a child, she had lost herself in it, so that her father had planted the tangle of blackberry bushes that still concealed the opening.

He grinned, 'Is it the eldarch's daughter speaking of humble folk? Your father will be taxing me double if he hears of this.'

She tossed her helmet of metallic hair. 'He will if he sees you in that Selui finery of yours.' Her eyes twinkled. 'For whose eyes was it bought, Hull? For you'd be better saving your money.'

'Save silver, lose luck,' he retorted. After all, it wasn't so difficult a task to talk to her. 'Anyway, better a smile from you than the glitter of money.'

She laughed. 'But how quickly you learn, mountainy! Still, what if I say I liked you better in tatters, with your powerful brown muscles quivering through the rips?'

'*Do* you say it, Vail?'

'Yes, then!'

He chuckled, raising his great hands to his shoulders. There was the rasp of tearing cloth, and a long rent gleamed in the back of his Selui shirt, 'There, Vail!'

'Oh!' she gasped. 'Hull, you wastrel! But it's only a seam.' She fumbled in the bag at her belt. 'Let me stitch it back for you.'

She bent behind him, and he could feel her breath on his skin, warm as spring sunshine. He set his jaw, scowled, and then plunged determinedly into what he had to say. 'I'd like to talk to you again this evening, Vail.'

He sensed her smile at his back. 'Would you?' She murmured demurely.

'Yes, if Enoch Ormiston hasn't spoken first for your time.'

'But he has, Hull.'

He knew she was teasing him deliberately. 'I'm sorry,' he said shortly.

'But – I told him I was busy,' she finished.

'And are you?'

Her voice was a whisper behind him. 'No. Not unless you tell me I am.'

His great roar of a laugh sounded. 'Then I tell you so, Vail.'

He felt her tug at the seam, then she leaned very close to his neck, but it was only to bite the thread with her white teeth. 'So!' she said gaily. 'Once mended, twice new.'

Before Hull could answer there came the clang of File Ormson's sledge, and the measured bellow of his Forge Song. They listened as his resounding strokes beat time to the song.

Then it's ho-oh – ho-oh – ho!
While I'm singing to the ringing
Of each blow – blow – blow!
Till the metal's soft as butter
Let my forge and bellows sputter
Like the revels of the devils down below – low – LOW!
Like the revels of the devils down below!

'I must go,' said Hull, smiling reluctantly. 'There's work for me now.'

'What does File make?' asked Vail.

Instantly Hull's smile faded. 'He forges — a sword!'

Vail too was no longer the joyous one of a moment ago. Over both of them had come a shadow, the shadow of the Empire. Out in the blue hills of Ozarky Joaquin Smith was marching.

Evening. Hull watched the glint of a copper moon on Vail's copper hair, and leaned back on the bench. Not the one near the pump this time; that had been already occupied by two laughing couples, and though they had been welcomed eagerly enough, Hull had preferred to be alone. It wasn't mountain shyness any more, for his great, good-natured presence had found ready friendship in Ormiston village; it was merely the projection of that moodiness that had settled over both of them at parting, and so they sat now on the bench near Vail Ormiston's gate at the edge of town. Behind them the stone house loomed dark, for her father was scurrying about in town on Confederation business, and the help had availed themselves of the evening of freedom to join the crowd in the village square. But the yellow daylight of the oil-lamp showed across the road in the house of Hue Helm, the farmer who had brought Hull from Norse to Ormiston.

It was at this light that Hull stared thoughtfully. 'I *like* fighting,' he repeated, 'but somehow the joy has gone out of this. It's as if one waited an approaching thunder cloud.'

'How,' asked Vail in a timid, small voice, 'can one fight magic?'

'There is no magic,' said the youth, echoing Old Einar's words. 'There is no such thing.'

'Hull! How can you say such stupid words?'

'I say what was told me by one who knows.'

'No magic!' echoed Vail. 'Then tell me what gives the wizards of the south their power. Why is it that Joaquin Smith has never lost a battle? What stole away the courage of the men of the Memphis League, who are good fighting men? And what — for this I have seen with my own eyes — pushes the horseless wagons of N'Orleans through the streets, and what lights that city by night? If not magic, then what?'

'Knowledge,' said Hull. 'The knowledge of the Ancients.'

'The knowledge of the Ancients was magic,' said the girl. 'Everyone knows that the Ancients were wizards, warlocks, and sorcerers. If Holland, Olin, and Martin Sair are not sorcerers, then what are they? If Black Margot is no witch, then my eyes never looked on one?'

'Have you seen them?' queried Hull.

'Of course, all but Holland, who is dead. Three years ago during the Peace of Memphis my father and I traveled into the Empire. I saw all of them about the city of N'Orleans.'

'And is she – what they say she is?'

'The Princess?' Vail's eyes dropped. 'Men say she is beautiful.'

'But do you think not?'

'What if she *is*?' snapped the girl almost defiantly. 'Her beauty is like her youth, like her very life – artificial, preserved after its allotted time, frozen. That's it – frozen by sorcery. And as for the rest of her – ' Vail's voice lowered, hesitated, for not even the plain-spoken valley girls discussed such things with men. 'They say she has outworn a dozen lovers,' she whispered.

Hull was startled, shocked. 'Vail!' he muttered.

She swung the subject back to safer ground, but he saw her flush red. 'Don't tell *me* there's no magic!' she said sharply.

'At least,' he returned, 'there's no magic will stop a bullet save flesh and bone. Yes, and the wizard who stops one with his skull lies just as dead as an honest man.'

'I hope you're right,' she breathed timidly. 'Hull, he must be stopped! He *must!*'

'But why feel so strongly, Vail? I like a fight – but most men say that life in the Empire is much like life without, and who cares to whom he pays his taxes if only —' He broke off suddenly, remembering. 'Your father!' he exclaimed. 'The eldarch!'

'Yes my father, Hull. If Joaquin Smith takes Ormiston, my father is the one to suffer. His taxes will be gone, his land parceled out,and he's old, Hull – old. What will become of him then? I know many people feel the way you – the way you said, and so they fight half-heartedly, and the Master takes town after town without killing a single man. And then they think there is magic in the very name of Joaquin Smith, and he marches through armies that outnumber him ten to one.' She paused. 'But not Ormiston!' she cried fiercely. 'Not if the women have to bear arms!'.

'Not Ormiston,' he agreed gently.

'You'll fight, Hull, won't you? Even though you're not Ormiston born?'

'Of course, I have bow and sword, and a good pistol. I'll fight.'

'But no rifle? Wait, Hull.' She rose and slipped away in the darkness.

In a moment she was back again. 'Here. Here is rifle and horn and ball. Do you know its use?'

He smiled proudly. 'What I can see I can hit,' he said, 'like any mountain man.'

'Then,' she whispered with fire in her voice, 'send me a bullet through the Master's skull. And one besides between the eyes of Black Margot – for me!'

'I do not fight women,' he said.

'Not woman but witch!'

'None the less, Vail, it must be two bullets for the Master and only the captive's chains for Princess Margaret, at least so far as Hull Tarvish is concerned. But wouldn't it please you fully as well to watch her draw water from your pump, or shine pots in your kitchen?' He was jollying her, trying to paint fanciful pictures to lift her spirit from the somber depths.

But she read it otherwise. 'Yes!' she blazed. 'Oh, yes, Hull, that's better. If I could ever hope to see that —' She rose suddenly, and he followed her to the gate. 'You must go,' she murmured, 'but before you leave, you can – if you wish it, Hull – kiss me.'

Of a sudden he was all shy mountainy again. He set the rifle against the fence with its horn swinging from the trigger guard. He faced her flushing a furious red, but only half from embarrassment, for the rest was happiness. He circled her with his great arms and very hastily, he touched his lips to her soft ones.

'Now,' he said exultantly, 'now I will fight if I have to charge the men of the Empire alone.'

4
The Battle of Eaglefoot Flow

The men of the Confederation were pouring into Ormiston all night long, the little dark men of Ch'cago and Selui, the tall blond ones from the regions of Iowa, where Dutch blood still survived, mingled now with a Scandinavian infusion from the upper rivers. All night there was a rumble of wagons, bringing powder and ball from Selui, and food as well for Ormiston couldn't even atempt to feed so many ravenous mouths. A magnificent army, ten thousand strong, and all of them seasoned fighting men, trained in a dozen little wars and in the bloody War of the Lakes and Rivers, when Ch'cago had bitten so large a piece from Selui territories.

The stand was to be at Ormiston, and Norse, the only settlement now between Joaquin Smith and the Confederation, was left to its fate. Experienced leaders had examined the territory, and had agreed on a plan. Three miles south of the town, the road followed an ancient railroad cut, with fifty-foot embankments on either side, heavily wooded for a mile north and south of the bridge across Eaglefoot flow.

Along this course they were to distribute their men, a single line where the bluffs were high and steep, massed forces where the terrain permitted. Joaquin Smith *must* follow the road; there was no other. An ideal situation for ambush, and a magnificently simple plan. So magnificent and so simple that it could not fail, they said, and forgot completely that they were facing the supreme military genius of the entire Age of the Enlightenment.

It was mid-morning when the woods-runners that had been sent into Ozarky returned with breath-taking news. Joaquin Smith had received the Selui defiance of his representations, and was marching. The Master was marching, and though they had come swiftly and had ridden horseback from Norse, he could not now be far distant. His forces? The runners estimated them at four thousand men, all mounted, with perhaps another thousand auxiliaries. Outnumbered two to one! But Hull Tarvish remembered tales of other encounters where Joaquin Smith had overcome greater odds than these.

The time was at hand. In the little room beside File Ormson's workship, Hull was going over his weapons while Vail Ormiston, pale and nervous and very lovely, watched him. He drew a bit of oiled rag through the bore of the rifle she had given him, rubbed a spot of rust from the hammer, blew a speck of dust from the pan. Beside him on the table lay powder horn and ball, and his steel bow leaned against his chair.

'A sweet weapon!' he said admiringly, sighting down the long barrel.

'I – I hope it serves you well,' murmured Vail tremulously. 'Hull, he must be stopped. He *must!*'

We'll try, Vail,' He rose. 'It's time I started.'

She was facing him. 'Then, before you go, will you – kiss me, Hull?'

He strode toward her, then recoiled in sudden alarm, for it was at that instant that the thing happened. There was a series of the faintest possible clicks, and Hull fancied that he saw for an instant a glistening of tiny blue sparks on candle-sticks and metal objects about the room, and that he felt for a brief moment a curious tingling. Then he forgot all of these strange trifles as the powder horn on the table roared into terrific flame, and flaming wads of powder shot meteor-like around him.

For an instant he froze rigid. Vail was screaming; her dress was burning. He moved into sudden action, sweeping her from her feet, crashing her sideways to the floor, where his great hands beat out the fire. Then he slapped table and floor; he brought his ample sandals down on flaming spots, and finally there were no more flames.

He turned coughing and choking in the black smoke, and bent over Vail, who gasped half overcome. Her skirt had burned to her knees, and for the moment she was too distraught to cover them, though there was no modesty in the world in those days like that of the women of the middle river regions. But as Hull leaned above her she huddled back.

'Are you hurt?' he cried. 'Vail, are you burned?'

'No – no!' she panted.

'Then outside!' he snapped, reaching down to lift her.

'Not – not like this!'

He understood. He snatched his leather smith's apron from the wall, whipped it around her, and bore her into the clearer air of the street.

Outside there was chaos. He set Vail gently on the step and surveyed a scene of turmoil. Men ran shouting, and from windows along the street black smoke poured. A dozen yards away a powder wagon had blasted itself into a vast mushroom of smoke, incinerating horses and driver alike. On the porch across the way lay a writhing man, torn by the rifle that had burst in his hands.

He comprehended suddenly. 'The sparkers!'* he roared. 'Joaquin Smith's sparkers! Old Einar told me about them.' He groaned. 'There goes our ammunition.'

The girl made a great effort to control herself. 'Joaquin Smith's sorcery,' she said dully. 'And there goes hope as well.'

He started. 'Hope? No! Wait, Vail.'

He rushed toward the milling group that surrounded bearded old Marcus Ormiston and the Confederation leaders. He plowed his way fiercely through, and seized the panic-stricken greybeard. 'What now?' he roared. 'What are you going to do?'

'Do? Do?' The old man was beyond comprehending.

'Yes, do! I'll tell you.' He glared at the five leaders. 'You'll carry through. Do you see? For powder and ball there's bow and

---

* The Erden resonators. A device, now obsolete, that projected an inductive field sufficient to induce tiny electrical discharges in metal objects up to a distance of many miles. Thus it ignited inflammables like gunpowder.

sword, and just as good for the range we need. Gather your men! Gather your men and march!'

And such, within the hour, was the decision. Hull marched first with the Ormiston men, and he carried with him the memory of Vail's farewell. It embarrassed him cruelly to be kissed thus in public, but there was great pleasure in the glimpse of Enoch Ormiston's sour face as he had watched her.

The Ormiston men were first on the line of the Master's approach, and they filtered to their forest-hidden places as silently as foxes. Hull let his eyes wander back along the cut and what he saw pleased him, for no eye could have detected that along the deserted road lay ten thousand fighting men. They were good woodsmen too, these fellows from the upper rivers and the saltless seas.

Down the way from Norse a single horseman came galloping. Old Marcus Ormiston recognized him, stood erect, and hailed him. They talked; Hull could hear the words. The Master had passed through Norse, pausing only long enough to notify the eldarch that henceforth his taxes must be transmitted to N'Orleans, and then had moved leisurely onward. No, there had been no sign of sorcery, nor had he even seen any trace of the witch Black Margot, but then, he had ridden away before the Master had well arrived.

Their informant rode on toward Ormiston, and the men fell to their quiet waiting. A half hour passed, and then, faintly drifting on the silent air, came the sound of music. Singing; men's voices in song. Hull listened intently, and his skin crept and his hair prickled as he made out the words of the Battle Song of N'Orleans:

Queen of cities, reigning
Empress, starry pearled
See our arms sustaining
Battle flags unfurled!
Hear our song rise higher,
Fierce as battle fire,
Death our one desire

      Or

The Empire of the World!

Hull gripped his bow and set feather to cord. He knew well enough that the plan was to permit the enemy to pass unmolested until his whole line was within the span of the ambush, but the rumble of that distant song was like spark to powder. And now, far down the way beyond the cut, he saw the dust rising. Joaquin Smith was at hand.

Then – the unexpected! Ever afterward Hull told himself that it should have been expected, that the Master's reputation should have warned them that so simple a plan as theirs must fail. There was no time now for such vain thoughts, for suddenly, through the trees to his right, brown-clothed, lithe little men were slipping like charging shadows, horns sounding, whistles shrilling. The woods runners of the Master! Joaquin Smith had anticipated just such an ambush.

Instantly Hull saw their own weakness. They were ten thousand, true enough, but here they were strung thinly over a distance of two miles, and now the woods runners were at a vast advantage in numbers, with the main body approaching. One chance! Fight it out, drive off the scouts, and retire into the woods. While the army existed, even though Ormiston fell, there was hope.

He shouted, strung his arrow, and sent it flashing through the leaves. A bad place for arrows; their arching flight was always deflected by the tangled branches. He slung bow on shoulder and gripped his sword; close quarters was the solution, the sort of fight that made blood tingle and life seem joyous.

Then – the second surprise! The woods runners had flashed their own weapons, little blunt revolvers.* But they sent no bullets; only pale beams darted through leaves and branches, faint blue streaks of light. Sorcery? And to what avail?

He learned instantly. His sword grew suddenly scorching hot in his hands, and a moment later the queerest pain he had ever encountered racked his body. A violent, stinging, inward tingle that twitched his muscles and paralyzed his movements. A brief second and the shock ceased, but his sword lay smoking in the leaves, and his steel bow had seared his shoulders. Around him men were yelling in pain, writhing on the ground, running back into the forest depths. He cursed the beams; they flicked like sunlight through branched and leafy tangles where an honest arrow could find no passage.

Yet apparently no man had been killed. Hands were seared

---

* Kohlmar's ionic beams. Two parallel beams of highly actinic light ionize a path of air, and along these conductive lanes of gas an electric current can be passed, powerful enough to kill or merely intense enough to punish.

and blistered by weapons that grew hot under the blue beams, bodies were racked by the torture that Hull could not know was electric shock, but none was slain. Hope flared again, and he ran to head off a retreating group.

'To the road!' he roared. 'Out where our arrows can fly free! Charge the column!'

For a moment the group halted. Hull seized a yet unheated sword from someone, and turned back. 'Come on!' he bellowed. 'Come on! We'll have a fight of this yet!'

Behind him he heard the trample of feet. The beams flicked out again, but he held his sword in the shadow of his own body. gritted his teeth, and bore the pain that twisted him. He rushed on; he heard his own named bellowed in the booming voice of File Ormson, but he only shouted encouragement and burst out into the full sunlight of the road.

Below in the cut was the head of the column, advancing placidly. He glimpsed a silver helmeted, black haired man on a great white mare at its head, and beside him a slighter figure on a black stallion. Joaquin Smith! Hull roared down the embankment toward him.

Four men spurred instantly between him and the figure with the silver helmet. A beam flicked; his sword scorched his skin and he flung it away. 'Come on!' he bellowed. 'Here's a fight!'

Strangely, in curious clarity, he saw the eyes of the Empire men, a smile in them, mysteriously amused. No anger, no fear – just amusement. Hull felt a sudden surge of trepidation, glanced quickly behind him, and knew finally the cause of that amusement. No one had followed him; he had charged the Master's army alone!

Now the fiercest anger he had ever known gripped Hull. Deserted! Abandoned by those for whom he fought. He roared his rage to the echoing bluffs, and sprang at the horseman nearest him.

The horse reared, pawing the air. Hull thrust his mighty arms below its belly and heaved with a convulsion of his great muscles. Backward toppled steed and rider, and all about the Master was a milling turmoil where a man scrambled desperately to escape the clashing hooves. But Hull glimpsed Joaquin Smith sitting statuelike and smiling on his great white mare.

He tore another rider from his saddle, and then caught from the corner of his eye, he saw the slim youth at the Master's side raise a weapon, coolly, methodically. For the barest instant Hull faced icy green eyes where cold, passionless death threatened. He flung himself aside as a beam spat smoking against the dust of the road.

'Don't!' snapped Joaquin Smith, his low voice clear through the turmoil. 'The youth is splendid!'

But Hull had no mind to die uselessly. He bent, flung himself halfway up the bluff in a mighty leap, caught a dragging branch, and swung into the forest. A startled woods runner faced him; he flung the fellow behind him down the slope, and slipped into the shelter of leaves. 'The wise warrior fights pride,' he muttered to himself. 'It's no disgrace for one man to run from an army.'

He was mountain bred. He circled silently through the forest, avoiding the woods runners who were herding the Confederation army back towards Ormiston. He smiled grimly as he recalled the words he had spoken to Vail. He had justified them; he *had* charged the army of the Master alone.

5

Black Margot

Hull circled wide through the forest, and it took all his mountain craft to slip free through the files of woods runners. He came at last to the fields east of Ormiston, and there made the road, entering from the direction of Selui.

Everywhere were evidences of rout. Wagons lay overturned, their teams doubtless used to further the escape of their drivers. Guns and rifles, many of them burst, littered the roadside, and now and again he passed black smoking piles and charred areas that marked the resting place of an ammunition cart.

Yet Ormiston was little damaged. He saw the fire-gutted remains of a shed or two where powder had been stored, and down the street a house roof still smoked. But there was no sign of battle carnage, and only the crowded street gave evidence of the unusual.

He found File Ormson in the group that stared across town to where the road from Norse elbowed east to enter. Hull had outsped the leisurely march of the Master, for there at the bend was the glittering army, now halted. Not even the woods runners had come into Ormiston town, for there they were too, lined in a brown-clad rank along the edge of the wood-lots beyond the nearer fields. They had made no effort, apparently, to take prisoners but had simply herded the terrified defenders into the village. Joaquin Smith had done it again; he had taken a town without a single death, or at least no casualties other than whatever injuries had come from bursting rifles and blazing powder.

Suddenly Hull noticed something. 'Where are the Confederation men?' he asked sharply.

File Ormson turned gloomy eyes on him. 'Gone. Flying back to Selui like scared gophers to their holes.' He scowled, then smiled. 'That was a fool's gesture of yours at Eaglefoot Flow, Hull. A fool's gesture, but brave.'

The youth grimaced wryly. 'I thought I was followed.'

'And so you should have been, but that those fiendish ticklers tickled away our courage. But they can kill as well as tickle; when there was need of it before Memphis they killed quickly enough.'

Hull thought of the green-eyed youth. 'I think I nearly learned that,' he said smiling.

Down the way there was some sort of stir. Hull narrowed his eyes to watch, and descried the silver helmet of the Master. He dismounted and faced someone; it was – yes, old Marcus Ormiston. He left File Ormson and shouldered his way to the edge of the crowd that circled the two.

Joaquin Smith was speaking. 'And,' he said, 'all taxes are to be forwarded to N'Orleans, including those on your own lands. Half of them I shall use to maintain my government, but half will revert to your own district, which will be under a governor I shall appoint in Selui when that city is taken. You are no longer eldarch, but for the present you may collect the taxes at the rate I prescribe.'   Old Marcus was bitterly afraid; Hull could see his beard waggling like an oriole's nest in a breeze. Yet there was a shrewd, bargaining streak in him. 'You are very hard,' he whined. 'You left Pace Helm as eldarch undisturbed in Norse. Why do you punish me because I fought to hold what was mine? Why should that anger you so?'

'I am not angry,' said the Master passively. 'I never blame any for fighting against me, but it is my policy to favor those eldarchs who yield peacefully.' He paused. 'Those are my terms, and generous enough.'

They were generous, thought Hull, especially to the people of Ormiston, who received back much less than half their taxes from the eldarch as roads, bridges, or wells.

'My – my lands?' faltered the old man.

'Keep what you till,' said Joaquin Smith indifferently. 'The rest of them go to their tenants.' He turned away, placed foot to stirrup, and swung upon his great white mare.

Hull caught his first fair glimpse of the conqueror. Black hair cropped below his ears, cool greenish grey eyes, a mouth with something faintly humorous about it. He was tall as Hull himself, more slender, but with powerful shoulders, and he seemed no older than the late twenties, or no more than thirty at most, though that was only the magic of Martin Sair, since more than eighty years had passed since his birth in the mountains of Mexico. He wore the warrior's garb of the southlands, a shirt of metallic silver scales, short thigh-length trousers of some shiny, silken materal, cothurns on his feet. His bronzed body was like the ancient statues Hull had seen in Selui, and he looked hardly the fiend that most people thought him. A pleasant seeming man, save for something faintly arrogant in his face – no, not arrogant, exactly, but proud or confident, as if he felt himself a being driven by fate, as perhaps he was.

He spoke again, now to his men. 'Camp there,' he ordered, waving at Ormiston square, 'and there,' pointing at a fallow field. 'Do not damage the crops.' He rode forward, and a dozen officers followed. 'The Church,' he said.

A voice, a tense, shrieking voice behind Hull. 'You! It is, Hull! It's you!' It was Vail, teary eyed and pale. 'They said you were –' She broke off sobbing, clinging to him, while Enoch Ormiston watched sourly.

He held her. 'It seems I failed you,' he said ruefully. 'But I did do my best, Vail.'

'Failed? I don't care.' She calmed. 'I don't care, Hull, since you're here.'

'And it isn't as bad as it might be,' he consoled. 'He wasn't as severe as I feared.'

'Severe!' she echoed. 'Do you believe those mild words of his, Hull? First our taxes, then our lands, and next it will be our lives – or at least my father's life. Don't you understand? That was no eldarch from some enemy town, Hull – that was Joaquin Smith. Joaquin Smith! Do you trust him?'

'Vail, do you believe that?'

'Of course I believe it!' She began to sob again. 'See how he has already won over half the town with – with that about the taxes. Don't you be won over, Hull. I – couldn't stand it!'

'I will not,' he promised.

'He and Black Margot and their craft! I hate them, Hull. I – Look there! Look there!'

He spun around. For a moment he saw nothing save the green-eyed youth who had turned death-laden eyes on him at

Eaglefoot Flow, mounted on the mighty black stallion. Youth! He saw suddenly that it was a woman – a girl rather. Eighteen – twenty-five? He couldn't tell. Her face was averted as she scanned the crowd that lined the opposite side of the street, but the sunset fell on a flaming black mop of hair, so black that it glinted blue – an intense, unbelievable black. Like Joaquin Smith she wore only a shirt and very abbreviated shorts, but a caparison protected the slim daintiness of her legs from any contact with the mount's ribs. There was a curious grace in the way she sat the idling steed, one hand on its haunches, the other on withers, the bridle dangling loose. Her Spanish mother's blood showed only in the clear, transparent olive of her skin, and of course, in the startling ebony of her hair.

'Black Margot!' Hull whispered. 'Brazen! Half naked! What's so beautiful about *her?*'

As if she heard his whisper, she turned suddenly, her emerald eyes sweeping the crowd about him, and he felt his question answered. Her beauty was starkly incredible – audacious, outrageous. It was more than a mere lack of flaws; it was a sultry, flaming positive beauty with a hint of sullenness in it. The humor of the Master's mouth lurked about hers as mockery; her perfect lips seemed always about to smile, but to smile cruelly and sardonically. Hers was a ruthless and pitiless perfection, but it was nevertheless perfection, even to the faintly Oriental cast given by her black hair and sea-green eyes.

Those eyes met Hull's and it was almost as if he heard an audible click. He saw recognition in her face, and she passed her glance casually over his mighty figure. He stiffened, stared defiantly back, and swept his own gaze insolently over her body from the midnight hair to the diminutive cothurns on her feet. If she acknowledged his gaze at all, it was by the faintest of all possible smiles of mockery as she rode coolly away toward Joaquin Smith.

Vail was trembling against him, and it was a great relief to look into her deep but not at all mysterious blue eyes, and to see the quite understandable loveliness of her pale features. What if she hadn't the insolent brilliance of the Princess, he thought fiercely. She was sweet and honest and loyal to her beliefs, and he loved her. Yet he could not keep his eyes from straying once more to the figure on the black stallion.

'She – she smiled at you, Hull!' gasped Vail. 'I'm frightened, I'm terribly frightened.'

His fascination was yielding now to a surge of hatred for Joaquin Smith, for the Princess, for the whole Empire. It was Vail he loved, and she was being crushed by these. An idea formed slowly as he stared down the street to where Joaquin Smith had dismounted and was now striding into the little church. He heard an approving murmur sweep the crowd, already half won over by the distribution of land. That was simply policy, the Master's worshipping in Ormiston church, a gesture to the crowd.

He lifted the steel bow from his back and bent it. The spring was still in it; it had been heated enough to scorch his skin but not enough to untemper it. 'Wait here' he snapped to Vail, and strode up the street toward the church.

Outside stood a dozen Empire men, and the Princess idled on her great black horse. He slipped across the churchyard, and around behind where a tangle of vines stretched toward the roof. Would they support his weight? They did, and he pulled himself hand over hand to the eaves, and thence to the peak. The spire hid him from the Master's men, and not one of the Ormiston folk glanced his way.

He crept forward to the base of the steeple. Now he must leave the peak and creep precariously along the steep slope around it. He reached the street edge and peered cautiously over.

The Master was still within. Against his will he glanced at Black Margot, and even put cord to feather and sighted at her ivory throat. But he could not. He could not loose the shaft.

Below him there was a stir. Joaquin Smith came out and swung to his white horse. Now was the moment. Hull rose to his knees, hoping that he could remain steady on the sharp pitch of the roof. Carefully, carefully, he drew the steel arrow back.

There was a shout. He had been seen, and a blue beam sent racking pain through his body. For an instant he bore it, then loosed his arrow and went sliding down the roof edge and over.

He fell on soft loam. A dozen hands seized him, dragged him upright, thrust him out into the street. He saw Joaquin Smith still on his horse, but the glistening arrow stood upright like a plume in his silver helmet, and a trickle of blood was red on his cheek.

But he wasn't killed. He raised the helmet from his head, waved aside the cluster of officers, and with his own hands bound a white cloth about his forehead. Then he turned cool grey eyes on Hull.

'You drive a strong shaft,' he said, and then recognition flickered in his eyes. 'I spared your life some hours ago, did I not?'

Hull said nothing.

'Why,' resumed the Master, 'do you seek to kill me after your eldarch has made peace with me? You are part of the Empire now, and this is treason.'

Hull could not keep his gaze from the emerald eyes of the Princess, who was watching him without expression save faint mockery.

'Have you nothing to say,' asked Joaquin Smith.

'Nothing.'

The Master's eyes slid over him. 'Are you Ormiston born?' he asked. 'What is your name?'

No need to bring troubles on his friends. 'No,' said Hull. 'I am called Hull Tarvish.'’

The conqueror turned away. 'Lock him up,' he ordered coolly. 'Let him make whatever preparations his religion requires, and then – execute him.'

Above the murmur of the crowd Hull heard Vail Ormiston's cry of anguish. He turned to smile at her, watched her held by two Empire men as she struggled to reach him. 'I'm sorry,' he called gently. 'I love you, Vail.' Then he was being thrust away down the street.

He was pushed into Hue Helm's stonewalled tool shed. It had been cleared of everything, doubtless for some officer's quarters. Hull drew himself up and stood passively in the gathering darkness where a single shaft of sunset light angled through the door, before which stood two grim Empire men.

One of them spoke. 'Keep peaceful, Weed,'* he said in his N'Orleans drawl. 'Go ahead with your praying, or whatever it is you do.'

'I do nothing,' said Hull. 'The mountainies believe that a right life is better than a right ending, and right or wrong a ghost's but a ghost anyway.'

The guard laughed. 'And a ghost you'll be.'

'If a ghost I'll be,' retorted Hull, turning slowly toward him, 'I'd sooner turn one – fighting!'

He sprang suddenly, crashed a mighty fist against the arm that bore the weapon, thrust one guard upon the other, and over-leaped the tangle into the dusk. As he spun to circle the house, something very hard smashed viciously against the back of his skull, sending him sprawling half dazed against the wall.

---

* Weed: The term applied by Dominists (the Master's partisans) to their opposers. It originated in Joaquin Smith's remark before the Battle of Memphis: 'Even the weeds of the fields have taken arms against me.'

6

The Harriers

For a brief moment Hull sprawled half stunned, then his muscles lost their paralysis and he thrust himself to his feet, whirling to face whatever assault threatened. In the doorway the guards still scrambled, but directly before him towered a rider on a black mount, and two men on foot flanked him. The rider, of course, was the Princess, her glorious green eyes luminous as a cat's in the dusk as she slapped a short sword into its scabbard. It was a blow from the flat of its blade that had felled him.

She held now the blunt weapon of the blue beam.It came to him that he had never heard her speak, but she spoke now in a voice low and liquid, yet cold, cold as the flow of an ice-crusted winter stream. 'Stand quiet, Hull Tarvish.' she said 'One flash will burst that stubborn heart of yours forever.'

Perforce he stood quiet, his back to the wall of the shed. He had no doubt at all that the Princess would kill him if he moved; he couldn't doubt it with her icy eyes upon him. He stared sullenly back, and a phrase of Old Einar's came strangely to his memory. 'Satanically beautiful,' the old man had called her, and so she was. Hell or the art of Martin Sair had so fashioned her that no man could gaze unmoved on the false purity of her face, no man at least in whom flowed red blood.

She spoke again, letting her glance flicker disdainfully over the two appalled guards. 'The Master will be pleased,' she said contemptuously, 'to learn that one unarmed Weed outmatches two men of his own cohort.'

The nearer man faltered, 'But your Highness, he rushed us unexpect –'

'No matter,' she cut in, and turned back to Hull. For the first time now he really felt the presence of death as she said coolly, 'I am minded to kill you.'

'Then do it!' he snapped.

'I came here to watch you die,' she observed calmly. 'It interests me to see men die, boldly or cowardly or resignedly. I think you would die boldly.'

'It seemed to Hull that she was deliberately torturing him by this procrastination. 'Try me!' he growled.

'But I think also,' she resumed, 'that your living might amuse me more than your death, and' – for the first time there was a breath of feeling in her voice – 'God knows I need amusement!' Her tones chilled again. 'I give you your life.'

'Your Highness,' muttered the cowed guard, 'the Master has ordered –'

'I countermand the orders,' she said shortly. And then to Hull. 'You are a fighter. Are you also a man of honor?'

'If I'm not,' he retorted, 'the lie that says I am would mean nothing to me.'

She smiled coldly. 'Well, I think you are, Hull Tarvish. You go free on your word to carry no weapons, and your promise to visit me this evening in my quarters at the eldarch's home.' She paused. 'Well?'

'I give my word.'

'And I take it.' She crashed her heels against the ribs of the great stallion, and the beast reared and whirled. 'Away, all of you!' she ordered. 'You two, carry tub and water for my bath.' She rode off toward the street.

Hull let himself relax against the wall with a low 'whew!' Sweat started on his cold forehead, and his mighty muscles felt almost weak. It wasn't that he had feared death, he told himself, but the strain of facing those glorious, devilish emerald eyes, and the cold torment of the voice of Black Margot, and the sense of her taunting him, mocking him, even her last careless gesture of freeing him – He drew himself erect. After all, fear of death or none, he loved life, and let that be enough.

He walked slowly toward the street. Across the way lights glowed in Marcus Ormiston's home, and he wondered if Vail were there, perhaps serving the Princess Margaret as he had so lately suggested the contrary. He wanted to find Vail; he wanted to use her cool loveliness as an antidote for the dark poison of the beauty he had been facing. And then, at the gate, he drew back suddenly. A group of men in Empire garb came striding by, and among them, helmetless and with his head bound, moved the Master.

'His eyes fell on Hull. He paused suddenly and frowned. 'You again!' he said. 'How is it that you still live, Hull Tarvish?'

'The Princess ordered it.'

The frown faded. 'So.' said Joaquin Smith slowly, 'Margaret takes it upon herself to interfere somewhat too frequently. I suppose she also freed you?'

'Yes, on my promise not to bear arms.'

There was a curious expression in the face of the conqueror. 'Well,' he said almost gently, 'it was not my intention to torture

you, but merely to have you killed for your treason. It may be
that you will soon wish that my orders had been left unaltered.'
He strode on into the eldarch's dooryard, with his silent men
following.

Hull turned his steps toward the center of the village. Everywhere he passed Empire men scurrying about the tasks of
encampment, and supply wagons rumbled and jolted in the
streets. He saw files of the soldiers passing slowly before
cook-wagons and the smell of food floated on the air, reminding
him that he was ravenously hungry. He hurried toward his room
beside File Ormson's shop, and there, tragic-eyed and mist-pale,
he found Vail Ormiston.

She was huddled on the doorstep with sour Enoch holding her
against him. It was Enoch who first perceived Hull, and his jaw
dropped and his eyes bulged, and a gurgling sound issued from
his throat. And Vail looked up with uncomprehending eyes,
stared for a moment without expression, and then, with a little
moan, crumpled and fainted.

She was unconscious only a few moments, scarcely long
enough for Hull to bear her into his room. There she lay now on
his couch, clinging to his great hand, convinced at last of his
living presence.

'I think,' she murmured, 'that you're as deathless as Joaquin
Smith, Hull, I'll never believe you dead again. Tell me – tell me
how it happened.'

He told her. 'Black Margot's to thank for it,' he finished.

But the very name frightened Vail. 'She means evil, Hull. She
terrifies me with her witch's eyes and her hellstained hair. I
haven't even dared go home for fear of her.'

He laughed. 'Don't worry about me, Vail, I'm safe enough.'

Enoch cut in. 'Here's one for the Harriers, then,' he said
sourly. 'The pack needs him.'

'The Harriers?' Hull looked up puzzled.

'Oh, Hull, yes!' said Vail. 'File Ormson's been busy. The
Harriers are what's left of the army – the better citizens of
Ormiston. The Master's magic didn't reach beyond the ridge,
and over the hills there's still powder and rifles. And the spell is
no longer in the valley, either. One of the men carried a cup of
powder across the ridge, and it didn't burn.'

The better citizens, Hull thought smiling. She meant, of
course, those who owned land and feared a division of it such as
Marcus Ormiston had suffered. But aloud he said only, 'How
many men have you?'

'Oh, there'll be several hundred with the farmers across the hills.' She looked into his eyes, 'I know it's a forlorn hope, Hull, but – we've got to try. You'll help, won't you?'

'Of course. But all your Harriers can attempt is raids. They can't fight the Master's army.'

'I know. I know it, Hull. It's a desperate hope.'

'Desperate?' said Enoch suddenly. 'Hull, didn't you say you were ordered to Black Margot's quarters this evening?'

'Yes.'

'Then – see here! You'll carry a knife in your armpit. Sooner or later she'll want you alone with her, and when *that* happens, you'll slide the knife quietly into her ruthless heart! There's a hope for you – *if* you've courage!'

'Courage!' he growled. 'To murder a woman!'

'Black Margot's a devil!'

'Devil or not, what's the good of it? It's Joaquin Smith that's building the Empire, not the Princess.'

'Yes,' said Enoch, 'but half his power is the art of the witch. Once she's gone the Confederation could blast his army like ducks in a frog pond.'

'It's true!' gasped Vail. 'What Enoch says is true!'

Hull scowled. 'I swore not to bear weapons!'

'Swore to *her!*' snapped Enoch. 'That needn't bind you.'

'My word's given,' said Hull firmly. 'I do not lie.'

Vail smiled. 'You're right,' she whispered, and as Enoch's face darkened, 'I love you for it, Hull.'

'Then,' grunted Enoch, 'if it's not lack of courage, do this. Lure her somehow across the west windows. We can slip two or three Harriers to the edge of the wood-lot, and if she passes a window with the light behind her – well, they won't miss.'

'Oh, I won't,' said Hull wearily. 'I won't fight women, nor betray even Black Margot to death.'

But Vail's blue eyes pleaded. 'That won't be breaking your word, Hull. Please. It isn't betraying a woman. She's a sorceress. She's evil. Please, Hull.'

Bitterly he yielded. 'I'll try, then.' He frowned gloomily. 'She saved my life, and – Well, which room is her's?'

'My father's. Mine is the western chamber, which she took for her – her maid,' Vail's eyes misted at the indignity of it. 'We,' she said, 'are left to sleep in the kitchen.'

An hour later, having eaten, he walked somberly home with Vail while Enoch slipped away toward the hills. There were tents in the dooryard, and lights glowed in every window, and before the door stood two dark Empire men who passed the girl readily enough, but halted Hull with small ceremony. Vail cast him a wistful backward glance as she disappeared toward the rear, and he submitted grimly to the questioning of the guards.

'On what business?'

'To see the Princess Margaret.'

'Are you Hull Tarvish?'

'Yes.'

One of the men stepped to his side and ran exploratory hands about his body. 'Orders of Her Highness,' he explained gruffly.

Hull smiled. The Princess had not trusted his word too implicitly. In a moment the fellow had finished his search and swung the door open.

Hull entered. He had never seen the interior of the house, and for a moment its splendor dazzled him. Carved ancient furniture, woven carpets, intricately worked standards for the oil lamps, and even — for an instant he failed to comprehend it — a full-length mirror of ancient workmanship wherein his own image faced him. Until now he had seen only bits and fragments of mirrors.

To his left a guard blocked an open door whence voices issued. Old Marcus Ormiston's voice. 'But I'll pay for it. I'll buy it with all I have.' His tones were wheedling.

'No.' Cool finality in the voice of Joaquin Smith. 'Long ago I swore to Martin Sair never to grant immortality to any who have not proved themselves worthy.' A note of sarcasm edged his voice. 'Go prove yourself deserving of it, old man, in the few years left to you.'

Hull sniffed contemptuously. There seemed something debased in the old man's whining before his conqueror. 'The Princess Margaret?' he asked, and followed the guard's gesture.

Upstairs was a dimly lit hall where another guard stood silently. Hull repeated his query, but in place of answer came the liquid tones of Margaret herself. 'Let him come in Corlin.'

A screen within the door blocked sight of the room. Hull circled it, steeling himself against the memory of that soul-burning loveliness he remembered. But his defense was shattered by the shock that awaited him.

The screen, indeed, shielded the Princess from the sight of the guard in the hall, but not from Hull's eyes. He stared utterly appalled at the sight of her lying in complete indifference in a great tub of water, while a fat woman scrubbed assiduously at her bare body. He could not avoid a single glimpse of her exquisite form, then he turned and stared deliberately from the east windows, knowing that he was furiously crimson even to his shoulders.

'Oh, sit down!' she said contemptuously. 'This will be over in a moment.'

He kept his eyes averted while water splashed and a towel whisked sibilantly. When he heard her footsteps beside him he glanced up tentatively, still fearful of what he might see, but she was covered now in a full robe of shiny black and gold that made her seem taller, though its filmy delicacy by no means concealed what was beneath. Instead of the cothurns she wore when on the march, she had slipped her feet into tiny high-heeled sandals that were reminiscent of the footgear he had seen in ancient pictures. The black robe and her demure coif of short ebony hair gave her an appearance of almost nun-like purity, save for the green hell-fires that danced in her eyes.

In his heart Hull cursed that false aura of innocence, for he felt again the fascination against which he had steeled himself.

'So,' she said. 'You may sit down again. I do not demand court etiquette in the field.' She sat opposite, and produced a black cigarette, lighting it at the chimney of the lamp on the table. Hull stared; not that he was unaccustomed to seeing women smoke, for every mountainy women had her pipe, and every cottage its tobacco patch, but cigarettes were new to him.

'Now,' she said with a faintly ironic smile, 'tell me what they say of me here.'

'They call you witch.'

'And do they hate me?'

'Hate you?' he echoed thoughtfully. 'At least they will fight you and the Master to the last feather on the last arrow.'

'Of course. The young men will fight – except those that Joaquin has bought with the eldarch's lands – because they know that once within the Empire, fighting is no more to be had. No more joyous, thrilling little wars between the cities, no more boasting and parading before the pretty provincial girls – ' She paused. 'And you, Hull Tarvish – what do you think of me?'

'I call you witch for other reasons.'

'Other reasons?'

'There is no magic,' said Hull, echoing the words of Old Einar in Selui. 'There is only knowledge.'

The Princess looked narrowly at him. 'A wise thought for one of you,' she murmured, and then, 'You came weaponless.'

'I keep my word.'

'You owe me that. I spared your life.'

'And I,' declared Hull defiantly, 'spared yours. I could have 'sped an arrow through that white throat of yours, there on the church roof. I aimed one.'

She smiled. 'What held you?'

'I do not fight women.' He winced as he thought of what mission he was on, for it belied his words.

'Tell me,' she said, 'was that the eldarch's pretty daughter who cried so piteously after you there before the church?'

'Yes.'

'And do you love her?'

'Yes.' This was the opening he had sought, but it came bitterly now, facing her. He took the opportunity grimly. 'I should like to ask one favor.'

'Ask it.'

'I should like to see' – lies were not in him but this was no lie – 'the chamber that was to have been our bridal room. The west chamber.' That might be – should be – truth.

The Princess laughed disdainfully. 'Go see it then.'

For a moment he feared, or hoped, perhaps, that she was going to let him go alone. Then she rose and followed him to the hall, and to the door of the west chamber.

7

Betrayal

Hull paused at the door of the west chamber to permit the Princess to enter. For the merest fraction of a second her glorious green eyes flashed speculatively to his face, then she stepped back. 'You first, Weed,' she commanded.

He did not hesitate. He turned and strode into the room, hoping that the Harrier riflemen, if indeed they lurked in the copse, might recognize his mighty figure in time to stay their eager trigger fingers. His scalp prickled as he moved steadily across the window, but nothing happened.

Behind him the Princess laughed softly. 'I have lived too long in the aura of a plot and counterplot in N'Orleans,' she said. 'I mistrust you without cause, honest Hull Tarvish.'

Her words tortured him. He turned to see her black robe mold itself to her body as she moved, and, as sometimes happens in moments of stress, he caught an instantaneous picture of her with his senses so quickened that it seemed as if she, himself, and the world were frozen into immobility. He remembered her forever as she was then, with her limbs in the act of striding, her green eyes soft in the lamplight, and her perfect lips in a smile that had a coloring of wistfulness. Witch and devil she might be, but she looked like a dark-haired angel, and in that moment his spirit revolted.

'No!' he bellowed, and sprang toward her, striking her slim shoulders with both hands in a thrust that sent her staggering back into the hallway, there to sit hard and suddenly on the floor beside the amazed guard.

She sprang up instantly, and there was nothing angelic now in her face. 'You – hurt – me!' she hissed. 'Me! Now, I'll – ' she snatched the guard's weapon from his belt, thrust it full at Hull's chest, and sent the blue beam humming upon him.

It was pain far worse than that at Eaglefoot Flow. He bore it stolidly, grinding into silence the groan that rose in his throat, and in a moment she flicked it off and slapped it angrily into the guard's holster. 'Treachery again!' she said. 'I won't kill you, Hull Tarvish. I know a better way.' She whirled toward the stair-well. 'Lebeau!' she called. 'Lebeau! There's – ' She glanced sharply at Hull, and continued, '*Il y a des tirailleurs dans le bois. Je vais les tireer en avant!*'* It was the French of N'Orleans, as incomprehensible to Hull as Aramaic.

She spun back 'Sora!' she snapped, and then, as the fat woman appeared, 'Never mind. You're far too heavy.' Then back to Hull. 'I've a mind,' she blazed, 'to strip the Weed clothes from the eldarch's daughter and send her marching across the window!'

He was utterly appalled. 'She – she – was in town!' he gasped, then fell silent at the sound of feet below.

'Well, there's no time,' she retorted. 'So, if I must – ' She strode steadily into the west chamber, paused a moment, and then stepped deliberately in front of the window!

Hull was aghast. He watched her stand so that the lamplight must have cast her perfect silhouette full on the pane, stand tense and motionless for the fraction of a breath, and then leap back so sharply that her robe billowed away from her body.

She had timed it to perfection. Two shots crashed almost

---

* 'There are snipers in the copse. I'll draw them out!'

together, and the glass shattered. And then, out in the night, a dozen beams criss-crossed, and, thin and clear in the silence after the shots, a yell of mortal anguish drifted up, and another, and a third.

The Princess Margaret smiled in malice, and sucked a crimson drop from a finger gashed by flying glass. 'Your treachery reacts,' she said in the tones of a sneer. 'Instead of my betrayal, you have betrayed your own men.'

'I need no accusation from you,' he said gloomily. 'I am my own accuser, and my own judge. Yes, and my own executioner as well. I will not live a traitor.'

She raised her dainty eyebrows, and blew a puff of grey smoke from the cigarette still in her hand. 'So strong Hull Tarvish will die a suicide,' she remarked indifferently. 'I had intended to kill you now. Should I leave you to be your own victim?'

He shrugged. 'What matter to me?'

'Well,' she said musingly, 'you're rather more entertaining than I had expected. You're strong, you're stubborn, and you're dangerous. I give you the right to do what you wish with your own life, but' – her green eyes flickered mockingly – 'If I were Hull Tarvish, I should live on the chance of justifying myself. You can wipe out the disgrace of your weakness by an equal courage. You can sell your life in your own cause, and who knows? – perhaps for Joaquin's – or mine!'

He chose to ignore the mockery in her voice. 'Perhaps,' he said grimly, 'I will.'

'Why, then, did you weaken, Hull Tarvish? You might have had my life.'

'I do not fight women,' he said despondently. 'I looked at you – and turned weak.' A question formed in his mind. 'But why did you risk your life before the window? You could have had fifty woods runners scour the copse. That was brave, but unnecessary.'

She smiled, but there was a shrewd narrowness in her eyes. 'Because so many of these villages are built above the underground ways of the Ancients – the subways, the sewers. How did I know but that your assassins might slip into some burrow and escape? It was necessary to lure them into disclosure.'

Hull shadowed the gleam that shot into his own eyes. He remembered suddenly the ancient sewer in which the child Vail had wandered, whose entrance was hidden by blackberry bushes. Then the Empire men were unaware of it! He visioned the Harriers creeping through it with bow and sword – yes, and rifle, now that the spell was off the valley – springing suddenly into the center of the camp, finding the Master's army, sleeping, disorganized, unwary. What a plan for a surprise attack!

'Your Highness,' he said grimly, 'I think of suicide no more, and unless you kill me now, I will be a bitter enemy to your Empire army.'

'Perhaps less bitter than you think,' she said softly. 'See Hull, the only three that know of your weakness are dead. No one can name you traitor or weakling.'

'But *I* can,' he returned somberly. 'And you.'

'Not *I*, Hull,' she murmured. 'I never blame a man who weakens because of me – there have been many. Men as strong as you, Hull, and some that the world still calls great.' She turned toward her own chamber. 'Come in here,' she said in altered tones. 'I will have some wine. Sora!' As the fat woman padded off, she took another cigarette and lit it above the lamp, wrinkling her dainty nose distastefully at the night-flying insects that circled it.

'What a place!' she snapped impatiently.

'It is the finest house I have ever seen,' said Hull stolidly.

She laughed. 'It's a hovel. I sigh for the day we return to N'Orleans, where windows are screened, where water flows hot at will, where lights do not flicker as yellow oil lamps nor send heat to stifle one. Would you like to see the Great City, Hull?'

'You know I would.'

'What if I say you may?'

'What could keep me from it if I go in peace?'

She shrugged. 'Oh, you can visit N'Orleans, of course, but suppose I offered you the chance to go as the – *guest,* we'll say, of the Princess Margaret. What would you give for that privilege?'

Was she mocking him again? 'What would you ask for it?' he rejoined guardedly.

'Oh, your allegiance, perhaps. Or perhaps the betrayal of your little band of Harriers, who will be the devil's own nuisance to stamp out of these hills.'

He looked up startled that she knew the name. 'The Harriers? How – ?'

She smiled. 'We have friends among the Ormiston men. Friends bought with land,' she added contemptuously. 'But what of my offer, Hull?'

He scowled. 'You say as your *guest*. What am I to understand by that?'

She leaned across the table, her exquisite green eyes on his, her hair flaming blue-black, her perfect lips in a faint smile. 'What you please, Hull. Whatever you please.'

Anger was rising. 'Do you mean,' he asked huskily, 'that you'd do that for so small a thing as the destruction of a little enemy band? You, with the whole Empire at your back?'

She nodded. 'It saves trouble, doesn't it?'

'And honesty, virtue, honor, mean as little to you as that? Is this one of your usual means of conquest? Do you ordinarily sell your – your favors for – ?'

'Not ordinarily,' she interrupted coolly. 'First I must like my co-partner in the trade. You, Hull – I like those vast muscles of yours, and your stubborn courage, and your slow clear mind. You are not a great man, Hull, for your mind has not the cold fire of genius, but you are a strong one, and I like you for it.'

'Like me!' he roared, starting up in his chair. 'Yet you think I'll trade what honor's left me for – that! You think I'll betray my cause! You think – Well, you're wrong, that's all. You're wrong!'

She shook her head, smiling. 'No. I wasn't wrong, for I thought you wouldn't.'

'Oh, you did!' he snarled. 'Then what if I'd accepted? What would you have done then?'

'What I promised.' She laughed at his angry, incredulous face. 'Don't look so shocked, Hull. I'm not little Vail Ormiston. I'm the Princess Margaret of N'Orleans, called Margaret the Divine by those who love me, and by those who hate me called – Well, *you* must know what my enemies call me.'

'I do!' he blazed. 'Black Margot, I do!'

'Black Margot!' she echoed smiling. 'Yes, so called because a poet once amused me, and because there was once a very ancient, very great French poet named Francois Villon, who loved a harlot called Black Margot.' She sighed. 'But *my* poet was no Villon; already his works are nearly forgotten.'

'A good name!' he rasped. 'A good name for you!'

'Doubtless. But you fail to understand, Hull. I'm an Immortal. My years are three times yours. Would you have me follow the standards of death-bound Vail Ormiston?'

'Yes!' By what right are you superior to all standards?'

Her lips had ceased to smile, and her deep green eyes turned wistful. 'By the right that I can act in no other way, Hull,' she said softly. A tinge of emotion quavered in her voice. 'Immortality!' she whispered. 'Year after year after year of sameness, tramping up and down the world on conquest! What do I care for conquest? I have no sense of destiny like Joaquin, who sees before him Empire – Empire – Empire, ever larger, ever growing. What's Empire to me? And year by year I grow bored until fighting, killing, danger, and love are all that keep me breathing!'

His anger had drained away. He was staring at her aghast, appalled.

'And then *they* fail me!' she murmured. 'When killing palls and love grows stale, what's left? Did I say love? How can there be love for me when I know that if I love a man, it will be only to watch him age and turn wrinkled, weak, and flabby? And when I beg Joaquin for immortality for him, he flaunts before me that promise of his to Martin Sair, to grant it only to those already proved worthy. By the time a man's worthy he's old.' She went on tensely, 'I tell you, Hull, that I'm so friendless and alone that I envy you death-bound ones! Yes, and one of these days I'll join you!'

He gulped. 'My God!' he muttered. 'Better for you if you'd stayed in your native mountains with friends, home, husband, and children.'

'Children!' she echoed, her eyes misting with tears. 'Immortals can't have children. They're sterile; they should be nothing but brains like Joaquin and Martin Sair, not beings with feelings – like me. Sometimes I curse Martin Sair and his hard rays. I don't want immortality; I want *life!*'

Hull found his mind in a whirl. The impossible beauty of the girl he faced, her green eyes now soft and moist and unhappy, her lips quivering, the glisten of a tear on her cheek – these things tore at him so powerfully that he scarcely knew his own allegiance. 'God!' he whispered. 'I'm sorry!'

'And you, Hull – will you help me – a little?'

'But we're enemies – enemies!'

'Can't we be – something else?' A sob shook her.

'How can we be?' he groaned.

Suddenly some quirk to her dainty lips caught his attention. He stared incredulously into the green depths of her eyes. It was true. There was laughter there. She had been mocking him! And as she perceived his realization, her soft laughter rippled like rain on water.

'You – devil!' he choked. 'You black witch! I wish I'd let you be killed!'

'Oh, no,' she said demurely. 'Look at me, Hull.'

The command was needless. He couldn't take his fascinated gaze from her exquisite face.

'Do you love me, Hull?'

'I love Vail Ormiston,' he rasped.

'But do you love *me?*'

'I hate you!'

'But do you love me as well?'

He groaned. 'This is bitterly unfair,' he muttered.

She knew what he meant. He was crying out against the circumstances that had brought the Princess Margaret – the most brilliant woman of all that brilliant age, and one of the most brilliant of any age – to flash all her fascination on a simple mountainy from Ozarky. It wasn't fair; her smile admitted it, but there was triumph there, too.

'May I go?' he asked stonily.

She nodded. 'But you will be a little less my enemy, won't you, Hull?'

He rose. 'Whatever harm I can do your cause,' he said, 'that harm will I do. I will not be twice a traitor.'

But he fancied a puzzling gleam of satisfaction in her green eyes at his words.

8

Torment

Hull looked down at noon over Ormiston valley, where Joaquin Smith was marching. At his side Vail paused, and together they gazed silently over Selui road, now black with riding men and rumbling wagons on their way to attack the remnant of the Confederation army in Selui. But Ormiston was not entirely abandoned, for three hundred soldiers and two hundred horsemen remained to deal with the Harriers, under Black Margot herself. It was not the policy of the Master to permit so large a rebel band to gather unopposed in conquered territory; within the Empire, despite the mutual hatred among rival cities, there existed a sort of enforced peace.

'Our moment comes tonight,' Hull said soberly. 'We'll never have a better chance than now, with our numbers all but equal to theirs, and surprise on our side.'

Vail nodded. 'The ancient tunnel was a bold thought, Hull. The Harriers are shoring up the crumbled places. Father is with them.'

'He shouldn't be. The aged have no place in the field.'

'But this is his hope, Hull. He lives for this.'

'Small enough hope! Suppose we're successful, Vail. What will it mean save the return of Joaquin Smith and his army? Common sense tells me this is a fool's hunt, and if it were not for you and the chance of fairer fighting than we've had until now – well, I'd be tempted to concede the Master his victory.'

'Oh, no!' cried Vail. 'If our success means the end of Black Margot, isn't that enough? Besides, you know that half the Master's powers are the work of the witch. Enoch – poor Enoch – said so.'

Hull winced. Enoch had been one of the three marksmen slain outside the west windows, and the girl's words brought memory of his own part in that. But her words pricked painfully in yet another direction, for the vision of the Princess that had plagued him all night long still rose powerfully in his mind, nor could he face the mention of her death unmoved.

But Vail read only distress for Enoch in his face, 'Enoch,' she repeated softly. 'He loved me in his sour way, Hull, but once I had known you, I had no thoughts for him.'

Hull slipped his arm about her, cursing himself that he could not steal his thought away from Margaret of N'Orleans, because it was Vail he loved, and Vail he wanted to love. Whatever spell the Princess had cast about him, he knew her to be evil, ruthless, and inhumanly cold – a sorceress, a devil. But he could not blot her Satanic loveliness from his inward gaze.

'Well,' he sighed, 'let it be tonight, then. Was it four hours past sunset? Good. The Empire men should be sleeping or gaming in Tigh's tavern by that time. It's for us to pray for our gunpowder.'

'Gunpowder? Oh, but didn't you hear what I told File Ormson and the Harriers, back there on the ridge? The casters of the spell are gone; Joaquin Smith has taken them to Selui. I watched and listened from the kitchen this morning.'

'The sparkers? They're gone?'

'Yes. They called them reson – resators – '

'Resonators,' said Hull, recalling Old Einar's words.

'Something like that. There were two of them, great iron barrels on swivels, full of some humming and clicking magic,

---

* The field of the Erden resonator passes readily through structures and walls, but it is blocked by any considerable natural obstructions, hills and for some reason, fog-banks or low clouds.

and they swept the valley north and south, and east and west,
and over toward Norse there was the sound of shots and the
smoke of a burning building. They loaded them on wagons and
dragged them away toward Selui.'

'They didn't cross the ridge with their spell,'* said Hull. 'The
Harriers still have powder.'

'Yes,' murmured Vail, drawing his arm closer about her. 'Tell
me,' she said suddenly, 'what did she want of you last night?'

Hull grimaced. He had told Vail little enough of that discre-
ditable evening, and he had been fearing her question. 'Treason,'
he said finally. 'She wanted me to betray the Harriers.'

'You? She asked that of you?'

'Do you think I would?' countered Hull.

'I know you never would. But what did she offer you for
betrayal?'

Again he hesitated. 'A great reward,' he answered at last. 'A
reward out of all proportion to the task.'

'Tell me, Hull, what is she like face to face?'

'A demon. She isn't exactly human.'

'But in what way? Men say so much of her beauty, of her
deadly charm, Hull – did you feel it?'

'I love *you*, Vail.'

She sighed, and drew yet closer. 'I think you're the strongest
man in the world, Hull. The very strongest.'

'I'll need to be,' he muttered, staring gloomily over the valley.
Then he smiled faintly as he saw men plowing, for it was late in
the season for such occupation. Old Marcus Ormiston was
playing safe; remembering the Master's words, he was tilling
every acre across which a horse could drag a blade.

Vail left him in Ormiston village and took her way hesitantly
homeward. Hull did what he could about the idle shop, and
when the sun slanted low, brought himself a square loaf of
brown bread, a great slice of cheese and a bottle of the still, clear
wine of the region. It was just as he finished his meal in his room
that a pounding on the door of the shop summoned him.

It was an Empire man. 'Hull Tarvish?' he asked shortly. At
Hull's nod he continued, 'From Her Highness,' and handed him
a folded slip of black paper.

The mountain youth stared at it. On one side, in raised gold, it
was the form of a serpent circling a globe, its tail in its mouth –
the Midgard Serpent. He slipped a finger through the fold,
opened the message, and squinted helplessly at the characters
written in gold on the black inner surface.

'This scratching means nothing to me,' he said.

The Empire man sniffed contemptuously. 'I'll read it' he said, taking the missive. 'It says, 'Follow the messenger to our quarters,' and it's signed *Margarita Imperii Regina,* which means Margaret, Princess of the Empire. Is that plain?' He handed back the note. 'I've been looking an hour for you.'

'Suppose I won't go,' growled Hull.

'This isn't an invitation, Weed. It's a command.'

Hull shrugged. He had small inclination to face Black Margot again, especially with his knowledge of the Harriers' plans. Her complex personality baffled and fascinated him, and he could not help fearing that somehow, by some subtle art, she might wring that secret from him. Torture wouldn't force it out of him, but those green eyes might read it. Yet – better to go quietly than be dragged or driven; he grunted assent and followed the messenger.

He found the house quiet. The lower room where Joaquin Smith had rested was empty now, and he mounted the stairs again steeling himself against the expected shock of Black Margot's presence. This time, however, he found her clothed, or half clothed by Ormiston standards, for she wore only the diminunitive shorts and shirt that were her riding costume, and her dainty feet were bare. She sat in a deep chair beside the table, a flagon of wine at hand and a black cigarette in her fingers. Her jet hair was like a helmet of ebony against the ivory of her forehead and throat, and her green eyes like twin emeralds.

'Sit down,' she said as he stood before her. 'The delay is your loss, Hull. I would have dined with you.'

'I grow strong enough on bread and cheese,' he growled.

'You seem to.' Fire danced in her eyes. 'Hull, I am as strong as most men, but I believe those vast muscles of yours could overpower me as if I were some shrinking provincial girl. And yet –'

'And yet what?'

'And yet you are much like my black stallion Eblis. Your muscles are nearly as strong, but like him, I can goad you, drive you, lash you, and set you galloping in whatever direction I choose.'

'Can you?' he snapped. 'Don't try it.' But the spell of her unearthly beauty was hard to face.

'But I think I shall try it,' she cooed gently. 'Hull, do you ever lie?'

'I do not.'

'Shall I make you lie, then Hull? Shall I make you swear such falsehoods that you will redden forever afterwards at the thought of them? Shall I?'

'You can't!'

She smiled, then in altered tones, 'Do you love me, Hull?'

'Love you? I hate – ' He broke off suddenly.

'Do you hate me, Hull?' she asked gently.

'No,' he groaned at last. 'No, I don't hate you.'

'But do you love me?' Her face was saint-like, earnest, pure, even the green eyes were soft now as the green of spring. 'Tell me, do you love me?'

'No!' he ground out savagely, then flushed crimson at the smile on her lips. 'That isn't a lie!' he blazed. 'This sorcery of yours isn't love. *I* don't love your beauty. It's unnatural, hellish, and the gift of Martin Sair. It's a false beauty, like your whole life!'

'Martin Sair had little to do with my appearance,' she said gently. 'What *do* you feel for me, Hull, if not love?'

'I – don't know. I don't want to think of it!' He clenched a great fist. 'Love? Call it love if you wish, but it's a hell's love that would find satisfaction in killing you!' But here his heart revolted again. 'That isn't so,' he ended miserably. 'I couldn't kill you.'

'Suppose,' she proceeded gently, 'I were to promise to abandon Joaquin, to be no longer Black Margot and Princess of the Empire, but to be only – Hull Tarvish's wife. Between Vail and me, which would you choose?'

He said nothing for a moment. 'You're unfair,' he said bitterly at last. 'Is it fair to compare Vail and yourself? She's sweet and loyal and innocent, but you – *you* are Black Margot!'

'Nevertheless,' she said calmly, 'I think I shall compare us. Sora!' The fat woman appeared. 'Sora, the wine is gone. Send the eldarch's daughter here with another bottle and a second goblet.'

Hull stared appalled. 'What are you going to do?'

'No harm to your little Weed. I promise no harm.'

'But – ' He paused. Vail's footsteps sounded on the stairs, and she entered timidly, bearing a tray with a bottle and a metal goblet. He saw her start as she perceived him, but she only advanced quietly, set the tray on the table, and backed toward the door.

'Wait a moment,' said the Princess. She rose and moved to Vail's side as if to force the comparison on Hull. He could not avoid it; he hated himself for the thought but it came regardless. Barefooted, the Princess Margaret was exactly the height of Vail in her low-heeled sandals, and she was the merest shade slimmer. But her startling black hair and her glorious green eyes seemed almost to fade the unhappy Ormiston girl to a colorless dun, and the coppery hair and blue eyes seemed water pale. It wasn't fair; Hull realized that it was like comparing candlelight to sunbeam, and he despised himself even for gazing.

'Hull,' said the Princess, 'which of us is the more beautiful?'

He saw Vail's lips twitch fearfully, and he remained stubbornly silent.

'Hull,' resumed the Princess, 'which of us do you love?'

'I love Vail!' he muttered.

'But do you love her more than you love me?'

Once again he had recourse to silence.

'I take it,' said the Princess, smiling, 'that your silence means you love *me* the more. Am I right?'

He said nothing.

'Or am I wrong, Hull? Surely you can give little Vail the satisfaction of answering this question! For unless you answer I shall take the liberty of assuming that you love me the more. Now do you?'

He was in utter torment. His white lips twisted in anguish as he muttered finally, 'Oh, God! Then yes!'

She smiled softly. 'You may go,' she said to the pallid and frightened Vail.

But for a moment the girl hesitated. 'Hull,' she whispered, 'Hull, I know you said that to save me. I don't believe it, Hull, and I love you. I blame – her!'

'Don't!' he groaned. 'Don't insult her.'

The Princess laughed, 'Insult *me*? Do you think I could be insulted by a bit of creeping dust as it crawls its way from cradle to grave?' She turned contemptuous green eyes on Vail as the terrified girl backed through the door.

'Why do you delight in torture?' cried Hull. 'You're cruel as a cat. You're no less than a demon.'

'That wasn't cruelty,' said the Princess gently. 'It was but a means of proving what I said, that your mighty muscles are well-broken to my saddle.'

'If that needed proof,' he muttered.

'It needed none. There's proof enough, Hull, in what's happening even now, if I judge the time rightly. I mean your Harriers slipping through their ancient sewer right into my trap behind the barn.'

He was thunderstruck. 'You – are you – you *must* be a witch!' he gasped.

'Perhaps. But it wasn't witchcraft that led me to put the thought of that sewer into your head, Hull. Do you remember now that it was *my* suggestion, given last evening there in the hallway? I knew quite well that you'd put the bait before the Harriers.'

His brain was reeling. 'But why – why – ?'

'Oh,' she said indifferently, 'it amuses me to see you play the traitor twice, Hull Tarvish.'

9

The Trap

The Princess stepped close to him, her magnificent eyes gentle as an angel's, the sweet curve of her lips in the ghost of a pouting smile. 'Poor, strong, weak Hull Tarvish!' she breathed. 'Now you shall have a lesson in the cost of weakness. I am not Joaquin, who fights benignly with his men's slides in the third notch. When *I* go to battle, my beams flash full and there is burning flesh and bursting heart. Death rides with me.'

He scarcely heard her. His gyrating mind struggled with an idea. The Harriers were creeping singly into the trap, but they could not all be through the tunnel. If he could warn them – His eyes shifted to the bell-pull in the hall beside the guard, the rope that tolled the bronze bell in the belfry to summon public gatherings, or to call aid to fight fires. Death, beyond doubt, if he rang it, but that was only a fair price to pay for expiation.

His great arm flashed suddenly, sweeping the Princess from her feet and crashing her dainty figure violently against the wall. He heard her faint 'O-o-oh' of pain as breath left her and she dropped slowly to her knees, but he was already upon the startled guard, thrusting him up and over the rail of the stair-well to drop with a sullen thump below. And then he threw his weight on the bell-rope, and the great voice of bronze boomed out, again, and again.

But Black Margot was on her feet, with the green hell-sparks flickering in her eyes and her face a lovely mask of fury. Men came rushing up the stairs with drawn weapons, and Hull gave a last tug on the rope and turned to face death. Half a dozen weapons were on him.

'No – no!' gasped the Princess, struggling for the breath he had knocked out of her. 'Hold him – for me! Take him – to the barn!'

She darted down the stairway, her grateful legs flashing bare, her bare feet padding softly. After her six grim Empire men thrust

Hull past the dazed guard sitting on the lower steps and out into a night where blue beams flashed and shots and yells sounded.

Behind the barn was comparative quiet, however, by the time Hull's captors had marched him there. A close-packed mass of dark figures huddled near the mouth of the ancient tunnel, where the bushes were trampled away, and a brown-clad file of Empire woods runners surrounded them. A few figures lay sprawled on the turf, and Hull smiled a little as he saw that some were Empire men. Then his eyes strayed to the Princess where she faced a dark-haired officer.

'How many, Lebeau?'

'A hundred and forty or fifty, Your Highness.'

'Not half! Why are you not pursuing the rest through the tunnel?'

Because, your Highness, one of them pulled the shoring and the roof down upon himself, and blocked us off. We're digging him out now.'

'By then they'll have left their burrow. Where does this tunnel end?' She strode over to Hull. 'Hull, where does this tunnel end?' At his silence, she added. 'No matter. They'd be through it before we could reach it.' She spun back. 'Lebeau! Burn down what we have and the rest we'll stamp out as we can.' A murmur ran through the crowd of villagers that was collecting, and her eyes, silvery green in the moonlight, flickered over them. 'And any sympathizers,' she added coldly. 'Except this man, Hull Tarvish.'

File Ormson's great voice rumbled out of the mass of prisoners. 'Hull! Hull! Was this trap your doing?'

Hull made no answer, but Black Margot herself replied. 'No,' she snapped, 'but the warning bell was.'

'Then why do you spare him?'

Her eyes glittered icy green. 'To kill in my own way, Weed,' she said in tones so cold that it was as if a winter wind had sent a shivering breath across the spring night. 'I have my own account to collect from him.'

Her eyes blazed chill emerald fire into Hull's. He met her glance squarely, and said in a low voice, 'Do you grant any favors to a man about to die?'

'Not by custom,' she replied indifferently. 'Is it the safety of the eldarch's daughter? I plan no harm to her.'

'It isn't that.'

'Then ask it – though I am not disposed to grant favors to you, Hull Tarvish, who have twice laid hands of violence on me.'

His voice dropped almost to a whisper. 'It is the lives of my companions I ask.'

She raised her eyebrows in surprise, then shook her ebony flame of hair. 'How can I? I remained here purposely to wipe them out. Shall I release the half I have, only to destroy them with the rest?'

'I ask their lives,' he repeated.

A curious, whimsical fire danced green in her eyes. 'I will try,' she promised, and turned to the officer, who was ranging his men so that the cross-fire execution could not mow down his own ranks. 'Lebeau!' she snapped. 'Hold back a while.'

She strode into the gap between the prisoners and her own men. Hand on hip she surveyed the Harriers, while moonlight lent her beauty an aura that was incredible, unearthly. There in the dusk of night she seemed no demon at all, but a girl, almost a child, and even Hull, who had learned well enough what she was, could not but sweep fascinated eyes from her jet hair to her tiny white feet.

'Now,' she said, passing her glance over the group, 'on my promise of amnesty, how many of you would join me?'

A stir ran through the mass. For a moment there was utter immobility, then, very slowly, two figures moved forward, and the stir became an angry murmur. Hull recognized the men; they were stragglers of the Confederation army, Ch'cago men, good fighters but merely mercenaries, changing sides as mood or advantage moved them. The murmur of the Harriers became an angry growl.

'You two,' said the Princess, 'are you Ormiston men?'

'No,' said one. 'Both of us come from the shores of Mitchin.'

'Very well,' she proceeded calmly. With a movement swift as arrow flight she snatched the weapon from her belt, the blue beam spat twice, and the men crumpled, one with face burned carbon-black, and both sending forth an odorous wisp of flesh-seared smoke.

She faced the aghast group. 'Now,' she said, 'who is your leader?'

File Ormson stepped forth, scowling and grim. 'What do you want of me?'

'Will you treat with me? Will your men follow your agreements?'

File nodded 'They have small choice.'

'Good. Now that I have sifted the traitors from your ranks — for I will not deal with traitors — I shall make my offer.' She smiled at the squat ironsmith. 'I think I've served both of us by so doing,' she said softly, and Hull gasped as he perceived the sweetness of the glance she bent on the scowling File. 'Would you, with your great muscles and warrior's heart, follow a woman?'

The scowl vanished in surprise. 'Follow you? *You?*'

'Yes.' Hull watched her in fascination as she used her voice, her eyes, her unearthly beauty intensified by the moonlight, all on hulking File Ormson, behind whom the Harrier prisoners stood tense and silent. 'Yes, I mean to follow me,' she repeated softly. 'You are brave men, all of you, now that I have weeded out the two cowards.' She smiled wistfully, almost tenderly at the squat figure before her. 'And you – you are a warrior.'

'But – ' File gulped, 'our others –'

'I promise you need not fight against your companions. I will release any of you who will not follow me. And your lands – it is your lands you fight for, is it not? – I will not touch, not one acre save the eldarch's.' She paused. 'Well?'

Suddenly File's booming laugh roared out. 'By God!' he swore. 'If you mean what you say, there's nothing to fight about! For my part, I'm with you!' He turned on his men. 'Who follows me?'

The group stirred. A few stepped forward, then a few more, and then, with a shout, the whole mass. 'Good!' roared File. He raised his great hard hand to his heart in the Empire salute. 'To Black – to the Princess Margaret!' he bellowed. 'To a warrior!'

She smiled and dropped her eyes as if in modesty. When the cheer had passed, she addressed File Ormson again. 'You will send men to your others?' she asked. 'Let them come in on the same terms.'

'They'll come!' growled File.

The Princess nodded. 'Lebeau,' she called, 'order off your men. These are our allies.'

The Harriers began to separate, drifting away with the crowd of villagers. The Princess stepped close to Hull, smiling maliciously up into his perplexed face. He scarcely knew whether to be glad or bitter, for indeed, though she had granted his request to spare his companions, she had granted it only at the cost of the destruction of the cause for which he had sacrificed everything. There were no Harriers any more, but he was still to die for them.

'Will you die happy now?' she cooed softly.

'No man dies happy,' he growled.

'I granted your wish, Hull.'

'If your promises can be trusted,' he retorted bitterly. 'You lied coolly enough to the Ch'cago men, and you made certain they were not loved by the Harriers before you killed them.'

She shrugged. 'I lie, I cheat, I swindle by whatever means come to hand,' she said indifferently, 'but I do not break my given word. The Harriers are safe.'

Beyond her, men came suddenly from the tunnel mouth, dragging something dark behind them.

'The Weed who pulled down the roof, Your Highness,' said Lebeau.

She glanced behind her, and pursed her dainty lips in surprise. 'The eldarch! The dotard died bravely enough.' Then she shrugged. 'He had but a few more years anyway.'

But Vail slipped by with a low moan of anguish, and Hull watched her kneel desolately by her father's body. A spasm of pity shook him as he realized that now she was utterly, completely alone. Enoch had died in the ambush of the previous night, old Marcus lay dead here before her, and he was condemned to death. The three who loved her and the man she loved – all slain in two nights passing. He bent a slow, helpless, pitying smile on her, but there was nothing he could do or say.

And Black Margot, after the merest glance, turned back to Hull, 'Now,' she said, the ice in her voice again, 'I deal with you!'

He faced her dumbly. 'Will you have the mercy to deal quickly, then?' he muttered at last.

'Mercy? I do not know the word where you're concerned, Hull. Or rather I have been already too merciful. I spared your life three times – once at Joaquin's request at Eaglefoot Flow, once before the guardhouse, and once up there in the hallway.' She moved closer. 'I cannot bear the touch of violence, Hull, and you have laid violent hands on me twice. Twice!'

'Once was to save your life,' he said, 'and the other to rectify my own unwitting treason. And I spared your life three times too, Black Margot – once when I aimed from the church roof, once from the ambush in the west chamber, and once but a half hour ago, for I could have killed you with this fist of mine, had I wished to strike hard enough. I owe you nothing.'

She smiled coldly. 'Well argued, Hull, but you die none the less in the way I wish.' She turned. 'Back to the house!' she commanded, and he strode away between the six guards who still flanked him.

She led them into the lower room that had been the Master's. There she sat idly in a deep chair of ancient craftsmanship, lit a black cigarette at the lamp, and thrust her slim legs carelessly before her, gazing at Hull. But he, staring through the window behind her, could see the dark blot that was Vail Ormiston weeping beside the body of her father.

'Now,' said the Princess, 'how would you like to die, Hull?'

'Of old age!' he snapped. 'And if you will not permit that, then as quickly as possible.'

'I might grant the second,' she observed. 'I *might*.'

The thought of Vail was still torturing him. At last he said, 'Your Highness, is your courage equal to the ordeal of facing me alone? I want to ask something that I will not ask in others' ears.'

She laughed contemptuously. 'Get out!' she snapped at the silent guards. 'Hull, do you think *I fear you*? I tell you your great muscles and stubborn heart are no more than those of Eblis, the black stallion. Must I prove it again to you?'

'No' he muttered. 'Got help me, but I know it's true. I'm not the match for Black Margot.'

'Nor is any other man,' she countered. Then, more softly, 'But if ever I do meet the man who can conquer me, if ever he exists, he *will* have something of you in him, Hull. Your great, slow strength, and your stubborn honesty, and your courage. I promise that.' She paused, her face now pure as a marble saint's. 'So say what you have to say, Hull. What do you ask?'

'My life,' he said bluntly.

Her green eyes widened in surprise. 'You, Hull? *You* beg your life? *You?*'

'Not for myself,' he muttered. 'There's Vail Ormiston weeping over her father. Enoch, who would have married her and loved her, is dead in last night's ambush, and if I die, she's left alone. I ask my life for her.'

'Her troubles mean nothing to me,' said Margaret of N'Orleans coldly.

'She'll *die* without someone – someone to help her through this time of torment.'

'Let her die, then. Why do you death-bound cling so desperately to life, only to age and die anyway? Sometimes I myself would welcome death, and I have infinitely more to live for than you. Let her die, Hull, as I think you'll die in the next moment or so!'

Her hand rested on the stock of the weapon at her belt. 'I grant your second choice,' she said coolly. 'The quick death.'

10

Old Einar Again

Black Margot ground out her cigarette with her left hand against the polished wood of the table top, but her right rested inexorably on her weapon. Hull knew beyond doubt or question that he was about to die, and for a moment he considered the thought of dying fighting, of being blasted by the beam as he flung himself at her. Then he shook his head; he revolted at the idea of again trying violence on the exquisite figure he faced, who, though witch or demon, had the passionless purity and loveliness of divinity. It was easier to die passively, simply losing his thoughts in the glare of her unearthly beauty.

She spoke. 'So die, Hull Tarvish,' she said gently, and drew the blunt weapon.

A voice spoke behind him, a familiar, pleasant voice. 'Do I intrude, Margaret?'

He whirled. It was Old Einar, thrusting his good-humored, wrinkled visage through the opening he had made in the doorway. He grinned at Hull, flung the door wider, and slipped into the room.

'Einar!' cried the Princess, springing from her chair. 'Einar Olin! Are you still in the world?' Her tones took on suddenly the note of deep pity. 'But so old – so old!'

The old man took her free hand. 'It is forty years since last I saw you, Margaret – and I was fifty then.'

'But so old!' she repeated. 'Einar, have I changed?'

He peered at her. 'Not physically, my dear. But from the stories that go up and down the continent, you are hardly the gay madcap that N'Orleans worshipped as the Princess Peggy, nor even the valiant little warrior they used to call the Maid of Orleans.'

She had forgotten Hull, but the guards visible through the half open door still blocked escape. He listened fascinated, for it was almost as if he saw a new Black Margot.

'Was I ever the Princess Peggy?' she murmured. 'I had forgotten – Well, Martin Sair can stave off age but he cannot halt the flow of time. But Einar – Einar, you were wrong to refuse him!'

'Seeing you, Margaret, I wonder instead if I were not very wise. Youth is too great a restlessness to bear for so long a time, and you have borne it less than a century. What will you be in another fifty years? In another hundred, if Martin Sair's art keeps its power? What will you be?'

She shook her head; her green eyes grew deep and sorrowful. 'I don't know, Einar. I don't know.'

'Well,' he said placidly, 'I am old, but I am contented. I wonder if you can say as much.'

'I might have been different, Einar, had you joined us. I could have loved you, Einar.'

'Yes,' he agreed wryly. 'I was afraid of that, and it was one of the reasons for my refusal. You see, I *did* love you, Margaret, and I chose to outgrow the torture rather than perpetuate it. That was a painful malady, loving you, and it took all of us at one time or another. 'Flame-struck,' we used to call it.' He smiled reflectively. 'Are any left save me of all those who loved you?'

'Just Jorgensen,' she answered sadly. 'That is if he has not yet killed himself in his quest for the secret of the Ancient's wings. But he will.'

'Well,' said Olin dryly, 'my years will yet make a mock of their immortality.' He pointed a gnarled finger at Hull. 'What do you want of my young friend here?'

Her eyes flashed emerald, and she drew her hand from that of Old Einar. 'I plan to kill him.'

'Indeed? And why?'

'Why?' Her voice chilled. 'Because he struck me with his hands. Twice.'

The old man smiled. 'I shouldn't wonder if he had cause enough, Margaret. Memory tells me that I myself have had the same impulse.'

'Then it's well you never yielded, Einar. Even you.'

'Doubtless. But I think I shall ask you to forgive young Hull Tarvish.'

'You know his name! Is he really your friend?'

Old Einar nodded. 'I ask you to forgive him.'

'Why should I?' asked the Princess. 'Why do you think a word from you can save him?'

'I am still Olin,' said the aged one, meeting her green eyes steadily with his watery blue ones. 'I still carry Joaquin's seal.'

'As if that could stop *me*!' But the cold fire died slowly in her gaze, and again her eyes were sad. 'But you are still Olin, the Father of Power,' she murmured. With a sudden gesture she thrust her weapon back into her belt. 'I spare him again,' she said, and then, in tones gone strangely dull, 'I suppose I wouldn't have killed him anyway. It is a weakness of mine that I cannot kill those who love me in a certain way – a weakness that will cost me dear some day.'

Olin twisted his lips in that skull-like smile, turning to the silent youth. 'Hull,' he said kindly, 'you must have been born under fortunate stars. But if you're curious enough to tempt your luck further, listen to this old man's advice.' His smile became a grin. 'Beyond the western mountains there are some very powerful, very rare hunting cats called lions, which Martin Sair says are not native to this continent, but were brought here by the Ancients to be caged and gazed at, and occasionally trained. As to that I know nothing, but I do say this, Hull – go twist the tail of a lion before you again try the wrath of Black Margot. And now get out of here.'

'Not yet Hull,' snapped the Princess. 'I have still my score to settle with you.' She turned back to Olin. 'Where do you wander now, Einar?'

'To N'Orleans. I have some knowledge to give Jorgensen, and I am homesick besides for the Great City.' He paused. 'I have seen Joaquin, Selui has fallen.'

'I know. I ride to meet him tonight.'

'He has sent representations to Ch'cago.'

'Good!' she flashed. 'Then there will be fighting.' Then her eyes turned dreamy. 'I have never seen the saltless seas,' she added wistfully, 'but I wonder if they can be as beautiful as the blue gulf beyond N'Orleans.'

But Old Einar shook his thin white hair. 'What will be the end of this, Margaret?' he asked gently. 'After Ch'cago is taken – for you will take it – what then?'

'Then the land north of the saltless seas, and east of them. N'York, and all the cities on the ocean shore.'

'And then?'

'Then South America, I suppose.'

'And *then*, Margaret?'

'Then? There is still Europe veiled in mystery, and Asia, Africa – all the lands known to the Ancients.'

'And after all of them?'

'Afterwards,' she replied wearily, 'we can rest. The fierce destiny that drives Joaquin surely cannot drive him beyond the boundaries of the world.'

'And so,' said Olin, 'you fight your way around the world so you can rest at the end of the journey. Then why not rest now,

Margaret? Must you pillow your head on the globe of the planet?'

Fury flamed green in her eyes. She raised her hand and struck the old man across his lips, but it must have been lightly, for he still smiled.

'Fool!' she cried. 'Then I will see to it that there is always war! Between me and Joaquin, if need be – or between me and anyone – *anyone* – so that I fight!' She paused panting. 'Leave me, Einar,' she said tensely. 'I do not like the things you bring to mind.'

Still smiling, the old man backed away. At the door he paused. 'I will see you before I die, Margaret,' he promised, and was gone.

She followed him to the doorway. 'Sora!' she called. 'Sora! ride!'

Hull heard the heavy tread of the fat Sora, and in a moment she entered bearing the diminutive cothurns and a pair of glistening silver gauntlets on her hands, and then she too was gone.

Slowly, almost wearily, the Princess turned to face Hull, who had as yet permitted no gleam of hope to enter his soul, for he had experienced too much of her mockery to trust the promise of safety Old Einar had won for him. He felt only the fascination that she always bound about him, the spell of her unbelievable black hair and her glorious sea-green eyes, and all her unearthly beauty.

'Hull,' she said gently, 'what do you think of me now?'

'I think you are a black flame blowing cold across the world. I think a demon drives you.'

'And do you hate me so bitterly?'

'I pray every second to hate you.'

'Then see, Hull.' With her little gauntleted fingers she took his great hands and placed them about the perfect curve of her throat. 'Here I give you my life for the taking. You have only to twist once with these mighty hands of yours and Black Margot will be out of the world forever.' She paused. 'Must I beg you?'

Hull felt as if molten metal flowed upward through his arms from the touch of her white skin. His fingers were rigid as metal bars, and all the great strength of them could not put one feather's weight of pressure on the soft throat they circled. And deep in the lambent emerald flames that burned in her eyes he saw again the fire of mockery – jeering, taunting.

'You will not?' she said, lifting away his hands, but holding them in hers. 'Then you do not hate me?'

'You know I don't,' he groaned.

'And you do love me?'

'Please,' he muttered. 'Is it necessary again to torture me? I need no proof of your mastery.'

'Then say you love me.'

'Heaven forgive me for it,' he whispered, 'but I do!'

She dropped his hands and smiled. 'Then listen to me, Hull. You love little Vail with a truer love, and month by month memory fades before reality. After a while there will be nothing left in you of Black Margot, but there will be always Vail. I go now hoping never to see you again, but' – and her eyes chilled to green ice – 'before I go I settle my score with you.'

She raised her gauntleted hand. 'This for your treachery!' she said, and struck him savagely across his right cheek. Blood spouted, there would be scars, but he stood stolid. 'This for your violence!' she said, and the silver gauntlet tore his left cheek. Then her eyes softened. 'And this,' she murmured, 'for your love!'

Her arms circled him, her body was warm against him, and her exquisite lips burned against his. He felt as if he embraced a flame for a moment, and then she was gone, and a part of his soul went with her. When he heard the hooves of the stallion Eblis pounding beyond the window, he turned and walked slowly out of the house to where Vail still crouched beside her father's body. She clung to him, wiped the blood from his cheeks, and strangely, her words were not of her father, nor of the sparing of Hull's life, but of Black Margot.

'I knew you lied to save me,' she murmured. 'I knew you never loved her.'

And Hull, in whom there was no falsehood, drew her close to him and said nothing.

But Black Margot rode north from Selui through the night. In the sky before her were thin shadows leading phantom armies, Alexander the Great, Attila, Genghis Khan, Tamerlane, Napoleon, and clearer than all, the battle queen Semiramis. All the mighty conquerors of the past, and where were *they*, where were their empires, and where, even, were their bones? Far in the south were the graves of men who had loved her, all except Old Einar, who tottered like a feeble gray ghost across the world to find his.

At her side Joaquin Smith turned as if to speak, stared, and remained silent. He was not accustomed to the sight of tears in the eyes and on the cheeks of Black Margot.*

---

* All conversation ascribed to the Princess Margaret in this story is taken verbatim from an anonymous volume published in Urbs in the year 186, called 'Loves of the Black Flame.' It is credited to Jacques Lebeau, officer in command of the Black Flame's personal guard.

DIVIDE AND RULE

L. Sprague de Camp
1

The broad Hudson, blue under spring skies, was dotted with
sails. The orchards in the valley were aglow with white and
purple blossoms. Beyond the river frowned Storm King, not
much of a mountain by western standards, but impressive
enough to a York Stater. The landscape blazed with the livid
green of young leaves – and Sir Howard van Slyck, second son
of the Duke of Poughkeepsie, wished to God he could get at the
itch under his breastplate without going to the extreme of
dismounting and removing half his armor.

As the huge black gelding plodded along the bypass that took
the Albany Post Road around Peekskill, its rider reflected that he
hadn't been too clever in starting out from Ossining fully
accoutered.But how was he to know the weather would turn hot
so suddenly? The sponge-rubber padding under the plates made
the suit suffocatingly hot. Little drops of sweat crawled down his
skin; and then, somewhere around Croton, the itch had begun. It
seemed to be right under the Van Slyck trademark, which, inlaid
in the plastron, was the only ornamentation on an otherwise
plain suit. The trademark was a red maple leaf in a white circle,
with the Van Slyck motto, 'Give 'em the works,' in a circle
around it.

Twice he had absently reached up to scratch, to be recalled to
the realities of the situation by the rasp of metal on metal.
Maybe a smoke would help him forget it. He opened a
compartment in his saddle, took out pipe, tobacco, and lighter,
and lit up. (He really preferred cigarettes, but the ashes dribbled
down inside his helmet.)

The bypass swung out over the New York Central tracks. Sir
Howard pulled over to his own side to let a six-horse bus clatter

past, then walked the gelding over to the edge and looked down. Up the tracks his eye was caught by the gleam of the brass rings on the ends of the tusks of an elephant pulling a string of little cars; the afternoon freight for New York, he thought. By the smallness of the animal's ears he knew it was the Indian species. Evidently the Central had decided against switching to African elephants. The Pennsylvania used them because they were bigger and faster, but they were also less docile. The Central had tried one out as an experiment the year before; the duke, who was a big stockholder in the Central, had told him about it. On the trial run the brakeman had been careless and let the lead car bump the elephant's hind legs, whereupon the animal had pulled two cars off the track and would have killed the chairman of the board if it had been able to catch him.

Sir Howard resumed his way north, relieved to note that the itch had stopped. At the intersection of the bypass with the connecting road to the Bronx Parkway he drew rein again. Something was coming down the road in long, parabolic leaps. He knew what that meant. With a grunt of annoyance he heaved himself out of the saddle. As the thing drew near he took the pipe out of his mouth and flipped his right arm up in salute.

The thing, which looked rather like a kangaroo wearing a football helmet, shot by without apparently looking at them. Sir Howard had heard of sad cases of people who had neglected to salute hoppers because they thought they weren't looking at them. He felt no particular resentment at having to salute the creature. After all, he'd been doing it all his life. Such irritation as he felt was merely at the idea of having to hoist his own two hundred and ten pounds, plus forty pounds of chrome-nickel steel plate, back on his tall mount on a hot day.

Seven miles up the Post Road lay Castle Peekskill, and Sir Howard fully intended to sponge a dinner and a night's sleep off his neighbor. Halfway up the winding road he heard a musical toot. He pulled off the asphalt; a long black torpedo on wheels was swooping up the grade behind him. He unshipped the duralumin lance from its boot, and as the car whizzed past, the maple-leaf flag of the Van Slyks fluttered down in an arc. He got a glimpse of the occupants; four hoppers, their heads looking rather like those of giant rats under the inevitable helmets. Luckily you didn't have to dismount for hoppers in power vehicles; they went by too fast for such a rule to be practical. Sir Howard wondered — as had many others what it would be like to travel in a power vehicle. Of course there was an easy way to find out; just break a hopper law. Unfortunately, the ride received in that was was a strictly one-way affair.

'Oh, well, no doubt God had known what He was about when He had made the rule allowing nobody but hoppers to have power vehicles and explosives and things. Men had been very wicked, so God had sent the hoppers to rule over him. At least that was what you learned in school. His brother Frank had doubts; had, very secretly, confided them to Sir Howard. Frank even said that once man had had his own power vehicles. He didn't know about that; the hoppers knew a terrible lot, and if that had been so they'd have had it so taught in the schools. Still, Frank was smart, and what he said wasn't /to be laughed off. Frank was a queer duck, always poking around old papers after useless bits of knowledge. Sir Howard wondered how it was that he got on so well with his skinny little elder brother, with whom he had so little in common. He certainly hoped nothing would happen to Frank before the old man was gathered unto his fathers. He'd hate to have the management of the duchy around his neck, at least just yet. He was having too much fun.

He swung off the road when Castle Peekskill appeared over the treetops, near the site of the old village of Garrison. He stopped before the gate and blew a whistle. The gatekeeper popped out of the tower with his usual singsong of: 'Who are you and what do you seek?' Then he said: 'Oh, it's you, Sir Howard. I'll tell Lord Peekskill you're here.' And presently the gate – a huge slab of reinforced concrete hinged at the bottom – swung out from the wall and down.

John Kearton – Baron Peekskill – was in the courtyard as Sir Howard's horse went *plop-plop* over the concrete. He had evidently just come in from a try for a pheasant, as he wore an old leather jacket and very muddy boots and leaned on a light crossbow.

'Howard, my boy!' he shouted. He was a short man, rather stout, with reddish-brown hair and beard. 'Get out of your tinware and into your store clothes. Here, Lloyd, take Sir Howard's duffel bag to the first guest room. You'll stay over-night with us, won't you? Of course you will! I want to hear about the war. WABC had an announcer at the Battle of Mount Kisco, but he saw a couple of the Connecticut horses coming toward him and pulled foot. After that all we could hear was the sound of his horse going hell-for-leather back to Ossining.'

'I'll be glad to stay,' said Sir Howard. 'If I'm not putting you out – '

'No, no, not a bit of it. You've got that same horse still, I see. I like entires better for war horses myself.'

'They may have more pep,' admitted the knight, 'but this old fellow does what I want him to, which is the main thing. Three years ago he took third in his class at the White Plains show. That was before he got those scars. But take a look at this saddle; it's a new and very special model. See: built-in radio, compartments in the cantle for your things, and everything. Got it at a discount, too.'

Sir Howard clanked upstairs after his host. The transparent lucite visor of his burganet was already up; he unlatched the bib and pushed it up, too, then carefully wriggled his head out of the helmet. His square, craggy face bore the little beard and mustache affected by his class. His nose was not all that a nose should be, as the result of an encounter with the business end of a billhook. But he had refused to have it plasticized back into shape, on the ground that he could expect more than one broken nose in his life, and the surgery would, therefore, be a waste of money. His inky-black hair covered a highly developed brain, somewhat rusty from disuse. When you could knock any man in the duchy out of his saddle, and drink any man in the duchy under the table, and had a way with the girls, there were few stimuli to heavy thinking.

Peekskill remarked. 'That's a nice suit you have. What is it, a Packard?'

'Yeah,' replied Sir Howard, pulling off a rerebrace. 'It's several years old; I suppose I'll have to trade it in for a new model one of these days. The only trouble is that new suits cost money. What do you think of the new Ford?'

'Hm-m-m – I dunno. I'm not sure I like that all-lucite helmet. It does give you vision in all directions. But if they make it thick enough to stop a poleax, it'll make you top-heavy, I think. And the lucite gets scratched and nicked up so quickly, especially in a fight.'

'Let's see your kicker, John,' said Sir Howard, reaching for the crossbow. 'Marlin, isn't it?'

'No, Winchester, last year's. I had my armorer take off that damned windage adjustment, which I never used, anyway. That's why it looks different. But let's hear about the war. The papers gave us just the bare facts.'

'Oh, there wasn't much to it,' said Sir Howard with exaggerated indifference. 'I killed a man. Funny: I've been in six fights, and that was the first time I really knew I'd gotten one of the enemy. I'm not counting that bandit fellow we caught up at Staatsburg. You know how it is in a fight: everybody's hitting at you and vice versa, and you don't have time to see what damage you've done.

'I shouldn't claim much credit for this killing, though. I signed up at Ossining because the city manager's a cousin of mine, and they pay well. The C. M. collected a couple of hundred heavy horses from lower Winchester, and he had the commons of Ossining and Tarrytown for pikes. He'd heard that Danbury was going to get a contingent of heavy horses from Torrington. So he put us in two groups, lances in the first only. I was in the second, so they made me leave my toothpick behind. That's a nice little sticker, by the way; Hamilton Standard made it.

'We found them just this side of Mount Kisco. Our scouts flushed an ambush, very neat; chevaux-de-frisse at the far end, horses on either side, crossbows behind every bush. The C. M. swung us south to smash one of their bodies of horses before the other could come up. When we shook out and charged, their left wing scattered without waiting for us as if six devils with green ears were after them. I couldn't see anything because of the lances in front of my group. But the ground's pretty rough, you know, and you can't keep a nicely dressed line. The first thing I knew was when something went *bong* on my helmet, and these red-shirted chaps with spiked helmets and shields were all around me poking at the joints in my suit. They were Danbury's right wing. He hadn't been able to get any heavy horses in Connecticut. They were crab-suited, with chain pants hanging down from their cuirasses.

'I swung at a couple of them, but they were out of reach each time the ax got there. Then Paul Jones almost stepped on a couple of dismounted red-shirts. I chopped at one, but he got his shield up in time. And before I could recover, the other one, who didn't have a shield, grabbed the shaft in both hands and tried to take it away from me. I was afraid to let go for fear he'd kill my horse before I could get my sword out. And while we were having our tug-of-war, some crab on the other side of me – the left side – grabbed my ankle and shoved it up. Of course, I went out of the saddle as pretty as a pay check, right on top of this chap who wanted my ax.

'I couldn't see anything for a few minutes because I had my head in a bush. When I got up on my knees there weren't any more red-shirts in sight. They'd found us pretty hard nuts to crack, and when they saw the pikes coming they beat it. I found I still had hold of the ax. The Danburian was underneath me, and the spike on the end of the shaft was driven under his chin and up into his head. He was as dead as last year's treaties. They had about half a dozen killed in that brush; we lost one man – thrust under the armpit – and had a couple of horses killed by kicker bolts. We took their dismounted horses and some of their crossbows prisoner. I climbed back on Paul Jones and joined up with the chase. We couldn't catch them, naturally. We chased 'em clear to Danbury Castle, and when we got there they were inside thumbing their noses and shooting at us with ballistae.

'We sat outside for a couple of weeks, but they had enough canned stuff for years, and threatening a seventy-foot concrete wall doesn't get you anywhere. So finally the C. M. and Danbury agreed to submit their argument about road tolls to a hopper court, and we went back to Ossining for our pay.'

During his story Sir Howard had gotten out of his armor and into his ordinary clothes. It was pleasant to sprawl in the freedom of tweed and linen, with a tall glass in your hand, and watch the sun drop behind Storm King. 'Of course, it might have been different' – his voice dropped till it was barely audible – 'if we'd had guns.'

Peekskill started. 'Don't say such things, my boy. Don't even think them. If *they* found out –' He shuddered a little and took a big gulp of his highball.

A flunky entered and announced: 'My lord, Squire Matthews, with a message from Sir Humphrey Goldberg.'

Peekskill frowned. 'What's this? Why couldn't he have written me a letter? Come on Howard, let's see what he wants.'

They found the squire in the hall, looking grimly polite. He bowed stiffly, and said with exaggerated distinctness: 'My Lord Peekskill, Sir Humphry Goldberg sends his compliments, and wants to know what the hell your lordship meant by calling him a double-crossing, dog-faced baboon in the Red Bear Inn last night!'

'Oh, dear,' sighed the baron. 'Tell Sir Humphry that first, I deny calling him such name; and second, if I did call him that, I was drunk at the time; and third, even if I wasn't drunk I'm sorry now, and ask him to have dinner here tonight.'

The squire bowed again and went, his riding boots clicking on the tiles. 'Hump's all right,' said Peekskill, 'only we've been having a little argument about my electric-light plant. He says it ruins his radio reception. But I think we can fix it up. Besides, he's a better swordsman than I am. Let's finish our drinks in the library.'

They had just settled when a boy in a Western Union uniform was ushered in. He looked from one to the other; then went up to Sir Howard. 'You Van Slyck?' he asked, shifting his gum to his cheek. 'O.K. I been tryin' to find ya. Here, sign, please.'

'Manners!' roared the baron. The boy looked startled, then irked. He bowed very low and said: 'Sir Howard van Slyck, will your gorgeous highness deign to sign this ... this humble document?'

Both men were looking angry now, but Sir Howard signed without further words. When the boy had gone, he said: 'Some of these commoners are too damn fresh nowadays.'

'Yes,' replied his host, 'they need a bit of knocking around now and then to remind them of their place. Why ... what's the matter, Howard? Something wrong? Your father?'

'No. My brother Frank. The hoppers arrested him last night. He was tried this morning, condemned, and burned this afternoon.

'The charge was scientific research.'

2

'You'd better pull yourself together, Howard.'

'I'm all right John.'

'Well, you'd better not drink any more of that stuff.'

'I'm okay, I tell you. I'm not drunk, I can't get drunk: I've tried. Right now I haven't even a little buzz on.'

'Listen, Howard, use your head. Lord knows I'm glad to have you stay round here as long as you like, but don't you think you ought to see your father?'

'My father? Good God, I'd forgotten about him! I *am* a louse, John. A dirty louse. The dirtiest louse that ever – '

'Here, none of that, my boy. Now drink this; it'll clear your head. And get your suit on.

'Lloyd! Hay, *Lloyd!* fetch Sir Howard's armor. No, you idiot, I don't care if you haven't finished shining it. Get it!'

Sir Howard spoke hesitantly; he wasn't sure how his father would take his proposal. He wasn't sure himself it was quite the right thing to do. But the old man's reaction surprised him. 'Yes,' he said in his tired voice, 'I think that's a good idea. Get away from here for a few months. When I'm gone you'll be duke, now, and you won't have many chances of gallivanting, so you ought to make the most of what you have. And you've never seen much of the country except between here and New York. Travel's broadening, they say. Don't worry about me; I have enough to do to keep two men busy.

'I'll ask just one thing, and that is that you don't go joining up in any more of these local wars. It's you I've always worried about, not Frank, and I don't want any more of that. I don't care how good the pay is. I know you're a mercenary young rascal; I like that, because I don't have to worry about your bankrupting the duchy. But if you really want to make money, you can try your hand at running the Poughkeepsie Shoe Co. when you get back.'

Thus it came about that Sir Howard again found himself riding north, and to his own mild surprise doing some heavy thinking. Luckily the hoppers hadn't made much red tape about the travel permit. But he knew they'd keep an eye on him. Even though he hadn't done anything, he'd be on their suspicious list because of his brother. He'd have to be careful.

Jogging along, you had plenty of time to think. He knew he had the reputation of being simply a large, energetic, and rather empty-headed young man with a taste for action. It was time he put something in that head, if only because of the prospect of inheriting the duchy.

He felt that something must be wrong with his picture of the world. In it the burning of people for scientific research was just. But he didn't feel that Frank's death had been just. In it, whatever the hoppers said was right, because God had set them over Man. It was right that he, Howard van Slyck, should salute the hoppers. Didn't the commoners have to salute him in return? That made it fair all around. He was bound to obey the hoppers; the commoners were bound to obey him. It was all explained to you in school. The hoppers likewise were under obligation to God to command him, and he the commoners. Again, perfectly fair.

Only there must be something wrong with it. He couldn't see any flaw in the reasoning he'd been taught; it all fitted together like a sheet of Chrysler super-heavy silico-manganese steel plate. But there must be a flaw somewhere. If he traveled, and kept his eyes open, and asked questions, maybe he could find it. Perhaps somebody had a book that would shed light on the question. The only books he'd come across were either fairy tales about the daring deeds of dauntless knights, which bored him, or simple texts on how to run a savings bank or assemble a cream separator.

He might even learn to associate with commoners and find out how they looked at things. Sir Howard was not, considering his background, especially class-conscious; the commoners were all right, and some were even good fellows, if you didn't let them get too familiar or think they were as good as you. What he had in mind was, for one of his class, a radical departure from the norm.

He squirmed in his lobster shell and wished he could scratch through the plate. Damn, he must have picked up some bugs at Poughkeepsie Manor, free of vermin though it was normally kept. That was the hoppers' fault.

It began to rain; one of those vigorous York State spring rains that might last an hour or a week. Sir Howard got out his poncho and put his head through the slit in the middle. He didn't worry about his plate, because it had been well vaselined. But the rain, which was coming down really hard, was a nuisance. With his visor up it spattered against his face; and with it down, he had to wipe the lucite constantly to see where he was going. Below the poncho, the water worked into his leg joints and made his legs feel cold and clammy. Paul Jones didn't like it, either; he plodded along with his head drooping, breaking into periodic trots only with reluctance.

Sir Howard was not in the best of humors when, an hour later, the rain slackened to a misty drizzle through which the far shore of the Hudson could barely be made out. He was approaching the Rip van Winkle Bridge when somebody on a horse in front of him yelled 'Hey!'

Sir Howard thought he wanted more room. But the strange rider sat where he was and shouted. 'Thought I'd skip the country, didn'tcha? Well, I been laying for you, and now you're gonna get yours!'

From his costume the man was obviously a foreigner. His legs were encased in some sort of leather trousers with a wide flap on each leg. 'What the hell do you mean?' answered the knight.

'You know what I mean, you yellow-bellied bastitch. You gonna fight like a man, or do I have to take your breeches down and paddle you?'

Sir Howard was too cold and wet and bebugged to carry on this lunatic argument, especially as he could see the town of

Catskill – where there would be fires and whisky – across the river.
'Okay foreigner, you asked for it. Have at you, base-born!' The
lance came out of his boot and was lowered to horizontal. The
gelding's hoofs thundered on the asphalt.

The stranger had thrown his sheepskin jacket into the ditch,
revealing a shirt of chain, and sent his wide-brimmed hat scaling
after it, showing a steel skullcap. Sir Howard, slamming down his
visor, wondered what form of attack he was going to use; he
hadn't drawn the curved saber that clanked from his saddle. With
that light horse he'd probably try to dodge the lance point at the
last minute –

The light horse dodged; the knight swung his lance; the dodge
had been a feint and the foreigner was safely past his point on his
left side. Sir Howard had a fleeting glimpse of a long loop of rope
whirling about the man's head, and then something caught him
around the neck. The world whirled, and the asphalt came up and
hit him with a terrific clatter.

To get up in full armor, you had to be on your stomach and
work your knees up under you. He rolled over and started to
scramble up – and was jerked headlong. The stranger had twisted
his rope around a projection on his saddle. The horse kept the rope
taut; every time the knight got to his knees it took a step or two and
pulled him down again. When he was down he couldn't see what
was happening. Something caught his sword arm before he had a
chance to get his weapon out. Rolling, he saw that the stranger had
thrown another noose around his arm. And down this second rope
loops came snaking to bind his other arm, his legs, his neck, until
he was trussed like a fawn.

'Now,' said the foreigner, coming toward him with a hunting
knife in his hand, 'let's see how you get into one of these stovepipe
suits –' He pushed the visor up and gasped. 'Sa-a-ay, you ain't the
guy at all!'

'What guy?' snarled Sir Howard.

'The guy what ducked me in the horse trough. Big guy named
Baker, over in Catskill. Your suit's like his, and you ride the same
kind of critter. I thought sure it was him; I couldn't see your face
with the helmet on in this bad light. It's all a mistake; I'm sure sorry
as all hell, mister. You won't be mad if I let you up, will you?'

Sir Howard conceded that he wouldn't be mad; the fact was
that his anger at his ignominious overthrow by this wild
foreigner's unfair fighting methods he had mixed a grudging
admiration for the man's skill and a great curiosity as to how it had
been accomplished.

The stranger was a lean person with straw-colored hair, some years older than Sir Howard. As he undid the rope he explained: 'My name's Haas; Lyman Haas. I come from out Wyoming way; you know, the Far West. Most folks around here never heard of Wyoming. I was having a quiet drink in Catskill last night at Lukas's Bar and Grill, and this here Baker comes up and picks an argument. I'm a peaceable man, but they's some things I don't like. Anyway, when it came to the punch, this Baker and two of his friends jump me, and they ducked me in the horse trough, like I told you. I see now why I mistook you for him: you had your trademark covered up under that poncho. His is a fox's head. This'll be a lesson to me never to kill nobody again before I'm sure who he is. I hope I didn't dent your nice suit on the pavement.'

'That's all right. A few dents more or less won't matter to this old suit. It's partly my fault, too. I should have thought of the poncho.'

Haas was staring at the Van Slyck trademark and moving his lips. 'Give . . . 'em . . . the . . . works,' he read slowly. 'What's it mean?'

'That's an expression they used a long time ago, meaning 'Hit them with all you've got,' or something like that. Say, Mr. Haas, I'd like to get somewhere where I can dry out. And I wouldn't mind a drink. Can you recommend a place at Catskill?'

'Sure; I know a good place. And a drink wouldn't hurt either of us.'

'Fine, I've also got to buy some insect powder. And when that's been attended to, perhaps we can do something about your Mr. Baker.'

The next morning the good citizens of Catskill were astonished to see the person of Squire Baker, naked and painted in an obscene manner, dangling by his wrists and ankles from a lamp-post near the main intersection. As he was quite high up and had been efficiently gagged, he was not noticed until broad daylight. Baker never lived the incident down; a few months later he left Catskill and shipped on a schooner in the chicle-and-banana trade to Central America.

3

'Say, How, I'd kinda like to hear some music.'

Sir Howard had not gotten used to Haas' calling him 'How.' He liked the man, but couldn't quite make him out. In some ways he acted like a commoner. If he were, the knight thought he ought to resent his familiarity. But there were other things – Haas' self-possession, for instance. Oh, well, no doubt the scheme of social stratification was different out West. He turned the radio on.

'That's a neat little thing you got,' Haas continued.

'Yep; it's nice when you're making a long ride. There's an aerial contact built into the lance boot, so this little toothpick acts as an aerial. Or, if I'm not carrying a lance, I can clip the aerial lead to my suit, which works almost as well as the lance.'

'Is they a battery in the saddle?'

'Yes, just a little light battery. *They* have a real fuel battery, but they don't let us use it.'

They topped a rise, and Albany's State Office Building came in sight. It was by far the tallest building in the city, none of the rest of which was yet visible. Some said it had been built long ago, when York State was a single governmental entity – and not just a vague geographical designation. Now, of course, it was hopper headquarters for a whole upstate region. Sir Howard thought the dark, square-topped tower looked sinister. But it didn't become a knight to voice such timid vagaries. He asked Haas: 'How is it that you're so far from home?'

'Oh, I wanted to see New York. You been to New York, I suppose?'

'Yes, often. I've never been very far upstate, though.'

'That was the main thing. Of course, they was that guy – '

'Yes? Go on; you can trust me.'

'Well – I don't suppose it'll do no harm, this being a long way from Wyoming. Him and me was arguing in a bar. Now, I'm a peaceable man, but they's some words I don't like, and this guy didn't smile when he said 'em, either. So we had it out in the alley with sabers. Only he had friends. That'll be a lesson to me, to make sure whether a guy has friends first before I fight him. I wanted to see New York, anyway, so here I am. When I ran out of money on the way, I'd make a stake doing rope tricks in the theaters. I made about six hundred clinkers in New York last week. It's purty near gone now, but I can make some more. They ain't nobody around these parts knows how to use a rope.'

'Why,' said Sir Howard, 'what became of it? Were you robbed?'

'Nope; just spent it.' The airy way in which this was said made Sir Howard shudder. The Westerner looked at him narrowly, with a trace of a smile. 'You know,' he said, 'I always had the idea that lords and knights and such were purty free with their wallpaper; threw it around like it wasn't nothing. And here you're the carefullest guy with his money I ever did see. It just shows you.'

'How did you like New York?' asked the knight.

'Purty good; there's lot of things to see. I made friends with a guy who works in a furniture factory, and he took me around. I liked to see the chairs and things come buzzing down the assembly line. My friend couldn't get me into the power plant though. They was a hopper guard at the door. They don't let nobody in there except a few old employees and I hear they examine them with this dope they got every week to make sure they haven't told nobody how the power machinery works.

'But I got tired of it after a few weeks. Too many hoppers. They get on my nerves, always looking at you with those little black eyes like they was reading your mind. Some says they can, too. I guess after what you told me about your brother it's safe for me to say what I think of 'em. I don't like 'em.'

'Don't they have hoppers out West, too?'

'Sure, we got some, but they don't bother us much. What they say goes, of course, but they let us alone as long as we mind our business and pay our hopperage. They don't like the climate – too dry.'

'They don't interfere too much with our local affairs, either,' said the knight, 'except that the big cities like New York are under their direct rule. That's how there are so many down there. Of course, if you – but I've already told you about that.'

'Yeah. And it's a crime the prices you pay for steaks around here. Out in Wyoming, where we raise the critter, we eat mostly that. It's the hopperage charges, and all these little boundary tolls and tariffs between here and there makes 'em so expensive.'

'Do you have wars out West, too?'

'Sure, once and a while us and the Novvos gets in a scrap.'

'The Novvos?'

'Folks who live down south of us. Stock raisers, mostly. They ain't like us; got sorta reddish-brown skins, like Queenie here, and flat faces. Hair as black as yours, too.'

'I think I've heard of these people,' said the knight. 'We had a man at the manor last year who'd been out West. But he called these red-skinned people Injuns.'

'That a fact? I always thought an Injun was what made the hopper cars and flying machines go. It just shows you. Anyhow, we get in a fight with the Novvos about grazing rights and such, now and then. Mostly mounted-archery stuff. I'm purty good at it myself. See.' He unfastened the flap of an elongated box that hung from his saddle, which proved to be a quiver. He took out the two halves of a steel bow. 'Wish I had one of those trick saddles like yours to pack my stuff in, 'steada hanging it all over me and my horse looks like a Christmas tree. But I travel purty light, at that. You got to, when you only got one little horse like Queenie. I suppose that high cantle's mostly to keep you from getting shoved off the horse's rump by some guy's toothpick.' Haas had been fitting the halves of the bow together. The bow had a sighting apparatus just above the grip.

'See the knot in that big pine? Now watch, *Yeeow!*' the mare jumped forward. Haas whipped an arrow from his quiver; the bow twanged. The Westerner swung his mount back, walked her up to the tree, and pulled the arrow out of the knot. 'Maybe I shouldn'ta done that,' he said. 'We're getting purty close in to Albany, and maybe they got a regulation about shooting arrows inside the city limits. What's they to see in Albany?' One of the hoppers' hexagonal glassy dwellings had come into view among the old two-story frame houses.

'Not much,' replied the knight. 'The first thing I have to do is to go the Office Building and have my travel permit stamped. How about you?'

'Oh, mine ain't that kind. I had it stamped in New York, and now I don't have to report to the hoppers again till I get out to Chicago. But I'll tag along with you. Far's I can see they ain't neither of us got to get anywhere in particular.'

They waited on the sidewalk in front of the Office Building for a quarter of an hour before they had a chance to go in, for, of course, they couldn't precede a hopper through the doors. By that time Sir Howard's steel-clad arm ached from saluting. A pair of the things passed him, chattering in their own incomprehensible tongue, which sounded like the twittering of birds. They smelled like very ripe cheese. He was startled to hear one of them suddenly switch to English. 'Man!' it squeaked. 'Why did you not salute?'

Sir Howard looked around, and saw that it was addressing Haas, who was standing stupidly with a cigarette in his mouth and a lighter in his hand. He pulled himself together, put away the smoking things, and took off his hat. 'I'm sure sorry as all hell, your excellency, but I'm afraid I wasn't looking.'

'Control your language, Man,' the hopper twittered. 'Being sorry is no excuse. You know there is a five-dollar fine for not saluting.'

'Yes, your excellency. Thanks your excellency, for reminding me.'

'Smoking is forbidden inside anyway,' the thing chirped. 'But since you have assumed a more respectful attitude I shall not pursue the matter further. That is all, Man.'

'Thank you, your excellency.' Hass put his hat back on and followed Sir Howard into the building. The knight heard him utter, 'I'm a peaceable man, *but* – '

Sir Howard found a man with a drooping white mustache at the travel-permit counter, who stamped his permit and entered his visit without comment. The man had the nervous, hangdog air that people got working around hoppers.

As they headed back to where their horses were tethered, Haas said, very low: 'Say, How, do you reckon that hopper that bawled me out was showing off to his girl friend?'

'They don't have girl friends, Lyman,' replied Sir Howard. 'They don't have sexes. Or rather, each one of them is both male and female. It takes two to produce a crop of eggs, but they both lay them. Hermaphroditic, they call it.'

Haas stared at him. 'You mean they – ' He doubled over, guffawing and slapping his chaps. 'Boy, wouldn't I like to have a couple of 'em in a cage!'

4

'Let's eat here, How; we can watch the railroad out the window. I like to see the elephants go by.'

'Okay, Lyman. I guess this is about as good as any place in Amsterdam.'

At the bar, men made way respectfully for the suit of armor. 'Two Manhattans,' ordered Sir Howard.

'Straws, Sir?' asked the barkeeper.

'Nope,' mumbled the knight, struggling with the helmet. 'At least, not if I can get this thing out of the way. Ah!' The bib came up finally. 'I'll have to take the damned hat apart and clean it properly one of these days. The hinge is as dirty as a secondhand hog wallow.'

'You know, How,' said Haas, 'that's one reason I never liked those iron hats much. For wearing, that is; I don't say nothing against them for flowerpots. I always figured, suppose a guy was to offer me a drink, sudden, and I had to wrassle all those visors and trapdoors and things out of the way. When I got ready to drink, the guy might have changed his mind.' He took a sip and sighed happily. 'You Yanks sure know how to mix cocktails. Out in Wyoming the cocktails are so lousy we take our poison mostly straight.

'It's a right handsome river, this Mohawk,' he continued. 'Wish I could say the same for some of the towns along it. I come up from New York through Connecticut; they got some real pretty towns in Connecticut. But the river's okay. I like to watch the canal boats. Those canal-boat drivers sure know how to handle their horses.'

Somebody down the bar said loudly. 'I still claim it ain't decent!' Heads were turned toward him. Somebody shushed him, but he went on: 'We all know he's been doing it for years, but he don't have to wave it in our faces like that. He might have taken her around a back alley, 'stead of dragging her right down the main street.'

'Who dragged whom down what street?' Sir Howard asked a neighbor.

'Kelly's been girling again,' the man replied. 'Only this time he had his gang grab her right here in town. Then they tied her on a horse, and Kelly led the procession right through the heart of town. I saw it; she sat up very straight on the horse, like a soldier. She couldn't say anything on account of the gag, of course. The people were sore. I think if somebody'd had a can opener he'd have taken a crack at Kelly, even though he had his lobsters with him. I would have.'

'Huh?' said Haas blankly.

'He means,' the knight explained, 'that if he'd had a bill-hook or a poleax he'd have gone for this Kelly, in spite of his having a gang of full-armored men at his back. A half-armored man is a crab.'

'You use some of the dangedest English here in the East,' said Haas. 'Who's this Kelly? Sounds kinda tough.'

Their informant looked at Haas' clothes and Sir Howard's trademark. 'Strangers, aren't you? Warren Kelly's tough, all right. He sells the townspeople "protection." You know, pay up or else. We're supposed to be part of Baron Schenectady's fee, but Schenck spends his time in New York, and there's nobody to do anything. Kelly has a big castle up near Broadalbin; that'll be where he's taken this poor girl. He hasn't got a title, though at the present rate he's apt to before long – meaning no offense to the nobility,' he added hastily. 'Gentlemen, have you ever thought of the importance of insurance? My card, if you don't mind. My company has a special arrangement for active men-at-arms –'

Sir Howard and Haas looked at one another, slow grins forming. 'Just like in storybooks,' said the knight. 'Lyman, I think we might do a little inquiring around about this castle and its super-tough owner. Are you with me?'

'Sure, I'm way ahead of you. They'll be a hardware store open after we finish dinner, won't they? I want to buy some paint. I got an idea.'

'We'll need a lot of ideas, my friend. You can't just huff and puff and blow a concrete castle in, you know. Strategy is indicated.'

The horse's hoofs clattered up to the side of the moat; the rider blew a whistle. A searchlight beam stabbed out from the walls, accompanied by a challenge. The light bathed Sir Howard van Slyck and his mount – with a difference. Paul Jones' feet had become white, and his black forehead had developed a big white diamond. On the rider's breastplate the Van Slyck maple-leaf insignia was concealed under a green circle with a black triangle painted in the middle of it. The red-and-white flag was gone from the lance.

'I am Sir William Scranton of Wilkes-Barre!' shouted the knight. (He knew that northeastern Pennsylvania was full of noble Scrantons, and there ought to be several Williams among them.) 'I'm passing through, and I've heard of Warren Kelly and should like to make his acquaintance!'

'Wait there,' called the watcher. Sir Howard waited, listening to the croak of frogs in the moat and hoping his alias would stand inspection. He was in high spirits. He'd had a moment of qualms about violating his promise to his father, but decided that, after all, rescuing a damsel in distress couldn't be fairly called 'joining up in a local war.'

The hinges on the drawbridge groaned as the cables supporting it were unreeled. He clattered into the yard. A blank-faced man said: 'I'm Warren Kelly. Pleased to meetcha.' The man was not very big, but quick in his movements. He had a long nose and prominent, slightly bloodshot eyes. He needed a haircut. Sir Howard saw him wince slightly when he squeezed his hand. He thought, why I could knock that little – but wait a minute; he must have something to make himself so feared. He's absolutely a clever scoundrel.

They were in the hall, and Sir Howard had accepted the offer of a drink. 'How's things down your way?' asked Kelly noncommittally. His expression was neither friendly nor otherwise. Sir Howard opened wide the throttle of his famous charm, no mean asset. He didn't want a kicker bolt between the shoulder blades before his enterprise was well started. He gave scraps of gossip as he heard from Pennsylvania, praised his host's brandy, and told tall tales of the dread in which he had heard Kelly was held. Little by little the man thawed, and presently they were swapping stories. Sir Howard dredged up the foulest he could remember, but Kelly always went him one better. Some of them were a bit strong for even the knight's catholic taste, but he bellowed appreciatively. 'Now,' said Kelly with a bleak little smile, 'let me tell you what we did to the hock-shop guy. This'll kill you; it's the funniest thing you ever heard. You know nitric acid? Well, we took a glass tube, with some glass wool inside for a wick –'

Some of Kelly's men were lounging about, listening to the radio and shooting crap. A bridge game was going in one corner. Sir Howard thought, it's time it happened. I mustn't glance up as if I were expecting something. If this doesn't work – He had no illusions about being able to seize the girl and hew his way through a score of experienced fighting men.

A faint tinkle of glass came from somewhere above. Kelly glanced up, frowned, and went on with his story. Then there was another tinkle. Something fell over and over, to land on the rug. It had a steel-tube arrow with duralumin vanes. The head had been thrust through a small bag of something that burned bluely with a horrible, choking stench.

'What the hell!' exclaimed Kelly, getting up. 'Who's the funny guy?' He picked up the arrow, making a face and coughing as he did so. He walked over to the wall and barked into a voice tube: 'Hey, you up there! Somebody's dropping sulphur bombs in here. Pick him off, nitwit!' 'A hollow voice responded something with: 'Can't see him!' A man was running downstairs with another arrow. 'Say chief, some bastitch shot this into my room, with a sulphur bag on it –'

They were all up now, swearing and wiping their eyes. 'All the lousy nerve –' 'This'll fumigate the place, anyway. The cockroaches is gettin' –' 'Shuddup, lug, the sulphur don't stink no worse'n you!' Sir Howard, coughing, pressed his handkerchief to his streaming eyes. Kelly blew three short blasts on the loudest whistle the knight had ever heard.

The men went into action like trained firemen. Doors in the wall were snatched open; behind each door was a suit of armor.

The men scrambled into their suits with a speed Sir Howard wouldn't have believed possible. 'Wanna come along, Wilkes-Barre?' asked Kelly. 'If we catch this guy, I'll show you some real fun. I got a new idea I want to try, with burning pine slivers. Hey, you guys! First squadron only come with me; the rest stay here. Stand to arms; it may be some trick.' Then they were half running, half walking to the court, where their horses already awaited them. They mounted with a great metallic clanging and thundered across the drawbridge.

'Spread out,' snapped Kelly. 'Butler, you take the north –'

'*Yeeeeow!*' came a shriek from the darkness. 'Damn yank robbers! Hey, Kelly, who's your father? Bethca don't know yourself!' Then they were off on the Broadalbin road, after a small shadowy form that seemed to float rather than gallop ahead of them.

Sir Howard pulled Paul Jones in slightly, so that man after man pounded past him, meanwhile loudly cursing his puzzled mount for his slowness. By the time they reached a turn he was in the tail. He pulled up sharply and whirled the gelding around on his hind legs –

In three minutes he was back at the castle, giving an excellent imitation of a man reeling in the saddle. Something red was splashed on his suit and on Paul Jones, and dripping from his left solleret to the ground. 'Ambush!' he yelled. 'Kelly's surrounded just this side of Broadalbin! I was in the tail and cut my way clear!' He gasped convincingly. 'Everybody out, quick!' In a minute the castle had disgorged another mob of gangsters. Again the black gelding didn't seem able to keep up with the headlong pace –

This time Sir Howard, when he reached the castle, tethered his mount to a tree outside the moat. There would be a few serving men in the castle yet, and they'd run out to take his horse and ask questions if he rode in. The sentries would be on duty, too. He peered into the dark, and couldn't make out either one in the battlements. It was now or never. Thank God, they'd left the drawbridge down.

The court was empty. So was the hall. So was the dining room. Jeepers, he thought, isn't anybody home? I've got to find at least one man! He tiptoed toward the kitchen, a rathur futile performance, as the suit gave out little scrapes and clashings no matter what he did.

Inside the door a fat, sweaty man wearing a high white cap was wiping a glass with a dishtowel. His mouth fell open, and he started to run at the sight of the naked sword, the glass shattering on the tiles. 'No, you don't!' growled the knight, and in four long strides he had the cook by the collar and the sword point over the man's right kidney. 'One squeak and it'll be your last. Where is everybody?'

'Y-yessir, chef's in bed with a cold, and the others have went to a movie in town.'

'Where is she?'

'She? I dunno who you – *eek!*' The point had been dug in an eighth of an inch. 'She's in the guest room on the second floor –'

'All right, show me. March!'

The guest room had a massive oak door, held shut by a stout Yale lock. The lock was in a bronze mounting, and was evidently designed to keep people in the room rather than out.

'Where's the key?'

'I dunno, sir – I mean, Mr. Kelly's got it –'

Sir Howard thought. He'd been congratulating himself on having thought of everything – and now this! He decided correctly that he'd only get a bruised shoulder trying to break down the door. He didn't know how to pick locks, even assuming that a cylinder lock was pickable. He'd have to hurry – hurry – Was that the hoofs of the returning troop? No, but they might be back any minute. If something happened to Haas – or if the second squadron caught up with the first –

'Lie down on your face next to the door,' he snapped.

'Yessir – you won't kill me, sir? I ain't done nothing.'

'Not yet, anyway.' He rested his sword point on the man's back. 'One move, and I'll just lean on this.' With his free hand he took out his dagger and began unscrewing the four screws that held the lock mounting. If only the narrow blade would hold –

It took an interminable time. As the last screw came out, the lock dropped with a soft thump onto the cook. Sir Howard opened the door.

'Who are you?' asked the girl, standing behind a chair. She was rather on the tall side, he thought. That was nice. She wore the conventional pajamalike clothes, and seemed more defiant than frightened. Her lightish hair was cut shorter and her skin was more tanned than was considered fashionable.

'Never mind that; I've come to get you out. Come on, quick!'

'But who are you? I don't trust –'

'You want to get out, don't you?'

'Yes, but – '

'Then stow the chatter and come along. Kelly'll be back any minute. I won't eat you. Yeowp, damn, that's done it!' The cook had rolled suddenly to his feet, and his cries of 'Help!' were diminishing down the corridor. 'Come on for God's sake!'

When they reached the hall, a man in half-armor was coming down the other stair – the one that led to the sentry walk. He was coming two steps at a time, holding a poleax at port arms.

'Stand clear!' Sir Howard flung at the girl, slapping his visor down. A second man appeared at the head of the stair; the first was halfway cross the room. The first lunged with his can opener. Sir Howard swayed his body to let the point go over his shoulder; then their bodies met with a clang. The knight snapped his right fist up to the man's jaw, using the massive sword guard as a knuckle duster. The man went down, and the other was upon him. He was even bigger than Sir Howard, and he brandished his poleax like a switch. At the business end the weapon had a blade like that of a cleaver. From the back side of the blade projected a hook – for pulling men off horses – and from the end extended a foot-long spike.

Sir Howard, skipping away from a stab at his foot, thought, if there's anyone else in the castle this anvil chorus of ours will bring them out quickly. There was a particularly melodious *bonggg* as the blade struck his helmet; he saw stars and wondered whether his neck had been broken. Then the butt end whirled around to trip him. He staggered and went down on one knee; as he started to recover, the point was coming at his visor. He ducked under it and swung. He couldn't hope to cut through the duralumin shaft but his blade bit into the tendons on the back of the man's unprotected left hand. Now!

But the man, dropping his poleax, was dancing back out of reach, flicking blood from his wounded hand. His sword came out with a *wheep* almost before the knight had regained his feet. Then they were at it again. Feint-lunge-parry-riposte-recover-cut-parry-jab-double-lunge. Ting-clang-swish-bong-zing. Sir Howard, sweating, realized he'd been backing. Another step back – another – the fellow was getting him in a corner. The fellow was a better swordsman then he. Damn! The sentry's point had just failed to slide between the bib and plastorn into his throat. The fellow was appallingly good. You couldn't touch him. Another step back – he couldn't take many more or he'd be against the walls.

The girl had picked up one of the light chairs around the card table. She tiptoed over and swung the chair against the back of the sentry's legs. He yelled, threw up his arms, and fell into a ridiculous squatting position, with his hands on the floor behind him. Sir Howard aimed for his face and put his full weight behind the lunge; felt the point crunch through the sinuses.

'The other one!' she cried. The other sentry was on his hands and knees across the room, feeling around for his weapon. 'Hadn't you better kill him, too?'

'No time; run!' They went, *clank, clank, clank,* into the dark. 'Never . . . mind . . . him,' the knight panted. 'Much . . . as . . . I . . . admire . . . your . . . spirit. *Damn!*' He had almost run off the edge of the drawbridge. 'Be . . . smart . . . to . . . drown . . . myself . . . in . . . the . . . moat . . . now.'

5

'Good heavens, I must have slept all morning! What time is it, please, Sir Knight?'

Sir Howard glanced at his wrist, then remembered that his watch was under his gauntlet and vambrace. It was a good watch, and the knight's economical soul would have squirmed at the idea of wearing it outside when there was a prospect of a fight. He got up and looked at the clock built into the pommel of his saddle. 'Eleven-thirty,' he announced. 'Sleep well?'

'Like a top. I suppose your friend hasn't appeared yet?'

Sir Howard looked through the pines at the gently rolling, sandy landscape. Nothing moved in it save an occasional bird. 'No,' he replied, 'but that doesn't mean anything. We're to wait till dark. If he doesn't show up by then we'll move on to – wherever we're going.'

The girl was looking, too. 'I see you picked a place without a house in sight for your rendezvous. I . . . uh . . . don't suppose there's anything to eat, is there.'

'Nope; and I feel as though I could eat a horse and chase the driver. We'll just have to wait.'

She looked at the ground. 'I don't mean to look a gift rescuer in the mouth, if you know what I mean . . . but . . . I don't suppose you'd want to tell me your real name?'

Sir Howard came to with a snort. 'My real . . . how the devil did you know?'

'I hope you don't mind but in the sunlight you can see that that trademark's been painted on over another one. Even with all that blood on your suit.'

Sir Howard grinned broadly. 'The gore of miscreants is more beautiful than a sunset, as it says in a book somewhere. I'll make you an offer: I'll tell you my real name if you'll tell me yours!'

It was the girl's turn to start, deny, and interrogate. 'Simple, my dear young lady. You say you're Mary Clark, but you have the letters SM embroidered on your blouse, and an S on your handkerchief. Fair enough, huh?'

'Oh, very well, my name is Sara Waite Mitten. Now how about yours, smarty?'

'You've heard of the Poughkeepsie Van Slycks?' Sir Howard gave a précis of his position in that noble family. As he was doing so, Paul Jones ambled over and poked the girl with his nose. She started to scratch his forehead, but jerked her hand away. 'What's *his* name?' she asked. The knight told her.

'Where did you get it?'

'Oh, I don't know; it's been a name for horses in our family for a long time. I suppose there was a man by that name once; an important man, that is.'

'Yes,' she said, 'there was. He was a romantic sort of man, just the sort that would have gone around rescuing maidens from captivity, if there'd been any maidens in captivity. He had a sense of humor, too. Once when the ship he commanded was being chased by an enemy, he kept his ship just out of range, so that the broadsides from the enemy's guns fell just short. Jones posted a man in the stern of his ship with orders to return each broadside with one musket shot. A musket was a kind of light gun they had in those days.'

'He sounds like a good guy. Was he handsome, too?'

'Well' – the girl cocked her head to one side – 'that depends on the point of view. If you consider apes handsome, Paul Jones was undoubtedly good-looking. By the way, I notice that *your* Paul Jones' coloring comes off when you rub him.' She held up a paint-smeared hand. The gelding had no desire to be scratched or petted; he was hoping for sugar. As none was forthcoming, he walked off. Sally Mitten continued: 'When I first met you, I decided you were just a big, active young man with no particular talents except for chopping up people you didn't like. But the whole way the rescue was planned, and your noticing the initials on my clothes, seem to show real intelligence.'

'Thanks. My family never credited me with much brains, but maybe I'll disappoint them yet. It just occurred to me that I needn't have told you who I was; I could have explained the trademark by saying I'd bought this suit secondhand.'

'But you'd hardly have repainted your horse, even if he was secondhand, also, would you?'

'Say, you're the damnedest young person. No matter what I

say you go me one better.' He thought a minute, and asked, 'How long were you in Kelly's castle?'

'Three days.'

Three days, eh? A lot could happen in that time. But if she wasn't going to tell him about it of her own accord, he certainly wasn't going to ask her. The question was, in fact, never referred to by either again.

'And where,' asked Sir Howard, 'did you get all that information about Paul Jones, and the times when men had guns, and so forth? '

'Out of books, mostly.'

'Books, huh? I didn't know there were books on those things, unless the hoppers have some. Speaking of the devil – '

He tilted his head back to watch a flying machine snore overhead and dwindle to a mote in the cloudless sky. There was the sound of a quickly indrawn breath beside him. He turned to the girl. Her voice was low and intensely serious. 'Sir Howard, you've done me a great service, and you want to help me out, don't you? Well, whatever happens, I don't want to fall into *their* hands. I'd rather go back to Kelly's castle. '

'But what – ' he stopped. She seemed genuinely frightened. She hadn't been at all frightened of Kelly, he thought; merely angry and contemptuous.

'You don't have to worry about me,' he reassured her. 'I don't like *them*, either.' He told her about his brother. 'And now,' he said, 'I'm going to catch a couple of hours' sleep. Wake me if anybody comes in sight.'

It seemed to him that he had hardly found a comfortable position before his shoulder was being shaken. 'Wake up!' she said, 'wake . . . up . . . oh, confound you, wake . . . up!'

'Haas?' he mumbled, blinking.

'No, one of *them*. I shook you and shook you – '

He got up so suddenly that he almost upset her. His sleepiness was as though it had never been.

The sun was low in the sky. Over the sand and grass a two-wheeled vehicle was approaching the group of pines. Sir Howard glanced at Paul Jones, nibbling contentedly at the tops of timothy weeds. 'No use trying to run,' he said. 'It would see us, and those cycles can go like a lightning flash late for a date. Three or four times as fast as a horse, anyway. We'll have to bluff it out. Maybe it doesn't want us, really.'

The vehicle headed straight into the pines and purred to a stop, remaining upright on its two wheels. The rounded lucite top opened, and a hopper got out unhurriedly. The two human beings saluted. They became aware of the faint cheesy odor of the thing.

'You are Sir William Scranton,' it chirped.

Sir Howard saw no reason for denying such a flat statement. 'Yes, your excellency.'

'You killed Warren Kelly last night.'

'No, your excellency.' The beady black eyes under the leather helmet seemed to bore into him. The pointed face carried no message of emotion. The ratlike whiskers quivered as they always did.

'Do not contradict, Man. It is known that you did.'

Sir Howard's mouth was dry, and his bones seemed to have turned to jelly. He who had been in six pitched battles without turning a hair, and who had snatched a robber chief's captive out from under his nose, was frightened. The hopper's clawed hand rested casually on the butt of a small gun in a belt holster. Sir Howard, like most human beings of his time, was terrified of guns. He had no idea of how they worked. A hopper pointed a harmless-looking tool at you, and there was a flash and a small thunderclap, and you were dead with a neat hole the size of your thumb in your plate. That was all. Resistance to creatures commanding such powers was hopeless. And where resistance is hopeless, courage is so rare as to lay the possessor thereof open to the charge of having a screw loose.

He tried another tack. 'I should have said, your excellency, that I do not *remember* killing Kelly. Besides, the killing of a man is not against the higher law.' (He meant hopper law).

That seemed to stop the hopper. 'No,' it squeaked. 'But it is inconvenient that you should have killed Kelly.' It paused, as if trying to think up an excuse for making an arrest. 'You lied when you said that you did not kill Kelly. And the higher law is what we say it is.' A little breeze made the pines whisper. Sir Howard, chilled, felt that Death was moving among them, chuckling.

The hopper continued: 'Something is wrong here. We must investigate you and your accomplice.' Sir Howard, out of the corner of his eye, saw that Sally Mitten's lips were pressed together in a thin red line.

'Show me your travel permit, Man.'

Sir Howard's heart seemed likely to burst his ribs at each beat. He walked over to Paul Jones and opened a pocket in the saddle stuffed with papers. He thumbed through them, and selected a tourist-agency circular advertising the virtues of the Thousand Islands. This he handed to the hopper.

The creature bent over the paper. The knight's sword whirled and flashed with a *wht* of cloven air. There was a meaty *chug*.

Sir Howard leaned on his sword, waiting for the roaring in his ears to cease. He knew that he had come as near to fainting as he ever had in his life. A few feet away lay the hopper's head, the beady eyes staring blankly. The rest of the hopper lay at his feet, its limbs jerking slightly, pushing the sand up into little piles with its hands and feet. Blue-green blood spread out in a widening pool. A few pine needles gyrated slowly on its surface.

The girl's eyes were round. 'What . . . what'll we do now? ' she asked. It was barely more than a whisper.

'I don't know. I don't know. I never heard of anything like this before.' He took his fascinated gaze away from the cadaver, to look over the dunes. 'Look, there's Haas!' His blood began to run warm again. The foreigner might not be able to help much, but he'd be company.

The Westerner rode up jauntily, his chaps flapping against Queenie's flanks. He called: 'Hiya, folks! Had the devil's own time gettin' rid of those lobsters, you call 'em. I had to drown –' He stopped as he saw the hopper, and gave a long whistle. 'Well . . . I . . . never. Say, boy, I thought maybe you had nerve, but I never heard of nobody doing *that*. Maybe you'd like to try something safe, like wrassling a grizzly, or tying a knot in a piece of lightning?' He smiled uneasily.

'I had to,' said Sir Howard. His composure was restored by the Westerner's awe. He'd mounted the wild stallion of revolt, and there was nothing to do but to ride it with what aplomb he could muster. 'He asked to see my permit, and I'd have been arrested for trademark infringement or something.' He introduced Sally Mitten, and gave a résumé of events.

'We've got to get rid of it, quickly,' the girl broke in. 'When they're out patrolling the way this one was, they report to their station by radio every hour or so. When this one fails to report, the others will start a search for it.'

'How will they do that miss?' asked Haas.

'They'll make a big circle around the place it last reported from, and close in, meanwhile keeping the area under observation from the air.'

'Sounds sensible. From what you tell me, this one was on an official mision or something, so his buddies'll have an idea where he was about the time he got whittled. So we'll be inside the circle. How'll we get rid of him? If we just buried him –'

'They might use dogs to locate it,' said the girl.

'Well, now if we could sink him in the river or something. This Hans Creek yonder ain't deep enough.'

Sir Howard was frowing at one of the large-scale maps he had bought in Amsterdam the previous evening. 'The Sacandaga Reservoir is over across those hills,' he said, pointing north.

'No,' said Sally Mitten. 'We've got to get rid of its cycle, too. You couldn't get it over the Maxon Ridge. I know: put it in Round Lake. That's just out of sight east of here.'

'Say, miss, do you carry a map of this whole country around in your head?' inquired Haas quizzically.

'I've lived near here most of my life. We'll put some clean sand and pine needles on the blood spots. And Sir Howard, you'll want to clean your sword blade at the first opportunity.'

'Your little lady's okay, How,' said Haas, dismounting. 'Only she ain't so little, at that. Fall to, folks. You take his head – I mean his arms; the head comes separate. Don't get any of that blue stuff on you. In we go! It's nice these things stand up on their two wheels even when they ain't moving; it'll make easy to push.'

'Punch some holes in the lucite,' said Sally Mitten. 'That'll let the vehicle sink more quickly.'

'Danged if she doesn't think of everything,' said Haas, getting to work with his knife on the thin cowling. He grinned. 'How, I'd sure like to hear the other hoppers, if they do find him, trying to figure out what happened to him. If I could understand their canary talk, that is. Say, miss, you got any idea how to get out of this circle if they start looking before we get away? And which way had we ought to go? '

'I'll show you, Mr. Haas. I think I know how it can be done. And if you desperate characters want to hide out, come with me. I know just the place. We'll have to hurry. Oh, you didn't bring any food with you, did you? I couldn't have eaten anything a few minutes ago, but I'm hungry again, now that *it* is out of sight. And I imagine Sir Howard is, also.

'Danged if I didn't forget. I stopped on the way and got some hot dogs. I figured you might be kinda hollow by now.' He produced a couple of Cellophane-wrapped sandwiches. 'They'll be kinda dry. But for flavor you might put a little of that blood How's got on his armor.'

The girl looked at the splotches on the suit. Sir Howard, grinning, wiped some of the sticky, almost-dry redness off and put his finger in his mouth. Sally Mitten gulped, looked as though she were going to gag. But she grimly followed suit. 'I'll show you humorists!' Her expression changed ludicrously. 'Strawberry jam!' Haas dodged, chortling, as her fist swept past his nose.

6

'There's another flier. They're certainly doing a thorough job. Can anybody see whether they've reached the water yet?' It was Sally Mitten speaking. They lay in a clump of pines, looking across the Sacandaga Reservoir, spread out in a placid sheet before them and stretching out of sight to right and left. An early bat zigzagged blackly across the twilight. On the far side of the water, little things like ants moved about; these were hopper vehicles. One by one their lights went on.

'I wish it would get dark more quickly, the girl continued. 'This stunt of ours depends on exact timing. They're almost at the water now.'

'Too bad we couldn't get farther away before they started hunting,' commented Haas. 'We mighta got outside the circle. Say, How, suppose they do meet up with us. Who'll we be?'

Sir Howard thought. 'I registered last at Albany, and gave my destination as Watertown and the Thousand Islands. Said I was going up there to fish, which I thought I was. And the hoppers will be looking for a William Scranton. So maybe I'd just better be myself.'

'Maybe,' said Haas. 'And then, maybe you better get rid of that fake trademark. Or will it wash out in the reservoy?'

'No, that's a waterproof lacquer. You need alcohol to get it off.'

'Well, what's wrong with that there bottle of snake-bite medicine you got in your saddle?'

'What? But that's good whiskey! Oh very well, I suppose this is more important.' Sir Howard regretfully got out the bottle. Haas found a sock in his duffle bag that was more hole than fabric, opined that it was purty near worn out, anyway, and went to work on the knight's plastron. 'Say,' he said, 'how do you reckon you're gonna swim over half a mile in that stovepiping?'

'He isn't', said Sally Mitten. 'We're going to strip.'

'Wha-a-t?' The Westerner's scandalized voice rose in pitch. 'You mean go swimmin' all nekkid – all three of us?'

'Certainly. You don't think we want to go running around on a cold night in wet clothes, do you? Or run into a hopper and have to explain how we got wet?'

Haas turned back to his work, clucking. 'Well, I never. I never. I knowed Yanks was funny people, but I never. It just shows you. Say, miss, you *sure* we couldn't get away by going around the end of the reservoy?'

'Good heavens, no. They'll be thickest around there. The whole idea is that the one time when there'll be a gap in the circle will be when they reach the water on the other side, and the ones who come up on the shore will separate, half of them going around each end of the reservoir, to re-form their circle on this side. If we're in the water when that happens, and it's dark enough so they don't see us, we'll find ourselves outside the circle automatically.'

'How we gonna get How's tin suit across if he don't wear it? The cayuses'll be purty well loaded down as 'tis.'

'We'll make a raft. You can cut some of the little pines and tie them together with those ropes of yours.'

'Guess we could at that. There, How, your breastplate's O.K. I guess it's dark enough so they wouldn't see us moving around, huh?' He got up, took out his saber, and began lopping branches from a sapling.

The knight did likewise. 'Wish I had an ax along,' he said. 'I didn't want to load Paul Jones down with too much junk. How big do we want this raft?'

'How heavy's your suit?'

'Forty-two pounds. Then there's my lance – we don't want that sticking up like a mast from its boot – and my sword, and all our clothes.'

'Better make it four by four, with two courses.'

'Hurry', said Sally Mitten. 'They're at the shore now; I can see the reflection of their lights on the water.'

'Who was it you drowned, Lyman?' asked Sir Howard.

'Oh, that. I had the dangedest time with those fellas. They were fast, in spite of their hardware. And the little one up front, who was ordering the rest around, could ride like the devil hisself. He had a flashlight and kept it on me. I kept going until Queenie began to puff, and I seen they was still coming. So – What's that little river that runs through Broadalbin?'

'Kenneatto Creek,' Sally Mitten told him.

'Well, when I got to a little bridge that goes over this Kenny . . . Kenneatto Creek – here, How, you pull tight on the end of that rope – I turned off into the water. I found a place under some trees where it was nice and dark, with the water about up to Queenie's belly. And then when these here lobsters hit the bridge I roped this little guy in the lead. He went off just as nice as you please into the creek. He was in about ten foot of water with that armor on. The only bad thing was I had to cut my good rope and leave most of it in the creek, because if I'd held it tight he mighta pulled hisself out with it, and his pals were beginning to hunt around to see why their boss went into the drink, naturally. I bought some more rope at the store on the way back to Round Lake. But I don't like it. It don't handle quite the same as a Western rope. I gotta practice up with it. And this holding a raft together won't do it no good.'

'I see,' said Sir Howard. 'That's why the hoppers think I killed Warren Kelly. They don't know about you, but they know I'd called at the castle – at least, that somebody calling himself William Scranton did.'

'You mean I drowned the big tough guy hisself? You don't say! I guess that raft's okay now. Look, miss, we'll put it on How's saddle, and you balance it while we lead the critters.'

Ten minutes later there was a metallic twang in front. Sir Howard called back softly: 'It's a wire fence; looks about ten feet high. I guess we can't see it from up on the bluff.'

'That's nice,' said Haas. 'We shoulda remembered that folks put fences around reservoys to keep critters from going and dying in 'em. Don't suppose anybody's got any wire cutters?'

'No', hissed the knight. 'We'll have to use that hunting knife of yours.'

'What? Hey, you can't do that! It'll ruin the blade!'

'Can't be helped. I've spoiled the point of my dagger getting Miss Mitten's door in the castle opened, so you oughtn't to kick.'

The knife was passed up, and there were low grunts in the dark from the knight as he heaved, and twang after twang as the strands gave.

'All right', he whispered. 'If we pull the horses' heads down we can get 'em through. Take my toothpick out of the boot, will you?'

They were through. Sir Howard said; 'Come here, Lyman, and hold these wires while I twist the ends back together. No use advertising to *them* which way we've gone.'

'Quiet,' said Sally Mitten. 'Sounds carries over water, you know. Hurry up; the hoppers are going off toward the ends of the reservoir. I can tell by their lights.' On the far shore the little needles of light were, in fact, moving off to the right and left.

'Say, miss,' came Haas's plaintive murmur, 'can't I leave my underwear on? I'm a modest man.'

'No, you can't,' snapped the girl. 'If you do, you'll catch pneumonia, and I'll have to nurse you. There's nothing but starlight, anyway.'

'I'm, c-cold,' continued the Westerner. 'How's gonna take all night getting that hardwear off.'

Sir Howard looked up from his complicated task to see two ghostly forms standing over him hugging themselves and hopping up and down to keep warm. 'You go ahead and fix the ropes,' he said. 'I'll be ready with this in a few minutes. I have to be careful how I pile the pieces or I'm liable to lose parts of it.'

The preparations were finally complete. The raft, piled with steel and garments, lay on the sand, connected to Queenie's saddle by a long rope. Another rope trailed from Paul Jones.

'All right, get!' Sir Howard slapped the gelding's rump and waded into the water. He and Sally Mitten each held the rope. Haas did likewise with the mare. The horses didn't want to swim, and had to be prodded and pulled. But they were finally in deep water, the ropes with their burdens trailing behind.

Sir Howard was thinking how warm the water gurgling in his ear was when something hit him in the left eye. 'Damn!' he whispered. 'Trying to blind me?'

'What did I do?' came the answer from up ahead.

'Stuck your toe in my eye. Why don't you keep on your side of the rope?'

'I *am* on my own side. Why don't you keep your face out of my foot?'

'So that's it, huh? I'll fix you, young lady! You're not ticklish, are you?' He pulled himself forward hand over hand. But the girl dived like a seal. Holding the rope, the knight raised his hand to peer over the starlit water. Then two slim but startlingly strong hands caught his ankles and dragged him under.

When he came up and shook the water out of his head he heard a frantic hiss from Haas: 'For gossake, cut out the water-polo game, you two. You sound like a coupla whales on a drunk!'

They were silent. The only sounds, besides the little noises of insect and frog, were the heavy breathing of the horses and the gurgle of water sliding past them.

Time ticked past slowly. The shore seemed to get no closer. Then suddenly it loomed before them, and they were touching bottom. After the quiet, the splashing of the horses through the shallows sounded like Niagara.

They lay on the beach. Sally Mitten said: 'Can you see?' She was making marks in the sand. 'Here's the reservoir, and here we are. My people and I live up in the Adirondacks. Now we can get there this way, by the Sacandaga Lakes. There's a good road up to Speculator and Piseco. But there's lots of traffic for just that reason. People going up to fish on the Sacandaga Lakes. And we want to be seen as little as possible. We'd better stay on this side of the Sacandaga River and follow the west branch to Piseco Lake. Then I know a trail from there to our place by way of the Cedar Lakes. It's hard going, but we're not likely to meet anybody.

'I normally come down to Amsterdam by way of Camp Perkins and Speculator; there's an old road down the Jessup in pretty good shape. We buy most of our supplies at Speculator; I only go down to Amsterdam once a month or so. And it would be just my luck to be there when they – ' She stopped.

'How do you get to Amsterdam?' asked Sir Howard. 'That looks like a pretty long walk.'

'It is; I have a bicycle. I mean I *had* a bicycle. The last I saw of it it was standing on the sidewalk at Amsterdam. It'll be gone by now. And I left my only decent hat at Kelly's castle. It's a good two-day trip. It'll take us much longer, since we're not following the good roads.' She carefully rubbed out the map 'We'll want to obliterate our tracks on the beach, and the horses', too.'

'Why do you suppose the hoppers are so concerned about Kelly?' he asked. 'They don't usually interfere in man-to-man quarrels.'

'Don't you know? They were backing him. Not openly; they don't do things that way. Schenectady's barony was getting too big, so they set Kelly up in business to break it up. *Divide et impera.*'

'What?'

'Divide and rule. That's their whole system – keeping men split up into little quarreling States the size of postage stamps.'

'Hm-m-m. You seem to know a lot about *them.*'

'I've been studying *them* for a long time.'

'I suppose so. What you say gives me a lot to think about. Say, do you suppose your . . . uh . . . people will want to have a couple of strangers with our fearful records?'

'On the contrary, Sir Howard – '

'I'd rather you dropped the "Sir".'

'Yes? Any particular reason?'

'Well – I don't know just how to say it, but . . . uh . . . it seems rather silly. I mean, we're all comrades together. Uh . . . you and

Haas are as good men as I am, if you know what I mean, in the time I've known you.'

'I think I understand.' She was smiling quietly in the dark. 'What I was saying was, you and he are just the sort of people we're looking for; men who have dared raise their hands against *them*. There aren't many. It sets you apart from other people, you know. You couldn't ever quite go back to the way you were.'

While they talked, the stars had been dimming. And now a mottled yellow disk was rising from behind the blackness of the skyline, washing their skins with pale gold.

'Good heavens,' said Sally Mitten, 'I forgot about the moon! We'll have to get dressed and get out of here, quickly. I'm dry, thank goodness. Lyman – why, he's asleep!' The Westerner lay prone, his head pillowed on his arm, his breath coming with little whistlings.

'You can't blame him,' said Sir Howard. 'It's his first in thirty-six hours. But I'll fix *that*.' He leaned over the recumbent form and raised his arm, the hand open and slightly cupped. Sally Mitten grabbed his wrist. 'No! That'll make a noise like a gunshot! They'll hear it in Amsterdam!' She gurgled with suppressed laughter. 'But it does seem a shame to waste such a chance, doesn't it?'

'You're limping, Howard,' said Sally Mitten. She was sitting in his saddle, with the bottom of her trousers gathered in by string tied around her ankles. Behind her the knight's armor, the pieces neatly nested together and lashed into a compact bundle, rode Paul Jones' broad rump. The pile of steel gave out little tinny noises.

'No, I'm not,' he said. 'At least, not much. It's just another blister.' He was walking in front of his horse, wearing a pair of riding boots from which four days of plowing through Adirondack brush had permanently banished the shine, and using his lance as an overgrown walking stick. He wore a red beret pulled down over his ears. Lyman Haas brought up the rear, swaying easily in the saddle and rolling a cigarette. Though the temperature was nearly eighty, all three wore gloves (Sally Mitten's being several sizes too large) and had their shirt collars turned up. They slapped constantly at their faces.

'Just another blister! You stop right now, young man, and we'll fix it. Have you any bandages? You don't do any more walking today. Those breeches and boots are all very well for riding, but not for walking around these parts.'

'It's nothing, really. Besides, it's my turn to walk. The schedule says I walk for half an hour yet.'

'Get your lasso out, Lyman; he's going to be stubborn.'

'Better do what the lady says,' said Haas. 'Sure, miss, he's got iodine and gauze in one of the pockets of that saddle. That there's a magic saddle. You just wish, and say hocus-pocus, and push a button, and whatever you want pops out. You see why How uses an outsize horse; no ordinary critter could carry all that stuff. I sometimes think maybe he oughta rented an elephant from the railroad.'

'Just like the White Knight,' said Sally Mitten. 'And me without even a toothbrush of my own!'

'The who?' asked Sir Howard.

'The White Knight; a character in a book called *Through the Looking Glass*. Does your equipment include any mousetraps or beehives? His did.'

'That a fact?' said Haas. 'Sounds to me like the guy was plumb eccentric. Now, How, you brace your other foot on this here root and I'll pull. Unh!' The boot came off, revealing two large toes protruding through a hole in the sock. 'Say,' said the Westerner, sniffing, 'You sure that foot ain't *dead?* Damn!' He slapped at his cheek.

'I should have warned you it was black-fly time,' said Sally Mitten. 'They'll be gone in a few weeks.'

'I haven't got a mousetrap,' said Sir Howard, 'but I have a clockwork mechanical razor and a miniature camera, if they'll do. And a pair of bird glasses. You know, my hobby's prowling around looking for yellow-billed cuckoos and golden-winged warblers. My brother Frank used to say it was my only redeeming trait.' He slapped at his jaw, decorated with streaks of dried blood from fly bites. 'Perhaps I ought to have kept my suit on. It would at least keep these bugs out, unless they can bite through steel.' He slapped again. 'This trail is more like a jungle than any I ever saw. Why doesn't somebody get an ax and a scythe and clean it out?'

Sally Mitten answered: 'That's just the point. If it were a nice clean trail everybody'd use it, and we don't want that. We've even planted things on trails we didn't want people to use.'

Haas said: 'It's thicker'n any bush I ever seen. It's different out my way; the timber, what they is, grows nice and far apart, so you can get through it 'thout being a snake.' He lit his cigarette and went on: 'This is what you call mountains, is it? I'm afraid you Yanks don't know what real mountains are. You take the

Mt. Orrey you showed me; in Wyoming we wouldn't bother to give a little molehill like that a name, even. Say, Miss, have we got much more swamps to wade through? It's a wonder to me how you can walk around at night in this country 'thout falling into some mudhole or pond. I'd think the folks would have growed web feet, like a duck.'

'No,' said Sally Mitten, 'We're through with the Cedar Lakes. If you look through the trees up ahead you can see Little Moose Mountain. That's where we're going.' She slapped her neck.

7

Sally Mitten said she was going to run ahead to warn her people. The next minute she was scrambling up the steep shoulder of the mountain, pulling herself up by branches and bushes. The two men continued their slow switchback ride. Haas said: 'Danged if I don't think it'd be easier to cut right across country than to try to follow what they call a trail around here.'

Sir Howard watched the girl's retreating figure. It dwindled to thumb-size. He saw no sign of human habitation. But a man came out of some poplars, and then another. Even at this distance the knight could make out embraces and backslappings. He felt a slight twinge of something or other, together with a devouring curiosity as to what sort of 'people' this mysterious girl might have.

When he and Haas finally reached the level space on which the three stood, she was still talking animatedly. She turned as they dismounted, and introduced them. 'This,' she said, 'is Mr. Elsmith, our boss.' They saw a man in his late forties, with thin yellow hair, and mild brown eyes behind glasses. He gripped their hands with both of his in a way that said more than words. 'And this Eli Cahoon.' The other man was older, with white hair under the world's oldest felt hat. He was dressed in typical north-woods fashion, his pants held up by one gallus and rolled up at the bottoms to show mud-caked laced boots. 'Lyman, you've been calling us York States Yankees; Eli's the genuine article. He comes from Maine.'

Sir Howard had been looking through the poplars. He saw that what he had first thought to be a cave was actually a good-sized one-story house, almost buried under tons of soil blending into the mountainside, and artfully camouflaged with vegetation. You couldn't see it at all until you were on top of it.

The man named Cahoon moved his long jaw, opened his thin mouth to show crooked, yellow snags, and spat a brown stream.

'Nice wuck,' he said, 'gettin' our Sally outa that castle.' His forearms were thick and sinewy, and he moved like a cat.

'Wasn't nothing to it,' drawled Haas. 'I just called 'em names to make 'em mad, and How, here, walked in and tuck her while they was out chasing me.'

Sir Howard was surprised to see that Elsmith was up and fully dressed already. The man smiled at him, showing a pair of squirrel teeth. Somehow he reminded the knight of a friendly rabbit.

'We keep early hours here,' he said. 'You'd better get up if you want any breakfast. Though how you can eat anything after the dinner you put away last night I don't just see.'

Sir Howard stretched his huge muscles. It was wonderful to lie in a real bed for a change. 'Oh, I can always eat. I go on the principle that I might be without food someday, so I'd better take what's offered. To tell the truth, we were all about ready to try a birch-bark salad with pond-scum dressing when we arrived. And we'd have been hungrier yet if Haas hadn't shot a fawn on the way up.'

During breakfast Sir Howard, who was not, these days, an unobservant young man, kept his eyes and ears open for clues to the nature of this menage. Elsmith talked like a man of breeding, by which the knight meant a member of his own predatory feudal aristocracy. In some ways, that was. Sir Howard decided that he was probably a decayed nobleman who had offended the hoppers and was hiding out in consequence. Sally Mitten called him Uncle Homer. On the other hand, Elsmith and the girl had something about them – a tendency to use unfamiliar words and to throw mental abstractions around – that set them apart from any people the knight had ever known. Cahoon – who pronounced his name in one syllable – was obviously not a gentleman. But on the rare occasions when he said anything at all, the statements in his tight-lipped Yankee accent showed a penetrating keenness that Sir Howard wouldn't have expected of a lower-class person.

After breakfast Sir Howard lounged around, his pipe going, speculating on his own future. He couldn't just sit and impose on these people's hospitality indefinitely, rescue or no rescue. He was sure they'd expect something of him, and wondered what it would be.

He was not left in doubt long.

'Come along, Van Slyck,' said Elsmith. 'We're putting in some potatoes today.'

Sir Howard's jaw sagged, and his class prejudice came to the surface with a rush. '*Me* plant potatoes?' It was a cry more of astonishment than resentment.

'Why, yes. We do.' Elsmith smiled slightly. 'You're in another world now, you know. You'll find a lot of things to surprise you.'

If the man had spoken harshly, the knight would have probably marched out and departed in dudgeon. As it was, his inchoate indignation evaporated. 'I suppose you're right. There's a lot of things I don't know.'

Bending humbly over his row in the potato patch, he asked Elsmith; 'Do you raise all your own stuff?'

'Just about. We have some hens, and we raise a shoat each year. And Eli pots a deer now and then. There's a set of vegetable trays around the mountain a way; carefully hidden, of course. You'd never find them unless I showed you the place. It's surprising how many vegetables you can raise in a small space that way.'

'Raising vegetables in trays? I never heard of that.'

'Oh, yes, once upon a time tray agriculture was widely practiced by men. But the hoppers decided that it saved too much labor and abolished it. They don't want us to have too much spare time, you know. We might get ideas.'

In Sir Howard's mind such statements were like lightning flashes seen through a window, briefly illuminating a vast country whose existence he had never suspected.

He asked: 'Are you Sally's uncle?'

'No. She's really my secretary. Her father was my closest friend. He built this place. Eli worked for him, and stayed on with me when Mr. Mitten died six years ago.'

In the afternoon Elsmith announced that that would be all the potatoes for today, and that he had correspondence to attend to. In the living room, Sir Howard noticed a stack of water-color landscapes against one of the the plain timber walls. 'Did you paint those?' he asked.

'Yes. They're smuggled down to New York, where an artist signs his own name to them and sells them as his.'

'Sounds like a dirty trick.'

'No; it's necessary. This artist is a good friend of mine. We don't need much cash here, but we've got to have some, and that's one way of getting it. Eli traps for furs in the winter for the same reason.

'Look, I've got to dictate to Sally for a couple of hours; why don't you look over some of these books?' He pointed to the shelves that covered most of one wall. 'Let's see . . . I'd recommend this . . . and this . . . and these.'

The books were mostly very old. Their yellow pages seemed to have been dipped in some sort of glassy lacquer. As a preservative, thought Sir Howard. He started reading reluctantly, more as a courtesy to his host than anything. Then sentence after startling sentence caught his attention.

He was startled when Elsmith, standing quietly in front of him, said: 'How do you like them?'

'Good Lord, have I been reading for hours? I'm afraid I haven't gotten very far. I've never been much of a reader, and I had to keep looking things up in the dictionary.

'To be frank, I don't know what to think of them. If they're true, they upset all the ideas I ever had. You take this one by Wells, for instance. It tells a story of where men came from that's entirely different from what I learned in school. Men practicing science – governments I never heard of running whole continents – no mention of hoppers ruling over them – I just can't grasp it all.'

'I expected that,' said Elsmith. 'You know, Van Slyck, there comes a time in most men's lives when they look around them and begin to suspect that many of the eternal truths they learned at their mother's knees were neither eternal nor true.

'Then they do one of two things. Some resolve to keep an open mind, to observe and inquire and experiment, and to try to find out what *is* the nature of Man and the universe. But most of them feel uncomfortable. To get rid of the discomfort, they suppress their doubts and wrap themselves in the dogmas of their childhood. To avoid any repetition of the discomfort, they even suppress – violently – people who don't share the same set of beliefs.

'You, my boy, are faced with that choice now. Think it over.'

After dinner Sir Howard said to Elsmith: 'In one of those books I was looking over, it said something about how important it was to get all the information you could before making up your mind about something. And what I've seen and heard in the last week makes me think I haven't got much information about things, after all. For instance, just who or what are the hoppers?'

Elsmith settled himself comfortably and lit a cigar. 'That's a long story. The hoppers appeared on earth about three hundred years ago. Nobody knows just where they came from, but it's fairly certain that they came from a planet outside our Solar System.'

'The what?'

'The – I suppose you learned in school that the sun goes around the earth, didn't you? Well, it doesn't. The earth and the other visible planets go around the sun. I won't try to explain that to you now; some of these books do it better than I could. We'll just say that they came from another world, far away, in a great flying machine.

'At that time the state of mankind was about what it tells about in the last chapters of those history books.

'The hoppers landed in an almost uninhabited part of South America, where there was nobody to see them except a few savages who didn't matter. There couldn't have been more than a few hundred hoppers in the ship.

'But, you see, they're very different from any earthly animal, as you might expect. Thy do look rather like overgrown jumping rats, but the resemblances are mostly superficial. An active land animal that size has to have his skeleton inside like a mammal, instead of outside like an insect, and he needs eyes to see with, and a mouth to eat with, and so forth. But if you ever dissected a hopper – I have – you'd find that its internal organs were very different from those of a mammal. Even their hair is different; under the microscope you can see each individual hair branches out like a little whisk broom. There are chemical differences, too; their blood is blue, because it has a blue chemical in it called haemocyanin, like an insect, instead of the red chemical haemoglobin, like a man or a bull-frog. So you couldn't possibly cross hoppers with any kind of earthly animal.

'It's thought among those like me who have studied the hoppers that the world they came from is much like ours in temperature, and that it has rather less oxygen in its atmosphere. It's also larger, and hence has a more powerful gravity, which is why the hoppers can make such enormous leaps so easily on earth. Being larger, it has an atmosphere deeper than ours and denser at the surface. That's why the hoppers' voices are so shrill; their vocal apparatus is designed to work in a denser medium.

'Most people know that they're bisexual and oviparous – they lay eggs about the size of robins' eggs. They grow very rapidly and almost reach their full size within a year of hatching. That's how they conquered the earth. In their ship were hundreds of thousands – perhaps millions – of eggs, together with knocked down incubators which they set up as soon as they landed. As they were in a heavily forested area, and as they are vegetarians, they didn't have any food problem.

'Their science at the time was quite a way ahead of ours, though not so far ahead that we probably wouldn't have gotten to that stage in time in the natural course of events. It took an advanced science to transform the wood, water, and soil in their neighborhood into weapons of conquest on a colossal scale. But it was their unexpectedness and their enormous numbers that helped them as much as their science.

'There was also the fact that to the people of the time they looked funny rather than sinister; it took a little while to learn to take them seriously. But people stopped thnking they were funny when they conquered all of South America within a week of the time they were first reported, and nobody's made that mistake since. Africa followed in short order. Their flying machines were faster than ours, their explosives were more destructive, and their guns shot farther and more accurately. They also had a lot of special gadgets, like the convulsion ray, the protonic bomb, and the lightning gun.

'As a matter of fact these gadgets aren't so mysterious as you might think. The convulsion-ray projector shoots a stream of heavy positrons, of Y-particles, which you'll read about in the books. They affect the human nervous system so as to greatly magnify every nervous motor impulse. For instance, suppose you were thinking of picking up a cup of coffee to drink. The thought would cause a slight motor-impulse in the nerves of your arm and hand. If you really wanted to pick the cup up, your brain would have to send out a much stronger motor impulse. Now suppose a convulsion ray were turned on you, and you merely thought about picking up the cup. Your muscles would react so violently that you'd dash the cup, coffee and all, into your face. So you can see why human beings' bodies became totally unmanageable when the ray was turned on them.

'Or take the protonic bomb. One of those bombs weighing a ton has a chunk of packed hydrogen ions in it the size of a marble, which really does the damage. The rest of the weight is caused by the coils and other apparatus necessary to keep the electrostatic field reversed, so the ions don't fly apart under the influence of their mutual repulsion. The minute you break down the field control, these ions go away from there in a hurry. They have a defense against these bombs, too, just in case men might steal one some day; we call it the X beam. It's really just a huge Roentgen-ray projector, thousands of times more powerful than a medical X-ray apparatus. It dereverses the field around the protons prematurely.

'But to get back to the story: Eurasia and North America, and most densely populated continents, held out for a while, and people began to think they might win. That was their mistake. The hoppers had merely paused in the attack while their second generation was reaching maturity. They can be fantastically prolific when they want to be, and as soon as the first crop had reached sexual maturity they'd laid another crop of millions of eggs. Remember, out of a given population of human beings only a fifth at most will be men of fighting age. But among the hopper everyone, practically, except the casualties, was available for the attack.

'They had another advantage. They seem to be immune to all the known earthly bacteria, though they have a few minor diseases of their own. But the converse unfortunately isn't true. It's probable that they deliberately turned loose a lot of their own exotic bacteria, and one of these found the human body a congenial environment. It caused a plague known as the blue madness. It was quite horrible. At least half the human race died of it. So – anyway, the hoppers won.'

Sir Howard asked, 'Have there been any more blue plagues since?'

'No; apparently part of the human race is naturally immune, and everyone who wasn't, died. So all of us today are immune, being descended from the survivors.

'The hoppers didn't exterminate us while they had the chance, for which we might give them some credit. Apparently when they saw the fairly high state of human civilization and its enormous productive capacity, they decided that it would be nicer to set themselves up a ruling species and use the rest of us to plow the farms and run the machines, while they enjoyed their own hopperish amusements, one of which seems to be ordering us around. They may even have felt sorry for us, though that's difficult to imagine. Anyway, that's the system they've followed ever since.' He looked at his watch and got up. 'Early hours here, you know. You can sit up to read if you want to, but I'm turning in. Good night.'

Up the trail from the camp was a grassy clearing, in the middle of which was a stump. On this stump sat Sally Mitten, smoking a cigarette and looking very much amused. Around the stump in a circle marched Sir Howard. He was looking not, as one might expect, at the girl, but at Lyman Haas. The Westerner was walking around the stump in the same direction in a still larger circle, with the expression of one who is putting up with a great deal for friendship's sake.

'Little slower, Lyman,' said the knight.

Elsmith appeared. 'What . . . what on earth, or off of it, is this? Some new kind of dance' 'No.' Sir Howard stopped. 'I was just checking up on that Cop . . . Copernican hypothesis. You know, about that motion of the planets – why they seem to go backward in the sky at times.'

'Retrograde motion?'

'That's it. Sally's the sun, I'm the earth, and Haas is Mars. I was looking at him to see whether he seems to go backward against the farther trees. You . . . uh . . . don't mind my checking up, do you?'

'On the contrary, my boy. I want you to check up everything you get from me, or from the books, every chance you get. Does he show retrograde motion?'

'Yep; he backs up like a scared crawfish every time I pass him.'

'What do you mean, backs up?' said Haas. 'I been walking forward all the time.'

'Certainly, but you're still going backward relative to me. I can't explain it very well; I'll have to show you the place in the book.'

Elsmith said: 'Do you read books much, Haas?'

'Sure, I like to read sometimes. Only I busted my reading glasses in New York, and I ain't been in one place long enough to get a new pair since. I was in a bar, and I had those glasses in my shirt pocket. And I got into an argument with a guy. He was saying it was a known fact that all Westerners are born with tails. Now, I'm a peaceable man, *but* –'

'That's all right, Lyman,' said Sally Mitten soothingly. 'We know you haven't a tail. Don't we, Howard?'

The upper, untanned part of Haas' face reddened a shade. 'Uh . . . ahem . . . Now, what's that again about those there planets? I want to get this straight –'

8

Sir Howard said; 'Are you going to tell me some more about the hoppers this evening?'

Elsmith blew out his match. 'I never lecture until I have a cigar going, and then it burns down to nothing while I'm talking and I don't get a chance to smoke it. Silly, isn't it?

'But to take up where we left off: The hoppers saw they'd have to remodel human society if they were going to keep human beings in check, especially as the human beings still greatly outnumbered them, and they apparently considered that ratio satisfactory from an economic point of view. They couldn't afford to let us become powerful again. Well, what sources of power did we have?

'We had powered vehicles; some ran on roads, some on railroad tracks, some in the air, and some on the water. So they abolished them, for us, that is. We had explosives, so they took them away. We had united governments over large populations; therefore, they broke us up into small units. Societies in which able people could rise to the top regardless of birth were a menace. They studied our history and decided that a feudal caste system would be the best check on that. Scientific research was, of course, outlawed, and all scientific practice except such engineering as was necessary to keep the productive machine going.

'They abolished every invention they thought might conceivably menace them. Did you know, for instance, that at one time you could talk over wires to people in all parts of the country? And that the telegraph companies owned vast networks of wires for sending messages almost instantaneously? Now they're just messenger-boy agencies, and deliver letters by horse or bicycle.

'That wasn't all. An empirical, materialistic outlook might enable us to see through the preposterous mythology that they were planning to impose on our minds through the schools. So the books expressing such a philosophy were put away, and the people who held it were destroyed. In its place they gave us mysticism, other-worldliness, and romantic trips. They used the radio, the movies, and the newspapers and books to do this, as these institutions continued to operate under their strict control. They'd have been foolish to destroy such excellent ready-made means of swaying the mass mind. Ever since then they've been filling us with 'Upright ignorance and stalwart irrationality,' as Bell, one of the pre-hopper writers, put it. And I must say' — here he leaned back, closed his eyes, and took a big puff on his cigar — 'that my species has come through it remarkably well. It's had a terrible effect on them, of course. But when I get most discouraged I can get some comfort out of the thought that they aren't nearly as crazy as they might be, considering what they've been through.'

'But,' said Sir Howard, 'But I was taught that God — ' He stopped, confused.

'Yes? Assuming for the sake of argument that there *is* a God, did He ever confide in you personally? Who taught you? Your schoolteachers, of course. And where did they get their information? Out of textbooks. And who wrote the books? The hoppers. Just assume I'm telling you the truth; what *would* you expect the hoppers to put in the books? The truth about how they conquered the earth and enslaved its inhabitants, to act as a constant irritant and incitation to revolt?'

Sir Howard was frowning at his toes. 'A couple of months ago,' he mused, 'I'd have probably wanted to make you eat my sword for some of the things you've said, Mr. Elsmith. No offense intended.'

'I know that,' said Elsmith. 'And if you'd been the man you were a couple of months ago, I wouldn't have said them.'

'But now – I don't know. Everything seems upside down. Why didn't the people revolt anyway?'

'They did; almost constantly during the first century of hopper rule. But the revolts were put down and the rebels were killed. The hoppers are microscopically thorough. As you probably know, they have a drug called veramin that makes you answer questions truthfully. Men had such a drug once, but this is much better, except that alcohol in the system counteracts it. They'd give an injection to every inhabitant of a suspected city, for instance, for the sake of catching one rebel. And there was just one penalty for rebellion – death, usually slow. So after a while there weren't any more rebellions. There have been practically none in the last century, so the hoppers have eased up their control of human beings somewhat.'

'Well,' growled the knight, 'what can be done about it?'

Homer Elsmith had seen that look in young men's eyes before. 'What would *you* do?' he asked gently.

'Fight!' Sir Howard had unthinkingly clenched his fist, and was making cut-and-thrust motions in the air.

'I see. You see yourself at the head of a charge of armored cavalry, spearing the hoppers like razorbacks and sweeping them from the face of the earth. No, I'm not making fun of you; that's a common reaction. But do you know what would happen? You've seen wheat stalks fall when a scythe passes through them? That's what you and your brave horsemen would do if the hoppers trained a rapid-fire gun on you. Or they might use the convulsion ray, and have the men and the horses rolling on the ground and writhing while they tied you up. The effect lasts for some minutes after the ray's been turned off, you know. Or they might use a cone transformer, setting up eddy currents in your plate and roasting you in your own lobster shells.'

'Well, what then?' Sir Howard's big fist struck his knee.

'I don't know. Nobody knows, yet. I don't know, though I've spent a good part of my life working on the problem. But that doesn't mean we shall never know. Man has solved knottier ones than that.

'We have some advantages; our numbers, for one. Then, the fact that the hoppers are spread out thinly over the earth makes them vulnerable to concerted uprisings. They're not an army, now, but a civilian administration and a police force. Take those hoppers at Albany; there are only a couple of hundred there. They're relieved frequently, because they don't like being stuck out in the sticks. If we were hiding out from human beings, this would be one of the worst places. But for the hoppers it's fine, because there are only two patrolling around the whole Adirondack area, and they seldom leave the main roads. Then there's the fact that they are not, really, very intelligent.'

'Not intelligent! Why, they – '

'I know. They know a lot more than we do, and have the sciences at their command, and so forth. But that's not intelligence. A bright hopper is about as intelligent as a stupid man.'

'But . . . but – '

'I know, I know. *But* they have three big advantages. First: they learn quickly, even if not intelligently. That's how the original conquering armies were trained to be competent soldiers so quickly. Second: they live long. I don't know what their average life span is, but I think it's around four hundred years. And third: the helmets.'

'The helmets?'

'Those leather things they wear. In their history, the helmets was invented by their god, whose name I can't give you because I can't imitate a canary. We'll call him X. As nearly as I can make out, this X was actually a great genius, a kind of Archimedes and Leonardo da Vinci and Isaac Newton rolled into one. They were some of the most brilliant men of ancient times. X may have been a sterile mutant. You can look that up later. I think it's likely, because the same strain of genius never again appeared among the hoppers, who were living hardly better than a wild-animal existence at the time.

'Early in life X hit upon the technique of scientific investigation: observing and experimenting to find what made things go. He invented their alphabet, which is a cross between a phonetic system and a musical score. He invented an incredible lot of other things, if we can believe the story. Instead of killing him, as human savages might have done, the hoppers made X their god, so he didn't have to work for a living any more. That was probably X's idea, too.

'Four hundred years is a long time, as I said. Toward the end of his life he invented the helmet. It's really an electrical apparatus, the effect of which is to give the hopper who wears it an enormous power of concentration. A man, for instance, can't keep his mind on one subject for more than a few seconds at a time. Try it sometime. First thing you know you'll be thinking about keeping your mind on whatever you're supposed to be keeping your mind on, instead of keeping your mind on the thing itself. I hope I make myself clear. But a hopper with a helmet can think about one thing for hours at a time. And even a chimpanzee could learn calculus if he could do that, I imagine.

'It may be that they're even stupider than stupid men, and that the helmets actually increase their reasoning powers. It's certain that without the helmets they're even more scatter-brained than chimpanzees, so that they're incapable of carrying out any complicated train of action. One reason I think they're so stupid is that their science seems to have remained just about static in the three centuries since the conquest. But it may be that having half a billion slaves of an inferior species to do their dirty work deprived them of ambition.'

'Then,' said Sir Howard, 'I'd think the thing to do was to rush them all at once and snatch their helmets off.'

'Yes? You forget the guns and things. If we could time an uprising as exactly as that, we could kill them with our bare hands. I tell you, wide conspiracies have been tried before. They haven't worked. For one thing, we have no sufficiently deadly, simple, and inconspicuous weapon. We're much worse off in that respect than we were at the time of conquest. We've got to have something better than gunfire, at least. Take those Albany hoppers again. They have a supply of small arms in the Office Building. The nearest heavy artillery is stored in the Watervliet arsenal. The really deadly things, like the protonic bombs, are down at Fort Knox, in old vaults where they used to store gold. If we could overwhelm even a large fraction of the hoppers, we could capture enough of their own weapons to redress the balance. But we'd need something to help us overwhelm that fraction first, and bows and bills wouldn't do it.'

'Well, how about getting them to take their helmets off of their own accord? Couldn't you send out some sort of radio ray or something?'

'That's been thought of: plans for blowing out the electrical circuits in the helmets; plans for heating up the wires to make them too hot for comfort: plans for interfering with their operation by static. Static doesn't seem to affect them, and we simply don't know of any form of ray or wave that would accomplish the other objects. Take the heating idea. It would require enormous power to heat up all those millions of helmets, and the amount that actually comes into your receiving set over the aerial is so slight you can't feel it. The biggest broadcasting station in existence doesn't send out as much power as the engine in one of the hoppers' two-wheel cycles develops. How are you going to erect a station to send out thousands of times as much power, without *their* knowledge?'

'Hm-m-m . . . it does seem hopeless. Maybe if you put on one of the helmets it would give you an idea.'

'That's been tried, too. I tried it once. It worked fine for about three minutes, and then I got the worst headache of my life; it lasted a week. The hopper's brains are cruder than ours; they aren't damaged by such treatment. You can't do it to a man's brain though, at least not with our present knowledge. Perhaps we shall be able to someday, when we've shaken off *them.*'

They sat silent for a while, smoking. Sir Howard said: 'If you don't mind me asking, where did you get all this information? And where did these books come from?'

'Oh, using my eyes and ears over many years. I might add that I'm an accomplished burglar. The books, together with much of the information about the hoppers, were partly stolen. The rest of them were picked up here and there, mostly by Thurlow Mitten before I joined him. The hoppers couldn't be expected to go into every corner of every attic and cellar of every old house in the country, you know, as thorough as they are.'

Sir Howard said, 'Some of your statements remind me of things my brother Frank used to say.'

Elsmith raised one eyebrow. 'Sally told me about him. That's . . . I'm sorry.' Something in his tone gave the knight the idea that Elsmith might know more than he cared to say about his brother. But he had too much to think about as it was to inquire any more just then.

9

'Well, he throws his knife at me, and it pins my big toe to the log so I can't get out nohow. But I says, "Mike Brady," I said, "I was

goin' to beat the gearin' out of you, and I still be." So I took after him
with my peavy. He runs, and me after him. But you know you can't
run fast with a twenty-foot log of hard maple nailed to your foot –
musta weighed nigh onto six hundred pounds – and after the fust
mile or two I seed he was gainin'! So I threwed my peavy, so the
point goes into a tree on one side of his neck and the cant dog goes
into the back on the other side, and there he was, helpless. So I took
my knife and cut his guts out. "Now," I says, "that'll be a lesson to
you to sass Eli Cahoon." He says, "Okay, I guess I was kinda hasty.
If you'll just put my guts back in I won't sass you no more." So I put
'em back in, and we been fine friends ever since. I still got the scar on
my toe.'

'That's a fact? I remember one time out in Wyoming, when me
and a fella was shooting arrows. We was shooting at horseflies.
Pretty soon a mosquita comes along. He says, "Bet you can't hit that
mosquita." I says, "What'll you bet?" He put up a hundred clinkers,
and I shot the mosquita. Then another mosquita comes along. He
says, "That was too easy. Let's see you hit this mosquita in the eye."
"Which eye?" I says, not stopping to think–'

The speakers were talking softly and casually in the firelight. Sir
Howard looked up from his book. 'Mr. Elsmith,' he asked, 'what
does this fellow mean? "Government of the people, by the people,
for the people." What people?'

' – and that's how I lost a thousand dollars, through getting the
right and left eyes mixed up. But I remember when I won this watch
on a bet. Fella named Larry Hernandez owned it, which is how it has
the same initials as mine. We wanted to see which could ride his
horse down the steepest slope – '

Elsmith spoke. Sir Howard wondered what there was about this
mild little man that gave his dry, precise words such authority. 'It
means that all the adults vote to select those who rule over them for a
limited time. When the time's up they have another election, and the
people can throw out their first set of officials if they don't like them.'

'All the adults? You mean even including the commons? And the
women? But that's a ridiculous idea! Lower-class person – '

'Why ridiculous?'

Sir Howard frowned in concentration. 'But they . . . they're
ignorant. They wouldn't know what was good for them. Their
natural lords –' He stopped in confusion again.

'Would you call me ignorant?' It was very quietly said.

'You? But you're not a – '

'My father worked in an iron foundry, and I started work as a
Postal Telegraph messenger boy.'

'But . . . but . . . but – '

'I admit that with a hereditary ruling class you get good men occasionally. But you also get some remarkably bad ones. Take Baron Schenectady, for example. Under this "government of the people" idea, when you find that your ruler is a scoundrel or a lunatic, you can at least get rid of him without an armed insurrection.'

Sir Howard sighed. 'I'll never get all these new ideas straight in my head. Thinking about them is like watching your whole world – all your old ideas and convictions – go to pieces like a lump of sugar in a teacup. It's . . . sort of awful. I should have come up here ten years ago to get a good start.'

'No.'

'Aw, come on, Sal; you like me pretty well, don't you?'

'That isn't it.'

'Well what *is* it?'

'It would be – expedient.'

There it was; one of those damned dictionary words again. He felt a surge of anger. Remembering Warren Kelly, an outrageously stinging remark formed in his mind. But his natural decency choked it off before it got to his lips.

'Well, why?'

She was baiting her hook. The boat rocked ever so slightly under the lead-and-snow cumulus clouds that towered over Little Moose Mountain and small Sly Pond.

'It's . . . this way. Maybe you haven't noticed, but we work hard at our job. Our job is the Organization, and we think that's literally the most important job in the world. Between that and keeping ourselves fed, we haven't time or energy for – personal relationships.'

'I'm afraid I'll never understand you, Sally.' He didn't either. She didn't act like a lower-class girl. He ought to know; base-born girls were pushovers for him. On the other hand, the upper-class girls he'd known would be horrified at the idea of baiting a hook with an active and belligerent crawfish, let along skinning and cleaning a mess of bullheads. But there wasn't any question of her being anything but upper-class. If necessary he'd stand the feudal system – for which he was feeling less reverence these days – on its head in order to put whatever class she belonged to on top.

'Another reason,' she went on. 'Uncle Homer tells me that you'll probably join us in a day or two. Officially, that is. I may say that I hope you do. But – this is important – you *mustn't* join us for personal reasons. And if you have any ideas of joining for such reasons, you can give them up right now.'

'But why? What's so awful about personal reasons?'

'Because if you changed your mind about the personal reasons, you might change your mind about the other things. You idiot, don't you see? What's one girl more or less, compared to the human race – everybody you've ever known and millions of others?' The reel sang for a second before she heard it. She caught up the rod in a smooth practiced movement and in a few more seconds had another bullhead in the boat. Sir Howard had already stabbed his hand on one of the fin spikes of the ugly brutes. But her hand gripped the fish's body as surely as his held a sword hilt. 'Damn them!' she said. 'They swallow the hooks, clear down to their stomachs. Someday we'll go out on Little Moose Lake and troll for bass.'

As they walked back to the camp with the fish, they passed Lyman Haas. He took one look at the gloom on Sir Howard's blunt features and grinned knowingly. Sir Howard thought afterward that he minded that grin more than anything.

Sir Howard asked: 'Hasn't your organization any name? I mean, you just call them "us" all the time.'

'No,' said Elsmith. 'It's just the Organization. Names are handles, and we don't want to give *them* any more handles to take hold of us by than we can help. Now if you'll just roll up your sleeve, please.' He held a hypodermic up to the light.

'Will that have any permanent effect on me?'

'No, it'll just make you feel slightly drunk and happy for a while. It's what the hoppers use in their third-degree work. It's much better than torture, because you can be sure that the prisoner is actually saying what he believes to be true.'

'Do I have to take an oath of some kind?'

'You don't have to. We go on the theory that a man's statement of his intentions, provided he actually says what he thinks, is as good an indication of what he'll do as any oath. People sometimes change their ideas, but when they do they almost always find excuses for breaking their oaths.'

'Tell me, was my brother Frank one of you?'

Elsmith hesitated, then said: 'Yes. He didn't go by that name in the organization, of course. We didn't have a chance to warn him. His immediate superior, who would normally have reported the state of affairs to me, had disappeared a couple of months previously. We knew what that meant, all right, but we hadn't succeeded in reestablishing communication with your brother.'

'This is the center of the whole business?' Sir Howard's eyebrows went up a little incredulously. Nothing much seemed to happen around the camp; certainly nothing that would indicate that it was the headquarters of a world-wide conspiracy.

'Yes. I see what you're thinking. Perhaps you hadn't noticed the number of times recently that you were tactfully lured away from the camp? There were conferences going on.'

The knight was slightly startled. He'd never thought of that. He began to appreciate the enormous pains to which these people went. You couldn't improvise something of this sort; it took years of careful and risky work.

'How do you feel?' asked Elsmith.

'A little dizzy.'

'Very well, we'll begin. Do you, Howard van Slyck –'

'You came through the test with flying colors, my boy. I'm glad of that; I think you'll make a good worker. I may add that if you hadn't you would never have left here alive.'

'What? Wh-why? How?'

Elsmith reached inside his shirt and brought out a hopper's gun. 'This, by the way, is the gun carried by the hopper you killed. We have some others. You didn't notice Sally take it from the body and hide it in her clothes, did you? You wouldn't. Sally knows her business.

'The reason I'd have used it, if necessary, is that you knew too much. Ordinarily it's only the old and tested workers who are allowed up here. Sally would never have brought you and Haas – who joined up last Tuesday, incidentally – if it hadn't been an emergency. You had to have a place to hide out, and you had too much good stuff in you to be allowed to fall into *their* hands. So we took a chance on you. If we'd been mistaken – well, we couldn't risk setting the Organization back years.'

Sir Howard looked at his toes. 'Would that have been right? I mean, according to your ideas. If I hadn't wanted to stay.'

'No, it wouldn't have been just. But it would have been necessary. I hope that some day we can afford to be just. It's treacherous business, this excusing injustice on grounds of necessity. People have justified or condoned the most atrocious crimes that way.'

'Try it again, Van Slyck.'

Sir Howard obediently turned and walked back across the room. He felt very silly indeed.

'No, that won't do. Too much swagger.'

'You can hear him clank,' said Sally Mitten, 'even when he hasn't got any armor on. I don't know what it is; something in the way the lower part of his legs snaps forward at each step.'

'Maybe I know,' said Haas. He was sitting with his feet in a bucket of hot water; he had gone for a hike with Cahoon, wearing ordinary laced boots instead of the high-heeled Western foot-gear he was accustomed to. As a result what he called his atchilly tendons had swollen up, to his acute discomfort. 'How's used to toting fifty pounds of stovepiping and other hardware with him. Maybe if you put lead in his boots it'd hold 'em down to the ground.'

'Look,' said Elsmith, 'relax your knees, so they bend a little at each step. And drop your whole foot to the floor at once, instead of coming down on your heel. There, that's better. We'll teach you to walk like a commoner yet. Practice that up.' He looked at his watch. 'They're due here any time. Remember, you're Charles Weier to members of the Organization. They'll be introduced to you as Lediacre and Fitzmartin, but those aren't their real names either. Lediacre *is* a Frenchman, however.'

'Why all the secrecy?' asked Sir Howard.

'Because, my dear Weier, if you don't know what a man's real name is, you can't betray it under the influence of veramin. The only people whose real names you're supposed to know are those directly below you. There's nobody below you yet, and for the present you're acting under my direct orders.'

When Lediacre and Fitzmartin arrived, they accepted their introduction to 'Weier' without comment. Lediacre was as tall as the Knight himself, though not as heavy; well-built, handsome in a foxy-faced sort of way, and exquisitely polite. He made Sir Howard feel like a hick. The other was a dark, nervous little man with a box to which he seemed to attach some great importance. When the rest were crowded around, he opened it and began to assemble a contraption of pulleys, belts, brass rods, and circular glass disks with spots of metallic foil on them. Sir Howard gathered that these men were important in the Organization, and was pleased to think that he was being let in on something big.

'Turn on the radio, somebody,' said Fitzmartin. 'The forbidden hopper wavelengths, can you?' When the set had warmed to the sinister chirping of a hopper station, he began turning a crank on his apparatus. Presently a train of blue sparks jumped from one brass knob to another in rapid succession. With the crack of each spark there was a *blup* from the radio, so that the twitterings were smothered. A program of dance music on one of the legal frequencies was similarly made unintelligible.

'You see?' said Fitzmartin. 'With an electrostat with wheels six feet in diameter, we can jolly well ruin radio reception within a radius of ten or more miles. If we cover the dashed country with such machines, we can absolutely drown the bloody hopper communications with static. They don't use anything but the blasted radio. They absolutely abolished all the wire communications centuries ago, and it would dashed well take them months to rig up new ones. Absolutely months.'

Elsmith puffed his cigar. 'Then what?'

'Well ... I mean ... my dear old man ... if we could absolutely disorganize them –'

'It would take them about twenty-four hours to hunt down our static machines and restore their communications. And you know what would happen to us. But wait –' Seeing the crushed look on Fitzmartin's face, he put out his hand. 'This is an excellent idea, just the same. I admire it. I merely wanted to remind you that the hoppers wouldn't commit mass suicide because of a little static. We won't build any of these yet. But we'll have a plan drawn up for the large-size machines, and we'll have a hundred thousand copies made and distributed to regional headquarters all over the world. Baugh can handle that, I think. Then, when we have something to give the hoppers the final push with, we'll have the machines built, and put them to work when the time comes. They'll be an invaluable auxiliary.'

The men stayed on several days. On the second day Sir Howard got a slight shock when he saw Lediacre and Sally Mitten strolling along a trail, apparently on the best of terms, and so absorbed in talk as to be oblivious of other things. He watched their figures dwindle, still talking, and thought, so that's it. He decided he didn't like the polished Monsieur Lediacre.

The next day he came upon the Frenchman smoking and looking at the view. 'Ah, hello, my friend,' said Lediacre. 'I was just admiring your scenery. It reminds me of the Massif Central, in my own country.'

'Are you going back there soon?' asked the knight, trying not to make the question sound too pointed.

'No – not for three or maybe four months. You see, I am in business. I am a what you call traveling representative for a French company.'

'Mind if I ask what sort of company?'

'Not at all, my dear Weier. It is perfumery.'

Perfumery! Good God! He didn't mind ignoble birth any more, but perfume! Out of the tail of his eye he saw Sally Mitten come out of the camp. Now if there were only some way he could show this perfume salesman where he got off. He had a reputation for prowess in the more spectacular forms of horseplay. Fencing, jousting, and steeplechasing weren't practical.

He said: 'I haven't been getting enough exercise lately; they've kept me so busy learning to jimmy windows and talk dialect. Do you wrestle?'

'I have not in a few years, but I should be glad to try some. I also need the exercise.'

'O.K., there's a grassy spot up the trail a way.'

When the Frenchman had peeled off his shirt and boots, Sir Howard had to admit that there was nothing soft-looking about him. But he knew he'd be able to squash this commoner chap like an undernourished mosquito.

They grabbed at each other; then Lediacre went down with a thump. He got up laughing with the greatest of good humor. 'I am getting stupid in my old age! I learned that hold when I was a little infant! Let us have another, no?'

Sir Howard tensed himself to grab Lediacre's left knee. He never knew quite what happened next, except he found himself flopping in midair, balanced across the Frenchman's shoulders. Then he came down with a jar that knocked the breath out of him. In a flash he was pinned firmly. His big muscles strained against the lock, but to no avail. It made him no happier to note that Sally Mitten, Lyman Haas, and Eli Cahoon were interested spectators.

'Again, yes?' said Lediacre. It was 'again,' quite literally. Sir Howard sat up and stretched his sore muscles. Lediacre, very solicitous, said: 'I did not twist too hard, did I? I learned that one from a Japanese man. I should be glad to teach it to you.'

The knight accepted the lesson with thanks but without enthusiasm. The man, in addition to his social graces, was a big noise in the Organization, whereas *he* was just a rookie. And his attempt to demonstrate physical superiority had backfired. What could you do against a combination like that? Oh, well, he thought, if she likes him better, that's all. We Van Slycks can't afford to let things like that bother us. After all, we have our self-respect to consider.

10

The two riders jogged south at an experienced horseman's long-distance pace; walk, trot, canter, trot, walk, over and over. A horse expert might have surmised that the enormous black gelding and the slim red mare were too fine a quality horseflesh to go with the somewhat shabby specimens that sat on them. Haas had grumbled about leaving his chaps and high-heeled boots behind, and had accepted the ancient felt hat with a couple of fishing flies stuck in the band in place of his seventy-five-dollar Western special only under vehement protest. Sir Howard likewise felt self-conscious as he never had when dashing about the country in alloy-steel plate. They had been allowed to tote their swords, as these would not attract the dangerous and unwelcome attention of hoppers.

'The idea,' the knight explained to Haas, 'is that my old man isn't supposed to know about this expedition. He thinks I'm up at Watertown or somewhere. Otherwise we'd just walk in and make ourselves at home. Personally I think they're making us do this play acting to see how good we are at it.'

'I don't mind the dressing up so much,' sais Haas. 'But every time I see a hopper I think he's gonna hop up and ask questions. It makes me uneasy as hell. I never noticed 'em before; just considered 'em a nuisance you had to put up with. It's got so I can't enjoy cheese sandwiches any more; the smell makes me think of hoppers.'

'Myself,' replied Sir Howard, 'I think I'd like that of a three weeks' corpse better. If they stop us, you know who you're supposed to be, and you've got a complete set of forged papers to prove it.' He was feeling much the same way. A human enemy, whom you could knock off his horse with a well-aimed toothpick thrust, was one thing; this invisible power with its mysterious weapons and ruthless thoroughness was another.

'Nothing in here,' whispered Sir Howard. They had gone microscopically over the little room in the back of the tool shed that Frank van Slyck had used as a laboratory. Their flickering pencils of light showed nothing but bits of twisted metal, wire gauze, and broken glass.

Haas murmured: 'Looks like the hoppers done a good job of cleaning up your brother's stuff.'

'Yes. They examined his poor little apparatus then smashed it up so its own mother wouldn't know it. They broke open the cases his bugs were in, and dumped the bugs out in the yard. They burned his notebooks, and took his textbooks away to put in one of their own libraries. Come on, there's nothing left to try but the manor house.'

'You sure they ain't no secret rooms around here?'

'Yes. This shed is raised up off the ground, and there's nothing but dirt under it. The wall here is nothing but beaver board. You can see through the cracks into the tool room, so there isn't any space between walls or anything. Come on.'

They calculated when the watchman would be at the other end of the grounds, then stole across the lawn. Sir Howard, being the heavier, boosted Haas up. Judicious use of a glass cutter gave him access to the latch, and the window opened with a faint squeak, no louder than the constant buzz and click and chirp of nocturnal insects. The slightly musty smell of the library mingled with the fragrance of the gardens.

'God help us,' said Sir Howrd, 'If my old man finds out what we've done to his roses. He'll be madder'n a hungry wolf with nine lambs and a sore mouth.'

They snooped around the room like a pair of inquisitive rats, running through desk drawers and wastebaskets. Sir Howard had almost despaired of finding anything when he remembered Frank's habit of putting papers between the leaves of books and forgetting them. His heart sank when he ran his flashlight over the well-filled stacks. There were hundreds of them, the books that had so bored him as a boy – poetry, fairy tales, romantic novels, theology. How different from the meaty Elsmith assortment! At least, he could use some selection. One shelf held books on farming, business, and other practical matters pertaining to the running of the duchy. If Frank had been reading any of the books, they'd be these. He and Hass began going through them.

Several blank pieces of paper were found, apparently mere place marks. Sir Howard put them in his shirt pocket. There was an exquisite drawing of a bee's head. There was a piece with several addresses on it. There was a piece with the cryptic notation:

Pulex irr.
M – 146 Attr. fac .17
M – 147 A. f. .88
M – 148 A. f. .39
M – 149 A. f. .99!!!

This was a volume entitled 'The Genetics of Stock Raising,' which was about as scientific a book as the hoppers permitted. There was another sheet, in a small dictionary, with an algebraic problem worked out. There was –

'Hands up, you two!' A yellow eye opened in the dark, flooding the burglars with light. Behind the eye, barely visible, was an elderly man in a dressing gown. He held a burglar bow, that is, a crossbow with a flashlight fixed to its end. The bow was drawn and cocked.

'Easy on the trigger, father,' said Sir Howard, getting up, 'unless you want to put a bolt through your heir and assign.'

'Howard! I didn't recognize you.' As a measure of disguise the knight had let his face alone for a week, and the resulting coal-black stubble was child-frightening.

'What on earth . . . what the devil . . . what in bloody hell are you doing, burgling your own home?'

'I was looking for something, and didn't want to get you up at this time of night. We can't stay, unfortunately.' Sir Howard knew the excuse sounded feeble.

'What's going on here, anyway? What are you looking for? And who's this man?'

Sir Howard introduced Haas. 'I was just looking for some papers I thought I'd left. It's nothing, really.'

'What papers? That doesn't explain this . . . this – '

'Oh, just some papers. I think we've about finished, eh, Lyman? It's nice to have seen you, father.'

'Oh, no, you don't. You don't stir out of here until you've given me a sensible explanation.'

'Sorry, father, but I've given you all I can. And I really am going.'

The duke was working himself up into one of his rare tempers. 'You . . . you young . . . you leave here, equipped like a proper gentleman, and say you're going on a pleasure trip. And six weeks later I find you dressed like a tramp, running around with commoners, and breaking into people's houses. What do you mean, sir? *What do you mean?*'

'Sorry, father; it's just my way of amusing myself.'

'It doesn't amuse *me!* You'll stop this nonsense now, or I'll . . . I'll cut you off!'

'That would be too bad for the duchy.'

'I'll stop your income! I still control most of your money, you know.'

Sir Howard was careful not to show how much this threat really jarred him. 'Oh, I can get along. If need be, we'll join a traveling circus.'

'You'll *what*? But you couldn't! I mean, that's preposterous. A Van Slyck working in a circus!'

'You'd be surprised. Remember Great-Uncle Waldo? The one who swindled those bank people? I can get a job as a strong man, and Lyman here can do rope tricks. We'll manage.'

The duke took a deep breath. 'You win. I don't understand you, Howard. Just when I think you're turning into a sensible, level-headed adult you act like this. But you win. Anything would be better than that! A circus performer!' He shuddered. 'By the way, how did you get over the wall?'

'Lyman threw his lasso over one of the merlons on the battlement. You know what a lasso is – a rope with a sliding noose. He's an expert. You remember, when you had the wall built, I advised you not to put those open crenelations on top.'

'They won't be there long!'

'Oh, while I think of it,' said Sir Howard casually. 'Are there any pups in the kennels just now?'

'Let me think . . . Yes, Irish Mist whelped about six months ago, and we have several that we haven't given away yet. Do you want one?'

'Yes, I'd like one.'

'Why – if you don't mind an old man's curiosity?'

'Oh, I just thought I'd give one to a friend.'

'Friend, huh? I hope she isn't another commoner wench?'

'Oh, you needn't worry about the Van Slyck escutcheon. It's nothing serious; just returning a favor.'

'Favor, humph! There are all kinds of favors.' The duke led them out to the kennels, and Sir Howard looked over the squirming Kerry-blue terrier pups with his flashlight. He picked one up.

'Don't you want something to carry him in?'

'Yes, if you have a basket or something.'

'Hm-m-m – I think this would do. Sure you and your friend won't reconsider and stay for the night?'

'No; thanks, anyway. I'll be seeing you. And by the way, better not mention our visit.'

'Don't worry! I don't want everybody to know that my son's gone squirrely! Take care of yourself, won't you? And try to come back in one piece? I couldn't stand having anything happen. Please, Howard. Good-by and good luck!'

11

'I hated to treat the old man like that. Hope I get a chance to explain some day.'

'H-m-m. He did seem kinda riled up. Say, How, maybe that wasn't such a good idea, us trying to make Renssalaer. Maybe we shoulda stopped the night at Hudson. It's gonna be blacker'n t'other side of hell. And I think she's liable to rain.' Haas pulled his damp shirt front away from his skin. 'Danged if I like your Yank summer weather, specially when it's fixing up to rain. Your clothes stick to you.'

'If it starts to rain we'll stop at Valatie. That's only a little way; we just passed Kinderhook.'

'Better use your flashlight, or you'll ride into the ditch. Is the little critter still in his basket? Cute little devil. Oh-oh, there goes a flash of lightning, off to the west. If I had my chaps, they'd shed the water.'

'The lightning's over the Helderbergs. The rain won't be here for hours yet. Trot!'

Plop-plop-plop-plop went the hoofs. Something – something – made the hair on Sir Howard's neck rise. Did he imagine it, or was there a faint smell of cheese?

'Halt, Man!' It was the familiar, detestable chirp. A blinding light was in his face. He looked around for Haas, but the Westerner and his mount appeared to have vanished into thin air.

There were two of *them*, in one of their two-wheeled vehicles. Or rather, one was in the vehicle, and the other was out and peering up at him. He slid his right foot out of the stirrup. 'Do not dismount!' There were chirpings and trillings in the dark and the command, 'Give me your reins!'

The vehicle purred ahead at a bare six miles an hour; Paul Jones trotted in tow. One of the hoppers had squirmed around in its seat to keep an eye on the rider.

He thought, these things belong to the road patrol. They're taking me to the station in Valatie – which the hoppers persisted in Calling Vallity, to the annoyance of the natives, who claimed they lived in Valaysha. They'll interrogate me, probably with the use of veramin. They'll want to know who I really am. They may

even want to know about Elsmith. I must not tell them. I ought
to kill myself first. But maybe there's an easier way out than that.
It's no use trying to run; they've got floodlights and guns. But if
that fellow would only get a crick in his neck for a minute. His
hand stole toward one of the saddle compartments –

The procession drew up at the Valatie station. There was a
hopper with a long gun by the door, a sentry. The two hoppers
in the cycle got out. Another came out the door, and there was
still another inside, using a typewriter.

'Dismount, Man.'

Oh, God, he thought. I mustn't stagger. I must keep my brain
clear. He scooped the small gray dog out of the basket on Paul
Jones's rump.

'Enter. Wait! Leave your sword outside.'

The knight unbuckled his sword belt fumblingly, and leaned
the weapon against the wall of the station.

'What is that?' The flashlight made the puppy blink. 'Dogs are
not allowed in the station. You must leave it outside also.'

'He'll run away, your excellency.'

'Place it in the basket, then.'

'The basket has not top, your excellency. He'll jump out.'

Twittering in the dark. Then: 'Leave it with the sentry. He
shall hold it.'

The sentry took the leash in one hand and tried to scratch the
dog's ears with the other. The dog backed as far as he could,
trembling. Sir Howard slouched into the station with his best
commoner walk.

'Your papers, Man. Sit here. Bare your arm.'

The needle pricked. The hoppers went through the papers.

He thought, I must talk right. I hope this works. If there's a
God, I hope He'll let me say the right things. Elsmith doesn't
seem to think there is a God; at least that's what he's implied at
times. But if there is one, I hope He'll let me say the right things.

There it was, that tingling, that dizzy feeling. I must say the
right things. If I start to say the wrong things, I've got my
pocketknife still. I could get it out quickly before they could stop
me. The throat would be best, I think. I'm not sure the blade's
long enough for my heart. Let me say the right thing –

It was beginning, now. The hopper who seemed to be boss
was looking up from the papers. 'You are Charles – Weier?'

'Yes, your excellency.'

'You are a professional hockey player?'

'Yes, your excellency.' If only they wouldn't ask him questions about ice hockey!

'Where were you born?'

The form of the question was different; there might be a catch to this one. He was supposed to tell them 'Ballston Spa.'

'Ballston Spaw, your excellency.' Thank God, he'd remembered in time! If he'd followed his natural impulse to use the downstate pronunciation of 'Spah,' he might have given himself away.

Twittering. Then: 'Do you know anything about a man, tall and dark like you, who has appeared in the Hudson-Mohawk region lately, and who sometimes passes himself off as William Scranton, and at other times pretends to be Howard van Slyck, the Duke of Poughkeepsie's son?'

'No, your excellency.' If only he didn't get his own name mixed up with his aliases! Scranton – Weier – Van Slyck – he wasn't sure he knew which was which himself.

'These papers appear to be in order. We are examining men of your physical type in an attempt to solve the disappearance of one of our troopers last month. Do you know anything about it?'

'No, your excellency.' Hot dog, he was winning!

More twitterings. If that was merely an order to check the stamps on his travel permit against the ledgers at Albany and Poughkeepsie, that was fine. The stamps were genuine. But if it was an order to check the permit itself against the central files in New York, that was something else.

'We are satisfied, Man. You may go.' The clawed, buff-haired hand shoved the papers at him across the table. I mustn't stagger when I get up – I mustn't swagger, either.

At the door there was no sign of the sentry. Its long gun lay on the ground. At the edge of the light from the open door lay its leather helmet.

Sir Howard was thunderstruck. He had no idea what could have happened. If they came out and found the sentry gone, they'd scour the country for it, and for him, too. He turned back to the door. 'Excellencies!'

'What is it, Man? You were told to go.'

'Your sentry has gone off with my dog.'

The four hoppers boiled out of the station like popping corn. They examined the discarded gun and helmet, sounding like a whole bird shop. A couple of them hopped off tentatively into the dark, trilling, then hopped back. They waved their clawed hands and wagged their ratlike heads, burbling. One hopped inside and began cheeping into a microphone.

'What are you waiting for, Man?' It was the boss hopper again. 'Your services are not required here.'

'My dog, your excellency.'

The hopper seemed to think for a moment. 'Man, your attitude has been admirably cooperative. In recognition, we will, as a special concession, keep your dog here, if we find it, until such time as you call for it. Provided of course, that you leave a deposit to cover the cost of keeping it. A dollar will suffice.'

Sir Howard's economy complex winced, but he paid up, buckled on his sword, and led Paul Jones away.

Out of hearing of the station he began whistling, softly at first, then more loudly. There was a click of claws on the pavement, the scrape of a trailing leash, and the sudden pressure of paws on his knee. He put the puppy, squirming with frantic joy, into the basket, mounted, and rode off. He hated leaving his dollar with the hopper, but the risk of going back to try to claim it was too great.

'Hey, How!' came a hiss from the blackness.

'Lyman! What happened to you?'

'I seen those guys laying for you, but I couldn't warn you because you was too far up front – right on top of them when I seen 'em. Before they turned the light on I jumped Queenie over the ditch and into a field. I watched the hoppers tow you off, and I followed through the fields so's they wouldn't hear me. What happened to *you*?'

Sir Howard told him.

'Is that a fact? The sentry fella just plumb disappeared? I never. But how did you keep from telling them the truth, if they doped you up with that stuff?'

'If anybody happens to notice an empty whisky bottle in the ditch near the Valatie station, they can put two and two together, perhaps. Alcohol in the system counteracts the action of veramin, Elsmith said, and it looks as though he was right. But between the two of them I don't feel so good. You'd better ride clear, Lyman. It looks as though I'm going to be sick from the liquor for the second time in my life.'

'Okay. Better aim to the right; that's downwind.' Thunder rolled overhead. 'Boy, there was a big drop on my hand. Looks like we're sure gonna get soaked tonight. But what the hell. I'd rather be wet outside a hopper house than dry inside one any day.'

12

'Oh, thank you, Howard, thank you ever so much. I've always wanted one.'

Not a bad reaction, he thought, especially considering that the pup didn't cost me anything, except that damned one-dollar deposit. I wonder what a new bicycle would do. Let's see – good bicycles are expensive – maybe I could get one wholesale. Oh, so *he's* here again, the knight thought disgustedly.

Lediacre appeared and began making French noises at the puppy, who seemed bewildered by all this attention.

'I don't know,' said Elsmith. 'If he can be trained properly, he'll be an asset, but if he turns out to be a yapper we'll have to get rid of him. He'd attract attention. Well, Weier, what have you to report?'

They went in, and Sir Howard spread out the papers he had found, meanwhile giving his story.

Elsmith stared hard at the pieces of paper. 'We'll test these blank ones for invisible writing, just to make sure, though I don't think there's anything on them. The sentry just disappeared, eh, leaving his hat and rifle? That's funny. What do you know about what your brother was doing with insects? Remember, we were out of touch with him for two months before his death.'

'Not a great deal,' said Sir Howard. 'I was away from home during most of those two months, too, and he never took me into his confidence. I didn't even know about the laboratory until I came home after I heard the news. And by that time they'd smashed up everything and confiscated what they hadn't smashed. They turned the bugs loose in our yard. We had a regular plague of insects for a week.'

'Hm-m-m. Hm-m-m.' Elsmith lit a cigar. 'Somehow I think your brother, and his insects, and the sentry's disappearance are all connected, though I don't see how.'

Sir Howard picked up the scrap with the cryptic heading 'Pulex irr.' 'Have you any idea that this means, sir?'

'I suppose it stands for *Pulex irritans,* the common flea. The M-146 might be the number of an artificial mutation, assuming that your brother was working on mutations. You know what they are, don't you? The thing to the right of it probably means 'attrition factor point one seven,' meaning that after a given length of time under certain conditions only one-sixth as many of the given batch of fleas were alive as would be with the normal nonmutated type. The exclamation marks oposite the M-149 presumably mean that he had found a type of flea that would stand those conditions, whatever they are, as well as the normal type stands normal conditions.'

Sir Howard thought. 'Fleas don't bite hoppers, do they? Everybody says that flies and mosquitoes never bother the things. There's – *WOW!*' Sir Howard thought afterward that it was the greatest moment of his life. He couldn't explain how he had done it. One moment there was confusion and bafflement, and then in a flash everything was clear. He saw in his mind the now-familiar picture of a small gray animal, scratching – scratching. 'It's the pup!'

'What? What? Don't ever do that again, my boy. At least, not indoors, unless you want to give me heart failure.'

'The puppy, the dog. Suppose Frank had found a mutation of the flea that liked hoppers. When they dumped all his bugs out, some of these special fleas found their way into the kennels, and, were on the pup when I gave him to the sentry to hold. A couple of them went exploring and got on the sentry.'

'Well?'

'Well, what would you do if you had a hat on and a flea crawled up under it and bit your scalp?'

'I'd take the hat – By Jove, I see. It's fantastic, but it seems to fit. Ordinarily insects don't bother the hoppers because the haemocyanin in their blood gives them indigestion. But if your brother developed a flea that thrived on haemocyanin blood as well as haemoglobin blood – and the hopper, never having suffered from insect bites, would be driven half crazy by them – they didn't bring any special parasitic insects from their own world – he'd take his helmet off and then not have sense enough to put it back on. With those synthetic minds of theirs concentrating on something else, they'd pull their helmets off to scratch without thinking – Where are you going?'

Sir Howard was already at the door. 'Lediacre!' he shouted. 'Where did the dog go?'

He went with Sally, my friend. Or rather, she took him. She said she was about to give him a bath.'

'Where? Where?'

'Up by the spring. You wish –'

Sir Howard didn't hear the rest of it; he was racing up the path to the spring. His heart pounded. At the end of the path a pretty picture came in view, framed by the trees; Sally Mitten on her knees, the sun in her hair, before a washtub. Over the washtub she held at arm's length a half-grown, smoke-gray, apprehesive-looking terrier.

'*Sally!*' His frantic yell, with all the power of his huge chest behind it, made the forest hum with echoes.

'Why ... Howard, what is it? Have the hoppers found our place?'

'No ... it's the dog.' He paused to catch his breath.

'The dog? I was just going to wash him. He's simply covered with fleas.'

'Thank God!' *Puff, puff, puff.*

'That he's covered with fleas?'

'Yes. Have you dunked him in that stuff yet?'

'No. Howard van Slyck, are you crazy?'

'Not at all. Ask your Uncle Homer. But I've got to have those fleas. C'mere, Mutt or Spike or whatever your name is.'

'I'm going to call him Terence.'

'All right. C'mere, Terence.'

Terence looked at the knight, wagged his tail doubtfully, sat down and scratched.

By the time he got the dog back to camp, ideas were sprouting like toadstools after a rain. Elsmith said: 'It's probable that only a fraction of Terence's fleas are the kind we want. We shall have to find some way of selecting them from the mass. There seems to be quite a mass, too.' Terence was nibbling at his silky flank.

Sir Howard said: 'If we had some of that haemocyanin blood, we could feed it to them, and the ones that didn't pass out would the the right ones.'

'Yes,' mused Elsmith, 'and that would give us a check on the validity of our theory. I don't know how we could get a supply of hopper blood, though.'

Haas drawled: 'Maybe we could kidnap one of the critters and take his hat off so he'd be harmless.'

'Bravo!' said Lediacre. 'That is the true American spirit, that we read about in France.'

'Too risky, I'm afraid,' said Elsmith.

'So,' continued Lediacre, 'does anything else have this special kind of blood?'

'It's almost identical with that of the anthropoda, especially the crustacea.'

'Crustacea? You mean like *les homards,* the lobsters?'

'Yes.'

'Then, my friends, our problem it is solved! One of our men is the manager of Vinay Frères, a retaurant in New York. Have

you ever eaten there? But you must! Their onion soup –
magnificent! I shall arrange with him to bleed his lobsters to
death before cooking them. It will not harm them as food. And
the blood we can smuggle up here. But how does one raise fleas?
One cannot call, "Here, flea; here, flea," at meal time.'

'One way,' said Elsmith, 'is to put them under a glass on your
wrist. They eat whenever they want to then. But perhaps if we
had the blood in thin rubber bladders, that they could pierce and
suck through –'

Once started, the flea farm grew by leaps and bounds. It took
an average of five weeks to raise a generation to maturity, but
there seemed to be no limit to their reproductive powers, at least
when they were coddled as they were at the Adirondack camp.
Sir Howard never had a chance to go to Amsterdam for a
bicycle. Men came and went. Little Fitzmartin departed happily
with instructions to have as many electrostats as possible built,
and talking about how they'd absolutely smear the bally
blighters. Lediacre was at the camp often. It was a crumb of
comfort to Sir Howard that if he was too busy to squire Sally
Mitten, the Frenchman was also. They drove from morning to
night. A chamber had to be cut out of the hillside to accommodate thousands of fleas.

There was a colored man from a place called Missouri, who
departed with several thousand peculiar pets concealed in the
lining of his battered grass suitcase. There was a red-skinned
man from the Southwest, a Novvo, who proved to be an old
friendly enemy of Haas. Whereat there was much backslapping
and reminiscing: 'Say, remember the time we beat the pants off
you guys on the South Platte?' 'What do you mean, beat the
pants off us? You had us outnumbered two to one, and even so
we retreated in good order!' There was Maxwell Baugh, the new
head of the Hudson-Mohawk branch of the Organization, to
report that the local hoppers hadn't shown any signs of suspicion, but that they were still worried about the sentry, who had
been picked up wandering idiotically, and was unable to give
any coherent account of his actions after his helmet had been put
back on.

Sir Howard began to appreciate what a big place the world
was. He'd have liked to question these men of odd sizes and
colors about their homelands. But there wasn't time; they came
and left by stealth, after staying but a fraction of an hour. A bark
from Terence, a shadowy form in the dark, passwords and
mutterings, and the man was gone.

'And now,' said Elsmith, 'we sit and wait. It's the damnable time lag.'

'What do you mean, sir?'

'The time it takes for our messengers to get to all parts of the world. In prehopper times you could get to any part of the world in a few days, by flying machines and ground vehicles. But with the fastest means of transportation available to us, it takes a full month to get to places like Central Asia. So we have to wait. Fortunately most of the messengers to the faraway countries got away early; we sent a lot of our own men to save time. But one of them, our man to Iberia, was picked up by the hoppers. He jumped into the Bay of Biscay and drowned himself before they got any information out of him. But we had to send another load of fleas.

'So, my boy, for the next five weeks you can plan to spend most of your time hunting, fishing, and gardening.'

'Sir, I'd like to run down to Amsterdam tomorrow –'

'I'm afraid not, Van Slyck. We'll have to lie very low for the next month. It would be intolerable to have something go wrong at the last minute. The hoppers haven't acted suspicious, but how do we know they're not playing cat-and-mouse with us?'

So, there wouldn't be any bicycle for Sally Mitten. And Lediacre was coming up again in a few days. Oh, to hell with it!

'About how many fleas have we raised altogether, sir?'

'I don't really know. Something like fifty million.'

'That doesn't sound like enough. There are twenty million hoppers. Seems as though we ought to have more than two hoppers per flea – I mean two fleas per hopper. Though the fleas hop, too.'

'We shall have. The messengers will establish stations for raising more generations of fleas in various parts of the world. Though one more generation is about all they'll have time for. Some of them are rasing their fleas on the way.'

'How will they keep them?'

'If everything else fails, there are always their own bodies.'

'When is M-day?'

'October 1st.'

The wait proved more difficult than the work, though Sir Howard did everything he could to make the time pass quickly. He threw himself into such occupations as were open to him with vicious energy, as when he walked five miles through the woods carrying across his shoulders an eight-point buck he had shot. He did little fishing. It wasn't active enough, and besides he was likely to arrive at Sly Pond to find the boat bobbing serenely in the middle of the lake with Sally Mitten and Lediacre in it. There was no fun in standing sullenly on the shore, and after the second occasion he hadn't taken any more chances. He'd rather take his bird glasses down to Little Moose Lake, and watch the local pair of ospreys dive for fish. He read voraciously.

Toward the end of September, when the maples were breaking out in scarlet and gold, Maxwell Baugh arrived to discuss detailed plans for the York State uprising. Sir Howard discovered to his surprise that he had been picked to lead a contingent of heavy cavalry against such of the Albany hoppers as were not affected by the fleas. The plans had long been drawn up; it remained but to fit individuals into their places in the pattern.

Sir Howard held up his helmet. 'This part,' he said, 'is the bowl. This is the visor. This is the bib or beaver.'

'Goodness!' said Sally Mitten. 'I suppose all those other pieces of armor have names, too.'

'Well, well, don't tell me that I've found one subject I know more about than you, my sweet? Yes, they all have special names, and they all have special purposes. And I know 'em all.'

'That's too bad, Howard.'

'Huh?'

'I mean, if we're successful, armor will go out of use pretty quickly, won't it? People will have guns then.'

'Good Lord, I never thought of that! I guess you're right, though.'

'And they'll have power vehicles, too. You wouldn't want to go somewhere on a horse when you can go a hundred miles an hour in a car.'

'I guess you win again, young lady. Here I've spent years learning to sit a horse, and hold a toothpick, and swing a sword, and jump around with fifty pounds of armor on. More tricks than a dead mule has flies. And now, I'm helping to make all that expensive knowledge useless. I suppose it's too late to do anything about it now.'

'Oh, I'm sure you'll get on all right. You're a resourceful young man. By the way, I never could see how men in full armor got around the way they do. I should think they'd be like turtles turned on their backs.'

'It isn't so bad. The weight's distributed, and all these joints and little sliding plates give you a good deal of freedom. But if you try to run upstairs with a suit on, you know you're carrying something.'

'I should think men would prefer chain armor. Isn't it lighter and more flexible?'

'That's what a lot of people think who never wore any. For equivalent protection it's just about as heavy. And there's a padding.'

'Padding?'

'Yes. Without an inch or two of cotton padding underneath, it wouldn't be much good. A blow would break your bones even if the edge didn't go through. And by the time you get all the padding on, the suit isn't much more limber than one of the plate, and it's hotter than the devil's private fireplace. Chain's all right for a little mail shirt like Lyman Haas'. That's just to keep some kind friend from slipping a dagger between your ribs on a dark night.'

He buckled his last strap, picked up his helmet, and stood up. The fire threw little red highlights on his suit. 'You boys ready?'

'Yeah,' said Cahoon. 'We be.'

'Been ready half an hour,' said Haas. 'That'll be a lesson to me, to allow more time for lobsters to get into their shells.'

'Howard –'

'Yes, Sally?'

'I wanted to ask you something –'

'Yes?'

'Be careful how you expose yourself. People who have never faced guns have no idea how deadly they can be.'

'Oh. Don't worry. I'm scared to death of the things myself. Be seeing you. I hope.'

13

Plot-plop-plop-plop went the hoofs. The fog was still rising off the Mohawk. You couldn't see anything but the other men in the troop and the glistening black road ahead. The mist condensed on their plate and ran down in little streaks.

Out of Schenactady, they passed the huge masts of the broadcasting station. A small fire near the base of the nearest mast made a spot of orange in the grayness. Three men were standing around the mast, and a fourth was kneeling at its base. He was chopping at a cable with a butcher's cleaver. *Chunk* went the cleaver. *Chunk. Chunk. Chunk*

'Here's McCormack Corners,' said a man.

'What's Weier taking us around this way for?' asked another. 'It's shorter by Colonie.'

'Dunno. Maybe they want to keep the Mohawk Pike open for somebody else.'

They halted. Up ahead was a pattering of many hoofs.

'Single file,' came back Sir Howard's baritone. 'Walk.'

They straightened out, and saw that a large troop of unarmored men with crossbows dangling from their saddles was trotting past along the Cherry Valley Pike. One of them called: 'Hey lobsters! What are you coming for? You'll be about as useful as real lobsters. We're the ones got to do the real fighting!'

'We're to fight the hoppers when they come out, and you guys pull foot,' retorted one of the armored men. 'Seen any hoppers?'

'Just one,' a crossbowman called back. 'Near Duanesburg, Funniest thing you ever seen. He just sat there on his cycle watching us go past. Didn't do nothing. Thought we was just a local war party, I guess.'

'Local war party! That's good!'

'He didn't do nothing. Didn't even say, 'Halt, men!' I bet he was surprised when Schuyler, up front, put a bolt through him.'

'What'd he do then?'

'Just keeled over and squeaked for a while. Then he didn't squeak any more.'

The crossbowmen pulled up ahead. It was getting quite light. The mist faded. In front of them the sun, orange on top shading to deep red underneath, threw cheerful lights on the plate.

'I see the Office Building,' said a man. 'Suppose any hoppers are in it now?'

'Prob'ly,' replied another. 'They get to work early. One reason I never liked the hoppers is the early hours they keep.'

'You call getting to work at seven early! You oughta work on a farm, mister.'

'Maybe they'll see us.'

'Maybe. They'll know something's wrong. That static machine oughta be going on any time.'

'They got guns in the Office Building?'

'Ayuh. I think so.'

'I mean big ones – artillery, they call 'em.'

'Well, this ain't Watervliet.'

'No. But the guns at Watervliet could shoot clear down to Albany if they had a mind to.'

'Huh? There ain't nothing can shoot that far.'

'Oh, yes. They can shoot clear down to Kingston if they got a mind to. But that's why they have the static machines. So the hoppers can't radio back and forth to tell where to shoot.'

'I hear we got guns, too.'

'I think we got some. Some they stole from the hoppers, and some they made. But the trouble is, there ain't anybody knows how to work 'em. I thought of trying to get in a gun troop, and then decided I'd liefer stick to my old toothpick.'

'Say, who's the twerp up front with Weier? Guy with a funny hat.'

'Dunno. He's from some place they call Wyoming. Down South, I think.'

'Don't see how he could make any speed with that hat. Too much air resistance.'

'Hey, wasn't that a shot?'

'Ayuh. Sounds like it.'

'They're shooting regular now. Weier better hurry up, or the fun'll be over before we get there.'

The windows of Albany rattled to continuous gunfire when Sir Howard led his troop behind the Education building across the street from the Office Building. Up and down Elk Street little knots of armed men waited. The knight told his men to wait, dismounted, and trotted around the corner.

Most of the gunfire was coming from the Office Building. All the windows on the lower floors of this building had been broken. From the nearer surrounding buildings came a stream of arrows and crossbow bolts. Barricades had been thrown up at the intersections. More crossbowmen, and a few men with rifles and pistols, stood behind these barricades shooting. Eli Cahoon was behind a near one. He was going from man to man, saying: 'Now, take your time, son; just squeeze the trigger slow.' In front of the shattered glass doors of the Office Building lay a pile of dead hoppers without helmets. Scattered over the broad Capitol Square were a score or so of dead men. A little puffy wind was rising. It picked up yellow and brown leaves from the piles raked together in the gutters and whirled them merrily around the square.

Sir Howard picked out an officer, a man in ordinary hunting clothes with a brassard on his arm. 'Hey, Bodansky! I'm on time, I hope.'

'Thank God you got here, Weier! You're in command.'

'*What?*'

'Yep; the whole shootin' match. Baugh's dead. He led the charge when they tried to get into the ground floor. Haverhill hasn't shown up; nobody knows what's become of him. And

McFee just had his arm all smashed to hell by a bullet. So you're it.'

'Whew! What's the situation?'

'So-so. We can't get in, and they can't get out. Olsen turned the fleas loose on schedule; they got most of the hoppers. But there was enough left to put the helmets back on the heads of some. The ones they didn't put the helmets on wandered out the front door like they were silly, and the boys potted 'em. I don't think you can get the boys to make another charge; they saw what happened to the first ones.'

'How about their cone transformers?'

'They've got a couple, but they can't use 'em because we turned the city power off. We got the power plant right at the start. They've got some convulsion rayers, too, but they're only the little kind, good up to fifty feet. Here's Greene.' Another officer ran up.

'The riflemen's ammunition isn't going to last much longer,' he gasped. 'Half of it's too old to go off, anyway. And they're shooting pretty wild.'

'Tell the riflemen to cease firing,' Sir Howard snapped. He was feeling both awed by the unexpected responsibility and tremendously important. 'We'll need them later.'

'The bows and kickers wont reach to the upper floors,' said Bodansky.

'We can't do much to the upper floors from here, anyway. We'll have to find some way of getting into the lower floors.' He thought for a minute. They were expecting him to produce some bright idea. If he didn't he'd be a failure. He raised his voice: 'Hey, Eli! Eli Cahoon!'

The old New Englander came over with his slinking walk. 'Yeah?'

'Think it's going to blow?'

'Hm-m-m. Maybe. Shouldn't be surprised.' He looked at the sky, at the dancing leaves. 'No' thwest, in about an hour.'

'All right. Bodansky, have another barricade thrown across the yard back of the Office Building. Use furniture, anything. Tell the boys to keep down close to it, so they won't be potted from the upper floors. Get all the crates and boxes in town. Pile 'em on the west side of the barricade. Get all the dead leaves you can.'

'Bonfire? Smudge?'

'Yes. And get every garbage can in Albany! We'll show them something about smells. Hey, St. John! Get out the fire depart-

ment. We're going to start a smudge, and when the smoke gets
thick we'll run the trucks up on the sidewalk alongside the Office
Building, and the boys will climb up the ladders into the
windows.'

He worked around behind buildings to the other side of the
square, checking dispositions and talking to harassed officers.
There were men in plate, men in overalls, men in store clothes.
There men with billhooks, men with bows, men with butcher
knives lashed to the ends of poles. There were a few dead men,
and an occasional wounded man being carried off.

The pile of assorted fuels grew, over beyond the Office
Building. The fire department hadn't appeared. Why, of course,
he thought, most of the firemen are on the firing line. I've been
dumb. There has to be somebody to hitch up the horses. I'll have
to get somebody to round 'em up. He gave orders; men ran,
hesitated, and came back to have them repeated.

The bonfire began to crackle and smoke. It smoked beautifully. The breeze was just strong enough to wrap the Office
Building in a shroud of pearly fumes, so that you could only see
parts of it. Sir Howard heard a man near him cough and say,
'Who the hell they trying to smoke out, us or the hoppers?'

There was a snoring buzz, and a flying machine swept over the
buildings. More and more men neglected their shooting to stare
up at it apprehensively. It circled and came back.

'They going to bomb us?' asked an officer.

'They'd like to,' replied Sir Howard. 'But they don't know
where to bomb. They're afraid of hitting their own people. Tell
your boys to pay attention to the Office Building; not to worry
about the flier.'

The machine appeared again, much higher and flying north. It
was almost out of sight behind the buildings when it disappeared
in a blinding magnesium-white flash. Sir Howard knew what
was coming, and opened his mouth. The concussion made men
stagger, and a few fell. It took the knight a second to realize that
the musical tinkle was not in his head but was glass falling from
thousands of windows.

Everywhere were scared faces, a few with nosebleeds. They'd
bolt in a minute. He trotted down the line, explaining: 'It O.K.!
We got Watervliet! We turned one of their own X beams on the
ship and set off the bombs! Everything's fine!'

'They're coming out!' somebody yelled.

Sir Howard looked around. It would be logical for the
hoppers to bolt, now that the arsenal had fallen. He ought to be

with his calvalry troop on the other side of the square. The shooting from the Office Building had slackened. It would take him all day to work around outside the zone of fire. He vaulted a barricade, almost fell when he landed under the weight of his plate, and started to run across the square with a queer, tottering run that armored men have.

He was halfway across when the hoppers boiled out of the Office Building by the front doors. He was right in front of them. There was a crash of shots from the guns they carried in their claws. Nothing touched him. He ran on. There were scattering shots from the hoppers, and something hit his right pauldron and ricocheted off with a screech. He spun half around and fell. Thank God, it was just a glancing hit, he thought. Better play possum for a few seconds. He thought he heard a groan from the human army when he fell, but that was pure self-conceit, as most of them had no idea who he was. He looked out of the corner of his eye toward the hoppers. They were bounding across the square toward the buildings. There must have been fifty; thirty-five, anyway. Arrows and bolts streaked toward them, mostly going wild. An arrow bounced off Sir Howard's backplate. God, he thought, is one of these idiots going to kill me by mistake? The hoppers had turned and were going back the way they had come.

Sir Howard scrambled up. In front of him men were dropping over a barricade and running toward him. They were shouting something and pointing. He looked around. Not thirty feet off was a hopper. It had a sort of gun in its hands, connected by cables to a knapsack thing strapped to its back. It was a lightning gun. It went off with a piercing crack, and a straight pencil of blue flash went past Sir Howard. It cracked again and again. A couple of the men who had run toward him were lying down, the rest were running back. The gun cracked again, and the flash ended on Sir Howard's breastplate. All his muscles twitched, and his bones were jarred. But he did not fall. The gun cracked again and yet again, with the same result. His suit was grounding the discharges. He got his sword out and took a step toward the hopper. The hopper went soaring away across the square after its fellows, who were bouncing along State Street.

People were dropping out of doors and windows and climbing over barricades. They came out quickly enough now that the hoppers were in retreat. If he didn't get his cavalry under way in a few seconds, the square would be packed and they'd be struck like flies on flypaper.

Just ahead of the crowd Musik, his second-in-command, and Lyman Haas appeared at a canter. The former was leading Paul Jones. The men were clattering in double file behind them. Sir Howard yelled, 'Stout fellas!' and climbed aboard. As he did so, Haas shouted: 'The cavalry from Pittsfield is coming up State from the river!'

'They can't get through here; you tell 'em to go around by the sound end of town and head west. Try to cut the hoppers off! All right, let's go!' They pounded diagonally across the square; men who had just run out ran back, like startled chickens, to get out of their way.

The barricade across State Street west of the Office Building was low, and had only a few men behind it. These shot wildly until the hoppers were two jumps away, then broke and scattered like flushed quail. The hoppers soared over the barricade and shot the men in the back as they ran. When Sir Howard arrived at the barricade the hoppers were far down State Street, their bodies rising and falling like overhead valves. Sir Howard put Paul Jones over the barricade. A terrific clang made him squirm around in the saddle. Musik and Musik's horse were standing on their heads on the west side of the barricade. Both got up quickly. Musik's horse ran along after the troop, and Musik ran after his horse on foot, yelling, 'Come back you, you bastitch!' and falling farther and farther behind. Far away they heard the sirens of the fire engines, arriving at last.

They cut across Washington Park and galloped out New Scotland Avenue, keeping the hoppers in sight, but not gaining much on them. People ran into the street, ran back when the hoppers appeared, ran out again, and ran back again when the cavalry came along.

They got out into the southwestern part of Albany, where New Scotland Avenue becomes Slingerlands Road. A few streets had once been laid down here, but very few houses had been built. It was mostly just a big flat area covered in weeds. There were other horsemen on their left, presumably the men from Massachusetts. These were swooping along drawing steel bows. The combination worked beautifully. An arrow would bring down a hopper, and by the time Sir Howard's lobsters had passed over it, each taking a jab at it with a lance, it didn't look like a hopper. It didn't look particularly like anything.

The hoppers were spreading out. The men, without orders, were spreading out to hunt them down. Sir Howard found himself alone and chasing a hopper. He wondered what he'd do if the hopper got to the edge of the plateau on which Albany stands before he caught it. He couldn't gallop Paul Jones down the slope that ended at Normans Kill. But this hopper seemed to be going slowly. As Sir Howard gained on it, he saw that it had an arrow sticking in its thigh.

Sir Howard squeezed his lance and sighted on the hopper. The hopper stopped, turned around, and raised a small gun. The gun went off, and something went off in the kinght's side. The saddle seemed to be lifted away from him, and he landed on his back in the weeds. His side pained horribly for a moment, so that he felt deathly sick.

He couldn't see for the weeds, which stuck up like a forest around him. All he could see was the hopper standing there. The hopper raised the gun again. The gun clicked harmlessly. Sir Howard thought, if I can get up I can finish it before it reloads. He tried to sit up, but his plate dragged him down again. The hopper was reloading, and he couldn't get up. He could hear the drumming of hoofs, but they seemed miles away. He thought, Oh, God, why do I have to die *now?* Why couldn't I have died at the start? The hopper clicked the gun and raised it again. His side hurt terribly, and he was going to die at the last moment.

Then there were hoofs, near, and something snaky hissed out of the air to settle around the hopper. The gun went off, but the hopper was bouncing away in grotesque positions. It gave a final bounce and disappeared behind the weeds.

14

The doctor at the door said: 'He'll be all right. It's just a broken rib. A bullet went through his plate and grazed his side. The broken ends cut him up a little when he fell. Sure, you can see him.' Then they all came in: Elsmith and Sally Mitten and Haas and Cahoon and Lediacre. The Frenchman was dirty and had a bandage over his left ear. He was very sympathetic.

They all tried to talk at once. Sir Howard asked how things were going. Elsmith answered: 'Fine. We got word by radio – we turned the electrostats off – that all the broadcasting stations in New York had been taken. There must have been at least a thousand hoppers in the RCA Building, but they mounted some captured heavy guns in Columbus Circle and blew them out of it. As far as I know, all the hopper strongholds in North America have been taken. There are some hoppers still at large, but they'll be killed on sight.

'There are quite a few holding out in Africa, but there's an Arab army on its way to deal wth them, completely outfitted with hopper guns. They even found some people willing to take a chance on running the captured flying machines. Mongolia never got any fleas at all, but there were only a few hoppers there, anyway. It's pretty much the same elsewhere. Some of them got away in their flying machines and used their bombs and rays. They blew Louisville off the map, for instance. But they had to come down eventually, and there wasn't any friendly place to land. In places where the most fleas were released, and all the hoppers took off their hats to scratch, the way they did at Watervliet, it was simply a slaughter of helpless animals. I'm trying to save a few of them.'

'Why?'

'Without the helmets they're quite harmless creatures, and rather interesting. It would be a shame to exterminate them completely. After all, they didn't exterminate us when they had the chance.'

'Lyman! You certainly saved my hash.'

'Wasn't nothing, really. That was a good cast I made, though. I'd used up all my arrows. Broke the hopper's neck with one yank. Guess that there helmet made it concentrate too hard on shooting you, or he'da seen me. Longest cast I ever made with a rope. The only trouble is they won't believe me when I get back home. I'll have to take the rope along to show them.'

'How did you happen to get there just then?'

'Oh, I caught up with you. Those truck horses you fellas ride ain't no faster'n turtles. It's a wonder to me you didn't get some big turtles to ride. The shells would stop arrows and things, and you wouldn't need to worry about being blown off backward by the wind.'

There will probably always be a Ten Eyck Hotel in Albany. They were standing in the lobby of the fifth building of the name.

'Are you going now, Howard?' asked Sally Mitten.

'Yep.' This was a final good-by, he knew. He managed to sound brightly conversational. 'I'll have to see how things are down at Poughkeepsie. You and Elsmith are going, too, aren't you?'

'Yes; we're taking a boat for New York tonight. We sail at nine, wind permitting. I've never made the Hudson River trip.'

'What are you gong to do?'

'Some people are talking about making Uncle Homer an earl, or king, or something. But he won't have it. He's going to organize a university. It's what he's always wanted to do. And I'm still his secretary. What are your plans? Go back and be a country gentleman again?'

'Didn't I tell you? We've both been so busy. I've got a career! You know all those books I read up at camp? Well, they set me to thinking. For three hundred years we've been standing still under the form of social and political organization the hoppers imposed on us – I'm getting pretty good at the dictionary words myself, huh? – and they didn't pack that form because they had our welfare at heart, or because they wanted us to get places. They picked it because it was the most stagnant form they could find in our history. What I mean is that our . . . uh . . . synthetic feudalism is about as progressive as a snail with arthritis. So I thought it might be a good idea to try out some of this government-by-the-people business. No classes; all comrades together, the way we and Lyman were.'

'I'm so glad. I was afraid you'd want to get back in the old groove.'

'I thought you'd approve. You know what it'll be like; a wild scramble for power, with every little baron and marquis trying to get everybody else by the short hair. You know what their cry will be: York State for the York Staters, Saratoga for the Saratogans, and Kaaterskill Junction for the whatever-you-cal'ems. But I'd like to see the whole continent under one government-by-the-people. Most of it was once. Or even the whole world, if we could manage it someday. Of course, a lot of our little lords won't like the idea. So I've got my work cut out for me. I don't anticipate a very quiet life.'

'How are you going about it?'

'It's already started. I got together with some of the boys who think the way I do – mostly people who were in the Organization – the other night, and we formed something called the Committee of Political Organization for York State. Copoys for short. They made me chairman.'

'Isn't that splendid!'

'Well, maybe the fact that I got the meeting together had something to do with it. I even made a speech.'

'I didn't know you could make speeches.'

'Neither did I. I stood there and said 'Uh . . . uh' at first. Then I thought, hell, they won't enjoy hearing me say 'Uh . . . uh.' So I told them what they'd been through, which they knew as well as I, and what a swell fellow the late Maxwell Baugh was. Then I repeated some of the things I'd read in those books, and said we might as well have left the hoppers in control if we weren't going to change anything. They tried to carry me around on their shoulders afterward.'

'Oh Howard! Why didn't you let them?'

'I was willing enough. But one of the carriers was the little Fitzmartin, the electrostat-man – his real name's Mudd, by the way – and he wasn't quite up to holding his half of my two hundred and some pounds. So the first thing I knew he was on the floor and I was sitting on top of him.'

She laughed. 'I'd like to have seen that!'

He laughed, too, though he didn't feel like laughing. He felt like hell. It was a very special kind of hell, new in his experience. 'It looks as though I'm cut out for politics. Jeepers, when I think of the snooty ignoramus I used to be! This may be the last time I'll wear the old suit.' He patted the maple-leaf insignia on his breastplate affectionately. 'I'm afraid my father won't approve of my program; I can just hear his remarks about people who are traitors to their class. But that can't be helped.'

'Are you riding Paul Jones down?'

'Yes. My slat's just about mended, though I'm still wearing enough adhesive to stop a bolt from a Remington highpower. I don't mind it, but I hate to think of the day it'll have to be pulled off.' He thought, come on, Van Slyck, you're only making it harder for yourself, standing here and gassing. Get it over with.

'You could go in one of the hopper vehicles, I should think.'

'Thanks, but until I learn to run one myself I'm not risking my neck with any young spriggins who thinks he can drive just because he's seen it done.' He added, 'It was fun, wasn't it?'

'It certainly was.'

It was time to go, now. He opened his mouth to say good-by. But she asked: 'Do you expect to get down to New York?'

'Oh, certainly, I'll be there often, politicking.'

'Will you come to see me?'

'Why, uh, yes, I suppose so.'

'You don't have to if you don't want to.'

'Oh, I want to all right. I want to worse than a fish wants water. But . . . you know . . . if you and Monsieur Lediacre . . . you mightn't want me –'

She looked puzzled, then burst out laughing. 'Howard, you idiot! Étienne's got a wife and four children in France, whom he's devoted to. Every chance he has he gets me off and tells me about them. Étienne's a dear fellow, and he'd give you his shirt. But he bores me so, with his darling little Josette, and his wonderful little Rene; such an intelligent child, Mamzelle, a prodigy! It was especially bad those last few weeks in camp; all the time I was wishing you'd butt in and interrupt his rhapsodies, and you never did.'

'Well, I . . . I . . . I . . . I never.'

'Were you really going to make it good-by forever on that account? I could never have looked at a maple leaf in the fall again without thinking of you.'

'Well, I . . . in that case, of course I'll come. I was planning to be down in a couple of weeks; that's . . . To hell with that! Where can I get a passage on this boat of yours? Never mind, there's a ticket agency right here in the hotel. I hope they ship horses; they'll ship my horse if I have to smuggle him aboard in my duffel bag. I see I've got some lost time to make up for. You once remarked, Sally, that you thought I had brains. Well, I admit I'm not a great genius like your Uncle Homer. But I think I have sense enough not to make the same mistake twice, thank God! What's more, I think I see how we can have a perfect revenge on our friend Lediacre.'

'What do you mean, Howard? The poor man can't help —'

'No. He's a nice chap and all that. But some day' — he smiled grimly — 'I shall take the greatest pleasure in getting him in a corner and feeding him a dose of his own identical medicine!'

WOLVES OF DARKNESS

Jack Williamson

1

The Tracks in the Snow

Involuntarily I paused, shuddering, on the snow-covered station platform. A strange sound, weird, and somehow appalling, filled the ghostly moonlight of the winter night. A quavering and distant ululation, which prickled my body with chills colder than the piercing bite of the motionless, frozen air.

That unearthly, nerve-shredding sound, I knew, must be the howling of the gray prairie or *lobo* wolves, though I had not heard them since childhood. But it carried a note of elemental terror which even the trembling apprehensions of boyhood had never given the voice of the great wolves. There was something sharp, broken, abut the eery clamor, far-off and deeply rhythmic as it was. Something – and the thought brought a numbing chill of fear – which suggested that the dreadful ululation came from straining human throats!

Striving to shake the phantasy from me, I hastened across the icy platform, and burst rather precipitately into the dingy waiting room. It was brilliantly lit with unshaded electric bulbs. A red-hot stove filled it with grateful heat. But I was less thankful for the warmth than for the shutting out of that far-away howling.

Beside the glowing stove a tall man sat tense over greasy cards spread on the end of a packing box which he held between his knees, playing solitaire with strained, feverish attention. He wore an ungainly leather coat, polished slick with wear. One tanned cheek bulged with tobacco, and his lips were amber-stained.

He seemed oddly startled by my abrupt entrance. With a

505

sudden, frightened movement, he pushed aside the box, and sprang to his feet. For a moment his eyes were anxiously upon me; then he seemed to sigh with relief. He opened the stove door, and expectorated into the roaring flames, then sank back into his chair.

'Howdy, Mister,' he said, in a drawl that was a little strained and husky. 'You sort of scairt me. You was so long comin' in that I figured nobody got off.'

'I stopped to listen to the wolves,' I told him. 'They sound weird, don't they?'

He searched my face with strange, fearful eyes. For a long time he did not speak. Then he said briskly, 'Well, Mister, what kin I do for ye?'

As I advanced toward the stove, he added, 'I'm Mike Connell, the station agent.'

'My name is Clovis McLaurin,' I told him. 'I want to find my father, Dr. Ford McLaurin. He lives on a ranch near here.'

'So you're Doc McLaurin's boy, eh?' Connell said, warming visibly. He rose, smiling and shifting his wad of tobacco to the other cheek, and took my hand.

'Yes,' I said. 'Have you seen him lately? Three days ago I had a strange telegram from him. He asked me to come at once. It seems that he's somehow in trouble. Do you know anything about it?'

Connell looked at me queerly.

'No,' he said at last. 'I ain't seen him lately. None of 'em off the ranch ain't been in to Hebron for two or three weeks. The snow is the deepest in years, you know, and it ain't easy to git around. I dunno how they could have sent a telegram, though, without comin' to town. and they ain't none of us seen 'em!'

'Have you got to know Dad?' I inquired, alarmed more deeply.

'No, not to say real well,' the agent admitted. 'But I seen him and Jetton and Jetton's gal often enough when they come into Hebron, here. Quite a bit of stuff has come for 'em to the station, here. Crates and boxes, marked like they was scientific apparatus – I dunno what. But a right purty gal, that Stella Jetton. Purty as a picture.'

'It's three years since I've seen Dad,' I said, confiding in the agent in hope of winning his approval and whatever aid he might be able to give me in reaching the ranch, over the unusual fall of snow that blanketed the West Texas plains. 'I've been in medical college in the East. Haven't seen Dad since he came out here to Texas three years ago.'

'You're from the East, eh?'

'New York. But I spent a couple of years out here with my uncle when I was a kid. Dad inherited the ranch from him.'

'Yeah, old Tom McLaurin was a friend of mine,' the agent told me.

It was three years since my father had left the chair of astrophysics at an eastern university, to come here to the lonely ranch to carry on his original experiments. The legacy from his brother Tom, besides the ranch itself, had included a small fortune in money, which had made it possible for him to give up his academic position and to devote his entire time to the abstruse problems upon which he had been working.

Being more interested in medical than in mathematical science, I had not followed Father's work completely, though I used to help him with his experiments, when he had to perform them in a cramped flat, with pitifully limited equipment. I knew, however, that he had worked out an extension of Weyl's non-Euclidian geometry in a direction quite different from those chosen by Eddington and Einstein – and whose implications, as regards the structure of our universe, were stupendous. His new theory of the wave-electron, which completed the wrecking of the Bohr planetary atom, had been as sensational.

The proof his theory required was the exact comparison of the velocity of beams of light at right angles. The experiment required a large, open field, with a clear atmosphere, free from dust or smoke; hence his choosing the ranch as a site upon which to complete the work.

Since I wished to remain in college, and could help him no longer, he had employed as an assistant and collaborator, Dr. Blake Jetton, who was himself well known for his remarkable papers upon the propagation of light, and the recent modifications of the quantum theory.

Dr. Jetton, like my father, was a widower. He had a single child, a daughter named Stella. She had been spending several months of each year with them on the ranch. While I had not seen her many times, I could agree with the station agent that she was pretty. As a matter of fact I had thought her singularly attractive.

Three days before, I had received the telegram from my father. A strangely worded and alarming message, imploring me to come to him with all possible haste. It stated that his life was in danger, though no hint had been given as to what the danger might be.

Unable to understand the message, I had hastened to my rooms for a few necessary articles – among them, a little automatic pistol – and had lost no time in boarding a fast train. I had found the Texas Panhandle covered with nearly a foot of snow – the winter was the most severe in several years. And that weird and terrible howling had greeted me ominously when I swung from the train at the lonely village of Hebron.

'The wire was urgent – most urgent,' I told Connell. 'I must get out to the ranch to-night, if it's at all possible. You know of any way I could go?'

For some time he was silent, watching me, with dread in his eyes.

'No, I don't,' he said presently. 'Ten mile to the ranch. And they ain't a soul lives on the road. The snow is nigh a foot deep. I doubt a car would make it. Ye might git Sam Judson to haul you over to-morrow in his wagon.'

'I wonder if he would take me out to-night?' I inquired.

The agent shook his head uneasily, peered nervously out at the glistening, moonlit desert of snow beyond the windows, and seemed to be listening anxiously. I remembered the wierd, distant howling I had heard as I walked across the platform, and could hardly restrain a shiver of my own.

'Naw, I think not!' Connell said abruptly. 'It ain't healthy to git out at night around here, lately.'

He paused a moment, and then asked suddenly, darting a quick, uneasy glance at my face, 'I reckon you heard the howlin'?'

'Yes. Wolves?'

'Yeah – anyhow, I reckon so. Queer. Damn queer! They ain't been any loafers around these parts for ten years, till we heard 'em jest after the last blizzard.' ('*Loafer*' appeared to be a local corruption of the Spanish word *lobo* applied to the gray prairie wolf, which is much larger than the coyote, and was a dreaded enemy of the rancher in the Southwest until its practical extermination.)

'Seems to be a reg'lar pack of the critters rovin' the range,' Connell went on. 'They've killed quite a few cattle in the last few weeks, and – ' he paused, lowering his voice, 'and five people!'

'The wolves have killed people!' I exclaimed.

'Yeah,' he said slowly. 'Josh Wells and his hand was took two weeks ago, come Friday, while they was out ridin' the range. And the Simms' are gone. The old man and – his woman and little Dolly. Took right out of the cow-pen, I reckon, while they was milkin'. It ain't two mile out of town to their place. Rufe Smith was out that way to see 'em Sunday. Cattle dead in the pen, and the smashed milk buckets lying in a drift of snow under the shed. And not a sign of Simms and his family!'

'I never heard of wolves taking people that way!' I was incredulous.

Connell shifted his wad of tobacco again, and whispered, 'I didn't neither. But, Mister, these here ain't ordinary wolves!'

'What do you mean?' I demanded.

'Well, after Simms' was took, we got up a sort of posse, and went out to hunt the critters. We didn't find no wolves. But we did find tracks in the snow. The wolves is plumb gone in the daytime!

'Tracks in the snow,' he repeated slowly, as if his mind were dwelling dazedly upon some remembered horror. 'Mister, them wolf tracks was too tarnation far apart to be made by any ordinary beast. The critters must 'a' been jumpin' thirty feet!

'And they warn't all wolf tracks, neither. Mister, part was wolf tracks. And part was tracks of bare human feet!'

With that, Connell fell silent, staring at me strangely, with a queer look of utter terror in his eyes.

I was staggered. There was, of course, some element of incredulity in my feelings. But the agent did not look at all like the man who has just perpetrated a successful wild story, for there was genuine horror in his eyes. And I recalled that I had fancied human tones in the strange, distant howling I had heard.

There was no good reason to believe that I had merely encountered a local superstition. Widespread as the legends of lycanthropy may be, I have yet to hear a whispered tale of werewolves related by a West Texan. And the agent's story had been too definite and concrete for me to imagine it an idle fabrication or an ungrounded fear.

'The message from my father was very urgent,' I told Connell presently. 'I *must* get out to the ranch to-night. If the man you mentioned won't take me, I'll hire a horse and ride.'

'Judson is a damn fool if he'll git out to-night where them wolves is!' the agent said with conviction. 'But there's nothing to keep ye from askin' him to go. I reckon he ain't gone to bed yet. He lives in the white house, jest around the corner behind Brice's store.'

He stepped out upon the platform behind me to point the way. And as soon as the door was opened, we heard again that rhythmic, deep, far-off ululation, that weirdly mournful howling, from far across the moonlit plain of snow. I could not repress a shudder. And Connell, after pointing out to me Sam Judson's house, among the straggling few that constituted the village of Hebron, got very hastily back inside the depot, and shut the door behind him.

2

The Pack that Ran by Moonlight

Sam Judson owned and cultivated a farm nearly a mile from Hebron, but had moved his house into the village so that his wife could keep the post-office. I hurried toward his house, through the icy streets, very glad that Hebron was able to afford the luxury of electric lights. The distant howling of the wolf-pack filled me with a vague and inexplicable dread. But it did not diminish my detrmination to reach my father's ranch as soon as possible, to solve the riddle of the strange and alarming telegram he had sent me.

Judson came to the door when I knocked. He was a heavy man, clad in faded, patched blue overalls, and brown flannel shirt. His head was almost completely bald, and his naked scalp was tanned until it resembled brown leather. His wide face was covered with a several week's growth of black beard. Nervously, fearfully, he scanned my face.

He led me to the kitchen, in the rear of the house – a small, dingy room, the walls covered with an untidy array of pots and pans. The cook stove was hot; he had, from appearances, been sitting with his feet in the oven, reading a newspaper, which now lay on the floor.

He had me sit down, and, when I took the creaking chair, I told him my name. He said that he knew my father, Dr. McLaurin, who got his mail at the post-office which was in the front room. But it had been three weeks, he said, since anyone had been to town from the ranch. Pehaps because the snow made traveling difficult, he said. There were five persons now staying out there, he told me. My father and Dr. Jetton, his daughter, Stella, and two hired mechanics from Amarillo.

I told him about the telegram, which I had received three days before. And he suggested that my father, if he had sent it, might have come to town at night, and mailed it to the telegraph office with the money necessary to send it. But he thought it strange that he had not spoken to anyone, or been seen.

Then I told Judson that I wanted him to drive me out to the ranch, at once. At the request his manner changed; he seemed frightened! 'No hurry about starting tonight, is there, Mr. McLaurin?' he asked. 'We can put you up in the spare room, and I'll take ye over in the wagon to-morrow. It's a long drive to make at night.'

'I'm very anxious to get there,' I said. 'I'm worried about my father. Something was wrong when he telegraphed. Very much wrong. I'll pay you enough to make it worth while.

'It ain't the money,' he told me. 'I'd be glad to do it for a son of Doc McLaurin's. But I reckon you heard – the wolves?'

'Yes, I heard them. And Connell, at the station, told me something about them. They've been hunting men?'

'Yes.' For a little time Judson was silent, staring at me with strange eyes from his hairy face. Then he said, 'And that ain't all. Some of us seen the tracks. And they's men runnin' with 'em!'

'But I must get out to see my father,' I insisted. 'We should be safe enough in a wagon. And I suppose you have a gun?'

'I have a gun, all right,' Judson admitted. 'But I ain't anxious to face them wolves!'

I insisted, quite ignorant of the peril into which I was dragging him. Finally, when I offered him fifty dollars for the trip, he capitulated. But he was going, he said – and I believed him – more to oblige a friend than for the money.

He went into the bedroom, where his wife was already asleep, roused her, and told her he was going to make the trip. She was rather startled, as I judged from the sound of her voice, but mollified when she learned that there was to be a profit of fifty dollars.

She got up, a tall and most singular figure in a purple flannel nightgown, with nightcap to match, and busied herself making us a pot of coffee on the hot stove, and finding blankets for us to wrap about us in the farm wagon, for the night was very cold. Judson, meanwhile, lit a kerosene lantern, which was hardly necessary in the brilliant moonlight, and went to the barn behind the house to get ready the vehicle.

Half an hour later we were driving out of the little village, in a light wagon, behind two gray horses. The hoofs broke through the crust of the snow at every step, and the wagon wheels cut into it steadily, with a curious crunching sound. Our progress was slow, and I anticipated a tedious trip of several hours.

We sat together on the spring seat, heavily muffled up, with blankets over our knees. The air was bitterly cold, but there was no wind, and I expected to be comfortable enough. Judson had strapped on an ancient revolver, and we had a repeating rifle and a double barrel shotgun leaning against our knees. But despite our arms, I could not quite succeed in quieting the vague fears raised by the wolf-pack, whose quavering, unearthly wail was never still.

Once outside the village of Hebron, we were surrounded on all sides by a white plain of snow, almost as level as a table-top. It was broken only by the insignificant rows of posts which supported wire fences; these fences seemed to be Judson's only land-marks. The sky was flooded with ghostly opalescence, and a million diamonds of frost glittered on the snow.

For perhaps an hour and a half, nothing remarkable happened. The lights of Hebron grew pale and faced behind us. We passed no habitation upon the illimitable desert of snow. The eery, heart-stilling ululation of the wolves, however, grew continually louder.

And presently the uncanny, wailing sounds changed position. Judson quivered beside me, and spoke nervously to the gray horses, plodding on through the snow. Then he turned to face me, spoke shortly.

'I figger they're sweeping in behind us, Mr. McLaurin,'

'Well, if they do, you can haul some of them back, to skin tomorrow,' I told him. I meant it to sound cheerful. But my voice was curiously dry, and its tones rang false in my ears.

For some minutes more we drove on in silence.

Suddenly I noticed a change in the cry of the pack.

The deep, strange rhythm of it was suddenly quickened. Its eery wailing plaintiveness seemed to give place to a quick, eager yelping. But it was still queerly unfamiliar. And there was something weirdly ventriloquial about it, so that we could not tell precisely from which direction it came. The rapid, belling notes seemed to come from a dozen points scattered over the brilliant, moonlit waste behind us.

The horses became alarmed. They pricked up their ears, looked back, and went on more eagerly. I saw that they were trembling. One of them snorted suddenly. The abrupt sound jarred my jangled nerves, and I clutched convulsively at the side of the wagon.

Judson held the reins firmly, with his feet braced against the end of the wagon box. He was speaking softly and soothingly to the quivering grays; but for that, they might already have been running. He turned to me and muttered:

'I've heard wolves. And they don't sound like that. Them ain't ordinary wolves!'

And as I listened fearfully to the terrible baying of the pack, I knew that he was right. Those strange ululations had an unfamiliar, an alien, note. There was a weird, terrible something about the howling that was not of this earth. It is hard to describe it, because it was so utterly foreign. It comes to me that if there are wolves on the ancient, age-dead deserts of Mars, they might cry in just that way, as they run some helpless creature to merciless death.

Malevolent were those belling notes, foul and hateful. Rioting with an infernal power of evil alien to this earth. Strong with the primal wickedness of the cosmic wastes.

'Reckon they are on the trail,' Judson said suddenly, in a low, strained voice. 'Look behind us.'

I turned in the spring seat, peered back over the limitless flat desolation of sparkling, moonlit snow. For a few minutes I strained my eyes in vain, though the terrible belling of the unseen pack grew swiftly louder.

Then I saw leaping gray specks, far behind us across the snow. By rights, a wolf should have floundered rather slowly through the thick snow, for the crust was not strong enough to hold up so heavy an animal. But the things I saw – fleet, formless gray shadows – were coming by great bounds, with astounding speed.

'I see them,' I told Judson tremulously.

'Take the lines,' he said pushing the reins at me, and snatching up the repeating rifle.

He twisted in the seat, and began to fire.

The horses were trembling and snorting. Despite the cold, sweat was raining from their heaving bodies. Abruptly, after Judson had begun to shoot, they took the bits in their teeth and bolted, plunging and floundering through the snow, dragging the wagon. Tug and jerk at the reins as I would, I could do nothing with them.

Judson had soon emptied the rifle. I doubt that he had hit any of the howling animals that ran behind us, for accurate shooting from the swaying, jolting wagon would have been impossible. And our wildly bounding pursuers would have been difficult marks, even if the wagon had been still.

Judson dropped the empty rifle into the wagon box, and turned a white, frightened face toward me. His mouth was open, his eyes protruding with terror. He shouted something incoherent, which I did not grasp, and snatched at the reins. Apparently insane with fear, he cursed the leaping grays, and lashed at them, as if thinking to outrun the pack.

For a little time I clung to the side of the rocking wagon. Then the snorting horses turned suddenly, almost breaking up the wagon tongue. We were nearly upset. The spring seat was dislodged from its position, and fell into the wagon box. I was thrown half over the side of the wagon. For another agonized moment I tried to scramble back. Then the grays plunged forward again, and I was flung into the snow.

I broke through the thin crust. The thick, soft snow beneath checked the force of my fall. In a few moments I had floundered to my feet, and was clawing madly at my face, to get the white, powdery stuff away from my eyes.

The wagon was already a hundred yards away. The fear-maddened horses were still running, with Judson standing erect in the wagon, sawing wildly at the reins, but powerless to curb them. They had been turning abruptly when I was thrown out.

Now they were plunging back toward the weirdly baying pack!

Judson, screaming and cursing, crazed with terror, was being carried back toward the dimly seen, gray, leaping shapes whose uncanny howling sobbed so dreadfully through the moonlight.

Horror came over me, like a great, soul-chilling wave. I felt an insane desire to run across the snow, to run and run until I could not hear the wailing of the strange pack. With an effort I controlled myself, schooled my trembling limbs, swallowed to wet my dry throat.

I knew that my poor, floundering run could never distance the amazingly fleet gray shapes that bounded through the silver haze of moonlight toward the wagon. And I reminded myself that I had a weapon on, a .25 caliber automatic pistol, slung beneath my shoulder. Something about the strange message from my father had made me fasten on the deadly little weapon, and slip a few extra clips of ammunition into my pockets.

With trembling hands, I pulled off a glove and fumbled inside my garments for the little weapon.

At last I drew out the heavy little automatic, gratefully warm with the heat of my body, and snapped back the slide to be sure that a cartridge was in the chamber. Then I stood there, in a bank of powdery snow that came nearly to my knees, and waited.

The dismal, alien howling of the pack froze me into a queer paralysis of fear. And then I was the horrified spectator of a ghastly tragedy.

The wagon must have been four hundred yards from me, across the level, glistening snow, when the dim gray shapes of the baying pack left the trail and ran straight across toward it. I saw little stabs of yellow flame, heard sharp reports of guns, and the thin, whistling screams of bullets. Judson, I suppose, had dropped the reins and was trying to defend himself with the rifle and shotgun, and his old fashioned revolver.

The vague gray shapes surrounded the wagon. I heard the scream of an agonized horse – except for the unearthly howling of that pack, the most terrible, nerve-wracking sound I know. A struggling mass of faintly seen figures seemed to surround the wagon. There were a few more shots, then a shriek, which rang fearfully over the snow, bearing an agony of pain and terror that is inconceivable . . . . I knew it came from Judson.

After that, the only sound was the strange, blood-congealing belling of the pack – an awful outcry that had not been stilled.

Soon – fearfully soon – that alien ululation seemed to be drawing nearer. And I saw gray shapes come bounding down the trail, away from the grim scene of the tragedy – toward me!

3

The Wolf and the Woman

I can give no conception of the stark, maddened terror that seized me when I knew that the gray animals were running on my trail. My heart seemed to pause, until I thought I would grow dizzy and fall. Then it was thumping loudly in my throat. My body was suddenly cold with sweat. My muscles knotted until I was gripping the automatic with painful force.

I had determined not to run, for it was madness to try to escape the pack. But my resolution to stand my ground was nothing in the face of the fear that obsessed me.

I plunged across the level waste of snow. My feet broke through the thin crust. I floundered along, wth laboring lungs. The snow seemed tripping me like a malevolent demon. Many times I stumbled, it seemed. And twice I sprawled in the snow, and scrambled desperately to my feet, and struggled on again, sobbing with terror, gasping in the cold air.

But my flight was cut short. The things that ran behind me could travel many times faster than I. Turning, when I must have gone less than a hundred yards, I saw them drawing near behind me, still vague gray shapes in the moonlight. I now perceived that only two had followed.

Abruptly I recalled the little automatic in my hand. I raised it, and emptied it, firing as rapidly as I could. But if I hit either of those bounding gray figures, they certainly were invulnerable to my bullets.

I had sought in my pocket for another clip, and was trying with quivering fingers to slip it into the gun, when those things came near enough, in a milky haze of moonlight, to be seen distinctly. Then my hands closed in rigid paralysis upon the gun – I was too astounded and unstrung to complete the operation of loading.

One of those two gray shapes was a wolf. A gaunt prairie wolf, covered with long, shaggy hair. A huge beast, he must have stood three feet high at the shoulder. He was not standing now, however, but coming toward me with great leaps that covered many yards. His great eyes glowed with a weird, greenish, unnatural light – terrible and strange and somehow hypnotic.

And the other was a girl.

It was incredible. It numbed and staggered my terror-dazed mind. At first I thought it must be a hallucination. But as she came nearer, advancing with long, bounding steps, as rapidly as the gray wolf, I could no longer discredit my eyes. I recalled the weird suggestion of a human voice I had caught in the unearthly cry of the pack; recalled what Connell and Judson had told me of human footprints mingled with those of the wolves in the trail the pack had left.

She was clad very lightly, to be abroad in the bitter cold of the winter night. Apparently, she wore only a torn, flimsy slip, of thin white silk, which hung from one shoulder, and came not quite to her knees. Her head was bare, and her hair, seeming in the moonlight to be an odd, pale yellow, was short and tangled. Her smooth arms and small hands, her legs, and even her flashing feet, were bare. Her skin was white, with cold, leprous, bloodless whiteness. Almost as white as the snow.

And her eyes shone green.

They were like the gray wolf's eyes, blazing with a terrible emerald flame, with the fire of an alien, unearthly life. They were malevolent, merciless, hideous. They were cold as the cosmic wastes beyond the light of stars. They burned with an evil light, with a malicious intelligence, stronger and more fearful than that of any being on earth.

Across her lips, and her cheeks of alabaster whiteness, was a darkly red and dripping smear, almost black by moonlight.

I stood like a wooden man, nerveless with incredulous horror.

On came the girl and the wolf, springing side by side through the snow. They seemed to have preternatural strength, an agility beyond that of nature.

As they came nearer, I received another shock of terror.

The woman's face was familiar, for all its dreadful pallor and the infernal evil of the green, luminous eyes, and the red stain on her lips and cheeks.She was a girl whom I had known. A girl whom I had admired, whom I had even dreamed that I might come to love.

She was Stella Jetton!

This girl was the lovely daughter of Dr. Blake Jetton, whom, as I have said, my father had brought with him to this Texas ranch, to assist with his revolutionary experiments.

It came to me that she had been changed in some fearful way. For this could be no sane, ordinary human girl – this strange, green-eyed being, half-clad, white-skinned, who ran over the moonlit snow beside a gaunt gray wolf, with dripping red upon her fearfully pallid skin!

'Stella!' I cried.

More a scream of frightened, anguished unbelief, than a human voice, the name came from my fear-parched throat. I was startled at my own call, hoarse, inchoate, gasping.

The huge gray wolf came directly at me, as if it were going to spring at my throat. But it stopped a dozen feet before me, crouching in the snow, watching me with alert and strange intelligence in its dreadful green eyes.

And the woman came even nearer, before she paused, standing with bare feet in the snow, and stared at me with terrible eyes like those of the wolf – luminous and green and filled with an evil, alien will.

The face, ghastly white, and fearfully red-stained as it was, was the face of Stella Jetton. But the eyes were not hers! No, the eyes were not Stella's!

They were the eyes of some hideous monstrosity. The eyes of some inconceivable, malevolent entity, from some frozen hell of the far off, night-black cosmic void!

Then she spoke. The voice had some little of its old, familiar ring. But there was a new, strange note in it. A note that bore the foreign, menacing mystery of the eyes and the leprous skin. A note that had a suggestion of the dismal, wailing ululation of the pack that had followed us.

'Yes, Stella Jetton,' the dreadful voice said. 'What are you called? Are you Clovis McLaurin? Did you receive a telegram?'

She did not know me, apparently. Even the wording of her sentences was a little strange, as if she were speaking a language with which she was not very familiar. The delightful, human girl I had known was fearly changed: it was as if her fair body had been seized by some demoniac entity.

It occurred to me that she must be afflicted with some form of insanity, which had given her the almost preternatural strength which she had displayed in running with the wolf-pack. Cases of lycanthropy, in which the suffered imagines himself a wolf – or sometimes a tiger or some other animal – and imitates its actions, have been common enough in the annals of the insane. But if this is lycanthropy, I thought, it must indeed be a singular case.

'Yes, I'm Clovis McLaurin,' I said, in a shaken voice. 'I got Dad's telegram three days ago. Tell me what's wrong – why he worded the message as he did!'

'Nothing is wrong, my friend,' this strange woman said. 'We merely desired your assistance with certain experiments, of a great strangeness, which we are undertaking to perform. Your father now waits at the ranch, and I came to conduct you to him.'

This singular speech was almost incredible. I could accept it only on the assumption that the speaker suffered from some dreadful derangement of the mind.

'You came to meet me?' I exclaimed, fighting the horror that almost overwhelmed me. 'Stella, you mustn't be out in the cold without more wraps. You must take my coat.'

I began to strip off the garment. But, as I had somehow expected, she refused to accept it.

'No, I do not need it,' her strange voice told me. 'The cold does not harm this body. And you must come with us, now. Your father waits for us at the house, to perform the great experiment.'

She said *us!* It gave me now horror to notice that she thus classed the huge gaunt wolf with herself.

Then she sprang forward with an incredible agility, leaping through the snow in the direciton in which Judson and I had been traveling. With a naked, dead-white arm, she beckoned me to follow. And the great, gray wolf sprang behind me.

Nerved to sudden action, I recalled the half-loaded automatic in my hand. I snapped the fresh clip into position, jerked back the slide mechanism to get a cartridge into the breech, and then emptied the gun into that green-orbed wolf.

A strange composure had come over me. My motions were calm enough, almost deliberate. I know that my hand did not shake. The wolf was standing still, only a few yards away. It is unlikely that I missed him at all, impossible that I missed him with every shot.

I know that I hit him several times, for I heard the bullets drive into his gaunt body, saw the animal jerk beneath their impact, and noticed gray hairs float from it in the moonlight.

But he did not fall. His terrible green eyes never wavered in their sinister stare of infernal evil.

Just as the gun was empty — it had taken me only a few seconds to fire the seven shots — I heard an angry, wolfish snarl from the woman, from the strange monster that Stella Jetton had become. I had half turned when her white body came hurtling at me like a projectile.

I went down beneath her, instinctively raising an arm to guard my throat. It is well that I did, for I felt her teeth sinking into my arm and shoulder, as we fell together into the snow.

I am sure that I screamed with the horror of it.

I fought at her madly, until I heard her strange, non-human voice again.

'You need not be afraid,' it said. 'We are not going to kill you. We wish you to aid with a greatly remarkable experiment. For that reason, you must come with us. Your father waits. The wolf is our friend, and will not harm you. And your weapon will not hurt it.'

A curious, half-articulate yelp came from the throat of the great wolf, which had not moved since I shot at it, as if it had understood her words and gave affirmation.

The woman was still upon me, holding me flat in the snow, her bared, bloody teeth above my face, her fingers sunk claw-like into my body with almost preternatural strength. A low, bestial, growling sound came from her throat, and then she spoke again.

'You will now come with us, to the house where your father waits, to perform the experiment?' she demanded in that terrible voice, with its suggestion of the wolf-pack's weird cry.

'I'll come,' I agreed, relieved somewhat to discover that the strange pair of beasts did not propose to devour me on the spot.

The woman – I cannot call her Stella, for except in body, she was not Stella! – helped me to my feet. She made no objection when I bent, and picked up the automatic, which lay in the snow, and slipped it into my coat pocket.

She and the gaunt gray wolf, which my bullets had so strangely failed to kill, leaped away together over the moonlit snow. I followed, floundering along as rapidly as I could, my mind filled with confused and terror-numbed conjecture.

There was now no doubt remaining in my mind that the woman thought herself a member of the wolf-pack, no doubt that she actually was a member. A curious sympathy certainly seemed to exist between her and the great gaunt wolf beside her.

It must be some strange form of lunacy, I thought, though I had never read of a lycanthrope whose symptoms were exaggerated to the terrible extent that hers appeared to be. It is well known that maniacs have unnatural strength, but her feats of running and leaping across the snow were almost beyond reason.

But there was that about her which even the theory of insanity did not explain. The corpse-like pallor of her skin; the terrible green luminosity of her eyes; the way she spoke – as if English were an unfamiliar tongue to her, but half mastered. And there was something even more indefinite: a strangeness that smacked of the alien life of forbidden universes!

The pace set for me by the woman and the wolf was mercilessly rapid. Stumble along as best I could, I was unable to move as fast as they wished. Nor was I allowed to fall behind, for when I lagged, the wolf came back, and snarled at me menacingly.

Before I had floundered along many miles, my lungs were aching, and I was half blind with fatigue. I stumbled and sprawled in the soft snow a last time. My tortured muscles refused to respond when I tried to rise. I lay there, ready to endure whatever the wolf might do, rather than undergo the agony of further effort.

But this time the woman came back. I was half unconscious, but I realized vaguely that she was lifting me, raising me to her shoulders. After that, my eyes were closed; I was too weary to watch my surroundings. But I knew dimly, from my sensations of swaying, that I was being carried.

Presently the toxins of exhaustion overcame my best efforts to keep my senses. I fell into the deep sleep of utter fatigue, forgetting that my limbs were growing very cold, and that I was being borne upon the back of a woman endowed with the instincts of a wolf and the strength of a demon; a woman who, when I had last seen her, had been all human and lovable!

4

A Strange Homecoming

Never can I forget the sensations of my awakening. I opened my eyes upon gloom relieved but faintly by dim red light. I lay upon a bed or couch, swathed in blankets. Hands that even to my chilled body seemed ice-cold were chafing my arms and legs. And terrible greenish orbs were swimming above in the terrible crimson darkness, staring down at me, horribly.

Alarmed, recalling what had happened in the moonlight as a vague, hideous nightmare, I collected my scattered senses, and struggled to a sitting position among the blankets.

It is odd, but the first definite thing that came to my confused brain was an impression of the ugly green flowers in monotonous rows across the dingy, brown-stained wall paper. In the red light that filled the room, they appeared unpleasantly black, but still they awakened an ancient memory. I knew that I was in the dining room of the old ranch house where I had come to spend two years with my uncle, Tom McLaurin, many years before.

The weirdly illuminated chamber was sparsely furnished. The couch upon which I lay stood against one wall. Opposite was a long table, with half a dozen chairs pushed under it. Near the end of the room was a large heating stove, with a full scuttle of coal and a box of split pine kindling behind it.

There was no fire in the stove, and the room was very cold. My breath was a white cloud in that frosty atmosphere. The dim crimson light came from a small electric lantern standing on the long table. It had been fitted with a red bulb, probably for use in a photographer's dark room.

All these impressions I must have gathered almost subconsciously, for my horrified mind was absorbed with the persons in the room.

My father was bending over me, rubbing my hands, and Stella was chafing my feet, which stuck out beneath the blankets.

And my father was changed as weirdly, as dreadfully, as the girl, Stella!

His skin was a cold, bloodless white – white with the pallor of death. His hands, against my own felt fearfully cold – as cold as those of a frozen corpse. And his eyes, watching me with a strange, terrible alertness, shone with a greenish light.

His eyes were like Stella's – and like those of the great gray wolf. They were agleam with the fire of cosmic evil, with the light of an alien, hellish intelligence!

And the woman – the dread thing that had been lovely Stella – was unchanged. Her skin was still fearfully pallid, and her eyes strange and luminously green. The stain was still on her pale face, appearing black in the somber crimson light.

There was no fire in the stove. But, despite the bitter cold of the room, the woman was still clad as she had been before, in a sheer slip of white silk, half torn from her white body. My father – or that which had once been my father – wore only a light cotton shirt, with the sleeves torn off, and a pair of ragged trousers. His feet and arms were bare.

Another fearful thing I noticed. My breath, as I said condensed in white clouds of frozen crystals, in the frigid air. But no white mists came from Stella's nostrils, or from my father's.

From outside, I could hear the dismal, uncanny keening of the running pack. And from time to time the two looked uneasily toward the door, as if anxious to go to join them.

I had been sitting up, staring confusedly and incredulously about, before my father spoke.

'We are glad to see you, Clovis,' he said, rather stiffly, and without emotion, not at all in his usual jovial, affectionate manner. 'You seem to be cold. But you will presently be normal again. We have surprising need of you, in the performance of an experiment, which we cannot accomplish without your assistance.'

He spoke slowly, uncertainly, as a foreigner might who had attempted to learn English from a dictionary. I was at a loss to understand it, even if I assumed that he and Stella both suffered from a mental derangement.

And his voice was somehow whining; it carried a note weirdly suggestive of the howling of the pack.

'You will help us?' Stella demanded in the same dreadful tones.

'Explain it! Please explain everything!' I burst out. 'Or I'll go crazy! Why were you running with the wolves? Why are your eyes so bright and green, your skins so deathly white? Why are you both so cold? Why the red light? Why don't you have a fire?'

I babbled my questions, while they stood there in the strange room, and silently stared at me with their horrible eyes.

For minutes, perhaps, they were silent. Then an expression of crafty intelligence came into my father's eyes, and he spoke again in those fearful tones, with their ring of the baying pack.

'Clovis,' he said, 'you know we came here for purposes of studying science. And a great discovery has been ours to make; a huge discovery relating to the means of life. Our bodies, they are changed, as you appear to see. Better machines they have become; stronger they are. Cold harms them not, as it does yours. Even our sight is better, so bright lights we no longer need.

'But we are yet lacking of perfect success. Our minds were changed, so that we do not remember all that once it had been ours to accomplish. And it is you whom we desire to be our assistant in replacing a machine of ours, that has been broken. It is you that we wish to aid us, so that to all humanity we may bring the gift of the new life, that is ever strong, and knows not death. All people we would change with the new science that it has been ours to discover.'

'You mean you want to make the human race into monsters like yourselves?' I cried.

My father snarled ferociously, like a beast of prey.

'All men will receive the gift of life like ours,' his strange voice said. 'Death will be no more. And your aid is required by us – and it we will have!' There was intense, malefic menace in his tones. 'It is yours to be our aid. You will refuse not!'

He stood before me with bared teeth and with white fingers hooked like talons.

'Sure, I'll help you,' I contrived to utter, in a shaken voice. 'I'm not a very brilliant experimenter, however.' It appeared that to refuse would be a means of committng very unpleasant suicide.

Triumphant cunning shone in those menacing green eyes, the evil cunning of the maniac who had just perpetrated a clever trick. But it was even more than that; it was the crafty look of supreme evil in contemplation of further victory.

'You can come now, in order to see the machine?' Stella demanded.

'No,' I said hastily, and sought reasons for delay. 'I am cold. I must light a fire and warm myself. Then I am hungry, and very tired. I must eat and sleep.' All of which was very true. My body had been chilled through, durng my hours on the snow. My limbs were trembling with cold.

The two looked at each other. Unearthly sounds passed between them, incoherent, animal whinings. Such, instead of words, seemed to be their natural speech; the English they spoke seemed only an inaccurately and recently learned tongue.

'True,' my father said to me again, in a moment. He looked at the stove. 'Start a fire if you must. What you need is there?' He pointed inquiringly toward coal and kindling, as if fire were something new and unfamiliar to him.

'We must go without,' he added, 'Light of fire is hurtful to us, as cold is to you. And in other room, called – ' he hesitated perceptibly, 'kitchen will be food. There we will wait.'

He and the white girl glided silently from the room.

Shivering with cold, I hurried to the stove. All the coals in it were dead; there had been nor fire in it for many hours, none, perhaps, for several days. I shook down the ashes, lit a ball of crumpled newspaper with a match I found in my pocket, dropped it on the grate, and filled the stove with pine and coal. In a few minutes I had a roaring fire, before which I crouched gratefully.

In a few minutes the door was opened slowly. Stella, first peering carefully, apparently to see if there was light in the room, stepped cautiously inside. The stove was tightly closed, no light escaped from it.

The pallid, green-eyed woman had her arms full of food, a curious assortment that had evidently been collected in the kitchen in a haphazard manner. There were two loaves of bread, a slab of raw bacon, an unopened can of coffee, a large sack of salt, a carton of oatmeal, a can of baking powder, a dozen tins of canned foods, and even a bottle of stove polish.

'You eat this?' she inquired, in her strangely animal voice, dropping the articles on the table.

It was almost ludicrous; and too, it was somehow terrible. She seemed to have no conception of human alimentary needs.

Comfortably warm again, and feeling very hungry, I went over to the table, and examined the odd assortment. I selected a loaf of bread, a tin of salmon, and one of the apricots, for my immediate use.

'Some of these things are to be eaten as they are,' I ventured, wondering what her response would be. 'And some of them have to be cooked.'

'Cooked?' she demanded quickly. 'What is that?'

Then, while I was silent, dazed with astonishment, she added a terrible question.

'Does it convey that they must be hot and bleeding from the animal?'

'No!' I cried. 'No. To cook a food one heats it. Usually adding seasonings, such as salt. A rather complicated process, requiring considerable skill.'

'I see,' she said. 'And you must consume such articles, to keep your body whole?'

I admitted that I did, and then remarked that I needed a can cutter, to get at the food in the tins. First inquiring about the appearance of the implement, she hurried to the kitchen, and soon returned with one.

Presently my father came back into the room. Both of them watched me with their strange green eyes as I ate. My appetite failed somewhat, but I drew the meal out as long as possible, in order to defer whatever they might intend for me after I had finished.

Both of them asked many questions. Questions similar to Stella's query about cooking, touching subjects with which an ordinary child is familiar. But they were not stupid questions – no indeed! Both of them evinced a cleverness that was almost preternatural. They never forgot, and I was astounded at their skill in piecing together the facts I gave them, to form others.

Their green eyes watched me very curiously when, unable to drag out the pretense of eating any longer, I produced a cigarette and sought a match to light it. Both of them howled, as if in agony, when the feeble yellow flame of the match flared up. They covered their strange green eyes, and leaped back, cowering and trembling.

'Kill it!' my father snarled ferociously.

I flicked out the tiny flame, startled at its results.

They uncovered their terrible green eyes, blinking. It was several minutes before they seemed completely recovered from their amazing fear of the light.

'Make light no more when we are near,' my father growled at
me. 'We will tear your body if you forget!' His teeth were bared;
his lips curled like those of a wolf; he snarled at me frightfully.

Stella ran to an east window, raised the blind, peered nervously
out. I saw that the dawn was coming. She whined strangely at my
father. He seemed uneasy, like an animal at bay. His huge green
eyes rolled from side to side. He turned anxiously to me.

'Come,' he said 'the machine which we with your aid will
repair is in the cellar beneath the house. The day comes. We must
go.'

'I cant' go,' I said. 'I'm dog tired; been up all night. I've got to
rest, before I work on any machine. I'm so sleepy I can't think.'

He whined curiusly at Stella again, as if he were speaking in
some strange wolf-tongue. She replied in kind, then spoke to me.

'If rest is needful to the working of your body, you may sleep
till the light is gone. Follow.'

She opened the door at the end of the room, led me into a dark
hall, and from it into a small bedroom. It contained a narrow bed,
two chairs, a dresser, and wardrobe trunk.

'Try not to go,' she snarled warningly, at the door, 'or we will
follow you over the snow!'

The door closed and I was alone. A key grated ominously in the
lock. The little room was cold and dark. I scrambled hastily into
the bed, and for a time I lay there, listening.

The dreadful howling of the wolf-pack, which had never stilled
through all the night, seemed to be growing louder, drawing
nearer. Presently it ceased, with a few sharp, whining yelps,
apparently just outside the window. The pack had come here,
with the dawn!

As the increasing light of day filled the little room, I raised my
self in the bed to scrutinize its contents again. It was a neat
chamber, freshly papered. The dresser was covered with a gay silk
scarf, and on it, in orderly array, were articles of the feminine
toilet. A few dresses, a vivid beret, and a bright sweater were
hanging under a curtain in the corner of the room. On the wall
was a picture – of myself!

It came to me that this must be Stella's room, into which I had
been·locked to sleep until night had come again. But what weird
and horrible thing had happened to the girl since I had seen her
last?

Presently I examined the windows with a view to escape. There
were two of them, facing the east. Heavy wooden bars had been

fastened across them, on the outside, so close together that I could not hope to squeeze between them. And a survey of the room revealed no object with which they could be easily sawed.

But I was too sleepy and exhausted to attempt escape. At thought of the ten weary miles to Hebron, through the thick, soft snow, I abandoned the idea. I knew that, tired as I already was, I could never cover the distance in the short winter day. And I shuddered at the thought of being caught on the snow by the pack.

I lay down again in Stella's clean bed, about which a slight fragrance of perfume still lingered, and was soon asleep. My slumber, though deep, was troubled. But no nightmare could be as hideous as the reality from which I had found a few hour's escape.

5

The Machine in the Cellar

I slept through most of the short winter day. When I woke it was sunset. Gray light fell athwart the illimitable flat desert of snow outside my barred windows, and the pale disk of the moon, near the full, was rising in the darkening eastern sky. No human habitation was in view, in all the stretching miles of that white waste. I felt a sharp sense of utter loneliness.

I could look for no outside aid in coping with the strange and alarming situation into which I had stumbled. If I were to escape from these dread monsters who wore the bodies of those dearest to me, it must be by my own efforts. And in my hands alone rested the task of finding from what evil malady they suffered, and how to restore them to their old, dear selves.

Once more I examined the stout wooden bars across the windows. They seem strongly nailed to the wall on either side. I found no tool that looked adequate to cutting them. My matches were still in my pocket, however, and it occurred to me that I might burn the bars. But there was no time for such an undertaking before darkness would bring back my captors, nor did I relish the thought of attempting to escape with the pack on my trail.

I was hungry again, and quite thirsty also.

Darkness fell, as I lay there on the bed, among the intimate belongings of a lovely girl for whom I had owned tender feelings –

waiting for her to come with the night amid her terrible allies, to drag me to I know what dread fate.

The gray light of day faded imperceptibly into pale silvery moonlight.

Apruptly, without warning, the key turned in the lock.

Stella – or the alien entity that ruled the girl's fair body – glided with sinister grace into the room. Her green eyes were shining, and her skin was ghastly white.

'Immediately you will follow,' came her wolfish voice. 'The machine below awaits the aid for you to give in the great experiment. Quickly come. Your weak body, it is rested?'

'All right,' I said. 'I've slept, of course. But now I'm hungry and thirsty again. I've got to have water or something to eat before I tinker with any machine.'

I was determined to postpone whatever ordeal lay before me as long as possible.

'Your body you may satisfy again,' the woman said. 'But take not too long!' she snarled warningly.

I followed her back to the dining room.

'Get water,' she said, and glided out the door.

The stove was still fairly warm. I opened it, stirred the coals, dropped in more fuel. Soon the fire was roaring again. I turned my attention to the food I had left. The remainder of the salmon and apricots had frozen on the plates, and I set them over the stove to warm.

Soon Stella was back with a water bucket containing a bulging mass of ice. Apparently surprised that I could not consume water in a solid form, she allowed me to set it on the stove to thaw.

While I waited, standing by the stove, she asked innumerable questions, many of them so simple they would have been laughable under less strange conditions, some of them concerning the latest and most recondite of scientific theories, her mastery of which seemed to exceed my own.

My father appeared suddenly, his corpse-white arms full of books. He spread them on the table, curtly bid me come look with him. He had Einstein's 'The Meaning of Relativity,' Weyl's 'Gravitation und Elektricität,' and two of his own privately printed works. The latter were 'Space-Time Tensors' and the volume of mathematical speculation entitled 'Interlocking Universes' whose bizarre implications created such a sensation among those savants to whom he sent copies.

My father began opening these books, and bombarding me with questions about them, questions which I was often unable to answer. But the greater part of his queries related merely to grammar, or the meaning of words. The involved thought seemed easy for him to understand; it was the language which caused him difficulty.

His questions were exactly such as might be asked by a super-intellectual being from Mars, if he were attempting to read a scientific library without having completely mastered the language in which its books were written.

And his own books seemed as unfamiliar to him as those of the other scientists. But he ran through the pages with amazing speed, pausing only to ask an occasional question, and appeared to gain a complete mastery of the volume as he went.

When he released me, the food and water were warm. I drank, and then ate bread and salmon and apricots, as deliberately as I dared. I invited the two to share the food with me, but they declined abruptly. The volley of questions continued.

Then suddenly, evidently concluding that I had eaten enough, they started toward the door, commanding me to follow. I dared not do otherwise. My father paused at the end of the table and picked up the electric lantern, whose dimly glowing red bulb supplied the only light in the room.

Again we traversed the dark hall, and went out through a door in the rear of the frame building. As we stepped out upon the moonlit snow, I shuddered to hear once more the distant, wailing ululation of the pack, still with that terrible note which suggested strained human vocal organs.

A few feet from us was the door of a cellar. The basement had evidently been considerably enlarged, quite recently, for huge mounds of earth lay about us, filling the back yard. Some of them were covered with snow, some of them black and bare.

The two led the day down the steps into the cellar, my father still carrying the electric lantern, which faintly illuminated the midnight space with its feeble, crimson glow.

The cellar was large, neatly plastered. It had not been itself enlarged, but a dark passage sloped down beside the door, to deeper excavations.

In the center of the floor stood the wreck of an intricate and unfamiliar mechanism. It had evidently been deliberately smashed – I saw an ax lying beside it, which must have been the means of the havoc. The concrete floor was littered with the broken glass of shattered electron tubes. The machine itself was a mass of tangled wires and twisted coils and bent magnets, oddly arranged outside a great copper ring, perhaps four feet in diameter.

The huge copper ring was mounted on its edge, in a metal frame. Before it was a stone step, placed as if to be used by one climbing through the ring. But, I saw, it had been impossible for one actually to climb through, for on the opposite side was a mass of twisted apparatus – a great parabolic mirror of polished metal, with what appeared to be a broken cathode tube screwed into its center.

A most puzzling machine. And it had been very thoroughly wrecked. Save for the huge copper ring, and the heavy stone step before it, there was hardly a part that was not twisted or shattered.

In the end of the cellar was a small motor generator – a little gasoline engine connected to a dynamo – such as is sometimes used for supplying isolated homes with electric light and power. I saw that it had not been injured.

From a bench beside the wall, my father picked up a brief case, from which he took a roll of blue prints, and a sheaf of papers bound in a manila cover. He spread them on the bench and set the red lantern beside them.

'This machine, as you see, has been, most unfortunately for us, wrecked,' he said. 'These papers tell the method of construction to be followed in the erection of such machines. Your aid we must have in deciphering what they convey. And the new machine will bring such great, strong life as we have to all your world.'

'You say 'your world'!' I cried 'Then you don't belong to this earth? You are a monster, who has stolen the body of my father!'

Both of them snarled like beasts. They bared their teeth and glowered at me with their terrible green eyes. Then a crafty look came again into the man's sinister orbs.

'No, my son,' came his whining, animal tones. 'A new secret of life have we discovered. Great strength it gives to our bodies. Death we fear no longer. But our minds are changed. Many things we do not remember. We must require your aid in reading this which we once wrote – '

'That's the bunk!' I exclaimed, perhaps not very wisely. 'I don't believe it. And I'll be damned if I'll help repair the infernal machine, to make more human beings into monsters like you!'

Together they sprang toward me. Their eyes glowed dreadfully against their pallid skins. Their fingers were hooked like claws. Saliva drooled from their snarling lips, and naked teeth gleamed in the dim crimson radiance.

'Aid us you will!' cried my father. 'Or your body will we most painfully destroy. We will eat it slowly, while you live!'

The horror of it broke down my reason. With a wild, terror-shaken scream, I dashed for the door.

It was hopeless, of course, for me to attempt to escape from beings possessing such preternatural strength.

With startling, soul-blasting howls, they sprang after me together. They swept me to the cellar's floor, sinking their teeth savagely into my arms and body. For a few moments I struggled desperately, writhing and kicking, guarding my throat with one arm and striking blindly with the other.

Then they held me helpless. I could only curse, and scream a vain appeal for aid.

The woman, holding my arms pinioned against my sides, lifted me easily, flung me over her shoulder. Her body, where it touched mine, was as cold as ice. I struggled fiercely but uselessly as she started with me down the black, inclined passage, into the recent excavations beneath the cellar's floor.

Behind us, my father picked up the little red lantern, and the blue prints and sheets of specifications, and followed down the dark, slanting passage.

6

The Temple of Crimson Gloom

Helpless in those preternaturally strong, corpse-cold and corpse-white arms, I was carried down narrow steps, to a high, subterranean hall. It was filled with a dim blood-red light, which came from no visible source, its angry, forbidding radiance seeming to spring from the very air. The walls of the underground hall were smooth and black, of some unfamiliar ebon substance.

Several yards down that black, strangely illuminated passage I was carried. Then we came into a larger space. Its black roof, many yards above, was groined and vaulted, supported by a double row of massive dead-black pillars. Many dark, arched niches were cut into its walls. This greater hall, too, was sullenly illuminated by a ghastly scarlet light, which seemed to come from nowhere.

A strange, silent, awful place. A sort of cathedral of darkness, of evil and death. A sinister atmosphere of nameless terror seemed breathed from its very midnight walls, like the stifling fumes of incense offered to some formless god of horror. The dusky red light might have come from unseen tapers burned in forbidden rites of blood and death. The dead silence itself seemed a tangible, evil thing, creeping upon me from ebon walls.

I was given little time to speculate upon the questions that it raised. What was the dead-black material of the walls? Whence came the lurid, bloody radiance? How recently had this strange temple of terror been made? And to what demoniac god was it consecrated? No opportunity had I to seek answers to those questions, nor time even to recover from my natural astonishment at finding such a place beneath the soil of a Texas ranch.

The emerald-eyed woman who bore me dropped me to the black floor, against the side of a jet pillar, which was round and two feet thick. She whined shrilly, like a hungry dog. It was evidently a call, for two men appeared in the broad central aisle of the temple, which I faced.

Two men – or, rather malevolent monstrosities in the bodies of men. Their eyes shone with green fires alien to our world, and their bodies, beneath their tattered rags of clothing, were fearfully white. One of them came toward me with a piece of frayed manila rope, which must have been a lasso they had found above.

Later it came to me that these two must be the mechanics from the city of Amarillo, who, Judson had told me on the evening of our fatal drive, had been employed here by my father. I had not yet seen Dr. Blake Jetton, Stella's father, who had been the chief assistant of my own parent in various scientific investigations – investigations which, I now began to fear, must have borne dreadful fruit!

While the woman held me against the black pillar, the men seized my arms, stretched them behind it, and tied them with the rope. I kicked out, struggled, cursed them, in vain. My body seemed but putty to their fearful strength. When my hands were tied behind the pillar, another length of the rope was dropped about my ankles and drawn tight about the ebon shaft.

I was helpless in this wierd, subterranean temple, at the mercy of these four creatures who seemed to combine infernal super-intelligence with the strength and the nature of wolves.

'See the instrument which we are to build!' came the snarling voice of my father. Standing before me, with the roll of blue prints in his livid hands, he pointed at an object that I had not yet distinguished in the sullen, bloody gloom.

In the center of the lofty, central hall of this red-lit temple, between the twin rows of looming, dead-black pillars, was a long, low platform of ebon stone. From it rose a metal frame — wrought like the frame of the wrecked machine I had seen in the cellar, above.

The frame supported a huge copper ring in a vertical position. It was far huger than the ring in the ruined mechanism; its diameter was a dozen feet or more. Its upper curve reached far toward the black, vaulted roof of the hall, glistening queerly in the ghastly red light. Behind the ring, a huge, parabolic mirror of silvery, polished metal had been set up.

But the device was obviously unfinished.

The complex electron tubes, the delicate helixes and coils, the magnets, and the complicated array of wires, whose smashed and tangled remains I had observed about the wreck of the other machine, had not been installed.

'Look at that!' cried my father again. 'The instrument that comes to let upon your earth the great life that is ours. The plan on this paper, we made. From the plan, we made the small machine, and brought to ourselves the life, the strength, the love of blood — '

'The love of blood!' My startled, anguished outcry must have been a shriek, for I was already nearly overcome with the brooding terror of my strange surroundings. I collapsed against the ropes, shaken and trembling with fear.

The light of strange cunning came once more into the glaring green eyes of the thing that had been my father.

'No, fear not!' he whined on. 'Your language it is new to me, and I speak what I do not intend. Be not fearing — if you will do our wish. If you do not, then we will taste your blood.

'But the new life came only to few. Then the machine broke, because of one man. And our brains are changed, so that we remember not to read the plans that we made. Your aid is ours, to restore a new machine. To you and all your world, then, comes the great new life!'

He stepped close to me, his green eyes burning malevolently. Before my eyes he unrolled one of the sheets which bore plans and specifications for the strange electron tubes, to be mounted outside the copper ring. From his lips came the curious, wolfish whine with which these monsters communicated with one another. One of the weirdly transformed mechanics stepped up beside him, carrying in dead-white hands the parts of such a tube – filaments, plate, grid, screens, auxiliary electrodes, and the glass tube in which they were to be sealed. The parts evidently had been made to fit the specifications – as nearly as these entities could comprehend those specifications with their imperfect knowledge of English.

'We make fit plans for these parts,' my father whined. 'If wrong, you must say where wrong. Describe how to put together. Speak quick, or die slowly!' He snarled menacingly.

Though I am by no means a brilliant physicist, I saw easily enough that most of the parts were useless, though they had been made with amazing accuracy. These beings seemed to have no knowledge of the fundamental principles underlying the operation of the machine they were attempting to build, yet, in making these parts, they had accomplished feats that would have been beyond the power of our science.

The filament was made of metal, well enough – but was far too thick to be lit by any current, without that current wrecking the tube in which it were used. The grid was nicely made – of metallic radium! It was worth a small fortune, but quite useless in the electron tube. And the plate was evidently of pure fused quartz, shaped with an accuracy that astounded me; but that, too was quite useless.

'Parts wrong?' my father barked excitedly in wolfish tones, his glowing green eyes evidently having read something in my face. 'Indicate how wrong. Describe to make correct!'

I closed my lips firmly, determined to reveal nothing. I knew that it was through the wrecked machine that my father and Stella had been so dreadfully altered. I resolved that I would not aid in changing other humans into such hellish monsters. I was sure that this strange mechanism, if completed, woud be a threat against all humanity – though, at the time, I was far from conceiving the full, diabolic significance of it.

My father snarled toward the woman.

She dropped upon all fours, and sprang at me like a wolf, her beastly eyes gleaming green, her bare teeth glistening in the sullen red light, and she was hideously howling!

Her teeth caught my trousers, tore them from my leg from the middle of the right thigh downward. Then they closed into my flesh, and I could feel her teeth gnawing . . . gnawing . . . .

She did not nake a deep wound, though blood, black in the terrible red light, trickled from it down my leg toward the shoe – blood which, from time to time, she ceased the gnawing to lick up appreciatively. The purpose of it was evidently to cause me the maximum amount of agony and horror.

For minutes, perhaps, I endured it – for minutes that seemed ages.

The pain itself was agonizing: the steady gnawing of teeth into the flesh of my leg, toward the bone.

But that agony was less than the terror of my surroundings. The strange temple of black, with its black floor, black walls, black pillars, vaulted black ceiling. The dim, sourceless, blood-red light that filled it. The dreadful stillness – broken only by my groans and shrieks, and by the slight sound of the gnawing teeth. The demoniac monster standing before me in the body of my father, staring at me with shining green eyes, holding the plans and the parts that the mechanic had brought, waiting for me to speak. But the most horrible thing was the fact that the gnawing demon was the body of dear, lovely Stella!

She was now digging her teeth in with a crunching sound.

I writhed and screamed with agony. Sweat rolled from my body. I tugged madly against my bonds, strove to burst the rope that held my tortured leg.

Fierce, eager growls came wolf-like from the throat of the gnawing woman. Her leprously pallid face was once more smeared with blood, as it had been when I first saw her. Occasionally she stopped the unendurable gnawing, to lick her lips with a dreadful satisfaction.

Finally I could stand it no longer. Even if the fate of all the earth depended upon me – as I thought it did – I could endure it no longer.

'Stop! Stop!' I screamed. 'I'll tell you!'

Rather reluctantly, the woman rose, licking her crimson lips.

My father – I find myself continually calling the monster by that name, but it was *not* my father – again held the plans before my face, and displayed upon his palm the tiny parts for the electron tube.

It took all my will to draw my mind from the throbbing pain of the fresh wound in my leg. But I explained that the filament wire would have to be drawn much finer, that the radium would not do for the grid, that the plate must be of a conducting metal, instead of quartz.

He did not easily understand my scientific terms. The name tungsten, for instance, meant nothing to him until I had explained the qualities and the atomic number of the metal. That identified it for him, and he appeared really to know more about the metal than I did.

For long hours I answered his questions, and made explanations. A few times I thought of refusing to answer, again. But the memory of that unendurable gnawing always made me speak.

The scientific knowledge and skill displayed in the construction of the machine's parts, once the specifications were properly understood, astounded me. The monsters that had stolen these human bodies seemed to have remarkable scientific knowledge of their own, particularly in chemistry and certain branches of physics – though electricity and magnetism, and the modern theories of relativity and equivalence, seemed new to them, probably because they came from a world whose natural phenomena are not the same as ours.

They brought, from one of the chambers opening into the great hall, an odd, glistening device, consisting of connected bulbs and spheres of some bright, transparent crystal. First, a lump of limestone rock, which must have been dug up in the making of the underground temple, was dropped into a large lower globe. Slowly it seemd to dissolve, forming a heavy, iridescent, violet-colored gas.

Then, whenever my father or one of the others wished to make any object – a metal plate or grid, a coil of wire, an insulating button, anything needed in building the machine – a tiny pattern of it was skilfully formed of a white, soft, wax-like substance.

The white pattern was placed in one of the crystal bulbs, and the heavy violet gas – which must have been disassociated protons and electrons from the disrupted limestone – was allowed to fill the bulb through one of the numerous transparent tubes.

The operator watched a little gauge, and at the right instant, removed from the bulb – not the pattern, but the finished object, formed of any desired element!

The process was not explained to me. But I am sure that it was one of building up atoms from the constituent positive and negative electrons. A process just the reverse of disintegration, by which radium decomposes into lead.First such simple atoms as those of hydrogen and helium. Then carbon, or silicon, or iron. Then silver, if one desired it, or gold! Finally radium, or uranium, the heaviest of metals. The object was removed whenever the atoms had reached the proper number to form the element required.

With this marvelous device, whose accomplishments exceede the wildest dreams of the alchemist, the construction of the huge machine in the center of the hall proceeded with amazing speed, with a speed that filled me with nothing less than terror.

It occurred to me that I might delay the execution of the monsters' dreadful plan by a trick of some kind. Racking my weary and pain-clouded brain, I sought for some ruse that might mislead my clever opponents. The best idea that came to me was to give false interpretation of the word 'vacuum.' If I could keep its true meaning from my father, he would leave the air in the tubes, and they would burn out when the current was turned on. When he finally asked the meaning of the word, I said that it signified a sealed or enclosed space.

But he had been consulting scientific works, as well as my meager knowledge. When the words left my lips, he sprang at me with a hideous snarl. His teeth sought my throat. But for a very hurried pretense of alarmed stupidity, my part in the dreadful adventure might have come to a sudden end. I protested that I had been sincere, that my mind was weary and I could not remember scientific facts, that I must eat and sleep again.

Then I sagged forward against the ropes, head hanging. I refused to respond, even to threats of further torture. And my exhaustion was scarcely feigned, for I had never undergone a more trying day – a day in which one horror followed close upon another.

Finally they cut me loose. The woman carried me out of the sullen crimson light of the temple, up the narrow passage, and into the house again; I was almost too weak to walk alone. As we came out upon the snow, the distant, keening cry of the weird pack broke once more upon my startled ears.

The pale disk of the moon was rising, cold and silvery, in the east, over the illimitable plain of snow. It was night again!

I had been in the subterranean temple for more than twenty-four hours.

7

When I Ran from the Pack

Again I was in the little room that had been Stella's, among her intimate possessions, catching an occasional suggestion of her perfume. It was a small room, clean and chaste, and I had a feeling that I was invading a sacred place. But I had no choice in the matter, for the windows were barred, and the door locked behind me.

Stella – or, I should say, the were-woman – had let me stop in the other room to eat and drink again. She had even let me find the medicine cabinet and get a bottle of antiseptic to use in the wound on my leg.

Now, sitting on the bed in a shaft of cold, argent moonlight, I applied the stinging liquid, and then bound the place with a bandage torn from a clean sheet.

Then I got to my feet and went to the window: I was determined to escape if escape were possible, or end my life if it were not. I had no intention of going back alive to the hellish red-lit temple.

But the quavering, dismal, howling of the pack came faintly to my ears, as I reached the window, setting me trembling with horror. I gazed fearfully across the fantastic desert of silvery snow, bright in the opalescent haze of moonlight.

Then I glimpsed moving green eyes, and I cried out.

Below the window was a huge, lean gray wolf, pacing deliberately up and down, across the glistening snow. From time to time he lifted his head, stared straight at my windows with huge, malevolent eyes.

A sentinel set to watch me!

With my hopeless despair came a leaden weight of weariness. I felt suddenly exhausted, physically and mentally. I stumbled to the bed, crept under the covers without troubling to remove my clothing, and fell almost instantly asleep.

I awoke upon a gray, cold day. A chill wind was whistling eerily about the old house, and the sky was gloomy with steel-blue clouds. I sprang out of bed, feeling much refreshed by my long sleep. For a moment, despite the dreary day, I was conscious of an extraordinary sense of relief; it seemed, for the merest instant, as if all that had happened to me was a horrible nightmare, from which I was waking. Then recollection came with a dull pain in my wounded leg.

I wondered why I had not been carried back into the terrible temple of blood-red gloom before the coming of day; perhaps I must have been sleeping too soundly to be roused.

Recalling the gray wolf, I looked nervously out at the window. It was gone, of course; the monsters seemed unable to endure the light of day, or any other save the terrible crimson dusk of the temple.

I wrapped a blanket about my shoulders, for it was extremely cold, and I set about at once to escape from the room. I was determined to win my liberty or die in the attempt.

First I examined the windows again. The bars outside them, though of wood, were quite strong. My utmost strength failed to break any one of them. I could find nothing in the room with which they might be cut or worn in twain, without hours of labor.

Finally I turned to the door. My kicks and blows failed to make any impression upon its sturdy panels. The lock seemed strong, and I had neither skill nor tools for picking it.

But, while I stood gazing at the lock, an idea came to me.

I still had the little automatic, and two extra clips of ammunition. My captors had shown only disdain for the little weapon, and I had rather lost faith in it after its puzzling failure to kill the gray wolf.

Now I backed to the other side of the room, drew it, and deliberately fired three shots into the lock. When I first tried the door again, it seemed as impassible as ever. I worked upon it, twisting the knob, again and again. There was a sudden snap, and the door swung open.

I was free. If only I could reach a place of safety before darkness brought out the weird pack!

In the old dining room I paused to drink, and to eat scantily. Then I left the house by the front door, for I dared not go near the mouth of that hell-burrow behind the house, even by day. In fearful desperate haste, I set out across the snow.

The little town of Hebron, I knew, lay ten miles away, directly north. Few landmarks were visible above the thick snow, and the gray clouds hid the sun. But I plodded along beside a barbed wire fence, which I knew would guide me.

Slowly the time-yellowed ranch house, an ugly, rambling structure with a gray shingle roof, dwindled upon the white waste behind me. The outbuildings, resembling the house, though looking smaller, more ancient and more dilapidated, drew toward it to form a single brown speck upon the endless desolation of the snow-covered plain.

The crust upon the snow, though frozen harder than upon the ill-fated night of my coming, was still too thin to support my weight. It broke beneath my feet at every step, and I sank ankle-deep in the soft snow beneath.

My progress was a grim, heart-breaking struggle. My strength had been drained by the nerve-racking horrors and exhausting exertions of the past few days. Soon I was gasping for breath, and my feet felt leaden-heavy. There was a dull, intolerable ache in the wound on my leg.

If the snow had been hard enough to support my weight, so that I could run, I might have reached Hebron before dark. But, sinking deep into it at every step, it was impossible for me to move rapidly.

I must not have covered over half the distance to Hebron, when the gloom of the gray, cheerless day seemed to settle upon me. I realized, with a chill of fatal horror, that it had not been early morning when I set out; my watch had stopped, and since the leaden clouds had obscured the sun, I had no gauge of time.

I must have slept through half the day or more, exhausted as I had been by the day and night of torture in the dark temple. Night was upon me, when I was still far short of my destination.

Nearly dead with fatigue, I had more than once been almost on the point of stopping to rest. But terror lent me fresh strength. I plodded on as fast as I could, but forcing myself to keep from running, which would burn up my energy too soon.

Another mile, perhaps, I had covered, when I heard the weird, blood-congealing voice of the pack.

The darkness, for a time, had been intense, very faintly relieved by the ghostly gleam of the snow. But the clouds had lightened somewhat, and the light of the rising moon shone through them, casting eldritch shadows of silver on the level snow.

At first the dreadful baying was very distant, low and moaning and hideous with the human vocal note it carried. But it grew louder. And there was something in it of sharp, eager yelping.

I knew that the pack which had run down Judson and me had been set upon my trail.

The terror, the stark, maddening, soul-searing horror that seized me, is beyond imagination. I shrieked uncontrollably. My hands and body felt alternately hot and fevered, and chilled with a cold sweat. A harsh dryness roughened my throat. I reeled dizzily, and felt the pounding of my pulse in all my body.

And I ran.

Madly, wildly. Ran with all my strength. Ran through the thick snow faster than I had thought possible. But in a few moments, it seemed I had used up all my strength.

I was suddenly sick with fatigue, swaying, almost unable to stand. Red mists, shot with white fire, danced in front of my eyes. The vast plain of snow whirled about me fantastically.

And on and on I staggered. When each step took all my will. When I felt that I must collapse in the snow, and fought with all my mind for the strength to raise my foot again.

All the time, the fearful baying was drawing nearer, until the wailing, throbbing sound of it drummed and rang in my brain.

Finally, unable to take another step, I turned and looked back.

For a few moments I stood there, swaying, gasping for breath. The weird, nerve-blasting cry of the pack sounded very near, but I could see nothing. Then, through the clouds, a broad, ghostly shaft of moonlight fell athwart the snow behind me. And I saw the pack.

I saw them! The pinnacle of horror!

Gray wolves, leaping, green-eyed and gaunt. And strange human figures among them, racing with them. Chill, soulless emerald orbs staring. Bodies ghastly pallid, clad only in tattered rags. Stella, bounding at the head of the pack.

My father, following. And other men. All green-orbed, leprously white. Some of them frightfully mutilated.

Some so torn they should have been dead.

Judson, the man who had brought me out from Hebron, was among them. His livid flesh hung in ribbons. One eye was gone, and a green fire seemed to sear the empty socket. His chest was fearfully lacerated. And the man was – eviscerated!

Yet his hideous body leaped beside the wolves.

And others were as dreadful. One had no head. A black mist seemed gathered above the jutting, lividly white stump of his neck, and in it glowed malevolently – two green eyes!

A woman ran with them. One arm was torn off, her naked breasts were in ribbons. She ran with the rest, green eyes glowing, mouth wide open, baying with other members of the pack.

And now I saw a horse in that grotesque company. A powerful, gray animal, he was, and he came with tremendous leaps. Its eyes, too, were glowing green – glowing with the malignant fire of an evil intelligence not normally of this earth. This was one of Judson's animals, changed as dreadfully as he and all the others had been. Its mouth yawned open, with yellow teeth glistening, and it howled madly with the pack.

Swiftly, hideously, they closed in upon me. The weird host sprang toward me from all directions – gray wolves, men, and horse. Eyes glaring, teeth bared, snarling, the hellish horde came closer.

The horror of it was too much for my mind. A merciful wave of darkness overcame me as I felt myself reeling to fall upon the snow.

8

Through the Disk of Darkness

I awoke within the utter stillness of a tomb. For a little time I lay with eyes closed, analyzing the sensations of my chilled, aching body, conscious of the dull, throbbing pain from my wounded leg. I shuddered at recollection of the fearful experiences of the past few days, endured again the overwhelming horror of the moment when the pack – wolves and men and horse, frightfully mutilated, eyes demoniacally green – had closed in upon me on the moonlit snow. For some time I did not dare to open my eyes.

At last, nerving myself against the new horrors that might surround me, I raised my lids.

I looked into the somber, crimson radiance of the ebon-pillared temple. Beside a dull jet wall I lay, upon a pile of rags, with a blanket thrown carelessly over me. Beyond the row of massive, black, cylindrical pillars, I saw the great, strange machine, with the huge copper ring glistening queerly in the dim, bloody light. The polished mirror behind it seemed flushed with a living glow of molten rubies, and the many electron tubes, now mounted in their sockets, gleamed redly. The mechanism appeared to be near completion; livid, green-orbed figures were busy about it, moving with a swift, mechanical efficiency. It struck me abruptly that they moved more like machines than like living beings. My father, Stella, the two mechanics.

For many minutes I lay very still, watching them covertly. Evidently they had brought me down into this subterranean chamber, so that I would have no chance to repeat my escape. I speculated upon the possibility of creeping along the wall to the ascending passage, dashing through it. But there was little hope that I could do it unseen. And I had no way of knowing whether it might be night or day; it would be folly to run out into the darkness. I felt the little automatic still under my arm; they had not troubled to remove a weapon which they did not fear.

Suddenly, before I had dared to move, I saw my father coming across the black floor toward me. I could not repress a tremor, at closer sight of his deathly pallid body and sinister, baleful greenish eyes. I lay still, trying to pretend sleep.

I felt his ice-cold fingers close upon my shoulder; roughly I was drawn to my feet.

'Further assistance from you must be ours,' whined his wolfish voice. 'And not again will you be brought back living, should you be the fool to run!' His whine ended with an ugly snarl.

He dragged me across toward the fantastic mechanism that glistened in the grim, bloody radiance.

I quailed at the thought of being bound to the black pillar again.

'I'll help!' I cried. 'Do anything you want. Don't tie me up, for God's sake! Don't let her gnaw me!' My voice must have become a hysterical scream. I fought to calm it, cudgeled my brain for arguments.

'It would kill me to be tied again,' I pleaded wildly. 'And if you leave me free, I can help you with my hands!'

'Be free of bonds, then,' my father whined. 'But also remember! You go, and we bring you back not alive!'

He led me up beside the great machine. One of the mechanics, at a shrill, wolfish whine from him, unrolled a blue print before me. He began to ask questions regarding the wiring to connect the many electron tubes, the coils and helixes and magnets, all ranged about the huge copper ring.

His strange brain seemed to have no conception of the nature of electricity; I had to explain the fundamentals. But he grasped each new fact with astounding quickness, seemed to see the applications instinctively.

It soon developed that the great mechanism was practically finished; in an hour, perhaps the wiring was completed.

'Now what yet is to be constructed?' my father whined.

I realized that no provision had been made for electricity to light the tubes and energize the magnets. These beings apparently did not even know that a source of power was necessary. This, I thought, was another chance to stop the execution of their hellish plan.

'I don't know,' I said, 'So far as I can see, the machine now fits the specifications. I know nothing else to do.'

He snarled something to one of the mechanics, who produced the bloody rope with which I had previously been bound. Stella sprang toward me, her lips curled in a leering animal snarl, her white teeth gleaming.

Uncontrollable terror shook me, weakened my knees until I reeled.

'Wait! Stop!' I screamed. 'I'll tell if you won't tie me!'

They halted.

'Speak!' my father barked. 'Quickly describe!'

'The machine must have power. Electricity?'

'From what place comes electricity?'

'There is a motor generator up in the cellar, where the other machine is. That might do.'

He and the monster that had been Stella hurried me down the black-pillared hall, and up the inclined passage to the old cellar. He carried the red-glowing electric lantern. In the cellar I showed them the generator and attempted a rough explanation of its operation.

Then he and the woman bent and caught the metal base of the unit. With their incredible strength, they lifted it quite easily and carried it toward the passage. They made me walk ahead of them as we returned to the machine in the black hall – blasting another hope for a chance to make a dash for the open.

Just as they were placing the heavy machine – gasoline engine and dynamo, which together weighed several hundred pounds – on the black platform beside the strange, gigantic mechanism, there came an interruption that, to me, was terrifying.

From the passage came the rustle of feet, and mingled whining, snarling sounds such as the monsters seemed to use for communication. And in the vague, blood-red light, between the tall rows of black pillars, appeared the pack!

Huge, gaunt wolves there were. Frightfully mutilated men – Judson, and the others that I had seen. The gray horse. All their eyes were luminously green – alight with a dreadful, malevolent fire.

Human lips were crimsoned. Scarlet smeared the gray wolves' muzzles, and even the long nose and gray jaws of the horse. And they carried – the catch!

Over Judson's livid, lacerated shoulders was hung the torn, limp, bleeding body of a woman – his wife! One of the gaunt gray wolves had the hideously mangled body of a man across his back, holding it in place with jaws turned sidewise. Another had the body of a spotted calf. Two more carried in red-dripping jaws the lax gray bodies of coyotes. And one of the men bore upon his shoulder the remains of a huge gray wolf.

The dead, torn, mutilated specimens were dropped in a horrible heap in the wide central aisle of the jet-pillared temple, near the strange machine, like an altar of death. Dark blood flowed from it over the black floor, congealing in thick, viscid clots.

'To these we bring life,' my father snarled at me, jerking his head toward the dreadful, mangled heap.

Shuddering and dazed with horror, I sank on the floor, covering my eyes. I was nauseated, sick. My brain was reeling, fogged, confused. It refused to dwell upon the meaning of this dreadful scene.

The mad, fearful, demoniac thing that had been my father jerked me roughly to my feet, dragged me toward the motor generator, and began plying me with questions about its operation, about how to connect it with the strange mechanism of the copper ring.

I struggled to answer his questions, trying vainly to forget my horror in the work.

Soon the connection was completed. Under my father's directions, I examined the gasoline engine, saw that it was supplied with fuel and oil. Then he attempted to start it, but failed to master the technique of choking the carburetor. Under constant threat of the blood-darkened rope and the warewoman's gnawing fangs, I labored with the little motor until it coughed a few times, and fell to firing steadily.

Then my father made me close the switch, connecting the strange machine with the current from the generator. A faint, shrill humming came from the coils. The electron tubes glowed dimly.

And a curtain of darkness seemed suddenly drawn across the copper ring. Blackness seemed to flow from the queer tube behind it, to be reflected into it by the polished mirror. A disk of dense, utter darkness filled the ring.

For a few moments I stared at it in puzzled wonder.

Then, as my eyes became slowly sensitized, I found that I could see through it – see into a dread, nightmare world.

The ring had become an opening into another world of horror and darkness.

The sky of that alien world was unutterably, inconceivably black; blacker than the darkest midnight. It had no stars, no luminary; no faintest gleam relieved its terrible, oppressive intensity.

A vast reach of that other world's surface lay in view, beyond the copper ring. Low, worn, and desolate hills, that seemed black as the somber sky. Between them flowed a broad and stagnant river, whose dull and sullen waters shone with a vague and ghostly luminosity, with a pale glow that was somehow unclean and noisome, like that of decaying foul corruption.

And upon those low and ancient hills, that were rounded like the bloated breasts of corpses, was a loathsome vegetation. Hideous, obscene travesties of normal plants, whose leaves were long, narrow, snake-like, with the suggestion of ugly heads. With a dreadful, unnatural life, they seemed to writhe, lying in rotting tangles upon the black hills, and dragging in the foul, lurid waters of the stagnant river. Their thin reptilian, tentacular vines and creepers glowed with a pale and ghastly light, lividly greenish.

And upon a low black hill, above the evil river, and the rotting, writhing, obscene jungle, was what must have been a city. A sprawled and hideous mass of red corruption. A foul splash of dull crimson pollution.

This was no city, perhaps, in our sense of the word. It seemed to be a sort of cloud of foul, blood-hued darkness, trailing repulsive tentacles across the low black hill; a smear of evil crimson mist. Mad and repulsive knobs and warts rose about it, in grotesque mockery of spires and towers. It was motionless. And I knew instinctively that unclean and abominable life, sentience, reigned within its hideous scarlet contamination.

My father mounted to the black stone step between the copper ring, and stood there howling weirdly and hideously, into that world of darkness — voicing an unclean call!

In answer, the sprawled, nightmare city seemed to stir. Dark things — masses of fetid, reeking blackness — seemed to creep from its ugly protuberances, to swarm toward us through the tainted filth of the writhing, evilly glowing vegetation.

The darkness of evil concentrate, creeping from that nightmare world into ours!

For long moments the utter, insane horror of it held me paralyzed and helpless. Then something nerved me with the abrupt, desperate determination to revolt against my fearful masters, despite the threat of the bloody rope.

I tore my eyes from the dreadful attraction that seemed to draw them toward the foul, sprawled city of bloody darkness, in that hideous world of unthinkable evil.

Realization came to me that I stood alone, unguarded. The green eyes of the monsters about me were fixed in avid fascination upon the ring through which that nightmare world was visible. None of them seemed aware of me.

If only I could wreck the machine, before those creeping horrors of darkness came through into our world! I started forward instinctively, then paused, realizing that it might be difficult to do great damage to it with my bare hands, before the monsters saw me and attacked.

Then I thought of the little automatic in my pocket, which I had been permitted to keep with me. Even though its bullets could not harm the monsters, they might do considerable damage to the machine.

I snatched it out and began firing deliberately at the dimly glowing electron tubes. As the first one was shattered, the image of that hideous, nightmare world flickered and vanished. The huge, polished mirror was once more visible beyond the copper ring.

For the time being, at least, those rankling shapes of black and utter evil were shut out of our world!

As I continued to fire, shattering the electron tubes and the other most delicate and most complicated parts of the great mechanism, a fearful, soul-chilling cry came from the startled monsters in human and animal bodies.

Suddenly the creatures sprang toward me, over the black floor, howling hideously.

9

The Hypnotic Revelation

It was the yellow, stabbing spurts of flame from the automatic that saved me. At first the fearfully transformed beasts and men had leaped at me, howling with the agony that light seemed to cause them. I kept on firing, determined to do all the damage possible before they bore me down.

And abruptly they fell back away from me, wailing dreadfully, hiding their unearthly green eyes, slinking behind the massive black pillars.

When the gun was empty, some of them came toward me again. But still they seemed shaken, weakened, uncertain of movement. In nervous haste, I fumbled in my pockets for matches – I had not realized before how they were crippled by light.

I found only three, all, apparently, that I had left.

The weird monsters, recovered from the effect of the gun flashes, were leaping across toward me, through the sullen, blood-red gloom, as I struggled desperately to make a light.

The first match broke in my fingers.

But the second flared into yellow flame. The monsters, almost upon me, sprang back, wailing in agony again. As I held the tiny, feeble flame aloft, they cowered, howling, in the flickering shadows cast by the huge, ebon pillars.

My confused, horror-dazed mind was abruptly cleared and sharpened by hope of escape. With the light to hold them back, I might reach the open air.

And to my quickened mind it came abruptly that it must be day above. It was morning, and the pack had been driven back to the burrow by the light of the coming sun!

As swiftly as I could, without extinguishing the feeble flame of the match with the wind of my motion, I advanced down the great hall. I kept in the middle of the wide central aisle, afraid that my enemies were slinking along after me in the shadows of the pillars.

Before I reached the passage which lead to the surface, a stronger breath of air caught the feeble orange flame. It flickered out. Dusky crimson gloom fell about me once more, with baleful green eyes moving in it, in the farther end of the temple. The howling rose again, angrily. I heard swiftly padding feet.

Only one of the three matches was left.

I bent, scratched it very carefully on the black floor and held it above my head.

A new wailing of pain came from the monsters; they fell back again.

I found the end of the passage, rushed through it, guarding the precious flame in a cupped hand.

In the great hall behind me, the blood-chilling wail of the pack rose again. I heard the monsters surging toward the passage.

By the time I had reached the old cellar, from whose wall the slanting tunnel had been dug, the match was almost consumed. I turned, let its last dying rays shine down the passage. Dreadful cries of agony and terror came again; I heard the monsters retreating from the tunnel.

The match suddenly went out.

In mad haste I dashed across the cellar's floor and blundered heavily into the wall. I found the steps that led to the surface and rushed up them desperately.

I heard the howling pack running up the passage, moving far swifter than I was able to do.

At last my hand touched the under surface of the wooden door, above the steps. Beyond, I knew, was the golden light of day.

And at the same instant, corpse-cold fingers closed about my ankle, in a crushing, powerful grasp.

Convulsively, I thrust upward with my hand.

The door flew up, slammed crashingly beside the opening. Above was soft brilliant azure sky. In it the white morning sun blazed blindingly. Its hot radiance brought tears to my eyes, accustomed as they were to the dim crimsom light of the temple.

Fearful, agonized animal wailing sounds came again from behind me.

The grasp on my ankle tightened convulsively, then relaxed.

Looking back, I saw Stella on the steps at my feet, cowering, writhing as if in unbearable agony, animal screams of pain coming from her lips. It seemed that the burning sunlight had struck her down, that she had been too much weakened to retreat as those behind her had done.

Abruptly she seemed to me a lovely, suffering girl – not a strange demoniac monster. Pity for her – even, perhaps, love – came over me in a tender wave, If I could save her, restore her to her true, dear self!

I ran back down the steps, seized her by the shoulders, started to carry her up into the light. Deathly cold and deathly white her body still was. And still it had a vestige of that unnatural strength.

She writhed in my arms, snarling, slashing at my body with her teeth. For a moment her green eyes smoldered malevolently at me. But as the sunlight struck them she closed them, howling with agony, and tried to shield them with her arm.

I carried her up the steps, into the brilliant sunlight.

First I thought of closing the cellar door, and trying to fasten it. Then I realized that the light of day, shining down the passage, would hold back the monsters more effectually than any locked door.

It was still early morning. The sun had been up no more than an hour. The sky was clear, and the sunshine glittered with blinding, prismatic brilliance on the snow. The air, however, was still cold; there had been no thawing, nor would there be until the temperature had moderated considerably.

As I stood there in the blaze of sunlight, holding Stella, a strange change came over her. The fierce snarling and whining sounds that came from her throat slowly died away. Her writhing, convulsive struggles weakened, as though a tide of alien life were ebbing from her body.

There was a sudden last convulsion. Then her body was lax, limp.

Almost immediately, I noticed a change in color. The fearful, corpse-like pallor slowly gave place to the normal pinkish flush of healthy life. The strange, unearthly chill was gone; I felt a glow of warmth where her body was against mine.

Then her breast heaved. She breathed. I felt the slow throbbing of her heart. Her eyes were still closed as she lay inert in my arms, like one sleeping. I freed one of my hands and gently lifted a long-lashed lid.

The eye was clear and blue – normal again. The baleful, greenish fire was gone!

In some way, which I did not then understand, the light of day had purified the girl, had driven from her the fierce, unclean life that had possessed her body.

'Stella! Dear Stella! Wake up!' I cried. I shook her a little. But she did not rouse. Still she seemed sleeping heavily.

Realizing that she would soon be chilled, in the cold air, I carried her into the house, into her own room, where I had been imprisoned, and laid her on the bed, covering her with blankets. Still she appeared to be sleeping.

For an hour, perhaps, I tried to rouse her from the profound syncope or coma in which she lay. I tried everything that experience and the means at hand made available. And still she lay insensible.

A most puzzling situation, and a surprising one. It was almost as if Stella – the real Stella – had been dispossessed of her body by some foul, alien being. The alien, evil life had been killed by the light, and still she had not returned.

At last it occurred to me to try hypnotic influence – I am a fair hypnotist, and have made a deep study of hypnotism and allied mental phenomena. A forlorn hope, perhaps, since her coma appeared so deep. But I was driven to clutch at any straw.

Exerting all my will to recall her mind, placing my hand upon her smooth brow, or making slow passes over her still, pale, lovely face, I commanded her again and again to open her eyes.

And suddenly, when I was almost on the point of new despair, her eyelids flickered, lifted. Of course, it may have been a natural awakening, though a most unusual one, instead of the result of my efforts. But her blue eyes opened and stared up at me.

But still she was not normally awake. No life or feeling was revealed in the azure depths of her eyes. They were clouded, shadowed with sleep. Their opening seemed to have been a mechanical answer to my commands.

'Speak. Stella, my Stella, speak to me!' I cried.

Her pale lips parted. From them came low, sleep-drugged tones.

'Clovis.' She spoke my name in that small, colorless voice.

'Stella, what has happened to you and my father?' I cried.

And here is what she told me, in that tiny, toneless voice. I have condensed it somewhat, for many times her voice wandered wearily, died away, and I had to prompt her, question her, almost force her to continue.

'My father came here to help Dr. McLaurin with his experiment,' she began, slowly, in a low momotone. 'I did not understand all of it, but they sought for other worlds besides ours. Other dimensions, interlocking with our own. Dr. McLaurin had been working out his theory for many years, basing his work upon the new mathematics of Weyl and Einstein.

'Not simple is our universe. Worlds upon worlds lie side by side, like the pages of a book – and each world unknown to all the others. Strange worlds touching, spinning side by side, yet separated by walls not easily broken down.

'In vibration is the secret. For all matter, all light, all sound, all our universe, is of vibration. All material things are formed by vibrating particles of electricity – electrons. And each world, each universe, has its own order of vibration. And through each, all unknown and unseen, are the myriad other worlds and universes vibrating, each with an order of its own.

'Dr. McLaurin knew by mathematics that these other worlds must exist. It was his wish to explore them. Here he came, to be alone, with none to pry into his secrets. Aided by my father, and other men, he toiled through years to build his machine.

'A machine, if successful, would change the vibration rate of matter and of light. To change it from the order of our dimension, to those of others. With it, he might see into those myriad other worlds in space beside our own, might visit them.

'The machine was finished. And through its great copper ring, we saw another world. A world of darkness, with midnight sky. Loathsome, lividly green plants writhed like reptilian monstrosities upon its black hills. Evil, alien life teemed upon it.

'Dr. McLaurin went through into that dark world. The horror of it broke down his mind. A strange madman, he came back. His eyes were green and shining, and his skin was very white.

'And things he brought back with him – clinging, creeping things of foul blackness, that stole the bodies of men and beasts. Evil, living things, that are the masters of the black dimension. One crept into me, and took my body. It ruled me, and I know only like a dim dream what it made my body do. To it, my body was but a machine.

'Dim dreams. Terrible dreams. Dreaming of running over the snow, hunting for wolves. Dreams of bringing them back, for the black things to flow into, and make live again. Dreams of torturing my father, whom no black thing took, at first.

'Father was tortured, gnawed. My body did it. But I did not do it. I was far away. I saw it only dimly, like a bad dream. One of the black creatures had come into my body, taken it from me.

'New to our world were the black things. Light slays them, for it is a force strange to their world, against which they have no armor. And so they dug a deep place, to slink into by day.

'The ways of our world they knew not; nor the language; nor the machines. They made Father teach them; teach them to speak; to read books; to run the machine through which they came. They plan to bring many of their evil kind through the machine, to conquer our world. They plan to make black clouds to hide the sun forever, so our world will be as dark as their own. They plan to seize the bodies of all men and animals, to use as machines to do that thing.

'When Father knew the plan, he would not tell them more. So my body gnawed him – while I looked on from afar, and could not help. Then he pretended to be in accord with them. They let him loose. He smashed the machine with an ax, so no more evil things could come through. Then he blew off his head with a gun. So they could not torture him, and make him aid them again.

'The black things could not themselves repair the machine. But in letters they learned of Clovis McLaurin, son of Dr. McLaurin. He, too, knew of machines. They sent for him, to torture him as Father had been tortured. Again my mind was filled with grief, for he was dear to me. But my body gnawed him, while he aided the black things to build a new macine.

'Then he broke it. And then. . .then. . .'

Her tiny, toneless voice died wearily away. Her blue eyes, still clouded with shadowed sleep, stared up unseeingly. Deep indeed was her strange trance.

She had even forgotten that it was I to whom she spoke!

10

The Creeping Darkness

An amazing and terrible story, was Stella's. In part, it was almost incredible. Yet, much as I wished to doubt it, and much as I wished to discount the horror that it promised our fair earth, I knew that it must be true.

Prominent scientists have speculated often enough of the possibility of other worlds, other planes, side by side with our own. For there is nothing solid or impenetrable about the matter of our universe. The electron is thought to be only a vibration in the ether. And in all probability, there are vibrating fields of force, forming other electrons, other atoms, other suns and planets, existing beside our world, yet not making their existence known. Only a tiny band of the vibrations in the spectrum is visible to our eyes as light. If our eyes were tuned to other bands, above the ultra-violet, or below the infra-red, what new, strange worlds might burst upon our vision?

No, I could not doubt that part of Stella's story. My father had studied the evidence upon the existence of such worlds invisible to us, more deeply than any other man, had published his findings, with complete mathematical proof, in his startling work, 'Interlocking Universes.' If those parallel worlds were to be discovered, he was the logical man to make the discovery. And I could not doubt that he had made it – for I had seen that world of dread nightmare, beyond the copper ring.

And I had seen, in that dark alien world, the city of the creeping things of blackness. I could well believe the part of the story about those strangely malignant entities stealing the bodies of men and animals. It offered the first rational solution of all the astounding facts I had observed, since the night of my coming to Hebron.

And it came to me suddenly that soon the monstrous beings would have the machine repaired; they could need no further aid from me. Then other hordes of the black shapes would come through. Come to seize our world, Stella had said, to enslave humanity, to aid them in making our world a planet of darkness like the grim sphere they left. It seemed mad, incredible – yet I knew it was true!

I must do something against them! Fight them – fight them with light! Light was the one force that destroyed them. That had freed Stella from her dread bondage. But I must obtain better means of making light than a few matches. Lamps would do; a searchlight, perhaps.

And I was determined to take Stella to Hebron, if she were able to go. I must go there to find the supplies I needed, and yet I could not bear the thought of leaving her for the monstrosities to find when night fell again, to seize her fair body again for their foul ends.

I found that at my command she would move, stand, and walk, though slowly and stiffly, like a person walking in sleep. It was still early morning, and I thought there might be time for her to walk to Hebron, with me to support her steps, before the fall of darkness.

I investigated her possessions in the room, found clothing for her: woolen stockings, strong shoes, knickers, sweater, gloves, cap. Her efforts to dress herself were slow and clumsy, like those of a weary child, trying to pull off his clothing when half asleep, and I had to aid her.

She seemed not to be hungry. But when we stopped in the dining room, where the remainder of the food still lay on the table, I made her drink a tin of milk. She did it mechanically. As for myself, I ate heartily, despite ill-omened recollections of how I had eaten at this table on the eve of my first attempt to escape.

We set out across the snow, following along by the wire fence as I had done before. I could distinguish my old foot prints and the mingled tracks of wolf, man, and horse, in the trail the pursuing pack had left. We followed that trail with greater ease now, for the soft snow had been packed by the running feet.

I walked with an arm about Stella's waist, sometimes half-carrying her, speaking to her encouragingly. She responded with slow, dull mechanical efforts. Her mind seemed far away; her blue eyes were misty with strange dreams.

As the hours of weary struggle went by, with her warm body against mine, it came to me that I loved her very much, and that I would give my life to save her from the dread fate that menaced us.

Once I stopped, and drew her unresisting body fiercely to me, and brought my mouth close to her pale lips, that were composed, and a little parted, and perfumed with sleep. Her blue eyes stared at me blankly, still clouded with sleep, devoid of feeling or understanding. Suddenly I knew that it would be wrong to kiss her so. I pushed her pliant body back, and led her on across the snow.

The sun reached the zenith, and began declining slowly westward.

As the evening wore on, Stella seemed to tire – or perhaps it was only that her trance-like state became deeper. She responded more slowly to my urgings that we must hurry. When, for a few moments, my encouraging voice was silent, she stood motionless, rigid, as if lost in strange vision.

I hurried her on desperately, commanding her steadily to keep up her efforts. My eyes were anxiously on the setting sun. I knew that we would have scant time to reach the village before the fall of night; haste was imperative.

At last, when the sun was still some distance above the white horizon, we came within sight of the town of Hebron. A cluster of dark specks, upon the limitless plain of glittering snow. Three miles away, they must have been.

Still the girl seemed to sink deeper into the strange sea of sleep from which only hypnotic influence had lifted her. By the time we had covered another mile, she refused to respond to my words. She was breathing slowly, regularly; her body was limp, flaccid; her eyes had closed. I could do nothing to rouse her.

The sun had touched the snow, coloring the western world with pale rose and purple fires. Darkness was not far away.

Desperately, I took the limp, relaxed body of the girl upon my shoulders and staggered on beneath the burden. It was no more than two miles to Hebron; I had hopes of getting there with her before dark.

But the snow was so deep as to make the effort of even unburdened walking exhausting. And my body was worn out, after the terrible experiences I had lately undergone. Before I had tottered on half a mile, I realized that my effort was hopeless.

Dusk had fallen. The moon had not yet risen, but the snow gleamed silvery under the ghostly twilight that still flooded the sky. My ears were straining fearfully for the voice of the dreadful pack. But a shroud of utter silence hung about me. I was still plodding wearily along, carrying Stella.

Abruptly I noticed that her body against my hands, was becoming strangely cold. Anxiously, I laid her down upon the snow, to examine her — trembling with a premonition of the approaching horror.

Her body was icy cold. And it had again become ghastly, deathly white. White as when I had seen her running over the snow with the gaunt gray wolf!

But her limbs, strangely, did not stiffen; they were still pliant, relaxed. It was not the chill of death coming over her; it was the cold of that alien life, which the sunlight had driven from her, returning with the darkness!

I knew that she would soon be a human girl no longer, but a weird wolf-woman, and the knowledge chilled my soul with horror! For a few moments I crouched beside her inert body, pleading wildly with her to come back to me, crying out to her almost insanely.

Then I saw the hopelessness of it, and the danger. The monstrous life would flow into her again. And she would carry me back to hateful captivity in the subterannean temple, to be a slave of the monsters — or perhaps a member of their malefic society.

I must escape! For her sake. For the world's. It would be better to abandon her now, and go on alone, than have her carry me back. Perhaps I would have another chance to save her.

And I must somehow render her helpless, so that she could not pursue me, when the dread life returned to her body.

I snatched off my coat, and then my shirt. In anxious haste, I tore the shirt into strips, which I twisted rapidly into cords. I drew her ankles together, passed the improvised bonds about them, knotted them tightly. I turned the frightfully pallid, corpse-cold girl upon her face, crossed the lax arms behind her back, and fastened her wrists together with another rope of twisted cloth. Then, by way of extra precaution, I slipped the belt from my trousers and buckled it firmly about her waist, over the crossed wrists, pinioning them.

Finally I spread on the snow the coat I had taken off, and laid her upon it, for I wanted her to be as comfortable as possible.

Then I started off toward Hebron, where a little cluster of white lights shone across the snow, through the gray, gathering dusk. I had gone but a few steps when something made me pause, look back, fearfully.

The inert, deathly pallid body of the girl still lay upon the coat. Beyond it, I glimpsed a strange and dreadful thing, moving swiftly through the ghostly, gray twilight.

Incredible and hideous was the thing I gazed upon. I can hardly find words to describe it; I can give the reader no idea of the weird, icy horror that grasped my heart with dread fingers as I saw it.

It was a mass of darkness, flowing over the snow. A creeping cloud of foul *blackness,* shapeless and many-tentacled. Its form changed continually as it moved. It had no limbs, no features – only the inky, snake-like, clinging extensions of its blackness, that it thrust out to move itself along. But deep within it were two bright green points – like eyes. Green baleful orbs, aflame with fiendish malevolence!

It was alive, this living darkness. It was unlike any higher form of life. But it has since come to me that it resembled the amoeba – a single-cell animal, a flowing mass of protoplasmic slime. Like the amoeba this darkness moved by extended narrow pseudopods from its mass. And the green eyes of horror, in which its unearthly life appeared to be concentrated, perhaps correspond to the vacuoles or nuclei of the protozoan animals.

I realized, with a paralyzing sensation of horror unutterable, that it was one of the monsters from that world of black nightmare, beyond the copper ring. And that it was coming to claim again Stella's body, to which it was still connected by some tainted bond.

Though it seemed only to creep or flow, it moved with a terrible swiftness – far faster, even, than the wolves.

In a moment after I saw it, it had reached Stella's body. It paused, hung over her, a thick, viscid, clinging cloud of unclean blackness with those greenish, fearful eyes staring from its foul mass. For a moment it hid her body, with its creeping, sprawling, ink-black and shapeless masses, crawling over her like horrid tentacles.

Then it *flowed* into her body.

It seemed to stream through her nostrils, into her mouth. The black cloud hanging over her steadily diminished. The infernal green orbs remained above, in the writhing darkness, until the last. And then they seemed to sink into her eyes.

Abruptly, her pallid body came to terrible life.

She writhed, straining at her bonds with preternatural strength, rolling from the coat into the snow, hideously convulsed. Her eyes were open again – and they shone, not with their own life, but with the dreadful fire of the green, malevolent orbs that had sunk into them.

Her eyes were the eyes of the creeping blackness.

From her throat came the soulnumbing, wolfish baying, that I had already heard under such frightful circumstances. It was an animal cry, yet it had an uncanny human note that was terrifying.

She was calling the pack!

That sound nerved my paralyzed limbs. For a few moments that it had taken the monstrous thing of blackness to flow into Stella's body, I had stood motionless, transfixed with the horror of it.

Now I turned and ran madly across the snow toward the dancing lights of Hebron. Behind me the werewoman still writhed in the snow, trying to break her bonds, howling weirdly – summoning the pack!

Those twinkling lights seemed to mock me. They looked very near across the ghostly, gleaming plain of snow. They seemed to dance away from me as I ran. They seemed to move like fireflies, pausing until I was almost upon them, then retreating, to scintillate far across the snow.

I forgot my weariness, forgot the dull, throbbing pain of the unhealed wound in my leg. I ran desperately, as I had never run before. Not only was my life at stake, but Stella's and my father's. Even, I had good reason to fear, the lives of all humanity.

Before I had covered half the distance, I heard behind me the voice of the pack. A weird, wailing, far-off cry which grew swiftly louder. The werewoman had called, and the pack was coming to free her.

On I ran. My steps seemed so pitifully short, despite my agony of effort, so pitifully slow. My feet sank deep into the snow which seemed to cling to them with maleficent demon-fingers. And the lights that seemed so near appeared to be dancing mockingly away before me.

Sweat poured from my body. My lungs throbbed with pain. My breath came in quick, agonized gasps. My heart seemed to hammer against the base of my brain. My mind seemed drowning in a sea of pain. And on I ran.

The lights of Hebron became unreal ghost-fires, false will-o'-the-wisps. They quivered before me in a blank world of gray darkness. And I labored on toward them, through a dull haze of agony. I saw nothing else. And nothing did I hear, but the moaning of the pack.

I was so weary that I could not think. But I suddenly became aware that the pack was very near. I think I turned my head and glanced back for a moment. Or it may be that I remember the pack only as I saw it in imagination. But I have a very vivid picture of gaunt gray wolves leaping and baying hideously, and pallid, green-eyed men running with them, howling with them.

Yet on I ran, fighting the black mists of exhaustion that closed about my brain. Heartbreaking inertia seemed to oppose every effort, as if I were swimming against a resisting tide. On and on I ran, with eyes for nothing, thought for nothing, except the lights before me, the dancing, mocking lights of Hebron, that seemed very near, and always fled before me.

Then suddenly I was lying in the soft snow with my eyes closed. The yielding couch was very comfortable to my exhausted body. I lay there, relaxed. I did not even try to rise; my strength was utterly gone, blackness came upon me – unconsciousness that even the howling of the pack could not keep away. The weird ululation seemed to grow fainter and I knew no more.

11

A Battle of Light and Darkness

'Pretty near all in, ain't you, Mister?' a rough voice penetrated to my fatigue-drugged mind. Strong hands were helping me to my feet. I opened my eyes and stared confusedly about me. Two roughly clad men were supporting me. And another, whom I recognized as the station agent, Connell, held a gasoline lantern.

Before me, almost at hand, were the lights of Hebron, which had seemed to dance away so mockingly. I saw that I had collapsed in the outskirts of the straggling village – so near the few street lights that the pack had been unable to approach me.

'That you, McLaurin?' Connell demanded in surprise, recognizing my face. 'We figgered they got you and Judson.'

'They did,' I found voice to say. 'But they carried me off alive. I got away.'

I was too nearly dead with exhaustion to answer their questions. Only vaguely do I recall how they carried me into a house, and undressed me. I went to sleep while they were examining the wound on my leg, exclaiming with horror at the marks of teeth. After I was sleeping they dressed it again, and then put me to bed.

It was noon of the following day when I awoke. A nervous boy of perhaps ten years was sitting by the bed. His name, he said, was Marvin Potts, son of Joel Potts, owner of a general store in Hebron. His father had been one of the men who had found me when their attention was attracted by the howling of the pack. I had been carried into the Potts home.

The boy called his mother. She, finding that I was hungry, soon brought me coffee, biscuits, bacon and fried potatoes. I ate with good appetite, though I was far from recovered from my desperate run to escape the pack. While I was eating, still lying in bed, raised on an elbow, my host came in. Connell, the station agent, and two other men were with him.

All were anxious to hear my story. I told it to them briefly, or as much of it as I thought they would believe.

From them I learned that the weird pack had found several human victims. A lone ranch house had been raided on the night before and three men carried from it. They told me, too, that Mrs. Judson, frantic with grief over the loss of her husband, had gone out across the snow to seek him and had not come back. How well I recalled now that she had found him! Bitterly I reproached myself for having urged the man to risk the night trip with me.

I inquired if any steps had been made to hunt the wolves.

The sheriff, I learned, had organized a posse, which had ventured out from Hebron several times. Abundant tracks of men and wolves, running side by side, had been found. There had been no difficulty in following the trail. But, I gathered, the hunters had not been very eager for success. The snow was deep; they could not travel rapidly, and they had owned no intention of meeting the pack by night. The trails had never been followed more than six or seven miles from Hebron. The sheriff had returned to the county seat, twelve miles down the railroad, promising to return when the snow had melted enough to make travelling easier. And the few score inhabitants of Hebron, though deeply disturbed by the fate of their neighbors who had been taken by the pack, had been too much terrorized to undertake any determined expedition on their own account.

When I spoke of getting someone to return with me to the ranch, quick evasions met me. The example of Judson's fate was very strongly in the minds of all present. None cared to risk being caught away from the town by night. I realized that I must act alone, unaided.

Most of that day I remained in bed, recuperating. I knew that I would need my full strength for the trial that lay before me. I investigated the available resources, however, and made plans for my mad attempt to strike at the menace that overhung humanity.

With the boy, Marvin, acting as my agent, I purchased an ancient buggy, with a brown nag and harness, to carry me back to the ranch house; my efforts to rent a vehicle, or to hire someone to take me back, had proved signal failures. I had him also to arrange to procure for me other equipment.

I had him buy a dozen gasoline lanterns, with an abundant supply of mantles, and two five-gallon tins, full of gasoline. Finding that the Hebron High School boasted a meager supply of laboratory equipment, I sent the boy in search of magnesium ribbon, and sulphur. He returned with a good bundle of the thin, metallic strips, cut in various lengths. I dipped the ends of each strip in molten sulphur, to facilitate lighting.

He brought me two powerful electric flashlights, with a supply of spare bulbs and batteries, extra ammunition for my automatic, and two dozen sticks of dynamite, with caps and fuses.

Next morning I woke early, feeling much recovered. The shallow, gnawed wound in my leg was fast healing, and had ceased to pain me greatly. As I sat down to a simple breakfast with the Potts family, I assured them confidently that, on this day, I was going to return to the den of the strange pack, from which I had escaped, and put an end to it.

Before we had finished eating, I heard the hail of the man from whom the buggy had been bought, driving up to deliver it and collect the ample price that Marvin Potts had agreed that I would pay. The boy went out with me. We took the vehicle, and together made the rounds of Hebron's few stores, collecting the articles he had bought for me on the day before – the lanterns, the supply of gasoline, the electric searchlights, and the dynamite.

It was still early morning when I left the boy at the end of the street, rewarding him with a bill, and drove alone through the snow, back toward the lonely ranch house where I had experienced such horrors.

The day, though bright, was cold. The snow had never begun to thaw; it was still as thick as ever. My brown nag plodded along slowly, his feet and the buggy's tires crunching through the crusted snow.

As Hebron vanished behind me, and I was surrounded only by the vast, glittering sea of unbroken snow, fear and dread came upon me – a violent longing to hurry to some crowded haunt of men. My imagination pictured the terrors of the night, when the weird pack would run again upon the snow.

How easy would it be to return, take the train for New York, and forget the terrors of this place! No, I knew that I could never forget. I could never forget the threat of that dread, night-black world beyond the copper ring, the fact that its evil spawn planned to seize our world and make it a sphere of rotting gloom like their own.

And Stella! Never could I forget her. I knew now that I loved her, that I must save her or perish with her.

I urged the pony on, across the lonely and illimitable desert of sunlit snow.

It was somewhat past noon when I reached the ranch house. But I still had a safe margin of daylight. Immediately I set about my preparations.

There was much to do: unpacking the boxes piled on the buggy; filling the dozen gasoline lanterns, pumping them up with air, burning their mantles, and seeing that they operated satisfactorily; attaching caps and fuses to the sticks of dynamite, testing my powerful flashlights; loading the little automatic and filling the extra clips; stowing conveniently in my pockets an abundance of matches, ammunition, extra batteries for the electric torches, the strips of magnesium ribbon.

The sun was still high when the preparations were completed. I took time then to put the pony in the stable behind the old house. I locked the door, and barricaded the building, so that, if any dread change converted the animal into a green-eyed monster, it would find itself imprisoned.

Then I went through the old house, carrying a lighted lantern. It was silent, deserted. All the monsters were evidently below. The door of the cellar was closed, all crevices chinked against light.

I lit my dozen powerful lanterns and arranged them in a circle about it.

Then I threw back the door.

A weird and fearful howl came from the dark passage below it! I heard the rush of feet as the howling thing retreated down the tunnel. From below came angry growls, shrill feral whines.

A physical wave of nauseating horror broke chillingly over me, at the thought of invading that red-lit temple-burrow, where I had endured such unnamable atrocities of horror. I shrank back, trembling. But at the thought of my own father and lovely, blue-eyed Stella, down in that temple of terror, ruled by foul monsters, I recovered my courage.

I stepped back toward the yawning black mouth of the den that these monsters had built.

The lanterns I had first intended to leave in a ring about the mouth of the burrow, except one to carry with me. Now it occurred to me that they would prevent the escape of the monsters more effectively if scattered along the passage. I gathered up six of them, three in each hand, and started down the steps.

Their powerful white rays illuminated the old cellar with welcome brilliance. I left one of them there, in the center of the cellar's floor. And three more of them I set along the slanting passage that led down into the deeper excavation.

I intended to set the two that remained on the floor of the temple, and perhaps return to the surface for others. I hoped that the light would drive the alien life from all of the pack, as it had from Stella. When they were unconscious, I could carry out Stella and my father, and any of the others that seemed whole enough for normal life. The great machine, and the temple itself, I intended to destroy with the dynamite.

I stepped from the end of the passage, into the vast, black, many-pillared hall. The intense white radiance of the faintly humming lanterns dispelled the terrible, blood-red gloom. I heard an appalling chorus of agonized animal cries; weird, feral whines and howls of pain. In the farther end of the long hall, beyond the massive ebon pillars, I saw slinking, green-orbed forms, crowding into the shadows.

I set the two lanterns down on the black floor and drew one of the powerful flashlights from my pocket. Its intense, penetrating beam probed the shadows beyond the huge columns of jet. The cowering, howling shapes of men and wolves shrieked when it touched them, and fell to the black floor.

Confidently I stepped forward, to search out new corners with the brilliant finger of light.

Fatal confidence! I had underestimated the cunning and the science of my enemies. When I first saw the black globe, my foot was already poised above it. A perfect sphere of utter blackness, a foot-thick globe that looked as if it had been turned from midnight crystal.

I could not avoid touching it. And it seemed to explode at my touch. There was a dull, ominous *plop*. And billowing darkness rushed from it. A black gas swirled up about me and shrouded me in smothering gloom.

Wildly I turned, dashed back toward the passage that led up to open air and daylight. I was utterly blinded. The blazing lanterns were completely invisible. I heard one of them dashed over by my blundering feet.

Then I stumbled against the cold temple wall. In feverish haste I felt along it. In either direction, as far as I could reach, the wall was smooth. Where was the passage? A dozen feet I blundered along, feeling the wall. No, the passage must be in the other direction.

I turned. The triumphant, unearthly baying of the pack reached my ears; the padding of feet down the length of the temple. I rushed along the wall, stumbled and fell over a hot lantern.

And they were upon me. . . .

The strange, sourceless, blood-hued radiance of the temple was about me once more. The thick, black pillars thrust up beside me, to support the ebon roof. I was bound, helpless, to one of those cold, massive columns, as I had once been before, with the same bloody rope.

Before me was the strange mechanism that opened the way to the other plane – the Black Dimension – by changing the vibration frequencies of the matter of one world, to those of the other, interlocking universe. The red light gleamed like blood on the copper ring, and the huge mirror behind it. I saw with relief that the electron tubes were dead, the gasoline engine silent, the blackness gone from the ring.

And before the ring had been erected a fearful altar, upon which reposed the torn, mangled, and bleeding bodies of men and women, of gaunt grey wolves, and little coyotes, and other animals. The pack had found good hunting, on the two nights that I had been gone!

The corpse-white, green-orbed, monstrous things, the frightfully changed bodies of Stella and my father and the others, were
about me.

'Your coming back is good,' the whining, feral tones of the
thing in my father's body rang dreadfully in my ears. 'The
manufacturer of electricity will not run. You return to make it
turn again. The way must be opened again, for new life to come
to these that wait.' He pointed a deathly white arm to the pile of
weltering bodies on the black floor.

'Then the new life to you also we will bring. Too many times
you run away. You become one with us. And we seek a man who
will act as we say. But first must the way be opened again.

'From our world will the life come. To take the bodies of men
as machines. To make gas of darkness like that you found within
this hall, to hide all the light of your world, and make it fit for
us.'

My mind reeled with horror at thought of the inconceivable,
unthinkable menace risen like a dread specter to face humanity.
At the thought that soon I, too, would be a mere machine. My
body, cold and white as a corpse, doing unnamable deeds at the
command of the thing of darkness whose green eyes would blaze
in my sockets!

'Quickly tell the method to turn the maker of electricity,' came
the maleficent snarl, menacing, gloating, 'or we gnaw the flesh
from your bones, and seek another who will do our will!'

12

Spawn of the Black Dimension

I agreed to attempt to start the little gasoline engine, hoping for
some opportunity to turn the tables again. I was certain that I
could do nothing so long as I was bound to the pillar. And the
threat to find another normal man to take my place as teacher of
these monsters from that alien world brought realization that I
must strike soon.

Presently they were convinced that they required more than
verbal aid in starting the little motor. One of the mechanics
unbound me, and led me over to the machine, keeping a painful
grip upon my arm with ice-cold fingers.

Unobtrusively, I dropped a hand to feel my pockets. They were empty!

'Make not light!' my father snarled warningly, having seen the movement.

They had awakened to the necessity of searching my person. Glancing about the red-lit temple, I saw the articles they had taken from me, in a little pile against the base of a huge black pillar. The automatic, spare clips of ammunition, flashlights, batteries, boxes of matches, strips of magnesium ribbon. The two gasoline lanterns that I had brought into the great hall were there too, having evidently been extinguished by the black gas which had blinded me.

Two gray wolves stood alertly beside the articles, which must have been taken from me before I recovered consciousness after the onrush of the pack. Their strange green eyes stared at me balefully, through the crimson gloom.

After fussing with the engine for a few moments, while my father kept his cold, cruelly firm grip upon my shoulder, and scores of hideous green orbs in the bodies of wolves and men watched my every move, I discovered that it had stopped for lack of fuel. They had let it run on after I wrecked the machine, until the gasoline was exhausted.

I explained to my father that it would not run without more gasoline.

'Make it run to cause electricity,' he said, repeating his menacing, wolfish snarl, 'or we gnaw the flesh from your bones, and find another man.'

At first I insisted that I could not get gasoline without visiting some inhabited place. Under the threat of torture however – when they dragged me back toward the bloody rope – I confessed that the fuel in the gasoline lanterns might be used.

They were suspicious. They searched me again, to be certain that I had upon my person no means of making light. And the lanterns were examined very carefully for any means of lighting without matches.

Finally they brought me the lanterns. With my father grasping my arm, I poured the gasoline from them into the engine's fuel tank. Under any circumstances it would have been difficult to avoid spilling the liquid. I took pains to spill as much as seemed possible without rousing suspicion – contriving to pour a little pool of it under the exhaust, where a spark might ignite the fumes.

Then they made me start the engine. Coils hummed once more; the electron tubes lit. Blackness seemed to pour from the strange central tube, to be reflected into the great copper ring by the wide, polished mirror.

Again, I looked through the vast ring into the Black Dimension!

Before me lay a sky of gloom, of darkness unutterable and unbroken, stagnant, lurid waters, dimly aglow with the luminosity of foul decay; worn black hills, covered with obscene, writhing, reptilian vegetation that glowed vaguely and lividly green. And on one of those hills was the city.

A sprawled smear of red evil, it was, a splash of crimson darkness, of red corruption. It spread over the hill like a many-tentacled monster of dark red mist. Ugly masses rose from it, wart-like knobs and projections – ghastly travesties of minarets and towers.

It was motionless. And within its reeking, fetid scarlet darkness, lurked things of creeping gloom – nameless hordes of things like that unthinkable monstrosity that I had seen flow into Stella's body. Green-eyed, living horrors of flowing darkness.

The monsters about me howled through the ring, into that black world – calling!

And soon, through the copper ring, came flowing a river of shapeless, inconvceivable horror! Formless monsters of an alien universe. Foul beings of the darkness – spawn of the Black Dimension!

Fearful green eyes were swimming in clotted, creeping masses of evil darkness. They swarmed over the pile of dead things on the floor. And the dead rose to forbidden, nameless life.

Mutilated corpses, and the torn bodies of wolves sprang up, whining, snarling. And the eyes of each were the malevolent, glaring green eyes of the things that had flowed into them.

I was still beside the rhythmically throbbing little engine. As I shrank back in numbed horror from the fearful spectacle of the dead rising to unhallowed life, my eyes fell despairingly upon the little pool of gasoline I had spilled upon the black floor. It was not yet ignited.

I had some fleeting idea of trying to saturate my hand with gasoline and hold it in front of the exhaust, to make of it a living torch. But it was too late for that, and the ruthless, ice-cold fingers still clutched my arm painfully.

Then my father whined wolfishly.

A creepy, formless, obscene mass of blackness, with twin green orbs in it, glowing with mad, alien fires, left the river of them that poured through the ring and crept across to me.

'Now you become one like us!' came the whining voice.

The thing was coming to flow into my body, to make me its slave, its machine!

I screamed, struggled in the cruel hands that held me. I cursed and pleaded – promised to give the monsters the world. And the creeping blackness came on. I collapsed, drenched with icy sweat, quivering, nauseated with horror.

Then, as I had prayed it would do, the little engine coughed. A stream of pale red sparks shot from the exhaust. There was a sudden, dull, explosive sound of igniting vapor. A yellow flash lit the black-pillared temple.

A flickering column of blue and yellow flame rose from the pool of gasoline beside the engine.

The things of blackness were *consumed* by the light – they vanished!

The temple became a bedlam of shrill, agonized howls, of confused, rushing, panic-stricken bodies. The fierce grasp upon my arm was relaxed. My father fell upon the floor, writhing across the room toward the shelter of a black pillar, hiding his green eyes with an arm flung across them.

I saw that the gray wolves had deserted their post beside the articles of mine they had been guarding, at the foot of the massive black column. I left the flickering pillar of fire and dashed across to them.

In a moment my shaking hands had clutched upon one of the powerful electric flashlights. In desperate haste I found the switch and flicked it on. With the intense, dazzling beam, I swept the vast columned hall. The hellish chorus of animal cries of pain rose to a higher pitch. I saw gray wolves and ghastly white men cowering in the shadows of the massive pillars.

I snatched up the other searchlight and turned it on. Then hastily gathering up pistol, ammunition, matches, and strips of magnesium ribbon, I retreated to a position beside the flaring gasoline.

This time I moved very cautiously, flashing the light before me to avoid stumbling into another bomb of darkness, like that which had been my undoing before. But I think my precaution was useless; I am sure from what I afterward saw, that only one had been prepared.

As I got back to the engine, I noticed that it was still running, that the way to the Black Dimension, through the copper ring, was still open.

I cut off the fuel, at the carburetor. The little engine coughed, panted, slowed down. The wall of darkness faded from the copper ring, breaking our connection with that hideous world of another interpenetrating universe.

Then I hastily laid the flashlights on the floor, laying them so they cast their broad, bright beams in opposite directions. I fumbled for matches, struck one to the end of a strip of magnesium ribbon, to which I had applied sulphur to make it easier to light.

It burst into sudden blinding, dazzling, white radiance, bright as a miniature sun. I flung it across the great black hall. It outlined a white parabola. Its intense light cut the shadows from behind the ebon pillars.

The cowering, hiding things howled in new agony. They lay on the black floor, trembling, writhing, fearfully contorted. Low, agonized whinings came from them.

Again and again I ignited the thin ribbons of metal and flung them flaming toward the corners of the room, to banish all shadow with their brilliant white fire.

The howling grew weaker, the whines died away. The wolves and the corpse-white men moved no more. Their fierce, twisting struggles of agony were stilled.

When the last strip of magnesium was gone, I drew the automatic, put a bullet through the little engine's gasoline tank, and lit a match to the thin stream of clear liquid that trickled out. As a new flaring pillar of light rushed upward, I hurried toward the passage that led to the surface, watching for another of those black spheres that erupted darkness.

I found the gasoline lanterns I had left in the tunnel still burning; the monsters had evidently found no way of putting them out.

On to the surface I ran. I gathered up the six lanterns I had left there – still burning brilliantly in the gathering dusk – and plunged with them back down the passage, into the huge, pillared temple.

The monsters were still inert, unconscious.

I arranged the powerful lanterns about the floor, so placed that every part of the strange temple was brilliantly illuminated. In the penetrating radiance, the monsters lay motionless.

Returning to the surface, I brought one of my full cans of gasoline, and two more of the lighted lanterns. I filled, pumped up, and lit the two lanterns from which I had drawn the gasoline.

Then I went about the black-walled temple, always keeping two lanterns close beside me, and dragged the lax, ice-cold bodies from their crouching postures, turning them so the faces would be toward the light. I found Stella, her lovely body still unharmed, except for its deathly pallor and its strange cold. And then I came upon my father. There was also the mangled thing that had been Judson, and the headless body that had been Blake Jetton, Stella's father. I gazed at many more lacerated human bodies and at the chill carcasses of wolves, of coyotes, of the gray horse, of a few other animals.

In half an hour, perhaps, the change was complete.

The unearthly chill of that alien life was gone from the bodies. Most of them quickly stiffened – with belated *rigor mortis*. Even my father was quite evidently dead. His body remained stiff and cold – though the strange chill had departed.

But Stella's exquisite form grew warm again; the soft flush of life came to it. She breathed and her heart beat slowly.

I carried her up to the old cellar, and laid her on its floor, with two lanterns blazing near her, to prevent any return of that forbidden life, while I finished the ghastly work left for me below.

I need not go into details . . . But when I had used half my supply of dynamite, no recognizable fragments were left, either of the accursed machine, or of the dead bodies that had been animated with such monstrous life. I planted the other dozen sticks of dynamite beside the great black pillars, and in the walls of the tunnel . . . .

The subterranean hall that I have called a temple will never be entered again.

When that work was done, I carried Stella up to her room, and put her very gently to bed. Through the night I watched her anxiously, keeping a bright light in the room. But there was no sign of what I feared. She slept deeply, but normally, apparently free from any taint of the monstrous life that had possessed her.

Dawn came after a weary night, and there was a rosy gleam upon the snow.

The sleeping girl stirred. Fathomless blue eyes opened, stared into mine. Startled eyes, eager, questioning. Not clouded with dream as when she had awakened before.

'Clovis!' Stella cried, in her natural, softly golden voice. 'Clovis, what are you doing here? Where's Father? Dr. McLaurin?'

'You are all right?' I demanded eagerly. 'You are well?'

'Well?' She asked, raising her exquisite head in surprise. 'Of course I'm well. What could be the matter with me? Dr. McLaurin is going to try his great experiment today. Did you come to help?'

Then I knew – and a great gladness came with the knowledge – that all memory of the horror had been swept from her mind. She recalled nothing that had happened since the eve of the experiment that had brought such a train of terrors.

She looked suddenly past me – at the picture of myself upon the wall. These was a curious expression on her face; she flushed a little, looking very beautiful with heightened color.

'I didn't give you that picture,' I accused her. I wished to avoid answering any questions, for the time being, about her father or mine, or any experiments.

'I got it from your father,' she confessed.

I have written this narrative in the home of Dr. Friedrichs, the noted New York psychiatrist, who is a close friend of mine. I came to him as soon as Stella and I reached New York, and he has since had me stay at his home, under his constant observation.

He assures me that, within a few weeks, I shall be completely recovered. But sometimes I doubt that I will ever be entirely sane. The horrors of that invasion from another universe are graven too deeply upon my mind. I cannot bear to be alone in darkness, or even in moonlight. And I tremble when I hear the howling of a dog, and hastily seek bright lights and the company of human beings.

I have told Dr. Friedrichs my story, and he believes. It is because of his urging that I have written it down. It is an historical truism, my friend says, that all legend, myth, and folklore has a basis in fact. And no legends are wider spread than those of lycanthropy. It is remarkable that not only wolves are subjects of these legends, but the most ferocious wild animals of each country. In Scandinavia, for instance, the legends concern bears; on the continent of Europe, wolves; in South Africa, leopards and tigers. It is also remarkable that belief in possession by evil spirits, and belief in vampires, is associated with the widespread belief in werewolves.

Dr. Friedrichs thinks that through some cosmic accident, these monsters of the Black Dimension have been let into our world before; and that those curiously widespread legends and beliefs are folk-memories of horrors visited upon earth when those unthinkable monstrosities stole the bodies of men and of savage beasts, and hunted through the darkness.

Much might be said in support of the theory, but I shall let my experience speak for itself.

Stella comes often to see me, and she is more exquisitely lovely than I had ever realized. My friend assures me that her mind is quite normal. Her lapse of memory is quite natural, he says, since her mind was sleeping while the alien entity ruled her body. And he says there is no possibility that she will be possessed again.

We are planning to be married within a few weeks, as soon as Dr. Friedrichs says that my horror-seared mind is sufficiently healed.

To Cynthia Manson, my amazing agent and friend,
with much love and gratitude

Acknowledgments

With many, many thanks to beta-readers Georgina Paterson, Vanessa Len, Sally McGrath, and Francesca Coppa, all of whom gave me incredibly helpful feedback and inspiration, and helped me improve this book in so many ways.

Thanks again to my wonderful agent, Cynthia Manson, and to my new editor, Anne Groll, who pounded this book into shape.

And now and always, all my love and thanks to my amazing husband, Charles, and also to Evidence, who doesn't quite get what mommy does yet, but is already fond of dragons.

PART

1

Chapter One

Water lapping salt at his cheek roused him, a fresh cold trickle finding its way into the hollow of sand where his face rested. It spurred him: with an effort he pushed to hands and knees and then up, to stagger indecorously along the shore and fall again at the foot of several gnarled old pines clinging to the edge of the beach.

His mouth was dry and cracked, his tongue swollen. His hands were clotted with sand. The wind bit sharply through the sodden wool of his coat, stained black with water, and he was barefoot. Slowly, he unfastened the remnants of a leather harness from around his waist: buckles and clasps of good steel, still bright, but heavily waterlogged; he let it fall to the sand. The sword-belt he kept. The blade when he drew it was bright Damascus steel, the hilt wrapped in black ray-skin, the collar the golden head of a dragon. He stared down at it, without recognition.

He rested it across his knees and leaned back against the tree, half-drifting. The empty ocean stood before him: water cold dark blue, the sky a thin grey; dark clouds receded into the east. He might have emerged onto the sand new-born. He felt as empty as the shore: of strength, of history, of name.

Thirst at last drove him onwards, when little else would have served to rouse him. The stand of trees gave onto a road, well-maintained and showing the signs of heavy use, recent tracks and disturbed dust. He walked slowly and mechanically until he found a narrow stream that crossed the road, traveling towards the sea, and he stopped and cupped water into his mouth urgently until the taste of salt had gone.

He held himself braced on hands and knees, water dripping from his face into the stream. The bank had a little new grass, though the ground was still cold. There was a smell in the air of pine-needles, and the stream ran over the rocks in a steady gurgle, mingling with the more distant sound of the ocean, the scent of salt on the wind. He felt inwardly the sense of something urgent and forgotten like a weight on his back. But his trembling arms slowly gave way. He lay down on the grass of the riverbank where he had knelt to drink and fell again into a heavy torpor; his head ached dully.

The sun climbed, warmed his coat. Travelers went past on the nearby road. He was distantly aware of the jingle of harness and slap of walking feet, the occasional creak of cart wheels, but none of them stopped to bother him or even halted by the stream. A small party of men went by singing off-key, loudly and cheerfully, not in any tongue he knew. At last a larger company came, accompanied by the familiar creaking of an old-fashioned sedan-chair. Some confused corner of his mind offered the image of an older woman, borne by porters through London streets, but even as it came he knew it wrong.

The creaking stopped abruptly; a voice spoke from the chair: a clear tenor with the directness of authority. Prudence would have driven him to his feet, but he had no reserves of strength. In a moment, someone came to inspect him—a servant of some kind? He had some vague impression of a youth bending down over him, but not so low that the face came clear.

The servant paused, and then withdrew quickly to his master and spoke urgently in a clear young voice. There was another pause, and then the master spoke again in yet another tongue, one which he could not put a name to and nevertheless somehow understood:

a rising and falling speech, musical. "I will not evade the will of Heaven. Tell me."

"He is Dutch," the servant answered in that same language, reluctance clear in every word.

He might have raised his head to speak—he was not Dutch, and knew that, if very little else; but he was cold, and his limbs heavier with every moment.

"Master, let us go on—"

"Enough," the tenor voice said, quiet but final.

He heard orders given in the unfamiliar language while darkness stole over his vision; there were hands on him, their warmth welcome. He was lifted from the ground and slung into a sheet or a net for carrying; he could not even open his eyes to see. The company moved on; suspended in mid-air, swinging steadily back and forth as they went on, he felt almost as though he were in a hammock, aboard ship, swaying with the water. The movement lulled him; his pain dulled; he knew nothing more.

"William Laurence," he said, and woke with his own name, at least, restored to him: out of a tangled dream full of burning sails and a strange weight of despair, a sinking ship. It faded as he struggled up to sit. He had been lying on a thin pad laid upon a floor of woven straw matting, in a room like none he had ever seen before: one solid wooden wall, the rest of translucent white paper set in frames of wood, and no sign of doors or windows. He had been bathed and dressed in a robe of light cotton; his own clothes were gone, and his sword. He missed the latter more.

He felt adrift, robbed of place and time. The chamber might have been a solitary hut or a room in the center of a great house; it might be set upon a mountaintop or the seashore; he might have slept an hour, a day, a week. A shadow abruptly loomed on the other side of the wall furthest from his bed, and the wall slid open along a track to furnish Laurence a glimpse of a corridor and another room across standing half-open, indistinguishable from his own, save for a window which looked out on a slim cherry-tree with bare dark branches.

A young man, not very tall but gangly with recent growth, perhaps sixteen, came through the opening and folded himself into the low-roofed chamber while Laurence stared at him blankly: he was Oriental. A long face with a sharp chin, clean-shaven and softened with the last remnants of puppy-fat; his dark hair was drawn back into a tail, and he wore an intricately arranged set of robes, creases as sharp as knife-edges.

He sat down on his heels and contemplated Laurence in turn, with an expression bleak enough to be aimed at a plague-carrier. After a moment he spoke, and Laurence thought he recognized the voice—the youth who had wished him left by the road.

"I have not the least notion what you are saying," Laurence said, his voice sounding hoarse in his own ears. He cleared his throat: even that much struck his head with fresh pain. "Can you speak English? Or French? Where am I?" He tried those tongues both, and then hesitating repeated the last over in the other language which the men had spoken on the road.

"You are in Chikuzen Province," the young man said, answering him in kind, "and far from Nagasaki, as you must well know."

There was a sharp bitterness to his voice, but Laurence seized on the one familiar name. "Nagasaki?" he said, half in relief, but the momentary gratification faded: he was no less bewildered to know himself in Japan, the other side of the world from where he ought have been.

The young man—too old for a page, and he wore a sword; an equerry of some sort, or a squire, Laurence could only guess—made no answer, only with a curt gesture motioned him off the mat.

Laurence shifted himself onto the floor, with some awkwardness and pain: the ceiling was too low to have permitted him to stand unless he had hunched over like a toad, and he ached in every part. Two servants came in at the young man's call; they tidied the

6

mat away into a cabinet and offered Laurence fresh garments, baffling in their layers. He felt a clumsy child under their valeting, thrust one way and then another as he put his limbs continuously in the wrong places; then they brought him a tray of food: rice and dried fish and pungent broth, with an array of startling pickles. It was by no means the breakfast he would have chosen, his stomach unsettled, but they had no sooner put it before him than animal hunger became his master. He paused only after having devoured nearly half the meal, and stared at the eating-sticks, which he had picked up and used without thinking of it.

He forced himself to go on more slowly than he wished, still queasy and conscious of being under observation, the young man regarding him coldly and steadily the whole of his meal. "Thank you," Laurence said at last, when he had finished, and the dishes were silently and deftly removed. "I would be grateful if you should give your master my thanks for his hospitality, and tell him I would be glad of an opportunity to repay it."

The youth only compressed his lips together. "This way," he said shortly. Laurence supposed he could have not looked anything but a vagabond, when they had found him.

The corridors of the house were not so stooped as the chambers. Laurence followed him to a back-chamber with a low writing-desk of some sort set upon the floor: another man sat behind it, working smoothly with brush and ink. His forehead and pate were clean-shaven, with a queue of his back hair clubbed tight and bound down doubled, over the bare skin; his garments were more ornate than the young man's, although of the same style. The young man bowed to him from the waist, and spoke briefly in the Japanese tongue, gesturing towards him.

"Junichiro tells me you are recovered, Dutchman," the man said, laying aside his brush. He looked across the desk at Laurence, wearing an expression of formal reserve, but with none of the dismay the young man—Junichiro?—had aimed at him.

"Sir," Laurence said, "I must correct you: I am an Englishman,

Captain William Laurence of—" He halted. Hanging from the wall behind the man's head was a large and polished bronze mirror. The face which looked back at him from it was not merely haggard from his recent ordeal but unfamiliar: his hair grown long; a thin white scar running down his cheek, long-healed, which he did not remember; and lines and wear accumulated. He might have aged years since he had seen himself last.

"Perhaps you would be so kind as to explain to me the circumstances of your arrival in this part of the country," the man said, prompting gently.

Laurence managed to say, reeling, "I am Captain William Laurence, of His Majesty's Ship *Reliant,* of the Royal Navy. And I have not the least notion how I have come to be here, except if my ship has suffered some accident, which God forbid."

Laurence did not much know what else he said afterwards. He supposed they saw his confusion and distress, for the questions stopped, and a servant was called to bring in a tray: a flask and small porcelain cups. His host filled one and gave it to him; Laurence took it and drank blindly, glad for the intensity: strong as brandy though light on the tongue. His cup was refilled promptly, and he drank again; the cup was small enough to be a single swallow. But he put it down afterwards. "I beg your pardon," he said, feeling acutely that he had lost control of himself, and all the more awkward in the face of their carefully polite failure to notice it. "I beg your pardon," he said, more strongly. "Sir, to answer your question, I cannot tell you how I came to be here: I must have been swept overboard, is the only possible answer. As for purpose, I have none; I have neither business nor friends in this part of the world."

He hesitated, yet there was no help for it; he could not help but recognize himself utterly a beggar. Pride should have to be sacrificed. "I am sorry to be so bold as to make any further claims on your generosity," he said, "when you have already been more than

8

kind, but I would be glad—I would be very glad indeed for your assistance in making my way to Nagasaki, where I may be reunited with my ship, or find another to return me to England."

But his host was silent. Finally he said, "You are yet too ill for the rigors of a long journey, I think. For now, permit me to invite you to enjoy the hospitality of my house. If there is anything you require for your comfort, Junichiro will see it is done."

All that was courteous, all that was kind, and yet it was a dismissal. Junichiro silently moved to hover behind Laurence at his elbow, plainly waiting for him to leave. Laurence hesitated, but he could not much argue: there was a low hollow thumping in his head, like the sound of bare heels coming down on a deck overhead, and the liquor already had thrown a further haze over his sight.

He followed Junichiro out and down the hall, back to the small chamber where he had awoken. Junichiro drew open the door and stood waiting; his face remained hard and unfriendly, and he fixed his eyes past Laurence like a grande dame giving the cut direct, though he said with cold hauteur, once Laurence had ducked inside, "Send for me if you should require anything."

Laurence looked about the chamber: the empty floor covered with straw mats, the bare and featureless walls, the silence of it; both the siren's promise of immediate rest, and confinement. "My liberty," he said, grimly, half under his breath.

"Be grateful for your life," Junichiro said with sudden venom, "which you have only by my master's benevolence. Perhaps he will think better of it."

He all but hurled the door shut, the frame rattling on its track, and Laurence could only stare after his shadow disappearing on the other side of the translucent wall.

The green, glassy wave broke against the shoals but flung itself rushing on even as it crumpled. The cold foam washed ferociously up Temeraire's hindquarters and left a fresh line of seaweed and splinters clinging to his hide as it finally fell back, exhausted. A low groaning came from the *Potentate*'s hull where she strained against the rocks, pinned and struggling; all around them the ocean stood wide and empty and grey, and the distant curve of land was only a smudge in the distance.

"You may say anything you like," Temeraire said, flatly, "but I do not care in the least. I will go alone, if I must, whether or not anyone will come and help me."

"Oh, Lord," Granby muttered, half under his breath; Captain Berkley, who was clinging to a stanchion to keep his balance on the badly slanted deck, did not bother to keep his own voice low, but bellowed up, "Listen, you mad beast, you don't suppose any of us like it better than you do?"

"I am quite sure I should like it less than anyone, if Laurence were dead," Temeraire said, "but he is not: he is certainly not dead. Of course I am going to go and look for him: I think it outside of everything for you to try and persuade me to any other course."

He did not bother to keep the reproach from his voice, and the anger. "And I do not see why you will all waste time arguing with me, when you had much better be helping me to organize a search: he cannot come to us, as long as we are still fixed out here in this useless position."

He was himself in an equally unpleasant position: perched awkwardly upon the long line of jagged black rocks, with his hindquarters half in the ocean, and peering over onto the dragondeck at the aviators. The *Potentate* had grounded during the storm: a terrific crash which had nearly sent all the dragons sliding off the deck into the ocean and tipped the ship up and over her ends.

There had been no time to think of anything but the mad scrambling effort to untangle themselves from the storm-chains in time, Laurence throwing himself up to where little Nitidus was pinned beneath three knots, frantically sawing them open and letting him at last wriggle free, so the rest of them had room enough to burst loose while the chains and tarpaulins slid down over the prow, into the churning ocean.

"When you are loose, take hold the anchor-chains at stern and bow!" Laurence had roared to him, before climbing up. "You must hold her back and off her beam-ends, else this cross-ocean will pound her apart on the shoals," and as soon as Temeraire had managed to break free he had done it: he and Maximus and Kulingile all working mightily together, straining against the anchor-chains and every rope that Nitidus and Dulcia could bring up to them, to keep the ship upright while the wind shrieked and tried to batter her and them against the rocks. And Temeraire had borne the brunt of it, for he could better maneuver than either of them: though it was quite impossible to hover properly in the storm, at least he could keep to his position more or less, without being flung down into the waves.

No-one had said a word to him, all that time—no-one had mentioned that Laurence was nowhere to be seen, and likely carried overboard with the chains—until he had finally been able to land exhausted on the deck, and look about, and Roland had slowly come and told him softly that Laurence was lost.

Temeraire did not mind admitting that it had been a very dreadful moment, and he had indulged himself in imagining consequences as dire as any of them. He had gone and swept frantically over all the neighboring ocean, every moment a torment as he found not the least sign of the tarpaulins or Laurence anywhere. But he had forced himself to stop searching empty waves—it had already been several hours, and Laurence would certainly not have stayed in the water, but would have struck right out for land, sensibly—and had gone back to the ship to consult maps to determine where best to find Laurence, and organize a better rescue.

It had not occurred to him that anyone would be so ridiculous as to throw some business of politics in his way: this nonsense of Japan being closed to foreign shipping, and unreasonably intolerant of visitors. Of course Hammond might be counted on to try offering him objections on such flimsy grounds, but Temeraire would have thought better of Granby and Captain Harcourt to lend themselves to it, or any of the other dragons' captains.

Temeraire was trying to be just: he did not hold it against anyone, much, that they had not noticed Laurence missing in the great confusion—although he had been trying to save the entire ship, and others had not been in quite so crucial a position; someone else might have looked sooner—"But I do not think it unreasonably selfish of me," he said, "that now the others should keep on without me, until I have found Laurence. And I will certainly go at once."

The storm was gone and the winds had died down, and Maximus and Kulingile could take it in turn to keep the ship from being smashed upon the shoals: Kulingile was aloft even now, doing his turn alone, and the ship was perfectly well. It did not signify if a few waves came over the side; sailors had to be prepared to get a little wet, now and again.

"I do not even mean to be gone very long," Temeraire said. "I am only asking to take perhaps twenty men, or thirty, and fly to the nearest shore and begin a search: certainly we will find him very soon. Particularly if we should make inquiries amongst the populace."

"We must do nothing of the sort," Hammond said, leaning over the rail and mopping his brow with his handkerchief: the weather was pleasantly hot now under the direct sun, which they had not seen for several days. "Nagasaki is the only harbor of Japan even open to any Western trade: the law utterly forbids the entry of any foreigners into the country, and if they should find Captain Laurence thrown up on their shore—" He stopped talking with a choking cough, as Granby stumbled with the swell on the shuddering deck, and knocked him in the side.

"If they do not want any foreigners about, they should be all the happier for us to find Laurence, and depart," Temeraire said, feeling himself on eminently solid ground. "And after all, we can tell them we do not want to be here, either: we are only on our way

12

to China, and if we had not run into that dreadful squall we should not have troubled them in the least."

"Perhaps instead you might proceed at once to Nagasaki," Gong Su said; he did not quail when Temeraire turned a cold glittering eye upon him, although he did add, "I beg your forgiveness for speaking of a course of action which is distasteful to you, but no good can come from failing to follow the proper forms of intercourse. I am sure that an inquiry laid with the harbormaster, with the proper respect, is most likely to yield the fruit which we all desire: the prince's safe return."

"Not much chance of that, certain sure," O'Dea muttered, from where he was sitting not far away, wrapped in an oilskin and huddled up to Iskierka's side for the warmth, pretending to be worming a rope usefully when really he was only listening. "Cruel, I call it, to keep up his hopes: the ocean keeps what she takes."

"Thank you, O'Dea, that is enough," Granby said sharply.

"It *is* enough," Temeraire said. "You need not silence him, when he is only saying what you all think. Well, I do not care. I am not going to Nagasaki; I am not going to China; I am not going anywhere without Laurence, and I am certainly not going to only sit here and wait."

"No, of course you aren't," Granby said under his breath.

"Oh, yes, you are!" said Iskierka cracking open an eye, now of all times. She had slept nearly the entire storm away fastened down in the most comfortable place, between Maximus and Kulingile, with Temeraire curled round and Lily, Messoria, and Immortalis all heaped on top; during the crisis, she had done absolutely nothing but huddle on an exposed rock and watch, grumblingly, while the rest of them had worked. And now the ship was more secure, she had slung herself, very inconveniently for everyone else, around the base of the mizzenmast to keep sleeping all the day.

"I am not, in the least!" Temeraire said to her, with strong indignation: if she were to tell him Laurence was dead, he would clout her across the nose. "Laurence is not dead."

"I don't see why he should be dead," Iskierka said, "what has that to do with anything? But you are not going haring off into the countryside when we are stuck here on these rocks, and anything at all might happen to the ship."

Temeraire thought this ridiculous. The storm was over, and the *Potentate* had not sunk yet; she would not sink now. "Whyever ought I stay here, when Laurence is lost somewhere in Japan?"

"Because I am going to have the egg tomorrow," Iskierka said, then paused and tilted her head thoughtfully, "or perhaps to-day: I want something to eat, and then we shall see."

"The *egg*?" Granby said, staring at her. "What egg? What—do you mean to tell me the two of you blighted fiends have been—"

"Well, of course," Iskierka said. "How else could we have made an egg? Although," she added to Temeraire, "it has been a great deal more trouble for me, so once it is out, I think it is only fair you should look after it: anyway you are not going anywhere, until it is quite safe."

Chapter 2

Another full day passed in sleep and eating restored Laurence to nearly all the outward semblances of comfort, and robbed him more with every passing minute of the inward: he could not conceive of any course which should have deposited him so unceremoniously on the highways of Japan. He could not even be grateful to find himself equipped, apparently by the hand of deity, with the Chinese language to hand: he would have preferred to have been made mute, and known in the confines of his own mind whence he came, even if he could not have communicated that knowledge to his captors.

And captors they certainly were: his request for transport to Nagasaki remained notably unanswered. He had learnt a little more of his situation from Junichiro, who had despite his earlier flash of resentment continued to wait upon him punctiliously. His host's name was Kaneko Hiromasa; his exact rank Laurence could not entirely work out, but he was at the least a reasonably wealthy man of some position, if judged by the size of his house and the number of servants, and engaged on important affairs by the quantity of papers in his study. A country-gentleman, managing his own estates, or perhaps even an official of some sort. Regardless of his rank, however, it was increasingly plain he did not view Laurence as a mere subject of charity, to be fed and washed and sent on his way.

Laurence had not been able to marshal his resources to pursue the matter on the previous day. Confusion and illness had overcome

him, and he had spent nearly all the day asleep, stretched his full
length upon the bare mats of the floor, rousing only for dinner. But
in the morning he awakened feeling himself again, in body at least;
and when the servants came with breakfast, he made plain he
wished to speak with Kaneko once again. The ordinary maids did
not speak Chinese, but when he had repeated their master's name,
they went away, and brought Junichiro back with them.

That young man came to the chamber door and stood outside,
his face hard and remote. "My master is presently occupied," he
said. "Permit me to address your needs." His voice was flat, and he
did not look Laurence in the face. There was a strange mingling of
formality and palpable resentment in his manner: all the outward
shows of courtesy, and no evidence of any real feeling which might
have motivated it.

Laurence could not make sense of it. If his presence had meant
some great burden for the household, he might better have understood, but Kaneko need not have picked him up from the ground if
so, and in any case the largesse which had been shown him, so far,
scarcely seemed of a kind which would have troubled the finances
of such a house.

But a full understanding was not his present concern: the meat
of the matter was that they did not mean to aid him to get back to
his ship. "I remain grateful for your master's hospitality," he said,
"but my health is recovered, and I will trespass on it no further: I
would ask you for the return of my clothing, and my sword, and to
show me the way to the road."

Junichiro looked at him with an expression briefly startled, as
though Laurence had asked him for a pair of wings. "What would
you do?" he said, with sincere confusion. "You cannot speak the
language; you are a foreigner and a barbarian—"

"And," Laurence said, cutting him off short; he could not have
said how he knew the word had the flavor of an insult, but he did,
"if I mean to go to the devil, that is my business, and surely no
concern of yours."

16

He would indeed have been glad of help, but not of the sort which would keep him penned in a room and plied with food and drink. So far, he seemed to figure at once as an unexpected but welcome guest, and a piece of highly inconvenient baggage: Junichiro plainly wished him gone—or never come at all—but even the servants eyed him with sidelong worried looks that required no translation.

At the very least, Laurence hoped his demand to leave might draw out some response which should illuminate matters, and let him know how better to proceed: and indeed Junichiro hesitated; he left and in a little while returned and said, "My master will see you."

Laurence hoped to make a better show of himself, at this second meeting; he had asked for a razor, and conquered the disquiet of looking at his strangely unfamiliar face in the glass long enough to clear away the several days' growth of beard. The servants had brought him to a bathing room, peculiarly divided with a wooden-slatted floor on which they insisted on scrubbing him in the open air, surely unhealthy in the extreme and inviting a chill, before permitting him to step into the large bath, itself excessively hot; at least, he had thought it so, but on emerging he could not deny it had done splendidly to ease his aches.

When ushered into the office this time, he was able to fold himself down in a better imitation of what was evidently the polite kneeling posture; his legs still complained of the position, but he was not so weak he was at every moment in danger of tipping over and having to reach out a hand to steady himself awkwardly against the floor with his fingertips.

Kaneko was frowning, however: Laurence's sword lay on the desk before him, unsheathed, and in the sunlight coming through the open window looked even more splendid than Laurence had recalled: jewels gleamed from the dragon's-head of the hilt, and the blade shone. His fingers itched to hold it again. "Where did you have this from?" Kaneko asked, touching the hilt.

Laurence could not bring himself to make the fantastic if honest answer that he did not recall: in any event, he did not feel himself compelled to answer such a question, personal and unjustified. "Are you proposing, sir," he said, "that I have stolen it? The sword is mine, as are the coat, the shirt, and the trousers you found upon me; I am sorry to be equally unable to provide you with the bills of sale for any of them, if you should require the same to restore them to me."

Kaneko hesitated. "This is a very fine blade," he said, finally.

He seemed to want something more, but Laurence could not provide it. "Yes," he said, unyielding, as he could not be otherwise. "I am a serving-officer of His Majesty's Navy, sir; I rely upon my sword."

He waited; he did not entirely understand what concerned Kaneko so about the blade. Finally, Kaneko said bluntly, "It is of Chinese make," and Laurence inwardly flinched not with surprise, but with the absence of surprise: he realized he knew as much, and had not even thought it strange, before.

"I have another of Spanish," Laurence said, swallowing his confusion, "and one of Prussian. Do you mean to keep it?"

Junichiro twitched as if with indignation, but Kaneko did not answer, only looking down still at the sword: Laurence had an impression he was dissatisfied with the answer, but why he should have cared where the sword had come from, Laurence could not say. "If not," he added, "I would be glad for its return."

"Ah," Kaneko said, and tapped his fingers once upon the desk, before stilling his hand. "The bakufu has directed that only a samurai may bear a long sword."

"If that is, as I suppose, a knight," Laurence said, "I am the third son of the Earl of Allendale and, as I have already said, a ship's captain: I must consider both my birth and my rank adequate to my arms by any reasonable standard. I will speak plainly, sir: if you mean to pillage me, I should be hard-put to prevent you under the circumstances, but I will thank you not to dress it up with justifications as ungentlemanly as they are unwarranted."

"How dare you speak so to my master?" Junichiro flared up, half-rising on his knees. "You should have died, but for his intervention—"

"I did not request your aid," Laurence said flatly, to Kaneko rather than to his squire, "and should rather have had none of it than a pretense at the same: I consider it no favor to be fed and clothed, and held against my will. If you are making yourself my jailor, sir, I should care to know on what grounds I am to meet with such treatment. So far as I know there is peace between our nations, and a shipwreck has in every civilized society all the claims to human sympathy which any man should care to receive, himself being the victim of such a disaster."

"One who breaks the law may desire sympathy and yet not deserve it!" Junichiro said, and then subsided: Kaneko had raised his hand a very little.

"If a man may break the laws of your nation merely by being hurled unwillingly upon your shore," Laurence said dryly, "then they seek to constrain not the will of man, but of God."

"Enough, Junichiro," Kaneko said quietly, when the young man would have answered hotly again. "The objection is just: I have not been of true service to you, as I vowed to be."

He sat in silence a moment, looking down at his desk, while Laurence wondered at *vowed:* he had done nothing to earn any promise of service himself; was Kaneko under some sort of religious obligation?

"The obligations of honor are many," Kaneko said at last, "and often contradictory."

Junichiro made a violent motion of protest, a hand chopped across the air, outstretched as if he meant to catch the words even being spoken. Kaneko glanced at him, and with affection but sternly said, "Enough, Junichiro."

"Master," Junichiro said, "not for *this*. Not—"

Laurence watched them, disturbed: the young man's voice was breaking, though Kaneko seemed as placid as a lake; he felt abruptly as awkward as though he had wandered into a stranger's house, and found it full of family quarrels addressed only obliquely, through hints.

"I must write to Lady Arikawa," Kaneko said, "and offer her my apologies. I see now that I have acted wrongly: I did not have the right to undertake an oath which might expose her to charges of disobedience to the bakufu. I regret that you must endure a delay in my answer," he added to Laurence. "It must be her will, and not mine, whether I am permitted to fulfill my vow with honor by offering you assistance, and then make her my amends."

"Pray Heaven she commands otherwise," Junichiro said.

"You will desire no such thing," Kaneko said, sharply, and after a moment, the young man looked away and muttered, "No."

Kaneko nodded once, and then dismissed them both silently but pointedly by returning his attention to his writing-work as thoroughly as if he had been alone in the chamber.

Laurence hesitated, but the decision seemed made: he followed Junichiro's shoulders, hunched forward a little as though he still felt his master's reproof, back through the corridors to his own chamber. "I should like my own clothing again, at least," he said abruptly, when they had reached the small room, and he had stepped inside, "if there is no objection to that."

"If you wish to look like a ragged beggar, I suppose it can be accomplished," Junichiro said, savagely, and closed the wall-panel behind him. But Laurence for the moment was as glad to be shut in with his own thoughts.

It seemed plain that the law here was inhospitable in the extreme to foreigners, and only some kind of vow—now-regretted—had impelled Kaneko to undertake the forms of charity towards him, evidently at real risk of his own disgrace. This Lady Arikawa, whoever she might be—perhaps his liege, certainly a person of authority—would be under no similar constraint. Kaneko might wish to leave his fate to the will of this lady, and so propitiate her, but Laurence felt not the slightest inclination to accommodate his plans. If return he owed, for hospitality so unwillingly given, then removing himself from the situation was all the return he was prepared to make.

The house was large, but hardly fortified, and he had seen only a few manservants. If the law generally barred the possession of blades, his own lack might not be an insurmountable obstacle if he could not get at the sword; although that, too, might be accomplished. The chief difficulty was not an escape, he thought, but its sequel. He could with an effort summon up the shape of the nation, on a chart, but he had never sailed this way in his life. If he had been asked to find Nagasaki by latitude and longitude, from memory, he might as well have made for Perdition straightaway.

But with any luck he could find his way back to the coast, whence perhaps some fisherman might be prevailed upon to carry him in secret to the port: and if he had not dreamt it in his delirium, the buttons of his coat had been gold. If not, in any case there might be a few coins in a pocket, or slipped through into the lining, if his things had not been pillaged.

They had not. Junichiro returned only a little while later with a servant trailing him, who set down on the floor just inside the room the bundle of clothing. And when the door had closed, and Laurence held the salt-stained and ruined clothes, he found the buttons, still firmly sewn on, were gold; and so, too, were the long narrow bars athwart each shoulder where the epaulettes had ought to be—

—and the coat itself was an aviator's green.

The first order of business was plainly to get the ship afloat again: a ship sitting on rocks was of no use to anyone. "But shan't the ocean get in, once those are underwater?" Lily said, her head tilted to examine the gaping holes where the rocks had pierced the hull and yet stood within, keeping the *Potentate* fixed upon the shoals.

"Oh! by no means," Temeraire said. "They will patch it, with some timber and oakum, I believe; or perhaps with something else, it makes not a particle of difference. That is not *our* affair: that is for the sailors to worry about."

He spoke with impatience, which he was aware Lily did not deserve, but he could not quite help himself. It was so very hard to stay here, especially when he was forced to overhear the officers, who insisted on speaking to one another in the certainty of Laurence's death; even Granby, of whom Temeraire would have expected better, had only said to Hammond, "For Heaven's sake, Hammond, let him think as he likes. It will take him dreadfully, when he *does* believe it."

"Well, I am *not* going to believe it, so there," Temeraire said, to himself; but it certainly did not improve his already-great anxiety to be away, searching for Laurence; and neither did Churki sitting there like a great unhelpful lump and wagging her head seriously and saying, "This is what comes of putting all your heart in just one person! Hammond, I should have mentioned before, I hope *you* are thinking of marriage, and do not fear that I am inclined to be unreasonable. As long as she is young enough to have a great many children, I will be very pleased, whatever your choice."

Temeraire snorted: Churki might be considerably older, and very experienced from her service with the Incan army, but what did she know of it, anyway. He was quite done considering her opinion as particularly worthwhile; at least, on *this* subject.

But he very badly wished to go look for Laurence, anyway: and after all, there was no egg *yet*; there might not be an egg for days, and until there was an egg, it was none of his business but Iskierka's, whatever she might say. And he would have gone, indeed—if only he could have persuaded himself that this explanation would hold the least weight with Laurence.

But Temeraire could just see himself trying to tell Laurence that he had left an egg on a ship swinging about on some rocks, with no-one to look after it but Iskierka. And not just any egg, but his very own egg and Iskierka's: a Celestial and Kazilik cross, which

Granby had said that very afternoon, to Captain Blaise, was likely worth more than the crown jewels of Britain—Temeraire had never seen these, but he was sure they must be impressive—and they must have a great deal of straw and a warm room set aside for it, if he pleased.

"But the ship is not in any *real* danger, at present," Temeraire argued, to an imagined Laurence, "and after all if it did sink, we are close enough to fly to shore. And it is not *only* Iskierka to watch over it: there are Maximus and Lily, too, who would not let anything happen to the egg; and the rest of our formation, and Kulingile and Churki, besides. Really it would be extraordinary if anything should go wrong—"

But the vision of Laurence was unpersuaded, and only looked at him with gentle reproof: it was not *their* responsibility; it was his, and not to be pushed off onto someone else. Temeraire's ruff drooped as he lost the argument with himself once again.

"Anyway," he said to Lily now, out loud, with apology in his tone, "I am sure they will manage that part of the business perfectly well: so pray let us think how we are to get her off the rocks, instead."

He had hoped, at first, that they might simply be able to lift the ship with all of them working together, but the ship's master Mr. Ness had categorically made this impossible as a matter of weight. When he had worked the figures large enough to see clearly, Temeraire had been forced to admit as much: why on earth anyone had put five hundred tons of pig iron and another four hundred of shingle at the very bottom of the *Potentate*'s hold was quite a mystery to him, and he could not in the least work out how she stayed afloat ordinarily, but lifting her straight up by even an inch would certainly be beyond their power.

"If only we might rig a pulley!" he added again, but his best ingenuity had failed at contriving any way to establish a pulley in mid-air, above the ship, out in the middle of the ocean. "Or a lever—"

"Well, what about a lever?" Maximus said, gingerly sitting back on his haunches on the shoals, giving over his own attempts to inspect the holes: the ocean was too rough to see them from any distance. "That is only a stick, put underneath and pushed, ain't it?" and Temeraire paused. He had been stopped, by the size of the ship, but perhaps—

"Where the devil are we to get a lever big enough to move her?" Mr. Ness called down at them, in exasperation. "Why, it should have to be taller than Babel."

"We do not want *one* lever," Temeraire said, with a sudden burst of inspiration. "We want three: one for me, and Maximus, and Kulingile, all to push on at once; and we will get trees from the shore to make them."

Laurence would have given a great deal for a pair of boots. He contented himself, in the meantime, by working out a way of lacing the sandals more closely to his feet with the unraveled remnants of his woolen stockings, braided to make thin ropes. The coat he made into a bundle with his trousers: at least in the native clothing, he hoped he would not be utterly conspicuous at a glance, when he had tied a rag over his hair.

The bundle he left in the corner of the room when the servants came with the evening meal, and despite the reawakening of his sense of taste, he forced himself to eat even the fermented fish with its sour, vinegared rice; he could not anticipate another meal, any time soon. When it was cleared away, and the noises of the house began to die away along with the light filtering in through the rice-paper walls, Laurence debated with himself the merits of going after the sword. All practicality argued against it. He could not be sure the sword would yet be in Kaneko's office, nor that the chamber would be unguarded; if he did retrieve it, the blade should then have to be concealed somehow, or draw unwanted attention. A sword wrapped in a bundle of clothing would be of little use if he

24

were confronted unexpectedly by a few pursuers; and only if he were taken so might he hope to escape.

"Well," Laurence said, standing, "I may as well have a look: if it does not come easy to hand, I may always withdraw." He felt awkward, uneasy in the decision: irrational, when so many sensible arguments stood against it. He could not have said why; some inarticulate feeling only revolted. He did not want to leave the sword.

He mentally told himself to wake at four bells of the middle watch, and slept until the deep of the night, rousing from another strange and unpleasant dream: great chains tangled around his wrists, dragging him through deep water. He took his bundle, slung over a shoulder by his belt, and stepped cautiously out into the hallway: the soft matting did not betray him as he walked, barefoot to keep the slap of the sandals from making any noise.

The walls were a faint luminescent grey, paler than their frames. He kept the very tips of his fingers lightly against the surface of the paper, guiding his steps through the dark. There was a yellow glow of lantern-light somewhere on his right—outside the house, he thought; within, all the rooms were dark. He came to Kaneko's office, and the door slid soundlessly open on its track. He thought at first he had mistaken the room: the desk was gone, and the room entirely bare at first glance. Then Laurence saw the furniture had all been tidied away against the walls, and the writing-desk stood atop a low chest.

He carefully lifted down the desk, and opening the lid found the blade wrapped in a soft silk cloth, which he left behind. He put the sword inside his bundle of clothing, pulling out folds to conceal it from hilt to tip, and restored the chest and desk to their places. He was comforted to have the sword again, and yet distressed for being so: too much as though he could not trust himself, his own feelings, to be as they ought.

Slipping back into the hallway, he looked for a way out, and followed a breath of air to the entryway: a very indifferent sentry drowsed in a corner, and Laurence was past him and had a foot in the gardens when a great roaring came from above, a sound at once familiar and bone-rattling, though he had not heard it since the battle of the Nile: a dragon, overhead, and the lights of all the house flared at his back.

"Buggering mad, the lot of you," Mr. Ness had said, rudely, but Temeraire had with some exasperation demanded a better suggestion of him and, failing to receive any, had nodded firmly.

"Then we shall at least try," he said, "and if it does not work, then I suppose you must begin to take out all that ballast and throw it into the ocean, along with the cannon, until we *can* lift the ship; and while you do that, Iskierka will go to the shore to be safe, and the other dragons will stay with her and the egg, and I will go and find Laurence. You *will* stay with the egg?" he appealed, turning his head.

"Of course we will," Maximus said stoutly, and Lily added, "All of us: except Nitidus will go with you, to carry messages back and forth," an excellent notion. Temeraire was quite sure no-one would give any trouble to Iskierka *and* Lily *and* Maximus.

"Anyway," Lily said, "perhaps it needn't come to that, and I am quite ready to be off these rocks: let us go by all means and fetch some trees."

But they were unable to leave immediately: "I want to come, too!" Kulingile called down, in protest. Certainly Temeraire could not stay, but Maximus stood on seniority and refused to stay behind, either, which bode fair to make a quarrel; and meanwhile Hammond began bleating of the necessity to avoid being seen. Well, Temeraire did not mean to go in blowing on trumpets, but after all, they did need to take away several large trees, and he supposed someone might notice: that would not be his fault.

"We had better come along, then, Hammond; and all your crews, also," Churki said.

26

Hammond, taken aback, said, "Certainly not—a martial presence, nothing more undesirable—"

But Churki shook her head censoriously at him. "If there are dragons here, they will certainly assume we are here to take their people away if they do not see we have any of our own. And if there are men, they will want men to talk to: that is only the natural order of things, and all the more so if they are like these peculiar sailors you have here on this vessel, who are afraid of dragons."

Hammond paused, doubtful; Temeraire could see the sense in what Churki said, but he did not mean to countenance the delay involved in getting all the crews aboard. He only had a scant few officers himself, but Lily and her formation-dragons had their full crews, and even the aviators could not easily go clambering aboard from the precarious surface which the ship presently offered.

"The captains shall come with us," Temeraire said, "and Ferris shall come with me, which will make a sensible number of men, and not any sort of threatening number; and," to Kulingile, "this time Maximus shall go, and if we cannot get the boat off, then *next* time, you shall: that is surely only fair. And," he added, very handsomely in his opinion, "I will take the lines when we come back to give you a rest before we lever her off, even though it will not be my turn yet."

"I do not need a rest," Kulingile said disconsolately. "This is not very difficult: it is only tiresome, and I want something better to eat, which you are sure to get when you are on land."

"Oh!" Iskierka said, raising up her head from the dragondeck, where she had lain down again, ignoring Granby and Maximus's surgeon Gaiters clambering about her hindquarters, consulting in low voices, "a cow! You shall bring me back a cow, Temeraire; do not forget it."

"Wherever am I to find a cow, which is not someone's property?" Temeraire said in exasperation, and Hammond at once began to speak again—likely the discussion should have been another hour, but Temeraire realized his mistake and said quickly, "but we will bring you both back something good to eat, if we should find anything without anyone seeing us, or objecting: we will save you the very best of what we find, you have my promise."

"Well, that is fair," Kulingile said, mollified, and Temeraire put out a foreleg on the dragondeck for Ferris, who hesitated only a moment before climbing into his grasp, and then launched them before anyone else could object further, or make any more unreasonable demands.

Ferris was very quiet, when he had got astride Temeraire's neck and buckled himself on, while they hovered waiting for the other dragons to take up their captains and come aloft—Temeraire was careful to keep out of ear-shot of the deck. "Are you quite well, Ferris?" Temeraire said, craning about his head.

Ferris hesitated; he looked a great deal better lately, Temeraire had even before now noticed and approved: he could not help but congratulate himself for it, and see in it evidence that he was not a careless guardian of his crew, despite all their trials amongst the Inca and since.

Certainly Ferris was happier than when he had first come back to them in New South Wales; he was not so weary-looking, and the ruddy blotches which had marred his face then had cleared. He looked nearer his four-and-twenty than he had, and if he did not wear a green coat—Temeraire did not understand why Hammond had not straightened out that matter yet—at least the coat which he did wear, brown, was neat and trim and with silver buttons; and he took excellent care of his linen, which was properly white.

"You ought have taken Forthing," Ferris said abruptly.

"Oh, Forthing," Temeraire said, with a flick of his ruff. "Whyever for? I do not see why I ought to be giving Forthing any special notice: he is very well, I suppose, for ordinary work."

"He is an officer of the Corps," Ferris said, "and I—I am not; he is your first lieutenant."

"You were, before him," Temeraire said, "except for Granby;

whom I cannot ask to come away from Iskierka under the circumstances. I do not take any notice of what some silly court-martial may have said, Ferris: I hope you do not think I do, and you ought not, either. Why, they declared Laurence should be put to death; you cannot imagine their judgment holds any water with me, or anyone of sense."

Ferris was silent, and then he said, "You wouldn't be taking Forthing up, no matter what, I suppose."

"Taking him up?" Temeraire said. "I am perfectly happy for him to ride, when the rest of the crew do," although this was not *entirely* true: with as much opportunity as Ferris had been given, during their brief stay in Brazil, Forthing had not bothered to repair any of his wardrobe but what had outright holes in it; his green coat was faded almost to grey, his neckcloth a disgrace, and his trousers frayed at hem and seams. It was an embarrassment, and all Temeraire's hinting had gone unheeded entirely.

"No, I mean," Ferris said, hesitated, and said, "if Captain Laurence—if we should not—"

Temeraire was still quite puzzled a moment; then he understood, and indignation swelled his breast. "I should not take that slovenly third-rate—*piker* for my captain if he were the last person to be had on the earth," he said, heatedly. "Oh! *Him,* to succeed Laurence: I should like to see it! If the Admiralty should dare to propose it, I should go to Whitehall and bring the Navy Offices down about their ears.

"Anyway," he added, in the teeth of his own anxiety, "I am sure Laurence will look after himself very well, until we can come get him: oh! Why are they taking so very long about getting aloft?"

The flight was not a long one, the coast rising ahead of them as they flew, the waters still depthless blue-black beneath. Dulcia and Nitidus sped on ahead in spite of Hammond's cries of protest, but they circled back to meet the rest of them shortly before they all came over the coast: they had seen a few small fishing-boats, they reported, and a great many large half-drowned rice fields, with the beginnings of green shoots.

"But nothing very nice to eat," Nitidus said sadly. "Why, I did not even see a sheep, or a goat."

"Thank Heaven," Temeraire could overhear Hammond say, foolishly: it would have been nice to know sheep might be had, even if they could not easily be got.

Captain Warren fetched Nitidus a buffet to the shoulder, and raised his speaking-trumpet to call over from his back, as they fell back into formation, "More to the point, there's a bay straight-away three points to the north, with pine-trees as handsome as you could like."

The bay was isolate, the glossy black water's surface broken with a great many lumpy protruding rocks which likely made it inconvenient for fishing-boats, and showed no signs of use except a low stone wall which did not seem to have any purpose at all; it only ran along the shore in either direction. Hammond let himself down from Churki's back clumsily but with haste the instant they had landed, and hurried to inspect: it was overgrown with a carpet of pale short green grass. "I see no sign of any other sort of traffic," he said, with great relief, when he had straightened up, "so now pray let us get the trees and be away: at once, at once. I shall account all arrears of Fortune paid off, if only we should escape without notice."

Lily cocked her head, considering, and said, "I suppose we should like them to fall inwards: stand back, all of you, if you please."

"And to the north," Captain Harcourt added, from her back, looking at the narrow wind-socks which stood up from Lily's harness at various points. "Sing out when you are all safe away."

Temeraire waited until Hammond with the rest of the company was moving, hastily, out of any chance of Lily's acid spattering, and then announced, "I will go aloft, and see if I can make out anything more of the countryside: I should not like to disappoint Iskierka."

In point of fact, he was quite willing to disappoint Iskierka if there were no cows to be had; but so long as they were here on land, Temeraire did not see any reason not to have a look around for Laurence. "Of course we are not *likely* to see him," he added to Ferris, over his shoulder, as he flew quickly away before he might have to hear Hammond shouting protests after him, "but if only we should happen to, how convenient that would be: even Hammond could not complain, then. And even if we do not, we will have saved some time, later; we will not have to search here again. We will not go far, we will only go along the coast—"

Indeed, he did not go so far that he did not hear the thundering crash of the first pine, coming down; he did not wish to risk overlooking any sign. The coast was mostly rocky, save for a few other inlets and narrow streams coming down, but not very high. "I do not think it would be *excessively* difficult to get safely ashore, for a man swimming," Temeraire said to Ferris.

Ferris said, "There aren't cliffs, at least," in a consoling way. "Shan't we turn back, now? Those fishermen there are sure to see us if only they look up, and I think that must be a harbor over there—"

"But there are a few more beaches in this direction," Temeraire said. "We shall go and have a look at those, from the air: I am sure they are too busy fishing to pay any attention to—"

He was interrupted in this optimistic speech by a sudden bellowing roar, loud and strangely gargled: he turned back hurriedly. "I do not see anyone in the air," Temeraire said, uncertainly, peering in every direction: the day was clear, and he could not imagine where the roar had come from. "Perhaps it was only another pine coming down—"

"That noise was no tree-fall," Ferris said, urgently, and Temeraire could not disagree however much he wished to do; he turned back towards the bay and crested the trees just in time to find, to his appalled surprise, Maximus and Lily and the others all mantling towards a monstrous sea-serpent rearing itself up out of the

31

bay. The rocks were not rocks at all; they were a part of its body, and it was twice as big as Maximus even only in the parts which Temeraire could see.

And then Temeraire realized he was wrong: it was *not* a serpent; it was a dragon, with forelegs out upon the sand: only it was very long, and with stubby wings. It opened its mouth and made another roaring noise, a deep angry growling demand at the formation, which carried over the water clear enough, but in some language which Temeraire did not recognize.

They stood all amazed a moment, regarding one another, very much like figures upon a war-table from Temeraire's distant view. When none of them answered, the serpent-dragon reached for the second tree, which had struck partway into the water. Lily sprang forward and put her talons upon it; the great dragon made a dismissive snort in her direction, which needed no translation.

Temeraire beat urgently towards them as Lily raised her wings and flared them out a little: the brilliant orange and purple would have warned any European beast, and their immense wingspan, but it was no surprise if the Japanese dragon did not recognize her as a Longwing, or did not know what that meant; and she was not a third his size. Temeraire saw Captain Harcourt, a tiny figure, lean forward on Lily's neck and point to the sand; Lily turned her head and spat a thin demonstrative stream of acid, to make her point.

The serpentine dragon drew back from the hissing black stench and the thin trails of smoke, its own small wings flattening against its back, and then it plunged its head into the water and opened its jaw wide. The dragon, already so massive but slender, began now to rapidly swell up and out to the sides: Temeraire could not understand in the least how he was managing it, and then the dragon reared itself back out and up, and up, and up, and it blasted Lily and all the others with a torrent of water.

"Oh!" Temeraire cried, "Oh, it is a Sui-Riu!" that variety of dragon being known to him from Sir Edward Howe's work on the Oriental breeds, but as he flew towards them as quickly as ever he could, he thought with some strong indignation that Sir Edward might have mentioned the immense—the truly immense—scale; and the book had not in the least conveyed the true impact of the water-spouting.

Even Maximus had been swept off his feet, and was now tangled and struggling up against the tree-line; Lily was coughing and sputtering, having taken the brunt of the torrent, jerking her head, and Nitidus and Dulcia had been carried into the bay itself and were floundering in the waves. Immortalis and Churki were a tumbled sand-clogged mess flung into the woods, trying to get their footing again; Sutton and Messoria, having stationed themselves back and apart, were a little better off and getting into the air.

But the Sui-Riu evidently had no intention of letting them get their bearings back: he had plunged his head back into the water and was inhaling again. He might blast them on the far side, and so sweep more of them into the water, where he would certainly have an advantage, since he could breathe through it: unsporting, except that to be fair he was one against eight.

However, Temeraire could not give him much credit for that: no-one had asked the Sui-Riu to be so unfriendly. Lily had given the most polite warning one could ask for—if *she* had liked to be similarly nasty, she might have taken the Sui-Riu directly in the eye with her shot. Temeraire worked his lungs as he flew, gathering breath, and even as the Sui-Riu drew himself up out of the water again, Temeraire dived towards him, roaring in full and terrible voice.

The waters of the bay shuddered from the divine wind, the surface going for a moment bowl-like and concave; the Sui-Riu was bowled over onto his side with an immense splash, and his torrent erupted involuntarily and spilled harmless over the water, merely adding more turbulence. But the distance was too great, or else perhaps the water somehow absorbed some of the impact; the Sui-Riu managed to right himself in the water, and did not look so dreadfully injured as did most dragons who had borne the direct brunt of the divine wind. Only a little blood trickled black from his right ear, over scales that were a deep greenish black the color of dry seaweed, and his eye on that side was bloodshot: otherwise he seemed quite all right, and great sharp fins were rising up angrily all over his back, like blades.

But Temeraire was hovering off the shore, now, closer; and Maximus and Lily were righting themselves. The others fell into line behind Lily, taking up their formation-positions. Temeraire did not much like formation-fighting, but one could not deny its tactical usefulness, and the Sui-Riu evidently did not have any difficulty recognizing his increasing disadvantage. Shaking away the last of the effects, he looked up at Temeraire, and his eyes—a great slitted pale grey that looked nearly white—drew thin and narrow.

The Sui-Riu rumbled some remarks in a most angry tone, sounding more like a distant thundercloud than anything else. "I do not have any notion what you are saying," Temeraire informed him loudly, in Chinese, "but you needn't complain of us, when you attack people out of nowhere—if you should—"

But as abruptly as he had emerged before, the Sui-Riu was gone: in one smooth motion he plunged beneath the dark murky waters of the bay, clouded even further now by silt and sand raised in their exchange. One long barnacled curve of tail breached the water, and was gone: though Temeraire held position a long time, he did not break the surface again.

Chapter 3

The lanterns were coming alight, one after another, all through the house. Laurence could trace the servants moving in waves as the glow spread behind the walls. The sentry at the door was waking with a snorting start and jerking to his feet, blinking around. Laurence for a moment considered: the man was paunchy and sleep-dazed, armed only with a short blade—a quick struggle might see him through—

But the dragon was descending from aloft—the dragons, rather, for there were two immense black shadows against the milky wash of the moonless night, coming into the lamp-light. One, the larger, had wide green eyes that glowed like a cat's: it was not looking at him presently, but if it could see in the dark, like the Fleur-de-Nuit, nothing could be easier than for the beast to hunt him down while he fumbled over unfamiliar ground in the dark.

Quickly, Laurence turned instead and thrust his small bundle into the ornamental bushes planted against the side of the house, and then went and stood by the door of the house to wait, as though he had been brought there. The sentry looked at him in confusion, but Laurence looked back at him with unmoving face, brazening it out, and the man was in a moment overwhelmed by a sudden flow of servants hurrying out into the garden. Junichiro appeared by Laurence's elbow.

"What are you doing out here?" the young man demanded, but

preoccupied himself did not wait for an answer; instead he seized Laurence by the arm and drew him along with the flow of people. "They have certainly come on your account," he said, "so you may as well stay here."

Kaneko was coming out of the house himself, dressed in formal robes; he wore two blades at his belt and came past his servants, who had arrayed themselves in a square as neat as any infantry troop. Two last men were hurrying around the perimeter of a great flagstoned courtyard, lighting lamps all around it, and then they all knelt together as the dragons came descending into the square, Kaneko out ahead of the rest of the party.

The dragons settled themselves neatly upon the ground; the larger, grey in body and something the size of a middle-weight, wore curious pale green silken dressings the color of its eyes wound about its neck and wing-tips and forelegs, which coming loose made graceful arcs about its body like sails spilling their wind. It had not a single man aboard. The smaller dragon, a brilliant yellow beast larger than a Winchester though not up to combat-weight, carried four: of these, the lead gentleman was dressed in elaborate and formal robes bearing signs of some sort of office, and the others were evidently servants who carried boxes and one an armful of scrolls, and preceding him down unfolded a set of steps to enable him to make a more ponderous and imposing descent.

The grey dragon bent its head towards Kaneko while the men dismounted. It spoke to him in the Japanese tongue, and he bowed more deeply and said something back. Laurence caught the name Arikawa out of it, but he saw no women; perhaps these were Lady Arikawa's emissaries, and he could see nothing to bode well for his future in their cold faces.

There was a little more formal exchange between them, which Laurence could not follow: he was all the more conscious of his utter isolation, of himself as a prisoner among strangers, unable even to pick out a word or to conceive their intentions. The servants were dismissed; the guests and Kaneko went inside the house;

36

Junichiro took him by the arm and drew him along after them. They turned immediately from the entryway into a chamber on the side, whose entire outer wall was slid back and left wide open to face upon the courtyard where the dragons had settled themselves.

The servants brought great kettles of steaming sharp-nosed tea out to bowls laid before the beasts. The official and Kaneko were served afterwards; they drank, making what Laurence assumed from their tone was mere small conversation, until abruptly he was drawn in front of them, and without hesitation or change of demeanor the official addressed him in Chinese and said, "What is your purpose in coming to our nation?"

"Sir," Laurence said, "I have no purpose but to be restored to my country-men, and my ship if at all possible."

It was the opening salvo of an interrogation which proceeded despite the hour of the night, and was as frustrating to Laurence as it was to his interlocutor. He could not but be conscious of the impossibility of avowing himself unable to *remember* his purpose. Better to be thought a liar than a lunatic, he was sure, but unable to confess this truth, he felt every other word hung upon a knife-edge of honor. He did not know why he was here, and therefore could not say with honest confidence that he meant them no injury. What if the Japanese sheltered some French ship, which he pursued?

"I am a shipwreck: I did not choose to be thrown on your shore, and my presence here is the merest accident," he said again, the best he could do. "And as you have received no declaration of war, from Britain, nor any envoy," he added, hoping as much was true, "then, sir, I hope you will believe I am not here as your enemy. You surely cannot imagine me intended in any way to be a spy, and His Majesty's Government does not behave in so underhanded a manner as to attack another nation with no warning or quarrel."

The official, who had been addressed by the others as Matsudaira, was an older man, with a narrow beard that framed his face in dark lines salted a little with grey; his mouth was thin and hard.

"Indeed," he said, and put down his teacup. "With your gracious permission, Lady Arikawa, we will take the Englishman to Hakata Bay, and consult him upon the evidence there."

Laurence looked in confusion for any new arrival; then the grey dragon answered, in Chinese, "Let it be done," with some reluctance in her tone. Kaneko, frowning slightly, looked at her: the dragon shook her head at him, setting the arcs of green fabric trembling.

The sun was rising, little by little, as they went. Kaneko alone went with the grey dragon—who, Laurence somewhat doubtfully supposed, *was* Lady Arikawa. She bent her foreleg and invited Kaneko upon her back: evidently some sign of great condescension on her part, and one of which Matsudaira did not approve, judged from the tightening of his lips. Laurence himself and the rest of the company went aboard the second, smaller beast.

Junichiro, left behind to watch the house, had watched them go aboard with his eyes darting anxiously from his master to Matsudaira: he, too, saw the magistrate's frowns. Yet he maintained his composure, or nearly so: when the dragons leapt aloft, his face turned up to follow them, betraying for a moment a boyish note of longing. Laurence recognized it as kin to the feeling which he had worn himself as a boy hanging on the prow of his uncle's ship, although he had never thought of attaching such a feeling to dragons.

Laurence was grateful to find both his stomach and his courage easily equal to the journey; he had been able to make his way up the harness without hesitation or awkwardness, and the wind cool and fragrant and crisp in his face was a pleasure despite the great rushing speed. They were near the ocean: dawn broke over the water brilliantly, sunlight a streaming silver path towards them so that Laurence's eyes teared with the glare. The green fabric on Lady Arikawa's back, which she had drawn taut about herself for the flight, was bordered with innumerable small gems which blazed in the new light. She averted her eyes from the sun, however, and dropped back so the smaller dragon's shadow could land upon her head and give her some relief from the light. Laurence noted it with some small gratitude: she would be no very effective searcher during the daylight, perhaps—if he could somehow still manage his escape.

The tenor of Matsudaira's interrogation had left Laurence in no doubt of the increasing urgency of flight. He could curse the ill-fortune that had brought the dragons down at so unexpected an hour, but not berate himself for failure. He had planned his attempt at escape as well as he could, and at least he had avoided giving rise to suspicion—he was neither bound nor chained at present, and Kaneko had not even missed the sword yet.

As soon as another opportunity afforded, even perhaps during this excursion, Laurence meant to try again. He had kept the gold bars tucked into the sash of his garment, so he was not wholly without resources even without his lost bundle. The flight indeed might aid him, for they were aloft more than an hour: Laurence had not realized he had been brought so far from the shore, but Kaneko's house evidently stood perhaps fifteen or even as much as twenty miles inland.

"Hakata Bay" was a promising sound, however: at least he should be on the coast again, and if there were any chance of slipping away, he could more easily hunt out some fishing-boat. So, at least, he told himself; he refused to listen to the grim internal voice which would fain have whispered in his ear at length of the impracticalities of any such plan, and the absurdity of escaping alone from a large and well-armed party accompanied by dragons, no less. Hopelessness was a worse defeat than any other; he did not mean to yield to it.

The countryside below was not unpromising for his purposes. At first the land below was settled; but towards the end of their flight, the dragons turned away from a bustling harbor full of shipping, following the line of an old low stone wall—some sort of coastal defense, perhaps? It resembled nothing so much as some of the defenses thrown up against Napoleon, on Britain's own shores.

It carried them along to a more isolate shore, hidden by the curving of the coastline, where there was only a mere fringe of sand leading up to a thick forest of tree-trunks, which Laurence thought might serve to hide him even from dragons.

But as they landed, the waters of the bay shuddered and broke open, and a monstrous creature came rising from the waves. It was something like the sea-serpents of half-legendary repute, but magnified to a size that put to shame the most outrageous and absurd sea-tales Laurence had ever heard passed off for truth by sailors; he had never even conceived its like.

The smaller dragons landed before it and bowed their heads low to the ground; the men slid to the sand and all knelt deeply before the creature. It climbed a little way out on the shore to meet them, its enormous talons digging great gouges in the sand, so deep that water pooled up in them as it lifted them to claw its way further up the shore. It made a rumbling speech to the party, permitting them to rise, and even inclined its head a very little to Lady Arikawa; but when at last it swung its heavy finned head towards Laurence, a glitter of angry malice shone in its pallid white eyes, one of them shot through with broken black vessels of blood.

"Pray be reasonable," Hammond said, leaning greenish over the rail; he was chewing a great lump of coca leaves in his distended cheek, an effort to make up for the wad he had lost when the Sui-Riu had swamped them: he was still in his sodden clothing. "We *must* go on to Nagasaki, as soon as we may, and there make amends. Only consider: if the beast was not some mere feral creature, and it should report our quarrel, any efforts to find Captain Laurence will certainly be grievously hampered by the opposition of the authorities—"

"What you mean is," Temeraire said, "you want us to run away from that big sea-dragon like cowards, only because you are afraid he will come after the ship."

He did not bother to be polite about it. Captain Blaise had not

40

been the least reluctant to express his own sentiments, when Temeraire and the others had returned, on the subject of the Sui-Riu as it was described to him—sentiments which did not in Temeraire's opinion do him the least credit. "We must get out of these waters at once," Blaise had said, and he had made all the men beat to quarters instantly, though there had not been any sign of the other beast all the long flight back.

"And," Temeraire added, "this after we blacked his eye for him quite thoroughly, to boot; it seems to me you might have a little confidence in us."

They were waiting now only for high tide to finish coming in: the great tree-trunks had been with enormous effort wedged slowly and painfully between the ship and the reef; the anchor-cables were woven in and around Messoria's harness and Immortalis's. Maximus would take one lever, Kulingile the other, and Temeraire the middle. Iskierka would lie about on the rocks doing nothing but criticizing—Temeraire snorted—and Lily would look on, and perhaps strike the shoals with acid, as they tried to get the ship off them, if that should seem useful.

"And if he does show himself, while you are working," Iskierka put in, yawning, "I am perfectly able to breathe flame, even if I do not mean to be exerting myself a great deal presently. He will certainly think better of attacking us, then."

"Dear God," Captain Blaise said, and seized Granby by the arm to object violently to any such proceeding: the sailors were really unreasonable on the subject of fire, Temeraire felt; it was not as though Iskierka had proposed setting the sails alight.

He withdrew along the line of the shoals to wait alone until the tide should rise, and simmered quietly beneath the steady cold wash of the waves. He would *not* go on to Nagasaki. He did not know where precisely Nagasaki was, but it was not near-by; he did not mean to abandon the search for Laurence an instant longer than the ship's rescue required. The egg would be quite safe, once they were afloat again.

The emptiness of the coast he had flown over with Ferris lingered in the back of his mind like an unpleasant aftertaste. It had been three days and nights since Laurence had been swept away—already any visible signs upon the shore might have been lost. Laurence would have gone inland for water, perhaps; or perhaps he had even been lying under some tree for shelter, or calling up to Temeraire from a distance, unheard. Temeraire still had not the least doubt of Laurence's survival, but that alone would be of little use if he could not *find* Laurence.

"Temeraire!" Dulcia landed on his back and knocked him on the shoulder with her head. "We have been calling and calling: it is time to get the ship off the rocks."

"Oh!" Temeraire said, rousing, and found himself very cold and stiff indeed coming out of the great dark circling of his thoughts; the water was almost halfway up his hindquarters, and the short harness about his shoulders was sodden and heavy and dragging as he went into the air, a reminder of his empty back.

Messoria and Immortalis launched themselves with the cables; Dulcia and Nitidus each took another cable, for what help they could give, and Captain Blaise gave the word to throw the sea-anchor over the side beyond them, to help if it might. The tree-tops had been wedged in carefully under the hull, and their long trunks were jutting up from the ocean, froth churning up around them.

"Are you quite ready?" Temeraire asked Maximus and Kulingile.

"I still say there is something strange about this," Demane said, from the dragondeck, gripping the railing hard; he had been reluctant to see Kulingile lent to the attempt at all. "Kulingile, you are sure you will do this? I don't see how it can work—"

"I've told you!" his brother Sipho hissed at him.

Temeraire flattened his ruff: he understood a little Demane's anxiety—there was every reason to believe the Admiralty would be delighted to push him and his brother off if Kulingile were lost: he had still not been confirmed in his rank, and Laurence had been his only patron. But it seemed to Temeraire that this was all the more reason to help him find Laurence and bring him back.

"Oh, I don't mind trying," Kulingile said easily, however. "If it don't work, we will only sit on those logs for a while, and nothing much will happen."

Temeraire drew breath to explain, yet again, why it *would* work, after all; then he forced himself not to argue. "If you are quite ready," he said, and together they flung themselves down upon the levers, and as one exhaled as deeply as they could, from all their air-sacs.

Temeraire had worked it all out on paper, or rather, Sipho had worked it out to his direction, with help from a still-doubtful Ness; but paper made nothing to the experience of plunging deep into the icy cold water, feeling his body pulling at him as though an anchor. He had to scrabble desperately to keep himself upon the lever; his own weight would have dragged him instantly deep beneath the surface of the water.

"Hold on, there, you damned lummox!" Berkley was bellowing, over the railing. "Breathe in again!" Maximus was struggling beside him, and Kulingile was sinking so deep the water was nearly to his fore shoulders.

"Oh, but it is working!" Lily cried, on the far side of the ship, and then with alarm, "Look out—" as the ship came up and off the rocks with almost startling ease, and began to slide down the levers towards them.

Laurence had made one of the party which had taken the *Tonnant*, at the Nile, after the Longwing formation above had made its pass. He remembered the great pitted smoking holes, which had gone through the decks, and the screams of the wretched seaman who had incautiously put his bare foot upon one small spatter, not the size of a shilling. One of his mess-mates had chopped his foot off at once, there upon the deck, and so saved the fellow's

43

life; although the wound had mortified and killed him three days later.

He recognized, therefore, the characteristic spattering of the Longwing acid upon the tree-stumps which they showed him, and the earth surrounding them, and although the stolen trees had provoked such hostility in his captors, Laurence could not help but rejoice that at last he could begin to understand; he could make sense of the intelligence these signs offered him. There was a Longwing near-by, and it had come and taken away three prime pieces of timber.

"Taken for masts, most likely," Laurence said, drawing a picture of a sailing ship in the wet sand to translate the word for them. Three masts on such a scale: a dragon transport for sure, which in any event should have been required to carry a Longwing and its usual formation; and *that*, surely, explained Laurence's own presence. The *Reliant* must have been traveling in company with the larger ship, to serve her as a more agile defender: no-one could call transports easy to handle, for all the massive weight of iron they could bring to bear.

The coat—the green coat—must have come off some aviator's back. Perhaps it had been thrown up on the shore beside him by the same storm that had wrecked the ship's masts, and in the first early moments of cold and delirium Laurence had put it on. He wondered now if the sword, too, had come from another man's hand; but he put that doubt aside. If it had, he could more easily restore it himself than could the Japanese—if he were permitted to go home.

And home was now a real possibility. There was a British ship here, in these very waters. She was not sunk; she was injured, but afloat, and her crew hoped to repair her. The *Allegiance*? Laurence wondered. Or perhaps the *Dominion*; although that ship was ordinarily on the run to Halifax. He still did not know what they had been doing with a transport so near Japan, but those questions were as nothing to the sheer inexpressible relief of knowing himself not, as he had begun to feel, wholly adrift, unmoored from any connection to his own life.

Laurence looked up from the sand, and addressed Matsudaira again. "Sir, I will say on behalf of my country-men that I am sure they intended no offense. They came ashore meaning only to take some necessary material for their ship's repair, from what they must have supposed to be a stand of unused timber."

"And where is this ship, now?" Matsudaira said.

His expression betrayed nothing but the same mild interest he had displayed throughout all the conversation, but the question came very quick. Laurence paused. He had just been thinking he might ask for a map of the coastline, or for a local fisherman to question. A transport had a draught near fifty feet: she could not anchor in shallow waters, and would not risk coming very near the coast. Some haphazard anchorage sheltered from the worst of the ocean by shoals was the most likely; near in straight line flight from this bay. He thought he might be able to guess a likely place, and even direct a boat thence, given some sense of the nearby waters.

He looked at the great serpentine creature looming overhead: the gleam of intelligence in its eye was plain, despite its monstrous size, and it was following their conversation with a keen, cold interest. It had come up from the bay with no warning—evidently it could breathe underwater. Laurence could easily imagine what such a sea-dragon could do to a ship, even one the size of a transport. Come up from below, throw her on her beam-ends, heave a loop of its body over the stern and drag her down—he could envision no easy defense. Perhaps the Longwing might be able to strike the beast, but in time to save the ship?

Its eye was fixed upon him, badly bloodshot. Was that merely some accident, or something else? Laurence glanced around the clearing. The ground was trampled into mud, as though after heavy rains; and when he looked he saw more damage to the trees around, smaller saplings crushed, branches fallen. There had been more than a mere dispute here—there had been fighting.

Laurence rose slowly to his feet. "I cannot hazard a guess," he said grimly, and watched Matsudaira's expression harden.

Temeraire was very cold. He did not know anything else, at first, and then his head was out in the air, and Iskierka was hissing at him ferociously, her talons sharp and clawing into his shoulders, saying, "Quick, quick, breathe in!"

The water held him like a vise, dragging. Temeraire tried to breathe and could not: his chest clenched and he vomited instead, gouts of water erupting painfully, dribbling away down his neck in long streams. Then at last Temeraire could draw in a thin, struggling stream of air. Lily was swimming beside him, trying to get her head under his foreleg. He clung to her, and scrabbled with his other foreleg at the great side of the ship, rising up before him; he managed to catch at a porthole, but the ship listed towards him alarmingly, and cries of warning came down.

"Oh! Why will you not listen to me?" Iskierka was saying impatiently. "You must get more air in, I cannot lift you if you will be so heavy!" She lowered her head and butted him.

"But I am trying," Temeraire said, only he could not speak for coughing; every breath was a battle. His sides were filling a little more, but the blood was running down his shoulders and he felt so very heavy. His head was ringing in a very peculiar way, and everything seemed colored with a faint greenish light.

Kulingile came up in the water beside him, bulling in under Temeraire's foreleg, so Temeraire could lean upon him and get out of the water a little more, though Kulingile grunted with the effort. "Get under his hindquarters, if you can," Berkley was calling down.

"Come on, Temeraire, scramble up, there's a good chap," Maximus said. Temeraire did not quite see his way clear to doing as much. He coughed again, and let his head sink against Kulingile's back; he was sliding back into the water, but he could not mind that so much. It did not feel so cold anymore, after all—

"Temeraire!" Roland said, leaning over the side, "if you drown, we shall all sail away and leave Laurence behind! You know no-one else thinks he is alive. You must get up, or else Hammond will make us all go."

Temeraire struggled his head up to protest: he was *not* going to drown, at all; he could swim excellently well. And as for leaving Laurence behind—

"You will, too, drown, and then we *shall* leave him, see if we don't!" Iskierka said, and bit him sharply. "Get out of the water. What else do you suppose you are doing?"

He tried to hiss at her, but he had to get another breath in to do it, and when he had that one, he got another. By slow measures, she and the others managed to help him heave up onto the line of the shoals, though the rocks crumbled as he clawed at them, and the waves tried to drag him back down. He crouched huddled on the rocks at last and breathed again in slow delicious sips of sea-air, splendid even though his throat ached badly, getting them in. His wings rattled against his back with cold.

"Well done, my dear one; let him have a rest," he heard Granby saying, faintly, to Iskierka. "We'll get him aboard as soon as he has filled his air out again." The *Potentate* was moving: Temeraire could see it out of one eye, a few sails rigged out on the mizzen, maneuvering away from the rocks. She was listing a little to one side, but not badly. He closed his eyes.

"Idiocy," he heard Gaiters saying, some indeterminate time after. The sun was beating on his back, now, but it did not seem to warm him. "Emptying your air—what made the lot of you take such a notion into your heads? I should have liked to come back to England with three heavy-weights having drowned themselves not fifty miles from shore; I suppose they would have hanged me and every other surgeon of the party for incompetence. Well, make yourselves of use, now: get him onto the deck at once. We must pack his sides with hot rocks, and fire up the galleys below. D'you think because he's a dragon he can't die of pleurisy?"

"I don't see why you fellows must always be complaining about something new," Maximus said. "We did get the ship back into the water, didn't we? And of course Temeraire will not die of a trifling little cold. But you ain't comfortable where you are," he added in Temeraire's ear, "so do let us get you aboard." His big blunt head came nosing at Temeraire's shoulder.

Temeraire would have preferred not to move very much, at present; his whole body seemed to ache from tail-tip to nose, and his side and his right foreleg felt especially tender and bruised. He did not quite recall what had happened: the ship had come sliding, and he had not been able to get out of the way—diving was quite impossible, and the rocks were too far away to grab a hold of, for he had been on the lever amidships. But nothing after that, except the water, and the cold, and the green glaze that still seemed to hang faintly over all the world.

"Come on, then," Iskierka said crossly, above. "I do not see why you must be making such a fuss at a time like this." She nipped at his hindquarters.

"I am *not* making a fuss," Temeraire wanted to say, but his throat ached so. He let them prod him up onto his haunches, and then Maximus and Kulingile put their shoulders beneath his forelegs.

"Just hop aloft, when you are ready," Maximus said, "and we will go with you, to take some of the weight off: we will see you over to the deck in a trice, see if we do not."

Temeraire did not feel ready, but Iskierka would keep complaining at him, and nipping, and making cutting remarks; and finally he gathered himself and jumped as best he could. "Oh!" he cried, "Oh," for he had *not* been ready, in the least; the pain flaring along his side was like being burnt with a hot poker, to sear a wound after cleaning, but it ran the whole length of his body. His wings snapped tight, and if Kulingile and Maximus had not been beneath him, he should have fallen into the ocean again.

"Ouhff," Kulingile said with a grunt, and wobbled beneath

him as they flew. "No, I am all right," he said; Temeraire heard it only distantly: everything had gone greenish and hazy again, and he felt very queer and ill indeed. He clung on blindly only, until they sank all three of them to the deck together and Maximus and Kulingile eased him gently down.

The planks were warm beneath him; the ship rocked with the familiar ocean swell. Temeraire put his head slowly beneath his wing, and shut his eyes, and knew no more.

"Enough!" Matsudaira struck the table before him with the flat of his hand.

They had taken Laurence back to Kaneko's house, and resumed his questioning in the open room off the courtyard, with Lady Arikawa listening in as she devoured the contents of an entire cauldron which had been brought to her smoking-hot and filled with rice, great bowls of beaten egg and fresh fish flung in to cook against the heated sides. The smell was fantastically appealing, enough to make Laurence a little light-headed; the servants had provided a similar meal, on a smaller scale, to Kaneko and Matsudaira, but he had been given nothing.

There had been no chance yet of escape or evasion, but Laurence told himself that at least now he had his bearings, a little. They were on the western coast of Japan—a pity, that; with Nagasaki on the west—and some seven miles as the crow flew from the nearest shore. Laurence worked the map in his mind while they questioned him; it was a refuge from the awareness that they were not likely to give him much future opportunity to put it to use, with a dragon at the door and increased suspicion.

"You persist in telling evident falsehoods," Matsudaira said. "I will be plain with you: Lord Jinai has told us of the true size of your force. He was attacked by eight dragons of war-like style and of great size. These did not come from England on a boat, and neither did a Celestial. Such a dragon has not been seen across the sea for

49

five centuries, since the servants of the Yuan emperor stole the last egg of the Divine Wind line from Hakozaki Shrine as he withdrew in ignominy from his attempt at conquest, his murderous beasts having slain the rest of that noble line."

The foreign names slid over Laurence's mind without purchase, unfamiliar. "A dragon transport is certainly equal to the task of bearing eight beasts; they are designed for twelve," he said. "As for the particular breed, I am no authority on dragons, and can offer you no explanation but to think your identification mistaken. Dragon-husbandry was not undertaken in my nation before the Norman Conquest, scarce eight hundred years ago; we certainly were not responsible for *that* theft."

He spoke dryly; he was beginning to think it not much beyond them to accuse him of such. The magistrate abruptly snapped shut his fan and pointed it at him. "Speak the truth! You are in league with the Chinese!"

Laurence opened his mouth to answer with heated denial, and then halted. The very tongue in his mouth seemed to give him the lie. He could speak Chinese—why? And Japan was not so far off the course for Guangzhou. Perhaps he *had* come here in league with the Chinese. It was not inconceivable that Britain should have sought an alliance with the mandarins—they were a byword for dragon-breeders, of course; Laurence was sure the Admiralty should have been delighted to purchase some of their beasts as breeding stock.

"Ha," Matsudaira said, in answer to Laurence's silence. "Now, Kaneko-san, let us see this Chinese sword, which you have described to me."

Laurence ruefully watched Junichiro leave the room at Kaneko's nod, knowing he would soon return with fresh provocation for his interrogators. "Sir," he said, "perhaps my information is out of date, but so far as I know, you are not at war with China?" Matsudaira looked at him coldly and said nothing, which Laurence took, perhaps with excessive optimism, for confirmation. "Then any friendship between my nation and China can be no concern of yours, if no offense is given you by either."

"No offense!" Matsudaira said. "Indeed, your brazenness knows no bounds. Permit me to inform you, if you imagine us to be so easily deceived, that I have the honor to be related to the governor at Nagasaki, where three years ago your vessel *Phaeton* by deceit took hostages and issued threats against the ships of the harbor, and fired upon the city."

That, Laurence could not conceal, was a blow; he had heard of no such action. The *Phaeton*—he could only vaguely recall the ship to mind. A frigate? Yes, *Minerva*-class, and he thought Captain Wood had her, but—

Matsudaira added coldly, watching his face, "That vessel's dishonorable captain and all his crew repaid their crimes with their lives." Laurence could not but envision with horror a ruin that might well have been achieved by that monstrous sea-dragon, or another such beast: like a kraken rising from beneath the waves, all unsuspected, to drag the ship down and down, shattered, and spilling the men into the waves to be devoured at its leisure, or by the ocean itself.

He shuddered for it, and for their fate; and more that he knew nothing of it. Three years ago? Could he have lost such a span of memory, and not be wholly mad? Certainly no such event could have escaped his notice—even if the events had gone unreported, he must have heard of the loss of the *Phaeton*.

"I cannot account for such an assault, sir, save by some grave misunderstanding, or if intended as an action against Dutch shipping in your harbor," he said, troubled. "They are French allies—"

"More excuses," Matsudaira said, cutting him off with a slash of the hand, and then Junichiro returned in haste, nearly running, to report the sword missing and launch a new uproar, which Laurence almost welcomed as distraction from the questions he was unable to answer even to himself.

"If I have taken it," Laurence said, when they demanded its

hiding place, "in doing so I have only been taking my own again, and I do not consider I owe you either apology or explanation in such circumstances. Nor could you rationally expect me to hand it back; yet if I should deny having it, you would call it a lie. I must beg to be excused: I have nothing to say upon the subject."

He had already decided to say as much, if he were questioned. He thought only a thorough and systematic search of the grounds would uncover his bundle: the ground outside had been trampled by too many feet, since his abortive escape the previous night, to show any trace of his actions.

Matsudaira was by no means conciliated by this reply. "We will see what you have to say when you have been more rigorously questioned," he said angrily. "I will send for a torturer at once—"

Laurence did not flinch, but regarded him with the flat disdain that any such threat merited. "You may question me as you wish," he said. "I have not lied; and I hope I can answer you and die like an Englishman."

To his surprise, however, Lady Arikawa raised her head and rumbled, low, making an objection. "I do not think that necessary yet," she said, a thin translucent ruff around her neck frilling out.

Matsudaira sat up a little further, with rigid shoulders, and said grimly, "I must with the utmost respect disagree, Lady Arikawa."

Laurence could not argue with the man's courage, at least, to so incite a dragon to anger; Lady Arikawa might easily have seized and broken him like a toy without even rising to her feet, and by the swift slitting of her eyes seemed tempted to do so.

"You are charged to carry out a full investigation," Lady Arikawa said. "We have yet no word from Nagasaki regarding any English vessel in the harbor, nor have the Kirin returned from their survey of the coastal waters, near-by. Surely we can wait for this intelligence to reach us before proceeding."

"The foreigner is certainly condemned by the law, regardless," Matsudaira said, after a moment. The grey dragon's wings flared from her back, unsettled, and folded again; the clawed tips shifted back and forth, restlessly.

Sitting beside Matsudaira and sipping tea, Kaneko had shown no expression but level calm all the while; now he said quietly, "My lady, I most deeply regret my error, and—"

"That is enough," she said, interrupting crisply. "What error can there be in the will of the heavens? Certainly it is only a great service to the bakufu that this barbarian is available to be questioned about these matters; it may be that much benefit to the nation may derive from his rescue. It would be a great impiety upon our part to disregard the means by which the gods have delivered him into our hands, through this vow which caused your eyes to light upon him where he lay in the road. If they did not intend him to be well-treated, they would not have arranged matters so. I cannot agree to a course which despises so clear a sign from the spirit world."

She delivered these arguments with an air almost of triumph. Laurence thought he detected in them rather more sophistry than true religious fervor. He remained unable to follow all the undercurrents, but he gathered at the least that she wished to spare her vassal Kaneko whatever embarrassment he might suffer at being forced to renege on his vow of assistance. Laurence could only suppose that embarrassment to have consequences more extreme than he imagined.

Matsudaira did not seem persuaded, but at least her vehemence gave him pause; he said more cautiously, trying to answer her in the same lines, "And yet as a magistrate, I must pursue my duty to the law by every means: the gods would not have delivered him in ignorance of so commonplace a fact."

"The gods would certainly not have expected you to disregard their wishes," Lady Arikawa returned, with scorn. "Which indeed, they may have meant as a warning. Consider: it is well-known that men of other races are weak. The torture which brings truth from a Japanese may perhaps even slay a Western barbarian, and deprive us of further information."

Laurence derived some black humor from the burst of indignation he instinctively felt at the nonsense of being any less fitted to endure pain: a fine and absurd thing it would be, to make a case for his own torture. However, the argument was ill-chosen on Lady Arikawa's part; Matsudaira and Kaneko could not forbear a doubtful glance in his direction. Laurence was a head taller than any other man in the room, and he could have given any of them thirty pounds or more.

Of course, from Lady Arikawa's perspective—near enough to twelve tons, Laurence would have guessed—the distinction was all muchwhatlike. In any event, Laurence closed his mouth on any retort he might have made, and stood wooden beneath their gaze; the weaker and more helpless they chose to think him the better, if they should set a commensurate guard upon him.

"It perhaps would be wise to employ a truly skilled practitioner," Matsudaira said, after a moment, in a conciliatory manner. "I will send to Edo for a specialist in questioning the sick and the elderly. That will necessitate a certain delay, of course. Perhaps in the intervening time, further intelligence will render the questioning unnecessary, or the foreigner may think better of his lies and confess freely."

Lady Arikawa inclined her head. "It will be convenient for you to keep charge of him here at Kaneko's house, in the meantime," she said—a rather strong hinting, there, and Matsudaira did not attempt to argue with her, but bowed his head in agreement.

Two guards were called in: Matsudaira's men, Laurence thought; they wore signs of authority matching his own. They escorted him, but only back to his original chamber; and there was a tray of food set on a low table in the middle of the floor. Laurence did not hesitate to devour it, and then lay himself down on the straw mat to consider and to rest.

He roused from a half-sleep a little while later; there were voices, coming faint but audible through the walls, and speaking Chinese: Lady Arikawa, and Kaneko with her. "There can be no more honorable fate than to die in the service of Japan, even for a barbarian," she was saying, in an anxious tone, low: Laurence could only surmise she preferred not to be overheard by the servants of the house. "Surely in delivering him to such an end, you will have assisted him?"

Kaneko did not immediately answer her, but then said, gently, "Most honorable lady, I regret to disappoint you. I vowed that whomever I found upon the road requiring assistance, whether a beggar or a digger of graves, I would serve him as I would my own grandfather, with honor. To see him dispatched as a low criminal—" He trailed off, and said no more.

"Oh!" Lady Arikawa said eagerly, "but that need not be so! I will speak with the magistrate. Why should he not be permitted *seppuku* instead? And then indeed you will have served him."

Laurence heard no more of the conversation: the heavy crunching tread of the dragon faded, as though they had wandered away through the gardens. The guards were sitting together at the far end of the chamber speaking in low voices over cards: some sort of game of chance. They were armed with short but serviceable blades, and wore a kind of light, handsome armor, crafted of small plates of wood which overlapped one another neatly.

They rose to attention when Kaneko ducked into the chamber, a short while later, and bowing deeply left the room when he dismissed them. Laurence had been engaged in exercising his right arm, which was yet bruised all along its length with markings as of chain links pressed hard against the flesh. He had the movement of it back, however, and he thought he had worked it limber. Laurence did not rise; he had already managed to crack his head on the ceiling several times, and if the King did not require his officers to rise for the loyal salute on board ship, in similar conditions, Laurence was damned if he would do it for his jailor, here.

Kaneko settled himself on the ground with easy grace and regarded Laurence somberly. "I have come to speak plainly with you, Englishman," he said.

"That, sir, cannot be anything but welcome," Laurence said, without much enthusiasm; he had heard enough of the conversation in the garden to guess at Kaneko's intentions: the man was looking for some means of eeling out of his vow, Laurence supposed, and meant to offer him some mean and cowardly alternative to death— imprisonment for life, perhaps, or a kind of indentured servitude.

Kaneko said, "Even if the bakufu had not decreed the death of all foreigners entering the nation without permission, the circumstances of your arrival would be dark. The shameful offense of your country-men in Nagasaki suggests a false character, and a league between your nation and China has been suspected for several years, now. Your ships have been reported in the northern waters near Peking, where no Westerners formerly were welcome—"

The existence of this traffic came as news to Laurence; so far as he knew, only the port of Guangzhou was open at all. "—and now, this appearance of a Celestial, in conjunction with yourself, and this British dragon you have mentioned," Kaneko continued, "more than confirms our most extreme suspicions: the Celestials travel only with the Imperial family."

Laurence could not disagree that such commerce indicated a more intimate connection formed between Britain and China than he recalled; this, however, pressed the bounds of credence. "I should be astonished beyond belief to learn that a member of the Imperial family of China were traveling with my ship. I must continue to believe it more likely that your witness, faced with unfamiliar beasts, mistook some rare British breed for the one you name."

"There is no mistake," Kaneko said. "Lord Jinai is the guardian of the West: he is four hundred years old, and he has seen Celestials before. He was not mistaken."

He spoke flatly, and Laurence did not propose that advanced years might render Lord Jinai's judgment questionable: he remembered too vividly the sharp, deadly look of the sea-dragon's eyes; no signs of creeping age there.

Kaneko added, "And your party have not only stolen timber

from our shores, but attacked him: so pronounced an insult cannot be anything but deliberate." He paused, and after a moment said, "You seem a rational man, and though your conduct is not correct, I imagine you are an honorable man, in your own country. Will you offer no explanation?"

Laurence would have liked to pace. He would have given a great deal to be on his quarterdeck, with the sails belled out overhead and wind in his hair, even just long enough to think his way through all the tangled evidence. Failing that, he would have been glad of a pot of strong coffee and a day of quiet—a chance perhaps to write out a letter to Edith Galman; he had often found the exercise to resolve his own thinking, when he had no trusted confidant to hand, as a sea-captain rarely might. Edith—he had a start for a moment; he had not thought of her. He looked at his hand, as yet without a ring.

He pushed that from his mind. He could not allow himself to dwell on such matters now. "I may as well be hanged for a sheep as for a lamb," he said aloud, in English, to himself, and steeling himself for incredulity, gave Kaneko to understand his loss of memory, in as succinct and unadorned a manner as he could.

Kaneko listened to his brief narrative with mingled bewilderment and suspicion; he asked a few questions only, in tones of extreme politeness, which Laurence ruefully feared covered equally extreme skepticism. "You do not recall why you are here," Kaneko said at last, "nor anything of an alliance between your nation and China."

"Whatever injury I have taken has robbed me of more than that," Laurence said. "I have lost years—how many, I cannot be sure, but certainly two or three. I do not suppose, sir, you can tell me what year it is, in the European reckoning?"

"By the latest report of the Dutch, they make the year 1812, if my recollection is not imperfect," Kaneko said, and Laurence stared at him, taken aback in real horror: eight years gone?

He looked away at once, but his distress, which he could not easily master, had at least some small beneficial effect: Kaneko was frowning at him, puzzled but a little more convinced, when Laurence managed to overcome his immediate feelings.

"If I may further trespass," Laurence said, "can you tell me anything of the war? Has Napoleon been defeated?"

Laurence tried as best he could to keep his spirits from sinking entirely, as Kaneko sketched for him the Japanese understanding of circumstances in Europe. Their news was certainly old, and as it came entirely from the Dutch also certainly colored by that nation's self-interest; it had been translated at least twice, and surely much was lost, in the way of nuance.

So he told himself, and Britain at least was free. Laurence clung to that, for what consolation it might be while hearing of Austria fallen, Prussia—Prussia!—fallen, Spain fallen, Russia half-allied with France—the shadow of the tricolor over all of them. Kaneko did not seem to know what had happened in the Netherlands, but Laurence could hardly imagine they had escaped, no matter what the Dutch representatives here might have said. Napoleon was the master of all Europe.

"I can well believe, sir, that you find my explanation difficult to swallow," Laurence said, when he could speak again, "for I can scarcely believe it myself; I have withheld it so far for that very reason, having no desire to figure either as an honest lunatic or a witless liar. But I have told you the truth, and you have served me a very heavy blow; I beg your pardon, but you could scarcely have given me worse news."

His voice failed him, broke, and he did not speak again. Kaneko also said nothing, so they sat together in silence, caught in their own private and separate distress, though by chance entwined. The sun was lowering. A branch outside cast a dappled silhouette upon the rice-paper wall, which lengthened little by little as it traveled over the wall. Soft footsteps moved through the hall outside now and again, the *shush-shush* of sandaled feet; the guards in their creaking armor shifted their weight on the other side of the panel.

At last Kaneko said, "Perhaps I am being foolish, and yet I do believe you. However, I cannot expect the magistrate to do so: indeed, it could scarcely be in keeping with his duty to do so. Nor would this explanation excuse you. A man who, out of his senses, commits a crime, is still guilty: and lacking memory of your own intentions, you cannot even defend them."

"Sir, you have taken it by the horns," Laurence said grimly. "And no, I do not expect him to believe my explanation in the least."

Kaneko nodded, and then said, quietly, "It may be I can do nothing. The magistrate may insist upon putting you to questioning. But—Lady Arikawa is generous, and her voice is not the least in the councils of the bakufu. She has offered to speak on your behalf, and to request for you the right to commit *seppuku,* if you should desire it—honorable suicide," he added, seeing Laurence's incomprehension. "I would stand for you as your second, if—"

"Good God, no," Laurence said, recoiling, and cut him off. "I will not pretend I have the least desire to be a martyr, sir, but I am a Christian: I will do my best to endure whatever torment God sees fit to try me by, and not turn to self-slaughter like—"

He paused; he had meant to say, like a heathen, but the remark seemed impolite, in addressing one who by his own expression found Laurence's own avowed preference as nearly unthinkable. Laurence abruptly wondered, then, if this same fate lay before Kaneko himself—

"If I cannot fulfill my vow," Kaneko answered, regarding him with somber surprise, "I hope that Lady Arikawa will be generous enough to grant me permission: I am her servant, and she may deny me the right."

"And if she refuses?"

Kaneko looked bleak. "I will be dishonored, and my family as well."

Laurence wished to press him further, to understand more, but refrained; a man's honor could only be in his own keeping, and

Laurence could understand, a little. He himself would gladly have accepted death as the price of escaping some dishonorable act, certainly before treason; and he would have preferred death to shameful torment, which would seek to break him. But to endure death was not the same as to seek it by his own hand.

"Sir," he said, "I know of no reason why you should consider yourself so. You *have* been of material assistance to me: without your aid, I should likely have died upon the road, sick and alone, without even what understanding has returned to me. I beg you not to commit such an act on my account. Indeed, if you wished to serve me, you would do better to grant me the satisfaction of knowing you stayed your hand, from what my own faith considers mortal sin."

"My vow was not to you," Kaneko said, cool and a little censorious, rising to his feet. He inclined his head a little and took his leave without another word; the guards came back in.

An evening meal was brought them all—Laurence noticed belatedly that his own meal, as sparse as he would have ordinarily thought it, was considerably more substantial than the simple bowl of soup and noodles offered the guards; he now understood a little better why he was confined in a hospitable and large chamber, waited upon with consideration. Nevertheless he was still a prisoner, and a condemned man. He looked at the guards: both wore short blades on their belts, and though he had reach and weight on them, they were by no means insubstantial fellows. But Laurence was determined, regardless, to hazard again an escape. His circumstances could hardly be the worse for it.

One of the guards lay himself down to rest; the other sat in the corner and yawned. Laurence lay down and closed his eyes to sleep a little while, until it was thoroughly dark.

He roused a few hours later and turned his head to look. The first guard yet snored; the other was idly humming to himself, tuneless, and rolling the dice.

Laurence turned back his head towards the ceiling, gathering himself. He closed his eyes and let his lips form soundlessly a prayer to the Almighty. Almost certainly he would be slain. He meant to try and overcome the first guard before the second awoke, get away the man's blade if he could, and then to somehow get out of the house—perhaps the window of the chamber across the hallway. Then he would fly for the woods. It was a reckless plan at best, given two men at his back and dragons in the courtyard, but better a clean death than to sit quietly in a room and await torture.

Laurence sat up from his bedding. The guard looked up, narrowly, but then turned away from him; Laurence halted as the door slid open. Junichiro stood outside, swords at his belt, and spoke coldly, gesturing at the sleeping guard. The second guard roused up, abashed; the two men muttered excuses, which Junichiro evidently cut short; he motioned them out of the room, and climbing in made to stand sentry in their place, his face hard and watchful. The men hang-dog went; the door slid shut. Their small light went bobbing away down the corridor, and vanished deeper into the house.

Laurence ought to have been glad of it: shorter odds by far, against one youth not yet at his full growth. But it left an evil taste in his mouth. He had not given his parole to his captors; he felt himself not in the wrong to make the attempt, and if necessary, he could have stomached killing a guard set upon him, in such circumstances. But not an over-eager young man, scarcely more than a boy, one who had done him not the least evil except to love his own master. Half-gathered to spring, Laurence hesitated. Perhaps if he waited, Junichiro might fall asleep himself, later in the night—

Junichiro said quietly, barely more than a whisper, "Get up. Once we are outside, we must go down the slope to the west, quickly, keeping near the stables—the dragons will not be there. Do you understand?"

"What?" Laurence said, taken aback.

Junichiro did not answer; he had taken a bound scroll out of his robes, and set it down precisely in the center of the floor. He went to the outer wall and began to work latches there: abruptly a large section of the lower half of the wall came loose, and the night air breathed in.

Laurence still did not understand in the least; but understanding might wait. He sprang to Junichiro's side and caught the heavy panel, lifting it aside; together they slid through the opening and into the gardens, small pebbles rolling underfoot and a fragrant smell of crushed leaves as they forced their way past a few small pines. Junichiro caught him by the arm. "Quickly, now!" he breathed.

Laurence had no idea what had possessed Junichiro to undertake his rescue, but he could still less easily imagine it some sort of deep-laid strategem. He turned aside for a moment, however, to hunt through the bushes, ignoring Junichiro's attempts to draw him onwards. Then he had the bundle out of the undergrowth where he had left it, and turning said, "Go!"

He followed Junichiro through the gardens, and past a low building smelling of cattle and horse piss; a gentle slope eased away into the woods. Junichiro unerring led them along paths he knew into the trees, jumping fallen logs and streams almost unconscious of their presence. Laurence fixed the bundle over his shoulder, and kept his attention for the forest floor: he had put himself into Junichiro's hands, and he would have certainly done no better evading pursuit alone.

They had been running for nearly half-an-hour when first a dragon roared, behind them and aloft somewhere. Laurence did not turn to look. If Lady Arikawa marked them out for pursuit, they were surely lost, even if she could not come down upon them herself while they remained within the trees. The snap of wings above, so like a sail belling in the wind, seemed strangely loud in his ears. They ran onwards.

Chapter 4

A sharp poke in his side roused Temeraire from his torpor; he lifted his head only slowly. The steady rocking of the ship had cradled him in comfortable withdrawal. They had put food in his mouth, from time to time; he had felt the sun creeping over his body, and the heat of the galleys below. "It is time you were awake," a voice said, in Chinese.

"Yes, I am awake," Temeraire said, and put his head back down and closed his eyes once more: the glare of the sun upon the waves ached.

"No, you are not," the stranger said, and prodded him unpleasantly with something sharp and cold in the pit of his shoulder; Temeraire flinched and looked around, frowning. The man, in long grey clothing, looked back at him with a severe expression; a long drooping beard with trailing mustaches hung down from his frowning mouth.

"Stop that," Temeraire said, irritably. "I do not wish to be prodded; take that away."

"Oho, next you will tell me how to mix your medicine," the man said, and poked him once more: he was using for the purpose a very long and narrow silver stick, with a sharpened end. "Up! Up! How do you expect to get well, lying around on hot rocks day after day?" He jabbed Temeraire sharply with the stick, in his hindquarters, and Temeraire indignantly pushed up.

"I am feeling *much* better for having lain here, and it is not hot rocks but the galley, anyway," Temeraire said. "And for that matter—" He stopped short, appalled: behind the stranger, three points to port, a merchantman flying the Dutch flag rode at anchor; and beyond this, only a little way off, the tight-crammed roofs of a city rose away from a curving and beautiful harbor. A ring of Chinese junks surrounded the *Potentate*, bobbing gently with the waves, like a garland made of ships.

"Where am I?" Temeraire cried. "Where have you brought me?" He turned to look furious reproach at Maximus, who was drowsing beside him and did not immediately open his eyes to be confronted: the other dragons were all further out to sea on the other side of the ship, all of them diving at the waves and plucking themselves up some fish.

"You are in Nagasaki Harbor," the stranger said, "and you have been here three days and nights."

Laurence was falling, wet leather slipping between his fingers and a smooth-scaled hide refusing to provide purchase, and he jerked up gasping from beneath the carpeting of leaves. Beside him, Junichiro slept on as soundly as if he had been upon a featherbed in a palace, his cheek pillowed on his arms and his face serene. Laurence ran a hand over his face, wearily, and pushed aside the remants of his covering. The sun was near making noon, he thought, though he could not see it very clearly for the leaves overhead.

They had continued on all the night, stumbling beneath the trees and over rocks. The dragon's roars had pursued them, but her flight had fallen behind; she had turned one direction and another away from their trail, it seemed to Laurence, perhaps led astray by some wild animals leaping in fear from her approach. Fortune had saved them, he could only imagine.

Junichiro had turned aside abruptly, near the dawn, and led Laurence down a narrow barely marked trail to their present resting place: overshadowed by a great standing gate, two enormous pillars joined by bars painted in an orange now faded and peeling. A little beyond it they had found a stand of trees grown wild and engulfed in vines, sheltered from the wind by a great smooth boulder. Laurence rose, brushing himself free of dead vines, and looked up at the gate again. The scale was immense, and yet it seemed to lead nowhere; as far as he could see through the frame in either direction was only wilderness.

In the dim light they had buried themselves beneath dry leaves and slept as the dead. Laurence was yet tired and footsore, but he did not think they dared linger for long. There was a little trickle of a stream running through the woods, ending with a little burbling over rocks in a great clear pool beside the gate. Laurence limped to it and drank deeply, washed hands and face, and took off his sandals and soaked his feet in the cold water as long as he could bear: it was a long time since he had scrambled barefoot over the ropes and planks of a ship as a boy, and the sandals had left him bruised and sore.

He rose at last and tied them back on, then turned to go back to Junichiro and halted, gone very still. The boulder he had noted last night had raised its head and was regarding him with enormous unblinking interest: it was a dragon, hide dark greenish black and with large eyes of pallid grey, which evidently had curled up to sleep against the comfort of the trees.

It yawned, widely, and said something to him in Japanese; Junichiro, still soundly asleep and huddled up against its side, woke with a start and scrambled up and away. The dragon turned and inquired of him, instead; Junichiro answered with a slightly evasive air, backing away towards Laurence. "What is it asking?" Laurence asked him, low, but the dragon overheard.

"Ah! So you can speak!" the dragon said triumphantly, in Chinese. "Are you," it leaned towards him with almost a longing air, "a *Dutchman*?"

"No, sir," Laurence said. "I am an Englishman."

"An Englishman?" The dragon rolled the sound around slowly, tongue flicking out to touch the air. It was only the size of a Yellow Reaper, perhaps, with a wide ruff and long dangling tendrils that hung down about its mouth: something of its appearance seemed strangely familiar, though Laurence had certainly never seen a beast anything like. "I have never heard any English poetry," the dragon announced, after some consideration. "You must tell me some! Come, let us go up to the temple and have something to eat and drink."

He uncurled himself and rose onto four feet, shaking himself out almost as might have a wet dog. He was long and as narrow in the chest as at the base of his tail, with feet widely spaced; his wings were short and peculiarly stubby, folded against his back. He ambled with a swaying stride through the gate itself, stopping briefly to knock his head against one of the posts three times, and went onwards up the rising slope beyond, where now Laurence saw the underbrush was lower, and trampled in places.

He glanced at Junichiro—he was not sure if they ought to take the chance and try to flee. But Junichiro was trailing wide-eyed after the dragon, and the promise of food was a powerful one. The beast at least did not seem to be immediately hostile.

The trail led a winding way through increasingly difficult undergrowth, where at last the dragon paused and looked back and said, "Why, you are falling quite behind. Up you get," and reached out a taloned hand to deposit them each in turn upon his back. Junichiro made a small sound almost of protest, and Laurence would have liked to question him—what was the beast, and why did it seem to have no fear of the same law which bound all others against a foreigner—but he could not find it politic to do so when aboard the very beast's back.

They continued on to a final steeper slope, where at the summit at last a small temple made of wood was found—a tall structure, enough that the dragon could comfortably walk inside, though not very large in plan; and in two great silver bowls at the center stood a pool of clear liquid, smelling very strongly of plums and spirits; and in the other a great heap of rice and meat, still steaming.

"Take cups! Help yourselves!" the dragon said, sprawling himself across the floor—or *herself*, Laurence belatedly corrected, when some portions of anatomy were thereby more exposed to view; he had been mistaken by a series of low finned spines which curved out from the dragon's body along its length. "We will drink to the good fortune of this meeting, and then you will recite some poetry for me. You do *know* some poetry?" the dragon asked, anxiously.

"Ma'am," Laurence said doubtfully, wondering where the attendants were, who had prepared this repast, and how he might hope to make a further escape, "I can give you a little Shakespeare, if that will suit you, but I do not know how it will do in Chinese."

"No, no," the dragon said, coiling back with an air of relief. "I do not want it in Chinese. I already know Li Bai and Wang Wei, and many more besides. I want English poetry."

"But—you cannot speak the tongue?" Laurence asked.

"You will translate it for me afterwards," she said, and nudged across to him with one talon a small empty cup, perhaps a little larger than a thimble, and another for Junichiro.

The excuses a rather shamefaced Granby provided Temeraire for their decampment were threadbare indeed. His health, the lurking unknown danger of the sea-dragon, the uncertainty of their position, the ship's need of further repair, the safety of the egg—

At the thought of the egg, he could not forbear putting his head over the side carefully and peering in, with a single eye, at the porthole which looked into the egg's chamber. This was below the galleys, carefully kept warm, and the egg itself was not visible for being swaddled in a great many velvet and silken dressings, and then hay, and then packed into a crate. But they had shown it to him, when he had first awoken: a splendid smooth pale-cream shell speckled with a very attractive pattern of red and violet spots, and one notable larger marking shaped roughly like a number eight.

"You must see it, surely." Temeraire had pointed it out to Lily, though she had looked at it doubtfully.

"It looks more like a cloud to me," she said, which was absurd; any shape might be a cloud. Temeraire pressed his other friends for their opinion, and finally Kulingile and Dulcia were brought to agree, when he had drawn them the shape of an eight, that it was not unlike; with this he was satisfied to consider his opinion confirmed, and nothing more propitious could be imagined.

Sipho had knocked him up quite a respectable watercolor on a large piece of discarded sailcloth, which was now draped over the crate and might be looked at in lieu of unpacking the egg again—a risk Temeraire quite agreed could not be taken under ordinary circumstances, although he was of course determined Laurence should see the egg as soon as he was found.

"And that," he said stormily, "will be as soon as I can fly back and manage it: I am very sorry indeed, Granby, to have found you so false as to allow the ship to leave Laurence behind; what he must be thinking of me, at present! You may be sure I will not be silent on the subject, when I have seen him again; he will know of this *treachery*."

"Oh! That is quite enough," Iskierka said, cracking an eye. "For Granby did *not* wish to go, at all. He said you would be very upset, and it could do you no good, but Captain Blaise would not stay and the ship is his; and Hammond egged him on, naturally."

"Pray be quiet, wretched creature, you are not making matters any better," Granby said, reproving, and called up, "Temeraire, old fellow, listen to me: you mustn't be so angry. You were very ill, and still are; you couldn't have gone searching for Laurence any road. And Hammond is at this very moment speaking to the local authorities of the port to have them bring us any news of Laurence, I promise you. He must have made a figure of himself, you know—he is a tall fellow, and they haven't yellow hair here; he will stand out

68

a mile. Someone is sure to have taken him up, if—if he has come to shore."

"If Hammond should come back with any news of Laurence at all, it will be a good deal more than I look for," Temeraire said, his resentment unabated, and all the greater for his indeed feeling very ill—very wretched. He did not like the thought of a long flight at present, and disliked still more feeling himself in so weak a condition. "And I *will* go back, if I must fly overland to get there," he added, in defiance of that consciousness.

Wen Shen, the physician, who had been hired to assist in his care, shrugged equally from the deck. "You will drop dead somewhere over the middle of the country, then," he said, and ate an enormous heaping spoon of the rice porridge, flavored with tunny from Kulingile's spare catch, which he had commanded to be worked up supposedly for Temeraire's benefit.

Temeraire did not think much of him, despite his physician's knot. He had insisted on Temeraire's drinking a great vat of some bitter and foul-tasting infusion, and on his flying a full circuit around the ship, though he did not feel at all like flying and his wing-joints ached fiercely afterwards. Wen Shen had also made a great many disparaging remarks on Temeraire's diet and general habits, some of them quite untrue: he did *not* eat an entire roast cow every day. Even if he had liked to, which he did not, they did not have enough cattle aboard for that.

Gong Su had dug up this physician, having rowed over to each one of the Chinese ships in the harbor on their arrival, where he had met with the greatest deference. Since he had openly avowed himself a servant of the Imperial court, he had exchanged his clothing for the formal robes of a scholar; he had shaved his head and put his hair into a severe topknot, with a blue button upon his hat, and now openly carried the pouch with the great red-sealed letter of his authority around his neck.

Temeraire knew Laurence had regarded this alteration of his costume coldly, as a reminder of injury—that Gong Su had deceived them all for so long, and spied, and passed on information. But in his own opinion, any injury could only be mitigated now by Gong Su's making amends and doing his best to make a good showing of himself; he was still, Temeraire considered, a member of his crew. And after all, why should Crown Prince Mianning not wish to send a messenger, a trusted servant, to accompany his brother? But Laurence had remained unconvinced by this argument, receiving it only with a snort.

In addition to digging up Wen Shen, Gong Su had spoken with the captains of the Chinese ships; all the vessels had subsequently weighed anchor and maneuvered, awkwardly, into places around the *Potentate,* evidently with the design of providing her some protection. Temeraire had heard this with some skepticism: the Chinese ships were so very much smaller, but Captain Blaise was very well pleased.

"At least it may give us some notice, if a monster like the one you knocked heads with decides to come up from under us," he said to Captain Berkley. "How we will come off in such an encounter, I am damned if I know, but we will give him a taste of hot iron down his gullet if only he gives us a chance, and see what he thinks of that," and he gave orders that men should be at some of the guns all hours of day and night.

Temeraire could not really disapprove of any measures for the egg's security; the sea-dragon had been so very unfriendly, even when there did not seem to Temeraire to be any excuse for such a cold reception. But he was not in the least pleased that Gong Su had also inflicted Wen Shen upon him, whatever any of them liked to say about the improvement in his condition since they had begun dosing him with the physician's recipe.

"For I am not well enough to go, yet," Temeraire said miserably to Lily, putting his head down again—somehow he had eaten up all the rice porridge, after all. "If I must be drinking medicine, at least it ought to work."

"Well, you are better already than you were," Lily said, consoling. "It was a great deal of time before I felt properly myself again, you know, after that nasty cough we all had a few years ago."

"You had better eat something more, and here: if you cannot go, in a few days, I will have a word with Berkley and we will go and have a look around for you, I dare say," Maximus said, which was very kind, but Temeraire did not believe it in the least: Berkley was like all the rest of them, quite insistent that Laurence was dead, and Temeraire was sure he would not be rigorous in any search.

"I only wish I knew where he was now," Temeraire said, low, and shut his eyes again.

"Kanpai!" the dragon cried, when Laurence had finished muddling through another passage, and dipped her own head into the silver bowl. Laurence was forced to at least moisten his lips in a show of accompaniment, and hope that he had indeed buried Caesar and not praised him, or for that matter raised him from the dead one act too soon; he was not perfectly sure. He did not think he had been this appallingly drunk since he had been a boy of twelve, trying to make good on every toast at his captain's table.

Junichiro had fallen asleep perhaps an hour ago, overcome with the liquor and the exertion of their night. He had by slow degrees eased to the floor, until his head had fallen onto Laurence's bundle and his eyes had closed, almost at the same time.

"I am delighted with it," the dragon continued, and hiccoughed. "*Neither wit, nor words, nor worth,*" this repeated unslurred and with a startlingly good accent, despite the truly remarkable quantity of liquor which the beast had consumed, "—that has a very pleasing rhythm. This is part of your funerary rites?"

"In the theater, when they have killed him," Laurence said, confusedly, trying to explain; he was beginning to find it difficult to make his tongue work in Chinese. "There is a dragon when he gives the speech," he added, with some vague sense that this might be of interest to another beast, trying with movements of his hands to convey some sense of the usual staging, which he had seen once as a boy of thirteen.

"I would be glad to see it," the dragon said. "I have lately seen a splendid performance by a troupe, who came by upon the road. I will give you a little of it."

She began to recite in a low melodious voice, rising and falling in the unfamiliar language. Laurence was not proof against so much inducement added to his own weariness, and before she had completed the third line he had fallen to sleep beside Junichiro. When he woke, the dragon was gone; Junichiro was stirring beside him, and the sun was going down. His head ached like the very devil.

"The guardian must have gone to the water," Junichiro said. "We should go onwards."

"Yes," Laurence said, wearily, "but we had better wait until the sun has gone, and eat," the bowl holding still a handsome share of leftovers, "and in the meanwhile, I will have a few answers: I am not ungrateful, but I would know what you are about. Did you— seek to escape Kaneko's service, yourself?" He spoke dubiously; he could scarcely imagine that to be Junichiro's motive. The boy's affection for his master had been too visible and sincere for that, and yet it seemed equally unlikely he had been motivated by any sense of injustice done to Laurence himself; there was certainly no personal attachment between them.

"Of course not," Junichiro said, bitterly; he was brushing his own garments clean as best he could. "I heard my master tell Lady Arikawa you were too much of a coward to take an honorable death. There was no course of honor left for him. If he gave you up for torture to the magistrate, he would have failed in his vow; and he could not disobey the bakufu to protect you. What else was there to do?"

"What *was* this vow?" Laurence demanded. "Why would he have sworn an oath to aid a perfect stranger?"

"He made the vow to Jizo," Junichiro said shortly, "who guards travelers, to ask him to look after his wife and son."

His manner did not invite further inquiry. But Laurence recalled the silence of the house, the absence of a chatelaine, Kaneko's black clothing, and thought he might understand: a wife lost in childbirth, and the child with her. Enough cause, surely, for a man to seek the consolation of religion, and to hold the oath he had made for their sake more dear than a mere promise to be put aside when inconvenient.

"So I will keep you alive, and get you away," Junichiro went on. "My master will not have disobeyed the law; he will not have brought shame on Lady Arikawa and his own family: the guilt will be on my own head."

Laurence shook his head in dismay: it was a solution which he felt could only have appealed to the excessive optimism of a young man, a wish to be the hero of the piece. "Unless that magistrate is a fool, he will hold your master accountable for your actions, and you will have only gained a crime to your account and his," he said.

"He cannot," Junichiro said. "Kaneko is my teacher, not my lord. I am not yet sworn to service. My family were—ronin." Laurence did not recognize the word, but Junichiro looked away and spoke as though ashamed. "He took me in. When my training was complete, he meant to present me to Lady Arikawa, to see if she would—" His voice died away, and he swallowed visibly: a dream plainly now lost. He straightened. "My family are dead. The shame of my behavior falls only on myself, not on him," he said. "Why do you think Lady Arikawa let us escape?"

Laurence paused and looked at him doubtfully. He had credited good fortune for the improbable success of their flight, but he could scarcely deny that a deliberate impulse on the part of their deadly pursuer was compellingly more plausible. "If so," he said slowly, "then you have achieved your aim. Listen: let me bind you here. That dragon will free you. You can tell them that I forced you to assist me—"

"And shame myself twice over, lying, and saying I yielded to you to preserve my life?" Junichiro said, with perfect scorn. "In

73

any case," he added, "you will never get to Nagasaki alone; and there will be no use in my having aided you this far, if I do not get you away," he added, and there was enough likely truth to that, to force Laurence to silence.

He could not like taking a clear advantage of the boy, even if Junichiro had chosen his own course: he was too much a young enthusiast to be trusted to make that choice clear-headedly. Even granting that the maneuver would spare Kaneko, Laurence could well imagine that gentleman's feelings on finding his young student had thus immolated himself to spare him; he knew what his own would have been, under similar circumstances.

But there was no answer to be made to Junichiro's refusing to lie: Laurence indeed could hardly encourage him to do so, when answered in such terms. The only saving grace was knowing the boy an orphan: at least he had not riven him away from family as well as home. Laurence could give him a place aboard ship—if they could either of them get to the ship, which was certainly more likely with Junichiro's guidance than without it. And if they could not, Laurence knew what his own fate would be; he could hardly imagine that Junichiro's would be any more merciful.

A low bubbling roar came from the river below, and Laurence looked down the hill from the temple to see the dragon emerge—at least, he thought it was the same dragon, but she had swelled out to nearly thrice her size, so wide that her very hide was stretched to a paler greenish silver. Laurence watched in astonishment as she spouted a great fountaining of water like a cascade that took illumination from the descending sun. The torrent of water continued a long time, the dragon reducing by degrees to her smaller size as she brought it forth.

"What sort of a dragon is she?" Laurence asked Junichiro.

"A river-dragon," Junichiro said, his tone implying strongly Laurence was a fool who required having the simplest of matters explained. "Like Lord Jinai!" the boy added pointedly, seeing Laurence had not followed.

"She is the same breed as that monster?" Laurence said, incredulous: the scale was so very different he could scarcely credit it.

"She cannot get big until she goes down to the ocean, of course," Junichiro said.

The water-dragon padded back up the hill towards them, stopping by the temple doorway to shake herself free of droplets again in a fine spray. "Now then," she said, stepping inside and ducking her great head beneath the lintel: Laurence recognized now the kinship between her appearance and the sea-dragon's, where her lines would spread out, as she grew in size. "I have refreshed myself, and I am ready to hear more of this Shakespeare."

Junichiro seated himself at once, as though this remark had the force of a command; Laurence hesitated, then said, "Madam, I beg your pardon: we cannot stay."

The dragon paused in the act of settling herself and regarded him with blank astonishment; Junichiro stared at him so appalled that Laurence supposed he had committed some enormous solecism. The sensation was discomfiting, but not so far, he was grimly certain, as would be their discovery and inevitable pursuit.

"We are bound for Nagasaki," he said firmly, "and cannot delay in our journey. I beg your pardon most sincerely if I do not express myself in the accepted mode, from unfamiliarity," he added. "I assure you I mean no offense."

The dragon sat for a moment, blinking; she seemed less offended than perplexed. "The river flows to the sea, whatever the wind says about it," she said, and reached up and rubbed a talon over some of the great swinging tendrils from her forehead, thoughtfully. "You have a long journey ahead," she said eventually. "Stay the night! In the morning we will go together, down to the Ariake Sea. You will not have so far to go from there."

Laurence had no notion of the geography, but he could well imagine that a dragon-back ride would speed their journey. He glanced at Junichiro, who wore a peculiar expression of mortification and longing mingled; as though Laurence had brazenly committed a crime, and been rewarded for it instead of condemned. He at least showed no disposition to reject the offer; and to be fair, Laurence did not see how it was to be refused. "Ma'am, I am honored by your condescension," Laurence said, bowing, and seated himself reluctantly again.

Hammond's boat rowed back three hours later, swiftly crossing from the harbor. Despite his avowed distrust, Temeraire could not help but watch her approach anxiously. The *Potentate* was very far from land, for the sake of her draught, and there were a great many small boats going to and fro in the harbor before them, betwixt which Temeraire could make no distinction. Captain Blaise came to the dragondeck and stood watching them for some time with his glass as Hammond's boat came nearer, and he said to Granby, "Well, it will be hot work, if they do try for us."

"Whatever do you mean?" Temeraire said, peering down.

"They have loaded up those boats there with tinder," Granby answered him, shading his eyes to peer at the shore. "They may come out and have a go at setting us afire, we think."

"What?" Iskierka said, rearing up her head abruptly, her eyes going very wide. "What? How dare they! I will go and fire *them*, at once!"

"Oh, no, you shan't," Granby said firmly. "Not until we have seen what they mean to do; you cannot blame them for having a lookout, when a transport loaded to the brim comes creeping into their harbor."

When Hammond had been put back aboard—he was so unhandy about coming up the side that Churki would no longer have it, pronouncing it a ludicrous and unnecessary risk, and insisted on reaching down to lift him up herself out of the launch—he did not say anything at all of Laurence, and nothing to reassure about the egg, either.

"The worst news imaginable," he said. "I had private conversation of Mr. Doeff, who is the commissioner here, and good God! Do you know a ship called the *Phaeton*?"

"Lost in the Pacific, two years ago," Captain Blaise said, automatically.

Laurence had thought well of Blaise—had called him a respectable and a sensible man, but in Temeraire's private opinion he was only a block: not the least imagination or interest as far as Temeraire had been able to discover in nearly the full year of their acquaintance. He was not afraid of dragons, which was the best Temeraire could say of him, and indeed he made a point of taking the air upon the dragondeck every day—after making a punctilious request of the most senior aviator on deck for the liberty—as a sort of gesture to reassure the hands. But his head was full of nothing but the *Naval Chronicle;* he had no other conversation but the weather, and that was not very much use as he insisted on always saying the prospect was very fair, even when it was plainly coming on to a three-days' blow.

"Pellew's second boy had her, if I recall aright, and she was looking in at the Dutch trade last anyone heard of her," Blaise added now. "Likely she went down in a gale—" and stopped as Hammond shook his head.

"She was sunk here," he said, "—*here,* after coming in under false colors, taking hostage two of the Dutch officials who went out to greet her, and threatening to fire the shipping in the harbor if the Japanese did not supply them. Her captain must have been a lunatic," he added bitterly.

The uproar this produced, Hammond had evidently not expected. He had meant to convey that the Japanese were not in the least pleased with the British, and that they naturally thought the *Potentate* had come to make a fuss over the sinking of the *Phaeton*. In this he had succeeded, but was dismayed to discover that Captain Blaise would have liked to confirm all the worst fears the Japanese might have entertained. When Hammond had finished, Blaise walked to and fro along the deck for an hour altogether in great fury, repeating that it was more than a dog could bear, that they should have sunk a British ship and receive no answer, even in the face of all Hammond's increasingly anxious remonstrations.

He was only at last persuaded to go inside to write a report of it to the Admiralty; Hammond turned at once to the dragondeck, so he might corner Captain Harcourt, who was senior, and try to make repairs by urgently pressing her in turn to disavow any possibility of action.

"Hammond, I haven't the least wish to start us another war in some hasty fashion," she said at last, in some irritation, "but no-one can blame Blaise for being distressed, and I am so myself. It is all very well to say her captain was provoking: whose word do you have for that, but this Dutch fellow, whose trade he would have gone after?"

She walked away from his importunities, and at last Temeraire could pin Hammond down with a clawed foot laid down in his path, when he would have dashed away from the dragondeck at once again. "Oh—no, no, they do not know anything of Laurence," Hammond said, distracted. "Pray will you move, I must go down and speak with Blaise again—"

"It is just as I thought," Temeraire said savagely, without giving way, "you have done nothing at all and it was all falsehoods, your promises to look for Laurence: did you even ask them about him? And what is he to do, now, when you tell us they all hate the British here, and he is all alone, and we are hundreds of miles away? I ought have let this wretched ship sink," he added, "and left you on it."

"I hope to God I will not wish as much, soon enough!" Hammond cried, taken aback by his violence. "But I *have* asked, I give you my word, and Mr. Doeff has promised me he should inquire among the Japanese. But you must see under these circumstances I was forced to proceed with the greatest caution. Imagine if they should know his value as a hostage against us? So I have only said we had a shipwreck, and we would be glad to have any news at all

78

of our sailors, if any sign had come up on the shore of any of them. I will bring you any word at once, I assure you: and pray consider that any opening of hostilities between us should certainly make his rescue a thousand times more difficult."

He added this last urgently, and though of course Temeraire saw straight through this transparent piece of manipulation, he could not argue with it; neither could he do anything, for good or ill, to forward the matter. "Maximus," he said, feeling quite desperate, when he had let Hammond go dashing away again towards the stern cabin, "I do not suppose *you* would go and look for Laurence? That sea-dragon cannot come out of the water. If you should keep away from the coast—"

But, "Enough of that," Churki said, overhearing. "Maximus had much better stay where he is, and you had much better eat another bowl of soup and take your medicine, so that when we *do* hear some word worth acting upon, you will then be able to do so. Do you suppose Laurence would be grateful if you have made yourself ill or lost one of our company, in the meantime, just to feel as though you were doing something when anyone can see there is nothing sensible to be done?"

This shot went uncomfortably home: Temeraire knew Laurence by no means approved of any rash or hasty action, and had spoken with him on several occasions about the need for sober reflection. "Particularly," Laurence had said, "when you must know the others will often heed your advice and attend your requests: how much more should that trust increase your obligation to serve them well in such circumstances, by the exercise of restraint? You must be careful not to abuse it, in trying to persuade them into a course against their own interest or that of the nation, for your own benefit."

And how eagerly Temeraire had agreed with him! He sank his head upon his forelegs. The truth was he did not know where to fly, even if he had been well enough to go himself; and besides that, Maximus was not the fellow anyone would have sent on a search mission. He would have to spend half of every day only hunting, and likely making all the people very angry for the quantity of food which he should be taking from them.

"But I *cannot* only lie here!" he burst out. "And do not tell me," he added, "—do not dare to tell me that Laurence is dead, so I might as well do so. If he *is* dead, then I cannot see any reason I should not go to the devil any way I like."

The water-dragon's name was Lady Kiyomizu, although much to Junichiro's horror she breezily told Laurence to call her Kiyo, and not to stand on formality. "You have no manners anyway," she said, "and there is no sense your trying to put out *sakura* blossoms, when you are a bamboo."

Laurence ruefully swallowed this friendly condemnation as the price of his rudeness: he was more than willing to accept it, in any case, to gain such assistance as she was ready to offer in exchange for the scraps of poetry and drama which he could dredge up out of his memory. Fortunately he had always cultivated literary entertainments on his ships, to improve both the education and conversation of his young gentlemen, and the spirit of his hands. They had only just concluded the performance of *A Midsummer Night's Dream,* and on the King's birthday last, Lieutenant Riley had given the officers a stirring rendition of the St. Crispin's Day speech, which Laurence did his best to repeat now. Fortunately his cabin abutted Riley's, and so he had heard the speech said over and over in the evenings for nearly a month beforehand.

"But I beg you will pardon me if you later learn I have mistaken any of the phrases," he said. "I have not heard it since—" and stopped, for of course, he had not heard it in eight years gone and more.

Indeed the *Reliant* herself was surely no longer his at all. It would have been a peculiar career which after such a period should have left him in a prime frigate, and yet not seen him advanced to the command of a ship-of-the-line. Either an unlikely disgrace or promotion must inevitably have been his lot—and then he wondered suddenly if the transport herself was his, something in between the two.

He found it hard to sleep that night, searching for some scrap of memory to be a rope-line which he might have climbed to get a look at himself, past horizons which seemed empty all around. But nothing came to hand, and he felt ever more strongly the anxious sense of something lost; he put his hand into the bundle beneath his head and closed it around the hilt of the sword, the ray-skin familiar and not at once. He slept at last fitfully, ill-at-ease, and startled awake when footsteps came into the temple: an old woman carrying a steaming pot, and she screamed when she saw his face and dropped it, fleeing into the early dawn.

"Why, that is a pity," Kiyo said, yawning tremendously: she seemed able to almost open her jaws in a straight line. "You have made her spill half the sake. Pour the rest in the bowl! It is a little early, but the morning is nice and wet. I do not mind getting up."

She put them on her back again, when they had eaten the rest of the rice dish, and she had drunk the rest of the wine, and she tramped down the hill through a faint cold drizzle towards the river. "Put the baskets on," she said, stopping on the shore, "and let us get under way! It's a long way to Ariake, and we will have to stop and get something to eat along the way."

There was a sort of harness resting upside-down underneath a little lean-to by the shore: two tightly woven baskets, watertight, lined thickly with straw and a final lining of fabric. These were joined to each other with straps which went about her body; each was big enough for a man to climb inside, and when Laurence and Junichiro had strapped it upon her and ensconced themselves so, Kiyo plunged into the river and swam out into the deep part of the current, very like a horse bearing saddlebags.

Almost directly they had left the curve of the river leading to the temple, they were in settled countryside: women and children on the banks, washing clothing and carrying water, waved to them with enthusiasm as they passed, and fishermen poled small vessels out of their way, yielding precedence. Laurence had bundled his hair beneath a scrap of his old shirt, and he hunched his shoulders and looked down as they sailed onwards to avoid any comment on his features: he was increasingly conscious that any journey overland would have offered scarcely any hope of success.

Junichiro for his part also kept his head down; from what Laurence could see of his expressions, he seemed to be caught in a confused welter of pleasure and misery. His delight in the dragon's company, and in the condescension she had shown them, was very plain; it was equally plain he did not feel himself deserving of it, and Laurence would not have been surprised to have him burst out in confession of his crime at the least encouragement.

Fortunately this was not immediately forthcoming. The two of them might have been traveling alone, for Kiyo's head was nearly always submerged beneath the surface as she carried on against the current, her long tendrils streaming away to either side around her like trailers of seaweed caught on a ship's hull. Her speed was indeed remarkable: better than six knots, Laurence judged.

"Will you tell me about the course we are on?" Laurence asked Junichiro, when they were on an isolate curve of the river, hoping as much to distract him as to learn more of his circumstances: they seemed to have been swept up beyond his control for the moment.

"You must have done something notable in a past life," Junichiro said, half to himself, as though trying to explain to his own satisfaction what had brought them so much undeservedly good fortune. Laurence, for his part, should have liked to know what he had done either evil or good so as to produce all the ills of his present situation, but as he did not accept Junichiro's explanation, he could only attribute it to some forgotten act of his lost eight years. "And we are on the Chikugo River, following it to the Ariake Sea," Junichiro added. "That is between Chikugo Province and Hizen Province—"

"Hold, you leap too far ahead," Laurence said, and made Junichiro explain a little more of the geography of the nation, a small country like his own; they were upon the island of Kyushu, which after a little description Laurence mentally classed with Scotland: it was not the largest, nor the site of the capital, but the home of considerable wealth and industry; and this divided into several provinces.

"Nagasaki is in Hizen Province, on the western side of Kyushu—and Hizen is on the Ariake Sea, like Chikugo, so it will be much easier to get to there," Junichiro added, and with a finger dipped in river water sketched him a very rough shape on the dry part of the dragon's back, which shortly evaporated but left Laurence with the comfort, not inconsiderable for a man who was used to knowing his precise latitude and longitude at nearly every moment, of having some approximation of his bearings.

Junichiro said it should require the entire course of the day, to see them to the shore of the inland sea; Laurence settled himself low in his basket and prepared only to wait: the rocking motion of their journey was familiar, and he was ready to yield himself to sleep when cries from the bank started him up. He looked and saw a small crowd of people urgently waving a banner bearing several large-painted characters in red, which they had been in the process of rigging out on the riverbank from a signpost.

"Oh," Junichiro said, taken aback, and Laurence, looking over, wondered if this were to their account—couriers, he supposed, might have carried around a warning to be posted to try to capture them. But after a brief hesitation, Junichiro reached down into the water and tugged on one of Kiyo's tendrils.

Her head burst from the surface, rivulets streaming away, and the people on the riverbank renewed all their clamor; she did not hesitate for an instant herself, but immediately shifted her course out of the river's current towards them, and as they neared Laurence could see the chief of the delegation, as he supposed, bowing deeply before they had even come to shore.

Kiyo climbed out partway onto the shore to speak with this man, balancing herself on forelegs in a pose reminscent of the great sea-dragon which Laurence had seen. The conversation, naturally, proceeded entirely in Japanese. Laurence crouched in his basket and tried as best he could to avoid any notice, which effort met with success only because no-one present showed the least interest in Junichiro or himself; all their attention was fixed on the dragon.

It struck him abruptly that Kiyo also had no captain, no master; as neither had Lady Arikawa nor Lord Jinai, nor even the light-weight who had ferried about the magistrate and his servants. Laurence was startled, and startled even more that he had not even noticed it before this moment; he had thought nothing of it at all.

It ought to have been certain proof of an untamed ferocity. Dragons required a captain, harness, crew, all the forms of control, to be tolerated anywhere near settled country, or they would rampage and destroy; any beast not so restrained could only be penned in breeding grounds and bribed with cattle to remain there. So Laurence had always supposed—so he had always known. But even as he articulated to himself this commonplace understanding, it rang false. Proof to the contrary was before him, of course—but that should have seemed peculiar, disconcerting, and did not.

He had not managed to explain it to himself when the discussion concluded and Kiyo turned her head over towards them and said, "Down you get!"

Junichiro obeyed at once, and leapt to unbuckle the baskets; Laurence had scarcely any alternative but to follow his example, and hide his face from the expectant delegation by keeping it turned towards her side. They at least did not immediately seize him. Unburdened, Kiyo plunged back into the river and opened her jaws: she began at once to swell up into that wide immensity which Laurence had witnessed the previous evening. This time when she had reached her full size she did not bring the water forth again, but swaying and ponderous dragged herself up onto the shore, and in a strangely gargled voice gave direction. The delegation all turned and set out along a track that led away from the river, carrying their banner with them.

"What is happening?" Laurence asked Junichiro quietly, as they trailed in Kiyo's wake; but he might have reserved his questions. The path turned quickly out of the trees and opened onto a truly splendid wide-open vista: a series of very wide terraces falling away from them down a sloping hillside, each full of water and faintly green with the earliest sprouting of rice plants, though surely the season was too early. There was yet a sharp chill of frost in the air, which Laurence thought must be inimical to any farming, although only to be expected at this time of year.

At the summit stood a great stone basin with a wide irrigation channel running away from it down the hill: peering over, Laurence could see more channels leading to either side into each terrace. The delegation here broke up, and most of the number went running swiftly down narrow pathways along the hillside, calling notice: workers in the fields, who were mostly busy staggering under yokes of water-buckets, raised their heads from beneath wide-brimmed hats and, seeing the dragon, hurried to take themselves out of the terraces until they were lining the hillside paths.

From a village visible at the base of the hill, a neat hamlet of thatch-roofed houses, more people were streaming to join the welcoming party, children running with a cheerful clamoring; more banners were being carried out of a larger house, perhaps ceremonial, and set at the foot of the hill in bright array.

Kiyo was leaning forward into the basin and dipping her face into it, shaking her head so the tendrils made a great cloud around her. Laurence could hear a peculiar gurgling and hissing from her side, an internal noise like a man digesting an excessive meal. She raised her head up and shook off the droplets, and then nodded to the anxiously waiting delegation. Two of the great banners had by now reached the summit and were fixed to either side of the basin, cracking in the wind. All were standing silent, in attitudes of tense expectation.

Kiyo adjusted her position, and then she opened her jaws wide and began to expel the water into the basin: not in any massive quantity at first, a thin stream like the jet of a small fountain, but Laurence was astonished to see the water so hot that it was steaming in the open air. Shortly the rime of white ice, half-an-inch wide, which edged the pool in the stone basin had melted entirely away, and water was running softly away down the channels. Kiyo paused in her work and put her face into the basin again—perhaps working out in some way the desirable degree of heat—and then she sat up again and began once more, in earnest.

The gush of water came out of her jaws as from a kettle, steaming-hot, and went running down to water all the fields— likely saving them from that very frost which Laurence had noticed. As he watched the process, he realized that the Japanese might well receive from this influence an entirely additional growing-season: if they might rely on such a rescue, when a frost threatened the crop, they might begin the first planting earlier, and take the second harvest later, and get two crops instead of one. Their urgency was easily explained, now; having drawn the attentions of a water-dragon so soon likely had saved more of the crop.

When Kiyo had reduced herself back to her original dimensions and closed her jaws again, and the men along the hillside had tried each shallow terrace and waved one after another their banners in signal of success, the general relief was nearly palpable. More bowing and ceremonial thanks ensued, and though there were no effusions, no broad beaming expressions, even so shoulders had straightened; anxiety had lifted. Laurence could not fail to interest himself in proceedings so foreign to his experience, and yet so familiar: he had ridden the estate with his father on occasion as a boy, and there was not so great a difference between the expressions of the tenants receiving relief in the case of some disaster to their crops or homes, and the present—though his father had not nearly so dramatic a support to offer.

Nor so general: the entire village had benefited, here, and it was at once apparent they meant to show their appreciation in proper form: an ox was led up the hill, lowing in anxiety as it came nearer the dragon, and was shortly butchered before them. The tender offal was flung immediately into a hot pan over coals: sweetbreads and heart and liver and brains, and these having been quickly seared were presented to Kiyo, who devoured them delicately while the great sides of beef were carried away to prepare some more elaborate offering. Other preparations were already in train—cooking-steam was issuing from many of the houses below and baskets of cooked rice beginning to emerge; the leaders of the delegation were seating themselves formally on mats placed around Kiyo's head.

"Well, we will be a little late getting you to the sea," she said cheerfully, looking around to Laurence at last, as she settled herself down to eat, "but at least we do not need to worry about eating. How delicious good, fresh beef is!"

The remark fell, unfortunate, loud. Whether they merely had more leisure now for interest, or her addressing him drew attention, several heads turned: the village chief, some other of the older men and women, and Laurence found himself regarded with dawning astonishment, in a widening circle of silence.

Chapter 5

Temeraire's spirits had been equal to the challenge of thinking Laurence swept overboard and flung onto the shore, even in the face of general doubt and disagreement; but he began to find it difficult to sustain his confidence, knowing Laurence in such dreadful circumstances: not merely a shipwreck in a strange country, alone, but with every hand against him—every man his enemy, every dragon.

Temeraire could not bring himself to choke down more than a few swallows of soup and rice to share room in his belly with the lump of anxiety, nor could he take any pleasure even in the egg, though Granby and Roland had spoken to him several times that afternoon, anxiously, and remarked upon how nicely it came along. Ferris also had complimented it, very prettily, while Forthing scowled at him and then only stammered out his own attempt—which no-one wanted, anyway; but in neither case could Temeraire raise much of either satisfaction or irritation. He lay unhappy upon the dragon-deck, watching the harbor traffic more from a dull consciousness of duty than from any real interest.

The Japanese boats which crowded the harbor, though not large, were well-handled: fishermen and porters and barges. Besides these and the Chinese ships, the Dutch ship stood out in the harbor: a clipper, with a long and narrow draught for her three masts; she would be a fast sailor, Temeraire thought vaguely. He did not much care about her; she was no danger, as she was all alone, and would scarcely have made a threat to the *Potentate* even without aerial support. He could not see that she had any guns at all.

She did have a dragon: at least, she had put out a pontoon-platform for one to rest upon, and he wore harness, so he was a Western dragon, surely, although his harness was a little strange and looked like nothing so much as a waistcoat, at this distance. But he was only a light-weight, a little bigger than Dulcia, and not very dangerous-looking: a very ordinary sort of brown speckled with cream, with a long and narrow snout and broad forehead. Certainly he did not look anything like the sea-dragon; if anything he looked more like Churki in the conformation of his body, though he was not feathered, of course.

He did not stay at the ship for very long at any one time, but flew busily back and forth to the shore several times over the course of the afternoon carrying substantial parcels away from the ship, which the crew delivered to him over the side with pulleys, and taking them to the shore, where he held several conversations with some party, whom Temeraire could not make out at the distance, before returning to his own ship.

On the fourth pass, Temeraire suddenly picked up his head. "Roland," he said, "that ship there, that is Dutch; she is lawful prize, is she not?"

"Oh?" Iskierka said interrogatively, waiting with interest for the answer.

"Oh," Roland said, looking sidelong, "well, I suppose she is, as she is under Dutch colors; but—"

"No, no," Temeraire said, "I do not mean to take her—"

"Whyever not!" Iskierka interrupted.

Temeraire snorted at her. "Because we have more important matters to consider than prize-taking, at present! But if she is lawful prize, then I suppose she is quite afraid of us; they are taking those parcels to shore, so we should not get them if we decide to demand she strike. Nitidus," he said, twisting his neck around and over Iskierka, to peer awkwardly at him, "would you be so kind as to go over to that dragon there, and invite him to come and have a cup of tea with us, if you please?"

"But," Nitidus said, "but you don't suppose they will shoot at me?"

"Of course they will not shoot at you," Temeraire said. "We are all here, quite ready to come over and answer anything they like to try against you; but if you like," he added, "you may hang out a flag of truce, so they are not worried when you come."

Roland looked a little anxious, and ventured that she might go and speak to Captain Warren before Nitidus should go; but Captain Warren and the others were at dinner: Hammond had in great haste arranged that all the captains should eat together that evening, as his guests. He only wanted to better argue with them all at once more conveniently, but that did not give anyone an excuse for refusing when Hammond was the King's envoy, no matter how rude his own behavior or late the invitation.

"Besides, I am not going to do anything: we are only going to have a conversation," Temeraire said, "so pray do go over, Nitidus," and he was persuaded to go, carrying a scrap of white sailcloth streaming away.

Temeraire watched the encounter anxiously: he *was* quite sure they would not fire on Nitidus, he hoped; but even so, perhaps the other dragon would not like to come; or perhaps he would not speak either English or French, which was all that Nitidus could do, although in such a case he hoped there might be a translator aboard the ship. But Nitidus was received, if not with visible pleasure, at least with no hostility; the brown dragon politely made room for him to land on the platform, and listened with attention to his message, as did several men leaning over the ship's side straining with ear-trumpets to overhear.

Temeraire nudged the others beside him, when he saw the brown dragon look over, to make an inviting open place for him to land on the deck. That was no easy feat—Captain Blaise did not like to put out their own pontoons when their position was so uncertain, and so they were very sadly crowded yet—but with a great deal of squirming and writhing it was accomplished, just as the brown dragon leapt aloft, following Nitidus, and came towards them.

"Oh, Gong Su," Temeraire said, turning as he came climbing up to the dragondeck, with Roland and Forthing and Ferris, "we are to have a guest: pray tell me, do you suppose is there any chance of our offering him a proper bowl of tea? And something to eat? I should be happy to see us offer that last goat, which I believe is marked out for me, if I might beg you to put a word in the ears of the cook," he added. Of course it was not really suitable, to Gong Su's proper rank, to ask him to cook anymore; but it was a sad fact that none of the British cooks seemed at all able to make a respectable meal for a dragon other than the plainest roasted meat, and Gong Su had hinted to Temeraire that so long as he should put the matter on the footing of a personal favor, no shame could attach to the act on his own side.

Gong Su bowed deeply. "I will make inquiries, and see what can be done, of course," he said, and instantly went; meanwhile Forthing could think of nothing better to do than to stamp up to the dragondeck and say, "Look, Temeraire, whatever are you about? We cannot be gabbing away with the enemy."

"How absurd," Temeraire said with scorn, "only look how small he is! An enemy of mine: I should say not. Anyway, I am only going to have a conversation with him. Hammond was closeted for hours with the Dutch commissioner, so I do not see why I should not have a chat with this fellow."

Ferris was trying to catch Forthing by the arm, murmuring to him, "Look, if it should bring up his spirits at all—"

Forthing shook him off and said, in cutting tones, "I know very well *your* motive to allow any degree of license whatsoever—" and Ferris flushed angrily, but Temeraire could not pay attention to them further, as he had to turn to meet their guest as he came in to land.

The brown dragon's harness was odd indeed, as it came into closer view: it was indeed made up of almost pouches of some ordinary fabric, brown wool perhaps, and these were overlaid upon and attached to a fine mesh which covered him nearly from the base of his neck to his tail almost like a shirt, made up of many thin chains—chains of *gold*, Temeraire realized with a real start, as the sun caught upon them, and so many! although almost entirely concealed by the dull fabric.

"But why would anyone wear gold chains in such a way, where you can hardly tell they *are* golden," he whispered doubtfully to Iskierka; they certainly would not be very handy, in a fight.

They could not discuss it: the dragon landed with an easy flip upon the deck before them, and settled himself in the waiting opened place, while Nitidus landed on Temeraire's back and made himself comfortable.

"Hello," Temeraire said, inclining his head. "How do you do? I am Temeraire, and also Lung Tien Xiang; and I am very pleased to make your acquaintance: thank you very much for coming."

"Well, it's kind of you to ask me," the brown dragon said, in perfectly good English although broadly accented. "And I am John Wampanoag, of Salem, Massachusetts, at your service," and he bowed his own head politely as well.

Temeraire said, a little uncertainly, "But surely that is not in Holland?" He was not perfectly sure of the geography of that nation, but there had been a great many places around Capetown, which had possessed Dutch names, and that did not sound in the least like any of them.

"Why, no," the dragon said, "I am American, you know. That is my ship, the *Lacewing*," and gave a flip of his tail in the direction of the Dutch vessel. "She is only under Dutch colors because we have been hired to bring in a cargo, since you have that Bonaparte fellow making hay of things in Europe."

"Oh, I see," Temeraire said, although he did not, at all: Bonaparte had conquered the Dutch, he was quite sure. "But is he not their emperor?" he inquired.

The American dragon shrugged. "The fellow in charge here

don't like to think him so," he said, "and he is the one who can sell my cargo for me and get me my copper for the return road, so I guess what he says is good enough for me."

"Your cargo," Temeraire said, a little perplexed, "and your ship—do you mean to say, she is your prize?"

"Prize?" Wampanoag said. "No; I paid to have her built, and I bought the wool cloth and the other trade goods in her belly. Well," he amended, "if you like to be precise, my firm did so: she is a venture of Devereux, Pickman, and Wampanoag: but as Devereux is in India, at present, and Pickman is back at Salem minding the store, you may as well call her mine."

Temeraire was staggered, and looked at the rather small and nondescript dragon with new respect: he was well aware that to outfit a ship, even quite a little one, was a very serious undertaking—thousands and thousands of pounds, at the least, and Wampanoag spoke of laying out the money for it as a matter-of-course, and buying cargo besides. "I do not suppose," he ventured, "—would it be quite rude of me to inquire, where you got the funds?"

"From other ventures," Wampanoag said. "I have been to the South Seas half-a-dozen times, and to India; we do a pretty brisk business in tea, I can tell you."

"Yes, but where did you get the money for the *first* one," Temeraire clarified, rather urgently. "—your capital, I suppose I mean."

He did not wish to be distracted from his original purpose for long, but he felt he could scarcely overlook such an opportunity as Wampanoag had just unexpectedly presented, of finding a way to restore Laurence's fortunes. A gauzy and splendid vision hung before him: Laurence rescued, Laurence back aboard the ship with him, on the way to China again, and very offhand, very casually, when they were alone on deck with the ocean slipping by Temeraire would say, "By the way, Laurence: I have brought you back your ten thousand pounds which I lost you, and I hope you will put them into the Funds, straightaway."

Of course it could be done with prize-taking—Temeraire knew

that, and Iskierka was forever nagging after finding some, but Laurence did not really approve of that. A prize taken legitimately, in the course of one's duty, he thought was very well; hunting after prizes for their own sake he frowned upon. Laurence would not be satisfied, if he were to ask where Temeraire had got the funds—and he *would* ask, Temeraire was glumly certain—should he hear, as answer, by taking prizes. And Temeraire had forfeited his own share of the perfectly correct prizes which he and his company had taken during the invasion of Britain, when he had been transported away with Laurence; those had all gone to building pavilions, back in Britain.

"I had a good bit from the tribe, when we formed the firm, which I have since bought out; but of course they would not go in with me until I showed I could raise some funds of my own," Wampanoag said. "I began with doing some cross-country carrier work, for other firms, and when I had shown I was a steady fellow and was not going to go haring off with someone's cargo, good old Devereux gave me my chance and hired me to be agent on one of his Indiamen, with two points of interest. When I had realized my share from that journey, the tribe went in with me, and Devereux's third son, and Pickman, to outfit our first ship; and we have done pretty well for ourselves since."

"Cross-country," Temeraire said, latching on to the first part of this nearly incomprehensible narrative, "—across your own country?"

"From Boston to the Kwaikiutl, on the West Coast," Wampanoag confirmed. "It's a good deal cheaper, you know, to carry things dragon-back instead of sailing all the way round." Then he sat back and looked at Temeraire with a tipped head. "I beg your pardon, am I being a dullard? Are you looking for work? There's not quite so much call for heavy-weights in shipping, as the cost of your feed is difficult to make back; but there is a particularly fine timber, on the West Coast, which I have been thinking might make it profitable to get a big fellow aboard."

"Why," Temeraire said, brightening, "that is very kind of you: how long a flight is it?"

"Not above a month," Wampanoag said, "once you are in Kwaikutl lands: that is three months' sailing, from here."

"Oh," Temeraire said, "I do not suppose I can: we cannot leave the war for four months. And then we should have to get *back*," he added, and sighed a small sigh; he ought have known that it could be no easy matter to build up a fortune, or else everyone would have done it already before now.

"But *anyone* can do this?" Dulcia ventured, from Maximus's back: they had all been listening raptly.

"If you know your book-keeping, so you cannot be cheated; and will do steady work," Wampanoag said, "and if you don't mind an empty belly now and again, and you are steady about avoiding fights and trouble and fuss, and showing away," rapidly diminishing the luster of the enterprise as he went on.

"An empty belly?" Maximus said, and snorted. "That is not for me: anyway we do very well, Temeraire. We *do* have pay now, you know, and it stacks up quite agreeably, when you ask to see it in coin."

"No—yes—I suppose," Temeraire said, though regretfully. "Still it is very generous of you to offer," he added to Wampanoag, "and I am very flattered, I am sure: will you stay to tea, if you please?" He saw with great relief that Gong Su was coming back up to the dragondeck with several of the galley cooks, the ship's boys carrying handsome brass bowls polished to a shine and steaming cauldrons of food, and upon a rack dripping over porridge the roasted goat, with what smelled like some fish liver in sauce to give it some interest.

"Thank'ee, I don't mind if I do," Wampanoag said. "If I am not putting you out: I can see you are crowded a bit," a sad understatement: Maximus was curled over all of the deck where Temeraire was not, and all the others heaped atop them both, whenever they were not aloft or swimming.

"We do very well, pray do not think anything of it," Temeraire said, of course.

"I suppose you fellows have come from England? Have you the latest news of the war?" Wampanoag asked, when they had settled themselves and begun to eat: there was of course fish and rice, to eke out the goat, but Temeraire had made sure—frowning down both Maximus and Kulingile—that Wampanoag received a haunch entirely for himself, as the courtsey due a guest.

"We have come from Brazil," Temeraire said, "and we have only a little news from there: the Incan Empress has married Napoleon, and we suppose gone to France with him." He hurried through this part of the story, and added, "But far more importantly, the Tswana have quite cast him off—they have made peace, in Brazil, and they do not mean to help him make war there any longer."

He finished on this, as the best note of triumph available; although the situation in Brazil had by no means been quite so settled as all that at their departure. The Portuguese owners had been as laggard as they could in freeing many of their slaves, and those released had not all been perfectly happy to find themselves subsequently claimed as the family of the Tswana dragons, however much cherished by the same. But so far the arrangement had held, at least in name; they had remained in Brazil several months to see it established, despite all their urgent wish to be on the way to China, and Temeraire counted it yet as a success.

"Why, that is very interesting, there," Wampanoag said, thoughtfully, though not as impressed as Temeraire might have liked by the news from Brazil, and rather more interested in the Incan side of things, asking, "Do they have so much gold and silver as they are supposed to do?"

"*Heaps*," Iskierka said, with a resentful and significant eye on Temeraire: she had not ceased to mutter quietly, where Granby could not hear, how much better everything should have been if he *had* married the Incan Empress instead, as she had busily tried to arrange. Temeraire paid her no mind. Granby had not wanted to marry the Empress at all.

"I must try and lay in some stock of silk, then, and pottery,"

Wampanoag said, which Temeraire did not follow at all, though he was too polite to say so; but Kulingile was not so shy of asking, and Wampanoag willingly explained, "Why, cotton will be cheaper soon, with this peace with the Tswana: the South shan't be looking to the sea-lanes and fearing to send out any ships, and gold and silver won't buy as much, if there is more to be had floating around. I will buy ten thousand dollars' worth of silk now, if I can get the Japanese to give it to me, and sell it for a hundred then: see if I don't." He gave a very decided nod.

"That," said Churki, when Wampanoag had flown back to his own ship, after tea, "is a highly respectable dragon, I am sure. And you see how many people he has, all his own! I wish you had asked him more about this tribe of his," she added, with a slightly censorious note, "instead of thinking only of his money. Money is very well and one must have enough, but it is not all that matters."

"That is not why I asked him, at all," Temeraire said, loftily, and well-pleased with the success of his opening gambit, swallowed his medicine in better spirits, and put himself to sleep with his new and private hope: if *he* could not go and find Laurence, and his friends could not, perhaps someone else might.

"He is just an Englishman going to Nagasaki," Kiyo said, eating a quarter of beef. "I am taking him as far as Seto. Pass that hot sake, if you please," she added to the headman, or something along those lines, Laurence gathered, picking out a few words and seeing the village chief looking between him and her helplessly and then turning to have the bowl of hot wine before her refreshed from a heated kettle.

There was very plainly an extraordinary degree of deference paid to the river-dragons, and Kiyo evidently considered herself—and likely was—above any considerations of the law. But the headman was not so, and his suspicions were not to be so easily allayed. He did not challenge Kiyo directly, but Laurence saw him speak to one of the other men, and shortly a few messengers slipped away from the celebration. He watched them go, grimly, and exchanged a look with Junichiro, who himself had been keeping back.

The headman came towards him shortly, to press him with smiling firmness to come down to the village and be housed there for the night. Laurence had not the least doubt there would be a guard on the house, and he did not mean to carve his way out of another prison through innocent farmers.

"Pray thank him for his kindness," Laurence said, casting for some way of deferring the entanglement, "and tell him I am honored to accept his invitation: we will come down very shortly, if Kiyo does not wish to get back on the water."

"Oh, I do not mind staying the night," Kiyo said, unhelpfully, without looking up from her gnawed bones. "We will not get to Ariake to-day, anyway, and there is not much moon to-night. We had much better sleep here, and get on the way in the morning."

By the morning, Laurence was sure, he would have no opportunity; but he bowed to the headman, and determined to wait for some small chance to get into the trees and out of sight. Kiyo abruptly compensated for her indiscretion by sitting up and belching enormously and noxiously, emitting a large diffuse cloud of greyish smoke that stung in the nostrils and left those near-by coughing and gasping: perhaps some aftereffect of her labors in heating the water, and the stink of it not unlike burning tar.

Many of the guests were wiping streaming eyes; the headman was distracted. Laurence seized his bundle in one arm and caught Junichiro with the other; they did not exchange a word, but together hurried as discreetly as they could back into the trees.

They ran as soon as they were out of sight, until they reached the banks of the river and pulled up again: there were a few small fishing-boats pulled up on the shore, with serviceable-enough oars. Junichiro balked. "We cannot steal from peasants," he said, but Laurence had already reached into the bundle and twisted off one of the gold buttons upon his coat.

He pressed it into the soft dirt of the bank. "Let us hope that will make adequate answer," he said. "I will tell you again, you may go back: it is not too late—"

"You know my course is decided," Junichiro said flatly, already climbing in.

"Very well," Laurence said, pushing off, and he bent his back to the oars with a will.

The river ran at a good pace, the boat was light; Laurence had labored harder, for less cause, and arms that took a regular turn at the pumps were not overly tasked by the steady pull. The day had been already long, even with Kiyo's assistance earlier, but Laurence thought it better to row through the night and seek some concealment for the day; the countryside would surely be roused after them, now. "How much further, to this Ariake Sea?" he asked Junichiro, as he rowed onwards.

"Another night after this one," Junichiro said, dully. He sat huddled low in the bottom of the boat: their narrow escape had been a fresh reminder to him of his crime, and there was no longer the pleasure of a dragon's company to distract him. He watched as Laurence rowed on and on; when at last they came to a quicker eddy, and Laurence shipped the oars to give himself a rest, he asked abruptly, "Are you truly a—nobleman?"

"What, because I can row?" Laurence said, half-amused. "Yes; my father is Lord Allendale. But I have been aboard ship since I was twelve years old. I dare say there is not a shipboard task I have not set my hand to."

The river was empty, for the most part, in the advancing night; only fishermen seeking a last piece of luck were out, and not many of those, mere shadows; one they passed was singing softly to himself, and raised a hand to them as they glided on past. Laurence felt the deep peacefulness of the countryside, its stillness, and the loneliness of being outside that quiet.

"Are we likely to meet anyone along the river?" Laurence asked quietly.

"Only at the fords," Junichiro said, "if we are unlucky." He paused and then said a little too quickly, as though he at once wanted very much to ask, and was conscious he should not desire it, "Have you been in a battle, at sea?"

"Three fleet actions," Laurence said, "and perhaps a dozen ship-to-ship. There is nothing very pretty in it. Have you never seen a battle?"

"The bakufu has kept the peace in Japan for two hundred years," Junichiro answered, with not-unmerited pride. "There are pirates and bandits, of course, but not near my mas—not near the honorable Kaneko's home." For all his satisfaction, there was a small wistful note in his voice.

"They are to be congratulated, then," Laurence said. "I do not think we have had peace in Europe for ten years together, in living memory: nor are like to have, with Napoleon roosting in France."

They fell silent together: there were a few huts approaching, and a lantern hung with a gleam of light. Laurence took up the oars again and fell into the easy rhythm of the work, no sound but the faint dripping patter of the water upon the river surface with each oar-stroke, the hush of the wind going by. The moon rose, gibbous and pale on the black water, and he drifted. He might have been on the broad deck of his ship at the prow, facing into the wind and the sails making a low *clap-clap* behind, the hands singing at the stern and a lantern throwing light in a circle on a book before him as he read aloud, looking up to speak to—

He started and looked over his shoulder: there *was* a light, and music, up ahead. A road came to cross the river at a ford, and on the left bank stood several houses lit up and festooned with lamps, women in long gowns at their doors calling out in a great noise to a party of travelers on the road, and several porters and two ferry-men perched upon both sides of the crossing, watching the approach of their small boat with interest and suspicion.

Temeraire had meant to send Wampanoag another invitation, the next day, but he did not need to; instead in the morning, when the hands had just finished holystoning down the dragondeck, the American dragon flew over of his own volition with a white scrap waving. Kulingile grumbled: it was his turn to sleep, after staying aloft during all Maximus's turn—as Temeraire could not presently take a turn aloft himself—and he disliked having to move.

"I am sorry to come shoving in amongst you," Wampanoag said, as he came down, "but as I can't ask you over to *Lacewing*, in turn, I hope you'll forgive me for making this answer instead for all your hospitality," and he lay down a large package wrapped in oilcloth, tied up with string.

"Oh!" Temeraire said, astonished but by no means displeased; Iskierka sat up and took notice. Maximus had been taking a swim, in lieu of going aloft, but he put his forelegs on the railing and peered over, and all the other dragons raised their heads to have a look; even Kulingile cracked an eye. "Roland, will you open it, if you please?"

She cut open the strings, and folding back the sheets revealed a glory of blaze, beautiful glass beads strung on silver chain, with pearls and gold beads scattered along the length, and how immensely long indeed—it might have made an anchor-chain for the *Potentate*, and a little more to spare.

"If you have a smith aboard, as I suppose you must," Wampanoag said, while they all gazed upon it in mute delight, "he can parcel it out for you all into lengths: I thought that might be better than my trying to cut it up beforehand. We wear it like so, in Salem," he added, and sitting up on his heels showed how a similar chain hung from one woolen pouch to another across his breast.

"Now that," Temeraire said, "I must call very handsome." No-one at all was inclined to disagree, and Temeraire considered it all the evidence which he required, of Wampanoag's being a very good sort of dragon, and to be trusted with important business. He knew perfectly well that Hammond might have a different view of the matter, of course—Hammond had complained a great deal of Temeraire's having spoken with Wampanoag yesterday at all—but Hammond had certainly forfeited any right to consideration after his shameful attempt to leave Laurence behind, and Temeraire did not mean to waste any time in useless quarreling with him where his own mind was made up.

It was too early to eat again, but Wampanoag was very ready to be persuaded to sit with them just for company, awhile, and when they had settled themselves as conveniently as possible, Temeraire delayed no longer in broaching the topic, very delicately. "For you see," he said, "I am afraid that Mr. Hammond may not quite have pursued the matter properly: it does not seem to me that any real search can have been put into train. And," he added, "I consider all the sailors of the ship to be our responsibility. I do not think it at all the thing for us to leave any of them here. We cannot sail away until we have found him: our lost sailor, I mean."

He was not entirely insensible to all Hammond's cautions: there was no need for anyone to know that Laurence should be a valuable hostage, so they might try to put him in prison; Temeraire much preferred for them only to know that if Laurence were returned, they would leave, and otherwise not.

"Are you sure he isn't only dead?" Wampanoag said, greatly diminishing Temeraire's opinion of his intelligence. "They usually are, if they get washed overboard."

Temeraire with an effort restrained himself from mantling. "I am *quite* sure," he said, repressively. "And I intend to remain so until I am offered *proof* otherwise."

Wampanoag had a trick of tilting his head a little to one side, as though he were looking you over from another angle to see if you seemed different, which Temeraire now found had the effect of making him feel under a too-sharp observation. But Wampanoag only said, "So you are only lingering to find him, this fellow you lost?"

"Yes," Temeraire said, eagerly. "And we should be *very* glad of any assistance in recovering him."

"But I beg your pardon," Wampanoag said, "aren't you here over the *Phaeton*?"

"No, for we hadn't any notion what had happened to her," Temeraire said. "We were only on our way to China: we have been invited to the court, you see."

Wampanoag was quite gratifyingly surprised to hear of their destination; he expressed himself very prettily on the matter indeed, calling it a remarkable honor. "And I will not scruple to say, that puts a very different shade on things here, it seems to me," he added, "if you are *not* here to quarrel."

"We are not, in the least," Temeraire said, although a stab of guilt, when he thought of what Laurence should say when he heard of the *Phaeton,* forced him to add, "although I do say we think it very hard that the *Phaeton* should have been sunk, so far from home with all her hands, and all because, we suppose, of some misunderstanding."

"Let us certainly call it that, for the moment," Wampanoag said. "That is a very good name for it, I must say."

He declared himself delighted to be of service in any way he could, promised to speak with the chief of the Dutch, a gentleman called Doeff, to forward the search, and even with the Japanese directly. "I have a bit of Dutch myself, you know," he said, "from the shell: my tribe adopted a good many of them back during the quarreling over New Amsterdam that was. So I can have a jaw with their translators, myself: that is why I hired us on here."

He was so ready to be obliging that Temeraire could not even be too angry with him for adding, "but pray do understand that it is more than I undertake, to return you your sailor. I don't mean to distress you, but my firm have lost a few ships entire ourselves, all hands, too. It is a dreadful sad wrench, I can tell you, to hear that a neat clipper with her hold packed full and three dozen men aboard has gone to the bottom of the ocean, to be gnawed by serpents, and a clear loss of twenty thousand pounds sterling."

Temeraire shuddered in real horror, his ruff flattening involuntarily down against his neck, and Churki exclaimed in passionate dismay; but Wampanoag made a prosaic flip of his wing in the air. "I don't complain: it is a hard business," he said, "and a necessary risk to run, if you mean to make your fortune at it. But what I mean to say is, not a scrap of sail or bit of timber do we have to show for any ship we have lost: we only know they are lost because they left the one port and never came in at any other, and after we had sat hoping after them a couple of years it was time to leave off saying, 'She will come in tomorrow.' So I cannot promise you we will find a trace to say, one way or another, what has happened to your sailor. But whatever I *can* do, I will, sure enough."

"I cannot hope for more than that," Temeraire said as politely as he could manage, rather wishing that Wampanoag would leave now before sharing any other ghoulish stories, and seeing before him a long empty stretch of days, waiting and waiting, while Laurence did not come.

The party about to ford the river was evidently the train of a lord on his way home from the capital, amongst them several armed retainers wearing two swords and more serviceable armor as well. Laurence kept his head bent down and rowed industriously but not, he hoped, too fast; Junichiro was silent in the boat's belly. Laurence thought for a moment they would manage it. The ferrymen and the porters lost interest when they saw that Laurence showed no intention to compete with their business, of which in any case there bade fair to be as much as they could manage with the sheer size of the lord's retinue, and the confusion and noise of the welcoming inns might have overwhelmed any interest in Laurence and Junichiro's quiet passage.

But luck turned against them: one of the lord's servants on the far bank, evidently in charge of getting the entire assembly across the river and looking exasperated and hot, with a few strands of hair straggled loose from his neatly swept-back arrangement, caught sight of the boat. He called out to them peremptorily, beckoning—*you there, you, the boat*—plainly wishing them to come and assist in the ferrying, despite the scowls of the ferrymen.

Laurence pretended not to hear, not to see; he rowed onwards with more vigor, trying to evade the clumsy-handled ferries, crammed too full of men. But an eddy pushed one of the waddling boats towards their little fishing-boat and bumped her, and a disapproving older woman in the prow took the opportunity to reach over and swat him reprovingly, gesturing back at the crowded bank as she chided him.

The swat dislodged the rag covering his hair; one of the samurai aboard the ship glanced over, and, after a moment of confusion, a recognition dawned. The samurai leaned over, and sought to grab him; Laurence shipped one oar and seized the other mid-stem, jabbing the handle hard into the man's belly, and tipped him over the side. Another was standing up in the ferry, trying to draw his sword, which he would have needed to practice a good deal more on the water before trying to accomplish it on a wallowing tub of the sort. Before he could get it out, Laurence swung up the flat of the oar and struck the man a hard and ringing clout across the head, knocking him down to the floor of the ferry.

The two boats were yet entangled. "Ma'am, I beg your pardon," Laurence said to the old woman, who was still sitting ramrod-straight in the ferry over the side from him and regarding him with a flat expression of utter disapproval and not the least evidence of fear; he put out a boot over the side and shoved the ferry off with a heave, and they were loose.

But the entire retinue were now alive to his presence, swarming out upon the banks, and a couple of the samurai wading out towards them with blades drawn: the ford was shallow enough to make attack practical, the river not waist-high on a man. "Take the oars!" Laurence said to Junichiro, who was hesitating with his hand on the hilt of his blade—he could scarcely have been eager to strike men of rank, of his own nation.

Junichiro looked even more torn; but he seized the oars and began awkwardly to pull. One of the samurai had reached them, catching at the boat's side: Laurence gripped the man's wrist to hold away the blade, and with his other hand closed hard struck him across the face and away from the boat. Another was struggling furiously through the current, almost there, but Junichiro had mastered the boat, and they were moving into deeper water.

Laurence ducked a last wild desperate swing of blade, and then he sat again and took the oars—pulled as urgently as ever he had pulled in his life: no longer the easy strokes he had used to move them along, but deep cupping sweeps, legs and back and shoulders all gone into every stroke. He had put a hundred yards between them and the ford before the first ferry could be emptied of her passengers, and a pursuit began to organize. Then he was further on, around a bend of the river, and they had vanished from sight.

He did not slacken his pace; he thought at first he might hope to escape the pursuit—the boats at the ford had by no means been very serviceable, and any rowers they had were like to be unhandy. But as he pulled them onwards, a blue flare went shooting up, back from the ford, and burst with a great thunderclap noise and a shining light on the water. A signal, and faintly he heard an answering roar—a dragon, alerted.

"They will set the patrols on us now," Junichiro said. "We will be taken," with a calm certainty, given almost in a conversational tone. He had straightened up in the boat, and looked as though he were already preparing himself to meet his fate.

"I do not propose to be quite so dull a fox as that," Laurence said. "Pick up that bundle, and jump for the shore when we are near enough." He turned them towards the left, where the bank came low to the water, with trees close together but not impassable.

Chapter 6

Laurence pushed the fishing-boat off, water already rising inside from the hole he had stove in her hull, and saw her go away down-river not without a qualm: even if remaining aboard would have been certain doom, she was still the quickest road to the sea, and the only one at all familiar. He had left the remains of his already-tattered old shirt wrapped around a bundle of branches to make a sort of scare-crow, standing up in the prow and fluttering out white; if only the boat evaded capture long enough to get some distance away before she sank, he hoped it might prove some source of confusion, if not long defer the pursuit.

At least it would conceal where they had gone, for a little while. Junichiro was already doing his best to obscure the marks their landing had made in the bank with more dead leaves and branches.

The going was slow among the trees, and slower still for lack of clear destination. Laurence could look up and catch a glimpse of the stars, now and again, which pointed him south-west generally, but besides this his progress was wholly blind. "Do you have any notion what is in the countryside near-by here?" he asked Junichiro, as they struggled onwards through the rough terrain.

"We are in Chikugo Province by now," Junichiro said. He paused and looked up over his shoulder: a sound of leathery wings, faint but carrying over the water, not far distant.

Laurence caught sight of a large old pine, gnarled and twisted,

roots erupting from the ground in low arches. They squirmed between two of these and pressed themselves back into the meager
shelter their intersection offered. The night was not bitterly cold,
but enough; they were wet, in thin cotton robes, and it would be a
long while for the hollow to have warmed with their bodies. The
dragon swept overhead a few times, with no particular direction,
merely having a general look, or so it seemed to Laurence; but they
huddled beneath the predatory search in silence, hearing the distant
noise of search parties.

A clamor was raised somewhere off, in the direction of the
river, and the dragon turned away towards it: perhaps the boat.
Laurence breathed, but did not yet live and move; too soon for
that. The sun was barely up, but had not yet penetrated the trees;
he only saw the sky lightened overhead. The voices left off, after a
while, and the dragon's searching resumed, but more distant—it
was looking somewhere on the other side of the river, Laurence
thought. In any case, this was the best chance which was likely to
come; a search would close in upon them soon enough if they
merely remained in hiding.

He stood, not very quickly or easily; all his muscles protested
the cavalier treatment he had served them, going from hot work to
a cold, crouching bed, and he could only ruefully envy Junichiro,
who bounded out of the hollow behind him as easily as a deer with
the limberness of youth. "Have you any notion of the best direction?" he asked.

"We should continue southward and make for the coast of the
Ariake Sea," Junichiro said, "and follow its shore around to Nagasaki." Laurence nodded, and followed him into the thicket.

They walked in silence most of the time, speaking only in low
voices; the woods were deep and hushed about them, and every
word seemed to ring out like a bell, inviting capture. But Laurence
asked Junichiro the distance to the sea when they made a brief halt
by a spring and they gave their feet a rest; blisters were already raising white upon his skin. The number meant nothing at first, as he

110

did not know how long a *ri* was, but when they began walking again, Junichiro did his best to tell Laurence when they had crossed the distance, and he made it something near two and a half miles. Ten miles to the coast and sixty around, if they could not find another boat and cut across: three days' forced march, for an infantry company—a company with boots and supply.

Laurence marched on after him and grimly did not make any close inspection of his feet: they would be worse before they were better.

"They are busy enough over *something,* there," Granby said, peering through his spyglass, which was rigged out with a loop into which he might slip his hook, and thereby use his hand to steady the front. Temeraire would have liked a spyglass himself; he could not see why one might not be made in dragon-size.

"Why would anyone bother?" Iskierka said, dismissively. "If I want to see what is happening, I will just go fly over and take a look; should you like me to do so, Granby?"

"Stay where you are, if you please," Granby said, "—or if you don't please, for that matter," he added. "The last thing I need is Hammond yowling at me some more; he leapt out at Berkley this morning directly he had put his head out of doors, before he had even swallowed a bite of breakfast: I think the fellow don't sleep."

Several dragons had come into the Japanese port. This alone was not unusual: they had seen several coming and going and in the town beyond, in the past several days, but those had been nearly all of them courier-beasts, or a few light-weights evidently engaged in the trade in some way. This party was led by a middle-weight, a grey dragon wearing an elaborate drapery of green, which had some sort of jeweled border that sparkled in the sunlight; Temeraire could not tell if it was diamonds, or beads, or something else, but it certainly looked very attractive. John Wampanoag had flown over a little while ago, evidently to meet the new party.

Temeraire observed it all with anxious hope: if only Wampanoag was right this moment explaining that they would leave should Laurence be found; if only the dragon were a person of substance, who might push things forward; if only she would listen to Wampanoag; if—if—if.

"Whyever has Hammond not been useful," he said, in rising impatience, "and got us aboard a translator? I might have begun to learn a little Japanese, and be able to speak with them directly. Can you see, is she speaking with Wampanoag?"

"I don't see, at all," Granby said, and Temeraire began to wonder if perhaps he had not ought to go ashore after all, just briefly, to speak with them. He felt a great deal better, indeed. He had drunk up all the medicine and eaten all the porridge resolutely, every day; and he had gone for a very long swim just this past evening, with not the least ill-effects.

"I am sure I could manage it without any trouble," he said, "and it only seems courteous that I should pay a call, while we are guests here—"

"Will you not ever have any sense?" Hammond said, when he had come running; Temeraire narrowed his eyes at Churki, whom he suspected of having made him some signal—perhaps they had agreed upon it in some way.

"They condemn us all as little better than pirates," Hammond continued, "and they must look upon this ship as the most rank provocation—a vessel of this size, this strength! Our armament! Bearing an entire formation's worth of beasts, and," he added, "you will note they do not have heavy-weights among them, so far as we have seen."

"That is perfect nonsense," Temeraire said. "I have never seen a dragon half as big as that sea-dragon."

"But he is confined only to the water!" Hammond said. "That is nothing to what a dragon of Kulingile's size could do, in the air, anywhere in the country he liked, if they have no heavy-weights of their own to check him: he might run rampant over them."

"I might, too," Maximus said, raising his head with a jealous gleam—he was not so inclined to quarrel with Kulingile as he had been, but he could scarcely be blamed when Hammond insisted on being so outright provoking.

"Good God, I hope I do not mean *that* in the nature of a compliment, I assure you," Hammond said, entirely missing the point, as usual.

"So much the better, then," Temeraire said. "I am very content for them to be worried, and to wish us gone: let them only find Laurence, and bring him to me, and we shall go."

"If they should even believe such a promise, and find it possible to fulfill your demands," Hammond said, "they will not fear us the less for going out of their sight, on such an endeavor. What do you imagine such a nation must think, with a vast neighbor so near-by, which has on previous occasions attempted their conquest, making alliance with another nation equipped with vessels of a size that might ferry a dozen dragons in a week across the China Sea? They cannot help but fear it."

"Then they must *be* afraid," Temeraire said, outraged. "You desire that alliance, you have said so again and again—"

"That does not mean I must be in a great hurry for the Japanese to *learn* of it," Hammond said, "and particularly not to think that more has been accomplished than has; it is better not to announce the wedding before the proposal has been accepted."

In Temeraire's opinion, this was quite absurd; if the Japanese wished to be anxious and imagine dreadful things happening, when no-one had done anything to them at all—bar taking a few trees which they had not been busy to use anyway—that was their affair. "Mine," he said, "is to see Laurence brought safe back to me, and if flying across and having a few words with that other dragon will persuade them, or our making some show of strength, I am happy to see it done: I would not hesitate in the least.

"Indeed," he added, with a sudden kindling impulse, and looked down to where Captain Blaise was consulting with Granby,

113

"Captain Blaise! Will you listen to me, if you please? I do not suppose we have exercised the great guns, in over a month—surely you ought to do it, do you think? If we cannot make answer for the *Phaeton* straightaway, at least we should like them to know we *might*—that we are not only sitting here because we cannot."

Captain Blaise did not look up at Temeraire directly, but he said after a moment, "Do you know, Captain Granby, I do believe we ought to exercise the great guns. And then at least those ruddy blighters will know we *might* answer them properly, if we liked."

Temeraire did not see why Blaise needed parrot what he had said, as though he had thought of it himself, but he did not very much care; Hammond's protests, swift to come, were not in the least heeded, and Temeraire had the pleasure, only a little while later, of hearing the drumroll as the ship beat to quarters, and every hand went to his rope or gun.

The eruption of flame and smoke and thunder was everything which he could have desired: the great dreadful roar of the broadside, the gouts of red and blue flame, the thick clouds of black powder smoke rolling away over the water before the wind, carrying towards the harbor. And then Captain Harcourt said, "Do you know, fellows, I think we will go up and have a bit of exercise, ourselves," and to compound Temeraire's satisfaction he could watch Lily and all her formation aloft, weaving through the intricate patterns of battle-maneuver. Even Iskierka took an interest, and capped the entire production by going aloft at the very end, and blazing a great circle of fire like a wreath around the ship. Ordinarily Temeraire by no means approved her rampant showing away, but in this case he forgave it. "*That* has shown them," he said with real joy.

"Yes," Hammond said, low and grim: he had not left the dragondeck all the while, but yet stood by Churki's side, his thin narrow hands clenched upon each other as though he wished to wring them out. "And now we must wait for what they will choose to show *us*."

A host of fiddler crabs, too small to be worth the attention of fish-ermen, scuttled away rapidly along the empty seashore at Lau-rence's approach: numerous enough that he and Junichiro were able to rake together a pile of them, with branches, onto a rock and away from their escape into the mud. They ate them raw, cracking the shells and sucking the large claw indecorously clean, without the least hesitation.

They went a little way towards easing the bite of hunger, and a small rivulet emptying into the sea near-by, running quickly over rocks, was fresh enough to drink. Laurence soaked his feet again in the salt water without removing the sandals, if he could even have done so without a knife at this point: the cords had sunk into his swollen flesh. He looked across the sea. The sun was setting at the far end, throwing an orange beam across a flat and level plain of water placid as glass, with scarcely a wave to be seen: broad gentle ripples only coming in to shore, nearly silent.

"I would undertake to cross it on a log, paddling with my hands," Laurence said to Junichiro. "It is not twenty miles across, here?"

Junichiro thought as much, when they had made some more calculations, and refreshed by their crab supper they plunged back into the forest and hunted out a few sturdy fallen branches, to be latticed together with saplings and the interstices stuffed with leaves. Three hours of work, by the fading light, gave them a raft serviceable enough for the distance—or so Laurence hoped.

"Can you swim?" he belatedly thought to ask, and was glad for Junichiro's nod; if she came apart beneath them, halfway across, the distance would not be insurmountable, if they could only hold on to a few of the larger limbs.

The moon had risen, brilliant full. "I will try her," Junichiro said, and carried the raft out upon the water and lay himself upon it flat, cautiously. She did not come apart at once; Laurence looked up from shore at his shout of triumph, and was very satisfied. The wind was in the west, gentle, a mere breath; he finished the last of the work, two branches crossed and tied with some strips of fabric cut, with a sharp rock, from the robe he wore; the rest of it he rigged on her as a sail, and striding out into the water he pushed the foot of the makeshift mast through the raft while Junichiro steadied her, and secured it beneath with another knotted length of fabric, filled with sand and pebbles.

He cautiously got himself upon her, braced his hip against the mast with Junichiro doing the same on the other side, slipped his finger into the loop of the cord he had tied around the end of the cross-yard, and drew her into the wind. The irregular sail stirred, and belled, and lifted; she began to move slowly but surely out upon the water.

"Well," Laurence said, after they had glided a dozen yards, and not yet sunk, "I would not like to meet even a strong breeze with this rig, but if we can contrive not to move very much, I suppose we may make it into sight of the opposite shore."

The sea was peculiarly still beneath them, broken more by the eddy of their passage than any waves. Laurence slept in fits and starts, rousing at the tug of the cord upon his finger to adjust the sail. Occasionally he glanced over the side and even saw fish moving, moonlight on dark scales through clear water, and watching them felt a curious sense of familiarity, something just out of reach.

"Have you any family?" Junichiro asked drowsy, drifting. "Any children of your own?"

"No," Laurence said; the lack of a ring upon his hand told him that much, enough that he could give the answer in confidence. "But I have my young gentlemen to look after, which is, as responsibility goes, not unlike: midshipmen, and some lieutenants, not your age," and as he said it he felt a name upon his lips—Roland, he thought, and was nearly sure of it; Roland. Hope filled him: that was not a name eight years old; that was something emerged from the lost depths.

They drowsed again and woke; they were nearing shore: the moon had been caught in the frame of the open volcanic cone of a high mountain: "Mount Tara," Junichiro said. "We should try and land to the south." He did not need to say why: directly ahead over the water, a cluster of bobbing lights shone in the distance, marking a fishing village or a settlement.

Laurence adjusted their direction. The mast gave them another few miles, but the wind changed a little, likely as they emerged from the sheltering bulk of the mountain: it came suddenly into their faces with more strength, and the sail was taken aback. Mast and sail both tipped; branches cracked; abruptly Laurence was in the water. He put his hand out blindly, trying to get his bearings, and touched sand, groped, straightened: he and Junichiro were standing, only knee-deep in water, and there were trees visible against the horizon perhaps a mile distant through the shallows.

They slogged through the remaining distance slowly, with the longest branches as walking-sticks. The thin cotton of the under-robe was soaked and plastered to Laurence's skin, chilling-cold, and broad sheets of dark seaweed tangled clammy about their ankles, but the stand of trees ahead was all the encouragement he might have wanted. He undid his bundle again and put on the green coat, the good wool staving off some cold. They staggered out through thick sheaves of sea grass, crawled up onto the sandy shore, and onwards just into the trees without getting up off their hands and feet.

There were dry leaves, rough branches, a large stone—this time, Laurence prodded it first with his stick to be sure it was nothing more. The sun was rising. They dug into the leaves, and Laurence shut his eyes; hunger gnawed, and thirst; his feet complained in earnest; but none of these proved able to stave off sleep. He slept as long as nature let him: the sun rising across the water warmed their resting place, and eased both ache and chill. He woke warm, and with only a tolerable amount of pain was able to get himself halfway up and knee-walk awkwardly a sufficient distance away to relieve himself.

Junichiro still slept, and Laurence let him continue; he crawled down to the shore again and put his feet back into the cold water

117

to numb awhile before he tried them. There were some fishing-boats out on the water, but at a long distance that made the men aboard them only stick-figures, in straw hats; when one waved, Laurence raised a hand in answer without fear. Sitting on the shore he worked out a loose thread from the green coat still in his bundle, to tie around the pin of one of the gold bars: bent in half, it made a serviceable hook, and he thought there might be a chance of some biting even so near the shore.

He took a mudskipper, by sitting still until they forgot to fear him, and with it as bait took a few better, and roused Junichiro to eat before they set out again. They had cut across a good deal of the distance: twenty miles left. Laurence counted it in quarter-miles and ignored his feet and the increasing heat of the day. He had bundled the coat back up around the sword, and wrapped the tatters of the sail around his head.

Junichiro said nothing, but eyed him sidelong, repeatedly; Laurence looked down at his bare chest, and realized Junichiro was looking at the many scars of pistol-shot and blade; mute testimony to Laurence's experience in battle. He did not recognize them all. He touched one long stroke along his shoulder, the white smooth long-healed line of it, then shook his head and let his hand drop.

When he had finished, Junichiro tried to press his own outer robe on him. "We look like beggars," he said urgently, in his persuasion.

"That," Laurence said, "I dare say we cannot avoid in any case; and it must be your task to approach anyone we must bespeak, while mine shall be to keep far out of sight. Keep it."

They struggled on through brush and trees, following a very awkward course well away from the road: but Laurence wanted only to find some coast, anywhere not settled, where they might approach Nagasaki cautiously. Any pursuit must expect the port to be his destination—the net would surely be waiting for him there, and his only hope should be to espy some European ship, or the Dutch commission, and strike out for it in some roundabout way.

118

An improbable goal perhaps, but he had come nearer than he had looked to do, in cold rational consideration.

And then—and then—but there was no sense in contemplating that future, and all its blank impenetrability, until he had come to it.

They found a little brackish pool, and drank, in the late afternoon. Junichiro dug up some wild radish, which he recognized as edible, and they gnawed its woody toughness as they walked. A few times they had to hide a little while crouching in brush, to avoid notice from other foragers; once they came upon a well-traveled road, and scurried across it like rabbits making a dash for safety, in a brief empty gap between walking travelers and sedan-chairs and ox-carts. A dragon went by overhead once, but flying fast, not searching; they listened huddled under concealing branches until its wingbeats faded.

The sun was sinking again, beginning to throw long shadows and wink at them through the branches. Laurence was trudging onwards, mind full of counting and steps, when Junichiro put out a hand to stop him. He lifted his face into the wind; he breathed in salt, and recognized belatedly the distant low crash of waves and voices both, not far off.

The trees were thinning ahead, approaching a road: a busy road, crowded with travelers and cargo. They crept up to a curve and looking down it saw before them the harbor laid out in a neat half-curve: a small island full of Dutch houses sat divided from the town by a narrow canal, and a great many boats filled the harbor together.

"Oh," Junichiro said, stifled, and Laurence followed the line of his gaze: there was a company of men standing off to the side of the road by a sort of tall signpost carved with characters, looking out upon the harbor. He at first did not understand Junichiro's exclamation, and then he recognized abruptly one of the party, standing to the side, armed: it was Kaneko, and down in a cleared field beside the port he saw Lady Arikawa resting, a grey-green curve of dragon.

"I thought she would have liked to let us go," Laurence said to Junichiro.

Junichiro made an impatient gesture: why would Laurence never understand? "Of course she wishes us to escape," he said. "But she cannot openly allow it, and my—and the honorable Kaneko would not merely stand by, either: it ought to have been the duty of the magistrate to secure you, but you were held in his house."

"Well, we must get around them, somehow," Laurence said, "and try to get there," indicating the tiny Dutch settlement. "They will hide us, I hope, even if they choose to ship me back to Europe a prisoner of war. Let us go south a distance, and see if we can get across the road: I would like a better look at the harbor."

Junichiro followed him back into the trees, not without a lingering look, regretful, back at his former master.

Temeraire looked dully down at the sodden scrap: white linen, very fine, with Laurence's mark plainly upon it; he had bought a dozen shirts like it, in Brazil, to repair his shipwrecked wardrobe, before they set out for China.

"I am sorry to give you bad news," Wampanoag was saying, "but I don't mind saying it is more than I hoped to turn up, whether bad or good. It must have washed up on the shore, I guess."

Maximus nudged at his shoulder, gently, a warm butting of his nose; Temeraire was aware of it, he supposed, and grateful distantly. "Did they tell you where they found it?" he asked, formally; he would pursue all inquiry—he would—

"You'll forgive my saying so," Wampanoag said, "but they weren't inclined to be talkative, after that show you lot put on. No-one could help but take it the wrong way: this whole city is full to the brim of warehouses, every last one of them built of nicely seasoned wood. I suppose if you just turned out this lady here," he dipped his head towards Iskierka, "the whole place would be burnt to the waterline in a couple of hours, even if you didn't care to lob over a few cannon-balls at the same time."

"Oh," Temeraire said, after a moment, "I am sorry to have occasioned them any concern. I hope——" He trailed off. He did not hope anything, really; he was only trying to be polite, since there was nothing else to do but try to behave in a civilized fashion, but he could not quite contrive something to say.

"*We* hope," Hammond said, jumping in at once into the breach of silence, when he saw that Temeraire had nothing more, "that you will be so kind as to convey our deepest apologies, to the governor, and to the shogun, for any action on our part which might have given rise to intimations—to false intimations—of hostility, and make plain to his Excellency that the Government of Britain desires nothing more than peace and future tranquility in the relations between our nations. And pray assure them," he added, "that we will at the *earliest possible moment,*" and he threw a hard look at Captain Blaise, "be taking our leave of them, with many thanks for their consideration in allowing us to remain so long in pursuit of our repairs, and our lost friend."

He carried on the conversation from there, for some time; Wampanoag seemed perfectly willing to listen to him, and to agree to carry more messages back and forth; Temeraire did not pay much attention.

The rest of the day passed away in useful, numbing minutiae. They had a wind already, as favorable as anyone could want; they had only to wait for the tide. There were the decks to be holystoned again, the sails to be slushed. Temeraire swallowed the medicine when it was brought him, and the physician looked him over again closely. He organized three of the stronger hands to pull down the lower edge of Temeraire's eye so he might inspect the dark flesh there, a particularly uncomfortable operation, but Temeraire made no objection.

Wen Shen sniffed, after prodding Temeraire a few more times, and said to Gong Su for translation, to Granby, "All right, he is well enough to fly; so do not let him sit there too long while you are sailing—he must fly a little every day, now, and swimming also cannot do him any harm."

So he was better, too, as though that mattered now. He might have been dreadfully ill for all the use he could hope to be, to Laurence. Temeraire felt the stirrings of resentment rising, suddenly, as he lay mute after the inspection—what had Laurence been about, after all, losing himself in such a stupid way? Anyone—anyone at all—might have cut apart the storm-chains. Anyone might have saved them, and the ship, if they had cared to do so—it had not been Laurence's duty alone, to do it. Laurence ought have let the ship sink, if no-one else had decided to cut the chains, and stayed with Temeraire. They had not been so far from shore. It would have been the work of a few hours to get them to land, and they might have saved all their crew and any number of sailors as well.

"I would rather have him back, than this whole ship and everything upon it," he burst out, without caring who heard him; and then Forthing, who was sitting by him, said, "I am very sorry, Temeraire, that he should have been lost—"

Temeraire snarled at him outright. "You are *not* sorry," he spat. "You think you may have your chance, now."

Forthing flushed alternately red and very pale, and then said, "I don't: you've made plain enough you've no use for me; and I *am* sorry, because he gave me my first lieutenant's step, when he might have left me on shore in New South Wales, and most men would have. If I live to get back to a covert, now I am like to have a chance for my own beast; and if I don't, my son will, when he is older."

Temeraire paused: "You have a son?"

"He is eight now," Forthing said, "and at Kinloch Laggan."

"Oh," Temeraire said. "Well," he added, "it does not make me like you any better; having a son is no excuse for looking like a shag-bag, and I dare say it is the opposite—you might consider you are reflecting on *him,* too, and not just upon *me.*"

Forthing stared at him and said, "What?" and looked down at himself.

"Why will you not buy a shirt?" Temeraire said. "Even if you do not buy a particularly decent one, you might buy something *clean;* and that coat is nothing like green: not at *all.* Whoever could wish to acknowledge you as a connection in any way when you look like an untended scare-crow? The hands before the mast have a neater appearance, and I *know* that Laurence has given you a hint, now and again—"

He stopped: *Laurence* rang in his ears, and the hot glow of temper died away beneath his spirits; he sank back low and put his head beneath his wing, as the bosun's bellowing cry went up, "Make sail! All hands to make sail!"

Laurence and Junichiro struggled away from the harbor, paralleling the course of the road for a short distance. The sun was lowering, and the traffic thinning out; at last it seemed worth the risk, and they came out of the trees and scrambled to the other side, heads down and shoulders hunched, between parties of travelers nearly lost in twilight; Laurence hoped they would see nothing more than a pair of lumpen beggars.

They climbed up the far side of the road, through the last thin ranks of trees to the shore: the narrow harbor still stretched out a long way southward to the open sea, and there at her mouth Laurence saw with a shocking, nearly painful sensation, the tremendous immensity of a dragon transport: four masts, the British colors flying stained to red with a last sun-beam, and a great horde of beasts upon her dragondeck tangled in a riot of serpentine colors.

She was making sail.

"Oh, God," Laurence said. "Fire—I must have some fire, at once—gather some kindling!"

He sprang back down through the trees to the road, all concern for disguise or concealment shed. An ox-cart was trundling along towards him, a lit lantern hung swinging from the seat, and ignoring the outraged bellow of the driver and the cut of his whip,

Laurence seized the edge and snatched it away. Another lash stung his back as he threw himself back up the hill, but Laurence cared nothing for that: the light was failing.

Junichiro had already begun to scrape together a heap of branches and dry leaves, though with an anxious look, and when Laurence bent to set them alight he snatched up another branch and began to turn up the earth in a wide channel around the fire, to keep it from spreading. Laurence worked in nearly a frenzy: the wind was fair to the east, and the tide was going out. She would be gone in half-an-hour, if he did not raise her.

The fire was climbing, making a pretty blaze; Laurence undid his bundle and stood before the fire with his coat, and flashed the signals desperately: *assistance required—assistance required—*

He made them a dozen times over, and then heard an outcry coming from the road; he wheeled and found Junichiro standing pale and stricken before Kaneko, who was regarding him with an expression utterly flat, but for a thin shine of tears standing in his eyes.

"Kaneko-sama—sensei—" Junichiro said, nearly inaudible, and something else in the tongue, reaching out a pleading hand, and half putting himself between Kaneko and Laurence.

Kaneko shook his head once, sharply, and simply drew his swords both: answer enough, and Laurence bent and seized his own from the ground, before catching Junichiro by the arm and drawing him gently away. "All that you could do," he said, "you have done. Go and keep making the signal there. The ship will send an answer, or they will not."

"You may surrender," Kaneko said, over the crackling fire, "if you wish. The shogun has directed you are to be brought to the court. You will be made prisoner, but permitted to live."

Laurence looked back at the ocean. The ship was under sail: the lanterns lit, beginning to move away over the water. They thought him lost, surely, and the Japanese could have informed them otherwise: they meant to make him prisoner, not ransom him. He would be held the rest of his days, perhaps, in a foreign prison.

He turned to Kaneko. "I am under an obligation to Junichiro," he said, quietly, "who you must know has aided me for love of you. If I surrender myself and am made prisoner in this way, will your honor be satisfied?"

Kaneko did not look at Junichiro, despite the faint suggestion of a flinch. He shook his head briefly. Laurence nodded and pulled off the thin and badly rent white cotton of his under-robe to free his limbs for movement. Kaneko waited poised and still, the fire now leaping and throwing his shadow up against the trees behind him, until Laurence was ready; then he struck.

They exchanged the first few blows, testing, and disengaged to circle. Kaneko had an unfamiliar and an elegant style, slashing: a kind of fencing. Laurence watched the two blades warily. He had six inches of reach on Kaneko, and could give him fifty pounds at least: advantages which, Laurence hoped, would be enough to give him a chance despite the handicap of his present condition, half-lame and spent. At least he had no need to husband whatever remained of his strength—in ten minutes, surely, assistance would come for Kaneko, and Laurence would be overwhelmed if not slain. Laurence could only hope to gain those minutes, a little more time for a rescue whose likelihood was diminishing with every moment—and which, if it did not come, would strand him here forever.

There was not the least hesitation in Kaneko's attack when it came again, flashing, though his victory meant his own death. Laurence met the long blade with his own, steel cracking sparks off steel, and grappled the shorter, gripping Kaneko's wrist and squeezing with all the force he could exert. His hands were hardened by rope and leather, and Kaneko's hand purpled; then they were falling—Kaneko had thrown them somehow to the ground. Laurence found his legs tangled, Kaneko nearly pinning him; only through sheer brute force did he manage to break the incomplete hold, and threw them over.

He had not lost his clenched grip; he smashed Kaneko's hand

against the ground, and the short blade sprang loose. Still half-entrapped, Laurence caught it and flung it away into the trees, and barely managed to deflect Kaneko's elbow when it came with crushing force towards his throat.

They broke apart and rolled back to their feet. Laurence had diverted the blow from his throat to his jaw, instead, which ached badly; broken, perhaps. Kaneko did not pause but came at him swiftly, both hands now on the hilt of his blade, with a series of rapid slashing cuts. Laurence parried and retreated, his pains fading into the queer, brief distance which so often accompanied battle. No opening was offered, no chance to shift the direction; Kaneko drove him around the leaping fire until Laurence, in grim desperation, forced the issue: he met Kaneko's sword with his own and stayed with it as he pushed it back, risking the chance of overbalancing, and threw his full weight against the blade.

For a moment both swords groaned, held; and then Kaneko's snapped with a loud crack like musket-fire, and he and Laurence fell to the ground heavily together. Kaneko rolled away swiftly and leapt back to his feet, still holding the jagged remnant of the blade, broken some six inches above the hilt. Laurence staggered up himself. A fine tremor ran up his arms, and he raised his sword only with difficulty; but now he had the advantage. Kaneko could not come into range of a blow without running himself into Laurence's blade.

They looked at each other, and Laurence knew Kaneko would in a moment do just as much: he would throw himself across the distance, and attempt another attack, though it meant his certain death. Laurence looked at Junichiro's despairing face, the boy standing with his own sword drawn and useless: whichever side he might have assisted, he condemned the master he loved.

And then a sudden roaring above, and Laurence flung himself to one side as Lady Arikawa came down upon the hill, her green drapes flaring and belling about her grey wings, talons coming down to strike: he barely evaded the blow and fetched up against the trees. "Wretched barbarian!" she said, furiously. "Will you cause no end of sorrow and misery? Kaneko, you are not hurt?"

Kaneko had taken already the first steps in his rush, and himself been nearly knocked flat by the force of her descent; he regained his feet and bowed. "I am not, Lady Arikawa, and the Englishman has fought only honorably—"

"I do not care!" she said. "Oh! Why did you ever make that dreadful vow; I should tear him to pieces!" She shook out her wings and glared the brilliant green of her eyes at Laurence. "You could not even manage to escape properly," she said bitterly, "and now what am I to do?"

"Lady Arikawa, we must deliver him to the governor," Kaneko said quietly, "and accompany him to the court in Edo, for the judgment of the shogun. The safety of the nation demands it." He hesitated and said, reluctantly, "It may be he will be exchanged back to his country-men, after all."

He spoke as one who did not believe what he was himself saying, offering a mere sop to feeling; and Lady Arikawa only shook her head and looked away in despair. She was silent a moment, but then she straightened, neck arched proudly over them, and looking coldly down. "I will do my duty," she said. "I will take you to Edo for judgment; and may the shogun sentence you to a traitor's death for the evil you have brought on my house!"

Yelling voices were nearing, through the trees, many men coming into the courtyard; Laurence, rising to his feet, looked around himself bleakly. There was no chance of resistance against so many, and Lady Arikawa reached out a taloned claw towards him.

Then: a noise too large to call roaring, a great tumult of rage above their heads. The trees upon the hillside behind Laurence were shattering like matchsticks, earth flying up in clouds, and a dragon came down upon that horrifying wreckage: thrice Lady Arikawa's size, pitch-black and with blue eyes. The noise stopped, and its absence left a dazed and muffling silence; in that hush the dragon bent over them with a savagery of bared teeth and said, in the clearest King's English, "How dare you! How dare any of you! Oh! I will kill all of you if you have done anything to Laurence!"

Even Lady Arikawa had drawn back, protective talons curled about Kaneko; and though she might not understand what the dragon had said, his wrath was by no means subtle, nor the threat implicit in his mantling. But she was not lacking in spirit, and drawing herself up said in Chinese, "Those who come as thieves and invaders to our country, and make threats, deserve no considerations of honor."

"Laurence is only here because he was lost overboard, saving our ship," the dragon said, answering her in that tongue, "and if you knew he was here, all along, it is a perfect outrage for you to call *us* thieves. We have taken but a few trees, and if you want us to pay you for them, we *shall:* that is nothing in the least to Laurence, whom you have tried to keep from me. I dare say we ought to have gone to war with you. If I had known of it, I should have, and I dare say the Emperor of China would have, too: it is too much to be borne!"

Lady Arikawa looked at Laurence with some doubt in her expression, which Laurence was inclined to share, at this particular piece of hyperbole. "And you need not look like that," the black dragon added, very coldly, "only because Laurence has been shipwrecked, and does not look his best at present. The Emperor adopted him, five years ago, and we are on our way to make a filial visit. He is a prince of China, and my captain."

"The devil I am," said Laurence.

Chapter 7

"I beg your pardon," Laurence said, interrupting, "but if you please, Captain, I would be grateful if you would begin earlier: the last—" He paused, not liking to give it voice, and then forced his way onwards. "The last I recall very clearly is in the year four."

"Oh, Lord," Captain Granby said. He was the captain of the fire-breather, an officer of twenty-and-nine years; tall and somewhat battered, short one arm, and a pleasant, likable fellow, if almost shockingly informal in his manners and his dress of peculiar ostentation: Laurence had not seen so much gold on an admiral of the fleet. "Well, I know you took the *Amitié,* and Temeraire's egg was on it—that news was all over the Corps; but as for the rest of that year, or how you came to be there, I haven't the faintest notion. I suppose Riley could have told us—"

"Riley?" Laurence said, with relief for a name he recognized: his second lieutenant. "Tom Riley? Do you know his direction? I might write him—" and then Granby's look of startled regret halted him, even before Granby spoke.

So Riley was dead—his ship the *Allegiance* lost. Laurence rose and went to stand by the stern windows, to breathe in the sea-air in great gulps. Granby was silent where he sat at the table, but Laurence felt his eyes upon his back.

There was a dreadful strangeness to sit across from a man who called him *Will,* a man who had been his first lieutenant, and yet have his face mean nothing; it was worse, somehow, than having been all alone and adrift. Granby had been all that was kind—they had all been so, and visibly gladdened by his return. Deposited on the deck, Laurence had been embraced with enthusiasm by a dozen strangers before he had been able to make his confusion known; since then, there had been nothing but the most generous anxiety for his health—an anxiety, however, which reminded him at every turn that he *was* ill, wounded, and in such a manner that he might never recover from it.

Outside the window, near the harbor mouth, he could see the curves of the sea-dragon's body where it dozed nearly hidden beneath the waves, its presence a warning. Their own dragons were on the deck, and on a few pontoon-rafts floating about the ship; he did not, at the moment, see the black dragon—his dragon. Temeraire. Granby was speaking in low voices with the ship's surgeon, a Mr. Pettiforth, behind his back. "I must insist we halt this interview, Captain Granby," Pettiforth said. "You can see for yourself the inimical effects of only this one shock. There can be no question that any further strain on an already-weakened mind must be dangerous. You must withdraw. I must insist; I do insist."

The surgeon had vociferously argued from the beginning against any attempt to repair the omissions in Laurence's memory by recounting the events of the intervening years, as more likely to do harm than good. "I consider it a most unique species of brain-fever," Pettiforth had said. "I have heard of only a few similar instances described; indeed, I am sure the Royal Society will be deeply interested, should I have an opportunity to set down the facts of the case—"

But Laurence had dismissed his advice: he longed for every scrap of intelligence, of knowledge. His feet had been bathed and bandaged; a night's rest had seen him back on them; he could scarcely imagine delaying any further. He turned back. "Sir, I cannot deny this news is an unpleasant shock, but I am by no means prepared to halt. Captain Granby, if you please—"

130

"I beg your pardon," Mr. Hammond broke in, anxiously. "I beg your pardon most extremely, Captain, but I think we must abide by Mr. Pettiforth's advice for the moment, and ask you to consider—I hope you will forgive my saying so—consider it the course most consistent with your duty."

"I can scarcely perform the least duty," Laurence said, "when I do not know what that duty is, sir: so far as I knew before yesterday evening, I was a sea-captain, not an aviator."

"At present," Hammond said, "our most pressing need is for your continued health. You can do nothing if you have been prostrated by an aggravation of your—your injury, and your presence is vital—utterly vital—to all the hopes of our mission."

Laurence hesitated. Hammond was the King's envoy, and evidently in charge of their mission to China; his urgency could not help but carry great weight. "Thank Heavens that you have not lost your facility with the Chinese language—I must credit," Hammond added, "the extent of our practice, the several months of our voyage—your dedication there, Captain, has been very commendable, and I consider this the reward; everything else can be managed. I assure you, we will manage. We will begin at once to review the likely ceremonies of welcome: our arrival at Tien-sing, the forms of your greeting to the crown prince, and to the Emperor—"

If anything had been likely to give him a relapse of brain-fever, Laurence thought it would be the programme of etiquette study which Hammond laid out, which would have been a punishment even if spread over the course of three years. How he intended to touch upon all its parts in the space of time required to sail from Nagasaki to Tien-sing harbor, Laurence had not the least notion.

"All the more need, sir," Mr. Pettiforth interjected, "not to add any additional strain upon your nerves. Avoiding any particular, any notable shock," he looked at Granby with a hard, meaningful look, which Laurence could not interpret, "must be of the utmost importance."

Granby looked at Laurence helplessly; Laurence drew and released a deep breath. "Very well," he said, grimly. "I will be guided by you, gentlemen."

He would rather have forgone the study, and closeted himself with Granby until he knew every detail that could be obtained of the last eight years from one who had been his close companion in nearly all of that time, from what he understood. But he could not refuse Hammond's request. His weakness of brain had already endangered their cause—it was incumbent upon him to do whatever he might to assist a mission whose urgency was evident.

Britain's situation, and that of all Europe, was more desperate than he had feared at the worst. Granby had, to his great comfort, been able to assure him of the health of his family, but little else of good could be said. The story of the invasion of Britain, of which he until now had received only the faintest outlines, had filled Laurence with horror: Nelson dead—Nelson, and fourteen ships-of-the-line sunk. Even so complete a victory over Napoleon as had been achieved could scarcely compensate for such a loss.

Indeed, Laurence was forced to give some credence to Pettiforth's concerns: if there had been more such disasters, in the years he had lost, he did wonder how well he might support the news. "But I must learn something of my duties," he said, "enough at least to carry them out: there is no telling but we may see battle, and at least the dragons must be exercised, surely? Captain Granby, who is the senior officer of our company?"

Granby rubbed his face with his good hand. "It has been all in the air, anyway—Harcourt has command of the formation, but you and I aren't formally assigned to her, or she to either of us, and—oh, damn it all," he muttered, at Laurence's bafflement—*her?*—and turning said, "look, Hammond, I must tell him *something*."

But even when Granby had explained, appallingly, that Longwings insisted on female captains, and that the slim young gentleman captaining that beast was indeed a woman, he had not much clarified their chain of command. "It goes by the beasts, you know," he said. "It's not much use our standing on ceremony, if they settle it otherwise amongst themselves; it don't matter if a Winchester's captain has twenty years on me when Iskierka gives a snort, you can be sure."

With four heavy-weights and a Longwing aboard, such a policy must surely have kept the command in a state of peculiar confusion: all the more so that the captain of the largest beast, an immense golden creature called Kulingile, was scarcely more than a boy, and not British at all but from Africa; Laurence could hardly imagine how he had been appointed to his post. "Well, he wasn't," Granby said, "Demane is from Capetown, you took him and his brother up when—" He halted abruptly, biting his lip. "You took them up," he continued awkwardly, leaving an ominous gap behind him, "as your runners, and he picked up the beast when no-one else would have it: came out of the shell deformed, and not the size of a lamb."

In any case, despite his size Kulingile did not seem inclined to assert his precedence particularly; and even after what little time Laurence had spent on deck amongst them so far, he could scarcely help noticing that the other beasts seemed inclined to give way to Temeraire, if to anyone. Laurence realized grimly he might well himself be the senior officer, by such a measure, and his injury all the more potentially disastrous: better in some way had he been wholly incapacitated, than presenting this peculiar mix of competence and confusion.

But he did not press Granby further for explanation. To have worked through an accounting of eight years all together would have been difficult enough, but it was still worse to acquire piecemeal details, and see the awkward hesitation on Granby's face as he tried to explain first one and then another chain of events, yet without conveying any information likely to cause distress, entangling the narrative at every turn. He faltered too often, and with a look almost pleading, as though he hoped Laurence would suddenly be recalled to himself: even while that same hope, privately but deeply held, quietly died away in Laurence's own breast.

"So far as the command is concerned, then, I will defer to you,

Captain Granby, at present," he said, cutting short the attempt, "and I trust you will feel not the least hesitation at correcting me in any failure to carry out my necessary duties. For the rest, my health has scarcely had a chance to recover, after the exertions of my escape; let us hope that in returning, it may restore my memory with it."

It was an empty sop, which he did not himself believe, though Granby seized upon it with eager relief and Hammond chimed in with eager agreement, although Mr. Pettiforth murmured quietly to himself, "Not at all likely—I wonder whether further degeneration ought to be expected, if anything. I must keep a journal of the progression—"

Laurence saw them out. He was glad to be left alone again in his cabin, though housed amongst things he did not recognize: even his sea-chest was unfamiliar to him, new and rough-hewn, a cheap construction which must have been bought in desperation and which should shortly have to be replaced; a green creeping stain was already to be seen growing upon the underside. The chest was full of books, though he had never been a great reader: *Principia Mathematica* so well-worn the corners of the pages were smooth where he evidently liked to turn them. There were only two pieces of correspondence: one letter from his mother, another, with the direction very badly scribbled and nearly unreadable, from the Peninsula: from a fellow-officer, then.

"Well," he said aloud, "I might be dead, or in a prison," and threw them back into his writing-desk, next to the log-book, which he also had not opened. He was resolved not to succumb to despair. He had the use of his limbs, and his reason; he had lost less than many another man in the service.

He belted his sword back on, went up to the dragondeck, and found Temeraire rousing from an exhausted sleep and looking for him. Hammond was there before him, trying to keep Temeraire's attention, and explaining in a loud voice, which could surely be heard across all the ship, "It is of the utmost importance that Captain Laurence be spared any unnecessary shock, which might further injure his weakened mind—I beg you to attend me, Temeraire! I assure you that we have every reason to expect his memory to return shortly, if you will only have a care not to—"

"Yes, yes, of course," Temeraire said, looking at him not at all. "Laurence!" he called, a ringing eager note in his resonant voice, which might be felt even through the deck: his ruff was standing up in a manner which somehow suggested to Laurence his excitement. "Laurence, how much more yourself you look: you must be better, I am sure," he said, when Laurence had mounted to the deck. There was an anxious question in the words, however. Temeraire had been lately injured himself, Laurence gathered, by some mishap in the rescue of the ship; and his spirits had been badly beset by the belief of Laurence's own death.

It seemed absurd to think of so terrible a creature as fragile in any way. The head bending towards him was nearly the size of a horse, the teeth standing in the jaws larger than his hand, serrated along their back edges and hard ivory. Strangely Laurence felt no fear, no instinct of alarm, though it seemed to him any rational man ought to; he had seen, only last night, what appalling devastation might be wrought by this beast.

But even without fear, it was difficult to think of Temeraire as vulnerable—and yet perhaps not so difficult: a first-rate off a lee-shore, and his the duty to keep her off the rocks. Laurence still did not wholly understand how he had come to harness the beast, to become an aviator; he did not know what might have impelled him to do such a thing. But for the moment, it would have to be enough to know that he *had* done so: that he had given up his naval rank, his ship, and all his hard-won prospects. No need to wonder, either, what had become of Edith Galman. She had surely wed another, a man who could offer her a respectable home and name. Laurence was determined to be glad of it; she deserved as much and more.

Duty remained: his country's need stood above his own concerns. "I am much better, indeed," he said. "I beg you have no concern for me. How is your own health?"

"Oh!" Temeraire said, "I am perfectly well, *now; I have* been a little ill, but that is quite done with; I am quite recovered. Laurence," he added urgently, leaning his massive head down to the deck, and peering at him with one anxious slitted eye, "of course you know that I would have come for you at once—I would not have permitted anything to interfere—if it had not been for the egg. I am so dreadfully sorry."

The rest of the afternoon was consumed in displaying this prize for him: the dragon insisted on Laurence's being taken below, on the crate and all its careful packing being undone to display the egg. It might have been made of gold and diamonds for the degree of passionate interest which Temeraire gave it, and not only he: the fire-breather, evidently the dam, roused herself and watched with equal attention, so that Laurence could scarcely make out the unremarkable shell for having one enormous eye peering in at either porthole, blocking the light.

He was invited to touch the shell, with great care and an open palm: a tender softness not unlike the head of his nine-day-old nephew, when that child had been laid carefully in his hands by a watchful mother. Having returned to the dragondeck and being pressed for his opinion, he used very much the same expressions as on that occasion. "A remarkable egg," he said, "perfectly hearty, and the size prodigious: I congratulate you both extremely, and I am sure it will do very well; extraordinarily well." He meant his compliments wholeheartedly: he could well imagine the worth to England of such a cross-breed. His effusions could not have satisfied Temeraire, however, if they had been ten times as enthusiastic, until Laurence gradually came to realize that half of the dragon's anxiety was to be sure that Laurence did not blame him, for not having come to his rescue.

"You could scarcely have found me, if you had tried," Laurence said. "I do not think I had been on shore half-an-hour before I was taken up."

"I would have contrived, somehow," Temeraire said. "I found

you in Africa, after all, when—oh; I am not meant to speak of that, am I? But in any case, Laurence, so long as you are satisfied—so long as you do not suppose I would have allowed any lesser cause to weigh with me."

Laurence was *not* entirely satisfied: the lesser causes had evidently included abandoning the ship, their mission, and perhaps even setting off a war with Japan: all for his sake, and here was Temeraire making apology to him for *not* doing any of these things. He began to feel there was an almost dreadful responsibility inherent in the rôle, a rôle for which nothing had prepared him, and which he felt wholly unsuited to carry out. The distance between this and a ship's command seemed a vast yawning gulf.

But he could not chide the dragon for his affection; particularly not when Temeraire had been under so great a strain, its evidence marked in the dull hide and the weary look in the dragon's eyes: his eyelids were heavy again already. Laurence lay his hand against Temeraire's warm breathing hide, its peculiar combination of resilience and softness at once familiar and not so. "I have been restored to you in defiance of all expectation and without, I hope, any evil consequence to our mission; we must both be satisfied with that outcome, and I beg you believe me so."

Temeraire sighed deeply, and lowered his head to his forelegs. "I am very glad to hear you say so," he said. "I was sure, Laurence, that you would not think it right of me to leave the egg—that you would tell me, if you were here, that it was my own responsibility, and I could not leave it to others no matter how much I might wish to go looking for you, not when the egg was not perfectly safe. I was quite sure, but oh! It was dreadful nonetheless, and I did fear that perhaps I had judged wrongly."

"You did not, at all," Laurence said, with a good deal of relief: so a dragon need not be insensate to duty at all. And then he was at a loss: what ought he do else, for the beast? Should he order aerial exercises? He did not see the other dragons engaged in such work, and indeed it might have been a provocation to the Japanese, to do so in harbor; besides this, he knew nothing of what his duties should be.

He looked for one of the ship's boys: a small creature was darting by him on the dragondeck, head full of yellow curls and in a patched green coat. When Laurence caught him by the shoulder, the boy looked up and said in a piping voice, "Aye, Captain?"

"Light along to my cabin and fetch my log-book, if you please," Laurence said, and pausing added, "And tell me your name again."

"Gerry, sir," the little boy said, giving him a peculiar look; Laurence sighed inwardly and made a note he should have to get all the names given him, at least. He thought he would read it over, and learn the daily routine thereby; perhaps he might thus advise himself.

"What a splendid notion," Temeraire said, unexpectedly, raising his head; his eyes had brightened. "Of course that must help your memory return more swiftly. Although I must tell you," the dragon added, "the log-book has not been very interesting at all. It has been nothing but fish and wind, these six months, before we ran into that storm. We have not seen a battle anywhere, since we had to run from the Inca, and that was ages ago."

He was regretful. Laurence's own thought: the Inca? And hard on that, it belatedly dawned upon him that the dragon himself, unlike a horse, or even a recalcitrant landsman pressed into service, might be relied upon to tell him of their work. "Temeraire," he said, "do you know the names of the rest of your crew?"

"Of course," Temeraire said. "You have always told me it is the duty of any good officer to know all the names of his officers and his crew."

"So it is," Laurence said grimly. "Pray will you tell me them, one after another?"

"He is already much better," Temeraire said to Maximus, anxiously, hoping for confirmation. "I know it is quite odd, when he does not remember someone's name, or a thing which happened in front of him, and quite lately; but you cannot say he is not better."

"Of course he is better," Maximus said reassuringly, lifting his dripping jaws from his share of the cod stew. "I dare say he will remember all the rest of it in a week or so, Temeraire; no need to fuss."

But Laurence was so very strange—so very stiff and awkward; it was not only that he had lost a great deal of his memory, which was bad enough and very inconvenient, but he did not seem to know Temeraire, either, or any of the other aviators, for that matter. He had spent nearly all the last two days closeted with Hammond, and had said very little to anyone. "But I am sure he will improve, once he has had a rest, and we are under way," Temeraire said to himself, uncertainly.

There was some little difficulty over their departure: Temeraire did not understand, himself; he saw no reason why they should not have sailed out directly they had Laurence again, and he would have liked to: what if the Japanese should have taken it into their heads to snatch Laurence back? And it was no use Hammond's trying to tell him they had no reason to do such a thing; they had kept him back in the first place, after all. And as for Lord Jinai—that was the name of the particularly rude sea-dragon—if he liked to stop them, he was very welcome to try. Temeraire felt himself quite equal to answering him, with Iskierka, and Kulingile, and all the formation at his backs; not to mention the guns of the *Potentate*.

But Hammond had objected to *that*, also; and so a great deal of communication had gone back and forth, passed through the Dutch commissioner, who evidently did not like Napoleon at all and persisted in considering himself a neutral party to the war. "And through us," said Wampanoag, having come over to share a bite, "which, I don't mind saying, has done some good: they have decided to give you a proper dinner, to say farewell politely, and see you on your way."

"That," said Temeraire somewhat baffled, "is quite absurd:

they would have been perfectly welcome to give us dinner, anytime they liked."

"They might give us more than one, too," Maximus put in somewhat wistfully: the cod had vanished.

"Why, it's not the dinner that matters, of course," Wampanoag said. "It is the timing of the thing: if you sail out before they have given you permission, then they will have lost face; if they should give permission and you shouldn't go, they will have lost face. And you shouldn't like it any better if they should try and stop you, or try and chase you, either way. This way, everything will be quite clear."

Temeraire still did not see very much sense in this: if all parties wished them gone, it seemed to him they might simply go: no-one was asking Lord Jinai to sit there in the harbor mouth, in their way. But Wampanoag seemed to think it entirely sensible.

"And I will say, I am pretty grateful to you," he said, "for opening the door, as it were. I like them very much, now they have decided to talk to me: very polite fellows, perfectly honest: easy to do business with. They don't like to say no, so you have to keep a sharp lookout to notice when they *mean* no, but that isn't so difficult: the older fellows of the tribe are like that."

"I do not understand," Temeraire said. "Why would they not have spoken to you before, when they do have these Dutch translators?"

"Well, their shogun wouldn't have it," Wampanoag said. "They aren't much for foreigners here, but I guess they have thought it over and decided, since the Chinese are throwing in with you lot, they had better start making some more friends." He snorted and waved his tail in the air. "They aren't wrong, either: those of us who don't want to get dragged into this mess you lot and Napoleon are brewing up all over the place had better stick together. I'll tell you, you ought to think better of it. Bad for business, that sort of thing."

That was not very fair, in Temeraire's opinion: *he* did not want war—he did not object to battles, of course, but war did seem a great trouble for everyone. "But we cannot very well just lie down before Napoleon: *he* is always provoking war, and trying to conquer his neighbors, and tell them how they are to go on; only someone very poor-spirited indeed could endure it."

Wampanoag shook his head doubtfully. "If you say so: it takes two to make a quarrel, in my experience." He shook out his wings. "But I cannot complain of the consequences for myself: they have given me license to buy more goods than they had meant to allow, on credit, and I suppose I will have a commission for Yankee ships to come in our own right before I go away again. I have promised them we will bring them a company of shipwrights straight from Salem, next season, if they will give us a treaty and let us trade, and I don't doubt the President will back me if I bring him terms for *that*."

"The President?" Temeraire said, and listened with mounting indignation as Wampanoag said, quite casually, "Yes: I have met him half-a-dozen times, and I am sure he will see the sense of a proper treaty with the Japanese for us. I should have rather had Hamilton in the job, of course, but there! You can't have everything, and for all that he isn't a Federalist, Tecumseh is a clever fellow."

He gave a final nod of his head, and leapt aloft, leaving Temeraire to simmer. "It is a good deal too much," he said to Maximus stormily, "that Napoleon sits in Lien's lap, and Wampanoag is off chatting with the President, and we must yell and make a great noise in Britain only to be seen by a general now and again. I have never met a minister in my life."

"Why would you wish to?" Maximus said, sleepily. "Berkley is always saying they are nothing but a lot of tiresome old windbags."

"Not to mention," Iskierka put in, as her own pontoon-raft drifted closer, "that if you hadn't interfered, Granby should have been a king himself: then you needn't have complained."

Laurence found the dinner, which he could not escape, a peculiarly constrained affair. It was held at the estate of the Japanese governor, in his gardens very near the shore, and the whole of it passed very nearly in silence. Hammond alone had anything to say to any member of the other company, having monopolized the conversation of the governor since the moment he had come ashore, through one of the translators; with an oblivious rudeness almost painful to witness, he had taken the seat at that gentleman's right hand, although the servants had made a very valiant effort to reserve it for Laurence himself. Laurence had then been established on the governor's other hand, making him unwilling witness to the rest of Hammond's performance: a mortifying experience, as all Hammond's too-anxious entreaties and half-apologies were met alike with silence, or responses brief and noncommittal: the governor betrayed by not the flicker of an eyelid his opinions on any of Hammond's remarks, and offered no encouragement whatsoever to his proposals for an exchange of envoys, or an opening of diplomatic communications.

The governor's safety was secured by the looming bulk of Lord Jinai, who hovered ominously overhead in the shallow waters just off the coast, and a dozen Japanese dragons also in attendance, most of them in polished armor. There were not very many friendly looks exchanged between them and the British dragons: Temeraire had come ashore, and Iskierka, to keep close watch on Jinai; she in particular kept a gimlet and suspicious eye upon the sea-dragon, and occasionally remarked audibly of her perfect willingness to set the entire city ablaze if he should make any motion towards the ship and its precious cargo.

Only Kiyo, who had hauled herself out of the nearby river mouth to attend the feasting, was in good humor. She had greeted Laurence cheerfully: no-one had dared to challenge her on the matter of the assistance she had given him. "No, why would anyone mind that?" she said, with perfect unconcern, when he had asked if she had been put to any distress. "I have been meaning to have a good look at one of these Western ships, anyway, that I have been hearing about the last century, and I am glad especially to have seen such a prodigious one, because I suppose most people would not have believed in it, otherwise. How large it is! I have swum all around it," she added, a piece of intelligence which would not have failed to horrify Captain Blaise, or for that matter any of their party, "and we must certainly have some like it.

"I petitioned the bakufu on the subject myself, and they have agreed we must let these Americans show us how to build them. And that good little fellow Wampanoag has promised that his crew will perform your *Julius Caesar* for me, before they sail away," she added, with great satisfaction. "So you see, it has all worked out splendidly. And there will be fireworks, after dinner!"

She put her head back into her wine-bowl and glugged away; but Laurence grimly realized she was by no means a mere carefree fool, pleasing herself, as he might have supposed before. He did not think Hammond would consider it a splendid outcome, to have the Japanese allied with the colonials, and busy at building a navy of their own.

The fireworks, set off above the harbor and splendid, were a relief to all present, as preventing any further need of conversation: all rose and stood gathered near the shore to watch the blooms of glittering light. Laurence took the opportunity however of speaking with Kaneko, who had been seated some distance down the table from him, at Lady Arikawa's side.

He bowed deeply, when Laurence approached him, and addressed him as a prince; Laurence received the title with dismay. "I beg your pardon," he said, "but I assure you I cannot consider myself deserving of the mode of address: I am not a prince, whatever fiction may have been invented for political necessity."

Kaneko said quietly, "A thing cannot be at once true and fiction: and this, I think, must be considered true, when it is the foundation of an alliance of two great nations."

He made no outward reproach, but Laurence could not help

but feel one: he *had* lied to Kaneko, even if not deliberately. He awkwardly made his apology, on that score, and hoped rather than thought he was believed: Kaneko received it only politely. "I wished also to promise you," Laurence said, "that I will do whatever is in my power to secure Junichiro's future. His familiarity with dragons—"

"The fate of the criminal you mention is none of my concern," Kaneko said with an unanswerable finality, although when he turned back towards the fireworks the spray of the lights shone wetly in his raised eyes.

Laurence did not press him. "May I ask you, sir," he said, "if honor is satisfied?"

Kaneko was silent, and then said, "Lady Arikawa insists it must be so," somewhat reluctantly. He paused and added, "She has honored me with an invitation to take up residence upon her estate."

Laurence wondered at the significance, and still more at Kaneko's evident doubts. Kaneko glanced at him and said, "The honor of dragons can only with great difficulty endure conflict with their affections. The authorities hold that their best and wisest course is to retain a proper distance from any particular individual. I fear I have been the instrument of diminishing her standing."

Laurence was silent, thinking of Temeraire's willingness to spring out a cause for war and all for his sake. "Perhaps I take your point," he said, soberly, and then had to raise a hand: as if knowing himself spoken of, Temeraire had broken off his own rapt contemplation of the fireworks, and looked over anxiously towards him, until Laurence went to his side.

"I do not see why you must be speaking with that fellow who tried to kill you," Temeraire said, putting out a foreleg, as if he would have liked to gather Laurence in close.

Laurence thought, with black humor, that there was every reason: he knew Kaneko better than any other man present. "That was merely his duty," he said, "and nothing ungentleman-like in his behavior: I have no reason to think he means me the slightest ill, as a personal matter. I can scarcely condemn him for trying to uphold the law of his nation, or its interest."

"*I* can," Temeraire said, "when he thought he would do so by putting a sword through you." He gave Kaneko, and Lady Arikawa behind him, a cold glare: Laurence shook his head and let Temeraire put him up. The sooner they were gone, the better; there was too much wrath still simmering, nearly palpable when he lay his hand upon Temeraire's neck. Laurence felt again unequal to the strength of Temeraire's affection: like a gift handed to him unexpectedly, and which he did not recall having earned.

He woke in his cabin early on the morning, to the welcome hurrying thunder of many feet on the ladderways, the bosun's shouts. Hammond was meant to breakfast with him—they were to review the order in which the presents carried aboard were to be delivered to the harbormaster, in Tien-sing; after that it would be on the order of the presents for the Imperial envoy, and how those should differ depending on the rank of the individual sent. Laurence struggled with temptation; temptation carried the day: he rose from his cot, dressed quickly, and called in O'Dea.

"Aye, Captain, it's a fine morning, and the wind and tide bid fair to get us under way," O'Dea said gloomily, as he helped Laurence into his coat. "Properly into the kraken's mouth: that seamonster is lurking ready there at the mouth of the harbor like Jonah's own whale, and it's sure enough the beast will try and have us down to the bottom if only it can."

Laurence swallowed down a cup of hot coffee, very bitter, and took himself to the dragondeck. There was no opportunity for conversation amid the cacophony, with every hand turned to clearing the dragondeck and making way for all the beasts to land. The dragons carried on their own negotiations, as to which should take a first turn in the air, to make the quarters more comfortable for all:

Iskierka and Kulingile leapt aloft, circling the ship; the rest arranged themselves in a complicated tangle on the deck, and the hands began to haul in the pontoons to be deflated and secured beneath the dragondeck.

Somehow it was managed in under an hour, and the massive anchors brought up by the beasts themselves while the men merely wound the chain back around the capstan. "Make sail!" the bosun cried, and they were under way: a cautious progress out of the harbor, past the raised and suspicious head of the sea-dragon, who paced the ship ominously while they crept past the harbor mouth and out to the open ocean, his great pallid eyes watching. But the wind held all the while, and they were in the clear before the sun had even reached its zenith. Blaise nodded to his first lieutenant, and the ship opened her own wings: "Make sail, make sail," the cry going up, the loud rumbling and snap of sailcloth unfurled, belling out with wind: coast and sea-dragon fell away behind them almost abruptly.

Laurence stood watching the whole from the railing of the dragondeck, at once glad and disquieted, feeling himself out of place. He had nothing to do, and no-one to speak with. Captain Blaise he recalled very vaguely, having met him some ten years before at an assembly in Mallorca: a sensible man and a proper sailor by reputation and who knew his work; not a blazing light by any means, but to be relied upon. There was not another soul aboard he knew even so distantly.

Save one: Junichiro stood by the taffrail, looking back at the shore. He ought not have been there, in the midst of the activity; it was a solecism, and several of the sailors cast him sour looks as they went past almost elbow-close, though on a transport there was no shortage of room, and he did not even understand their pointed muttering. He stood with hands clasped behind his back, and expression stoic, peculiarly isolated and standing out sorely despite his Western dress: a borrowed aviator's coat, and trousers.

"Gerry," Laurence said, catching that young boy where he

leaned over the rail into the rising wind of their passage, his tow hair blown up into a cloud, "light along to Mr. Junichiro, there, and invite him to the dragondeck, if you please; and be sure you bring him back along the port side."

The sea-dragon was vanished beneath the waves, a handful of fishing-boats on the water receding, the low mountains of the coast rapidly diminishing. Junichiro lingered for one final uncertain and lonely look back at his native shore before he turned and followed. His steps dragged. In the morning, Laurence intended to find some work for him—surely there could be no shortage of it, on a ship so heavily burdened with dragons—and see him worked to exhaustion for a few weeks. It would strengthen his appetite and dull his capacity for imagination: both ends much to be desired, at present, where his health was concerned. A ship's ration did not suit the palate of most landsmen, even ones not so gently reared; thankfully Junichiro was still young enough to adapt. And of an age with some few of the aviators, including one young sandy-haired fellow whom Temeraire had named Roland, in Laurence's own crew, who according to Hammond spoke the Chinese tongue: Laurence would have his young gentlemen to dinner, to-night, and introduce Junichiro around.

He turned his face back to the prow, and tried to persuade himself to be content. A transport was no graceful sailor, but the *Potentate* was answering beautifully to the wind so directly at her back, nearly her one good point of sailing. Surely no heart could fail to rise beneath so vast and brilliant a spread of sailcloth: four great masts rigged out from mainsail to topgallants. They might well be going twelve knots, a glorious rushing of wind upon his face and everything calculated to delight.

The dragons were still chattering amongst themselves behind him, speaking with pleasure of the entertainment they had lately seen, and their dinner: the equal of any party of drunken officers after a revelry, with two bottles of port in their bellies. Laurence was hard-put not to laugh. It ought have occurred to him, he supposed, that creatures gifted with speech would of a certainty proceed to gossip. He was an old hand at not eavesdropping upon shipboard conversations, but the flow of their strange, resonating voices, which seemed somehow to issue from the base of their throats and not their lips, was a comfortable rumble in the back of his mind, until gradually he became aware that there was an absence. Temeraire was scarcely speaking, and when he did answer some inquiry put to him directly, his voice was quiet and subdued; he lay facing the prow, looking ahead, and apart from the others.

Laurence slowly went to him; he felt uncertain—what could one say, to a dragon? He had no orders to give. But Temeraire's head lifted and turned to meet him, something half-hopeful and wary in his looks; Laurence said, "If you are not otherwise occupied, may I bear you company?"

"Oh!" Temeraire said, "as though you had to ask, Laurence. Would you—perhaps would you care to have out the dear old *Principia Mathematica,* and have a look into that? If you have forgotten it, you may at least have the pleasure of reading it afresh."

Laurence was taken aback: it had not occurred to him a dragon might be a great reader, although belatedly he recalled Kiyo's fascination with poetry. Gerry was sent for the book, and returned quickly; Temeraire dragged a foreleg forward, out from beneath the heap of dragons, and held it forth. He plainly meant it as a couch, and when Laurence put his hands to it, he found he knew how to climb up, and his body remembered the seat in the elbow's crook as though he were going blindfold up into the rigging. Laurence sat still a moment with the book open upon his lap, struggling with a kind of horror between bone-deep familiarity and endless strangeness.

"Laurence?" the dragon asked, anxiously. "Are you well? Shall I send for the ship's surgeon?"

"I am well," Laurence said, drawing his breath deep; for what alternative was there? "Where should you like me to begin?"

PART

2

Chapter 8

Despite a disquieting lack of any shipboard duties, Laurence had very little leisure on their journey: every hour was consumed by Hammond urgently cramming a thousand details of a foreign court into his head, with the assistance of the Chinese nobleman who was the envoy of the crown prince, Gong Su. Laurence felt himself dragged unwilling back to schoolboy days, with two tutors far more zealous than his own had been—and he had fled the schoolroom for the sea.

Worse yet, the tutoring only increased his impatience with himself. The most absurd sorts of minutiae came to him easily: he could navigate a formal dinner of nine courses, walk without a stumble in the elaborate formal dress, incline his head in the correct degree, all as though he had known these things from childhood; he could repeat over long and flowery phrases in the foreign tongue as though he had been their author, and meanwhile his own history remained unfathomable.

Three days dragged by before he had so much as an hour to himself, on the occasion of Mr. Hammond's having been asked to dine by Captain Blaise. Laurence was in turn asked to Captain Harcourt's table and found that anticipated relief worse than the endless study: he could take no pleasure in being surrounded by those who so frequently checked their anecdotes, and hushed one another, and looked at him anxiously, lest he should have heard anything to distress him. Nor was it any comfort when Dulcia's Captain Chenery said heartily, "Do you know, Laurence, I knew a fellow who was knocked off his beast at the Nile—landed on his head on the deck of the *Tonnant,* and could not speak a word at all for three years; but then one day he woke up and asked for coffee," as on further inquiry, it turned out that this was the extent of the gentleman's recovery, and he had died in a sudden fit two years later on.

Laurence excused himself as soon as he could, and sought the solitude of his cabin as preferable; there in a kind of rebellion against the coddling he took out his writing-desk and opened it to read his letters. But he was only disturbed further by his mother's strange and half-stilted letter, and when he found amongst its general awkwardness a wholly incomprehensible passage:

> And I trust that Miss Emily Roland is in good Health, and pray that you will assure her of my Interest in her Progress; I have enclosed a set of Ear-Rings, which she might enjoy, when not Impractical in the course of her Duties . . .

Laurence read these words some four times over before he was perfectly convinced of having them correctly, though he could read his mother's hand as easily as print, and then laying the letter down sat back in his chair, very blank. He did not know what to make of it in the least.

He had been surprised enough himself to discover that Mr. Roland was in fact *Miss* Roland: Temeraire had not seen fit to make note of the fact while giving him the names of his officers, and so Laurence had suffered several uncomfortable moments on finding a young lady so unexpectedly at his dinner table that first evening. He could not think how she should be addressed, much less treated; whether she ought to be given precedence at the table, as the only lady present, or left halfway down the side as her midwingman's rank would have her. He had in some confusion resolved on treating her as an officer: she had come in uniform, wearing trousers, and was evidently destined for command of a Longwing, from what Granby had told him. But Laurence had not been easy with the decision, though Roland herself had shown not the least consciousness of any peculiarity.

She seemed, indeed, a perfectly respectable officer, from what little he had seen of her since then. But Laurence could not imagine he would have confided such a peculiar aspect of the service to his mother; and if he had done so, he would scarcely have made Roland personally known to her; and having done *that,* he could still not reconcile his mother's taking so particular and forthright an interest in a junior officer under his command, and sending her gifts of so personal a nature.

The ear-rings were gone, evidently having been delivered when the letter was first opened. Laurence looked into the writing-desk again, and drew out the other letter, which when he studied the direction more closely was revealed to be from an *Admiral* Roland: perhaps a close friend, he wondered, whom he had forgotten entirely? Eight years might have made enough intimacy to offer some explanation—if this Admiral Roland were of a family distantly related to his own, somehow? He could not remember any such connection, but as he read the letter through, he grew convinced: the letter, quite short and written in an unlovely hand, was generally not that of a superior to a subordinate, save in a few lines surely intended jokingly, that directed him by no means to run Britain into another war or two, or undertake a fresh Crusade. It was a frank note, and it quickly formed in Laurence's mind a decided portrait of its author: an officer not very much older than himself, confident in his own judgment, secure in his position and influence; a gentleman of perhaps forty-and-five, writing him a brief note amid the consuming routine of his duties, a serving-officer and not some mere retired admiral, and Emily's father, this last confirmed by the mention of a dragon named Excidium, who sent Emily his affection.

All seemed plain, easy to understand, until Laurence came to the end of the letter and this comforting portrait was entirely exploded by the scribbled signature, "Yours, etc., Jane."

Laurence could scarcely avoid the only, the obvious conclusion, about Miss Emily Roland's origins: a conclusion made all the more certain when he had looked in at the rest of his papers, and found in his brief accounts the salary of Mrs. Pemberton, Miss Roland's chaperone, paid directly from his personal funds. Badly staggered, he went up to the dragondeck: Miss Roland was returned from her own dinner and at the moment engaged, at his own request, in trying to teach English to a silent and largely unresponsive Junichiro. Mrs. Pemberton, a composed lady of not quite thirty years of age, her dark hair tucked neatly beneath a cap, was sitting on a coiled cable and sewing as she supervised; she nodded as he came up the stairs. "Captain," she said, politely: Laurence touched his hat and said a few words to her while he watched her charge: *could* the girl be his own natural-born child?

He saw no great similarity of feature: Roland's face was round and she was stocky rather than tall. But to counterbalance this, she did have rather a look of his aunt Stourland in the chin, a stubborn determination; and there was very little difference between her fair hair and his own, if one made allowances for the effects of sun-bleaching. Roland certainly had not treated him as a father, but as her commanding officer; however, as this was how he would have expected any son of his to behave in similar circumstances, whether illegitimate or no, he could not argue himself out of it on those grounds alone.

He crossed over to her and Junichiro. "How do your studies go?" he asked, to be answered only by a half-bow and silence, on Junichiro's part, while Emily said, "I am sure he will soon have the trick of it, sir," rather doubtfully.

Junichiro too plainly did not care to learn; he had a dull look of resignation. "I intend," Laurence had told him, "to seek you a commission with the Aerial Corps; you have no fear of dragons, I know, and I think you will do very well: there is no reason you

154

should not be assigned to serve dragon-back, and advance through the ranks; you might aspire to a beast of your own, at length. Or I will buy your commission in the army, if you prefer: once you have learnt English."

Junichiro had expressed no preference, no enthusiasm at all; he had said only, briefly, "It does not matter." He had carried out any small task he was put to, silently and quickly, and took no initiative; he otherwise remained a solitary fixture on the deck.

Laurence shook his head privately; sensible of his own debt, he still did not know what else to do. "Carry on," he said to Roland, and went to the forward railing, near where Temeraire dozed after his own meal.

"Why yes, of course Admiral Roland is Emily's mother," Temeraire said sleepily, when Laurence could not resist quietly inquiring of him, "and whyever would she be married? She has Excidium, of course. There is not the least reason for her to be married."

Laurence could not conceive how Emily should have been got: she was sixteen, so her birth ought not have been lost from his memory, and he did not remember any incident for which he should have had to reproach himself, involving a Jane Roland. But the weight of evidence was too damning, and he now wondered with alarm whether he could not trust his memory of earlier dates any better than that of the later. He ran a hand through his hair: he could feel no trace of the injury; what swelling there had been, had vanished quite, without bringing any relief of his condition. The ocean streamed away before the ship to either side, very familiar and home-like—if only he stood in the bow and did not look behind him to see the dragons, the vast decks of the transport, the crew that were not his own.

He turned and found Temeraire grown more wakeful, and regarding him with an anxiety as great as that of his fellow-officers. Laurence meant to summon up a more cheerful expression, but Temeraire said abruptly, before he could put on a better face, "Laurence, shall we not go up together? I suppose that fellow Pettiforth knows what he is about," this said with as much doubt as Laurence felt, "but there is nothing which could be distressing about *flying*; and we needn't talk about the past at all. We might practice some more of those maneuvers Churki has taught me, that the Inca squadrons use: we might try some which I do not know very well, and work out our own counters for them, together."

Laurence surprised himself by finding this offer, though from so unexpected a quarter, intensely appealing; Gerry went running for his harness, which Laurence found himself able to sling on as easily as an old favorite coat, and Temeraire put him up to his neck. The carabiner clasps were comfortable in his hands. Laurence harnessed himself to the heavy and well-secured chain of the breastplate Temeraire wore, and felt the enormous leap that took them off the deck like a springing away from care: wind tearing by and the curving vastness of the world opening wide beneath them, even the massive *Potentate* diminishing into toy-like insignificance as Temeraire circled higher; they seemed almost level with the enormous cloudbanks that broke up the sky a little way north.

Laurence drew a deep breath of the thin cold air, gladly, and Temeraire turned his head at the end of his long neck, looking back at him, and called, "Is this not splendid, Laurence? Shall we try a first pass?"

"I am ready whenever you should care to make the attempt," Laurence answered him, and held on with real delight as Temeraire flung himself into a spiraling course.

He was all the happier to find that he could offer some thoughts—tentative, but he hoped not foolish—on the subject of the maneuvers: several points at which Temeraire's head had been concealed from him, by the contortions of his body, which he thought might open a dragon to being taken by surprise with an attack aimed at the vulnerable back. Temeraire agreed with his conclusions, and after some further exercise, they settled it they should ask Churki to practice, on the morrow—"If Hammond can spare me," Laurence was forced to add.

"We might invite him to come aloft also," Temeraire said, a notion which Laurence privately could not very much imagine that gentleman appreciating: Hammond spoke rather dismally of Churki, whose affections had evidently been bestowed upon a very unwilling subject, and he was regularly to be found chewing enormous wads of coca leaves, which he evidently considered a sovereign remedy for sea-sickness, even when the swell was not above ten feet.

"I will have a word with Churki on the subject," Temeraire continued. "I am sure it cannot be healthy for him to be always closeted inside that stuffy ship, any more than for you: there is a much better color in your face now. And perhaps you will stay on deck with me to-night, Laurence? I have heard the ship's officers saying the hands would be turned up to sing, and a couple of the fellows exchanged books with Wampanoag's officers, which they might be asked to lend us: I believe Immortalis's Lieutenant Totenham has a new novel called *Zastrozzi*, which he has already finished, and pronounced remarkably good."

"By all means," Laurence said, and though he found the novel, a dreadful gothic with an appalling villain, wholly distasteful, he was more than content with his company: if Temeraire had no great quarrel with the novel's moral turpitude, which he seemed to find less shocking than peculiar, he roundly condemned its construction and what seemed to be several omitted chapters, so they had the pleasure of disliking it together, for their several reasons; and Temeraire did not treat him as an invalid, and shut his mouth on every other word. By the time they had finished out the novel, Laurence stealing an hour here and there from his studies as he might, he found he preferred Temeraire's society above anyone else's, dragon or no.

"I am glad to have had something quite new," Temeraire said, "even if it was not really satisfactory," when they went aloft for exercise again: a morning flight had already become their settled routine, "and now we are sure to have something better to read soon: I think those are the Changshan Islands, over there."

Laurence put his glass up to his eye and looked out along the line of Temeraire's gaze: a scattered archipelago of green and white islands, dotting the sea. Two days to Tien-sing harbor, if the wind stayed fair.

The flooring of the palace was constructed peculiarly on two levels: the lower of hard smooth-polished stone, great flags of green marble shot with deep veins of gold, joined by the thinnest mortar, on which the dragons walked, and above this a network of slightly raised platforms of dark amber-colored wood and gold, for the people. Laurence had been given ample opportunity to examine it, in performing his reluctant obeisances before Crown Prince Mianning, who sat upon a great throne of gold on a dais set at the very end of the great hall. A great host of scarlet dragons and dark blue were gathered on either side of the aisle approaching the dais, with a pair of sleek beasts of pitch-black coloration one to either side of the throne.

The value of the wooden floor, to those kneeling, was certainly very great, particularly those poor souls of rank so lowly they evidently were not permitted to raise their heads while royalty remained within the room. It had an echoing quality from the gap and the stone beneath, not unlike that of the hollow deck of a ship. Laurence found it comforting: the jewel-encrusted silken robes weighed on his shoulders enough to have made him feel a king in truth and not merely in play-act; he was grateful to have anything to remind him of his true and proper place.

When he saw the round incendiary rolling across the planks beside him with its fuse smoking, that same habit came to his service: he recognized the rumbling clatter of its progress, and automatically put down the thick, low-hanging sleeve of the robe in the path of the ball, and snatched it hot from the ground.

And there he was forced to stop an instant: the nearest windows, behind the throne, were latticed over with heavy wooden shutters. "Temeraire!" he called, without thinking: and indeed

Temeraire was already in motion, reaching forward to hook with a talon a pair of the shutters and tearing them away. Laurence leapt forward upon the dais and flung the incendiary outside as though heaving a rock. Even as it flew, the charge took fire and erupted, flame licking in at the frame of the window; long splinters from the wood, smoldering, scattered upon the floor.

Laurence ducked away from that furious hail, and only belatedly realized his shelter was none other than the throne. "What was that?" Temeraire said, and added, "ow!" in protest: the explosion had ceased, and Laurence looked around to see the dragon's side sprouting half-a-dozen red-enameled splinters the size of rapiers, dug in between the scales.

The first moments of blank surprise gone, abruptly the guards sprang into action: they surrounded the crown prince bodily, and Laurence found himself enveloped in their protective ranks as well. A deep-voiced man somewhere beyond them was shouting orders to get the prince away, to hide him—

"Laurence!" he heard Granby shout, but Laurence had no opportunity to answer over the noise: the enormous orange-red dragons in their armored plates, who had been arrayed at the back of the room, were running forward to make formation around the throne: smashing to pieces the wooden floor, bowling men and dragons to either side in their haste: there were twelve of them, heavy-weights all. Four of the beasts seized the elaborate carved borders of the dais, which Laurence had thought mere decoration, but now seemed to be intended almost as handles. A shout came; that deep voice—one of the dragons, Laurence belatedly realized—counted three, and they heaved; the entire dais swayed up into the air and they were moving, the dragons' heavy four-taloned feet thumping upon the ground as they began to run.

Laurence, holding on to the throne for very life, had only time to throw one startled look back at Temeraire, who had been shouldered out of the way by the pack and was only just righting himself. The back wall of the palace fell before the red dragons as they bulled forward; it went down not smashed but in a single piece, as though by design; then there were wings everywhere blotting out the sky, the translucent skin glowing orange-red with the sun above them, and with another heave they were aloft. The palace grounds fell away: off the side of the dais, Laurence could see the yellow roofs glowing in the late-morning sun, and the silver-grey brick of the vast plazas, rapidly dwindling away below.

Laurence said to Prince Mianning, "Where are they taking us?" He supposed it was a violation of all etiquette, but at present there was no-one to object to that: they were quite alone upon the dais. The platform was carried low, beneath the dragons' sides; each one clutched a handle, and their wings beat wildly overhead. Laurence could not even catch sight of a single officer, nor see the dragons' heads.

Mianning's face was composed, despite the assassination attempt and his having been swept pell-mell away in such a fashion. "To the Summer Palace," he answered, as calmly as though he had only gone for a pleasant stroll, but then he paused: he leaned forward from the throne and looked down at the ground that spilled away beneath them, and then towards the position of the sun.

Laurence caught sight of his look, of the frown that suddenly touched the crown prince's forehead. Mianning put his hand on the hilt of his long blade: though the sheath was adorned with jewels and gold, when Mianning drew a few inches of the blade to loosen it, they gleamed good serviceable steel. Laurence watched him: he missed his own sword painfully at the moment. "What is it?" he asked grimly.

"We are being taken in the wrong direction," Mianning said.

He fell silent, and Laurence could think of nothing to propose. He glanced over the side: they were already past the city limits, and the pale green fields of spring spilling away below were so far distant they were merely squares upon a chessboard. There was nothing to be done but wait. Laurence looked back: was there a small speck that might have been a dragon, to their rear? He could not be sure: it might as easily have been a bird. Temeraire would surely have followed them as soon as he was able, but he might have been held back somehow, or misdirected.

"Did you see the assassin?" Laurence said to Mianning, who regarded him thoughtfully a long moment; Laurence did not know what to make of his expression, until Mianning said, "He was of your own party: he wore Western clothes."

"What?" Laurence said. "That is impossible. Hammond, myself, your own servant Gong Su—Captain Granby, Captain Berkley—that was the sum of our party. It is perfectly impossible any one of them should have done such a thing. We were searched, in any case, before we came into the room, and required to leave our swords."

"And yet six of you entered," Mianning said. He raised a hand, when Laurence would have protested. "You misunderstand me. The sixth man was surely introduced to your party as you entered the pavilion. If his attack had succeeded, and I had been slain, your party would surely have been blamed."

Laurence paused. "And *will* be blamed, if, for instance, we should be found to have died of wounds taken in the attempt?" he asked grimly. Mianning inclined his head in answer.

Hammond had been deeply anxious over the preparations for this mission not least because its outcome was by no means certain: a substantial conservative faction of the Imperial court passionately opposed anything they called foreign adventures, and had made an attempt to unseat Mianning as the Imperial heir on the occasion of their last visit. It had not occurred to Laurence that this passion might extend so far as to openly murder their crown prince, but he could imagine no-one else who might have arranged such an incident. Napoleon might have a long arm, but not so long as this.

"Lord Bayan was given the right to oversee the preparations for our meeting," Mianning said. "The conservative party raised a great protest at your coming at all within the walls of the Forbidden City, and suggested I am excessively partial towards your nation, and might be inclined to allow you too much license." He looked towards the sun, which lay ahead of their flight. "His estate lies west of the city."

The dragons carried them towards the lowering sun for nearly an hour. At last they began a descent over what seemed to Laurence a sprawling country estate: a great wilderness of gardens in the Chinese style—meandering paths and great pitted boulders amidst running streams crossed by graceful arched bridges, and a large pavilion which might have accommodated a horde of dragons beside the house.

Their dais was set down in a wide courtyard with great care, and a gentleman dressed in embroidered robes of great magnificence came out of the house to meet them, prostrating himself with all correct formality. "Lord Bayan," Mianning said, calm but watchful; there were a dozen blank-faced guards on either side, besides of course the dragons.

"My humble abode is honored beyond measure by your visit, Your Highness," Lord Bayan said. "I am full of desolation that the peace and tranquility of your days should have been profaned by so desperate an attack upon you by the Westerners, whom I am told have infested the palace grounds like so many evil termites gnawing away at live wood." If this speech were not enough to make his position plain, the look he gave Laurence, sidelong, would have sufficed alone: a mingling of disgust and disdain. And beneath that, something of terror; there was a dew of sweat scattered upon the top of his broad shaven forehead, and he had the look of a man who knows he has gone too far.

"My poor home will be your shelter," Bayan continued, "and I pledge my own life to your safety from attack. I have three most beautiful young concubines, all virgin, who will attend you, and a troupe of actors are in attendance for your entertainment."

"We are indebted to you for your concern for our well-being, and our brother's," Mianning said. "We must at once however write to our father, who even now shall have heard such news as will make him concerned for our health."

162

"You shall be given pen and ink at once, Your Highness," Bayan said; after a few more stilted pleasantries and fencing exchanges they were with inexorable courtesy escorted inside the house with the guards trailing, deep within to a spacious chamber, nobly appointed, with a great writing-desk. Brushes and ink and paper were already laid out waiting. Mianning seated himself as easily as though he were in his own house and favorite chair, and taking up the brush began to write.

Lord Bayan hesitated, but after a moment kowtowed again and left them, the practiced smile already falling from his face as he went out the door. They were left alone.

Laurence himself remained standing by the desk. Mianning had given him the shorter of his blades; it was hidden yet beneath his robes, thrust into the waist of his trousers—for what use a single blade might be.

Mianning tapped his brush against the inkwell, noisily; Laurence glanced down and saw upon the sheet a message written in clear simple characters: *Having gone to such lengths, they likely cannot let me leave alive.*

Laurence inclined his chin halfway to his collarbone slowly, only once, to show he had heard and seen. Any act so overt as this would put the conspirators far beyond the pale, and surely demand reprisals. Except of course, if their plot succeeded. Laurence met Mianning's eyes, in defiance of all Hammond's laborious tutelage on the subject: in the moment they were no longer marionetting the forms of Imperial etiquette, representatives of states, but mortal prisoners together, and in that exchanged look shared the understanding of their likely fate.

Too many witnesses had seen them carried away alive, surely not all of them suborned, and the bomb had not wreaked much damage inside the building; Bayan could not easily claim they had been brought to him already dead, victims of the assassin. But some other deadly outcome might now be engineered: perhaps Mianning murdered by Laurence's own hand, the supposed culmination of a

British plot to slay the crown prince, and Laurence slain in reprisal and wrath by Bayan's guards.

That would be a good story, and the Emperor would have little alternative but to accept such an explanation on its face to keep the peace in his own court, to gain the time for the laborious process of grooming another heir. And in doing so, he would be forced as well to treat the British as the murderers of his son and heir, despite their having come under pretense of seeking friendship: betrayers of the worst kind. There would be no alliance; instead the reverse entirely, all the wrath of the Imperial armies flung upon their party and on the *Potentate* in Tien-sing harbor, and every last man of their company put to torture and death for so outrageous a crime.

Laurence went to the door and looked out of the room. Two dozen guards were lined against the walls to either side. Too many to fight: if they wished, they could put a knife in Laurence's fist, close their hands around his arm, and force him to thrust the blade into Mianning's breast. They did not meet his eyes, nor even turn their heads to look at him. He closed the door again.

Mianning was taking his scribbled note off the scroll-handles and putting it to the lamp to burn; Laurence looked at it catching the flames, at the oil, at the jug of rice wine standing; and then he took up another of the blank scrolls from the table and unrolled it into a long sheet at his feet. Mianning watched him, and then silently joined him: soon they had laid all the scrolls down in rows stretching from one end of the long chamber to the other. There were two lamps burning in the room. They each took one and poured the oil out, spilling it in a glossy line across the parchment, and after that splashed on the contents of the jug of wine, and dropped the first burning sheet down. Blue flame went leaping across the wooden floor.

They took scraps of flame, burning pieces of paper, and spread the fire to the delicate scrolls hanging on the walls, to the silken draperies and furnishings. Smoke began to fill the room; the furniture, beneath its enamel, was catching. Laurence covered his mouth with a fold of his robe and kept to the work; the fire was climbing to a steady yellow-red crackling in a few corners of the room as the seasoned wood took light. His face was streaming sweat already, and Mianning's was made distant and blurred by the smoke: Laurence had the strange unpleasant itching of a memory he could not quite grasp, something he should have remembered—flame and smoke, voices shouting, a crammed struggling belowdecks. A ship in flames, a ship burning; but he could not remember her name, or what had happened, or when.

He pushed the sensation aside and flung cushions down into the building blaze, and then at last the door opened: the nearest guard looked in and cried out. Others came running to the doorway: Laurence leapt for the narrow entry with the short sword in his hand and stabbed the first man coming through in one eye, and got away his longer sword. Mianning took the other side of the door, his own blade drawn. They took the first three easily and backed the rest away from the door for a moment's hesitation: realizing the opposition that faced them, the guards began to group themselves together for a united rush, to bull through the door.

But the smoke was thickening now, and the sickening charred smell of human flesh rose as corpses fell amid the kindling: the opened door had fed the fire with a rush of air, and flames were now climbing the walls, leaping for the rafters. The house had caught, well and truly. Laurence drew a gulp of air from the doorway and then, catching Mianning by the arm, pointed to the fallen guards. Together they stripped off swiftly the slain guards' helms and retreated into the grey haze of smoke even as more guards came pouring through the door.

Laurence threw off his elaborate robes behind the veil of smoke, dropping them into another corner of the fire. The milling guards were shouting to one another as they swiftly organized a defense: already buckets of water slopping were being brought from the kitchens. The disorder was great. Laurence was dizzy and ill with smoke and struggling not to breathe; stinging burning cinders were falling into his hair, onto his bare chest and shoulders. He jammed on his helm, saw Mianning doing so as well beside him; Mianning caught his arm and they pushed out into the hallway together through the din of shouting and panic, and snatched empty buckets from the serving-boys who carried them.

They ran through the hallway towards the back of the house, where more servants came staggering under tubs and buckets; shouts pursued them almost at once. Laurence knocked down a burly cook's assistant who tried to thrust an arm in his path, and reaching for the pots and deep-bowled skillets standing on the stoves flung them behind him, leaving a greasy slick of steaming water and cooking-oil upon the floor. They burst out through the back door of the kitchens and were in the courtyard in back of the house, looking out upon the grounds; more guards were running towards them. Laurence did not suppose they could defeat so many; together he and Mianning drew their swords, however, and ran towards the stables. If they could but get horses—

Laurence stopped and caught Mianning's arm to halt him; he flung off his helm and bellowed aloft, "Temeraire!" waving his hand; and the guards slowed hastily and backed away as Temeraire landed in a rush of thundering wings, in the courtyard.

"Whatever is happening?" Temeraire said. "Why is that house on fire? Laurence, you see I did *not* let them keep me from coming after you, this time: although they tried; some fellow of the guards even had the gall to say that one of our friends threw that bomb, if you can credit it. But you may be sure I quite silenced him: I caught the fellow who threw it, though he was trying to put off his clothes, and he was not from our ship at all."

"'Ware above you!" Laurence cried out: the four scarlet dragons who had abducted himself and Mianning were descending towards him, claws outstretched, bulkier than Temeraire himself and plainly bent on his destruction.

Temeraire, startled, sat up on his haunches, fanning back his wings. "What do you mean by this?" he demanded, and then had to make a writhing leap, twisting himself away from their talons and teeth as he got himself aloft again, eeling between two of them. "Oh," he said indignantly, "I do not know in the least what you are doing, but if you mean to get between me and Laurence—!"

He beat up and away, drew breath, and roared at the foremost beast coming towards him: that terrible earth-shattering resonance again, which Laurence heard yet lingering in his dreams from the moment upon that hill in Japan, familiar and dreadful at once, and the scarlet beast's eyes quite literally burst in their sockets, blood erupting in a sickening rush. The dragon plummeted from the sky. It was already dead when its corpse smashed into the roof of the house and in its sprawl tore down half the north wall: smoke and flame leapt out around it like a massive pyre, and other rooms left gaping open to the air, cries of horror and men and women looking out in astonished dismay.

The three other dragons fell back in dismay and horror, and dropped to the ground cowering: they flattened themselves before Temeraire as he came down, and remained there with their wings nearly covering their heads.

Temeraire still did not quite understand what had happened. First that wretched assassin had nearly slain Laurence, and then the Imperial guards had flown off with him—Temeraire had tried to be understanding; Hammond had shouted urgently to him that they meant only to protect Laurence, to protect Mianning, and take them to a place of safety. That sounded well enough, until several of the courtiers had begun to cry out that the British had tried to kill the crown prince; fortunately Temeraire had already snatched up the bomb-thrower, as that fellow tried to creep out a side door, and he could see that it was only a fellow dressed in Western clothes, which were anyway not quite right: his too-long wool coat dyed royal blue, instead of navy or bottle-green, and no waistcoat, and his hair lightened somehow; he had been wearing a dented hat drawn low down his face.

Temeraire had been forced to knock down several guards, who had tried to advance on Mr. Hammond and the rest of his party with swords, to make them all listen to him; he had even been forced to roar—awkwardly; it had brought down a portion of the roof—and it had required the better part of an hour to straighten out the matter, and persuade the Imperial dragons to take charge of the scene. "Mr. Hammond," Temeraire had said, at that point, having handed over the assassin to Mianning's guards with what he considered was extraordinary restraint; he had not killed him straightaway, "I perfectly understand those fellows did not mean anything terrible by carrying Laurence away, and I will try not to be *very* short with them, but they certainly ought to have consulted my opinion on the subject of his protection, and you may be sure I will make that quite plain to them: I do not mean to have any repetition of such a misunderstanding. Now, someone had better tell me which way they have gone."

To the Summer Palace, someone had told him; but Temeraire remembered the Summer Palace quite well, and it was not due west of the city at all; they had *not* gone to the Summer Palace, so it was no use his flying that way. So he had been forced to chase them down directly, even though his flying strength was not entirely recovered; when he had gone out of the city limits, he had at last been able to distinguish them from the ordinary traffic, a cluster of specks in the distance, but he fell further and further behind. Once he had even lost sight of them entirely, and panic had clutched his breast a little while, driving him to a speed greater than he could comfortably maintain, until he had passed a small porter flying in the opposite direction who, chirping, had said, "Oh, they are going to Lord Bayan's estate, I am sure: he lives just over those hills. He is very rich," the porter added, "and a great servant of the Emperor."

"I am very grateful to you," Temeraire said, and, feeling relieved to hear that Laurence was in such good hands, he had flown onwards at an easier pace, though even more irritated at the guard-dragons: there was no call for them to have made such haste. They ought to have considered, it seemed to Temeraire, that in taking Laurence further away from him, they were *not* improving his safety: and where, he wondered, was Mianning's companion? Lung Tien Chuan certainly ought to have been there, at their meeting, and Temeraire would have felt a good deal happier to rely on *his* judgment, and not some soldier-dragons who had not even managed to stop an assassin getting into the room in the first place.

But still he had not been very anxious, and then he had sailed into the courtyard to find the house burning, the red dragons attacking *him* of all absurdities, and to cap everything Laurence fleeing the disaster stripped to the waist; his beautiful robes were gone. "Good God, that does not matter," Laurence said impatiently, when Temeraire anxiously inquired after them. "I imagine they have burnt by now; I dare say no-one has the least concern for my costume at present."

To his horror, Temeraire could hold out no hope for their rescue: even as he turned to look, bitter smoke and flames were boiling out of the windows, licking from under the eaves at the roof wherever the scarlet dragon had not smashed it to pieces. He leapt to action at once, and worked as quickly as he could, calling out instructions to the other dragons, who had cowered down now and were not behaving so stupidly: soon they were ferrying great loads of water back and forth from the nearby pond, while Temeraire himself tore down and stamped out the worst bits of the fire, and roared down other parts of it.

But it was no use. One wing of the house they managed to save; all else was a smoldering ruin, damp and stinking, the body of the scarlet dragon lying amid it blackened and surrounded by puddles. All the household stood huddled aside and watched it collapse, women with children in their arms and the servants still clutching dully at the small buckets they had been trying to use against the flames, and not even a scrap of silk left of Laurence's gown. Lord Bayan himself, the owner, did not do anything to help; he only stood surrounded by his guards watching his house burn, and when the flames had at last been conquered, Temeraire turned back and found the lord prostrating himself before Prince Mianning.

"I am desolate that my house should have been the scene of such events," Lord Bayan said, "when you ought to have been confident of safety here."

"Oh!" Temeraire said, glaring down upon him; his eyes were smarting from the smoke and ash flying through the air, "you may well apologize: how dare you have taken Laurence away from me, and the crown prince, too, when this is the consequence? And I should like to know what those dragons of yours meant, leaping upon me when I came in; it is absurd to say they did not know who I was, or thought I should be a danger."

Lord Bayan did not even answer, or rise from his kowtow; Prince Mianning only said to him, "Your service will be rewarded as it deserves." It was a small consolation to Temeraire that the crown prince himself was in no better state than Laurence: half-naked and smirched with a fine layer of black soot, except for the trickles of sweat and one pale smudged handprint across his back with the fingers stretched improbably long, as though someone had tried to grab hold of him and the grip had slid off.

Lord Bayan still kneeling said, "I would be honored to offer you escort and shelter—"

"Lung Tien Xiang will escort Prince Lao-ren-tse and myself," Mianning said and turning away gestured to Temeraire slightly, asking for a leg up. Temeraire was more than glad to provide it: he wanted nothing more than to get Laurence, and Mianning, too, well away from here; there was certainly no reason to stay. Laurence hesitated oddly, looking at Bayan as the lord rose up again; then he turned and climbed aboard as well.

As glad as Temeraire was to leave, questions pressed in upon him as soon as he was aloft again and Laurence securely with him; he turned his head to ask Laurence and only then received the full and appalling explanation. "What?" Temeraire cried, halting mid-air. "Whyever did you not say so! I should have torn him to pieces, at once; why did you not say he was a traitor and a murderer? I only thought he was a fool who had made a great mess of things."

He felt truly indignant: indignant, and wounded, and all the more by hearing that Laurence had set the dreadful fire himself. Why had Laurence not relied upon him? Surely Laurence should have expected Temeraire to follow, to come to his rescue—or perhaps not. Temeraire was painfully conscious he had not saved Laurence in Japan; he had not found Laurence and brought him safe away.

But on this occasion, Temeraire thought, he might at least avenge Laurence's ill-usage: he almost turned back at once, but Mianning said, "No: I can use Bayan's life better than his death, at present."

"Do you truly mean to allow a man who has failed once to slay you to get another chance at the prize?" Laurence said to Mianning, echoing Temeraire's own feelings on the subject: Temeraire did not see that Bayan's life was any use to anyone at all. "There can be no question of guilt, here—Bayan suborned your guard, abducted you, held you against your will. That the assassin came from him, at the first, can scarcely be in doubt.

"I beg you will forgive my frankness, Your Highness," Laurence added, "but this matter affects our own mission as much as you yourself. We both know how Bayan would have chosen to use this: not merely to destroy us personally, but to destroy all hope of alliance between our nations."

Laurence spoke very soberly; Temeraire knew Hammond had spared no efforts to impress upon him the urgent necessity of the alliance, and that Laurence felt very anxious for his part in achieving it, very doubtful of his own efforts. Temeraire had tried to assure Laurence that he would do splendidly, that there could be nothing wanting in his performance, but of course, Temeraire had not suspected that there would be assassins throwing bombs at him, and treacherous dragons abducting him; he had not expected such things in China, of all places.

He did not see any reason not to kill Bayan at once, as the author of these calamities, but Mianning answered Laurence, "And so, too, must I use his failure: to ensure that alliance, and the future of my nation and my reign. I have had no certain evidence, no sword to hold above their heads, until now, but they have over-reached at last." He leaned forward. "Lung Tien Xiang, take us back to the Forbidden City: I will return to my own palace."

"With so many of your nearest guard turned traitor?" Laurence said.

"Those were not my nearest guard," Mianning said. "I did not have free choice of my attendants at our meeting, as I told you; I have others whom I can better trust. But in any case, there is no alternative. One who yields, always yields; I will not come to the throne in the minds of my enemies as one who may be moved by threats or danger. I have withstood worse than this, at their hands; far worse. Better if I die than permit them to hold my leash."

Temeraire thought this an appalling choice of alternatives, and one he scarcely imagined Mianning's own dragon Chuan would approve. "I cannot think my brother would permit you to go into such danger," he said. "Why was he not there, to-day? If only he had been by your side, I am sure together we should not have allowed those treacherous lizards to snatch the two of you away: I would certainly have done no such thing," he added, for Laurence's benefit, trying not to let his tone convey too plainly his sense of injury, "if only I had had the least notion, before now, that someone should be trying to kill you. I do not think I can be blamed, when we have just arrived, and no-one told me: but Chuan should have known; he should have been on his guard."

"Lung Tien Chuan is dead," Mianning said.

Chapter 9

Mianning evidently did not care to discuss the matter further. It fell to Gong Su to convey the details: he seemed high in the councils of the crown prince, and spent nearly all the day closeted with his own associates within the government; later that evening he rejoined their small and wary party in Laurence's chambers, and quietly told them, "Lung Tien Chuan was slain six months ago. He was served with poison in his tea."

Laurence was appalled by the act: a dreadful waste, and it seemed to him pure cruelty, to punish the dragon for merely loving his master, and over a political quarrel with the latter, which the former should have had very little to say to, he imagined. "There are only eight Celestials in full, are there not?" Laurence said.

"Yes," Gong Su said. "There is no other to be the prince's companion."

Laurence only belatedly took the deeper meaning of this intelligence that evening, when he was alone again: he had been quartered in another part of the Imperial palace grounds under Mianning's control and surrounded by watchful guards loyal to him.

Laurence had closeted himself to write his report of the strange and convoluted events of the day, which yet he preferred to struggling through more of the letter he had not yet sent to his mother to acquaint her with his condition. But he set his pen down abruptly and, sitting up, looked out the window into the courtyard where

Temeraire slept, in arm's reach—in a dragon's arm's reach at least—recovering from his exertions.

Hammond had conveyed to him from the other side the necessity of Laurence's adoption: a Celestial might only be companion to a member of the Imperial family; and Temeraire's egg had been sent away from China in the first place only to avoid setting up a rival to Mianning. Therefore—the heir to the throne required a Celestial? Perhaps *required* was too strong: many things might be bent at the will of the Emperor. But tradition had its own power. If Mianning had no Celestial companion—if he had lost his own dragon—

Shipboard, Temeraire had spoken censoriously to him of Hammond. "I do not say he is not clever, in his own way," Temeraire had said, "but I am very sorry to say, Laurence, that he is not to be relied upon. When last we were here, he wished to insist upon your giving me back to the Chinese only so they would open another port to us."

Surely that request would come again, now, Laurence realized, and was disturbed by his own reaction to the possibility—a reaction which owed more to the viscera than clear rational thinking. Sensibly considered, he ought to be grateful for such an excuse to be restored to his respectable Navy career and a ship of his own; and if he were not grateful, if he had not wished to do it, nevertheless it would be no less than his duty. And yet—and yet he discovered he had begun to think of Temeraire as his own man, as it were. Such persuasion, coming from one trusted as a friend, would only be honorable if meant sincerely, if given from the heart and in expectation of its advancing Temeraire's real happiness.

Laurence did not think he could, even at the direct request of the King's envoy, consent to deceive a friend. To lie in such a cause would be contemptible, a kind of personal treachery. But Laurence felt himself on unsteady ground. It was surely his duty as a captain in the Aerial Corps to use the bond between himself and Temeraire to be both a check and a goad upon the beast, and that bond was one which many another aviator would willingly have taken on in his stead. Perhaps it was a kind of folly to think of a dragon as a friend, as a companion-in-arms; would he skate perilously close to treason to refuse such a demand?

Granby listened willingly enough as Laurence began to outline the situation for him, but Laurence did not reach the question: no sooner had he explained Mianning's need than Granby broke in, snorting, and said, "Oh, Lord! Yes, Hammond will be after you straightaway, I am sure; I dare say their Lordships would give him a peerage if he managed anything so neat as giving them a treaty and being shot of Temeraire all at once."

Laurence stared: shocked, silenced; Granby caught his eye, and a slow crimson flush overspread his cheeks. "Well—" Granby said after a moment. "Well—he is too independent by half; he's thought too clever for his own good—a little troublesome, perhaps—but you see," he added hurriedly, "you must see I've no room to criticize. Iskierka is a demon and a half, and it's not as though Temeraire hadn't any provocation, for that matter, you know—"

Laurence made him no reply; he could not conceive of any reply which should be fitting. He did not know: he did not know at all, that he was the captain of a troublesome beast; he did not know that the Admiralty should have been glad to see the back of his dragon, though Britain was desperately short on heavy-weight beasts, even ones of less remarkable capability.

Granby made a hasty and threadbare excuse of having to go see to Iskierka; Laurence mechanically said, "Of course," and rising left Granby's quarters. A fine thin rain was presently falling. Granby and the rest of the formation were quartered in one of the guest palaces to the south of Mianning's personal quarters, where Laurence had been invited to stay; the dragon-wide pathway between the buildings was grey and misty, blurred, and deserted but for a handful of servants, errand-boys, dashing quickly through. Laurence stood beneath the eaves; across the path another great palace stood, with a dragon's-head as gutterspout giving out a steady clear stream of water washing over the paving-stones.

The guards behind him, Mianning's chosen escort, shifted their weight behind him; he heard the creak of their armor, their boots on the stone, the nearly stifled sighs. The scene was wholly unfamiliar, wholly strange; in the distance was the great blue bulk of a dragon crossing the pathway, its wings half-furled to its back. It was something from a fairy-tale, nothing he would ever have imagined into his life. It gave his mind no purchase. He did *not* know, he did not remember, what could have made Granby ever say such things.

Laurence had never studied—to his recollection—to know much of aerial combat or of dragons, beyond learning the signals to bespeak them from his ship, but this much he remembered from the battle of the Nile: the formations wheeling, like flocks of birds, above them in the sky. In modern warfare, dragons fought in formation; and yet Temeraire did not seem to have a place in one. Laurence had not thought on it before: but a dragon so gifted, so powerful, so agile—he must have been placed in formation, if it could be done. If the dragon were not—were not a recalcitrant, mismanaged beast.

He had always prided himself on being a reliable captain, one who did his duty with honor, neither haring off after prizes or unreasonable glory nor guarding his ship too jealously from danger; he had prided himself on a well-run crew. It now bore in on him with sudden force that his crew was strangely depleted, and of a peculiar nature; he had paid little mind to that, struggling as he did merely to learn all the names of those men he did have, but by comparison to the complement Maximus bore, Temeraire had not half so many. His ground crew consisted entirely in a dozen men—several of them, Laurence now realized, former sailors. His officers were a motley and an awkward lot: Forthing, his first officer, was not a gentleman, nor of any particular brilliance which should excuse the same.

Laurence could scarcely imagine whom he might approach on the subject; Granby had certainly been most unwilling to speak.

His subordinates he could hardly insult in such a manner, either, as to ask them whether they served on an inferior crew, and why.

Finally he strode out into the rain and returned to his own quarters, to speak with Temeraire himself: if he could not ask for a direct answer, he could ask where they stood with the Admiralty, together, he and the dragon. If Temeraire had some memory of chastisement, some punishment—

Temeraire was awake, in his courtyard, awake and spangled a little by the rain, which he shook off with a rippling shiver of the scales. "Laurence!" he exclaimed with relief. "I wish you had not gone away when there are assassins about: I was on the point of going to look for you. Wherever have you been? Surely you might have stayed here with me, and waited until I woke?"

He sounded an anxious mistress more than anything else, an odd mixture of plaintive and accusatory. "I left word," Laurence said, a little surprised. "I have been speaking with Captain Granby—"

"Granby had much better come and visit you," Temeraire said, "than the reverse: no-one is trying to assassinate Granby."

"No-one is trying to assassinate me, either," Laurence said dryly. "I had merely the misfortune of being near the crown prince."

"If they want to kill the prince, I dare say they may want to kill you just as well," Temeraire said. "After all, you are his brother and the Emperor's son as well; and if they do not like his being a friend to Britain, how much less must they like your being British, to begin with. But," he added, in tones which implied he was making a handsome gesture, "I do not mean to fuss: come and let us have a bowl of tea, and then you can read to me; that would be much better than wandering all over this palace."

"Temeraire," Laurence said, while the servants leapt without further instruction into a rush about them, bringing out a great porcelain bowl of deep red for Temeraire, and a small ironwork table and chair for himself, with a cup and saucer to match, and kettles full of steaming and fragrant tea. "—Temeraire," he repeated, unsure how to broach the subject: would a dragon even care anything for the Admiralty, for what men and government should think of him?

"No, of course I do not give two sous for the Admiralty, or the Government," Temeraire said, straightaway answering all Laurence's worst fears. "How could anyone, who has known anything of their folly? Why, Laurence, you know that perfectly well.

"I suppose you do not remember this," he added, "but Perscitia writes me they have still not made all the pavilions, which Wellington promised us during the war; but they are also upset if ever a dragon should chance to sleep by the road, on the way from London to Edinburgh, and perhaps eat a pig left wandering loose. But that is perfectly stupid: if there is no pavilion, and no provender, then how else is one to make a long flight? And nevertheless they complain.

"As far as I can tell, there is no-one in it who is worth two pins; well, except for you, Hammond," Temeraire added, as that gentleman entered in haste. "You are not a bad sort of fellow; but if you should attempt to do anything scaly underhand, such as tell me I ought to remain here to replace Chuan, I shall be very cross with you."

Laurence was thwarted in pressing his inquiry by Hammond's arrival, that gentleman in some disarray, his formal robes far from neatly pressed and showing sharp folded creases in the silk; his hair was disordered. "No, no, not at all," Hammond said. "I assure you, nothing could be further from my wishes. We cannot afford to lose you. The tie is too valuable to sacrifice, save of course in utter extremis. Without your connection, Captain Laurence's adoption may be too easily disavowed, and it is that bond which forms the foundation of all our negotiations.

"Naturally we must make some gesture, some effort; but I have had a hint, I believe, from Gong Su; with your permission, of course, I should propose Temeraire's favoring them with an egg. As I understand it," Hammond added, "your engaging in relations with an Imperial dragon would be the ordinary way of arranging such things."

"I should like to know," Iskierka said, with a hiss of steam and a roiling eye, "what is wrong with *our* egg. If an egg of yours were wanted, why should anyone look further than that?"

They were being served their dinner in Temeraire's courtyard: a truly splendid dinner, of stewed oxheads and bowls of live eels, seasoned expertly with pepper and vinegar, which unfortunately Maximus did not seem to much enjoy, nor Immortalis and Messoria; they poked a little anxiously at the squirming masses and then nudged the bowls aside, although they were pleased enough with the oxheads, so tender the meat fell off the bones and with the skull cracked open so one might take them into one's mouth and suck upon them for the excellent brains.

"I am afraid," Temeraire said, a little loftily, "that they do not think much of fire-breathers, here in China—and in any case," he added, "it is a matter of certain particular superior qualities, which belong to the Celestial breed only, and distinguish us from all others, which must be present in the next Emperor's dragon."

"Dear one," Granby said to her, "we don't at all want to give them your egg: we want to take it back with us, to Britain, and see it in the hands of some proper captain of the Corps."

"I do not see any reason why it should not stay here and belong to the Emperor of China," Iskierka said stormily. "No reason at all; it is ten thousand miles back to Britain, and who is to say we will not run into some trouble along the way—someone might steal the egg, or it might be cracked. Of course my egg would be very valuable, in the war," she added, "but I do not believe in taking foolhardy risks—"

Granby choked heavily upon his own dinner, coughing, and had to be rescued with a steady thumping upon his back, and several glasses of wine.

Iskierka was in no better mood even after their meal had ended with a marvelous shaved ice, flavored with a syrup of plums and studded with the same, imparting delightful tiny bursts of flavor upon the tongue when one happened across them in a swallow. However, she did not hesitate to eat all her share and then some.

"That is something like, I will admit," Maximus said, licking out his enormous silver bowl, "but I don't suppose you could ask them for us, Temeraire, what they have done with the rest of those cows? I haven't any objection to those cow's heads, very tasty, but I would be glad of a side of beef, or perhaps two," he added, with a slantwise look at Kulingile—who had at last stopped getting longer, but had only just yesterday sprouted the beginnings of a pair of horns, much to everyone's bafflement: neither the Chequered Nettle nor the Parnassian, his progenitors, possessed any similar adornments.

"I wouldn't mind one, either, if they are just lying about somewhere," Kulingile said, raising his own head; and stifling his own remonstrations, Temeraire addressed the servants and conveyed the request. It was met with some confusion and a great deal of delay; when the beef was at last delivered two hours later, it was presented in the form of a false cow, the meat having been roasted, stuffed with grains and dried fruit, tied up with string, put into a wrapping of dough, and propped up on legs made of sticks; the head was a separate lump of meat, adorned with horns made of bread. Maximus sighed but ate it anyway, particularly after Kulingile had devoured his own share in a few bites.

As the servants began to bring out the bowls for tea, one came to Temeraire's side and murmured that a visitor had come and sought admittance. "Oh!" Temeraire cried. "Lung Qin Mei! Pray ask her to join us at once: how delighted I shall be to see her again," and he looked himself over anxiously. If only there were time to send Roland for his talon-sheaths, and if only they had a little black enamel paint—

Mei landed gracefully in the courtyard, though they were

crowded and there was little space—but then, she did everything gracefully. Temeraire straightened himself up to meet her, abruptly conscious that he was now more cut-about than when last she had seen him; there was that very nasty scar upon his breast, where the barbed ball had taken him, before the sinking of the *Valérie,* and he had not filled back out from the long dismay of the sea-voyage and Laurence's disappearance. He had not had much appetite, of late, and it was difficult to be always competing shipboard with Maximus and Kulingile; one felt a little awkward taking anything more than one urgently needed, with the two of them casting mournful looks at their own share.

Iskierka said rudely, "I do not see why she is come; who wants her, anyway?" when Temeraire presented Mei to the company, but naturally Temeraire did not translate this remark. Iskierka drew herself up and raked Mei with a cold eye. "So that is an Imperial? Skinny, if you ask me; I dare say *she* could not go eye-to-eye with a Copacati. I don't see she has any scars at all."

"Mei," Temeraire said coldly, "is a great scholar, and took highest honors in the Imperial examinations."

"Oh!" Iskierka said, dismissive, "say nothing more! She does not fight at all; I see. I hope you have a splendid time talking over books together while you are making this egg of yours: I hope it don't leave you any more out of frame than you already are. Granby, I should like a flight before bed: pray let us go aloft, and then we shall go have a look in at *my* egg," she added, "and I take your point entirely; we shouldn't want to leave it in this country, where they don't value courage as they ought."

Temeraire was ruffled to indignation by this speech, and would surely have made a particularly sharp rejoinder if Iskierka had not gone away directly. The others were more polite to Mei, and looked with respectful interest on her jewels—this evening a collar-like delicate netting of pearls and silver wire, brilliant in the lamp-light against her dark blue scales. Although Temeraire writhed a little inwardly to see Maximus look up from the indelicate gnawing of a leg bone between two teeth and greet her with a mere joggle of the head, scarcely even a nod, saying jocularly, "How d'ye do," before going back to rattling the bone around in his mouth in what seemed to Temeraire a particularly noisy way.

And then Berkley *would* say, coarsely, "Put down that leg, you mannerless gobbler: we had better be going along and let the two of them have at their business. Laurence, will you come and have a hand of whist?" which even if Temeraire did not translate it for Mei had too obvious an effect: the dragons and all their captains getting hurriedly up and leaving the tea-bowls half-full, rudely. Even Laurence rose and, speaking softly with Berkley, made to climb aboard Maximus's back.

Temeraire would rather Laurence had not left, either; he did not see why Laurence should go anywhere. He caught Lily as they departed and whispered, "Lily, you will keep a lookout for Laurence, will you not? Pray do not let him wander off, or be assassinated; or lose any more of his memory."

"Of course," Lily answered, stoutly. "I will make sure he stays with Catherine and Berkley, and do not let Iskierka trouble you. I am sure you will make a perfectly splendid egg with this Imperial."

"Lily, I do not look too wretchedly scarred, do I?" Temeraire asked.

"No," Lily said, with a quick critical look. "—no; and you will fill out again very soon, with good eating. She must know you have come from a long way."

This was not terribly reassuring, but there was nothing to be done for it; the others were all leaping into the air: it was only Temeraire and Mei left in the courtyard. The servants laid out fresh bowls and poured the tea again.

Then they withdrew as well, to the hallway where they might hear a call; with a desperate leap into the ensuing silence Temeraire said to Mei, "How well you look—those jewels are particularly becoming."

"You are very kind," Mei said, and then to his horror and

dismay added, in quite respectable English, "I am glad to see you so well, Lung Tien Xiang: too many times has the moon turned since we last saw one another beneath the boughs of the peach-trees, in the Summer Palace."

"Why," Temeraire said, wretchedly, "you have learnt English."

"Yes," Mei said, and with her usual tact added, "but I still cannot follow it very well, if someone speaks quickly: I have not had enough chance to practice."

"I must have words with Iskierka," Temeraire said. "I *will* have words with her; oh! I am so very sorry, Mei, that she should have been so rude. I only wish you hadn't known of it."

Mei ruffled out her wings a little, but did not pretend any longer that she did not know exactly what he meant. "I do not take any notice of it," she said. "She must be very attached to you, I suppose: I do not fault her for that. One cannot expect civilized manners from barbarians."

"She is not very attached to me, in the least," Temeraire said. "She is only attached to showing away, and annoyed she cannot do it so well as usually." He fell silent; he was not sure how to approach the matter. Diffidently he added, "I imagine—I expect Hammond has told you—" and then paused helplessly; this was not the breeding grounds of Pen y Fan in Wales, where everyone treated the matter with an easy coarseness, and everyone understood what they were about and merely wished to have the matter over with as quickly and easily as they might.

He had never expected to regret anything of those conditions, anything of being treated as a dumb bestial creature good for nothing else, but at the moment, if old Lloyd had appeared from nowhere to say, "Here now, why don't the two of you share a nice cow, and then have yourselves a splendid time," and Mei had acquiesced, Temeraire might almost have managed gratitude. If only Laurence had stayed: Temeraire might have introduced him to Mei, and they might have conversed awhile; they might have been quite comfortable and easy, and the subject of eggs might have been allowed to rise naturally, in the flow of conversation. But that seemed quite impossible now: Temeraire found himself adrift and speechless.

Mei took pity upon him, and said gently, "I have not spoken to Mr. Hammond; I have come at the request of the crown prince. But I will be frank with you, dear friend: your minister's thoughts have run along behind his, it seems, for I have come to ask if you would consider doing me the very great honor of permitting me to attempt to bear a Celestial egg to you."

Temeraire felt rather heaped with coals of fire by this gracious speech, and made haste to convey to Mei his own willingness, and gratitude. He hesitated to go too far, in expressing the latter; after all, though he might be cut-about, he had come by his wounds honorably; and he was a Celestial: he did not want to abandon his dignity. Nothing could be less pleasing, he thought, to Mei; he did not want her to feel that she condescended. But he felt he could say, and did, "Nothing should give me greater pleasure than to make the attempt, if you were willing. I am very honored that His Imperial Highness would look to myself, to sire a companion for his reign."

And then he heaved a sigh of relief, to have escaped the rocky shoals and come safe to harbor; now they could be easy together. He asked her if she had read any English books. "I hope you will let me make you a present of some," he added, "if you haven't many here: I do not suppose you have had a chance of seeing the *Principia Mathematica*? It is of all books my favorite," and they passed a very pleasant hour discussing the poetry which Temeraire's mother, Qian, had lately sent him.

"Mei," Temeraire ventured, "pray tell me, if I might ask—is there not—is there a reason that Qian should not have had another egg?"

Mei said quietly, "The physicians think it inadvisable: she suffered greatly in bearing the twin eggs, last time, and in Imperials, where such a birth has happened once, it oft occurs a second time; the Empress does not wish Qian to risk her health."

"Oh," Temeraire said, sadly. "I am very sorry, I am sure; and my uncle?"

Mei shook her head. "A dozen attempts have come to nothing," she said. "We have been breeding a great deal amongst ourselves," she added, "—we Imperials, that is, in hopes of another Celestial arising, but without success. I assure you, Xiang, no-one will think any less of you, should we fail: it is well known that Celestials often cannot produce issue."

Temeraire was glad of an excuse to preen a little; he coughed, and gave Mei to understand he was not in the least concerned, at all. "For Iskierka, you see, has had my egg," he said. "That is why she is making such a fuss: she does not care to see it passed over, for yours."

He trailed off, a little puzzled, by the expression of open surprise upon Mei's face: she stared at him unblinking a moment and then said, in cautious tones, "Is it—perhaps the egg is yet in the shell?"

"Yes," Temeraire said. "It is in our quarters, under guard, of course."

Mei hesitated even longer and then said, "Is it not possible the egg should be—the gold dragon's, perhaps, the very large one? There are many young males in your company—"

"What?" Temeraire said, taken aback. "Why, no; Iskierka particularly wanted *my* egg; it is not as though just anyone's would have done for her. She followed me to New South Wales to get it, and threw over an Incan royal dragon for me," he added, a little wounded that Mei should not think him worthy of such dedicated effort.

"I beg your pardon very much," Mei said, bowing her head deeply in a courtesy, her wings spread a little. "I would not for the world give offense; only it is not to be heard of, that a Celestial might get an egg on anyone but an Imperial. I have always heard it described as impossible. The divine wind is a great burden, which often defies the powers of the body to support it."

185

A little mollified by this explanation, Temeraire forbore to stay offended, and when they had finished their tea, he and Mei repaired to the gardens, to walk awhile, and at length to enjoy a little sport before going on with the breeding: Mei might not be a fighting-dragon, Temeraire silently told Iskierka in his head, with some hauteur, but she was certainly very lithe and agile, and no-one could have complained of the experience.

Afterwards, a little out of breath, they ambled together to the courtyard again and had a refreshing second helping of shaved ice. "We must see the crown prince safely to the throne," Mei said soberly, when the servants had retreated again. "I know your heart is divided, Xiang, and I am grateful already for what you have given; but I will not conceal from you that I fear deeply for the sake of the nation. The death of Chuan was a grievous crime against the throne, and yet those responsible dare name themselves defenders of the law and of right thinking. What can it portend if such twisted people should gain control over the Celestial Throne? And they will let nothing stand in their way; they have shown as much time and time again."

"Mei, surely the Emperor must do something to Lord Bayan," Temeraire said. "Why, I would have slain him myself, if only Laurence and the prince had told me what mischief he had been about; and I would not have let anyone stop me, either."

"It is not enough to cut off the serpent's head," Mei answered. "This one grows another, and another after that. There are too many now who refuse to think of the future. They think only of what will enrich them—what will make them comfortable—what will guard their precedence and their estates. They wish to keep China preserved in glass, and if it could be done, they would not be wrong! I have seen a little of the rest of the world, through your eyes, and I do not think there is anything to compare.

"But so of course the world will be envious, and come knocking at our door. I have seen your monstrous ship in Tien-sing harbor; I have seen men felled by guns. We also must have ships, and more guns, and cannon. Our army must be renewed in strength, and the banners must be brought back to their old strength and discipline."

She spoke passionately, the tips of her wings nearly trembling with urgency, and leaning towards him rested her neck across his shoulders, coiling loosely about him. "I fear greatly, Xiang," she said, low, "even if I should bear this egg, if that will be enough. So many things can happen to an egg! They may persuade the Emperor to grant it to one of the other princes; or they may try—they may try—"

She shuddered, silently, and Temeraire bent his own head and nosed at her comfortingly. "I do not blame you in the least for worrying," he said. "If they are mad enough to try and kill Laurence, and the crown prince, and to murder Chuan, they might do anything at all."

"That is my own thought as well," Mei said unhappily. "Xiang, will you forgive me: would you not stay? Let the alliance be made, let China send legions to this war; might you not remain here in their stead, where you alone can act? I do not ask you to forsake your companion," she added swiftly, "but you might stay to keep watch over your own egg, quite reasonably; you might demand that it go only to the crown prince, and perhaps even—"

She faltered, and then said, low, "I have thought that perhaps the egg might even be bound to him at hatching; though it is not the proper way."

"Well, I have never found anything to complain of in it," Temeraire said. "I am very glad indeed to have had Laurence all my life, from the beginning; even if he did not know much about dragons, and nothing at all of China. I see nothing against it, provided that one ensures the captain is quite the right sort of person, which of course Laurence is, and not some wretched fellow like Rankin; that is where it goes all wrong."

Mei flew away not long afterwards, and Temeraire had just been deciding to go and find Laurence, when he came back into the courtyard: the captains had seen Mei go. "I hope," Laurence said to him, "—I hope you have had—a pleasant evening."

"Oh! A splendid evening," Temeraire said, reassuringly as he could: Laurence sounded so doubtful. "Mei is a magnificent lover," he added, "whatever Iskierka likes to say about her, and I dare say we may already have made a very handsome egg."

"Ah," Laurence said, in a slightly stifled voice. "I—Temeraire, I beg your pardon; I do understand that this is—ordinarily considered in the normal course of your—your duty, but I should hope—that is to say, I should have been certain—"

Temeraire listened a little puzzled, but he soon worked out that Laurence only feared he might not like making the egg. "Oh, I certainly do not mind obliging Mei," Temeraire said. "I only minded in Wales, when they would set me to every female dragon in the Corps, it seemed, and only the meekest ones at that: some of them only middle-weight, for that matter. It was not what was due to me, I felt; I only obliged them for your sake," for at the time, of course, Laurence had been a prisoner aboard the ship *Goliath:* a prisoner, convicted for treason, and sentenced to die.

Temeraire shivered a little; he did not like to remember that dreadful time of separation. He hurried on. "But pray do not think this anything like: after all, this is quite an especial compliment to me, that the crown prince should want my own egg—even if he hasn't any other choice," he added.

"Very—very well," Laurence said, still awkwardly, and then said, "Pray shall I read something to you, this evening?"

"Shall I not read to you, Laurence, instead?" Temeraire said. "Mei has brought me a new book of poetry, which we read into only a little way; I should be glad to read it with you."

He felt a little craven in making the suggestion: it was merely a delaying tactic. Temeraire could scarcely imagine that Laurence would be willing to stay here in China, with the war in Europe from all reports going badly and Britain in such dire straits; even if an alliance was formed, Laurence would wish to be there. And yet, if they remained, and so protected Mianning and saw him to the throne, *that* would serve Britain and China both.

He marshaled his arguments in one corner of his mind while they read several of the lovely poems together, and Temeraire explained to Laurence his sense of the meaning; and then as the moon climbed overhead and bathed the courtyard stream in white, Temeraire drew a deep breath and broached the subject at last.

Laurence was silent a long while afterwards, as silent and grave as Temeraire had feared. His ruff drooped against his neck. He could not press Laurence; he was still painfully conscious of the great debt between them yet to be repaid: the loss of Laurence's reputation, of his countenance, and most sharply and terribly of his fortune of ten thousand pounds. At least Temeraire had seen him restored to his rank—with seniority—but that did not make up for all the rest. Temeraire still woke occasionally with a start from dreams in which he heard Roland saying again, "He has lost his fortune," and found the eyes of all his friends upon him accusingly, horrified, as they all repeated in unison, "*Ten thousand pounds.*"

He felt still low and guilty, and so he said hurriedly, "Laurence, I would not for the world distress you—"

"No," Laurence said, rousing, "no; I was only considering— but no. I beg your pardon. You must consult your sense of what is right, not my feelings. God forbid I should lean upon friendship to stand between you and your duty: it could not be borne. I would not for the world act in so false a character, towards any man— towards anyone. All feeling revolts at the idea."

"That is just how I feel myself," Temeraire said, a little puzzled, but relieved: Laurence was not angry. Perhaps Laurence *would* consider their remaining? It occurred to Temeraire belatedly that if they should remain, then perhaps the Emperor would grant Laurence an estate, and at least surely some finer clothing and jewels might be arranged.

Relief, gladness surged; he meant to add this handsome suggestion to his persuasions, to expand upon them, and then all was shattered—all turned at once dreadfully wrong, for Laurence added, "I hope having said as much, I may add I should most deeply regret the parting," and Temeraire realized, in slow-rising horror, that Laurence meant he would not stay himself. Laurence would leave him.

Laurence was taken aback by the violence of Temeraire's response; and only after a sharp recrimination did he understand that Temeraire had meant to propose not a separation but their remaining in China together, as though Laurence had anything to do here but make a cake of himself, prancing about in false honors bestowed for mere politics and luxuriating in a wealthy foreign court, while on the other side of the world, his country-men fought and died to defend their country against an encroaching tyrant.

It had not occurred to him even as a possibility that he should remain. Failing that, he had therefore made the only answer he felt endurable: and he had felt only ashamed of the reluctance which had slowed it coming from his lips—a reluctance which had not even the excuse that he had thought of his duty and Hammond's wishes. His reluctance had been wholly selfish and irrational: a disquieting pang at the thought of losing Temeraire. But such sentiments had even less place, in a question of duty, than the political considerations which Hammond had put forward.

"But you must see," Laurence said bewildered, "I cannot contemplate remaining. While Britain stands on the brink of subjugation, my remaining behind, to serve no purpose, could be nothing better than rank cowardice. *Your* remaining may indeed have some beneficent effect; mine, none. I should be a mere supernumerary, and useless here, just when every able-bodied man in Britain ought beat to quarters, as it were."

"You said once before we should remain if I liked," Temeraire said, accusatory, to Laurence's broad astonishment, "and you needn't look at me that way, as though you did not believe it, only because your memory is all ahoo; so I do not think I am in the least foolish for having *asked*. I did not propose keeping you from *your* duty, which properly considered ought be *our* duty. Of course I did not. Only, I thought you might have felt as I did, that our duty might lie here. *I* did not propose we should be parted—that you should go back to those wretched fools at the Admiralty, who do not want us, anyway; not really. And I dare say if I *did* let you go back without me, they would only hang you."

So concluding his wild outburst—the most singularly irrational thing Laurence had heard Temeraire say—the dragon flung himself aloft and vanished into the night sky with a rattle of black wings, leaving Laurence calling, "Temeraire—!" after him into the air.

Disheartened and impatient all at once, Laurence turned to his quarters; a cup of tea was offered but he rejected it to pace instead. That he had misstepped, and badly, was plain; but he had no idea how he had gone wrong, and where the fault lay. Temeraire's final words rankled, as well: that the Admiralty should not want them echoed yet again all Laurence's worst fears, and hinted at an almost mutinous disposition.

And the absurdity, to talk of the Admiralty hanging him—or perhaps not, if one treated the loss of a dragon like a captain's loss of his ship; Laurence supposed that he might be court-martialed over it, and yet he could not envision any reasonable jury finding against him in such a case. A ship had not her own mind, and could not decide to run herself onto rocks, or be captured and go over to the enemy, or be sunk in battle or by incompetence. A dragon, possessing its own will, who chose to remain behind, could scarcely be compelled by any man.

He sat down upon the bed, troubled suddenly: and yet that seemed untrue. Temeraire's anger and their misunderstanding had this real and understandable root: where Laurence had not contemplated remaining, Temeraire had for his part not contemplated separation; he had viewed their connection as indissoluble. In such a case, Laurence realized, he indeed did have the power to compel—he had the power to say, I will go, whether you will or no; and it seemed perforce would Temeraire go as well.

That was a strange and even disturbing power to possess over so great a creature: one which demanded a respect that Laurence was unhappily conscious he had not shown, just now. When in an hour's time he heard wingbeats returning, and Temeraire settled himself into the courtyard again, Laurence went out to him, ignoring the head curled pointedly beneath its wing. "I hope you will forgive me," he said, to the dark grey translucence of the membrane, which hid the great blue eye from his view.

"I hope you will forgive me," he said, "and accept my assurances that I would not for the world have wounded you: I see I have not understood how matters stood between us, and that we may only be stationed together, as it were. I can only beg your pardon and assure you that I stand ready to be persuaded, on the subject."

Temeraire made him no answer, but there was a shift of the wing-joint, and beneath the membrane as it spread out, Laurence could dimly make out a large narrow-slitted eye watching him.

"I cannot—I cannot pretend," he added, "that I feel I ought easily be swayed to see it our joint duty to remain here, taken all in all, in the present circumstances. I do not doubt you in the least that, on a prior occasion, I should have been willing to remain; I can only suppose that the circumstances of the war must have been considerably different, at the time. But I will do my best to consider the matter, if you wish to—"

The wing lifted away. "No," Temeraire said, shortly, "no; I do not see any sense in it. Pray forget I mentioned it," and he thrust his head back beneath the wing, and was silent again.

Laurence hesitated, torn, and at last gave way and went inside the house again. He did not immediately attempt to sleep: his mind was in an excess of disorder. The guilt of having caused pain to one deserving only consideration at his hands mingled with unanswered disquiet. He wondered if he had been wrong now; or if he had been wrong before: had he spoilt Temeraire? Temeraire was a high-spirited creature, with a remarkable intellect; Laurence could not deny that he took great pleasure in his company, and in the camaraderie that had endured even his loss of memory. Had he indulged that pleasure, and Temeraire's spirits, at the cost of discipline—at the cost, perhaps, of character?

A dreadful notion, and yet—Temeraire was so certain they should not be missed by the Admiralty; Granby also. It seemed a settled matter with them, scarcely to be questioned. If that were simply a matter of old men preferring more docile breeds, the sort of political caution that saw dull and predictable officers advanced over brilliant ones, Laurence might not have cause to blame himself: God knew he did not find the Admiralty faultless. But if there were something else—

Laurence looked out at Temeraire, who had not stirred out from under his wing. He could not think how he might question Temeraire on the subject, not after this unhappy misunderstanding; he could not make Temeraire feel still more wretched, perhaps without just cause. So he said nothing, while he thought what he might say; and he had still said nothing when a knock upon the door of his chamber interrupted his considerations, and Hammond without invitation thrust his head within, most anxiously. "Captain, I beg your pardon, we must intrude," he said, and opened the door for a messenger in pale green livery who followed him into the courtyard, and prostrating himself with a quick efficiency presented a letter bearing elaborate seals. Laurence took it up and opened it, and found therein a brief missive from the Emperor himself—a piece of enormous condescension which he supposed had been merited by the assassination attempt.

It contained wishes for his good health, an expression of outrage at the recent events, and concluded with a mild hope of seeing him, at some time. "His Majesty is most generous," Laurence said to the still-prostrate and waiting messenger, who seemed to be waiting for some immediate answer; but this did not satisfy him: or, at least, it did not make him rise. "Hammond, will you pray tell me how I am to answer this?" He held out the note.

Hammond read the letter through more swiftly than Laurence had managed to puzzle it out, and paled. "Good Heavens," he said, "we must go at once: and I suppose we have not the first thing for you to wear."

The Emperor did not look well: a heavy-set man and jowled, fatigue was writ upon his face; he breathed stentoriously and sweat gathered upon his thin mustaches and glistened to the sides of his chin and upon his forehead. Laurence began to realize what particular urgency had driven the conservative party to strike at Prince Mianning so blatantly: they foresaw him coming shortly to the throne. But the Emperor's ill-health did not place bounds on his temper; his expression was set in grim lines and a glitter of anger that revealed itself plainly when the formalities had been quickly dispensed with.

He was not enthroned in state, but received Laurence in a courtyard with his own Celestial, Temeraire's uncle Chu, coiled watchful and heavy along a raised dais behind a chair that was a simple and comfortable affair of wood. Temeraire had been permitted to accompany them only so far as the outer court of the pavilion; Laurence had been conscious of that anxious gaze upon his back as they had been ushered away into the inner halls of the palace, and thence to the great central court.

Laurence was not the sole guest; Mianning and Lord Bayan both had preceded him and were seated before the throne. Mianning was the nearer; Laurence followed Hammond's hissed whisper to seat himself at a distance between the two, and they all three faced the Emperor as if defendants at a trial. Nor was the simile inapt: with the flick of a hand the Emperor dismissed nearly all his attendants, save the well-armed and watchful guards; Hammond, too, was forced to go trailing reluctantly away, leaving Laurence to rely upon nothing but his own uninformed and lately doubtful wits. There was at first no difficulty, however, no call for decision; he had merely to sit and be thundered at in company.

"I scarcely know who to blame the more," the Emperor said, "for this upheaval of the Imperial court and therefore of the state, its mirror; for whatsoever evil begins here, it will show itself reflected tenfold throughout the nation! What madness should have permitted any man to lay a plot within their hearts upon my chosen heir and my adopted son? What reckless actions, in pursuing foreign involvement and disregarding the sage wisdom of centuries and respect for tradition, should have driven otherwise loyal servants of the court into such madness?"

Laurence wished badly for Hammond, adrift and struggling to pierce the veil of the Emperor's terms; but despite his inexperience he felt he understood this much: whatever the Emperor might choose to say officially, he knew in private all that had transpired. He surely knew: the cold rage in his eyes, beneath which Bayan flattened his head, was not merely that of a ruler jealous of disruption in his palace, but that of a father. He knew Mianning's intentions; he knew of Bayan's assault; what power struggle here transpired, he permitted, to some extent.

But only to some extent: and evidently that extent had been exceeded; he meant to rope them in one and all. Laurence felt cold anxiety settle stone-like in his belly: he did not need Hammond to tell him deadly shoals lurked beneath these waters, and he had neither pilot nor chart nor even soundings to tell him where they lay. One misstep and he might ruin all their hopes as effectively as Bayan might have wished to do. Laurence resolved to shut his mouth and say nothing, so far as he might; he would offer nothing but the meekest response. Mianning should have to speak for their side, if at all.

"I will hear your explanations," the Emperor said, concluding his tirade, and slumping angry back into his throne; he held a hand out and a cup bedewed with cold was placed within it. He drank heavily and put it aside.

Mianning prostrated himself, and quietly said, "My honored Imperial father, my trespasses against the wisdom of my elders would be unforgivable, save if by respecting that wisdom I should neglect my greater duty to the nation: surely it is my obligation to plant and tend the seed for a future harvest of peace and prosperity, that the fortune of Heaven will continue to smile upon our land. Though in summer the winter storms seem far away to those who must labor on the present harvest, they are coming nonetheless; and one whose shoulders do not yet bow over the sweep of his scythe may look towards the West, and see them approaching from afar."

Bayan said, "And in looking afar, mislead himself that the distant clouds he sees, which soon will disperse of their own accord, are grave dangers; and worse yet, in chasing a defense against them will forget what nearer danger threatens, and let the crow plunder his fields."

"This can only be the argument of all men who will not raise up their eyes at all," Mianning said. "For these clouds have lingered now long years, and the storm grows ever larger."

He made a quick gesture, and two servants scurrying unrolled a great map of the world over the floor: not entirely accurate as to shape, with China outsize and the other continents somewhat awry, but plain enough to recognize. "My father, already the Emperor of France, Napoleon, has stretched forth his hand to make alliance with mighty nations across the sea." France itself and all Europe were stained a dark green color; so, too, the Incan Empire and Africa: they stood like dark blots against the pale canvas. "His appetite knows no bounds, and already once have the evils of this foreign conflict crossed our borders, bringing the pestilence which struck at the ranks of our dragons, the breath of our nation. If not for your own foresight in having secured my brother's service with the bonds of filial devotion, and his courage on that occasion," he gestured to Laurence, who could only wonder what he had done to merit such an encomium, "who can say how many would have perished?"

"And yet what worse sickness, what worse miasma," Bayan said, "could enter our nation but the poison which their ships carry unchecked into Guangzhou? How many lives and souls have they destroyed with the crushed seed of the poppy, which makes men drown themselves by their own hand? Thrice have you commanded a reduction in this evil trade; thrice have they obeyed only with sullen reluctance, like disobedient children, and then stealthily permitted it to resurge. And it is the British, those to whom you have in your generous love given most license, who do the most evil in this regard by far. They are poisoners, and liars, and should all be banished from our shores.

"And, Dread Lord," he added, and Laurence glancing saw him press his forehead to the ground again, "I pray you forgive my humble words: I wish to offer no disrespect to the crown prince—"

Mianning's shoulders were stiffening, and the Emperor's eyes narrowed; Laurence had one moment to realize, *Now we come to it,* and then Bayan concluded, "—but I have received a report of General Fela, whom you charged with repressing the remnants of the White Lotus rebellion, and ensuring they did not flourish to regrow, that he has seen the British bringing those evil traitors aid, in the form of this evil drug."

"By God," Laurence said, too outraged to restrain himself, "—that is an outright lie."

He at once regretted having uttered a word, however justified; Mianning threw him a short unreadable glance, and the Emperor's eyes turned towards him. Laurence only at the final moment remembered to drop his own gaze, but he was caught: plainly he was now expected to speak. He saw from his lowered eyes Mianning flick his fingers towards the ground, and belatedly made another prostration himself, however reluctant. As he had dug himself a hole, he could only jump into it without complaining.

"Your Majesty," Laurence said, speaking to the ground, "I must beg to be excused from speaking on behalf of His Majesty's Government, for which I have insufficient authority; but I have not the least hesitation in most heartily repudiating the scurrilous accusation which Lord Bayan has made against my country which, if true, would be injurious not merely to her honor but to her sense, and which should defy all rational consideration. We have come here for no lesser cause than alliance against Napoleon. How could it profit us in any manner to create turmoil and distress within your borders, which should make you less able to aid us, even were we not the guilty culprits?"

He halted there, hoping at least he had not made matters worse; neither Mianning nor Bayan spoke immediately, which, Laurence rather dismally suspected, meant that he had spoken so far out of turn they had neither of them been prepared to respond to an outburst of the sort. The Emperor gave no sign of his own thoughts yet; but he left the field to them, and after a moment Lord Bayan bent forward and said, "Your Majesty's adopted son, who to do him credit has shown all the instinct of proper filial respect—"

The instinct only: Laurence supposed this was meant to hint at the deficiencies of his training and education in the same. "—all the instinct of proper filial respect," Bayan went on, "would scarcely be the confidant of those of his country-men intent upon such dishonorable behavior: even within a band of thieves one man of good character may be found."

"But not to deceive himself that his fellows are themselves honest men," Mianning said, "unless we are to believe him a fool."

They feinted back and forth a little further along these lines, it seemed to Laurence very much like two fencers feeling out their way onto unfamiliar ground, trying to ascertain which of them should take the better advantage from it, in which direction and what manner they wished to press the attack. And then abruptly Bayan made his lunge, adding, "And if nothing else, what he has said is surely true: China can ill afford to involve herself in the disputes of a foreign nation while strife rends the state from within."

"I am surprised to hear that you have so little confidence in General Fela's ability to put down the White Lotus resurgence," Mianning said.

"When a hidden hand props the foe from behind, and he is

forbidden to strike at the true source of danger, even the greatest general cannot be expected to easily find success," Bayan said. "Perhaps," he added, with a false air of having been suddenly struck with a new idea, "the foreigners should be tasked to go to his aid, under the command of the Emperor's son and Lung Tien Xiang. If the British are responsible, they may correct their own wrongdoing. If they are not, they may do a singular service to the nation, and thereby properly merit some acknowledgment."

Laurence heard this proposal with dismay: he could well imagine what Hammond should say to their entire party being sent away from the heart of Imperial power to the hinterlands of China, silenced and expected to clear away a provincial rebellion that might be as much whisper and legend as armed force, and nearly incapable of defeat. Let a man be robbed on the road, and the conservatives might claim rebels had done it. And if the rebellion were real, were some truly dangerous insurgency against the throne, Laurence could scarcely imagine that their own party would be of particular use, stumbling over themselves in a foreign land. They might well merely be in the way, and in so being might make Bayan's accusations almost true.

He was all the more dismayed, then, to hear Mianning slowly say, "While rising from questionable suppositions, nevertheless Lord Bayan's proposal has merit."

Laurence could not help but stare at him, while Mianning serenely continued, "Though the remnants of the White Lotus may not yet have become truly dangerous, the creeping vine is best pruned back early, and with greater zeal than necessary. To send my brother—with a force appropriate to his rank—to see them put down and restore harmony, would be a wise course and a duty befitting his dignities."

It was little comfort to Laurence to see Bayan as taken aback as himself by Mianning's unexpected yielding. "What escort could the prince require other than his own company?" Bayan said at once, urgently. "General Fela and the army are there already—"

"And yet have so far been insufficient to halt this insurgency, by your own report," Mianning said. "Surely you would not propose that such a risk be taken with my brother, nor the honorable Lung Tien Xiang, who have not had the blessings of proper military training. When I myself first led men into battle, I was arrayed not only in armor, but with the wisdom of the senior officers who advised me."

Laurence could not like the proposal any better for Bayan's evident dismay; but neither he nor Bayan had any opportunity to object further: the Emperor had straightened in his seat, and it was plain the audience had reached its conclusion.

"My son Laurence," the Emperor said, "taking General Lung Shao Chu, and consulting at all times his advice and wisdom, you will gather three *jalan* of dragon bannermen and go south with them, to deal with the rebellion and uncover the source of these strange and evil rumors about your country-men, proving them false if you can. Return swiftly and victorious home."

He had scarcely finished speaking when one of the half-a-dozen scribes working busily by his side, the one nearest the throne, rose and kneeling before the throne presented him a clean copy of the orders upon a writing-desk. The Emperor took up a brush and signed, swiftly, and taking up the red seal pressed it down; the sheet was folded over thrice by the scribe's skillful hands even as he turned to offer it to Laurence, who with a sense of numb disaster bowed his head before it.

Chapter 10

"Hm," said General Chu, deep in his throat, when he had been presented to the rest of the formation, and to Iskierka and Kulingile. Temeraire eyed him uneasily. His yellow crest had evidently with age sprouted a great golden-colored mane, which framed his broad flat jaws and the curving horns which bent away from his forehead, and the edges of his vermilion scales were tipped with translucence. He was not quite so large as Temeraire himself, smaller considerably than Maximus and Kulingile, and he was not a Celestial, of course; but somehow that did not seem to matter very much.

He had been very polite, of course—very gracious—on their introduction; he had bowed quite formally and correctly to Laurence and to Temeraire himself, with all the respect due to the Imperial connection. No-one could possibly have faulted his manners, only Temeraire could not quite help but feel that the general did not think very much of their company.

"Hm," General Chu said again, after a moment's silence in which they all stared at one another. "Well, we will not get to Xian any sooner. Let us be going."

"Oh," Temeraire said, a little taken aback. "Do you mean, now?"

Chu peered at him from under the bristling fringe of his mane, with an air of raised eyebrows. "Are you ill?" he said, with a hint of waspishness. "Is the chill of the day too great?" The day was in fact not in the least cold, an early-spring pleasantness in the air.

"No, only," Temeraire said, "are we not to take a great many soldiers with us?"

"Three *jalan*," General Chu said, and paused as if waiting for Temeraire to go on; but since Temeraire did not know in the least what to say, after a moment Chu added, "Of course you would not expect them to gather all here and fly along the entire way with us," in heavy, pointed tones.

Temeraire had expected just that. He had been on fire, in fact, to see a proper Chinese aerial company assembled; and he knew Laurence and the other aviators were as deeply interested as he was himself. "Of course not," he said, a little abashed, and turning his head down murmured to Laurence, "Can we be ready to leave very quickly, Laurence, do you think?"

"He means us to leave on the moment?" Laurence looked at Hammond, and at the other captains; no-one spoke a moment in their confusion. Laurence had only returned two hours before, and had scarcely even had enough time to explain to everyone the Emperor's command.

Then Captain Harcourt said, "I suppose there's no reason to wait, if we *are* going. Have we any better notion of what to do?"

She looked around, and no-one answered her: they had all been debating just that, vigorously, before General Chu's abrupt arrival; but while disliking the orders, no-one could work out an alternative. Hammond had just been saying, "We *cannot* refuse this direct Imperial command—at least, Captain Laurence cannot, not and maintain any thin fiction of familial connection: and having lost that tenuous connection, they will assuredly not merely refuse our requests for alliance, but order us out of the capital forthwith, and revoke all those particular and unusual trading privileges which have so benefitted our nation, in the last five years—"

Temeraire, for his part, had no objection to taking Laurence away from here, where assassins lurked around every corner and he was not even to be permitted to deal with Lord Bayan as that treacherous coward deseved. Temeraire was sure that they should certainly be able to quash this rebellion handily, and it seemed to him as good a means as any for ensuring they should gain the alliance they required.

"Well," Harcourt said, when no-one had anything else to offer, "let us call it settled: I don't say we shall *stay*, but I don't suppose it will hurt us to *go*. Mr. Hammond, you would oblige me greatly if you would dash a few words to Captain Blaise in the *Potentate*, so he knows where we have got ourselves off to; and I dare say we can be off in a trice."

She turned and called to her first lieutenant, "Richards, we must get aloft: and there is not a moment to lose, if you please."

The aviators went into the tremendous scrambling rush of getting away: gear tumbled pell-mell into chests, the ground crewmen hauling up the belly-netting to the shouts of, "Heave! Heave!" and the officers leaping aboard. Temeraire watched with a little disgruntlement as his own crew went aboard Kulingile. Of course he understood that, according to the Chinese way of thinking, there was a loss of dignity in carrying so many men and going under harness, and for a Celestial to be so burdened was unthinkable; as a consequence, they had devised this arrangement for their journey to the capital from Tien-sing harbor. And while certainly Temeraire did not want to look undignified, he still could not like it in the least; he sighed.

"Will I come with you?" Junichiro was asking Laurence. Temeraire did not quite know what to think of him: he had been very ready to take Junichiro to his heart, when he had learnt everything that young man had done, to see Laurence safely back; but Junichiro had been so very standoffish; he had spurned Temeraire's thanks, saying, "I did nothing for *his* sake," and when Temeraire had asked him for lessons in Japanese, shipboard, he had refused with a flat, unfriendly, "Of what use could such instruction be to you? We will never return there again," and he had walked clear away across the dragondeck. He did nothing all day but sit and stare across the ocean, or, since they disembarked, at a wall, it seemed to Temeraire; and though Laurence had asked Emily Roland to teach him English, Junichiro did not seem to be making any progress at all: he scarcely answered when she tried to make him repeat the most basic words.

Even now, he did not ask with any interest, only a cold question, as though he did not care either way, and did not very much *want* to come; but Laurence said only, "We are all going; stay with Midwingman Roland, if you please," and sent him up to Kulingile's back after her.

"Have a little patience: he has been a great deal bereft," Laurence said, as he climbed into Temeraire's cupped talons to be put up. "And I cannot give him any real work to do, until he has learnt English; we must let time work on him, and isolation. He is a young man: I dare say he will lose his taste for solitude, soon enough, and want some more society than he can get speaking only Chinese."

Laurence latched his carabiners on: Temeraire did not even need to shake himself and settle his own harness, as he had none but his polished breastplate, which O'Dea had looked over for him. "It is sure to tarnish sooner or late, with all this sea-air and flying," O'Dea had said, alarmingly, but when pressed had added, "though not yet: the rot lies far off in wait, for another day."

Leaning over to speak to General Chu, Laurence asked, "Sir, may I inquire, are there arrangements we ought make for our supply?"

"No particular arrangements will be necessary until we are closer to Xian," Chu answered, without even looking up. He had sighed heavily, watching their preparations, and had shut his eyes and lay his head down upon his forelegs to rest.

Those preparations were accomplished in under half-an-hour; he cracked one enormous green eye and peered out. "Are you ready at last?" he said, and heaved back up to his feet. "Very well, then," and coiling himself up on his hindquarters launched himself into the air. His wings were short, the veins and ribbing in green, and his body long and sinuous, so he went undulating as he flew.

"I do not see in the least what he has to object to; we went very quickly indeed," Temeraire said to Laurence, grumbling, and leapt after the general's dwindling figure.

A quartet of Jade Dragons, the tiny light-weight couriers scarcely much larger than a man, rose from outside the Imperial grounds to join them: the four of them bore long fluttering banners, red emblazoned with golden characters, and preceded General Chu in the air in a straight line. They led the way southward out of the city, the broad avenues and teeming marketplaces falling away to narrower streets thronged with men broken with the occasional great pavilion crammed with dragons sleeping or amusing themselves. Temeraire saw from aloft, as they passed an immense complex upon the outskirts of Peking, a handful of the most common sort of blue dragons playing some sort of game with stones, which he made a note to inquire about when he had anyone more sympathetic to ask than Chu.

The city yielded to settled sparse towns and then all at once to farmland and fields. Temeraire noticed large square markers set at regular intervals beneath them, dark grey stone engraved with white-enameled characters: they all bore the name of Peking, the direction to that city, and the distance. He pointed them out to Laurence. "That is very convenient," he said, "and I wonder we do not have them in England; it is much less trouble than having to follow a road, only to know where you are; I can see these from quite far away without the least difficulty."

"It is a clever notion," Laurence said, peering down over Temeraire's shoulder with his glass, "although I suppose it is no use at night."

But that proved not to be the case: as the evening fell, the letters still came onwards, taking on a pallid glow, faint but enough to make them legible for a little while as they swam out of the dark. "I cannot imagine how they are arranging it," Laurence said, trying to look through his glass. "Perhaps when we land we may have an opportunity to examine them. Temeraire, we must ask him for a halt in any case, not long from now; those fellows in the belly-netting must be allowed to stretch their legs. We are not flying to a battle."

They had gone nearly ten hours straight, without a pause; but even as Laurence spoke, abruptly General Chu and the Jade Dragons turned their course and began to descend gradually from the sky towards a pavilion, its eaves hanging with shining white lanterns and a thin trailing column of smoke rising from the roof, and they came to ground in a broad hard-packed courtyard before it.

There was a splendidly appetizing smell of roasted pig coming from within. The Jade Dragons stepped aside and bowed their heads, and Chu also stepped to one side waiting for Temeraire to precede him in, which was as satisfying as anyone could wish, and when he had gone in he found a high-roofed hall, splendidly formed of what looked to be entire tree-trunks bound at intervals with polished bronze, and a handsome dinner laid on for them already.

At the head of the table, waiting, was Prince Mianning; and to his either side several dragons, both Imperials and the scarlet war-dragons, but that was not the important, the very important point: one of the dragons was Mei.

"The dangers of your charge are many, I am aware," Mianning said, "and the chance of failure is great; but the rewards of victory will be commensurate."

His servant was pouring the tea with great carelessness; it slopped freely to every side, leaves and liquid spattering hot across the table and even to the ground. The dragons had sated themselves all upon roasted pork, and most of the aviators as well, and fallen into a stuporous sleep well-earned by their day's long exertions; it was surely almost the middle of the night. Laurence alone had been invited to join Mianning within the inner chamber, for this final leavetaking, although he half-suspected Hammond of sitting by the door outside with his ear pressed to a crack.

"My intention is to send Lung Qin Mei with you," Mianning

went on as the servant with ceremony handed him and then Laurence a cup, of a brew which had a peculiarly smoky and strong flavor, bitter on the tongue. "This will ensure further opportunities for conception; and should we be fortunate and an egg produced, will also enable you to keep the news concealed from the capital as long as possible. With your company, sheltered amongst foreign dragons and away from the Imperial household who are ever-watchful for such signs as mark the coming of an egg, she may conceal her state a long while. You and your fellows may then hide away the egg, and perhaps bring it back to the palace in secret.

"For the rest, I hope you have seen the advantages of the situation. You will travel under our banners, and with a company of three *jalan*. Should you succeed in your mission, nothing will be more natural than to send a similar force westward with you, to your war against Napoleon."

Laurence did appreciate that advantage, but not in the least the high-handed way in which the situation had been thrust upon them. Hammond's endless strictures still rang in his ears, but he and Mianning had gone through fire together, quite literally, and though the crown prince could not at all be said to have a manner which encouraged license, Laurence determined to take the bull by the horns. "Your Highness, I beg your pardon for speaking plainly, but I cannot undertake to commit even myself, much less my country-men, to this mission: not for any length of time and certainly not for the time required to produce an egg. We are certainly *not* responsible for the resurgence of this native rebellion; we cannot contribute materially to its end. Mr. Hammond has urged our going, rather than defy the Emperor's will openly; but I cannot conceive our long remaining, kicking our heels in your back-country. There is open war in Europe, and if our party seems to you insignificant to that effort, I assure you by the standards of our own nation it is not. If you desire this alliance as much as we do, then I must tell you that we will require some excuse for our returning, sooner rather than late, if you do not mean us to give it up."

Laurence had no idea how this was received: Mianning heard him out with no evidence of either impatience or sympathy. "We must permit events to unfold," Mianning said only. "The situation of your army in the West is naturally of great concern to you." Polite enough, but making no promises. "I suggest that you take this opportunity to observe the work of General Chu, and of our *jalan:* this will afford you opportunity to gain a better understanding of the management of aerial warfare as its principles are understood by our nation." He did not say outright that he felt their understanding of those principles was far superior to the British, but he hardly needed to.

"When we have actually seen scale or tooth of any other dragon in this so-called company," Captain Warren said, with some asperity, when Laurence had recounted his conversation, "it will be soon enough for us to be amazed. I suppose we have managed well enough against Boney, even with that Chinese worm of his whispering advice in his ear. If these fellows will only give us a few dozen beasts, I will thank them well enough, and they can keep their principles."

"Pray not so loud," Hammond said, glancing worried over his shoulder: he had nearly suffered an apoplexy at Laurence's account. Mianning and his escort had already departed, but Chu droned in sleep in a warm forward corner of the pavilion, and the Jade Dragons lay in a neat row against the entry wall. Laurence did not think they were in any state to overhear, despite the thin gleaming slits of their eyes still cracked ajar, but the impression of being observed lingered, and he could understand Hammond saying, "Perhaps we ought to retire, gentlemen; we will surely have a long flight ahead of us again on the morrow."

They parted, the captains each joining their own beasts; Laurence went first to see how his crew were settled. A folding screen, pilfered in haste from their quarters in the Imperial palace, made at least the illusion of a private space for Mrs. Pemberton and Emily in the corner, although when Laurence tapped and was invited to look in, he discovered that rather in defiance of their respective rôles, Emily had placed herself nearer the open floor, and her hand rested in her sleep upon her unsheathed sword.

Mrs. Pemberton yet sewed by the light of a candle. "Yes," she said ruefully, "I am afraid she insisted, and asked what I would do if someone did choose to come in. As I had no answer to give but that I would certainly raise a cry, she told me I could do that perfectly well from behind her, while she taught the fellow a sharper lesson."

"I am sorry to subject you to such a journey," Laurence said; she had been swept along in their general pell-mell departure, but now he wondered if he ought send her by some escort back to the *Potentate*. He made the offer, but she avowed herself quite willing to endure the hardship.

"Emily has offered to teach me how to shoot her pistols, and to reload them," she said, "and I believe I will take her up on the offer if you have no objections, Captain. Not that I am truly concerned at present, but as I understand it, we expect to be joined by a large force of soldiers?"

"How large," Laurence said dryly, "remains to be seen."

He bowed and took his leave of her, making note to speak to Forthing about arranging some guard of steady and respectable men for the ladies. He had not yet decided what to think of his first officer: it was perhaps the worst of his loss of memory, to have no measure, no sense, of those on whose judgment he had to rely; and he was the more disturbed to have some cause to doubt them. At least Forthing so far seemed steady enough—he was no gentleman, it was true, but that was a charge which many a good officer of the Navy could not answer. But Laurence knew nothing of him in any difficult circumstances, under exigency.

The rest of his men were sleeping on the other side of the folding screen, bundled into rough blankets and bedrolls. O'Dea and a few of the ground crewmen were engaged in a muttered game of cards, their legs stretched out around them and their deck so worn that the faces could scarcely be distinguished.

Baggy was sitting with them; Laurence silently caught him by the ear and drew him up and away, the boy scrambling to his feet wincing and stifling a yelp. "Take his cards, will you, O'Dea?" Laurence said. "Sleep well, men; we will do what we can tomorrow to see you do not have so cramped a time of it."

"Ah," O'Dea said, scooping up the cards, "and two queen in his hand; well, 'tis the wages of sin." He tossed them into the discards. "No call to go to great lengths, Captain, when we are flying into a hive of very iniquitous rebels: the Old Nick can make us dance even if our legs are stiff when we get to him."

The other ground crewmen did not look very enthusiastic about this description of their prospects; Laurence sighed inwardly, but only nodded them good night and hauled Baggy away. "Sir, I didn't think there were no—any harm in it; they're only playing for pence," Baggy said, tipping his head sideways to ease his ear, and trying to peer at Laurence out of the corner of his eye at once.

Laurence let him go at his empty bedroll, near the other officers. "You have been advanced before the mast, as it were," he said, "so I will make allowances this time, Mr.—" He stumbled; he realized he did not even know Baggy's real name. "—sir," he substituted. "But you are an officer now: you cannot sit to cards with the ground crew at night, with men twice and more your age, and then make them give you precedence in the morning. Nothing could be less respectful." He paused, glancing over: Junichiro, who shared quarters with the junior officers, was sitting yet awake on his own bedroll; he was looking steadfastly down at his hands, and pretending not to observe the lecture.

"You will show Mr. Junichiro the ropes," Laurence said abruptly to Baggy, "beginning tomorrow. We will put a little more harness on Temeraire, and you will come aboard, as my servants; I dare say the Chinese cannot object to that. You will take him above and below while we are aloft."

"How am I to learn from *him*?" Junichiro said, with at least some sort of a spark, even if it was of dismay, when Laurence had conveyed this programme to him in Chinese. "He does not know any civilized language, and he is—" Junichiro hesitated, for lack of the word, but Laurence did not require it said aloud: Baggy was indeed not very prepossessing, and no-one could have called him gentleman-like.

"As you must learn English, however uncivilized, before I can seek a commission for you," Laurence said, "that must not be a bar; and Baggy is an officer of the Corps, regardless of his manners. You will sit together on the left shoulder, and inquire of me if you require a translation now and again: you will have to climb over to my position to do so, but it will be as well for you to have that practice." He left them staring at each other, satisfied himself if they were not. At the very least Junichiro would be diverted some more from his desolation, and Baggy from seeking inappropriate society; and Laurence relied on the power of boredom to make them learn to talk to each other eventually, trapped aloft for ten hours at a time: Baggy was a sociable creature, and might with his very lack of sensibility wear down Junichiro's resistance.

A separate inner chamber of the pavilion had been set aside for Temeraire's use; but as he had withdrawn to it with Mei after their dinner, Laurence was far from wishing to interrupt them. He had delayed as long as he might, however, so tentatively he looked inside. To his relief, the two dragons slept already, with their noses only touching; and he found a separate sleeping alcove set aside where his own things had been laid out, the archway leading to it closed off by heavy drapes.

He roused early and found the main chamber empty: going outside he saw Temeraire at some distance from the pavilion, an enormous bulk in the midst of a bare field peering intently at something on the ground; he looked up when Laurence called his name and came towards him. "Pray come and see," he said, "I admire it very much." It was one of the carved numbers, and at this close range Laurence could see the white paint lining the sides of each carved channel had in it a great many silvery flecks, polished to a mirror-shine, which evidently caught whatever starlight or moonlight offered and brightened the characters thereby.

Everyone was awake when they returned to the pavilion, and rousing for the day. "Is there more of that pork, anywhere?" Maximus asked, yawning, his eyes half-open.

"Pork!" General Chu said, when Temeraire ventured to ask him, and snorted disapprovingly. He bounded across the chamber to Maximus and, seizing in his jaws one of the tall reeds from the wall, which carried a banner, thwacked him soundly on the hindquarters.

"Oi!" Maximus said, rousing up, "what does he mean by that? Temeraire, tell that fellow to stop, or I will pin him down."

"Hah! Will he!" General Chu said. "Well, if he is awake, then, tell him to get aloft and stop looking for more food: we will eat tonight, not weight our bellies down for a long day of flying, and if he is sleepy and hungry in the air, perhaps that will remind him to eat more porridge to-night, instead of only gulping meat as though he were a dog. We are on campaign!"

With this rejoinder he put down the reed and stalked outside to make ablutions: a large fountain stood outside gushing from a tall stone pillar, fed somehow from underground; he drank thirstily and deeply from the gush, then thrust his head into the deep pool which it fed, and flinging it back let the water pour off his mane and cascade down his back to the ground. Then he flew some short distance to the nearby midden.

"It don't make any sense to me; we've always stuffed them full as they could hold, when we were going to be doing any long flying, if there was food to be had," Granby said doubtfully, when Laurence asked him his opinion. "But we can't drum them up some pigs from thin air, and I don't see any here, so we must lump it for now whether it's good advice or no."

They followed Chu's example at the fountain, and got themselves aboard again, not without some stifled sighs from the ground crewmen, who could see ahead another day of endless crammed-in flying. "Pray forgive us, Larring," Harcourt said, to her own ground-crew master. "I don't mean to use you all so unkind. While we fly to-day, piece out the spare leather into belt-harnesses for you all, and beginning tomorrow we'll have you take it in turn to latch on to the back harness yourselves. It will be good for the officers to have some exercise climbing about, anyway; it's been too long since we had maneuvers."

She added to Laurence and Granby afterwards, before they themselves mounted, "But it will slow us down, if they have to be clambering all over creation while we fly, with only belt-harness. Will there be any more dragons, any time soon, so we could let the fellows ride?"

That question was answered late that afternoon: beneath them the markers changed, and instead of Peking the name of another city was shown, unfamiliar to them all; General Chu glancing down saw it, and said something to one of the Jade Dragons. The green dragon nodded, with three quick efficient jerks rolled up her banner, handed it on to the second, and wheeling shot away into the upper air and south-easterly, vanishing with almost unbelievable speed.

She returned scarcely an hour later, dropping back into place, and took up her banner again. They flew on another two hours, and as the sun descended Laurence saw in the distance four dragons, three red and a blue, gathered at a marker up ahead. Even as their own company approached, the party leapt aloft to meet them and fell into place off their left flank and slightly above, in a simple arrow-head formation, the blue dragon at the rear and center. The leader, who wore a thin flat band of silver about his neck, bobbed his head respectfully to Temeraire and to Chu, but not a word was said: they all flew onwards together.

Laurence could crane about to peer at them more closely, at least at their underbellies, and could see the other aviators doing so all amongst their company. The three red dragons wore a kind of light armoring, thin hammered plates sewn together and bound very near the skin; it was heaviest at the pockets where the legs met the body, padded a little there. They carried not a single man amongst them; Laurence had seen a few upon their backs, but those were not visible from below, and did not at any time come climbing into view.

The blue dragon, on the other hand, wore no armor but bore a silken carrying-harness, some thirty men aboard in rows down its sides, and long nets between those rows bulged with supplies. It flew a little below the red dragons, and Laurence realized after a time observing that where the three red beat their wings in time, the blue beat his at a pace off-set and quicker, three to each stroke of the larger beasts. "I wonder if it improves his speed," Laurence said.

The next day two more such groups joined them; the day after, another. By the end of the first week, as they crossed the border into the neighboring province, they flew with forty dragons at their back.

Chapter 11

Chu called halts now two hours earlier, and these occurred in staggered fashion: first he landed, and the formation with him, accompanied by one of the four-dragon clusters; the rest of the body flew onwards, and might be observed for some distance ahead landing two groups at a time in sequence, spreading themselves out across a wide territory.

No sooner did these land but the crew were leaping off the blue dragons, bringing with them the packed nets, then the blue dragons all went aloft again and flew off to either side of the course of their flight, returning an hour later with motley supply acquired, Laurence could only guess, at storehouses and villages around them, which all of it went into cooking-vats already prepared by the crew and full of boiling water. Bags of grain formed the largest part of this supply, with only a few oxen or sheep or pigs to leaven the porridge, and there was now no opportunity to pick out the meat: all went into the pot and was cooked an hour, then served out.

"It does not seem right they should all have to work so hard when we only sit and wait," Temeraire said, observing their labors, but Chu, overhearing him, shook his head.

"We are too big to spend our time on supply," he said. "We must save our energies for the heat of battle."

"But it is far more pleasant to do the fighting, and have someone else bring your dinner," Temeraire said. "I do not understand why anyone should agree to do it."

Chu shrugged. "They are paid twice, of course."

"Oh," Temeraire said, with a nearly longing sigh. "Twice?"

"General," Laurence said, listening to their exchange in some surprise; it had not occurred to him that dragons might be paid at all, "might it be possible to bring on a few more such dragons to aid with our own company's supply?"

Chu immediately bowed to him formally and said, "It will be done at once," and vanished off issuing orders before a startled Laurence could even say he had only meant to ask, and not to command. By dawn the next day three more blue dragons had joined their own party, bringing carrying-harnesses, and the much-relieved ground crewmen were given leave to be carried on their backs.

Laurence began to suspect that he had merely given Chu an excuse for what the general must have longed to do: the blue dragons and their crews managed to snatch away all the supply meant to go in the belly-netting while the British dragons were refreshing themselves at the fountain, and they were already packed and waiting expectantly for boarding before anyone had seen what they were about. Harcourt uncertainly said, "Well, I suppose it would be churlish of us to insist they give us back our baggage," and the dragons went aloft with only their officers, with a marked increase in speed.

"I would be glad to be enlightened," Chu said to Temeraire as they flew that day, "why the rest of those men may not go and ride aboard the porters also."

"Well," Temeraire said, "the officers are needed in battle, of course: if we should be attacked by surprise, we would not like to be taken aback."

"Ah," Chu said. "And may I inquire why we are to expect an ambush under the present circumstances?"

This was a fair-enough question. Their company had ceased to grow day by day, but it did not need to grow any further; it was difficult to envision so massive a force meeting with any kind of truly unexpected attack. Laurence had not known what three *jalan* would be, neither had any of them: it was staggering to think that a company of this size might be so casually assembled, and sent to deal with a mere provincial unrest. He did not think he had heard of forty dragons being brought together in England since the Armada.

"We had sixty at Shoeburyness," Granby said that night, over their own helpings of porridge, "during the invasion; and Napoleon brought over a hundred, though he had to send a good number of them back. So it's been done, but not at the drop of a handkerchief, I will say."

It was plainly the substitution of porridge for raw cattle which made so vast a difference in what force could be fielded, Laurence supposed: he would have expected it to take more of a toll on the size and strength of the beasts, but though none of the Chinese soldier-dragons approached the sheer massive bulk of Kulingile or Maximus, they were by no means undersized.

"For my part, I should not mind sending our men onto those porters," Sutton said: Messoria's captain, the oldest of them, and a fellow of much seniority. "I expect Chu would like us all to fly lighter, and I cannot blame him; we are bounding their speed."

Captain Berkley grunted his own agreement, setting down his mug of beer. "I will tell the fellows to strip Maximus bare," he said, "and have them go aboard those blue dragons: I can cling on to a neck-strap well enough by my own solitary self. Do you suppose they will really let us take these beasts, after this rebellion of theirs is put down, only because we've pranced about and waved a sword with them?"

"If so, I would call the help cheap at the price," Sutton said, and all the aviators murmured in agreement. "I would be glad to see Boney's face if we show up on his eastern doorstep with these forty fellows at our backs: a nasty shock for him, I would say, and all the more so with the Army in the Peninsula nipping at him from that side. He won't be looking for us to have so many beasts, not after—"

He halted; the conversation fell into an awkward silence; all eyes turned towards Laurence. Laurence had meant to ask how matters stood in the Peninsula. "You will excuse me, gentlemen; good night," he said instead, and went away from the fireside; shortly their conversation resumed at a louder and a happier pitch behind his back.

He could not blame his fellow-aviators for preferring his absence; their situation was a complex and a precarious one, and they could not be glad for any reminder of the disordered state of his mind when he made so crucial a member of their company. He was uneasy himself; about too many things. He stood in the cool night air, looking out past the fires. They were sheltering this night in an open field, dotted with their handful of tents and the great lumps of the sleeping dragons. At the center of the camp stood the one enormous and—to his mind—absurd silk-draped pavilion erected for Temeraire: a cleverly contrived sheet of wooden shingles sewn together, which could be rolled for carrying; unfolded and stiffened with poles, and mounted on tall shafts, it formed a high roof from which enormous drapes of red silk hung billowing in the wind. It was wreathed also in thin wispy trailers of fog: Iskierka lay not far away, upwind of it, glaring at the elaborate structure and emitting envy and steam together.

Laurence's own tent, a gaudy but more prosaic affair, stood directly beside. At the moment, though, Temeraire and Mei lay entwined within the pavilion still; Laurence could not immediately seek his bed without intruding. He turned aside instead, and went slowly through the avenues of their small encampment, until he saw Hammond's tent on the lee side of a small rise, with Churki sleeping half-curled about it.

"A moment, please, I beg your pardon," Hammond said, rummaging urgently in his packs, which had only just now been delivered him from their luggage; he did not enjoy flying, and had still less enjoyed the last strenuous stretch. "Ah, there." He took out a sheaf of folded and mostly dry leaves, which he moistened with water and put into his mouth to chew. "I ought never have left them with the baggage; those porters took it away, and I have not had a leaf all day. Thank Heavens," he said, lowering himself to sit upon one of the camp-stools. "Forgive me, Captain: what did you say?"

"That I cannot account for it, sir," Laurence said, remaining himself standing. "The size of this force is nothing short of extraordinary. Lord Bayan ought have moved Heaven and earth to keep them from being assigned to my command. He ought have retracted his accusations, and protested, sooner than promoting this expedition in any way.

"I should not like to think he or this General Fela had any cause to believe such a thing," Laurence added, "—that we should be offering aid to these rebels; much less any proof."

"He can have none, none at all," Hammond said, with a firm nod, "and indeed I scarcely know how we are supposed to have managed it: that we should have somehow supplied the wants of a gang of rebels from so distant a position."

"By the sale of opium, as I understand it," Laurence said, watching his face, "shipped to their shores, the profit of which is also meant to be our motive, as little as that ought to answer for any honest man. Mr. Hammond, do our factors in Guangzhou knowingly disregard the prohibition on the importation of this drug?"

He asked it abruptly, half-ashamed to ask; his suspicions, as inchoate and confused as his memories, troubled him. He did not wish to accuse, he did not think any accusation merited.

But, "Oh," said Hammond, with an easy shrug, "no more than you might expect. There is scarcely any market here in China for most of our goods, and enormous markets for their goods in the West: the deficit was quite unmanageable, until opium was introduced. His Majesty's Government was very alarmed by the quantity of specie flowing out at the time, very alarmed indeed; the drug quite reversed the situation.

"Naturally," he said hastily, glancing at Laurence's expression, "naturally, that does not mean—that is, I do not mean at all to say that we are promoting any evasion of the official regulations. Only, there is a certain ebb and flow, in these matters. A limit is established which is excessively severe—it drives prices higher—we make our best efforts to impress it upon the merchantmen—but Captain, you must know it is difficult to make men restrain themselves when they have risked their lives to go around the world, and they can double the profit of their journey by smuggling in a chest or two—"

"Thank you, I have heard enough," Laurence said grimly. "I dare say it is difficult to make men restrain themselves, when you wink at them."

Hammond flushed. "I must reject such a characterization of the work of our factors," he said, "—utterly reject it, Captain; I wish you would not insist on reducing such tangled matters to angels and devils. And in any case," he added, "I do say categorically we have not the least interest in promoting this rebellion: I assure you I myself have scarcely heard of it, save as a piece of distant history; they were put down years before I ever came to my post.

"On that, I am happy to give you my word: and if that does not suffice, sir, I am afraid I cannot satisfy you," Hammond finished defiantly.

Laurence left him without courtesy; he thrust the drape of the tent out of his way and strode out angrily into the darkening camp, voices mostly fallen silent. He was *not* satisfied; he was by no means satisfied. He remembered his vigorous words in the Emperor's chambers, to Mianning himself: they now felt like more than half a lie. He would not have spoken so if Hammond had told him this much beforehand. It had not occurred to him that any representative of the King, or even the officials of the East India Company, would endorse maneuvers so deceitful; and if they would, what more else might they not do? It had not occurred to him—

But after all, it had. Laurence slowed his steps and halted. He had doubted, and felt that doubt gnawing at his belly, when he ought not have. Even now he was merely unhappy; he was not surprised.

He had reached Temeraire's pavilion. Temeraire lay within, Mei beside him, both of them heavily asleep after their dinner and their congress. Laurence stood silently by Temeraire's head, listening to the sighing breath with all its sussurations; he half-wished to wake him, to unburden himself. But Laurence did not feel he could confide in Temeraire with Mei mere paces away; he scarcely wished to speak any of it aloud at all. If Hammond were lying—

Laurence shook his head to himself; no, he would not think so, even in the back of his mind, of a man he had no right to believe vicious. Hammond had spoken to him frankly and then given him his word, when he might as easily have concealed all. But he need not be lying, merely himself unaware. What if there *were* some more vicious and less official plot under way?

Laurence could too-easily imagine opium smugglers, already subtly encouraged by their own government and eager for more profit, might well decide to fuel an internecine conflict to open fresh markets for their wares; and perhaps to undermine the Imperial authority which was too plainly their only real restraint, if they knew the British Government would applaud them so long as they brought back shiploads of silver and gold, regardless how obtained.

In three days' time, they would be in the mountains, hunting for whatever traces might be found of the rebellion. Laurence hoped that they would not find any condemning evidence of British involvement—a wretched, cowering thing to be forced to hope for. But if such a plot were under way, if any proof were to be found, that would destroy any chance of alliance—would condemn them all, and very likely bring Mianning down with them.

Laurence tried to persuade himself he was wrong, that he was unreasonable even to fear; and yet he was unsuccessful. "I would almost wonder if I am fevered," he said, low, "if this is some lingering consequence of the injury to my mind; that I now entertain thoughts of the darkest nature—"

"Captain, I cannot think it at all likely," Mrs. Pemberton said.

Laurence had unburdened himself to her only hesitantly, unsure what counsel she could give him; he could not disclose to her all his thoughts. He could not confide any particulars to her which should in any way tend to discredit their country. He had said nothing of opium, nothing of smugglers, nothing of the accusation that British plotters might support the rebellion; he spoke only in the most general terms, and of his own mind.

But he had begun lately to find her company a balm against his own confusion of mind and spirit: a relief from questions and from the anxious tension of his fellow-officers; her conversation a welcome change from the constrained silence that fell upon the others so often. Her cool and sensible nature was itself a worthy solace, but better than that, she was no close connection of his own; she had been employed for Emily's protection only a little more than a year, and they had not been intimates previously, his own time preoccupied by his duties and his fellow-officers his true companions.

She said, "I cannot speak with very much authority on your past; however, sir, I will speak for your present: you are a rational man, and if you have fears, they are founded on sensible causes. I do not mean to say you may not be mistaken: certainly you may, and you speak in such forboding terms to make me hope you are, whatever it is you fear; but you are not in the least given to building castles in the air.

"I am no physician," she continued, "but I have had to do a great deal of nursing in my life; and I have seen illness and injury alter a man's character or a woman's to no little extent. But not in such a wise that you would appear yourself in every other respect, act according to your former character at all times, and remain competent, save in this one particular instance. That, I must find too remarkable to believe—I am sorry if that opinion should distress you, in this circumstance, more than please you."

He was silent; she was not wrong, that was the heart of it. He would willingly have heard himself called a lunatic to find his fears unfounded. "I must always value your honest opinion," Laurence said, "whatever its conclusions; I thank you, sincerely, and for imposing on you in such a manner."

"There is no imposition felt, Captain Laurence, I assure you," she said, and looked up as footsteps came: a moment later, Emily had put her head around the corner of the folding-screen to see them sitting outside the tent, before the fire.

"Oh," she said, "Captain, I didn't know you were here; did you want me for something? I have just been over at the next fire over those rocks: and you needn't frown, Alice, they are all girls there."

"Oh, dear," Mrs. Pemberton said, with a sigh.

"Not that sort!" Emily said. "I mean soldiers: more than half of them on the dragons are girls. Not just the captains, though some of them, too; but nearly all those fellows who manage the baggage. I dare say we ought to just bunk in with them instead of perching out here away from everything."

For safety, their campfire had been established at the very edge of camp; their tent was of double thickness and sheltered further by the folding-screen: Laurence had solicited a pair of pistols, from the aviators, for Mrs. Pemberton, and had shown her how to send up a flare, if need be.

Laurence stared at Emily. "Do you mean to tell me half their army is women?" he demanded, to his dismay recalling he had without the least consciousness stripped and bathed at several of their previous nightly halts, in full view of Chinese companies. "Are the dragons so insistent upon it?"

"It's not the beasts at all," Emily said. "They tell me they can come instead of their brothers, if their families like, so they don't have to spare the boys from the fields."

"Well," Laurence said, helplessly. He found it difficult to accept, and yet he was no pot to be calling names for kettles: if not his daughter, then a young woman under his tutelage was in the service; he could scarcely condemn those families, if it were the accepted mode. But he should have to tell Forthing and also his fellow-captains at once: if the men should work out they were surrounded by an encampment full of young women, they would surely run riot and make nuisances of themselves, given half an opportunity.

"Are they willing," he began to ask, and then Emily leapt at him, in one straight bound across the small campfire, and knocked him to the ground as a sharp blade thrust down through the air towards him.

Emily rolled away from him, and came up drawing her sword; Mrs. Pemberton with a cry had fallen back upon the tent. Laurence drew his own sword: five men were descending upon them, drawn metal gleaming in firelight. Their sabers were peculiarly workmanlike: a wide blade at the tip and tapering to the hilt, and they wore black that made them almost invisible against the dark; one scattered the fire with the end of his sword, stamping out embers. Laurence swung a wide circle leaping forward to press them back, and seized one still-burning branch; he thrust it towards the nearest man's eyes and then fell back with Emily, putting the tent at their backs before the men closed in.

The steady rhythm of sword-strokes occupied his next moments to the exclusion of thought: no room for anything but answering to one strike and another. He and Emily had the reach of them, their own blades the longer and the better, but they were outnumbered. She fought well at his side, matching his pace. There was a brief opening; he shouted, "Ho, the camp!" at the top of his lungs, "Murder!" and they were fighting again.

Laurence bent to parry low, and only just in time brought his sword back up to catch a slash meant for his throat. Another did catch him in the shoulder, but he wrested himself away before he felt more than the tip scoring his flesh; he heard the thick wool ripping away around the blade, and dropping the burning brand managed to reach up and wrench the blade away from the man's grip.

But he was forced to pay for it: the third man, on his left flank, lunged for Laurence's exposed side with two knives in his hands, feinting one at his eyes. Laurence turned to slash back, but Emily was there, her sword flying upwards, and she sheared away the man's hand halfway to the elbow, blood spurting from the stump; she reversed her grip on the blade and jammed it brutally through his chest, and booted his corpse off with a shove of her foot into the other standing beside him.

Now there were four: Laurence whirling back struck one of the men upon the bridge of his nose with the pommel of the short sword he had taken, and then ripped the man's throat with the blade as his head tipped back.

A pistol-crack came jumping-loud from over his shoulder, deafening in his ear; Laurence felt a few hot flecks of burning powder on his chin, and saw a thin thread of smoke rise from his sleeve; a hole stood in the chest of the man on Emily's left. Mrs. Pemberton stood pale with the smoking pistol in her hands a moment, then she let it fall and reached to raise the other from the pocket of her skirt; Emily, turning, snatched it from her hands and shot another.

"Captain!" a shout came, "Captain Laurence—" and a young man, his personal servant Ferris, came scrambling over the rocks; Forthing was on his heels.

The last attacker looked at the corpses of his fellows and the approaching men; Laurence caught for his arm, but too late. The man turned his blade inwards and throwing himself away fell upon it; when Laurence turned him over with his foot, his eyes beneath the sooty mask were staring blind and dead.

"Good God," Ferris said panting, coming to a halt; he held a pistol, which he carefully uncocked and put back onto his waist. "You are not hurt, sir, I hope?"

"Nothing to signify," Laurence said, looking at Emily, who did not show blood anywhere. He was a little torn: surely it ought to have been his own duty to shield her from danger, and yet in the moment he had not the least difficulty classing her with himself as a combatant, and he could not help taking a degree of pride in her skill and courage; she had been as resolute a fighter as he could have wished at his side. "Ma'am, I trust you are well?"

"I must be," Mrs. Pemberton said, though she had not let a tight grip on Emily's arm. "I am perfectly untouched; only, very shaken. Emily—"

"It takes you so, the first time," Emily said to her, consolingly. "Pray don't give it a thought; that was a very pretty shot. What? Oh! No, I am fine; they didn't get a touch on me. They scarcely tried: I don't think they cared a lick about the two of us; they meant to kill the captain."

"And it will be wonderful, at this rate," Iskierka said with mean satisfaction, "if these assassins do not get their way, when you are always busy making up to this Imperial flirt of yours, and paying no attention."

Temeraire would have hissed her down, but he hardly could; wretched guilt silenced him. He ought have been there; no assassin ought ever have been able to get so close to Laurence. "Only," he said unhappily, "Laurence ought to have been asleep—or at least, safe within the camp; I do not understand how he ever came to be so exposed."

He clawed the dirt of the clearing; whyever had he gone to sleep without seeing Laurence properly settled? He thought Laurence had only gone to have supper with the other captains; Laurence had told him to rest and be comfortable—surely Temeraire ought have been able to rely on him. Laurence could not have imagined Temeraire would be in the least comfortable, knowing that Laurence was endangering himself.

Iskierka snorted. "It is easy to say, he *ought* to have been asleep: he wasn't, he was nearly being stuck with swords," she said. "I

226

don't see that you should be blaming him, when you didn't take the trouble to look out for him properly. You may be sure, Granby," she added, "if you ever are a prince, I will not begin to neglect you; not that I am very sorry anymore that you are not, since all it would mean is that people were always trying to kill you."

"Come, dear one, pray don't stir up Temeraire," Granby said, coming from the tents. "Temeraire, there's no harm done: Laurence hasn't a scratch."

"He does too have a scratch," Temeraire said, "—upon his shoulder; and his coat has been ruined. Whatever was he doing so far from the pavilion?"

"You cannot go calling a mere pinprick a scratch," Granby said, "and I am sure we will put him in the way of a new coat, soon enough. He went out there to have a word with Roland, that's all."

But Laurence had *not* gone out to speak with Emily. "Why, I wasn't there," Emily said, when Temeraire asked her later, as they packed for resuming their flight, what had been so urgent as to induce Laurence to go so far upon the outskirts of camp. "I only came upon them later; I suppose he wanted to talk to Alice. Mrs. Pemberton, I mean," she added.

"What?" Churki said, lifting her head up abruptly from her sniffing over the packs, and ruffling up the feathers of her collar. "What is he doing with Mrs. Pemberton?"

"Lord, *I* don't know," Roland said. "He likes to talk to her, I suppose because she's a gentlewoman; you know he is ever such a stickler."

"Hrmmr," Churki said, frowning, but then she smoothed down her feathers. "Well," she said to Temeraire, "I do not have a *real* claim, and I suppose Laurence is older; although I *had* thought of her for Hammond. But I do not mean to interfere," she said, as though making a handsome concession.

"Interfere with what?" Temeraire said, in alarm. "Whatever do you mean? I am sure Laurence does not think of her like *that,* at all—"

227

"Why should he not?" Churki said. "She is a hearty young woman: she might bear him children for twenty years, if they begin quickly. Certainly they should neither of them wait any longer; a man should begin to have children at twenty, in *my* opinion, and a woman at sixteen."

Temeraire stalked away from them and back to the pavilion. "I do not see why she must always be on about Laurence marrying," he complained in some irritation to Mei, who very kindly put aside the poetry she was reading to comfort his distress. "Laurence has quite enough to do, as it is. He has his crew to oversee, and there is the war, which we must contrive to win; and when that is done, there will be our valley, and I dare say I will find him another fortune, sooner or later, which he will have to manage. I do not see that he at all ought to marry."

"Well," Mei said, "if he is not married already, certainly he ought not without the Emperor's approval, and the choice must be carefully made. There is no call for a prince to marry in haste; concubines may suffice him quite well."

"Aren't those a sort of whore?" Temeraire said, doubtfully. "I know Laurence does not hold with visiting those—"

"No, no," Mei said, "a concubine, bound to him and him alone; surely that woman who travels with you, who is under guard by your young soldier, is one of his?"

Temeraire flattened down his ruff. "No!" he said. "That is Mrs. Pemberton; she is Emily's chaperone, and why we must needs have brought her along, I am sure I do not in the least know! Laurence hasn't any concubine, at all."

"What, none?" Mei said, staring at him with her eyes widening.

"No," Temeraire said, suddenly wary.

"None!" Mei cried. "Prince Mianning has seven: one has borne him a promising boy of four already, with another child coming soon. However is he to have heirs?"

So Temeraire spent the day's flight in high dudgeon, speaking to no-one. Why would everyone see Laurence married? He did not see that it was anyone's concern, other than his own. "You are quite well, Laurence?" he asked, turning his head around. "Are you certain you are not feverish, and warm through?"

"I am perfectly comfortable, I thank you," Laurence said, tiredly, and fell silent again. They had searched the camp through and searched again, of course, all the rest of the night and in the early hours of the morning, looking for any trace of the assassins—whence they had come, what their purpose, but without a trace at all.

By the end, General Chu had shrugged and said he supposed the men were mere outlaws, having made the attempt only to get at Mrs. Pemberton and Emily. Which was perfect nonsense: Emily was quite a remarkable young officer, but Temeraire did not see that there was anything out of the ordinary about Mrs. Pemberton, nor why anyone should have gone to particular lengths to get at her.

"I must suppose," Laurence had said to him and to Hammond, after they had given up the futile search, when morning light at last coming had uncovered nothing more of use, "that this is another endeavour of the conservative faction."

"I will make the argument, sir, if I may," Hammond had said to Laurence with a somewhat stiff tone, "that *this* explains their willingness to permit this expedition. To separate you from the Imperial court, exposed to such blatant attempts as these upon your life which their partisans may nevertheless easily explain away, must be sufficient good in their eyes, and preclude the notion that they must have some *real* complaint to make.

"I suppose," he added, "that we may expect more of these assaults, when we have reached camp: General Fela is, we know already, one of their partisans; and they must rely on your death, in severing the one formally acknowledged tie between our nations, to remove the impulse to alliance."

"Then we ought not go any further," Temeraire had said, in high alarm. "We ought to return at once to the court; and then I *will* squash Lord Bayan, and that will put a stop to these assassination attempts."

But Hammond had protested at once, and Laurence shook his head as well. "Prince Mianning has had the right of it: the reward we seek is proportionate to the risk we run," he said. "An alliance between our nations might well change the course of the war and the fortunes of all Europe, if not the world entire: we cannot give up the chance of it merely for a personal fear. This force alone, if we can bring it to bear smartly, may well make the difference between victory and defeat."

He had gone to sleep then in his tent having been awake all the night; and now when Temeraire glanced back towards him, Laurence had drifted once more to sleep again. Temeraire wished he had made Laurence promise to keep close to him at all times henceforth, and in particular not to go speak with Mrs. Pemberton again: when Laurence woke, he would discuss it with him, perhaps. He was only not entirely certain how to open the conversation: he shied from the thought that Laurence might object, might dislike the request.

"Temeraire," Baggy said, calling out to him through cupped hands, "be a good fellow: will you tell me how to say 'spend the night with me'?"

Temeraire obliged him, but asked, "But why should you need to ask Junichiro that? You are already quartered together."

"No, no," Baggy said hurriedly, "I didn't mean to ask him; I don't mean to ask anyone; I was only curious."

"He means to ask one of those soldier-women, I suppose," Junichiro said, contemptuously, "in defiance of your captain's orders: a shameful lack of discipline."

"Oh!" Temeraire said. "I dare say he is right; what are you about?"

"What did he say?" Baggy said, eyeing Junichiro doubtfully.

"That you mean to pester the Chinese soldiers," Temeraire said, "even though you know very well Laurence has said not to."

"I don't!" Baggy said, with a quick furtive look over at Laurence, who yet slept. "Only we are coming up on a city, and I dare say there will be a girl or two about; that is all. And what business is it of *yours*," he hissed, to Junichiro.

Temeraire had been drifting himself, with more attention to the air currents than to the landscape; now he looked ahead. There was a blue smudged haze on the horizon, a long narrow blot. "That is Xian," General Chu said, peering ahead, "and we have all made good time, I see."

"We all?" Temeraire said, and squinted. There were five small clouds converging upon the city—clouds which might each of them have been a flock of birds. "Baggy, perhaps you might wake Laurence," he said uncertainly.

Baggy clambered carefully over to rouse Laurence; Junichiro was standing in his own straps, his eyes shaded with one hand, staring. Laurence came awake at once and opened his long spyglass; he gazed through it in silence. "Yes," Laurence said finally. "Those are dragons. Temeraire, will you ask Chu if those companies are coming to join us?"

They were all nearing the walls of Xian, at almost the same pace; already Temeraire could make out the long banners flying before each of them, and the steady rhythmic beat of the wings: each one a company the size of their own.

"Of course; did the Emperor not command three *jalan* attend to this task?" Chu answered over his shoulder, absently; he himself was eyeing the companies on their way, critically. "But Commander Li is a couple of *niru* short, I see. Well, we will recruit them from the city outpost here: it is good for fat guardsmen to get a little exercise."

That evening, Temeraire looked down from an enormous pavilion, established upon the fortified city wall: two hundred dragons and more sleeping beneath him, many in other pavilions, some draped over the walls, others on the open ground at their base; several of the companies had gone to encamp some distance from the city, and their fires might be seen dotting the low hills. Laurence stood beside him, a hand upon his foreleg, with Forthing near-by and Ferris also; scarcely any man of the aviators had said a word, since the company had assembled.

"I understand from General Chu that we leave early on the morrow, Mr. Forthing," Laurence said finally. "Pray encourage the men to go to their sleep, if you please, and let us get those camp-followers out of the pavilion; they will never get any rest otherwise."

"Yes, sir," Forthing said, touching his hat; he lingered looking for a moment more, and turned away.

"We cannot reach the mountains in less than another week, I suppose," Temeraire said to Laurence, trying for nonchalance: he felt a little daunted, though he did not like to admit it, by the size of their assembled force. "We must be a little slower, with so—so very many dragons."

"I imagine so," Laurence said, soberly. He gave Temeraire's flank a pat and sought his own bed, and Temeraire settled himself; the only one left awake was Junichiro, who was standing half-hidden against one of the pavilion columns, nearly at the edge, still looking down at the great crowd of dragons. "You had better go to sleep also," Temeraire said, yawning. "Not that you are doing anything much, but you will have to get up and go aloft, anyway."

Junichiro said, low, "I have never heard of so many dragons gathered."

"Well," Temeraire said, glad to exchange his own private surprise for authority, "of course China is a very large country, and they know dragon-breeding very well here, and dragon-husbandry. There is really nothing very unusual in the size of this force; it is nothing to be amazed at, after all, when there are so many dragons here. I dare say the Emperor could call together an army ten times the size, if he liked."

Junichiro was quiet again; Temeraire half-shut his eyes and had just begun to drift off comfortably, before Junichiro abruptly asked, "That transport ship we came upon, the large one—how many are there, in Britain?"

"Well, we captured two French, only last year," Temeraire said, "so I think we are up to twenty; they take a good deal of building." He yawned again, pointedly, but Junichiro did not take the hint, and only kept standing there; and then Gong Su came climbing up the stairs from the ledge below, and bowed. "I hope I am not intruding, Lung Tien Xiang; I only wished to see that you and His Highness have everything you might require, and that you are satisfied with our preparations, and the humble force under your command."

Temeraire sighed; he could hear Maximus snoring away behind him, and he was very ready to go to sleep himself. "Yes, there is nothing wanting, thank you very much," he said politely, however. "I understand we will be leaving very early in the morning? It is very kind of you to look in on us, but I am sure you should be asleep as well: Laurence has already gone to bed.

"And if you have any questions," Temeraire said to Junichiro, hitting upon the notion to divert him, "I am sure Gong Su can tell you anything you would like to know, about the *jalan;* I was only just telling him," Temeraire added, "that of course, this is not an exceptionally large force: that China has so many dragons, that one cannot really be astonished."

Gong Su looked at Junichiro thoughtfully. "Indeed. If you are interested in such matters," he said to that young man, "perhaps I will speak with His Highness. There might be a place for you in the service of the crown prince: it may well be that relations with your nation will at some point assume a closer character than at present, and I do not believe we have very many officials with knowledge of your tongue."

Junichiro paused, then bowed. "I am honored by your consideration, but I cannot think of leaving the service of Captain Laurence."

"As you wish," Gong Su said, and made his good nights, retiring formally and disappearing again down the stairs; Temeraire meanwhile had roused up again to eye Junichiro doubtfully.

"I cannot see why you would say such a thing, when you have not the least interest in doing anything, or even learning English: it seems to me you would do very well to stay here and help the crown prince, if he means to make better friends with your country."

"China is no friend of my country," Junichiro said flatly, and looking one last time down at the immense dragon-horde below turned and vanished into the back of the pavilion, to bed down amongst the other officers.

They woke early and the aviators breakfasted only lightly; there was nothing but a bit of porridge for them, and water for the dragons. "I cannot conceive how such a force is to be supplied or maintained at all," Laurence said to Temeraire, as he went up again. "We must surely strip the countryside bare as we go."

But as they all began to go aloft, several dragons of varying colors in green-and-gold trappings took up positions throughout the flying armada, and raised a strident chant to which the larger dragons all matched their wingbeats: they began at once to set a grueling pace, greater by far than their speed before. Temeraire had not been hard-pressed so far, during all their journey. Even now, of course, he was not at all *struggling,* but he had to keep his head down and think about every stroke to keep up their speed.

Before the sun had reached its zenith, they had covered a hundred miles of distance, Laurence told him: they were flying nearly fifteen knots. Temeraire would not at all have minded a pause for rest or drink or food, but none was called, and he did not at all mean to be the one to propose it. General Chu himself did not seem to be having any difficulties, and he was a great deal older. Poor Maximus and Kulingile were both of them having a bad time of it, however, and late in the afternoon Berkley raised signal-flags to say he was dropping behind, and would catch them up shortly. He signaled Demane, too, to keep with him; the two huge dragons sank towards the ground. Temeraire privately would not have minded at all stopping to rest with them, if only he could have thought of a way to suggest it, between one wingbeat and the next.

The mountains grew before them all afternoon. In the foothills, as they drew near at last in the late evening, Temeraire glimpsed below a supply depot prepared for them, surely over weeks: pens holding cattle and swine, and enormous granaries; oh, how he would have delighted in a cow, that very moment. The very thought of the sweet gush of juicy blood upon his tongue made his ruff prick forward for a moment.

Their force, he abruptly realized, was breaking apart again into smaller parties, three or four groups splitting away from the main body at one time, the blue dragons diving to take up some supplies from the pens below, and each such company then vanishing into the craggy mountains, to some ledge or cavern or hidden valley. They overflew a few of them already busy making camp, and Temeraire was wondering how much further it would be to their own, when at last they came over a ridge and saw outspread below the bowl of a valley full of tents, and in the middle of an open landing ground several men in armor, one of them in the lead with a splendid cloak, and with them a large wooden chest.

The Jade Dragons with their banners had already landed, and disposed of themselves to either side of the landing grounds; General Chu was stooping towards them. Temeraire came to earth beside him, making a great effort to descend gracefully, easily, as though he were not in the least tired; but he *was* glad to fold his wings. And then General Chu said sharply, "What is that smoke coming from, there to the west?"

The man in the cloak bowed low and said, "Honored General Chu, we have this very morning destroyed a stronghold of the rebels: and if those in your company are British, we gladly await their explanation for *this*."

He turned and beckoned: the chest, nearly six feet long, was carried forward; Temeraire saw to his surprise it was a sea-chest, the front painted with a banner reading LYDIA. They flung the lid open, and inside to the very lip was loose sackcloth, and the chest was heaped with large round balls, wrapped in faded brown petals. "What is that?" Temeraire said over his shoulder, to Laurence, who was gazing down upon it with a hard and grim expression.

"Opium," Laurence said.

Chapter 12

General Fela was young for his rank, but his hands and his face were those of a man who had spent his life not in drawing rooms but in the field, hardened and sword-callused and leathery with sun; his mustaches and his queue were trimmed to an efficient length. His pistol-belt and swords all of them showed heavy use.

He led the way personally up through the silent ruins of the village: a small creeping terraced place, ancient and clinging to the mountain-side, grey stone mortared to make the walls and steps of the narrow lanes that wound between the houses. The door of the largest house stood thrust open, and blood spattered the floor; the bodies had been removed. Laurence followed Fela and his soldiers inside, grimly, and stood looking in the courtyard: two dozen chests and more, stacked upon one another to the height of a man's head.

"We followed a British dragon to this place," Fela said, coldly, "bearing more such chests. The guilty culprits fled before our approaching forces, however, and left their allies to their destruction."

Laurence looked at Hammond, who did not answer, but only stood in pallid silence.

They went back out through the village. The attack had evidently come in the early hours before dawn, and the town had been brutally punished for its support of the rebels: cattle and goods stripped, citizenry put to the sword. The streets echoed emptily beneath their boot-heels, and the doors stood open, ruined.

A poor mountain village, worth nothing to anyone but its citizens; and now all of those were dead. Laurence could see the marks of talons and jaws, where roofs had been ripped away, walls torn down; and through one gaping hole as he walked along the dusty, smooth-cobblestoned lane he saw a cradle, empty and overturned, blackened with smoke. Laurence was not unused to blood nor to brutality; God knew he had seen more than enough men dead, falling corpses into the ocean or hacked apart with saber and cannonfire. And yet when he stood looking over the empty and ruined village, his stomach twisted wrenchingly with disgust: a passionate horror.

"Was there more opium there?" Temeraire asked, from where he stood nearly upon the outskirts of the village, leaning anxiously over the roofs.

"Yes," Laurence said shortly. "Twenty thousand pounds' worth, or near to it; a monstrous amount."

"Oh?" Iskierka suddenly raised her head. "Is opium worth so much? I have never heard that, before. What do they mean to do with it, now that they have taken it?"

"Burn it," Laurence said.

"*That* seems a great waste," she said, in disgruntled tones.

"I cannot—I cannot by any means account for it," Hammond said, in much agitation, when they had returned to the encampment.

The British party had been directed to establish themselves on the western side of the valley, separated pointedly from the rest of the forces by a wide furrowed line of open dirt, with sentries posted along it and a dozen of the red dragons encamped surrounding them. "To do honor to the prince, and to Lung Tien Xiang, and ensure none should trouble them," Fela had said, coldly, paying lip service to the fiction of Laurence's command.

"I thank you," Laurence had said, and did not argue; he was himself savagely angry. Across the camp, Chu was directing that his own pavilion be raised up at the farthest point from theirs, beside Fela's tent.

Their baggage had been heaped carelessly at the boundary, and the cauldrons of porridge: not a generous allotment of the last, particularly when Maximus and Kulingile dragged at last into the camp; the dragons were snappish and sharp at one another over the pots. Spent from their long and arduous flight, however, they were too weary to quarrel long; the porridge was eaten quickly, and they all collapsed into sleep almost at once.

Hammond's tent had been put up near the center of their encampment, surrounded for privacy by the tents and pavilions of their own men; Churki slept now half-circled round it, the steady heaving of her side gently swelling the back panel of the tent.

"It will be a wretched mess, if we have to fight our way out of this," Catherine Harcourt said to Laurence, low, as they ducked inside Hammond's tent together, with the other captains. "If those twelve can hold us long enough for any reinforcements to come up, which I suppose is what they are thinking, we will be sunk. Our only chance will be to bull out through them as quickly as we can—Lily in the middle, Temeraire and Iskierka on her either flank, one pass to clear out anyone before us, and then they give way to Maximus and Kulingile, and we all fall in behind the two of them and make due west. How we are to contrive to win home, with no supply—"

"Pray keep your voice down!" Hammond said. "There can be no call to begin planning so disastrous a course. I grant you the circumstances are awkward—"

"Awkward!" Harcourt said. "Hammond, we are landed in the middle of the largest aerial army of which I have ever heard tell, and now they are only waiting for word that they may put us to the sword and claw."

"Word that will not come," Hammond said. "It is preposterous, the idea that we should have provided opium to these rebels—that we should have somehow delivered it here." He blotted his forehead with the back of his hand and looked around his tent, anxiously. "Where are—ah." He dug after his pouch of leaves. "I assure you," he said, folding over a hunk of crumbling leaves with hands that shook, "there must be a misunderstanding. In the morning, I will consult with Lung Qin Mei—we will draft a reply. There are any number of possible explanations. Perhaps these rebels meant to sell opium in order to fund their efforts; it does not follow that *we* must have been involved in their crimes."

"And I suppose," Laurence said, reaching the end of his temper, "that this ragged band of rebels have somehow contrived in their small and impoverished territory to acquire the funds to purchase so enormous a supply?"

He rose to his feet; Hammond stepped back from him, warily. "What use do you imagine it will be to defend ourselves against other charges, when we have already been proven so demonstrably false?" Laurence said. "Twenty chests of Indian opium, of the same make, packed together and certainly from a single British ship. This is no private, no individual endeavor; this was not concealed from the eyes of our factors. This is no secret winking. This is deliberate, orchestrated defiance of the law, and our guilt *there* is undeniable."

Laurence was grimly aware that a courier had already flown for the Imperial City with the news of this latest discovery. He would be obliged to follow it with his own; he would have to make excuses, to scrape and connive at justification. He would have to let Hammond put falsehoods into his mouth, or see his men and fellow-officers condemned, his country-men in Guangzhou chased out, all hope of alliance ruined. And he could scarcely see any hope for averting that fate even if he did all this.

"You have made me a liar, and yourself," he said, bitterly, and stalked from the tent.

Outside the last of the tents had gone up, and the night had gone quiet: the quiet of a prison camp. The ground crewmen and the junior officers were sitting wearily at their fires, supping on the remnants of the provided food. Several knots of officers stood looking across the boundary line at the rest of the camp and the twelve red dragons drowsing along it: not with more caution than was deserved.

Granby ducked out of the tent and joined him, watching them. "Laurence, I don't mean to tell you not to be angry: this is a rotten hole for us to have been put into, all because some fellows in Guangzhou want to line their pockets," he said, after a moment. "But there's a stink to this all around. Fela hasn't told all the truth, either."

Laurence looked at him. Granby said, "Where is this British dragon supposed to have come from, that he says was lugging these chests? It's the sort of thing he might imagine: I dare say all their merchants ship goods dragon-back, here. We don't; we haven't any merchant dragons. Even our courier-beasts don't come to China: we can scarcely get one to India four times a year."

"And yet those chests are from Guangzhou, and from a British ship," Laurence said slowly. "They were conveyed here somehow."

"I suppose so," Granby said, "but they weren't brought by a British dragon, and if Fela says they were, he's a bare-faced liar."

"I beg your pardon; I am distracted," Laurence said, to Mrs. Pemberton: she had spoken to him, and he had not attended, for the lingering turmoil in his mind. "Thank you, tea would be most welcome."

He had not slept easily or well. The ruined village lingered in his mind, in his dreams; he saw again and again the cracked stone houses, the mill fallen silent, the walls blackened with smoke and the claw-marks standing pale against them. Again and again he had walked through the street, hearing somewhere distantly the roar of dragons, with a strange and dreadful sense of familiarity: perhaps because it might almost have been an English village, a village of Nottinghamshire on his own father's estates, pillaged so and broken. He had woken unsettled, cloudy.

The day stood before him without direction. He had still the charge, in theory, of finding this rebellion and putting it down, but it was hard to imagine how he ought to carry that out. His command had never been more than a nominal fiction, and if Chu's sympathies had not been with Lord Bayan and the conservative faction from the beginning, they were surely fixed in that direction now.

He had contemplated crossing the camp to Chu's pavilion and speaking with him. "I hope you will pardon me, Captain," Hammond had said, cool and formal with him after the previous day's reproof, "but I must urge against it. Let us not forget the attempts upon your life. In the present—difficulties—your death would surely be the cap to the efforts to sever relations between our nations. I must ask you to remain within the camp."

Hammond had spent the rest of the morning in Temeraire's pavilion, drafting the letter to the Emperor, with Mei offering him advice on the choice of argument and phrase. Mei had regarded the chests of opium with a stony expression as they were brought out of the ruined village, and afterwards had curled herself to sleep without any word to Temeraire, or any of them; but at least she had remained in his pavilion. She had met Hammond's request for assistance that morning without pleasure, but with a nod of her head.

She had as little choice as he did, Laurence supposed: the conservative faction would surely try to use this to topple the crown prince, if they could, and certainly to undermine his plans for modernization. But to her, the British could be now nothing more than a gang of ruffians, smuggling poison into her nation and conniving at treason; she could scarcely have liked any better than Laurence did, to attempt to defend their acts.

But Hammond had written the letter; she had helped him; Laurence had signed his name to it, and one of the Jade Dragons had borne it away. Then they had all three of them retired, separately: Hammond, with a short bow, to his tent; Mei curled into a corner of the pavilion in pointed silence. Laurence had gone to see Mrs.

Pemberton settled: he had ordered that her tent be pitched as near Temeraire's pavilion and his own as possible, and had begged the most reliable men from the other captains' crews to stand guard.

She gave him a cup of tea: to his surprise, with milk. "There are some sheep down there below," she said, with a ghost of a smile, "and Emily has made several acquaintances amongst the young women. They were kind enough to find us a milch one and liberate her. The ewe is picketed down that crevasse, over there, so she needn't be troubled by seeing the dragons, poor creature. The flavor is not quite right, but at least it is something."

She had also somehow assembled and kept a service, though a small and motley one: her two cups were now the handle-less Chinese sort, and the saucers wide and smooth; the sugar bowl was of Portuguese make, evidently acquired in Brazil; the teapot, plain earthenware, had been given her by the American merchant in Nagasaki. She stirred her cup with a chop-stick inverted, and her hands did not shake, though she looked still drawn: it had been only three days since the attack, and those full of wearisome travel.

"I find nothing wanting, I assure you," Laurence said. "I hope you are recovered?"

"I would be ashamed to be anything else," she said, "when I was of so little use, and in less danger. I hope I am not so poor-spirited as that."

"More than a little, of both danger and use, ma'am, I must protest," Laurence said. "But I am glad if you are well."

She drew a breath and sighed, then looked away across the camp. "May I confess something to you, Captain?" she said. "I hope it will not make you very angry, but I should like to clear the air, on my side—I should like to be quite frank."

Laurence paused and set down his cup upon his knee. "By all means; I hope you need never even ask, to speak so," he said.

"I was shocked, very shocked, when I first understood Emily's position," Mrs. Pemberton said, "when I first knew she was an officer. I thought it the most outrageous thing I had ever heard, to see a mere girl imposed upon in such a manner, from childhood; and I must admit, sir, I thought—I assumed—she was surely imposed upon in the other manner, as well."

"I cannot reproach you," Laurence said grimly. "What else is anyone to imagine, who knows a little of the world?"

She nodded. "If she had given me the least encouragement, I should have taken her away with me at the first opportunity—the first ship we met—and laid suit in court to see her respectably established," she said. "I was quite ready to name you a villain, and all the Corps with you."

Laurence looked at her in surprise, and some respect; he could not fault her impulse, even if he knew it could hardly have found a less willing object. "*That* encouragement," he said, "I know very well you did not receive."

"No," she said. "She quite abused me for an idiot."

She laughed and exchanged a rueful glance with Laurence, who could well imagine the nature of Emily's reaction, and her scornful answer; she had griped to him often enough, in only the last month, about being saddled with a chaperone at all.

"And now instead I must say I do increasingly see the justice of her complaint," Mrs. Pemberton said, "though I would be sorry to lose my post; I cannot see that I am of the least use to her."

She fell silent, and after a pause quietly added, "I dare say I would not at all like to be an aviator. But there is nothing quite so unpleasant as to find oneself so wholly dependent on another's protection, in such dreadfully visceral circumstances. I would cheerfully have exchanged a life of hard service to be able in that moment to defend myself."

Laurence offered her his handkerchief; she waved it away, and drew out her own to press to her eyes briefly. "I beg your pardon," she said, "and I am done with being a watering-pot. I will have Emily teach me to fence, if I can learn; and oh! I am sorry now I sold my husband's guns after he died, for I would be happy indeed to have a pair of pistols of my own."

"I should be happy to be of service to you in the matter," Laurence said, "when we next have the opportunity."

"Thank you, Captain," she said. "I would be grateful."

He took his leave of her to return to his own tent, pausing when he saw Temeraire standing watching him, his tail lashing in so uncontrolled a manner as to threaten the supports of his pavilion. "Is there something wrong?" Laurence asked him, in some concern; Granby had given him to understand that the danger he had been under was likely to provoke some long repercussions of watchfulness and anxiety, but Temeraire could hardly suppose him to be in danger from a conversation with Mrs. Pemberton.

"Oh!" Temeraire burst out. "Do you *wish* me to stay in China, then, and let you go away from me, so you *may* be married, and have as many children as you like, and a house again?"

Laurence stared, astonished and bewildered. "What?" he said.

Temeraire was nearly trembling with resentment and indignation, which Laurence could scarcely understand. "*Her,*" Temeraire said. "Whyever are you always speaking with her, and going to her tent? And why has her tent been moved so close to your own?"

"Do you mean Mrs. Pemberton?" Laurence said, in no diminished confusion. "She is under my protection, and was lately abused by ruffians—" He stopped, helplessly: he had not expected to find jealousy in a dragon, and still less so much imagination. "Do you—I beg your pardon, have you any reason for supposing I mean to marry her?" he asked, in sudden alarm. "Had I—before my loss of memory, had I—had I made her any promises, or expressed to you any intentions, in that quarter—"

"Oh! None at all," Temeraire said, "but what does that signify, when you are so dreadfully altered, and everyone thinks you should marry; even Mei does, even if she does not call it marriage. She thinks you ought take a concubine, and *ten* of them at that."

"I may confidently promise you to do no such thing," Laurence said, much relieved and beginning to be half-amused, "and I have not the least notion why anyone should concern themselves with my marriage, save myself and my nearest relations."

Temeraire calmed a little; at least his tail settled slowly to the ground. "And you do *not* want to marry her?" he said.

Laurence looked round; it was an outrageous subject for conversation, and Temeraire's voice could not be called discreet. "Pray let us go inside," he said, "if you wish to speak any further on the subject," and went as far to the back of the pavilion as he could, and seated himself on the cushions there. Temeraire sat before him coiled tightly, and curled his tail around his limbs, still radiating wary distress.

"I should begin," Laurence said cautiously, unsure *how* to begin, "by asking you whether you object to the lady in particular, or to the—to the event, in a general way?"

"I do not see anything particularly remarkable about Mrs. Pemberton at all," Temeraire answered, "which should make her in the least suitable for you. After all, you are a prince of China, and my captain, and you have been in a great many battles. Whatever has *she* done, to brag of? But I do not at all mean to be rude," he said, in succession to this piece of outrageous rudeness. "I should not like it in the least if you were to marry anyone else, either."

"Pray explain to me a little further," Laurence said, wondering if it would console Temeraire to be assured of his own ineligibility; few gentlewomen would contemplate throwing themselves away upon an aviator. "I would by no means distress you, but I had not been aware of any objections you might have, nor that my marriage—not that I contemplate any such step at present—should be any bar to my continuing to serve. So far as I knew, while aviators make poor material for an eligible woman, we are not barred from establishing a home, and—and I beg your pardon, but Roland has given me to understand that providing you an heir is rather in the nature of my duty."

"Well, *I* have never wanted an heir," Temeraire said, snorting. "I should certainly never wish to replace you with another, no matter the circumstances. I understand Excidium feels differently about the matter, and I do not at all mean to criticize, but that is *his* business. For my part, I do not see why I ought to be expected to like it if you should be married, only because it means that someday, if you should die, there might be another person I might like. It is all very airy and unreasonable, it seems to me, and I do not care for it at all."

"Well," Laurence said, "if it will relieve your mind, I will promise you not to marry without seeking your consent: I must consider your feelings as engaged in the matter as those of my family, and I can conceive of few circumstances in which I would proceed over any objections you might express."

He hesitated, then; he could conceive of one: namely, an obligation which could not be escaped. "Temeraire," he said, "before I can make you such a promise, however, I must ask you whether I should be obliged by decency to—that is—" He drew a deep breath and bluntly asked, "Do I owe Admiral Roland an offer? Is she—is Miss Roland my daughter?"

"Why no, she is not, at all," Temeraire said, in surprise. "Her father is some aviator in the North: we have never met him, and I do not think Emily has seen him over three times in her life. Whyever would you suppose she were your daughter?"

"You have relieved me greatly," Laurence said, but the relief was short-lived. Temeraire went on, "After all, Admiral Roland has only been your lover since the year five, and Emily was nine when you met; how could the two of you have made her? But it doesn't signify," Temeraire added in tones of reproach, "for you have already asked her, and she wouldn't have you, because she was your commander."

So Laurence hardly knew whether to laugh or be mortified: it seemed his life the last eight years had been a succession of scandals and outrages, which he ought have blushed to think of. To have intrigued with an unmarried gentlewoman, and a fellow-officer no less—

But Temeraire, perceiving his distress, misread the cause; he said in a small voice, "Why, Laurence—do you *wish* so to be married? I knew that you were quite unhappy that Miss Galman would not have you, after—after I was hatched."

"Did I offer for her, then?" Laurence said, glad that at least he had been decent enough to give *her* the opportunity to refuse him.

"—yes," Temeraire said, with a hitch. "So—so I suppose you do wish to be married, whatever you have said." He fell silent, and then with a very evident summoning of all his resources said in determined tones, "Well, then I suppose, if Mrs. Pemberton will be sensible and not wish you always to be leaving me to go and be with her, and will not expect you *always* to be having children, and if she will not mind coming back to live in our valley, in New South Wales, after we have won the war—"

"I beg your pardon!" Laurence said, raising his voice to stem this torrent of conditions. "Temeraire, I have not the least desire to be married to Mrs. Pemberton, I assure you. And when should we have been living in New South Wales? There can hardly be any call for dragons, there."

"—when we were transported," Temeraire said in surprise, "Oh," he added, "I suppose you do not remember *that,* either? Laurence, it is very inconvenient you should recall nothing at all."

Chapter 13

Laurence could see Granby speaking softly with Harcourt and Berkley; they had trailed him to the edge of the escarpment and stood now at a distance together, all of them looking at him warily as though they imagined he might fling himself over, and as though they would have been sorry for it if he had. Even though he was a traitor—a convicted traitor. Even though he had carried aid and comfort to the French, deliberately, of his own free will, and undermined thereby a stroke which might have averted the invasion of Britain.

An appalling stroke, one which would have meant the slow and dreadful death of a thousand dragons or more, a deliberate plague-bearing—but notwithstanding this, a stroke which had been commanded by his officers, by his Government, and through them by his King. He had betrayed them all, and the invasion of his country might be laid at his door.

"Laurence," Granby said, low, coming to his side, "—pray will you come back to my tent? Temeraire is frayed like a torn rag already, and he'll be worse the longer you stand out here. He is watching you."

Laurence did not answer; he could scarcely yet form thoughts in his own head. The worst of the matter was to be unable to recall what should have shaped his choice: he had committed no mere act of passion. He had acted with deliberation. He had also been pardoned, Temeraire had urgently told him, pardoned and even restored to the list of officers; but Laurence felt that he would have given up that pardon, given anything, only to *feel* again the sentiments that had driven him to such an extremity.

But he did not; he did not remember, and only now understood that he did not know himself any longer. He did not know how he ought to feel. Temeraire had evidently driven him to the act; a court-martial had condemned him; the Government had pardoned him. But none of these facts could tell Laurence whether he had condemned himself, or ought to, and whether he should long since have separated himself from Temeraire as ought a sailor shut his ears to the Sirens.

Granby gently took his arm, and Laurence after a moment let himself be drawn away. They walked slowly back across the encampment, past the watchful, suspicious looks of the red dragons. Laurence did not look towards Temeraire's pavilion, but ducked into Granby's tent; there he took the glass of strong rice liquor Granby offered him and swallowed it straightaway.

"I'm damned sorry," Granby said, sitting on a chest. "We ought have found some other way to break the news to you, whatever Pettiforth and Hammond said; we must have known you could not go forever, not learning of it. I suppose we have all been telling ourselves you would remember, surely, any day now." He leaned over with the bottle, and filled Laurence's glass again.

Laurence took another hot, too-bitter swallow. "I think I can scarcely blame myself," he said, low, "if having forgotten, I did not wish to remember *this*." He downed the rest of the glass and asked abruptly, "I beg your pardon: may I ask your opinion of the act; of the—" He stopped; he did not put a word to it. He did not know what name to give it; he did not know why Granby should consider his feelings, in the least, nor tolerate his company, in the face of it. But he desperately wished to know.

Granby hesitated a moment and then said, "I haven't anything to say, Laurence. I was damned glad the French had the cure, and so was any aviator worth his salt, in my opinion. They asked me, you know, if I'd had a part in it; they asked all of us, and all I could tell them was you wouldn't have taken any help, and I wouldn't have thought of it. And that's too paltry for words. Anyway," he added, "you wouldn't have, either; Temeraire came up with the notion."

"Yes," Laurence said.

"I don't deny it was ugly," Granby said, "and I dare say it has given you a sad turn now, but—but do recall, we have all come about. Boney would have got his hands on the cure sooner or later anyway, and he would have come over anyway. And he'd be in England still if Temeraire hadn't brought half the dragons out of the breeding grounds and to the war with him. You've your pardon, now, and you're restored to the list."

"A pardon cannot restore a man's reputation," Laurence said, "and still less his honor, if lost." He was silent, and then said, "I suppose I was pardoned for Temeraire—that the Corps should continue to have the use of him."

"Well," Granby said.

Laurence nodded. He wondered bleakly if such a motive had kept him by Temeraire's side; if he had clung to his post to save himself from hanging. But even as he had the thought, some instinct rejected it. He finished the glass and put it aside. "I beg your pardon," he said quietly, "I cannot suppose I concealed my feelings from Temeraire at all well, and he was distressed already. I must go and speak with him."

Temeraire huddled in his pavilion, as wretched as ever he had been; it seemed to him disaster followed directly on disaster. First their shipwreck; Laurence's peculiar brain-fever; the assassination attempts which so nearly had succeeded; then the discovery of the opium, which might ruin everything—might prevent an alliance and leave them at a standstill. Mei had been very stiff and withdrawn, since then. She said she had accepted Temeraire's assurances

251

that *he* had known nothing of the smuggling, and neither had Laurence, but she had not wanted to try again for the egg since then; and all the other dragons in the encampment kept a cold distance.

But all that paled before this. Temeraire could not conceive how Laurence had forgotten the treason—the treason, which had so deeply wounded him. It seemed wretchedly unfair. If only Temeraire had known, he would never, never have said a word; how gladly he would have joined Laurence in forgetting, and Laurence need never have known anything about it ever again.

And if Laurence had forgotten the treason, surely he had forgotten everything else, as well. He had forgotten about the loss of his fortune. Temeraire would have to confess *that* to him, all over again; he would have to explain to Laurence that he had lost him ten thousand pounds, and that loss Temeraire had not repaired. Laurence would have all the pain of it afresh, and Temeraire should have to face all his justified blame. Temeraire huddled his head beneath his wing and tried not to think of it.

Forthing had tried to speak with him, half-an-hour ago; Temeraire had paid him no attention. He returned now with Ferris, who came by Temeraire's head and said quietly, "Come, Temeraire; it will come out all right, you will see. The captain will come round. Will you eat something, or would you like Sipho to read to you?" He turned his head and called out the pavilion's side, "Sipho! Will you bring that book over here, of poesy?" and added, "What you need is some distraction—"

"How can you speak of distraction to me?" Temeraire said, lifting his head up. "If I had paid better attention—if I had properly understood—oh! I am distracted, far worse than I ought to be. Where is Laurence?" He reared up his head, and tried to see him. Laurence had walked away across the camp, and his eyes—his eyes had looked half-blind—

"He is with Captain Granby," Forthing said. "He will be all right, Temeraire; it's all that knock on the head he took—"

"It is not!" Temeraire said. "I dare say he *wished* to forget, and whyever would he not wish to? I have lost him his fortune, and his rank, and his ship, and his wife—"

"What?" Ferris said. "Whenever was the captain married?"

"Never!" Temeraire said. "That is what I mean; and everyone *will* have it that nothing could be more splendid than marriage, and he has put it aside for my sake—that, and everything else, and he regrets it so that he has forgotten all of it, so he needn't think of it."

"Lord, Temeraire!" Forthing said. "You can't suppose he has chosen to drop a hand of years out of his head."

Temeraire turned his narrowed gaze sharp on Ferris. "Would *you* not, if you could?" he demanded. "Ferris! Would *you* not rather be shot of me? If you had anywhere else to go? It was my fault you were dismissed the service—"

Ferris flushed and said shortly, "I shouldn't reproach you or the captain for any of it, if only you had asked me to take a part. I should have been happier hanged for such a cause than dismissed for a cowardly liar."

"Oh," Temeraire said. "But—but I am very glad you are *not* hanged," he added awkwardly, "and I dare say if you had helped, you should have been, so I cannot be sorry for that." His ruff drooped against his neck.

They were all silent a moment; Forthing stared at the ground, and Ferris, his cheeks still hot, looked away from the pavilion. Sipho came trotting in with the large scroll of poetry, and paused to eye them all doubtfully.

"I do not want it," Temeraire said. "Pray take it away. I must *do* something," he added, and heaved himself to his feet. "I will go flying, over that burnt town—I will see if I cannot find some trace of the rebels—"

"Wait!" Forthing said. "There's no call for you to go venture yourself like that, and not in this mood, if you please. Let me go and fetch the captain—"

"*No*," Temeraire said, fiercely; he could not bear to speak with Laurence at the moment, not when so many dreadful things might possibly be said. Whatever Ferris might feel, whatever Laurence himself *had* felt, before he had lost his memory, too plainly he did not feel those same things any longer. Laurence did not remember anything, and would be happier not remembering. What if Laurence were to come back and indeed tell him they should part? "No. I am going straightaway."

He walked out of the pavilion; Ferris caught with a desperate leap at his foreleg, and scrambling went up the side to get hold of the breastplate chain, which Laurence ordinarily used to latch himself upon Temeraire's back. "I am coming with you," Ferris said. "Sipho, will you go and—"

"Oh!" Temeraire said, and caught Sipho and Forthing and put them up onto his back as well. "You will *all* come with me, and not run tattling; I do not see any reason that anyone ought go and tell Laurence. If we do not find anything, there is no reason at all."

"A flight won't hurt him," Ferris said to Forthing in an undertone.

"I can't like it in the least," Forthing said, hissing back. "Half this camp is ready to leap on us and tear us to pieces for the least excuse, and if we did find some rebels, they'd like to do the same. We oughtn't let him go anywhere away, and without a word to anyone."

"These fellows are hunting the rebels, aren't they?" Ferris said. "If there were anything to be found at that town, they would have found it by now. We'll go for a flight there and back, and then likely enough he'll come down and let Sipho read to him awhile."

"I don't think they have been looking very hard," Sipho said unexpectedly, in his still-high voice, "when they think we are guilty, and want us to be," which gave Forthing and Ferris both pause; Sipho added, "I don't mind going to have a look, either, and seeing some more of this country. But I don't think Demane will like it if I go off without him for a long while," in rather cheerful tones: he did not have a very great distaste for upsetting his brother, who was somewhat given to a smothering and anxious degree of affection.

"Well, I am going, and so are you," Temeraire said, "so latch on

254

your carabiners," and he delayed only a moment longer before he threw himself aloft. Privately, his thoughts were urgently turning, even as he beat up and turning flew away from the encampment. Surely it was not himself, but Laurence who required distraction; Laurence ought above all things be distracted from thinking of his losses. Perhaps General Fela's men had missed something, some sign—perhaps he *would* find some trace of the rebels. If only Temeraire returned in some victorious accomplishment, perhaps having smashed a rebel army or at least discovered one, Laurence could hardly reply to it with chiding, with a desire to part from him.

The destroyed village, when he reached it, no longer smoldered; the last of the fires had gone out. The opium had been taken away, and the streets cleared; now it was merely abandoned to time. There was no trace, so far as Temeraire could see, of rebels. There were no weapons scattered, and when he flew in widening circles around, the old worn road bore few signs of any traffic at all: the stones were overgrown with grass.

But Temeraire paid no mind to Ferris and Forthing already importuning him to go back to camp; he did not mean to swallow defeat so easily. "After all," he said, "the rebels would not keep their opium in a village they did not come to, now and again; and if they have not come by road, I suppose they must have dragons as well."

"If they have, all the more reason we ought go back to camp and not encounter them on our own," Ferris said.

"Well, we do not know for certain that they do," Temeraire said hastily. He was already aloft again and hovering, looking around at the nearby mountains, trying to decide where he might have liked to perch, if he had been coming to and from the village, or wished to observe it unseen. "What do you think of that mountain, over there—the one with the double ridge. I suppose anyone might have hidden between the two."

Ferris had a glass in his belt, and he took it out and looked as Temeraire flew towards the ridge. "He isn't wrong," he said to

Forthing, and passed him the glass; but Sipho was the only one who was of any real use, for as Temeraire flew along the ridge he said, "Is that a trail, over there?" pointing downwards.

It *was* a trail: with at one end a clearing full of gnawed bones, and fresh claw-marks on the rock. "We must get back to camp," Forthing said. "Temeraire, you must see—"

"Why, those could be anyone's markings," Temeraire said, outwardly dismissive; inside his heart leapt with excitement. By the signs there had not been very many dragons, perhaps even only one, and not very large; he was sure he could win out over one, or even a few. "We cannot merely waste everyone's time. If you like, you may wait here, and I will go and have a look."

"Give over," Ferris said to Forthing, grimly. "He's looking for a fight. Have you anything to make a light with, or some noise? Blast this notion of not having Celestials in harness; we ought to have half-a-dozen flares to hand."

Forthing had his pistols. "Whatever are you doing?" Temeraire said in irritation, looking round, as he shot them off one after another into the air. "If there *is* anyone, you will warn them off."

"I hope I do, before you run yourself into their teeth," Forthing returned, and he fired again. He was sitting on Temeraire's back directly between his wing-blades, where Temeraire could not conveniently reach around to stop him.

Temeraire snorted in irritation, and beat on quicker following the trail, and coming round had to pull up hard as it descended abruptly between two jagged rising walls of stone. He caught an updraft and threw himself up along the wall and caught onto the summit so that he might take a quick look over, unsuspected from below—he did not at all mean to be foolishly reckless, whatever Forthing and Ferris might think.

And then "Oh," Temeraire said, in astonishment, and pulled himself up higher to peer over the ridge and into the valley below. "Arkady? Whatever are you doing here?"

Arkady stood in the midst of a small encampment otherwise hastily and very recently abandoned: tents left pitched and a fire-pit still smoking; ragged bundles of supplies everywhere and one bleating sheep staked out at the far end of a gully.

"Why am I here?" Arkady said. "I am looking for *you*, and see what it has got me." He did present an appearance very unlike himself, drooping and his grey hide dull and grimed with dust.

Temeraire landed beside him, baffled extremely. The last he had seen Arkady, they had parted on the shores of Britain, not long before Temeraire had embarked on his transportation and taken ship with Laurence for New South Wales. Arkady and his feral band of dragons had been persuaded to take up service with the Aerial Corps in exchange for a regular payment of cattle; but they were natives of the Pamirs, nearly two thousand miles west of China. If he had decided to throw over the Corps, Temeraire could not imagine why he would have come here; and in any case, he was still under harness.

Under harness, and something else: "Whatever is that thing upon your back?" Temeraire said, nosing at it cautiously. Temeraire had never seen its like: iron bars linked together in a long chain, the ends of two bars pierced through Arkady's wings, and others dangling down to Arkady's back—and then Temeraire drew his head back in horrified disgust: the ends were barbed spikes, and they had been planted into Arkady's flesh.

"They put it upon me," Arkady said, "so I cannot fly; it is dreadful if I even move my wings a little. Take it off me at once!" And he leaned against Temeraire miserably.

Forthing and Ferris had already leapt cautiously from Temeraire's back to his, to inspect the chains. "I don't dare touch that," Forthing said to Ferris, "do you? We want a surgeon, double-quick: I dare say we could spoil him for ever flying again, if we took it out wrong."

Ferris was looking with grim disgust at the bindings also. "We ought try and get the links open, if we can," he said. "Then at least he won't be forever pulling on it."

"But who put it on you?" Temeraire said, still bewildered, "and what did you want with me? And if you were looking for me, why would you be here? *I* was not here, until presently; are you saying you have just come from Peking?"

"Why do you say such ridiculous things?" Arkady said. "As though I meant to be here, in this dreadful condition! We were going to Peking: there was some letter you sent, that you meant to go there, or so Admiral Roland said. And as for what did I want with you, how dare you ask me such a thing. What has happened to *my egg*?"

"Your egg!" Temeraire said, with a guilty start of remembering.

Arkady was rousing up despite his miserable state, and he blazed on reproachfully. "I left it in your charge, on that great ship, to take to New South Wales; then I hear you are in Brazil instead, and going on to China. Why are you not there, keeping watch upon it?"

"Oh," Temeraire said, writhing a little in shame and discomfort; he did not know how to tell Arkady what had happened. His egg had been treated with the greatest of care; but that had not availed anything: it had hatched out Caesar, a most disagreeable dragon, who had taken as captain none other than the paltry Jeremy Rankin. "I did assure Caesar," Temeraire offered desperately in his own defense, "that he needn't take on anyone he didn't like; that I should not have permitted Rankin to force harness on him—only Caesar would have it, because he learnt that Rankin is the son of an earl, and, I believe, very rich—"

"Ah! Why did you not say so at once?" Arkady closed his eyes in relief. "Then all is well. I am sorry I doubted you," he said handsomely. And by way of heaping coals of fire on Temeraire's conscience went on, "Only some very strange stories came to us, that you had lost an egg—that someone had stolen it from under your nose—"

Temeraire squirmed even more wretchedly. He had indeed lost an egg to thieves, though not Arkady's, and it was not much excuse

258

that he had found it safely hatched in the end; the egg had not hatched in British hands, and anything might have happened to it during the long dreadful chase across the desert. He seized upon the quickest excuse to change the subject. "Well, I did not lose *your* egg, at all," he said hastily, "and I am very happy to have been able to reassure you on the subject. So that is why you came from England?"

"Yes," Arkady said, "for Wringe is brooding again," triumphantly, "and you may be sure we were not going to let go another egg, when the first had not been properly looked after. But now that it seems there was right care taken, I suppose we will let the officers have it, after all."

"Well, I am sure they will look after it properly," Temeraire said, relieved to have escaped with so little of the scolding he guiltily felt he deserved, "but now pray tell me, *how* did you come here? I suppose you took transport to Guangzhou?"

He had already worked out the picture: surely General Fela's men had seen Arkady being taken prisoner by the rebels, and had misunderstood; they had thought *he* was bringing the opium, when instead he had been their helpless prisoner.

But Arkady said, "No, of course not! It is eight months at sea; there was no time for that! I suppose you would have gone somewhere else by the time we came, the way you have been running all over the world. We came by the Pamirs, and to Xian, because we thought this would be a quicker way to Peking. Instead here I am all chained up, and you *have* gone on somewhere else."

"I do not see that you have any business complaining about my having gone on," Temeraire said, a bit indignantly, "as I have gone on here, and otherwise I dare say the rebels would have kept you chained up here forever."

"Rebels?" Arkady said. "What rebels?"

"The White Lotus," Temeraire said, "who took you prisoner. But it will all be all right now," he added, "for this proves you were not bringing them opium: if you were, they would certainly not have chained you up."

"I was not bringing opium to anyone, but I do not know anything about this White Lotus, or any rebels," Arkady said. "I was chained up by some great red dragons, a dozen at least. I fought them very bravely, but there were too many of them: they held me down for the men to put those chains on me, though we were only flying through and asking them the way to Peking."

"Red dragons?" Temeraire said, puzzling. "Like the dragons in the army?"

"Yes," Arkady said, "in jeweled collars, and their men shouted at us a long time, but I do not understand how they talk, nor do I want to."

"What is he saying?" Forthing said, looking up from his search of the camp, as Sipho came scrambling out of one of the tents with an odd blade in his hand, wide at the end and narrow at the hilt, and brought it over to them.

"Look what I found," Sipho said. "There are more of them, inside."

"That might do, to pry these open," Ferris said, reaching for it.

"That is not what I mean!" Sipho said. "These are the same kind of swords those fellows used when they tried to murder the captain."

"Oh!" Temeraire said, whipping his head around. "Oh, these are not the rebels; these are the assassins! Where did they go?" Temeraire demanded of Arkady. "How many of them were there—"

"How many of who?" Arkady said, opening his eyes again to slits and glaring sullenly: he had drooped weakly against Temeraire's side again. "I did not count them: there were enough to chain me up. Hundreds, I suppose! Why do you not get this thing off my back so I can fly again?"

A low rumbling of distant thunder came, and came, and came, growing louder and more near. Temeraire looked up in alarm, and saw the narrow shelf of rock above them crumbling. "Look out!" Ferris called out, but there was no time to get him aboard, to get any of them aboard: the rock was coming down in a roaring torrent.

Temeraire lunged and put himself above Sipho and Ferris, and scraped Forthing in quickly beneath him as well with one foreleg; then the rockslide was upon them, boulders pounding Temeraire's hips and back painfully as a rain of pelting pebbles and sand roared down with them. Arkady pressed up against his side, taking less of the brunt though squalling furiously nonetheless.

The noise died away first; then the rocks settled, though the air was still full of choking, clouding dust. Temeraire sneezed and sneezed, and coughed, and said hoarsely to Arkady, "Do stop yowling; it does not make matters any better." He shook his head to cast off the worst of the dust; he would have liked to wipe his eyes against his forelegs, but the pebbles and stones had buried him up to his withers.

"*You* are not wearing this monstrosity," Arkady returned, "and you are half out of the rocks," with some justice, for the rocks cascading over Temeraire's back had covered Arkady to the base of his neck, so only his head and his wing-tips poked out. "Aren't you strong enough to heave out of them and get us loose? It hurts," he added plaintively.

"I am sure it does hurt; I am not at all comfortable myself," Temeraire said. "And I dare say I might get us out," he added, although he was not in the least certain; he felt very unpleasantly pinned, "but I cannot risk shifting these rocks. I am sure if I moved they would kill Ferris and Sipho, and Forthing, in a trice. There is nothing to do for it but wait until someone should find us," he finished glumly.

He did not in the least look forward to being found in such an absurd position, having done nothing whatsoever heroic, and found only Arkady, who was of no use to anyone; and Temeraire supposed that now the assassins would have fled to some new hiding place long before he should ever be dug out.

"I do not see why that mountain should have chosen now of all times to fall down on us," he added resentfully, and looking up saw some men peering down upon him from the ruined summit: men in

261

soldiers' uniforms. "Oh!" he said. "You there," he called, raising his voice, "send word to the camp—"

"Why are you talking to them?" Arkady said. "Hurry and get loose, and never mind about your men, I am sure they will be all right! Those are them, those are the ones who put these chains on me!"

Temeraire jerked his head around to stare at Arkady. "What?" he said. "But those are soldiers from the army—" and broke off, in understanding and in swelling wrath. "I *will* kill General Fela, I *will*," he vowed.

"You will not kill anyone if you are stuck under those rocks," Arkady said, "Quick, quick!" and looked with fear as the soldiers began to pick their way down the loosened slope, with long sharp pole-arms in their hands.

"And you have seen nothing of him since?" Laurence asked, frowning.

O'Dea shrugged. "Mr. Ferris was aboard, and Mr. Forthing, too," he said, "and that young black fellow. I suppose they may have run into a thunderstorm, or gone afoul of some mountain current; ah, it's sure there's many a dragon's bones littering these peaks, Captain. And those pernicious rebels out there somewhere, no doubt looking for a choice target."

"Yes, thank you, O'Dea," Laurence said. The more likely, and perhaps worse possibility, was that Temeraire had fled the camp in misery, and wished to avoid Laurence entirely; that Temeraire did not wish to return. Laurence stood a moment in the pavilion, worrying the straps of his well-worn harness in his hands, the carabiners hanging empty. He should not have cared so much as he did; his heart ought not have been bound up so completely, and yet he could not but recognize that it was. There, perhaps, was his answer: loving Temeraire, and seeing in him all dragonkind, he had not been able to take refuge behind some comforting fiction of their being mere beasts. He wondered now that he had ever thought them so. It had outweighed treason, in his heart; he was not sure he had been wrong.

He looked hesitantly over the camp. They were still under guard, the scarlet dragons watching from their posts, and the British dragons had not tried to go on maneuvers. Chu had evidently ordered patrols of the region, but only by the other dragons under his command. Laurence had seen them overhead, flying in small groups.

To take Iskierka up, or Lily, or one of the heavy-weights, would at once be provoking and leave their own party too bare. But one of the Yellow Reapers was sleeping near-by, Immortalis, and his captain, Little, was sitting beside the drowsing beast and sketching a little upon a writing-desk—an illustration of a Chinese pistol, which he had evidently got somehow from one of the soldiers, perhaps in exchange for his own. He had a neat hand; Laurence paused and Little looked up from his work and straightened.

"Captain Laurence," he said, formally.

"Captain," Laurence said, "I would not disturb you, but Temeraire has been gone some time, and I—I have some reason for believing him in some distress. May I presume so far as to ask you to take me up in search of him?"

"Ah," Little said, and was silent, obviously hesitant. Laurence recalled too late that Little had been awkward about him and had avoided conversation whenever conversation might be avoided. Easy to understand, now: Little of course had known of the treason which Laurence had committed, even when Laurence himself had not. Little had known the stain upon his character, and perhaps cared more than the other aviators; because Granby sympathized, and Harcourt, did not mean they all did so.

"I beg your pardon," Laurence said. "I have not the least desire to impose on you; pray consider the request withdrawn." He would have gone, at once, but Little rose hastily.

"No, no," Little said. "I do beg your pardon. Of course we ought to go and find him."

They had flown a couple of widening circuits of the camp when Immortalis turned his head over his shoulder and said to Little, "Augustine, what is that there, do you think?" A plume of smoke and dust was rising from a knot of mountains not far in the distance.

"That is no ordinary rockfall; that is black powder," Laurence said, when they had gone close enough for the sulfurous smell to reach them.

"The rebels, do you suppose?" Little said. "We had better have a quick look," he told his dragon, and came rounding over the smoke, cautiously, to find Temeraire buried in stones up to his collarbone with a small grey dragon by his side, its head marked with a bright crimson patch like a birthmark.

"Good God, is that Arkady?" Little said.

"Do you know that beast?" Laurence said, startled. "Is he is one of ours?"

"Yes, but what the devil he is doing in China, I should like to know," Little said. "Immortalis, take us down there. What they have been doing to get themselves buried like that—"

There were some soldiers already clambering over the stones towards the two imprisoned dragons; but Temeraire whipped his head around on his long neck and snapped at them, his jaws clashing on empty air: the men were beyond even his reach. "Temeraire!" Laurence called out surprised as he leapt from Immortalis's back.

"Laurence!" Temeraire cried, catching sight of them, "Laurence, look out! They are assassins, all of them."

"What?" Little said, himself just slid down from Immortalis's back.

A shadow was growing on the ground beneath them, and Laurence, seeing it, turned and shouted to Immortalis through cupped hands, "Aloft again, quick!" while he and Little both dived for safety. A great scarlet beast in armor came heavily down where Immortalis had just in time darted away, its claws digging furrows in the rock; the beast roared and swung its head narrow-eyed over them all.

Laurence scrambled away over the loose stones, towards Temeraire and Arkady. The red-patch dragon looked down at him and said in a strange tongue, which Laurence only a little followed, "Make Temeraire move! They will all be squashed anyway, if those men kill him."

"Laurence, be careful," Temeraire called anxiously. "Do not get anywhere near these fellows; and that is for you," he added, snapping again at one of the soldiers, who had lunged at him, a weapon a little like an old-fashioned halberd in his hand, a curved and wicked blade bound to the end of a long staff, which he jabbed at Temeraire's eyes. "Ow!" Temeraire added, and Laurence saw one of the other soldiers had climbed up onto his back and was stabbing the blade down towards Temeraire's spine.

Laurence realized then in sudden horror that Temeraire was not merely buried but helpless to free himself; Temeraire could not move, and the soldiers might carve him at their leisure like a side of slaughtered beef. He drew his sword and leapt for the would-be murderers. The ground was perilously uncertain, a loose slide of pebbles beneath his feet. Still, he scrambled for the top of Temeraire's back and charged the man jabbing at the great column of the spine.

There were several other men drawing close down the unsteady slope, but Laurence thought for the moment of nothing but the enemy immediately before him. He dived under the man's swing, that already-bloody blade shaving painfully along the back of his head, taking skin and hair with it; but Laurence came up inside the man's guard and, seizing his shoulder, drove his sword up between the loose plates of armor, through and through the man's body to his back. The soldier was a young man, only a scruff of beard yet grown; his eyes and open mouth stared and clouded, and the halberd fell away with a clatter to the rocks as Laurence heaved the body off his blade.

Laurence looked down at Temeraire's wound: the scales had resisted, but the flesh was hacked enough to let grey bone show through, stained with the dark dragon blood that ran away in rivulets down Temeraire's back. The enormous lump of the backbone, the size of Laurence's trunk nearly, had defied the halberd's strokes so far, but five men more were nearly upon him, and if unopposed they could hack away at it, like woodsmen together felling some great monster of the forest.

"Laurence!" Little called, and Laurence reached down to catch the end of the halberd, which Little had taken hold of, and was holding outstretched to him. Little used it to scramble more easily up the slope of rocks to Laurence's side; he drew a pistol from his belt, and his own sword.

Above them, Laurence saw Immortalis feinting bravely around the Chinese beast, which outweighed him so greatly. But the red dragon was not merely the stronger but the more maneuverable, its long lanky body snapping with great agility back upon itself almost, allowing it to turn sharp in mid-air, and its wings had something in common with the structure of Temeraire's own, which allowed him to hover. Immortalis could merely hold it off briefly, and not hope to defeat it.

"If Immortalis went back to camp, to raise the alarm?" Laurence said to Little.

Little looked up at Immortalis with a grim expression, and back at Laurence, shaking his head. "That last day of flying, those fellows could manage twenty knots," he said. "A Yellow Reaper can't get above sixteen. If he turns tail, he'll only be brought down by the hindquarters."

He spoke with a hard flat tone, as though he were not speaking of the death of his beast, but when one of the soldiers came down off the slope, Little leveled his pistol and fired with a look of very savagery, distorting his face which in ordinary repose bore almost a poet's half-dreamy look. He hurled the pistol into another man's face, and sprang forward to meet the halberd and cut him down.

Laurence leapt with him, to take advantage of the unsteady footing the men would have as they came off the slope. He felt all the same useless fury he saw in Little's face: to see Temeraire brought so low, so hideously, and by a pack of cowards and traitors—murderers indeed—burned through him with an intensity that came from no rational font. Laurence had seen his ship sink; he had suffered that—he was sure he had suffered it, though the name slid from his mind. He remembered sea-water pouring in waterfalls through the gunports; he remembered sitting in a boat rowing, rowing, while the masts slid in ragged tatters beneath the waves.

The *Goliath*, he suddenly thought, as his sword met the halberd-stave with a clanging; and he jerked his head in a shake to send away the false memory—he had not served on *Goliath* since the Nile; *Goliath* had not sunk there. But the feeling stayed on his tongue: black powder ash and the smell of burning sails, and the roaring torrent. And yet that pain, that sorrow, was distant and removed by comparison.

He set his teeth and flung his enemy's weapon wide by sheer brute force, heaving it up and clear, and risked the brief opening, overbalancing himself for an extra inch of reach, so that the tip of his sword tore open the man's throat. Blood spilled down his neck along a bloody line, but as Laurence completed the stroke and stumbled away, it suddenly spurted red with ferocious energy. The soldier clapped a hand up to the gush and then fell to knees and toppled away over the side.

Laurence caught himself on Temeraire's back with one hand and tried to twist himself up to his feet; but not quickly enough, and he felt another blade catch his sword-arm and bite into the meat of the muscle. He jerked away from the hot pain, falling, and rolled along Temeraire's back hearing Temeraire above roaring in fury.

"Laurence!" Temeraire cried, and did manage to heave himself a little despite the weight of stones, tumbling all of them off their feet together, and straining he brought his head around and snatched the soldier with the dripping pole-arm in his jaws.

There was something dreadful in watching a man broken between those enormous jaws; Temeraire cracked his body like walnut shells, and flung the wreck of him to the ground. He roared again, that terrible shattering roar, and the soldiers involuntarily cowered back from it.

But he could roar only to the sky. He could not turn that power upon them, not without breaking apart the unstable slope and burying them one and all in a shared tomb, and aloft, the red dragon was closing in on her tiring adversary. Immortalis darted low beneath her, and tried to claw at her belly, but with striking speed she reversed herself again and caught him, claws tearing into Immortalis's shoulders, driving him with a powerful thrust of her great body into the ground.

"Immortalis!" Little cried, anguished. The red dragon had seized him with her jaws by the back of the neck, just below his skull, and was shaking him like a rat terrier, a great clawed foot holding his thrashing body pinned. She would break his neck in a moment; then she would be free to do as she wished, and Temeraire and Arkady yet pinned into helplessness.

Then a roaring above, and a monstrous shadow falling: Kulingile came down with Demane and Junichiro and Baggy all three upon his back and his claws outstretched, the scarlet dragon an easy target for him. She gave an undignified squawk of alarm and let Immortalis go, but too late: Kulingile smashed her down into the ground. He closed his jaws midway down along her throat and wrenched her neck away from her body with brute force. Laurence heard the audible crack, and she collapsed into dead weight.

"Captain," Demane cried from Kulingile's back, his voice sharp and high with anxiety, "where is Sipho?"

"I have not the least idea," Laurence said, grimly anxious himself; there was no sign of the boy, nor of his officers, and the cascade of rock that had buried Temeraire and Arkady would have crushed them like insects.

The would-be assassins were trying to flee, too late. Laurence had heretofore thought Kulingile of a remarkably placid nature, but that was not in evidence now as the great golden beast turned towards them: having been roused to violence and with Demane's fear driving him, he hissed and swept the soldiers into a broken heap onto the ground with a few swipes of his massive talons, careless of them as a child with its toys; only a few of them groaned and moved a little, and soon they, too, were still. Junichiro leapt down from Kulingile's back and drawing his own sword stood over the bodies, while Baggy cautiously collected away their blades.

"Sipho is here," Temeraire said, "underneath me; I will keep him quite safe, only get Laurence back to the camp where he will be safe, at once; hurry!"

"I am certainly not leaving until I see you freed," Laurence said.

"Are you sure you hadn't better go, after all?" Little said to him, doubtfully, and Laurence, startled, looked at him. "Your head is all over blood."

Laurence reached up to wipe the grime from his face, and finding his hand come away red with gore felt back to where his scalp hung open and wet. "Help me fold it up again," he said. "A head wound is always a bloody nuisance; but unless my brains are out in the air, I suppose it will not kill me."

Little gave him his neckcloth, to tie it up with; and Laurence settled himself by Temeraire's side to wait out the slow, cautious labor. Kulingile scraped away the loose crumbling rock only a little at a time, so as to free Temeraire without risking the death of the trapped men below, if they had survived so long, buried alive; meanwhile Junichiro and Baggy wordlessly helped Little to get thick bandages from Immortalis's belly-netting, to pack into his sluggishly bleeding wounds; the poor dragon lay heavily and breathing in gulps.

Temeraire also was silent, his head resting awkwardly upon a heap of loose-piled rock, breath wheezing a little through his nostrils; the rocks pressed in upon his sides and drove them inwards, forcing him to struggle for his air. Laurence stroked the soft muzzle while he waited. He had longed for the feelings which might have driven him to treason, having only the stark barren knowledge of it; here, seeing Temeraire so vulnerable to murder and treachery, he had instead been roused to sentiments of great violence, unexplained by reason. He groped after the truth of himself like a prisoner in Plato's cave, watching shadows.

The grey dragon, Arkady, was rather the worse for wear; his eyes were drifting half-shut and groggy, and his breath came noisily: the weight of stone had pressed still more of the breath out of him. Laurence watched him with concern, seeing Temeraire's fate looming ahead if he was not quickly freed, and only with an effort held himself back from urging Kulingile to work faster. Demane had as much right to fear for his brother, and the dragons were not yet in truly dire straits.

"Laurence," Temeraire said, hoarsely, breaking the silence suddenly. "Laurence, I must beg your pardon."

"There is no cause, as far as I know," Laurence said. "I hope you know I do not hold *you* responsible for my own actions— where I have allowed myself to be persuaded, the decision must in the end have been my own. And where apologies between us may have been merited, in the past, and there made, I hope you do not imagine me so unreasonable as to expect you to repeat them."

"Oh! That is very easy to say," Temeraire said, unhappily, "when you do not know the half of it. You do not know—" He heaved a breath, which rolled a cascade of pebbles from his back. "Laurence, it is not only the treason; it is not only your rank: I lost you all your fortune," he said. "I lost you—ten thousand pounds. A court took it away from you, because you could not answer the charge."

Laurence waited, but this seemed the sum total of Temeraire's great confession. "I hope you do not think me so wretchedly mercenary as to weigh that in any wise with the rest," he said, more than half outraged.

270

"I suppose you have forgotten *that*, as well," Temeraire said. "But ten thousand pounds is an enormous sum! Why, Gentius said to me it should be worth a dozen eagles, like we took from Napoleon."

"I am perfectly aware of the size of the sum; and as it might be ten times the greater and still not buy me a thimbleful of honor, I must beg leave to continue to disdain it by comparison," Laurence said. "I suppose I have been in the way of twice that sum, in prize-money, if I had chosen to ask for a prize-cruise or to chase shipping, instead of harrying the enemy's forces if ever I could."

"But *that* is all the worse," Temeraire said, with a heaving gasp. "For you got it just so, honorably, and it was all your own. You had won it, by yourself, before ever I was hatched; it was not *our* fortune, at all; it was yours. I had not the shadow of a right to do such a dreadful thing, and after you had built me a pavilion as well. I did offer you my talon-sheaths," Temeraire added wretchedly, his voice sinking low, "but oh—you would not take them; as though I could not even repair the injury."

Laurence struggled to make sense of it. He had seen Temeraire gloating over the prized sheaths, to Laurence's mind a singularly absurd piece of adornment which made any sort of eating ten times the more awkward and battle impossible; and he thought Temeraire would have seen his wings clipped off his back before surrendering them. "I suppose if you imagine it a kind of theft," he said slowly, "I can better comprehend your misery; but if I have been plundered by a court, either it was unjustly, which cannot be your fault, or for some act of my own. In any case," he added, with as much energy as he could, "I do assure you I do not regard it; I am not made in the least wretched by *that* loss."

Temeraire was silent, and then said low, "Very well. Not by that, perhaps; but certainly by—" He halted, and then said even more softly, "Surely you would be happier, if you had—if you had never found my egg; if you had not harnessed me at all."

Laurence hardly knew how to answer; it seemed to him true as well. Temeraire dragged in a breath and added with a strange rasp like the hum of bee-wings beneath it, "If you would prefer—I will stay in China, alone; if you would like. You may go wherever you like. Or, or you may stay here, where no-one would call you a traitor, and I—I will—"

He halted, evidently fumbling for some alternative, but Laurence said, "No." It came easily to his mouth, as easily as anything: that itself would have to be answer enough. "I would not make the exchange," he said, "even now; what I have done, what I have chosen, I would not unmake, even if I could."

Chapter 14

Another hour passed; night had come. Enough of the rocks had been drawn away, by now, that Temeraire could breathe freely once more; but he scarcely noticed the relief, by comparison with the rest, although he was very glad when Arkady—who had begun by then to feel well enough to complain incessantly and fidget—was freed from his side and helped away. Immortalis had stolen back to the camp, under cover of dark, to tell the others what had happened; Nitidus had flown back carrying Maximus's surgeon Gaiters, who now was studying the dreadful chains and considering how they might best be removed.

Temeraire could not quarrel with his situation despite the discomfort. It was worth, oh, everything! to know that Laurence did not wish to leave him. Temeraire was with some difficulty trying to comprehend Laurence's disgust of his own lost fortune—he could scarcely call it anything else—only because it could not buy him honor. The fortune *could* have bought him a great many other things, all of them very splendid, so that did not really explain it to Temeraire's satisfaction. But he was not so determined to be unhappy that he would insist on Laurence's being so, having been given such assurances.

"Why is he taking so long about it?" Arkady demanded of Temeraire, breaking in on his thoughts. Temeraire jerked his head up, for he had been drifting in a half-doze, dull with fatigue even though he could breathe now more easily. "Tell him to finish and take it off me. I do not see why he is waiting."

Temeraire looked over. Gaiters had already drawn the hooks which had been driven through Arkady's wings, by cutting them and pulling them away; his point of concern seemed to be how to cut out the barbs in Arkady's shoulders so that the flesh would not be torn so badly that he could not fly.

"Well, I will have a go at it, at any rate. Horrocks, get me my knives," Gaiters said, calling down from Arkady's back to his assistant, and Kulingile was pressed from the work of digging to hold Arkady still for the operation. Arkady indeed shrilled loudly in protest and shuddered all over while the cruel knives dug around in his flesh; Horrocks pointed, now and again, and Gaiters, without taking his eyes off his work, grunted and nodded in answer, while the blood welled up continually around his hands. Horrocks mopped about them with a rag, and three of the midwingmen stood holding the bar of the barb steady.

Temeraire tried not to watch; it was gruesome, and he did not like surgery at all. But some fascination drew his eyes again and again to the spectacle, until at last Gaiters gave the word. "All right, fellows, lift away," and he and Horrocks together reached within the wound to guide the barb out as the midwingmen raised up the bar. It emerged little by little—a thing of horror with curling spikes and gobbets of flesh still clinging to them.

The second one was extracted more quickly: not five minutes, and then Horrocks was finishing the sewing while Gaiters washed his hands. "What a vicious piece of work," Gaiters said, looking it over laid out upon the ground. "I have never seen the like. I suppose they have so many dragons here they don't mind if they ruin a number of them."

Temeraire was very glad to have it bundled up and taken away, in any case; Arkady was coaxed limping away to a corner of the encampment, as he had been warned away from any exertion until the wounds had healed, where he collapsed almost at once into slumber, snoring loudly.

Kulingile turned back to help with the digging. Nitidus had

been working industriously on the stones directly before Temeraire's chest, clearing a safe path; he suddenly exclaimed, "Oh! I hear them; I am sure I do," and in another quarter of an hour Sipho scrambled out of the first narrow opening, and a little while after Ferris and Forthing came staggering out over Temeraire's forearm, which was still pinned in place.

Then at last Temeraire could heave himself free, the last of the stones pouring away from his hindquarters as he lunged out, and he collapsed wearily with a sigh beside Arkady. "Oh! how tired I am," Temeraire said, closing his eyes, only for a moment, as Laurence came to his side and stroked his muzzle again. "But I am not going to wait an instant. We must get back to camp, and I *will* squash General Fela, and I do not mean to let Hammond or anyone else talk me out of it, either."

But somehow his eyes did droop shut; they closed, and he heard Laurence saying, "He must have some water, and something to eat. Can we get it out of the camp, without being observed?"

He woke again with Mei nosing at him anxiously, and an even more anxious cow lowing in his ear: fortunately this second might be dealt with in the most summary fashion, if somewhat indecorously. Temeraire swallowed down the last bite of the head, spat out the horns, and said, "I beg your pardon: I was extremely hungry."

Arkady himself was still sleeping, and Laurence was drowsing as well beneath the remains of one of the encampment's tents, ragged and much abused by the landslide. Immortalis and Kulingile had gone back to camp. "We do not at all want General Fela to know you have uncovered his treason," Mei said, much to Temeraire's outrage. "We must find proof of his treachery which can be demonstrated to the Emperor, first. You have killed everyone here, so we have no-one to obtain a confession from."

She sounded faintly reproachful about the last. "Well, they were trying to kill us, so I do not see how you can complain of that," Temeraire said. "It is the outside of enough to say that we must have *more* proof. They are soldiers, they are under Fela's command, and they were holding Arkady prisoner here, hidden away from all of us, and pretending that *he* brought the opium."

"But you must see that Fela can make any number of excuses," Mei said. "He will say that he did not know of these soldiers, that they are some small band of deserters; or he will say that Arkady *did* bring the opium, and is a false witness, and demand that he be put to torture."

"What is she saying about me?" Arkady said, pricking up his head, his eyes sliding open. "And what is there to eat? I smell blood: have you not left me anything?" he added accusingly.

Temeraire did not think it was very prudent to tell Arkady that there might be any question of torture. "She is saying we must have more proof that General Fela is guilty, and that you did not bring the opium here," he said. "And you needn't complain; there is a nice goat, right there." He also did not think it needed to be mentioned there had been a cow, too, just lately; anyway he was much bigger than Arkady, and needed a larger meal.

"Hm," Arkady said, and reaching out seized the tethered goat with a practiced blow, to break its neck. "I do not see that question is sensible at all," he said, around a mouthful. "Where would I have got any opium, and why would I have brought it here if I had? What good is it? Is it worth a lot of money?"

"Well, it is," Temeraire said, "but General Fela would have it that you brought it here to give to some rebels."

"He could scarcely have brought so many chests, alone," Laurence said, coming out of the tent and buckling on his sword as he did. "Temeraire, pray inquire where he was intercepted, and how long ago? Why did he not come through Guangzhou?"

Arkady was disinclined to be helpful; he was already sagging back into exhausted sleep, and complained that he was tired after his meal, but after a little prodding muttered fretfully, "A month, and all this while I have been alone, and in chains, and now you will not let me sleep. Why would we have come so roundabout a way as the ocean? We had to come quickly: we have an important message for you."

"Who does he mean by 'we'?" Laurence asked.

"Oh," Arkady said, lifting his head abruptly, looking more wide-awake and to Temeraire's instant suspicion guilty; then he said in feigned tones of great surprise, "Why, Tharkay was with me, of course; haven't you rescued him yet?"

"My God," Granby said, springing up with dismay, when he heard the name. "You don't remember," he added to Laurence, "but he is a damned good fellow; he has saved all our necks more than once. I suppose Roland must have asked him to play the courier. He knows those roads backwards and forwards; his people on his mother's side are in Nepal. He took us to Istanbul overland, the last time we were in this country."

Laurence briefly caught at an elusive twist of memory: running beside someone through dark half-deserted streets, and a great echoing vaulted chamber half-drowned in water, drops striking like bells; but it meant nothing, and slid from his grasp without leaving him a face or a voice, though from what Granby said they had known the man five years and more.

"It was some human thing, about the war," was all Arkady could tell them, maddeningly, of the message Tharkay had carried, "—something that fellow Napoleon means to do." This ominous news might have encompassed everything from another invasion to offering peace on terrible terms, but Arkady flipped one wing in a small shrug when they pressed him. "It did not seem very important to me; I had my *egg* to think about. You will have to ask Tharkay."

"If he is even alive," Granby said, "and we can find him: Fela and his crew have been torturing him, no doubt, to get a confession out of him to use against us."

"What we're to do about it is the question," Captain Harcourt said, later that night. They had gathered in her tent, as secretly as they might, to discuss the matter; Mei had smuggled Laurence back to the camp, under cover of dark, while Temeraire and Arkady remained hidden in another valley. "We haven't the faintest notion where they are keeping him, and if we challenge Fela, he will claim it is all a lie and he has no idea where Tharkay is; and like as not will kill him.

"I suppose Fela must be wary already," she added. "Those guard-dragons are his, that much is sure enough. They are watching everything we do: they will have noticed Temeraire has been gone more than a day, and have seen Immortalis and Kulingile and Mei flying back and forth as well. If anything, we are giving him all the cause he needs to accuse us of going about and giving more aid and comfort to the rebels, in the meantime."

"Rebels," Hammond said slowly, from the chest upon which he sat, "—rebels, of whom we have seen not the least sign, and have no evidence for, but General Fela's own reports," and they all regarded him in surprise. "Oh! It is the prettiest arrangement," he added, answering their growing astonishment, "I wonder I did not guess at it before. The conservative party required some excuse, some argument, to resist an alliance and to undermine Prince Mianning's growing influence at court. They trumped up this rebellion, General Fela sent in a few false reports—"

"The devil," Berkley said. "Are you saying there are no damned rebels at all?"

"I dare say there are some number of malcontents, and some quantity of small banditry here and there: enough to make reports plausible," Hammond said. "But we have not heard a peep of any kind of truly organized force—no rebel army, no real fighting."

They none of them spoke a moment; the implications hideous: "Good God, Hammond: if it is true, he put that village to the sword without cause," Laurence said.

"Pray consider the desperate nature of Fela's situation," Hammond said. "He might have expected to vanish away a false rebellion as easily as he had created it, with no such measures required. Yet quite unexpectedly, the crown prince proposed your superceding him in command, with a substantial force and an experienced senior officer to back you. From that moment, he has known the lie of the rebellion could not long be preserved. His only hope is to quickly discredit us, and have General Chu and his force recalled— and he has made excellent headway on that front. But if Prince Mianning had *not* made the suggestion, and we had been sent here alone as the conservatives wished, I am sure he would have been delighted to keep us traipsing about these mountains looking for mythical rebels until the end of days."

"Doing his best to arrange Laurence's murder in the meanwhile," Granby said. "But how are we to prove any of it?"

There was scarcely any hope of their finding Tharkay, or any other evidence, so unfamiliar with the territory as they were; General Fela and his own forces knew it far too well themselves, from having been stationed here for some time. "We must have help," Laurence said.

Temeraire could not but feel the most dreadful awkwardness, marching coolly past the guard-dragons to General Chu's tent, and summoning him out of it. Of course Laurence was nominally in command, and he himself as a Celestial technically took precedence over any other breed, but oh! What did that matter when everyone *knew* perfectly well that General Chu was a most senior dragon, a great general, and really meant to be in command; he could feel the outrage of the other dragons' eyes upon him, and writhed inwardly to be behaving so rudely.

General Chu came out of his pavilion, between the two scarlet dragons whom Fela had appointed his personal honor-guard, and very stiffly bowed his head. "How may I be of service?" he said shortly.

Temeraire did not know how he could have answered; but Laurence had not the least hesitation. He said in quite a calm voice,

"General Chu, have you found any trace of the rebels that the Emperor has commanded us to destroy?"

Chu's mane bristled. "As yet we have not discovered their base of operations," he said, even more shortly. "The search continues."

"Then you would oblige me greatly by coming with us to discuss how we may improve that search," Laurence said, and nothing more—no explanation, no polite adornment. One of the guard-dragons flattened his own heavy brows, and Temeraire avoided their eyes.

Chu's eyes narrowed under the forward ridge of his mane. "If I may propose to Your Highness, there is no reason we cannot discuss the matter profitably here," and indicated with his claw the great maps laid out just inside his pavilion, with clustered markers of red upon them showing the maneuvers of the dragons.

"I prefer to be surveying the territory directly, with my own eyes," Laurence said. "We will seek out a higher vantage point, if you please. You there, you may keep your places," he added, when the honor-guard would have risen. "We do not need an escort." He touched Temeraire's side; Temeraire was desperately glad to leap aloft and escape the mortification and the cold glares. He hovered just out of ear-shot, pretending not to notice the outraged expressions on the other dragons, and their flattened wings and spines, as General Chu heaved himself into the air and followed.

Arkady was not yet well enough to fly, but that dawn they had loaded him onto Kulingile, who was good-natured enough not to mind his ongoing sighs and restless shifting. He had shown them the way to a pass through the mountains, not far from the encampment where he had been chained, and a valley at its end with a small and glacier-cold pond fed by a trickling cleft in the rock.

"Here," he had said, "this is where they took us. We saw them having a drink, so Tharkay thought we should ask them for direction; but after he climbed off my back, and spoke with them, suddenly they sprang on him."

"What did you do?" Temeraire said.

"Oh, well," Arkady said, "I thought it would be a very good thing if I could only get away, so I could come round and free him later, of course—so I tried to fly away as quick as I could; but those red fellows are fast, even if they do not look it much," he added disgruntled.

"As though he had any right to be," Temeraire had said indignantly to Laurence, after, "once he turned tail and left poor Tharkay, and I am sure would never have given him another thought."

Arkady and Kulingile were waiting for them there in the valley when they descended with Chu; Temeraire had been sure to fly on ahead as quickly as he could, without pausing for conversation. "What is this?" Chu demanded. "Who is that peculiar dragon, and why have we come here?"

"Sir," Laurence said, "I beg your pardon for the maneuver which has brought you here. We have reason to believe we have all been practiced upon, to an extent difficult to swallow; but we have not a hope of demonstrating it, without your assistance."

But Chu received the explanation of Arkady's presence, and of Fela's treachery, with enormous skepticism; Temeraire laid back his ruff to see it, and said angrily, "I suppose you would rather believe that we are all liars—that *I* am a liar, and Laurence as well, even though he is the Emperor's adopted son."

Chu snorted a little. "*That* does not disqualify anyone to be an emperor's son, or an emperor for that matter: what is an emperor but one who tells a lie that all the world believes?"

Temeraire was rather taken aback by this remark, which made an uncomfortable sort of sense, and did not quite know how to answer it. Chu waved a wing-tip dismissively and said, "But in any case, I do not think you liars; I think you want China to make alliance with this foreign nation of yours, and so you are willing to believe the lies of others. General Fela, to have committed such treachery? To have sent false reports, and connived at the attempted murder of the crown prince?"

"Sir," Laurence said, "*have* you seen any evidence at all, of the rebellion which he claimed was so greatly resurgent as to challenge his own forces?" General Chu was silent in answer, frowning; in the cold mountain air, the breath from his nostrils drifted forth in pale clouds.

"Then I ask you to indulge us this far," Laurence went on. "You yourself commanded the army which cleared away the last insurgency. You are well acquainted with these mountains, and whatever rebel fastnesses were taken and secured by the army at that time. Is there anywhere close-by, where they might have taken and concealed a prisoner? If we can find our man, we may find answers with him; his guards may be questioned, and other evidence found."

"Hm," Chu said, after a moment, and then he said, "Well, it will not hurt for us to take a look."

He leapt aloft, Temeraire after him, both dragons beating far up to where the air grew thin and cold. A thin clouding layer of haze reduced the mountains to faded blue, but the sharp and angular lines of their peaks might be clearly seen below. Temeraire heard Laurence's breath coming quickly; his own was laboring in his chest, and his wings working mightily to keep with Chu.

Chu did not keep them so high long, but soon dropped to a more comfortable height. There he flew in ruminative circles a while, and then beat up a second time, as though to confirm some conclusion; then he swung in easy circles back down to the clearing. He plunged his head into the cold pool and drank deep, then raising his head shook water from his mane vigorously.

"It is a long while since I hunted these mountains," he said, half-aside to himself, "but I have not forgotten all the bolt-holes of the rabbits yet. There was a White Lotus fortification, a cave, near Blue Crane mountain. And there is some smoke coming from the mountain-side now."

"Ha, this makes me feel like a young soldier again," Chu said, peering over the mountain's ridge, "flying over the northern plains looking for the enemy, under the great Kang-Xi Emperor! It is not at all respectable, of course," he added, "for either of us; but it can be excused in this case, I think."

There was some sort of activity at the cave, certainly: as Temeraire raised his head cautiously to peek over, alongside, he could see that the fortifications by the mouth of the large cavern had been rebuilt, and fresh traces of cart wheels tracked through the dust of the slope and into the entryway.

"Either we *have* found your nest of traitors, which I do not suppose in the least," Chu said, "or we have found the rebels. But we will soon find out. We will go back to camp, and send ten *niru* here to investigate thoroughly—"

"Temeraire!" Laurence said sharply, and Temeraire sprang for Chu and bowled him over the slope, only just in time as three dragons plunged towards them from a concealed height above, talons outstretched, and plowed dirt and stone into a cloud where they had been: three scarlet dragons, the very honor-guard which had been appointed to Chu by Fela.

Though flung off his feet, Chu nimbly rolled his entire body over itself and got up roaring. "What is this outrageous behavior?" Chu said, rearing up onto the slope and bellowing at them. "You *are* traitors! Lost to all decency and right thinking!"

The scarlet dragons half-cowered from him a moment, plainly hesitant, as well they ought to have been, but Temeraire could see that they did not mean to stop. He gathered his breath, his chest swelling, and as the red dragons steeled themselves to leap he roared, shaping the thunder of the divine wind into their path, and the slope crumbled away and left them tumbling down in a heap of stones and broken shale, falling trees entangling their limbs. That seemed poetic justice to him, after his own half-burial. "It serves them all very well," he said, dropping down to his own feet.

"Temeraire!" Laurence called to him. "We must away at once,

before they can call more assistance. If you and Chu only return to camp, with this evidence, Fela is undone; they must slay you at once, or face disaster."

"The disaster they have made for themselves!" Chu said angrily. "Come: your companion is right, we must get back to camp." But there was no chance; more of the scarlet dragons were spiraling down from the clouds, all the dozen dragons and more who had been guarding them in the camp: Fela's loyalists, and all too plainly a willing part of his conspiracy.

"Let me down!" Arkady was squawking, further down the slope, where he and Kulingile had waited for Temeraire and Chu to finish their spying.

"Well, hurry up then!" Demane said, as Arkady scrambled off Kulingile's back and crept hastily away into a narrow crevasse, peering out and up at them with only the tip of his grey nose showing.

Still they were three against a dozen, and Temeraire struggling to gather his breath again. Chu said, "Quickly, behind me!" and leapt aloft. Temeraire and Kulingile dropped in behind him. Chu darted into a gap between two mountain ridges, angling himself sharply to pass his wings through the space, and led them onwards through a dizzying rush of mountains: thick green slopes and grey stone flying past at such a speed that Temeraire could only blindly follow, twisting himself to meet every new gap and losing his sense of direction all over again at every third turning.

Kulingile was gasping, but at last they burst out between two peaks into the air over a valley, and beneath them, chasing through the very channel they had fled along, were the traitorous dragons. "Now!" Chu said, and Temeraire gathered his breath and roared out, and the peak before him shattered; boulders toppling. Kulingile flung himself down after them, and bore two of the red dragons to the ground beneath his wickedly long talons, drowning them in the rockslide before he sprang aloft again.

The enemy had split up their ranks, however, and still more

beasts were coming; six and six from either side approaching, and another six descending from above. The odds were too great. "We must try and fight a way through for you," Chu said to Temeraire. "You must return to camp, with the Emperor's son," and while Temeraire could appreciate that sentiment, his heart recoiled at the idea that he should flee and leave others to fend off the enemy. He felt very sorry suddenly he had ever criticized Laurence for risking himself; he had never properly understood how dreadful it would be.

"We cannot on any account desert you, General," Laurence said. "Your own survival must be of paramount importance: if you can win back to camp, you will be trusted and obeyed, where we may be considered too partial, and your death somehow laid at our door by further machinations."

"Laurence," Temeraire said, "perhaps you ought to go with General Chu, and——"

The knot of dragons was closing in upon them; but shrieks and cries erupted, as a torrent of flame enveloped their hindquarters and Iskierka burst through their ranks behind it, her talons raking along their sides in either direction. "What are you all hovering about here and talking for?" she demanded, whipping about them mid-air. "Don't you see you are under attack? Hurry up and do some fighting! The others are coming as quick as they can."

She whipped away again, and Temeraire dived after her, indignant at her reproaches; he roared as she flamed, and together they broke apart the other side of the closing net just as the arrow-head formation massed behind Lily came diving towards them all. "Hah," Maximus called, as he swung by, "we thought you might have got yourselves into trouble, after those guard-dragons slunk off: we followed them here, and so you have."

"We did not get ourselves into trouble, at all," Temeraire said. "It came to us, without any effort on our parts."

Chu was falling in on his left flank, calling to Temeraire, "Hurry! Tell them to send up a signal! Blue lights and red, together!"

Temeraire was inclined to think, himself, that they were quite enough to manage the enemy; together their formation had dealt with quite more than a dozen dragons, and the red dragons were not as large as himself, much less Maximus and Kulingile. But Laurence shouted the word on to Granby, through his cupped hands, and in a moment the flares went up: blue lights bursting against the mountain-side, and Iskierka followed them with a torrent of red flame.

Dodging another pass from the red dragons, Temeraire noticed that the fighting had doubled back over the cave, and too late realized they had been neatly herded. Soldiers were coming out of the cave-mouth and hoisting into the air bundles which, when the scarlet dragons dived to seize them, proved to be enormous weighted nets.

Four of the scarlet dragons threw themselves in a tumbling pass through the narrow gaps in the formation, their crews lashing out with long barbed whips in either direction that threatened the British dragons' wings and managed to cut the formation apart, while others in groups of three pounced with the nets. Nitidus and Immortalis were falling off in one direction, a net catching at Nitidus's wing and leg, so that he would have plummeted into the jagged mountains but for Immortalis giving him support.

Another three of the dragons managed to entangle Lily and Messoria and flung nets over them both, carrying them to the ground, wings and limbs thrashing as they roared, men of their crews broken and bloody beneath them as they fell. Three of the scarlet dragons were feinting at Maximus, drawing him in one direction and another, their crews carving up his flanks with the long whips while the British riflemen fired volleys that the twisting and darting of the dragons sent astray.

The scarlet dragons were fighting too well together, Temeraire realized in dismay: being so nearly alike they all might take any position in the fighting, and exchange places, and alter their formations to suit any particular moment of the fighting. Meanwhile

Maximus and Dulcia were the only ones left, and Dulcia could not do very much to help Maximus, outweighed by the scarlet beasts as she was.

He could not go and help; he and Iskierka were struggling to keep together as the enemy beasts came towards them, and even with her fire, it was proving dreadfully difficult: he could not build up enough force behind the divine wind to use it to proper effect over and over. Iskierka only just turned her head over his back and burnt up a net as it flew for his wings; he managed to dive beneath her belly and roar away three dragons coming from beneath with their crews aiming for her with stakes topped by pointed steel caps.

Below, he heard terrible screams, and smelled the acrid bite of Lily's poison: she had righted herself. The spray of her acid had gone through the net and spattered the defenders before the cave-mouth, and with a great heave, she and Messoria burst free, themselves bellowing as they brushed against a few lingering drops.

But Temeraire could see Kulingile being driven down: one of the scarlet dragons had flung herself at him in a sacrificial roll, hurtling into his chest heedless of his clawing talons. As he reeled back, three others seized on him with jaws and talons closing over his wings and his legs, tearing at the membranes. Temeraire wanted to fly to his rescue, but he could not gather the divine wind, or drag himself free: he was being dragged down as well. "Laurence!" he cried in alarm, thrashing, trying to see if Laurence was still on his back, still hooked on and safe, as three dragons pinned him to the mountain-slope.

Chu roared, coming down upon the back of one of the red dragons, and seized the younger beast by the neck and wrenched it expertly sidelong; the dragon shrieked and fell off Temeraire's shoulder. "Hah!" Chu said, and seizing one of the fallen trees from the slope flung it at the dragon on Temeraire's other legs, and Temeraire managed to heave up; the last of the three dragons fled aloft. "Come along!" Chu said. "It is time for us to get out of the fighting."

"What?" Temeraire said, gasping for breath, and then looked

up as a thrumming noise came sharply from overhead: more of the red dragons were wheeling into view, but these were not Fela's beasts; these were Chu's soldiers, their armor polished and fresh, gathered in two formations of six and nine.

"This way," Chu said, and led Temeraire to a flattened peak, broken earlier by the divine wind, high enough to let them see the wheeling, fighting dragons clearly.

"Come upon their left flank," Chu roared to the smaller formation, and "Zhao Lien, bar their escape," he shouted to the leading dragon of the other, then sat back on his haunches with satisfaction as the dragons moved skillfully and methodically to begin bringing down the traitor-beasts. "Where are you going?" he demanded, when Temeraire would have gone back aloft. "No, no: there is no excuse for that anymore. We have won the battle: it is only a matter of time, now."

Temeraire flattened his ruff to his neck in irritation, especially when he saw Iskierka dart by, flaming another two beasts. But he could not quarrel with it; they were winning, that was plain enough.

"Temeraire," Laurence said, and to his alarm Temeraire saw him unclasping his carabiners, and Forthing and Ferris with him. "We must get down and look into those caves: we must find Tharkay. When the traitors see the fighting going against them, they might well kill him rather than leave him to be witness against them and perhaps General Fela himself. General Chu," he added, "you would oblige me if you might send down some soldiers with us, from your beasts."

"Oh," Temeraire said unhappily as Chu roared the command to his dragons: the cave-mouth was indeed not at all large enough to let him or another dragon go inside. He had only just resolved not to condemn Laurence for wishing to go into fighting, but he had not thought that resolve would be put to the test quite so soon. "Pray be careful," he said, steeling himself to it, and watched in anxiety as Laurence plunged within the caves, Ferris and Forthing on his heels, and a number of Chu's soldiers with them.

And then he could do nothing but sit and watch the battle, and wait, while Iskierka and Lily and Maximus and Kulingile helped knock about the traitors, as they well deserved; Temeraire clawed the slope in frustration.

"Hm! I must have a better look at that fire-breather of yours," Chu said to Temeraire, adding insult to injury. "It is the accepted understanding that they cannot be bred without a grievous lack of balance, but I see she is a most skillful flier. Her temperament, I have observed, is not ideal, but one may make some allowances. Where was she hatched?"

"She is Turkish," Temeraire said, rather coldly, as Iskierka went showing away again with a great corkscrewing spiral turn, flame sweeping the air like a banner. "She is a Kazilik dragon. I suppose you are quite an expert, on these matters."

"I am indeed," Chu said, equably. "I am a minister of the breeding office, and I have served three terms as overseer of the Imperial breeding programme."

The ground before the cave-mouth still smoked with the Longwing acid, several crates burnt through: Laurence caught a glimpse, in one, of balls of opium charred through and wafting a thick rope of pale grey smoke into the air. He plunged between them and over the deserted fortifications, dead soldiers sprawled over the ground, one with a face half-eaten-away and stiffened hands still clutching at his own head stared as he went past and into the darkness of the cave-mouth.

Laurence's eyes took a moment to adjust: a few lanterns hung from a thin rope strung overhead, and a honeycomb of tunnels dividing away in front of him. "Sir," Forthing said, "we had better mark the way we've gone." He took down a lantern, and tearing it open fetched out the candle.

Laurence nodded, taking a piece of the candle. "Each of you take a side," he said, "and do not go down more than five branchings, for the moment." He spoke grimly; if the tunnels did go so deep into the mountains, they might search months without finding a concealed prisoner.

He shouted Tharkay's name, and called in English as he led the way down the first tunnel; distantly for a little while he heard Forthing and Ferris doing the same, until the rock swallowed their voices. He dragged the softened wax across the rough rock wall, at each division of the passage, choosing always the rightmost way; it left a smudge of pale yellow that showed clearly in the light of the torch one of the soldiers carried by his side. The wind currents brought other noises: he heard shouts and footsteps, echoing queerly along the hallways, and his mouth held the unpleasant taste of bitter smoke.

They looked into storerooms, mostly empty and disused. By any fourth or fifth branching, the tunnel would begin to take on more the character of what the place had once been, Laurence supposed: a mine, the tunnels rough-hewn and pickaxed; when they reached a dead end in one, the torch gleamed on a thin line of silver, the remnant of a vein pursued to its end.

In one chamber, somewhere near the third branching, they found a writing-table, with a handful of scattered letters and pen and ink: but old; the ink dried to a black crumbled clot. Laurence glanced at the topmost sheet, a work broken off mid-stream, and then held it to the soldier nearest him, an officer he thought; the man wore a mark of senior rank. "Can you make anything of it?"

The soldier studied it and said, "This is a letter written to Ran Tian Yuan: I believe he was a chief of the rebels," in a woman's clear voice. "He was executed ten years ago." Laurence with a start looked at her: deep lines about her eyes, her face not very old but leathered from sun and wind, and a peppered scar of burnt-in powder upon her cheek.

The woman took up the papers and held them out to one of the other soldiers, to be bundled up together; she fell in again with Laurence as they went through the tunnels. Laurence glanced back at the other soldiers behind them. Their hair was bound up beneath snug caps, with wrappings bound down beneath their chins, likely for warmth when aloft; in the dim light he could not tell whether they were men or women.

The tunnel died shortly after, and they retreated towards the entry, to take another branch; before they could go down this, footsteps came towards them running. Laurence was appalled to find the soldier thrust him behind her arm as they drew their swords, and another of the soldiers push through the hallway to take her side instead.

The enemy soldiers coming had a look of desperation, drawn blades wet with blood, and pulled up short to see them; then it was a sudden, close struggle in the passageway. Their numbers were even, Laurence thought, but he could not easily tell; the tunnel was too narrow to see clearly, and the soldiers at the front, of both parties, had dropped their torches to free their hands for fighting. He took a blow from a fist to his temple and shook his head to clear it; then thrust back high, his long blade coming over the other's guard. Then he caught another arm descending, and the woman soldier drove her own blade, a shorter one, into the man's arm-pit beneath his thick jerkin. She grunted abruptly with pain and fell: one of the enemy had thrust a sword into her thigh. Laurence stepped into the gap. He killed three more, and then a sword took him hot in the meat of his arm; he dropped back and let another step into his place.

Abruptly the enemy soldiers gave over the fight: they made one heaving push, and then withdrew hurrying down the hall. Laurence said, "Let them go." Twelve lay dead in the corridor, and five of their own party. The waste of it made him sorry, with the battle above already decided. They bound up their hurts as best they could. The woman officer was limping; another soldier, Laurence thought a man, looked dazed: his cap and its bindings were wet through with blood, and a trickle coming down his cheek. Two soldiers stood with him; he swayed between them and did not speak.

Laurence looked down the branching they had been on the point of taking: he wished to get the wounded to safety, but the enemy soldiers had been coming this way. "Come with me, if you please," Laurence said, to two of the unwounded soldiers, one of them a torch-bearer, "and the rest stay here. We will have a quick look, then return to the entry."

The passageway smelled of smoke: burning wood, a torch, acrid. His head ached. Blood was wet and sticky upon his arm and on his fingers, and the orange glow of torchlight played from behind his back and over the corridor walls, leaping like a bonfire. There was a strange familiarity to it: the narrow walls in around him. And when he came to a wooden door set in the wall, he put his hand upon it and pushed it open.

There was a room, and a pallet inside it; a small torch burned low in a socket upon the wall. A man lay upon the cot, his face bruised and battered, his hands curled against his chest bloody: and Laurence knew him; knew him and knew himself. He remembered another door opening, in Bristol, three years before, and a voice asking him to come outside his prison, in a Britain under siege.

"Tenzing," Laurence said, and, as Tharkay opened feverish eyes, went to help him stand.

Chapter 15

"La Grande Armée, he is calling it," Tharkay had said, lying exhausted and thin against the cushions which propped him, in Laurence's own camp-bed: they had carried him gently and carefully dragon-back, in a hammock of netting, back from the caves. "They have been mustering all winter; he will march into Russia in three months—in two—" He stopped, breathing hard, and asked, "What is the day?"

"It is the third of May," Laurence said, quietly. The abuse had not marked Tharkay excessively: fortunately they had wished to preserve the appearance of a more honest confession, perhaps, when they had wrung one from him. But he had been lashed more than once, judging by the half-healed marks; there were burns upon his limbs as from a hot poker, and his hands were badly mangled.

"In a month," Tharkay said. "He will march in June; that was our latest intelligence."

"With near a million men?" Laurence said, low.

Tharkay nodded, minimally. "And some hundred dragons."

It was indeed a message terrible enough to bring a man racing flat-out halfway around the world. The largest army ever heard of, and with it Napoleon meant to crush the last embers of resistance out of Europe: first Russia, and then he would turn all his attention to the Peninsula. Hammond was already rising, pale. "I must go speak with General Chu at once, and with Qin Mei: we must—these events must require our immediate return to the capital. Oh! We must return at once." He left unceremoniously, and Tharkay closed his eyes.

Laurence sat silently with him in the growing dark of the tent, groping back through patchwork scenes of memory. He remembered the *Goliath* sinking more clearly now; he remembered the faces of the officers at his court-martial; he remembered the cold bleak desperation of the flight across the Channel, to take the plague-medicine to France.

"I hope you will forgive my mentioning it, Will," Tharkay said, eventually, rousing Laurence from his reverie. "—I recognize there is a certain pot-calling quality to my doing so under the circumstances, but have you noticed that the top of your head appears likely to come off?"

Laurence put up a hand: he had taken off his hat. The scalp-wound had crusted over, and the bandages had come loose in the fighting; he had not had an opportunity to repair them, and the scabbing made a gory line of dried blood around half his skull. "It is only an inconvenience," he answered. "Will you try and take a little wine?"

He eased Tharkay up, and gave him the glass; Tharkay held it awkwardly between his bruised and bloody hands, drank thirstily, and sank back again.

Temeraire peered in through the tent-opening, with one enormous platter-like eye. "I have seen to General Fela," he said, with an enormous and glittering satisfaction which made unnecessary any questions about that gentleman's fate, "—General Chu acknowledged I had every right to do it; but how is poor Tharkay?"

"Not yet expired," Tharkay said, dryly, without opening his eyes again. "Though I would be glad of some rest; and that, I think, I cannot rely upon."

"No," Laurence said, quietly. "We will have to leave at once; and, pray God, bring some of these legions with us."

"Be careful, there," Iskierka called, a hiss of steam escaping her spikes, and Temeraire craned his head over a little further, just to be sure there was not good cause for her concern. The egg was supported in a nest of furs, within a well-tried net, and there were three dozen handlers directly beneath it, their fingertips lightly touching the surface, in case the net should break, but still anything might happen; one could not be too careful. Temeraire was glad when the maneuver was complete, and the egg transferred at last from his back to the waiting, ceremonial dais where it would await its hatching.

He nosed at the dais again, to be sure it was just the right temperature. With his head close, he could hear the low gurgle of water running through it, which the head of the Imperial household had explained to him brought the heat, from a cistern below. It was indeed very pleasantly warm without being excessively hot, and a gentle breeze played through the hall in which the egg now stood: the central hall of Prince Mianning's palace, where they had first made their bows on arriving in China; but in attendance now there were only Mianning's trusted retainers, as well as Mei and a handful of Imperial dragons, and Temeraire's own mother, Qian.

Iskierka finished her own re-inspection of the dais, and drew her head back to snort with satisfaction. "That is well enough, I suppose," she said. "I hope you will make a point to those fellows, Temeraire, that they will answer for it, if anything should go badly. You may be sure I will not listen to anyone telling me that I cannot squash this fellow, or that fellow, if anyone should hurt the egg; I will certainly come back and answer it."

Temeraire had already expressed similar sentiments to the handlers, very delicately, a few dozen times; but he did agree, of course, that on this point he could not repeat himself too often. He had a final reminding word with Huang Li, the minister who would oversee the egg's protection and nurturing; that gentleman took it very kindly, and assured Temeraire that everything would go well.

"We will send you dispatches every week," Huang Li said, "with a report upon the egg's progress, until it is hatched."

"Oh!" Temeraire said, with delight. "That would be of all things wonderful. But do you suppose those will reach me, in Britain?"

"The Emperor has commanded it," Huang Li said, which was indeed heartening.

Iskierka nodded in satisfaction when Temeraire had translated this for her. "That is just as well," she said. "I want to be quite sure they are taking proper care of *my* egg," with a pointed stress on the possessive, and throwing a smugly superior look towards Mei before she pranced across the room to Granby's side.

Temeraire went to Mei to make his own farewells; they were leaving in the morning. "I am sorry we did not manage an egg together," he said, "but I am very glad to have seen you again, Mei. I hope you can forgive me," he added, "for the opium; I promise we will put a stop to it somehow, even if the Government does not like to. Laurence and I will make them give over."

Laurence and Mianning were speaking quietly together, near the dais. Laurence had been permitted to keep his sword, and a second one, a shorter blade, now sat upon his other hip; he wore a splendid set of new robes, in red satin, the gift of the Emperor himself. Temeraire rested his eyes upon him in tremendous satisfaction. If only he could persuade Laurence to wear them always, or at least on special occasions.

"I hope it will be so," Mei said, "and yes, I do believe you, Xiang, that you did not know. In any case," she added, "the crown prince means to send me there, in the company of the minister Ruan Yuan. We will soon begin to search the ships when they come in to Guangzhou, and burn the opium when we find it."

Temeraire was well aware this new policy would not be received with equanimity by the British Government, and the East India Company, but with a guilty glance over his shoulder, he decided he did not wish to spoil the parting, and he would just forbear to mention it to anyone else, except perhaps to Laurence once they were already on their way. After all, if the East India Company wished to complain, they might stop the opium coming, themselves. If there *were* no opium upon the ships, there would be nothing to burn.

Mei leaned out and rubbed her head against his, affectionately. "And perhaps you will return and we can try again, when you have won this war of yours. This egg might not breed true Celestial, after all, although we must hope for the best."

Temeraire flattened his ruff a little; he was quite sure the egg would hatch splendidly, regardless: one needed only look at its magnificently pearlescent shell and exquisitely proportional dimensions to see that it was something out of the ordinary. "I am sure that all will be well," he said, dignified, "and the egg will make a most notable companion for the prince."

"Oh! Yes, of course," Mei said hastily. "Only, one does not wish to see the true Celestial line disappear; another line may equal, but not surpass it."

Temeraire thawed; *that* he could accept. "If my honor and duty permit me, I would be very happy to return," he said, with only a little loftiness.

He would be, too, he thought, and sighed a little, looking around the gorgeously appointed hall, the comfortably high rafters, as he went back to Laurence. "You must admit, Laurence," he said, "that they do things very properly, here; no-one can complain of the hospitality, or the arrangements."

"I do not deny it in the least, my dear," Laurence said, resting a hand upon his flank. "And I will once again make you my promise we shall return, if fortune permits it; but you could not wish us to remain now, in these circumstances."

"No, certainly not," Temeraire said. "It is the outside of enough, for Napoleon to be beginning another war, and only just after he stole the Incan Empress, and caused so much trouble for us in Brazil."

They had undertaken the return to Peking in a blazing rush, as swiftly as dragons could go; but even so the weeks seemed to Laurence to melt away and run through their fingers. By now, they were all dreadfully aware, Napoleon might already have crossed the Niemen; if the Russians had chosen to give battle, the fate of Europe might already have been decided.

The speed of the Jade Dragon couriers, within China, depended on their intricate system of relays; traveling so far as Moscow was no easy matter, and they labored without intelligence. They could only muster with all possible speed and go, hoping. Laurence had wondered how swiftly the assembled *jalan* could be brought back north from the mountains, but Chu had shaken his head in some bemusement even to be asked. "There is no sense bringing those soldiers all that way," he said. "Those *niru* will go back to their usual stations; we will muster up fresh as we fly north. You Westerners seem to insist on thinking of dragons as though we were infantry. Telling ten thousand where to go is very difficult. Telling three hundred is not! Now, *feeding* them, that is another matter."

Tharkay had not wholly recovered, but he had preferred to come with them than to remain behind for his convalescence. Laurence now stopped into his bedchamber in the palace, returning from the ceremony of handing over the egg. They had made use of the sickroom, which gave out upon the courtyard, to spread a great many maps upon the floor and consult upon the quickest route towards Russia's borders.

Gong Su and General Chu had come three mornings ago to look these over, bringing with them a nondescript middle-weight dragon, one of the common blue sort, who was distinguished however by a silver headdress featuring two cabochon amethysts nearly the size of her own eyes, and who was introduced to them as Lung Shen Shi.

They looked over the maps, the dragons' heads thrust through the open wall; withdrawing, Shen Shi had shaken her head doubtfully as though casting off water; the movement set the silver jingling. "I suppose we cannot rely on them to have any proper depots?" she asked Chu. "We must rely entirely on forage?"

"I am sure the Tsar will be pleased to put his resources at your disposal," Hammond began.

"Herds of cattle, I suppose," Chu said, with a snort. "We cannot rely upon them."

She nodded her head. "In such circumstances as these, Honored General," she said to Chu, "I regret most deeply that supply will be somewhat difficult to assure."

Chu grunted. "How many dragons will this Napoleon have?"

"No more than a hundred?" Laurence said. "He can scarcely muster and supply a force larger than that which he brought across the Channel to England, so much nearer to home."

"That is something, at any rate." Chu said, not very enthusiastic. "Well, I hope he is not as clever as all of you seem to think."

"I had not thought, sir, that you thought so highly of our Western tactics," Laurence said, a little dryly, but wondering truly; he himself would not have given much for Napoleon's chances in the air against the Chinese legions, so outnumbered and in hostile territory.

"I am not worried about the fighting," Chu said, "when we have any. I am worried about time. I do not like to think what it will be if we have not defeated him before the harvest season. As the Emperor has commanded, however, so it must be." He heaved himself up. "There is no time to lose, but I suppose you will not want to go until you have seen the egg safely conveyed," he added to Temeraire. "We had better go the day after that, then. I will send on the word to the *jalan*-commanders, and we will rendezvous at Moscow."

"And I myself must leave at the earliest possible moment," Shen Shi said. "I ought to have been there six months ago, to assure proper supply."

Gong Su nodded and turning to Hammond said, "Mr. Hammond, will it be convenient for you to leave at once?"

"Oh," Hammond said, dismally. "I thought I—that is, I had expected, in the new circumstances of amity between our nations—surely I ought remain, as our standing ambassador—" He looked around as though for rescue. He had spoken with much enthusiasm of the opportunity of promoting the fragile new alliance, of cementing closer ties with Britain; and Laurence suspected he would be equally enthusiastic to be done with flying from one corner of the earth to another.

But Gong Su said gently and implacably, "The crown prince desires me to serve as the envoy of the court to His Imperial Majesty the Tsar, and relies upon you to provide the necessary introductions."

"Perhaps a letter—" Hammond said, half-desperately: he had already written three of these, in French and English both, and sent them on ahead by courier to Moscow, to inform the Tsar of the approaching windfall of dragons.

But he could scarcely deny that a single envoy appearing, in the company of several unharnessed dragons and claiming to be from the Emperor of China, should find it difficult to gain the confidence of the Tsar; and Gong Su pointed out he himself had not the advantage of the French language, nor could he rely upon finding an English interlocutor at the Russian court. "No, yes, of course, your point is well taken, only—" Hammond said, until at last with an unhappy look he had gone away to gather what few things he could assemble before being swept away: amongst these Churki, who shook her head disapprovingly at the prospect of the war herself.

"Three thousand miles to cross before we even come to the battle?" she said. "I do not deny the Chinese managed things very nicely on this last journey: I do not know that I have ever seen a neater job of supply. But that was in *their* country, with all the arrangements and storehouses they have laid up. It is unwise to fly so deep into a strange country without making arrangements in advance. But," she added, "in any case, Hammond, yes, it will be for the best if we go on ahead with this advance party. If I do not like the look of things, we will be closer to Britain, at least."

Her pleasure at the prospect of returning to Britain had very little to do with having absorbed Hammond's loyalties. He had in desperation, to prevent her trying to keep him back at her own mother's estate in the Incan Empire, explained his unwillingness to be severed from contact with his family. This being large and numerous, and by Incan tradition Churki's right to claim under her own protection, had changed her mind entirely; she spoke of them already in a possessive light at regular intervals, and had made Hammond teach her the names of all his nieces and nephews.

Hammond had given over trying to detach her, by now; he merely threw her a look of anxiety, and said to the rest of them as he made his hasty farewells, "Gentlemen, I trust I will see you in Moscow, not very long from now," a little grimly, as if he *hoped*, rather than promised, to be there.

"Hammond," Captain Harcourt said abruptly, "I beg your pardon, but I don't think you will see all of us." Laurence looked at her in surprise; he saw the other captains turn to look at her as well. "I have read over our orders, and they are clear enough: we are to get help to the Russians. But we have done that; I don't think our formation will make a particle of difference with three hundred Chinese dragons there, and we *will* make a good deal of difference in the Peninsula."

She turned to the other officers. "As soon as we have seen the egg safe delivered, gentlemen, I am taking the formation back to the *Potentate,* and we are going to make the best time we can for Portugal."

She spoke with decision; she was senior, as Lily headed the formation, and the right was hers. In any case Laurence could not quarrel with her judgment. In company with the Chinese legions, the formation could only be incidental, accompanying a force already more powerful than anything they would face in the air. In the Peninsula, they would represent very likely a substantial alteration in the balance of power. He could see at a glance, in Berkley's face and Sutton's, the immediate agreement, the eagerness almost at once to be gone where they might do so much good, and rejoin their own ranks; Laurence himself was hard-pressed to regard their prospects without envy.

"You must go with them," Laurence said to Demane, later that same evening, and found as he spoke that he knew Demane would not wish to go; that he knew, remembered, that Demane would not wish to be parted from Emily Roland. "I trust," he added, when Demane drew a breath, "that you do not propose to offer me an argument against your departure that would be as ungentlemanly as it would be ill-advised, when she has refused your offer."

Demane hesitated, and Laurence softened his tone a little. "No better chance is likely to offer itself to establish your career and see your rank confirmed properly: away from the Ministry and political concerns, on a battlefield, under Admiral Roland's command and Wellington's. Resolve to win their confidence, to behave as an officer and a gentleman, and you may hope to be treated as one: there are not so many heavy-weights on a scale as Kulingile that the Corps can easily let you go begging.

"And you could hardly hope for a better encomium in the eyes of the one whose good opinion you most desire," Laurence added, "than Admiral Roland's approval—nor should Excidium's feelings towards Kulingile be of small concern to you."

Demane was silenced by these last arguments more than the rest, Laurence was regretfully aware; but the point was won. Temeraire had then to be reconciled to being parted from Sipho, obstinately refusing to grant Demane's greater claim to his brother's company. "For after all," Temeraire objected, "it is not as though Demane is going anywhere that he should need someone who can read Chinese, and whatever else has he for Sipho to do, but hang aboard Kulingile's back, and perhaps be shot by some French soldier? I cannot like it in the least."

"What he can do," Laurence said, "if confirmed as a captain, is give Sipho his step to midwingman; and like as not to lieutenant. In any case, you must see that we cannot propose to separate them."

"I do not see whyever not," Temeraire said sulkily, though the two brothers had not spent a day apart from each other likely since the half-remembered occasion of their orphaning; Demane had been as much parent as sibling, since then. "I do not see why *either* of them must go," Temeraire added. "Demane can be confirmed as a captain very well here. If Kulingile considers him a captain, I do not see why anyone else ought to quarrel: you and Granby and the others have not in the least argued."

Laurence was well aware that *his* opinion on the matter should weigh with the Ministry not as much as a lofted feather; Granby himself was half-disgraced from their association and, unhappily, by Iskierka's general recalcitrance. As for Captain Harcourt, she had said nothing, but Laurence was well aware she and the other captains of the formation regarded Demane doubtfully: still too much a boy, still too much given to distempered brawling, and of foreign birth and race. They had not witnessed Demane's rescue of Kulingile as a misshapen hatchling when every other aviator would have seen the beast put to a quick death, nor the daily lengths to which the boy had gone to feed a ravenous young dragon in the midst of the Australian desert.

They had deferred to Laurence's judgment, and to the practical consideration that they none of them had the right to speak. Kulingile was unassigned to any formation, and too large to naturally acknowledge himself or his captain subordinate to any other beast of their company, for all his easy-going temper. But Laurence could not pretend to himself that they would not have been delighted to see Kulingile shift his affections, for instance to one of their own junior officers.

"He deserves the chance to show what he can do," Laurence said, "before the eyes of senior officers whose preferment can assure him the acquiesence of the Ministry. You cannot doubt that they, at least, *would* be full willing to quarrel with Kulingile's choice."

"Oh! I can believe anything of them, certainly," Temeraire said, "but I do not see why we must pay them any mind: after all, we have resolved *not* to do so, haven't we, when we think they are mistaken."

Temeraire was only at long slow length convinced that perhaps such a half-vagabond and uncertain existence as their own should not be the only nor yet the ideal course for a young man only beginning on his career to follow. "And one," Laurence added quietly, "who has not the advantages of family and name which both you and I possess, even if not in such measure as you might desire. Recollect he is an orphan, alone in the world, divided from the country of his birth and from his very tribe: even if he wished now to return, the port of Capetown is closed to our ships, and he is not of the Tswana; his own people have no dragons among them, and would scarcely welcome him and Kulingile back."

All now was nearly in readiness for the moment of parting, come upon them so swiftly and, Laurence only hoped, not too late to bring them to the aid of the Russian armies. The egg was now safely in Mianning's keeping; at dawn they would make their last farewells, the dragons of the formation taking wing for the harbor, Kulingile and Iskierka with them; and Temeraire and Arkady flying north with General Chu.

Laurence ducked into Tharkay's chamber again. The maps had been rolled into their cases and the meager baggage packed; Tharkay was lying in the bed, his eyes closed, dressed but for his swordbelt and his boots as though he meant to sleep in his clothing before waking for the journey. "It will be just as well not to be fumbling to dress in the dark, with these hands of mine," Tharkay said, dispassionately, working them gently open and shut as Laurence sat in the chair beside him: bruises still darkened the skin, and half the fingers were splinted.

Granby came into the room to join them and said, "You're

determined you won't take ship with us?" while perching upon the end of the bed. "It won't be an easy road. You'll be flying cold, Laurence, I'm afraid: I dare say the Chinese would have a fit if you tried to put up a tent on Temeraire's back. Have you got a new flying-coat, yet?"

"I have, thank you," Laurence said. Mianning had made him free of his own purse, towards repairing his wardrobe, and Laurence had swallowed his half-remembered irritation and begged Gong Su for assistance in navigating the etiquette of commissioning a garment from one of the local tailors in such a way that would not oblige the poor tradesman to proffer the item as a gift.

The coat had been delivered with sufficient alacrity to mean that the fellow had however stayed up night and day working upon it. But Laurence was grateful for the speed, which should let him take the coat with him; and more so that the garment did not make a guy of him. The leather was a supple black and the sleeves darted cleverly at shoulder and elbow with padded dark blue silk: a little outré, perhaps, but when Laurence had discovered how the contrivance served to ease the sweep of a sword, he had no objections to make. There were a few more ornate embossed decorations than he might have liked upon the sleeves, but these were subtle and easily to be missed at a distance.

His memory had begun more steadily to come back to him—flashes of recollection and emotion, conversations and actions: still with blank spaces full of surprise between them, but he felt no longer that strange sense of division from himself. Even that, he now recognized, was not so great a distance from the state of his mind these last several years. He *was* divided from the man he had once been, and by a gulf he could no longer cross.

"I fear there is something of cowardice in it," he admitted, meaning his loss of memory. "A retreat, and weak-minded at that, when I can no longer be what I was even if I wished; there is no pretense, no masquerade that could achieve it. I thought I had faced up to it; I had not thought to be so easily overcome."

"I am of the opinion," Tharkay said, "that you ought not assign to free will something more likely the consequence of a sharp blow to the skull."

Granby snorted. "You are the only fellow I can think of, Laurence, whose notion of a weak-minded retreat would be to cast your own head ahoo and slog onwards confused beyond everything, and nearly kill yourself thrice over."

He rose and gave Tharkay a bow in lieu of shaking hands: as he was short one, and Tharkay's still in sorry condition. Together they left him to his rest, closing the courtyard door behind them as they stepped out. The dragons of the formation were engaged in post-dinner ablutions—a final enjoyment of that pleasure which they would not so easily find after leaving the Imperial precincts, where enormous dragon's-head spouts were placed at the eaves of the buildings through which torrents of pleasantly hot water might be pumped over the dragons' backs.

"What an ungodly flood: we will be lucky if we are not all carried away," Captain Little said, as he sprang up onto one of the stone benches to save his boots, after Nitidus had grown too enthusiastic in his pumping: a broad gushing stream developed, running down Immortalis's back to the drain. "John, we will need Iskierka to toast their rumps before we get them back under harness, or we will all be flying wet," he said, offering a hand to pull Granby up by his good arm; and then, after a moment's hesitation, Laurence afterwards.

Laurence took it in an equally awkward spirit. The return of his memory had belatedly clarified all Little's avoidance: of course Little knew, for Granby had surely told him, that Laurence had by misfortune and Iskierka's indiscretion been brought into not only Granby's guilty secret, but his own.

And not, as one might learn of such a thing aboard a ship—not by whispered ship's gossip, and eavesdropping through her wooden walls, and one suspicious circumstance laid upon another like bricks to make a wall of certainty. Laurence could by that sort of testimony have denounced a score of men, in the Navy, and would nevertheless cheerfully and with a sense of perfect honesty have sworn, under oath, that he knew nothing of their predilections and personal habits, and denied any knowledge of a crime, even if Admiral D— had maintained an entire troop of particularly beautiful young men who could not reef a sail or pull upon a line, and Captain K— had so passionately greeted his first lieutenant of ten years, that man returning wounded from a boarding party, as to require all present to avert their eyes.

No: in this case, Granby had confessed it to him, outright, and thus made him complicit; and Iskierka had as plainly marked out Little's guilt. Laurence could not argue to himself that he did not know, and that he had no duty to speak.

The man he had been eight years before, Laurence realized, would have acknowledged that duty; perhaps would even however reluctantly and unhappily have denounced them to a superior, and set in motion all the machinery of the courts-martial to destroy them. That man would have put duty above not merely personal sentiment and attachment, but above the natural sense of justice which revolted at the idea of exposing to ruin and misery any man for such a crime.

He would have not valued his own feelings, on such a matter, higher than the law and the discipline of the service. If he *had* kept silent, either from affection or a sense of having received a confidence, or a more practical consideration of the damage the loss of two skilled captains and their beasts would do to the service, he would have felt a painful and bitter guilt at doing so. And so aside from an ordinary mortification at having his intimate concerns so exposed to a man not his close friend, Little had indeed a cause to fear; and especially a partial and stumbling return of Laurence's memory.

Laurence ruefully admitted to himself that he *had* been a great deal happier in this instance not to remember: it was wretchedly awkward to know that which he ought not know, and to know that Little and Granby should both know he knew it, while none of them might utter a word on the subject. But he felt no guilt; he was done with that subtle species of cowardice which hid behind the judgment of other men. He said to them, "I had better take my leave of you now, gentlemen; you will have a difficult time enough getting away, I think," and offered Little his hand. "My most sincere regards, and good fortune, to you both," he said, as close as he could come, he felt, to conveying a reassurance without being so plain as to embarrass them both. Granby he embraced, and added, more lightly, "And for Heaven's sake, John, have a care for that other arm."

"Trust me! Though I can't very well complain," Granby said. "I did say that I would have given an arm to have Iskierka a little more biddable, so if I have been taken at my word, that is not the fault of Fortune. So at least this time, you may indeed hope to be shot of me: I have Iskierka's word she will go quietly to the *Potentate*, and no more haring off madly."

"I am sorry for the pains she has put you to," Laurence said, "and I will refrain from expressing the sentiment to her, but for my own part, I must be grateful to her: I cannot think what we should have done, these last two years, without you both. Godspeed!"

He took his leave of them and navigated from one stone bench to another, making his farewells to the other captains as he passed them and their beasts in the flooded courtyard, until at last he was across, and stepped through the house and out to the palace lanes, returning to Temeraire's courtyard. "What is all that noise, over there?" Temeraire asked, raising his head from his book. The ground crewmen were bundling up their supplies, and the house servants were busily engaged in packing all Laurence's things under Temeraire's watchful eye, including the scarlet robes of silk and velvet. Laurence sighed inwardly to see them; he would gladly have left them behind by oversight.

"They are making something of a lake," Laurence said. The stones of Temeraire's court were still a little damp from his own bathing, and his hide still speckled with drops that had not run off him; Laurence took one of the large soft silken rags from their basket in the corner of the courtyard and dried a small pool which had accumulated in the crook of Temeraire's foreleg. Temeraire nudged him with pleasure and thanks, and Laurence seated himself upon the arm.

They sat together a little while without a word required, in silent contentment, a peace that would vanish soon enough; and yet would still be there to be found again, Laurence thought. How nearly he had lost it, entirely, without even knowing what he lost.

"Laurence," Temeraire said after a little while, "Napoleon will be quite outnumbered in the air, will he not?"

"So we hope," Laurence said. "And he will not be able to bring his full infantry and cavalry to bear against us, either. He will have to leave detachments behind to hold his lines open. Numerically, we should have the advantage, and the advantage of fighting on Russian soil."

"It does sound so very promising," Temeraire said. "Surely we shall have him this time. And you need not make that noise, either, O'Dea," he added. "We will have three hundred dragons with us: I am quite sure even Napoleon and Lien cannot have anything to say to them."

O'Dea, sitting on a rock and sewing links of mail back onto Temeraire's armor, had given a lugubrious snort. "Why, it's true enough we've a great many dragons *here;* I suppose we can hope that most of them will still be with us when we're *there.* We must hope for it, sure, seeing how Boney has sent the Russians scampering more than once before now. 'Tis a cold winter in that country, so I've heard: a cold winter to be out on the barren plain, haunted by wild beasts, without a fire to sit beside and all the French Army on our heels."

"I do not think you ought to speak so discouragingly," Temeraire said disapprovingly. "Why, Maximus and Lily and even Iskierka would not be going away if they thought there were any chance of our being beat: you see how sure they are we will win."

O'Dea wagged his head. "Ah, indeed; 'tis a pity, all those fellows going away by ship, and like as not to the bottom of the ocean."

Temeraire flattened his ruff, and maintained a dignified silence until O'Dea had gone back into the house, as the lanterns were dimmed; then he said to Laurence, "Laurence, what *will* we do, if Napoleon should defeat us?"

"Starve," Laurence said, dryly.

PART

3

Chapter 16

The room was ablaze with candles, many standing before mirrors of gilt and shining on gold and silver; the guests an equal brilliance of jewels and silks and velvet, their voices rising and falling in steady rhythm over the delicate threads of music. There might be a hectic flush on some cheeks, a nervous edge to laughter too quickly suppressed, but no-one surveying the company would have imagined that four hundred miles away, St. Petersburg was occupied by Napoleon's army; nor from overhearing their conversation.

"They say that one could walk across the Seine on the backs of those foreign dragons, so closely were they crammed in upon one another outside Notre Dame," Countess Andreyevna said, in tones of solemn horror more appropriate to the discussion of a funeral than a baptism. "We see now where all this dreadful revolution leads, and what a monster has taken hold of France! He will not content himself with regicide and self-aggrandizement, but will tear down the Christian faith with everything else: he is a heathen, that is plain to see.

"And not seven months since the wedding," she added, with a flavor of spitefulness. "I hope that Bonaparte may be confident of his paternity."

The new *Roi de Cusco,* as he had been styled, was by now four months old and reportedly thriving: he had been christened Napoleon Joseph Pachacuti Yupanqui—by Cardinal Fesch, and quite in accordance with Catholic rites, despite the complaints of the countess.

Laurence had not held much hope of some event preventing the marriage. The Incan Empress had shown plainly she had as much quick decision in her nature as ever did Bonaparte, and having made her choice to accept his suit, she had already flung all the resources of her own vast Empire behind that course. Her dragons had driven the British out of the Incan Empire the very same day, and she had taken ship for France with Bonaparte not three months later, from the reports which had reached Laurence in Brazil.

Evidently, Anahuarque had also chosen to anticipate the rites, and thus had Napoleon so quickly gained the heir required to secure the loyalty of the Incan dragons and the future of his dynasty— the only thing which might have been wanting to further spur his relentless ambition. But however much the child's birth might be deplored, Laurence had not the least desire to engage in gossip about it. Napoleon's son could as yet do nothing; his army, everything.

Laurence quitted, without much ceremony, the company gathered around the countess in some impatience, and went seeking Hammond. He had been raised amid political dinners, gatherings of men either in power or soon to be, and his sense of such things was finely tuned: this was nothing of the sort—merely society, not politics, nor even the mingling of the two. There were a handful of aristocrats with some influence, each of them courted by a subtle band of hangers-on seeking personal advantage; a few staff officers and adjutants, none as high as a general. The rest of the company were merely the wealthy or titled or connected to the same, and of not the least significance.

"Hammond," Laurence said, having cut him out of his own conversation with an elderly dandy of a baron with a brusque swiftness of which he would have been ashamed under less dire circumstances, "why the devil are we here?"

He and Temeraire had arrived the previous evening, with Chu

and a couple of *niru*, and joined Shen Shi at the supply depot outside Moscow: enormous granaries piled high with wheat and cured meat, which she had displayed to them with an attitude of deep embarrassment. "I regret that my preparations have been so inadequate," she said.

They could not in justice be so called; but they were not, however, what one might have wished for a force of three hundred dragons: the Russians had been recalcitrant in providing assistance. "I am trying," Hammond said now, with some asperity, "to catch someone's ear: they will not listen to me; not even our own ambassador," he added bitterly, "the wretched old fool! There are a thousand adventurers all over the city, peddling miracles to anyone that will give them an audience; they have decided I am to be classed with these charlatans.

"My only hope," Hammond added, "was that your arrival would bring an end to their doubts—that they could scarcely deny the evidence when you had appeared—but I called at the department of state this morning, and a staff-officer told me that if you would fight, you might go westward down the New Smolensk Road and report for duty to whichever colonel you found first; but if I did not leave, he would lay hands on me and kick me all the way to the door. They have not received any report whatsoever, from the east, of any force of dragons approaching. Where *are* the rest of the beasts?"

"That is not a new question, to be asked of the British," a man said, approaching their corner, and Laurence looked at him startled: an extraordinary intrusion, and the note of rancor as palpable as the thick Prussian accent.

"I beg your pardon," Laurence said, grimly, wondering if he was on the point of facing a challenge, a wretched trap between honor and duty; and then there was something familiar about the man, the face. Laurence had a brief, vivid memory of gunpowder smoke in his nose amid a clear and brilliantly blue sky: of a vast army pouring over fields, tricolor flags billowing; a great dragon lapped in heavy scales almost like mail, a bellowing laugh; and he found he did know the man, despite his greying hair and his paunch. "Captain Dyhern, I believe?" he said, slowly.

They had fought together, briefly, in the disastrous campaign of the year six. Dyhern had been taken prisoner at Jena, he and his dragon Eroica, an impressive Prussian heavy-weight, both of them among the many victims of the revolution in aerial tactics which Lien had brought to Bonaparte's service.

Dyhern's face was hard and sour and scarred, thinner than last they had met and aged far more than the intervening years could account for; but they had been allies, once, and had done him no injury of which to be ashamed: Laurence and Temeraire had given what aid they could, even in the midst of that overwhelming rout. The anger was not personal, but general, then; Laurence looked steadily into his face, and Dyhern after a moment looked aside, as one who knows himself in the wrong and does not care to admit it.

"I am glad to see you at liberty, sir," Laurence said; he felt no obligation to press for any more satisfaction. "I hope it is not—I hope the cause is not an unhappy one." A captain would not ordinarily be paroled or released by the enemy, save if his dragon were slain; although in the legal sense Napoleon and Prussia had made peace, Napoleon had neither withdrawn his occupying troops nor released the dragons, nor his most valuable hostage: the crown prince of Prussia, who lived yet in Paris under his supposed guardianship.

"I escaped prison a year ago," Dyhern said, briefly for what could only have been a long and a dreadful tale. "As for Eroica—I know not. I have sought him in the breeding grounds. But they did not know of him. They sequestered many of our beasts deep in France—some we hear they have persuaded to turn coat and join their ranks: you may be sure he will never be seen among *those*," he added, with a touch of fierce pride. "But of anything else—" His hand moved a little sideways, limply, as though to convey that the sum of his knowledge was insufficient even to be put into words.

So he was an aviator without a beast, grounded and unable to be of any use, and burdened by the wretched knowledge that if Eroica did live, he was yet kept a prisoner by his fear for Dyhern's own safety: a cause for bitterness Laurence had himself tasted, enough to make him sympathetic. But the twenty dragons that Britain had promised to the Prussian war effort, in the campaign of 1806, had only been held back due to the deadly plague which had descended so mercilessly on Britain's dragons, and would not even when healthy have made any material difference to the disaster.

"Yes, perhaps it is true," Dyhern said, with a snort. "But it is no wonder if the Tsar and his generals think very little of British promises now, and little of this story, this fantasy, of three hundred dragons from nowhere, from the hordes of the East. I have heard your story: you bring eight dragons, and call them three hundred."

Laurence shook his head: he did not himself know where the bulk of the Chinese forces were, nor why they had not yet arrived in Moscow, and in truth he would have felt doubtful himself if he had not already seen once with his own eyes the rapidity of their mustering. Dyhern was not wrong: with a few seeds of doubt sowed already, particularly if many other Prussian officers were also refugee among the Russians, and the British ambassador himself unconvinced, it was no wonder any longer if they could gain no ear.

"We had best go and speak with Chu," Laurence said to Hammond. "The remainder of the dragons cannot be far distant now: we might persuade the Russians to send a courier to confirm the approach of at least one cohort, if he can tell us their direction."

There could be no question of their merely departing for the front: the armies might be anywhere in a square five hundred miles across. An aerial force with no ground support, even one of their extraordinary size, would be perilously vulnerable to any encounter with a substantial French force mingling dragons and artillery; three hundred dragons was not so many that they could afford to lose half of them.

Laurence hesitated, on the point of departing, and then quietly said to Dyhern, "Captain, if you are not otherwise engaged in the war effort, I hope you will permit me to say that Temeraire and I would be glad of your assistance: we are short-handed, and my crew have many of them not seen aerial combat." Several of them indeed were former sailors, recruited from the survivors of the wreck of the *Allegiance*; his officers were a wretchedly scanty bunch, most of those having also perished in that disaster. Forthing was brave and competent enough, but not by any means a star in the firmament; Ferris could not be called a lieutenant, though he deserved the place; besides them Laurence had only a few ragged midwingmen and ensigns.

Dyhern was silent; the lines of resentment and misery stood out upon his face more strongly for a moment it seemed, in the candle-light of the room; then abruptly he said, "My God! I will not sit by the fire while there is a dragon to fly and fight; yes, I will come with you. Of course I will come. Do you go now?"

Laurence would have gladly made arrangements for his later joining them, but Dyhern refused: "I have with me my boots, my coat, and my sword. What else do I possess?" He accosted a servant to write a hasty note of apology to his host, begging for his things to be delivered to Hammond's care at the embassy when it should be convenient. "Baron Sarkovsky will understand: his mother was a Prussian, a cousin of my father," he said, "and he has been kind enough to give a home to a few of us who have not been able to stomach bending our necks beneath the Corsican's boot-heel: even those like myself for whom the army has had no use." The treaty which the King of Prussia had signed with Napoleon had been humiliating in the extreme.

The streets of Moscow were silent and humid, heat lingering in the late air of August, thick even at night, and the moon above them shone through an aureole of pale haze. "Napoleon is near Smolensk," Dyhern said, "or so they say; but he might be outside the gates of Moscow tomorrow, for all that damned coward Barclay has done to slow him down. He has not given a single battle.

318

He flees and flees, like a rat evading—Oh, it is Davout! Run to the east! Ah! Murat is there! Fly to the south! My God, Napoleon himself! And he faints away like a maiden," with a contemptuous sweep of his hand, his deep voice descending again from high-pitched mimicry. "It is enough to turn one's stomach. They let St. Petersburg fall without a shot fired; and still he flees. But Barclay must defend Smolensk; he cannot let it fall: so my friends say."

The streets had wound through a narrow and unpleasantly scented warren of crammed-in impoverished buildings, approaching the gates of the small main covert of the city. Hammond had at least gained them the use of the British embassy's courier Placet, a glum Winchester of middling years whose captain, a man named Terrance, contented himself with his isolate post through a good-humored drunkenness: they could not presently fly their usual routes with the French Army blocking them to east and north. Dragon and man were both snoring in harness, and were roused only with difficulty for the flight out to the encampment: this lying some ten miles and more beyond the city limits.

"*Three* of you, now?" Placet said with a sigh at Dyhern's addition to their party, though he outweighed an elephant handily and could have taken several more passengers without any real trouble. "Well, I suppose you had better lock yourselves on; we won't get there any sooner."

The encampment was barely respectable, by Chinese standards, though its appearance astonished Dyhern to silence. Shen Shi and her escort, eight of the common blue dragons and their numerous crews, had labored extensively: large cooking-pits were covered with rough-hewn stone lids, and over these enormous mats of wood and metal had been unrolled, on which dragons might sleep warm: more stood yet unused and waiting. Wells had been sunk up on a hill, near-by, and channels dug to bring the water rolling downstream, diverted into distinct pools for drinking and for bathing, and continuing on towards the cattle pens.

Above all this stood the great gauzy pavilion which had been erected once more for Temeraire, and beside this the one for Chu, where the general was napping; as they approached he raised his head, peering narrowly at Dyhern, and before Hammond could address him on the subject of the missing beasts demanded in tones of irritation, "Well, is *this* a Russian general, finally? Where are his maps? Will he tell me where the enemy is? My army cannot travel any slower than they already are."

Hammond, mouth half-opened, recalled himself and stammered, "Sir, no, this is Captain Dyhern, a Prussian officer, a friend of Captain Laur—that is, I mean, of His Imperial Highness. But so far as the army goes, we had come to ask you that very—that is to say, to inquire of you, where your army might be. I am afraid the Russians have had no reports, from the countryside, of any substantial forces approaching—"

He trailed off, in the face of Chu's stare, and fell silent. "Your remarks are very peculiar," Chu said. "Are you complaining because we are *not* spoiling the territory of our allies? My troops are not undisciplined yearlings."

"I beg your pardon," Hammond said, "but surely by now many of the—of the *niru* will have joined up, in preparation for the final muster? Even a quarter of a *jalan* could not escape notice—"

"No," Chu said, "nor travel more than twenty miles in a day, through this barren and unsettled countryside, before they had to stop to be sure they could feed themselves; certainly stripping the farmers bare to do so."

Laurence could not but recognize the plain sense of Chu's remarks: he realized in dismay he had unconsciously gone too far in assigning to the Chinese legions some fantastical power of supplying their wants, by the example he had seen within China itself, where undoubtedly there had been, unseen, supply depots and warehoused goods in the near distance available to the building force. "Sir," he said, "do you mean they are traveling in their individual *niru*? Keeping some substantial distance from one another?"

"Twenty miles, at least," Chu said, agreeing: indeed a sufficient separation to permit even many groups of dragons, traveling four at a time, to make themselves nearly invisible within the vastness of the Russian countryside. "It will require four days to muster the full force upon the battlefield: but that," he added in some heat, "must be presently!

"I have already sent the couriers to delay their pace, having seen the inadequacy of our supply here, but they cannot merely halt where they are, nor slow very much: the countryside is too poor. We must find the enemy, concentrate to defeat him, and disperse again to return."

Hammond cleared his throat and said, "Sir, I am—I entirely take your point, and—and I beg you do not suppose I in the least mean to question your arrangements; but perhaps if—perhaps if some fraction of the force might be assembled, and summoned hence—"

Chu lowered his head to stare at him. "Why?"

"The Russians think us liars," Laurence said bluntly, when Hammond would have continued to evade. "They do not believe that the force is coming."

Chu snorted and shook out his fringed mane with disgust. "They will certainly believe it when they have three hundred dragons eating every last scrap of wheat in twenty miles around this city, but they will not be very happy, and less so when I will have to send all my *jalan* away again before we have even seen any fighting!"

"I am very glad to see you, Captain Dyhern," Temeraire said, "and oh! It is the greatest shame, about Eroica: we must try and find out where he is, and I dare say then we can get word to him that you are at liberty. Perhaps we will take some French dragons prisoner, and I will ask them: I am sure no dragon could fail to be sympathetic to his situation, nor wish him to be denied a reunion with you."

"Temeraire," Laurence said, "you could not ask them to commit treason against their own nation."

"I do not see why it should be treason," Temeraire said, "when their nation has no business keeping Dyhern away from Eroica: you might as well say Moncey committed treason, because he told me you were on *Goliath,*" recalling with a shudder his own dark days in the breeding grounds of Wales; Moncey and his fellow feral Winchesters had been his only hope of himself being reunited with Laurence, then.

"But if they do not like to talk to me about it," he added, "I will speak to Moncey himself when we are back in England. I do not see any reason why one of the Winchesters mightn't nip across and have a word with some of the unharnessed French dragons, from their own breeding grounds. They did as much only to gossip; indeed, Captain, I am sure we will be able to find him for you."

Dyhern flushed red, when Temeraire had finished; he said, "I will thank you, if it can be done," very shortly, and then stepped away; Laurence said to Temeraire quietly, "My dear, pray do not raise false hopes: a thousand things may arise to prevent our being able to assist him."

"Well, I will not say anything more about it, at present," Temeraire said, but privately he did not see why it should be at all difficult: after all, Eroica must be somewhere, very likely with other dragons about, and it seemed very poor-spirited to be getting in the dumps without having at least asked properly. So far as Temeraire could see, Dyhern had only ever spoken to other men, and not tried to ask any dragons at all, much less the couriers or better yet the unharnessed dragons of the breeding grounds, and the ferals, who had the most chance of flying about as they liked.

"I don't suppose you know any of the unharnessed dragons in this country?" he asked Placet.

"You suppose rightly," Placet said. "I haven't seen hide or wing of a feral, and as for their couriers here, they are rudesbys; they speak some outlandish stuff and don't care to even nod their heads, in a friendly way, when they see you. They only go and take their pig, and sit in a corner and stare at you, as though they supposed you meant to come and steal it from them." He sighed heavily. "Not all of us get to go gallivanting about the world to charming places, with fancy dinners, and gewgaws; but one would think that perhaps the Admiralty might let a fellow come home, once in a while. But I don't complain, of course," he added.

"Well, there must be a breeding ground here, somewhere," Temeraire said, "and at the very least, they must have a bigger covert near-by for their own beasts: and," he added in sudden inspiration, "Laurence: surely we ought to go and speak to them in any case. I dare say the dragons will know all that Chu would like, about where the French Army is; they must be hearing of it from their officers every minute."

Dyhern could speak the Russian tongue, and direct them to the main covert of the Russian beasts, some twenty miles from the city, on the opposite side from their own encampment. It seemed a peculiarly inconvenient arrangement, in its relation to the encampment they had been allocated: when he drew it upon a map for them to see, there could hardly have been a greater distance, and yet keep both in an hour's flight of the city. Temeraire flattened his ruff at this discourtesy.

"Let us be a little more generous than that," Laurence said. "We have claimed the approach of three hundred beasts; even doubting us, they may well have wished to give us as much room as possible. I can conceive of no other reason that would place us at opposite ends. They can hardly imagine that we should seek a quarrel with their own dragons, when we are come as their allies."

"No, indeed," Temeraire said in some irritation, a state which only increased upon their arrival: the Russian covert was far better placed than the ground which they had been allocated, with better drainage, several small ponds and lakes sharing ground with a series of low craggy foothills, into which hollows had been dug and large roofs built out to make neat and comfortable dens, and from aloft many of these looked quite deserted but for small bands of men: Temeraire felt he and Chu might at least have been invited to take up residence, as a gesture of courtesy to the senior officers of their force, even if there were not enough room for all the dragons which were coming.

He descended through a brush of low straggly trees and scrub and nudged his way to the hollow nearest the border of the covert, and then he halted short, staggered, as the morning sun crept through behind him and broke like a stream upon the mass of a mighty and glittering hoard.

Gold—jewels—silver—Temeraire did not know where to look. Heaps of brass pieces, long chains of thick links of bright metal, dazzling great chunks of polished stone and glass, long carved sticks of polished ivory and mahogany and ebon, great cups and plates—dented and scratched from lying in a heap, but what did that matter when there were so many of them! so large!—and swords, and helms, and even huge bolts of cloth—velvet and silk, stained perhaps and torn, but still luxurious—enormous carved chests of wood heaped high with glinting shards of glass in colors, huge blocks of marble carved—

"Temeraire!" Laurence said, and Temeraire shook himself all over and jerked up his head. A low rumbling hiss of warning reached his ears, and he saw only then the huge dragon sprawled over the ground—she was lying upon the very heap itself, as though she had so much treasure she might make a bed of it.

She had a peculiar appearance: her body was sheathed in great plates of bony armor overlapping one another, not unlike the Prussian dragons Temeraire had met before, but to a far greater extent, and she seemed to bulge strangely underneath them: thick rolls swelled over her shoulders, and a large hump upon her back. Steel spikes and great steel rings had been bolted to her natural armor, silver over the natural green coloration of her hide, and were bristling all over her body; she was enormous, larger than himself and nearly as great as Maximus.

She reared herself up with a great heave; several other dragons scrambled away from between them. Temeraire had not noticed them before, either: small frightened-looking creatures, light-weights, mostly grey and white; they did not have the same armor plates, but the steel rings were planted in their bodies as well.

"Temeraire," Laurence said again, "she must fear you are here to quarrel over that treasure; we must reassure her at once."

"Oh," Temeraire said, "oh—yes. Of course. Of course I am not here to challenge her. Pray tell her so, Dyhern," a little wistfully: only look how much treasure there was! And he could surely have made a successful challenge, and perhaps won some of it for Laurence—"But we are allies," he said, mastering himself with an effort, "and we must think of our duty first. I am not at all going to challenge her, no matter how much treasure she has."

"We had better go away at once," Dyhern said to Laurence, low, in French. "The beast will pay no mind to us: why should she? We are not her captain, nor her officers; you will do your cause no good if you provoke a quarrel."

"Sir," Laurence said, "dragons cannot be blamed for not speaking to us, if we do not address ourselves to them. Pray translate for Temeraire, if you can, and let us make the attempt; we will certainly not engage. If she attacks, we must withdraw at once, Temeraire, without offering a blow in return."

Temeraire did not at all like the notion that if she should strike him, he should be obligated to run away; she would think him a terrific coward, and all those other dragons who were watching as well. "I do not see any reason she should attack me," Temeraire said. "I have done nothing to her, and I do not mean to; nothing at all."

Dyhern spoke to the dragon in Russian; Temeraire pricked his ears forward to listen to it: quite different from any tongue he had ever learned. But the enormous dragon did not pay him any attention, nor even look at him: instead she bared her teeth at Temeraire and hissed again, taking a step towards him that required no translation at all. He swelled up his chest, his ruff flaring: "I am not to be hissed at, if you please," he said coldly in French, "as I am perfectly able to manage you, if you *do* want to be quarrelsome."

"Temeraire—" Laurence began, but one of the small dragons, who had ducked behind the great one, put out his narrow white head, arrow-shaped, and said something timidly in a queerly accented French, "What do you want, please, if you are not here to fight?"

"Oh, you speak French, do you?" Temeraire said. "Well, we are here to find out where the French Army is: Napoleon, I mean. We are your allies," he added, "and might have expected a more polite welcome than this, I must say; I do not know what you are about, when someone cannot even land to pay a visit, without being hissed at and treated like a thief. And you may tell *her* so, anytime you like." There was a great deal of righteous satisfaction in making this speech, which a little consoled Temeraire for *not* being able to fight.

The little dragon turned and spoke to the larger in a tongue that was very much like Durzagh, the dragon language which Arkady and his ferals spoke, in the Pamirs. Temeraire could follow it better than not, and understood quite plainly when the large dragon snorted and said, "That is nonsense. Tell him to go away at once, or I will crush him, and take that breastplate of his for myself."

Temeraire flattened his ruff and snapped, "I should like to see you try—" But Laurence's hand upon his neck reminded him, so with a great effort he straightened his neck and with chilly condescension went on. "—but we are not here to pick a quarrel: so if you do want me to go away, you need merely answer my question, and we shall leave; I do not in the least wish to remain in the company of a dragon whose wealth is by no means sufficient to excuse her poor manners."

"And why would you ask me such a question?" the dragon said coldly.

"Well, I do not mean you must know where the *French* Army is, I suppose," Temeraire said, "but you can tell me where the Russian Army is, and that will be where the French are, soon enough; so that will do."

"What Russian Army?" the enormous dragon said. "What is this to me?"

Temeraire drew back his head upon his neck, in some confusion. "Laurence," he said, turning his head, speaking in French, "and Captain Dyhern, is there perhaps some mistake? This dragon is not in the army, at all."

"Of course she is," Dyhern said. "There is her regiment number, upon her shoulder," and indeed, Temeraire saw where he pointed to a large 26 painted in bright red that stood out upon one of the armor plates, and beside it the number 8.

"The captain is in a regiment," the little dragon interjected, a little uncertainly, "—I believe? I have heard him speak of the regiment."

The enormous dragon shrugged when this had been relayed to her, and said without moving her suspicious eye from Temeraire, "So this is some human matter. I do not care about that. If you want an army, you had better go find some humans and talk to them; and while you do it, you may go far away from me and *my* treasure."

She reached out her foreleg and jealously scraped a few spilled coins back into her heap: her talons were sheathed in bright caps of polished steel, which had been nailed on; she certainly *looked* as though she were a fighting-dragon. But Temeraire felt quite at an impasse: how could she not know if she were in the army, and not care about it in the least? Before he could ask her anything further, however, a man appeared in an officer's uniform: out of breath and red in the face, with several other younger officers running behind him, and shouted up at Laurence in French, "Who the devil are you? How dare you come stir up my beasts?"

"Sir—" Laurence said, and slid down from Temeraire's back,

to go and speak with the gentleman, who coldly deigned to give his name: Captain Ivan Rozhkov, of the Twenty-Sixth Regiment of the Air. He had a luxuriant mustache and beard, brown shot through a very little with silver, and a narrow face fixed presently in anger; he held in one hand a peculiar sort of short whip, with a heavy silver handle. The little white dragon had sidled over towards him, and was murmuring quietly to him; but he waved the dragon off. "As far as I am concerned," Rozhkov said, "you are a pack of spies: you will go, or I will set Vosyem upon you."

"If you mean that dragon there," Temeraire said, interjecting, "I have fought bigger dragons than her, without the least difficulty," although privately he did admit to himself that she would present a notable challenge: the armor might, he feared, stand up to the divine wind; and those spikes and her tipped claws would certainly be quite nasty at close quarters. "So you needn't be threatening. We are only asking so we can go and fight alongside you, after all."

Rozhkov only looked up at him halfway through this conversation, and then snorted and said to Laurence, "You English, you make your dragons into house-pets and parrots: keep your three hundred fairy tales, and take this trained dog of yours away to them, also! There are ten fighting-beasts in this covert all her size; I will rouse them all up if you are not on your way at once."

Temeraire reared up on his hind legs, to take a quick look around, and indeed he saw two more of the hollows in sight, and then he realized that in each of them a gleam might be spied out, through the treees—ten dragons! Ten dragons, all of them with so much treasure, it nearly could not be borne. "Oh," Temeraire said, longingly. "Oh; but how can they all be so rich?"

"If you think you will be pillaging here, you are very wrong," Rozhkov snapped to Laurence.

"That is enough," Laurence said shortly. "More than enough, sir; I am sorry to have distressed your beast, and to have disturbed your morning. I hope to God you will have no greater cause to regret the occasion. Temeraire, we will be on our way; there is nothing to be gained here. We must rely on Hammond to procure the intelligence for us."

"Certainly," Temeraire said, as haughtily as he could manage, dragging his eyes away; he reached out to put Laurence up. "It seems very peculiar to me, to find dragons so perfectly uninformed about the war they ought to be fighting in; but as their officers do not seem to be much better, one cannot blame *them*, I suppose."

He paused, with Laurence in his talons, and raised up on his haunches again: a heavy clanging bell had begun to ring, not far away, and cries were going up across the covert. Vosyem had lifted her own head in fresh suspicion. In the distance, approaching swiftly, a knot of five dragons were flying, unsteadily and on a wavering course. One was a beast on Vosyem's scale, enormous and armor-plated; the others were smaller, in motley colors, trying to support him as they went. He left a thin spattering trail of blood behind him.

Temeraire swung Laurence to his back and sprang aloft, even as Rozhkov shouted some commands, cracking the whip, and the small white and grey dragons all went up together alongside him. "Why is Vosyem not helping?" Temeraire demanded of the little one who spoke French, as they flew up. It would have been a great deal handier to have a beast or two that size, when there was one so large to manage landing; the poor fellow did not look as though he could come down properly on his own.

"But what if one of the others took her treasure?" the little dragon said, looking at Temeraire dubiously. "There are no guards posted, and it has not been locked up properly."

While that argument could be said to have a great deal of sense, it was also distinctly selfish, in Temeraire's opinion. At least there were a great many of the smaller dragons, and together they caught the huge beast from beneath and managed to get him landed safely in a vacant clearing. His head hung forward listlessly, and he seemed as though he only wished to lie down. But an officer aboard his back cracked his whip, and he continued to hold himself up while a rope ladder was flung down, and men scrambled off: he was carrying a crew of nearly thirty, and many of them officers.

They were met by the officers of the covert, running to help; several men in bandages stained badly with blood, some being let down from the belly-netting strapped down to flat cots; they were all carried away. A man in a captain's uniform staggered off, took a rag from a colleague and mopped his bloody brow, said in French, "Give me a drink, for the love of the Holy Mother," and took a cup from another and drank it down. He wiped his mouth and said, "I must get back aloft and to the city. Rozhkov, will you get Tri settled and get that belly-wound stitched up? By God! I didn't think we would make it in the end, even though I swore to General Tutchkov we would manage."

He took another gulp; his crew were already busily re-harnessing one of the smaller dragons, a white creature stippled with spots of grey and black, for him to ride, while dragon-surgeons scrambled for the beast. "For God's sake, Vasya," cried a younger officer, "don't keep us all holding our breath: what has happened? Has there been fighting?"

"Fighting!" the captain laughed, a harsh noise, hoarse. "If you want to call it that. We have been run out of Smolensk. We are falling back on Valutino, and if not there on Usvyatye, and if not there, on Tsarevo Zaimische—and if not there, God help the Tsar!"

Chapter 17

Half-a-day's flight, and a pillar of smoke rising in the distance: another Russian town burning. As Temeraire beat towards it, Laurence saw the Russian Army straggling by, the small dragons flying past scarcely to be made out beneath the infantry soldiers clinging all over their bodies, being borne back with the retreat more swiftly than their feet could carry them. Officers were astride at the neck or in some cases being dangled beneath from a sort of swinging chair.

"Too much for their weight," Chu said, observing the flocks of smaller beasts, "although they are performing well, but infantry-dragons ought to be one hundred and fifty *picul*," this measure being roughly on the order of nine tons; the white dragons were not more than six or seven, to Laurence's eye: barely light-weights. In the far distance, he could see a melee of courier-weight dragons skirmishing: Cossack troops, he supposed, tangling with the French scouts; the pursuit was not far behind. It was the thirtieth of August.

The army was in disarray; beneath them, Laurence saw the men marching in long columns, bedraggled, dusty; heads bowed with exhaustion, sullen. Endless numbers of men; Chu himself fell increasingly silent and astonished by the numbers, the further they flew; when they had come to rest upon a hill, near a trickling spring, he shook his head and said, "The ant can devour a mountain," and then plunged his head deep to drink.

Temeraire continued futilely to search for the high command;

there was nothing which might have been called a headquarters visible to the eye. They flew over an artillery company rattling sluggish upon the road; Dyhern caught sight of Prussian soldiers and clambered down from Temeraire's neck, and went to speak with them. He returned to say, "Barclay de Tolly has been replaced: it is General Kutuzov, now, and they say he is in Elnya, to the south."

Kutuzov was not in Elnya; but much of the army had concentrated north of the town, and spilled into its limits. Laurence and Dyhern and Tharkay went into the streets together, to try and find some senior officer. A deep smoldering atmosphere emanated from the soldiers and officers alike, somewhere between misery and wrath; the burning of Smolensk was on every tongue, a collective mourning, and Laurence heard Kutuzov's name repeated every few steps with more desperation than hope. They at last found a ferociously busy colonel engaged in directing the fortification of the northern approach to the town. "General Kutuzov is in Vyazma," he said: another fifty miles, back the way they had come.

"I begin to see," Chu said in dry irritation, "why you use such heavy couriers; they must carry enough men to hunt down the one you are looking for, who may be under a table, or in a basket." The Jade Dragons might have flown the distances trivially, at much less cost to their joint energies, but speaking neither Russian nor French could not themselves communicate, even if Russian officers would have deigned to speak with them; they could serve only as couriers among Chu's own forces.

Temeraire and Chu reached the town as night was falling, weary. Two of Shen Shi's supply-dragons had accompanied them, carrying sacks of wheat and a dazed pig, for which they had ample cause to be grateful: the few Russian dragons they saw, their encampments merely crushed fields, were snarling and hissing at one another with belligerence over a scanty supply of dead cavalry-horses. They made their own camp upon a low hill not yet tenanted by any other company, and the supply-dragons dug a cooking-pit. "If you will come with me," Laurence said to Dyhern, "we will try again: I suppose when we have looked in every town between Smolensk and Moscow, we will find him eventually."

He scarcely hoped for success, but they made Kutuzov at last, his pavilion planted atop a low rise among three companies of artillery, with two courier-dragons, red, drowsing beside it and a great flag waving brilliant white and red. But the way was still barred. Dyhern attempted to persuade the guards to let them through the perimeter without success; Laurence's French gained them no better result.

"Well," Chu said, when they had returned to report their failure, "this general can talk to me, and we can settle upon our ground, and I can summon the three *jalan* to assemble there in four days. If he does not want to talk to me, I can call together ten *niru,* here, and let them feed themselves off the countryside for three days. And if he does not talk to me *then,* we will turn around and go home, and I will apologize to the Emperor. I will not spend my soldiers for fools, nor expose them to those guns for no purpose."

He said this last very flatly: to have failed his orders so thoroughly would certainly condemn him to disgrace and exile from the Imperial court, even if the fault had been none of his own. But Laurence found he could not argue the decision. He had recalled too clearly, as Chu spoke, the dreadful slaughter of the French dragons at Shoeburyness: the smell of sulfur and fresh loam overturned, the rain of dirt flung high into the air as the British guns brought down the Grand Chevalier. He could scarcely fault Chu for not wishing to hazard his soldiers to such a fate without some assurance of support and the achieving of some desirable end.

"Laurence," Tharkay said abruptly, "do you have those particularly magnificent robes with you somewhere?"

"Oh! Oh, yes! That is a splendid notion," Temeraire said, lifting his head with as much eagerness as might be needed to supply the want of Laurence's own. "Of course they will not turn you away, Laurence, when they see you properly dressed. And I have the robes with me; at least, I ought to: Roland, you have made them quite safe, I suppose?"

"Yes, of course; they are wrapped in oilcloth and in the batting chest," Roland said, before Laurence could begin to protest. "Shall I fetch them out?"

"At once, if you please," Temeraire said, while Laurence drew breath. However desperate the circumstances, all feeling revolted at the notion he should trick himself out in the panoply of the Imperial court and use it to present himself as a prince of China—and not merely in that court, where all involved knew and perfectly understood the polite and fictional nature of his status, but brazenly to the government of a foreign state, to none other than the commander-in-chief of the Russian Army, appointed by the Tsar himself.

"Besides which, you can scarcely expect the Russians to believe me a prince of China on sight," Laurence said, "and they are not likely to listen or accept so fantastic a story as my adoption must seem, on first blush." But Temeraire was inclined to be mulish; Temeraire did not see any reason why anyone should doubt Laurence's claims.

"I beg that you will forgive my presuming to raise a small difficulty, Lung Tien Xiang," Gong Su said, coming quite unexpectedly to the rescue, "but there can be no question of His Imperial Highness presenting himself in such a manner."

Temeraire paused, his ruff flattening, but undeterred Gong Su added gently, "I am sure that if not for the urgency of our situation, and the small amount of time your duties have permitted you to enjoy at the Imperial court, you would recall that the honor of a formal Imperial visit cannot be lightly bestowed, and requires most careful arrangements. The foreign officials should have to be instructed in correct protocol," meaning of course they should have to agree to prostrate themselves before Laurence, an event unlikely in the extreme, "and appropriate gifts should have to be presented on the Emperor's behalf and offered in return. Of course such a remarkable mission cannot be sent forward without the Emperor's will."

"Certainly not," Laurence said, with deep relief. "Temeraire, you would not in the least ask me to do such a thing."

"But when the war depends upon it," Temeraire said, "I am sure the Emperor would understand if one were to make an exception—and all to carry out his orders," he added quickly, with the air of one seizing upon an excellent argument.

"I think we must be guided in such matters by Gong Su," Laurence said hastily, "whose experience of the Imperial court dwarfs our own."

Temeraire turned to Chu in appeal, but he shook his mane vigorously. "Oh, no," he said. "You are not going to get me to quarrel with the crown prince's envoy: I am keeping out of it. You are a Celestial and he is a prince; *you* can disagree. I am just an old general who wants a quiet life, and to retire to a place in the mountains."

Temeraire snorted at this. "But how otherwise are we to get in to see Kutuzov?" he said, turning back to Laurence, who was grimly aware he had no answer, other than perhaps bringing Temeraire down over Kutuzov's pavilion and pulling it up into the air, which should certainly provoke a response of some kind: more likely a cannonball than an invitation, however.

"If I may cut your Gordian knot," Tharkay said, with a glint in his eye. "Bring down the robes, Roland. You are not going to wear them, Will. You are going to lend them to me."

"I do not see why anyone other than Laurence should wear them," Temeraire grumbled, while they unpacked the indeed very thoroughly wrapped garments from their layers and layers of oilcloth and sacking. "They are *his* robes, and *he* is the Emperor's son; it seems to me quite wrong that you should present yourselves in any other manner. Laurence, if you are worried about causing the Emperor any distress, I am sure he should object to your lending out his gift. And is it not in any case quite illegal for Tharkay to wear them?"—half-pleadingly.

"Tharkay can hardly be considered guilty of violating the sumptuary laws of a nation of which he is neither citizen nor servant, and when we are not even within its borders," Laurence said, "and I will present myself to General Kutuzov, as I am, a British serving-officer, here with our nation's allies to assist in the war effort; Gong Su will present himself as the Emperor's envoy. We will not *claim* any position falsely for Tharkay. Whatever conclusions the Russians might choose to draw, from his looks, and his having borrowed certain garments of mine, will create no obligations of state on either side."

He spoke to convince himself as much as Temeraire: but his conscience smote him badly for this undeniable piece of sophistry, and still more when Tharkay had been rigged out in the red robes: he did indeed look a very imposing potentate. "You look as wretched as a cat, Will," Tharkay said. "You need not borrow so much trouble; I dare say we will be run out of camp at bayonet-point before ever we announce ourselves."

When he ran so dreadful a risk, Laurence could hardly begrudge him the right to extract what black humor might be found in the situation: they were far more likely to be shot, than laughed at, in the prevailing mood of the Russian Army, and Tharkay, in assuming a deceptive rôle, most likely to be held culpable. "Are you certain you wish to go forward with this?" Laurence said to him quietly. "If the Russian command are determined to reject help offered with an open hand, it need not be our concern to deliver it to them in the face of all obstacles which they put before us."

"And go back to China, with three hundred dragons at our back?" Tharkay said. "No, Laurence; it would be an unconscionable waste, and I find I have committed too much to the enterprise to see it fail now." He paused, and with less levity added, "You must know, Laurence, that if we cannot stop Napoleon here, likely we can never stop him. If he has time to establish a Kingdom of Poland, and feed it the rest of Prussia little by little; if he can ship over a hundred Incan dragons—" The sentence required no completion; Laurence nodded. With the wealth and power of the Incan Empire merging with his own, and his conquests in Europe secured, Napoleon's position would grow the more unassailable; his fist would close ever tighter. Russia was the last great counterbalance left in Europe; if it fell, Napoleon would turn all his attention to Spain. And when Spain had been crushed—he would look to Britain once again.

He settled on his own sword, then flanked Tharkay on one hand; Gong Su took the other, with Dyhern, Forthing, and Ferris behind, all of them in the best show they could arrange. They were preceded into the camp by two Jade Dragons: the size of draft-horses and utterly foreign with their lean vulpine heads and dragging wings, bearing suspended between them, on chains slung from their necks, a fence-post on which they had rigged Chu's banner, framed on either side by lanterns in the Chinese style.

Their procession met with bewildered astonishment as they began it, and collected up a number of strays and camp-followers in their train as they went through the encampment: boys running alongside staring and calling in Russian. One of them, rather daring, darted forward to touch with a finger the wing of Lung Yu Fei, the Jade Dragon nearest the side; she whipped her head on her long narrow neck around and hissed at him for this effrontery. With her jaws of serrated teeth scarce inches from his face, the boy paled and fell backwards in alarm, scuttling away on hands and feet like a beetle while his friends jeered him good-naturedly.

They were very nearly as good as a circus coming up the hill for pageantry, and the very growing noise of their approach removed the necessity of passing some challenge: the inhabitants of Kutuzov's pavilion came out themselves to see and to stare as they climbed the hill towards them: the field marshal himself a portly and beribboned gentleman in front, white-haired and with a large, high-browed face, the nose and cheeks and jowls bulbous, one eye milky; epaulettes and medals and sash proclaiming his identity. Beside him was a tall lean man with a smooth-pated head: Barclay de

Tolly, Laurence thought. Their party came to a halt some several arm's-lengths away, and the Russian high command regarded them in silent astonishment while not a word was said.

Tharkay carried the event in high aplomb, his face set in the sternest lines as he regarded the assembled Russian company with a searching air, and then said over his shoulder, in Chinese, "I think that will do; you had better be the first to break the silence."

"Gentlemen," Laurence said to them in French, "I am Captain William Laurence, of His Royal Majesty's Aerial Corps. I am here on behalf of our ally, the Emperor of China, in the company of his envoy, and I have the honor to offer you three hundred of the Chinese aerial legions, who can be on the battlefield in four days: if you will use them."

Temeraire could not help but feel a little dissatisfied the next morning, even though Kutuzov had personally come to see them, accompanied by several of his staff officers: the general inspected them all with an air of suspicion, studying Chu and Temeraire especially with narrowed eyes. He looked over the supply-dragons and the Jade Dragons, and then demanded of Laurence, "The numbers of this force are in these proportions? Two middle-weight to eight light-weight and four of these—"

He gave a wave of his arm up and down, baffled by the Jade Dragons, who regarded him and the Russian officers with doubtful expressions of their own; Lung Yu Li said to Temeraire very quietly, "Surely that man has forgotten to put on all his clothing?" Kutuzov was wearing snug trousers and a waistcoat all of brilliant white, excessively tight upon a figure which was not good and showed to even less advantage as he lowered himself into a field chair put down for him, low to the ground, and stretched forth his legs and reclined back so as to make the mound of his belly protruberant under his folded hands.

"No, sir," Laurence said to him. "There are only a few more of the couriers, and they are not counted in our numbers; it is three middle-weight fighters to one light-weight for supply."

"Well, well. You are generous fairies, indeed. All the more so that he has brought almost no heavy-weights, himself," Kutuzov added, meaning Napoleon. "All right, so where is this Chinese general of yours? As long as I am here, let me talk to him. Why is he hiding?"

"I beg your pardon, sir," Laurence said, "*this* is General Chu."

An absurdly long amount of time was required to make Kutuzov believe that Chu was indeed their commander; the Russians looked increasingly disdainful, and several of them began to speak in low voices to Kutuzov, again proposing that the whole force was imaginary, until Temeraire, still smarting at *middle-weight*—he was by no means middle-weight; no-one could possibly have called twenty tons *middle* weight even if he were not as enormous and lumpen as the Russian beasts—broke in.

"If we were inventing it all, for what reason I cannot imagine," he said coldly in French, "you would not be any worse off believing us than you are now, with Napoleon chasing you across your own country, and, it is plain to see, giving your dragons a drubbing. If you *did* have a dragon general yourselves, I dare say he would have put matters into better train."

With morning, Temeraire had been able to see a little more of the arrangements of the Russian beasts in the rough coverts they had arranged for themselves: they were all outrageously quarrelsome with one another, at least the heavy-weights were. There did not seem to be very many of them, and all had wounds of some sort, some of which had not yet been treated properly: he had seen at least three with swollen bulging places where a pistol-ball had not been extracted, although he remembered quite well his own surgeons Keynes and Dorset saying that it was of great importance to remove them swiftly.

Vosyem and her regiment had been summoned up overnight, and Temeraire had seen the small dragon from her clearing again, laboring under a heavy tun of water which he was bringing her to drink, though she certainly could have more easily carried it herself, or for that matter gone to the pond to drink.

The little dragon had stopped by their own camp: his was the only friendly greeting they had from any of the Russians. "I am glad you have found us after all," he said, in his small chirping voice, "and that it is all cleared up: so you *are* here to fight with us?"

"Yes, of course," Temeraire said, "but pray tell me, whatever are you doing with that water?"

"Oh, I will bring you some, too, I promise—only pray do let me get a little supper, first," the little dragon said, misunderstanding. He spoke with his head tilted, peering sidelong up at Temeraire as though he expected to be cuffed, and then glanced with even more anxiety over to where several other of the small dragons were now picking over the remnants of the carcass of a large moose which had just been abandoned by one of the heavy-weights.

"I do not need any water," Temeraire said; the Shen Lung had jointly chosen a campsite near a small stream, which had taken not the work of half-an-hour to divert into forming a convenient pool, "and if you are hungry, you may have some of our breakfast, if you like; we have plenty. Only I have seen you fly back and forth seven times in the last hour past our camp. I beg your pardon," he added, "if I seem rude for inquiring, but I cannot make any sense out of it."

"Oh, I am doing whatever Vosyem would like me to do," the little dragon said, meanwhile turning to stare at the immense pit full of porridge and meat. "Is that really food? But there is so much of it."

Shen Lung Chi, who could not understand him, nevertheless could read his hungry expression perfectly well, and dished out a large bowl of the porridge; after having devoured this and licked it bare, and refreshed himself at the pool, the small dragon was induced to reveal that his name was Grig, though he seemed half-alarmed even to confess he had one at all. It seemed that the light-weights were meant to answer to the whims of the bigger dragons, and ordinarily fed only on what leavings they could snatch.

"She wanted some water," Grig said, "and then she wanted me to fly back to camp and be sure that her treasure was under proper guard; but Captain Rozhkov would not give me leave to do that, so I had to go back and tell her so," he hunched his shoulders as if in the memory of a blow, as he repeated this, "and then she had me carry him a message, and say that if he did not let me go, she would go herself; so then I had to come back and tell her that if she left, he would call off the guard and let *all* her treasure be stolen—"

"Well, it seems to me a perfectly wretched arrangement," Temeraire said, "and I do not see how any of you are going to fight properly, when we have any fighting: you will be too tired."

"Oh," Grig said, "but I will not be *fighting*; I am too small to fight."

"You aren't smaller than those Cossack dragons, over there," Temeraire said.

"No; but they are irregulars, and I am too big to join them; they cannot feed a dragon my size," Grig said. Temeraire looked over at the Cossack camp: it seemed a far more hospitable place, their dragons tucked around the campfire in amongst the people, and if they did not have enormous heaps of treasure at least had neat harness, and most of them wore handsome woven blankets. But it was certainly true they were considerably smaller: the size of Winchesters, courier-weight beasts by British standards.

Certainly the Russian heavy-weights all looked very imposing—no-one could deny it, and Temeraire had observed that, despite their size, they demonstrated a remarkable speed. Their steel-taloned claws and long necks lashed out very much as though, as Forthing put it, there was gunpowder lit behind them. But as they demonstrated their fighting qualities, for the most part, by quarreling with one another and knocking about the smaller beasts, Temeraire nevertheless felt entirely justified in making his criticisms now, although the Russian officers evidently did not enjoy hearing it, and several of them scowled and spoke again to Kutuzov in their own tongue instead of French, with passion; but the general waved his hand and silenced them.

It seemed that the Russian Army had been retreating all this time, ever since Napoleon had crossed the Niemen—all summer long. Their first plan of battle, which to Temeraire sounded quite sensible, had evidently been to give battle at Vilna and then withdraw a little way into their countryside, luring the French to a final battle at a fortified encampment, where the Russians should have had the advantage. Why they had decided instead to only run away, Temeraire could not in the least understand, when they did have a very substantial army; surely it would have been better to at least try and fight, even if it did seem that Napoleon had a much larger army than anyone had expected.

Evidently many of the Russian officers shared his sentiments, and General Barclay had been superseded as the senior commander for having failed to give battle; but it did not seem to Temeraire that Kutuzov was in a great hurry to fight, either: they were still arguing whether the battle should be given here, or at the nearby town of Tsarevo Zaimische, which evidently offered good ground, or somewhere else entirely.

In any case, though they had been running away as hard as they could, Napoleon's army had nearly caught them a dozen times. He had refined still further the use of dragons in his operations. From what the Russians described, each regiment now traveled with its own beasts, infantry and artillery alike. Men and light-weights foraged, while the heavier dragons leap-frogged companies down the road, and occasionally bore up the guns and heavy loads. Napoleon had eschewed larger magazines; his supply depots were instead numerous and lightly defended, each of them vulnerable perhaps, but as a whole able to withstand even many losses.

"He builds them in the woods, where there are no roads at all," General Barclay said. "A heavy-weight knocks down a few trees for them and goes on; the middle-weights come, deposit some

342

goods and cattle, assist in building a little fortification, and go on; a few light-weights strike out across the countryside for whatever of substance they can steal, leave it, and go on; then a company remains with a couple of light guns and a few couriers, enough to carry supply forward. If our Cossacks strike, they defend themselves. If we come in force, they snatch whatever they can carry and flee, dispersing to the nearest other depots and reinforcing these, and call for a heavier beast to strike in return."

The Russians had only evaded Napoleon through good luck and desperate contortions, and because he and his generals had thrown away several chances by arguing with one another. Napoleon's own brother Jerome had simply run away from his corps on the eve of battle in a temper and gone back to France; or so the Russians said—they had evidently learned of the incident from their spies, and it was repeated with great enjoyment. Then, too, thanks to heavy rains, the Russian roads had become quite impassable with mud at several points, slowing the French advance and forcing Napoleon's dragons to carry the guns nearly all the way by air. Temeraire had carried a twelve-pounder himself once, in the retreat from London, and it had been quite exhausting; one could not lug something so heavy and then fight again straightaway, particularly not without a healthy dinner.

It seemed that Napoleon had tried to repair the sluggishness of his advance, as much as he could, by personally flying about to the different parts of his army, when he could, to take command directly; he had been at the battle of Kliastitzy, and smashed the Russian corps there, opening his Marshals' road to St. Petersburg; and a week later at Smolensk, where by the narrowest of margins the Russian Army had escaped him. And now he was closing in ever more swiftly; he would be on them within a day, perhaps two, and it seemed the Russians had decided at last to fight.

Chu, when Temeraire and Laurence had finished translating the Russian accounts of the campaign so far, hummed deep in his throat, skeptically. "Are they sensible men?" he demanded.

"I know it seems peculiar that they have been running away all this time," Temeraire began, but Chu snorted.

"Nonsense," he said. "What is peculiar is that they have been planning to fight an army larger than theirs in every way, with inferior air support. If they did not know we were coming, they had much better have kept running!"

Temeraire was taken aback; Laurence said, "General Chu, Moscow is in some sense the central city of their nation—it is not formally the capital, but the Tsar is crowned here; they cannot let it fall without some resistance."

"Oh, I see; politics," Chu said. "Well, at least find out for me why they have organized their aerial forces in such an absurd way, for there must be *some* reason. I see they do not have any proper system of supply, but they could at least field forty middle-weights, instead of those fifteen hulks and so many of those little fellows."

The Russians looked irritated to be questioned on this point. "Does this beast of yours not know how long an egg takes to hatch?" General Tutchkov said to Laurence, impatiently. "How does it suppose we should have got fifty middle-weight beasts under harness since they crossed the Niemen?"

"You might have gone to your breeding grounds," Temeraire said. "I dare say if you had offered even a little of all that immense treasure to your retired beasts, or your ferals, they would have been delighted to fight for you." This suggestion met only with stares, and a great comprehensive snort from Kutuzov out of his bulbous nose, which was quite rude; but at any rate, it answered Chu's remaining concern: the Russians had not thought to do so.

"So, they are *not* sensible men," Chu said with finality. "How do they expect to properly oppose a nation whose aerial forces so outweigh their own? They may be victorious in this war, thanks to our assistance, and yet find themselves in the gravest difficulty in the next season once again.

"But," he added, "that is not my business, but theirs! My business is to win now, and if that is the only reason, and these numbers are correct, I am satisfied with our prospects for battle. But I must yet have four days to concentrate upon the battlefield."

Kutuzov was silent a moment, when this information was conveyed: the great massed corps of Napoleon's army were hard upon their rear, and even falling back might not gain them sufficient time along the road to Moscow. "Well," he said finally, "if we cannot win the time from our enemy, we must ask him if he will be so kind as to give it to us." And he called over one of his pages, and took up a pen and paper, to write swiftly a letter to the Tsar.

A large tent had been erected upon neutral ground outside Vyazma, a field cleared half-a-mile in either direction and policed watchfully by dragons of both parties: for the French part, Laurence saw, nearly all middle-weights of no breed which he recognized, most of them with large broad foreheads. Deep chests and heavy shoulders were common as well, but their hides were of peculiarly motley appearance, muddied greens and yellows and browns.

He thought grimly that he detected Lien's hand at work there, though there was no sign of her either at present or reported by the Russian scouts; at least one spy report not three weeks old had positively placed her at the Château de Saint-Cloud, outside Paris, in the company of the new Empress and the infant heir. "I can believe nearly anything of her," Temeraire said, "but she cannot have let Napoleon go to war without her: I am sure she cannot. I dare say she is hiding somewhere, and will find some way to do something dreadful to us before the end. Not," he added, "that I will not be entirely ready to meet her, Laurence, of course."

Gong Su had not disagreed with him openly, but quietly told Laurence afterwards, "It is considered the foremost duty of every Celestial to guard the Emperor's line, a duty which precedes even the ties of companionship: and Napoleon has now but this one child. I think it likely that Lung Tien Lien has indeed remained in Paris, to protect him and to forward his education," a stroke of great good fortune for which Laurence could not but be grateful.

But Lien had now had charge of Napoleon's aerial forces and his breeding programme for a full five years, and the fruits of her labor were everywhere to be observed not only in the looks but in the wide intelligence and education of the French dragons. These were frequently to be seen sitting up high on their haunches and peering into the distance, getting the best look they could at the disposition of the Russian troops, and then putting their heads together to murmur and exchange thoughts. They were all of them under harness, but many of them bore no evident captain, and several of them emblems which might have been symbols of rank.

Indeed one of the dragons, a grey-and-green beast not quite a middle-weight, sat quietly and unobtrusively in the corner of the field, unremarked; but Laurence saw with disquiet that besides a very cursory harness, only enough to take up perhaps a few riders, it bore a wide red sash pinned with a large silver star: a Marshal? Napoleon had granted Lien the baton years before, establishing the precedent; a dragon of sufficient military gifts to have merited another such grant would surely make a deadly opponent.

There were also three heavy-weights beside: a Petit Chevalier and a Chanson-de-Guerre, each holding one corner of the French line, and anchoring the center was a dragon as different from every other beast upon the field as could be imagined: an Incan dragon, with its long lapping scales like feathers gleaming a brilliant sky-blue and tipped with scarlet, looking more like some immense sort of brooding phoenix, wearing a kind of golden headdress and its belly armored in a mesh washed with gold and bearing many decorations: surely an officer in the Incan armies, and if not yet wholly familiar with Western warfare, likely to be an able commander in the air.

But there were enough signs of weakness visible to hearten a Russian ally, too: hard use had worn many a harness-strap and tarnished many a buckle; the men aboard the dragons looked thin, and they were fewer in number than they ought have been, for so many beasts. However skillfully they had stretched their supply, however swiftly they had moved, still their ranks had dwindled during their long march, and Napoleon could not easily get more men to swell them out again. Laurence had taken a short flight aloft with Temeraire, earlier, and spied out a little of the enemy's artillery: nearly all nine-pounders or lighter, although there were many of them, and the number of cavalry astonishingly small; Bonaparte was relying heavily upon his aerial advantage.

And to this encouragement, Hammond had sent a welcome dash of joyful news: Placet had arrived breathless from Moscow the night before, with Captain Terrance, wide-awake sober for once, spilling off his back; he had seized Laurence by both arms. "Wellington has smashed Marmont, at Salamanca," he said. "On July the twenty-second. Routed him foot and horse and wing: the French lost thirteen thousand men, and they say Marmont is dead, or at least so gravely wounded we will not see him again in the field this year."

If that news had yet reached Napoleon, or his men, to discourage them, there was no evidence of it to be found in their soldierly demeanor across the field; but it had been inexpressibly heartening to men facing the might of France. Laurence would have been drunk still this morning if he had swallowed every toast offered him the night before, in Wellington's health and the King's.

Chu had under cover of darkness taken himself and the rest of his forces to the back of their lines, out of sight of French spies; he now napped comfortably, too old a campaigner to fear the event and satisfied with his arrangements, while Shen Shi and her staff, even further back, had begun the work of organizing cooking-pits and water, and medical stations; the blue dragons were ferrying supplies from the depot near Moscow. The Jade Dragons had gone already to pass the word amongst the *jalan* to gather.

Temeraire stood anxiously amongst the dragons on the Russian side of the field: incongruous in his smooth black and clean-lined conformation when lined up with the bristling, armored Russian heavy-weights, whose own suspicious attentions were nearly all devoted to him and to one another, rather than the enemy. The Russian beasts were laden with men, grim officers in thick leather coats, who held thick riveted straps of leather which had been chained on to the rings driven into the heavy plates of horn that grew upon the dragons' shoulders. Others dangled from grotesque bridles, made of chainmail with spiked steel bits, which Laurence no less than Temeraire could only regard with disgust.

Vosyem was of their number; Temeraire had tried to speak with her, and propose helping her remove it. She had snarled at him around the bit, and fiercely said, "You would like it, that I should be shamed, and refused a chance to do battle and win my share; one less to divide the plunder with, is that it?"

"That is a very quarrelsome beast," Temeraire said in some irritation, withdrawing, "and if anyone could be said to deserve to wear a muzzle, I suppose she does; but no-one *can* be said to deserve it, Laurence. What are they about?"

"I cannot tell you." Laurence watched the line of Russian dragons: the snarling, savage twists of head giving them a look of restive cavalry-horses; the crews gripping hard upon the lines with their faces as set as men facing down artillery, as men looking into the maw of death, though they stood upon no battlefield: they were afraid of their own beasts. "I have always heard the Russian aerial corps mentioned as one to fear," he said, low. "The dragons, it is reputed, will not cease fighting if their captains are taken and cannot be seized by boarding; they have often been seen to fight wholly unmanned."

He had thought, by that reputation, that they might expect to find some greater degree of enlightenment here in the treatment of dragons, perhaps some influence from the East; instead it was plain the dragons would fight on in such circumstances because they had no affection for their officers, or their crews, at all. They cared nothing for the cause of battle, and only for the reward which might be theirs at its conclusion.

348

"I cannot deny," Temeraire said, "that their treasure is magnificent beyond anything; but it is not enough for any sensible dragon to put up with *this*. No wonder they did not think any of their ferals would fight for them. Laurence, I must say, if only he were not such a tyrant, and always beginning wars, and invading people's countries—"

"Yes." It was hard indeed, for anyone who had affection for a dragon, to look upon this field and not feel the keenest sympathy with the French and their emperor's more enlightened regime, in that regard at least. And yet behind the noble ranks of that army lay a track of near ten thousand miles of wasteland, of death and ruin for man and dragon alike, and if Bonaparte were not stopped, it would march across another ten thousand. There would never be an end to his ambition. "It is time," Laurence said.

From the northern end of the field, the French dragons had made way for a small company to come out: three courier-weight dragons, bearing the flag of France and the standard of the Imperial Guard; a company of the Imperial Guard on foot watchful behind them, polished and brilliant in their red cloaks. And sitting on the center dragon, a man in a grey coat, with his bicorn hat worn athwart.

"Pray do be careful," Temeraire said to Laurence. "Even if Lien is *not* here, I dare say Napoleon will think of something dreadful to do, if only you give him the least chance."

"Recall that for once, this is our trap, not his," Laurence said, "and we can only be grateful that he seems to be walking into it." The grass of the field was yet wet with dew and left streaks upon his Hessian boots as he strode across it towards the gathering Russian party.

Napoleon was altered still further from the last occasion Laurence had seen him, in the Incan capital city of Cusco: older, fatter, and more tired; his voice was thick with a bad cold, and he pressed a handkerchief often to his face, coughing. He showed all the ill-effects of the strain which he had placed upon himself, by flying at

349

such frequency from one part of his army to the next. Standing to greet him, Tsar Alexander was the taller by a head, his face set in stern lines and handsome, though his curling hair drew back a little already from his high brow; young and vital and with an intensity in his looks, romantic in flavor, and a flush on his pale cheeks that stood stark against the high black collar which he wore. The contrast they offered to the eye only increased the impression, looking upon the French Emperor, of fatigue, of a man past the days of his youth, and perhaps his prime.

And yet somehow when Napoleon entered the pavilion he diminished his company, rather than the reverse: a subtle and yet sensible movement traveled around him, a shifting of weight, eyes turning towards him, which made him somehow the center of the stage.

He discarded formality: reached out his arms and embraced the Tsar and kissed him upon both cheeks, though Alexander received the gesture only stiffly, and with a set mouth. "*Mon cher,*" Napoleon said to him, and keeping a hand upon his arm spoke to him directly of his regret, disregarding quite all other men in the room: all sorrowful familiarity, nearly paternal. "You have desired this war, I think," he said, "as little as I have. I know the love you have for your people and your country; no less than mine for France, and so dreadfully have both suffered from our disagreements, and to what end? To whose satisfaction?"

He turned and beckoned forward one of his young aides-de-camp, who carried a long, thin draped package forward. "I have the honor," Napoleon said, "to return this to you: a token, if you will take it as such, that we would gladly be not your enemies, trespassers and thieves in your land, but your guests, cherishing your possessions as dearly as those of any well-loved host."

It was indeed the icon of Smolensk, the frame a little blackened with smoke, carefully laid on a bed of white velvet. "It was saved from the fire by Murat himself," Napoleon said, "who ran into the cathedral to snatch it from the smoke and amidst the falling timbers:

a scene of such destruction I yet am anguished to recall, and had no power to prevent; God forbid another such occasion."

The threat, standing as they did not a hundred miles from Moscow, could not have been more pointedly delivered nor received, and Alexander, though handling the icon reverently, gave only short thanks; he had it swiftly removed from the tent, when an aide had been sent out to bring a Russian priest to carry it away. "I think you know Mikhail Illarionovich," the Tsar then said, meaning Marshal Kutuzov, and made punctilious introductions to every other officer of the general staff present, even through the ranks of brigadiers: at once serving to make a greater delay, and to deflect Napoleon's attentions from himself.

Napoleon addressed Kutuzov with a jovial note, congratulating him on his recent appointment to the command, and a little slyly saying, "It is a long while since we met, you and I, on the field outside Austerlitz," an unnecessary reminder of that devastating victory, which had first established him as the master of Europe.

He had for nearly every man there a word of recognition, most without any malicious flavor behind them. He knew their battles and their decorations, and when a brigadier general named Tzvilenev was presented to him, he said thoughtfully, "Ah! I hope you will permit me to congratulate you, young man," and kissing him added, "You have a son. Your wife was in St. Petersburg when it fell to us, for her time came upon her and she could not flee; I am happy to be able to tell you they were both in excellent health, and under the protection of Marshal Oudinot there."

That poor young man, who had labored under a preoccupied and anxious look which Laurence now could well understand, stood dazed by the intelligence and the low congratulations of his fellows, who looked a little wary at venturing to make them in the present circumstances. But Kutuzov made his own loudly, clapping the young man upon the shoulder, and calling at once for a toast, which necessitated glasses and bottles and camp-tables; so through Russian machinations and Napoleon's vanity in turn, the introductions alone were so prolonged as to devour nearly two hours of time.

Napoleon paused during the long proceedings, on seeing Laurence standing behind the ranks of the senior officers, and called him forward to be embraced. "My gratitude," he said solemnly, "does not fail. I have not forgotten what I and perhaps all the world owe to you, Captain Laurence, though I must yet deplore your presence here and the influence of your masters, who sit upon their island fomenting these quarrels amongst nations, and destroying from their fastness the peace and security of Europe. Would that you were now a subject of France! You know well," he added to Alexander, with a hint of reproach, "how the efforts of England have been bent to divide us from one another, and how I have spent myself and France, to try and remove their power to do so."

Laurence could hardly receive Napoleon's sentiments with satisfaction: well might the Emperor regret having failed, in his invasion of Britain; Laurence could only rejoice at it, and the wound which it had inflicted on Napoleon's dominion. And yet with all the cause in the world to hate the man before him, Laurence could not deny the power of his presence. If there had been any smaller advantage to be won by this conference than a force of three hundred dragons, if they had played for lesser stakes, anything not so sure to bring them victory, he thought this encounter might have been as destructive to the morale of the officers as if Napoleon had brought poison to put into their cups.

Alexander himself was not unaffected; evilly so, while the meeting proceeded through drawn-out paces. Impossible not to see that he felt even now a kind of instinctive yearning towards the conqueror as Napoleon concentrated all his attentions, all his intent focus, towards him, not unlike the direction of batteries of artillery; and yet he was resentful of his own feelings, a resentment silenced but diminished not at all by the necessity of deceit.

He played his rôle thoroughly and well, speaking at length and only of intangibles—of the honor of Russia, of his duty to his patrimony, of philosophy and of religion—so that all the while the conversation was kept carefully inconclusive. Napoleon, it was evident to see, saw himself a seducer; and to oblige him Alexander made himself out a maiden to be courted, and as coy as any skillful courtesan played off his suitor's ardent attempts to reach a consummation.

He deferred any explicit offers, which should have to be rejected; he made none himself; and yet he conveyed appealingly all the willingness to make peace which Napoleon, at the head of a tired army thousands of miles from their homes, might hope for. His reward was the success of their aim. When the sun began to sink, nothing had been resolved upon, and they agreed to meet again: Napoleon departed, and they had won the first day.

But Alexander afterwards was in a rage of humiliation, so overcome that he sat silently and unmoving, saying not a word, until the word came that Napoleon was well away with all his escort. Then Alexander flung the camp-table with a savage jerk of his hand upwards and over, startled men scattering away before the toppling dishes and the smoking candles, and rose to pace the opened space like a tiger upon a leash.

His ministers hastily made efforts to clear the pavilion, ushering out the aides and junior officers; Laurence half wished to leave himself, but there was no easy way to do so, standing as he was with the senior officers.

"As though," Alexander said low, "as though Holy Russia were to be bought like a girl, for the price of a few compliments—as though we were to come like the cringing dog to heel, servile beneath him, and allow him to march forward this vile philosophy, this blasphemy, across all Europe—to overthrow all Christianity, and set a—"

The men who remained were all silent before the tirade, their heads nearly bowed; only one of the diplomats, a Greek nobleman named Kapodistrias, at last ventured to step forward and speak to the Tsar quietly, reminding him the goal had been achieved. "Buon-aparte's vanity and contempt will soon receive their just reward," he said.

But Napoleon was not to be deferred so easily for a second day. As though he felt he had paid sufficient lip service to his courting, the next morning he grew swiftly more insistent, and Alexander's patience was by no means equal to fending off his approaches. They had not yet made noon when Napoleon cut short the diplo-matic dance, thrusting aside with a sweep of his arm the carefully wrought speech which Kapodistrias and several of Alexander's other diplomats had engineered, outlining without commitment the nearly innumerable small points of conflict and how these might perhaps be resolved—a catalogue which, if permitted to continue, might have consumed another day all on their own.

But Napoleon interrupted with a brusque, "Enough; enough of this," and leaning forward to Alexander said bluntly, "Come, Your Majesty: these matters are for other men. Oudinot governs in St. Petersburg, and we speak here less than one hundred miles from the great city of the Moskova. Must the very throne of your ances-tors fall into the hands of my army before you will cease to listen to warmongers? Shall we not again be friends? Give me only your oath that you will uphold again the Continental System, that you will recognize the Kingdom of Poland, and we will proclaim peace to these brave assembled soldiers. Then let the diplomats argue what they will!"

"In the sight of the Holy Mother," Alexander said, springing from his chair, "I will chop the throne into kindling with my own hands before you sit upon it, and for the rest, you may take what you can. But before I give you peace while you stand with an army on my soil, I will grow my beard to my belt and go and eat potatoes with my serfs!"

The conference was shattered. The diplomats on both parts made small abortive attempts to bring their monarchs back to the table, for their several causes; but Alexander could scarcely make apology now without becoming a liar, and Napoleon, at first only surprised, grew swiftly choleric when he understood Alexander's intransigence had not been a mere flourishing of temper but an expression of true feeling, and an outright rejection of the most central terms which should have formed naturally the core of any serious negotiation.

Napoleon's face colored; he looked as though he would have liked to upbraid the Tsar like a junior officer, and nearly took a step towards him; Berthier put a hand upon his arm, prudently. Still hot with anger and breathing quickly, Napoleon said to Alexander's back, "When you have thought better of your choice, I will not let this harden my heart against you," and turning stormed from the pavilion.

The Russian courier-riders outside the pavilion had of course heard all the proceedings; Laurence saw one young enthusiast, as angry as Alexander himself at the indignity offered the Tsar, jerk deliberately upon the chain of his dragon's bridle, and jab it with a spur, so the dragon snarling lashed its head forward to pull the rein loose, placing its jaws directly in Napoleon's path scarce half-a-foot from his head. Napoleon jerked back from the gnashing teeth, many of them jagged and broken and stained; two of his aides caught him, else he would have fallen, and the French couriers opposite their Russian counterparts all rose snarling on their haunches.

For a moment, the battle might have been joined directly, on the field before the pavilion; Laurence put his own hand on his pistol, and saw many another officer do the same. Then Napoleon said, "No," sharply, and waved his own couriers down; he gave one look to the brazen young officer, who defiantly raised his chin and made no apology, though he had better have hung his head at so nearly breaking the state of truce; and then another harder to the dragon, who had pulled its head in towards its chest, and was mouthing the bit with sullen irritation and a cold look for its own handler. "No," he said again, more thoughtfully, and turning went to mount up on his own courier, and departed for his lines.

"More than the heart could bear, Sire," Kutuzov said to Alexander, out of the silence; they were all of them aware that the hammer of the French Army stood ready to fall upon them. "But the point has not been lost. We have been falling back all this day; they will not catch us to-night or tomorrow. Bagration's men have been making fortifications at Borodino. We can hold him there—until the dragons arrive."

He glanced at Laurence as he spoke, a narrow gleam in his one good eye, which Laurence did not wholly know how to interpret. But he and Temeraire carried the report back to Chu, with a borrowed map to show him the location of the little village: scarcely a pinprick on the outskirts of Klin, a little way off the road to Moscow.

"Well, it will have to be good enough," Chu said philosophically, when he was given the news, and dictated new orders to one of the Jade Dragons, instructing half of the first *jalan* to concentrate and approach at a quicker pace. "I would rather have the entire force at the outset, and in the meantime a frightful number of these men will die, I imagine, but ah well! There are a great many of them, and we can manage for a day," he added, a little callously.

"Sir," Laurence said after a moment, "I must tell you I think the Russians as yet doubt the arrival of our oncoming forces. I fear they may not intend to organize their forces so as to provide that ground support which they have promised." He spoke half-reluctantly: his duty to bring the Chinese aerial forces to bear warring with his sense of what was owed them.

"I do not see why they should not support us properly," Temeraire said; he turned to look at Grig, who had become something of a fixture of their encampment, drawn by the regular helpings of porridge. "Grig, surely they do believe us *now,* they must know we are telling the truth."

"Oh," Grig said, doubtfully, looking up from his bowl, "I would not know about that. Are you *sure* that all these dragons are coming? It does seem very strange that there are so many of them, and we still have not seen them on the way."

Temeraire flattened his ruff. "Of course I am sure," he said, "and anyway, Laurence," he added, "even if they *don't* believe us, they may as well prepare: after all, they must give battle somewhere."

Tharkay had been sitting beside the dragons, reading; he looked up and raised an eyebrow. "Why?"

Temeraire paused, doubtfully. "But they cannot simply keep running away," he said.

"Why not?" Tharkay said, and Chu gave a snort of laughter; Temeraire put back his ruff.

"Ha ha," Chu said, to Temeraire, "young fellows like you are the only reason why not, and probably that Tsar of theirs is clamoring for a fight, too. Well, I see that fat old general is not so stupid after all. If we come, why then, he will win a great battle and the war will be over; and if we don't, we have given him an excellent excuse to run some more without losing face."

"But if we did *not* come, and he ran, then Napoleon would win the war!" Temeraire protested.

Chu snorted. "We had to fly over three thousand miles of this country just to get here!" he said. "This Napoleon would have a long way to go to conquer the whole thing, a long and hungry way. No: I begin to think a little better of this Kutuzov fellow, even if these people don't know anything about dragons."

Chapter 18

Laurence slept only ill, the night of the seventh September; his head was pillowed on his folded coat, where he stretched on Temeraire's arm, and he raised it at a dozen sounds, a dozen noises, all his mind alive to the wide road of possibilities opening before them. In the distance there was the occasional sound of musketry, now and again a faintly heard roar: the Cossacks on their dragons and horses were harrying the French lines.

The Russians had previously established a small redoubt at the town of Shevardino, a meager fortification of only a few logs piled atop one another, which now Kutuzov meant to use as a lure to dangle before the French—another day's distraction before the great conflict unfolded, and another day which might allow him to slip away if the dragons did not materialize.

Laurence slept again, woke again, this time to the sound of resonant dragon voices near-by. He roused to see another of the scarlet dragons, wearing the symbols of a *jalan* commander, speaking low with Chu and bowing deeply. "No, Shao Ri, it is not to be supposed we might travel without attracting any attention," Chu said. "You have done all that you could. Establish your camp and bring forward your troops."

"As you command, General," Shao Ri said, and with a final bow went aloft again; Laurence sat up as Temeraire lifted his own head, and Chu looked over at them.

"So you are awake? It's just as well," Chu said, "for we have had some bad luck. A patrol of those French dragons came upon the leading edge of Shao Ri's *jalan*, late last night, and three of them escaped. He says," he added, "they are good fliers: too bad! You had better go and tell Kutuzov. The French will be falling back at once, of course, unless they are very stupid; but if he moves quickly enough there may be a chance to strike him on the road."

Temeraire flew very quickly indeed. "It would be the outside of enough," he said as they went, the air tearing with great violence at Laurence's hair and the skirts of his coat, "for Napoleon to escape, after all the trouble we have gone to, and when he has come all this way."

"We will bring him to battle sooner or late," Laurence answered, but he felt as much urgency as Temeraire did, and sprang down from his back with jarring haste directly they had landed, to push his way into the camp; he waited impatiently while a cold, reluctant aide went to rouse Kutuzov, and counted every dragging minute as a blow.

There were many of these: he stood for nearly three hours in the cold, damp morning air, watching others go in and out, all the while the sky lightened; the coming day's heat was still only a distant promise. At last the tent-flap was raised, and he was admitted; Kutuzov was not yet finished dressing, and sat at the remnants of his breakfast in the company of several Russian officers, nobles all, and most of them to Laurence's eye useless hangers-on. "Good morning, Captain?" Kutuzov said, very placidly, almost sleepily, but there was a hard note to the words.

"Sir," Laurence said, without preamble, "we have been made: the French reconnoitering behind us spied the first *jalan* on the approach. They will have fallen back at once, certainly, unless we move to engage. It may already be too late."

One man, a colonel named Toll, gave a half-snorted laugh, stifled; a few other men of the company smiled with a kind of gentle condescension, as though to say that Laurence's little joke had been amusing enough, but wasn't it stale by now? Kutuzov folded his hands together over his belly, leaning back in his chair, and contemplated Laurence with the careful expression of a scholar at a rare specimen, trying to make it out properly. "Hahm," he said. "I wonder if Napoleon is so easily to be put off the battle he has been seeking for so long."

"By all means," Laurence said grimly, "if his alternative is destruction, and if by doing so he can fall back on better ground, knowing that *we* will now make ourselves the pursuers, and come to meet him on a position of his choosing."

"Be that as it may," Kutuzov began, in mild noncommittal tones, which Laurence might with pleasure have shaken out of him; already the candles in the tent were growing dim and unnecessary. The sun was up outside.

The tent-flap was thrust aside, impatiently; a young captain of hussars pushed inside and said, panting and breathless, "Sir, the Cossacks report the French have left their pickets; they are gone— there is a cloud on the road for ten miles, going west. The French are falling back everywhere."

Kutuzov paused; the tent was silent. Laurence saw every man of the company staring at him in return, as though they began at last to believe: it was nearly anticlimax when scant moments later a young courier captain stumbled in, pale, and blurted, "There are a thousand dragons coming from the east."

The weather was choking-hot and the clouds of dust upon the road, stirred up by many marching feet, rose so high that Temeraire coughed and coughed as he flew; he could make out nothing at all of the French Army, and very little even of their own directly below.

It was splendid nevertheless to be flying once more at the head of the assembled *jalan,* and flying now not to some contrived mission but to a real battle, where he and these dragons should fight properly and win a magnificent victory and defeat Napoleon at last. He would like to see what the Ministry should say to Laurence *then*, Temeraire thought with an intense private sensation of delight.

Nothing could have been more satisfying than the behavior of the Russians, when at last they had seen the ranks of the *jalan*. The heavy-weights had been quite abashed into silence, looking overhead as the legions came on, singing their flying-song and the beat of their wings making a great hollow rushing sound like the wind in the tops during a gale. The Russian soldiers had many of them formed, quite without orders, into their defensive squares with bayonets held aloft bristling, until General Kutuzov had sent men around to tell them all that these dragons were their allies, and some old men in very long beards and robes had gone out amongst the troops and made loud speeches.

"Those are priests," Dyhern said, "and they are telling them that you are sent by God to smite the enemies of Russia."

"Oh," Temeraire said in strong indignation, "we are not; why should they suppose God had anything to do with it? We are sent by the Emperor. I do not see why God should get the credit of it, at all." But in spite of his objections on this score, he could not deny being pleased when slowly the soldiers instead began to cheer lustily, and clash their bayonets together in an unmusical sort of welcome. Kutuzov was even so kind as to order a salute fired, from the great guns; although this startled the dragons nearest those guns a great deal and caused a degree of confusion as they recoiled and tangled with the *niru* nearest them, and it required half-an-hour to quite smooth out the resulting disarray.

"Of course they had no business not to believe us," Temeraire said to Laurence, "but I cannot deny they are proving ready to make handsome amends for it, and I do not know it is not more gratifying to have such a change."

"I should be more ready to enjoy it," Laurence said, "if not bought at such a cost: Napoleon will make us pay dearly for this mistake."

Napoleon had evidently no sooner received the news of his deadly danger than he had at once leapt into action and flung his men back onto the road—an immense gamble on his part: if Kutuzov had only moved more quickly, the French should have been vulnerable to an attack in their rear. But with the crisis upon him, as so often before, Napoleon had disdained the smaller course and seized the one avenue of obtaining some compensatory advantage, which the choice of ground might give him, against the suddenly altered balance of power between himself and his enemies.

And he had been rewarded, for the moment of great danger had passed. The bulk of the French Army, falling back west by forced marches, had been already well away before the Russians had roused, and as soon as the sky had grown even a little light, the French dragons had begun their quick hop-scotch portage of men and guns, and sped them even further away.

Temeraire could not but regret the opportunity lost, but after all, they would win in any case, and in some way it seemed more sporting, that Napoleon should know what force would meet him, and have a chance to do his very best, and then be defeated anyway. "Not, of course," he said hastily, "that I mean we ought not have taken advantage of the opportunity, or that it would have been unfair; this is war, after all, and I do not mean to be romantical—but as it has been lost, anyway, we may console ourselves that the quality of our victory will be the greater, if no-one can say Napoleon did not have a fair chance to win, that he was only taken by surprise."

"When we are in battle with the greatest general of this age, and perhaps of any," Laurence said, "I will be glad enough for victory of any kind; we can ill afford to sacrifice this chance or any other."

Temeraire refused to be so pessimistic: Napoleon was not trying to get away entirely, which would have been maddening; he had only fallen back on a nearby town, Tsarevo Zaimische, and soon the battle would be joined properly—although it seemed, not today, but tomorrow. Kutuzov was advancing their army, but they would not be in position properly until late, and then there would not be enough time to engage the enemy.

Chu growled deeply in his throat. "And where are we to get supply, if we do not defeat him the next day?" he demanded, and summoned Shen Shi to join him and Temeraire in proceeding to Kutuzov's tent; although at least General Kutuzov came out at once to speak to them now, and listened with attention to their difficulties.

"We have four days' adequate supply on hand, and of that we require three to reach our nearest resupply point," Chu said, his tone glacially polite.

"Which means, sir," Laurence said, having translated this, to the perplexed pause which received it, "that the legions should have to quit the field by mid-day tomorrow, regardless of the circumstances of the battle."

Kutuzov at once sent for his own quartermasters, and an urgent conference was held. "General, we cannot procure three hundred head of cattle overnight!" one of these worthies protested. "Not unless you mean to starve the entire army for three days to feed them."

"What do we want with three hundred head of cattle?" Chu said, with a disparaging snort.

"Twenty would serve excellently, if they are animals like this one," Shen Shi said, indicating an unhappy bullock in the near distance, intended for the Russian couriers, "and ninety tons of grain. A hundred and ten, if we must transport it ourselves, so long as the supply is within forty miles."

This list of requirements was so at war with the understanding of the Russian supply-officers that some argument was required even to persuade them to believe it correctly conveyed to them; then at last with some doubtful reluctance one said to the others, "The magazine at Mozhaisk is sufficiently supplied. We might get pigs from the farms near Kozhukhovo—"

Some seven of the supply-dragons set off at once, with a few rather alarmed Russian officers flung aboard with the crew to smooth the paths of the requisition, and the immediate crisis was averted; but Chu shook his head disapprovingly as they went back to their own campsite. "If they don't have enough dragons for their infantry, of course this kind of sluggish maneuvering must be the consequence," he said, "but what a mess! I expect those French will have dug in like moles by the time we get started in the morning."

Indeed, when Temeraire went aloft shortly afterwards to have a look, he could see the French working frantically on earthworks and fortifications—the heavier dragons were holding entire trees in place, lengthwise, piled upon one another while men lashed them with rope and the middle-weights heaped up dirt to either side. "That is an inordinate number of trees," Tharkay said to Laurence, as they took their turns peering down through the glass.

"Those trees have been cut, not torn up," Laurence said, after some further study. "How the devil have they managed to cut down a hundred trees—"

"They are cutting down another, over there," Gerry piped up, and looking Temeraire saw not a heavy-weight but three light-weight dragons instead, who were using a kind of saw which was little more than a long toothed chain with one end run around a wheel, which two of them turned rapidly by a crank while the third steadied the tree; the trunk was being torn through at extraordinary speed, and when it had been reduced to only a thin sliver, a heavy-weight was waved down; when she had seized it, several men chopped at the remaining portion with axes until she was able to break it off and carry it away.

"They will have a palisade by morning, at this rate," Laurence said.

As they returned towards their own encampment, towards the Russian rear, Temeraire stopped briefly to speak with Grig, who with his fellows was perched on a hill watching not the preparations for the battle, but the Chinese supply operations, behind their lines: the thirty cooking-pits, spaced at intervals so three *niru* might gather to eat around each one; two pigs and a great deal of wheat had gone into each one, and the bubbling stews were now being attended by five of the Shen Lung, who were stirring at occasional intervals, while another five were busy digging additional watering-holes with the assistance of their crews; the rest were napping while their crews worked on spare harness or cleaned them, or tended to the fighting-dragons who had come back with wounds to be tended.

"How *many* of you there are," Grig said to Temeraire, in amazement, "and how well all of you eat! I haven't seen so many dragons ever, except in the breeding grounds when I was hatched, and no-one gets enough to eat there."

He looked down at his own covert as he spoke. The twenty Russian heavy-weights were presently feasting on what Temeraire could not deny were some very handsome cows, which would have been splendid if properly roasted, or perhaps stewed with some potatoes. But the Russian aviators plainly had no notion of anything of that sort, and the resulting scene was little better than an abattoir, the heavy-weights all tearing the cows apart violently, snapping and hissing at one another in arguing over the best bits of the innards in a very showy way, meanwhile scattering and wasting a great deal of the meat, and most of the blood sinking into the ground. Temeraire sniffed and turned aside.

"There is no reason that a great many dragons cannot partake in battle, and eat well, too, if only things are managed properly, and everyone has a fair share," he said. "Our supply-dragons are paid for their work, too," he added to the assembled dragons, who had cautiously edged a little closer to hear, "which is like being given treasure."

Grig and several of his companions tittered softly together at this, as though Temeraire had made an excellent joke; Temeraire put back his ruff and said severely, "I am not making fun! They are paid wages, which are put into a bank account, and which they can take out as gold and silver, whenever they should like. Look!" He pointed at one of the Shen Lung just then flying in with a load of rocks, which she meant to use for damming up a stream. "Look, you can see for yourselves, Lung Shen Mei, there, has a very handsome gold chain about her neck."

The Russian dragons looked, and were silent; one of them said, low, "It is enough to make one think," and many of the others rustled their wings uneasily, and eyed Temeraire and one another sidelong; they edged in towards one another and away from the speaker, who flung his head back defiantly, though he also threw a nervous look at Temeraire.

"Well, you should think," Temeraire said, "that you needn't live in such a wretched manner as you do. You ought to have liberties, and be paid wages if you *do* choose to obey orders—which you needn't, if you do not want to—"

"But if we do not obey, they will send us back to the breeding grounds," one said, "to go hungry."

"If they do not give you enough food, they cannot complain if you go and take some, elsewhere," Temeraire said. "It is not as though they can make you stay there, if you do not like to."

They all stared at him, as though he had said something very peculiar; but before Temeraire could inquire further, a Russian aviator came out from his tent and saw them speaking together, and began shouting and pointing at them, cracking his short whip. He jerked on the chain of one of the heavy-weight dragons, rousing him up and turning him towards the assembled group, and the small dragons burst away in a frightened cloud, dispersing.

"Come away, Temeraire," Laurence said, "before that fellow comes up here, and demands to know what we are about. I am damned if I will apologize to him for interference, and more so if I will tell him what you were saying to those beasts: the poor wretches have enough to bear, without being cuffed about further."

"Laurence," Temeraire said, leaping aloft, "do you suppose that they *do* keep the dragons in the breeding grounds, somehow, even if they are hungry?"

Laurence was silent, then heavily said, "I imagine they might set the heavy-weights upon them, if they try to leave."

"But how could the heavy-weights agree to hurt a dragon so much smaller than they are, and who was only hungry, and not taking anything of theirs?" Temeraire said. "Surely they would feel perfect scrubs for doing such a thing. Although I do see," he added, "that it would be hard to refuse anyone who had given you *so* much treasure, and helped guard it; one would feel the most extraordinary sense of obligation. Laurence," he said suddenly, with dawning realization, "Laurence, is that why you do not care anything for fortune?"

"I cannot claim to be so unworldly as to care *nothing* for fortune," Laurence said, "but I hope that I am unwilling to be a slave to it."

The notion that fortune might enslave had not previously occurred to Temeraire, and it did not sit very well, but he could not deny that the Russian heavy-weights seemed to be quite willing to put on chains, all for treasure. "But I cannot believe," he decided, "that they are so dreadful as to pen up small dragons for it; not, at least, without giving them a chance to refute it: I will ask Vosyem."

"Pray save your inquiries for after the battle," Laurence said. "We cannot hazard a division among our forces now. *That* might indeed offer Napoleon an advantage he would be quick to seize; and you may be sure that no argument or quarrel could have so powerful an effect, towards your ends, as the demonstration you and the legions—and for that matter, the enemy—are presently setting forward before the eyes of the Russian high command and so many of their young officers, of the immense advantage to be gained by an honorable and just treatment of dragons."

Temeraire did see the necessity of defeating Napoleon, first, before they tried to do anything else; but that only made it all the more aggravating that Napoleon refused to be properly defeated. Anyway he did not see why the Russian dragons had let things get into such a fix, in the first place: even if the heavy-weights *did* behave so badly, surely the little dragons could sneak out, one after another—or they might mass themselves into groups, and all but a few dash past—there were any number of ways Temeraire might imagine, for them to slip out of the breeding grounds, and once out, they might go anywhere they liked.

He devised several dozen such strategems, that afternoon, while there was nothing to do but wait: Laurence had urged him to rest, but Temeraire found he could not sleep properly with the enemy so very close—with victory so very close. He drowsed only a little, and ate his porridge unenthusiastically—he did appreciate, of course, how efficient porridge was, and how necessary to supply a force as large as their own, but he was growing rather tired of it— and then looked around for distraction: but Laurence was closeted with Tharkay and his officers, discussing their positions in the coming battle. That was a somewhat delicate matter, with Tharkay and Dyhern and Ferris not properly officers, although in Temeraire's opinion that ought not count for much when one considered how ragged the proper officers were, and anyway—he sighed—it seemed they would very likely not have much to do. General Chu had hinted very strongly that Temeraire needn't expect to do a lot of fighting, himself. It did not seem fair, somehow, that he and Laurence should have made it at all possible for them all to have such a splendid battle, and now have no real share of it themselves.

He decided to discuss his thoughts with Grig—in an entirely hypothetical manner; he would not at all provoke a quarrel—and looked for him; Grig was for once not directly in their camp, but sitting on the edge of it, and watching a couple of other Russian dragons hanging about with the long and messy supply-train of the army. They were a sort of dragon Temeraire had not seen at all amongst the Russians before, closer to middle-weight and without any bony plates, colored in green and fawn brown, and they wore only light harness.

"Why," Temeraire said, coming over to join Grig, "those fellows look likely: why are *they* not fighting? I dare say they would be more use than those heavy-weights, if we had enough of them: where did they come from?"

Grig gave a start when Temeraire came down. "They aren't Russian dragons, at all," he said, ruffling his wings to his back, and indeed Temeraire had scarcely landed before a man, very portly and red-faced, in high boots and a brown waistcoat and no coat at all, was stomping over with an angry expression, from the waggons, to shout in broad colonial English, "I've already told you fellows to be off: they aren't for sale, and I'll be damned if—" only to halt in some surprise when he saw that neither Grig nor Temeraire had any officers.

"Why, you are Americans," Temeraire said, rather doubtfully. "Whatever are you doing here?"

"You may be sure we aren't here by any choice of mine, that is blasted certain," the sweating man said. "Where else can we be, with Oudinot and Saint-Cyr in St. Petersburg all but confiscating goods, and standing between us and our ship? I would rather get thirty cents on the dollar for my wares than ten; but if you scaly brutes and your rotten pack of whip-happy overseers don't keep off Josiah and Linden, I *will* take my cargo back to Boney's gang and make them welcome to it, and I'll call in my ship and sell them every last bale of wool in the hold, too, see if I don't."

It seemed that the Russians had already made several attempts to buy the merchant's dragons, who eyed Temeraire with some understandable nervousness and edged back from him, refusing to say a word, even though he explained quite clearly he had not the least interest in delivering them to the Russian service. "I don't suppose," he said at last, "that you are acquainted with John Wampanoag?" which produced something of a thaw.

"We are out of New Jersey, ourselves," the fat waistcoated merchant said, mopping his forehead, when he had at last sat down, somewhat more assured of their peaceable intentions, "but I have heard his name, of course; I don't suppose there's many Yankees who haven't. Well, if you are a friend of John Wampanoag, I guess you are all right; and it's true you don't have a look of those other big fellows, always snapping and yelping in that queer gabble of theirs that a man can't fit his tongue around. But what are you doing mixed up in this business, then?"

Explanations made, Temeraire wished to be introduced to Josiah and Lindy, but they only spoke a language called Unami and not English; their employer was a Mr. Calvin Jefferson, and when Temeraire tentatively asked that man, he stridently denied their having any interest in taking part in the battle. "Get themselves shot, all for someone else's quarrel; I should think not," he said, bristling.

"Well, I will not pretend to understand it," Temeraire said, somewhat doubtfully; he wondered if maybe the dragons would have expressed different sentiments, if only they could have spoken for themselves in the matter, "but naturally they should not fight if they do not like; I suppose the Shen Lung will not be fighting, either. Only it seems a shame for them to be here, just when we are sure to win a splendid victory, and not have a share in it."

Jefferson snorted. "It's soon enough to brag of your victory after you've won it," he said. "I don't set myself up as an expert on the matter, but it seems to me that Bonaparte's done pretty well for himself on these occasions in the past."

He gave them a very nice cup of tea, however, and he had some very fine woolen cloth, of which he made Temeraire a present large enough to make Laurence a new coat; as a sample, he said. "I have three thousand bales of it," he said very mournfully, "sitting just out of cannon-shot of St. Petersburg harbor; and if these Russian fellows would only make me a reasonable offer, I guess I could land it north of the city, and they could ship it down to Tver: if the French don't take *that*, pretty soon."

"I do call that handsome," Temeraire said to Grig, as they flew back to his own camp, very pleased with the use of his afternoon, "and I am sure I do not know why your people have not bought his wool."

"Well, he has no-one else to sell it to," Grig said, "except Napoleon, who is offering less," which was a point that Temeraire had not quite considered. "Of course, I do not know much about these things," Grig added.

Laurence received the gift with pleasure, although he professed himself surprised by the presence of the traders. "I suppose I ought not be," he said. "They seem to be everywhere in the world, these days; and in the article of speed their ships are scarcely to be outmatched. Blaise told me he crossed paths with one of their schooners, in his Atlantic crossing to Brazil, and he would have sworn she was doing fourteen knots, in a light wind.

"But this merchant may have gambled badly," Laurence added, "if he was hoping to see his price driven up: God willing, we may end the war tomorrow. Come, my dear, you must try and get some rest."

Chapter 19

Temeraire jolted out of sleep the next morning with a start: the thunder-roll and the low terrible whistling of the field guns. It was just dawn. "Twelve-pounders," Laurence said, listening: not as great a noise as the enormous sixty-eights which could be carried by a dragon transport like the *Potentate,* or even the thirty-six-pounders which had made up most of the guns of the *Reliant,* on which Temeraire had hatched, but they were certainly loud enough for all that. When Temeraire put his head out of the pavilion, he saw many of the other dragons sitting up on their haunches, looking a little uneasily to the west where the noise of the guns came steadily.

"How they go on!" Chu said. The guns were firing in nearly a continuous stream; as soon as the reverberation of one shot had died away, here came another. "At least when dragons roar, we have it over with, and then you can hear yourself think again. But I am ready to bear the noise, if that means we can get started. Come, we had better go and have a look."

They had encamped at the Russian rear, as they could reach the fighting more easily than might the infantry or the cavalry, and this way refresh themselves during the battle and tend to injured dragons without being exposed to the artillery. As Chu issued his orders, the *niru* began at once to go aloft; Temeraire flew alongside him swiftly the five minutes to the front, and there halted to hover: the battlefield looked quite different than the previous afternoon. The

French had thrown up three rows of fences nearly all about the highest ground, constructed as they had seen of heavy logs and piled stones and dirt. And as a final insult, they had even seized and improved upon the very fortifications which the Russians had built and abandoned, not a week before.

The ranks of infantry stood arrayed now behind the heavy fences, deployed into broad lines, and great batteries of artillery stood upon raised ground behind them, with several redoubts piled up; their felling of trees had removed the few obstacles which remained to their clear prospect in every direction, while the Russians had been obliged to take up positions crowded up against a heavy stand of timber to the north and with marshy ground not distant from their rear. But the French dragons were massed towards the center, in a peculiar concentration, which it seemed to Temeraire should make it possible to encircle them entirely.

He ventured to point this out to Chu, who said, "Yes, so why has he done it?"

"You have forgotten the guns," Laurence said, pointing: many of the great massed batteries of smaller guns stood behind the infantry ranks, aiming skyward. "Those will surely be firing on us: they are elevated too high to fire on the Russian infantry."

As the Russian dragons made their own first pass, carrying heavy loads of bombs meant for the French infantry positions, the raised artillery began to roar: canister-shot, filling the air with smoke and the flying balls and scraps of metal, and even though these nearly all fell harmlessly into the field between the armies, the hail barred an approach to the French forces from more than half the sky: only the center, where the French dragons were massed, was open air.

"Hah," Chu said, "so he is making a mountain pass, out of gunfire. Yes, I see; we will have a hard time coming at him." The Russian heavy-weights were already being stymied, their approach towards the French falling back before the blistering fire, which would have torn their wings apart if they had continued.

But Chu signaled nevertheless, and Temeraire watched with rising joy as six *niru* flew forward to make the first sortie, and two other wings of four *niru* apiece broke away to either side of the battlefield, to probe at the French defenses. They were fighting, at last they were fighting, and then Chu said, "Well, let's go back and sit down and have a morning drink; is there any tea, Shen Lao?"

"What?" Temeraire said, outraged. "But the battle is joined! Everything has begun!"

"And it will be a long while going, too," Chu said, unperturbed, "as long as we can't come at them more than twenty at a time." He waved towards the engagement: the *niru* had closed with the front ranks of the French dragons, and were skirmishing with them skillfully though as yet cautiously, all the dragons on both sides working out a sense of their unfamiliar enemies. There was indeed no room for any other Chinese dragons to attack. One of the *niru* was already falling back a little from the fighting to give the rest more room for maneuvering.

"But then surely we ought do something to open a wider front, on which we might attack," Temeraire said. "We might—" He paused, and looked upon the field: perhaps they might go around to the west—but there were guns on the heights there covering the French rear, with a forest of sharpened stakes rising up around them. "Well, we ought to do *something*, anyway," he finished a little lamely, even if he could not immediately see what that something might be.

"Certainly," Chu said. "Go find that Russian general, and tell him we had better arrange supply for another two days." And then he turned around and flew back towards the campsite, as though there were no fighting going on at all.

The rest of the morning was equally deflating. Even Laurence only said, "We could scarcely give Bonaparte a better gift than to accept the extraordinary losses which it would require on the part of the Chinese legions to seize and overwhelm those artillery positions as they stand: pray notice, if you will, that the French have secondary guns waiting against just such an attempt, and crews of pikemen in support.

"Time is our ally: they cannot hold against us indefinitely. They have sixty dragons here, you five times that number. Even if we allow the French dragons to be the equal of the Chinese, which we ought not, as the day progresses we can send fresh beasts against tired, and by slow tide wear them down; and all the while, the Russians will be executing their own assault upon the French ground positions."

This was a very sensible and practical explanation and by no means satisfying. Temeraire without much enthusiasm agreed to Laurence's suggestion that they should indeed go and assure additional supply, for the Chinese legions, largely in hopes that the Russians should protest and insist on some more useful course of action. But Kutuzov was sitting in his own low chair with no more hurry in his manner than Chu; he only nodded to Laurence's request and said, "I think Colonel Ogevin has already put it in train. Vasya," he added to one of his aides, "see that it is done."

So Temeraire, with enthusiasm still more diminished, returned to the campsite, where Chu was now eating a large helping of porridge as placidly as—as a *cow*, Temeraire thought, meanly; he scornfully refused the bowl which Shen Lao offered him. He had not in the least regretted Iskierka's absence, all this while, but in the moment he missed her quite acutely. He was certain *she* would not have tolerated merely sitting about, but would have insisted on their going to join in somehow or other.

He ventured quietly to Laurence that perhaps they might try a pass against the French artillery. "For I am quite sure," he said, "that I would be able to break some of those earthworks, with the divine wind, and bowl over a great many of the gunners, so the Russians might be able to come at them."

"Yes," Chu said, having overheard and demanded to know what Temeraire was saying, "and you could also go and dig some ditches, for latrines; and I dare say if you wanted, you could try and cook our dinner, though it might not taste very well; and also you could go and dance for the troops, which at least would entertain them. None of that is your business: it is your business to stay here, and learn how a battle is managed properly, and then *if* a moment should arise where you may, through a decisive action, alter the course of the battle, you will be ready to act, and not worn out and too distracted to observe it."

Temeraire flattened his ruff, but even Laurence did not disagree, saying gently, "My dear, you must see that in the present situation, where the enemy's positions mean we cannot bring to bear even the better part of the forces which we have, it would be folly to risk you to no purpose. Recall that we are here not merely as soldiers, but as envoys; it would be as wrong for us to go foolhardy into battle now, when our destruction could cast into serious disarray all the cooperation between the Russian army and the legions we have asked to follow us here, as it would be in another situation for us to evade battle out of cowardice."

So Temeraire had nothing to do but sigh, and put down his head, and wait, while the Jade Dragons darted back and forth, bringing Chu reports of endless tedium, and the sun crawled by overhead.

"What a hideous noise," Tharkay said. The artillery had not ceased to fire, all this time.

Temeraire went aloft again after noon had passed, only to have a look; although privately he thought perhaps he *might* see an opportunity, of making a particularly significant attack. The battle-field was so thickly obscured by smoke, by now, that it was nearly impossible to see what any of the soldiers were doing on the ground. One could only guess at it, by listening to the roar of the guns, which went on and on and on. His own ears rang with it, the unpleasant brassy noise: he had never heard anything like, save at the battle of Shoeburyness, during the final great bombardment, which had lasted half-an-hour; here so far it had gone on more than half the day.

"Oh, there," Temeraire said, when a breath of wind stirred and blew a great rolling cloud of powder away from before the French earthworks on their left flank, "now we will be able to see something, at any rate." And then he paused, and was silent. The ground was littered thickly with the shattered bodies of horses and of men in both uniforms.

"Dear God, what a slaughter," Laurence said, low. And the soldiers were yet fighting, bitterly, around the fence: the Russians had seized one end now and were striving forward with bayonets and swords and even in some instances bare fists to push back the French further along it.

"Surely we might help them," Temeraire said, unhappily, but even as he half-stooped towards the struggle, involuntarily, another roaring sounded below, and he backwinged, recoiling instinctively: a hail of canister-shot went whistling by not a hundred feet distant.

"We have already helped them," Laurence said to Temeraire, as they drew back. "We have put a stop to Napoleon's aerial attacks: the French would otherwise be enacting a terrible bombardment against the Russian troops. And the guns which he is using to keep the Chinese legions off, he cannot direct against the infantry."

"But he seems to have enough of them to do both," Temeraire said: there were hundreds and hundreds of field guns, it seemed, on both sides. "Laurence, whyever is Napoleon insisting on such a battle? Surely *he* can see, as well as we can, that he is lost: that he is only dragging things out dreadfully, for everyone, and killing so many on all sides."

"He has little alternative," Laurence said, "save if he chose to abandon his army, and flee back to France in a state of ignominy: in a pursuit, our aerial advantage would shortly begin to tell ruthlessly against him; we would have been able to overwhelm his rearguard, and catch him and his army strung out upon the road. Most likely he yet hopes for some mistake upon our part, which would permit him to use his own advantage in artillery and in ground troops." But the Russians were being quite careful to avoid that: as the fortifications and the heavy woods kept them from coming at the full body of the French Army, General Barclay had positioned his soldiers along the road to Moscow to the south, to guard against any attempt on the part of the French to slip away again during the night, or to sneak some substantial portion out to flank the Russian Army.

Junichiro had unexpectedly begged to be allowed to come aloft with them, on every one of Temeraire's passes: he had become, to Temeraire's gratification, quite a reformed character, and in the course of their journey from China to Russia had acquired a great deal not only of English but of French; to-day he had been avidly studying the order of battle of the armies on both sides. He ventured now, from Temeraire's shoulder, to say, "This seems something between a battle and a siege," and Laurence nodded in agreement.

As a siege might take months or even years to lift, that was by no means encouraging, and it was only meager consolation when Laurence said, "They cannot have the supply to hold out for more than a few days, Temeraire, even if they eat the cavalry-horses: you can see for yourself they have virtually no cattle amongst their baggage."

It did not make Temeraire feel much better, either, to see Vosyem and the rest of the Russian heavy-weights sitting disgruntled in their own encampment, sullenly tearing at the ground and snapping at one another, when he came past them: Chu had sent a word to the Russian generals hinting that perhaps it would be easier for the Chinese legions to operate if they were not being fouled and harassed by their own allies. The Russian heavy-weights had several times bulled through the *niru* formations to engage the enemy directly, with nothing but ill-effect all around.

Temeraire sighed and looked back towards the battlefield: the guns had begun roaring more energetically. The front row of the fences had at last fallen, but the French had got away their guns, and raced back behind the shelter of the second row; the artillery were now pounding away at the Russian troops who had seized the first row, before those men might even have enjoyed a moment's respite from their victory. The batteries of artillery aimed against the sky were yet sheltered behind a third row of fences, and overlooking them were the massed ranks of Napoleon's Imperial Guard, as yet withheld from all the fighting. But aloft, the *niru* were battering steadily and systematically away at the French dragons.

"Ah, there you are," Chu said, when Temeraire came down in the encampment. "This is Colonel Zhao Lien, commander of the third *jalan*," he said, presenting Temeraire to one officer, a heavy-set dragon of pale green, with a bristling spine of tendrils and a mane not unlike Chu's own, in scarlet; she bowed her head politely before continuing her report.

"The quantity of smoke produced by the guns has made it most difficult to obtain a clear understanding of the organization of the enemy's forces," she said, "but their reserves are substantial, and I have determined their supply may be a great deal better than we have supposed to be the case. I sent a small foray against their rear, upon the ground, which was repulsed swiftly by the repositioning of their guns, but one of my dragons was able to seize a packet from their supply-waggons—"

She indicated this, a large square bundle which had been hastily rewrapped; when one of her crewmen opened it up again, Temeraire bending down to sniff found it full of long hard strips of some dark brown stuff that smelt strongly of spice; pieces were handed around, and when Temeraire chewed it, he found that it was meat: quite tough and dry and salty, but perfectly good to eat.

"Hm," Shen Shi said, inspecting it. "That is very clever: they do not need cattle, then."

"No," Zhao Lien said, "and they had fifty pallets of a similar style on hand."

Chu made a low grunt. "Well, then they can hold out at least a week," he said, "but why would they have had so much meat, for this number of dragons—" He fell silent, scratching at the ground ruminatively.

"I will say, General," Zhao Lien said, "that it seems to me the enemy are fighting very conservatively."

"Hm," Chu said. "Colonel, I wish you to take four *niru* and scout—where are those maps? What is to the north of our position?"

Temeraire looked back and forth between them, conscious that he had not quite followed their train of thought, and wondering how he might ask without looking somehow foolish. Chu was bending low over his maps, and then suddenly, very near-by, a blasting of thunder erupted, a cannonball-whistling. Temeraire looked up and around, in surprise, and then recoiled with a cry as something hot and terrible seared along his side. Roars of pain went up on all sides of him—canister-shot was flying down all over the rear of the camp. "Aloft!" Laurence was shouting from his back, through his speaking-trumpet. "All aloft, at once! Get into the air!"

Temeraire flung himself up, blindly, backwinging, and took up the cry himself as he went, roaring it out as loudly as he could; as soon as he was up, and out of the flight path of the balls, he could see the guns firing upon them: a tiny clearing, some four hundred yards to the north, where the French had established a small battery of three-pounders. They were firing at a furious pace: not even pulling their guns back into place after they fired, nor even trying to aim, merely reloading and firing again and again; all they cared for was to hit anything in the Russian rear at all, and even more guns were being dragged out from the trees behind them.

But they had as yet no covering-fire, nor aerial defenders; Temeraire hissed in fury and circled towards them, out of their line of fire. Plunging towards them, he drew in his breath, once and twice and three times, swelling all his chest with air, and roaring fell upon the line of guns, sweeping them and seeing men and horses fall screaming to the ground before the divine wind, while he caught at the hot guns and tipped them over into a clanging, tumbling heap.

Musket-fire spat against his flank, hot stinging bursts of pain, but he was through and pulling up and away, the guns silenced, their crews shattered. Looking back he saw the wreckage they had already made in that brief span of time: the cooking-pits clogged with dirt and smoking metal, many spoilt; a dozen of the Shen Lung moaning upon the ground, bleeding, many of the wounded dragons injured again also; and near the half-collapsed pavilion—

Temeraire flung himself down again next to Chu: the general's great scarlet side was heaving, and with each breath a gush of blood rose up and spilled black from three gaping wounds, clustered near the top of his back; his wings lay limp against his sides. "No, no," Temeraire said, wretchedly. Five of the Chinese dragon-surgeons were already at work, digging their arms within to bring out the shot: one was calling for long tongs to be brought. Another managed to draw out one, which had struck upon a rib; the ball had burst like a star, and another torrent of blood followed it when the surgeon pulled it out.

Chu's eyes were closed; he coughed, rattling, and blood trickled from the sides of his mouth; one of the surgeons was thrown from his back. Temeraire almost nosed at him, but timidly held back; he did not know what to do. Zhao Lien landed beside him and said, "I have ordered five *niru* to the north, accompanied by couriers, to scout for more of the enemy attempting to flank us, as General Chu directed. What are your commands?"

She was speaking to him, Temeraire realized; she was asking him for orders. Abruptly, Temeraire felt rage swelling hot in his breast; he imagined with burning satisfaction throwing himself to the front, commanding all the legions to fall in behind him and overturn the French defenses, smash their artillery and then slaughter all their ranks, no matter what the cost. He would drive them forth with the divine wind, and avenge—

"Temeraire," Laurence said softly, a hand on his neck, and

Temeraire dragged in a breath; he looked at Zhao Lien, and saw her regarding him narrowly, warily, as though she feared what he might do. He swallowed and said to Laurence, in English, "Laurence, what ought I do, now?"

"If you will be counseled by me," Laurence said, "we will determine which of the three *jalan* commanders is senior, and appoint them to the command."

Temeraire took another breath, and nodded; he said to Zhao Lien, "Who is the senior commander, of the three *jalan?*"

She sat back upon her haunches, relaxing a little. "I am," she said.

"Then—then you shall take command, until General Chu is quite recovered," he said, though he could not help but think longingly, one more time, of the glorious vision of his charge. "And I am quite sure," he added savagely, "that there *are* more soldiers coming; it is just the sort of thing Napoleon likes to do, so you had better plan as though there were."

Zhao Lien turned to a limping Shen Shi, who had one badly torn wing, and conferred with her about supply; then she turned and said, "If the soldiers who approach are a substantial force, our situation will be extremely precarious."

"But we still outnumber them so heavily in the air!" Temeraire said, uncertainly. "Of course we must still beat them, surely."

"We cannot be assured of doing so in the present position," Zhao Lien said. "An immediate assault upon the artillery must lose us half our fighting troops. This, having diminished our aerial advantage, may permit the enemy to hold their well-fortified positions against us. If they have sufficient ground forces to strike against the flank of our allies' ground soldiers—"

Interrupting her explanation, Lung Yu Fei came blazing into the camp as swiftly as a rocket, skidding in the dirt as she pulled up: Temeraire regarded her with dismay even before she opened her mouth and said, "There is a whole army coming, from the north-east: they are coming through the trees on foot."

Once again now the advantage changed hands, as abruptly as before; but Kutuzov's caution had not deserted him even in an apparent moment of triumph: he had placed his rear-guard to cover the road to Moscow, and had kept a great many of his forces uncommitted to the battle. Even before the French reinforcements had completed half their advance, the Russian Army was melting away again eastward, escaping the trap.

Laurence and Temeraire scarcely touched ground the next four hours, trying as best they might to create a unified action with the Russian forces: a coordination almost impossible to achieve when the two of them were nearly the sole interlocutors between the two bodies of troops. The battle had lent itself to a sharp separation between commands; the retreat by no means did so, for the Russians badly needed air cover, and the French had been reinforced by some forty dragons more, under the command of the very dragon Laurence had noted at the false negotiations: Marshal Ombreux.

"We cannot keep flying about in this manner," Laurence said, when they had made the fourth frantic pass back to Kutuzov's headquarters, trying for some clarification in orders which had already seemed inapplicable. "Temeraire, see if you can find Grig, and persuade him and the rest of those Russian light-weights to go-between for us."

What the officers of those dragons should think, of his summarily appropriating their beasts, Laurence cared little; he had already privately resolved that if their conditions were not ameliorated, he should ask Temeraire to offer the poor creatures safe passage back to China, with the *jalan*, on the conclusion of the hostilities. "And if the officers at headquarters do not care to listen to them," he added, "I dare say they will be persuaded, at the next moment when they wish to send us orders."

Grig was easy to find: he had been trailing them, and he and several of his companions were by no means unwilling to help once

Temeraire had assured them of sharing the dinner of the Chinese dragons that night; they soon worked out for themselves an effective rotation whereby each dragon went in turn to the high command. To the credit of Kutuzov's staff, whatever dismay they might have felt at seeing their old order overturned, they did not allow it to deter them: Grig returned from his flight carrying a Russian officer with him, a young man of noble family from Kutuzov's staff, who had with real courage tied himself onto the smaller dragon's harness-rings with nothing but his belt, the better to convey the orders.

As the withdrawal advanced, the *jalan* were pressed into service to carry away the guns and thereby speed the pace of the retreat. The Cossacks carried out a whirling and ferocious defense in their rear; but the heavier French dragons massed for a sortie now and again, and in such occasions, Temeraire would quickly call out and send back a few *niru* to engage and drive them away.

But Laurence was well aware of the dangerous falseness of their position: if the French surged forth from their defenses, and flung all their strength upon the Russian ground troops, success might well be theirs: a quick shattering blow could give them the complete mastery in artillery which should make them impervious even to the continuing disadvantage in the air.

He half-waited for Bonaparte to act, to move; waited at every moment for the French to come pouring forward over their fences; but the moment did not come, and then the ground had opened wide between the armies, and at last the guns fell silent.

The army was yet moving, all that night. Laurence came to ground with Temeraire in Mozhaisk. "Remain here," he said quietly, laying a hand on Temeraire's muzzle. Temeraire had been aloft, flying and maneuvering vigorously, without a halt for seven hours; they had come fifty miles. Temeraire did not answer aloud, but let his eyelids sink shut; Forthing slid down from his back and said, "I'll see about his dinner, sir; will we encamp here?"

"Assume a short halt only, for the moment," Laurence said.

"Roland," he added, beckoning to her; her command of Chinese, having unwillingly suffered Temeraire's tutelage in that language for several years, was by far superior to Forthing's. "Have a word with the supply-officers, and see what they can tell you about our circumstances."

Tharkay fell in with him, as they walked towards the headquarters established in a large farmhouse, some half-a-mile distant; the night was still hot, and the air thick with dust. All around, Laurence heard soldiers coughing, heavily, and long lines stood at all the wells, of men desperately thirsty from dust and gunpowder in their mouths. But the lines were patient, well-ordered; the ranks had not disintegrated, though the circumstances might have been discouraging enough to depress the spirits and morale of any army.

"I can only wonder," Laurence said, "why Bonaparte did not come forth. Even if he were ever to have another chance at smashing their army, he could scarcely hope to find himself at better relative strength. Can he be seriously ill, perhaps?"

"As pleasant a possibility as that might be to contemplate," Tharkay said, "I hope you will forgive me for discouraging it. A man who has seen three hundred enemy dragons appear without warning does not need to be on his death-bed to discover a little caution, even if he is a Napoleon."

The farmhouse was the scene of enormous activity: officers rushing in with reports on the number of troops, the losses; the activity observed among the French by the Cossacks on their light dragons and horses. Bonaparte's army had certainly been reinforced by more than twenty thousand men: now identified as the Sixth Corps, which had last been sighted in Petersburg not a week before. General Saint-Cyr had managed to bring them south so quickly they had outdistanced even the reports of their travel, which uselessly had trickled in that very day. Three separate witnesses had glimpsed him upon the field, that evening, as Napoleon had embraced him and bestowed on him a Marshal's baton, which he had won by the enterprise.

The initial goal of those troops had likely been Moscow itself: a neat pincer-trap for the Russian Army, which would have cut off their supply and likely secured for the French the great magazines of the city, full of food and munitions, which they themselves so desperately required. Napoleon had sacrificed that ambition for the rescue of his army.

In the dining chamber of the house, Kutuzov and his senior generals had gathered about the table; Barclay was speaking impassionedly of the necessity of retreating, and therefore of sacrificing Moscow. "We cannot take the wholly unjustified risk of the destruction of the army—the only way in which this war can now be lost. We know Bonaparte's numbers have already been diminished by half during this campaign; he has lost more cavalry even than that. He can take Moscow, but he cannot hold it; he cannot hold St. Petersburg. He has overreached—"

"Overreached!" Another general, Bennigsen, was already roaring at him, before he had finished. "You would let him walk through the gates of Moscow without giving battle, without challenge—" He broke here into a torrent of Russian, savage, which made Barclay's cheeks flush hot with color, before he returned to French. "Listen to me, General," Bennigsen said, turning towards Kutuzov, "it will not be so simple a matter to get Bonaparte out again, once we have let him in. He may be diminished in numbers, but those who remain to him are the best of his army, seasoned men. If we give him so splendid a resting place as Moscow, his stragglers will gather in to him, he will secure his supply with all the stores laid up for the use of our own army—dear God! If any of us had ever thought there should be danger of them falling into the enemy's hands!"

The argument could not fail but be impassioned, in such circumstances as these: the Chinese legions were still enough advantage to make the Russian Army seem the superior, though on the ground they were as yet perilously outnumbered, and the losses on the previous day had been immense. The French had known they fought a holding action; Bonaparte at every turn had conserved his men, and yielded ground judiciously to preserve them: ground which the Russians had bought dearly in blood while exposing themselves to the withering French artillery.

But no man could easily have borne sacrificing, even in worse circumstances, the very heart of the nation; though the government had been seated in St. Petersburg some years now, Moscow remained to nearly all of them its foremost city. "To have lost Petersburg was bad enough; if we lose Moscow as well, without a shot fired, you may as well send a courier to ask Napoleon which of his brothers we shall see upon the throne, by the New Year!" General Docturov said bitterly: his infantry had borne the brunt of the day's hot work; his own arm was bandaged, and his face spattered with powder-burns.

Another officer, a younger man named Raevsky who had led the assault upon the French fences, said quietly to Kutuzov directly, "We must cover the southern provinces to permit General Chichagov and General Tormassov to unite their forces. Without Saint-Cyr's forces at Petersburg, Wittgenstein has sufficient numbers to drive back the French there—"

"Before we are subjected to more of these counsels of—let us say retreat, instead of surrender," Bennigsen said to him, with acid bite, "perhaps we might first ascertain if the retreat can be accomplished. If Bonaparte were to overwhelm the rear-guard—"

Kutuzov sat impassively while they argued it out, his heavy-lidded bad eye giving him an appearance almost half-slumbering and his face resting upon his fist, elbow propped against the arm of his chair; the fingers of his other hand touched gently the many reports which had gathered up before him, and now and again he lifted one of these to his eyes. But Laurence did not think he read them; and when at last the voices fell silent, he did not answer them, but looked to Laurence. "What is the state of your legions?" he said.

"Sir," Laurence said, "we remain at your service, constrained only by supply. General Chu's injuries are grievous, but I have every confidence in Colonel Zhao Lien, and our losses otherwise were slight: ten fighting-beasts and seven supply wounded past flying."

"Will they carry infantry?" Kutuzov asked; Bennigsen made a small jerk, a half-abortive movement.

"Certainly, for a short distance," Laurence said. "For any longer march, sir, that may materially alter the requirements of supply."

Kutuzov nodded, a little. "We must be in Moscow by tomorrow," he said, "and we will take the road to Riazan," he held up a hand, to forestall argument, "and then cross to the Old Kaluga Road, and make for Tarutino."

Bennigsen checked his first reply without speaking; Raevsky nodded. Laurence looking at the map upon the table picked out the roads, the cities, and understood: Kutuzov would make it seem as though he were retreating eastward, deeper into the Russian steppes, the safest course; and then would turn south again sharply while the French were busy with their occupation of Moscow—and surely its looting as well—and seize a strong position to the south, protecting the supply of food and munitions coming to his army from the rich southern provinces, and ensuring his communications with the large portion of the Russian Army which yet remained in the Empire's south.

There was much to like, in the strategy, and nothing better recommended itself; only sentiment stood in its way—only sentiment. Barclay's own expression was of relief and weariness combined; the other officers remained silent, giving a dull and unhappy consent.

Kutuzov looked around at them and nodded. "To yield Moscow is not to lose Russia," he said. "And if Bonaparte should think otherwise, so much the better."

But if Bonaparte did, he was not alone: so, too, plainly did the soldiers as they marched through the streets of Moscow, sharing the roads at every turn with a terrified and appalled peasantry and merchants all desperately trying to evacuate themselves and their goods before the French arrival. The great square before the red walls of the Kremlin was a solid mass of people, the glorious twisting domes of the splendid cathedral rising like an island out from among lowing cattle, struggling horses, waggon-carts loaded with goods.

Temeraire had insisted on taking a carrying-harness himself with all the rest of the dragons; he bore nearly two hundred Russian soldiers over the city, and Laurence saw many of the young officers openly weeping with rage as they looked down and saw the thronged streets, the masses of men and horses and carts pouring out of the city, the River Moskva crammed with barges and smaller boats. To the west behind them, guns yet spoke sporadically, all the day, and the French advance guard under Murat continued harassing the rear.

They left their load of soldiers on the far side of the city, the *niru* behind them descending each in turn and practicing a maneuver Laurence had never before seen. As they came close to the ground, the dragons' crews went below and detached the lower straps of the carrying-harness; much to the alarm of the soldiers craning their heads to look. Each dragon then made a quick expert hop just before landing, flinging the sides wide—the soldiers shouting wildly as they swung out—then immediately flattening themselves low upon the ground, so the startled men at the ends found themselves already down, and even the soldiers higher up on the dragons' backs might the more easily clamber off.

"How clumsy they are," Laurence overheard one of the dragons murmuring to another, not unjustly: the Russian infantry were not even skillful at mounting their own dragons, plainly as yet uneasy with the entire business, and often tripped over one another in their haste to disembark even without the addition of acrobatics.

The morale of the Chinese forces was as yet untarnished: they did not suffer those same pangs as did the Russians, on seeing the city fall, and they had come off the better in their skirmishing against the French dragons. They plainly were confident in Zhao Lien, although Laurence overheard a little soft grumbling by the first *jalan* that their own commander Shao Ri ought have been the choice: there was a little rivalry, it seemed, between the scarlet dragons who made the bulk of the southern troops, and the green ones who preferred the northern climes.

The attack upon their rear had not disheartened but inspired all the legions with the desire for revenge. General Chu had been gently and tenderly borne to the new camp on a litter by four dragons: he had not yet roused, save to ask for a little water, now and again, and his body was hot with fever; his loud labored breathing was a constant reminder to them all of the treachery which had struck them. But for all that, when they encamped at last for the night, Laurence heard many of the dragons and their crewmen murmuring softly, doubtfully, about the retreat and their allies.

"I cannot like it at all," Temeraire said, unhappily. "It seems to me nearly wicked, Laurence: do you know, Grig has told me his captain was saying the French will take *a hundred million* rubles in treasure out of the city—which I suppose are like pounds—"

"Nothing like," Laurence said, "—not in the least; five in one, my dear."

"Well, I am very glad to hear it," Temeraire said, only a little mollified, "but even so that is more money than I have ever heard of, and they can settle in very comfortably, and eat well there all winter if they like as well: it certainly looked a very splendid city, from above."

The retreat continued, the next day, although a temporary armistice held off the French advance behind them. It was tiring work, and sorrowful; as the day went on the dragons began to be loaded with the wounded, and had to witness their agony at being put aboard. And yet they were the fortunate, not to be dragged over the dreadful roads in horse-carts. Temeraire was drooping before the last flight, as the bloodied and weary men dragged themselves aboard, or were heaved up by their few able-bodied comrades; night was coming on, and the sun had sunk low. He gathered himself and heaved aloft, wings beating, and slowly began to fly. A deep red-orange glow rose against the sky ahead of them; the wind had grown stronger yet again. The riot of color did not diminish as they went, though the sky was sweeping to black above, the stars emerging, and as they drew near the city they heard a great crackling noise, punctuated by sharp explosions like shattering glass.

"*Boze Moje,*" one of the men said, low. "*Onii goryat Moskvye.*"

Laurence put the glass to his eye as they came overhead, a rolling wave of baking heat rising, lifting Temeraire soaring high: a handful of Russian soldiers were dashing through the city streets ahead of the line of leaping, hungry flames, carrying torches; there were heaped piles of hay and tinder at corners, and they were firing them as they went. They were burning their own city. Napoleon would find no shelter in Moscow, after all.

Chapter 20

Laurence paused a long moment in the empty street, caught by the sight of a swinging, blackened lantern and the shape of steps leading up to a gutted doorway, opening onto the rubble of a house. For a moment he thought it another old memory returning, some flash of the destruction of Portsmouth; then he recognized abruptly the home of Countess Andreyevna, where he had dined his first night in Moscow. Of the palatial house there was nothing left but jagged timbers thrust up into the sky, heaps of tumbled brick and cinders, one corner in the back where a narrow servants' staircase and a corner of the second floor stood alone, a few feet of space.

"Do you see something?" Tharkay asked quietly. His own face was half-covered; only his eyes looked out above the scarf he had wrapped over his nose and mouth: not too incongruous a costume in the city, for there were yet quantities of dust and ash lingering in the air.

"No," Laurence said. "No, it is nothing; let us go on." He put his shoulder back to the yoke of the small cart they were dragging behind them, with its few bags of grain: their safe-passage and the only one required; the French had mastered their own marauding troops and now were offering urgent and enthusiastic welcome to any of the local peasantry who offered to sell them any food—there being very few such offers; those who made them were meeting with savage reprisals from Russian partisans.

The streets of Moscow bore little resemblance to the thronged narrow lanes which Laurence had seen from aloft, only a month before: now half-deserted, frequented more by rats than men and full of rubble, lined with ruined houses and gardens still choked with ash. Some three-quarters of the city had burned, and if that disaster had denied the French its comforts and supply, Laurence found it hard to accept the price. Little better illustration could be wanted of the cost of Napoleon's pride.

A troop of grenadiers marched past in good order, though their uniforms were an unholy mess: coats in a dozen different colors, most of them threadbare and patched, boots cracked and wrapped about with string; only their muskets still shone brightly. Their eyes drifted to the cart as they passed, with an interest more than academic; when they turned the corner, one man even detached himself from the end of the column and came back, and pointing at the bags said, "*Qu'est-ce que c'est là?*"

Without answering him, Tharkay silently presented him with a paper which had been prepared for them by one young Russian aide-de-camp, in that alphabet, and embellished with all the official art which his creativity had permitted; the name *Louis-Nicholas Davout* was the only legible Latin on the sheet. It was a name to conjure with, for Davout's harshness with indiscipline was legendary, and reports had reached even the Russian camp of the executions he had ordered for pillaging. The soldier thrust the paper back and assumed an officious mien, saying coolly, "*Le Maréchal est avec l'Empereur, en la place Rouge,*" and pointed them along another street before hurrying to rejoin his vanished troop.

Tharkay raised an eyebrow to Laurence as he put away the paper: should they take the chance? Laurence hesitated a moment, but nodded. They had intended only a general reconnoiter, to gain a sense of the French strength and the imminence of action—a sense which could not presently be gained, not reliably, from their Russian allies.

Morale in the Russian Army had rebounded and even swelled

as the French showed no inclination to foray past Moscow, and steady reports of the disintegration of their supply reached the Russian camp every day—often at the same time as their own supply-waggons arrived from the south, loaded with shipments of bread and boots and uniforms. Even the rank and file now had gradually come to share Barclay's view: that Napoleon had indeed overreached, and delivered himself and his Grande Armée into as neat a trap as was ever devised for an enemy. Each day meant the death of another hundred of his cavalry-horses, and three days before he had sent away fifteen of his dragons, traveling together to defend themselves against Cossack harrying: their departure had been observed, and had occasioned great cheer amongst the Russians.

But even as the soldiers grew more satisfied, their commanders grew less so. The intrigue at the Russian headquarters had risen to a fiery pitch; despite having managed the singularly effective retreat through the city, General Barclay had at last resigned his command entirely, in indignation at the disrespect he had met from both Kutuzov and Bennigsen, and those two men were at logger-heads themselves.

Kutuzov's position was an unsettled one: he had been nearly forced on Alexander to begin with, and he had sacrificed Moscow to the enemy. With both Moscow and Petersburg lost, the enemy everywhere west of the Volga and north of Moscow, the Russian nobility had been scattered upon the countryside, many of them cut off from their estates and fearing personal ruin. It was his task not merely to plan the Russian counterattack, when time had done its work, but to keep those nobles and even the Tsar himself placated, and fight off all the loud and urgent cries for an immediate battle.

He was resorting to a kind of outrageous propaganda: mere skirmishes between his men and Murat's advance guard were magnified into great victories—even if his forces came back with but a single prisoner and having lost several men themselves—and he exaggerated even the already-heartening reports of the French decline, filling his dispatches with such numbers as would have shortly ended with Napoleon sitting in Moscow alone but for a single mule and a barrel of beer.

And he was concerned, above all, with ensuring that the Chinese legions remained with the army. If Napoleon were to once again have the advantage in the air, the French position would by no means be so desperate as it was. They had great magazines of their own at Smolensk, and elsewhere through the south. If they did not need to fear being pounced upon by half-a-dozen *niru*, Napoleon's dragons might have been put to supply work, or even to swiftly relocate his army to Smolensk, there to winter and regroup for a fresh campaign in the spring.

Laurence did not wish to abandon Kutuzov in the least, but neither could he feel it at all consistent with the duty he owed the Emperor of China, to strand his borrowed legions in the midst of Russia with inadequate supply during the oncoming winter. October had so far been beautiful, warm and mild; but in the last two days the trees had with startling speed begun to shed their leaves. The Russian countryside was taking on a grey and gloomy character, unrelieved by the enormously tall pine trees looming with their cold dark needles, the increasingly barren birches rattling in the wind.

With the full cooperation of the Russians, Shen Shi had now established depots to the east and west both, which she estimated could carry the legions at their full strength for a month. But there was no reason to expect that Kutuzov would have struck even then: the old general was perfectly willing to permit Napoleon to sit in Moscow as long as he wished. And once they had begun the counterattack, the road back to the Niemen was a long one.

"How much longer will we be required?" Zhao Lien had asked Laurence bluntly, two days before. He could not tell her, and he felt too strongly that he could not trust whatever answer Kutuzov might make him.

"Bonaparte is our best hope, for the campaign to begin," he had said ruefully to Temeraire that evening. "If he has any sense, he must try and fight his way back to Smolensk sooner than late, and westward on from there swiftly. He cannot long suppose that the Russians will make peace with him now."

Such a peace would have allowed Napoleon to withdraw without humiliation, surely all that he could now hope for; but that peace was as surely to be denied him. Alexander, with his government-in-exile in Tula, was intensely, savagely delighted by the growing evidence of French discomfiture: he had already written out many long ambitious schemes to Kutuzov and his other generals for retaking Moscow, for the pursuit and destruction of the remnant of the French Army, and indeed even the capture of Napoleon himself.

Kutuzov received these directives placidly, and stayed just where he was. He had done his best to assist Napoleon in deceiving himself about the prospects of peace: he had received a French envoy affably, and agreed to a temporary armistice, but the false negotiations of Vyazma had done much to close that door. Alexander refused to receive such an envoy himself, or to write so much as a note, feeling that he had already stretched his own honor to bear as much as he could. Napoleon's pride alone could keep him in Moscow—but of that, he had an ample supply. When desperation and the growing certainty of disaster would overcome it, was nearly impossible to tell.

"We could hope for no better opportunity to learn his mind," Laurence said softly to Tharkay now, in the ruined street; together they dragged the cart onto the main street leading towards the Kremlin.

Here the devastation altered in character: the buildings had been more preserved than not, evidently by the labors of the French dragons; great puddles of dirty water yet stood in the gutters. Yet they had still been looted: scraps of silk and shattered porcelain might be seen on the steps, broken furnishings. How the French supposed they should carry away such an immense store of plunder, Laurence could hardly imagine.

The street itself was better tended; looking west towards the bounds of the city, Laurence could see a troop of dragons laboring to clear away the rubble and men behind them repairing the worst of the damage to the cobblestones: perhaps making ready the road for retreat? He and Tharkay went plodding on with their heads down into the vast square around the onion-domed cathedral which, though blackened with smoke, had also been saved: Laurence saw in some disgust that the building was evidently being used for a stable.

The remains of many smaller wooden buildings still lingered at its base, and resting against the high walls of the Kremlin some forty dragons were drowsing together in heaps, while their crews silently prodded at large cauldrons simmering with their poor thin dinner: they were eating dead horses mostly half-starved or sick, stewed with flour. The dragons looked too weary to be called indolent, slumped in the heavy attitudes of exhaustion.

One more-alert beast stood before the cathedral, beside the great city fountain, while some few peasant women, cringing, took their buckets of water before hurrying away: a heavy-weight Papillon Noir in black with iridescent stripes. "That is Liberté," he murmured to Tharkay. He had seen the beast once before, during the invasion of England: he was the personal beast of Marshal Murat, and beside it stood the man himself.

The pair were standing beside one of the Russian light-weights, white-grey. Laurence thought for a moment it might be a prisoner, but as he and Tharkay drew their cart a little closer, he saw the poor beast had no harness and was nearly skeletal in appearance, deep concavities between its ribs. It had a bowl of thin soup, which it was licking up with slow, painstaking care, one foreleg curled around the bowl and a wary watchful hostile eye turned up towards Liberté. Its wings were drawn up tight to its body, as though it might at any moment flee.

Murat was evidently waiting to see the Emperor, and following the line of his gaze Laurence saw him: Napoleon was near the

Kremlin gates, in his dust-grey coat and flanked by the still-glittering ranks of his escort, the Imperial Guard. Davout was a tall thin figure beside him, and his chief of staff Berthier as well.

A French officer then approached the cart, and they were forced to stop: Laurence engaged the man before he could notice Tharkay's foreign looks, pulling back the cover to show him the ten sacks of grain, pantomiming numbers with his hands to indicate many more than these were on offer. "*Cinq cent?*" the Frenchman asked. Laurence nodded, and then held out a hand flat and tapped his palm, asking for an offer; the officer said, "*Attends,*" and went away to confer with another.

Napoleon looked himself as heavy and morose as the dragons of his army; he seemed to only be giving half his attention to an anxious speech which Berthier was making him, full of gestures and intensity; the Emperor glanced away often at the somnolent dragons, at the few companies of soldiers equally dispirited and yawning against the walls. He knew, of course; surely he knew the hopelessness of his position. He was not a fool. He had his hands clasped behind his back, his chin lowered upon his breast; Berthier gestured, down the square, and following his arm, Laurence saw a nearly medieval train of waggon-carts, already loaded and with their covers lashed down.

Bonaparte stood a moment more, and then gave a short nod; Berthier, after a speaking look of relief exchanged with Davout, hurried away back into the Kremlin. Davout seemed as though he wished to say something; Napoleon jerking a hand forestalled him and turned abruptly away, his face hard, and strode out across the square towards Murat, who rose to meet him.

The French quartermasters were still discussing amongst themselves. Laurence looked at Tharkay and, receiving a nod, hazarded the risk. He strode across the square towards the city fountain, as though to have a drink of water, where he could overhear a little.

Napoleon had put his hand on Liberté's side, patting the dragon with easy familiarity as he spoke with Murat; the beast nosed at him with pleasure. "Well, brother," he was saying, with a ghost of a smile, "the last die is thrown, we must stand up from the table! We will have to fight our way back to France, and no rest after that."

"What else is a soldier for?" Murat said, with a wave of his arm: more generosity than Bonaparte deserved, having pressed them all on towards destruction. "We'll sleep a long time in the end. Will you want us to give them a bite on the flank before we draw back?"

Fortune did not smile on Laurence's adventure to so great an extent as to permit him to overhear such invaluable intelligence; Bonaparte only raised his hand a little and wagged it to either side, noncommittal, and jerked his head towards the small Russian dragon, asking Liberté in a deliberate tone of levity, "What is this, your prisoner? A fine battle you must have had!"

"I have not fought her at all," Liberté said, in some indignation, "even though she tried to steal one of our pigs, when we camped near the breeding grounds; and I carried her here myself."

"I couldn't stomach leaving her to starve, poor beast," Murat said to Napoleon, "and it's not as though she could do us any real harm. I've sent for one of the surgeons. Look at what they do to them."

The surgeon, a man in a long black frock coat carrying the grim instruments of his trade, still stained with the blood of some recent patient, came past the fountain even as he spoke; Laurence averted his face, quickly, until the man had gone around him. The dragon hissed at the surgeon and snapped as he approached, only to subside when Liberté put his foreleg on her neck and pinned it to the ground. The man climbed carefully upon her back, between the wings.

Laurence could not see, at first, what the surgeon was doing there; the dragon bellowed in pain and tried to thrash, but Liberté held her fast. A few minutes passed, perhaps three, and then the man flung down over the dragon's side a chain, dripping black blood, with two large barbed hooks on either end still marked with gobbets of flesh: a hobble, simpler but not unlike the one which had held Arkady, when they had found him held prisoner in China. The dragon made a low keening noise, shivering still, but her wings gave a small abortive flutter, as if suddenly freed.

Napoleon made an exclamation of disgust, looking down at the hobble. "And she was not the only one?"

"All of them, in the breeding grounds," Murat said. "And they look as though they do not get enough food to keep alive a cat; I wonder they get any eggs out of them at all."

Temeraire could not but fret anxiously at Laurence's absence, though he had for comfort a splendid dispatch newly arrived from Peking, in which Huang Li had not only reported the egg's continuing perfect condition, but even, to Temeraire's delight, enclosed a small illustration of the pavilion in which the egg was housed, at the Summer Palace, showing it attended by four ladies-in-waiting and four Imperial dragons, and being fanned by servants against the late summer's heat.

"Of course I must keep the original," Temeraire said to Emily, "but perhaps we might make a copy of it, for Iskierka. Surely one of those aides could knock something up?" He was dictating her a letter to pass along the comforting reassurances he had received, and trying as best he could to describe their own success, giving it better terms than he really felt it deserved. "Do you suppose they have reached the Peninsula by now?" he asked wistfully. It was very hard to think that Iskierka might at this very moment already be with the Corps in Spain, which was evidently winning one brilliant battle after another, and he could report nothing for his own part but one battle, from which they had retreated.

"I don't think so," Emily said, with sufficient promptness to suggest that she had thought about the subject before. "They left China in July, just as we did. They might have gone by air from Persia, if they stopped there, and have just been able to reach

Gibraltar. But if they have gone round Africa, they cannot be in Spain before Christmas."

Temeraire did not say, but felt, that this was a small relief: perhaps they would have had another battle before Iskierka did finally have a chance for one of her own. But Emily herself sighed and said, "So it isn't surprising, that we shouldn't have had word from them yet," and looked down at the letter she was writing with a discontented expression, fidgeting with her quill in such a way as to scatter ink across the page.

While she was blotting up the spots, Temeraire said a little anxiously, "I hope you are not changing your mind—I hope you have not thought better of refusing Demane. I am sure that marriage cannot be so wonderful."

"No," she said, downcast. "No, at least, not marriage; but—I suppose I am sorry, a little; I wish I'd had him, while I had the chance."

"Emily," Mrs. Pemberton said, raising her head from where she sat near-by, working on her sewing. "I must beg you not to say such things."

"Oh, I know it isn't my duty; and it should have been a monstrously stupid thing to do," Emily said, "and so I didn't. But I shan't see him for years now, I suppose; if we ever serve together again at all." She sighed. "And one gets curious," she added.

"I ought to be turned off without a character," Mrs. Pemberton said to herself, half under her breath, and then to Emily said, "Even if you must think such things, you needn't *say* them, at least not where anyone might hear you. The last thing a young gentleman requires is any encouragement in that direction."

Temeraire was entirely of like mind with her. He had considered briefly whether perhaps it might be just as well to have Emily marry one of the officers of his own crew, but after some cautious inquiries about the etiquette of the matter, he had determined that this could not really serve to keep her with him when Admiral Roland decided to retire, and it was perfectly likely that she would instead take her own husband away to Excidium with her: so it was not at all to be wished under any circumstances.

He raised his head, alertly, catching some movement through the encampment: Laurence and Tharkay had come back, he saw with much relief, although Laurence's expression was dreadfully grim, and as he came near, already stripping away his peasant cloak, Temeraire asked anxiously, "Napoleon will not retreat?"

Laurence did not answer at once, only shook his head to say he could not immediately answer, and went into the pavilion, and into his tent; Temeraire in surprise went after him and lowered his head anxiously to peer inside: Laurence was putting on his uniform again, his movements short and sharp, angry. He said to Temeraire briefly, savagely, "They are chaining their dragons in the breeding grounds; they are keeping them hobbled."

Temeraire did not understand, at first, until Laurence had explained; and then he scarcely could believe it, until he had found Grig again and demanded a confirmation. "Well—well, yes," Grig said, edging back and looking at him sidelong with some anxiety at Temeraire's anger, though it was not directed at him. "If one won't go into harness, they don't let one fly. Whyever would anyone stay in the breeding grounds, otherwise?"

"It is quite beyond anything," Temeraire said, furious. "Laurence—"

But at that very moment, the courier arrived from headquarters, breathless, with fresh orders: the clamoring demands for action had at last overcome Kutuzov's inertia. They were ordered to attack.

Laurence regarded the orders silently, Temeraire peering down beside him. He knew his duty; it was not to liberate the miserable and wretched Russian dragons, nor to tell the Russians how they were to manage their own beasts: it was to secure the defeat of Napoleon and his army, and see them reduced beyond the ability to threaten either a renewed invasion of Britain, or further warmongering upon the Continent. That defeat was now within their grasp.

"But afterwards," he said to Temeraire, "—afterwards—" He stopped, and then sent for Gong Su and asked him, "Sir, would the Emperor consent to receive these dragons into his Empire?" He gestured to Grig, who looked back with an uncertain expression.

Gong Su looked at Grig with a cool, assessing eye. "He speaks more than one tongue?" he asked. "Will you inquire at what age he acquired them?"

"Well, the dragon-tongue, I learnt that in the breeding grounds before I was hatched," Grig said, doubtfully, "and as for Russian, and French, I cannot rightly say; I suppose I have just picked them up bit by bit the same way that the others have: one does, hearing them every day."

As this was by no means characteristic of most dragon breeds, particularly not in the West, Gong Su nodded in some appreciation. He said to Laurence, "Of course I cannot speak with any official weight. But these beasts appear to be of respectable qualities, and moderate size. There is a great hunger for village porters in the countryside. If they did not consider laborer's work in such small settlements beneath their dignity, then there should be no difficulty in finding employment for them."

"Will you write and inquire if I may extend an offer of such hospitality?" Laurence asked bluntly; Gong Su bowed.

Laurence nodded and said to Temeraire, "Then afterwards, when we have done, we will go to all the breeding grounds which Grig can lead us to—you will explain to them the conditions of their welcome in China, of their employment there—and those who wish to depart, we will free from their hobbles and take with us on our own return to China.

"And if the Russians do not care to lose all their breeding stock," he added, low with anger, "they may amend their treatment."

He knew the condition of the Russian peasantry, very little removed from slavery, was nearly as pitiable as that of the dragons;

and yet there was something intolerable in the spectacle of hundreds of beasts so hobbled that they might not even fly as was their nature, but instead were confined to scrabbling in pits; save for those beasts who, cowed by the horror of their circumstances, would consent to be slaves for scraps and at least a little freedom of movement. The sensation was much as though, laboring with all his might upon the rigging of a ship and in her upper decks, keeping company with her crew, Laurence had suddenly seen through an open ladderway the faces of captives chained and looking up at him with accusation, and discovered himself in service upon a slaver.

He and Temeraire flew together to the headquarters, where a ferment of activity was going forward: Bennigsen and his staff were in an ill-suppressed condition of delight, Kutuzov more phlegmatic; he had appointed Bennigsen and Colonel Toll to the command of the operation. Their target would be Murat himself and his corps, encamped not far from Tarutino, who had grown incautious after a month-long informal truce, their patrols slack: a heavy forest near-by offered cover for a surprise attack.

"Ah, Captain," Kutuzov said, and beckoned him out of the tumult, "come and let us discuss your orders."

"Sir," Laurence said, following him into a separate chamber, formerly the private library of the master of the house, "I will carry out your orders, if you continue to desire our assistance; but I must beg permission to speak frankly, as the price of that assistance may no longer be one you willingly accept."

Kutuzov settled himself comfortably in his chair and waved a hand for permission, his face settling into its habitual slack lines; he listened in silence while Laurence laid out both his objections to the abuse of the Russian ferals, and his intentions towards them. "I hope you will understand, sir, if Temeraire and the other dragons should have that fellow-feeling towards their own kind, which absolutely must have prohibited their making themselves allies of a nation which so maltreated them. This project is the only manner in which I can conceive of reconciling that repugnance with our continued service to you.

"But I am by no means willing to provoke a confrontation between nations, wholly undesirable to either; if you should wish us to depart at once, without engaging in what you may call interference in your affairs, we will do so," Laurence added, "and I hope you will believe me nevertheless entirely desiring your victory over Bonaparte, in such a case."

He finished slowly, a little surprised to find Kutuzov still listening to him with an attitude almost of complacency. The old general snorted at his look and said, "Grig is a clever little creature, you know: Captain Rozhkov raised him from the egg."

While Laurence with a sense of strong indignation digested this, Kutuzov continued, "It is not as though we have not heard of you, Captain Laurence. We have all had a great many arguments, whether your aid would not be too expensive, to begin with."

"Sir," Laurence said, now baffled, "I beg your pardon; however should you know me from Adam?"

"If the world had not heard of you, after your adventure at Gdansk," Kutuzov said, meaning Danzig, where they had rescued the garrison from the wreck of the Prussian campaign, "or after the plague, we should certainly have heard of you after Brazil. Where you go, you leave half the world overturned behind you. You are more dangerous than Bonaparte in your own way, you and that beast of yours.

"It is awkward you should have seen that feral just now, in Moscow, but in the end, it seems it will not make so much difference. The Tsar means us to chase the French all the way to Paris, and I cannot do that without four hundred dragons or more. I must get them out of the breeding grounds somehow.

"So! You will show us how to feed dragons on grain, and I will speak to Arakcheyev," the Tsar's chief minister, "and we will cut them loose."

Laurence almost did not at first quite comprehend Kutuzov's

answer; he had long felt—long known—the many practical advantages offered by a more humane and just treatment of dragons; he had recognized the danger to Britain and any other nation in the stark comparison between the increasing consideration offered to French dragons, and the ill-treatment of their own. He had indeed made these practical matters his argument on many occasions, but he had grown so used to failure, to meeting with only a stolid, blind resistance, that to find not only a tolerant ear but agreement left him more nonplussed than rejection; he did not at once know what to say. "Sir," Laurence said, and halted, overwhelmed by a perfect reversion of feeling, as though he had faced a mortal enemy, and been offered from his hand a priceless gift; he could cheerfully have embraced the old general with Slavic passion.

He with difficulty tried to express his sentiments; Kutuzov waved them away. "Don't be too quick to rejoice," he said. "We can't cut them loose until we can be sure we can feed them. It hasn't been so long since the Time of Troubles, you know; half the country would rise up if they saw dragons flying all over unharnessed." He indicated with one thick finger a painting upon the wall, which depicted a band of pikemen heroically massed and their commander pointing aloft at a looming, snarling dragon, which stood with outspread wings over the broken body of a horse and clutched in one taloned hand a screaming maiden, her trailing white gown a banner stained with blood and her arms outflung in supplication as she cast her eyes up to the heavens.

"Sir," Laurence said dryly, "permit me to assure you that the most vicious beast in all Russia would not prefer to make its dinner out of a lady of six or seven stone over a horse of one hundred."

Kutuzov shrugged. "There were not always horses," he said bluntly.

Laurence was nevertheless able to return to Temeraire with a spirit no longer weighed down with guilt, and share with him the satisfaction not only of having carried their point, but having won it in such a manner as founded the victory on the most solid of ground: that the Russians had freely recognized the necessity of reforming their treatment of their native dragons. "Well," Temeraire said, "I am very glad to see that they have some real sense, Laurence; Kutuzov must be quite a good fellow, particularly as he means us to attack. And now we can do so wholeheartedly.

"Although," he added, with a lowering frown, "I cannot like hearing that Grig has been carrying tales of us: whatever did he mean by it, and pretending that he was so wretched, if he is really quite the pet of his captain? I do not know what to make of it at all."

"You must take it as a compliment," Tharkay said, "that you are of sufficient importance to have spies set upon you." He had expressed just such a sentiment on first learning that Gong Su had been all the while an agent of Prince Mianning; Laurence could not partake in those feelings, however, and was not in the least sorry to find the little dragon had prudently taken himself off and vanished into the general mass of the Russian forces.

But it was nevertheless with a gladdened heart that Laurence went to his tent, to clean his guns and sharpen his sword before the engagement, and was surprised to find Junichiro there. "I have neglected you, I find," Laurence said, in apology: it had not escaped his notice that Junichiro had made extraordinary progress in his study of English, and had furthermore devoted himself with great attention to mastering not only aerial tactics, but learning as much as he could of all others as well: he had seen the boy make persistent overtures to the Russian artillery-officers, in particular, and questioning any he found who could speak at least a little French.

He had in short done all that anyone might have wanted, to make him an officer; but Laurence had realized, too late, that he was by no means a valuable mentor: the Aerial Corps would be more likely to scorn Junichiro than embrace him, for having Laurence's good word.

"But," he said, "I will write to Admiral Roland, and see if I can solicit her influence on your behalf—"

"Sir," Junichiro said quietly, "I beg you do not concern yourself further with this matter: I cannot serve in your Corps."

Laurence paused, startled, and was even more so when Junichiro added, "I have come to ask your permission to depart; and if you refuse it, I must nevertheless end my service to you, even if by a final means." Laurence realized with appalled astonishment that Junichiro spoke of ending his own life: that he would die, by his hand, rather than continue with them.

"Good God," he said, "whatever should make you even contemplate so desperate a course of action? I know of no reason why I should refuse you the right to depart; I might counsel you against it, but you are a free man, and you have made no oath of service to the King: indeed, I am rather indebted to you, than the reverse."

"Captain," Junichiro said, "you may feel differently when I have explained, but it would be dishonorable of me to conceal my purpose from you: I intend to go to France."

"You mean to take service with Bonaparte," Laurence said, half-disbelieving: although he did now see why Junichiro had thought he would object. It sounded like treachery, and yet the confession made it not so; a true traitor would have gone, silently, slinking away. But if Junichiro truly meant to go to Napoleon now, with so much intimate knowledge of their force, their positions—

"No." Junichiro shook his head. "I mean to ask him to send an envoy to my country."

Laurence sat down slowly on the camp-chair, disturbed. "Pray explain yourself."

"I am masterless," Junichiro said, "—a criminal and an exile. But it is still my duty to serve the Emperor—*my* Emperor. It is still my duty to serve Japan. And your nation is not the friend of mine."

He gestured a little, towards the tent entrance. "Your position in this war is now superior," he said. "It is likely that you will be victorious, and cement your alliance with China. And long have they coveted dominion over Japan. I have seen the might of their dragons. Soon they will have Western ships, and Western guns.

409

And we must have them, too—and if not from you, it seems we must have them from France."

"We need not be your enemy, only to be China's friend," Laurence said, but Junichiro raised his eyes and looked at him straight-on.

"You require alliance with them," Junichiro said. "You require their dragons. Whatever you might hope to get from us, you do not need, not in the same way. If they demand that you choose, you will choose them." He made a short cutting gesture with one hand. "My decision is made. I have only waited so long because I did not wish to depart while your situation was yet uncertain, or bleak: I would not leave you in defeat. If you wish to prevent my leaving, you can. I will not attempt to steal away like a thief in the night. But I will no longer serve Britain."

Laurence was silent. He knew what Hammond would have said, to the prospect of sending so priceless an ambassador as Junichiro would make straight into Napoleon's hands: a man not merely versed in the language of Japan but intimately familiar with its customs, and of high birth; a man who despite his exile still had friends among the nobility of that nation, and whose opinions might be privately respected, even if he could not officially be pardoned. It could easily be as much as handing Napoleon a new ally, one who could threaten China's coasts and British shipping.

"You have sacrificed everything," Laurence said finally, "home, position, friends; and if not for my sake, to my benefit. I have no right to keep you, and I cannot dispute your conclusions. But my first duty is to see this war won. If you will give me your word of honor, not to reveal any information about our forces or those of the Russians, I cannot stand in your way."

Junichiro said, "I swear it," very simply.

Laurence nodded a little; he had no doubt of that promise being kept. "Then I will bid you Godspeed," he said quietly, "and I hope with all my heart that your fears will not come to pass."

Junichiro bowed to him deeply, and slipped away; Laurence sat

410

silently in the tent with his sword across his knees, and wondered if they would next meet again as enemies, across a battlefield.

Temeraire was all the more relieved, that Kutuzov's good sense meant that he could properly continue to fight: he was sure now of their ultimate victory. The strike against Murat's forces proved a great success, although a great many of the Russian infantry got themselves lost in the woods and did not reach the battlefield in time: but that scarcely mattered, when Shao Ri came back with not only four captured dragons, and all their crews, but a golden eagle still with tatters of a tricorn attached and sixteen guns; and the rest of the infantry had done well for themselves also, having taken nearly two thousand prisoners and twenty guns, and three eagles. One could not compare, of course, for there were so many more of the French infantry that Napoleon was obliged to give them more eagles to carry, and the eagle which Shao Ri had captured was nearly three times the size—perhaps a little closer to twice—and in any case truly splendid. Temeraire had rarely felt so much delight as when Shao Ri lay the captured standards before Laurence and himself, with a low bow: he felt his breast quite bursting with pride and satisfaction.

The mood in the Russian camp was also nearly exaltation, and everyone was pleased, except the generals, who were quarreling again: General Raevsky, whom Laurence thought a great deal of, and who had dined with them on several occasions, even told Laurence he avoided headquarters as much as ever he could. "It is a nest of vipers," he said, "and they have not yet reorganized the command, even though Barclay is gone."

But however much they quarreled, at least they had won their first real and clear victory, unquestioned, and in the shadow of this defeat, Napoleon had to begin his own retreat from Moscow at last, quite as humiliated as the most ardent Russian patriot might have desired. Of course, they had only defeated his advance guard, but for the moment it seemed as good as if they had routed his entire army, and Temeraire now looked forward with the most eager anticipation to an opportunity to do just that. The question before them now was which way Napoleon would withdraw, along which road; and only a few days later, Temeraire was woken a little way into the evening by a courier coming: there was fighting in Maloyaroslavets, a little town south of their camp along the Kaluga Road, and Napoleon's whole army was there.

"Nothing could be better," he said to Laurence jubilantly. "Now we will properly fall upon him; and perhaps he will be there himself, and we can take him prisoner."

Of course, they had been obliged to disperse the second *jalan* back to the east, because Shen Shi felt too uncertain of supply. But Temeraire privately felt that was all the better, because it should mean more of an excuse for him to take part in the battle, directly; however little he wished to disregard General Chu's last advice to him, he could not help but think he would have quite an awkward time of it explaining, when next he saw Iskierka, if he did not have at least a little fighting himself.

"And we cannot be blamed now, Laurence," he said, "for Kutuzov has got those aides who can speak Chinese, even if their accents are perfectly dreadful; so I do not see that we must sit about behind the lines. Indeed, they are by far the better placed to do it, since they can speak Chinese and Russian, and I have not worked Russian out yet."

He had been very careful to avoid doing so: he did not in the least want to be able to go-between any more than he already did.

"So long as we can be of material use," Laurence said, "I will not scruple to say I share your feelings: and God willing, this battle will see Napoleon's army broken."

Laurence had a note from General Raevsky, while the *jalan* were assembling: *Will you carry us?* was all the message, and he was glad to return an affirmative answer. Raevsky had ten thousand men in his corps, lately denied the opportunity to partake in the attack upon Murat and all of them filled with passion; they flung themselves aboard the Chinese dragons with a will, as enthusiastic seeking battle as they had been miserable in retreat.

The dragons snatched up the guns, and launched aloft: Temeraire nearly trembling with excitement beneath him and only with difficulty keeping to the pace that Zhao Lien watchfully set, to avoid wearing out her forces under their burden; the Russians began to sing as they flew on, deep young joyful voices, and traded off with the Chinese crews, one after another, all the length of their flight.

"He must have meant to march on Kaluga," Raevsky said to Laurence, as they flew: that city being presently the main supply base of Kutuzov's army, and the gateway to the munitions factories of the south. "God favors Russia at last: if Dokhturov had not caught him, he could have done us some more mischief yet."

The distance was only twenty miles: two hours put them in sight of the town, and the plumes of smoke rising; several of the buildings were burning, and the cannon roared ferociously on both sides. Zhao Lien brought them around wide, to the south behind the Russian advance guard which was ferociously holding the small town against Napoleon's advance. More prepared this time for the hop-skip of the Chinese landing, Raevsky's corps were disembarked in not half-an-hour; his sergeants were already bawling for order and forming the men into their regiments as the Chinese dragons lifted off again, to form up aloft.

Temeraire hovered longingly beside Zhao Lien as she sent forth the first *jalan* through the climbing smoke. Dokhturov had only one aerial regiment of six heavy-weights, and with them two dozen light-weights whom, in defiance of tradition, he had flung into battle to give his men a little cover against the French skirmishing attack. The French dragons, some twenty in number and wearing the emblem of the corps of Eugène de Beauharnais, had been handily outfighting them and dropping bombs upon the Russian troops, who were taking a dismal shelter against a handful of buildings now all of them in flames.

The Chinese legions drove in and at once turned the tide in the air: the French infantry fell back and dug themselves grimly into the stone monastery at the center of town behind their guns, and the French dragons turned tail and simply fled, as quickly as they could go. "Look, Laurence, you see they are just running away!" Temeraire said, in rather exultant tones, as they watched the retreat from the southern end of the town.

Five *niru* set off in pursuit; but the crews of the French middle-weights abruptly swung below and cut loose their belly-netting, dropping their munitions. And thus lightened, the French middle-weights could just barely outdistance the Chinese and began to pull away. One *niru* did manage to pounce on a lagging beast, however, and skillfully dragged him down to the ground. The remainder escaped: but meanwhile the soldiers below were now exposed, and the Russian supply corps had labored to some purpose in these intervening weeks to provide the Chinese legions with their own bombs, which now their crews began to hurl down on the entrenched Frenchmen.

The French answer came in the form of round-shot. The French used stones and bricks from the shattered walls and streets of the town to elevate their guns until they were pointing nearly directly over their heads, and in so doing managed to inflict a casualty of their own: a ball tore into the belly of one of the Shao Lung and erupted through its back, and the poor creature fell stone-dead from the sky, smashing through a burning building and leaving its wreck sprawled across the streets of the town. Raevsky's men had now dragged their guns into position, with the aid of horses snatched from Dokhturov's corps: the battlefield was no place for cavalry, with fire on every side and the narrow streets choked with rubble nearly impassable even for men on foot. Their guns began to thunder in company.

The French—whom Laurence realized, when the smoke cleared well enough to see their uniforms, were not Frenchmen but Italians, recruited from another of Napoleon's conquests—would surely have retreated in the face of their disadvantages, if any opportunity offered them; but as they were behind the only stone walls in their vicinity, they could get no better shelter than where they were, and by removing themselves from it would have exposed themselves both to the relentless artillery and to the snatching talons of the dragons above.

From necessity they held their position, answering as best they could, and so valiantly that they could only be winnowed down a little at a time, and the fires of the town crept ever closer towards them.

They held for an hour, pushed back slowly, and then Laurence through his glass saw movement through the immense towering clouds of smoke. "Temeraire," he said, "take us aloft, if you please," but Zhao Lien's scouts were already darting back to report to her: Davout's corps had arrived, with fifty French dragons in support.

For the next four hours, the battle roared back and forward through the town: at first the French fell back, under their newly arrived air cover, and the Russians with a shout charged into its narrow lanes and took possession; then they themselves were forced back by the terrible weight of the French artillery and their advantage in infantry. The town changed hands five more times, that dreadful afternoon: many of the wounded could not be rescued, and a sudden change in the wind drove the spreading flames abruptly further on. As those who could not walk were engulfed by the spreading flames, the shrieks of the dying rose like a noise out of perdition from the smoke.

"Dear God," Laurence said. "Temeraire—Temeraire, can you interrupt them? For God's sake, we must have a cease-fire, and get those men out of the way."

They passed the word to Zhao Lien, and then Temeraire flung

himself aloft and roared terribly, shatteringly: so hugely that all those below halted a moment and covered their heads against it. Emily and Baggy flung out a great white trailing sheet and waved it in the wind, and for a moment the guns fell silent; Zhao Lien sent in four of the supply-dragons, to snatch up the wounded of both sides, and bear them limp and half-scorched out.

The pause stretched on for a moment, for a minute, for three. Laurence half-wondered if perhaps it might go on, no-one wishing to continue: if a little space might break through whatever illusion it was permitted men to desire battle and to give it. It seemed as though all the world held its breath; and then a small company of artillery from de Beauharnais's corps touched off a primed gun, near the center, and the conflict was rejoined even as the wounded—and the many dead which had been taken up from among them—were laid out moaning upon the ground.

"Laurence, when we do not even want this town anyway, particularly," Temeraire said, looking sadly over the miserable wretches. "There is nothing splendid in it; if there ever were, it is surely quite ruined now, and if we *did* win this battle, we should have gained nothing but to say that we had won: that cannot be enough."

"The town may not be of significance in itself," Laurence said, "but it is immensely so as a gateway to our main sources of supply and beyond that to the Russian munitions-factories; if Napoleon managed to seize a great magazine for himself, and so hamper our own supply, he might well cripple the Russian Army."

As the battle continued, Zhao Lien directed her dragons steadily and conservatively: their advantage against the French was no longer so overwhelming, for besides the removal of the second *jalan*, they had been reduced by injuries: the Chinese armor, though excellent against talon and tooth, which it deflected easily, did not withstand rifle-fire as did chainmail. Of the 200 dragons of the remaining *jalan*, 150 were fighting-beasts, of whom nearly 30 were presently in the care of the surgeons; and their scouts and spies had recorded nearly 80 beasts in fighting trim still to Napoleon's tally, though not all of those were to be seen. So she was careful not to commit her entire force: 50 beasts presently were napping on the ground below, conserving their strength, leaving them 70 against 50 in the air.

Laurence had kept all this time scanning the town with his glass: even with all the advantages of elevation, he could scarcely make out anything for the smoke, layers upon layers of it, white and grey and smudged black, except when the blaze of cannon-fire briefly illuminated a company. "The French are presently heavily committed to those streets in the north-east," he said, having made out their positions, "and I do not see any of their guns pointing to their rear. If we should come around for a single pass, and level the buildings behind them with the divine wind, we should likely roll them up: and they are supporting the right flank of their army."

"I will ask Zhao Lien at once," Temeraire said, eagerly, and shot to her side; she looked more than a little anxious—small wonder; Laurence could well believe she would not like in the least to return to China with the news she had lost a Celestial, and even a dubious sort of Imperial prince—but there were nearly twenty guns established in the exposed position, and she could not fail to see the advantage of knocking such a hole in the French artillery.

"Very well," she said, reluctantly, at last, "—only wait a moment: the seventh and the fifteenth *niru* have performed with particular excellence, and deserve the honor of escorting your pass." She waved aloft two companies from the resting dragons below, and recalled those two named companies from the battle; surrounded thus by six beasts flying in protective pattern, Laurence almost felt himself back in England, formation-flying, as they swung out around the town.

Sweeping his gaze over the battlefield as they flew, Laurence saw, aboard one of the French middle-weights, a tall captain in flying-leathers looking at them through his own glass who plainly recognized the danger they posed; his ensign began at once putting out urgent signal-flags. The smoke concealed these from the men below, however; and the French were too hard-pressed to send enough relief to overcome Temeraire's escort. The captain bent forward over his dragon's neck, and the beast fell back from the fighting and turning flung itself gallantly towards the ground, going to warn the artillery-men in person.

"Quickly," Laurence said, "quickly, before they can turn round the guns—"

Their course by necessity was taking them wide around the town, as French artillery range covered nearly every inch of it and beyond its limits; Temeraire increased his speed, while his escort struggled to keep pace with him. Below, the middle-weight had managed to perch for a moment upon a collapsed building, hopping from one foot to the other and trying to keep her bell-men from being scorched while the captain shouted down to the artillery company.

The men were frantically dragging round several of the guns, to aim towards their approach, but their horses were stumbling with drooping heads, already weak, and the guns were surely scorching-hot from their work. Temeraire threw himself forward, roaring, and the buildings, weakened already by fire, began to shatter as the divine wind struck: the center of the walls collapsing inwards and the half-burnt roofs falling after them, until the whole went tumbling forward in a sudden crashing wave of burning tinders, a great blinding rush of orange sparks and ash spraying up, very much as from a fire stuck by a poker and stirred, and buried the guns and the men with them.

The French dragon had snatched one gun from the wreck, crying out with pain at the heat; the bell-men stretched their hands out to seize a few of the soldiers as she flung herself aloft. She was laboring away as Temeraire pulled up again, and Laurence alarmed called, "Temeraire! Temeraire, we must pull back!" for Temeraire was plainly unsatisfied with the immense success of his maneuver and half-instinctively had begun beating in pursuit, though this course should bring them too close to another battery of French artillery.

"Oh—" Temeraire said, stifled, and turned away: but a little sluggishly, and the roar of guns came from beneath as they came briefly into range.

Laurence caught Baggy, when he would have ducked, and kept him standing straight; the boy abashed glanced to see if anyone else had noticed his brief lapse. But his nearest neighbor, Roland, was hanging halfway out over Temeraire's shoulder, her carabiner straps extended to full length, and shouting enemy positions down to Forthing below: he was directing Laurence's handful of bell-men in flinging bombs down.

A whistling of round-shot came nearly past Laurence's ear; behind him another struck one of the dragons on Temeraire's left, scored its side, and as it jerked away, crying, tore a terrible gaping rent through its wing. Temeraire nearly turned back to catch him, but the other dragons of the *niru* were already closing in to support their wounded comrade. "Onward straight!" Laurence shouted through his speaking-trumpet: the other dragons would try to stay with Temeraire, and if he turned backwards they would find themselves snarled and vulnerable. The guns below had been meant for firing on the enemy infantry, at the other end of the town, but in a moment they would be reloaded with canister-shot, and a second volley would be sure of doing terrible damage among them.

Temeraire put on a burst of speed, and carried them back out of range; they swung back to Zhao Lien, who said nothing, but looked at the wounded dragon as he was helped tenderly to the ground; Temeraire hung his head, and as plainly did not require the lecture. He flew down to stand beside the wounded dragon, asking his name unhappily—"Lung Zhao Yang, Honorable One," the dragon said, trying despite his injuries to bow his head.

"I am very sorry I should have led you too close to the guns," Temeraire said, low, and stayed watching anxiously while the surgeons inspected the terrible damage to the wing, shaking their heads with concern.

"Do not wholly reproach yourself," Laurence said quietly. "We have silenced eighteen guns, and made a material change to the course of the battle; their position has been badly weakened. It must be counted worth the cost."

Temeraire nodded a little, unhappily, but did not say anything; he went back aloft watching, until abruptly a small panting Russian dragon came flying wildly towards the village from the north-east, and threading their own ranks dropped himself unceremoniously onto Temeraire's back amidst the crew, sending them all scrambling and himself nearly trembling with his speed and the effort of his flight: it was Grig.

"Oh," Temeraire said, coldly, having craned his head around in astonishment to be so boarded, "—you."

"Yes, but pray," Grig said, between his gulped breaths, "pray don't be angry, not now: they are all coming. I couldn't stop them; they won't listen to me. If only you can persuade them—"

"What has happened?" Laurence said sharply, and looked back the way that Grig had come: a low grey cloud, moving fast, approaching.

"Murat went to the breeding grounds on the Motsha River," Grig said, "and let them all go. He told them—"

The cloud was resolving into a great mass of dragons, most of them grey-white beasts with also a handful of smaller black dragons like the Russian couriers, flying raggedly and slowly but coming onward for all that: not towards the battlefield, nor towards their army, but heading directly for the supply-train in their rear. Temeraire flung himself towards their path, but even as he tried to intercept their course, they were already flying past like hurtling comets, lean and swollen-bellied and hollow-ribbed, some of them with eyes nearly shut and others dripping a kind of trailing slime from the sides of their mouths.

The Shen Lung, though ordinarily not combatants, were nevertheless well prepared to guard the supply against enemy attack: the twenty of them in the rear rose up swiftly to form a knot of protection over the cooking-pits, but preparation was no match for the number and desperation of the loosed ferals, in a battle whose sole question was, whether the supply should be ruined, or not. Some ferals blindly flung themselves heedless of claws and teeth down, and dragged quartered pigs dripping from the pits, then fled with their prizes away; others avoided the defenders and threw themselves instead further on to fall upon the rearing, terrified cart-horses of the supply-train stretched down the road to the south.

These, too, were defended promptly by their drivers, who despite the little warning they had been given with courage unshipped their pikes and began to thrust at the snatching ferals; but there were not dozens of dragons, but a hundred and more, and though maddened with hunger they were not dumb beasts. They quickly began to form impromptu bands: one beast or two would draw the defenders, and the other snatch a horse away in that brief opening; then all three together would dart off bearing their trophy.

In the span of ten minutes, all had been reduced to utter chaos in the Russian baggage: carts unhorsed or overturned, and the rest trying both to defend themselves and keep their frantic horses from destroying themselves with their plunging, desperate attempts to break loose from their traces and escape. The Cossack aviators were trying to do what they might, but even massed, their small beasts could not stand against the grey dragons when the latter were so blindly determined to bull their way through.

The ferals were indiscriminate in their hunger: Laurence saw, looking back, that there was some chaos also in the French rear, where a few knots of starving dragons had hurled themselves against their supply-train; but Murat had evidently aimed the beasts well, and the general course of their flight was leading directly to the Russian rear. A dozen afflicted the French; it seemed near a hundred and more had fallen upon the Russians.

The *niru* who had been held in reserve had now come aloft. "Pray do not hurt them, if you can help it!" Temeraire called to them, as they joined him and began to swiftly work to envelop the rampaging cloud of ferals. "Let us try and force them to the ground:

421

I am sure if only we can, they will listen to us, once we give them a little food."

But the ferals had no intention of staying either to listen or be recaptured, as surely they must have feared. Those who had already snatched some food were darting away in every direction, like fish escaping from a closing net; only an especially ragged few, who had not been able to seize a prize and had reached the limits of their strength, were borne down. Others yet unsuccessful began to abandon their attempts, and then, to Laurence's horror, he saw them turning away from the well-defended supply, and falling upon the rows of the prone and bloody ranks of the wounded soldiers in their hospital.

Temeraire roared in protest, and led the *niru* in a scattering charge: but a dozen dragons fleeing carried off men screaming for aid and rescue in their talons. "God in Heaven," Laurence said, sickened, as he saw one wild-eyed creature raise a thrashing man to its jaws even as it flew, and with a snap of teeth and a savage jerk tear him in half.

Temeraire with a surge caught two of the beasts, and seizing them by the necks with his talons dragged them down to the ground. Laurence saw Ferris raise his rifle to his shoulder and take aim at one of the dragons, who was still trying even pinned to the ground to eat its victim. They were perhaps twenty yards distant. The gun spoke, with a burst of grey smoke; the dragon's head jerked back like a kicking horse, a spurt of blood and ichor coming from its eye, and fell limp. The man it had seized fell to the ground with it, and began to drag himself sobbing away, pulling his leg from between its teeth.

Nine dragons of the *niru* at Temeraire's rear together managed to bring down another five, along with their hapless captives; but by the time they could save the men and go aloft again, there was no hope of catching any more. The ferals were all of them vanishing again, as swiftly as they had come, dispersing to all corners of the countryside.

The battle was dying behind them, in the confusion and horror brought on by the unexpected swarming attack. The day was drawing to a close; the Russians began to fall back to the south, taking up positions across the road to Kaluga, and left the French to possession of the streets, choked with bodies and running with blood.

Their dinner that night was a thin and scanty one. The ferals had not acted with malice: they had not deliberately spoilt the cooking-pits nor the supply they could not themselves carry off, save accidentally, but accident had been more than enough. Their attack had taken or ruined more than half the army's food, for that night. Reports were yet coming in, from all around the countryside, of further depradations against the farmers and nearby villages: terrified peasants were even coming to the army, with their children and their cattle, begging for protection.

"And there are breeding grounds also on the Ugra River," one Russian aviator said: a river which ran on past Kaluga itself. "Heavy-weight breeding grounds."

The Cossacks were laboring valiantly all that evening, despite nightfall, to bring them further intelligence of the movement of both the French Army and the feral beasts. Late in the night, while Kutuzov yet sat looking heavily over his maps, one of their captains came in weary and in his dirt, his mustaches stained with tobacco, and reported to him in Russian. Kutuzov nodded a little.

"The French have put out cooking-pits for them," Kutuzov said briefly to Laurence.

Despite all the barriers of language, evidently the French had managed to make a simple bargain understood: if the ferals brought them grain, which they could not ordinarily digest, the French added some meat to the stew, and shared it out between them and their own dragons.

"And like as not throwing our prisoners and our slain into the pits, the monsters," another Russian said, a grotesque fantasy, but one which Laurence heard more than once repeated in the camp.

Kutuzov said heavily, "We fall back towards Kaluga, at once. Captain," he said to Laurence, "will you go to the Ugra grounds, and secure them?"

Laurence was silent a moment: to make himself a gaoler, for starving and chained beasts, was work he could scarcely bear to contemplate, and yet the faces of the screaming wounded haunted him. "We will, sir," he said.

Temeraire did not disagree; he and all the Chinese dragons, and their crews, had been very silent and shocked since the battle: what was yet a lurking fear in the heart of most Westerners, who had grown up on tales of maurauding dragons and heroic knights standing forth to slay them, and who thought of aviators as the handlers of savage beasts, was to them so unthinkable and vile as to be unacceptable even as a subject for fiction.

They left at once, despite the late hour; so, too, did the army. They saw a few torches moving upon the road below for guidance, the light reflected here and there off pikes and bayonets that bristled in every direction; in the hospital-waggons, those less grievously wounded rode sitting up, holding weapons aloft. There was no sight of French pursuit or forward motion: they remained ensconced around Maloyaroslavets, or what was left of that town after the ruinous combat.

Three roads now stood open to Napoleon: he might retreat himself towards Moscow and from there retire to Smolensk along the road which had brought him, or he might instead try and take a southern route; or if he had not yet lost the heart for a final adventure, even strike out for Kaluga after all, and throw a gauntlet once more in the teeth of the Russian Army.

"I could scarcely imagine it, even of Bonaparte," Laurence said to Tharkay, as they flew through the night; he had sent most of the officers below to sleep, as much as they might, in the belly-netting, "after he was halted in his tracks yesterday, except—"

Tharkay nodded minutely. Dragons could not fly long distances day in and out without steady provender, and their assembled host was so large that if their supply were destroyed, even an instant dispersal to all directions with the liberty of pillaging could not feed them all. And their own supply depots, intended as they were for the feeding of great numbers of dragons, would in any case now be appealing targets for the ferals. Shen Shi already looked grave, and after private consultation that night, Zhao Lien had sent away some twenty dragons to be a guard upon their nearest depots—and with instructions that should they be overwhelmed, they were immediately to begin to retreat eastward instead of trying to rejoin the main body of their *jalan*.

So at a stroke, Napoleon had already managed to whittle down their aerial advantage to a thin margin, now composed not very much of numbers but only of the greater experience and skill at maneuvering which the Chinese forces brought to battle, as compared to his young legions.

The night was very clear, and very cold: Temeraire's breath streamed away behind them in long trailing gusts as he flew on. The first hard frosts had come at last; before they had gone aloft, the ground had been frozen beneath them to a depth of seven inches, and many of the Shao Lung, unused to the cold climate, had been grumbling. It was the twenty-fifth of October. Laurence had to check their course against the stars, several times, until at last they struck the line of the Ugra River and turned to follow it southeast; a gibbous moon hung pale white, shining off the water and more translucently the skin of ice forming over its surface.

"When we arrive," Laurence had said to Temeraire and Zhao Lien, "we must first give them something to eat; we cannot expect beasts who are starving to hear any reason, but having been fed might listen, when Temeraire and Grig can speak with them in their own tongue."

Shen Shi had looked even more grave, but had at last agreed to release an additional quarter-day's ration from her already-strained depots; the grain and drugged cattle were now being carried by the dragons following them along with their own supply. The sixty remaining dragons of the first *jalan,* under Shao Ri, were coming with them; the rest, and Zhao Lien, had remained with Kutuzov's army to cover the withdrawal south. A withdrawal which could all too easily end in disaster, if Kaluga's storehouses were struck.

"Temeraire," Grig said, laboring to catch them up, "Temeraire, there is someone there on the river, I think."

"Where away?" Temeraire asked, and stooping they landed to find a Cossack dragon, barely the size of a Winchester, lying smashed and dying upon the bank half in and half out of the water: his side riddled with bullets, and his two riders both broken beneath his body. The dragon was already nearly gone; one man, who had been half in the frigid water, was dead; but the other opened his eyes and turned his head to look Laurence in the face.

"We will have you out in a moment," Laurence said to him, kneeling to put a hand on his shoulder, the best comfort he could give; ribs were protruding from the man's flesh, and the dragon lay over his legs. The Cossack only seized him by the collar with a desperate final straining effort and tried to pull him close; Laurence leaned in, and the man whispered, "*Murat,*" and released him, falling back; a little gush of blood came from his lips, and he was still.

Laurence rising to catch at the harness and climb back aboard said, "Temeraire, we must go at once. Send half the *niru* along the river, quietly, until they see the other end of the breeding grounds, and then we must close in on all sides: and let us pray the quarry has not yet escaped us. And pass the word: douse all lights."

Lanterns all extinguished, they flew low and quietly over the tree-tops, until coming over a hill they reached a wide shallow valley of the breeding grounds; a massive Russian heavy-weight nearly the size of a Regal Copper was crouched low, its head hanging to the ground, as four men labored frantically upon its back, working on a massive chain of iron stained with rust. They were not surgeons, but blacksmiths: Laurence realized abruptly that the French had forgone removing the barbs for the practical expedient of merely cutting the chains off them, and leaving the difficult hooks where they were.

A small portable forge glowed orange-red where they hammered on the second link, having already broken the first; the dragon was already moving its right wing, experimentally, and looking over with a craning head at its own back to watch the work: it was nearly quivering. The beast did not look quite so starved as had the grey light-weights: if maddened past fear of maiming by starvation, a heavy-weight might have been able to break even the strongest hobble, and then could have done enormous damage. But it certainly looked lean and hungry enough, and eager for its freedom.

The smiths were working with desperate urgency, and around them all the crew and company of twelve dragons in harness were looking anxiously in all directions, around Liberté himself; but on the ground before him, as nonchalant as if he was in the midst of Paris instead of engaged in a wildly reckless and dangerous enterprise behind his enemy's lines, Murat walked back and forth whistling unconcerned. Laurence put a restraining hand silently on Temeraire's neck, and kept his glass stretched out, watching the far side of the breeding ground, for any glint of the other half of their own company; he did not mean to lose this chance through excessive haste.

At last he caught a glitter of moonlight on a bared sword-blade waved at him. The smiths had nearly cut through the second link, below. "Ready arms, and on them," Laurence said, and with a glad and terrible roar, Temeraire surged forward, while below them the French dragons sprang desperately for escape.

The Russian heavy-weight, jerking up its head, saw them approaching and tried its other wing: the smiths were thrown off their feet as the chain went flying from beneath their hands, and with their smoking, sparking forge went sliding down its back to the ground as the massive dragon reared up. It bent down and snatched them all up together in one claw, four men and forge tumbled together, and with the other caught the loose hanging end of the chain; and then it flung itself into the air.

Laurence signaled to let the beast go—he had not the heart to return the creature to its chains, and they had better prey before them. Liberté had snatched Murat off his feet and flung himself into the air, and all the other dragons of the division were doing their best to make of themselves a screen between him and their attackers.

But the net had been drawn too tight: one *niru* after another skillfully surrounded and carved away each French dragon, nearly in minutes, with the skill of a surgeon cutting away limbs: until Liberté was all exposed, flying desperately, but not quickly enough. Ten more dragons surrounded him and began to cut off his flight, no matter which way he turned, tiring him and slowing his movement: a great stag, surrounded by wolves. Then one of the Shao Lung, especially large and with a jagged pale white scar running enormous the length of his left flank, made a full-body leap onto Liberté's back and with a roar knocked his crew off their feet; he sank both foretalons deep into Liberté's back, behind his wings.

Liberté shrilled with agony, and his wings faltered. Another Chinese dragon made a raking pass at his side, knocking air from his body; a third caught his tail and then they all closed in upon him and above him: he sank down at last helpless from the air, and having fallen to the ground resorted to curling his entire massive body tight around Murat, still held within his talons, with a pitiful hunted desperation.

Temeraire landed before him, nearly quivering with excitement, and murmured, "Laurence, I have never taken anyone so important prisoner: what ought we do?"

"Nothing more nor less than with any other man or beast: we must require Liberté's surrender," Laurence said, "and his giving Murat into our hands; and we must have both of their paroles."

Temeraire straightened, sweeping back his wings, and rather grandly said to Liberté, "We will accept your surrender, if you please; and your parole."

428

"Do you swear you will not hurt Murat?" Liberté demanded anxiously, looking at them both, though he could scarcely have prevented it. Murat's own opinion on the circumstances as yet could not have been obtained, because only a faintly muffled noise was emerging, from the tight coils of Liberté's body, to confirm that he was still even there.

"I am confident the Russians will treat him with all the consideration due to a prisoner of his rank," Laurence said, "and I will give you my own word, he will be neither abused nor pillaged."

A faint voice was heard saying, in French, "Damn you, you silly python, let me out!" and Liberté unwillingly uncoiled himself; Murat pulled himself up and over one great foreleg, and sprang down to the ground in the open. Laurence slid from Temeraire's back to meet him.

Laurence bowed and said, "Your Majesty—" Napoleon had put him on the throne of Naples, "—I am obliged to require your parole."

Murat reached out and seized him by the shoulders. "What are you saying," he said. "Can *you* truly mean to prevent us?" He turned Laurence almost bodily, and flung out an arm to where Laurence saw a heap of five broken chains scattered on the ground, massive and monstrous links of brutal iron. "Have *you* a heart to see these magnificent beasts chained and starved like rats, for even another minute? I know you, Captain Laurence—I remember when you brought the cure to France, and saved my own Liberté thereby, and so many others. Once you had the courage to seek justice, more than only obey; will you not find that courage again?

"You and these," he gestured to the hovering and watchful dragons, "ought to aid us, not stand in our way. Will you truly make common cause with men as would do such things?"

Laurence said, quietly, controlled, "You are right, sir, that this treatment cannot but appall any sense of justice and decency. But what *you* have done, in merely striking their chains and throwing them upon the army and the innocent peasantry of their own country, is to set them upon a course whose certain event is their destruction at the hands of a furious and determined nation. And you have done this, not for their benefit, but to make them weapons to serve your own unjust ends and thirst for conquest."

"Oh, villain!" Murat cried. "Where else should they turn, but on the holders of their whips? I told the Emperor I would not walk out of this country, without striking the chains off every beast I could find, if it cost me my life and him my service. March me away, then, and have me shot if you like; *I* have no regret. *Vive la France!*"

He flung his saber at Laurence's feet, delivering this speech in parade-ground tones; it roused an answering cheer from his men and their beasts, despite their captivity. Laurence could not but shake his head: he found he did not question Murat's sincerity; so wild an impulse seemed all of a piece with the very recklessness which had led him to expose himself and his men so deeply in enemy territory.

Roland with a quick jump leapt forward, and picked up the sword to give to Laurence, so he would not need to bend down and pick it up. "Sir, if you will give me your parole, I should be glad to return it," Laurence said, mastering his own anger, and when Murat haughtily acquiesced, did so: he could not take insult from a man made prisoner, and Murat's courage could hardly be denied; he had been at the fore of the French dragons, at Tsarevo Zaimische, time and again.

The *niru* had been swiftly going over the breeding grounds, in the meantime; and now one of Shen Shi's lieutenants, a man named Guan Fei, quietly approached Laurence. "I must advise against preparing our cooking-pits here," he said. "This place is unhealthy: there are many dead, who have not been properly buried. We should go along the river to the south, and find some clean ground."

"The remaining dragons here will be unable to fly," Laurence said, "and we ought still to feed them; and then free them ourselves and take them along with us, if they will come. If we can catch any of the rest, perhaps their fellows will be able to induce them to pause and listen, rather than fight."

But Guan Fei said, "There are only four dragons we have found yet remaining within the grounds: we can arrange to transport them a short distance, but they are in any case ill and close to death. I have arranged for them to be tended."

"There ought to be fifty dragons here," Temeraire said in alarm. "Where are all the others?"

Laurence looking at Murat's face, which showed no small degree of satisfaction, said grimly, "Kaluga. He has set them on Kaluga."

It was not until the next day that Laurence had the pleasure of delivering his prisoner to Kutuzov in Kaluga: a thin and insubstantial pleasure, in the face of the disaster which had unfolded about them.

The town had been utterly unprepared for the sudden and thunderclap descent of forty heavy-weight beasts: the great magazines had been smashed open and ruined, immense quantities of munitions and grain taken, cattle and horses slaughtered and devoured; and much of the town itself smashed in the frenzy of destruction.

Temeraire and his fellows had driven on the last few miles from the breeding grounds to Kaluga, despite their fatigue and hunger. But even so they had come too late, and found a scene of wreckage only: the heavy-weights had come, the townspeople told Laurence, and plundered swiftly, and as swiftly fled back towards the north— perhaps carrying their stolen goods towards Napoleon's army.

Temeraire had tried to go aloft again, in pursuit; he and his fellows had gone half-a-mile, heads drooping progressively lower, and then Shao Ri had roused up and shaken his head and turning towards Laurence and Temeraire had said, "We must halt."

Laurence himself started from a half-doze and realized the folly of their attempt: after a day of hard fighting, little food and less

431

rest, followed by a cold flight in the dark and a battle to end it, the dragons were at the limits of their strength. "Put out the signals, Gerry, if you please," he said, and to Temeraire's half-drowsing protest said quietly, "We cannot throw ourselves at nearly our own number of fresh heavy-weights, in this state; we would be destroyed. You must all have some rest, and something to eat, before we can continue on."

The exhausted dragons slept eight hours, in four watches, with the French dragons always under a wary eye; Laurence had put their captains and crews aboard the swiftest of the dragons of the *niru*, and kept Murat himself aboard Temeraire, but he was mindful that not all the French dragons might have been harnessed from the shell, and might not feel the intensity of attachment to their captains which ordinarily served to render a captured beast meek. He was well served by his caution: a little while after dawn, he roused to find two of the French dragons being wrestled to the ground again, having made an attempt to creep away.

In the morning, they returned to Kaluga, where the army was slowly marching in, and Laurence delivered their noble prisoner to the headquarters. Murat had been considered by the Russians an honored foe; they saluted him in the air and on the field, when they saw him: a great horseman, a great swordsman, a great soldier, fearless in battle and gallant in his personal manner, he was in most respects the romantic ideal to which young Russian officers aspired.

But now as Laurence escorted him past many of those who had cheered him, not long before, and into the building of the headquarters, silence followed them: a hard, angry silence. In his office, Kutuzov said, very briefly, coldly, "Your Majesty," and then paused; he then said, "The Tsar has commanded that you be sent to Tobolsk," a city which Laurence recalled: they had passed it, in the earlier stages of their journey from China, deep in Siberia's wastes, "there to await the conclusion of the war; you depart in the morning."

Murat's courage, to do him credit, flagged not a moment; he

only said, cheerfully, "I am sorry to miss the rest of it! May I write a letter to my wife?"

He did not wait for permission, but brazenly reached for pen and paper on Kutuzov's desk, and scribbled out a careless note:

My darling Caroline! My luck has gone sour; I have been taken prisoner and am being shipped away to some distant corner of beyond, whose name I have already forgotten—

"Tobolsk, was it?" he asked, and scribbled it in.

I am perfectly well; Liberté has not a scratch; tell your brother to win the war as quick as blazes and bring me home before I die of boredom. Ever yours, Joachim.

He folded it once and handed it over. "You are welcome to read it over, but I promise there are no secrets," he said. "I've no head for ciphers. I don't suppose there are any pretty women in this country?"

Laurence could not but feel some sympathy, seeing him sent away: he knew the bitter pang of being sent away from the field to linger in remote exile in an alien land, and felt an echo of the misery of his own transportation, the heavy bowing weight upon his shoulders, the knowledge that he and Temeraire would be denied the chance to be of any use. And Murat had not even the comfort of his own dragon's company; Liberté would be kept imprisoned far from him, and very likely in one of the same dreadful breeding grounds they had emptied.

But Laurence felt nothing but coldness for Murat's acts: the impulse to free the dragons might have been a noble one, but it would not have been carried out, if it had not so neatly aligned with his interests and those of Bonaparte, and if truly motivated by disinterested affection would never have been done in so crude a way, which showed so much disdain for the evil consequences that would fall on those dragons themselves.

"Sir," Laurence said to Kutuzov, when Murat had been escorted away to await his transport, "will you tell me where we stand?"

Kutuzov shook his head. "Thirty ferals were seen at Maloyaroslavets this afternoon, with cartloads of grain from Kaluga." Answer enough: that meant the Russian dragons were accepting the lures which the French had thrown out to them. Laurence was silent. He could no more reproach the beasts for pursuing a course of liberation, than the Russians for wishing to defend themselves against Napoleon's invasion.

He returned to his own encampment and found an unhappy Grig lingering there, having managed to beg Temeraire's pardon, and wanting company: twenty Russian light-weights had vanished from the muster. "They are leaving," he said, low. "I think—I think they are going over to Napoleon."

"How many of them speak French?" Laurence asked, grimly.

"So many of our officers speak it," Grig said, "I dare say nearly all of us know a little, at least."

Meaning that by serving as go-betweens, they might permit Napoleon to turn the ferals into more than simply a wild foraging party, scarcely under his control; they might allow him to weld them into a true fighting force, and use them effectively in battle.

The day was drawing on; Laurence spoke long with Shen Shi, and several officers of the Russian general staff, upon the one essential note: supply, supply, supply. The roads from the south were slow and choked with mud, and more attacks had already been reported, against their supply depots. At last he fell asleep for a few hours of rest, on Temeraire's arm; at eleven in the night, Roland woke him.

"I'm sorry, sir," she said, quietly, "but there's a dispatch," and handed him the note; he broke it open and read: Napoleon's army had begun to move south, along the Kaluga Road. He was coming. He had chosen the great gamble. A cold and stinging wind was blowing into Laurence's face; he rubbed away sleep, and found his hand wet; he looked up. Snow was falling.

Winter had come.

GR 5114